GHOSTS

The Lost

COLONEL-COMMISSAR IBRAM Gaunt and his regiment, the Tanith First-and-Only, are known across the Sabbat Worlds as the most resourceful and dogged of the Imperial Guard. In *The Lost* they face their toughest challenge yet, pitched against the powers of Chaos with their honour, their sanity and their very lives at stake.

Traitor General: When Gaunt arrives on the Chaos-held world of Gereon, the local rebels believe redemption is at hand. But Gaunt has his own mission to achieve – one even more crucial than the fate of an entire planet.

His Last Command: After their escape from Gereon, the Tanith First-and-Only are sent to the battlefield at Sparshad Mons. With the Blood Pact pressing from all sides, and darker creatures stalking the war zone, will Gaunt and his men be victorious this time?

The Armour of Contempt: Gaunt's orders take him back to Gereon and reopen old wounds. This time the mission is one of liberation, but what cost must be paid to free the world from the Ruinous Powers?

Only in Death: On the world of Jago, Gaunt and his men are sent to defend an abandoned outpost. With the Blood Pact relentlessly on the offensive and supplies running low, the situation grows desperate. Only by facing their own ghosts can the Tanith First hope to survive…

GAUNT'S GHOSTS

The Lost

Dan Abnett

BLACK LIBRARY

A Black Library Publication

Traitor General copyright © 2004, Games Workshop Ltd.
His Last Command copyright © 2005, Games Workshop Ltd.
The Armour of Contempt copyright © 2006, Games Workshop Ltd.
Only in Death copyright © 2007, Games Workshop Ltd.
All rights reserved.

This omnibus edition published in Great Britain in 2010 by
The Black Library,
Games Workshop Ltd.,
Willow Road, Nottingham,
NG7 2WS, UK.

10 9 8 7 6 5 4 3

Cover illustration by Clint Langley.
His Last Command map by Nuala Kinrade.

A CIP record for this book is available from the British Library.

UK ISBN: 978 1 84416 818 7
US ISBN: 978 1 84416 819 4

See the Black Library on the internet at
www.blacklibrary.com

Find out more about Games Workshop
and the world of Warhammer 40,000 at
www.games-workshop.com

Printed and bound in the UK.

IT IS THE 41st millennium. For more than a hundred centuries
the Emperor has sat immobile on the Golden Throne of Earth.
He is the master of mankind by the will of the gods, and master
of a million worlds by the might of his inexhaustible armies. He
is a rotting carcass writhing invisibly with power from the Dark
Age of Technology. He is the Carrion Lord of the Imperium for
whom a thousand souls are sacrificed every day, so that he may
never truly die.

YET EVEN IN his deathless state, the Emperor continues his
eternal vigilance. Mighty battlefleets cross the daemon-infested
miasma of the warp, the only route between distant stars, their
way lit by the Astronomican, the psychic manifestation of the
Emperor's will. Vast armies give battle in his name on uncounted
worlds. Greatest amongst His soldiers are the Adeptus Astartes,
the Space Marines, bio-engineered super-warriors. Their comrades
in arms are legion: the Imperial Guard and countless Planetary
Defence Forces, the ever-vigilant Inquisition and the tech-priests
of the Adeptus Mechanicus to name only a few. But for all their
multitudes, they are barely enough to hold off the ever-present
threat from aliens, heretics, mutants – and worse.

TO BE A man in such times is to be one amongst untold
billions. It is to live in the cruellest and most bloody
regime imaginable. These are the tales of those times.
Forget the power of technology and science, for so much has
been forgotten, never to be re-learned. Forget the promise of
progress and understanding, for in the grim dark future
there is only war. There is no peace amongst the stars,
only an eternity of carnage and slaughter, and the
laughter of thirsting gods.

CONTENTS

CONTENTS

AUTHOR'S INTRODUCTION

Of Ghosts

IT SEEMS TO me that I spend an awful lot of my time surrounded by ghosts. I'm not complaining, you understand. I'm just stating a fact.

I'm not just talking about the three or four months I spend, every year or so, in the company of Tanith's finest. No, the thing is, I appear to be haunted. The house I'm living in (for the last can-you-believe-it *ten* years) is the third house in a row that's had – okay, I'm just going to come flat out and say it – a ghost. Actually, the last one I lived in had at least two, and they used to argue, but that's beside the point.

I live in a house that was built in 1812 as accommodation for an NCO in the nearby barracks, which was, at the time, a cavalry regiment. A horseman lived here, with his batman. We still have the vestiges of a copper in the basement, the old hot water boiler that the batman would use to keep his master's life ticking over.

As regular readers of my blog will know, I call the presence in my house *The Hussar*. He's not any trouble to live with. There is no ill feeling. When he's visible, it's fleetingly, at the very limit of peripheral vision. I've seen enough of him to know he wears a cavalry officer's frogged jacket.

He seems to enjoy watching, and making loud footsteps, and occasional sub-vocal utterances. He is very good at 'apports' (the random materialisation of objects), particularly keys. He also likes to make garden gates squeak. Especially when they're not *actually hung on their gate post anymore*. But that's quite another story…

I don't believe in ghosts. I like the idea of them, but I didn't grow up believing in them, and I'd never experienced anything to make me believe otherwise, until I was in my thirties, and then, like buses, three haunted houses came along in a row. It's very strange… it's not scary or even weird.

It hasn't made me question life or my place in the universe. It hasn't even made me begin to consider the notion of post-mortem survivals or the concept of supernaturality. It just *is*.

I have written most of Ibram Gaunt's adventures in this house. This is simply a coincidence. The four novels in this omnibus, which are collected under the arc title 'The Lost', were all written here, and all of them were written in the basement chamber which is my office (and where the batman's copper resides). It's a good house to write in: ghost or no ghost, it breathes its age and its tranquillity. It makes you want to sit down and quietly imagine… something. Anything. Everything.

This is a bleak arc. It starts with the intense 'Where Eagles Dare' claustrophobia of *Traitor General* (the corollary of which, *Blood Pact*, forms the start of the next arc), divides the Ghosts, gives some up for dead, reunites them, introduces the Belladon in *His Last Command*, and ends on the double whammy of *The Armour of Contempt* (which I consider to be my hardest yet most lyrical novel) and the siege/ghost story of *Only In Death*.

I am very proud of this sequence of stories. *Traitor General* is, I believe, a tight and page-turning thriller. *His Last Command* has some of the most poignant moments in *any* of my books, especially the end. *The Armour of Contempt* has the best title and is the most harrowing. *Only In Death* is… well, readers I've met have named it the best book so far. This isn't true. The best book so far is the one I'm writing, but I take the point.

It's a ghost story, you see. It's a ghost story about ghosts. It's a haunted house story. They always say, write what you know. Well, this is where I live, and this is what I know. Location informs the creator.

I hope you enjoy this collection. I think you will. The Hussar has yet to comment, but I hardly think he'd have let me write all these books, uninterrupted (almost), for this long, without approving just a little bit.

I think he recognises kindred spirits.

Dan Abnett
Maidstone, May, 2009

TRAITOR GENERAL

FOR TANITH · FOR THE EMPEROR

For Mrs Abnett
XDX

'TOWARDS THE CLOSE of 774.M41, the nineteenth year of the Sabbat Worlds Crusade, Warmaster Macaroth seemed to be consolidating the victories he had finally secured after several desperate years of tactical brinksmanship. The leading edge of the Crusade host had at last toppled the fortress world Morlond, and was now driving onwards into the Carcaradon Cluster and the Erinyes Group, to wage what Macaroth had declared, with typical arrogance, would be the final phase of the war against the Archenemy overlord ('Archon'), Urlock Gaur.

'Crucial to the prosperity of this advance was the fact that the savage attempts by two of Gaur's warlord lieutenants to bisect the Crusade force at the Khan Group had failed. Enok Innokenti's assault on Herodor had been repulsed, and Innokenti himself slain. Anakwanar Sek's counterstrikes had been denied at Lotun, Tarnagua and, most particularly, Enothis.

'But Sek and his forces remained a threat to the Crusade flank. In retreat, the magister's host had seized a tranche of worlds in the margins of the Khan Group, and dug in. Macaroth charged the Fifth, Eighth and Ninth Crusade Armies to annihilate the warlord's disposition in that region.

'Macaroth may have underestimated the scale of this endeavour. The war to dislodge Sek raged for several years, and saw some of the most massive and bloody battles of the entire Crusade. However, documents recently declassified by the Administratum reveal that one of the most vital actions during that period was undertaken on a far less monumental scale...'

– from *A History of the Later Imperial Crusades*

PROLOGUE

THE LAST OF the daylight was fading, and the fields of windflowers beyond the mansion walls had turned to violet shadow. From the terrace, in the evening cool, it was possible to see the redoubts of the Guard camps on the far side of the river, the elevated barrels of the defence batteries sticking up into the pale sky like thorns.

Barthol Van Voytz set his drink down on the terrace wall, and adjusted his fine, white gloves. They were loose. He'd lost weight since he'd last worn them for a formal occasion like this. He yearned for battlefield armour, not this ill-fitting dress uniform, starched and heavy with medals. Tomorrow, he told himself, tomorrow he could put on his wargear. Because tomorrow at oh-five thirty Imperial, the war to retake Ancreon Sextus would begin in earnest.

'My lord? The chamberlain wonders if they might begin serving dinner.'

Van Voytz turned. Biota, his chief tactical officer, stood behind him attentively. He too was gussied up in white, formal dress regalia.

'You look like a game-bird's behind in the moonlight,' said Van Voytz.

'Thank you, lord general. You are no less splendid. What shall I tell the chamberlain?'

'Are we all here?' asked Van Voytz.

'Not quite.'

'Then tell him to wait. If we're going to do this, we're going to do this right.'

They wandered back up the stone terrace together, and went in through the glass hatches. The banquet hall appeared to have been made of gold. Hundreds of yellow glow-globes lit the long room, casting everything in a golden light. Even the white cloth on the long table and the flesh of the men present seemed to be gilded.

There were forty places set at the table, and Van Voytz counted thirty-eight officers in the room. They clustered in groups, stiff in their formal attire, filling the room with the low murmur of their conversations. Van Voytz noted General Kelso of the Crusade Eighth Army, and Lord Militant Humel of the Ninth, mingling with the other regimental leaders and senior officers.

Luscheim had been killed on Tarnagua, so now Van Voytz had command of the Crusade Fifth Army. He felt the honour was overdue, and hated the fact that it had taken the death of his old friend Rudi Luscheim to make his promotion possible.

'Can we not begin, Van Voytz?' Kelso asked grumpily. He was a squat, elderly man with heavy jowls, and his brocaded dress uniform made him look even wider than he actually was.

'We're not all here yet,' Van Voytz replied. 'If we're going to endure the indignity of a formal staff dinner to mark the eve of war, we might as well make sure everyone suffers.'

Kelso chuckled. 'Who are we missing, then?'

'The commissar and commanding officer of the Tanith First, sir,' Biota said.

'Well, I suppose we could take our seats at least,' Van Voytz conceded.

Kelso gave a signal, and the assembled officers began to move to their places at the long table. Servitors passed among the company, charging glasses.

The outer door opened, and two men entered. One was a tall fellow, dressed in the uniform of an Imperial commissar. The other wore the black number one issue of his regiment.

'At last,' said Kelso.

'Gentlemen, please,' Van Voytz said, pointing the newcomers to their seats. The Tanith officers crossed to the places reserved for them.

'A toast, I think. Van Voytz?' Kelso suggested.

Van Voytz nodded and rose to his feet, glass in hand. The distinguished company rose with him, chairs scraping back.

Van Voytz considered his words for a moment. He looked across the table at the commanding officers of the Tanith regiment: Commissar Viktor Hark and Major Gol Kolea.

Van Voytz raised his glass and said: 'To absent friends.'

ONE

ON THE SIX hundred and fourth Day of Pain, the two hundred and twenty-first day of the Imperial Year 774, Gerome Landerson left his place of work at the sounding of the carnyx horn. The horn signalled the change from day-labour to night-labour.

He was weary, hungry and drenched with sweat. His arms and spine ached from swinging a hammer, and his hands were so numbed from the constant impacts that he could no longer feel his fingers. But he did not trudge towards the cookshops or the washhouses with the other day-labourers from the Iconoclave, nor did he begin the long walk back to the consented habitats along the river wall of Ineuron Town.

Instead, he walked west, down through the fractured arches of the town's old commercia. Markets had once thrived there – the daily cheaps of food-stuffs, grain, livestock, instruments – and the licensed mercantile houses had once raised their lavish silk tents and displayed the gewgaws and trinkets of their trade.

Landerson had always loved the commercia for its flavour of the faraway. He'd once bought a small metal plaque with an engraving of an Ecclesiarchy templum on Enothis just because it had travelled so far. Now the faraway seemed even more remote and unreachable, even though it was his business tonight.

The commercia was a ruin these days. What remained of the vast roof vault was smoke-blackened and rotten, and the rows of metal stalls where the traders had congregated for the daily cheaps were twisted and corroding. On the rubble-strewn ground, a few furtive dealers lurked by oilcan fires, bartering luxuries like marrowbones and bent cutlery for ration coins and consent wafers. Every time there was a hint of an excubitor patrol passing nearby, the scavengers melted away into the shadows.

Landerson walked on, trying to rub some life back into his soot-caked hands. He left the commercia via the wide flight of white marble steps, steps still riddled with the black boreholes of las-fire, and began down the Avenue of Shins. That wasn't its real name of course, but the yoke of oppression bred black humour in the conquered. This had been the Avenue of the Aquila. Long and broad, it was lined on either side by rows of ouslite plinths. The statue of an Imperial hero had once stood on each. The invaders had demolished them all. Now only splintered stone shins rose from the proud feet planted on those plinths. Hence the name.

Talix trees, tall and slender, grew along the outsides of the avenue. At least two had been decapitated and remade into gibbets for the wirewolves. There was no point trying to avoid them. Landerson walked on, trying not to look up at the skeletal mannequins hanging limply from the axl-trees on their metal strings. They creaked, swinging slightly in the breeze.

Daylight was fading. The sky, already hazy with the perpetual canopy of dust, had taken on a sheen as if a fog were closing in. To the west, the furnaces of the meat foundries glazed the low clouds with a glow the colour of pomegranate flesh. Landerson knew he had to hurry now. His imago consented him only for activity during daylight.

He was crossing the square at Tallenhall when he smelled the glyf. It stank like a discharged battery pack, an ionized scent, the tang of blood and metal. He huddled down in the overgrown hedge by the tangled iron railings and watched. The glyf appeared in the northern corner of the square, drifting like a balloon eight metres up, slow and lazy. As soon as he had located it, he tried to look away, but it was impossible. The floating sigils, bright as neon, locked his attention. He felt his stomach churn at the sight of those abominable, intertwined symbols, his gorge rising. At the back of his mind, he heard a chattering, like the sound of swarming insects rubbing their wing cases. The imago in the flesh of his left arm twitched.

The glyf wavered, then began to glide away, out of sight behind the shell of the town library. As soon as it was gone, Landerson sank onto his hands and dry-heaved violently into the burned grass. When he closed his eyes, he could see the obscene symbols shining in meaningless repeats on the back of his eyelids.

Unsteady, he rose to his feet, succumbed to a spell of giddiness, and slumped against the bent railings for support.

'Voi shet!' a hard voice barked.

He shook his head, trying to straighten up. Boots crunched across the brick dust towards him.

'Voi shet! Ecchr Anark setriketan!'

Landerson raised his hands in supplication. 'Consented! Consented, magir!'

The three excubitors surrounded him. Each was two metres tall and clad in heavy buckled boots and long coats of grey scale armour. They aimed their ornate las-locks at him.

'I am consented, magir!' he pleaded, trying to show them his imago.

One of them cuffed him down onto his knees.

'Shet atraga ydereta haspa? Voi leng haspa?'

'I... I don't speak your–'

There was a click, and a crackle of vox noise. One of them spoke again, but its coarse words were obscured by a rasping mechanical echo.

'What is your purpose here?'

'I am consented to pass in daylight, magir,' he answered.

'Look at me!' Again, the barbarous tongue was overlaid with augmetically-generated speech.

Landerson looked up. The excubitor leaning over him was as hellish as any of its kind. Only the upper half of its head was visible – pale, shrivelled and hairless. A dripping cluster of metal tubes and pipes sprouted from the back of its wrinkled skull and connected to the steaming, panting support box strapped across its back. Three huge, sutured scars split its face, one down through each eye socket – in which augmetic ocular mounts were now sewn – and the third straight down over the bridge of a nose from which all flesh had been debrided. A large brass collar rose in front of the face, mercifully obscuring the excubitor's mouth and most of the nasal area. The front of this collar mounted a wire-grilled speaking box, which the excubitor had switched to 'translate'.

'I... I look upon you, and I am graced by your beauty,' Landerson gasped as clearly as he could.

'Name?' the thing snapped.

'Landerson, Gerome, consented of day, b-by the will of the Anarch.'

'Place of industry?'

'The Iconoclave, magir.'

'You work in the Breaking House?'

'Yes, magir.'

'Display to me your consent!'

Landerson lifted his left arm and drew back the sleeve of his torn workcoat to reveal the imago in its blister of clear pus.

'Eletraa kyh drowk!' the excubitor said to one of its companions.

'Chee ataah drowk,' came the reply. The sentinel drew a long metal tool from its belt, the size and shape of a candle-snuffer, and placed the cup over Landerson's imago. Landerson gasped as he felt the thing in his flesh writhe. Small runes lit up on the shank of the tool. The cup withdrew.

The third excubitor grabbed Landerson by the head and turned it roughly so as to better examine the stigma on his left cheek.

'Fehet gahesh,' it said, letting him go.

'Go home, interceded one,' the first excubitor told Landerson, the machine words back-echoed by the alien speech. 'Go home and do not let us catch you out here again.'

'Y-yes, magir. At once.'

'Or we will have sport with you. Us, or the wirewolves.'

'I understand, magir. Thank you.'

The excubitor stepped back. It covered the grille of its speaking box with one hand. Its brethren did the same.

'We serve the word of the Anarch, whose word drowns out all others.'

Landerson covered his own mouth quickly. 'Whose word drowns out all others,' he repeated quickly.

The excubitors looked at him for a moment longer, then shouldered their massive las-locks and walked away across the overgrown square.

It was a long while before Landerson had recovered enough to get back on his feet.

IT WAS ALMOST dark when he reached the abandoned mill at the edge of the town. The dimming sky was lit by fires: the burning masses of the distant hives and the closer glows of the ahenum furnaces that powered the town's new industries. On the wide roadway below the mill, torches were bobbing and drums were beating. Another procession of proselytes was being led to the shrines by the ordinals.

Landerson tapped on the wooden door.

'How is Gereon?' asked a voice from within.

'Gereon lives,' Landerson replied.

'Despite their efforts,' the voice responded. The door swung open, revealing only darkness. Landerson peered in.

Then he felt the nudge of an autopistol muzzle against the back of his head.

'You're late.'

'I ran into trouble.'

'It had better not have followed you.'

'No, sir.'

'Step in, nice and easy.'

Landerson edged into the darkness. A light came on, in his face.

'Check him!' a voice said, as the door swung closed behind him.

Hands grabbed him and hustled him forward. The paddle of an auspex buzzed as it was passed up and down his body.

'Clean!' someone said.

The hands withdrew. Landerson squinted into the light, resolving his surroundings. A dank cellar of the old mill, figures all around, flashlights aimed his way.

Colonel Ballerat stepped into the light, holstering his pistol.

'Landerson,' he said.

'Good to see you, sir,' Landerson, replied.

Ballerat moved forward and embraced Landerson. He did so with only one hand. Ballerat's left arm and left leg had been ripped away in the foundries. He had a crude prosthetic that allowed him to walk, but his left arm was just a nub.

'I'm relieved you got the message.' Ballerat smiled. 'I was beginning to worry you hadn't.'

'I got it all right,' Landerson said. 'Dropped into my food pail. It was difficult getting away. Is it tonight, sir?'

Ballerat nodded. 'Yes, it is. They're definitely down. We need to make contact so we can move to the next stage.'

Landerson nodded. 'How many, sir?'

'How many what?' Ballerat asked.

'I mean… what sort of numbers, sir? Disposition? What sort of size is the liberation force?'

Ballerat paused. 'We… we don't know yet, major. Working on that. The key thing right now is to make contact with their recon advance so we can lead them in.'

'Understood, sir.'

'I'm sending you, Lefivre and Purchason.'

'I know them both, sir. Good men. We served in the PDF together.'

Ballerat smiled. 'That's what I thought. So you know the area well. Rendezvous is an agri-complex at the Shedowtonland Crossroads. Contact code is "Tanith Magna".'

Landerson repeated the words. 'What does that mean, sir?'

Ballerat shrugged. 'Damned if I know. A Guard code. Ah, here they come.'

Lefivre and Purchason approached. Both were dressed in the ragged, scrabbled-together remnants of PDF combat gear. Lefivre was a short, blond man with a scrappy beard. Purchason was taller, leaner and dark-haired. Both shook hands with Landerson. Both carried silenced autorifles.

Another member of the resistance hurried over with a set of fatigues, equipment and weapons for Landerson. Crouching, Landerson began to sort through the stuff.

'That can wait,' Ballerat said. 'We have to strip you out first, son.'

Landerson nodded and rose to his feet. Ballerat led him into an adjoining chamber that stank of animals, chyme and dung. The air was warm and heavy. Landerson could hear grox snorting and farting in the gloom.

'Ready?' Ballerat asked him.

'I'd just like to get it over with, sir,' Landerson said. He pulled up the sleeve of his left arm.

Several other men appeared and took him by the shoulders, holding him tight. One offered him a bottle of amasec. Landerson took a deep swig. 'Good boy,' the man said. 'Helps dull the pain. Now bite on this. You'll need it.'

Landerson bit down hard on the leather belt that was pushed into his mouth.

The chirurgeon was a woman, an old lady from the habs. She smiled at Landerson, who was now pinned by four men, and poured more amasec over the imago.

Landerson felt it squirm.

'They don't like that at all,' the chirurgeon muttered. 'It numbs them. Makes them sleepy, dull. Makes them easier to withdraw. Steel yourself, boy.'

She produced a scalpel, and quickly slit open the huge blister on his forearm. It popped, and viscous fluid poured out. Landerson bit down. It hurt already. The coiled black thing in the meat of his arm, now exposed, fidgeted and tightened in the sore, red cavity. He tried not to look, but he could not help it.

The chirurgeon reached in with long-handled tweezers.

She began to pull. Most of the glistening black grub came away in the first tug, but the long, barbed tail, dark and thorned like razor-wire, resisted. She pulled more firmly and Landerson bit down harder, feeling his flesh tear. The grub began to squirm and wriggle between the tips of the tweezers. Agony pulsed down Landerson's arm. It felt like a barbed fishing line was being drawn out down an artery.

The chirurgeon doused the wound with more alcohol, and yanked hard. Landerson bit through the belt. The whipping grub tore free, jiggling at the end of her surgical tool.

'Now!' she cried.

One of Ballerat's men had already slit open the haunch of one of the grox in the stalls. The old woman stabbed the twitching grub into the wound, and then, as she released it, clamped the wound shut with a wadding of anaesthotape and bandage.

She held it tight, fighting as if something was trying to get out from under the wadding.

'We're all right,' she said finally. 'I think it's taken.'

Everyone fell silent for a few long minutes, listening intently for the sound of an excubitor alarm or worse. Landerson realised he was shaking hard. The old woman beckoned to one of the men to hold the wadding tight to the animal's flank, and came over to Landerson to bind his wound.

She cleaned it carefully, sealed it, bandaged it, and then gave him a shot of painkillers and counterseptic agents.

Landerson began to feel a little better, though he was slightly distressed to note an odd sensation of absence. All those months, longing to be rid of the foul, twitching thing under his skin, and now his body seemed to miss the imago.

'Are you feeling all right?' Ballerat asked him, emerging from the shadows.

'Yes, sir,' Landerson lied.

'I'd like to give you more time to recover, but we don't have it. Set to move?'

Landerson nodded.

Ballerat showed him a crumpled, hand-drawn map. 'Take a moment to study this. Memorise it, because I can't let you take it. This is the route I suggest you follow. These are the times and locations of the patrols we know about.'

Landerson studied the information hard, looking away from time to time and then back at the map to test his recall. Then Ballerat handed him an envelope, and Landerson glanced inside.

'What's this for?' he asked.

'You never know,' the colonel replied. Landerson put the envelope inside his jacket.

'Right,' said Ballerat, nodding Lefivre and Purchason over to join them. 'Rendezvous is set for twenty-three fifteen. Find out what they need from us and do your best to provide it. Contact with us is via the usual methods. We'll be staging a diversion event about forty minutes prior to rendezvous that should draw surplus attention away from your zone. Any questions?'

The three men shook their heads.

Ballerat couldn't make the full sign of the aquila, but he placed his right hand over his heart as if he were. 'Good fortune, and for the sake of Gereon, may the Emperor protect you.'

THE NIGHT WAS cool and damp. Landerson had almost forgotten how it felt to be outside in the dark. They made good progress out of Ineuron Town, smuggling themselves through the western palisades, and then headed out across the old ornamental park called the Ambulatory. The lights of the town flickered behind them, and once in a while they heard distant horns and kettle drums.

The bloodiest phase of the battle for Ineuron Town had been fought around the precincts of the Ambulatory and the ground, now fully overgrown, was littered with machine debris and pathetic scatters of human bone. The three men made no sound. Ballerat hadn't picked them for this mission simply because of their local knowledge. All three had been in the ranger-recon brigade of the PDF.

Halfway across the Ambulatory they had to take cover behind a thicket of juvenile talix trees as a patrol went by: two half-tracks, blazing with hunting spotlights, the lead one resembling an ice sled because of the long string of fetch-hounds straining ahead of it on chains. The animals growled and rasped, pulling at their harnesses. They were trained to scent imagos and also human pheromones. The last thing Landerson and his companions had done before leaving the mill was stand under a crude gravity shower that soaked them with scent-repellers.

The patrol moved away. Landerson signalled the other two men forward. He used the sign language fluently, like his last ranger-recon mission had been the day before. But he noticed that his left arm felt curiously light. Had the old woman got it all out? Or was there some piece of the grub still inside him, yearning for–

Landerson dismissed the thought. If even a scrap of the imago had been left behind, corposant would be crackling over every gibbet in the town and the wirewolves would be gathering.

They left the Ambulatory, and picked their way through the silent ruins of the tiered hab blocks that ran down the slopes of Mexley Hill. This suburb was an agriculture district, marking the point at which the heavy industry of the inner conurbations gave way to the farmland disciplines of the town's rural skirts. Behind the habs, strips of crop fields were laid out across the hillside and over into the next valley. Landerson could smell silage, plant rot, and the distinctive perfume of canterwheat. But the crop, unharvested, had gone over, and the smell was unpleasantly strong, with a sickly tinge of fermentation.

Purchason stopped dead and signed a warning. The trio melted into cover behind the yard wall at the rear of one of the habs.

Thirty metres away, a glyf hung, almost stationary, above the lane.

In the dark, the glyf was even more terrifying than the one that had passed Landerson by in daylight. Its coiled, burning symbols seemed to writhe like snakes, forming one unholy rune then another, bright against the night sky as if they were written in liquid flame. Landerson could hear it crackling like a log fire. He could hear the thick, nauseating insect noise. This time, he managed to look away.

He was suddenly aware of Lefivre next to him. The man was shaking badly. Glancing round, Landerson saw that his companion had his eyes locked on the infernal glyf. Tears were trickling from eyes that refused to blink. Landerson reached out quickly and took Lefivre's weapon just moments before it slithered out of the man's nerveless hands. In the half light, he could see Lefivre's jaw working and his adam's apple bobbing. Lefivre's lips were pinched and white. He was fighting not to scream, but it was a fight he was about to lose.

Landerson clamped his hand over Lefivre's mouth. Realising what was happening, Purchason grabbed Lefivre too, hugging him tight to keep him upright and pin his arms. Landerson felt Lefivre's mouth grind open, and squeezed his hand tighter, fighting back a cry as Lefivre's teeth bit into his palm.

The glyf trembled. The insect noise increased, purring, then sank away. The glyf drifted off to the north, hissing over the shattered roofs of the hab terrace and then away across the park. Landerson and Purchason maintained their grip on Lefivre. Ten seconds later, five excubitors ran past along the lane, heading towards the town. The glyf had found something, and now the patrol was drawing in. After a few minutes, they heard the dull bark of las-locks discharging.

Some poor unconsented, no doubt, hiding in the rambles of the park.

Landerson realised he was now unconsented too.

He took his hand away. Blood pattered onto the stony path. Lefivre slumped over, panting like a dog. In his terror, he'd lost control of his bladder.

'I'm sorry... I'm sorry...' he gasped.

'It's fine,' Landerson whispered.

'Your hand...'

'It's fine,' Landerson repeated. His hand really hurt. Lefivre had bitten a large chunk out of his palm. Now he smelled of blood, Lefivre smelled of piss, and they all stank of the sweat the tension had engulfed them in.

Landerson wrapped his hand in his neck cloth, and prayed they would not meet any fetch-hounds.

IT WAS ALMOST twenty-two thirty when they reached the Shedowtonland Crossroads. Left untended and unirrigated, the paddies had dried up, and now great areas of fertile land were reduced to caked mud mouldering with neglected, blighted crops. The air was ripe with mildew and corruption.

Thunder rolled in the distance, out beyond the agriculture belt, out in the untamed swampland of the Untill. Once, those miasmal regions had been seen as danger zones. Now, post intercession, they seemed safe compared to the populated areas.

They skirted wide round the bulky prefabs of the agri-complex and then turned back into them, weapons ready, long suppressor tubes fixed. They crept through the shadows, between immobilised tractor units and dredge-harvesters in the low garages, and on past iron pens where swine had been slaughtered and left to decompose. More than once they disturbed carrion mammals feeding on refuse, local fauna lured out of the swamps by the scent of decay. Squalling, the small creatures bushed their tails up and started off into the darkness.

Lefivre was still spooked. He swung his gun at every last forager.

'You gotta calm down,' Landerson whispered.

'I know.'

'Really, friend. Deep breaths. I can't have you jumping.'

'No, major. Of course not.'

Apart from the foragers, there were rats everywhere. Everywhere in the Imperium, Landerson imagined. The starships of Holy Terra had spread many things across the galaxy – faith, colonists, technology, civilisation – but nothing so comprehensively or so surely as the indomitable *rattus rattus*. Before the Intercession, he had heard learned men joke that the Imperium was actually forged by rats, and humans were just along for the ride. On some worlds, the accidentally imported rat had overmastered all other life forms. On other worlds, they had interbred and created monsters.

The three men completed a circuit check, and found nothing except some sickening runes daubed on the outer fence that might have been charged to become glyfs. Landerson didn't want to risk it, so he doused each one he found with the flask of consecrated water that had been issued as part of his kit.

Purchason helped. Lefivre held back. He didn't want to look at the marks. He didn't want his mind to lapse that way again.

They reached the main buildings. It was twenty-two thirty-seven. Pretty much on cue, they heard a boom from the town behind them. A fiery glow slowly rose into the sky. Then a buzzing filled the air. In the valley below them, they saw glyfs floating like ball lightning, drawn to the commotion.

The colonel's diversion was underway.

'Emperor protect you,' Landerson muttered.

Landerson checked the main door. It was unlocked. Weapon braced, he crouched his way in as Lefivre pushed the door open. Purchason stood to his left, rifle raised to cover.

The prefab hallway was dark. There was an intense smell of dry fertilizer. Rats scurried.

Landerson signalled Lefivre to watch the door, then he and Purchason swept up the hallway, covering each other door by door. The place was deserted. Chairs and tables were overturned, agricultural cogitators smashed, seed incubators and nursery racks destroyed.

There was a dim light ahead. Cautiously, they prowled on, signing to each other, weapons set. The light was coming from a central office area. A single candle, guttering on a desk.

Landerson glanced at Purchason. Purchason shook his head. He had no idea what was going on either.

They slid inside. The room was empty apart from broken furniture and the desk with the candle. The windows were locked. There was only one door.

'This is the place,' said Landerson as loudly as he dared.

'What the hell's that candle about? Are they here already?'

Landerson looked around for a second time. 'I don't know,' he whispered. 'Go check on Lefivre.'

Purchason nodded and slid back out into the hallway. Landerson stood by the desk, his weapon aimed at the doorway. A minute passed. Two. His hands began to sweat.

He heard a faint noise.

'Purchason?' he called quietly.

The candle suddenly went out. An arm locked about his body, pinning his weapon. He felt a blade at his throat.

'Say it now and say it right,' said a voice in his ear.

'T-tanith Magna...'

The grip released.

Landerson turned in the darkness, terrified.

'Where are you?' he gasped.

'Still here,' the voice said, behind him again. Landerson switched round.

'What are you doing?' he breathed. 'Show yourself!'

'All in good time. You got a name?' The voice was behind him yet again. Landerson froze.

'Major Gerome Landerson, Gereon PDF.'

There was a click of tinder sticks and the candle on the desk relit. Landerson swung round to look at it, gun raised. The candle fluttered, solitary. There was no sign of whoever had lit it.

'Stop it!' Landerson said. 'Where are you?'

'Right here.' Landerson froze as he felt the cold muzzle of a weapon rest against the back of his neck. 'Put the gun down.'

Landerson gently placed his silenced rifle on the desk.

'How did you get in?' he whispered.

'I was here all the time.'

'But I searched the room–'

'Not well enough.'

'Who are you?'

'My name is Mkoll. Sergeant of scouts, Tanith First-and-Only.'

'Could you take the gun off my neck?'

A man appeared in the candlelight in front of Landerson. He was short, compact, shrouded in a camouflage cloak that seemed to melt into the darkness. 'I could,' he said softly, 'if it was my gun. Ven? Let the poor guy off the leash.'

The pressure of the gun-muzzle went away. Landerson glanced round and saw the second man. Just a shadow in the extremity of the candlelight. Taller than the first, a murmur of a shape.

'W-what are you?' Landerson stammered. 'Ghosts?'

By the light of the single candle flame, Landerson saw the eyes of the man calling himself Mkoll crinkle and glint. A smile. That was the most unnerving thing of all, for clearly this was a face unaccustomed to smiles.

'You could say that,' Mkoll said.

TWO

THEY LED LANDERSON back into the yard. The amber glow in the sky was still bright and defined. He could feel the distant agitation of the enemy on the night air, like the balmy pressure of a closing storm.

Lefivre and Purchason were on their knees facing the stockade fence, hands behind their heads. A third soldier in black stood watch over them.

'Bonin?' Mkoll asked.

'These seem to be the only other two, sir,' the third soldier replied.

'Three of you, is that correct?' Mkoll asked.

'Yes,' said Landerson. He heard the muffled click of a vox-com. 'One, this is four. Move in,' Mkoll said quickly. Then he glanced at the tall man. 'Mkvenner? Take Bonin and secure the perimeter.'

Mkoll's two comrades moved off and disappeared into the darkness at once. Then other shapes loomed, detaching themselves from the night. At least a half-dozen figures. The tallest strode right up to Landerson and looked him up and down. He was a lean, powerful man dressed in black boots and fatigues, a black leather jacket, and a dark camo-cloak wrapped tightly around his throat and upper body. There was a pack on his back, and a soot-dulled bolt pistol strapped across his chest in a combat rig. Under the brim of his plain, black-cloth cap, his face was slender and sharp.

'Which one is the leader?' he asked.

'I am,' said Landerson. He froze as he felt the man Mkoll lean close to his ear. 'Under the circumstances, I advise you not to speak unless we give you permission,' Mkoll said.

Landerson nodded.

'Say to him what you said to me,' Mkoll instructed.

'Tanith Magna,' Landerson said quietly.

'Tell him your name.'

'Landerson. Major Landerson.'

'And address him as sir,' Mkoll added.

'Sir.'

The tall man in the cap made the sign of the aquila and then saluted. 'Major,' he said. 'My name is Gaunt. I have command of this operation. You're in the right place at the right time and you've given the correct code, so I'll presume for the moment you're the man I've come to see. You've been instructed to meet us by the commander of the Ineuron cell.'

Landerson swallowed. 'I have liberty to discuss certain things, sir. They don't include the possible activities, movements or even existence of any resistance cells.'

'Fair point,' said Gaunt. 'But the next stage of our business involves establishing contact with a colonel called Ballerat, or any of his chief officers.'

'Regard me as such, and then we'll review,' Landerson replied.

A man appeared at Gaunt's side. He was shorter than Gaunt, but a little more robustly proportioned, as dark as Gaunt was fair. There seemed to Landerson something sleekly cruel about the man's face.

'Want me to beat the crap out of him, sir?'

'Not at this stage,' Gaunt replied.

'Just to loosen his tongue, you understand.'

'Wouldn't want you to get your hands dirty, Rawne.'

The man smiled. It was not a little chilling. 'I wouldn't. I'd get Feygor to do it.'

'Full marks for delegation. Now step off, Rawne.'

The man shrugged and walked away. Landerson could see the others now, quite plainly. There were seven of them, apart from Mkoll, Rawne and the commander, all dressed in black camo-gear and packs. Most of them were tattooed. A large, rough-looking man hefted an autocannon; a slight, older fellow carried a marksman's weapon. The four other troopers had lasrifles. The seventh, Landerson realised, was a female. She too was clad in pitch-black combat gear, but the only weapon she carried was a compact autopistol in a holster.

Gaunt looked at Landerson. 'Major, in your estimation, how long can we remain here safely?'

'Another thirty minutes would be pushing it.'

'Do you have secure fall-back positions?'

'I know a place or two where we could avoid the patrols.'

'And they're safe?'

Landerson stared at him. 'Sir, this is Gereon. Nowhere is safe.'

'Then let's get on with this,' Gaunt said. 'Doctor. Check them out, please.'

The woman moved forward, pulled off her pack and produced a small narthecium scanner. She began to play it across Landerson.

'Lily of Thrace,' said Landerson.

'What?' she asked, stopping and looking at him.

'Your perfume. Lily of Thrace. Am I right?'

'I haven't used perfume or cologne for three weeks,' she said firmly. 'Part of the mission prep–'

'I'm sure you haven't,' said Landerson. 'But I can still smell it. That, and counterseptics, and sterile rinse. The fetch-hounds would have you in a second.'

'That's enough,' said Mkoll. The woman shook her head at the scout and stared at Landerson. 'These... hounds. They'd detect my scent even though I have been scrupulous not to use anything that might give me away?'

'Yes, mamzel. You're too clean. All of you.'

'These hounds would find me because I don't smell like shit, like you?'

'Exactly, mamzel. Gereon gets in the pores. Into the flesh. The smoke, the dust, the taint.'

'Speaking of taint,' the woman said, reading her scanner. 'You have elevated B-proteins and a high leucocyte count. What exactly has been bonded to your metabolism?'

Mkoll immediately raised his rifle and aimed it at the side of Landerson's head.

'I'm going to show her my arm,' Landerson said, very aware of the gun barrel pointing into his ear. He raised his left sleeve and revealed the bandage. 'The Archenemy brands all citizens with an imago. I've had mine removed, so have Purchason and Lefivre. Can they get up, by the way? I'm not really happy with the way you're depriving my men of their liberty at this point.'

'Want me to get Feygor?' Mkoll muttered.

'No,' said Gaunt. 'Is he clean, Curth?'

'Clean is a strong word. In so many ways,' said the woman. 'But... yes, I'd say so.'

'Check the other two. If they're clean, get them up. Major Landerson, walk with me.'

Gaunt led him back into the prefab, down to the room where the candle still burned.

'Have a seat,' he offered.

'I'll stand, sir.'

Gaunt frowned, and sat down himself.

'What is your rank, sir?' Landerson asked.

'Colonel-Commissar.'

Landerson felt his heart skip slightly. 'I see. You're very cautious.'

'I'm landing a mission team on a Chaos-held world, Landerson. Do you blame me?'

'No, sir, I suppose I don't. How did you reach the surface?'

'I don't think I'm going to tell you that.'

'Uh huh. Can you tell me your force disposition?'

'I shouldn't do that either, not until I trust you a little better. But you can count.'

'I've counted a dozen of you.'

Gaunt said nothing. The candle fluttered.

Landerson nodded to himself. 'The advance party. I understand that. I also understand you're not going to tell me anything about the main force, where they're concealed, what armour they've got, but–'

'But?'

'At least tell me when it's going to start.'

'When what's going to start, major?'

'The liberation, sir.'

Gaunt looked up at him. 'Liberation?'

'Yes, sir.'

Gaunt sighed. 'I think,' he began, choosing his words, 'I think perhaps the understandably tortuous lines of communication between the Gereon resistance cells and Guard Intelligence have been even less adequate than we'd hoped.'

'I don't understand,' said Landerson.

'Twelve mission specialists, major. Twelve. You've seen them all, you've counted them yourself. We're not the advance. We're it.'

'Sir?'

'No one else is coming. We're not meeting here tonight to pave a way for a triumphant liberation army. Your priority is to link with my team and get us underground so we can achieve our mission parameters.'

Landerson felt a slight buzzing in his head. A dizziness. He pulled a chair out from the table and sat down heavily.

'I don't understand,' he repeated. 'I thought–'

'I realise what you thought. I'm sorry to disabuse your hopes. We're all that's coming, major. Now I need you to do your part and get us inside. Can you do that?'

Landerson shook his head.

'Is that a no?'

'No, no.' Landerson looked up. 'I just… it's not what I was expecting. It's not what anyone was… I mean, I assumed. The colonel said… I…' He tailed off. 'What mission?'

'I'm not going to tell you that either, Landerson. Not even going to hint until I know you better. Even then, maybe not. I'm as scared of what you might be as you are of what I might be. Let's not fight about it. Right now, I need you to do as you were instructed so we can get on. I can tell you that I need to establish face contact with Ballerat, or his proxy, or with the leader of another cell in the Ineuron Town region. I can also tell you that, unless any senior resistance contact can inform me otherwise, I'm going to need a clear and secret line of deployment to the Lectica heartland. And I can tell you that my mission parameters were given to me directly by Lord General Barthol Van Voytz of the Crusade Fifth Army, as ratified and instructed personally by Warmaster Macaroth himself.'

'This is so much shit,' snapped Landerson, rising.

'Sit down.'

'This isn't what we need! This isn't what Gereon was waiting for–'

'Sit. Down.'

Landerson turned to face Gaunt, his fingers curled like hooks, tears in his eyes. 'You come here with this crap? Some half-arsed stealth mission that you can't breathe a word of? Screw you! We've suffered! We've died! Millions have died! Do you know what those bastards have done to us?'

'Yes,' said Gaunt quietly.

'I don't bloody think so! The invasion? The slaughter? The extermination camps? The things they buried in our flesh to keep us tame? The foul propaganda they blast from the speakers every hour of the day and night? The few of us left who can think straight, the bloody few of us, risking our lives every day to keep the resistance alive! A raid here, a bombing there, comrades massacred, dragged off for interrogation or worse! What kept us going, do you suppose? What the hell kept us going?'

'The thought of liberation.'

'The thought of liberation! Yes, sir! Yes screw-you sir! Every day! Every day for six hundred and four days! Six hundred and bloody five now! Days of Pain! We have a calendar! A bloody calendar! Six hundred and five days of pain and death and torment–'

'Landerson–'

'Do you know what I do?' Landerson asked, wiping his mouth, his hands shaking. 'Do you know what the bloody ordinals make me do? I am consented to work in the Iconoclave! Do you know what that means?'

'No,' said Gaunt.

'It means I am allowed to go to what was the town hall for twelve hours every day and use a sledgehammer to break up any symbols of the Imperium that the bastards drag in! Statues... plaques... standards... insignia... I have to pound them to scrap and rubble! And they allow me to do this! They permit me! It's seen as a special honour for those of us consented to do it! A perk! A trustee's luxury! Because it's that or file into the maws of the meat foundries and, you know, somehow I'd rather splinter a statue of Saint Kiodrus into chippings than be dragged off there!'

'I understand–' Gaunt began.

'No, you don't!'

Gaunt raised his black-gloved hands. 'No, I don't. I don't begin to understand what that's like. I don't begin to understand the pain, the misery, the torment. And I certainly don't understand the choices you've had to make. But I do understand your disappointment.'

'Yeah?' laughed Landerson, bitterly.

Gaunt nodded. 'You wanted us to be your salvation. You thought we were the front markers of a crusade force come to free you. We're not, and I can understand why that hurts.'

'What do you know?'

'I know I left a world to Chaos once.'

'What happened to it?' Landerson asked quietly.

'What do you think? It died. But the few men I saved from it have now spared a thousandfold more Imperial citizens from suffering than I would have managed if I'd stayed there.'

Landerson stared at the candle flame.

'Some of those men are with me here tonight,' said Gaunt. 'Look, major. This is the Imperium of Man. There is only war. It has edges and corners, and all of them are hard. If I could save Gereon, I would, but I can't and that's not why I'm here. Gereon must continue to suffer. In time, there may be a liberation effort. It's not for me to say. Right here, right now, I have a mission. Its success is important to Lord General Van Voytz, to Warmaster Macaroth, and to the Imperium. Which means it's important to the God-Emperor himself. What I have to do here is bigger than Gereon.'

'Damn you to hell.'

'Very likely. But it's true. If my team fails here, we're talking about the possible failure of the entire Sabbat Crusade. One hundred inhabited systems, Landerson. Would you like them all to end up like Gereon?'

Landerson sat down again.

'What,' he whispered. 'What do you want me to do?'

'I'd like you to–' Gaunt paused and put his hand up to the micro-bead vox plug in his ear. 'Beltayn, this is one. What do you have?'

He listened for a moment, then rose to his feet. 'We'll have to finish this later, major,' he said.

'Why?' asked Landerson, getting to his feet too.

'Because something's awry.'

OUTSIDE, EVERYONE HAD disappeared. Landerson felt a slight rise of panic, but Gaunt strode out into the yard. As if conjured by some sorcery, Mkoll appeared from nowhere.

'Report?'

'Movement on the road. Perimeter is secure.'

'Have we made them?'

'I'm waiting for Mkvenner and Bonin now, sir,' Mkoll whispered.

'Where are the–' Gaunt paused. Landerson knew he'd been about to say prisoners. 'Where are the major's associates?'

'Varl's moved them to the shed there,' Mkoll pointed.

'Take the major to join them,' Gaunt instructed.

'I can be more use here,' said Landerson.

'Major, this is n–'

'Do you know what you're facing?'

Gaunt breathed deeply. 'All right, with me. Stick close. Do exactly what Mkoll and I tell you.'

They headed for the gateway. Landerson realised that two of the visitors – the man with the marksman's rifle and the devil who'd offered to beat him up – were concealed by the fence stakes, wrapped in their camo-capes. He didn't see them at all until he was right on them.

Landerson ducked low and tucked in behind Gaunt and Mkoll as they went up the ditch to the road wall.

The vox pipped. Mkoll listened and replied softly.

'Two carriers, coming this way. Ven counts twenty-three heads. Dogs too, in a chained pack.'

'Standard mechanised patrol,' whispered Landerson. 'It wasn't on my expected schedule.'

'They know we're here?' asked Gaunt.

'I doubt it, sir. If they knew there were insurgents at this location, they'd have beefed up the numbers. We staged a diversion in the town tonight to distract from this meeting, but there was always the chance they'd step up the patrols as a consequence. The enemy is not stupid.'

'That's been my experience too,' said Gaunt darkly.

'You don't want an open firefight with a patrol,' Landeron said.

'Delighted to see you grasping the meaning of the phrase "stealth mission",' said Gaunt. 'We need to peel out and find a back door. What's that way?'

'Agricultural land. Field systems. Too open.'

'That way? Over there?'

'Open ground for about five hundred metres, then woods.'

'We'll take the woods,' said Mkoll.

Gaunt nodded.

'Make it fast,' said Landerson. 'Once the fetch-hounds have your scent – and they will get your scent – we're screwed.'

'Let's get going,' said Gaunt, and Mkoll turned and simply vanished into the night. Landerson followed Gaunt back down the ditch to the gate.

'Up and out that way, Rawne,' Gaunt said. 'Lead them out. Head for the woods.'

'On it.'

'Larks?' Gaunt said, turning to the marksman.

'Sir?'

'You'll be out last with Ven. Cover us. But remember engagement rules. Keep your finger off that trigger unless there's no other choice.'

'Yes, sir.'

'The Emperor protects, Larks,' Gaunt said and moved Landerson into the yard. Purchason and Lefivre were coming out of the shed escorted by two of Gaunt's troopers.

'I request you return our weapons,' said Landerson.

'I will, if you promise not to use them,' Gaunt said.

'Still grasping that meaning, colonel-commissar.'

'Good,' said Gaunt. 'Varl?'

One of the troopers came over. His broadly grinning face was smeared with filth.

'Fall on your face?' Gaunt asked.

'Pig dung,' said Varl. 'I fething hate dogs. I'd rather they smelled you first.'

'Your loyalty knows no beginning, Varl. Give these men back their weapons.'

'Sir.'

Landerson immediately felt more confident with his muzzled autorifle back in his hands. He followed Gaunt and the others to the perimeter fence, climbed it, and dropped into the waste ground beyond. They all started to run towards the dim treeline half a kilometre away.

The ground was rough and scrubby, thick with ground vine and fronds of cupwort. Landerson glanced back. Beyond the fence and the silhouette of the agri-complex, he saw the twitching radiance of lights on the road.

He should have been looking where he was going. The loop of ground vine yanked his ankle and he went down on his face.

'Get up, you clumsy gak!' a voice hissed at him, and Landerson was pulled to his feet. It was the other trooper who'd been guarding his men with Varl. He was a she.

'Move it or I knife you and leave you!' the female trooper snarled.

Landerson ran after her.

They reached the trees. The thick canopy cut out what little ambient light the night sky provided. It was as dark as the void. The woman made no sound as she moved through the knee-deep vegetation. Landerson felt like he was making as much noise as a charging foot patrol.

'Down!' she said.

He got down. There was silence, apart from the breeze in the leaves, and a distant engine note coming from the agri-complex.

As his eyes adjusted, Landerson saw Gaunt's team was all around him, in cover, weapons raised.

'How long before your point men pull out?' Landerson whispered.

'They already have,' said Gaunt. Landerson realised the marksman and the tall, thin scout were with them. How in the name of Holy Terra had they done that?

They heard the sound of dogs on the night air. Eager, frantic, whining and howling.

Landerson knew that sound.

'They've got the scent,' he whispered, his heart sinking.

'Feth!' spat Gaunt.

'Lily of Thrace, I suppose,' said the female medic.

Landerson shook his head. 'No. Blood. Blood is the one thing they fix onto more than anything else.' He held up his hand. His fall had torn the bandage off the bindings, and blood was weeping again from the bite in his palm.

'I'm sorry, sir.' He rose to his feet. 'Get your men away. I'll draw them off.'

'No,' said Gaunt.

'It's me they've scented. I–'

'No,' Gaunt repeated. 'If they've got us, they'll be on us all night, no matter how heroic and stupid you decide to be. We'll end this quickly here and get clear before anyone comes looking for a missing patrol.'

'You're mad,' said Landerson simply.

'Yes, but I'm also in charge.' He looked round at the mission team. 'Straight silver. Let the dogs come and do them first. Then switch live and take out the rest. Understood?'

A whispered chorus of affirmatives answered him.

'For Tanith. For the Emperor.'

The sound of the dogs grew louder. Down by the agri-complex, an engine revved and a section of the outer fence stoved out and collapsed, driven down by the front fender of a large half-track. Its spotlights blazed out across the waste ground. Around it, through the gap, the unleashed hounds dashed out.

They were big. Some kind of semi-feral mastiff breed sired in the holds of the Archenemy fleet. A dozen of them, each one so thickly muscled it weighed more than an adult human male. They could hear their paws thumping on the rough ground, hear their slavering growls.

Gaunt slid out a long silver dagger dulled with soot.

'Let them in,' he whispered. 'Let them come right in…'

The first bounding animal crashed through the treeline, heavy and stinking with spittle. Landerson heard it barking, heard it–

Whine. A meaty thump. An interrupted whimper.

The next came, and then the next. Two more frenzied dog-voices suddenly stilled away in pathetic squeals.

Then the rest. The other eight. One came in through the tree trunks right for Landerson. He saw its dull eyes, its gaping, wretched maw, the fleshy, drooling lips bouncing with the impact of its stride. He gasped out and raised his weapon.

Two metres from Landerson, as it began the pouncing leap that would bring him down, it jerked sideways in the air. Using his lasrifle like a spear, Mkoll wrestled the hound to the ground on his bayonet. It howled and writhed. He put a foot on its distended belly to free the blade, and lanced it twice more.

Around him, Landerson heard a quick series of dull, wet impacts, like ripe fruit being hacked by a machete. One human cry of pain.

A moment's pause.

'All done?' Gaunt asked, wiping dog-blood off his warknife.

'Clear. They're done,' Mkvenner replied from nearby.

'Everyone all right?'

'Fething dog bit me!' complained Varl in a whisper.

'Must've liked the idea of pig for dinner,' replied the female trooper who had dragged Landerson up.

'Imagine my surprise that he didn't go for you then, Criid,' Varl said.

'That's great. Talk some more so the enemy knows where the feth we are,' said the man Gaunt had called Rawne.

'Here they come,' said Mkoll, his voice just loud enough to be heard.

'Safeties off,' said Gaunt. 'Mkoll. Circle the scouts round to the right and pincer. Brostin, Larkin? The transports. Ana? Keep your head down please.'

'But–'

'Keep it the feth down! Everyone else. On my word. Not a moment sooner. That goes for you too, major. You and your men.'

'Yes, sir. Lefivre? Purchason? Don't shame me, you understand?'

Landerson looked back across at the fence. Both half-tracks had moved out through the collapsed section and were advancing across the rough ground at a slow lick, searchlights sweeping. He saw a dozen excubitors dismounted alongside them, walking forward, las-locks raised.

'Looking for their fething pooches,' muttered Varl.

'Noise discipline!' Rawne snapped.

The patrol came closer.

'Not yet....' Gaunt whispered. 'Not yet... let the foot troops get into the trees.'

So close now. Searchlight beams washed in through the trees, dappling off the shrubs and low boughs. Landerson could smell the spice and sweet unguents of the excubitors. There was no way they could take them all. Two to one, not counting the vehicles.

He raised his autorifle to his shoulder.

He saw the first excubitor enter the hem of the trees, a lanky black shape, las-lock right up to aim. He could hear the knock and thump of the bastard's respirator box.

The excubitor disappeared. It had bent down. It had found one of the gutted fetch-hounds.

'Voi shet tgharr!' the excubitor yelled, rising.

'Now,' said Gaunt. His bolt pistol banged and the excubitor flopped backwards violently.

The edge of the woods went wild. Las-fire streamed out between the trees, shredding the low foliage. It was suddenly so bright it was as if the sun had come up.

The noise was extraordinary. Landerson saw at least four of the excubitors cut down in the opening salvo. He started to fire, but the air was suddenly thick with smoke wash and water vapour from the burst foliage.

The patrol began to answer, charging and firing weapons into the hail of fire from the woods. The half-tracks gunned forward. A heavy bolter on the top of the closest vehicle began to flash and chatter. Small trees in the woodline were decapitated and deep wounds tore the trunks of the more mature trees.

'Larks! The lights!' Gaunt yelled.

The sniper close to Landerson sat up and fired his long-las, reloading and refiring with amazing precision. The searchlights on the vehicle rigs exploded one after another like cans on a shooting gallery wall, spraying out glass chips and stark thorns of shorting electricals. Another sniper round took the head off one of the excubitors manning the lamps.

Landerson saw Gaunt striding forward, shouting to his men though the roar of the intense combat drowned him out. He had a compact bolt pistol in each hand and was firing both of them. What Landerson had taken to be a single chest holster had evidently been a doubled pair.

Shots screamed through the trees. Branches exploded. Landerson could smell wood pulp and sap, fyceline and blood. He crawled to the nearest trunk and tried to get a better angle.

'Brostin!' Gaunt yelled. 'Nail that first track!'

The big, rough-looking man calmly advanced with his massive autocannon cradled like a baby in his arms. He dropped the long telescope monopod to brace and then let rip, feeding ammo on a belt from one of two heavy hoppers strung to his hips.

The half-track plating buckled and twisted. This Brostin seemed to be aiming for the main chassis of the vehicle rather than the upper crew compartment. Why the hell would he be aiming for the most heavily armoured section, the engine bearing, the–

The half-track ignited like a fuel-soaked rag. Flames gushed out from underneath it and wrapped it in a cocoon of fire. The steady flow of armour-piercing rounds had ruptured the deep-set fuel tank. Landerson saw two excubitors, swathed in flame, tumble screaming out of the crew well.

'Holy Throne of Earth...' Landerson mumbled.

'He's got a thing about fire, our Brostin,' said the man next to him. It was the sniper. Larks. Larkin. Something like that. He had a face as lined and creased as old saddle leather. 'Plus, he's ticked off he wasn't allowed to bring his precious fething flamer. Whoop, 'scuse me.'

Larkin raised his long-las, panned the barrel round and snapped off a shot that destroyed the head of another excubitor.

Pincer fire suddenly ripped in out of the right-hand quarter. Lasrifles on rapid, but devastatingly precise. Some of the excubitors tried to turn and were smacked off their feet. Landerson saw a chest explode, scale-mail pieces flung out. A las-lock was hit as it fired and blew up in a crescent of torched energy. Another excubitor was hit in the head and stumbled blindly across the wasteland like a jerking puppet until another shot put him down. Mkoll, Mkvenner and Bonin appeared out of the dark, coming in from the side, firing from the chest.

The last of the excubitors went down. The second half-track tried to turn and reverse. A tube-charge spun in from Rawne – a long, precise throw – and blew it apart.

Landerson lowered his weapon. He was breathing hard and his mind was reeling. How long? Thirty, forty seconds? Less than a minute. A whole patrol slaughtered in less than a minute. How... how was that even possible?

'Cease fire!' Gaunt yelled.

The area was bright with the burning wrecks of the vehicles.

'Douse them?' Varl asked Gaunt.

'No, we're out of here. Now.'

'Into the woods!' Rawne shouted. 'File of two, double time! That means you too, Varl, feth take your dog bite! Come on! Keep our new friends with us!'

'Stick with me,' the sniper said to Landerson. He smiled reassuringly. 'Stick tight. The Archenemy's not found a thing yet that can kill Hlaine Larkin.'

'Right,' said Landerson, hurrying after him. For an older man, the sniper could move.

'What's your name?' Larkin called back over his shoulder.

'L-Landerson.'

'Stick tight, Landerson. The woods await.'

'The woods?'

He heard Larkin laughing. 'We're Tanith, Landerson. We like woods.'

THREE

THEY HAD REFUSED, from the very start, to refer to him by his name or rank. He was pheguth, which his life-ward told him meant something like 'one that commits base treachery' or 'one for whom betrayal has become a way of life', only less flattering. It was a slur-word, a taboo. They were letting him know what they thought of him – vermin, filth, the lowest of the low – which was rich coming from them.

And it was fine by him. He knew what he was worth to them. Calling him a pariah was the worst they could do.

'Awake, pheguth,' commanded his life-ward.

'I'm already awake,' he replied.

'And how is your health this morning?'

'I'm still pheguth if that's what you mean.'

The life-ward began to open the chamber shutters and let in the daylight. It made him wince.

'Could you leave that for now?' he asked. 'I have a headache, and the light hurts my eyes.'

The life-ward closed the shutters again, and instead lit the glass-hooded lamps.

'This is because of the transcoding?' the life-ward asked.

'I would imagine so, wouldn't you?'

His life-ward was called Desolane. It (for he had not yet been able to determine its gender with any conviction) was two metres tall, lean and long-limbed. Its slender, sexless body was sheathed in a form-fitting suit of blue-black metal-weave that had an iridescent lustre, like the filament scales of a bird's wing. Around its shoulders, a gauzy black cloak drifted rather than hung. It was light and semi-transparent, like gossamer or smoke, and moved with Desolane's movements even though it did not seem quite attached to the life-ward. The smoke-cloak almost but not quite concealed the pair of curved fighting knives sheathed across the ward's thin back.

Desolane had been the pheguth's constant companion now for six months, ever since his transfer to the custodianship of the Anarch and his removal to Gereon. The pheguth had begun to think of the life-ward as human, as far as that term would stretch, but this morning it was especially hard to ignore the xeno-traits, particularly the way Desolane's long legs were jointed the wrong way below the knees and ended in cloven hooves.

And Desolane's face. He'd never actually seen Desolane's face, of course. The polished bronze head-mask had never come off. Indeed, it looked like it was welded on. It fitted around the ward's skull tightly, smooth and featureless except for four holes: two for the eye slits and two on the brow through which small white horns extended.

The eyes themselves, always visible through the slits, were very human, watery blue and bright, like a young Guard staffer the pheguth had once had in his command. So very human, but set far too low down in Desolane's face.

'Do you wish to eat?' it asked.

'I have little stomach for food,' he answered. He wondered how Desolane ate. The bronze mask had no mouth slit.

'The transcoding?'

He shrugged.

'We were warned that the transcoding process would unsettle your constitution,' said Desolane. Its voice was soft and pitched on a feminine register, which the pheguth decided was the reason he couldn't determine the life-ward's precise gender. 'We were warned it might make you… sick. Should I fetch a master of fisyk to attend you? Perhaps a palliative remedy could be manufactured.'

He shook his head. 'We were also warned that I should imbibe nothing that might interfere with the transcoding process. I imagine that if a safe palliative existed, I would have been offered it already.'

Desolane nodded. 'A drink at least.'

'Yes. A cup of–'

'Weak black tea, with cinnamon.'

He smiled. 'You know me very well.'

'It is my job to know you, pheguth.'

'You tend to my every need with perfect decorum. I've had personal adjutants who've taken less care of me. It occurs to me to wonder why.'

'Why?' asked Desolane.

'I am a senior branch officer of your sworn enemy's armies and you are – forgive me, I'm not entirely sure what you are, Desolane.'

'You are pheguth. You are atturaghan–'

'That's something else I don't want to know the meaning of, right?'

'You are enemy blood, you are flesh-spoil, you are of the Eternal Foe and you are the most shunned of those that must be shunned. I am a sept-warrior of the Anarch, trophied and acclaimed, consented and beloved of the High Powers, and the winds of Chaos have breathed into me splendid magiks by which I have achieved the rank of life-ward, so as to stand amongst the Anarch's own huscarls. Under almost every circumstance, my duty and choice would be to draw my ketra blades and eviscerate you.'

'Almost every circumstance?'

'Except this one. This strange one we are in.'

'And in this circumstance?'

'I must attend your every need with perfect decorum.'

The pheguth smiled. 'That still doesn't tell me why.'

'Because it is what I have been ordered to do. Because if one harm comes to you, or you suffer for one moment, the Anarch himself will scourge me, bleed me ceremonially, and eat my liver.'

The pheguth cleared his throat. 'A fine answer.'

'You do so love to taunt me, don't you, pheguth?' said Desolane.

'It's the only pleasure I get these days.'

'Then I'll allow it. Once again.' The life-ward walked towards the door. 'I'll bring your tea.'

'Could you release me first?'

Desolane stopped by the chamber door and turned back.

'Of course,' it said, producing the keys from under the smoke-cloak and unshackling the naked man from the steel frame.

AN HOUR LATER, Desolane escorted him out of the chamber and down the long, drafty steps of the tower. The pheguth was dressed in the simple beige tunic, pants and slippers that his captors issued him with every morning.

In the long basement hall at the foot of the steps, where Chaos trophies hung limp in the cloying air, the pheguth turned automatically towards the chamber set aside for the transcoding sessions.

'Not that way,' said Desolane. 'Not today.'

'No transcoding today?'

'No, pheguth.'

'Because it makes me sick?'

'No, pheguth. There's something else to do today. By the order of the Plenipotentiary.'

'What's going on?' he asked.

Two antlered footman came up, las-locks slung over their stooping shoulders. One carried a dagged foul-weather cloak of selpic blue rain cloth.

'This may be added to your garments,' said Desolane, taking the cloak and handing it to the pheguth.

He put it on. He could feel his pulse racing now.

Desolane led him out into the daylight of the inner courtyard. The bulk of Lectica Bastion rose like a cliff behind them. At a barked command, a waiting squadron of excubitors shouldered arms and announced their loyalty to the Anarch. One of the footmen scurried forward and opened the side hatch of the transport.

'Where are we going?' asked the pheguth.

'Just get in,' said Desolane.

THEY DROVE FOR an hour, down through the steep cliff passes away from the bastion, onto a highway that had been repaired after shelling. The squadron of excubitors escorted them in their growling half-tracks. Deathships, fat-winged and freckled with gunpods, tracked them overhead.

'There is a function,' said Desolane, sitting back in one of the transport's ornate seats.

'A function?'

'For which your presence is required.'

'Am I going to like it?' he asked.

'That hardly matters,' the life-ward replied.

They passed through some burned-out towns, through tenement rows of worker hab-stacks that the enemies of the Imperium had turned their meltas on. Finally, the cavalcade drew to a halt on the head road of a massive dam that curved between the shoulders of a craggy mountain range. The daylight was cold and clear, and water vapour hung like mist.

About three hundred battle troops stood in files along the dam top, weapons shouldered. Several pennants fluttered in the wind. As he dismounted from the transport, pulling the cloak around him for warmth, the pheguth saw the waiting group of dignitaries. Ambassadors, stewards, division commanders, warrior-officers, chroniclers, all attended by their own life-wards.

And the Plenipotentiary Isidor Sek Incarnate himself.

'By the Throne!' the pheguth gasped as he saw him.

The troops and excubitors in earshot cursed and ruffled, some spitting against ill-omen.

'Try not to say that,' said Desolane.

'My apologies. Old habits.'

'This way.'

Desolane walked him down to the waiting group. There was some back-and-forth formal ceremony involving Desolane and the other life-wards. Challenges were shouted, antique oaths and ritual insults, a drawing and brandishing of weapons.

Isidor waited until the performance was done, and then beckoned to the pheguth.

He'd met Isidor twice before, once on arrival on Gereon, then again the night before the transcoding sessions had begun. Isidor Sek Incarnate was a short, plump human male wearing long black robes and a grey cowl. His pale, hairless face presented a permanent expression of disdain. He was the Anarch's instrument of government on Gereon.

There was nothing about him that was at all intimidating or frightening, and that's why he terrified the pheguth. This little man was surrounded by monsters – a veritable minotaur held a black parasol over his head deferentially – and massive Chaos Space Marines paid him fealty, yet there was no visible clue to his source of power. He was just a little man under a parasol.

'Welcome, pheguth,' the Plenipotentiary said. His voice was like a sharp knife slicing satin.

'Magir magus,' the pheguth responded as he had been rehearsed, bowing.

'There are two persons I would like you to meet,' said the Plenipotentiary. 'You will be spending a lot of time with them in the next few months.'

'What, may I ask, about the transcoding, magir magus?' he asked.

'That will continue. Transcoding you is our foremost agenda. But other issues will grow in importance. Otherwise, there is no point keeping you alive. Meet these persons.'

'Of course, magir magus.'

Isidor made a signal. Something vast and vaguely female crawled forward. She was immense and swollen, like the effigies of the Earth Mother early humans had fashioned, so morbidly obese that all the features of her face had vanished into folds of skin except her loose mouth. A wide-brimmed Phrygian hat perched on her scalp and swathes of green and silver fabric enveloped her bulk and flapped loose in the wind. Four midget servitors, squat and thick, clung around her lower body in the folds of her gown, to support her weight. Two hooded life-wards, both women, both skeletally thin, walked beside her, their long fingers implanted with bright scalpels.

'This is Idresha Cluwge, Chief Ethnologue of the Anarch,' said the Plenipotentiary. 'She will be interviewing you over the coming weeks.'

'I…' he began.

The female slug spoke. A barbaric clutch of consonants burst from her fat mouth like a burp. Immediately, her two female life-wards translated, in chorus.

'This is the pheguth, Isidor? How intriguing. He is a little man. He looks not at all like a commander of soldiers.'

'I'd like to say you don't look like an ethnologue,' said the pheguth. 'Except that I have no idea what one of those is.'

The female life-wards hissed and raised their blade-fingers towards him.

'Oh, have I erred on the protocol front?' the pheguth asked dryly.

'Show respect, or I will slay you,' Desolane warned him.

'He'll eat your liver…'

'I'll take that chance. The chief ethnologue is a person of consequence. You will evidence respect for her at all times.'

'Just playing with you, Desolane. Can she at least tell me what an ethnologue is?'

'It is my duty to learn in all detail about the life and culture of the enemy,' the life-wards said in unison the moment the female thing had stopped burping out more noises.

'I'm sure it is,' said the pheguth.

'All will become evident,' said the Plenipotentiary. He nodded, and a second figure stepped forward. 'This is the other person I wish you to greet.'

The man was a warrior. The pheguth recognised that at once. Straight-backed, broad, powerful. He wore a simple coat of brown leather, insignia-less army fatigues and steel-shod boots. His head was bald and deeply, anciently scarred. Ritually scarred. The warrior took off one glove and held out an oddly soft and pink hand to the pheguth.

'I believe this is how one warrior greets another in your part of the galaxy,' he said in clipped, learned Low Gothic.

'We also salute,' said the pheguth, shaking the man's hand.

'Forgive me. I can clasp your hand, sir, but I cannot salute you. That would result in unnecessary liver-eating.'

The pheguth smiled. 'I didn't catch your name, sir,' he said.

'I am Mabbon Etogaur. The etogaur is an honorific.'

'I know,' said the pheguth. 'It's a rank name. The Guard had pretty damn good intelligence. It's indicative of a colonel rank or its equivalent.'

'Yes, sir, it is. General, actually.'

'It's a Blood Pact rank.'

Mabbon nodded. 'Indeed.'

'But you present to me unmasked and your hands are clean of rite scars.'

Mabbon pulled his glove back on. 'You appreciate a great deal.'

'I was a general too, you know.'

'I know.'

'And you're going to be talking to me?'

Mabbon nodded.

'I look forward to it, sir. I wonder if at some point we might explore the meaning of the word "pheguth".'

Mabbon looked away. 'If needs be, that might happen.'

The pheguth looked back at the Plenipotentiary.

'Are we done?' he asked.

'Not even slightly, pheguth,' the magir magus replied. 'Nine worlds in the Anarch's domain lack water sources. They are parched, thirsty. Today, here, we conduct a ceremony that will access Gereon's resources to aid them. The process has already been done at four sites on the planet already. I wanted you to oversee this one.'

'Another test of my resolve?'

'Of course another test. Wards, bring the cylinder.'

With Desolane and the minotaur at their heels, the Plenipotentiary led him to the wall of the dam overlooking the vast reservoir beyond.

'Eight billion cubic metres of fresh water, replenished on a three-day cycle. Do you know what a jehgenesh is?'

'No, magir magus, I don't.'

Isidor smiled. 'Literally, a "drinker of seas". That's quite accurate. It leaves out the warp-fold part, but other than that...'

Two goat-headed servants clopped up to the wall, and held out a glass canister in which about three litres of green fluid sloshed. Deep in the fluid suspension, the pheguth could see something writhing.

Isidor Sek Incarnate took the cylinder and handed it to the pheguth. 'Don't be misled by its current size. It's dormant and infolded. Released into the water, it will grow. Essentially, it's a huge maw. On one end, flooding in, this water source. The jehgenesh is a warp beast. The water that pours into its mouth will be ejected through the holy warp onto another world. The arid basins of Anchisus Bone, for example.'

The pheguth gazed at the cylinder in his hands. 'This is how you plunder?'

'It is one way amongst many.'

'But this is why so many worlds we find have been drained?'

The Plenipotentiary nodded. 'The drinkers swallow water, also fuel oil, promethium, certain gas reserves. Why would we conquer worlds if we didn't actually use them? I mean, literally, use them?'

The pheguth shrugged. 'It makes perfect sense. What do I have to do?'

'Unscrew the lid. Release it.'

'And prove I am loyal?'

'It's another step on the way.'

The pheguth turned the steel cap of the canister slowly. He felt the warp-thing inside writhing, agitated. The lid came off. There was a smell… like dry bones. Like desert air.

'Quickly,' said the Plenipotentiary. 'Or it will drink you.'

The pheguth up-ended the canister, and the green water poured out into the reservoir, along with something slithering and coiled.

'Two days,' said Desolane. 'Then it will grow.'

'I'd like to go back to the bastion now,' the pheguth said, turning away from the lake.

FOUR

GAUNT OPENED HIS eyes. It was early still, and only a thin suggestion of light bled through the woodland canopy. In the violet twilight of the forest, it was cold and damp, and dawn mists fumed like artillery smoke.

They'd found the glade late the previous night and had bedded down to steal a few hours' rest. Gaunt had settled into a half-waking doze, more meditation than actual slumber, ready to snap alert at the slightest cue. He got like that during intense combat rotations. Sometimes true sleep would elude him for days or weeks at a time, and he survived on these snatches of subsistence rest. 'Sleeping with one eye open,' that's what Colm Corbec had liked to call it.

It was at times like this – the quiet, tense interludes – that Gaunt missed Corbec the most.

He realised his awakening had been triggered by a shadow next to him. Gaunt looked up. It was Mkvenner. The tall scout was standing so still he seemed to be part of the tree behind him.

'Ven?' Gaunt whispered.

'Everything's fine, sir,' Mkvenner replied. 'But it's time we were waking. Time we were moving.'

Gaunt got to his feet, his joints stiff and aching. A campfire was a luxury they couldn't afford. Nearby, Beltayn, Varl and Larkin were huddled up, drinking soup through the straws of self-heating ration packs. Brostin was still asleep close to them, bundled up under his camo-cloak with his arms around his autocannon.

'Wake him up,' Gaunt told Beltayn, and his young adjutant nodded.

Tona Criid sat against a large, sprawling tree root further up the slope. She was cleaning her lasrifle and keeping watch over the three locals. They were curled like children in the underbrush, slumbering deeply. Gaunt took three ration packs from his own kit and handed them to Criid.

'Wake them in a few minutes,' he told her, 'and give them these. Make sure they eat properly.'

'All right,' she said simply, not commenting on the fact that Gaunt was giving away some of his own precious supplies.

'Did you get any sleep?' he asked.

Her hands fitted the lasrifle sections together, wiping each one with a vizzy cloth. She didn't even have to look at what she was doing.

'Not much,' she admitted.

'In the night. Anything?'

She shook her head.

'That's good.' He paused. 'He'll be all right. All of them will. You know that, right?'

'Yes, sir.'

'Because you trust my word on that?'

'Because I trust your word, sir,' she said.

Tona Criid's lover was a Tanith trooper called Caffran. Both of them were excellent soldiers, amongst the very best in Gaunt's regiment. Competition for a place on this mission had been gratifyingly fierce. Gaunt had been forced to turn down many fine Ghosts he would have loved to bring along. Both Criid and Caffran had qualified easily for the final cut. It had been a hard choice, but Gaunt had accepted he could take one or the other, so he'd switched Caffran out in favour of Feygor, Rawne's adjutant.

Criid and Caffran had two kids in the regimental entourage, waifs they'd rescued from the urban wastes of Vervunhive. He couldn't and wouldn't risk both parental proxies on a mission that the Departmento Tacticae officially rated 'EZ' – *extremely hazardous/suicidal*.

Gaunt made his way on up the slope. He couldn't see Mkoll or Bonin, but he knew they were out there, invisible, covering the perimeter.

Rawne and Feygor sat with Ana Curth, the team's medicae, in the shadow of a moss-skinned boulder. She was giving them both shots using a dermo-needle from her field kit. Curth was technically a non-combatant, but she had guts and she was fit and it was essential they had a medicae with them. Gaunt knew he'd have to look after her, and he'd asked Mkoll to keep a special eye out for her safety.

Curth had voluntarily undergone intensive field training for the mission, and Gaunt was already impressed with the discipline she displayed. She'd been the only viable choice for the medicae place anyway: Dorden, the regiment's chief medic, surpassed her in ability, but he was too old and – after the grievous injuries he'd taken on Herodor almost a year before – too frail for this kind of operation.

'Everything all right here?' Gaunt asked, joining them.

'Dandy,' said Murtan Feygor. Rawne's adjutant was a rawboned rogue whose voice came flat and sarcastic from an augmetic voice box thanks to a miserable throat wound he'd taken on Verghast. He was a mean piece of work, vicious and disingenuous, but he was a devil in combat. He'd made Gaunt's cut because Gaunt figured his relationship with Rawne would work better if Rawne felt he had a crony to complain to.

Major Elim Rawne had become Gaunt's number two following the death of Colm Corbec. Rawne was darkly handsome and murderous. There had been times, especially in the early days, when Rawne might have sheathed his silver Tanith warknife in Gaunt's back the first chance he got. Some among the Tanith – a precious few, these days, and getting fewer all the time – still blamed Gaunt for abandoning their homeworld to its fate. Rawne was their ringleader. Hate had fuelled him, driven him on.

But they had served together now for the best part of nine years. A kind of mutual respect had grown between the major and the colonel-commissar. Gaunt no longer expected a knife in the back. But he still didn't turn his back on Rawne, nevertheless.

'Feygor's showing signs of the ague,' Curth said, cleaning and reloading her dermo-needle. 'I want to give everyone a shot.'

'Do it,' said Gaunt.

'Arm please,' she said.

Gaunt rolled up his sleeve. This was to be expected. The ague was a broad and non-specific term for all kinds of infections and maladies suffered by personnel transferred from one world to another. A body might acclimatise to one planet's germ-pool, its pollens, its bacteria, and then ship out on a troop transport and plunge into quite another bio-culture. These changes required adjustment, and often triggered colds, fevers, allergies, or simply the lags and fatigues brought on by warp-space transfer. Gereon was going to make them all sick. That was a given. Potentially, they might all get very ill indeed, given the noxious touch of Chaos that had stained this world. It was Curth's primary job to monitor their health, treat any maladies, keep them fit enough to see out the mission. Treating wounds and injuries they might sustain was entirely secondary to this vital work.

She gave him the shot.

'Now you,' Gaunt said.

'What?'

'You're looking out for us, Ana. I'll look out for you. Let me see you self-administer before you go to the others.'

Ana Curth glared at him for a moment. Even annoyed, even smeared with dirt, her heart-shaped face was strikingly attractive. 'As if I would jeopardise this operation by failing to maintain my own health,' she hissed.

'As if you would withhold preventative drugs because you decided others needed them more, doctor.'

'As if,' she said, and gave herself the shot.

Gaunt rose, and drew Rawne to one side.

'What's the play?' Rawne asked quietly.

'Unless I hear a good reason, the same as before. We use our contacts to penetrate Ineuron Town and contact the resistance cell. We've got to hope they can give us what we need.'

'Right,' said Rawne.

'You have concerns?'

'I don't trust them,' said the Tanith.

'Neither do I. That's why I've disclosed as little as possible.'

'But you've told Lanson–'

'Landerson.'

'Whatever. You've told him there's no liberation coming.'

'I have.'

Rawne took off his cap and smoothed his hair back with one gloved palm. 'They're jumpy. All three of them. Fething dangerous-jumpy, you ask me.'

'Yes, strung out. I noticed,' said Gaunt.

'They've had things in them too.'

'The implants, you mean? Yes, they have. They call them imagos. It's the Archenemy's way of tagging the populace.'

'And the marks on their faces.'

Gaunt sighed. 'Rawne, I won't lie. I don't like that either. The stigmas. The brands of the Ruinous Powers. Makes me very uneasy. But you have to understand, these people are Imperial citizens. They had no choice. To remain active, to keep the resistance running, they had to blend in. They had to submit to the authorities. Take the brand, play along.'

Rawne nodded. 'Troubles me, is all I'm saying. Never met anyone or anything with a mark of Chaos cut into its flesh that wasn't trying to kill me.'

Gaunt was silent for a moment. 'Major, I doubt we'd find a man, woman or child on this world that hasn't been scarred by the Archenemy. This is intruder ops, nothing like anything we've ever faced. The point is, sooner or later we're going to have to trust some of them. If not trust them, then work with them at least. But your point is well made. Consider operational code Safeguard active from this time. Command is "vouchsafe". Tell Feygor, Criid and the scouts.'

'All right then,' said Rawne.

'But only on the word, and it had better be mine, you understand me? These people, and any others we meet, are to stay alive unless there's a fething good reason.'

'I hear you.'

'Look at me when you say that.'

Rawne fixed Gaunt's eyes with his own. 'I hear you, sir.'

'Let's round up and move out. Ten minutes. Make a personal check that Curth's given everyone a shot of the inhibitors.'

Rawne saluted lazily and turned away.

'I'VE BEEN DISCUSSING things with my men,' Landerson said. His eyes were still puffy from sleep. 'We're uneasy.'

'We're all uneasy,' Gaunt said.

'You're telling me you want us to get you into Ineuron Town?'

'Yes.'

'And broker contact with the cell there?'

'Yes.'

Landerson paused for a moment. 'I'd like you to reconsider this, sir. I'd like you to think again.'

Gaunt looked at him. 'I'm not sure I know what you mean.'

'Gereon requires liberation, sir. We're dying. I don't know what your intentions are here, sir, but whatever they are, it's not what we want or need. I'd like you to reconsider your mission, perhaps even withdraw if necessary. I'd like you to contact your forces and coordinate a full counter-invasion.'

'I know you would,' Gaunt said. 'We've been over this. Last night, I thought you understood—'

Landerson reached into his shabby jacket and produced an envelope. 'I'm authorised to give you this, sir.'

'What is it?' asked Gaunt.

'An incentive, sir. An incentive to get you to aid us in the way we need aid. Right now.'

Gaunt opened the envelope. There were twenty hand-drawn paper bills inside, each one notarised and issued to the value of one hundred thousand crowns. War money. Bonds that promised to pay the bearer the full stated amount once Imperial rule and monetary systems had been re-established.

Gaunt put the bills back in their envelope.

'I wouldn't for a moment describe this as a bribe, Landerson. I know we're not talking in those terms. But I can't accept this. There are three reasons. One: I have no way of withdrawing now or making contact with my superiors. I can't coordinate any kind of deal. Two: even if I could, there is no deal to coordinate. At this time, my lord general, who I am privileged to serve, has no means or manpower to orchestrate the sort of mass operation you're talking about. There will be no liberation, because there are no liberators to achieve it. Three – and this is the one I need you to truly understand – my work here is more important than that. More important, it pains me to tell you, than the lives of every citizen currently enslaved on this world. And that's the up and down of it.'

Gaunt handed the envelope back to Landerson. Landerson looked as if he'd been slapped.

'Put them away, and let's not speak of it again. Now, I'd like you to get my team into the town and get us face to face with your cell leader.'

A few metres away, in the treecover, Feygor glanced round at Brostin.

'You see that?' he whispered.

Brostin nodded.

'The bonds, I mean?'

Brostin nodded again. 'I ain't blind, Murt.'

'Did you see how much he just turned down?'

'A real lot,' said Brostin quietly.

'Feth yes! A real lot.'

Brostin shrugged. 'So what?'

Feygor looked back at the envelope Landerson was tucking away in his jacket. 'I'm just saying, is all,' he muttered.

* * *

A FILMY SHEEN of sunlight filled the air. Through the mists, they made their way along the limits of the woodland into the dykes and ditches of the Shedowtonland pastures. The day seemed opaque. Gereon's parent star was hot and white, but the atmosphere was dirty with ash and particulates, and it deadened the pure light down to a tarnished amber.

Landerson had told Gaunt that the town was about two hours' walk away by road, but the roadways were not an option. He mentioned patrols, and other hazards that Gaunt made a mental note to quiz Landerson about when the opportunity came. So they stuck to the watercourses and the overgrown embankments of the agricultural landscape. The going was slow, because the ditches were choked with weed. Horrors lurked there too in the foetid, slippery ooze. Vermin, again in great profusion, and wildly swarming insects. On two occasions, they were forced to turn back and find a new route because the dyke path ahead was blocked by a buzzing mass of insects, the overhanging vegetation bent over by the weight of their molten, dripping numbers. It had been common for farmers in this region to use entomoculture techniques. Specially reared and hybridised swarms were employed seasonally to pollinate the field systems. Unmanaged since the invasion, these hive populations now roamed feral.

There were other horrors too. Rat-gnawed skulls bobbed and rocked in the pools, yellowed bones jutted from the mire. War dead had been dumped here, or refugees had fled here and died lingering, famished deaths as they hid from the patrols.

They walked for three hours, in virtual silence except for the occasional verbal or manual instruction. The mists began to burn off as the heat of the day increased, but the sky above, glimpsed through the overhanging brambles and gorseweed, slowly set into an arid, baked strata of yellow and ochre cloud, like the ribbed sands of an open desert. It was as if the touch of Chaos had caused the atmosphere to clot and fossilise.

Mkoll held up his hand and everyone stopped dead. A moment's pause. He looked back at Gaunt.

'Did you hear that?'

Gaunt shook his head.

'A horn of some kind. Not close, but clear.'

'That's the town,' Landerson whispered. 'The carnyx sounding a labour change. We're close. Within a kilometre.'

They continued for another ten minutes, down a particularly dark and overhung stretch of marshy ditch. Then Mkoll signalled again, this time adding the gesture that ushered them low. Everyone hunkered down, Beltayn pulling down Lefivre, who seemed slow to understand.

Mkoll, a shadow in the gloom, signed to Gaunt and indicated Bonin. Gaunt signed affirmative. The two scouts slipped away ahead of the group.

They waited for five minutes. Six. Seven. Gaunt distinctly thought he caught the sound of a combustion engine, a passing vehicle.

Then he heard two flicks on the vox-channel.

Gaunt waved the group on slowly. Their boots were sticking in the sucking black muck, and it was hard to walk without slopping the water. Landerson and his comrades seemed particularly inept. Gaunt saw Rawne's look. He shook his head.

Mkoll and Bonin were waiting for them at the end of the ditch, where it opened out into an overgrown morass, some kind of pen or farming yard. The broken, peeling shapes of four large bunker silos faced them, festooned with climbing ivy and brightly flowered merrymach. Beyond the silos, a stand of trees followed the line of a track.

'There was a patrol,' whispered Mkoll. 'But it's gone by now.'

'Let's get out of sight,' said Gaunt, and they hurried across the squelching morass into the nearest of the silos. It was dark and dusty inside, with a noxious, yeasty smell. The grain reserves heaped up against the backboards were rotten, and they all tried to ignore the weevils writhing through the mass. Mkoll sent Mkvenner and Bonin outside to cover the approach, and Larkin up onto the grain mound to take a firing position from the open slot of the feeder chute.

'You know where we are?' Gaunt asked Landerson.

'Parcelson's agri-plex. West of the town. This is where I should leave you.'

'I beg your pardon?'

'You want me to make contact for you? Then I have to get into the town and make arrangements. You stay here and–'

'No, we won't,' said Gaunt flatly.

Landerson glanced away in frustration. 'Do you want my help or don't you?'

'It would be good.'

'Then listen to me. I can't get a dozen people into Ineuron without having somewhere to hide them at the other end. It doesn't work like that. I have to slip in, make contact, and then bring you all in.'

Gaunt thought about it. 'Fine, but you're not going alone. Mkoll and I are coming with you.' Something in Gaunt's face made Landerson realise there was no room for negotiation.

'All right,' he sighed.

'How long will this take?'

'We should be back by tomorrow. Arrangements take time. Things will need to be checked. Remember, you're asking me to make contact with people who don't want to be found.'

Gaunt nodded. He called Mkoll and Rawne over to him and took them to one side. 'I'm going with Landerson to arrange a handshake. Mkoll, you'll be with me. Rawne, you're in charge here. Keep everyone low and contained. Move only if you have to.'

'Got it.'

'Landerson's guys are in your care. If they're not still breathing by the time I come back, you'd better have a feth of a good reason that can be vouched for by Mkvenner and Curth.'

'Understood,' said Rawne.

'If we're not back by this time tomorrow, figure us as dead and move on. The mission will be yours then, Rawne. Don't come looking for us. Get out and get it running, try and establish contact of your own. I suggest you use Landerson's men to get you to another town and try somewhere fresh. If Mkoll and I don't come back, Ineuron's probably a dead end.'

Rawne nodded. 'Codes?' he asked.

'Code positive... "Silver". Code negative... How about "Bragg"?'

'Works for me.'

'Go tell the others,' Gaunt said, and Rawne moved off.

'Sir–' Mkoll began.

'Save it, old friend,' Gaunt smiled.

'Save what? You don't know what I was going to say.'

'You were about to tell me that this was a job for the scouts, and that I should stay here.'

Mkoll almost grinned. He nodded.

'This is not the normal order of things,' said Gaunt. 'We're all front-line here. Right?'

'Sir.'

'Unless you have some concerns about my abilities?'

'None whatsoever, colonel-commissar. But if this is a stealth insertion, I'm calling the play. Ditch your kit. Bare minimum. And switch one of your bolt pistols for the auto I gave you.'

'Agreed,' Gaunt said.

Gaunt took off his pack and went through it, transferring a few essential items into his uniform pockets. He took one of the bolt pistols out of his holster rig and slipped it, along with half his bolt-ammo allowance, into the pack. Then he gave the pack to Beltayn's safekeeping.

Except for Larkin, none of the team was armed with their usual weapons. Ordinarily, the Tanith Ghosts carried mk III lasrifles, finished with solid nal-wood stocks and sleeves, with a standard laspistol and silver warknife as back-up. For this mission, it had been decided they needed to be light and compact. They'd swapped their rifles for hand-modified versions of the so-called 'Gak' issue weapon: wire-stocked mk III's supplied to the Verghastites in the regiment. The wire stocks made the weapons lighter, and could be folded back to make them significantly shorter. The special modifications had also shortened the muzzle length, strengthened the barrel, and increased the capacity of the energy clip. These were insurgence weapons, tooled for commando work, with the power and range of a standard lasrifle but about a third less overall length. The Ghosts had kept their trademark warknives, of course, but the laspistols had also been ditched in favour of compact autopistols. These pistols lacked the stopping power of a lasweapon, but a lasweapon was hard to keep muffled and it was impossible to keep flash suppressed. Each autopistol had a fat drum silencer screwed to the muzzle.

Gaunt checked the fit of the suppressor on his auto, slipped four spare clips onto his coat pocket, then cinched the weapon into the adjustable holster he'd taken the bolter from.

One item remained for consideration: the long, flat object, wrapped in camo-cloth, that Gaunt had strapped across his shoulder blades. Reluctantly, he removed it and handed it to his adjutant.

'Look after this,' he told Beltayn.

'I certainly will, sir.'

'If I don't come back, give it to Rawne.'

'Yes, sir.'

GAUNT, MKOLL AND Landerson left the silos, and followed the rutted track down to the edge of the trees, turning west through the thickets and saplings that had flourished along the edge of the road. It was hot and dusty, and the sunlight had a strange, twisted quality that unsettled Gaunt. So many worlds he'd been to in his career, some Imperial, some wild, some touched by the Archenemy of man. But he had never been to a world before where the Archenemy held total sway. It was more distressing than any battle zone, any fire field or bombarded plain. More distressing than the pandemonium of Balhaut or Verghast or Fortis.

Here, he suspected everything. The mud on the path, the starving birds in the silent trees, the wild flowers glittering along the verges. He noticed the way the hedges and thickets were browning and dying, slain by the atmospheric dust. He noticed the pustular livestock shuddering in spare fields. The twitching vermin in every gulley and ditch. The very perfume of the place.

Gereon was not a world that could be trusted in any detail. It was not a world where Chaos could be fought back or displaced. Chaos owned every shred of it.

And how long, Gaunt wondered, before it owned him and his men too? He'd read his Ravenor, his Czevak, his *Blandishments of Hand*. He'd read a double-dozen treatises from the Inquisitorial ordos as recommended by the Commissariat. Chaos always tainted. Fact. It infected. It stained. Even into the most sturdy and centred, it seeped osmotically and corrupted. That was an ever-present danger on the battlefield. But here... here on what was by any measure a Chaos world... how long would it take?

Before departure, Gaunt had spoken to Tactician Biota, a man he trusted. Biota had reckoned – in consultation with the Ordo Malleus – that Gaunt's men had about a month.

After that, no matter what they felt or thought about themselves, they would most likely be corrupted beyond salvation.

The thought made Gaunt wonder again about Gerome Landerson.

THEY HUGGED THE roadside thickets as traffic approached. Motorised transports, growling in towards the town. An excubitor patrol that left them cowering in a foul-smelling gutter for fifteen minutes. A convoy of traders, and a line of high-sided carriers laden with grain drawn by puffing traction engines.

'Vittalers,' Landerson said of these last. 'Food supplies from the midland bocage. They've maintained crop production up there, because the land is easily harvested. Grain is needed to supply the cookshops. The working population must be fed.'

Ineuron Town now lay below them, a pattern of habs and derelict mills, towers, ruined stacks and snail-horned temples that, Gaunt knew without asking, had been desecrated and reordained to god-things whose very murmured name would make him weep.

They faced the western palisades, a towering shield wall that circuited the western hem of the town. There were two gates, well guarded, accessed by metal-frame bridges that spanned the deep, murky ditch at the foot of the wall. In cover, in the leached undergrowth, Gaunt took out his scope and played it over the scene. The palisade was solid, but in poor repair, patched after the invasion. Excubitor teams sentried the gates. On the fighting platforms of the wall itself, he could make out troopers of the occupying force, glinting in the dead light like beetles as the weary sun caught their polished, form-fitting green combat armour.

Beyond the wall, inside the town, he saw distant manufactories, pumping black smoke into the air.

'What are those?' he asked.

'The meat foundries,' Landerson replied.

'Where they–?'

'Yes, sir.'

'Right,' said Gaunt, and stowed his scope. 'How do we get in?'

'The same way I got out,' said Landerson. 'The vittalers.'

Landerson and his comrades had hopped on an empty, outbound wagon the night before. Now they had to stow away on a laden one.

The excubitors helped them. At the wall gate, the sinister guardians were checking tariff papers, stigmas and imagos carefully, and the long convoy of high-sided carriers had come to a standstill, tractors panting. Mkoll led them down to the roadway and, after checking both ways, hurried them over to the tail gate of the rear wagon. They monkeyed up the tailboards and dropped over into the grain piles.

'Bury yourselves!' Mkoll snapped, and they wriggled down into the moving mass of loose grain, spading it over their backs with open hands.

The carrier started to roll forward again, its traction engine puffing. Another halt. Steam hissed. More checks ahead. Then they were shunting forward again, and the shadow of the gate-mouth fell across them.

Choking in loose grain, Gaunt listened hard. A challenge, an exchange of voices. The gurgling rasp of the excubitor voices. Questions.

Then a rattling of chains and the sniffling whine of hounds.

More orders, shouted.

They're searching the carriers, Gaunt realised. They're looking for scents. The hounds. The fetch-hounds.

His hand closed around the grip of his holstered autopistol and he thumbed the safety off. There were loose kernels of grain and chaff in his nostrils now. He felt a sneeze building.

Gaunt clamped his mouth shut. His throat constricted with the pressure. His eyes teared up. He tried not to breathe. Dust tickled his larynx.

A shouted order. A sudden jolt. They were moving again.

The panting chuff of the tractor was so loud that Gaunt risked a cough. Across the grain heap, Mkoll raised his head and glared at him.

They were in. Feth, they were in!

Landerson was already getting to his feet, the grain pouring off him like sand in a glass.

'What are you doing?' Mkoll hissed. 'Get the feth down!'

'No time!' said Landerson. 'Trust me, we can't wait until we roll into the market. There's only one section of roof low enough to exit on and it's coming up fast!'

They scrambled up and got to the left-hand side of the carrier. Below, narrow low-hab streets hurtled by. Gaunt looked back. On the palisade, the guards were visible… looking outwards.

'Where?' Mkoll asked.

'Here! Quickly! It's coming up!' Landerson urged. He pointed. A low roof section, two metres lower than the wagon's side, badly-tiled.

'There! That or nothing else!'

They swung their legs over the edge of the wagon's side, hands gripped to the lip. The street, five metres below, rushed past. Certain, broken death: a mis-jump, a glancing fall against the gutterwork…

'Now!' Landerson cried.

They jumped.

IT WAS ALMOST balmy now. The amber sunlight baked the soil, and clouds of drowsy insects murmured around the silos.

Rawne slithered down from his check on Larkin. Varl, sitting in a corner, looked at him.

'How do you think they're doing?' he asked.

Rawne shrugged.

MKOLL FOUND A grip and held it. The impact had all but winded him. The old tiles were rotten, and they shredded under his fingertips. He dug in with his knife and got a good purchase. He looked back.

Gaunt had landed well. Landerson had slipped, and was sliding back down the low roof, scrabbling for a hand-hold.

Gaunt stabbed his own knife home, then threw out the end of his camo-cape to Landerson. The man grabbed it and his slide ceased.

'Help me,' Gaunt grunted.

Mkoll edged back down the roof, and threw his own cape out to Landerson. Between them, Gaunt and Mkoll dragged Landerson up to join them. 'My thanks,' he gasped.

'How do we get in?' Gaunt asked.

'Skylight on the far side.'

* * *

THE BUILDING WAS an old scholam primer. They dropped down into the gloomy interior, and walked past half-sized desks and alphabet murals. Gaunt paused briefly and gazed at the scatter of tiny wooden building blocks and forgotten dolls.

Landerson led them to the back exit, out into a dingy alley that led back along a series of rents and low-habs. Filthy water gurgled down the central gutter.

'Where to?' Gaunt whispered.

'Just shut up and follow me,' Landerson replied.

They chased him through a series of gloomy vacant lots and under the rough timber scaffolding that had been erected to shore up the sagging wall of a manufactory.

At the corner of the aged building they stowed themselves in cover and waited until Mkoll gave them an all clear.

Then they sprinted across the cobbled thoroughfare and ran down the stone steps beside a public water syphon.

The air was dank. Landerson headed on through the dim blue shadows until he reached a chainlink fence.

'We're blocked,' Gaunt started to say. Landerson shook his head, and took off his coat, wrapping it around his hands so he could grab the filaments of razorwire knotted into the fence without ripping his palms open. He hefted hard and a section lifted away.

'Through. Now!' he barked, and Mkoll and Gaunt ducked under the partition. Landerson followed, and settled the section back in place. He put his coat back on. It had a number of fresh tears.

He beckoned them. They jogged down a low pavement, flanked on either side by the plaster-finished walls of public buildings, and then across a small yard where a dried-up fountain stood forlorn. A left turn, another alley, and then up a flight of worn stone steps to the next street.

Mkoll hushed them back hard.

They clung to the mossy wall and watched the steel-shod feet of an excubitor patrol stride past on the street level.

Mkoll put his silenced pistol away again and nodded them on.

'We have to cross here,' Landerson said.

Mkoll nodded, and took a look out. The side-street, cobbled and shadowed, was empty.

'Go!' Mkoll said.

They darted across the street and into an adjacent alley. Ten metres down from the alley mouth, there was a door of heavy wood, painted red.

Landerson waved the Ghosts back. He knocked once.

A slit opened.

'How is Gereon?' a voice asked from inside.

'Gereon lives,' Landerson replied.

'Even though it dies,' the voice responded.

Landerson stiffened abruptly and turned away from the door. He started walking back towards Gaunt and Mkoll.

Dan Abnett

'What's the matter?' asked Gaunt.

'Move. Move,' Landerson whispered urgently. 'It's not safe.'

They began to hurry away.

The red door opened wide and an excubitor stepped out, its las-lock raised to fire.

Mkoll spun around, dropped to one knee and fired three shots with his silenced autopistol. It made a *phut! phut! phut!* noise.

The excubitor slammed backwards as if it had been yanked back by a rope.

'Run!' said Mkoll.

FIVE

GAUNT STARTED TO run, but heard Mkoll's weapon spit again. He looked back. Another excubitor had fallen awkwardly away from the red door, its las-lock clattering onto the flagstones.

'Come on!' Gaunt shouted.

Mkoll raced to join him. Landerson was already heading out onto the side street.

'Which way?' Gaunt hissed.

'Down here...' Landerson began. He shut up quickly. They heard the squeaking clatter of vehicle treads, and a half-track swung into view at one end of the street. Dark figures leapt out, long coats flying. Gaunt heard challenges shouted through augmetic voice boxes.

They turned immediately, but three excubitors were emerging from the alley they had just left. Gaunt wrenched out his auto. Mkoll was already firing.

One excubitor keeled over, speaker box blown out in a spurt of acrid sparks and synthesised howls. Gaunt's auto bucked as he put three muted shots through the hip and ribs of a second, punching holes in the grey-scale armour coat and spattering the wall behind with gore. The third got its long, ornate weapon up to fire but Mkoll crashed into it, bearing the excubitor down onto the cobbles under him. The silencer of Mkoll's auto pressed against the excubitor's sternum and he executed it with two quick rounds before it could get up.

Then the three of them started to run down the street away from the half-track and the oncoming patrol. Landerson led the way, sprinting, his autorifle bumping against his hip. Gaunt and Mkoll followed him. Gaunt presumed Landerson had some sort of plan, that he was working on local knowledge.

Then again, maybe he was just fleeing in blind panic.

He heard a shot. The hyphenated *zzt-foff* of a las-lock firing. The bolt blew stones and brick chips out of a wall. Gaunt glanced back. The gang of excubitors was closing fast. They seemed like figures from a nightmare: their armour coats billowing out behind them, their grotesquely long, thin legs carrying them in huge, headlong strides. Gaunt fired a couple of shots in their direction then pounded on after Mkoll and Landerson.

The street opened out into a wide yard with a pillared stone colonnade along one side. On the far side of the yard, the mouth of the adjoining street was blocked by a battered troop transporter. The excubitors lined up in front of it swept their weapons to their shoulders.

'Feth!' Gaunt cried. The three men hurled themselves into the scant cover of the colonnade as the las-locks started to blast. Bolts smacked off the old pillars, or flew between them and detonated against the colonnade's inner wall. Mkoll got his back to a pillar, and Landerson scrambled on hands and knees for cover. Gaunt threw himself down behind another stone column. His nostrils burned with cooked stone and burn-dust. The las-lock fusillade sounded like whipcracks. They were pinned, and in a second they were going to be outflanked. For in a second, the foot patrol was going to round the corner, with a clear field of fire down the shadowed colonnade.

Gaunt pressed his back against the pillar, his leather jacket scratching on the rough stone. He pulled out his bolt pistol so he had a weapon in each hand.

'I've got our backs! Take them!' he yelled.

Landerson heard the shout. He was still on his hands and knees, shielding his head from the lock-fire. What the Throne did Gaunt mean by 'take them'? There were just three of them, cornered like rats, and the excubitors were everywhere.

'Use that fething weapon!' Mkoll snapped at him. The scout had holstered his pistol and was swinging the lasrifle off his shoulder. He didn't even bother extending the wire stock. He leaned out from behind the pillar and let off a burst of las-fire, rapid auto. The line of excubitors by the transport on the far side of the yard scattered for cover. Mkoll chuckled at the sight of it, and raked them again, cutting two down in a flurry of sizzling bolts.

'Come on!' he shouted.

Landerson struggled up onto his knees, and started firing his autorifle. The shots coming out of the suppressed muzzle sounded like wet kisses. He saw a row of raw metal holes punch into the side of the transport and raised his aim, knocking an excubitor off the back of the truck.

The patrol ran into view, shouting. Gaunt stepped out of his partial cover behind the pillar and opened fire with both handguns. The first three figures jerked and fell backwards. The clip of his auto out, Gaunt aimed the boltgun steadily and boomed out four more loud reports. Another dark shape folded violently, as if struck by a sledgehammer.

Gaunt ducked back behind the pillar, reloading. Las-lock rounds squealed down the colonnade. Behind him, he heard the furious crackle of Mkoll's las, and the splutter of the resistance fighter's old rifle. Gaunt peered out to the left of the pillar and fired his bolt pistol, then jerked back as las-locks answered him, before popping out to the right to fire his autopistol. The hard rounds smacked an excubitor in the face and forehead and walloped it onto its back. Then he leaned out to the left side again, and fired a bolt shell that pulped the chest of another excubitor who was trying to make a dash down the colonnade.

'Moving,' he heard Mkoll yell. The air around the colonnade was thick with dust and gunsmoke. Gaunt fired a few last bright flashes into the pall and turned to run after his chief scout.

Mkoll and Landerson had emerged from cover, firing their weapons from the hip as they ran across the yard. Their hammer-fire was forcing the second excubitor squad to cower behind walls and ragged heaps of trash and masonry. Gaunt caught up with Landerson. Mkoll had spotted a boarded door in the far wall of the yard. He reached it, kicked it savagely several times until it splintered open and then knelt down to deliver wholesale blasts across the yard with his lasrifle as Landerson and Gaunt charged in through the gaping doorway. As soon as they were inside, he barked off a final burst and plunged after them.

It was some kind of storage shed, unlit apart from the daylight slanting in through holes in the tiled roof. Old furniture was piled up against the walls. Gaunt edged his way in, with Landerson close behind. Mkoll paused in the doorway and pulled a tube-charge from his pack. He wedged it on one side of the splintered door, tied a length of monofilament wire to the det-tape, and then played the almost invisible wire out taut across the doorway at shin height, wrapping it off around a broken hinge on the other side.

Then he hurried after Gaunt.

'Know this place?' Gaunt whispered to Landerson. Outside they could heard guttural shouts and the occasional shot as the relentless patrols regrouped.

'Tillage Street bunkers. They lead into the manufactory district.' Landerson peered around in the gloom. 'Let's go that way. We want to come out on the south side of Rubenda.' Landerson sounded a little frantic, and Gaunt had a feeling it wasn't only the fun and games they'd just experienced.

'Where do we head for–' he began.

'Shut up. Please,' Landerson said. 'This is really bad. Really bad. We're not doing anything right now except finding a place to hide.'

'Of course,' said Gaunt.

'You don't understand,' Landerson said.

'What the feth is that?' Mkoll said behind them. They froze, listening. They could still make out the noises of the excubitors in the yard outside, but there was something else now. Horns were blowing, harsh and strident. And behind them, a rustling, like a gathering wind. A moaning that threatened to become a howl.

'Is it just me, or is that a sound no one wants to hear?' Mkoll whispered.

'Wirewolves,' said Landerson. 'Oh Throne. We've woken the whole place up.'

'What are–' Gaunt started to ask and then stopped. He didn't want to know. 'Your call, Landerson. A place to hide, you said.'

'I'll do my best,' said Landerson.

They found another door on the south side of the store, pulling broken tables aside to clear it. It let out into a dingy alley that was running with sewage from a broken drain. The moaning in the air had become a howl now. A keening.

Mkoll had slung his lasrifle again, and was leading the way with his silenced pistol raised. Behind them, in the store, they heard a dull, reverbarative *crump*, and a good deal of augmetic shrieking. An excubitor's shin had snagged Mkoll's tripwire.

They sloshed away through the muck. On a nearby street, transports rumbled by, their badly maintained engines rattling and coughing. Another booming note echoed from the city horns. More keening howls shrilled in the damp air. Gaunt felt his skin prickle. He could smell the unholy magic loosed on the wind.

Mkoll gestured with his pistol to a dark alley to their left.

'No,' Landerson said, without breaking stride. 'That's a dead end. This way.'

They turned right up a steep cobbled street and then Landerson immediately darted left into a covered alley between two boarded premises. The alley led through into a ramshackle clutch of overgrown walled gardens behind the tenement row. Only then did Landerson slow down.

'How did you know?' Gaunt asked.

Landseron beckoned the Ghosts after him. They followed a weed-infested path behind a row of broken cold frames and cultivator shacks, and into a yard piled with hemp sacks full of nitrate fertiliser.

'How did you know?' Gaunt repeated. 'Back at the red door.'

'They gave the wrong response. The warning response. The excubitors must have had them at gunpoint.'

'They knew you were coming,' said Mkoll.

'They knew someone was coming. That house was a key contact point. We'll have to use another. If there are any left they haven't found.' Landerson slid the bar on the rotting wooden door of a workshop and they went in. It was dirty, and piled with junk and machine parts.

'What's here?' Gaunt said.

'Nothing. It's a way through. We have to keep off the streets.'

Landerson led them to the far end of the workshop and moved some old cans of paint and sheets of fibreplank so he could pull a section of the flakboard wall aside. The dust he disturbed spilled up into bars of pale light slanting in through the windows and made mote galaxies.

They ducked through and came out into a stone shed that, judging from the promethium stains on the floor, had been used until recently to garage vehicles. Landerson checked the street door.

Outside, the sound of howling had risen a notch. The air was charged. Gaunt felt nauseous. In the corner of the shed, an old engine block rested on a wooden pallet.

'Help me with this,' Landerson said. With Mkoll's aid, Landerson shifted the pallet load and exposed a trapdoor. He yanked it open and dropped down into the darkness.

Mkoll and Gaunt followed. Landerson closed the hatch with a rope-pull and they were plunged into darkness. Mkoll lit his lamp pack. By the light of it, they moved on through a series of cellars. The brick walls were mildewed and rotten. Clumps of black fungus sprouted from the mortar. Vermin scuttled from the wavering light beam.

They reached a flight of dank steps, and edged down into a narrow tunnel that was flooded knee-deep with cold, noxious water. Landerson sloshed ahead, and located a set of iron rungs fixed into the tunnel's brickwork. Dripping, they clambered up it into a dry, vaulted cellar where the roof was so low they couldn't stand up straight. By the light of Mkoll's lamp, Gaunt could see there was a pile of old equipment crates and sacks of dried provisions heaped against one wall.

'Where are we?' he asked.

'The undercroft of the Ineuron flour mill. It's one of the bolt holes the cell uses.'

'Are we safe here?' Gaunt asked.

Landerson laughed. 'Of course not. But it's safer than other places. Safer than out on the streets. Pray to your Emperor that it'll be safe enough.'

'The Emperor protects,' Mkoll whispered.

'He's your Emperor too,' Gaunt said.

'What?'

'Pray to your Emperor, you said. As if he wasn't yours.'

Landerson shrugged. 'This is my world, Colonel-Commissar Gaunt. And I love it dearly. My family line dates back to the original colonist-founders. Landerson. Sons of the First Landers here. I am true to the God-Emperor of Mankind, but honestly... do you think I trust him to protect me any more? Where was he when doom came to Gereon?'

'I can't answer that,' said Gaunt.

'How long must we stay here?' Mkoll asked.

'Until it's safe to show our faces,' said Landerson.

'Which means–'

'Later tonight at the earliest. When things have calmed down.' Landerson leaned his rifle against the undercroft wall and sat down. 'Then, maybe, we can start trying to hook up with the underground again. If we're not found in the meantime.'

THE SUN WAS setting. In the dry, starchy air of the silos outside the town, the rest of the insertion team waited fitfully.

'You hear that?' Bonin asked.

Larkin nodded. He was drooped as if asleep over his long-las. 'Been hearing it now for a good few minutes.'

'What the feth is it?'

Larkin didn't like to say. It was a distant howling sound, murmuring from the town below them. It sounded just like his worst nightmares. It made the noise of his migraines, the chatter of his darkest thoughts.

'I say we try the link,' announced Tona Criid, rising to her feet.

Beltayn shook his head. 'Nothing like range. Not with micro-beads. My set won't pick them up.'

'We wait,' said Rawne, emphatically. 'That was what his orders were.'

'I hear that,' said Feygor.

Varl looked as if he was about to say something then just shook his head.

Mkvenner paced into the silo, just finishing his latest sweep. He stood in the doorway, backlit by the sinking sunlight. 'Something's wrong,' he said.

'We figured that much,' Bonin replied.

'Have you heard the noises?' Mkvenner asked.

'Yes, I have,' said Rawne. 'Worst case scenario, our beloved leader has run into seriously shitty trouble and is either dead or about to be.'

'Right. Best case, major?' Ana Curth asked.

Rawne shrugged. 'Best case? Our beloved leader has run into seriously shitty trouble and is either dead or about to be. Sorry, was that a trick question?'

'Screw you, Rawne,' Curth sneered.

'I look forward to it,' smiled Rawne, and got to his feet. 'Listen up, Ghosts! We wait until tomorrow. Then we do things my way.'

SIX

NIGHT CAME, AND was no safer than the day.

A silence fell. Even the horns went quiet. Spectres haunted the town, snuffling and whining in the dark, and terror stiffened the air. In the deep stone undercroft, the three men waited it out.

At Landerson's instruction, they had turned the lamp off, and made no sound, uttered no word. Gaunt felt the cold through the thick walls. The undercroft was so massively built it would have withstood an artillery bombardment, but in the dark it felt fragile and insubstantial, as if no more than a canvas field tent sheltered them.

And there were things moving in the night.

The chill ebbed and flowed through the stones, as if transmitted by some fluid, tidal motion outside. Sudden cold spots froze the air, and frost foamed on the dank ceiling. Gaunt heard distant moaning, mumbling noises from the streets outside, the slow slide and squeal of metal blades or claws tracing along tiles and outer walls. Once in a while, there came a long scream or a sudden, truncated shriek.

He tried not to imagine what might be outside, what manner of abomination was loose in Ineuron Town. In the biting dark, his mind played wicked tricks. His hand clamped around the grip of his boltgun. He fought to arrest his own anxious breathing.

Every now and then, they heard marching feet in the distance, the rumble of motor engines, the bark and fuss of hounds. Those were dangers too, but somehow they seemed honest and solid. Dangers they could face down and deal with.

The drifting, half-heard sounds of the spectres were something else again.

Then utter silence fell outside. By his chronometer's luminous dial, Gaunt saw it was two hours past middle night.

Landerson lit the lamp pack. The sudden brilliance hurt Gaunt's eyes.

'They've called them off,' Landerson announced, speaking for the first time in over eight hours.

'You're sure?' asked Mkoll. It dismayed Gaunt to see how pale and worried his stoic chief scout looked.

'Sure as I can be,' Landerson replied. 'Once they're summoned, the wire-wolves bleed power quickly. They've gone for now.'

'Gone?'

'Folded back to replenish their energies.'

'Folded back where?' Mkoll asked.

'Into the warp, I suppose,' Landerson replied. 'Oddly enough, I've never had the chance to ask.'

He got up on his feet, his head hunched down under the low roof. 'Come on,' he said. 'We've got a window of comparative safety between now and dawn. Let's not waste it.'

He led them back down the iron rungs into the flooded tunnel, and they churned along through the cold water. The tiny, frail bones of rats floated in the channel, forming a brittle skin. Thousands and thousands of rats, rendered down to buoyant bone litter. The lamp pack's beam lit them as an undulating white crust.

They reached steps and clambered up out of the cold flow. The steps were slimy and treacherous. Wet-rot clung to the walls.

As they climbed, the steps became drier and the rot receded. They came up through a wooden storm door onto a narrow back street. The night was still, and feeble stars glimmered in the narrow patch of sky visible between the close-leaning roofs above them. To the west was the ruddy glow of the ahenum furnaces.

Landerson beckoned them on, down to a junction between two quiet streets. At a crossroads up ahead, they could see a barrel fire burning, scattering flame-light and shadows back down the cobbles. Two excubitors stood by the fire, chafing their hands.

The trio slipped to the left, and ran down through the darkness of an adjoining street. Then right, up a shallow hill where the cobbles were worn and buckled, and left again into a silent court where ornamental plants had overgrown and wrapped around the brickwork. At Landerson's direction, they sprinted across the court and made their way along a sloping alley that ran down between a furniture manufactory and a defunct distillery. There was an iron gate at the end of the alley, fletched with moss and weed. Landerson shooed them down into cover.

A patrol rumbled by. Not excubitors, a military unit. Behind the weeds, cowering, Gaunt saw the grinding treads of a light tank, the pacing feet of the enemy. A searchlight flashed their way, breaking its light on the bars of the iron gate.

Then it was gone, and the patrol had passed on too.

'Come on,' Landerson whispered.

THEY MADE THEIR way down around the skirts of the commercia into the depths of the town. On one of the main avenues, a torch-lit parade was winding past, filling the night with the din of drums and cymbals. A mixture of excubitors and battle-troops formed the vanguard. Many of them held aloft spiked, racemose standards and filthy banners on long poles. The bulk of the procession was citizenry, shackled in long, trudging lines, singing and clapping.

These were proselytes. It saddened Gaunt to see so many. Every day, more and more members of the cowed populace elected to convert to the wretched faiths of the enemy. Some saw it, perhaps, as their only chance to survive. Others regarded it as a way of securing a better life, with greater liberties and consents. For the most part, Gaunt thought darkly, they converted because Chaos had swallowed their bewildered souls.

Ordinals led the parade towards the temple. Landerson had told Gaunt that 'ordinals' was a blanket term for the senior administrators of the enemy power. Some were priests, others scholars, bureaucrats, financiers, merchants. They wore elaborately coloured robes and headdresses, and their be-ringed fingers hefted ornate staves and ceremonial maces. Some were female, some male, others indeterminate, and many displayed horrifying mutation traits. Gaunt couldn't tell – didn't want to tell – what the variations in dress and decoration denoted. They were all enemies. But they intrigued him nevertheless. In his career, he had faced the warriors and the devotees of the Ruinous Powers in many guises, but this was the first time he had properly laid eyes on the dignitaries and officials who ordered their culture and society. These were the fiends who followed the smouldering wake of battle and established rule and control over the territories conquered by their warrior hosts.

Once the parade had passed, the three men hurried on into the low pavements where the town's administratum buildings had once stood. Here, the faces of the broken walls and chipped plasterwork were covered with paint daubs and scribbles that made nonsense words and strange designs. In one large square, lit by fierce bonfires, hundreds of human slaves laboured under the attentive guns of excubitor squads. The slaves, some on makeshift ladders, were painting more designs on the open walls.

'Petitioners,' Landerson whispered. 'Or criminals trying to atone for minor infractions. They labour day and night until they either drop of exhaustion, or make a mark that is deemed true.'

'True?' Mkoll echoed.

'The enemy does not teach its signs and symbols, except to the converted. It is said they believe that those touched with Chaos will know the marks instinctively. So the petitioners make random marks, scribing anything and everything their imagination comes up with. If they make any mark or sign that the ordinals recognise, they are taken away for purification and conversion.'

Amongst the gangs of excubitors, three ordinals lurked, overseeing the insane graffiti. One of them sat astride a mechanical hobbyhorse, a bizarre machine whose body rose above its small wheels on four thin, strut-like legs. The ordinal trundled around on his high perch, shouting orders. He looked like a child with a nursery plaything, as dreamed up in a nightmare. There was nothing childish about the twin stubber pintle-mounted in place of the hobbyhorse's head, though.

Avoiding the square, they darted from cover across an empty street and into the breezeway opposite. This was a narrow rockcrete passage, which smelt of urine. At the far end of it, behind a row of overflowing garbage canisters, was a low hatch.

Landerson glanced at Gaunt. 'Let's pray they haven't found this one too,' he said.

'Let's,' Gaunt said, and looked round at Mkoll. At his commander's nod, Mkoll vanished into the shadows.

Landerson stepped up to the hatch and knocked. After a moment, it opened slightly.

'How is Gereon?' asked an echo from behind the hatch.

'Gereon lives,' Landerson replied.

'Despite their efforts,' the echo responded. The hatch opened.

Landerson and Gaunt stepped into the darkness.

They'd gone no more than five paces into the darkness when rifle snouts poked against their backs.

'On your faces! Down! Now! On your faces!'

'Wait, we–' Landerson began. He grunted as a rifle stock rammed his neck. 'Down! Now! Now!'

They got down. Hands clawed at them, fishing out weapons, forcing shoulders flat. Boots came in and kicked their legs apart.

'Get on your faces, you bastards!' a voice barked.

A lamp pack suddenly flicked on and bathed the chamber in light.

'I so, so wouldn't be doing that if I were you,' Mkoll said from the doorway, his lasrifle aimed.

'MY APOLOGIES, COLONEL-COMMISSAR,' said Major Cirk.

'Not necessary,' Gaunt replied. 'I understand the rigorous nature of your security.'

She shrugged. 'Your man would have had us dead even so.'

They looked across as Mkoll, who was sitting with his back against the chamber wall and his rifle across his lap, observing the scene.

'Yes, he would,' said Gaunt. 'But as far as I know, he's the best there is, so don't beat yourself up.'

The chamber was small, and lit by a single chemical fire in the corner. Six ragged resistance fighters sat in a huddle with Landerson, talking quietly. Another two, armed with homemade charge-guns, watched the door.

'The scare today,' Cirk asked. 'Did you trigger it?'

'I'm afraid so,' Gaunt replied. 'We got into a duel with a couple of patrols. We were trying to make contact.'

She nodded. 'They've closed a lot of our outlets down. After last night.'

'What was last night?' Gaunt asked.

Cirk sighed. She was a tall woman in her early forties, with cropped brunette hair and a face made fabulous by high cheekbones and a full mouth. She might once have been beautiful, voluptuous. Food shortages had thinned her frame, drawing her face and emphasizing her breasts and hips. Her fatigues were ill-fitting. 'Last night,' she said, 'we staged a diversion.'

'A diversion?'

'To get you in, sir.'

Gaunt nodded. The idea stuck painfully.

'The cell deployed, and staged attacks at various key locations to occupy the attention of the Archenemy forces. The idea was to draw focus away from the team contacting you. We were successful.'

'Define success.'

'Three tactical targets hit. Forty per cent casualties. The reprisals shut down a lot of our active houses. Four out of nine in Ineuron Town. Another half dozen in the agri-burbs.'

'How many dead?'

'Dead? Or captured, sixty-eight.'

'I was supposed to link up with a colonel called Ballerat,' Gaunt said.

'Dead,' she replied. 'Killed last night in the firebomb raid on the Iconoclave. I'm cell leader now.'

There was no emotion in her voice, and nothing on show in her face. Like Landerson, like everyone on Gereon, Cirk had been through too many miseries to register much of anything any more.

'We've actually closed up shop here,' Cirk said. 'Ineuron's too hot now. What's left of the underground here has fled. Except for a few skeleton units like mine.'

Gaunt nodded. 'Waiting for us.'

She nodded back. 'Contacting and aiding you was a vital function. That much was passed down the line to Ballerat and me.'

'From where?' Gaunt asked.

'Not for me to say, sir. The underground only survives by compartmentalising its strengths. No one gets more than they need to know. That way, if anyone is captured...'

She let it hang.

'I understand,' said Gaunt. 'And I'm grateful to you.'

'Don't be,' she said simply.

'All right. But understand that my gratitude comes from a much higher place.'

'That's enough for me,' said Cirk. 'So, what do you need?'

'Immediately? I need to get word to the rest of my outfit. Let them know we're good.'

'Are they voxed?' she asked.

Gaunt nodded.

'All right, we have access to a set. I don't like to use it, but it's better than trying to get a runner out of the town just now. Can your message be short?'

'Yes. Two words. "Silver" and "standby".'

'Good. Channel?'

'Anything between two-four-four and three-one on the tight high-band.'

Cirk beckoned over one of her team, a thin blonde girl who looked no more than a teenager.

She gave her careful instructions, and the girl slipped out into the night.

'Right,' said Cirk. 'What else?'

Gaunt paused. He thought for a moment about the bitter wranglings he'd already had with Landerson. 'Let me ask, first of all, what are your thoughts about liberation?'

Cirk stared at him. She was truly beautiful, he realised, but the mix of lingering pain and beauty was almost too hard to look at. The stigma mark cut into her cheek both marred her beauty and reminded Gaunt of the poison infecting Gereon. 'I understand it's not coming any time soon, sir,' she said.

'You do?'

'First off, I'm not a fool. Second, Ballerat briefed me. We didn't share the information with too many of the cell members. Bad for security and bad for morale. But I know you're here for an insertion mission, not as the vanguard of some glorious counter invasion.'

Gaunt sighed. 'I'm relieved. Breaking that to Landerson was hard. I'd have hated to see the same disappointment on your face.'

'Why?' she asked, interested.

'Not for me to say,' he replied.

She smirked and sat back. 'So what is next?'

'You don't know what we're here for?'

'Compartmentalised, remember? Ballerat and I were privy to the fact you were an insertion mission, but I don't think even he knew what that might be.'

'I'm here to kill someone,' Gaunt said quietly.

'Anyone in particular?' she asked. 'From what I've heard Landerson say, you've been clocking up quite a body count already.'

'Yes,' said Gaunt. 'Someone very particular. An old friend.'

Cirk stroked her cheek and grinned. 'There were inverted commas around that word, if I'm not mistaken.'

'You're not.'

'Who is he?'

'I didn't even say it was a he.'

'Compartmentalising, colonel-commissar?'

'Indeed.'

'Fine. I'd rather not know, actually. This old "friend"… I imagine you want to find him?'

'I do,' said Gaunt. 'I need the underground to furnish me and my team with passage into the Lectica heartlands.'

She exhaled heavily. 'Shit! You don't want much, do you?'

'Is that going to be a problem?'

Cirk leaned forward again. He could smell her stale sweat and the grease in her cropped hair. 'If you needed to get into the heartlands, you could have picked a better starting point than Ineuron Town.'

'Because?' asked Gaunt.

'Because you're about three hundred kilometres south of where you want to be.'

'I know,' Gaunt replied. 'But this is a slow-burn operation. Guard Intelligence was conferring secretly with the Gereon underground for months before we set off. A safe drop point was the first priority. The underground advised that the marshes south of Shedowtonland would be the safest territory to make a rapid drop from a lander. Anything closer to Lectica would have been too hazardous.'

'True enough,' she said. 'You came in by lander?'

'By grav-chute from a low flyby over the marshes, actually.'

'Holy crap, that can't have been any fun.'

'It wasn't. When the time came, my marksman refused at the hatch. His name's Larkin. He's not the most together man in my command.'

'What did you do?' asked Cirk.

'I had Brostin – the biggest man in the team – throw Larkin out of the lander. He's come to terms since then.'

Cirk laughed. He liked her laugh.

'What were you, Cirk? Before the enemy came, I mean?'

She hesitated and looked at the flames of the pallid chemical fire. 'I was a farm-owner, sir. My family held two thousand hectares west of the town. Canterwheat and soft fruit. The bastards torched my orchards.'

'What's your name?' he asked.

'I'm Major Cirk of the Ineuron undergr–'

'I asked your name. Mine's Ibram.'

'My name is Sabbatine Cirk,' she said.

Gaunt paused, as if he had been slapped.

'What is it?' she asked.

'Named after the Saint, I imagine?'

'Of course,' she said.

'Everywhere I go, she's there to lead me...' Gaunt murmured.

'Sir?'

'Nothing. So, what about Lectica?'

'I'll see what I can do. We have a line of contact with the Edrian cell. They might be able to get you cross country and into Lectica. After that, we'll be relying on their contacts in the field.'

'That's a start,' Gaunt said.

SEVEN

ANOTHER DAY ROSE, languid, above the bastion. The pheguth had been undergoing transcoding for the better part of the morning. Desolane had heard his screams rolling up and down the windy halls.

Desolane went to the day room to review security. Light spilled in through the barred windows. Assisted by a half-dozen warriors in enamelled green armour, three ordinals were sorting the report dockets and adjusting the light-pins on the chart table.

'Anything interesting?' Desolane asked.

One of the ordinals looked up. 'A lively night, life-ward. Insurrectionists torched the temple in Phatima, and an underground cell assassinated two ordinals in Brovisia Town. A firebomb. Excubitor reprisals have been rapid and thorough. A decimation order has been placed on Brovisia Town.'

'Anything else?' Desolane wondered.

'This, from the south provinces,' said another ordinal, holding out a data-slate. Desolane took it and reviewed it. 'Ineuron Town? Where the hell is that?'

'South of here, life-ward, in the marshlands, along the edge of the Untill. A minor farming centre. Last night there was a flurry of insurrectionist attacks. A great deal of damage. It is now contained.'

'You think so?' Desolane asked.

'Life-ward?'

Desolane tapped the slate. 'Did you not study the detail? An excubitor patrol slaughtered in the farm lands. Las-weapons used. And a firefight against unknowns in the town itself that was so furious it woke the wire-wolves there.'

'Local governance has control of the situation, life-ward,' said one of the ordinals.

72

'They don't know what they're dealing with,' Desolane growled. 'Las-weapons? You simple fools! Since when has the underground been using las-weapons?'

The ordinals fell silent. They were powerful beings of great substance, but they quailed in fear before one of the Anarch's own life-wards.

'Inform the office of the Plenipotentiary, but advise him we have the matter in hand.'

The ordinals bowed their heads and covered their mouths with one hand. 'We serve the word of the Anarch, whose word drowns out all others,' they chorused.

'And once you've done that,' said Desolane, 'get me Uexkull.'

DESOLANE WAITED FOR Uexkull in the annexe outside the day room. Two of the bastion's antlered footmen appeared at the far end of the annexe, dragging the pheguth between them from the transcoding chamber. The pheguth was shivering and retching, barely conscious.

'Be careful with him, you idiots!' Desolane shouted. 'Take him to his chamber.'

The footmen nodded, and began heaving the limp human up the marble stairs towards the tower room.

Fifteen minutes passed, and then Desolane heard boots thumping across the inner hall. Desolane rose, expecting Uexkull, but it was Mabbon Etogaur.

Desolane had divided feelings about the etogaur, but was prepared to admire him. Mabbon Etogaur had commanded many signal victories for the Anarch.

'Etogaur, good day,' Desolane said.

'Life-ward, my greeting. Is this fair time to talk with the pheguth?'

'Not the best. He's been in transcoding all morning. He'll be weak.'

'Even so.'

'Go on up. Wait for me, and I will take you in to see him.'

Mabbon nodded. 'Thank you.'

The etogaur had been gone for five minutes when Uexkull arrived. Attended by a coterie of four Chaos Space Marines, Uexkull clanked down the long hall in his burnished power armour, vapour wisping from the smoke-stacks rising from his back. He towered over Desolane, but still made an effort to bow.

'Life-ward,' he creaked. Uexkull's voice was hard as leather. Dry, stiff, calloused. 'You sent for me?'

'Yes, magir. I'd like you to look at this.' Desolane handed him the data-slate.

Uexkull's massive armoured hand took hold of the device almost daintily. He reviewed it. 'Las-fire,' he creaked.

'Indeed.'

'A patrol annihilated.'

'It speaks volumes, does it not?' Desolane said.

'Ineuron's a backwater.'

'Yes, but someone's there. Probably because it's a backwater.'

'Astartes?'

'No, I don't think so.' Desolane said. The huge warrior looked disappointed. 'But mission specialists. Guard. You know what to do.'

Uexkull nodded. 'Find them. Kill them. Gnaw on their bones.'

'The last part is optional,' Desolane said.

'Consider it done, life-ward,' said Uexkull.

AT DESOLANE'S INSTRUCTION, the footmen had taken the pheguth out onto the terrace. The fresh air and sunlight seemed to rouse him from his sickness a little, but there was still a palsied droop to one side of the pheguth's face that concerned Desolane. Perhaps they were pushing the transcoding too hard. The life-ward would consult a master of fisyk.

The terrace was a machicolated parapet crowning a huge talus at the north end of the bastion. The grey stone of the talus dropped away three hundred metres into the dark and ragged gorge beneath. From the terrace, unaided, it was possible to see nearly a hundred kilometres out across the heartland. The mountains rose, hard and angular, to all sides, and off to the west climbed higher than the perilous bastion itself, forming great, snow-capped summits that framed the distance in veils of icy mist and bright low cloud.

Beyond the rampart mountains, the vast farmlands of the midland bocage covered the land to the horizon with a lush green patchwork.

Desolane brought the pheguth a cloak. It was chilly on the exposed terrace, with a fresh, buffeting wind. The life-ward was sure that the pheguth would do nothing foolish, but instructed the footmen to lock the pheguth's ankle-cuff to an iron ring.

'You think I might end my life, Desolane?' the pheguth asked. 'Hurl myself into the oblivion of the gorge below?'

'I think it unlikely,' said Desolane. 'To have suffered and contended with so much only to submit now would seem… weak. And I do not believe you are a weak man. However, even strong men have moments of weakness, and the transcoding has not been kind.'

'You're right,' said the pheguth. 'Oblivion is quite attractive to me just now.'

'Perhaps conversation will divert your mind. The etogaur craves audience.'

The footmen led Mabbon Etogaur out onto the terrace. One carried a tray of refreshment. Then Desolane withdrew, leaving one footman to watch the entry.

Mabbon Etogaur looked out over the towering scene for a moment, then offered his pale, soft hand to the pheguth as he had done the day before.

'Sit down,' said the pheguth. Mabbon took a place at the other end of the iron bench.

'How is your health, sir?' he asked.

'Not as rude as I would like. I'm sure the psykers are trying to be gentle, but every session leaves me feeling as if I have been adrift in warp space.'

'Transcoding is a necessary evil,' said Mabbon. 'Why do you smile, sir?'

'It surprises me to hear you use the word "evil". I am well aware of its importance. My life depends upon it. If my mind cannot be transcoded, and its secrets unlocked, I am of very little use to you or your masters.'

'I believe you will be useful to me,' said Mabbon.

'Indeed? What shall we talk about then?'

'The one thing we both know,' said Mabbon Etogaur. 'Soldiering.'

ANA CURTH RINSED her mouth with the last water in her flask and spat in the weeds. They'd been confined to the grain silos for a day and a night, and the rancid dusty interiors – which by day became hot, sweltering, rancid dusty interiors – had made her hoarse and plugged her sinuses. She hoped to the God-Emperor that prolonged exposure to yeast mould and other airborne spores had not complicated the agues they would all be suffering from soon.

It was good at least to be outside for a spell. Bonin had found a small stone well at the edge of the ramshackle property from which issued water that, if not exactly potable, could be efficiently refined using the decontam tabs they carried in their packs. Curth, desperate for air, had volunteered to go and fill all the water bottles.

It was nearly midday. The sun was harsh and bright, and she was grateful for the shade along the track. Sickly trees clustered together along the side of the muddy yard, and insects sizzled in the merrymach and the hanging flowers. The yard, the morass, was slowly baking hard in the sunlight and exuding a strong, fecal odour. A stronger scent still came from a plank-covered silage pit halfway down the track.

But her mood was better, and it wasn't just the open air. After a night of waiting, they'd got the message by vox just before dawn. Curth had been beginning to think that they'd never see Gaunt or Mkoll again. The sounds that had been coming from the town during the night...

Even Rawne had seemed alarmed. On another occasion, the news that Gaunt was dead and he was in charge would have been like all his paydays rolled into one. But not here. Not now.

The well was a little stone post over a drain grate, with an iron tap fastened to the post. Curth found it easily enough, clutching the empty water bottles to her body to stop them knocking. She pulled a few strands of weed away and turned the tap. After a moment, brackish water began to spatter out.

She unstoppered the first flask, filled it from the flow, dropped in one of the tabs from her pocket, then rescrewed the top and gave the flask a good shake to mix the contents. That was one. She started on the second.

Just as she was about to start filling the fourth bottle, she heard a sound that made her turn off the faucet and listen in silence. An engine. She was sure she'd heard an engine from the direction of the road. Traffic had come and gone through the morning, and each time they'd laid low.

Nothing went past. Just her imagination then, or the sound of the splashing tap coming back from the leaves.

She picked up the fourth bottle and reached for the tap.

A hand closed over her mouth.

Curth went rigid with fear.

'It's me,' a whisper said into her ear. 'Don't make a sound.'

The hand came away. Curth looked round. Varl stood behind her, his finger to his lips. He saw the question in her eyes and pointed towards the roadway. She couldn't see anything.

Varl edged round the well. His rifle was slung over his back, but he'd drawn his autopistol. He beckoned her after him. She followed, forcing her feet to remember the basic stealth techniques Mkoll had drilled into her before the mission.

They moved into the thicker undergrowth under the trees. The road was a sun-bathed space beyond the black trunks. Varl suddenly went so still she almost bumped into him. He pulled her down until they were kneeling in the weeds.

A figure moved past on the road, little more than a silhouette. The silhouette had hard edges – a pack, a helmet, shoulder guards, a weapon. It was moving slowly in the direction of the silos. In less than minute, a second figure passed the same way.

This time Varl got a better look. Gleaming green combat armour, unit patches of a shouting or singing human mouth on the shoulder guards.

A military outfit.

Varl squirmed forward through the foliage and got a view out down the dusty, sunlit road. About two hundred metres down the rutted trackway, a quad-track troop carrier was parked in the shade of some mature talix trees. A squad of enemy troopers – Varl counted at least a dozen – was fanning out along the road towards the silo.

What was this? A chance patrol? A betrayal? Or had they somehow given their hiding place away? Varl screwed his body back into the undergrowth and thought hard for a moment. Curth was looking at him, rising panic in her eyes. He couldn't risk the vox, even a simple mic-tap. The hostiles had comm-sets and might well be listening.

He beckoned her again, and they slithered back the way they'd come, heading down to the path where the well stood. They'd have to sneak back around through the yard and carry the warning in person.

Curth grabbed his arm. Another hostile had just stepped into view on the overgrown path, near to the well. They'd put part of their force in through the treeline to encircle the silos. There was no way, no fething way in creation, that Varl could get himself back to the agri-plex now without being seen.

He closed his eyes. *Think, man, think…*

Varl cupped one hand around the other in a curious conjunction of grips and raised them to his mouth. Curth stared at him as though he was a lunatic.

He blew.

* * *

AT THE REAR of the silos, Brostin stood in the shade of the eaves. He'd told Rawne he was going out to take a leak, but he really just wanted to quell his cravings. He slipped one of the lho-sticks from their waterproof packet and put it between his lips. Ven had been straight as silver about this: no smoking, under any circumstances. What Brostin wouldn't give to light the thing. And not for the draw of smoke. Not so much. Really, what he craved to see was the tiny flame cupped in his gnarled hands. Larkin often called him a pyromaniac. Like it was a bad thing.

'Of course, you weren't going to light that, were you?' Bonin asked quietly. Brostin started. Fething scouts, popping out of nowhere.

'Course not,' he said.

'Course not,' Bonin echoed, leaning against the silo's side in the shade beside him.

'Just reminding myself of the feel of it.'

'That's fine.'

Bonin suddenly straightened up, listening. 'You hear that?' he hissed.

'What?'

'That. Just then.'

'Mmm. Yeah, Just a treecrake. Nesting, probably.'

Bonin drew his pistol. 'Get inside. Tell Rawne.'

'Tell Rawne what?'

'Since when were there Tanith treecrakes here… or anywhere else, for that matter?'

EIGHT

Close to the well, the enemy trooper paused and looked round into the undergrowth. He'd heard the odd, warbling call. He raised his weapon to his chest and began to advance.

Varl and Curth lay as flat in the brambles and weeds as they could. Slowly, very slowly, Varl slid his warknife out of its sheath.

The armoured trooper stopped suddenly, glancing down. Curth knew exactly what he'd seen. Ten Guard-issue water bottles on the grass beside the well.

Bending, the trooper reached up to activate his helmet vox.

Varl slammed into him, knocking him off his feet. The silver blade plunged in but glanced sideways off the shoulder armour. The trooper fought back, shoving Varl sideways. Undeterred, Varl punched the knife up under the helmet's chinstrap. The trooper rolled away, clutching his throat. Blood was pouring out more copiously than the water had flowed from the tap. The man got upright, gurgling. Varl grabbed him by the shoulders and slammed him, face-first, against the top of the well post. There was an ugly crunch.

Varl caught the deadweight before it hit the ground and dragged it into the undergrowth. Then he went back for the water bottles, pausing briefly to make the call again.

Silently, spurred by quick hand signals, the troop patrol came up around the silos. Insects ratcheted in the noon heat. The heavy boots of the combat detail made only slight, dull sounds on the dry earth. Some fanned out along the front of the silos, others slipped down the track and came around the rear, panning their weapons. In teams of two, they came up to the flaking doors of the silos.

* * *

THE LONG FIELD ended in a line of trees, and was covered down its entire length by rotting propagation frames around which soft fruits had once been trained. A rotten organic mulch festered in the trenches under the frames.

Cirk took a quick bearing and moved the team into cover in the field's hedge. They crouched down with her, two of her own cell members, as well as Gaunt, Mkoll and Landerson.

'We're close,' she said. 'The road's beyond those trees, and the agri-plex is down that way, about a kilometre.'

Mkoll nodded. That agreed with his own mental map, which was seldom wrong. The shifting forests of Tanith bred an unerring sense of direction in its sons.

'We should have range now,' Gaunt said. He adjusted his micro-bead.

'One,' he said. There was a pause.

Then a single word reply. 'Bragg.' Then the vox-channels went entirely dead.

'We've got trouble,' Gaunt said to Cirk.

THE PATROL COMMANDER, who bore the distinguished rank of sirdar, moved down the track from the road, checking his team's disposition. He was sweating in the heat inside his taut combat armour and presently wished a doom upon this stinking world worse than the one his kind had already visited upon it. His unit, along with a dozen like it, had been called up from the Ineuron garrison first thing that morning with orders to sweep the surrounding countryside. A job for excubitor crews, not combat troops, surely? Still, the alerts in the night had been extreme, and word was the martial response had been ordered by a senior ordinal. Another report said that Uexkull himself was en route to take charge, and the last thing the sirdar commander wanted was to be found shirking his duties by that monster.

They'd searched six deserted farmsteads that morning already. This one promised no more than the last, but the sirdar had remained true to his briefing. They'd left their transport back down the road and advanced on foot in a quiet, spread operation.

He reached the yard, and was about to give the signal to enter. The pincer squad had now moved up from the treeline ditches, and the place was pretty much surrounded, although it seemed as if one of the squad was missing. Lost in the woods, probably. The sirdar decided that when the trooper turned up, he'd shoot him himself and save Uexkull the bother.

He raised his hand, then paused. He'd distinctly heard a vox-signal, and it wasn't from his squad. Only the resistance had vox-sets...

The sirdar commander felt a prickle of anticipation. They were on to something. He drew his sidearm, and then made three quick hand gestures: contact suspected, lethal force, go.

His troops went in.

* * *

A SILO DOOR splintered open. Two armoured troopers thrust into the gloom, weapons raised. They crunched forward. Just heaps of mouldering grain. One looked up. Rafters, crossbeams. Shadows and cobwebs. The place was empty. They turned to leave.

Bonin and Feygor, knives drawn, rose up out of the spoiled crop heaps behind them, grain streaming off them in hissing rivulets, and seized them by the throats.

THE LATCH ON the storage outhouse parted at a kick. The first trooper in the gloom lit a lamp pack and played it around as his companion covered him with his assault weapon. They advanced into the main shed, which was stacked with old wooden crates. Piles of old hemp sacking covered the floor. The second two troopers went left, into a lean-to area where a rusted threshing machine sat up on blocks. They heard a thump from the main shed and backed up to check it.

The store shed was now empty. There was no sign whatsoever of the duo that had split that way. The troopers edged forward. A shadow seemed to flicker across one of the yellow, dirt-crusted window slits, and they turned rapidly to face it.

But Mkvenner was behind them.

He grabbed one by the edges of his tightly-strapped helmet and wrenched hard, snapping the neck in one twist. The corpse collapsed into the sacking Mkvenner had spread on the floor, its impact muffled. Before it had even landed, Mkvenner had turned, bent low at the waist, and driven the heel of his right foot into the throat of the other hostile. The trooper staggered backwards, unable to breathe, unable to even cry out. He dropped onto his knees, head bowed over, and Mkvenner drove the tip of his fingers down into the man's neck, finishing him off with a click like bone dice knocking together. The man collapsed forward onto his face, and Mkvenner dragged the bodies behind the crate stacks where the first two already lay.

THE END SILO also seemed empty. The two troopers sent in to check it approached the pungent, mildewed grain, searching for somewhere anything bigger than a rat could hide.

The cable shivered down out of the roof space and the noose on the end hooked neatly around the neck of one of them. Before he could exclaim his surprise, it had pulled ferociously tight and he was leaving the ground, feet kicking, hands to his throat.

Criid let gravity do the rest. As she jumped down off the rafter, she dragged the cable after her, and the trooper rose like a counterweight as the cable slid tight over the crossbeam, friction sawing it into the wood. The other trooper turned, astonished, as his companion shot up vertically into the roof, and she pendulumed into him, kicking him backwards onto the grain. Criid let go of the cable. The slicing noose had already finished the first man. Twitching, his body fell hard from the loosed cable.

Criid landed on the other one. She pinned his shoulders and shoved his face down into the polluted grain, her hand clamped around the back of his helmet. After a brief struggle, he went limp.

A trick? Her warknife made sure it wasn't.

THE PATROL'S SIRDAR suddenly realised something wasn't right. There were no signals of contact, no shots, but his men weren't coming back out of the silos and the sheds.

With a violent gesture, he moved the remainder of his unit in across the yard. Those positioned to cover the front now circled in too, down the side of the end silo.

The trooper next to the sirdar commander fell over on his back. Furious, the sirdar turned to reprimand him, then saw the small, bloody hole in the man's glare visor.

On the silo roof, sheltered by a vent hood, Larkin braced his aim and fired again. Using the silenced autopistol was no fun, but at least it was a challenge. It wasn't just a matter of hitting the targets. They were armoured and would easily shrug off a small cal round, especially one underpowered by a silencer. The art was to aim really well and hit them where they were soft. Visor. Throat. The armpit gap between chest plating and shoulder guard. Larkin fired off three more shots, and dropped two more of the hostiles in the caked mud of the yard.

Coming down the side of the silos from the road, one of the troopers turned at the sound of a heavy impact behind him. He saw the man at his heels had been felled by a devastating blow to the head that had cracked his helmet. Gleeful, Brostin swung the old threshing flail he'd found in the shed and smashed the second man into the clapboard siding of the silo. Wood seams popped and burst. Rawne rose up out of the undergrowth and cut down the last two before they could take a pop at Brostin. His silenced gun spat.

Then he and Brostin hurried down to the end of the path and added their quiet firepower to Larkin's. The final few troopers crumpled in the yard.

The sirdar had started running, along with his last surviving man. The silent sniper on the roof shot the man through the neck just short of the outbuildings, but the sirdar made it into cover, struggling with his helmet vox, trying to get a clear channel. He had to warn someone. He had to get a call out to the other units and–

Nothing. The vox was dead. Like it was being jammed. How was that even possible?

On the straw-littered floor of the shed in front of him, the sirdar saw an Imperial field-vox-set, infantry issue. It was powered up and active, the dials set to a white noise broadcast that would wipe vox contact, at least anything in the locality of the farm.

The sirdar commander took a step towards it.

The silencer of an autopistol pressed into the side of his head.

'Something awry, sir?' Beltayn asked, and pulled the trigger.

NINE

'ONE,' GAUNT SAID softly. They'd been lying low for over fifteen minutes, and this was the third time he'd tried the link. Now at least there was a background fizzle on the channel that suggested the link was finally live again. The sudden, jammed deadness had made his heart race.

'One,' he repeated.

'Silver.'

They moved off quickly, along the drainage ditch on the field side of the road, with Mkoll at the front. A little way down, they sighted the quad-track carrier parked on a dusty verge under the trees.

Mkoll shot a look at Gaunt.

'Occupation troopers,' whispered Cirk.

They pushed on and cautiously crossed the dry road-pan to the silos of the ruined agri-plex. The place lay still and silent in the hot afternoon. Insects buzzed. The hazed, polluted sky had broiled to a toxic ochre laced with sickly clouds.

Mkoll suddenly brought his weapon up. Bonin appeared from behind a low fence. He smiled. 'Good to see you,' he called.

They jogged up to join him. Bonin clapped his hand against Mkoll's briefly extended palm in a simple acknowledgement, then led them down the track to the rear of the silos.

Rawne and the others were dragging the enemy corpses into the yard and heaping them up. Feygor and Brostin were busy pilfering pockets and packs for anything useful. Or valuable. Most things they tossed aside: ugly charms, unholy texts printed into tiny chapbooks, inedible or inexplicable rations. Even gold coins lost their lustre to seasoned looters like Feygor when they came stamped with a mark of the Ruinous Powers.

'Been busy, major?' Gaunt asked.

Rawne looked up and shrugged. 'They came looking, so we showed them some Tanith hospitality.'

'Any survivors?' Mkoll asked.

Rawne gave the scout sergeant a withering look. 'Mkvenner's sweeping the area to double-check, but I think we were pretty thorough.'

'And very discreet,' Feygor added.

Cirk looked at the crumpled bodies and raised one eyebrow. 'That's... a whole unit,' she said.

Rawne shrugged. 'They didn't get off a single shot. And we didn't make a sound.' He turned to Gaunt. 'Who's this?' he asked.

'The contact we were after,' said Gaunt. 'Major Rawne, Major Cirk.'

They nodded to each other.

'The others are with her. Acreson and Plower. That's right, isn't it?'

Cirk nodded again. The two cell members who had accompanied her were greeting Purchason and Lefivre. The underground was a close-bonded group.

'As soon as they're listed overdue, the enemy will come looking,' Cirk said, gesturing to the dead.

'We'll be long gone,' Gaunt assured her. 'Rawne. Assemble the team and make ready to move out. Major Cirk's here to direct us to our next point of contact.'

'Good. I'm tired of waiting,' Rawne said.

'Anywhere we can dump these bodies out of sight?' Gaunt asked.

'The silos?' Bonin suggested.

'First place they'll look,' Cirk said.

'There's a silage pit down that way,' Varl said, walking over and wiping his dagger on a handful of straw.

'Let's do that,' Gaunt agreed. Brostin, Varl, Feygor and Bonin began hefting the corpses away down the track.

'What about the transport?' Landerson asked. 'That's not so easy to hide.'

'We could use a transport,' Mkoll said quietly. Gaunt looked at him.

'It's big enough,' Mkoll added. 'And they're less likely to stop a military vehicle.'

Gaunt paused thoughtfully and glanced sidelong at Cirk. She shrugged. 'It's a risk, but then so's everything. It would certainly shave some time off our journey. Edrian Province is a good sixty kilometres away. I was anticipating a couple of days to reach it on foot.'

'We'll take the transport,' Gaunt decided. 'At least for now. We can ditch it if needs be. Varl and Feygor both have some experience handling heavy rides.' He turned and called out down the track towards the men sliding bodies into the pit. 'Varl! Save two sets of armour. Helmet and shoulder guards at least!'

'Sir!' Varl called back. 'Can we wash them first?'

'Do what you have to.'

Gaunt walked across the yard and joined Curth. She was seated on the cross-spar of an abandoned mouldboard plough, checking her narthecium. 'Good to have you back,' she said. There was real feeling in her voice.

'Any trouble?' he asked.

'Apart from the obvious?' she said, with a nod to the dead.

'I mean the sort of thing a military surgeon shares with her mission commander.'

'Ague's taking a hold. Beltayn and Criid are both complaining of head colds, like pollen fever. Feygor's running a temperature, though he won't admit it, and he seems to be developing an infection in the flesh around his augmetic voicebox. I've given him another shot, and I'm keeping an eye on it. Larkin says he's fine, but he's sleeping badly. Nightmares. I heard him. He was talking to Bragg in his sleep. Talking to the dead. Can't be a good sign.'

'With Larks, that's borderline normal.'

She smiled at his cruelty. 'Brostin's just edgy. Bad-tempered.'

'Again, borderline normal. That's just withdrawal. Brostin would be chain-smoking lho-sticks under usual circumstances.'

'Ah,' she said. A pause. 'I know the feeling.'

'Anything else?'

'Everyone's tired. More than ordinary fatigue. And everyone's got this.' She pulled back her cuff. Her pale forearm was dotted with a prickle pattern like angry heat rash. 'Allergic reaction. I was wondering if it was the spores in those damn silos.'

Gaunt shook his head. He yanked down his own collar and showed her a comparable rash along the base of his neck and collarbone. 'We've all got it. It's an allergic reaction, all right. To this world. To the taint here. Major Cirk says it afflicted everyone on Gereon in the first few weeks after the invasion. When it fades... that's when I'll worry. Because that's when we're acclimatised.'

'When we've become tainted?' she asked.

He shrugged.

'Major Cirk,' Curth said, squinting across the yard at the resistance officer, who was standing in conference with her men and Landerson. 'She's... a good looking woman, don't you think?'

'Can't say I gave it any thought,' Gaunt replied.

'I'd better check you over,' Curth said, getting up. 'It would appear the taint of Gereon is suppressing your hormones.'

He chuckled. 'Check yourself too, Ana. Gereon may have a contagious strain of jealousy.'

She smacked him on the arm. 'In your dreams, colonel-commissar,' she smirked, and walked away.

Gaunt watched her go. He thought about his dreams. For so long now, they had been haunted by the beati, by Saint Sabbat. It felt as if she'd been in his mind forever, from the aching alpine vistas of Hagia to that small, neglected chapel in the woods on Aexe Cardinal. Guiding him, leading him, confusing him. Sometimes he dreamed of Sanian, and sometimes poor

Vamberfeld appeared, bleeding from the nine holy wounds he had taken at the Shrinehold as the Saint's proxy.

Gaunt's life and his destiny was tied to the Saint now, he knew that. It had been ordained by some higher power, and he hoped with all his soul that power sat upon a golden throne.

Herodor, bloody Herodor, just a year gone by now, had been a watershed. Gaunt had presumed that a face to face encounter with the Saint Incarnate might have exorcised his dreams. But, if anything, the dreams had grown worse in the time since then. His sleep was visited by the Saint in her glory, so beautiful it made him weep and awake with tears streaking his face. Figures attended her, half-seen in the mists of his swirling visions, people he missed dearly. Old Slaydo sometimes, hunched and pale. Bragg, dear Try Again Bragg, looking around himself in wonder at the enfolding darkness. Sometimes, very occasionally, Colm Corbec, laughing and calling to Gaunt to join him. Behind Corbec, every time he came, a proud honour guard of ghosts waited, rifles shouldered... Baffels, Adare, Lerod, Blane, Doyl, Cocoer, Cluggan, Gutes, Muril...

Gaunt shook the memory away. Despite the stifling heat in the silo yard, he felt cold sweat leak down his spine. Ghosts. Ghosts he had made, and then made ghosts.

Most chilling of all, he remembered, was the screaming. The dream where there was only darkness and a man's voice screaming piteously through it. Who was that? Who *was* that? He seemed to recognise the voice, but...

It seemed so helpless and so far away.

And not once, not once since Herodor, had he dreamed of the one face he missed more than any other, more even than Colm. Brin Milo had never featured in any of his dreams.

There was one final fact that nagged at his mind. From the moment he had set foot on Gereon, he had not dreamed at all. Months of dreams and faces and hauntings, and now not one, as if the watchful spirits could no longer reach him on this poisoned planet.

That was why he had responded so strongly to Cirk. To Sabbatine Cirk.

It had been the first clue he'd had since his arrival that the Saint had not forgotten him.

'Do WE REALLY have to go through this again today?' the pheguth sighed.

'We do,' said Desolane, walking him down the stone hallway. 'You do, pheguth.'

'I'm tired,' the pheguth said.

'I know,' Desolane replied. There was something close to compassion in the life-ward's musical voice. 'But demands are being made. Plenipotentiary Isidor is under pressure from host-command. It is said that the Anarch himself, whose word we serve and whose word drowns out all others, is frustrated at the lack of progress. As a resource, you promise much, pheguth, but you have yet to deliver. Great Sek may yet regard you as a waste of energy and have you executed if you don't yield up your secrets.'

The pheguth considered this, a slight smile creasing his face. His conversation with Mabbon Etogaur had revealed much about Magister Sek's plans. Too much, perhaps. It was clear to the pheguth now that Magister Anakwanar Sek, lord of hosts, Anarch, chosen warlord of the Archon Urlock Gaur himself, had ideas above his station. Sek wanted power. Control. Command. And the bastard considered the traitor general a key instrument in obtaining that power.

The pheguth remembered some of the briefings he had sat through as a high commander of the Imperial Guard. At Balhaut, the Crusade had destroyed Nadzybar, who had been the Archon of the Chaos host. Broken in retreat, the Archenemy forces had been riven by a succession struggle as Chaos factions warred to elect a new Archon. Many of the notorious magister-warlords had been in contention – Nokad the Blighted, Sholen Skara, Qux of the Eyeless, Heritor Asphodel, Enok Innokenti. Rumour had it that more of the Archenemy numbers were killed in that internecine war of succession than had been lost to the Crusade armada at that time.

Of all the contenders, Nokad had the charisma, Asphodel the temperament, and Qux the sheer weight of loyal servants. But Sek, Anakwanar Sek (whose word we serve, the pheguth reminded himself, and whose word drowns out all others) was the obvious choice. No other magister was quite so brilliant a battlefield technician. Sek's command of tactics and leadership was peerless, better than Slaydo, better than Macaroth himself.

Damn the Warmaster's life and name.

But Gaur, an obscure warlord from the fringes of the Sabbat Worlds, had become Archon. Why? Because he possessed the one thing that all the other magisters lacked. Even the great and blasphemous Sek.

What Urlock Gaur brought to the table was a refined, trained and disciplined military force. All the other magisters commanded vast legions of zealot cultists and insane worshippers. Hideous forces, but utterly without focus, and vulnerable to the rigid drive of the Imperial Guard.

Urlock Gaur's host was known as the Blood Pact. They were sworn to him, utterly loyal, their bodies ritually scarred by the serrated edges of Gaur's own armour. They had discipline, armour, tactical ability and great combat skill. They were, in fact, an army, not a host.

The pheguth had never encountered the Blood Pact in action, but he knew of them from intelligence reports. They were mankind's worst fear, a force of the Ruinous Powers guided and orchestrated on military models. They could meet with and defeat the Imperial Guard on its own terms, outfighting them.

For the simple reason that the Blood Pact was modelled directly on the structure of the Imperial Guard.

They borrowed their weapons and armour, they stole their uniforms, they seduced Guardsmen into their ranks and made them traitors, stealing their skills. They were a force the Imperium must reckon with, and they had secured Gaur the rank of Archon.

Throne take them, they might even have the skill to drive Macaroth's Crusade back out of these stars.

And that, very simply, is what Sek wanted. He reviled Gaur for his success. Sek wanted, yearned, longed, to be named Archon. He was biding his time, playing the part of a loyal magister to the most high Archon. But he prized that rank as his own. He felt he deserved it. He was, by any measure, a finer leader than Gaur.

And the first step along the way was to build a Blood Pact of his own. A fully and finely trained military force as good as, if not better than, the Blood Pact.

This was the delicate matter Mabbon Etogaur had spoken to him about. Mabbon – and how very much the pheguth had warmed to the fellow – was a traitor in his own right. Etogaur was a Blood Pact rank. Mabbon had, by means the pheguth could not imagine, been tempted away from Gaur's service and employed by Sek to use his knowledge of the Blood Pact's workings to forge a similar force.

Gereon was the base for this work. The pheguth, with his intimate knowledge of the Imperial Guard, an invaluable tool. Alongside Mabbon, the pheguth was to use his skills, training and abilities to build the Sek's force.

Mabbon had given it a name during their conversation on the windy terrace: the Sons of Sek. A force of warriors that would eclipse the Blood Pact and defeat, without quarter, the vaunted Imperial Guard.

'Pheguth?' Desolane said. The hatch stood open.

'Are they ready for me?' the pheguth asked.

Desolane nodded.

'Desolane… please understand, I do so want them to learn my secrets,' the pheguth said. 'It's just this…'

'Mindlock,' answered Desolane. The life-ward tapped one finger against its own bronze mask as if to indicate the skull beneath. The taps sounded alarmingly hollow, as if the bronze mask was empty.

The pheguth stepped through the hatch and walked into the small stone chamber. He sat down in his seat. It had been scrubbed and sterilised since his last visit. He settled. The electric cuffs snapped down over his wrists and ankles. The chair rotated backwards until he was staring at the arched roof.

'Pheguth,' a voice whispered.

'Hello,' he replied.

'Again, we begin.'

The pheguth could not see the alien psykers, but he could hear them shuffling close. The chamber went cold. Icicles formed above him. He braced himself, and his augmetic hand clenched hard against the steel restraints. The psykers edged closer.

Scabby hands reached up and plucked the little rubber plugs from the pre-drilled holes in his skull.

'Gods, how I hate this…' the pheguth murmured.

There was a mechanical whine of servos, and a high pitched shrill. The delicate psi-probe needles, mounted on a bio-mechanical armature, approached his shaved skull and slipped into the holes.

The pheguth convulsed. His mouth opened wide.

'Let us start again at the beginning,' the psi-voice commanded.

'Gaaaah!' the pheguth responded.

'Your rank?'

'Ngghh! General! Lord general!'

'Your name?'

'Nghhh! I can't... I can't remember! I- aghhh!'

'Unlock! You must unlock! Unlock!' the voices called.

'Nyaaaaa! I can't! I can't! I can't!'

Desolane listened for a while, then when the screaming became too much for even the life-ward to bear, it closed the hatch on the transcoding chamber and walked away.

TEN

FOLLOWING CIRK'S GUIDANCE, they drove north, avoiding Ineuron Town and its outlying agri-habs, and joined a major arterial route that ran in a long, straight line across a flat immensity of pasture land. Varl drove, quickly becoming accustomed to the quad-track's spare, functional controls.

There was little traffic. They passed a couple of slow convoys of vittaler wagons plodding towards Ineuron, and a few battered trucks running errands for the occupation with consented locals at their wheels. Once in a while, they sighted figures on the dusty road ahead – refugees and vagabonds – but these ragged souls fled into hiding in the overgrown pastures at the sight of a military transport.

They'd been going for about an hour when Larkin, sharp-eyed as ever, warned them that a vehicle was coming up behind them. Gaunt told Varl to maintain speed and took a look. It was an armoured car, a STeG 4, lighter and faster than the quad-track. The Ghosts immediately checked their weapons.

Thundering along on its four, big wheels, the STeG came up behind them and sounded its horn.

'Feth!' Varl said. 'Do they want me to pull over?'

He dropped his speed slightly and edged over towards the gutter. The armoured car immediately accelerated and went round them, blasting its horn again. Two armoured troopers stood in the top of the SteG's cabin well and waved salutes to their 'comrades' in the quad as they overtook. Standing up in the quad-track, Bonin waved back. He was wearing the borrowed helmet and shoulderguards. His lasrifle was just out of sight behind the handrail.

The armoured car quickly shot past and pulled away, leaving pink dust in its wake.

THE PASTURE FLASHING by on either hand was, like so much of the fecund agri-world's premium land, sadly neglected. The grasses had grown out, springing tall and lank, and had dried to straw. The pastures appeared bleached, like silver wire. Profusions of weed flowers had flourished: hot red emberlies like spatters of blood, and millions of white grox-eye daisies. Gaunt stared at the passing view. The Archenemy had broken Gereon, and tainted it, but even in its undoing there was accidental beauty like this. A transient glory, seen by very few, had been produced by miserable neglect. Not for the first time, Gaunt reflected that whatever the actions of mankind and the foes of mankind, the cosmos asserted its own nature in the strangest ways.

The afternoon began to fade. The seared sky became a darker, acid green, and then dark clouds began to heap in the west. Thunderstorms fizzled into life, and mumbled in the distance. The air became heavy and charged.

They drove on for another half hour, until Varl was forced to switch on the transport's running lights. The sky had now bruised a dark, unhealthy brown. There was rain in the wind. They drove through several burned-out villages, and then the land became more hilly and they reached the fringes of a belt of forest.

'We're just crossing into Edrian Province,' Cirk said. 'A little further, and we should stop for the night.'

During the invasion, fighting had been fierce along the province's borders. The roadway had been repaired in many places. Stretches of forest had been bombed or burned flat and the road wound through scorched wildernesses where only the splintered, black trunks of trees poked from the ash. They saw the wreckage of abandoned war machines, most of them PDF armour, and dry, shrivelled heaps that had once been bodies. Elsewhere, the forest had been mutilated by acid rain. The team aboard the quad had been chatting amiably on the open road, but now they fell silent, their faces solemn.

They had just reached another village on the woodland road when the rains began. Beltayn and Criid raised the tarp roof over the transport crew compartment, and they heard the caustic rain sizzling as it ate at the treated canvas.

Drum fires had been lit along the roadway. Ahead, beside a grim ouslite customs house, a roadblock had been set up. A small queue of vehicles was drawn up to it, headlamps on and engines running as the guards checked consent papers and imagos.

Varl slowed down. 'What now?' he asked.

'Just a routine inspection post,' said Landerson. Cirk nodded agreement.

'Go round,' she said. 'Follow my lead.' She picked up the helmet and shoulderguards Bonin had used. Varl downshifted the transmission, and rolled the quad-track round the tail-end of the queue. Peering out, Gaunt could see a lot of hostiles on the ground under the awnings of the checkpoint. Excubitors and occupation troops. Several officers. He wondered if they had dogs, or worse. By the roadside just ahead, the rotting corpses of executed law-breakers hung on display from a wooden scaffold.

Varl overtook the line of waiting trucks and came up to the barrier. A trooper in a rainslicker poncho approached, holding up one mailed hand.

'Voi shet! Ecchr Anark setriketan!' he shouted above the drumming downpour.

Cirk stood up, disguise in place. 'Hyeth, voi Magir!' she called, pitching her voice low. 'Elketa sirdar shokol Edrianef guhun borosakel.'

'Anvie, Magir!' the trooper replied, and waved them through at once. The checkpoint barrier lifted smartly, and Varl gunned the quad forward.

'What did you tell him?' Gaunt asked Cirk as she sat down next to him and pulled the helmet off.

'That my commanding officer was late for a meeting in Edrian thanks to the damn rain, and was in the mood to shoot the next idiot who delayed him.'

Gaunt nodded and then thought for a moment. 'Major?'

'Yes?'

'*How* did you tell him that?'

'I used their language, colonel-commissar. You pick it up. It's essential for underground work.'

'Right,' said Gaunt. He leaned back, not at all reassured. Rawne sat across the compartment from him, facing him. Gaunt knew the look in his number two's eyes. 'Vouchsafe?' Rawne mouthed.

Gaunt shook his head.

Plower, one of Cirk's people, got up and took a look out ahead into the dismal night. 'Next turning left leads to the Baksberg ornithons. We can find shelter and a good place to lie low.'

Cirk agreed. 'Give Mr Varl instructions,' she said, then turned to look at Gaunt. 'If that's all right with you.'

'Carry on,' said Gaunt.

THE TRACK TURNING led them off the main arterial into the festering darkness of the woodlands. The heavy rain had turned the track into a mire, but the quad's big tread sections coped well. White smoke drifted from the acid-bitten trees around them, and there was a pungent stink of halides and sulphur.

The headlamps picked out a cluster of buildings up ahead. The ornithon, typical of the poultry farms common in that woodland region, comprised a low-gabled main house, stores, feed bins and the long, mesh-walled hutches of the batteries. The place was ruined. A loading tractor, stripped to its bare metal by months of corrosive rain, slumped in the main yard on decomposing tyres.

The main house had lost its roof, but the batteries were still intact and relatively dry. They reeked of birdlime and decay. The mission team and its allies dismounted and dashed into the shelter. While the scouts checked the area for security, Larkin, Criid and Feygor cleared some floor space of the foul-smelling straw, and Brostin set up a few lamps. Beltayn went to work preparing food. Landerson and Plower volunteered to help him, setting up the portable stove, and fetching water from the outside pump for purification. Cirk sat down in a corner, in deep conversation with Purchason and Acreson. Lefivre settled alone in the shadows, lost in his own thoughts.

'Check everyone,' Gaunt told Curth. She nodded. 'Including our associates,' he added.

'What do I tell them?' she asked.

'Tell them I'm concerned for the health of everyone in my team.'

Curth began to prepare her kit.

Varl came in from the rain, having parked and shut down the quad-track. He was heading for the stove to warm his hands, but Gaunt caught him by the sleeve as he went by.

'Sir?'

'Find a good reason to lurk in earshot of Cirk. I want to know what they're talking about.'

'You got it,' Varl said.

Gaunt turned to Rawne. 'Arrange a watch. But make sure everyone gets a decent rest.'

'Right,' said Rawne. He paused.

'Something else on your mind?'

Rawne shrugged. 'I was just thinking,' he whispered. 'If we didn't need their help so badly, I'd kill them all.'

'But we do need their help.'

'Maybe,' Rawne said. 'Keep your eye on that one, though,' he said quietly, indicating Lefivre with a roll of his eyes. 'I mean, Landerson seems all right, and Cirk knows what she's about, it would seem. But that one…'

'Strung out?'

'And then some.'

'I noticed. Landerson seems to be carrying him, as if he's close to losing his nerve.'

'One word, that's all it takes. One word from you.'

'I know,' said Gaunt. 'For what it's worth, major, I'm inclined to agree. If we didn't need their help so badly, I think I'd kill them too.'

'WHO'S IN CHARGE here?' Uexkull growled as he burst into the room. The light from the hovering glow-globes shone off his ribbed copper armour. Chief Sirdar Daresh rose quickly to his feet, scraping back his chair. He put his fork down next to his half-finished supper and hurried to swallow the mouthful he was chewing.

'I am, lord,' he said. The dining hall of Occupation Headquarters, Ineuron, fell silent, and the other officers sprang to their feet from the long table in a terrified hush. Rain beat against the shutters. Uexkull was so massive he'd had to turn his shoulders sideways to pass through the doorway.

'You are an incompetent weakling,' Uexkull said, and shot Daresh through the head with his bolt pistol. The single shot made a deafening boom in the close confines of the chamber. Daresh's almost headless corpse cannoned backwards from the end of the table, knocking over his chair. A blizzard of blood and tissue spattered the officers standing to attention at the table. They winced, but none of them dared move, not even to wipe clots of brain matter from their faces.

Uexkull walked down the length of the table, his armour's hydraulics clicking and whirring. The wooden floor creaked under his great weight. Two of his warriors took up positions at the doorway.

Uexkull reached the head of the table. He rolled Daresh's limp body out of the way with his foot, and set the chair upright. Then he sat down on it. The chair groaned under the monster's bulk.

Uexkull put his engraved bolt pistol on the table beside the place setting. Pale wisps of smoke still fluted from the muzzle.

'Who is,' Uexkull asked, his voice like the slither of dry scales, 'second in command? Say, for instance, if the garrison commander is suddenly deprived of brain activity?'

There was a nervous silence. Uexkull picked up Daresh's fork, speared a piece of fatty meat off the half-finished plate, and popped it into his mouth, oblivious to the speckles of fresh blood that dotted the food, the fork, the plate and the table.

He chewed. Swallowed. 'Do I look like I have all night?' he creaked.

'I... I am, lord,' said the officer standing to his left.

'Are you? Name?'

'Erod, vice sirdar.'

Uexkull nodded, toying with his fork. Then he swung round and impaled Erod through the throat with it. Erod staggered backwards, hands to his neck, face contorted, and collapsed backwards, writhing and vomiting blood.

'Lesson number one,' Uexkull said over the sounds of a man drowning in his own body fluids. 'When I ask a question, I expect an immediate answer. Vice Sirdar Erod would not be in that pretty fix now if he'd just spoken up when asked. I am not, by nature, a dangerous man...'

The warriors at the door sniggered.

'Oh, all right. I am. I really am. I am bred, trained and equipped for one purpose. To kill the enemy. I understand that I lack subtlety. Subtlety was not part of my training. I am not a governor, an ordinal, an arbiter of laws, a calculator of tariffs. The Plenipotentiary keeps me here as part of the Occupation force for a single reason. To kill the enemies of the Anarch.'

There was a long pause.

'Who is third in command?' Uexkull asked.

'I am, lord,' said the officer to his right, an older trooper whose face was heavily spotted with Daresh's blood.

'Good,' Uexkull nodded. 'Quick. Obedient. And your name is?'

'Second Vice Sirdar Eekuin, lord.'

'You answered promptly, Eekuin. You have learned. I will not kill you. Unless you are an enemy of the Anarch. Are you, perhaps, an enemy of the Anarch, Eekuin?'

'I am not, lord. I am true to the Anarch, whose word we serve–'

'And whose word drowns out all others,' Uexkull finished, raising one hand to cover his mouth. 'Eekuin, you're now in charge. Command of the Ineuron Town occupation is in your hands. Your first task will be to explain to me why the enemy insurgents have not been located and destroyed.'

'Lord, we have searched the town. During the night, the wirewolves were roused and they found nothing either. Checks have been doubled, house to house–'

Uexkull raised his hand. 'I have been in the town now for three hours. I have seen the patrols, the search sweeps. I know what's being done. What concerns me is what is *not* being done.'

'Yes, lord.'

Uexkull slid a data-slate out of his belt pouch and speed read the display. 'An excubitor patrol slaughtered at the Shedowtonland Crossroads. A terrorist campaign. Bombings. A firefight in the midtown areas yesterday that left the better part of two more excubitor squads dead. Las-weapons used. This is not the work of the resistance cells.'

'No, lord. I did not suppose it was.'

'So… something more dangerous than a resistance cell has been active in this backwater. Call me old-fashioned, but wouldn't that make it a priority for the senior staff here to find the interlopers and obliterate them?'

'I believe it would, lord,' Eekuin replied.

'Yet… and yet, you're sitting down to dinner.'

Eekuin risked lifting his right hand to wipe away blood that was beginning to trickle into his eye. 'I request permission, lord, to rectify that at once and organise the senior staff into a hunting pattern.'

'That would be good,' said Uexkull. 'Permission granted.'

Eekuin stepped back from the table, saluted, and turned to issue an order to the frozen officers around him. Uexkull picked up his bolt pistol.

'Eekuin?'

The man halted, shaking.

Uexkull expertly swung the pistol over in his hand so that the grip was pointing at Eekuin. 'Before you start with that, shut Erod up, will you? He's making a bloody awful noise down there.'

Eekuin took the bolt pistol, cleared his throat, and walked round the table. Erod, his face blue, thrashed on the floor in a pool of blood. He clawed at Eekuin's ankles. Trying to look dismissive, Eekuin shot him between the eyes. The shot's impact punched the impaling fork up into the air.

It landed with a clatter. The ghastly gurgling fell silent.

Eekuin handed the weapon back to Uexkull.

'Find me something,' Uexkull told him. 'Find me something in the next fifteen minutes, or I'll be asking after the next in line.'

* * *

THE GHOSTS WERE settling down to sleep, weary and fed well enough from the stew Beltayn had concocted. Acid rain still belted against the ornithon's low roof. Curth came over to Gaunt, nursing a cup of caffeine.

'Anything?' he asked.

'Not here,' she said, and drew him away towards the back of the long hutch. Brostin and Feygor chuckled as they observed the game of regicide Criid was playing with Varl. Everyone else was dozing.

'What?' Gaunt asked.

'I checked them all out,' Curth said. 'Your lady friend, and her man Acreson... they have parasites embedded in their forearms.'

'You sure?'

'Ibram, they made no effort to conceal them. Throne, they're filthy, awful things. Bedded deep. Landerson and the others had theirs cut out.'

'Right,' Gaunt said. 'Go find Mkoll for me.'

EEKUIN STRODE INTO the control room and saluted Uexkull. Around them, by lamplight, the ordinals and servitors manned the clanking codifiers and instruments of the command annexe.

'What do you have for me, chief sirdar?' Uexkull asked.

Eekuin held out a data-slate.

'A military patrol has not reported in, lord. It went out this morning, searching farms along the Shedowtonland road. Garrison lists it as missing.'

Uexkull studied the chart. 'A full unit? How is that possible? And where's their damned vehicle gone?'

'Vox log records the unit's last check was just before midday. They were dismounting to search Parcelson's agri-plex.'

'Where the Eye is that?'

'Just out of town on the foreroad. I've sent another unit to check it out.'

'There's something else, isn't there, Eekuin?'

'Lord?'

'You look pleased with yourself.'

Eekuin produced another data-slate. 'The unit was using a quad-track, pool serial II/V. A vehicle bearing that mark was passed by the border checkpoint at Baksberg earlier tonight.'

'Baksberg? Location?'

'On the Edrian provincial border, lord.'

Uexkull smiled. The sight of his teeth made Eekuin feel unwell. 'Contact Edrian Occupation. Tell them I want a vox-link to their area commander. Tell them about the mood I'm in, Eekuin. Tell them how I murdered your senior officers without compunction. Tell them I'm inbound. Have the link relayed to my ship. I want a full battalion mobilised and ready at Baksberg by the time I arrive.'

'Yes, lord,' Eekuin replied. As Uexkull marched out of the room, Eekuin sagged a little. He was still alive.

'Get me Edrian Command,' he snapped.

* * *

'COLONEL-COMMISSAR?'

Cirk stepped into the feed store under the low doorway. A single lamp burned. The rain fell outside.

'Hello, Cirk,' Gaunt said, appearing from the shadows.

'What is this?' she asked, her attractive face tilted inquisitively. 'I need to sleep. We've a long day ahead of us.'

He stepped closer. 'The day can wait,' he said. 'Sabbatine… may I call you that? Sabbatine, there's something about you. Something that utterly intrigues me.'

She smiled. 'Well, I have felt it too. But this isn't the time or the place…'

'Why not?' he asked. He was in her face now. Tall, thick-set. Warm. His nose almost touched hers. His hands went around her waist.

'Sabbatine…'

'Really, I… I don't think this is…'

His strong hand gripped her arm. Twisted. She yelped.

'Gaunt, what?'

'What indeed. What the Throne is this, Cirk? Answer me that?'

He had pulled up her sleeve. The imago, in its dark blister, throbbed against her pale skin.

'You bastard!' she said.

'Oh, please,' he snapped, pulling her arm around so the lamplight caught it. 'Why don't you explain–'

Her punch caught him by surprise. Base of the neck. Nerve point. As he folded, he cursed himself for being so stupid. His knees hit the straw. Wrenching free, she kicked him for good measure, right in the ear.

'Feth!' he snarled, hurt.

'And that's about all I'll let you get away with,' said Mkvenner, sliding out of the shadows.

She whipped round to face him. He was holding a two-metre length of slender-gauge fence post, a ready-made quarter-staff. One end smacked round and knocked the autopistol away even as she drew it. The other end winded her and, as she doubled over, the staff dropped down over her shoulders and pinned her arms.

'Thanks, Ven,' Gaunt said, getting back on his feet.' Obviously, in future, I won't want you to constrain my dates like this.'

Ven laughed.

'You have an imago,' Gaunt said to Cirk. She spat at him, wrestled tight by Mkvenner's horizontal staff.

'You bastard! I thought we had a degree of trust!'

'We did. We have. But I want that explained.'

'This?' she said, looking down at the grub in her arm.

'Yes, Cirk,' Gaunt replied, pulling one of his bolt pistols out of its chest holster and cocking it. 'I'm a commissar, first and foremost. The next words you speak had better be fething good.'

'This imago is consented for day and night, you idiot. I'd have been a fool to let it be removed. How the hell do you think the resistance remains active? We need to use everything we have to beat their glyfs and their scanners. You think I like having this thing eating into my arm? You bastard! I can't get you into Edrian without this. I can't get you anywhere! It's all about consent! Some of us have them removed if they're restrictive, but Acreson and me, we have full clearance.'

She stopped. 'Acreson. What have you done to him?'

'Nothing, yet,' Gaunt said.

She looked at him. 'We have to work their system, Gaunt. Please believe me. That's the only reason I haven't had this thing taken out of me. It's too useful. Ibram... please.'

Gaunt reholstered his weapon.

'Let her go, Ven,' he said.

JUDDERING THROUGH THE torrential rain, the pair of deathships swung in towards Baksberg. In the lead ship, Uexkull readied his weapons. Seated with him, his four warriors did likewise. They'd been through the fires of many war-theatres with him. He knew them, trusted them.

Uexkull latched his autocannon against his shoulder plate and connected the servo feeds.

'Baksberg, coming up now. Four minutes,' the pilot voxed.

Uexkull slammed a sickle mag home in his bolt pistol.

'Prep for exit,' he hissed.

The vox beeped. 'Lord, this is Eekuin.'

'Go ahead.'

'The search unit has reported back. They found the entire patrol in a silage pit. All dead. A variety of wounds.'

'Commando tactics, Eekuin?'

'Most certainly, lord.'

'Understood. Uexkull out.' The monster turned to his warriors. 'Imperial Guard. Specialists. Damn good at what they do, it would appear. But still, just men. This will be over quickly.'

His warriors growled their agreement.

'Do we have a location yet?' Uexkull barked.

The pilot came back smartly. 'Baksberg checkpoint directs us on a likely target zone, lord. There are a number of abandoned ornithons in the back-woods off the main road here, and activity has been reported at one.'

'Poultry farms?' Uexkull questioned.

'Yes, lord,' the pilot said.

Uexkull smiled. 'Consider them plucked.'

ELEVEN

THERE WAS NO quarter. The first of the deathships, its thrusters whining, dropped low until its hull was brushing through the wood's wet canopy, and then opened fire with its forward gunpods. The rainy night suddenly lit up with strobing flashes of bright yellow radiance that captured rapid snap-shots of the slanting rain like stop-frame playback. Clouds of steam billowed off the gunpod vents as they heated. The hail of heavy fire disinte-grated the walls of the main house and threw tiles and broken stone high into the air.

The deathship steadied, and swung around on a low hover above the ornithon's yard. Its gun pods started up again, pulverising a row of store sheds.

The other ship dropped in low on the approach track and opened its hatches. Uexkull was first out, splashing along the muddy lane in the dark. Augmetic sensors embedded in his collar-plate and the side of his cranium automatically selected low light scoping. Nictating filters slid over his eyes. The world resolved into a ruddy blur, the crimson wash of cold areas grad-uating to the palest pink tells of heat sources. The muzzle flash cones of the hovering deathship up ahead read as searing white blinks that overlapped as their after-images gently faded.

Uexkull reached the edge of the yard, his squad at his heels. He heard the first hand-weapon discharge: bolter rounds whipping like small comets through the night to his left as Czelgur began firing on the rear of the main dwelling. Uexkull's enhanced aural sensors heard the bat-squeak pain of a human voice behind the furious noise of the guns and the lifter jets. Gut-tural vox interplay chattered back and forth between the monstrous Chaos Space Marines.

'Main dwelling secure,' Gurgoy voxed. 'Three kills.'

'Stores cleared. Another two dead here,' Virag reported.

A grenade detonated, filling the edge of Uexkull's vision with a bolus of light. More bat-squeaks, and a single, lingering wail of agony. The downwash of the hovering deathship spattered liquid mud across him, and he felt the delicious sizzle of the acid rain on his flesh. He smashed through the loose plank wall of the nearest hatching battery. Something scrambled in the shadows to his right, but he saw only heat and cold. His cannon slammed into life, licking out a sizzling flash, the recoil smacking it back against the locking harness in his upper body armour. Something made of meat and bone atomised. Another heat spot, right ahead, moved against the cold-streaming fuzz of the rainwater drizzling in through the roof. Uexkull fired his bolt pistol and saw a human-shaped pink outline crash over onto the floor. He strode forward, smelling blood now over the birdlime, the acid and the driven smoke.

Nezera burst into view to his left, shredding chain-link mesh aside with his powered claw, his bolt weapon barking into the depths of the battery as he broke his way inside.

'Go left!' Uexkull grunted. He took another few steps and then paused as a burst of small-arms fire – small calibre solid rounds – was stopped harmlessly by his carapace armour. Tracking round, he unloaded his cannon again, ripping down part of the hutch roof. He saw the shooter's shape on his optics briefly, spinning away, torn, just before the roof collapsed on it.

More pathetic gunfire came his way. Resistance at last, though hardly the sport he'd been looking forward to.

BONIN POINTED. THERE wasn't much to see – just a distant flashing that delineated trees against the encompassing night. But the sounds were enough, carried through the rain. The dull thwack of heavy cannons. The whistle of lift-jets.

'Feth,' Gaunt murmured. 'How far?'

'No more than two kilometres,' the scout replied.

Gaunt hurried back into the battery. 'Up now! Everyone! We're moving now!'

The party began to stir from sleep, cold and numb.

'Come on! By the Emperor! Now!'

The Ghosts needed no further urging. Cirk also leapt to her feet and shook her fighters into shape. Lefivre woke up screaming, and Cirk clamped her hand over his mouth, trying to get him to remember where he was.

'The quad?' Varl asked Gaunt as he ran up.

'No, we can't risk starting it. On foot, out the back. Mkoll! Get those lamps off! Ven! Find us an exit path. Consult Cirk!'

Mkoll and Beltayn gathered up the lamps and killed their glow.

'Sound off!' snapped Rawne, shouldering his pack.

He got a curt reply from everyone except Larkin.

'Lead them out,' Gaunt said to Rawne. 'Double-time it. I'll find him.'

Larkin was curled up in a straw-filled roosting pen. He'd slept on through the fuss. Gaunt shook him.

'Larks! Come on!'

Larkin's face was a pale, thin shape in the gloom.

'Is it time, Try?' he whispered.

'Come on, Larkin!'

'What's it like being dead?'

Gaunt slapped the sniper across the face. 'Larkin! Wake up! We're in trouble.'

Larkin roused with a start and moaned quietly as he realised his surroundings.

'Get your kit. Don't leave anything. Come on, Larks, I need you to be sharp.'

'Feth this,' Larkin whimpered. 'I was dreaming I was dead and now I wake up and find things are much worse.'

RAWNE AND MKVENNER led the group out through the back yard of the ornithon towards the trees. It was pitch black, and they'd wrapped their camocapes around themselves against the burning rain. The wet air was caustic and caught at their throats. Criid came close behind, urging Cirk's men along.

Last out of the ramshackle farm were Gaunt and Larkin. In the distance, the gunfire had stopped.

CZELGUR RAISED A spitting flare in his left paw and by the light of it Uexkull crouched and turned over the nearest body. Bolter fire had mangled it, but not so much that Uexkull couldn't see the rag clothing and the emaciated, malnourished build. The others were the same.

'Fugitives. Unconsented,' Uexkull muttered, his voice stiff and dry like caked mud cracking. One of the bodies clutched an old vermin-gun, a rusting small calibre weapon. There was no sign of any lasguns.

'Unless standards have dropped, these are not soldiers of the False Emperor,' Uexkull said. Czelgur snorted at his leader's ironic scorn. 'We've wasted the night tracking unconsented outlaws.'

Static warbled on the vox-link.

'Go,' said Uexkull, rising to his feet.

'Auspex is showing a large metallic contact in the woods two point three-one kilometres east of us, lord.'

'Let's move!' Uexkull shouted.

THEY WERE A good way into the acid-bitten woods when they heard the sound of the deathships behind them. The machines circled over the ornithon, playing their stablights over the ruined outbuildings.

'They'll find the transport,' Varl said.

'No helping that,' Rawne replied.

'Let's just keep going,' said Gaunt. His skin itched from the rain, and the vapour drifting up from the dissolving leaf mould under their feet was making them all short of breath.

According to Cirk, deeper forest lay to their west, and then something she called the Untill, which didn't seem to be an option. She directed them north. They were, she insisted, about ten kilometres short of one of the main arterial routes through Edrian Province, and once they hit that they would be close to the outer townships. In one of those, she hoped, they could make contact with the local cell.

'But handling your team north through the province isn't going to be easy now,' she said. 'The enemy is likely to be fully alerted. The garrisons will be mobilised. But we'll have to risk it.'

'Is there an alternative?' asked Mkoll.

'We could go wide to the east, maybe up through hills. But that's a long detour. On foot, a month. And that's without trouble. The search zones will widen if they don't find us around Edrian.'

Gaunt said nothing. He'd expected trouble from the outset, but this was bad luck. The occupation was tighter than he'd hoped and he doubted the enemy would take long figuring out what they were doing on Gereon.

Unless, he thought, they could manage a little misdirection. But putting that notion into effect would take a little time. They had more immediate problems to deal with.

'THAT'S THE MISSING transport,' Gurgoy said. Uexkull nodded. Clutching an overhead handgrip, he leaned a little further out of the hovering deathship's open hatch and peered down. The shifting stablights flickered through the rain below, lighting up the abandoned ornithon.

'Life signs?'

'Nothing human, lord,' the pilot voxed.

'Move us north,' Uexkull ordered. 'Slow and low.'

'Yes, lord.'

The two gunships began to prowl forward above the woodlands. Uexkull knew there was no point trying to track the insurgents on the ground. The acid rain would have obliterated any traces or spores already. He activated his heat vision again, gazing down at the canopy, hoping to pick up some pale flicker of bodywarmth in the wood. He got nothing but a vague pink fuzz. The acid decomposition had raised the background temperature of the leaves and the woodland floor as it digested the organics. Nothing was reading back. A human could be standing in plain view down there and be invisible against the ambient radiation.

'Where's the local battalion now?' he asked.

'At the Baksberg checkpoint as per your orders, lord,' the pilot responded. 'Another brigade strength force is in transit along the Edrian road.'

'Transmit my orders. The battalion moves into the woods and fans out. Search pattern, northward sweep. The brigade forms a picket along the road way and holds for anything the sweep flushes out.'

'Yes, lord.'

'This will be done in the name of the Anarch, whose word drowns out all others,' Uexkull said. He felt a hint of failure. That was something he did not enjoy, and seldom experienced.

By dawn, perhaps he would have made that feeling go away.

DARK SHAPES AGAINST a darker sky, the two deathships passed overhead, the long white beams of their searching lights penetrating the rotting tree cover. Their downwash made the branches stir and rustle.

Once they had gone by, the Ghosts stirred out of hiding. They'd covered themselves with their camo-capes, huddling down with the resistance fighters so they could share the concealment.

'Thank you,' said Landerson. He'd sheltered under Criid's camo-cape.

She shrugged. 'They find you, they find me,' she said.

'No chatter,' said Rawne. 'Let's get moving again.'

At the back of the file, Mkoll paused, his head slightly cocked, listening. Behind them, to the south, fetch-hounds had begun to bay.

TWELVE

WHEN THE PHEGUTH woke up, he noticed three strange things.

The bastion seemed very quiet, that was the first thing. It was early still (he guessed, he had no chronograph), and his tower chamber remote, but even so, there was no sound at all.

The second thing was that the door to his chamber stood ajar.

That was truly odd. The life-ward would never do something so careless. One of the bastion footmen, maybe? If so, the moron would not enjoy Desolane's reprimand.

Still, for whatever reason, the door was open. The pheguth could feel a draft blowing through it, cool air against his skin. An open door...

The pheguth sat up on the steel frame that served him as a bed. As soon as he was upright – rather too suddenly – the lingering, cumulative pain of the transcoding sessions ambushed him. It felt as if the back of his skull was being used as a regimental dinner gong. Pain gusted against the back of his eyes and he felt a pounding in his ears. Naked, he half-stepped, half-fell off the frame and threw up violently into the steel pot that served him as a toilet. His retches were violent, and by the time they had subsided, blood was running from his nostrils.

Shaking, his head still churning, he got to his feet. And that was when he realised the third strange thing.

He was not shackled to the frame.

He stood, puzzled, for a long moment. Then he hobbled over to the chair in the corner and pulled on the tunic and trousers lying folded on the seat.

Very slowly, he approached the door.

'Desolane?' he said quietly, his throat hoarse from the retching. No one answered. He reached out and touched the door, and, when it didn't simply slam shut, he pulled it open warily.

'Desolane?'

The anteroom beyond was empty. Strong, cold sunlight lanced down through the high window slits. On the far side of the anteroom, the reinforced shutter into the hallway was also open.

The pheguth took one more step forward.

'Desolane?' he called.

FORTY-FIVE MINUTES LATER, Desolane found the pheguth. He was in his chamber, seated on the wooden chair, facing the open door.

'Good morning, pheguth,' Desolane said.

'The doors were all open. I was unshackled.'

'Indeed?' The life-ward said. 'Someone has been remiss.'

'I didn't know what to do. I called out for you, but you did not answer. So I sat down here.'

'The doors were open and you were unshackled, pheguth. Did you not think to make your escape from this prison?'

The pheguth looked appalled at the suggestion. 'No. Of course not. Where would I go? I know I'm only in here for my own protection.' He paused and looked up at the life-ward. 'Was this...' he began, 'was this another trick? A test?'

'You may care to call it that, pheguth,' Desolane admitted, summoning the footman with the tray of breakfast. 'Last night, I spoke with the psykers. They reported that yesterday, for the first time, the transcoding bore fruit. Outer mnemonic barriers were erased. An entire layer of engrammatic suppression was removed.'

'What... what did they learn?' the pheguth asked.

'Nothing. Nothing yet. But they have removed the, if you will, casing of your mindlock at last, and can see its inner workings. They estimate that within a week, precision transcoding will have unlocked your memory entirely.'

The pheguth thought about this. 'Then why this test today?' he asked.

'It was considered prudent. The psykers conjectured that, as your mindlock was loosened, your personality might reassert some measure of free will. They wondered how this might affect your loyalty, and your decision to side with us.'

'So you left the door open?'

'Yes, pheguth.'

'To see if I suddenly became loyal to the Golden Throne again?'

Desolane winced. 'Yes, pheguth. Please, try not to use that phrase.'

The pheguth smiled. It was a curious, bleak expression. He held up his augmetic hand. The prosthetic implant was over five sidereal years old, but time had not softened the ridges of scar tissue where it was married to the wrist stump. 'You see this?' he said.

'Yes,' said Desolane.

'For this, and for so much else, I can never go back. Do not test me again. It's beneath us both.'

BY FIRST LIGHT, the Ghosts had reached the northern boundary of the woods. What lay beyond – rolling arable land, apparently – was obscured in a thick blanket of fog. The rain had stopped before dawn, but the air remained wet and ripe with acidic rot.

In the middle distance, like a row of behemoth sentries lining the borders of Edrian Province, gigantic air-mills rose up out of the fog, their great sails motionless in the still air. Dormant since the invasion, the mills no longer ground flour. Vast, lank banners hung from some sets of sails, adorned with the mad emblems of the Ruinous Powers.

They took a brief rest at the edge of the treeline. From the sound of it, the hunting parties that had been scouring the woods at their heels all night were less than half an hour behind them.

The arterial road ran along the bottom of the vale below the trees, some half a kilometre away. For most of its visible length, it was set on a raised causeway. Though partly obscured by the fog, vehicles and figures could be seen along this causeway. Hostile troopers. Transports. They had the road hemmed close. This was the other edge of the pincer, the trap that the hunting parties were driving them towards.

'We've got no choice but to go forward,' Gaunt said.

'Have you seen the numbers down there?' Landerson replied. Cirk just shook her head.

'Correction,' Gaunt said. 'We have two other choices: we stay here and die, or we turn back into the woods and die. We have to cross that road, get beyond the trap. And I'm not asking for your approval. I'm telling you what's going to happen.'

He looked at Cirk. 'Once we're over that highway, which way is our ideal heading?'

She deferred to Plower, who seemed to have a better knowledge of the district. He pointed to the north-east. 'Edrian Town is about ten kilometres that way. If I had a choice, I'd head in that direction. There's a greater chance of contacting the local cell there.'

'But that's the way they'll expect us to be going,' said Cirk. 'More chance of capture.'

Plower pointed north-west. 'Two smaller settlements over that way. Millvale and Wheathead. We might find a contact there, I suppose. No promises. Last time I came this way, the excubitors had tightened up on the smaller communities.'

'We go that way, then,' said Gaunt. He gestured to the waiting Ghosts. 'Close up, listen good. We're going to try and run the picket. Get beyond that road. Now's the time, while the fog's still with us. Everyone see that air-mill?'

He pointed to one of the nearest structures to their left, three kilometres away. It looked like a cathedral spire breaking the white mist. A scarlet banner was draped across its sails.

'The one with the red banner on it,' Gaunt said. 'That's our rendezvous point. We'll cross the road directly below this point, so we're in the open for the shortest possible time. And we'll be covering Major Cirk's people. That means sharing capes. Criid, look after Landerson. Beltayn, take Acreson. Varl, you'll have Purchason. Feygor, Plower. Rawne, you'll cover the major. I'll take Lefivre with me.'

'I think I should–' Rawne began.

'It's settled,' Gaunt interrupted. 'Now, we need a diversion. Mkoll?'

The scout-sergeant scratched his upper lip. 'I'll take Ven and Bonin east. We'll think of something.'

'Sir?' It was Larkin. He'd been scanning the road with the scope of his long-las. They turned to see what he'd spotted.

Some way over to their right, a truck was approaching along the causeway. A fuel bowser. It stopped every now and then to replenish the tanks of the picket vehicles.

Mkoll looked at Gaunt and raised an eyebrow.

'All right then,' Gaunt said. 'The Emperor provides. Take Brostin with you. Leave me Bonin.'

Mkoll nodded.

'See you at the mill,' Gaunt said.

BEFORE THE FOG could dwindle any further, they slid out of the treeline and down the slope through the long, wet grass towards the causeway road. It seemed a short distance, but the effort was great. They moved on their hands and knees with their camo-capes tied over them. Bonin led the way, followed by the teamed pairs awkwardly sharing cloaks. Curth followed, under her own cape, with Larkin crawling along at the rear.

It was hot under the camouflage and they began to sweat. Before long it became an effort not to pant, an effort to keep their advance unhurried and smooth. Huddled up with Purchason, Varl was finding it particularly onerous. He was carrying Brostin's heavy weapon lashed to his belly and chest. They'd swapped so that Brostin could move more lightly. The ammo hoppers were draped around Purchason's shoulders. He'd volunteered to carry them. In the half-light under the camo-cape, Varl wiped perspiration from his brow and grinned at the resistance fighter. Purchason just closed his eyes and edged on, droplets of sweat dripping off the end of his nose.

They closed on the roadway, one gentle hand-set at a time. By now, they could hear the low conversations of the troopers up on the causeway. An occasional crunch of footsteps. A vehicle door slamming. Curth swore she could smell a lho-stick.

Gaunt felt Lefivre beginning to tense up beside him. The man's breathing became more shallow, and he kept pausing to fidget at his face. Gaunt had to keep checking his crawl. If Lefivre stopped suddenly, Gaunt risked dragging the cloak off him and exposing him.

Somewhere above them, an officer called out to his men. The voice was loud, harsh. Lefivre froze. Gaunt could feel him trembling. The man stank of sour sweat under the cape. His jaw ground, and his mouth moved, forming noiseless words.

Gaunt took hold of the man's shoulder and pulled Lefivre's face round to look at him. Gently, Gaunt shook his head.

The officer called out again. Gaunt saw the panic attack vicing on Lefivre and rolled the man over into the grass, his left hand pressed to Lefivre's mouth.

'Breathe,' he whispered, 'nice and slow. Breathe. Fill your lungs. A sound now, and we're all dead, so breathe, for the Emperor's sake.'

Lefivre's breathing wasn't slowing. His eyes were wild, drawn white in the gloom beneath the cape.

He began to shake.

MKOLL, MKVENNER AND Brostin hurried through the thickets of the treeline, keeping an eye on the fuel truck. The scouts disturbed nothing, but Brostin, big and clumsy, kept snapping twigs and swishing wet fronds with his shins.

Mkoll glanced back at the trooper, his expression disapproving.

'Do better,' he hissed.

Brostin shrugged.

'You're a fething Ghost. Use your skills!'

'I'm trying!' Brostin whispered back. 'Fething scouts,' he mumbled to himself.

Mkvenner turned and placed his open hand against Brostin's neck. Brostin swallowed hard. He was a brute of a man, packed with muscle, and the pressure was light, but there was no mistake at all. One twitch of the wrist, and Mkvenner would snap his spine.

'Do as the sergeant says,' Mkvenner mouthed. 'We need you for this, but not that badly.'

Brostin nodded. Mkvenner withdrew his hand. They crept on.

BROSTIN CUDDLED VARL's lasrifle up under his armpit and stared at Mkvenner's back. The scout had a rep, a real rep, and all the regiment respected him. One of Gaunt's chosen, one of the favoured, like all the fething scouts. Brostin, whose loyalties lay with Rawne, despised every one of them. One more trick like that, Brostin thought, and someone's going to get unlucky in the confusion of the next firefight.

Mkoll came to a halt and made a signal. They pulled their capes up over their shoulders and began to belly down the slope towards the road.

DIRECTLY BELOW THE causeway embankment, the sloping pasture of the woods rolled down into a waterlogged culvert. Bonin reached it first and, wading gingerly into the cold pool, got to his feet. He pulled back his cape. The shadow of the bank fell across him, and the mist was streaming. Gradually, the others reached him: Rawne and Cirk, Criid and Landerson, Beltayn and Acreson. Then Curth, then Feygor with Plower. Then Varl and Purchason, struggling with the heavy weapon in its canvas boot.

Bonin fanned them out behind him with a gesture, and made a swift signal for them to prep weapons. They leant in the ooze, their backs to the bank. Larkin appeared out of the grass, and scuttled in beside Bonin, his boots making the merest ripple in the standing water.

Bonin nodded to him.

Where's the boss? Larkin signed.

Bonin felt his heart skip and looked round. Twenty metres up the slope, he could just see a huddled shape covered by a camo-cape in the long grass. It wasn't moving.

* * *

'CONTROL IT! CONTROL your fear!' Gaunt hissed. 'Feth it, Lefivre, don't lose
it now!'

Lefivre's eyes rolled back. Choking, suffocating on Gaunt's hand, Lefivre
began to convulse.

THERE WAS A RICH stink of promethium in the air. Voices gabbled. They could
hear the sound of a chattering pump running off the tanker's idling engine.

Mkoll, Mkvenner and Brostin slunk along the culvert with the shadow of
the causeway over them. The sun was rising hard now, casting the roadway
shadow out across the grassy slope. They could see the elongated shapes of
the vehicles above them, the huddled figures, stretched like giants.

Mkoll and Mkvenner slung their lasrifles across their backs and took out
their silenced handguns. Mkoll looked at Brostin.

Ready? he signalled.

Brostin breathed in the fuel stink again and smiled.

He nodded.

BONIN STARED AT the huddled shape in the grass. It was still in the causeway
shadow, but at the rate the sun was climbing, it wouldn't remain so for
much longer. The cape was twitching, quivering. What the feth...?

'Lefivre's lost it,' Rawne whispered.

'I'm going back–' Bonin began.

Rawne shook his head. 'You'll blow us all. Stay here.'

Bonin glared at him. 'But–'

'You heard me.'

Above them, on the roadway, the voices came again.

'Voi alt reser manchin?'

'Eyt Voi? Ecya ndeh, magir.'

What? What had they seen? Rawne glanced at Cirk. She shook her head
and made the signal 'stay put'.

Rawne drew his warknife all the same.

GAUNT HAD NO choice. With his free hand, he tugged out one of his bolt
pistols and smacked Lefivre across the temple with the butt. The cell fighter
slumped unconscious.

And still. At last.

THERE WERE TWO half-tracks on the stretch of roadway, the bowser truck, and
a cluster of troopers. They were starkly lit by the sunlight. Around them,
below the lip of the causeway, the white fog drifted like smoke.

Mkoll rolled up over the causeway edge, and scurried into cover behind
the nearest track. He could smell the fuel, hear the thump of the cycling
pump. He slid under the half-track's chassis, into the greasy shadow, as two
troopers crunched past.

He smelled smoke.

'Akyeda voi smeklunt!' a voice shouted.

'Magir, magir, aloost moi!' another voice protested. The figures moved past the other way. Two troopers, smoking lho-sticks while they waited, rebuked by their sirdar to stand clear of the bowser. They wandered over to the edge of the causeway and looked out at the woods.

Under the track, Mkoll heard a rattle. The pump had stopped, and the feed line was being withdrawn. He heard more voices, and a cab door open.

The fuelling was done. The tanker was leaving.

He looked back at the edge of the roadway.

Mkvenner rose behind the smoking, chatting troopers, tall and lean, like a spectre from the mist. He caught one in a choke hold, and knifed the other in the small of the back. As the stabbed trooper fell backwards off the roadway silently, Mkvenner twisted his grip and snapped the other's neck. He lowered the corpse to the ground gently and raised his silenced pistol.

Brostin clambered into view behind him, getting up on the roadway. Somehow, he had caught one of the half-smoked lho-sticks the men had dropped. Upright, nonchalant, as if he were taking a morning constitutional, Brostin leaned back, and put the smoke to his lips.

He drew deeply, inhaled, exhaled, and smiled in satisfaction.

Two occupation troopers came around the rear of the half-track and saw them.

'Voi shet-' one began to cry.

Mkvenner was already down on one knee, his pistol raised in a two-handed grip. The weapon popped rapidly and both men tumbled over with a clatter.

'Doess scara, magir?' a voice called.

Mkvenner ran forward until he was snuggled in behind the rear fender of the half-track. He winced as a salvo of las-fire ripped the air behind him.

Mkvenner looked round. Three more troopers had appeared behind him. Lasrifle cradled in one meaty arm, Brostin had cut them down, the lho-stick pressed to his mouth with the finger and thumb of his other hand.

The roadway went mad. Troopers appeared from all around, alerted by the sound of gunfire. Alien voices bellowed and screamed.

Brostin leant into the recoil and fired another burst, one-handed, that sent two more Archenemy troopers over onto the road. Las-shots chopped his way.

Mkvenner holstered his pistol and swung his lasrifle out, firing as the muzzle came up. He kept it on single-shot. He seldom wasted ammo on blurts of auto.

The gun up to his shoulder, he ran forward, aiming and slaying. Each bolt was a perfect kill-shot. Men dropped.

Mkoll was still under the half-track. He had crawled forward until he was under the front fender. His pistol spat. The officer who had, until recently, been chatting beside the bowser went down. Then so did his adjutant. Another trooper ran for cover and dropped on his face.

'Brostin!' Mkoll yelled.

* * *

BONIN LOOKED UP. Gunfire echoed down the causeway. Fierce gunfire. The figures above them began to break and run. Engines started. Trucks rolled away.

'Diversion,' he said to Rawne.

'Let's take them over,' Rawne said.

'Do it yourself,' Bonin snapped, and began to run up out of the culvert towards the figure in the weeds.

'Let's go!' Rawne called, and the main force began to scramble up the embankment onto the road.

Bonin reached Gaunt.

'Come on, sir!' he yelled.

'Help me with him,' Gaunt protested, trying to drag Lefivre's dead weight.

'There's no time, sir!' Bonin exclaimed.

'Now, Bonin! The Emperor Protects!'

With a curse, Bonin grabbed a limp arm.

MKOLL GOT UP from under the track and started firing his lasrifle. Mkvenner was covering his back. Serious fire was coming from both directions along the causeway. Squads were closing on foot, and trucks were approaching too.

'Brostin!' Mkoll yelled. 'Brostin, now or never!'

He looked round. Rifle under his arm, Brostin stood beside the fuel bowser. The driver hung, limp and shot, from the cab. Brostin had unhooked the hose and started the pump again. Promethium flooded out over the road, gushing across the hardpan, trickling down the embankments, pooling under the halftracks and the crumpled bodies.

Brostin was still smoking the lho-stick. It was down to the stub almost.

Mkoll skidded to a halt.

Brostin smiled at him. 'All right, sarge. I got it from here. This is my thing.'

Mkoll gaped. 'But–'

'Seriously, take a fething hike. You and Ven. *Now*, you got me?'

Firing off the last of their clips, Mkoll and Mkvenner threw themselves off the causeway into the deep grass on the mill side of the road.

The stink of promethium in the air was now unbearably strong.

The occupation troopers closed from both sides, stumbling to a halt as their boots splashed into the edges of the widening lake of liquid fuel ebbing out over the roadway. Hurriedly, they stopped firing and began to back away.

They all saw the man. The big-built, hairy man, standing beside the fuel bowser with the flooding pump in one hand and lho-stick in the other. He glistened from head to toe, as if he had dowsed himself in fuel as well.

'That's it,' Brostin grinned. 'Guess what's cooking.'

He took one last, long drag on the lho-stick, exhaled a sigh, then flicked the butt away.

It circled twice in the air.

Then two hundred metres of causeway went up in a wall of fire.

THIRTEEN

Rising, dazed, Mkoll and Mkvenner toiled up through the long grass away from the road, the furnace-heat of the fire on their backs. Patches of the field around them were ablaze, and sparks and burning cinders fluttered down out of the sky. Glancing back when they dared, shielding their eyes against the blazing light, they saw the ruin of the causeway stretch away. An inferno, in which the vague outlines of consumed vehicles could just be made out. The blast had been so intense it had conjured up a swirling doughnut of flame that mushroomed into the sky and even now was spilling out in a wider and wider halo.

On the road, they could see the picket line disintegrating as men rushed to aid their comrades and then were beaten back by the unquenchable heat.

'Holy Throne,' Mkoll muttered.

'Let's get to the mill,' Mkvenner said. His voice was cold. Nothing ever seemed to ruffle the stoic scout, not even a spectacle of this magnitude.

Then he paused. At long last, something penetrated his reserve and produced a response.

'Feth me...' he said.

Mkoll looked. A figure, trailing flame, was staggering through the grass below the causeway. It fell, and rolled, trying to stifle its own burning clothes. Then it got up again and began to limp towards them.

It was Brostin. His clothes were scorched, his hair and eyebrows singed, his skin blackened and blistered.

But he was alive. And smiling.

They hurried down the slope to him and helped him along.

'I'm fine,' he said, his voice hoarse and wheezing.

'How the feth... how the feth are you not dead?' Mkoll asked him.

Brostin hesitated before replying. There had been a drum of detergent gel on the back of the bowser, retardant material carried in case of spills. Just like the stuff Brostin had used back in his days on the fire watch in Tanith Magna. He'd poured it over himself just before his trick with the lho-stick. It wouldn't stop him burning, not in an inferno like that, but it would protect him long enough to get clear. Brostin considered explaining this to Mkoll and Mkvenner, but he realised that, for the first time, he had shown skills and secrets that impressed the unimpressable scouts. He wasn't about to waste that moment of superiority with a mundane explanation.

He said: 'I know fire. Been waging war with it for years. It wouldn't dare harm me, not after all we've been through together.'

The scouts looked at him, suspecting they were being hoodwinked, but lost for an answer. Brostin clambered on up the slope.

'Come on,' he said. 'We haven't got all day.'

'THANK YOU, SIR,' Landerson said.

Gaunt turned to look at him. 'For what?'

'For Lefivre. You could have left him. By rights, you should have killed him. He nearly blew it for everyone.'

'He was scared. I can't blame him for that.'

'We're all scared,' Landerson said. 'We all deal with it. Lefivre's nerves are shot and he's a liability–'

Gaunt held up a hand. 'Listen, Landerson. You and Lefivre and the other cell members have risked everything to help my team. I can't repay you the way you'd like me to. I can't save your world. But I'll damn well save any of you if it's in my power to do so. If we don't look out for each other, we might as well quit now.'

'You're not at all what I expected,' Landerson said.

'I know.'

'No, I mean… you're a Guard commissar. I've heard stories. Stories of ruthlessness. Brutality. Iron rule and unflinching punishment.'

'I'm all of those things,' said Gaunt. 'When I have to be. But I have a soul too. I serve the beloved Emperor, and I serve mankind. I believe that service extends to the weak and the frightened. If I'd executed your friend or left him to die, what kind of servant of mankind would that make me?'

Throughout Gaunt's career, the ability to turn out an inspirational phrase had served him well. A key part of any commissar's job was to inspire and uplift, to make a man forget the privations he suffered or the horrors he faced. He was good at it. Right now, with some distaste, he realised he was playing on that skill, saying what Landerson needed to hear. The truth was he hadn't wanted to leave Lefivre's body behind, nor any other clue the Archenemy could exploit. If he was going to pull Lefivre out, it might as well have been alive.

But Gaunt wanted to keep Landerson on his side. The Ghosts needed the resistance now, more than ever. Without their cooperation, the mission was doomed. Gaunt had serious misgivings about Cirk, and by extension her associates Plower and Acreson. But Landerson seemed the soundest of them. Solid, dependable, driven. And loyal. Gaunt didn't want to breed any resentment between the mission team and the cell fighters by treating them as expendable.

So he did what commissars had been doing since the inauguration of the Officio Commissariat. He put a positive spin on things. He inspired and kindled trust.

They had been at the air-mill now for twenty minutes. Ruined and derelict, the structure rose above the thinning mist at the top of the fields. There was a decent view down across the three kilometres to the causeway. Gaunt could see the shimmering light of the huge fire, and with his scope he could pick out the commotion along the enemy line.

So far there was no sign of the diversion team. Cirk was pressing to move on. 'They'll be scouring the area before the hour's out,' she'd told Gaunt. Gaunt decided to give Mkoll's team another ten minutes.

He prayed they were alive. The fireball had been vast. Had it been the promised diversion, or an accident?

'Go check on Lefivre,' Gaunt said to Landerson. 'Tell him... tell him we're fine. Him and me, I mean. No hard feelings.'

Landerson turned and went back inside the mill, leaving Gaunt in the stone doorway. Gaunt looked up at the winch window twenty metres above him in the tower's side.

'Anything?' he called.

Larkin's head appeared and shook.

'Keep watching, Larks.'

Gaunt wandered around the mill's vast base and entered the loading yard. Feygor stood watch on the gate, and nodded to his commander. Criid had found a rusting water tank and was purifying water to refill their flasks.

'Any sign of the sarge?' she asked Gaunt. Criid was a sergeant herself, a platoon leader, the first female sergeant in the Tanith First. But everyone called Mkoll 'the sarge'.

'Not yet, Tona.'

She shrugged. 'I had a dream last night,' she went on. 'Saw Caff and the kids. They were fine.'

'Good,' he smiled. They were all suffering from vivid, sometimes delusional dreams. Tona Criid had been a gang-girl on Verghast, hard-forged by that tough and uncompromising life, but she still displayed a wonderful naïveté. The florid dreams Gereon was fermenting in their minds were not illusions to her. She reported her dream as a matter of fact, as if she'd had a pict message from home. Gaunt wasn't about to contradict her. Criid was one of the most dependable and four-square people in his team, up there with Ven and Mkoll.

'How light are we getting?' he asked. Criid and Beltayn shared responsibility for supervising the team's supplies of food and ammunition.

'Down to two days on rations,' she said. 'Four if we switch to emergency conservation. I don't recommend that. Doc Curth agrees. We'll get slow and tired. Time to start foraging.'

Gaunt nodded. There had been no way they'd have been able to bring enough rations for the entire mission. Foraging was a necessary evil, and he'd been putting it off. Once they started eating the native resources, it would likely accelerate the effect of Chaos in their systems.

Time was running out.

'Ammo?' he asked.

'Plenty for the heavy, and almost a full set of charges. Las down by a third. Hard rounds is a different story. Pretty short. We've been into a gak of a lot more firefights than we were expecting at this stage.'

Gaunt pursed his lips. They certainly had. The stand-off in Ineuron Town alone had almost cleaned him out of bolt and slug clips.

'Sir?'

'Yes, Tona?'

'Do you know someone called Wilder?'

'Wilder? No, I don't think so.'

'A Colonel Wilder. He has dark hair, and is a good looking man.'

'No, sergeant. I don't believe I do. Why?'

She smiled, screwing the lid onto one of the flasks. 'He was in my dream too. Caff kept calling him "sir".'

'I'm afraid I don't know what that's all about, Criid,' Gaunt said.

'Oh well,' she said. 'I'm sure Caff will tell me.'

Feygor called out from the gate. Out of the mists, Mkoll, Mkvenner and Brostin had just come into view.

A WRETCHEDLY THICK pall of smoke hung over the causeway. Uexkull swung down out of the deathship hatch and walked along through the jumble of transports until he reached the point where the road surface became black and blistered. Behind him, the occupation troopers cowered on their knees.

Before him lay a stretch of destruction. Buckled rockcrete, charred heaps, the torched, molten residue of vehicles.

'A fuelling accident?' he asked.

At his side, Virag cleared his augmented throat. 'Lord, we think not. There was a report of gunfire just before the ignition. A firefight.'

Uexkull turned slowly to look up-country at the air-mills now slowly being revealed as the fog breathed away. 'Then they died here. Or they used the confusion to slip past the picket.'

'They have shown themselves to be devious and resourceful thus far,' Virag said. 'I think we have to presume they are beyond the road. Some of them, at least.'

'Agreed,' said Uexkull. 'Start a point by point search of the region. Begin with the mills and the nearby villages. I have a nasty feeling they have played me for a fool, and that is not a sensation I wish to prolong. Find them, Virag. Find them, or at least point me at them. I want to kill them myself.'

'Yes, lord.'

'One last thing,' Uexkull said. 'Summon all the sirdars and other seniors in charge of the picket line. Have them come to me in the next five minutes.'

Virag nodded. Uexkull drew his bolter and checked the clip load.

'The next five minutes, you hear me? I wish to discipline the morons who let this happen.'

IDRESHA CLUWGE HAD been belching at him for three hours now. True, her skeletal hand-maids had been translating her guttural questions, but the pheguth felt like he'd been burped at for long enough.

'I'm tired,' he said.

The Anarch's chief ethnologue leaned back in her grav-chair and steepled her massive fingers across her domed chest.

'We have barely begun, pheguth,' she said, via one of her life-wards.

The pheguth shrugged. The ethnologue bemused him. Not as a person – she was a grotesque monster, and that was bafflement enough. No, it was her purpose. It was her 'duty to learn in all detail about the life and culture of the enemy'. That's what she'd told him on the dam. She asked him curious questions like:

'How does a man make the sign of the aquila, and what does it represent?'

or

'Eggs, when fried, are popular amongst men of the Imperium, are they not?'

or

'How old must an Imperial child be before he or she is considered fit for military service?'

or

'Explain simply the financial mechanisms of the Munitorum.'

THEY KNEW NOTHING. Nothing! It made the pheguth laugh. For all its might, for all its frightening power, the Archenemy of mankind understood virtually nothing about the day-to-day workings of the Imperium.

The ethnologue was, in his opinion, the Archenemy's most formidable weapon. The forces of the Ruinous Powers might lay waste to worlds, conquer planets, and burn fleets out of the void, but they did not even begin to understand the mechanisms of their sworn enemy.

Cluwge was an instrument in that subtle war. She asked the questions that were unanswerable during the heat of combat. She asked about the little details, the small particulars of Imperial life. The hosts of the Archon might crush the warriors of the Imperium, might drive them to rout, but Cluwge's understanding offered them true mastery. Defeating the enemy was one thing. Comprehending the workings of its society so that it might be controlled and suppressed – that was quite another.

Idresha Cluwge was a tool of domination. What she learned informed the higher powers and armed them for rule.

The pheguth had answered his best.

'I want to go now,' he said. The nagging pain of transcoding soaked his brain. 'Tomorrow, or the day after, we can take this up again.'

Cluwge shrugged.

The pheguth rose. 'A pleasure,' he said and walked out of the room.

He had expected to find his antlered handlers in the anteroom, but there was no sign of them. The door stood open and bright sunlight beckoned from the gallery beyond.

The pheguth walked through the door and out onto the gallery. Daylight spilled in through the windows. The gallery was empty right down its length. At the far end, the next door was also open.

'Desolane, Desolane,' the pheguth tutted as he scurried down the gallery in his slippers. 'When will you stop these tests of my loyalty?'

A figure stepped in through the doorway at the end of the hall. It was not Desolane. The pheguth had never seen this person before. He came to a halt, eyes narrowed in curiosity.

'Who-?' he began.

The man was tall and clad in dark khaki fatigues. He was sweating, as if he was scared.

'Are you the pheguth?' he asked in a curiously accented voice.

The pheguth began to step backwards. 'That is what they call me...' he replied, his voice tailing off.

The man in khaki produced a laspistol from his tunic and aimed it at the pheguth's head.

'In the name of the Pact and the Archon!' he said.

And fired.

FOURTEEN

THE PHEGUTH STOOD where he was and blinked. There was an odd, stinging pain in the left side of his face, and a warmth on his left shoulder. The man in khaki continued to point the pistol at him, his hand shaking, his eyes wide.

The pheguth glanced down slowly. Blood was soaking his left shoulder and the front of his tunic. *His* blood. He raised his hand and gently prodded the fused mess of his left ear. His fingertips came away bloody. The man in khaki had been so scared, so worked up that he'd botched the point-blank headshot.

The pheguth was simply stunned. He blurted, 'God-Emperor of Mankind!'

The words saved his life. The would-be assassin, already hyped up on adrenaline, flinched at the sound of the heretical phrase and took a step back, raising his hands to his ears. In that moment, the pheguth felt his own adrenaline surge. He swung his fist and broke the man's nose with an audible crack.

The assassin fell to one knee, snorting blood. The pheguth turned and ran.

'Murder!' he shouted. 'Murder!' There was a door to his left. He threw it open and ran through as the first las-bolts spat after him. The assassin was on his feet again, running after him, firing his pistol and spitting blood.

The room was a well-appointed retiring chamber, dressed with many pieces of antique furniture and elegant floor-length wall-tapestries. There was an open door on the far side of the room, but the pheguth knew he'd never reach it and clear it before he came into the firing line again. Instead, he threw himself down and crawled behind a chaise on his hands and knees.

117

The assassin ran into the room making an ugly gurgling, panting noise through his split nose. He crossed to the far door and peered through. The pheguth could see his feet from under the chaise.

The assassin turned back from the door and began to search the chamber. From his hiding place, the pheguth watched the man's feet as he pulled back chairs and peered behind tapestries. In another few moments, he'd turn his attention to the other side of the room.

A second set of feet entered the chamber, booted like the first.

'Did you kill him?'

'He ran in here,' the first man replied, agitated.

'You fired. Did you kill him?'

'He ran in here!' the first man repeated. 'I wounded him…'

The newcomer cursed. His feet disappeared from view. The pheguth heard a heavy sideboard scrape on the floor as it was pulled out.

'You mean he's hiding?'

'Yes! Help me look for him!'

The second man mumbled something else. A chair moved. 'Look. Look! Is this your blood? Here, on the rug?'

'No.'

'He's behind that chaise,' the second man said.

The pheguth dropped flat on the floor and pulled his arms around his head. Two laspistols fired, and multiple shots perforated the back of the chaise, punching through the fabric into the tapestry and the wall behind, puffing out blossoms of kapok stuffing. One shot, low, kissed across the pheguth's left hip and made him squeal in pain. He writhed forward, scurrying from the cover of the chaise until he was behind a hand-painted spinet.

But one of them at least had spotted him moving. Now the shots renewed, tearing into the instrument. Strings burst and broke in weird jangling discords; box panels splintered, and pieces of the keyboard flew into the air.

A weird howl filled the room and the rain of las-shots stopped abruptly. A man cried out. Then there was a bright shriek of pain. Something was switching the air like a whip. The pheguth raised his head, hearing solid impacts and muffled weights striking the floor. Liquid spattered across the tattered spinet, as if shaken from a loaded sponge.

A final las-shot. A final scream. A final wet impact.

Shaking, the pheguth looked out from under the spinet's stand. He saw a pair of hooves. He rose, and peered out over the top of the broken instrument.

Desolane faced him. The life-ward's arms were extended. Blood dripped from the fighting knives brandished in each hand. The smoke-cloak wreathed about Desolane's torso like a swarm of insects. A few tiny dots of blood glinted on the bronze mask.

Through the mask slits, the life-ward's watery blue eyes fixed on the pheguth. 'You can come out now,' Desolane said.

The pheguth blinked. He got to his feet. To say that the two assassins were dead was as much of an understatement as saying that a supernova is the end of a star's life. It conveyed nothing of the catastrophic violence involved.

The room was wet with great quantities of blood that had been spilled with explosive force. It soaked the tapestries and the soft furnishings, ran down woodwork and pooled on the floor. The rug was drenched crimson. The two killers had been dismembered with such sharp frenzy that not even their skulls remained intact. The pheguth had seen his share of horror, but even so he decided not to look at the surgically split and severed remains. He focused instead on a bloody laspistol that had been cut cleanly in two.

Desolane sheathed the twin ketra blades. 'Pheguth, my humble apologies,' the life-ward said.

THEY REACHED THE village Plower called 'Wheathead' in the early part of the afternoon. It was dark and cold, with a constant threat of rain from the east. The sky churned in sulphurous, lightless patterns. Cirk led them down through a sparse copse of trees towards the hedgeline that flanked the main road into the place. To either side lay raw fields of decaying vegetable crop and rows of collapsed incubation cloches.

From the trees, Gaunt used his scope to study the village. 'I see two troop trucks,' he said.

'A search will be underway already,' Cirk replied.

'There, by the granary. What are those masts?'

Cirk took a look. 'The local excubitor house. The vox-links belong to them.'

'I have a plan in mind,' Gaunt said. 'I've been discussing the practicalities with my adjutant, Beltayn. We'll need your help to make it work.'

'What sort of plan?' Cirk asked.

'You won't like it. Not at all. We need a diversion.'

Cirk snorted without much humour. 'I've seen what you and your kind do as a diversion, colonel-commissar. Set half the world alight. No wonder you think I won't like it.'

Gaunt shook his head. 'I mean a real diversion. One to put the enemy off the scent. Otherwise, it's not going to be long before they figure out why we're here.'

'Go on,' she said, dubiously.

'In a moment.' Gaunt adjusted the scope's focus. 'There, to the north of the village. That space there. What is it?'

He had pinpointed a wide acreage of freshly-turned earth surrounded by a long chain-link fence. Clusters of hooded figures moved slowly about the broken ground.

'A boneyard,' Plower said. 'There's one in almost every settlement. Thousands died during the invasion. Many were left to rot on the battlefields, but in towns and villages, the enemy heaped the dead in mass graves.'

'Those people look like mourners,' Gaunt said.

'That's right, sir,' Plower replied. 'The Archenemy understands that certain allowances must be made to placate a conquered population and keep it in check. They permit the consented to visit the boneyards, provided they do not break any laws governing religious worship. Of course, no one knows who exactly is interred in any given pit, but it helps some people to be able to pay their respects at a graveside.'

Gaunt closed his eyes briefly. Once again, the abominable foe had surprised him. It was almost an act of humanity to allow public mourning at the mass burials. Or was it merely another way of reminding the people of Gereon how little their lives were worth?

'Let me get this straight,' Rawne said quietly. 'The fething enemy forces allow people to come here and visit the grave?'

'Yes,' said Cirk.

'That's our way in,' said Rawne. 'Posing as mourners, I mean.'

'I thought that,' Gaunt replied.

'Our first priority is to try and establish contact with the resistance here,' Cirk said.

'Agreed,' said Gaunt. 'My other plan can wait.'

AN INFLUX OF mourners had gathered around the headroad into the village. Most were dressed in filthy travelling robes. A few rang hand bells, or rattled wooden beads. Lost in their own little worlds of misery, they paid little attention to the clutch of shrouded mourners who joined them from a side path.

Cirk and Acreson – with their damnable consented imagos – led the group. Rawne followed with Bonin, Criid, Feygor and Lefivre.

There had been what Colm Corbec had once called 'robust discussion' about who should make up the team. Gaunt insisted on being part of it – this was his show, after all, and every Ghost knew it. But Rawne had been sidelined at Ineuron, and didn't want to be left waiting again. He and Gaunt had argued fiercely.

'One leader goes, one stays!' Gaunt had said. 'We must maintain the viability of the mission. If both of us die–'

'Then Mkoll takes over! You treat him like a fething senior as it is, and we both know he can do the job. I want to be part of this! I want to know what's going on!'

Gaunt had looked at Rawne coldly. Maybe it had been a mistake bringing him in the first place.

'With respect to Mkoll, that's not an option. We do this by the book.'

Rawne just nodded. 'In that case, sir, it's my turn.'

Rawne had picked Feygor and, on Cirk's advice that women were less frequently checked than men, Criid.

They'd been all set to go when Lefivre asked to join them. Gaunt and Rawne had both said no at first, but Lefivre, looking stronger and more determined, had insisted. It seemed to Gaunt that the cell fighter desperately wanted to prove himself to the Guardsmen after his foul-up at the causeway.

'There is another thing,' Lefivre had said quietly. 'I come from this region originally. There's every chance my mother, father and both my brothers are buried in that boneyard.'

Not even Rawne could argue with that.

FROM THE TREES, Gaunt watched their slow advance through his scope.

'You can trust Rawne, you know,' Mkoll said quietly.

Gaunt looked round. 'I know. I just wish he could trust me.'

Mkoll smiled. 'He does, sir. In his way.'

'Sir?' Larkin's call was no more than a whisper. He was laying the sight of his long-las across the low roofs of the dismal village. 'What the hell are they?'

Gaunt adjusted his own scope. Near the central crossroads of the village, there rose several talix trees, shorn of their branches, transformed into gibbets. A pair of broken, puppet-forms dangled from them, swaying in the breeze.

'Landerson?' Gaunt handed the cell fighter his scope and pointed.

'What are those?' he said.

'WIREWOLVES,' SAID CIRK. 'Don't look at them.'

Rawne turned his gaze towards the muddy track. He had a lasting memory of puppets, two life-size mannequins loosely made of metal parts, strung together on wires.

'They're dormant now, but don't look at them,' Acreson whispered. 'It provokes them.'

Fine by me, Rawne thought.

They moved on. A glance told Rawne that Bonin and Criid were doing fine, heads bowed under their hoods. Feygor too, if he'd only relax his fething shoulders. He was the most damn upright and rigid mourner in the history of grief.

Rawne looked at Lefivre. He inwardly cursed Gaunt for his decision to allow the man into this play. Gaunt had even had the brass balls, before they left, to draw Rawne aside and tell him 'vouchsafe' was not an option as far as Lefivre was concerned.

'You want this lead, Rawne, all right. I'm giving it to you. But Lefivre comes back alive if any of you do. Got me? I owe them this much.'

The mourners with them moaned and rang their bells.

You and me both, Rawne thought.

Wheathead was a miserable place. They passed what had once been an inn before an artillery shell had closed it down. Only the sign still swung.

Loose, in the wind, like the wirewolves.

The procession of mourners drew to a halt. Up ahead, excubitors were checking the line. Rawne reached in under his cloak and took hold of his mk III.

He heard the rank voices of the grim excubitors. They barked and cursed in their foul language, not even bothering to let their voice boxes translate.

He saw them check Cirk's imago with a funny, paddle-like device.

'You are a long way from home, consented,' one excubitor said, suddenly translating in a delayed crackle.

'I am come to visit my dead, magir. I have walked a long way, and paid the tariffs,' he heard Cirk reply.

The excubitors waved the rest of them by. Rawne could smell the excubitors. Sweat, grease, and some other odour too rank to describe. The mourners trudged on up the hill towards the boneyard.

Cirk dawdled until she was alongside Rawne. 'There is a house off to our left. I think we can contact the cell there.'

He nodded.

They slipped away, leaving the road and the plodding mourners. Behind them, the excubitors at the checkpoint showed no sign of noticing. Hugging the shadows, the mission team hurried along the side street and stopped at a stone porch. Acreson reached up and turned one of the loose stones in the gate post around.

'We'll go to the boneyard now,' said Cirk. 'If the resistance is active here, there'll be a feather under that stone by the time we come back.'

'All right,' Rawne nodded.

They began to climb the hill towards the boneyard. Rawne kept looking back. He could see the parked troop transports, and the Occupation troopers going from house to house.

And then he saw something else.

'What the feth is that?' he asked.

Cirk turned. She uttered a low gasp. 'It's a glyf,' she murmured. 'Look away. For the God-Emperor's sake, look away!'

'I'VE LOST SIGHT of Rawne's group,' Gaunt said. 'I think they went down that street there, left of the main road. But the buildings are blocking my view.'

'Be patient,' said Mkoll.

'Is that a lantern? What is that?' Larkin murmured.

'Where?'

Larkin suddenly jerked back, as if he'd been stung. He pulled the sniper scope down from his eye. Larkin was deathly pale and his eyes were wide with fear. 'Emperor protect me! Feth! What did I just see?'

Gaunt panned round. He saw the light, a glowing mass, bright as neon, the size of a trooper's backpack, drifting along at the height of the eaves. It made no sense. But it seemed to have some kind of glowing structure. He–

The scope went black.

Gaunt looked up. Landerson had clamped his hand around the end of Gaunt's scope, blocking his view.

'What the feth are you doing?'

'It's a glyf,' said Landerson. 'Believe me, the last thing you want is a good, magnified view of it.'

'What the feth is–' Rawne began.

'Shut up, Rawne!' Cirk hissed. 'Keep walking. No one look at it!'

'But–'

'No talking!'

Rawne did as he was told. He turned back to make sure everyone was following, struggling to keep his eyes off the strange, curling light that lingered over the street behind them.

Everyone had obeyed Cirk's order. Everyone except Feygor.

Murtan Feygor stood transfixed, gazing at the illuminated symbols that coiled and chittered against the sullen sky. So bright, like words written in lightning, and such words! He did not understand them, but they made his flesh crawl.

In his head, the sound of scuttling insects grew louder and louder.

'Murt!' Rawne called as loud as he dared. There was an edgy pitch to his voice. Everyone turned.

'Oh shit!' Cirk gasped as she saw how the Guardsman was transfixed.

Rawne reached Feygor's side and pulled at his arm. Feygor was frozen like a statue. His eyes were wide and almost glazed. His mouth lolled open and drool hung from his slack lips.

Rawne dragged harder. He was panicking. The worst part of it was he wanted to look too. He wanted to tilt his head and understand what his old friend was staring at. There was a buzzing sound in the air, like the burr of the swarms they'd found in the Shedowtonland fields.

Bonin appeared, his eyes also deliberately turned towards the ground. He grabbed Feygor too, and together they heaved at the rigid man. Feygor refused to budge. Without thinking, Bonin slapped his hand across Feygor's eyes.

Feygor let out a strangled moan as his view was blocked. He staggered backwards into their arms and there was a sharp stink as his bladder let go. He began to struggle, shake, like an obscura addict in the throes of withdrawal.

'Come on!' Cirk called. 'Carry him if you have to!' She had a hand raised to blot out the glyf as if she was shielding her eyes from bright sunlight. The team began to move again.

But now Lefivre had looked at the glyf too.

'EXPLAIN TO ME what it is,' Gaunt said to Landerson bluntly. Landerson shrugged.

'I can't… I mean, I'm no magister, no sorcerer. I don't understand the workings of Chaos.'

'Try!' Gaunt snapped.

'It's an expression of the warp,' Plower said. 'That's what I was told. The Archenemy has branded our world in every way, even the atmosphere. A glyf is the way Chaos makes its mark on the very air. A glyf is a thought, a concept, an idea… an utterance of the Ruinous Powers somehow conjured into solid form. Some say they're sentient. I don't believe that. Glyfs are Chaos runes, sigils, symbols, whatever you want to call them. The ordinals summon them into being and release them to watch over the populace. They drift, they patrol, they lurk…'

'Great,' cut in Curth sourly. 'But what do they *do*?'

Plower looked at her. 'I suppose you could describe them as tripwires. Sensors. Alarms. They react to human activity. I've no idea how. Certainly, they respond to imagos. If they detect anything unconsented, they… they react. They summon.'

THE FIRST SIGIL was hooked like a crescent moon, but also coiled somehow. The second was like the pattern a spider's steps might make in dust. The third, like the valves of a human heart. Bright. So bright. So cold. There was no order to the sigils, no arrangement, because they constantly switched places or transformed. There were more than three. Less than one. A thousand, twisted into a single light.

Lefivre knew he should be doing something other than looking at this wonder. He tasted acid reflux in his mouth. The sore wound on his forearm where the imago had once been buried ached and throbbed.

The memory of his previous encounter with a glyf came back to him. He remembered biting Landerson's palm. He remembered fear.

He wasn't frightened now. Not now. Because now he understood the symbols that crackled in the air before him. He understood what they meant. He couldn't think of a human word that meant the same thing, but that didn't matter.

He understood.

Acreson was closest to Lefivre. As Bonin and Rawne dragged the thrashing Feygor back down the muddy street, Acreson ran forward, waving at Cirk to get the others clear.

Acreson's own imago jerked and tightened. He felt it fidget in the flesh of his arm. He loathed the grub with every atom of his body, but now he counted on it, and counted on his decision not to have it removed. It consented him for night and day. Maybe it would appease the glyf and distract it from poor, unconsented Lefivre.

Acreson slammed into Lefivre, knocking him to the ground. Averting his eyes from the trembling light-form, Acreson raised his arm and exposed his imago.

The sight of it seemed to still the glyf's crackling noises for a second. Was it backing off? Had he diverted it?

There was a hard sound, like a stick breaking. Acreson gasped. Time seemed to slow down. He felt a hot pain in his belly, as if a white-hot skewer had been rammed through it. Then he felt his feet leave the ground. He was flying…

Flying backwards. Impact recoil snapped through his body like a whip-crack. For one long, silent moment, Acreson saw glittering drops of blood drift lazily up into the air before him.

His own blood.

Acreson hit the ground hard in a concussive blur of pain and sudden real-time. The las-lock bolt had blown clean through his belly and thrown him three metres backwards. Down the narrow street, summoned by the glyf, a pack of excubitors was running forward, weapons raised. Several more bolts stung down the street. Prone, rigid with pain, Acreson watched them flash over him.

'Oh. God. Emperor,' he sighed.

Its work done, the glyf was already drifting away across the low rooftops, as if bored with the game. Calling the alarm, the excubitors ran on. A carnyx horn blasted, echoing across the dismal streets of Wheathead.

The mission team was already running. Cirk and Criid led the way, with Bonin and Rawne close behind, struggling with Feygor. Lock-bolts ripped around them.

Thirty metres behind them, Lefivre got to his feet, puzzled and dazed. He felt as if he were waking from a deep sleep. What the hell was going on? He couldn't remember.

Nearby, Acreson lay on his back, twitching. The man's belly was a crater of gore. Darts of light crisped through the air.

Lefivre turned. He saw the excubitors charging towards him. By some freak of fate, they had not yet managed to hit him.

Instinct took over. PDF ranger programme training. Lefivre calmly pulled the shoddy old autorifle out from under his ragged clothing and opened fire.

His jury-rigged silencer snorted like a pressure cooker valve. Lefivre's first shots killed the two excubitors leading the charge stone dead, blowing them over onto their backs. He winged a third and then hit another in the forehead as he raked his cone of fire across the street.

The excubitors dived for cover. A las-lock bolt took off Lefivre's right earlobe and another dug a searing gouge through his left shoulder. Lefivre emptied the last of his magazine and dropped two more of the skeletal foe face-down in the mud.

Change clip. He had to change clip. His hands fumbled, dropping the empty, reaching into his belt back. A passing bolt lased off his left shin and burst the meat of his calf.

Swaying, Lefivre found a fresh magazine and rammed it home.

Autofire licked down the street. At first, Lefivre thought it must be him, but then he saw Acreson. The man had sat up, his legs crooked under him, and he was blasting with his assault weapon. The man's hands, belly and lap were soaked with blood. Ghastly black and purple spools of entrail were pushing out of Acreson's exploded stomach.

'For the God-Emperor of Mankind!' Lefivre screamed. 'For Gereon! For Gereon!' He opened fire again. The two resistance fighters hailed their fire down the narrow street. Several more excubitors toppled and died. The rest were driven back, trying to reload their slow, single-shot light muskets.

Lefivre ran to Acreson.

'Come on!'

Acreson looked up at him. Blood leaked from the corners of his mouth. 'I'm not going anywhere,' he said.

'Yes, you are. Yes, you are!'

Acreson looked up at Lefivre strangely. 'You don't remember, do you?'

'Remember what? Shut up and let me help you!'

'The glyf,' said Acreson. 'You triggered the glyf.'

Lefivre hesitated. He remembered something, a light, a word. But not...

'I didn't mean to do anything,' he said.

'I know,' said Acreson, blood bubbling around his lips. 'Run.'

'But–'

'Run, Lefivre. Save yourself.'

The excubitors had suddenly stopped shooting. A clammy chill fell across the street. In the lingering quiet, the wind rose, and the carnyx horn started to boom again.

Down at the talix tree gibbet, ball lightning seethed into being, curling and licking around the axl-beam. The wired mannequins began to tremble and quiver.

'Dear God-Emperor who protects us all...' Acreson murmured. 'We've woken them up.'

FIFTEEN

THE EXCUBITORS SCATTERED, wailing. Townsfolk and mourners fled for cover in a blind panic. Even the Archenemy troopers, who had been mustering at the sudden alarm, now began to run. Some dropped their weapons.

There was a taste of ozone in the air. A dry, bald scent, like a heated wire. The clouds closed in over Wheathead, blooming fast like ink in water. Thunder boomed.

On the stark gibbet, the ball lightning frothed and bubbled, brighter than any sun. Warp-light shone out of it. The lightning mass sputtered and then began to drip down from the cross-beam like lava, like molten, white-hot rock, pouring down into the hollow metal puppets, filling them with light.

The wired puppets twitched as they filled. Metal segments ground against each other. Wires hummed like charged cables. The air temperature in Wheathead plunged. Frost powdered the roof tiles and the muddy streets became stiff with ice.

The wirewolves woke.

The glyf had summoned them. Arcane practices had made the space above the gibbet thin so that the immaterium could finger its way through the aether when the correct command came. Now the crude metal puppets, engineered to contain the energies of the warp and coalesce them, vibrated into life.

There were two of them. They took the form of men simply because the puppets had been fashioned to bottle them in that shape. Jerking spastically from their wires, they looked like ancient knights in full plate armour, illuminated from within by the brightest lanterns ever lit. The suspending wires shivered and sang, taut with power.

The puppet hosts had not been fashioned well. Just crude metal shoes, shin-guards, thigh plates, hauberks. Hungry radiance speared out through the gaps and chinks of joints and seams. The arm sections jerked. Light speared out through the helmet eyeslits as bright as a Land Raider's stablights.

The arms of the puppets were unfinished. Shoulder plates, metal sections for upper and lower arms. They had no gloves or hands. The supporting wires suspended loose bouquets of razor-sharp steel blades from the fore-arm cuffs that tinkled together as the rising wind stirred them. Extending, controlled by governing magicks scratched into the armour, the baleful light sprouted from the wrists and made long, crackling claw shapes of solid light into which those blades became embedded like fingernails.

'Run!' gasped Acreson.

Lefivre took a step or two backwards on the suddenly brittle mud. His heels cracked panes of ice. He could not believe what he was seeing. He felt his bowels turn to water.

'Run, Lefivre! Run, for Throne's sake!' Acreson pleaded.

The gibbet wires, whining frantically like live telegraph lines, trembled and then snapped.

The wirewolves dropped from the gibbet.

Shedding ghastly light from every joint, they landed hard, then stood upright. Slowly. Very, very slowly.

The first one took a step. There was a sound like a tank's tracks as it moved. The second one followed.

Grating metal noises, blistering power.

Their bright eyes, lancing like target beams, swept across the scene ahead of them. They began to snuffle, then whine.

Then they began to howl.

'Oh my God-Emperor…' Lefivre began.

The wirewolves started forward, moving faster than any man. A deathly chill surrounded them. Their blade fingers scraped and squealed against the stone walls as they slithered along, feeling their way down the village streets with lascivious caresses.

'Please… run,' Acreson repeated.

The howling was growing so much louder.

An excubitor, caught in the open, fell to its knees before the oncoming wirewolves. One of them slashed at it with its claws of light and steel. The excubitor fell in a haze of violet light and came apart, torn into pieces. Smoke wafted from its sliced remains.

Lefivre started to run.

'WHAT THE FETH is that noise?' Rawne cried.

'Ignore it. Ignore it!' Cirk jabbered. 'We have to find cover and we have to find it now!'

Feygor had fallen again. Now Criid joined the effort to lift him.

'For Throne's sake, come on!' Cirk yelled.

They were at the edge of the village now, the sky black above them. Hideous light shone from the narrow street they had just left.

'Head for the treeline!' Cirk ordered and they began to race across a bare field that sloped away from Wheathead's western edge.

'WHAT THE HELL are you doing?' Landerson cried. 'We have to get out of here!'

'I have people down there,' Gaunt replied, shaking off the cell fighter's grip.

'Not any more,' said Landerson. 'Trust me, sir. The wirewolves are loose now. If we run, we might make it out of here with our lives.'

Gaunt looked Landerson in the eye. He knew the man wasn't lying. He had no idea what he was getting himself into. The mission was too important, too vital. Every one of his team was expendable. That's what Van Voytz had stressed. All that mattered was getting to the prize.

Gaunt had believed that was acceptable at the time. But now, as his faith was put to the test, he realised it wasn't. Rawne was down there. Feygor. Criid. Bonin.

Bonin. 'Lucky' Bonin, who'd offered his life to take Heritor Asphodel on Verghast and survived to earn his nickname. One of Mkoll's finest.

Criid, dear Tona, the punk-girl ganger, who'd come out of Vervunhive and become not only a Ghost but the First's first female officer. She had Caffran's heart. And then there were the children, of course...

Feygor. Gaunt owed nothing to Feygor except that he'd always been there and always fought like a brazen bastard.

And Rawne. His nemesis. His shadow. The man who would, Gaunt was sure, one day kill him more certainly than the forces of the Archenemy.

But Rawne was Rawne. Without him, there would be no Tanith First. And now Corbec was dead and buried on distant Herodor, Rawne was the last remaining strand of that founding spirit that had been born years ago on Tanith.

Gaunt wasn't going to lose that. He wasn't going to lose any of them.

Feth take the mission.

'Mkoll!' he shouted. 'Get the team up and moving. Get them clear. If I don't come back, you know what we've come to this world to do and I trust you to get it done.'

Mkoll nodded. 'I'll do my job, sir. For what it's worth, I don't think you should be leaving us, sir.'

'Neither do I,' said Gaunt, 'But I must. Rawne's down there.'

'The man who you said never trusted you?'

Gaunt nodded. 'Consider this my way of proving him wrong.'

Mkoll smiled. Then he raised his voice. 'Varl! Brostin! Get the group moving! Turn south into the woods. No noise, you understand?'

Mkoll paused. 'Mkvenner... go with the commander.'

'I don't need–' Gaunt began.

'Ven's going with you, sir. My instructions.'

Gaunt nodded. He'd already drawn his bolt pistols and was hurrying down the bank out of the trees.

'Bring him back, Ven,' Mkoll said.

Mkvenner nodded and turned to run after the Tanith's colonel-commissar.

Mkoll hurried into the trees. 'Move it! Move it now, you bastards! Come on!'

LEFIVRE HAD GONE. Acreson, close to passing out from blood loss, maintained his sitting position and aimed his weapon down the street.

The wirewolves slithered and bounded towards him, keening. Acreson retched involuntarily at the sight of them. Wiping bile from his mouth, he opened fire.

The frantic bullets spanked off the armour of the nearest wolf, and where they hit solid light at the junction of limb armour, they melted into steam.

Acreson fired again, and again, until his clip was out.

'Oh Emperor Emperor Emperor…' he began.

The first wirewolf was on him. It sliced around with its savage claws. Acreson's head flopped sideways, his neck almost severed. The claws bit deep and lightning seethed. A violet glow suffused the body of the cell fighter. In a second, Acreson was reduced to a skeleton, coated in blue-white ash, his exposed bones smoking.

RAWNE'S PARTY FLED Wheathead through the edges of the field, the sky swirling with dark clouds overhead.

'Run!' Rawne ordered. Cirk was already sprinting through the coarse grass. Criid and Bonin were struggling with Feygor.

Rawne took a tube-charge out of his jacket and plucked the det-tape upright between finger and thumb.

The howling was getting closer now. The sky looked like blood.

They were all going to die. Fact.

How well they did it was up to Rawne.

SCREAMING AND FIRING his weapon, Lefivre reached the end of the street. Over the fence behind him, the lifeless fields rolled away to the woodline.

The first wirewolf lunged at him and he opened fire, emptying his clip into its chest. The kinetic force of the bullets drove it back.

But the second one had slithered up at Lefivre's right hand. It didn't strike. It reached out with its claws and the smoking blades sank into Lefivre's shoulder.

He shuddered. His mouth opened in pain. A violet aura lit up around his body.

Then his flesh evaporated in a drizzle of blue dust and his blackened, cooked bones clattered onto the pathway.

SIXTEEN

LANDERSON WAS RUNNING through the gloomy trees. He was close to panic. Purchason and Plower were ahead of him, sprinting headlong. The Ghosts were–

Landerson skidded to a halt and fell over into the loam. He looked back. The Ghosts had stopped. They had stopped and they were arguing.

In the name of the Throne! Death is at our heels! What are you doing?

'You let him go? Alone?' Curth was yelling.

'I sent Ven with him…' Mkoll said.

'This isn't right. We shouldn't be running,' Beltayn announced.

'Thanks for sharing, trooper,' Mkoll growled. 'Now move it.'

'You heard the sarge,' Brostin said. 'Let's go!'

'No,' said Larkin.

'Well then, feth you, Larks!' Brostin said, and began to run on anyway.

Mkoll looked at Varl, Curth, Larkin and Beltayn. 'I've given you an order. Gaunt's own order. Don't do this. Not now.'

'My dear sir,' Curth hissed. 'If not now, when?'

She turned, and started hurrying back through the undergrowth towards the village.

'Stop it! Stop it, woman! Ana!' Mkoll cried. No one had ever seen the master of scouts display such open emotion. It didn't stop Varl, Beltayn and Larkin from following her.

'Sorry, sir,' Beltayn called back over his shoulder. 'He needs us. Something's awry.'

'Stop where you are!' Mkoll shouted. He almost raised his weapon to aim at them, then he thought how ridiculous that would be. 'Please!' he called. 'Gaunt told us to go!'

The four Ghosts stopped and looked back at him. Beltayn stared at the forest floor, unwilling to catch Mkoll's fierce gaze. Curth shrugged. Larkin kept looking back towards the village, listening to the howling that rang up the fields towards them.

Varl just smiled. 'Sarge... since when did Ibram Gaunt go into a fight and not expect the Ghosts to be right behind him?'

'We have a mission here,' Mkoll began. 'We have a duty. It's important. We can't just...'

His voice tailed away. 'Feth, I'm not even convincing myself.'

He turned and looked at the departing form of Trooper Brostin heading away through the trees. 'Brostin! Get back here! Now! For Tanith and for the Emperor, we're going back! Move it, trooper!'

They turned, raised their weapons, and began to run back towards Wheathead.

'WE'RE WHAT?' BROSTIN said. Panting, he set down his heavy cannon and looked back through the trees. 'You've got to be fething kidding me...'

'You need a hand with that?' Landerson said, slipping through the undergrowth behind him.

'What?'

'The cannon. It's awful heavy if we're going back all that way.'

'Feth! You too? Has everyone gone fething mad?'

Landerson was sure they hadn't. Once in a lifetime, an officer came along who was worth following. Call it love, call it respect, call it duty, it was something about the man that made you want to push yourself, right to the limit, even in the face of horror. Ballerat had been that sort of man, Throne rest him. And Gaunt was that kind too. Landerson had seen the look in the faces of Varl and Curth, Beltayn and Larkin. That was all he had needed to know.

He looked over his shoulder. Plower and Purchason were long gone. Brostin looked like he might just follow them.

'Coming?' Landerson asked. 'If you're not, let me take the heavy. They're going to need it.'

Brostin glared at him. 'Feth you. Feth you, you stupid gak. Are you all fething crazy?'

STREAMING RIBBONS OF light in their wake, the wirewolves leapt the perimeter walls of Wheathead and swept down into the fields. Rawne turned again and saw them coming.

'Move! Move!' he yelled at Bonin and Criid as they stumbled with Feygor. The treeline was so far away. They'd never make it. Rawne swivelled the tube-charge in his hand like a baton and decided that this was the moment to stand his ground. The field's dry grasses swished around his legs.

The wirewolves came for him, wailing.

CIRK WAS STRUGGLING up the rise towards the treeline when she saw Gaunt and Mkvenner leap past her, dashing the other way.

'Where are you going?' she cried. 'In the name of Terra, run, you idiots!'

They ignored her.

Fools, Cirk decided, and ran on. She tripped over a root and fell hard. Getting up again, she looked back down the field and saw Rawne, isolated amid the dry grasses, facing down the warp monsters that were bounding towards him.

RAWNE COULD SMELL their fury. Taste their evil. The wirewolves thrashed through the spent corn to meet him, daemons bottled in clanking suits of metal.

Rawne pulled out the det-tape, raised the charge, and threw it.

The blast knocked him off his feet. His timing had been perfect. The tube had gone off right under the leading wirewolf. It disappeared in a volcano of fire and exploded earth.

The dust cleared. The wirewolf came on. He hadn't even slowed it down. Not even sightly.

Rawne's fingers slid into his jacket and grabbed his last tube-charge.

The wirewolf pounced at him, its claws slicing the air.

No time. No time. No–

Bolt rounds hit the monster in mid-leap and blew it back into the grass. It got up again immediately, and then was felled a second time by sustained bolter fire that thumped off its chest plating like hailstones off a tin roof.

Rawne looked up. Gaunt ran past him up the field, firing a bolt pistol in each hand. Every round slammed home, twisting the daemon back again and again, buckling its armour sleeve.

But it refused to die.

And the second one was right on them. It reared up, its claws unfurled.

Rapid las-fire knocked it over into the grass. Mkvenner arrived, right on Gaunt's heels, blasting at the thing with relentless rifle shots.

The second wirewolf shrugged, rising again. Where it had fallen, it had burned a patch of dry grass black and scorched the earth. It flew at Mkvenner.

His mag was spent. He spun the lasrifle like a staff and hit the attacking daemon in the face plate with the butt-end of his weapon, jerking it back. Then he ducked and jumped sideways as the claws cut for him. Another jab with the butt-stock into the crackling breastplate and the wirewolf recoiled again.

Darting back, legs wide and braced, Mkvenner drew his warknife and fixed it to his rifle's muzzle. As Rawne looked on, awe-struck, Mkvenner spun the weapon a second time, the straight silver gleaming in the dull light, and speared it at the wirewolf's renewed attack. Lunge, stab, block, sweep, another blow with the stock.

It had been rumoured that Mkvenner had somehow received training in the ancient art of *cwlwhl*, the martial art of the long-vanished Tanith wood-warriors, the Nalsheen. In the old days, it was said, the Nalsheen had banded together in the oblique forests of Tanith and, armed only with fighting staves tipped with silver knives, had overthrown the corrupt Huhlhwch Dynasty, ushering in the age of modern, free Tanith.

A lot of old balls, Rawne had thought. All part of some mythic and patriotic legend from Tanith's past. There were no Nalsheen any more, no wood-warriors. It was all a load of old crap and Mkvenner played it for all he was worth to boost his rep as the mysterious, quiet type.

Rawne rapidly revised his opinion. He watched in quiet wonder as a lone man, armed only with an exhausted rifle, fought hand to hand with a daemon from the warp, blocking, striking, sweeping, stabbing. Mkvenner's movements were like some violent ballet. He was matching the thing's every blow, every slice, fending it off, driving it back, avoiding every lethal hook it swung at him with sheer agility and grace.

Until his luck ran out.

The wirewolf ripped, and Mkvenner tumbled over, legs pinioning, his lasrifle staff shorn in two by the murderous claws.

The wirewolf leapt at the sprawling scout.

Rawne reached for his last tube-charge, knowing he would be too late.

A hotshot round hit the monster in the jaw plating and blew it sideways violently. It rolled and writhed, burning the ground.

Up at the treeline, Larkin reloaded and re-aimed.

'Wanna go again?' he breathed, and fired his second shot. Beside him, Mkoll and Beltayn opened up too.

THE OTHER WIREWOLF had launched itself at Gaunt again, howling fit to break the sky apart. His bolters spent, Gaunt holstered them and unslung the weapon he had asked Beltayn to care for during his mission into Ineuron Town.

The power sword of Hieronymo Sondar.

He triggered the ignition stud. It lit up like a firebrand in his hands. Gaunt swung it at the wirewolf and sent the creature staggering away, a deep gouge hacked into its chest plate.

But that was nothing like enough to kill it. It came back at him with renewed fury.

Gaunt knew he wasn't going to get his sword up to block in time.

'MY MASTER,' VIRAG said, and handed the printout wafer to Uexkull. The warrior read it.

'Is this correct?' he asked, his voice creaking like a dry tree in a slow wind.

'Yes, lord,' said Virag. 'Intelligence reports that the wirewolves have woken at Wheathead.'

'That's what… ten kilometres from here?'

'A dozen at most.'

Uexkull hurried towards the waiting deathships. 'We have them now. I just hope something's still alive by the time we get there.'

THE WIREWOLF'S ARM swept round, its luminous claws whistling towards Gaunt's throat. But the blow didn't land.

A bright stream of heavy cannonfire ripped into the wirewolf, hurling it backwards a good three metres. Some of the hammerblow shots broke the metal threads articulating the daemon's arm, and its claws and wristguard ripped away. Blinding energy began to spit and bleed out of the broken limb.

In the treeline, close to Larkin, Beltayn and Mkoll, Landerson squeezed the autocannon's stirrup trigger again and hit the stricken wirewolf for a second time.

It juddered backwards, weeping warp-power out of its stump in a flurry like welding sparks.

'You'll probably need these,' a voice said.

Landerson looked up. Brostin hunkered down beside him, pulling feeder belts out of his ammunition hoppers.

'Load me,' said Landerson.

HEAVY FIRE WAS streaking out of the trees, along with las-blasts and devastating shots from a long-las. But the wirewolves weren't beaten. Shuddering from the impact of incoming fire, shrugging off hard rounds and las-bolts alike, they drove themselves forward to get at Rawne, Gaunt and Mkvenner.

Gaunt had seen what the cannon shots had done to the arm of one of them. Already, the wirewolf seemed to be moving more sluggishly, its inner light dimmer. Gaunt remembered Landerson saying, back in Ineuron Town, that the things used up their power quickly. The precious sword held in a two-handed grip, Gaunt swung at the damaged wirewolf. The powered blade slashed into the metal threads of the thing's neck.

The taut wires snapped. Its containment armour now entirely broken open, the wirewolf released its channelled energy.

It ignited, blasting ferocious white flame out in a wide shockwave that smashed Gaunt, Rawne and Mkvenner to the ground.

Struggling up from the detonation, Gaunt shook his head. His ears were ringing. The grass around them was burned and scorched, and littered with pieces of the daemon's metal suit. The flesh of Gaunt's face tingled. It felt like sunburn.

He shook his head again and his hearing began to return.

That was when he heard a rumbling sound.

SEVENTEEN

A MILITARY TRUCK was thundering across the field towards them. It was an Occupation force troop transport, painted matt green, churning up the rough surface of the field with its six big tyres. It had come from the outskirts of the village, and demolished at least one low wall in its urgent effort to reach them.

Great. Now they had troops closing on them too.

Gaunt tried to get Rawne and Mkvenner up. Both were badly dazed, concussed, and had red heat burns on their faces.

'Come on!' Gaunt urged. He was none too steady on his feet himself.

The second wirewolf was still intact. As the smoke from the blast drifted around it, it halted for a second, as if trying to work out what had happened to its twin. Then it lifted its iron-cased head, its eyeslits blazing pits of light, and began to stride towards the stumbling Ghosts. Its pace increased. In a moment, it was bounding along, closing fast.

Rawne still had hold of his last tube-charge. He threw it behind them, and the charging wirewolf vanished in a veil of grit and flame.

Rawne, Gaunt and Mkvenner ran towards the trees. Back on its feet, the wirewolf leapt through the thick black smoke from Rawne's munition and gave chase.

The truck slammed through the smoke behind it and drove straight into the wirewolf, mashing it down. It vanished under the bellowing transport. Gaunt heard metal screech and grind.

The truck swung round and came to a halt. There was a figure standing in the open back. It was Curth.

'Get on!' she yelled.

They ran towards her. She helped Rawne and Mkvenner clamber up into the back. Gaunt struggled into the cab to find Varl behind the wheel.

'What the feth are you doing?' Gaunt said.

'Improvising,' Varl replied, and threw the vehicle in gear. 'It was the doc's idea, actually. The others were giving you cover-fire, and she had no weapon, so she said, Varl, she said–'

'Spare me the details,' Gaunt said.

Varl slammed the heavy machine forward. Criid and Bonin were ahead, approaching the treeline with Feygor slumped between them.

'Pick them up first. Then we have to g–'

There was a rending noise, metal on metal, and the truck lurched as a savage shudder ran through it.

'What the feth–' Varl began.

Electric discharge lit up the cab, crackling across the metal dash in lambent blue, jellyfish patterns.

The wirewolf wrenched its way up over the tailgate, its talons gouging the bodywork, and landed in the back. Its armour was buckled and dented, and power spurted out of the cracks. It swung its claws at Rawne. Mkvenner threw himself forward and tackled the major out of its way. But the force of the desperate bodyslam carried them over the side of the still-moving truck, and they hung there, scrabbling for handholds. Rawne slipped. Mkvenner had one leg and one arm hooked over the truck's sideboarding and managed to grab Rawne's wrist. If he let go, the Tanith officer would disappear under the rear wheels.

Curth stumbled back away from the advancing wirewolf. 'Feth you!' she yelled and hurled her narthecium case at it. The daemon-thing swatted it aside, and the case bounced across the cargo space, its contents spilling. The truck lurched violently again, and even the wirewolf staggered. Curth fell, knocked her shoulder, and reached for something – anything – to use as a weapon.

Her hand closed over something small and hard. A flask of inhibitor suspension from her case. She hurled it.

It smashed against the wirewolf's dented chest plate. The inhibitor solution contained a number of compounds manufactured by the Departmento Medicae to counteract the effects of warp-contact on the human metabolism. The fluid they were suspended in was blessed water from the Balneary Shrine of Herodor.

The wirewolf screamed. It staggered backwards, clawing at its face and chest, wounding itself with its own claws. The inhibitor solution ate into the thing's armour where it had sprayed, gnawing like molecular acid.

Eyes wide, Curth looked round, found another flask, and threw that too.

The wirewolf screamed again.

Curth saw her dermo-needle gun. It had fallen out of the spilled narthecium. She grabbed it and loaded a third flask into the gun's dose reservoir.

Fuelled by a stubborn courage that surprised even herself, Curth lunged forward and jammed the dermo-needle tip into the wirewolf's left eyeslit. Her finger squeezed the activator.

The wirewolf shook, as if it were suffering from a grand mal seizure. Liquid energy, terribly bright and sickeningly viscous, bubbled and frothed out of its eyeslits. Its face plate began to fester and melt like paper in the rain.

It staggered backwards, limbs twitching, and fell back over the tailgate.

Then it exploded.

The blast threw Curth back down the length of the cargo space. The truck itself was almost thrown over. It skidded to a halt, spraying up soil.

Silence. Smoke billowed.

Still half-hanging over the sidewall of the transport, Mkvenner gasped and let go of Rawne's wrist. The major dropped down onto his feet and looked back up at Mkvenner.

'Thanks,' he said.

THE GHOSTS IN the treeline were running down towards them. Cirk and Landerson were with them. Gaunt climbed up into the back of the truck and helped Curth to her feet.

'You all right?'

She nodded. She was still holding the dermo-needle. It was broken and smoking.

'What did you do?' he asked.

'I… I think I used up our entire medical supply in about thirty seconds,' she said ruefully.

'Right now, I don't think that matters,' he replied.

Varl got the truck restarted and the mission team hauled themselves aboard. There was no sign of Plower or Purchason.

'Do you want us to wait?' Gaunt asked Cirk. 'To look for them?'

She shook her head. From across the field, the horns of Wheathead were blowing, and troopers were emerging, fanning out into the grass.

'We have to get out of here now,' she decided.

Varl drove the battered truck up the slope and into the trees, zigzagging them through brambles and brushcover until they reached a narrow trackway.

East or west? There was no choice now. The enemy forces were closing from the east. In the distance, they could hear the drone of deathship engines. West was the only way now.

Varl put his foot down and they rattled away along the track.

Sitting in the cab beside Varl, Gaunt turned round and opened the small window through to the cargo bay.

'Cirk?' he called.

She made her way over, and leaned close to the other side of the window.

'We'll use this ride as far as we can, to put some distance between us and that place. Earlier, you told me west wasn't an option. Something called the Untill. What is that?'

'Marshland,' she said. 'We're heading into the deep forests now, and that marks the boundary. Beyond it lie the marshes themselves. Vast areas, unnavigable. The word "Untill" comes from the earliest maps of Gereon, the colonists' maps. Gereon was found to be a fecund, fertile place, hence its reputation as one of the chief agri-worlds in the cluster. But some regions, like the marshes, were unfarmable. "Untillable". That's what the name means.'

'So there's no way through?'

Cirk shook her head. She seemed tired and edgy, and the stigma on her cheek more raw than ever. It pained Gaunt to see her beauty so irretrievably spoiled.

'I'm afraid, sir,' she said, 'that your mission is now over. There's no way to achieve it. Not for a long time, at least. We might be able to hide in the Untill, I suppose. Right now, it's as good a place as any. Even the forces of the Occupation avoid the Untill. A few months lying low, maybe, and we might risk coming out. Once the fuss has died down. Maybe start trying to hook up with a resistance cell.'

'A few months,' Gaunt echoed. He knew they had nothing like that. The mission was desperately time-sensitive. And besides, a few months and they would all have succumbed to Gereon's taint. Especially now Curth's medicines had gone.

'We'll see,' he said.

'We won't,' she replied. 'You asked me to face up to hard truths when you enlisted my help, sir. I did that. Now face up to hard truths yourself. Your mission has failed. There is no chance now we can accomplish it.'

'We'll see,' Gaunt repeated.

SLEEK AND UNLOVELY, like carrion birds, the two deathships circled Wheathead. Wan smoke drifted from the dry fields under the trees where patches of grass were burning. Uexkull used a scope to scan. Below, squads of troopers and excubitors were extending out in a wide search pattern into the forests. They had packs of fetch-hounds, and some rode in half-tracks. On Uexkull's orders, a full brigade strength was moving in on the village to bolster the units.

He turned back to the report Gurgoy had given him. The Wheathead wirewolves had been woken, but they had not returned to their gibbet when their power was spent. That made no sense. They always returned to sleep again, unless they were destroyed.

And nothing could destroy a wirewolf, surely?

Uexkull felt uneasy, as if the nature of the cosmos was out of balance. He hated impossibilities.

Was it plausible that the False Emperor had sent warriors to this world who were actually capable of destroying the merciless implements of Chaos?

'My lord?' said Virag suddenly. His face was alarmed. He was staring at Uexkull.

'What?'

'Are you unwell, lord? Have you ingested poison?'

Uexkull blinked. 'Of course not! Why do you ask me that?'

'Your face, great lord. It was twisted into a rictus, a grimace, as if toxins infected you. And you were gurgling and choking, like you were dying of some foul–'

'I was laughing,' said Uexkull.

'Oh,' the warrior said. He paused. 'Why, lord?'

'Because we have prayed for a test, have we not?' The warrior pack all grunted *yes*.

'We have yearned to face down the bright Astartes in war, but our beloved Anarch, whose word drowns out all others, decided in his wisdom such glory was not for us. He did not send us to the frontline. Instead, he honoured us with the task of overseeing this wretched occupation. Now it seems we might have worthy prey here after all. Rivals in war. Soldiers who can destroy wirewolves and make the common troopers and the excubitors chase their own tails.'

Uexkull looked at his men. 'We have grown lazy. Now there is a true challenge. I will enjoy killing them.'

The warriors began to beat their steel-clad fists against their chest plates and bark out approval. Above the din, Uexkull heard the link chime.

'Report?'

'My lord,' the pilot's voice crackled over the intercom. 'The auspex has detected a metal object twenty-four kilometres west of this position, moving into the forests. A vehicle, lord.'

'Lock on,' Uexkull said. 'Hunt speed. Take us to it.'

THE LONG DAY was drawing to a close, and they were running out of road fast. A dark, sludgy brown light filled the sky, and the forests were growing increasingly dark and forbidding. The trees were closing around the track, which had now dwindled to an overgrown rut, and branches swished and flapped against the truck's sides. Varl had dropped his speed.

Beside him in the cab, Gaunt was talking to Mkoll. Like Cirk had done before, Mkoll was leaning to speak through the cab's little rear window. He could only see Gaunt's mouth through the slit. Both of them realised it was unpleasantly like a confessional booth. Mkoll knew he was owning up to his sins as surely as in any Imperial templum.

'I gave you an order,' Gaunt said.

'Yes, sir. I know you did.'

'Get the team away.'

'Yes, sir. I take full responsibility. We should have gone like you said.'

'But you came back, all of you. You abandoned the mission and you came back.'

'Yes, sir. We did that. Like I said, I take full responsibility. The others were just doing what I told them to.'

'Like feth!' Curth called out.

'Shut up,' Mkoll snapped. He looked back through the slit at Gaunt. 'My fault, sir. I'll gladly remove my rank pins. Mkvenner can take scout-command and–'

Glimpsed through the window slit as the truck bounced and jarred, Gaunt's mouth was smiling.

'I can pretty much guess what happened,' he said softly. 'We wouldn't be here now but for you.'

'Sir,' said Mkoll. 'Sir,' he added.

'Cirk says we're doomed, Mkoll,' Gaunt went on. 'She says we're heading into a marsh waste and that there's no hope of finding our way through. Feel like proving those rank pins to me?'

'I do, sir. Me, Ven and Bonin. We'll get us through.'

'I'm counting on it.'

'Sir?' It was Beltayn. He shuffled forward along the rattling cargo bay and Mkoll slid aside so he could reach the window slit. Beltayn had his vox-set's phones around his neck, and dragged the set behind him.

'What have you got, Bel?' Gaunt asked.

'Monitoring enemy traffic, sir.' He paused to blow his nose. His eyes were swollen and red. 'They're spread out in force behind us, closing out the woods. I'm picking up chatter from at least two airbornes. Three maybe. They're tracking in fast. I can't get a triangulation, but I think they're close.'

'The boy's right,' said Mkoll. 'I can hear jetwash. East of us, low and fast.'

In the cab, Gaunt turned to look at Varl. 'We won't get much further, will we?'

'Does the God-Emperor sit much?'

'Pull us over, Varl. Let's ditch the truck.'

THE TEAM JUMPED down the moment Varl brought the truck to a halt. There was no real trackway any more. The truck's wheel arches were throttled with torn strands of bramble and choke-weed.

'Make sure we've got everything,' Gaunt told Rawne.

'Everything?' Rawne replied sarcastically. 'Gee, what will everybody else carry?'

He was right. They were in poor shape. Ammo was perilously low. Gaunt had only a clip or two left for his bolt pistols, and everyone else was down to their last few las cells. The cannon had fired off so many rounds at the wirewolves Brostin had barely half a hopper left. Mkvenner didn't even have a rifle. The wolves had destroyed it. He had his autopistol, and he'd salvaged his warknife. Rawne had no tube-charges left. Varl still carried the team's last six in a satchel. They were low on food, and down to half on drinking water. Except for a few basics, Curth's narthecium was empty.

And that was the worst part, really. The ague was gripping them all now. Rashes, ulcers, headaches. Everyone seemed to have a head cold, especially Beltayn and Criid, who were sniffling. Feygor was still so dazed from exposure to the glyf that he had to be helped to walk. Curth told Gaunt quietly that the infection around Feygor's voice box implant seemed to be getting a great deal worse, and spreading.

'Whatever you've got, give it to him,' Gaunt said.

And that was just the start. Brostin had weeping burn blisters from his pyrotechnics on the causeway. Rawne, Mkvenner and Gaunt himself had a bad case of what seemed like sunburn from the wirewolf immolation. Curth nursed her badly bruised shoulder. Rawne's wrist was sprained from Mkvenner's life-saving grip. A hundred other knocks and cuts and–

Gaunt sighed. *It won't be easy.* That's what he'd said. It won't be easy. He could picture himself saying it. Standing to attention in a sunlit hall on Ancreon Sextus, with the windflowers nodding in the breeze outside the mansion walls. Biota had just finished his briefing, and Van Voytz had risen to his feet.

'I know it won't, Ibram,' Van Voytz had said. 'But do you think you can do it?'

Gaunt had glanced sideways to his waiting officers. Rawne, Daur, Mkoll, Kolea and Hark. Rawne had just folded his arms. Mkoll had nodded. One tiny nod.

'Yes, general. The Ghosts can do this,' Gaunt had said.

'There's a fast picket already prepped to leave high anchor,' Van Voytz remarked. 'What's it called, Biota?'

'The *Fortitude*, lord.'

'Ah, yes. That's an appropriate word, don't you think, Gaunt?'

'Yes, general.'

'Tac suggest you should choose a team of no more than twelve. The groundwork's been laid. Intelligence has made contact with the local underground to welcome you. Ballerat. Ballerat, right?'

'Yes, sir,' Biota replied.

'He's the man to find. So… any first thoughts about who you'll take?'

Both Kolea and Daur had raised their hands, interrupting each other.

'I'd be anxious to–'

'If I could offer my–'

'Thanks,' Gaunt said, looking at them. 'I'll pick the team tonight.'

'Just as you say, Ibram… this won't be easy.' Van Voytz had turned to stare out of one of the hall's deep windows. The sunlight fell across his face. It betrayed nothing. 'There's a good chance you won't come back.'

'I realise that, general sir. I'll make sure a strong command structure for the Tanith First remains in my absence.'

'Of course. Just so. Look, Ibram…' Van Voytz turned to face him. 'This is a messy business. But crucial. I won't order you to do it. If you want to back out, say so right now and we'll forget this meeting ever took place.'

'No, general. I won't. I feel this is down to me, sir. But for my decision, this situation would never have occurred. I'd like the chance to clean it up.'

'I thought you might. Because it's him?'

'Yes, general. Because it's him.'

'Sir?'

Gaunt blinked and came out of his thoughts. Night was closing in. The team was ready to move out.

'I'm coming, Criid,' he said. She nodded, and moved up to the head of the file.

'Let's go!' Gaunt called. They started to march away into the dense, dark forest.

Cirk was beside him. 'Gaunt, there's one other thing I think you should know.'

'Really? More bad news?'

'Yes,' she said. 'The Untill. It's not safe. Not at all safe.'

'Because?'

'Apart from the predators and the toxic plants… there are the partisans.'

'The what?'

'Partisans, sir.'

'Oh great,' he replied.

EIGHTEEN

DESOLANE DREW ONE of the vicious ketra blades from under the drifting smoke-cloak and set it down on the table beside the pheguth.

The pheguth turned slowly to look at it. His ear and hip were wrapped in surgical wadding. He had been given pain-killers for the first time, on the advice of the doctors of fisyk. They hadn't helped with the headache.

'What's this for?' he asked.

Desolane spread one hand on the table, fingers splayed.

'For punishment. Punish me, pheguth.'

'What?'

'I failed to protect you. You were injured. You are now permitted to exact punishment.'

'I'm sorry?' The pheguth looked up into the pale blue eyes behind the bronze mask.

'For failure. For my failure of charge as a life-ward. You are allowed to exact punishment.'

'What sort of punishment? Am I supposed to kill you?

Desolane shrugged. 'If that is what you desire. For this type of failure, a master would ordinarily sever one of his life-ward's digits.'

The pheguth sat up sharply. 'Let me get this straight. You're suggesting I should hack off one of your fingers?'

'Yes, pheguth.'

'Because I was attacked?'

'Yes, pheguth.'

'Don't be so silly, Desolane. It wasn't your fault.' The pheguth settled back against his pillows. They made a fine change to his usual sleeping conditions. He was quite enjoying the luxury.

'I was absent, and you were left vulnerable,' Desolane said. 'I don't think you understand. I am a life-ward. I am bred to protect my charges. You are my charge. Please punish me.'

'I'm not about to chop off one of your–'

'Please!'

The pheguth looked up at Desolane again. 'You seem very anxious to be maimed, life-ward.'

'The Plenipotentiary is outraged by today's attack. He is insisting that I am not fit to guard you.'

'Well, I don't believe that's true. I believe you're very fit. You saved me from those gunmen.'

Desolane shrugged slightly. The life-ward's hand remained splayed on the table. 'Please,' Desolane said again.

'No,' said the pheguth, turning away. 'This is just stupid.'

'Pheguth… understand me. If you don't punish me, the Plenipotentiary will decide I am not fit to guard you. He will replace me. You hate me, pheguth. You fear me. But you will hate and fear the ones who might replace me even more.'

'What do you mean?'

'The other life-wards available for assignment. They would not… treat you as well as I do. They would make your life harder. Don't let them. I have grown to like you, pheguth. I would hate to see you… discomforted.'

The pheguth sat up and swung his legs over the side of the bed. 'So, unless I maim you, I will subject myself to greater cruelties?'

Desolane nodded.

'Great Throne!' the pheguth murmured. Desolane flinched. The pheguth picked up the blade and balanced it in his palm for a moment. 'You want me to do this?'

'For your own sake, pheguth.'

The pheguth raised the ketra blade and–

Put it down again.

'I can't. The truth is, I have grown to like you too. You look after me, Desolane. You understand me. I couldn't begin to hurt you.'

'But… please, pheguth…?'

'If it's so important to you, take off your own digit. I couldn't possibly do something that coarse.'

Desolane sighed. The life-ward reached out and took the ketra blade, and very quickly lopped off the smallest finger of its right hand. Blood, bright blue-red, spurted out of the stump. Desolane quickly closed a surgical clamp around the wound.

The pheguth stared in astonishment.

'Thank you, pheguth,' Desolane said. The life-ward picked up the severed finger and sheathed the blade.

The pheguth rolled away so he was facing the far wall. Unseen by Desolane, there was a smile on his face.

Now that, he thought to himself, that's real power.

'Desolane,' he said quietly. 'How did two Imperial agents get so close to me? I mean, on a world like this.'

'They didn't,' Desolane replied. 'The two assassins were not Imperial agents.'

'What are you talking about?' the pheguth asked, looking round sharply.

'The matter is closed,' said Desolane, and strode out of the chamber.

THEY SPENT AN uneasy night in the cold blindness of the forest, and then started west just before daybreak.

To the west, the land shelved away in a deep gorge of black earth and broken rock. They descended into the cave-like gloom, screened from the sky by the towering forest. The trees were ancient, twisted things, massive forms that clung to the steep slope with gnarled clusters of thick roots. A furry grey lichen coated most surfaces, and where it didn't, treebark and boulders were caked with foul black moss. Strange fungal forms sprouted from the soil, some fleshy and pink-lipped, some rough and hard like stale bread or shoe leather. The largest of them were several metres wide.

There was no birdsong and no breeze, but the still upper spaces of the sinister forest rang with woodtaps, buzzes, clicks and odd purring clacks. The only sign of animal life was the occasional long-legged fly that hummed past like an intricate clockwork toy set running and slowly winding down.

And the moths. They were everywhere. Some were tiny, and speckled the air like floating wheatchaff. Some were as big as birds. When they flew by, their dusty wings made a sound like the pages of a book being flicked. When they landed, they vanished, their wings perfectly camouflaging them against lichen and crinkled bark. Brostin misstepped and disturbed a fallen log, and hundreds of them took flight into the air, lazy and sluggish, like a flock of birds startled up in slow motion.

It made Brostin jump in surprise, and that amused the scouts. But Curth became jittery.

'I've got a thing about moths,' she confided to Gaunt.

'What do you mean, a thing?'

'They give me the creeps.'

'Ana, yesterday you faced down a wirewolf.'

She grimaced. 'Uh huh. But it wasn't all furry and dusty, was it? I'm just squeamish about them, that's all.'

'You? Squeamish? Feth, woman! You're a surgeon. You regularly deal with stuff that makes even my stomach turn, and–'

'Yeah, yeah, it's all very funny and ironic. Duhh!' She flapped her hands as an albino-white moth beat past her face. 'We've all got something, and mine is moths. All right? And on the subject, isn't it your job as mission leader and, oh – I don't know, *commissar*? – to say something reassuring at this point to keep up the spirits of a valued team member like me? Something along the lines of "everything's fine, they can't hurt you, Ana, they're just moths and I swear by the Throne of Terra to personally swat any that come near you"?'

'Everything's fine, they can't hurt you, Ana, they're just–'

'Ha ha. Too late. I'm creeped out.'

Gaunt looked at her. 'Everything is fine. Ana, if the worst thing I have to do on Gereon is keep you moth-free, I'll be happy. Be thankful your "thing" is moths and not, let me think... Chaos.'

She grinned. 'You'll do,' she said.

Ahead of them, down the steep, black slope, Cirk paused and looked back up the group. 'I forgot to say,' she called. 'The moths are poisonous. Don't touch them or let them touch you.'

Curth glared at Cirk, then at Gaunt. 'She was listening. She's got it in for me.'

'She wasn't and she hasn't.'

'Yes, she has.'

'Well, you killed a wirewolf. It's probably an alpha-female assertion thing.'

'You think?'

He nodded.

'Yeah,' Curth said, almost to herself. 'You're probably right. She's probably making it up to mess with me.'

Without even looking back, Cirk called, 'I'm not making it up.'

THE DEEPER THEY went, the darker and hotter it got. The gorge seemed to drop away into the belly of the earth. It was humid, and an increasing odour of putrefaction filled the close air. Their faces began to bead with sweat. The thick foliage of the trees around and above them was glossy black and moisture dripped from it. Parasitic vines and veiny epiphytes knitted about the trees. The weird sounds grew louder and more frequent.

By the time the steep slope began to level out, most of the team had stripped down to their vests and undershirts. Their arms shone with sweat and their throat-hollows gleamed wet. Feygor was still fully clothed.

'You feeling all right, Murt?' Rawne asked him quietly. Feygor was walking unaided now, but the trauma of the previous day had not left him yet. There was an unblinking, unfocused look in his eyes, and his face was pale.

'I'm cold,' he said. 'This place is so cold and wet.'

Rawne, sponging perspiration out of his eyes with the corner of his cape, just nodded.

Feygor was shivering. The flesh around his throat implant was swollen and angry, and when he spoke the augmetic tone sounded like it was drowning in phlegm. Casualties of war, Rawne thought. There were always some. It was the price of combat, and this time it was going to be Murt.

Beltayn and Criid kept stopping to catch their breath. The humid air combined with their streaming head colds made breathing a real effort. Both were hyper-fit, but now both seemed to have the endurance of the aged or the frail.

The ground underfoot had become spongy and waterlogged. The ancient trees populating the forest and the gorge slope were giving way to an infestation of spider-rooted mangroves and bulbous cycads. But these tree forms were just as abundant, and still screened out the sky with their meaty leaves and groping tendrils. Down here, the moths were fat and dark-coloured.

'This is the Untill?' Gaunt asked Landerson.

'Not quite. We're in the fringes of the marshland. Another few kilometres, and we'll reach them proper.'

'Tell me what you know about these partisans.'

Landerson shrugged. 'Been here as long as anyone can remember. They call themselves the Sleepwalkers.'

'Sleepwalkers?'

'Don't ask me. Apparently their name for themselves is something like noctambulists. Sleepwalkers. Anyway, they're outlaws, essentially, that's what I understand. They believe in an independent Gereon. They want no part of the Imperium.'

'They deny the Emperor?' Gaunt asked.

'Yes,' said Landerson. 'They're descendants of religious radicals who came here on the colony ships. There was a war, early on, in the first histories. The partisans lost and were driven out into the Untill. Into any places that were agriculturally worthless. They've been out here ever since. Sometimes they used to raid, or mount terrorist attacks. We used to worry about them terribly, you know? Inquisitors came here to purge them, but got lost in the marshes and never returned. They were always Gereon's embarrassing secret. A fine, upstanding Imperial world that harboured a secret population of secessionists.'

Landerson glanced at Gaunt. 'I used to hate them. They were an insult to my family name and my birthright. And like I said, they were an ongoing problem. The bogeymen out in the swamps. And then the real enemy came.'

He looked away and took a deep breath. Gaunt knew the man was trying not to let emotion overtake him. 'The real enemy. And suddenly worrying about a few deranged backwoodsmen in the marshes seemed like a luxury. Throne take me, I long for the days when the partisans were our biggest problem.'

Three black moths fluttered across the gloomy path ahead of them, as dark and heavy as Imperial hymnals.

'If they're anti-Throne, have they sided with the Archenemy?' Gaunt asked.

'No idea. Maybe. The Untill is so impenetrable, even the Occupation forces leave it alone. Far as I know, the partisans are still out there. They may not even know the world outside has changed.'

'MY LORD, HE's here,' said Czelgur.

Uexkull climbed down from the parked deathship and walked through the misty dawn out across the woodland clearing. The shuttle descended out of the rosy sky, lights blinking, vector jets shuddering. Uexkull's warriors came out to meet it, standing alongside their master.

In a final flurry of downwash, the craft landed. After a long pause, the side hatch opened pneumatically and a hydraulic ramp unfolded. Climate-controlled cabin air billowed out into the cold morning as steam. Two excubitors ran down the ramp and took up position to either side of it, their las-locks shouldered.

Ordinal Sthenelus had to duck his head to emerge from the hatch. He was old, wizened, and his shrunken body had long since atrophied. One emaciated arm still appeared to function. His withered head lolled back against a neck rest. He walked towards them over the wet grass on six long, stilt-like limbs.

Sthenelus sat in a braced seat, secured by a harness, surrounded by intricate brass devices that he manipulated with his one good arm. Sighing gyros balanced the seat on a small augmetic unit from which the elongated limbs extended. Perched on top of the slender legs, he towered over the huge Chaos Space Marines, almost four metres tall. He seemed frail to Uexkull. One sweep of his hand would demolish Sthenelus and his delicate walking carriage.

But Sthenelus was a senior ordinal, one of the Plenipotentiary's chief advisors. Respect and deference were in order.

'Nine point three metres from ramp base to this place. An incline of two per cent. Terrain soft. One hundred and eighty metres above local sea level. Sixteen hundred cubic metres of forest and–'

'My ordinal,' Uexkull said.

'Hush! I am recording.' Sthenelus adjusted some of his complex instruments. His voice was a dry whisper. 'Subject one, Lord Uexkull, masses five hundred and thirty-three–'

'My ordinal!' Uexkull said. 'I have not called you here to chart and record.'

Sthenelus's creased face frowned. 'But that is what I do. In the name of the Anarch, whose word drowns out all others. I am his planetary assessor. I make precision maps, and assay every measurable detail of the conquered worlds. I was busy in Therion Province when your call came through, busy measuring hectares of arable land for plantation seeding. The topography there is very interesting, you know. No more than eight per cent variation–'

'Ordinal, I have summoned you for a special purpose.'

'One, Lord Uexkull, that I trust involves codification. That is my duty. That is how I serve the Anarch, whose word drowns out all others. It had better be important. Plenipotentiary Isidor requires a full survey of Therion by the end of the fortnight. Show me this urgent and special purpose. Do you require me to count the trees in this region? To label their forms and species? Do you perhaps wish me to survey and sound a lake or other body of water? I smell water. Humidity of eleven over five, with a rising gradient–'

'My ordinal, no. I require you to track and locate someone for me.'

Sthenelus was so astounded that he blinked. As his parchment lids closed and opened, tiny augmetic wires whirred forward from his temples and puffed lubricating moisture into his dry eyeballs to stop the lids from sticking.

'There has been some mistake,' Sthenelus said. 'I do not track. I am no common bloodhound. This is a regrettable waste of effort. In the time it has taken to travel here from Therion, I calculate that I could have charted fifteen point seven hectares of–'

'This is the Anarch's work, ordinal,' Uexkull said. 'This is a matter of world security. Nothing – not even your scrupulous labour of measurement – has more priority. Check with the Plenipotentiary, if you must, but he will surely reprimand you for wasting time on such an urgent concern.'

'Indeed, lord.' Sthenelus paused. 'Explain this matter to me.'

'Insurgents, ordinal. Dangerous men, agents of the False Emperor. They are loose on Gereon, and they have murdered many brave servants of the Anarch. They must be found and they must be stopped before they achieve the purpose for which they have been sent here.'

'Which is, lord?'

Uexkull hesitated. 'Which is something we will discover as we torture the last of them to death. They have fled into the Untill beyond. We must find them.'

'Ah, yes. The Untill. A marsh and/or swamp region covering nine hundred thousand square kilometres of land from–'

'Ordinal.'

'I was told the Untill was to be left unmapped for now. Because of the difficulties involved. It is not tenable land. Compared to the crop production of, say, the Lectica bocage, which runs at an annual average of eight billion bushels per–'

'Ordinal!'

'Though I must say, I was itching to map the Untill, Lord Uexkull. A search, you say? It sounds rather vigorous.'

'My warriors and I will supply the vigour.'

Sthenelus licked his thin lips with a pallid, slug-like tongue. 'I have no doubt. But why would you request me, lord? I am no soldier.'

'At the feast to celebrate the first month of Intercession, the Plenipotentiary chatted with me. He told me of your talents and your matchless instruments. Designed for mapping and measuring, of course, but they have a side benefit, do they not? Nothing escapes your scrutiny. Not one bent blade of grass, not one broken twig. You have tracked fugitives before, he said. On Baldren. On Scipio Focal. Located men who believed themselves lost. Picked out the veritable needle in the wheat.'

'I admit I have. As a diversion.'

Uexkull nodded. 'The Untill is a trackless waste, and it is said that no one can chart it. Except, I would think, you. Find these enemies for me, ordinal. Lead me to them, and the Anarch himself will thank you.'

THE MARSHES SPREAD out before them, vast and mysterious. Yellow mist fumed beneath the tortured, spidery trees. Moths and flies flickered in the scant shafts of etiolated sunlight that speared down through the dense canopy. Everything smelled of rot.

They were wading now. The land had vanished, and only pools of stagnant water remained. Mkoll and Bonin led the way, probing the liquid with long poles, like the steersmen of punts. Every few minutes, the party had to turn onto a new course as a stabbing pole revealed no detectable bottom to the water ahead.

The mangroves lowered over the thick water on their crusted rafts of roots. Algae coated the water's surface, and bubbles of gas flopped up from the rot. It felt like they were wading on through a flooded cave, except that no cave would be so swelteringly hot. There was only a vague suggestion of daylight.

Leeches wriggled in the fermenting water. Curth had to remove several from bare arms. They were fat and black, and fought against her pliers. Things moved under the surface, darting and sliding. Varl got a glimpse of something half-fish, half-eel that was so ugly he nearly shot it. Long-limbed insects dappled the surface tension as they ran upon the water top.

Larkin raised his long-las suddenly.

'What?' Gaunt hissed.

'Movement,' the sniper replied. Something emerged out of the dark. It was a wading insect, the sized of a small dog, stalking the swamp water on long, stilt legs, its bladed mouthparts tilted downwards, ready to duck and stab any submerged prey. There were several more behind it. When they became aware of the human intruders, they took flight, opening wing cases and soaring into the hot air, trailing metre-long legs beneath them.

Larkin lowered his weapon. 'Feth that,' he said.

Criid had to stop again. She could barely breathe. Curth used the last of her inhibitor shots to relieve the trooper's discomfort.

Mkvenner had cut a long stave like Bonin and Mkoll. He'd fixed his silver warknife to one end, like a spear, and was using it to slash down overhanging plants. Some vines writhed back like snakes from his blade.

No one saw whatever it was that attacked Cirk. She suddenly fell, pulled down into the water, thrashing. She vanished. The Ghosts splashed through the water towards her last position and she abruptly surfaced several metres away, fighting and wailing.

Something had her. She went under again. Cursing, Gaunt stabbed into the water with his sword and Mkvenner jabbed with his spear. Cirk came up again in a rush, coughing and gagging, covered with weed and algae, and Landerson grabbed her. Something long, sinuous and dark rippled the water as it swam away.

Cirk's left calf was ripped and bloody. A tooth had been left in one bitemark. Five centimetres long, thin, transparent.

'Can you walk?' Gaunt asked her.

'Yes!'

'Sabbatine…'

'I'm fine. Let's get on.' She tried to wipe the sticky algae out of her hair.

'Curth can bind your wounds and–'

'Let's get on,' she snapped. 'Tell your lady friend to save her bandages.'

'My what? Ana's not my lady friend. She's a–'

'A what, Gaunt?'

'A valued team member.'

'Yeah?' Sitting on a root bole, Cirk reached down and pulled another, smaller tooth out of her leg. Her fingers were running with diluted blood. She tossed the tooth into the undergrowth. 'I've seen the way she looks at you. I've seen the way you treat her.'

'Cirk–' Gaunt began, then stopped and looked away. 'I don't have time for this. It's redundant. If you can walk, fine. We have to get on and–'

A piercing scream echoed across the dank water.

'That's your lady friend,' Cirk said.

Gaunt was already moving, churning up septic water as he ran. The others were closing in too, weapons raised.

Curth hadn't meant to scream. She really hadn't. But what she'd seen, in the shadows of the undergrowth. What she'd seen…

She'd sunk to her knees. The water was up around her chest.

'Ana!' Gaunt cried as he reached her, one bolt pistol drawn. 'What is it?'

She pointed with a shaking hand. 'There. In there. I saw it.'

'What?'

'A m-moth.'

Gaunt holstered his gun and made to wave the others back. 'For feth's sake, Curth, I told you–'

'You don't understand, it was big, Ibram.'

'Yes, but.'

'I mean big! Big, you bastard! The size of a man!'

'What?'

He turned and pulled the pistol out again.

'It was crouched there, looking at me. Those fething eyes…'

'Get up. Curth, get up. Beltayn, move her back. Help her.'

Beltayn waded forward.

'Come on, doc. Up we go,' he said, getting her arm around his neck.

Gaunt took another step forward. There was something in the dim undergrowth ahead all right. A grey shape.

Bonin arrived at Gaunt's side, his lasrifle aimed.

'What did she see?' he whispered.

'Something. In there. I can make out–'

Gaunt's voice trailed off. The shape stirred. He saw glinting multi-facet eyes and furry grey wings. They unfolded. A moth. A moth man.

Who was aiming a las-lock right at him.

'Feth me,' said Bonin. 'I think we've found those partisans.'

'Actually,' said Landerson, raising his hands and barely daring to move. 'I think they've found us.'

NINETEEN

'Nobody,' murmured Gaunt, 'make any sudden moves.'

'Should we drop our weapons, sir?' Beltayn whispered.

'No. But nobody aim anything. If your guns are on straps, let them hang.'

'What are we doing?' Rawne hissed, the outrage in his voice barely contained. 'Are we surrendering? Feth that! Feth all of–'

'Shut up, major,' Gaunt told him through gritted teeth. 'Can't you feel it? They're all around us.'

Rawne fell silent and slowly turned his head. The members of the mission team were spread out across the pool. Grey shapes seemed to lurk and stir within every root ball and behind every tree surrounding them.

'Dammit!' he spat, and let his weapon swing on its strap.

His weapons sheathed, Gaunt kept his eyes on the figure facing him, and slowly raised his hands to show his open palms. The figure stiffened slightly, the grip on its own aimed weapon tightening.

'Pax Imperialis,' Gaunt said. 'We intend no fight with you.'

The figure kept its las-lock raised. It said something, but Gaunt couldn't make it out.

'I'm not your enemy,' Gaunt said, hands still open. Landerson shot him a look. From what the cell-fighter had told him earlier, that wasn't exactly true. But the partisans – if that's what these beings were – had them trapped and pinned down more completely than anything the forces of the Archenemy had managed since they'd arrived on Gereon. Talking was the only way out of this. Any attempt to fight would lead to two things and only two things: their deaths, and the end of their mission.

'Pax Imperialis,' Gaunt repeated. 'We are not your enemy. My name is Gaunt.' He tapped his own chest. 'Gaunt.'

The thing in the shadows still did not lower its aim. But it spoke again, more clearly now. 'Hhaunt.'

'Gaunt. Ibram Gaunt.'

'Kh-haunt.' The voice was glottal and wet, thick with a strange accent.

'They say,' Landerson whispered, slowly and very carefully, 'that the Sleep-walkers still use the old tongue. Old Gothic. Or a dialect form of it.'

Gaunt's mind raced. The principal language of the Imperium was Low Gothic, with a few regional variations, and the stylised High Gothic was used by the Church, and other bodies such as the Inquisition, for formal records, proclamations and devotions. All strands had their roots in a proto-Gothic that had been the language of mankind in the early Ages of Expansion. Like most well-educated men, Gaunt had been required to study Old Gothic as part of his schooling. At the scholam progenium on Ignatius Cardinal, High Master Boniface had taken an almost sadistic pleasure in testing his young pupils on such Old Gothic epic poems as *The Voidfarer* and *The Dream of the Eagle*. So many things had filled Gaunt's head since then, so many things, forcing the old learning out.

Think! Remember something!

'Histye,' Gaunt began. 'Ayeam… ah… ayeam yclept Gaunt, of… er… Tanith His Worlde.'

'What the feth?' Bonin muttered, glancing at his commander.

Gaunt's brow creased as he concentrated. He could almost see old Boniface now, smell the musty scholam room, Vaynom Blenner at the desk beside Gaunt, doodling cross-eyed eldar on the cover of his slate.

'No looking at your vocab primer now, Scholar Gaunt,' Boniface called. 'Parse the verb form now, young man! Begin! "Ayeam yclept… Heyth yclept…" Come on, now! Blenner? What's that you're drawing, boy? Show the class!'

'Histye, soule,' Gaunt said, more deliberately now. 'Ayeam yclept Gaunt of Tanith His Worlde. Preyathee, hwat yclepted esthow?'

'Cynulff ayeam yclept,' the partisan replied. 'Of Geryun His Worlde.' His voice dripped like glue in the sweaty air.

'Histye, Cynulff,' said Gaunt. 'Biddye hallow, andso of sed hallow yitt meanye goode rest.'

'Are you off your fething nut?' Rawne whispered.

'Shut up, Rawne,' Curth spat. 'Can't you see he's getting somewhere?'

Gaunt dared another step forward. The marsh water slopped and bubbled around his boots. 'Biddye hallow,' he repeated. 'Biddye hallow andso of sed hallow yitt meanye good rest.'

The partisan gradually lowered his las-lock and took a step forward himself. He emerged from the mangrove shadows. Gaunt heard Curth gasp.

The partisan was not, as Gaunt had begun to fear, some mutant hybrid of human and moth. At first sight at least, he appeared to be essentially human.

That made him no less frightening. He was tall, a head taller than either Gaunt or Mkvenner, the tallest members of the party. He would have towered over even Colm Corbec or Bragg, Throne rest the both of them. But as much as he was tall, he was thin. Big boned and powerful, but starvation-lean, his long shanks encased in tight, fat-less muscle. What Gaunt had at first mistaken as the bulging multi-facet eyes of an insect were revealed to be oval arrangements of glittering scales, fixed like a mosaic around his kohl-edged eyes and spreading up across his shaved skull. The eyes themselves were tiny, glittering slits. His wings were a segmented cloak that appeared to have been fletched with masses of grey feathers. The cloak hung from a harness around the man's throat and shoulders. His clothes were wound rags, and both these shreds and his skin itself were caked with some clay-like material that glowed a sheened, iridescent grey colour. Silver pendants were strung about his neck, and silver bands decorated his fingers and his long, slender arms. He had a long, lank moustache, also stiffened and slathered in grey woad, which resembled an insect's mandibles and added to the impression that he was a moth in human form. His long, trinket-dangling weapon was not, as Gaunt saw it clearly, a las-lock. It was an actual musket of archaic design, as long as the partisan was tall. A wound-back hammer mechanism with a lump of flint in the claw served as a firing lock. The muzzle-end of the long, thin rifle had a dirty, serrated blade built into it.

Holding the weapon steady in one hand, the partisan raised his other and opened his grey palm to Gaunt.

'Cynulff ayeam yclept, of Geryun His Wolde, ap Niht. Biddye hallow Khhaunt and otheren kinde, andso of sed hallow yitt meanye goode mett wherall.'

'I…' Gaunt began. 'That is to say… I mean… I am… I mean, ayeam…' He struggled, panicking, trying to think. High Master Boniface had, many times, told his students that 'a lack of good learning will kill a man more surely than a thousand guns.'

I hope you're happy now, you old coot, Gaunt thought, because you're about to be proved right.

'Ayeam yclept Gaunt…' he began again. No, already done that. Think. Think!

The partisan stiffened, wary, and his open hand returned to its grip on the preposterously long musket.

Feth, I've blown it, Gaunt thought.

'Histye, Cynulff ap Niht,' a voice suddenly called out behind him, 'and so beyit akinn. Sed hallow seythee, yitt be wellcomen into thissen our brestas owne us, and of fulsave yitt be hered. Well mettye, Frater, wherall so withe yeall!'

Gaunt looked to his side. Mkvenner had walked up to flank him, his long, makeshift spear trailing in the mire, his left hand held palm-up. The partisan nodded to him.

'Ven?' Gaunt breathed.

'A moment, sir.' MKvenner paused and then said, 'Histye, soule, so beyit pace twine us eitheren kinde. Brandes setye aparte, withe rest alse, as yitt meanye goode mett wherall. Council yitt shall sey akinn, preyathee.'

The partisan seemed to notice the Tanith warknife fixed to Mkvenner's spear.

'Preyathee, seolfor beyit?'

'Yclept beyit so,' Mkvenner nodded.

The partisan lowered his rifle and splashed into the pool until he came face to face with Mkvenner. He studied the blade with great interest, and Mkvenner calmly allowed him to take the spear in his hand. They exchanged words, too fast and too complex for Gaunt to keep up.

'I don't like this at all,' Bonin whispered to Gaunt. 'What the feth is this about?'

'At the moment, it's about us not getting mown down in a hail of musket balls. Wait, just wait,' Gaunt urged. He looked around. Rawne and Brostin were close to snapping, and ready to reach for their weapons. Cirk too, damn her. The others just seemed alarmed or confused. All except Feygor. He had sat down with his back to a treebole, up to his waist in the swamp, his head leaning forward.

'Ven?' Gaunt called.

Mkvenner looked at him, and saw his gesture at Feygor. The tall scout exchanged some further words with the towering partisan and the fellow nodded.

'Curth can look to him,' Mkvenner called.

'Thank you,' Gaunt replied. 'And thank him for me. Ana?'

Curth slopped through the marsh water to reach Feygor and began to examine him. Beltayn went with her.

Gaunt turned his attention back to Mkvenner and the partisan. They were still talking, fast and unfathomably.

'Seolfor beyit!' Mkvenner suddenly called out. 'Show him your knives,' he added. 'Quickly!'

The Ghosts quickly brandished their warknives. Some of them had to unfix them from the bayonet lugs of their rifles. Gaunt held his own up.

The partisan – Cynulff – nodded, as if pleased.

'Sheathe them now,' Mkvenner ordered. He bowed his head to the partisan and splashed across the pool to Gaunt.

'He's agreed to a parley. You and his leader. It seems they are impressed with our silver.'

'How safe is this?' Gaunt asked.

Mkvenner shrugged. 'Not safe at all, sir. They'll kill us in a second if we make the wrong move. We may even be walking into a trap. But I think it's the best chance we've got.'

Gaunt nodded.

Cynulff made a sign, and almost forty partisans, clad just like him and just as tall, emerged from the smoky shadows. Grey and sinister, winged with articulated capes, they were armed with muskets and curious, crossbow-like weapons.

'Aversye wherall!' the partisan cried, gesturing with his rifle.

'He wants us to move,' Mkvenner said.

'Thanks,' said Gaunt. 'I actually got that one.'

* * *

THE PHEGUTH SUBMITTED to the next transcoding session that morning, but when Desolane informed him that during the afternoon, instead of resting, he was expected to make a visit to Mabbon Etogaur, the pheguth refused.

Desolane stared at him for a moment. 'This is not for discussion, pheguth.'

'I'm tired, and my head feels like it's about to split, Desolane,' the pheguth replied. He sat on the simple chair in his tower cell, trying to staunch a heavy nosebleed with some surgical dressing the life-ward had given him. 'I want to cooperate, of course I do. But the transcoding is wretched enough as it is. You force me to take meetings, undergo interviews that are little short of interrogations. I think you should cut me some slack.'

'Cut you some slack?' The life-ward repeated the words as if they were unclean.

The pheguth nodded. This was a dangerous game, and he knew it. He had a certain pull over Desolane now, but the life-ward was still quite the most dangerous being he had ever encountered. The pheguth had to test his new-won power, but not too far. There was a line even Desolane would not cross.

'What use will I be to you if I'm exhausted, Desolane? Burned out? I am already weary to my bones. I feel sure the transcoding is taking longer because of my fatigue.'

'That is possible, I suppose,' Desolane said uncertainly.

'Have I not been obliging in every way possible?' the pheguth asked.

'You have, pheguth.'

'And I'm only thinking of the grand scheme of things. I know my potential value to you and your Anarch. Believe me, I'm looking forward to the day when I can offer my full help. But I have to consider my own health.'

The pheguth let the words hang. He had deliberately not mentioned the attempt on his life, or made any reference to Desolane's oversight in allowing the killers to get so close. But the implication was clear by its very omission. *You owe me, life-ward. Because you failed me and I didn't even punish you. Don't push me.*

Desolane was still for a few seconds, and then nodded. 'I'll see what can be arranged,' it said, and left the cell.

THE PHEGUTH WAS allowed his afternoon of rest. Food was brought. In truth, despite the nosebleeds and a lingering headache, and despite the wounds the assassins had inflicted, the pheguth felt better than he had done in months. Clear-headed, calm, purposeful.

The transcoding was finally unlocking the shackles that the psykers of the Imperial Commissariat had placed on his oh-so-valuable mind. The pheguth had known how much of his memory had been repressed by the mindlock, and very little of that had been recovered yet, but he hadn't realised how much of his own self had been repressed too.

That was what was returning to him now, with each passing day. His character. His personality. He felt like a man of distinction again. He felt like a leader, a commander, a lord general. He remembered what it was like to be respected and feared. He could taste the addictive flavour of power again.

He relished it. It had been a long, long time. Years. He had been an officer of great import, a master of the Imperium. Hosts of men had charged into battle at his merest word. And then that bastard, that jumped-up bastard, had taken it all away from him and reduced him to this enfeebled misery.

That bastard's name had been the one thing he'd never forgotten. Even the mindlock had failed to dim its echo in his brain.

Ibram Gaunt.

The pheguth relaxed, and sipped some more tea. Fortune was turning to favour him again. He would rise once more, and become a master of armies. Different armies, perhaps, but power was power. Already Desolane was his willing pawn, and Mabbon, the pheguth fancied, his ally. He had a great destiny again, when for so long he had presumed his life over.

Desolane returned near nightfall. 'Pheguth. Once I appraised the etogaur of your weary state, and postponed your visit to him, he insisted he would visit you.'

'That's kind of him,' the pheguth replied. 'But I think I might sleep now. Give the etogaur my apologies. Like you, I'm sure, he knows how much Great Sek values my wellbeing.'

Desolane took a step forward. Its cloven foot rang hard on the stone floor of the chamber.

'Pheguth, there are some words I cannot allow you to speak with your heathen lips and tongue. The name of the Anarch, whose words drown out all others, is chief amongst them.'

The pheguth sat up sharply. He realised immediately he'd gone too far. The life-ward was in his thrall only so much.

'I apologise,' the pheguth said quickly. 'Please, show the etogaur through.' *Appease the creature, win it back…*

'I will. Thank you, pheguth. I will warn him not to stay too long and tire you.'

Mabbon Etogaur entered the chamber a few moments later. He shook the pheguth by the hand very formally, and then sat down on a second chair that had been provided by the footmen.

'Your life-ward tells me you are indisposed, sir,' he said, settling the tails of his brown leather coat.

'A fatigue, no more. Thank you for your concern. I apologise for missing our appointment this afternoon. Was it something important?'

'It can wait,' Mabbon replied. 'I had drawn up the first trainee regiment to parade for you. I thought you might like to look them over.'

'By trainee regiment, you mean… the Sons of Sek?'

'The Anarch, whose word drowns out all others, has charged me to establish the first training camp here on Gereon. It lies in the heartland bocage, about thirty kilometres from here. The men are doing well. They keenly anticipate your arrival to oversee training.'

'I look forward to my first review.'

The etogaur opened a despatch case and took out a sheaf of high resolution picts. He passed one to the pheguth.

'Here you can see them in file order, sir.'

The pheguth looked at the pict. He was impressed. It was a remote-view shot of some three hundred men in rank, to attention. They were all big brutes, shaven-headed but for a cock's comb of hair across their skulls. They were wearing fatigues that were unmistakably Guard issue, but dyed ochre.

'They seem a fine body of men, etogaur,' the pheguth said.

'They are. Hand-picked.'

'By you?'

'Naturally, sir.'

Mabbon arranged some more shots and passed them to the pheguth. 'When you called off your visit this afternoon, I decided to run an exercise instead. The men were armed, and given an objective. As you can see, they accomplished the task well.'

The pheguth slowly turned through the pictures. His hands began to quiver slightly.

'What–' he began. 'What objective did you give them, etogaur?'

'A village in the bocage. It's called Nahren Town. Population sixteen thousand. That's consented, of course. Nahren is a known centre for the resistance and the unconsented.'

'They... they really took the place apart, didn't they?'

Mabbon nodded. 'Expertly so. In this shot, and in this, you'll see the fire-fight that began when the resistance showed themselves. I think those poor fools were actually trying to stop the civilian slaughter.'

'I suppose so...'

'Bad tactics, in my opinion,' the etogaur said lightly. 'The resistance here has prospered by keeping its head down and remaining covert at all costs. The raid on Nehren brought them out like rats. An elementary combat mistake. Better to flee and retain your secrecy. They were outmatched. You see? Here... and here too.'

'You killed them all.'

'All of them. Fifty-nine resistance cell fighters. With no losses on our end.'

'No, I mean... you killed everyone.'

'Oh, yes, sir. The entire population was accounted for. A fine showing, do you not think?'

The pheguth stared for a moment more, then shuffled the picts back into a block and handed them to Mabbon. 'Excellent. Excellent work. Simply excellent.'

Mabbon smiled. 'The men will be so pleased when I inform them of your pleasure, sir.'

'Sixteen thousand...?'

'Yes sir, and the bodies are burning now. The Sons made a pyre of them. Dedicated it to our beloved Anarch.'

'Whose word drowns out all others...' the pheguth said.

'Indeed so. Pheguth? Are you all right?'

'Just… just a little weary. Don't mind me, etogaur. That's quite a… quite a display your men put on today. Very… ruthless.' The pheguth looked up and met Mabbon's eyes. 'I'm very impressed,' he said.

Mabbon seemed pleased. 'I'm ordering another exercise for the day after tomorrow. A town called Furgesh. Population forty thousand. Does that meet with your requirements?'

'That would be perfect,' the pheguth sighed.

Mabbon slid the picts back into his case and got to his feet. 'I thank you for your time, sir. I know you're tired. I… I was told about the attack. Are your wounds troubling you?'

'Not at all,' the pheguth replied.

The etogaur nodded, and turned to go.

'Mabbon?' the pheguth called out. The warrior paused and turned back. 'Sir?'

'My life-ward told me that the assassins were not Imperial agents. Why would that be?'

'Sir, I'm not at liberty to–'

'Tell me, Mabbon.'

Mabbon walked back and resumed his seat. His voice was low. 'The assassins were men from the Occupation force, sir. Men whose loyalty to the Archon exceeds their loyalty to his lieutenant, Great Sek. You are considered by some to be a heresy and a monster of the enemy that should not be entertained in any wise. In short, sir, you are still an Imperial general to them, and that makes you a target.'

'I have renounced the Imperium of Man. I am a traitor general.'

'I know that, sir. But many believe… what's bred in the bone. Some individuals loyal to the Archon fear you'll betray him by aiding the Great Sek. Others simply cannot understand why a man who has made a career out of fighting us can now be watered and fed as a friend.'

'But you understand, don't you, Mabbon?'

Mabbon nodded. 'Yes, sir. I understand, because I am a traitor myself.'

THE SLEEPWALKERS' ENCAMPMENT covered over an acre of marshland, but very few parts of it touched the ground. It had been built in a glade of particularly old and massive mangrove trees, and was essentially a series of wooden platforms suspended like stages between the trunks. The lowest were supported on root balls, or wedged onto islets of land that rose from the stewing bog, often with a tree or two projecting from their tops. Others, the larger stages, had been constructed between the tree boles, some two metres above the surface of the mire. They were supported by a mix of stilt-beams sunk into the ooze and heavy wooden brackets dovetailed into the living tree trunks. Higher up, smaller platforms depended from the heavy branches on frames of rope. Plank walkways connected the lower stages, and woven ladders ran up to the higher platforms. Their dwellings dotted the stages, domed tents woven from some pale fabric and articulated like the partisans' cloaks.

The encampment had an eerie glow to it. Braziers were burning to light the place, and the glow reflected back off the water and the foliage gave the place a grey-green cast.

Brostin smiled when he saw the brazier flames. He sniffed the air. 'Promethium…' he said.

The nearest Sleepwalker glared at him to be quiet. Brostin shrugged.

It had taken more than three hours to reach the encampment, and they had trudged in forced silence. Gaunt was dying to speak with Mkvenner, but the partisans made it clear they would tolerate no talking, so he kept his mouth shut. He didn't want to antagonise them now.

Besides, they were outnumbered almost four to one. The Sleepwalkers had allowed them to keep their weapons, but there was no mistaking who was in control. And Gaunt was certain that the partisans' weapons, however primitive, would be quite lethal. He was particularly interested in the crossbows which, on closer sight turned out not to be crossbows at all. In structure, they bore a superficial resemblance to machine bows, but they were not strung in any way. Each one was handmade and individual, though they all followed the same basic pattern: a long, hollow tube of metal or hardwood with a trigger grip set behind it, and a shoulder-stock behind that. As far as Gaunt could tell, there seemed to be a power cell built into the shoulder stock. The arms of the bow coiled back sharply on either side of the tubular barrel, more sharply than any crossbow's, even under tension, and were made of metal, with metal weights on the end of each arm. The weapons were a puzzle. A lack of visible hammer or lock suggested they were not firearms, not bows either. Some form of energised launcher, perhaps. The Sleepwalkers who bore them were also slung with what looked to Gaunt like satchel quivers.

Beltayn and Varl were half-carrying Feygor, who seemed to be lolling in and out of consciousness feverishly. Cirk was limping badly, and kept shooting Gaunt evil looks as if the particular situation was somehow all his fault.

Gaunt ignored her. The 'sunburn' on his face was becoming raw and painful, and seemed to attract the local bugs. He was sure it was the same for Rawne and Mkvenner.

He wondered what lay in store for them now. The mission to Gereon had seemed an overwhelming challenge right from the outset, but for a while there, they had seemed to be getting somewhere. Now he seemed to have lost sight of the mission entirely. Bad luck had driven them further and further away from their goals, and now they had fallen into this surreal world. It was like a dream. En route to Gereon, he'd imagined many fates that might befall them there. This was so unlike any of them it almost made him laugh.

The partisans brought them through the pools to the encampment. Many more Sleepwalkers, silent and pale, watched them approach from the platforms. The watchers were mostly male, but Gaunt saw womenfolk and children too. All of them were tall, slender and grey-skinned.

Cynulff ap Niht, or whatever his name was, led them up the walkboards onto the lower stages, and they trudged up into the camp, the silent figures gazing at them. He took them to where a heavy wooden chest sat bolted to the platform and lifted the lid.

'Setye brandes herein,' he ordered in his strange, thick voice.

'Weapons,' Mkvenner said. 'He wants us to put them here in the coffer.'

'Is that an order?' Gaunt asked. Mkvenner asked Cynulff and listened to the reply.

'It's their law,' he told Gaunt. 'Guests are not permitted to carry firearms in the camp. We must leave them here, where they will be safe. We can keep our blades, apparently, and he doesn't seem bothered by your sword.'

'Do it,' Gaunt told the team. Lasrifles and pistols went into the chest, along with Brostin's cannon and the autorifles Cirk and Landerson carried. Larkin sighed and kissed his long-las before he put it in.

Cynulff closed the lid and then beckoned them again. They followed him up onto a larger platform, and he pointed up a woven ladder that dangled from a much smaller hanging stage suspended from the canopy.

'He wants us to wait up there while he consults his leader,' Mkvenner said.

One by one, they climbed the ladder. It took a few minutes to get Feygor up onto the platform. Once he was there, he laid down and fell asleep on the mossy boards almost at once. The others sat down and rested wherever there was space. The platform swayed slightly under their moving weight.

Gaunt stayed by the top of the ladder and looked down into the camp. Cynulff and the other partisans who had brought them in were moving away towards the dome-tents on the main platform. No guard had been set on the Ghosts, but Gaunt knew they were absolutely expected to stay on the small stage until Cynulff returned.

Mkoll crouched down beside Gaunt. 'Well, this is all pretty odd,' he said.

'It could be worse,' Gaunt began.

'We could be dead,' Mkoll finished. They both smiled.

'If you like, I can slip away. Up that tree there, maybe. Take a look around. Get some weapons back.'

Gaunt shook his head. 'We're up here in trust, I think. Throne knows, Mkoll, we could turn this to our advantage. If we could get them to help us...'

'They don't look to me much like the helping kind, sir,' Mkoll replied.

'What do they look like?'

'The freaky dangerous kind who just happen not to have killed us yet.'

'Uh huh. That's my reading too. But let's give them the benefit. It's clear to me that if they wanted us dead, we wouldn't even have known about it until it happened. I think we intrigue them. They're curious. Speaking of curious, get Ven over here.'

Mkvenner came across to them at Mkoll's signal.

'Sir?'

'Ven, I believe we're only alive now because you possess a previously undisclosed facility with proto-Gothic.'

Mkvenner shrugged.

'A shrug isn't going to cut it, Ven. I need to know.'

'It's a personal matter, sir. Private. I'd prefer not to speak of it.'

'I'd prefer not to have to ask you, but I'm asking. The needs of this mission supercede any private issues any of us might have. That's the way it is.'

Mkvenner took a deep breath.

'I'll be over there, checking on Feygor,' Mkoll said, and got up quickly to leave them alone.

'So,' said Gaunt. 'Even the sarge doesn't know the secrets of his best scout?'

'He knows some. More than anybody else. But not everything.'

'You can speak the old tongue.'

'Yes, sir.'

'Because…?'

'I learned it as a child on Tanith, sir.'

'I learned it as a child too, in a classroom on Ignatius Cardinal. But you speak it like a native, Ven.'

'Maybe.'

Gaunt took off his cap and ran his fingers though his lank hair. 'I'm not a dentist, you know, Mkvenner.'

'A… what, sir?'

'This is like pulling teeth. We haven't got much time. Talk to me, for feth's sake. Is this to do with the Nalsheen?'

Mkvenner seemed wary suddenly. 'It is, sir. Who's been talking?'

'Ven, there have been rumours about you since the day of the First Founding. There's not a man in the regiment who hasn't heard them. And not a single man who's seen you fight hand to hand that doubts them. Your skills are like no one else's.'

'Sir.'

'The Nalsheen are supposed to be extinct, Ven. A memory from the feudal days of Tanith. As I heard it, the Nalsheen were wood-warriors, a fighting brotherhood who dwelt in the nalwoods and who overthrew the old tyrants. Some think them a myth. Some think they never existed at all. But they did, didn't they, Ven?'

'Yes, sir.'

'Come on, man. I'd like to think that you can trust me.'

Mkvenner sat down next to Gaunt. Their feet hung over the edge of the platform. 'The Nalsheen existed, sir. Right up until the day Tanith died. They continued their traditions in the remote woods, passing on the lore of *cwlwhl* from father to son. There were very few of them, but they had sworn to keep the brotherhood alive in case tyranny ever rose again on Tanith. My family line has been Nalsheen as far back as records go.'

Gaunt nodded, and waited for Mkvenner to continue.

'I was trained from an early age, three or four, I think. I was taken to the old master in the nalwoods by my father, and the lore was passed to me. The fighting skills, the woodcraft, the faith itself. And the language. The Nalsheen had always used the old form of Gothic as their private tongue. The same language the first woodsmen spoke when they settled Tanith in the Early Times.'

'Just the same as here,' Gaunt said.

'Yes, sir. When I heard the partisan speak, it chilled my blood. It was like hearing the voice of my father again.'

Mkvenner stared silently out across the marshland trees for a long moment, lost in his own memories.

'That'll do, Ven. You've answered my questions. Not all that I'd like to ask, but enough.'

'Thank you, sir. But you should ask the rest of them, I think. You deserve to know. I don't believe I should have secrets from my commander.'

'Right. Are you Nalsheen, Mkvenner?'

'No, sir. I have many of their skills and craft, but I never finished my training. My father wanted me to, and so did the old master. But I was a headstrong youth. I... thought I knew better. I wanted to serve the Emperor, you see. I joined the militia of the nearest city and, when the Founding was called, signed up to the Guard. The last of the Nalsheen... men like my father and the other wood masters in the remote places... died when Chaos burned our world.'

Gaunt nodded. 'Ven,' he said, 'if you hadn't been that headstrong youth, if you hadn't quit the woods and joined the Guard, you'd also have died with Tanith. And if that had been the case, two men would have been very sorry.'

'Sir? Who?'

'Me, for one, because without you so many of the Ghosts' battles would have been lost. How many times have you saved me? Just yesterday, on that field, against the wirewolves. I owe you. The Ghosts owe you. I know Corbec owed you to his dying day.'

'Is Colm the other man, then, sir?' Mkvenner asked.

'No, Ven. The other man is your father. If you had stayed in the nalwoods, and died with him as Tanith died, there wouldn't have been a Nalsheen to guide the last men of Tanith today.'

BROSTIN SAT ON the far side of the hanging stage, looking out over the swamp and mock-smoking one of his precious lho-sticks. He didn't care who saw him.

'Can I bum one of those?' Curth asked, sitting down beside him.

Brostin grinned. He was a massive brute, but his smile was infectious. He hooked the pack out of his tunic pocket and let Curth take one.

They sat for a while, pretending to smoke.

'Mmmm... tastes good,' she murmured.

'Finest rolled Imperial grade,' he agreed, playing along with the charade.

'Of course,' she said, 'as a Guard medicae, I ought to warn you of the health risks. Smoking lho-sticks is very, very bad.'

'Oh, I know, doc. Really, I do. Filthy things.'

'Exactly. Smoking lho is, frankly, stupid. Only stupid people do it. Really, really stupid people.'

'You know,' Brostin said, hooking the heel of his right boot up on the edge of the stage and making another, laborious fake draw on the smoke. 'You know what's really stupid though?'

'Tell me, trooper.'

'It's people pretending to smoke.'

She laughed. 'I hear that, Bros. What I wouldn't do for a light.'

He glanced at her and raised his thick eyebrows suggestively. She laughed again.

He chuckled too, then pointed out across the camp. 'There's a light,' he said.

He was pointing to one of the camp braziers, throbbing with flame.

'Too far away,' she said.

'Its burning promethium,' he said. 'Crude prom, not refined stuff. They use it here for fuel. In fact, that's why their camp is here.'

'What do you mean?' Curth asked, momentarily forgetting to keep up her pantomime of smoking.

'Over yonder,' Brostin replied, nodding towards the swamp pools west of the stage-camp. The water there was murky and brown, and bubbled lazily. The Sleepwalkers had planted several marker poles in the centre of the pools.

'A natural well,' Brostin said. 'Gushing up from the silt. Raw, mind you, not synthesised. My guess is the moth-freaks built this camp at a place where they could dredge up fuel for burning.'

'Are you sure?' she asked.

'I can smell it, doc,' he said, tapping the side of his fleshy nose with a dirty finger. 'Besides, just look at the oil patterns on the water there. Like a rainbow, they are. That's crude prom, coming up from the deposits. Sure as I'm not a petite blonde lass called Ana.'

She looked at him. 'I'm guessing, but you have an overwhelming desire to set fire to it right now, don't you?'

'Doc,' he replied, 'many call it arson. Many call me a pyromaniac. I just think of it as fun with matches. But I tell you this: I'd toss my whole pack of lhos into the marsh for a chance to light that baby up. Fire, y'see. It's what I do.'

Curth pretended to flick ash from her lho-stick. 'Let's just keep pretending, shall we?' she said.

THERE WAS ACTIVITY down on the lower platforms suddenly. Cynulff ap Niht reappeared with a gang of armed Sleepwalkers, and gestured for Gaunt to descend.

'Ven, with me,' he said, getting up. 'Rawne, you're in charge.'

For the life of him, Gaunt had wanted to give Mkoll command of the group he was leaving, but Rawne had rank.

'Just don't do anything stupid,' Gaunt told Rawne.

'As if.'

'You, or anyone else.'

Gaunt climbed down the rope ladder onto the lower stage, Mkvenner behind him. They followed Cynulff's men towards the main platform.

'So, they call themselves sleepwalkers?' Gaunt whispered to Mkvenner.

'No, sir. They call themselves *nihtgane*, which means "those who go about in the night". Simply put, they are *nightwalkers*.'

Gaunt nodded. How easily the locals had translated that word into *noctambulists* and therefore *sleepwalkers*. They'd missed the point entirely.

'The niht is the darkness of these marshes,' Mkvenner said. 'That's all they know.'

THE MAIN TENT, articulated like a giant umbrella, was lit from within by a single large promethium burner, hanging from a chain. The partisans had packed in, surrounding the chieftain, who looked more like a gigantic moth than any of them. His cloak was long and thick, and trailed out across the platform around him. His eyes glinted from within the mosaic ovals. His woaded moustache was so long it was plaited.

His name was Cynhed ap Niht. He was 'of the night', that was a thing he insisted on making clear through Mkvenner's translation. He introduced his sons: Eszekel, Eszebe, Eszrah and almost a dozen others. Gaunt lost track. In their grey skin paint and capes, they all looked alike.

When his turn came, Gaunt tried to explain his identity and his purpose. It was slow work. Mkvenner did his best to translate, but the chieftain kept asking questions and interrupting.

'Gereon has changed,' Gaunt found himself repeating. 'The world outside the niht has changed. The Imperium is no longer your enemy. Chaos has come.'

'Khh-aous?' the chieftain repeated. 'Hwat yitt meanye thissen werde?'

'The Archenemy of us all,' Gaunt tried to explain. 'My team, my men, we are here on an important mission. It is vital to the Imperium. Many will die if we don't–' he looked at Mkvenner, who was still translating.

'This is getting us nowhere, isn't it?'

'Keep going, sir,' Mkvenner said.

'Tell him… tell him I want the help of the partisans. The nihtgane. I want guides to lead us through the Untill so we can reach Lectica and the heartlands. Tell him many lives–'

'Many lives will be saved, Yes sir. I've told him that. Twice. He seems fixated on the notion of another enemy.'

'Another enemy?'

'Chaos, sir.'

'Preyathee,' the chieftain said, leaning forward. 'Hwat beyit thissen khh-aous, soule?'

'Ven, tell him that the Archenemy is a murderous beast, one that seeks to murder him and his kind as much as it wants to kill us. We are here to fight it. In the name of the God-Emperor.'

Mkvenner translated again. The chieftain listened with interest.

'Tell him–'

Cynhed ap Niht interrupted, holding up a grey hand. 'Histye, lissenye we haf. Council beyit takken, preyathee. Goye from heer, withe rest alse, as yitt meanye goode mett wherall. On yitt we shalle maken minde.'

The Sleepwalkers led them out of the tent.

'Well?' Gaunt said.

'Now, we wait,' said Mkvenner. 'They're going to consider what we've said and decide what to do about it.'

ONE OF THE ordinal's excubitors had accidentally inhaled a moth. It writhed in the thick water, splashing and vomiting itself to death.

Uexkull looked down at it. It wasn't worth a bolt round to put it out of its misery. The ordinal had five more. Hell knew why he'd brought them in the first place. Sthenelus had an escort of five warrior Space Marines. What did he need with excubitors?

The ordinal stalked his way over to the dying excubitor. The choking wretch clawed at Sthenelus's slim metal limbs with slippery hands, hoping for benediction and relief. The ordinal simply extended a thin sampling hook and took a swab of the excubitor's bloody froth.

'Toxin levels at eight point one on the Fabius scale. Air humidity now nine parts to level. Land is pooled to a half metre, and shelves away at two degrees. Flora sampling now follows.'

The ordinal's pict-coders began to click as they recorded the surrounding tree mass. The excubitor convulsed one final time and expired.

Around them, in the gloom, Sthenelus's remote mapping psyber skulls hovered and recorded.

The ordinal continued his non-stop vocal cataloguing, engaging the flimsy brass sensors of his walker frame to chart. The articulated rods reached out in all directions.

'Thick-husked berry fruit with red exocarp, toxic, but with potential commercial value for seed oils. Small pendule fruit with brownish pith, approximately–'

'My ordinal,' Uexkull said. 'Please concentrate. The enemy. Where is the enemy?'

One of Sthenelus's long brass samplers lifted from the ooze, sucking.

'One moment, lord Uexkull. Hmmm… one part in ten million, but human blood nevertheless. Someone was bitten here. I detect an odd concentration of moth venom too. Curious. An artificial compound.'

'Which way?' Uexkull demanded.

Sthenelus pointed.

ON THE HIGH, suspended platform, the members of the mission team waited. Minutes swelled into hours. Time seemed to pass at the most laborious rate. Around them, the quiet camp and the slow, swirling fogs of the vaguely illuminated marsh seemed to match the crawl of time.

'This is worthless!' Rawne announced.

'Sit down,' said Gaunt.

'This is a waste of–'

'Rawne, sit the feth down. I won't tell you again.'

'For feth's sake, we should get our scouts out at least. Mkoll's boys could cover the area, secure weapons. They–'

'No, Rawne.'

'But–'

'I said no and I believe I meant it.' Gaunt looked up at his flustered second. 'We wait, Elim. We wait and see what they have for us. If it's nothing, so be it. But if it's something, I'll not be ruining our chances with hasty measures.'

'I agree with Rawne,' Cirk said.

'Gee, no surprises,' Curth muttered. Varl sniggered.

'Shut up, female,' Cirk said, looking at Curth.

Curth got to her feet and faced the cell leader. 'Maybe I was imagining it, but I think I was part of this mission team long before you came along. I have rank–'

Cirk shrugged disparagingly. 'Really? We all know the reason you're here, female.' She jerked her head in Gaunt's direction.

'The pack leader only keeps his mind on the job if he's happy and serviced on a regular–'

'Whoa, lady!' said Curth, coming forward. 'Your mouth just doesn't know when to stop, does it?'

Cirk drew to her full height. She was significantly taller than the Ghosts' medic. She smiled. 'Touch a nerve, did I?'

'I can locate and trigger more nerves than you've ever dreamed of, you b–'

'That's enough. Both of you,' Gaunt said.

'Mamzel Curth... Doctor Curth... is here because of her medical training,' Landerson said, getting to his feet. He got in between them and stared Cirk in the eyes. 'To suggest anything else would be unbecoming of a Gereon soldier.'

Cirk glared. 'Landerson, you're a sycophantic piece of sh–'

There was a dull crack. Curth had landed her small, tight fist right on Cirk's mouth. The cell leader reeled back, and only the urgent hands of Beltayn and Criid stopped her from toppling off the platform.

'You little witch!' she snorted.

'Want some more?' Curth laughed.

'Shut up! Shut up!' Larkin spat. 'Shut them up, for feth's sake! They're coming back!'

Below, Cynulff and several other Sleepwalkers were striding towards the ladder.

'You'll keep,' Cirk simmered.

'Uh huh. Bite me,' Curth whipped back.

'Shut up,' Gaunt said.

'Well now, the ladies are fighting over you...' Rawne clucked.

'You can shut up too.'

'Oh, how I relish these moments,' Rawne said.

Cynulff pointed up at Mkvenner and gestured.

'He wants you,' Gaunt said.

Mkvenner nodded and jumped down onto the lower platform to join the partisans. He looked back at Gaunt briefly as he was led away. Gaunt splayed his hands across his chest and made the sign of the aquila.

'I'M SORRY,' CURTH said quietly. 'I apologise.'

'Right. Think you could apologise to her?' Gaunt asked, nodding across at Cirk, who sat on a corner of the platform, her faced turned to the marsh beyond.

'If you ask me nicely,' Curth replied.

'I shouldn't have to. Cirk's a superior officer. Other commissars would have shot a soldier for striking a superior, without question.'

Curth stared at him. 'You're kidding me.'

'It's true. I've seen it happen.'

'You'd shoot me?' Curth whispered. Her eyes were very wide.

'Not in a million years,' Gaunt said. 'So go and make nice.'

'I don't think that's going to be very easy,' Curth said. She opened her battered narthecium and rooted around in the remains of its contents. 'I ran a test. Using the last of my kit. It's not definite. I haven't got the equipment left for it to be definite. But I trust the result.'

'Which is?' Gaunt asked.

'The mood swings. The intolerance. It's all part of the Chaos taint here. It's infecting us. Changing us. Rawne's at your throat. Cirk is completely off her chuff.'

'Who did you test?' Gaunt asked.

'Me,' she replied. Tears welled in her eyes. 'I hit her because... because it's in me now. It's making me... different... It's making me violent. It's affecting our hormones. Altering them, boosting some of the repressed aggressional–'

'Ana. Shush.' Gaunt hugged her to his chest. Curth started to cry. 'If what you say is true, it's too late for us all. But I think we can overcome it. I think we can be strong. You stood up for me because you cared and because you hated to hear her slurs. We'll make it.'

She said something, but it was muffled by his chest. He pulled back. 'What?'

'I said, you're doing that commissar thing, aren't you? Saying the right things, the way you were trained.'

Gaunt smiled. 'If I say no, you'll think that's just part of the training too, won't you?'

'Maybe.'

He sat down beside her. 'Then I'm damned if I do and damned if I don't. Ana, we'll be fine. If the taint is affecting us, then it's slow. We've only been here a short while.'

'Cirk hasn't. She's been here from the start.'

Gaunt thought about that. 'Yes, she has,' he said. 'Yes, she has.'

* * *

'WE GAVE YOU everything,' Sabbatine Cirk said, as Gaunt crouched beside her. 'We'd lost our world, and you brought no word of liberation with you, and still we gave you everything we had. The entire cell was destroyed getting you in. Ballerat. So many others. For what? This nonsense. This madness.'

'I'm sorry,' Gaunt said. 'If it's any help, most of what I do… most of what my Ghosts do… appears to be madness in the doing of it. I have a mission and a goal still. We will get there, I firmly believe that.'

'You're a liar.'

'And so many other things besides. Stick with me, Sabbatine. I need you.'

Beltayn called out.

Mkvenner was coming back.

'THEY SAID NO,' Mkvenner announced as he climbed up onto the platform.

'No?' asked Brostin. 'No what?'

'They're not going to give us guides. They're not going to help us find our way out of the marshes. We're the old enemy. They've fought us for so long they're not going to aid us now.'

'Feth,' moaned Rawne.

'Ven,' said Varl. 'Where's your fething cap-badge gone?'

'I don't know. I must have dropped it.'

'They really said no?' Curth asked.

'Bel,' Mkvenner said, ignoring her and gesturing to the team's vox-man. 'Tune your set to my channel.'

'What?' Beltayn asked.

'I dropped my earplug and transmitter out of sight in the chieftain's lodge. Tune it in.'

'I'll do my best.'

Mkvenner looked at Gaunt. 'They're up to something. They're not going to help us but I got the impression they don't want us to leave either.'

'Getting nothing… just fuzz…' Beltayn said, the phones clamped to his head.

'The bastards are going to sell us out,' Rawne said.

UEXKULL CAME TO a halt. His lowlight vision was scoping nothing in this miasmal world. Heat on heat. But he trusted his eyes.

Figures were emerging out of the pools and root balls ahead of him. Tall, dusty-grey figures, flimsy as ghosts.

'Hold fire,' Uexkull ordered his men.

The spectres approached.

'How fascinating,' Sthenelus announced. 'Locals, indigens…'

'Quiet!' Uexkull barked.

The lead figure approached, wading through the stagnant pool. He was draped with a cloak of moth fur, and carried some sort of crossbow.

Peasant, Uexkull thought.

But he raised his massive gauntlet in greeting.

'Hail to you,' he called out.

'Preyathee,' the lead figure replied. 'Beitye Khhaous, soule?'

'What is he saying?' Uexkull snapped over his shoulder.

'Extraordinary,' replied Sthenelus. 'The being appears to have no concept of what we are. Indeed, he appears inquisitive.'

'Khhaous? Beitye Khhaous? Preyathee?' the partisan repeated. He held out one grey, long-fingered hand and showed them the glinting skull-crest Tanith cap-badge he had stolen.

'They have contact with the insurgents,' Uexkull cried as soon as he saw it. 'Ordinal, can you track these beings to point of origin?'

'Of course, lord. Pheromonally, and also by the wake of concentrated moth toxin they leave behind them.'

'Excellent,' Uexkull said, racking his storm bolter. 'These grey souls have come looking for… what was it again? "Khhaous"? Was that it?'

The lead partisan nodded eagerly and held the cap badge out again.

'Let us show them what "khhaous" means,' Uexkull cried.

The five Chaos Space Marines opened fire. Their shots mowed down the first rank of the partisans, exploding them backwards in wretched drizzles of crimson. Some ran, and were cut down. A mist of blood fumed the air.

The Tanith crest cap-badge tumbled out of a dead hand and sank quickly into the churning silt.

TWENTY

'THERE,' SAID BELTAYN, concentrating as he made minute adjustments to the dial of his vox-set. 'I'm picking up voices. Very faint…'

He handed the headphones to Mkvenner, who pressed them against his ears and craned to hear.

'The bastards are going to sell us out,' Rawne repeated.

'Shhh!' Mkvenner said. 'I can barely… Bel, can you boost the signal at all?'

'Trying,' Beltayn replied. 'Better?'

'A little.' Mkvenner listened hard. 'Hnh. Yeah. There's talking. I hear the chieftain. Couple of other voices. Talking about waiting. Waiting to learn something. Hang on.'

Everyone except the still-sleeping Feygor grouped around Mkvenner in silence, even Cirk. It seemed to take an age for Mkvenner to hear enough. Finally, the scout looked up at Gaunt.

'It's not good,' he said. 'The partisans have located another group moving into this area. Other outsiders.'

'Searching for us?' Gaunt asked.

Mkvenner shrugged. 'That's a good bet. The chieftain has sent a group of his warriors to make contact and find out more about them.'

'I told you!' Rawne snapped. 'Sell us out! They're going to sell us out!'

'The sort of monsters who are looking for us won't be interested in doing deals,' Gaunt said.

'Whatever,' said Cirk. 'The partisans will lead them right to us, whether they mean to or not.'

'Right,' said Gaunt. 'This is a bust. We tried, and it didn't come off. Time to cut our losses. Let's retrieve the weapons and get mobile. If the partisans don't like it, tough. Be ready to-'

Mkoll was suddenly ignoring him. The scout leader turned and looked out off the platform into the foggy darkness. 'Gunfire,' he said.

UEXKULL AND HIS warriors came in out of the swirling marsh mists, wading through the soupy water and firing indiscriminately. Their weapons' flash lit up the gloom. Bolter and cannon shot lashed from Uexkull, Nezera and Virag, plasma shots lanced from Czelgur and roaring cones of fire belched from Gurgoy's flamer. Ordinal Sthenelus followed them, fanning out his excubitors to lend support.

The western end of the encampment withered under the remorseless assault. Tree trunks splintered, foliage shredded, platforms shook as they were punctured, tents burst into flames.

Sleepwalkers died. Many of the grey-skinned people watched in a mystified daze as the attack came on, baffled by the massive warriors invading them. Uexkull's warriors cut them down: men, women, children. Others began to run. Czelgur raised his plasma weapon and speared bright, purple beams of energy at the encampment site. An entire platform section collapsed into the water, sending dozens of partisans tumbling into the swamp. Thrashing and struggling, they were mown down in the next hail of fire.

Uexkull strode up one of the walkways, which groaned under his weight. He fired his cannon and ripped down three fleeing partisans. Burning scads of grey feathers drifted like ash from their torn segmented cloaks.

'Fan out,' he ordered. 'Kill everyone. Find the Imperials and bring their bodies to me.'

'MOVE!' GAUNT YELLED. He could see the flashes and hear the ugly roar of the assault breaking across the far end of the encampment. 'Rawne! Brostin! Larkin! Recover the weapons! Beltayn and Landerson... pick Feygor up! Move!'

'We have to run!' Cirk yelled.

'They're massacring these people!' Gaunt replied.

'Oh, for feth's sake,' Rawne shouted, already halfway down the ladder. 'These people were going to sell us out, and they're not even Imperial citizens anyway!'

'Follow my orders!' Gaunt shouted back. 'We need our weapons! No more damn running! We face them here!'

Ignoring the protests behind him, Gaunt leapt off the platform and landed on the lower staging with feline grace, rising from his bended knees and drawing the power sword. 'The Emperor protects!' he yelled, and ran towards the attack.

Partisans fled past him, running the other way. Gaunt realised that one crucial thing was missing from this terrible scene. There was no screaming, no cries of horror. Even the Sleepwalker children were silent.

The guns weren't. He heard plasma fire, a flamer's crackling hiss and spit, and bolter weapons. Heavy stuff...

Pushing ahead, he got his first sight of the attackers as they strode forward through the camp, firing wholesale.

And he realised he had made a bad call. A very bad call. Maybe Curth had been right. Maybe the taint was so deep in them now they were acting rashly and irresponsibly. They should have run. Just run. Forgotten the weapons. Just fething run for their lives.

The attackers were giants, clad in the whirring power armour of Space Marines. Gaunt glimpsed ceramite plates as polished and luminous as mother of pearl, gold laced with filigrees of rust, adorned with abominable badges.

Chaos Space Marines. The most grotesque, most powerful warriors in the Archenemy's host. Imperial Guard didn't fight Space Marines. They left that job to the superhuman Astartes, for the simple reason that there was precious little a Guardsman could do that would even annoy a Chaos Space Marine. On the battlefield, brigades of well-armed Guardsmen regularly fell back in rout when even a few Chaos Space Marines appeared.

Gaunt had about a dozen Guardsmen in his team. They were unarmed, their weapons shut up in a coffer somewhere. Outclassed didn't even begin to cover it.

Bad call. Bad, bad call.

BELTAYN, LANDERSON AND Curth were struggling to get Feygor down off the platform. Criid and Varl jumped down past them. The others had already taken off in the direction of the coffer.

'He's gone in alone,' Criid was insisting. 'Gaunt's gone in alone and it's Space Marines.'

'You're kidding me,' Varl said.

'Look for yourself.'

'Holy feth. We are dead. We have to get our guns...'

'Why?' snapped Criid. 'So we can fluster them a little?'

'Tona–' Varl warned.

'Give me your satchel. Now, Varl. Right now!'

Without thinking, Varl tossed her the satchel containing the last six tube-charges. She caught it and started to run after Gaunt.

'Tona! Don't be a total gak!' Varl shouted. But she was already gone.

Varl started to run in the direction of the weapons chest, then came to a halt. 'Feth!' he cussed, and turned back to chase after Tona Criid.

GREY BODIES LAY everywhere amongst the burning tents and damaged trees. Some hung from the edges of the platforms, draping dead limbs into the green water, their segmented cloaks broken and disarrayed like the wings of dead birds, or swatted moths. Nezera, nearly two and a half metres tall in his hulking carapace armour, thumped up the walkboard bridgeway onto a higher level, and turned his cannon on a group of partisans who were trying to cower behind the remnants of a buckled tent dome.

Gaunt came out from behind the thick tree that provided central support for the platform's weight. He put all his strength into the two-handed sword blow. One chance.

Nezera had just enough time to realise a figure had appeared to his right. Then the scalding power sword of Heironymo Sondar sliced round and through him. Ceramite armour could withstand just about anything... lasfire, bolt rounds, even cannon shot. But it was like paper to the powered blade. Gaunt's lacerating blow cut through Nezera's chest plating, through the torso inside, and out through the spine in a fog of gore. His body half-severed at mid-rib height, Nezera stumbled, amazed, his system trying to manage the pain and repair the traumatic damage.

It was far too grievous. Blood poured out of the huge fissure in the plating like water over the edge of a wide cascade, jetting wildly in places. The cut edges of the armour plate glowed and crackled.

Nezera fell, heavy and dead, face down on the platform. The impact was so great that the platform shuddered and wobbled.

Gaunt looked at the cowering partisans. Their mosaic-edged eyes were wide in awe.

'Get up!' he yelled, not even trying to use their language any more. 'Get up and fight back, or they'll kill us all!'

SOMETHING'S CHANGED, UEXKULL thought, raking bolt fire through a cluster of tents and bursting open more grey flesh in bright splashes of blood. He could feel it. Like the change in the air before a thunderstorm. He–

The first shots came at him. Metal quarrels, hissing in the air like angry hornets. They pinged off his carapace armour, stopped dead by the bonded ceramite casing.

So, the peasants are fighting back, he smiled.

Then an iron quarrel smacked through the flesh of his left cheek.

There was some pain, but his bio-motors countered it. Uexkull closed his jaw and plucked the metal arrow out in a spurt of blood. Immediately, he felt his body glanding antivenin at a furious rate, the product sluicing through his system. The arrows were poisoned. An extremely lethal compound, no doubt derived from the local moths. An ordinary man would have been stone-dead in a second or two.

Uexkull was not an ordinary man. Not even slightly. His body-system rejected the formidable poison. He savoured the burning rush of the antidote. Shrugging off the rain of quarrels that spattered against his armour, he moved forward.

And continued to kill.

INSPIRED BY THE example of sheer, thoughtless bravado Gaunt had displayed taking down the Chaos Space Marine, the Sleepwalkers began to rally. Many continued to flee, guiding the womenfolk and children into the waters to get clear of the doomed encampment. But others took up their weapons and turned back against the attackers. Muskets fired, their loads glancing off the Space Marines' power armour. The crossbows fired too.

Moving forward through the smoking devastation that the enemy had wrought on the camp, Gaunt witnessed the crossbows in use. Drawing a poisoned iron quarrel from his quiver satchel, each partisan dropped the projectile down the snout of his bow's barrel and then shouldered the weapon to fire. The bows made no sound, just a whistle of release as they launched the iron darts with huge force.

Magnetics, Gaunt realised. The heavy lobes on the end of each bent-back bow arm were powerful magnets. They sucked the quarrels down into the weapon and, at a flick of the trigger, the charged polarity reversed and spat them out. Simple, perfect.

But utterly useless against Chaos Space Marines in full armour, warriors who could gland against toxins if they took a scratch.

If this battle were to be won – and Gaunt doubted there was a tactician in the whole cosmos who would predict that outcome in his favour – it had to come another way.

Unarmed Guardsmen and locals packing primitive weapons would not, could not stop a pack of Space Marines. But Gaunt had slain one, thanks to the sword. And he'd do it again.

Even if that meant facing them one by one.

STALKING FORWARD ON his high seat, Sthenelus blinked as two of his excubitors fell face down into the stinking water and did not get up. Metal quarrels hissed around him, and two plinked off the base of his walker.

He used his articulated probe limbs to retrieve one from the water.

'Crudely-fashioned projectile, perhaps deserving the name "quarrel", fifteen centimetres in length, smelted from poor-quality iron ore. Latent polarisation indicates magnetic delivery, tip reveals evidence of a resin compound manufactured from the toxic wing scales of the local moth-forms.'

The excubitor beside him walloped over into the thick water with a splash as a musket load burst its skull. The two remaining excubitors fired their laslocks and then began to reload.

Before they had even half-finished the job, they had been felled by quarrels too.

Sthenelus glanced down at the bodies of the excubitors floating lank and limp in the filthy water around him.

'Said toxin has a rapid effect on humaniform biosystems, suggesting–'

He stopped. He looked down. A passing quarrel had torn through the fabric covering his malformed belly. There was a single long scratch in the flesh from which blood welled in ruby beads.

'Lord Uexkull?' he said. 'Lord Uexkull!'

Ordinal Sthenelus tried to call the name a third time, but his mouth had filled with clogging foam by then. The tiny measure of poison killed him an instant later, turning his blood to sludge. His little body spasmed violently, and then fell still. A moment later, two more quarrels smacked into his torso, but they did nothing more than knock his walker carriage over. The misshapen man on the tall machine toppled backwards into the bog, and the stinking water rolled in to cover his face.

SHE SAW THE partisans were fighting back now, but knew it wasn't going to be enough. The four remaining Chaos Space Marines were reducing the camp to blazing wood pulp. Criid clambered higher into the boughs of one of the main trees, her hands tearing on the damp bark. The satchel of tube-charges swung about her slender body on its strap.

Below her, she saw one of the monsters, the one with the plasma weapon. He was storming forward, shrugging off the rain of quarrels and musket balls, vapourising everything in his path.

Don't look up. Don't look up, Criid willed.

RAWNE KICKED OPEN the chest's lid and started throwing weapons out. Mkoll, Mkvenner and Bonin caught their lasrifles and took off towards the mayhem. Brostin pulled out the heavy cannon and started to feed in the last rounds in his hopper.

'Long-las!' Rawne yelled. Larkin caught it neatly and smacked home a hotshot pack. If anything could dent a Chaos Space Marine's armour, it was a high-yield hotshot. Larkin knew he'd have to place it right. Between the plate joints. That's the one chance he had.

Brostin was suddenly firing. The cannon was kicking out a huge, vibrating sound. One of the enemy monsters was right on them.

Not even fazed by Brostin's cannonfire, the Chaos Space Marine thundered forward. His swinging power fist crumpled the autocannon like tinfoil and sent Brostin flying. Limp and spinning over in the air, Brostin splashed into the swamp water off the platform.

'Larks!' Rawne yelled.

Larkin raised his long-las. The Chaos Space Marine brought his flamer to bear. The world vanished in a blaze of white flames.

UEXKULL PAUSED IN his onslaught, and knelt down, smoke wreathing from the muzzles of his overheated weapons.

He had come upon a body. One of his own.

Nezera was dead, his corpse split open. Dead? How was that possible? Uexkull reached out with his steel fingers and touched the steaming innards that had spilled out of his warrior's sliced armour.

A true challenge. That's what Uexkull had said. That's what he'd boasted of to his warrior band. That, it seemed, was just what Nezera had found. By the laughing gods, what waited for them here?

Uexkull's inhumanly sharp senses suddenly warned him he was about to find out.

Gaunt launched himself out of the shadows and swung the power sword at Uexkull. Jerking back at the last moment, Uexkull raised one gauntlet to deflect the blow. The sword clanged off in a flurry of sparks, the savage rebound stinging Gaunt's forearms. He tried to reprise, but Uexkull was up on his feet again now. The scything blade cut the end off Uexkull's bolter. The severed edges of the metal sizzled.

With a deep roar, Uexkull lunged forward, dropping the mutilated weapon and reaching for Gaunt.

Gaunt threw himself flat and rolled away.

'You little bastard!' Uexkull creaked, smashing his fist at his human prey. Stage planking split and cracked. Gaunt was already up again, clambering up a rope ladder onto the next platform.

'You can't escape me!' Uexkull roared, and opened fire with his shoulder cannon. The furious salvo punched upward through the stage, and shredded the wet canopy overhead. Gaunt rolled sideways, wincing as huge holes exploded in the wood beside him.

Uexkull fired again, raking the upper stage, and decapitating several of the supporting trees. With a terrible shriek of wrenching timber, the entire stage platform buckled and collapsed. Gaunt flew into the air, falling with it.

HER BREATHING SHORT and panicky, Criid balanced herself between two branches, legs splayed, and looked down. The Space Marine was almost directly beneath her, firing on anything that moved. Criid plucked the satchel off her shoulder, weighed it in her hands as a test, and then pulled out one of the tube-charges. She knotted the satchel strap around the charge as a counterweight, then pulled off the twist of det-tape and threw the bag down.

It spun in the air. Her aim was dead on. The loop of the satchel landed around the Space Marine's neck.

The tube detonated. A millisecond later, the other five in the bag went off too.

The Space Marine vanished in the blinding flash.

Criid had a brief moment to enjoy her success. Then the rushing, rising fireball rippled upwards through the trees and engulfed her.

Screaming, she fell into the expanding flames.

LARKIN WAS DOWN, felled in the concussive rush of the Space Marine's flamer-surge. Dead? Unconscious? There was no time to check. There was fething little time for anything at all.

Not even a prayer.

Rawne grabbed the fallen long-las. Smoke and wood fibres swirled in the air. The Chaos Space Marine turned, saw him through the haze, and began to raise his weapon.

One chance. One shot. Rawne was no marksman, not like Larkin. He wasn't even practiced with the long-las. But it had a hotshot loaded and Rawne knew he had to make it count. He wouldn't get another.

The Chaos Space Marine's flamer came up to roar again.

Rawne relaxed into the butt stock and fired.

Range was almost point-blank. The searing round took the Chaos Space Marine's head clean off.

CANNON FIRE CHEWED the swamp water behind him. Clutching his sword, Gaunt surfaced with a splutter, and fought his way up onto a walk-board. He ran, dripping, across the next platform, trying to stick to the shadows.

But Uexkull saw him and followed, wading into the mire, his cannon barking out tongues of muzzle-flash. Gaunt frantically got a heavy tree bole between him and the line of fire. He heard shots slam into the body of the ancient cycad. Leaves, insects and droplets of water rained down from the shaken canopy above. He started to run again, up a walk-bridge onto the next stage.

Uexkull's weight quaked the staging behind him as he got up out of the ooze onto the boards. Filthy water streamed off the lower half of his ceramite armour. Gaunt heard a distinctive clatter as the enemy's suit-loaders automatically engaged a fresh ammo supply to the smoking cannon. He looked for cover, moved, slipped and fell hard. Cannon shots zipping over his head.

Gaunt rolled violently, shots chewing into the old wood, and ducked down behind one of the anchor posts from which several of the platform's supporting ropes ran. The ropes were old and hand-wound, and had been treated with some kind of lacquer to harden them. He sliced his blade through the central knot. The platform trembled, creaked, and fell, one end first.

Uexkull toppled back into the water as his end of the stage dropped down violently. His wild cannon shots ripped up into the canopy as he fell, and churned up a showering downpour of leaf-mulch.

Gaunt slithered down the shelving slope of the stricken platform. He got a purchase, and began hauling himself up onto the next stage section. Making deadly, almost feral sounds now, Uexkull dragged himself out of the marsh water, thrashing up from the stagnant liquid like some rising swamp-beast. Festooned with weed and algae, he seemed to be a hideous, primeval daemon of the marshes, submerged for eons, and woken to anger now by the tumult of war.

Uexkull ascended the slumped stage after Gaunt.

CRIID LANDED BADLY on the splintered platform. The impact drove the breath right out of her. Limp, winded, she rolled over. The boards beneath her were hot and smouldering. Right next to her, the steaming Chaos Space Marine lay crumpled and dead. The combined satchel charge had burst it open, its armour fractured like an egg shell, the bloody interior oozing out like yolk.

Criid tried to get up. She was dazed and close to grey-out. She couldn't breathe. Gasping, trying to refill her lungs, she writhed, her vision dim and starred with lights. Little circling lights, like moths in the night.

A partisan, grey-faced and silent, was pulling at her to move. A second partisan, armed with a crossbow, stood over them, uttering something urgent in their guttural language.

Criid began to roll to her feet.

'All right,' she choked. 'All right...'

The partisan pulling at her smiled. Then he vanished from the chest up in a boiling cloud of blood and tissue. His ruined corpse fell over to one side. He was still holding her hand.

A second Chaos Space Marine came roaring out of the smoke, bolter still firing. Criid felt the scorching heat of shells zipping past her head.

The second partisan fired his bow weapon and died a moment later as one of the bolt rounds struck his chest and detonated. But the partisan's quarrel had punched through the radiator vanes of the Chaos Space Marine's helmet. He staggered backwards, dropping his bolter with a heavy thud. Blood was gushing from under the snout of his helmet where the quarrel had stuck, transfixed. He clawed at his snout with both hands, making monstrous, squealing noises that were amplified by his suit's vox-system.

As Criid tried to crawl away, she heard a twang of snapping, parting metal. The Chaos Space Marine had pulled the arrow out. He came forward, unsteady, reaching his huge paws at Criid as she flinched back. The Space Marine's armoured gauntlets were immense, each one big enough to enclose her head, and strong enough to crush it like a berry.

'Feth you!' she shouted.

One steel hand grabbed her around the lower leg and began to pull. She kicked back, pointlessly.

Varl appeared from somewhere. He grabbed the Space Marine's fallen bolter and raised it, grunting under the weight of the thing. Varl jammed the fat muzzle up under the lip of the Space Marine's helmet.

And fired.

Varl kept his finger depressed. The huge, antique weapon shook as it emptied its clip, threatening to knock him down with its gigantic recoil. He braced against it, his augmetic shoulder locking in place.

On the fifth shot, the Space Marine's helmet began to deform and buckle from within.

On the seventh, the helmet burst. Varl, Criid and the now headless Space Marine were saturated in the glistening material that sprayed out. Small shards of helmet metal tinkled down around them.

The Space Marine's mighty form swayed for a second, and then fell backwards.

UEXKULL HESITATED, LOOKING around. The platform area was dark and hot and his enhanced vision was useless. He listened instead, hearing moisture drops rolling down leaves, the thrum and tick of insects, the creak of the support ropes, the nearby hum of his cannon's autocoolers as they steamed and hissed.

Close, close.

A good fight, better than he had expected. A true challenge. But over now. The power sword, that had been a dangerous surprise, but the man who had carried it...

Just a man. A lump of flesh and bones. An eminently destroyable thing.

Uexkull took another step. He deliberately started glanding an adrenaline-based stimm, feeling the killing lust rise in his biosystem. This would be a precious kill, one to celebrate. One to compose songs about. The murder-mist began to cloud his vision, the hunger for blood engorging his soul.

His senses became acute. He smelled sweat dripping from a man's raw knuckles, smelled the tang of an ignited blade, heard the drumming of a frantic heartbeat and racing breath that could not stifle or disguise itself.

'Who are you?' he called. Insects chirruped. Flames crackled. Water rippled.

'Who are you, warrior?' he called again, prowling forward. 'I am Uexkull. You have fought well. Beyond the measure I had expected of you. For that, I make you a promise.'

Bird calls. Insects. Slapping water. A heartskip, somewhere close now.

'Did you hear me? A promise. A mark of respect. Surrender now, and tell me who you are, and I will kill you quickly, without lingering pain. That is my promise, one warrior to another.'

Insects shrilled. Branches creaked. Leaves fluttered down. Each leaf impact sounded like a gunshot to Uexkull. The smell of human sweat was strong now. So close. He could hear the fizzling power of the accursed sword now. He could actually taste meat, wet boot-leather, silver.

Lure the enemy out, make him show himself...

Leering, still moving forward, Uexkull clapped his steel palms together slowly. 'Bravo, warrior. Bravo, I say. Guardsman, are you? Bravo! Quite a dance you have led me. It ends now, of course, and I swear to make that end brief.'

Right there. Behind that tree to his right. The rank salt-wet of a man, the quick-tempo thump of his heart. Right there...

'But I tell you, I have not met so fine a warrior in all the ranks of the enemy Guard that I have killed.'

'You should get out more,' Gaunt snarled, and came out around the other side of the tree. His sword raked in and sliced the cannon off its shoulder mount in a crackling discharge of severed cables.

Uexkull roared as he came about. His furious cry shook the platform and shuddered water and leaves, like heavy rain, from the canopy above. His fist swung at Gaunt.

Gaunt ducked, rolled, and came up again to plant a killing stroke through the Space Marine's armoured torso.

But Uexkull was much, much faster.

His fist hit Gaunt and sent him flying across the platform, blood spattering from a torn cheek. Gaunt landed awkwardly, and the power sword of Heironymo Sondar skittered out of his hand and slipped away across the wet boards.

Gaunt tried to rise, his head swimming. His knees refused to lock and his legs shot out from under him, dropping him onto his belly. He clawed with his hands, feeling the platform jump as Uexkull stormed towards him.

Covering his head, he rolled away instinctively. Uexkull's armoured fist mashed a hole in the boarding. The giant warrior cursed, turned and rose to his full height to smash both hands, fingers interlaced, down onto his prone foe.

With an ugly thwack, an iron quarrel suddenly impaled his nose. Uexkull staggered backwards, mewling with pain. A moment later, and the undergrowth began to hiss. Three more quarrels clattered off his shoulder plating. Another speared his cheek like a darning needle. Another smacked through his chin.

Then yet another lanced itself in his left eyebrow.

His face streaming with blood, Uexkull cried out and tried to move forward. The iron quarrels were smacking into him like rain now, bouncing off his plates or burying themselves between the segments. An arrow popped his left eye and remained there, rigid and embedded.

Uexkull began to scream. The sound was deafening, abhuman. It tore through the clearing. It made the Untill marshes shake to their waterlogged depths.

Another quarrel embedded itself in his cheekbone. Uexkull stumbled forward, his continuing scream unbroken. His mouth was wide open in a raw, carnassial rictus.

Gaunt was on his feet. He had retrieved the power sword, but there was no need for it any more.

The partisans were emerging from the shadows all around, swathed in their grey cloaks, firing and reloading their mag-bows, then firing again. They were aiming for the bare, exposed head.

Uexkull stopped screaming because he couldn't any more. His head was a head no longer. It was a distorted mass of meat and broken bone so thickly stuck with iron barbs that many of the bow-shots ricocheted back off the close-packed metal stalks.

Blood ran down his chest plate and shoulder guards. Lord Uexkull, his skull just a malformed pincushion, sank down onto the decking and died.

TWENTY-ONE

'WHAT THE FETH did you do to my las?' Larkin muttered.

'Saved your life, so shut the feth up,' Rawne replied.

'Only asking...' Larkin said, nursing and tweaking the long-las, and shushing at it like it was a girlfriend of his who'd been goosed while his back was turned.

'Well, don't,' said Rawne. 'Feth, I don't even know if this is over.'

'It's over,' Mkoll said, emerging from the thick smoke that billowed from the burning tents upwind. That much was evident from the quiet that had settled over the shattered camp. The gunfire had stopped.

The Ghosts regrouped, numbed by the ferocity of the savage fight, and quietly dazed at the simple magnitude of what they had accomplished. Between them, they had taken out five enemy Chaos Space Marines, and with no losses of their own. Criid and Larkin were both bruised, but the closest they had come to losing a man was Brostin, who had nearly drowned. In the midst of the mayhem, Landerson had dived in after him and dragged his unconscious form to safety.

'Five,' breathed Rawne. 'Five of the bastards. How the feth did we manage that?'

'Luck?' Bonin suggested.

LUCK DIDN'T SEEM to have favoured the partisans. The Archenemy warriors had slaughtered over forty of them, including women and children. Their platformed encampment was devastated. Gaunt ordered his team to help them in any way they could, and the Ghosts spread out, running triage under Curth's direction. She collected up the remaining supplies in her kit and all the field dressing sets in their own packs to treat any manageable wounds. But some injuries were too extreme even for her abilities.

'There'll be another five or six dead in a few hours,' she told Gaunt.

He nodded. His own cheek was a bloody mess where Uexkull's armoured fist had torn it, but he refused a dressing. 'I'm all right. Others need it more.'

The partisans seemed not to understand the Ghosts' intentions at first, but Mkvenner did his best to explain, and they reluctantly permitted their wounded to be taken to Curth. Brostin, still belching up swamp water occasionally, supervised the extinguishing of those parts of the camp set ablaze in the attack. His knack with fire was as impressive when it came to quelling flames as it was when making them thrive.

Landerson assisted the Ghosts as best he could. Only Cirk refused to involve herself with the partisans. She sat on one of the lower stages, keeping watch over Feygor's supine form.

The surviving partisans, silent and sombre in their segmented cloaks, seemed to be gathering up the salvageable items from their campsite. The cleverly constructed dome tents – those that had not been shredded or burned – were collapsed into portable spindles of tight-wrapped fabric. Sewn-leather packs were filled with possessions, and gourd flasks brimming with crude prom sealed so they could be carried on shoulder yokes.

'They're leaving,' Gaunt observed.

Mkoll nodded. 'As far as Ven can make out, they're nomadic anyway. There are many platform camps like this dotted all through the Untill. All of them built an age ago. They move from one to the next, stay a few weeks, move on again. Apparently, they're not likely to return to this one again. It's been... polluted, I suppose is the word. Polluted by what just happened here.'

'We brought this doom on them,' Gaunt said.

'No, sir, we didn't. They brought it on themselves. Rawne doesn't even think we should be helping them now.'

'Funny thing, Mkoll,' said Rawne, appearing from the shadows behind them. 'I have a rank.'

'My apologies, major,' sniffed Mkoll.

'That true, Rawne?' asked Gaunt.

'Yes, sir. You made me major yourself.'

'I meant the other thing. And you know it. Don't feth around right now, Rawne. I'm not in the mood.'

'Sir.'

'You honestly can't understand why we're helping them?' Gaunt asked.

Rawne shrugged. 'They refused to help us. They tried to sell us out. I don't understand why we fought to defend them. I don't understand why we're wasting the last of our field dressings treating their wounded.'

'Because the Emperor protects, Rawne,' Gaunt said.

'Even those who don't recognise his majesty?'

'Especially those, I should think,' Gaunt said.

Rawne huffed and walked away. 'This place is getting to you,' he muttered.

Is it, Gaunt wondered? That was perfectly likely now. They'd won the battle – somehow – but it had been a mistake to fight it in the first place. Was his leadership now suspect? Was he making irresponsible decisions? Was the taint of Gereon now so deep in him that he was thinking wrong?

He tried to put the nagging fear aside. His mind felt clear and true. He felt fine. But wasn't that how it always started? Men weren't drawn to the madness of Chaos because it seemed like a viable lifestyle change. The clammy influence of the Ruinous Powers wormed inside a man, changed him slowly and subtly without him ever realising it, making the insanity of the warp-darkness seem like the most natural thing in the cosmos.

All his life, as a commissar, Gaunt had understood that. That was why a commissar had to be so vigilant. And so harsh. Right to the end, on Herodor, Agun Soric had seemed like the most reasonable, loyal man. Gaunt had trusted him, loved his spirit, adored his simple courage.

But the man had gone over. The mark of the psyker had been in him. There had been no choice but to send him to the black ships.

Gaunt had dutifully read all the scholarly texts as a young man, and still reread many. Some of them, like the poetic philosophy of his favourite, Ravenor, writing nearly half a century earlier, had implanted this understanding in his mind. Especially where Ravenor wrote so eloquently, so heartbreakingly, about the fall of his master, Eisenhorn. Gregor Eisenhorn's ultimate, terrible fate was an object lesson in the seductive power of the warp.

But Gaunt tried to focus on one memory, a lesson taught to him what seemed a lifetime ago by his own mentor, Delane Oktar. It had been Oktar's deepest belief that a man should simply strive to do what seemed right. Gaunt remembered the thawing snowfields of Darendara, just after the liberation, the best part of thirty years before. They had been fighting secessionists, not Chaos, and there was great debate as to the appropriate punishment of the prisoners taken. Several commissars urged a thorough purge and a programme of execution. Commissar-General Oktar had argued for a different way. More lenient.

'Let us be firm, but let us re-educate. Blood is not always the answer.'

Three of the senior commissars opposing Oktar's view had leaned on Cadet Gaunt, hoping to get the young man to use his pull to influence Oktar's decision. Gaunt had taken supper with his master in one of the lamp-lit rooms of the Winter Palace, and during dinner, he had brought the matter up.

Oktar had smiled patiently. 'My boy,' he said at length – he had always referred to Gaunt as 'Boy'. 'My boy, if we execute everyone who disagrees with us, the galaxy will quickly become an empty place.'

'Yes, but–' the Boy had started to say.

'The Emperor protects, Ibram. He watches us all, no matter what dark corner we lurk in. It should be our sworn duty to convey that message to others, to the lost and the disenfranchised, to the ignorant and the troubled. We should be finding ways to help them learn, to help them come to terms, and benefit from the God-Emperor's goodness, just as we do. There are plenty of things in this thrice-accursed galaxy that we have no choice but to fight and kill, without turning on ourselves too. Think of this... if we do no more than what we feel is the right thing, then the Emperor is watching, and he will see it. And if he approves, he will protect us and let us know he is pleased with our service.'

'You know, sir, some would say–'

'Say what, boy?'

'Some would say that's heresy, sir,'

Throne, had he really said that? Gaunt winced as he remembered uttering those idiot words to his mentor. A few short years after the Darendara Liberation, the new governing council – many of them politicos spared thanks to Oktar's mercy – had formed a new allegiance and renewed their vows to the Imperium. Darendara was now one of the most staunchly loyal worlds in its subsector. Oktar's views had been vindicated.

Gaunt wandered alone along the smouldering platforms, and lingered for a while on the highest stage still intact. He gazed out over the marshes of the Untill.

'The Emperor protects,' he murmured to himself. 'The Emperor protects...'

Judge thyself first, then judge others. That was the first law of the Commissariat. Gaunt took out one of his bolt pistols. He had very few rounds left for either. As long as he still had one shot, he could yet make the most important judgement of all.

THE FOLLOWING DAWN, he was vindicated.

They had all slept badly on the hard platforms. The night had been humid, and the swamp air especially close. Curth had stayed awake until after midnight, tending two partisans who died despite her efforts. Brostin, his cannon destroyed, had been busy all night fiddling with the flamer that one of the Chaos Space Marines had been carrying. It was a crude thing and, in truth, rather too large and bulky to be carried by anyone without the support of power armour. But he persevered, stripping it of all but the basics, and chiselling away the more offensive Chaos symbols and badges. Finally, he fashioned a shoulder harness from some of the severed lengths of platform cable to distribute its weight. He practised lugging it around, and quickly decided he could only manage one of the three fuel canisters the Space Marine had carried. More adjustments. Just before first light, he had waded out from the platforms and filled the canister from the natural well.

'Will it work?' Varl asked him.

'You fething betcha!' Brostin snorted, and test-clacked the trigger spoon. A coughing, faltering gust – part flame and mostly steam – exhaled weakly.

'Right,' Brostin said, scratching his head. 'Right. A few adjustments, and you'll see.'

When the Ghosts woke, unsteady and weary, they found the partisans about to leave. All their camp belongings were packed and shouldered. The wounded had been lifted up on makeshift stretchers. The dead were laid out on the broken stages, with swamp flowers on their faces.

Cynhed ap Niht, the chieftain, came to speak with Mkvenner, and brought several of his warriors with him. They talked for a long time. Finally, Mkvenner wandered back to the waiting Ghosts, with one of the warriors at his side.

'What's going on?' Gaunt asked.

'They're leaving now. But the chieftain has had a change of mind. He's decided to help us, after all. After what happened here. It seems we impressed them with our efforts to defend them.'

'Great. What does that mean, Ven?'

'He's given us one of his sons.'

'What?'

Mkvenner gestured to the tall partisan at his side. The grey man seemed like a statue, so silent and still.

'This is his son. Eszrah ap Niht. He's going to act as our guide and lead us through the marshes to the heartlands.'

Gaunt looked up at the towering, thin man. 'Really?'

'Yes, sir.'

And if he approves, he will protect us and let us know he is pleased with our service.

'Then let's get moving,' Gaunt said.

He looked round, and saw that the partisans had already started to leave. They were vanishing slowly into the mist. Eszrah ap Niht didn't even look round to see them go.

Some few, last figures, like phantoms in their segmented cloaks, waited to perform the last rite of leave-taking. Brostin saw them, dumped his heavy pack with the not-yet-working flamer, and jumped off the stage into the water, splashing across to join them.

'Can I?' he asked. 'Can I do this?'

Not really understanding his words, but understanding his urgent intent and his bright eyes, one of the partisans handed the flaming torch to Brostin.

'Quethy?' the partisan said.

'You've no idea,' Brostin replied. The partisans murmured several ritual prayers, heads bowed.

'Are we done? Are we all done? Can I do this?' Brostin asked eagerly.

One of them nodded.

With a swing of his thick, tattooed arm, Brostin threw the torch. It landed near the centre of the natural well in the mire. The well lit up with a fizzling suck followed by a solid bang. In a moment, lambent yellow flames were boiling out and ripping into the ruined wooden camp. The glade burned. The dead were consumed and sent to whatever god or gods they had worshipped since the dawn of the colony.

Brostin waded back to rejoin the group, who were already backing away from the fierce heat.

'That's the stuff,' he chuckled.

'Move out!' Rawne cried.

Gaunt looked back one last time. It was hard to see against the glare of the inferno, but there was no sign of the partisans now. The Sleepwalkers had vanished into the Untill.

Eszrah ap Niht still did not look back. He said nothing. He raised one dove-grey hand, and gestured.

So they followed him.

'How DID HE tempt you to his cause, etogaur?' the pheguth asked as they walked down the field from the roadway where the transports were parked.

'What do you mean, sir?' Mabbon replied. Desolane was walking ahead of them, and the pheguth was certain the life-ward could hear their conversation, but he didn't care.

'The Great Anarch, whose word drowns out all others,' the pheguth said, raising his hand to mask his mouth in a coy imitation of the Archenemy ritual. 'You were a lord of the Blood Pact.'

'I cannot really say, sir,' Mabbon replied.

The pheguth nodded. 'I understand, if it's a private thing...'

'No, it's not like that. I mean I really can't say where my dissatisfaction began. I was a sworn lord, as you say, and I had made the Pact, blooding myself on the sharp edges of the Gaur's own armour. It was a privilege. The Blood Pact is a superb fighting force. To be a commander in their ranks, to be an etogaur, it was all the honour a man might hope for.'

They walked on a little further. The day was sunny but cheerless. Cloudbanks loomed against the sky like blotches of mould on stale white bread. The field was broad, and contained nothing except grit and short, wiry stubble.

Desolane was taking no chances since the attempt on the pheguth's life. The life-ward had insisted on careful security for the day's outing. Twelve soldiers of the occupation force walked with them, surrounding them in a wide, loose circle, weapons ready. Others guarded the road approach, and the line of the hedge. Two deathships hovered, watching, over a nearby field. The pheguth could hear the lazy rush of their lift-jets.

'I suppose,' Mabbon said at length, 'it all changed when I met the Anarch. The Pact division I was commanding was sent into the Khan Group to assist Great Sek. He impressed me at once. He has great personal charm, you see. A ferocious intelligence. The insight to see what needs to be done and the ability to accomplish it. Archon Gaur is a matchless leader in so many ways, but what he achieves, he achieves by brute force. He is a killer of worlds, a dominator, a feral thing. Not once in all the years that I served him as etogaur did he listen to my thoughts or even solicit my opinions. He takes no advice. On many occasions, officer-commanders of the Blood Pact, myself included, were ordered to engage in rash and costly actions at his whim. I've lost many men that way, been forced to send units to their deaths, even when I could plainly see a better way of defeating the forces of the False Emperor. When Archon Gaur gives an order, there is no opportunity for discussion.'

'I see,' said the pheguth. He was only half-listening. The constant, post-transcoding headache simmered within his skull. The fresh air seemed to help a little, but not much.

'Great Sek is different,' Mabbon continued, 'He possesses subtlety, and actively looks to his commanders for suggestions and ideas that he can incorporate into his strategy.'

'I've heard he has brilliance in that regard.'

'You will enjoy meeting him, when the time comes,' Mabbon said.

'I'm sure I will,' replied the pheguth.

'Serving under the Anarch, I won three worlds in quick succession. Each victory was due, in great part, to the active cooperation between Great Sek and the field commanders. It opened my eyes to possibilities.'

'Such as?'

'Such as... that the successful prosecution of this war against the Imperium depends on more than raw strength and fury. Our victory in these Sabbat Worlds will require guile and cleverness. Your Warmaster is a clever man.'

'Macaroth? Why, I suppose he is. A gambler, though. A risk-taker.'

'Audacious,' said Mabbon. There was surprising admiration in his voice. 'That is his strength. To fight as much with daring and intelligence as with iron and muscle. Great Sek has a good deal of respect for your Macaroth.'

The pheguth smiled. 'Not my Macaroth, Mabbon. Not now.'

'Forgive me, sir,' the etogaur said. 'But the Anarch certainly watches Macaroth's moves closely. He has told me that he relishes the prospect of matching his prowess against Macaroth's directly, when the time is right.'

'You make it sound like a game of regicide!' the pheguth laughed.

Mabbon looked at him. 'A bigger board, a billion more pieces, and those pieces alive, but...' The etogaur smiled.

They were approaching the brake of sickly trees that screened the end of the field from the valley beyond. The pheguth glimpsed the hedgerow outlines of the field system covering the heartland bocage all around them.

'So,' the pheguth wondered, 'you felt you might be backing the wrong horse?'

'I beg your pardon?'

'My idiom, I'm sorry. I meant... you made your choice because you felt the Archon might not be the best Archon for the job?'

'Wait here,' Mabbon told the troop detail and they came to a halt. 'You may wait too, life-ward,' Mabbon added.

Desolane glared at the etogaur.

'I will guard him, Desolane. You have my word.'

Reluctantly, Desolane halted too. Mabbon led the pheguth down into the trees. Some form of lice or blight had afflicted them. Their leaves were withered and sere, and their trunks wet with black decay. There was a powerful stench of decomposition.

'We must watch our words,' Mabbon said to the pheguth as they wandered in through the dead stand. 'Desolane vets your guards carefully, but as you have already found, there are some amongst the host who might consider our opinions heresy. The Archon is still the Archon. He is master of us all, even Anarch Sek.'

'But you seek to change that balance of power?'

Mabbon Etogaur paused. He raised his hand and idly touched the deep, old scars that decorated his face and bald head. It was as if he was considering the best way of replying. That, or remembering some past pain and the promise it had contained. 'Many believe that if Gaur remains in command of our forces, he will squander our strengths with his fury, wear our host down with relentless assaults against Macaroth, and ultimately lead us to nothing but defeat and annihilation. Many believe that Sek should have been Nadzybar's successor after Balhaut. Many believe that particular mistake must be corrected, and soon, before we lose the Sabbat Worlds forever.'

'And the first step?' asked the pheguth. 'To give Sek a martial order to rival the Blood Pact?'

Mabbon nodded. 'You know that much already, sir.'

'Yes, I know. But I think it's just really sinking in now. The… the scale of this. The audacity.'

Mabbon chuckled. 'That concept again. I told you, Sek admires the quality.'

'But the Archon could have us all killed. This is tantamount to insurrection. Gaur was my enemy for a long time, and now I've come over, I don't relish the irony of it happening again.'

'As far as the Archon is concerned,' said Mabbon, 'we are helping Magister Sek to improve his forces, and thus the quality of his service to the Gaur. We are not the simple brutes you Imperials seem to think, sir. We are not beyond politicking and intrigue. We will disguise and misdirect, and behind those lies, build our forces. The rest, the dangerous part, can wait. It may be years until Sek is ready to make his move. We have years. This war is old, and it isn't going anywhere.'

'So that's why you turned pheguth too?'

The etogaur laughed out loud. 'Traitor, eh? Traitor to the Archon. Yes, that's why. I believe in the future. And the future is not Urlock Gaur.'

'You renounced the Pact?'

'I did,' said Mabbon. 'My heart and mind were easy to change. My ritual scars were not.' He held up those pale, soft, unblemished hands of his. 'The meat foundries gave me new hands to erase the marks of my pledge.'

The pheguth found himself looking down at his own, augmetic hand. 'It's strange, don't you think, Mabbon? That we both celebrate our treasons, the break of long-held loyalties, in our hands?'

'You must tell me your story sometime, sir,' Mabbon said.

'My dear Mabbon, I will. As soon as I remember it.'

* * *

THEY CAME OUT through the trees into the lower field and the pheguth saw what he had been brought there to witness. It was an impressive sight.

Some three hundred men, stripped down to ochre combat trousers and brown boots, were training in paired teams down the length of the field. They were sparring with dummy rifles, roughly-shaped wooden blanks, refining bayonet work. The air was filled with grunts and gasps and the crack of wood on wood. Every man wore a distinctive amulet on a chain around his neck. The badge of the Anarch.

These were the Sons of Sek.

Mabbon led the pheguth down towards the clattering rows. The practice weapons were toys, but there was nothing playful about the practice itself. Dummy rifles splintered under the repeated blows, sweat glistened on the huge backs and thick arms of the trainees. Broken wood drew blood. Scratches bled freely down chests and bellies. Some men were down, fysik attendants treating deep gashes and gouges. Two men were actually unconscious. Discipline masters – Mabbon called them scourgers – walked the lines with whips and whistles, punishing any half-hearted efforts. The scourgers were brutish men dressed in blue chainmail and iron sallet helms.

'The Gaur based the Blood Pact formation on the structure principles of the Imperial Guard,' Mabbon explained. 'But he did not duplicate all aspects. The Blood Pact has no equivalent of the… what is the word?'

'Commissars?'

'Exactly. This is something my magister seeks to correct in the Sons. The scourgers have been selected from veteran units, and are trained separately from the Sons, along with my officer cadre. The scourgers' duties are discipline, education and morale.'

'The Magister is perspicacious,' said the pheguth. 'Without the Commissariat, the Guard is nothing.' The pheguth watched as one burly scourger lashed a man's back with his whip for slacking, and then turned and gently advised another on technique. Just like the bloody commissars, he thought, one hand teaching, one hand striking.

'You approve, sir?' Mabbon asked.

The pheguth nodded. The martial excellence on display was undeniable. The sheer savagery. But his headache was growing worse. Pain flared and ebbed behind his eyes. Perhaps it was the sunlight. He'd been out of it so much recently. He wondered if he should have asked Desolane for a hat.

They strolled down the lines, admiring the display. The noise all around was hard and brutal: clacking weapon-dummies, snorts of breath, whip cracks.

'How many?' the pheguth asked, rubbing his aching brow.

'Sir?'

'In the first year, how many men do you think you'll raise?'

'This is the trial unit, pheguth. My officers intend to establish two more camps of similar size here in the heartland in the next few weeks. But I plan to have a force of at least six thousand come winter, here, and in camps on two nearby worlds. Subject to your advice and assistance, obviously.'

'Obviously.'

The pheguth winced as the fighting pair next to them ended their latest bout with one man on his back, his nose mashed by a well-placed stock.

'Fysik here!' a scourger called, blowing his whistle for emphasis.

'We'll begin the exhibition this afternoon, sir,' Mabbon said. 'Furgesh Town is just over the hill. Before then, I was hoping you'd address the men. Say a few words.'

'I'd be happy to.' The pheguth massaged his pulsing head again. Colours seemed very bright suddenly, sounds far too stark.

'I'd also appreciate it if you'd talk with the senior scourgers. Maybe a little insight into the workings of the Commissariat?'

'No problem,' the pheguth replied. Damn the pain. Right behind his eyes. Like hot needles. Nearby, one of the sparring Sons lost a chunk of meat from his shoulder as his partner sliced in with a dummy bayonet. The man cried out as his wound squirted into the warm air.

The pheguth shivered. The cry felt so loud, like a physical slap, and it seemed to echo in his head, over and around.

'Are you all right, sir?' Mabbon asked.

'Fine. I'm fine,' the pheguth said, realising he was sweating profusely. 'Fine. Just the effects of transcoding. All this talk of commissars, I think. Touched a nerve, Mabbon. I have a thing about...'

...about

about

about

a thing about

about...

A rushing sound, like water down a drain. A humming. No light. Darkness. No light. A taste of blood.

And then Gaunt. Ibram Gaunt, in the full, brocaded uniform of a commissar, his eyes like slits, that damned superior expression he so loved to inflict on others. Gaunt was holding something. A bolt pistol. Holding it out, butt-first.

'Final request granted,' Gaunt said. Damn him, damn him, who did he think he was? Who did he think he was...

...he was

was

was

he was...

He wasn't.

It wasn't Gaunt at all. It was Desolane. The pistol was a flask of water. The light came up, as if lamps had been lit. Sound returned. So did the dry smell of the bocage field. Distantly, the pheguth could hear Mabbon ordering the men back.

'Into groups! Groups, now! Scourgers, get them back in line!'

'Pheguth?' Desolane said.

'Nhhn.'

'You fell, pheguth. You passed out.'

'time a lord–'

'What? Pheguth, what did you say?'

'I said… the only time a Lord General passes out is on his graduation review.'

'Are you all right?'

The pheguth sat up. His head swam. But the ache had gone. He breathed deeply and looked around. Silent, staring, the Sons of Sek stood all about him, their dummy weapons lowered. Desolane knelt down and offered up the flask to the pheguth's lips.

The water was deliciously cold.

'You fell–' Desolane began again.

'So help me up,' the pheguth said. His head was amazingly clear suddenly. Clearer than it had been in a long, long time.

Desolane lifted him to his feet. 'Your nose is bleeding,' the life-ward whispered.

The pheguth wiped his nose and smeared blood across his cheek. He looked at the rows of warriors. There was suspicion and disgust in their perspiring faces. Now that just wouldn't do.

'I'm sorry you had to see that,' he said, his voice suddenly strong, and carrying the way it had once done over the Phantine parade grounds. 'Weakness in an officer is not a thing for soldiers to see. And you are most certainly soldiers of the highest quality. You are the Sons of Sek.'

A murmur ran through the assembly.

'That was not weakness,' he cried. It was all returning now, the manner, the effortless rhetoric, the art of voice-pitch, the confidence of command. He'd forgotten how wonderful it felt. He'd forgotten how good he was at it. 'Not weakness, no. That was an ugly aftershock of a process known as mindlock. Can I trust you, soldiers? Can I trust you, friends, with the truth?'

The Sons hesitated, then they began to snarl out a wild assent.

He smiled, acknowledging them, playing them. He raised a hand, his real hand, for quiet. A hush immediately fell. 'You see,' he said, 'your enemy decided my brain was too valuable, my secrets so awesome, that you should never know them. Psykers placed a cage around my mind, a cage that months of careful work is now, finally, undoing. My mind is almost free again. My secrets are almost yours. Yours, and our beloved Anarch's!'

The men roared their approval. Wooden rifle blanks clattered together furiously.

'Pheguth?' Desolane whispered above the rapturous tumult.

Dabbing at his bloody nose, the traitor general turned towards the life-ward. 'Don't call me that. Not ever again. My memory is returning fast now. Like a rockslide. I have remembered things, Desolane. Even my own name. And that's how you'll address me in future.'

'H-how…?' Desolane asked.

Lord Militant General Noches Sturm didn't bother to reply. He turned to face the uproar coming from the ranks of the Sons of Sek. This time, he raised his augmetic hand, clenched in a fist. 'For the future!' he bellowed.

They began to cheer. Like animals. Like daemons.

Like conquerors.

TWENTY-TWO

NIGHT AND DAY had no particular delineation beneath the dank canopy of the Untill.

They walked, waded, and clambered, moving on through a permanent gloom fraught by warm fogs and miasmas of marsh gas. The sluggish green pools pulsed and bubbled, and unimaginable things snaked through the slick water, betrayed only by their rippling wakes. Other life clicked and fretted in the lowering black canopy above. What little light there was seemed as hard and unyielding as green marble.

This was not a place for men, for men had no mastery of it. They hadn't had it when they first arrived on the planet and named it Gereon, and they didn't have it now. Not even the Sleepwalkers, seasoned to the Untill's murky dangers. Though they had dwelt here for generations, they were only tenants, tolerated by the true rulers of the marshland.

For this was the domain of the insects. They were everywhere. They were lice in the hair, parasites on the skin, formations of tiny waders, a billion strong, hurrying upon the surface tension of the water. They were crawlers on tree bark, marching in formation, burrowers in mud, gnawers into wood. They criss-crossed the humid air on dank, trembling wings.

And in the swelter of the Untill, they had not been told when to stop growing. Moths swooped amidst the upper canopy like hawks, taking flying beetles as air-prey. Dragonflies thrummed across the glades, primordial gliders the size of vultures. Stalking grazers, bloated like balloons, stilted their way through the waterbeds, gorging on silt-dwelling creatures that they raked up with their mouthparts and then sucked dry.

Treading onwards, the Ghosts saw skaters the size of small deer, travelling over the water surface on hundreds of long, paired legs. They saw grubs like fat, pallid, glistening fingers, waving as they extruded from rotten trees. They saw mantis-spiders as big as hunting dogs dancing slow, jerky tangos with wasp-worms.

The wet air stank of gossamer. Gossamer, wood-rot, steam and stagnation.

The three scouts moved on ahead, trailing Eszrah ap Niht, who seemed to know where he was going. To Mkvenner's quiet disgust, Larkin had decided that the partisan's name was 'Ezra Night'. The nomenclature would undoubtedly stick. Larkin had a knack for coining simple names. They had become 'Gaunt's Ghosts' because of him, after all.

The tail end of the party was lagging. Feygor had not recovered consciousness, and Beltayn, Curth, Landerson, and sometimes Gaunt himself, took turns carrying him.

Rawne was tense. Gaunt had ordered him to keep the group together, but the slower the back-end got, the further the scouts led away.

He slopped to a halt in a glade where engorged, fist-sized aphids suckled in their hundreds around the albino taproots of a fallen mangrove. The forward party was now out of sight, and the only sign of the rest of them was some distant splashing behind him.

'Feth this,' he said.

'Agreed.' Cirk appeared, her weapon over her shoulder. Her skin was glowing with sweat, and dark half-circles stained the armpits of her jacket. Rawne didn't like her at all, but he found himself admiring her. And not for the first time. She was a damned attractive woman. Fully loaded, that would have been Murt Feygor's description. Her jacket was unbuttoned and loose, and her damp, clinging undervest accentuated her bosom as she strode towards him.

Cirk came right up to him, face to face. He swallowed hard. He could smell her musky perspiration. Her generous mouth curled in a slight smile. She tilted her chin down slightly and coyly widened her eyes.

'Uh, seen something?' she inquired.

Rawne realised he was staring at her. This was wrong. He knew it. She couldn't be trusted. That mark on her cheek. That... brand of Chaos. He forced himself to look at it. He tried to curb his libido by thinking about that sickening thing inside Cirk's arm. That did the trick. The fething imago. Rawne was at a loss to know why Gaunt hadn't just executed her. She was dangerous. For a while now, Rawne knew Cirk had been playing him off against Gaunt. She'd picked up on their old enmities, and since then she'd been siding with Rawne on every call, every argument. The woman was trying to build an alliance that Rawne wanted no part of. Ibram Gaunt would never, ever be Elim Rawne's friend, but for the good of the mission, there was no way he'd let this–

'Rawne? What's the matter?'

He glanced up and their eyes locked. Her gaze was full of simmering heat, hotter than the damn marsh itself. A promise of something illicit and taboo. Rawne tried to tear his eyes away to the cheek-brand. But now even that wretched mark on her cheek seemed to be just part of her allure. He wondered what it would feel like to touch the scars of the stigma. He–

Shocked by his own desires, he looked away. He was a soldier of the God-Emperor, feth it! Not the purest, he'd be the first to admit that. But he was an officer of the Guard. And he had a woman of his own. Since Aexe Cardinal, he'd enjoyed a liaison with Jessi Banda, the Verghast girl serving as a sniper in three platoon. Their affair was secret, but it meant something to him. For Throne's sake, Rawne had a lock of Banda's hair in a spent cartridge case around his neck!

'They're falling behind, major,' Cirk said.

'I know, major,' he replied.

What was wrong with him? According to Curth, the taint of this world was now so deep inside them, it was affecting their hormonal balance, their emotions, their self-control. Was that it? Were they all beginning to lose it, him included?

'Time to cut the poor man loose,' she said, wiping the sweat from her forehead on her jacket cuff. Her raised arm accented her full breasts.

'What?' he said.

'I said time to cut the poor man loose. What's the matter with you?'

Rawne hesitated. 'Nothing. Nothing. Not a thing. I just thought I saw a bug. There. On your... throat.'

'Is it gone?'

'Your throat?'

'No, idiot!'

'Yeah, it's gone.'

Rawne tore his eyes away from her considerable appeal. He thought of the mark. The brand on her cheek. He tried to remember Banda's face.

'You mean Feygor?'

'That's right. He's... lost.'

'We're not leaving Feygor behind,' Rawne replied, looking at the trees behind her. That was no better. The arrangement of the coiled branches seemed to mimic the shape of the mark on Cirk's cheek.

'Really? Why not?'

'Because we look after our own.'

Cirk laughed darkly. 'Tell that to Acreson. To Lefivre.'

'Give me a break, Cirk. Gaunt stuck his neck out to get them clear. So did I. They died well.'

'No such thing, major.'

'Whatever.'

Cirk shrugged. Throne, she was really beautiful, Rawne thought. Luminous. And the swirling mist behind her... for a second, the wafting vapour made shapes, pictures. Figures entwined. A man and a woman.

'Anyway, what I think hardly matters,' Cirk said. 'Your commander is about to ditch Feygor.'

'What?'

'I heard him say it.'

That, finally, snapped him out. He felt a new emotion, as primal as lust. Rawne started to move. 'Stay here. No, go get the scouts. Get them back.'

He ran back the way they'd come.

BELTAYN AND LANDERSON laid Feygor's body on a bulging root-mass, and tried to make him comfortable. Beltayn was trying to shoo the blood-flies away from Feygor's face.

'We can't carry him,' Gaunt said.

'We can, sir,' Beltayn said. 'All the way.'

'No, Bel,' said Gaunt. 'I mean we can't afford to carry him. It's slowing us down badly. Exhausting all of us.' He looked over at Curth, who had sat down on a muddy tussock and was cleaning the leeches off her calves. He'd never seen her look so tired. She was like a faded pict of herself, drained and bleached out.

'He's not dead yet,' she said, without looking up.

'I know, Ana–'

Curth got to her feet and sloshed over to them. She pushed Landerson and Beltayn aside and ran another check on Feygor's vitals.

'Murt's a feth-hard son of a bitch,' she said. 'It's gonna take a lot to kill him.'

Gaunt peered over her shoulder. Feygor's skin was abnormally pale and waxy. His eyes – closed – had sunken back into deep, dark pits and the flesh of his face was slack. Brown liver spots freckled his shoulders and arms, and Gaunt was rather afraid to ask Curth what they were. He suspected some kind of mould. A sweet, corrupted scent came out of the dying man with every shallow, ragged breath, and the flies seemed drawn in by it. Worst of all was Feygor's throat. The flesh around his implanted larynx augmetic was swollen and sore, and it was beginning to fester. It looked like the soft, expanding rind of a rotting ploin, about to burst with its own putrescence. Stinking yellow mucus threaded out of Feygor's chapped lips. Every weary breath rattled phlegm in the man's throat.

'He's going to die soon, isn't he Ana?' Gaunt asked.

'Shut up,' she snapped, sponging Feygor's infected neck.

'Ana, for my sake, and for Feygor's, tell me the truth.'

Curth looked around. There were tears in her eyes again. 'Shut up, Gaunt!'

'Just tell me one thing, ' Gaunt said. 'Is there anything else you can do for him?'

'I can–' She trailed off.

'Ana? Is there really anything else? Anything?'

Curth turned and punched at Gaunt. The blow struck his shoulder. She threw another punch, another, and then began pummelling against Gaunt's chest, hammering with the balls of her clenched hands. She was too weary to do any damage. He put his arms around her and pulled her close, pinning her thumping fists. She started to weep into his chest.

'There's nothing else, is there?'

'I've got… I've got nothing… nothing left… no drugs… no stuff… oh Throne…'

'All right,' he said, embracing her tightly. 'It's all right. This is just the way it goes sometimes.'

'Sir?' It was Landerson.

Gaunt slowly let go of Curth and allowed Beltayn to lead her over to a root-clump where she could sit and recover.

'Yes, Landerson?'

'I'd like to volunteer to carry Feygor, sir.'

'Noted, but–'

Landerson shook his head. 'I understand this, sir. I understand you need to ditch Feygor because he's slowing the team down. I understand the importance of your mission. But I'm not one of your team. If I fall behind, so be it. I'd just like to try, to give that man a chance.'

Gaunt looked Landerson in the eyes. He was amazed to feel tears of his own welling up. The man was offering such a sacrifice, and after all that–

'Landerson,' Gaunt began, sniffing hard and fighting to stay in control of himself. 'You'd be dooming yourself and I won't have that.'

Landerson was about to answer when Gaunt heard a snarl behind him. Rawne appeared out of nowhere and crashed into Gaunt, smashing him down into the water.

'Holy feth!' Beltayn cried.

Struggling, thrashing, the two figures surfaced. Rawne had Gaunt by the throat and was forcing him back down into the swamp. 'Feth you! Leave him to die? Feth you!' Rawne was screaming, water spraying from his face. 'You'd leave us all to die! Like you left Tanith to die!'

Blowing bubbles, Gaunt went under again.

'Holy feth!' Beltayn yelled again, and splashed forward to break up the fight. Landerson was with him.

'Let him go, sir!' Beltayn yelled, pulling on Rawne's arms.

'Feth you too!' Rawne shouted back.

'Major Rawne, stop it now!' Landerson cried. He grabbed Rawne by the collar and yanked hard. Rawne twisted backwards and Gaunt surfaced again, spluttering for air.

'Get off me!' Rawne bawled, and chopped Landerson across the windpipe so hard, he buckled and fell over, gasping.

Curth rose to her feet. 'What, now?' she said. 'Now? Right now? Are you fething kidding me, Elim?'

Rawne was too busy drowning Gaunt and fighting off Beltayn. Curth ran over to the floundering Landerson and propped him up out of the marsh water.

'Stop it! Stop it!' Beltayn yelled, yanking as hard as he could. Rawne swung round and smacked a fist into Beltayn's face. The adjutant blundered backwards.

Rawne locked both his hands around Gaunt's neck and dunked him yet again into the thick, green water.

'I don't fething believe this,' Curth barked. 'This is it, is it? The moment you finally decide to settle your score? Rawne, you're fething unbelievable! How many years have you waited and you choose now? Thanks a fething lot, you stupid bastard!'

'What?' Rawne said.

'Your feud with Gaunt! You decide to settle it now?'

Rawne swayed and blinked. 'What?' he repeated. He let go of Gaunt's neck. 'This isn't about him and me, this is about Feygor–'

Released, Gaunt came up out of the water and punched Rawne across the clearing.

Rawne slammed into a tree-bole, scraped his face on the bark, and then turned back.

Gaunt had the point of his warknife aimed at Rawne's throat. Straight silver.

'Are we really going to do this, Rawne?' Gaunt asked.

'I won't let you just leave him,' Rawne said, wiping his mouth.

Gaunt slowly put his blade away. 'I'm going to make allowances, Rawne. This place is making us crazy. We all knew that would be a risk when we signed up for this. I don't think any of us is really thinking straight any more. Gereon is screwing us up. Do you understand?'

Rawne nodded.

'But we have to try and hold this together. We have to try and keep our minds on the mission. Have you forgotten the mission, Rawne?'

'No, sir.'

'Have you forgotten the mission's classification?'

'No.'

'And you remember what that means? The mission is paramount. Everything else, everyone else, is expendable. We all understood that at the start. We all knew that a bad business like this might come along and we'd have to deal with it. Feth knows, we may yet face choices even harder than this one. But this is how it has to be.'

Rawne sighed. 'Yes. I know. Fine.'

Gaunt nodded. He looked at the others. 'Let's break here for thirty minutes. Rest and collect our wits.' To Rawne, he said 'Thirty minutes. Then I'll make the final decision on Feygor.'

'Don't just… leave him here to die,' Rawne said.

'I won't. I wasn't going to,' replied Gaunt. 'If the Emperor can't protect, then he can at least show mercy.'

The scout party appeared, brought back by Cirk. Brostin, Varl, Criid and Larkin were with them. Sensing that something had happened, Mkoll looked at Gaunt.

'We'll take a short rest here,' Gaunt said. Mkoll shrugged, and the scouts found places on the roots to sit.

'I'm sorry,' Curth said quietly to Gaunt. 'That's twice now I've lost it completely. I'm crying all the time, I don't know what's wrong with me–'

'Yes, you do,' Gaunt said. 'It's not you. So we'll forget about it.'

'All right, b–' Curth broke off. 'Hey, what's he doing?'

Gaunt looked round. Eszrah ap Niht was standing beside Feygor's body, studying him curiously.

Gaunt and Curth waded across to him, and Gaunt signalled Mkvenner to join them.

'Preyathee?' Gaunt asked.

Eszrah regarded the colonel-commissar with his dark, unreadable, mosaic-edged eyes and muttered something as he gestured to Feygor. It was too complicated for Gaunt to follow.

'Slow down,' Gaunt urged.

The Sleepwalker began to repeat himself, but it was still too complex. Mkvenner asked a question in proto-Gothic, and they exchanged a few words.

'He says his people have seen several cases of infections like this in the last few months,' Mkvenner said.

'Since Chaos came,' said Gaunt.

'Exactly,' Mkvenner nodded. 'The partisans had a way of treating it that sometimes worked. He's offering to try that, if you permit him.'

Gaunt glanced at Curth.

'Look,' she said, making a helpless gesture with her hands, 'I'm standing on the edge of Imperial medical science, gazing into the dark. At this point, anything's worth a try.'

'Right,' said Gaunt. He nodded to Eszrah. 'Do it.'

The Sleepwalker drew back the folds of his segmented cloak, and revealed a number of small gourd flasks suspended from his waist-belt. He selected one, opened the stopper, and wiped two fingers around the inside rim. When his fingers withdrew, they were smeared with a grey paste, the same colour as the pale dye that covered every centimetre of his skin. He leaned forward, and gently smudged the paste around Feygor's swollen throat. Feygor stirred slightly, but did not wake.

'What is that stuff?' Curth asked.

'Hwat beyit, soule?' Mkvenner asked and listened to the reply. He looked back at Gaunt and the doctor. 'It's… um… it's essentially moth venom.'

'What?' Curth spluttered. 'Moth venom?'

'Basically,' said Mkvenner.

'Fantastic,' said Curth. 'Maybe we could help Feygor by stabbing him as well.'

'Look,' said Mkvenner. 'As I understand it, the stuff works. The only way the partisans have survived over the centuries in an environment this toxic is to understand it. Their skin dye, that's for camouflage, and for ritual show, but it's made from ground-up scales from moth wings. It's built up an immunity in them. There are very few venoms in the Untill that can actually affect them now. They use a more concentrated version to tip their quarrels. That paste stuff has enough in it to purge taint infections.'

Curth exhaled as she considered this. 'There might be some sense in it,' she admitted. 'But what works for them may not work for us. Feygor's got no immunity.'

'Feygor's got no other chance, either.'

Eszrah finished his treatment and restoppered the flask. Then he crouched down beside Feygor, folded his arms, and waited.

THE REST PERIOD Gaunt had set was over. He'd let it overrun a little, in the hope that they might see some change in Feygor's condition. Forty minutes, forty-five. He was about to get up and call them all to order when he heard a strange, chilling moan.

Feygor was suffering some kind of violent fit. His body convulsed and his back arched. The noises coming out of him were made all the more distressing by the flat tone generated by his implant.

'Feth!' Curth cried. Everyone was already getting up and coming close. The partisan was gently trying to restrain Feygor.

Abruptly, Rawne's adjutant writhed to his feet, slithering down off the root ball. His flailing hands lashed out and knocked the Sleepwalker off him. His head was tilted back and his howling mouth was flecked with foam. Feygor's eyes had rolled back into their sockets.

'Grab him!' Gaunt yelled. 'Hold him down!'

Bonin was nearest, but the lunatic strength in Feygor's arms took the tough scout by surprise. Feygor threw Bonin back into the water.

And began to run.

Wailing, arms waving like a man on fire, he ran blindly, crashing into trees, tearing through undergrowth. Clouds of moths burst up into the air like confetti, disturbed by his frantic progress.

Gaunt and Rawne ran after him. Rawne shot a threatening, malevolent look at the Sleepwalker as he ran past him. 'Hold the team here!' Gaunt yelled over his shoulder to Mkoll.

They ran out into the marsh, ducking under fibrous branches and shawls of lank moss, their boots churning up the muck. Already, Feygor was out of sight in the gloom, but they could still hear him, and still see his footprints in the water.

Dark brown blooms of disturbed sediment stained the green pool in a long, twisting line.

'Well, that's it then,' Rawne spat as they ran on.

'I was trying to help him,' muttered Gaunt.

'Good work,' said Rawne.

'Wasn't anything better than nothing?'

'I suppose.'

'The toxin must have been too much.'

The miserable screaming came from off to their left now.

'He's doubled back,' said Rawne. 'Feth, he sounds like he's in agony.'

'There he is!' Gaunt cried.

Feygor's pale, ragged figure had stumbled to a halt in the next clearing. His awful moans had subsided and he had slumped forward against the trunk of a leaning cycad. His scabbed hands clawed and dug weakly at the bark.

Gaunt and Rawne slowed down as they approached. Gaunt glanced at Rawne and took out his silenced autopistol.

'He won't know a thing,' Gaunt said. 'Better it's quick, than a drawn-out death by poison.'

Rawne blocked Gaunt with a raised hand. There was a terrible look of fatalism in his eyes.

'Better it's me,' he said.

Gaunt hesitated.

'For this sort of kindness, it should be a friend.'

Gaunt nodded, and handed the pistol to Rawne.

Rawne waded across the pool, clutching the pistol to his chest. 'Golden Throne of Earth, forgive me...' he whispered. Feygor had slumped down in a heap, his face against the tree, his trailing arms, curled around it.

Rawne racked the gun and aimed it at Feygor's head.

At the sound of the slide, Feygor suddenly looked round. He stared at the gun Rawne had levelled at him.

'What the feth is that for?' he asked.

TWENTY-THREE

'Is THIS GOING to take much longer?' Sturm asked. Desolane looked at the hunch-backed master of fysik and the man quickly shook his head.

'Not much longer now, pheguth,' Desolane said.

'Desolane…?' There was a warning note in Sturm's voice.

'My apologies, ph– My apologies, sir. I am having trouble getting used to the new name.'

'Old name, Desolane. My old name.'

The master of fysik completed his battery of tests. He lifted the articulated chrome scanner hood away from Sturm's head and removed the needles from his scalp.

'You may sit up,' the master of fysik said.

Sturm sat, small motors whirring the examination couch back upright to support him. The traitor general gazed with some distaste across the hall of fysik. Ornate medical apparatus was arranged all around: sensoriums, transfusers, servo-surgery tables, wound baths, blood drains and metal frames for laser scalpel assemblies. Steel surgical tools were laid out on bright red silk. Bottles and flasks containing fibrous organic specimens in urine-coloured fluid lined the shelves, and on the walls were charts and parchments, maps of nerve distribution, blooding points, trepanning techniques and other anatomies described in brown ink. Articulated skeletons, some human, some sub-human, hung from metal frames, their bones and joints labelled with parchment tags.

The master of fysik pulled open Sturm's right eye and peered in, reading the capillaries of the retina through a lensed scope. 'Your headache?'

'Barely there.'

'And the anomia is passing?'

'I remember my own name. The names of others who were just blank figures in the fog that clouded my memory until this morning.'

'There is considerable improvement in brain activity,' the master said to Desolane. 'But I can detect very little physiological trauma. I recommend the psykers see him as soon as possible.'

'More transcoding?' snapped Sturm, getting to his feet.

'We must make sure the collapsing mindlock has left no nasty surprises,' Desolane said. 'This is the most critical time.'

Sturm was naked, but he did not cower. The change in him was quite startling. Even his posture had altered. There was a marked difference in his bearing and even the tone of his voice. Confidence, and a regal arrogance that had straightened his back and squared his shoulders.

Desolane held out his tunic.

'No,' said Sturm. 'Not those rags. I can't abide them. Find me something suitable to wear, or I'll go naked.'

Desolane turned and barked orders to the footmen at the door of the hall. They vanished in a hurry.

'I take it the Plenipotentiary has been informed,' Sturm asked, idly inspecting some of the bladed chrome tools laid out on a nearby trolley.

'He has. He is making arrangements to come here as soon as possible. Command echelon leaders, strategists and other key ordinals have also been summoned. After the transcoding, you will need to rest well. The next few days will be demanding.'

Sturm nodded. 'I want a better room. With a proper bed in it. And no more shackles.'

'Sir, I–' Desolane began.

'I want a better room, a proper bed and no more shackles. Is that clear?'

'Yes,' said Desolane.

THE FOOTMEN RETURNED with a uniform. It was the dress garb of a sirdar of the Occupation force, though all rank pins and badges had been removed. Black boots and shirt, green breeches and a long green jacket. Sturm dressed quietly and then admired his reflection in a looking glass hanging on the wall of the fysik hall.

He stared at his image for some time. He'd seen his own face in mirrors several times since entering custody, indeed the transcoders had often shown him his reflection in the hope that it might aid the loosening of his memory. That had been frightening. The face he'd seen had been unknown to him, an alien thing.

Now it was like an old friend. Every line and fold and crease had a comfortable familiarity. He scratched at his stubbled chin.

'I want to shave,' he told the life-ward. 'This is unacceptable.'

'Yes, sir,' said Desolane. 'But first, the psykers.'

THEY WALKED TOGETHER along the echoing halls and galleries of the bastion, passing hurrying servants, patient soldiers, lean excubitors and chattering gangs of ordinals. Desolane noticed that the pheguth no longer shuffled. He marched, back straight.

An impish little creature was waiting for them at the door of the loathsome transcoding chamber. He was little more than a metre tall, his bent, simian frame shrouded in a red velvet robe with gold-thread decoration. The hem of the robe spread out over the flagstones. He wore a mechanical harness around his torso, the front of which formed a lectern that was braced against his chest. Fastened to this was a black metal printing machine, with rows of wiry letter levers and a thick roll of parchment wound into the spindle-lock. The little man had the lever section hinged up as they approached, and was carefully applying ink to the back of the letter press using a suede paddle. He looked up. His eyes were beady and he had nothing in the way of a nose, but his mouth was a lipless grimace of exposed gums and discoloured, spade-like teeth. In place of ears, he had augmetic microphones sutured into his flesh, and a wire armature from each secured flared brass ear trumpets to either side of his head.

His name was Humiliti, and Desolane had summoned him.

'What for?' Sturm asked.

'He is a lexigrapher. He will accompany you at all times, and record your comments so that nothing can be lost.'

Humiliti closed his machine's lever section with a sharp metallic clatter, put the suede paddle back in a pouch at his side, and flexed his long bony fingers for a moment. Then he began to type on the keys, a jangling sound, and the parchment roll began to turn.

Desolane opened the door, and Sturm entered. The little lexigrapher waddled after him. Sturm sat down on the seat and the electric cuffs immediately closed over his wrists and ankles.

'They will not be necessary,' he said, and heard the lexigrapher record the words. After a moment's pause, the cuffs disengaged. The chair tilted back until he was looking at the arched roof.

'Pheguth,' a voice whispered.

'Not this time,' he replied.

'Again, we begin.'

Sturm heard the shuffling, and felt the chamber go chill. Foetid fingers picked the rubber plugs from the holes in his skull. Then, making their distinctive high pitched squeal, the psi-probe needles swung in and slipped into the holes.

Sturm grunted slightly in discomfort.

'Let us start again at the beginning,' the psi-voice commanded.' Your rank?'

'Lord militant general.'

'Your name?'

'Noches Sturm.'

'How do you come to be here?'

Sturm cleared his throat. Over the murmuring acoustics of the warp filling his head, he could hear the damned lexigrapher jabbing away at his machine. 'As I understand it,' he replied, 'I was a prisoner aboard a military transport ship that was caught in an ambush near Tarnagua. When the attackers realised they had captured a senior branch officer of the Imperial Guard, I was taken directly to a safe world for interrogation. That was where the mindlock was discovered. I was then sent here to Gereon, away from the front line, so that the mindlock could be undone.'

'What do you understand of the mindlock, Noches?' another psi-voice asked. This one sounded distressingly like a small child.

'It is a standard provision. In cases where a subject knows sensitive information. The guild can blank a man's mind entirely, but that does not allow for any future recovery of his memory.'

'Your mind is full of secrets, Noches,' the male voice said. 'Intelligence of the highest level of confidentiality. Why would they not have just blanked you?'

'I've no idea,' Sturm said. *Chatter chatter* went the lexigraph machine.

'That is not true,' an old, female voice asked. 'Is it? Think about it. This is a memory you can reach.'

Sturm closed his eyes. He realised he could remember now. It felt amazing. 'I was being prepared for trial. Court martial. The Commissariat did not want my mind wiped, because I would not be able to face their cross-examination. But until the trial date, it was considered too risky to leave me... accessible. The Guild Astropathicus placed the mindlock on me, securing my secrets. They intended to remove it at the time of the trial.'

'You didn't like that much, did you, Noches?' the child-voice asked.

'I hated it. I implored them not to do it. But they did it anyway. It was monstrous. Numbing. Afterwards, I had no idea what they'd done. Just the nagging memory that something barbaric had been accomplished in my mind. It took everything away. I'm only now just understanding quite how much was stolen.'

'Your memories are returning rapidly.'

'Yes, but I'm not just talking about facts and figures, names and dates. I'm not talking about the empirical data they shut away. I had forgotten myself. My character. My nature. My soul. They had taken my personality. The man you have been transcoding these last few months was just a shell. He was not Noches Sturm. I'd forgotten even how to be myself.'

There was a pause. The acoustic murmur circled around him.

'Hello?' Sturm called.

'Why were you in custody, Noches?' asked the male voice. 'Why were you facing trial?'

'It was a mistake. I was betrayed.'

'Explain.'

'I was serving in the defence of Vervunhive, on the planet Verghast. It was a bitter fight, and for a while it seemed we would be overrun. But my worst enemy was a commissar in the Guard. Our paths had crossed before, and there was some animosity between us. I was prepared to let it go – we had a war to win, no time for petty squabbles. But he manipulated the situation and accused me of forsaking my post. Trumped up charges. But he was a commissar, and enjoyed some popularity in that dark time. He made the charges stick, and, with the backing of his superiors in the Commissariat, kept me incarcerated and forced me to trial.'

'Doesn't the Commissariat ordinarily perform summary executions?' the child-voice asked.

'On low-lifes and dog-troops. Not on lord militant generals. My family has powerful connections to the High Lords. There would have been uproar if he'd taken my life.'

'What was his name?'

Sturm smiled. The one thing that the mindlock had never closed off was that name. 'Ibram Gaunt. May he burn in hell.'

The voices swooped and whispered around him.

'Are we done?' Sturm asked.

'We are pleased with the state of your mind, Noches. Your memory has almost entirely returned. The last tatters of the mindlock are falling away from your psyche. Our work is all but finished.'

'And I thank you for it,' said Sturm. 'Even on the days you made me scream. I'm glad to have myself back.'

'There is one last question,' the female voice asked.

'Ask it.'

They asked it together, all three voices as one chorus. 'When you first came to us, you swore allegiance to the Anarch. You promised that once we had unlocked your mind, you would renounce the cause of the False Emperor and fight with us against his forces.'

'I did.'

'But today you have admitted that you are a different person now. You have told us that the pitiful wretch who swore that oath was not Noches Sturm. So, we ask you... have you changed your mind?'

'You have changed my mind,' Sturm said. 'If I'm lying, you'll read this in my head. So listen well. I served the Imperium loyally, and devoted my life to the Throne. But the Imperium turned on me, and kicked me down like a dog. There is no going back. The Imperium has made me its enemy, and it will live to wish it hadn't.'

Behind the chair, Humiliti's type-levers were clattering almost frantically.

'I swear allegiance to the Anarch, whose word drowns out all others,' said Sturm. 'Does that answer your question?'

THE SLEEPWALKER LED them up through the great basin of the Untill, through the steaming glades of the Niht. They skirted vast thickets of crimson thorn, so dense that there was no way through. They waded through green water, through stinking amber bogs. When the water level finally began to drop, where the land shelved up and away, the world became a mire of thick, grey mud. White globe fungus clustered on the black bark of the gnawed trees. Some of it was photoluminous, and created clearings of frosty blue-white radiance that the moths flocked to in their millions. Blizzards of them swirled through the air. There was still no sunlight. The canopy above was an impenetrable black roof.

The team pushed on. It had taken them two full days' march from the partisan camp to reach these upland marshes. The temperature had dropped by several degrees, and the humidity was less. Consequently, they felt chilled. Their clothes, soaked from hours in the thigh-deep water, clung to them. They were hungry and they were exhausted. They had regular rest-breaks, but it was almost impossible to find a place to sleep in the liquid mud.

However, some spirit had returned to them. Feygor was alive. His health was still poor, and he was by far the weakest member of the team. But he was conscious, lucid and walking. The infection in his throat was less angry. Eszrah ap Niht's poison paste may have nearly killed him, but it had saved his life too. Neither Rawne nor Gaunt spoke of how close they'd come to the mercy killing.

Their route led on through the thick grey sludge and the rank trees. These higher marshes were the haunt of lizards: bright tree scurriers, and balloon-eyed amphibians that lurked under stones and fallen logs and took moths out of the air with whipping, adhesive tongues. A bladdery, burping chorus of amphibian voices bubbled and popped all around them as they walked.

Their rations were all gone, and hunger would have long since killed them all, leaving their picked bones forgotten in an Untill glade. But Eszrah provided. He showed the scouts some basic tricks for finding game, and taught them what was edible and what should be shunned. The Sleepwalker made most kills himself, using his mag-bow. He allowed each scout in turn to try his hand with it. Mkvenner took to it best.

Curth used the remnants of her medical kit to analyse the partisan's poison pastes, and also scrutinise the prey that was brought in. Some things, she ruled, only Eszrah's immunity could deal with. But there were certain types of mud-eel, and a rat-like tree lizard that they could all ingest, provided they were carefully roasted or boiled. Brostin's flamer, still misfiring, at last had a use as a cooking tool. Gaunt had considered ordering Brostin to ditch the weapon. It was a Chaos thing. But in the circumstances, given the taint inside them all, it had seemed ridiculous to worry. He was glad now he hadn't. Without it, they would not have eaten.

On one occasion, Gaunt sat with Eszrah as they finished a meal. The partisan allowed him to examine his weapon.

'Preyathee, soule,' Gaunt asked, tapping the bow. 'Hwat yclept beyit?'

'Reynbow, beyit,' Eszrah replied. He was delicately picking meat from a spindly frog-bone with his small, white teeth.

'Reyn-bow, seythee?' Gaunt repeated.

Eszrah nodded. 'Thissen brande sowithe yitt we shalle reyn yron dartes thereon the heddes of otheren kinde, who gan harm makeyit on us.'

A rain-bow, to rain quarrels on the heads of the enemy. Gaunt smiled. He'd seen that. Emperor bless the nightwalkers.

* * *

THE TRAIL LOOPED north-west now, following the lip of another deep miasmal basin. They kept to the upper ground, the piled mud, slithering along the edges of the frog territory, their legs caked with clay. They passed another forest of crimson thorns, this one the largest they had yet seen, and then wandered the fringes of an eerily silent woodland, crisp with leaf mulch, where the trees were straight and tall and thin, like spears planted into the ground. Beyond that, reed beds furred a quagmire where flies billowed, then rose onto a crusty black slope of forest that stretched for several kilometres.

The trees here were ancient and gnarled, twisted into grotesque shapes and leprous deformations. There was a constant creaking sound, and Gaunt realised it was the canopy in motion. The trees were moving in the wind. He was painfully tired, but this roused him. That was a good sign, surely?

A little further on, Eszrah hushed them down into cover. Higher up the slope from them, something wandered past in the gloom. No one saw it clearly, but they all felt its footfalls shake the ground and heard its snorting breath. The drier uplands of the Untill were evidently the hunting grounds of the marshland's most massive predators.

Three hours later, Bonin was the first of them to see the light. He was scouting ahead through the mossy groves, and at first he thought it was a strange, white-barked tree, perfectly straight and branchless. Then he realised it was a single shaft of daylight spearing down through the interminable dark canopy.

He walked under it, and turned his face upwards, circling slowly, smiling, as the precious light flooded into his eyes.

'This way!' he called. The others quickly joined him, several cheering the sight. They gathered around it for a short while, some of them just daring to reach their fingertips out into the beam, others doing what Bonin had done and basking under it. Even Cirk touched the beam, as if for luck.

Only Eszrah ap Niht kept well away.

UPLIFTED, THEY PRESSED on, making better time. They found other shafts of light, then they became commonplace as the tree cover finally began to thin. The Niht reduced to a pale twilight. The ground became firmer.

Surely, we've begun to reach the far edge of the Untill now, Gaunt thought. Many of the Ghosts were laughing and joking about their trek being at an end.

'Ask him,' Gaunt said to Mkvenner. 'Ask him how much further before we reach the end of this place.'

Mkvenner nodded, and phrased the question to Eszrah. He frowned at the answer.

'Well?' asked Gaunt.

'He doesn't know, sir,' said Mkvenner. 'He's never been this far before.'

TWENTY-FOUR

DAY WAS BREAKING over the Lectica heartlands, revealing the misty patchwork of the endless bocage in soft russets, greens and yellows. This vast territory was the breadbasket of Gereon, the most productive of all its agricultural provinces. In the distance, like a blue mark against the horizon, lay the heartland massif, an upthrust of mountains crowned with cloud. So far away and yet, at last, in sight.

The early sky was glassy, and threaded with ropes of jumbled clouds like twists of cotton. Rawne lay in the long grass and watched them. Every damn one had a discernable shape. There, a woman on a horse. There, a larisel. That one was a bird, or maybe a pair of narrowed eyes. That one, a hand holding a knife.

He was going mad. He knew that now. He rolled over onto his back and closed his eyes, not wishing to see any more. The frail sunlight fell on his dirty face. It felt hot after their days in the sunless Niht.

They were all sick. All of them. Some, like Feygor, physically infected. Some, like Curth, emotionally disturbed. They'd been warned about it, by the medicae and the priests, before they'd embarked, but a warning is only ever a warning. There was no way they could have prepared for the reality.

Rawne was seeing symbols everywhere he looked. He knew it was the taint doing it to his mind, but that didn't make it any easier. He saw images in clouds, in leaf-patterns, in shadows, in the grass, in the shape of stones. Every one was specific and could be given a name. Every one had a specific meaning.

Even now, with his eyelids closed, he could see symbols made by the spots and shapes drifting against the red. An eel, a ploin, a full-breasted woman. A stigma.

He opened his eyes.

Everywhere, he saw the obscene mark Cirk wore on her cheek. There it was again, in that clump of grass. There, in the dried grey clay adhering to his toecap. There, in the lines of his palm, the whorls of his fingerpads.

'Rawne!'

He looked up. 'What?'

Gaunt was calling. Rawne got to his feet and went over to the others. The way they were grouped around Gaunt made the shape of the mark too. Except one part was missing. And by stepping up to join with them, he would make the shape complete.

IT HAD TAKEN another full day's march to travel between that first shaft of light Bonin had found to this, the edge of the heartland proper. The way had led through miserable woodland and deep gulches of caked earth where weeds grew in thickets, waist-deep. They had been drawn on to the light, to the promise of actual day behind the thinning trees.

Then had come the ascent up the shoulder of the Untill's deep bowl, through blasted uplands thick with scrub and loose stone. The trees here were bare and dead, thorny antlers of desiccated wood breaking from the steep ground. They saw emaciated grox and other livestock turned feral that had clearly run free from the adjacent heartlands and were now foraging in the flinty heath. One made a good supper, the best they'd yet had on Gereon.

Beyond the heath land, the ground became grassy and they entered the boundary forest of old woodland that fringed the western edge of the Untill. Gaunt could see how unnerved Eszrah ap Niht had become. He kept stopping to sniff the strange new air, and sometimes lingered behind, blinking up at the sky.

'He's never seen it before,' Mkvenner advised Gaunt.

'I realised that.'

'He's crying all the time,' Mkvenner added.

'It's just the light,' Curth said. 'He's not used to the light. His eyes are watering.'

Varl raked through his battered pack, and produced his prized sunshades. He liked to wear them to look cool off duty. Throne alone knew why he'd brought them.

He gave them to Eszrah.

'There you go, Ezra Night,' he said. 'Take them. They're yours, mate.'

The partisan was puzzled, and kept trying to give them back, until Mkvenner slowly explained their purpose. Eszrah put them on. An odd smile flickered across his face. More than ever, with the dark, gleaming lenses masking his eyes, he looked like a human moth.

'Ven, tell him he can go back now. He can go back and rejoin his kind. Thank him for me, carefully. He's done more for us than I could ever have expected.'

Mkvenner came back a few minutes later. 'He won't go, sir,' he said.

'Why not?' Gaunt asked.

Mkvenner cleared his throat. 'Because he's yours, sir.'

'What?'

'He's your property, sir.'

Gaunt went over and talked to Eszrah himself. Mkvenner had to join them to help out. The Sleepwalker was quite definite about it. In return for the efforts made by Gaunt and his team in defending the partisan camp, Cynhed ap Niht had given them one of his sons. It appeared that the partisans were terribly literal people. When Gaunt had originally asked them for a guide to lead them through the Untill, Cynhed had understood him to be requesting permanent ownership of a Sleepwalker. No little wonder he had refused.

But Eszrah's father had felt duty bound after the battle with Uexkull's murderers. He'd given them the guide they had been asking for. Literally given Gaunt one of his sons. Forever. As a gesture of thanks.

'You go back now,' Gaunt told Eszrah. 'You've done all I asked of you. Go back to your father.'

Mkvenner translated. Eszrah frowned and queried again.

'Please, go back,' Gaunt said.

Eszrah made to take off the sunshades.

'He can keep those,' Varl said.

They left Eszrah ap Niht standing alone in the skirts of the forest.

BUT HE FOLLOWED them, at a distance.

'He's not going away,' Mkoll said.

'Ven, go talk to him again,' Gaunt said. 'Make him understand.'

When Mkvenner came back, Ezra Night was with him, wearing his sunshades like a trophy.

'He won't be told, sir,' Mkvenner said. 'I think it's a cultural thing. A matter of honour. His father told him to come with you and guide you, and that's what he's going to do. Quite possibly forever. Don't ask him to go back again. He's never been this far before, and he's not entirely sure of the way. Besides, asking him to go back is the same as asking him to disobey his father's strict instructions. He loves his father, sir. He's made a vow. I don't think you should expect him to break it.'

Gaunt nodded. He turned to Eszrah and held out his hand. Eszrah ap Niht took it gently.

'You're one of us now,' Gaunt said. Eszrah seemed to understand. He smiled.

It was a strange moment of union that Gaunt would remember for the rest of his life.

SO, AT DAWN, under the hem of the woodland, Gaunt gathered his battered team around him. Beyond, the bocage beckoned, tranquil. He knew that the tranquility was an illusion. Briefings had reported the heartland to be the most securely held territory on Gereon.

And also, the location of their target.

'We need good rest, food and resupply,' Gaunt began.

'There's a village about three kilometres north-west of here,' Mkoll said. 'It appears to be deserted.'

'We'll start there. More importantly, we need to find out where we are exactly. Cirk?'

She shrugged. 'Lectica, the eastern fringe. Beyond that, I have no idea.'

'Mr Landerson?' Gaunt asked.

'That town in the distance could be Hedgerton. But then again, it could be half a dozen heartland communities. I'm sorry.'

'Let's head for the village,' Gaunt said.

THE PLACE WAS no more than a clutch of abandoned farmhouses, a farrier's shed, a grain store and a small templum. All of it was overgrown, the windows shattered, weeds festering around the doorposts.

They approached cautiously in the warm sunlight. Insects buzzed. The scouts spread wide, circling the place. There was no sign of life. The village had been vacated months before, probably at the time of the invasion, and no one had visited it since.

They split up and searched a few of the dwellings, recovering some dried goods, salted meats and jars of preserves from the pantries. Beltayn found an old shotgun and some kerosene lanterns. In one upstairs room, Curth discovered a doll in an empty cot. It made her cry again. She swore and raged against the weakness that the taint had bred into her. Criid found her and tried to calm her down. Then she saw the empty cot and began to cry too. It was a blessing for Curth. She forced her emotions into check so she could comfort her friend.

Feygor and Varl searched another house. As soon as they were inside, Feygor saw an old bed with a ratty straw mattress. He laid himself down on it.

When Varl came back to find him, Feygor was fast asleep. Varl sat down on the end of the bed and watched over him.

Rawne pushed his way into the next farmhouse and found a table set for dinner. Six places, cutlery, plates. A charcoal mass sat in the pot on the cold stove. Dinner had been abandoned in a hurry.

Rawne sat down at the head of the table and gazed at the settings. They made the shape of an oared boat. Here was the shape of a rising sun. Rawne reached out and rearranged some of the cutlery, and pushed plates into new positions.

That was better. Now they made the mark of the stigma.

IN THE FARRIER'S shed, Larkin and Bonin found a half-empty tank of promethium that had been used to fuel the smithy furnace.

'Go get Brostin,' Bonin said.

The big man appeared a few moments later and, with a delighted chuckle, began to replenish his canister tanks.

The micro-bead pipped.

'One,' Gaunt acknowledged.

'Mkoll. Come to the templum, sir. Bring Landerson.'

GAUNT AND LANDERSON walked into the gloom of the village templum. Like all the buildings in this remote farm community, it was little more than a wooden shack. Sunlight pierced in through holes in the wallboards and lit up the dust the visitors were disturbing. Rough wooden chairs were arranged in rows, facing down the nave to the brass aquila suspended over the altar. Gaunt walked forward and knelt before it. He made the sign of the eagle, and began to utter the *Renunciation of Ruin*.

There was a good chance this was the last undesecrated Imperial shrine on the planet.

Gaunt closed his eyes. In the last few nights, he had started to dream again, for the first time since his arrival on Gereon. These recent dreams had been so vivid; they played back now across his mind. Sabbat, always beckoning him, although sometimes she looked like Cirk. That was fine. As long as the beati was with him, it didn't matter what guise she took.

But there were noticeable absences in these renewed dreams. Some of his long-lost friends were no longer coming to him during slumber. Slaydo was still there, though faint and transparent. Gaunt had seen Zweil too, and the wizened priest had been laughing. But there had been no sign of Bragg. No Vamberfeld either. And Gaunt couldn't remember the last time he'd seen Colm Corbec's face.

Worst of all, Brin Milo still hadn't appeared to him. Gaunt still hadn't seen Milo in his dreams since leaving Herodor. But, and this made him uneasy, there was always the screaming. The man screaming in the void. Who the hell was that? He was quite certain he knew the voice...

Ibram Gaunt took dreams seriously. He believed they were the only conduit through which the God-Emperor could make his purpose understood to the common man. Gaunt hadn't always thought that way, but the visions that had led him and the Ghosts to Herodor had been so real, he now regarded every single dream as a message.

He was glad they had come back at last, no matter how disquieting they seemed.

'Sir?'

Mkoll called him over to a massive book he was leafing through.

'What is this?'

'Parish records, sir,' Mkoll replied. 'Look here.' He opened a dusty page and tracked a dirty finger down the copperplate entries. 'Births and deaths. Marriages.'

'This is what you wanted me to see?'

Mkoll folded shut the heavy, brass-cornered volume and then reopened it on its title page.

'See?'

'Parish registry of Thawly Village,' Gaunt read. 'Landerson?'

Landerson hurried over to them.

'Thawly? Know it?'

Landerson shook his head. 'Sorry, sir. I don't. I could ask Cirk...'

'Never mind that,' said Mkoll. 'There's more.'

He unfolded the page and spread it out. It was a flaking chart of the parish boundaries. It showed Thawly and the nearby bocage towns.

'Great Throne...' Gaunt said. 'We've got a map.'

THEY GATHERED IN the porch of the templum, and Gaunt showed them the old chart. 'Mr Landerson was right. The town over there is Hedgerton. And that's Leafering. Take a look. We're located now.'

'So, where's the target?' Rawne asked.

'Just off the map this way, beyond Furgesh, here. You see?'

Rawne saw all too well. He saw the way their shadows made the shape of a mantis on the porch floor.

And he saw the mark on Gaunt's cheek, the one Uexkull's knuckles had gouged, and which Gaunt had refused to allow to be bandaged. It was scabbing over now, but the shape was unmistakable. The witchmark of Chaos. The stigma. Just like the one that daemon-beauty Cirk wore so proudly.

Gaunt had been branded.

'Isn't it about time you let us in on your mission, sir?' Cirk was asking.

'Soon, major. Very soon,' Gaunt replied. 'Look at the map, tell me what you know.'

Landerson bent forward. 'Hedgerton is a small place. All we're likely to find there are glyfs and excubitors. Leafering is more important. Its a large community, and last I knew there was a cell faction active there. Major Cirk?'

'Landerson's right.' said Cirk. 'There's a good chance of making a connection in Leafering. But it's garrisoned. A well-maintained hab, with a vox-base and lots of Occupation troopers. Not to mention wirewolves.'

'I can do wirewolves,' Curth retorted. 'They don't scare me.'

Gaunt decided not to mention the fact that the reason Curth had beaten the wirewolf was long gone.

'A vox-base? Are you sure, Cirk?'

She shrugged. 'Last time I checked.'

Gaunt smiled. To Rawne, that twisted the witchmark into even more obscene shapes.

'Leafering's the one,' Gaunt announced. 'Definitely.' He paused. 'Varl, where's Feygor?'

'I left him sleeping, sir,' Varl said.

'Good advice,' Gaunt said. 'Let's all get some decent sleep and move in the morning.'

NIGHT FELL OVER the hamlet, cool and black. In the various dwellings, the Ghosts had found beds and were sleeping deeper than they had since planetfall. Nobody cared about the musty smell of the cot sheets, the dampness. Compared with the grey ooze of the Untill, it was luxury.

Eszrah ap Niht didn't sleep. He took off his sunshades and hooked them carefully over his belt. It was night now, something he understood.

He saw movement in the hamlet's narrow street and followed it. It was the man called Rawne. He was slipping between the houses, a silver knife in his hand.

Eszrah slid an iron quarrel into the mouth of his reynbow.

GAUNT HAD CHOSEN a bed in the upper floor of a cottage. The sheets were rank and mildewed, so he lay down on top of them and slept in his clothes.

He was vaguely aware of the chamber door opening. He looked up, into the dark, and saw a woman framed against the starlight from the window.

'Ana?'

She took off her jacket and dropped it onto the floor. Then she sat down on the end of the bed and yanked off her boots. The rest of her clothes quickly followed.

'Ibram,' she whispered. He took her in his arms and they kissed. They both laughed as she struggled to pull off his clothing.

'Ana...' he whispered.

'Shhh...' she said.

HIS STRAIGHT SILVER in his hand, Rawne edged up the cottage stairs in the dark. From above him came faint noises. He trod up the next few steps. Now he could hear orgasmic cries through the thin lathe walls of the cottage.

Then silence.

Rawne went up the last few stairs, quiet as a shadow, and carefully opened the chamber door.

He looked in.

Naked, sleeping, Gaunt and Cirk lay wrapped in each other, their limbs entwined. Just like the symbol Rawne had seen in the Untill mists.

He shut the door and went downstairs again. The business end of Eszrah ap Niht's mag-bow suddenly loomed in his face.

Rawne sheathed his warblade.

'Go to sleep,' he told the partisan. 'Just go to sleep.'

GAUNT WOKE WITH a start. It was early, dark still. He had been dreaming that he was sharing his bed. Confused memories flooded back. He reached his hand out and found the mouldering sheets were still warm to the touch.

Someone had been there with him. He had vivid recall now of soft skin. Of urgency. Of heat.

'Ana?' he called out. 'Ana?'

THEY LEFT THAWLY as the sun rose, hazy and red, above the fields. Decent rest and the chance to wash out clothes and kit at the village pump had lifted their mood. Even Feygor seemed a little better, with some colour back in his face.

Mkoll set a brisk pace. They followed the village track until it joined a lane between fields, which in turn linked to a country road. For the first two hours of the day, they saw no one, but as the sun climbed higher, a few transports came up and down the road, so they left it and cut out across the fields, making a direct line for Leafering.

The heartland fields were in a much better state of repair than the farmlands around Ineuron had been. The invaders had maintained horticulture, and there was evidence of extensive planting programs and the use of pesticides. The bocage was a resource the Archenemy intended to use to keep its Occupation force fed, perhaps even generate food supplies that would be shipped off-world to help feed their front-line hosts.

As they got closer to Leafering, they saw signs of more disturbing land use. Huge field zones, some created by the systematic clearance of the old hedgerows to join smaller fields together, had been turned into industrial plantations. The air stank of fertilisers, and the fields were coated with a thick crust of pinky nitrates. Out of this grew row after row of thick, black, fleshy stalks on which millions of bulbous mauve fruits were developing.

'These aren't local production measures,' Cirk said.

'Nor a local crop, I'll bet,' Gaunt replied. Over the years, he'd read many reports of the Archenemy mass-planting xeno-crops on captured agri-worlds like Gereon. Highly resistant to disease and climate, perhaps hybridised for accelerated growth, these plantations rapidly tripled or quadrupled the planet's crop yield, but at huge cost to the planet's eco-sphere. After a few decades of xenoculture, the planet would be left barren and infertile, all the organics stripped from the topsoil. He wondered if Cirk had any idea what these plantations would mean for the future of her world.

'If you ever get the chance,' he said, 'advise the resistance to target these plantations. You don't want them here, even more than you don't want the Archenemy.'

She regarded him with a strange expression. There'd been an odd look in her eyes all morning, come to that. Gaunt was about to ask her about it when Bonin raised a warning and they all sought cover in the thick hedges that ran along the length of the plantation. A machine was approaching down the field. It looked a little like a stalk-tank, its central body-sections propelled on eight arachnoid limbs. But these limbs were more than twenty metres tall, so that the vehicle towered over the ground, as if on stilts. It straddled the plantation rows, a set of feet on either side of the planting line, so its body hung above the crop. As it walked, it exhaled noxious clouds of pesticide from ducts in its belly.

The Ghosts slipped away through the hedge, along the quiet roadway, and crossed the next plantation field instead.

THEY MADE THEIR way through at least ten kilometres of plantation land. Gaunt wondered just how many thousand square kilometres of the heartland had been infested with the alien crop. The team avoided the other stilted sprayers, and what seemed to be mechanical cropper machines at work in the distance.

Leafering was less than half an hour away now. It looked like a big place with old, grand stone buildings. Once they were close enough, the scouts would conduct a quick appraisal and they'd decide how to move in.

The roads were now quite busy with traffic, mostly transports and tracks, so they kept to the hedge paths, crossing in the open only when they had to. During a rest stop under a copse of talix trees, when the sun was high and hot, Gaunt sat down next to Curth.

'How are you doing?'

'Today? Better. Not feeling quite so overwrought.'

'Me too, I think,' Gaunt said. He took a drink from his water bottle. 'You left.'

'I left what?' she asked.

'You left. This morning.'

'What the feth are you talking about?' she asked. 'Have you been out in the sun without your cap on again?'

'Never mind,' Gaunt said. He decided there was no point pushing it when Curth was quite so vulnerable and prone to mood swings. He got to his feet.

'Let's go,' he called. 'Let's get this done.'

TWENTY-FIVE

THREE EXCUBITORS WANDERED down the yard, the long barrels of their slant-wise las-locks swinging. They exchanged a few words, then turned right through the gate arch and disappeared up the flagged street towards the commercia.

Bonin waited until they were well clear, then slipped out of the shadows, ran the length of the yard and ducked down behind a tall stack of paper bundles. Some of the loose papers were sticking out, and Bonin pulled one free and read it. It was a crudely printed leaflet encouraging 'citizens of the Intercession' to become proselytes and convert. Bonin stuffed it back where he'd found it.

It was early evening in Leafering, and the street lighting was beginning to flicker on, though the streets themselves were still quite busy. Another hour and the curfew would sound, ordering all those consented only for day to their habs. From his vantage point behind the stacked propaganda leaflets, Bonin had a good view along the rear of the yard. The large ouslite building to his left was being used as a station house by the Occupation forces. Around the front, there was a lot of troop activity, and a line of half-tracks was parked in the thoroughfare.

But this small yard area, enclosed by a high stone wall, ran around to the rear of the building. There were several smaller annexes out here, one of which had a roof festooned with vox-masts and aerials.

No one in sight. And no sign of any nasty glyf-like surprises either. They'd had to shrink past wirewolf gibbets in the outskirts to get into the town, and at least once had seen the shimmer of a glyf behind a nearby row of buildings. The sight had made Feygor shake.

But this little yard was clean enough.

Bonin made the signal.

Mkoll and Mkvenner came in over the wall, dropped down and crossed to the far side of the yard until they had overlapped Bonin. All three had their suppressed pistols drawn.

As Bonin backed up the yard, his weapon hunting left and right, Mkoll and Mkvenner reached the annexe with the masted roof. Mkvenner covered Mkoll as he ducked inside.

Thirty-five seconds later, he came out and gave the all clear.

Bonin nodded, and keyed his micro-bead.

'Silver,' he said.

A door in the back of the main building suddenly opened onto the yard. Mkoll and Mkvenner had slipped inside the annexe doorway, and Bonin threw himself back into the shadows along the outer wall. A uniformed sirdar, accompanied by a junior officer and four excubitors, emerged and began to walk down the yard.

'Bragg! Bragg!' Bonin hissed.

IN THE SHADOWS of an alleyway on the far side of the yard wall, Gaunt listened hard to his earpiece.

'Bonin? Bragg or silver? Which is it?'

A long pause.

'Bonin?'

'Bragg,' the whisper came back.

Rawne and Beltayn were all set to go over the wall.

'Hold it,' Gaunt said. 'It's not clear.'

'I heard Bo call "silver",' Rawne said.

'Well, he's changed his mind,' Gaunt said.

'I'm going anyway,' Rawne said, gesturing for Varl to cup his hands and boost him over the wall. 'We'll be here all night otherwise.'

'Can't you control your people?' Cirk hissed.

'There's been no evidence of it so far,' Gaunt replied.

'Silver. Silver!' Bonin called.

'Right, go,' Gaunt said.

THE SIRDAR AND his escort had gone out through the gate. Bonin signalled again, and Rawne and Beltayn appeared over the wall and slithered down into the yard. They ran towards Bonin, who ushered them up to the annexe, where Mkvenner was waiting at the door.

The annexe was the vox office for the station house. Inside, in a dingy room lit by yellowed glow-globes, sat a large, non-portable vox-caster unit. Coils of trunking and sheaves of cable sprouted up through the roof to connect it to the mast array. It was part of the Occupation's principal communications network, tuned to the Archenemy's main command channels and data relays. Most important of all, it was equipped with a cipher module that decrypted the network's confidence codes. Two operators had been staffing the annexe. Mkoll had left their bodies in the corner of the room.

Beltayn hurried in, and swung his vox-set off his shoulder. He pulled the cover off, and unlatched the door of the cable port in its side.

'Fast as you can,' Rawne urged.

'Don't fuss me when I'm working,' Beltayn answered without looking up. He'd unbuttoned a pouch of tools, and was playing out a connector cable. Then he turned his attention to the enemy machine.

'Sonegraph 160. Really, really old, and clearly modified. I haven't messed with one of these in a long time.'

'Fascinate me further, why don't you,' Rawne growled. He glanced at the outer door where Bonin and Mkvenner were watching for interruptions.

Beltayn test flicked a few of the switches on the big caster, and studied the wavelength display. Then he used a watchmaker's screwdriver to remove the pins holding an inspection plate in place. The plate came away, exposing loops of wire and small plug-in valve shunts. Using small pliers and a volt-meter from his kit, Beltayn tested and then exchanged several of the wire connectors and took out one of the valves. Then he attached one end of the connector cable to his set and the other to an output socket on the caster.

'Hurry up,' Rawne said. He was getting jumpy. The cluster of wires Beltayn had exposed precisely formed the shape of the stigma. He looked at something else.

Beltayn switched on his set's power pack, made an adjustment to its dials, then crossed back to the big machine. He tentatively pressed several keys on the main console and, as gauges glowed amber and needles quivered, he started to scroll down through a column of data presented in trembling graphic form on a small sub-screen.

'Got it,' Beltayn said. 'Yep, I've got it. The transmission log. How much do you want?'

'How much is there?' asked Rawne.

Beltayn scrolled down some more, peering. 'Mmm… about eight months at least. It'll take a while to get all that.'

'How long are we talking?'

Beltayn shrugged. 'Probably five, ten minutes per week.'

'Feth!' said Rawne.

'Take the last week,' Mkoll said. 'We don't have time for more. Let's just pray there's something usable in it.'

Beltayn looked at Rawne.

'Do as he says,' Rawne agreed. Beltayn set the device, pressed activation keys on both the main caster and his own portable, and information began to stream down the connector into the set's recording buffer.

'Quiet!' Mkvenner called from the doorway.

Outside, two Occupation troopers had wandered out into the yard and were loitering, smoking lho-sticks. They were making idle conversation.

'Come on,' whispered Bonin. 'Smoke up and get lost.'

Beltayn got up and crept over to his set, studying the small display.

'Something's awry,' he whispered.

Rawne felt his heart go cold. 'What do you mean?'

Beltayn reset his vox and hurried back to the main caster to do the same.

'It's transferring, but the data's encrypted. I'll have to start over. What I've got so far is useless.'

'Feth it!' Rawne hissed.

The troopers in the yard were still smoking and chatting.

'Think, think…' Beltayn said to himself. He located the cipher module and examined it. 'Why aren't you working? Why the feth aren't you working?'

He turned to Rawne and Mkoll. 'It's got a security lock-out. The cipher needs a key to start it running.'

'A code?'

'No, an actual key. Goes in here.'

Mkoll went over to the bodies of the operators. He searched their pockets and finally found a small steel key on a thin chain around the neck of one of the dead men.

'This it?'

Beltayn tried it. As the key turned, the cipher module began to hum. Two monitor lights came on.

'We're back in business,' he said, and set the transfer going again.

Bonin was pretty sure the two troopers were close to leaving. Then the yard door opened again, and a uniformed junior ran out with a sheet of paper in his hand. He was heading for the annexe. A runner, bringing an urgent message for the operators to send.

'Someone's coming,' Mkvenner said.

'Here?' asked Rawne.

'Right here,' Bonin replied.

Mkoll came towards the door. 'Let him in,' he said. 'Let him right in and then take him. No noise.'

The runner came up to the annexe door. Then he did the one thing they weren't expecting. He knocked.

The Ghosts looked at each other blankly.

The runner knocked again. Waiting at the door, bouncing eagerly on his toes, the runner turned and grinned at the two troopers. One of them called out something. The runner replied and laughed. Then he knocked again.

'Voi sahn, magir?' he called out.

Everyone was looking at Rawne. 'I don't know!' he mouthed indignantly. How the feth did you say 'Come in'? All Rawne could think of was that Cirk would have known.

In desperation, he called out some made-up sounds, deliberately strangling them into an unintelligible bark.

It did the trick. The runner opened the door and stepped inside. His smile melted. He saw three enemy troopers in filthy black fatigues grouped around the main caster. He didn't see the other two either side of the door behind him. Bonin closed the door. Mkvenner's left hand clamped around the runner's mouth before he could utter a word and his warknife punched. He held the wide-eyed runner tightly as he twitched and shook. When the twitching had stopped, he lowered the body sound-lessly to the floor with Mkoll's help.

Bonin gently reopened the door a crack and peered out. The troopers were leaving.

Mkoll looked down at the runner. 'He was in a hurry. He may have been expecting to take back a quick reply. I'd lay money he's going to be missed within the next fifteen minutes.'

Rawne looked at Beltayn. 'How long?' he asked.

Beltayn was watching the set display. 'It's slow. Ten, maybe twelve minutes more.'

Those minutes tracked by painfully slowly. Bonin and Mkvenner crouched by the door. Mkoll sat, perfectly still, in one of the operator chairs. Rawne paced, drumming the fingers of his right hand against the knuckles of his left. He became aware that Mkoll was staring at him, his eyes nar-rowed. Rawne's fidgeting was really getting to the calm, quiet chief scout.

Rawne glared at Mkoll. 'I'm a major,' he snapped. 'I can do what I fething like.'

'And therein, so often, lies our problem,' Mkoll replied coldly. Everyone looked round. With the possible exception of Mkvenner, Mkoll was the most collected, reserved man in the Ghosts. No one had ever heard him rise to the bait and throw out a jibe like that.

'You say something?' Rawne said, taking a step forward. Mkoll's chair scraped back and he got to his feet. Rawne was a good deal taller than Mkoll, but their eyes locked murderously.

'Do you honestly want some, you asshole?' Mkoll breathed.

Mkvenner and Bonin had both risen, flanking Rawne from behind. Sur-rounded by three of the most dangerous men in the Tanith First, Rawne seemed utterly unfazed. His eyes never leaving Mkoll's, he said, 'You know, feth-face, I believe I do.'

'Oh for feth's sake!' Beltayn cried, so loudly it made them all start. 'What's the matter with you, major? Is it your plan to pick a fight with everyone on the mission team before we're done?'

All four men looked at him sharply. Beltayn shrank back, raising his hands. 'Or I could just carry on minding my own business.'

His expression made Bonin snigger.

Rawne's shoulders relaxed slightly. 'Boy's right. Feth's sake,' he murmured. 'What am I doing?'

Mkoll backed off too, staring at the floor, his fingers to his temples. 'Holy Throne,' he said. 'That was me, wasn't it? That was me.' He looked up at Rawne. 'I'm sorry, sir,' he said. 'I don't know where that came from.'

Rawne bit his lip and shook his head sadly. 'It's all of us,' he said. 'It's all of us.'

'Transfer's complete,' Beltayn called. He started to uncouple his equip-ment and stow his kit.

'Let's go,' Rawne said.

'To quote my friend the vox-man,' Bonin said. 'Something's awry.'

A truck, painted in the livery of the Occupation forces, had pulled up in the yard while they had been idiotically facing off. Four men had jumped down and, under the supervision of a fifth, an obese, older man in a sirdar's uniform, they were loading the bundles of propaganda pamphlets onto the flatbed from the pile.

'This we didn't need,' Bonin remarked.

Rawne took a look. 'Emperor kiss my arse,' he sighed. 'It's going to take them ages to get that crap loaded. We're stuck here until they've finished.'

'Or until someone comes looking for the messenger,' Mkoll said.

'Or until we go out there and kill them,' suggested Beltayn. 'Not me, obviously. You guys are the mean, tough types who do that sort of thing.'

'Last thing we want now is a fight that could escalate,' Mkoll said.

TWILIGHT WAS SLIDING into night now. The curfew had sounded, and the streets were clearing. Mkoll's team was taking far too long.

Gaunt had withdrawn the rest of them from the alley, where they were too exposed, and they'd holed up in the back parlour of a derelict tailor's store a few doors down. Larkin was covering the front, Varl the back, and Criid was lookout on the side door of the premises. Gaunt waited with Cirk, Landerson, Feygor, Curth and Brostin in a room full of headless fitting dummies, dusty cloth samples and crinkled paper patterns. Eszrah ap Niht lurked in one corner, slowly leafing through a heavy catalogue book, his grey fingers tracing in wonder across the pictures of fine gentlemen and ladies modelling the styles of the latest season.

'What did you mean, I left?' Curth said suddenly.

'Not now, Ana,' Gaunt said.

'No. What did you mean?'

Gaunt got up quickly and walked away. He went into the back hall. 'Anything?' he called down to Criid.

She shook her head.

'Dammit,' he said and turned back. Cirk had followed him out. She was blocking the doorway.

'What is it?' he asked.

'Your woman didn't leave,' she said quietly.

'What?'

'I left, Ibram.'

Gaunt stared at her. He was about to reply, when his micro-bead blipped. Rawne had been told only to use the link in an emergency.

'One?'

'This is two. We've got the stuff. But we're pinned in the annexe. Some idiots are loading a truck in the yard.'

'Can you deal, two?'

'I'd say "Bragg" to that, sir. We could take them, but it could get complicated fast. However, we don't want to be sitting here much longer either.'

'Understood. Stand by. When you hear "silver", get out into the alley. One out.'

'Problem?' Cirk asked. She reached out a hand and placed it against Gaunt's chest. He brushed it aside.

'Not now, Sabbatine. We'll talk about this later.'

'What's to talk about?' she asked.

'Stop it.' Gaunt walked back into the parlour. 'Everyone up,' he said. 'It seems to be time for one of those events Major Cirk dreads.'

'A planetary invasion?' she quipped smartly.

'A diversion,' he replied.

'Throne's sake!' she growled, her jaw stuck out pugnaciously. 'Fine, just so long as it doesn't involve your pyromaniac.'

'Bad news part two,' said Gaunt. 'Brostin, you're up. That fething burner work yet?'

'We'll see, sir,' Brostin replied, pulling the harness of the hefty weapon over his wide shoulders.

'Varl?' Gaunt called.

Varl responded quickly, running back into the parlour with his lasrifle ready.

'I'm going out front with Brostin. Gather the team, get out into the alley, and wait for Rawne's bunch. Cirk?'

'Yes, Ibram?'

He ignored the familiarity. 'The next stage is up to you and Mr Landerson. The Leafering cell. How do we find them?'

'Things may have changed, but there used to be a contact point at the Temple of the Beati, just west of here,' Cirk replied.

The Temple of the Beati, Gaunt smiled. *How entirely appropriate.* 'All right,' he said. 'Talk to Varl, explain how to get to it. I want the two of you ready to lead the team through as soon as we rejoin you. If you hear the code word… uh… "Sabbat", let's use "Sabbat"… if you hear that, go on without us. No questions. Varl, at that point, the senior ranking officer has command of the mission.'

'Yes, sir.'

'Stop smiling, Varl,' Gaunt said. 'If things go arse-up now, it could be you.'

'The Emperor protects,' Varl said sweetly. 'And also dumps on us from a very great height.'

GAUNT LED BROSTIN out through the shop front onto the empty street. The public lighting was poor in this area, though streetlamps glowed beyond the street corner, flooding the boulevard that the station house fronted. They could hear motor traffic and, somewhere, a gong beating.

That was all right. There were several sounds Gaunt didn't want to hear, and foremost amongst them was the howling of wirewolves. He never wanted to hear that particular noise ever again.

'What's the plan?' Brostin whispered.

Gaunt was about to reply when a figure came up behind them. He wheeled round, his silenced auto aimed.

It was Eszrah.

'Go back!' Gaunt hissed. 'Go back with the others!'

The Sleepwalker frowned, not comprehending. Clearly his bond was with Gaunt specifically, not with the party in general. Gaunt owned Eszrah ap Niht, and therefore Eszrah ap Niht would go wherever Gaunt went.

'Preyathee, soule... uh...' Gaunt began. 'Ah, feth it. Come on. Aversye wherall!'

Eszrah nodded. Gaunt didn't bother trying to say 'and be quiet'. The partisan seemed incapable of being anything else.

The trio hurried up the street. As they passed the open gateway of the yard, they peered in and saw the troopers loading the truck by the light of the vehicle's stablight.

Gaunt waved Brostin and Eszrah on and they dashed across the opening and up towards the main boulevard.

'That one,' said Gaunt, pointing to another derelict shop that faced the station house across the street.

'That one what?' Brostin asked.

'I want you to burn it down, Brostin.'

A huge smile split Brostin's face. 'Sir, that's the nicest thing anyone's ever said to me.'

They went over to the shop's doorway, and Gaunt forced the door. It was a cloth merchant's – evidently, this was the haberdashers' quarter of the town.

'All right?' he asked.

'Perfect,' replied Brostin. 'Plenty of ignition sources, plenty of wick.'

'Wick?'

'It's an arsonist thing. Don't worry. Just be set to go when I say.'

Gaunt grabbed Eszrah by the arm and pulled him back to the doorway. Brostin circled the shop front, touching bales of cloth and dusty bolts of material as if assessing them for value. He settled on a thick, velvet fabric.

'Here we go,' he said.

He nursed the feed trigger of his flamer so that liquid promethium spilled out of the snout and dribbled the fuel across the bale, and the others beside it. Almost daintily, he dabbed spots of fuel on other bundles, and trailed it down the shop's walls.

Then he backed off to the doorway, leaving a track of liquid fuel across the floor behind him. He pushed his flamer around behind his back, pulled out his tinderbox and crouched down.

'You're not going to use the flamer?' Gaunt asked from behind him.

'A burst of flamer would take this place up like a furnace. I was assuming you wanted it to look like an accident.'

Gaunt nodded.

'Say hello to Mister Yellow,' Brostin murmured, and struck his match. It fizzled between his fingers. 'And get ready to run like hell.'

Brostin flicked his hairy, tattooed arm, not so hard that it would extinguish the match, but hard enough to send it flying. It landed on the prom trail on the shop floor. And took immediately.

Crackling, flames leapt up and raced along the fuel path towards the bales of soaked fabric.

'I'd love to stay and watch,' Brostin muttered. 'But we should go. Running will help.'

They ran back down the street towards the mouth of the alley behind the yard. Behind them, there was a sucking sound and then a hard bang that blew the glass out of the shop front. A swirl of fire engulfed the shop's ground floor, and rippled up into the night air through the broken windows.

Gaunt, Brostin and Eszrah slid into cover behind the wall end. Already they could hear shouting above the crackle of the fierce flames. Figures rushed out of the yard, shouting cries of alarm. Two, three, five. The obese sirdar was the last to emerge.

'Silver,' Gaunt voxed.

Firebells began to ring. Brostin stood at the wall end and watched the conflagration eating into the facade of the old shop.

'Now isn't that just lovely,' he breathed.

'Will you come the feth on?' Gaunt barked.

REGROUPED, THE MISSION team ran through the dark alleys, leaving the furious fire behind them. More firebells were ringing now, and the glow lit up the night sky.

'You got it?' Gaunt asked Rawne.

'We got it. But there are three bodies back there that will raise some questions.'

'Understood. Cirk? Where's this temple?'

'This way!' she called.

They crossed two more side-streets, and then ran down an empty boulevard for twenty metres. Abruptly, Cirk and Varl pulled them into cover. They cowered in the shadows, pulses thumping. Half-seen, a glyf drifted past the head of the road, its obscene light reflecting off the polished flagstones. Curth had to jam her hands across Feygor's mouth to stop him crying out.

The glyf was gone. They started to move again, footsteps clattering over the hard cobbles.

'Oh, crap!' said Varl.

Five excubitors had suddenly rounded the end of the street. They blinked at the gang of figures before them and then began to raise their las-locks.

'Cover!' Gaunt cried. Everyone split left and right.

Everyone except Eszrah ap Niht. He'd seen these creatures before. He raised his reynbow and planted an iron dart through the forehead of the lead figure. The excubitor flew backwards and fell down. Eszrah reloaded. The iron quarrel made a clinking noise as it rattled backwards down the bow's barrel, pulled into place by the powerful magnets. He fired again.

A second excubitor tumbled down, its arms flailing. It made a heavy sound as it hit the flagstones, and its las-lock snapped under its weight.

Calmly, the partisan reloaded again. *Sklink-ptup*.

The remaining excubitors were firing now. Their weapons cracked and sizzling lock-bolts kissed past the tall grey figure. He didn't even flinch.

Criid and Varl, enjoying the best of the street-side cover, leaned out and let go with their auto-pistols. The stammering, silenced bursts slammed two more excubitors over on their backs.

The last excubitor started to run. Eszrah took a step or two forward, settled his aim and fired.

It was a long shot. The excubitor had all but disappeared around the street corner. The poisoned quarrel smacked into the back of its shaved skull and dropped it on its face with a bone-breaking crack.

'The temple?' Gaunt urged Cirk.

'Down here,' she said.

THE TEMPLE WAS empty and silent. It was the saddest thing Gaunt had yet seen on Gereon. Labour gangs from the local Iconoclave had rendered its icons to debris and shattered the statuary. The murals had been defaced with obscenities.

Guns ready, the team prowled in through the shadows. Ragged bodies, long decayed, lay on the marble floor of the inner shrine where they had been killed months before. Women and children, craving sanctuary from the Saint. Gaunt closed his eyes.

That was exactly what they were doing now.

He walked towards the ruined altar and sank to his knees. The face of the Beati was just visible through the daubings and smears the Occupation forces had inscribed.

'Please,' Gaunt whispered to the defaced image. 'Please.'

'She's not listening,' Cirk snapped, and walked past him. 'I'm the only one here.' Cirk took hold of a battered golden candelabrum, and swung it so it faced north.

'Now we hide and we wait,' she said.

A TEMPLE PRIEST came in just after midnight, to perform his furtive, unconsented worship. When he saw the candelabrum, he made the sign of the aquila and retreated fast.

An hour later, he returned.

'Hello?' he called. He was hunched and old, and his voice was thin. 'Hello? Is anyone here?'

Gaunt rose to his feet and slid out of the shadows.

'Hello,' he said.

TWENTY-SIX

'THIS IS UNACCEPTABLE,' said Colonel Noth. 'Quite simply unacceptable.'

'Well, I'm sure you're going somewhere with this,' Gaunt replied. 'But I wish you'd get there fast.'

They were in the basement of a municipal store in the north-west of Leafering. The local cell, fifty-strong and surprisingly well armed, had brought them out of the temple into hiding. The mission team was all around, relaxing, sleeping or drinking the broth that had been prepared over the basement's crackling drum-fires.

Maxel Noth was a short, well-built man in his late forties. His black hair was long and dank, and tied back in a ponytail.

'You come here with this incredible story. Incredible. And you have the gall to ask me to believe you?'

'You might want to have a word with Major Cirk there,' Gaunt suggested. 'She's cell too.'

'So she says. Of the Ineuron cell. But it's common knowledge that the Ineuron cell was exposed and annihilated over a week ago. You could be anyone. You could be well-briefed informers.'

'Noth,' Gaunt said wearily. 'I need your help. I am here to do the Emperor's work. I need friends.'

'To do what?' the cell leader asked bluntly. 'You claim to be Guard. Are you here to liberate my world?'

'Not this again…' Gaunt sighed.

Landerson came over. 'Colonel Noth? I think we should square this away. The colonel-commissar and his squad are here on a mission of extreme priority.'

'What sort of mission?' Noth asked.

'I have no idea. I haven't been told. But I trust him, sir. Ballerat himself ordered me to bring him and his team in.'

'Ballerat, eh? A good man.'

'He's dead, sir,' Landerson said.

'Is he? Dead?'

'Died getting Gaunt's people in, so that should tell you something of the importance he placed on them.'

Noth shrugged. 'That's not the point. We're on the anvil here in Leafering as it is. We can't be expected to–'

'The Emperor expects, sir,' Gaunt said.

Noth glared at him. 'Understand this, sir. We have been engaged in covert fighting these last months. We have used our anonymity to target grain stores, trackway junctions and power plants. Nothing we have done has been… vulgar or visible. Vulgarity and visibility lead to discovery and death. Now, tonight, you have blundered into Leafering, set fires, killed Occupation officers by your own admission. It's a wonder the wolves are still slumbering. Throne, sir! You'll reveal us all.'

'Maybe he will,' said Cirk, sitting down beside Gaunt. 'Colonel, it's hard to hear… believe me, I know… but you have to understand that the colonel-commissar is here for a reason that's much bigger than you or me. Much bigger than this cell. Much bigger than Gereon. By the Emperor's will, we might all go to our deaths, and it would still be worth it if Gaunt succeeds. Please, take this seriously. This is about the Imperium, and if Gereon burns to make it happen, then so be it.'

Noth frowned. 'I've been taking things seriously since the Archenemy came to my planet. Everything is about life and death. Don't lecture me on responsibility.' He looked at Gaunt. 'What would you need from me?' he asked.

'Some supplies. Rations, field dressings, hard rounds, grenades if you have them. I understand your resources are thin to begin with. After that, transportation. You must have covert ways to move personnel from place to place.'

'Transportation to where?' Noth asked.

'I hope to be able to tell you that shortly,' Gaunt replied.

'Anything else?' asked Noth.

'He'll probably ask you for a diversion too,' said Cirk snidely. 'He's very fond of them.'

'That's quite likely,' said Gaunt.

NEARBY, MKOLL SAT beside one of the drum-fires, carefully sliding the power cells of the team's lasrifles into the flames. Every team member was low on energy munitions, and though cells were simple enough to recharge, the local power supply was less than reliable. Exposing a cell's thermal receptor to heat in a fire was a drastic but effective method of recharging. However, it shortened the life of the power packs badly. Mkoll was resigned to that. He had a feeling their life expectancy was down to days now, if not hours.

Mkvenner came over with the last few packs he had collected up from Criid and Varl. He helped Mkoll feed them into the fire.

'That shouldn't have happened,' Mkoll said.

'What?'

'That nonsense with Rawne. I can't believe I did that. It wasn't me there for a moment, you know, Ven? Not me at all.'

'Curth says we should all expect it. We've been exposed to this world for long enough, and its blight's soaked into us now. She says our personalities will change. Our moods will switch. You've seen it.'

Mkoll sighed. 'I have. I just thought I'd escaped its touch so far.' He looked at his own hands as he dropped the last pack into the fire. Like all of them, his skin was speckled with a rash, and his fingernails had started to mottle. 'We're not coming out of this one, Ven. Our bodies are falling apart and we're losing our minds.'

'But on the bright side…' said Mkvenner.

Mkoll smiled. *That Nalsheen fortitude…*

'I don't think it does destroy us,' Mkvenner said thoughtfully, after a long pause.

'What?' Mkoll asked.

'Chaos. We're warned so often that the taint of the Ruinous Powers destroys a man like a disease. But that's not what it feels like, is it?'

'What are you talking about, Ven? I feel sick to my bones.'

'It's changing us,' Mkvenner said. 'That's what it does. That's why it's so… dangerous. Look at Rawne.'

'Do I have to?'

'Rawne's never trusted anyone. Now the taint's got to him, it's brought that part of him to the forefront. Magnified it. He's paranoid now. You can see that. So jumpy. And Doctor Curth. She was always hard-nosed, but she also always kept her outrage at the cost of war shut away, so she could concentrate on saving lives. Chaos is letting all that hidden anger out like a flash flood. Beltayn too. The lad's always had a cocky streak he works to keep in check. Now he's answering back and wising off. And you…'

'Me?' replied Mkoll.

'You're finally saying to Rawne all the things you always wanted to. Chaos doesn't destroy us, it finds the things that were always there inside us and brings them out. The ugliness, the flaws, the worst parts of us. That's why mankind should really fear it. It brings out the worst in us, but the worst is already there.'

'You could be right,' said Mkoll.

'I could be,' agreed Mkvenner. 'Or that idea might just have been Chaos bringing out the worst in me.'

ON THE OTHER side of the basement, Beltayn was working on his vox-set. Larkin sat down next to him.

'How's it going?' he asked.

'Slow. There's so much stuff to sort through. It's killing my eyes.' Beltayn was scrolling through the transmission log he'd copied out of the Archenemy's vox-caster. The set's display screen was small, and he was straining to make out the data. 'It's decrypted, but I'm still having to run everything through the set's translator system, and you know how hopeless that is. Only a rudimentary grasp of the enemy language forms. Loads of words are coming up as *not found*.'

'How much did you get?' Larkin asked.

'Just the last week's worth, but that alone is thousands of transcripts. I'm going through the record of the enemy's primary data-broadcasts first. That seemed the most likely place to start. '

'Want a hand?' Larkin asked.

Beltayn glanced at him.

'Sharpest eyes in the Ghosts, me,' Larkin grinned. 'Go get yourself some of that vile broth and let me have a go.'

GAUNT HAD BEEN asleep for about three hours. The sleep had been dreamless at first, then the pictures had begun to come. He saw ice and snow, which may have been Hagia, the Shrineworld. A silver wolf ran across the snow fields, leaving no trace behind it. It reached a stand of lonely black timbers and looked back. The wolf had Rawne's eyes.

From somewhere, the screaming started up. Distant, but clear. A man's voice, screaming and screaming in such pitiful pain. He knew that voice. Who was it?

The wolf had vanished. For reasons of dream-logic, a door opened in the middle of the trees and a figure stepped out. It was the Beati, but it was also Cirk. The stigma on her cheek was an aquila.

Her mouth moved as she spoke, but the sounds were oddly out of synch with her lips.

She said, 'Under the skin. What matters is on the inside.'

Then she backed away through the door again, like a pict-feed running in reverse, and the door closed.

That was when the screaming began to get louder, until there was no snow, no ice, no door, no trees, no dream at all. Just screaming.

Then Beltayn woke him up, which suited Gaunt just fine.

He yawned and stretched. Larkin was beside Beltayn.

'Well?'

'I think we've got it,' Beltayn said. 'Larkin spotted it.'

'And?'

'It was on the primary command channel. Several transmissions yesterday and the day before. Activity at the Lectica Bastion. As best as I can make out, a lot of senior ordinals are gathering there. The transmissions use codenames for VIPs. Some sort of high level security meeting.'

'Right,' said Gaunt. 'But the bastion is one of the chief fortresses on Gereon. A meeting of senior ordinals would not be an unusual event.'

Beltayn nodded. 'One of the codenames is "eresht". That means parcel or package. Whoever is codenamed "eresht" seems to be there at the bastion already. The others are coming to see him. They've been summoned to see him. Sir, in some of the early intel gathered prior to the mission, "eresht" was used as a codeword for our target.'

Gaunt stroked his hands down his cheeks and stared at the ground. 'He's still there?'

'Yes, sir.'

'Holy Throne. He's still there.' Gaunt looked up at Beltayn and Larkin. 'Well done, both of you. Let's talk to Colonel Noth. And get Cirk and Mr Landerson too. It's time they learned the truth.'

'OUR MISSION HERE on Gereon is to find and eliminate one individual,' Gaunt said.

The assembled Ghosts sat or stood around Gaunt in a semi-circle. None of what their leader had to say was news to them. This was for the benefit of Landerson, Cirk, Noth and four of Noth's senior lieutenants.

'One individual?' Noth asked. He laughed. 'Who? The Plenipotentiary? I can't think of anyone important enough to warrant these efforts. Not even the Plenipotentiary, come to that. The Anarch would just replace that toad Isidor with another lord...' His voice trailed off. 'Holy Throne, he's not here is he?'

'Who?'

'The bloody Anarch! He's not here on Gereon is he?'

'No,' Gaunt replied. 'Our target is a man named Noches Sturm.'

'A man?' said Landerson. After all his patience and trust, he felt disappointed.

'A prisoner, in fact. He's being held by the Archenemy at the Lectica Bastion.'

Noth got to his feet. 'I said this was all a load of nonsense! You're out of your mind!'

'Sit down, colonel,' Gaunt said.

'I want no part of–'

'Colonel Noth, the man I've just told you about has a rank too. Noches Sturm is Lord Militant General Sturm of the Imperial Guard.'

Noth blinked and sat down again. Landerson exhaled a long, whistling breath.

'They've got a lord general?' Noth asked.

'They've had him for many months now. As you can imagine, this represents a critical security risk to the Crusade armies. It's no exaggeration to say that it could change the tide of the entire war here in the Sabbat Worlds. A lord general knows... well, where do I start? Guard codes, cipher patterns, force distribution, army deployment, fleet dispersal, tactical planning, communication protocols, weaknesses, strengths, secrets.'

'How the hell did they get to him?' Landerson asked.

'Accident,' said Gaunt. 'And, to a certain degree, because of a misjudgement I made.'

'What?' Cirk grinned. 'Is that why you ended up with this nightmare mission? To make amends for letting him get captured?'

Gaunt glanced at her. 'No, Cirk. I'm here to make amends for not killing him when I had the chance.'

'I don't understand,' said Noth.

'Sturm is a traitor, colonel. Several years ago, he and I were responsible for the defence of a hive-city on the planet Verghast. It was a close-run thing, hard won. At the darkest hour, fearing for his own hide, he tried to abandon the hive and make his escape. His actions weakened the defence and almost cost us the fight. As senior commissar, I had him arrested for desertion and cowardice. He chose to take the honorable way out, but then turned that opportunity into another attempt to escape. I cut off his hand and put him in detention. I should have executed him, right then and there.'

'Why didn't you?' asked Cirk.

Gaunt hesitated. 'After all he had done, Cirk, I think I wanted him to suffer. I wanted him to endure the humiliation of a court martial, of public disgrace. A simple, summary execution on the field of battle, something quite within my power to exact, would have been too easy. Besides, the commissar in me could see the political value of a court martial. The public disgrace, trial and execution of a lord general would send out a message to any other over-zealous, over-ambitious commander that the new Warmaster was not someone to be trifled with. Sturm was transported for detention pending trial. The trial was scheduled for the middle of last year, but the events of the counter-attack through the Khan Group got in the way. Disastrously, Sturm was en route to the court martial when his ship was captured by an enemy squadron. They quickly realised what a valuable trophy they had accidentally won.'

One of Noth's officers raised his hand. 'Sir, isn't it too late now? I mean, surely Sturm will have already divulged all of his secrets?'

'Especially if they torture him,' Noth agreed.

'Sturm was placed under mindlock by the Guild Astropathicus during his detention. It's standard practice in these cases. The guild would have removed the lock at the trial, so that Sturm could be properly cross-examined.'

'So he can't tell them anything?' Landerson said.

Gaunt shrugged. 'Not willingly, Mr Landerson. But the Archenemy has powerful psykers of its own. A mindlock is hard to remove, but not impossible. No, I'm afraid the only way of ensuring Sturm reveals none of his secrets is if they die with him.'

'If it's this vital,' said Noth, 'why only send in a team of troopers? Why not engage the fleet and flatten the bastion from orbit?'

'The same reason the liberation of Gereon has not yet begun, colonel,' Gaunt said. 'The counter-attack is still being fought back. The fleet is stretched to its limits. And besides, there'd be no guarantee. With a bombardment, we could never be sure we'd actually got Sturm.'

'You know the Lectica Bastion isn't the sort of place you just walk into?' Noth said quietly.

Gaunt nodded. 'It's going to take scrupulous planning and a lot of luck.'

'You're sure he's there?' asked Cirk.

'As sure as we can be. Intelligence gathered prior to this mission positively identified the bastion as the place the enemy had sequestered Sturm. There was every chance he'd be moved. But my vox-officer has managed to access and read recent transmissions made on the Archenemy command channels.' Gaunt looked at Beltayn.

Beltayn cleared his throat. 'Sturm is referred to by the enemy codeword "eresht", which means a package or parcel. He's definitely still there. In fact, it looks like something big is going down. A large number of senior ordinals is gathering at the bastion to meet with him.'

'Something big?' Noth said. 'Like... the breaking of the mindlock, perhaps?'

Beltayn shrugged. 'Not for me to say, sir. A lot of the transmissions are untranslatable. But we know he's there. Several codes are used to refer to him. Eresht is the main one. They also use "pheguth", but my system can't supply a meaning for that word.'

Rawne nodded across the room. 'Maybe Major Cirk can tell us?'

Cirk glared at Rawne. 'Don't ask me for a literal translation. The word is a slur. Extremely unpleasant. In simple terms, it means "traitor".'

Noth got to his feet. 'I'll assemble what maps and charts I can get hold of, sir,' he said. 'We'll start devising an entry plan. Cirk also spoke of a diversion. It seems to me that's vital. A big noise to draw the enemy's attention. I'll make contact with the other cell leaders in the heartland tonight. Together we can field upwards of six hundred fighters. It wouldn't be hard to coordinate a joint attack on the bastion, especially if I tell my fellow commanders that there's a chance to destroy a whole crowd of the enemy's senior ordinals in one go. That's a target of opportunity the resistance can't afford to miss.'

'Colonel,' Gaunt called out. 'You do realise that's a lie, don't you? Even with six hundred men, the chances of getting through the gate are slim. You're not likely to get anywhere near the ordinals.'

Noth nodded. 'I know it's a lie. But I've got to tell the commanders something if I'm going to persuade them to sacrifice their entire cells just to get you inside.'

TWENTY-SEVEN

'WHAT THE BLOODY hell is that noise?' Sturm asked. At his heels, Humiliti the lexigrapher jabbed out some more keystrokes.

'Don't type that, you idiot!' Sturm snapped. 'Desolane?'

It was late afternoon, but the light outside was already failing, as if a storm was drawing in. Servants with tapers hurried down the long hallways of the bastion, lighting the lamps. There was a general bustle of activity everywhere in the fortress. Transports and aircraft had been arriving all day, and the primary courtyards were swarming with newly-arrived troops. Sturm basked in the knowledge that it was all in his honour. All this fuss, and the formal ceremonies to come. For him.

'Desolane!'

The life-ward was at the far end of the marble gallery, talking with sirdars of the Bastion Guard. The officers were dressed for the evening in extravagant formal uniforms, dripping with gold frogging and silver buttons. The gorgets at their throats were encrusted with gemstones, and the silver helmets they held under their arms were festooned with white feather combs.

Hearing Sturm's voice, Desolane dismissed the sirdars, and hurried to the general's side.

'Sir?'

'That bloody awful noise, Desolane. What is it?'

'It is the martial band of the First Echelon, sir, rehearsing for tonight's reception. High Sirdar Brendel insisted the band played when the Plenipotentiary arrived.'

'This Brendel's an idiot.'

'He is high sirdar of the Occupation army, sir. And he will be one of the senior dignitaries asking questions of you when the formal interviews begin.'

'I'll tell him what he wants to know,' Sturm snorted. 'And I'll tell him his marching band's a bloody disgrace to boot.'

'You must do as you see fit, of course,' said Desolane.

They walked together down the gallery, the lexigrapher hobbling after them. Humiliti had recently cut another flapping swathe of typescript off the printing machine's roll and handed it to a servant to be taken for filing. The lexigrapher had been following Sturm about the bastion all day, recording the general's every comment. He'd had to change paper rolls twice already.

Sturm had been in a magnanimous mood, eager to talk, even though he affected a contempt for the dwarfish servant. Memories were returning now all the time: some small and fragmentary, others long and involved. Sturm took delight in recounting everything that occurred to him for the lexigrapher to take down. He recalled the events of certain actions, uniform details of the regiments he had served with, events from his childhood, the characters of men he had known, his family background, his first battlefield success.

At one point, earlier that afternoon, he had stopped in his tracks and announced, 'Roast sirloin of grox. Bloody, not over-done. That is my favourite dish. I've just remembered. Fancy not remembering that.'

He laughed. Desolane made a note to make sure grox was on the menu for the banquet. Bloody, not over-done.

It seemed to the life-ward that Sturm was desperate to get his memories down on paper. Sturm had speculated about 'composing a full autobiography' as a work of that nature was only fitting for a man of such note and substance. 'History must know me, Desolane. For history will take its shape because of me.'

Desolane had nodded dutifully. The life-ward had no wish to discourage Sturm's urgent recollections, as he seemed to remember more and more with each returning memory. One thought set off another, one idea reminded Sturm of a dozen other new things to say.

But in truth, there was desperation. It was as if Sturm dearly wanted to get everything down in case he forgot it all again. The mindlock had been cruel indeed. Sturm never wanted to feel so lost again.

The general was wearing the plain Occupation force uniform Desolane had found, but he had already insisted on 'something more dignified' for the evening's formalities. 'Something with braid, please, Desolane. A long jacket, a sash. An officer's cap too, or is that too much?'

'I will arrange these things,' Desolane had replied.

Now, as the daylight faded, they wandered out from the gallery onto the wide marble landing that overlooked the double sweep of the grand staircase in the bastion's main hallway. The crystal chandeliers were lit, and huge silk banners decorated the walls, displaying the insignias of various echelon units, the symbols of the High Powers, and, centrally, the badge of the Anarch himself.

Sturm was talking again, something about a formal ceremony like this that he had once attended. Humiliti rattled it all down, pausing only once to re-ink his levers. Down below them, servants and troopers hurried back and forth across the wide floor of the hall, pushing trolleys laden with crystal glasses, bringing food stuffs from the unloading freighters.

Desolane had plenty to think about. Security in the bastion had to be perfect. Apart from Sturm himself, and the exalted Plenipotentiary, three hundred and eight senior ordinals and staff officers were due to arrive before nightfall. Most would have their own life-wards or bodyguards, but Desolane felt ultimate responsibility for the safety of all of them. Since the attempt on Sturm's life, the life-ward had personally overseen every aspect of security. Desolane didn't dare delegate to any of the sirdars, and didn't feel comfortable relying on anyone else to get the job right.

'More seniors are arriving now,' Desolane said, pointing down towards the hall's huge outer doors.

'Do I have to greet them?' Sturm asked.

'No, you will be presented formally at the reception, once the Plenipotentiary has arrived,' Desolane said. 'There. That man is Ordinal Ouflen. He is an expert in lingua-forms, and will want to question you about Imperial battle languages. With him, that is Ordinal Zereth, who specialises in propaganda. He will be interviewing you on Imperial morale, and what methods might be employed to undermine the confidence and motivation of the average Imperial Guardsman. Coming in through the door, that is Sirdar Commander Erra Fendra Ezeber of the Special Echelon. She has interest in tactics and also in cunning and subterfuge.'

'What's that?' asked Sturm, gesturing at a hulking figure dressed in fur-edged robes that had just come in through the door escorted by two silver servitors.

'Aha. That is Pytto, an agent of Flotilla Admiral Oszlok. There will be a lot of questions from him. Imperial Battlefleet tactics, ship weaknesses, possibly even dispositions. It's been a while since you were privy to such information, but the admiral hopes you will be able to pinpoint safe harbours, and secure high anchor points used by Imperial warships. A surprise assault on an Imperial safe harbour could cripple a significant portion of the Warmaster's space power.'

'I spoke about that earlier. Didn't I?' Sturm looked down at Humiliti, who nodded eagerly.

'Earlier today, I remembered some details of hidden high anchor stations in the corewards portion of the Khan Group. The midget wrote it all down. Make sure the appropriate sections of my transcript are passed to your beloved admiral with my compliments.'

'Perhaps you should rest for a while, sir,' Desolane suggested.

'I'll try, if that bloody band agrees to shut up.'

Desolane bowed slightly in consent. 'His highness the Plenipotentiary is due to arrive in three hours, at which time the formalities will begin. I understand he wishes to start by having you swear an oath of allegiance to the Anarch, whose word drowns out all others. After that, I believe he intends to bestow an honorary rank upon you – sirdar commander, I think

– and award you a ribbon of merit to acknowledge your efforts and coop-eration.'

Sturm nodded sagely. 'Wise. It would be good to reinforce the perception that I am a man of significance to these commanders.'

Desolane was amused. Sturm could not disguise the flush of pride that filled his face. Respect, admiration, power, after all this time, restored to him.

'I will have a bath drawn in your quarters, sir,' Desolane said, 'and send the footmen to lay out your attire. I will come for you fifteen minutes before the ceremonies begin. Now, if you will excuse me, sir.'

Desolane bowed again, and hurried down the stairs, pausing to issue instructions to a group of excubitors. Then the life-ward descended to the hall floor and walked towards the guest most recently arrived.

Mabbon Etogaur was wearing his usual, understated garb of brown leather, but his boots and buttons were polished, and he had affixed a golden badge of the Anarch to his throat button. He wore an expensive laspistol in a belt holster, and a short, curved power sword in an ornate scabbard.

'Etogaur,' Desolane nodded.

'Life-ward. You asked me here early.'

'You understand why?'

'Security, it said in your message.'

'Indeed.'

Mabbon Etogaur turned and nodded at the two men who had accompa-nied him in. They were both huge, heavily-muscled troopers, wearing ochre uniforms with gold sashes and bone-white helmets that came down in a half-visor over their faces. They stood to attention, rigid, eyes forward, their polished lasrifles crossed in front of their chests.

'It's going to be a fine night,' Mabbon said, 'and I see no reason why it shouldn't be an appropriate time for the worthy commanders of the Anarch's forces to get their first glimpse of the Sons of Sek. I've brought a force of sixty, the best in the camp. I trust that will help you with your secu-rity issues?'

'I'm gratified,' said Desolane. 'Most should assemble in the upper court-yard, ready for review. I'd like a few ready to reinforce the front gates and the curtain wall during the banquet. Might you also spare two of the most trustworthy to stand guard over the pheguth's... I'm sorry, over Lord Sturm's private apartments?'

Mabbon nodded. 'You say two of the most trustworthy, life-ward, but I'll tell you an odd thing. Over the weeks of training, I've been speaking from time to time to the men about the... the pheguth, and how he would even-tually empower them with knowledge and wisdom. In their expectation, they came to almost worship him. And then, the other day, when we went to inspect them on the field, when Sturm collapsed in front of them... I was afraid they would lose all respect for the man. The Sons despise weakness, you see.'

'And?' asked Desolane.

'You were there, life-ward. You saw how Sturm recovered, got back on his feet, faced them without a hint of shame. And the speech he made, just like that. It was humbling. The man has true charisma. He is a born leader. No wonder he achieved such a high rank in the army of the False Emperor.'

'I agree,' Desolane said. 'It was inspirational.'

'It was stunning,' said Mabbon. 'So, you see, when you ask for the most trust-worthy, I'm stumped because I don't know who to choose. The Sons of Sek adore General Sturm. They almost worship him. And they would die to keep him safe.'

'The general will be delighted to hear it,' said Desolane.

'Isn't that him, up there on the landing?' Mabbon asked.

Sturm was still where Desolane had left him. He was talking animatedly, recounting some new-remembered detail to the lexigrapher.

'It is. He's been wandering the halls of the bastion all day, remembering.'

'Remembering what?' Mabbon Etogaur asked.

'As far as I can tell,' said Desolane, 'everything.'

THE BASTION WAS enormous. In the dying light, it seemed to be part of the giant mountain range that surrounded it, discernible only because of the thousands of window lights that speckled its flanks. It was built as a tow-ering central donjon, flanked by two smaller towers that sat like broad shoulders against the main keep. There was an upper courtyard, ringed by a bulwark wall, and then a lower ground, encircled by a massive curtain wall.

As they got closer, they could see the defence batteries along both wall cir-cles, enough to see off a brigade-strength attack with the slightest effort. Aircraft were coming in towards the landing fields inside the inner bulwark, their running lights winking in the cold mountain air. Deathships, shuttles, lavish transporters. The cream of the Archenemy hierarchy was coming to the glowering bastion tonight.

The single approach road ran up through the deep valley below the bas-tion, winding around hard turns. There was frost on the road, and only a thin barricade rail defended the sheer drop on one side of the track. A gorge loomed below, so deep its floor was lost in inky shadows.

The wheels of the heavy cargo-10 slithered.

'Keep your eyes on the road,' she said. The hooded driver nodded.

The approach road itself was busy with traffic. Troop transporters, freighters, armoured cars, and the more splendid motor carriages of the ordinals arriving by land, all of them heading up towards the fortress. A tail-back was forming at the checkpoints below the main gate as excubitors and Occupation troopers checked each arriving vehicle.

They slowed down, joining the queue. The transport's big engine sput-tered and coughed.

'Don't you dare let it die!' she snapped.

'Enough, will you?'

She glanced in the door mirror. Already more vehicles had bunched up behind them, waiting in line.

'Heads up,' the driver said.

Two excubitors, their breath steaming from their speaking grilles, were crunching back down the line of waiting vehicles, barking orders.

'Voi shet! Ahenna barat voir! Mej! Mej!'

'What is this?' the driver asked.

'They want us to pull over. To the side there. We have to make room.'

'Ahenna barat voir! Mej! Avar voi squen? Mej!'

'Pull it over! Come on! They want us all to make space for something.'

'Trying, all right?' the driver complained. 'This heap of junk is… junk.' He revved the engine and hauled on the heavy wheel, pulling the massive truck over against the cliff side of the road. Ahead of them, and behind, under the shouted orders of the excubitors, the rest of the line was doing the same.

They waited. After a minute or two, a huge transport with four outriders as escort purred past. It was waved on towards the checkpoint and entered the main gates without stopping.

'That was somebody very important,' she said.

'Remind me to find out who so I can kill them later,' the driver said.

The line began to move again, crawling forward. 'Keep cool. Just keep cool,' she said. 'Just do what I tell you and leave the talking to me.'

'And if that doesn't work?' the driver asked.

'Kiss your arse goodbye,' she said.

It took another ten minutes for them to reach the head of the queue. The guards at the outer checkpoint were inspecting every arrival. She saw that at least three transports had been pulled off the side of the checkpoint and were being searched. The crews of the transporters were waiting in the cold, their hands on their heads, weapons aimed at them and fetch-hounds pulling at their leashes to attack.

'If that happens to us…' the driver whispered.

'It won't,' she said, 'because we're going to do this right. Right, here we go.'

They rolled to a halt at the lowered bar. Occupation troopers strolled out to slowly surround the truck. She saw a lascannon emplacement to her left, the barrels trained on her cab. Three excubitors came forward, one of them wrangling a pair of snarling fetch-hounds.

She lowered the window as the lead excubitor came up.

'Voi shet? Hakra atarsa?'

'Consented, magir. I am consented.'

The excubitor switched his speaker to translate.

'What are you?'

'Delivery, magir. From Gornell. Foodstuffs. We have to get them into the kitchens before they spoil. The ordinals will be most displeased if their meat is rotten and–'

'Shut up,' the excubitor said. 'You talk too much, consented.'

'Yes, magir.'

The excubitor with the dogs was walking them round the vehicle. They barked and snuffled.

'Stigma?' the excubitor by the cab asked.

She turned her cheek and showed him.

'Display to me your consent!' it demanded.

She rolled up her sleeve and held her arm out of the cab window.

'Eletraa kyh drowk!' the excubitor said to its companions.

'Chee ataah drowk,' the other replied. It drew the long metal tester from its belt, and placed the cup over her imago. She stiffened as the thing in her arm twisted and seethed. Rune lights on the tester lit up.

'Fehet gahesh,' the excubitor told its companion.

'You may proceed, interceded one,' the first excubitor said.

She nodded to the driver who started to put the vehicle in gear. But the barrier did not raise.

'Wait!' the excubitor commanded.

The pair of fetch-hounds were agitated, growling and sniffing around the back gate of the cargo-10. The hound-master shouted a few words, and the excubitor answered.

Then it looked back up into the cab at her. 'The hounds have smelled something. We must search your transport. Back up and park over there.'

'Of course they've smelled something, magir,' she said quickly. 'The cargo is raw meat. Steaks and brisket, also some chops and four whole grox. They smell blood. It's a wonder they haven't broken down the hatch.'

The excubitor thought about it. It turned and shouted something she didn't catch to the hound-master. An answer came back.

'You may proceed,' the excubitor said.

A nod, and the barrier swung up.

'Thank you, magir,' she said.

The truck gunned forward, up the slope and in under the towering arch of the main gate.

Inside there was a noisy jumble of vehicles, all with lamps blazing. The night shadow behind the curtain wall was especially dark. Excubitors with lighted poles directed traffic to the appropriate destinations. She leaned out of the cab, told her business to one of the excubitors, and was given instructions.

She sat back and closed the window. 'To the right. Up there, where those lowbeds are going.'

'Right,' the driver replied.

They approached the inner bulwark, and entered it by one of several smaller gatehouses. Inside, directly below the massive walls of the bastion itself now, they drove into a smaller courtyard that served the loading docks of the kitchens.

'Pull over there. There, behind those other trucks. Get us in tight, against the yard wall.'

The driver nodded and obeyed. He pulled the cargo-10 to a halt and switched off the engine. They both let out long sighs of relief.

Varl sat back from the wheel and pulled down his hood. He grinned at Cirk.

'That was tight,' he said.

'I know,' she replied.

'Fething tight. For a moment there–'

'I know,' she repeated.

'You were great,' Varl said. 'Talked up a storm to those bastards. Were you born a liar, or does it just come naturally?'

'We haven't even begun, trooper,' Cirk said.

'Yeah, but that was a rush. I could kiss you.'

'Don't,' she said.

Varl did anyway.

Cirk smiled. 'Let's get on,' she said, and rapped her fists against the partition wall behind them.

In the container section of the transport, bloody carcasses swung from hooks and the finest cuts of meat were stacked in trays, wrapped in grease-paper. The stifling air stank of blood.

Gaunt heard the knock.

'Let's get ready,' he told the Ghosts. They got up, gathering their kit, and filed down towards the rear doors.

'All right?' Gaunt asked Landerson.

The cell fighter was carrying a brand new autorifle Noth's people had supplied.

'Sir,' he said. 'I want to thank you again for letting me–'

Gaunt put a finger to his lips. 'You've come this far, it would have been rude to leave you out, Mr Landerson.'

Gaunt looked over at Eszrah ap Niht, the other stranger in their midst. Gaunt hadn't wanted to include the partisan in this, but it had proved impossible to dissuade the Sleepwalker from staying by Gaunt's side. During the journey up through the heartlands, Gaunt and Mkvenner had spent a long time carefully explaining to Eszrah what was at stake and what was expected of him.

'Opening the doors,' said Mkoll.

'Go,' Gaunt replied.

The truck's big freight doors squealed open and the Ghosts dropped out into the darkness, one by one. Gaunt was last out. Keeping low, they joined Cirk and Varl, and hurried down the dark space between the parked transporters and the yard wall.

It had taken the best part of a day to travel up to the environs of the bastion from Leafering. Noth's people had arranged it. They'd used vittalers' wagons, and crawled through the heartland bocage to a town called Gornell, in the foothills of the rampart massif. There, the local cell, commanded by a woman called Thresher, had taken them in. Going with the details Noth had forwarded to her through the underground network, Thresher had been working hard to design a way into the bastion for the team. A cell contact at one of Gereon's butchery firms had reported that a last minute order for grox had been sent down from the bastion staff, and a truck was being prepared to deliver it.

From there, they had been on their own.

Hugging the wall shadows, draped in their camo-cloaks, the Ghosts edged towards the brightly lit entrances of the kitchen bay. Porters were rumbling in trolleys of food, and they could hear shouted orders and chatter. The smell of heat and cooking filled the cold mountain breeze.

Mkoll and Mkvenner went ahead. They checked one entrance, hands raised for caution, and then snapped off quick gestures to move.

The team raced forward into the bright light of the entrance way. A corridor, stone-built, with doorways to the right out of which steam and cooking smells billowed.

Mkoll waved them on, and they hurried down the corridor to a junction. Left or right, or up the stairs ahead?

Up, Gaunt signalled. Up they went, taking the stairs a turn at a time, silenced pistols in their hands.

Five floors up, they broke left along a draughty hall lit by taper lights. They hugged the walls and moved from shadow to shadow. The diagrams of the bastion that Noth had been able to obtain had been poor and incomplete, but enough to tell Gaunt that the kitchens were in the base of the right-hand tower, and any guest as significant as Sturm would be secured in the main donjon, probably in the upper levels.

Music rolled distantly from somewhere. Awful, jarring martial music. Bonin ushered them on across the next open junction, staying on watch, pistol raised, until the last of them was across. Was that cheering he could hear?

There were slit windows here. Rawne crossed to one, and peered out.

'We're in the main tower,' he whispered.

Now the hard part begins, Gaunt thought. As if everything they'd been through so far had been easy. The bastion was huge, with thousands of rooms. Sturm could be almost anywhere.

They ascended another series of staircases and came out in a high gallery. The gallery had once been lined with huge oil paintings of Gereon's nobility and army commanders. Only the gilt frames remained on the walls. The canvases had been hacked out. In the centre of each vacant frame, a sign of Chaos had been daubed on the stone wall.

Wind moaned down the long stone hallway. They could hear snatches of the triumphal music again, far away below them.

At the end of the gallery, an arch led through into another broad staircase landing. Gaunt was deciding which way to turn when three patrolling Occupation troopers came around the corner.

Landerson winced. The killing was so quick. He hadn't even registered the enemy troopers before they were dead. The three scouts wiped their silver knives and concealed the bodies in a dingy garderobe off the landing.

The team headed on, across the landing, and down a long hallway lined with doors to private bedrooms.

Mkoll raised his hand.

'What is it?' Gaunt whispered as they halted.

'I dunno, sir. Singing?'

Gaunt signalled the main group to stay where they were and edged forward down the cold hallway with Mkoll. He could hear it now too. Singing, laughing. Voices chatting.

One of the doors was open.

It was a regal bedchamber, lit by glow-globes. Two antlered mutants, household servants, were making the bed. One was singing a tuneless refrain, the other gibbering about something as it smoothed the coverlet of the four-poster. There was a wooden cart near the doorway, stacked with brooms and dustpans, flasks of bleach, nosegays of scented herbs, and piles of laundered sheets.

Gaunt nodded to Mkoll and stepped into view. His silenced autopistol was raised.

'Sturm,' he said carefully. 'Where is he?'

The mutant by the bed defecated in fear and threw its lamp-trimmer at Gaunt. Gaunt ducked, and shot it dead. The other scampered for the door, mewling. Mkoll tackled it, but the beast was surprisingly strong and threw him off. Gaunt turned quickly and his silencer coughed twice. The fleeing servant crashed into the wooden cart and brought it over as it fell.

'Sorry, sir,' Mkoll said, rising to his feet. 'Must be getting slow in my old age.'

Gaunt knew it wasn't that. He didn't want to think about the real reason that Mkoll's reactions were down.

Criid and Mkvenner moved up and helped them to drag the mutants' corpses into hiding behind the bed. Criid also collected up the spilled trolley.

'Sir?' she called. She'd found a roll of parchment that had fallen out of the cart. She passed it to him.

It was a long list of names or titles, and numbers were attached to them. Other than that, it made no sense.

'Cirk?' Gaunt called softly. She came forward.

'Can you read it?'

Cirk studied the parchment. 'It's a room registry,' she said. 'This here is a list of ordinals, dignitaries and senior officers, and this is a chart of the rooms they've been assigned for accommodation. Whoever wrote this wanted there to be no slip-ups. Everything's detailed. Every particular need accounted for. See, here, it says, "Ordinal Cluwge requires a south-facing room". And here, "The high sirdar's bed must be made up with hemp sheets, and a single lamp placed on his night table"'

'Yes, but–' Gaunt began.

'Way ahead of you,' she replied. 'Here. It says that the grand apartment on the sixteenth floor is to be prepared for *the pheguth*. A bath must be drawn. There are some details about a uniform. Blah blah. Seems he wants cotton sheets.'

Cirk looked at him.

'And the sixteenth floor?' he asked.

'According to this, we're on the ninth,' Cirk said.

Gaunt nodded. 'Close up!' he called out. The team gathered round. 'This is where we split up,' Gaunt told them.

LACED WITH STABLIGHTS, the Plenipotentiary's shuttle settled in to land in the upper courtyard. The band began to play, horns droning loud above the thundering kettledrums. An honour guard formed to greet him. Behind them, the long avenues of the Occupation troopers stood to attention, and the phalanxes of the ordinals, heads bowed.

Plenipotentiary Isidor Sek Incarnate stepped down out of his hovering flyer. Two massive Chaos Space Marines flanked him, snarling, their weapons brandished high, and behind them came four minotaurs, snorting in the cold air, their thick arms supporting the posts of the umbrella shield above the Plenipotentiary's disdainful head.

He waved indifferently at the hallowing crowd, the troopers rattling their weapons. The high sirdar came forward and bowed. Beside him, Desolane made reverence.

Isidor nodded, and allowed them to kiss his hands as another fanfare broke out.

'Does General Sturm await my pleasure?' Isidor asked above the thrashing music.

'He does, magir,' Desolane said.

It took twenty-seven minutes for the Plenipotentiary to walk the length of the long carpet. He stopped frequently to acknowledge the sirdars in the ranks, and then began to greet the ordinals, allowing them to kneel and kiss his fingers.

By then, Desolane had sent a runner to bring the pheguth.

STURM STOOD AND admired himself in the long looking-glass. He shook out his cuffs.

'Not bad. The coat is a little tight, but the sash is glorious.'

The lexigrapher hammered on the keys.

'Don't write that, you maggot!' Sturm snarled.

Humiliti cowered and, taking out his eraser, started to scrub out the lines he had just scrolled back.

'Where was I?' Sturm asked, pacing.

The lexigrapher showed him the sheets that spooled out of his printing machine's clamp.

Sturm read back. 'Ah yes. Vervunhive. So close as it was to my barbaric mindlocking… are you getting this, ape?'

Humiliti nodded, typing furiously again.

'So close as it was to my unreasonable, inhuman mindlocking, I find I have difficulty remembering the details. I had overall command, naturally. Gaunt was a makeweight. He had no talent for soldiering. What he had was a talent for mischief. He was a commissar, you see, as I think I have said. Have I said that?'

The lexigrapher read back quickly and then nodded.

'He was a member of the Commisariate, the discipline division. That's all politics, if you ask me. The man was a self-serving bastard. And the charges? I tell you this, was ever a man so wrongly accused? Desertion? Is it any wonder I hate the Imperium so? All my life, serving the God-Emperor… and then what does he let his minions do to me? Bastards! I was a lord militant general!'

There was a knock on the apartment door.

'Come!' Sturm yelled.

The door opened and one of the Sons of Sek leaned in. 'Magir,' he said. 'The Plenipotentiary awaits your pleasure.'

Sturm put his cap on.

'Let's go,' he said.

IN THE RAGGED slip beyond the approach road, Colonel Noth buckled his helmet in place and looked down the line of waiting men and women.

'On my word,' he whispered into the vox-link. 'Three, two, one… go!'

The Gereon resistance stormed towards the gates of the Lectica Bastion, weapons blazing.

'Gereon resists!' Noth screamed. 'Gereon resists!'

TWENTY-EIGHT

THE CHARGING WAVE of underground fighters swept like a tidal flood through the checkpoint at the head of the approach road, mowing down the excubitors and the post guards. The troopers in the roadway weapon emplacements didn't even get a chance to return fire. Rifle grenades swiftly ended their contribution to the occupation of Gereon.

The blizzard of fire from the hundreds of cell fighters was so fierce that the last few transports waiting at the barrier for admission to the bastion rocked as they were riddled with shots. One caught fire.

'Move in! Move in!' Noth yelled above the crackling gunfire. 'The walls and the gate!'

Hundreds of rifle grenades pelted the steep curtain wall, drizzling it with explosions. Some lofted high enough to drop cleanly onto the wall top itself and blow out manned batteries. But the massive array of wall defences had now begun to fire back, decimating the crowds of cell fighters approaching the foot of the wall. Steam winches were slowly pulling the vast gates shut.

The heartland cells had pooled their resources and were fielding every last man and every last, precious weapon left in their combined caches. At least a dozen shoulder-launched rocket tubes and twenty portable mortars answered the barrage blazing from the wall-top. The swishing rockets impacted in savage fire-flashes, and one actually blew out a section of the battlement. Chunks of stonework and pieces of body rained down the flank of the curtain wall.

But if the main gate closed, nothing else counted. Running forward, Noth looked around desperately. Las-shots lanced the air around him. A cell fighter just ahead of him buckled and fell. Another was blown off his feet by a cannon shell.

Noth saw the truck. Just another supply transport heading up the road to the bastion. Except it wasn't.

Gaining speed, it swerved around the shot-up vehicles at the checkpoint, splintered through the barrier, and rattled up the last stretch of road towards the still-closing gates.

From the top of the wall, the Bastion Guard raked it with fire, blowing out the cab windows, puncturing the bodywork, destroying a rear wheel. But it was still going. Noth saw the driver hurl himself out of the cab.

The transport rammed into the gates with a terrible wrench of metal. The winches continued to close the gates, but the mangled transport was now wedged between them. Its metal hull and chassis twisted out of shape as the massive gates closed tighter, but then the steam winches began to struggle and falter.

What's taking so long, Noth thought? What's taking so–

Nearly a tonne of fyceline-putty explosives – the entire combined supplies of the heartland cells – at last went off in the transport's freight bay.

There was a pink haze, bright enough to hurt, and when the hammer blow of sound and shock came a second later, it was so hard it knocked Colonel Noth and many of the cell fighters onto the ground. Some of the underground attackers too close to the truck vaporised with it.

But vast chunks of the bastion's main gates were atomised too.

Wretched, eye-watering smoke billowed all around and the air was full of streaking gunfire. Noth got up.

'Into the gates! Go! Into the gates!' he yelled. 'Gereon resists! Gereon resists!'

THE FIRST EXPLOSIONS backlit the curtain wall like sheet lightning. Then a huge blast spewed flame and debris high into the night air in the direction of the main gate.

On the inner courtyard, the assembled masses froze and turned. The band stopped playing. There was a sudden, general consternation, voices rising, ordered ranks breaking up. Everyone could hear that the bastion's defence batteries had opened up.

Desolane ran forward. The Plenipotentiary's life-wards were already hurrying him back towards the safety of his flyer. Behind them, there was mounting uproar from the assembled worthies.

'Troops to the curtain wall!' Desolane ordered. 'Now! Excubitors, get the ordinals back into the bastion! Get them to safety!'

Men rushed around the life-ward in all directions. Desolane seized a sirdar of the Bastion Guard.

'Assemble your detail,' the life-ward told him. 'General Sturm is on his way down. Intercept him and escort him back to the safety of his quarters. I will be there shortly.'

'HEAR THAT?' BONIN whispered. Mkoll nodded. Even through the massive stone fabric of the bastion, the shudder of explosions was distinct.

'The attack's started,' Landerson said, and made the sign of the aquila. Part of him, his fervent patriotism, wished he was out there, fighting alongside the resistance. But Gaunt had selected him for this greater honour.

'Are we set?' Mkoll asked.

'Almost,' said Varl. He was working carefully to attach a shaped charge low on the wall of the hallway. Criid and Brostin were covering one end of the corridor, Beltayn and Bonin the other. Under Mkoll's command, this half of the team had split from Gaunt's. Their job was to sow confusion and cause as much damage as possible. Colonel Noth had reserved one box of fyceline-putty charges from the giant payload that had gone on the transport, and Varl now carried it in a canvas satchel. Thirty charges, plus detonator pins. Mkoll's team had descended through the fortress as Gaunt's had headed upwards, laying charges at strategic intervals. The satchel was a third empty already.

Varl pressed a det pin into the soft putty. 'Done,' he said. The pins were set on a ten-minute delay. In another five minutes, the first of the charges would start going off.

'Move!' Mkoll ordered. The squad headed down the hall and reached another stairwell. Bonin pulled them all back into cover as a platoon of Occupation troopers clattered past down the staircase. Alarm bells were ringing. The noise of warfare from outside was getting louder.

The Ghosts entered the stairwell as soon as the troopers had disappeared, and silently descended another two floors.

'Here,' Mkoll said to Varl, pointing at a section of wall. Varl got to work as the others stood guard.

'Footsteps,' Bonin warned. 'From above.'

'Varl?' Mkoll asked.

'I'm right in the middle of it!'

'Feth!' Mkoll growled. He pointed at Bonin and Criid and gestured up the stairs.

The pair let their lasrifles swing and drew their suppressed autopistols. Bonin led the way. Criid could hear the footsteps too, now. Boots, several pairs, running.

Criid and Bonin braced their weapons.

Six bastion troopers hurried down around the wide stair-turn. Criid and Bonin thumped rapid shots into them. The enemy troopers went over like skittles. Criid had to side-step as one body somersaulted past her down the stairs.

Five were dead outright. The sixth, fallen and wounded, managed to get his hands on his autorifle before Bonin shot him cleanly between the eyes.

But the man's spasming fingers clawed the trigger and the autorifle blurted out a burst of automatic fire.

Criid and Bonin glanced at each other. Both had ducked and neither had even been scratched. The burst had nailed a long line of craters up the curved wall of the staircase. Smoke drifted.

In the confines of the stairwell, the gunfire had been deafeningly loud. From above them, they heard shouts.

STURM CAME TO such an abrupt halt that the Sons of Sek who had been in walking step went several paces past him. Humiliti nearly waddled into Sturm's legs.

'What is that?' Sturm asked.

'Sir?'

'Can't you hear it, man? That's gunfire. Detonations.' Sturm threw open the door of a nearby apartment, and strode over towards the narrow windows that looked out over the inner yard. The apartment was unlit and not in use. By the time Sturm reached the window, the amber glow from outside lit his features.

'The bastion is being assaulted,' he murmured in astonishment. 'There is a great fire at the gate, and other explosions…'

He swallowed hard. The sight was kindling other recollections now. Feelings. The apprehension of battle, the rush of adrenaline.

The Sons looked at each other.

'We should take you back to your quarters, sir,' one said. 'You will be safe there.'

Sturm nodded. 'That would be for the best, I think. Until the situation is under control.'

They went back out into the corridor and turned around the way they had come. Both of the Sons unslung their weapons and carried them ready.

Humiliti sighed, turned about face, and hobbled after them again.

ON THE SIXTEENTH floor, far removed from the conflict outside, Gaunt's squad stole down an almost silent hallway towards the door of a stateroom. Gaunt led the way, one bolt pistol drawn, flanked by Mkvenner, who carried an autorifle the resistance had given him.

Behind them came Eszrah ap Niht, his reynbow aimed, alongside Ana Curth who had drawn her silenced pistol. Further back, the rest of the group – Rawne, Larkin, Feygor and Cirk – covered the hallway back down to the landing.

Gaunt and Mkvenner burst through the door, weapons sweeping from side to side. The lamps were lit, but there was no one around. It was a handsome sitting room, with richly upholstered chairs, a card table and a tall looking-glass. An adjoining door led through to a bedchamber. Garments lay scattered on the floor. Parts of an Occupation force uniform. There was also an elegant brass bath tub, full of used water. Mkvenner touched the side of the tub.

'Cooling. Used not long ago. We've missed him.'

'If this was his room at all,' said Gaunt. 'Let's check the rest of the floor.'

BONIN AND CRIID came bounding back down the stairs.

'We have to go! Now!' Bonin cried. Stray shots were following them down the steps, slapping off the curving wall.

'Move out!' Mkoll ordered.

'Done! Done!' Varl yelped, and gathered up his gear.

The squad scrambled down the next long hallway, a wide, panelled gallery. Mkoll was at the back, waving the others on. They were halfway down when the first bastion troopers appeared in the stair doorway behind them.

Mkoll dropped to one knee and opened fire with his lasrifle. 'First and only!' he yelled.

Several of the enemy troopers pitched over, struck by his searing las-bolts. The others began blasting with their rifles.

Criid and Landerson both turned and added their firepower to Mkoll's. Hard rounds and las-shots chopped up and down the great gallery for a few furious seconds, tearing into the wood panelling and shattering lamps. Landerson felt a bullet graze his left thigh, but he kept firing.

A dull bang shook the floor. Somewhere, the first of Varl's charges had gone off.

More bastion troopers appeared. The doorway area was littered with dead, but still they surged to get through.

Firing, hugging the gallery walls, Mkoll, Landerson and Criid backed off towards the rest of the squad, who had now made it to the far end of the gallery.

Beltayn was the first to the exit.

'Check it!' Bonin yelled, but the vox-officer had already gone through.

A sizzling shot from a las-lock hit Beltayn square in the back and threw him down on his face.

'Beltayn!' Bonin yelled. He ran forward, firing his lasrifle one-handed as he tried to drag Beltayn back into cover. Troopers and excubitors were pouring up the steps ahead.

Mkoll's squad was trapped.

GAUNT HEARD THE thump of Varl's second charge come up through the floor from far below. He was about to suggest they might be on the wrong floor, when three figures came round the corner not ten metres away. Two big soldiers, dressed in menacing ochre fatigues, with another man between them.

It was Noches Sturm.

For one nanosecond Sturm's eyes met Gaunt's. One fleeting heartbeat of shocking mutual recognition.

Then the soldiers in yellow were shooting.

Gaunt felt a bullet go through his left shoulder. He crashed against the door of a nearby room. Mkvenner had thrown himself at Gaunt, bringing them both down in the partial cover of the doorway to avoid the withering fire from the strange enemy troopers.

Behind Gaunt and Mkvenner, the others scrambled for cover. By the time Rawne had got himself into some kind of firing position, the two warriors in ochre had expertly backed off around the hall-turn, covering Sturm every step of the way.

'Him! It was him!' Gaunt yelled.

'GAUNT? GAUNT? How could... how could he be here?' Sturm was saying. Humiliti didn't know if he should be recording this, but he did anyway. Guns smoking, the Sons of Sek hustled the general roughly towards the nearest apartment, kicked the door open, and pushed him inside.

'How is this possible?' Sturm demanded. 'How is this happening?'

The Sons didn't reply. Rawne, Mkvenner and Feygor had already appeared around the corridor turn and were firing down the passageway. The Sons slid into hallway doors, using the heavy sills as cover, and replied with quick, calculating bursts that forced the Ghosts back into cover.

'How?' Sturm was yelling. 'How?'

GAUNT REACHED THE corner, ignoring Curth's attempt to dress the wound in his shoulder. Shots were zinging past the end of the wall.

'There's only two of them!' Rawne was yelling.

'There only needs to be,' replied Mkvenner. 'They've got the whole passageway covered. And they're fething good.'

Gaunt knew that already. Sturm's bodyguard had reacted with the speed and tenacity of elite force troopers.

'Two or two hundred, we're taking them now,' Gaunt said.

But suddenly there was gunfire coming from behind him too.

The Bastion Guard detail that Desolane had sent to intercept Sturm had just arrived at the other end of the sixteenth floor. Drawn by the sound of weapons fire, they were rushing down the corridor to engage.

Larkin, Cirk, Eszrah and even Curth had opened fire.

THE DIN OF battle echoing from the outer courtyards was immense. It trembled the cold night air and echoed off the surrounding mountains. A large stretch of the curtain wall around the main gate was ablaze, generating an infernal radiance that lit the vast plume of white smoke rising off the gate itself. Inside, between the curtain wall and the inner bulwark, a flickering mass of flashes, bursts and tracer fire stitched the night.

Desolane reached the bulwark. Reserves of bastion troops, along with visiting companies, were drawn up behind the inner wall, checking their weapons.

Desolane approached the senior officers. 'Report?'

'Somehow, they've breached the gates and got into the outer yards,' said one sirdar.

'We've sealed the bulwark,' another reported, 'but they're hitting it hard.'

'Numbers? And who are they?' asked Desolane.

'Several hundred. Unconfirmed reports say it is the resistance,' a senior excubitor stated.

'Of course it is!' snapped Desolane.

'This is an unforgivable outrage,' High Sirdar Brendel announced. 'I will of course present his highness the Plenipotentiary with my abject apologies for this miserable failure of security.'

There was a rapid, whistling noise, and a crunch. The officers all flinched. One of Desolane's ketra blades had cleaved the high sirdar's head and helmet in two. His corpse fell backwards.

'I'll save him the bother of accepting them,' Desolane whispered. The lifeward turned to the other seniors. 'That idiot was mistaken. The security of the bastion, the Plenipotentiary and the pheguth is mine to uphold. Mine alone. You will follow my orders and contain this disgraceful exhibition at once. Where is the etogaur?'

'I'm here, life-ward,' Mabbon stepped into view.

'I need a commander I can trust to crush this uprising immediately. Are the Sons of Sek ready?'

'Eager, life-ward.'

'Command of the field is yours. Sirdars and seniors? You answer to the etogaur.'

There was a hasty chorus of affirmatives. 'Prepare to deploy!' Mabbon yelled out. 'In the name of the Anarch, whose word drowns out all others! Now!'

'Life-ward?'

Desolane turned. A junior officer was approaching, panting hard.

'What?'

'Reports of explosions, life-ward,' the junior gasped. 'From within the bastion.'

Desolane pushed the junior aside and began to run across the inner yard towards the keep.

'GET THE FETH down!' Brostin bellowed and squeezed the trigger-spoon of his captured flamer. The weapon gurgled, coughed and then sent a dazzling spear of liquid flame out through the doorway into the stairwell. Voices began to scream.

Mkoll, Criid and Landerson had now rejoined them, still duelling hard with the Archenemy troopers coming in through the gallery's far end.

'I'll clear us a way,' Brostin said, firing through the doorway again.

'Make it fast!' Mkoll snapped. Shots were raining down around them, ripping into the walls and carpet. Mkoll saw Beltayn lying on his face, Bonin crouching over him.

'Oh, feth! No!' the scout-sergeant cried.

'It's all right,' said Bonin. 'He's alive.'

Beltayn rolled over, gagging. The potent las-lock shot had hit him squarely in the vox-caster strapped to his back. The sheer force had winded him badly, but he was completely intact.

The same could not be said for his vox-set. Bonin pulled it off him. It was a blackened ruin, smoke wisping out of the shattered cover.

'I need that...' Beltayn gasped.

'Not any more, Bel,' Bonin said. 'It's junked. Come on, on your feet.'

With Criid, Varl and Landerson forming a rearguard, blazing away down the now devastated gallery, Brostin led them through the doorway. The stone stairwell radiated heat from the torching and soot caked every surface. Smouldering bodies, most of them so reduced by fire they were charcoal lumps, littered the stairs. Brostin sent another searing blast down the stairwell for good measure.

'Let's shift!' he cried.

From somewhere overhead, they felt the thump from another of Varl's charges.

THERE WAS SMOKE in the air. It drifted lazily along the empty hallways of the bastion. From far below echoed the sounds of the battle outside, and the pandemonium amongst the ordinals cowering in the main halls.

But this smoke, up here... It was coming from inside the fortress, from higher up. Desolane paused as a tremble ran through the stone floor. Something had just exploded, a few levels above.

The life-ward swept out its ketra blades.

'RAWNE!' GAUNT YELLED. 'Take the squad and drive those bastards back! Ven and I will go in after Sturm!'

There was no time to argue. The hammer of gunfire from the battle with the bastion detail made it almost impossible to hear anyway. Rawne nodded and rolled to his feet. Cirk, Feygor, Curth and Larkin had taken up firing positions along the sixteenth floor's main hallway, and were trying to keep the troopers at bay. The partisan was backing them up, thumping quarrels at the ceremonially-attired enemy soldiers. One of the iron darts hit a man in the face, and he toppled over, his huge helmet-plume of white feathers swishing like a game-bird brought down in flight.

Rawne edged forward. Somehow, Cirk had ended up in charge of the defence, and Rawne had to admit she was doing a good job. She'd arranged the Ghosts into a decent cover formation using doorways and pillars as shields, and they were, for now, holding the enemy back.

Only Curth – inexperienced in combat – was ignoring Cirk's instructions. Curth's anger had broken loose again. She was blasting away wildly with her pistol. It pained Rawne to see the strong, wilful medicae so broken and mad.

'Cirk!' he yelled. 'I want to try and drive them back through the stair head doorway! We can hold that much more securely!'

'Agreed!' she shouted.

Rawne dropped down, and pointed to Cirk, Feygor and Larkin in turn, indicating each position of cover he wanted them to move up to when he gave the order. He and Cirk would move first.

'Larks!' he called. 'Smack a hotshot down through the centre of them and get them ducking!'

Larkin nodded, and loaded a fresh cell into his long-las. The powerful hotshot clips each delivered one super-heated shot before they were spent. He was down to his last three. After that, he'd be using his pistol.

'Set!' he yelled.

'Go!' Rawne cried.

The long-las cracked and the gleaming bolt stung down the passageway. Rawne and Cirk were already moving.

But as he came out of cover, Rawne hesitated. The smoke swirling in the air in front of him had formed the precise shape of the stigma mark, and behind it, the figures of the regal enemy troopers somehow matched it perfectly. The creeping madness was on him again, the paranoia. They were going to fail and die and–

A shot tore through his left thigh and he went down on one knee with a grunt. Confused for a moment by Rawne's hesitation, Larkin wavered too, and was smacked over onto his back by a shot that broke his collarbone.

Larkin writhed on the floor, wailing, blood soaking out of him into the hall carpet.

'Larks!' Feygor bawled, and ran through the hailing fire, head-down. He grabbed Larkin by the straps of his webbing and began to drag him back towards the cover of a doorway, oblivious to his own safety. A shot ripped through his left triceps, another cut the flesh above his right knee, a third glanced off his forehead so savagely it almost scalped him. Blood pouring into his eyes, Feygor screamed out and continued to drag the helpless sniper backwards. At every jolt, Larkin shrieked as his broken bones twisted and ground together.

Rawne crawled into cover, cursing his own frailty. Their effort had been completely unsuccessful.

Worse than that, Cirk had dashed forward ahead, assuming they were all behind her. Now she was pinned down, alone and entirely helpless.

THIRTY METRES BEHIND them, Gaunt and Mkvenner edged back to the corner. The shooting had stopped. Gaunt risked a glance, in time to see the two warriors in ochre rushing Sturm away around the next hallway turn. A curious little hominid in long robes was waddling after them.

'Come on!' Gaunt yelled. With Mkvenner at his side, he began to run after the man he had crossed light-years and risked everything to eliminate.

ON THE NEXT landing, Desolane paused again. The smoke was thicker now. Somewhere in the bastion there was a considerable fire. The life-ward felt yet another vibration. Another explosion. How many was that now? Six? Seven?

Who was doing this? Surely this was beyond the scope of the local resistance. All they ever seemed to manage to do was blow up roads or set fire to granaries.

Desolane thought of Lord Uexkull. He and his band of warriors were now long overdue, along with Ordinal Sthenelus. In his last report, Uexkull had spoken of 'Imperial killers', specialist soldiers who had fought off everything the Occupation had thrown at them. Were they here now? Were they the ones who had so entirely shamed the life-ward and the bastion's regiments?

There could be only one reason an elite squad of the False Emperor's soldiers was here on occupied Gereon. Desolane knew it. That reason was the pheguth. Desolane's beloved pheguth. The life-ward had sworn before Isidor himself to protect the life of the Anarch's precious *eresht*. Other life-wards had refused the duty, spurning it. A traitor, they believed, an enemy, hardly deserved the sort of protection usually reserved for the most high-ranking ordinals. But Desolane had not. Desolane had seen it as a true challenge of its abilities. Life-wards were bred from birth to be the ultimate protectors. Nothing was more important than the safety of the charges they pledged themselves to.

And Desolane was the very best. It had been a mark of pride to accept this task from the Anarch, whose word drowns out all others, and to carry it out faultlessly.

There was another side to it too. Over the months they had spent in close company, often just the two of them alone for days at a time, Desolane had come to care for the pheguth. A bond had grown between them. The pheguth had seemed to Desolane a kindly, sorrowful man, broken down by the harsh hand fortune had dealt him, always respectful of the life-ward, always appreciative of every special attention Desolane paid to make his incarceration more bearable. When the attempt had been made on his life, the pheguth hadn't blamed Desolane. He'd actually refused to dish out the ritual punishment. It had been then that Desolane had realised the pheguth cared for the life-ward too.

Of course, it had been difficult when the mindlock collapsed, and the pheguth had become Sturm again. Sturm was a pompous, arrogant soul, and he had shown far less respect for the life-ward. But even then, Desolane had been able to see the man it had sworn to protect. The humble pheguth, in his slippers and gown, shackled to a steel bed, smiling as he sipped a cup of weak black tea as if it was the most precious thing in the galaxy.

Desolane would protect its pheguth now. Against anything. The life-ward took a little golden scanner-wand out from under its smoke-cloak. The pheguth didn't know, but early on a tracker had been embedded in his right buttock, so that Desolane would always know his location.

Desolane checked the wand's reading, and then leapt up the staircase, four steps at a time.

THE RESISTANCE WAS at the bulwark. Thresher reported that one of the gates was about to break. Gunfire licked in all directions, most of it coming off the top of the bulwark itself. Around Noth, cell fighters were dying, cut to pieces by the lethal defences.

But they were still advancing. If there had been any time to consider it, Noth would have marvelled at their success so far. There was still a chance.

If the bulwark could be breached, they would be into the inner yards of the bastion. In amongst the damned ordinals and the other dignitaries, killing the bastards in the name of a free Gereon.

'Move in!' Noth yelled above the gunfire, his own weapon chattering in his hands as he ran forward. 'Take the gate! Tube launchers! Come on, we've got them! Gereon resists! Gereon resists!'

Noth staggered as the backwash of an explosion struck him from the left-hand side. Grit flew into the air and pattered onto the yard. Through the smoke, Noth saw movement. One of the other bulwark gates had opened from the inside, and troops were charging out to counter-attack them.

They were daemons, dressed in ochre. Noth had never seen anything like them before.

A cell fighter to his left folded as gunfire ripped through her belly. Another man went down howling, his leg shot off below the knee. Still more collapsed under the streaming fire.

'Rally! Rally!' Noth yelled. 'Come about! Line order!'

He turned himself, firing his rifle on auto, and saw at least one of the ochre figures shudder and fall.

'Form on me! Resist!'

The man beside him reeled sideways, as if caught by a whip. A shot had destroyed his jaw. Others ran to take his place. Thresher's cell turned back from the vulnerable gate and laid down fire too.

'Form a line! A line!' Noth yelled. 'Gereon resists!'

To his left, he heard Major Planterson bellowing as he tried to control his formation. Colonel Stocker was already dead. Thresher was trying to re-form her milling troops.

The ochre-clad warriors came on through the smoke like a storm, tearing into Noth's still-forming line. Bayonets lashed and stabbed.

Noth had read the resistance reports on Furgesh and Nahren, bocage towns that had been mysteriously exterminated in the last two weeks. There had been unsubstantiated rumours that the killing had been done by soldiers dressed in ochre, warriors who had howled the words 'Sons of Sek!' as they slaughtered.

Noth's line buckled under the impact of the charge. The colonel saw men and women he'd known all his life cut down, murdered, dismembered as they tried to stave off the feral attack. Thresher's cell was trying to engage, but now the bulwark emplacements were cutting them down in their dozens.

Noth saw Thresher fall.

So close, he thought. One of the ochre bastards came right up at him, and Noth shot him apart. Another smashed his bayonet right through the skull of the man at Noth's side, and Noth put five rounds into the killer's chest.

'Gereon resists!' he yelled. 'Gereon resists!'

Another one was on him. Noth's magazine was empty. He lunged with his bayonet, screaming. The ochre warrior smashed Noth's weapon aside with a supremely practiced flick, as if he had been drilling for months on end.

The enemy bayonet impaled Noth through the sternum. He coughed up blood as it was wrenched out and staggered forward.

He knew he was dead. He tried to make the battle cry of the resistance one last time, but his lungs were full of blood.

The Sons of Sek didn't even let him fall. Cackling like jackals, they hacked Noth limb from limb with their blades.

'Down! Go on!' Mkoll yelled, urging his squad down the next winding staircase. Up was not an option. What seemed like a division of Occupation troopers was hard on their heels, hammering fire down the stairwell after them. Every single member of Mkoll's team, himself included, had picked up at least one flesh wound now, and Bonin had been hit badly above the right hip.

Besides, there was fire up above them. The charges Varl had managed to plant had set several floors in the midsection of the fortress alight. The air was filmed with drifting smoke, and there was an alarming scent of burning. Mkoll wondered if Gaunt had been successful. He prayed so.

Varl and Criid were leading the way down. Blood was running from a cut on Varl's shoulder, and Criid was bleeding from a wound under her hairline.

Landerson was helping Bonin along.

Shots suddenly began to spray up at them. They ducked back. Varl peered down. Dozens of excubitors were lurching up the stairs below.

'We need another way out!' Varl yelled.

Mkoll ran back up the stairs a little way, firing shots up at the first Occupation troopers that poked their faces around the stair bend, and kicked open a door. It led into another hallway. They were crossing back into the side tower adjacent to the main keep.

'Get moving!' Mkoll shouted, blasting up at the troops trying to press down the stairs to get at them. Several fell, hitting the stone steps hard and slithering down, limp.

Varl and Brostin were the last two through the door. Brostin's flamer had accounted for many of the enemy so far, and added to the conflagration in the bastion too. Now his prom tanks were wheezing and almost empty.

'You saving the rest of those charges?' he asked Varl.

'Not particularly,' said Varl. 'But I don't have time to set the det pins–'

'Just fething toss them!' Brostin yelled.

Varl turned and hurled the satchel down the stairwell.

'Now run, Varl. Run like a bastard and don't look back.'

Varl did exactly what Brostin told him to do. Brostin shook the flamer's tanks and drooled up the last of the accelerant. Then he aimed the weapon down the stairs.

'Say hello to Mister Yellow,' he murmured, and belched off his last spear of flame.

Brostin threw the heavy weapon aside and started to run. Most of Mkoll's squad had already reached the end of the hallway. His long legs pumping,

Brostin moved fast for a heavy man. He had almost caught up with Varl when the fire in the stairwell ignited the satchel.

There was a strange, drum-like thump. Then a fireball rushed up the stairs and boiled along the corridor, throwing Varl and Brostin right off their feet.

IN THE OUTER yards, the Sons of Sek were beginning to howl out their victory. Mabbon Etogaur moved forward, slapping men on the back, stepping over the butchered dead. Sporadic gunfire still rattled from either side.

He heard something and looked up. Dark against the night sky, the bastion was suddenly illuminated. Some kind of furnace light had split its midriff, spilling flame up into the air from dozens of windows. Mabbon looked at it in astonishment. The right-hand side of the bastion was on fire, and so were the upper storeys of the side tower.

Mabbon keyed his vox-bead. 'This is the etogaur. Primary orders. All units evacuate the bastion. You are charged with the safe removal of the ordinals. Do it now and do it properly!'

He looked back at the vast fortress. Fire was belching from the entire right-hand side. What in the name of the Anarch had happened up there?

'CIRK! CIRK, STAY down!' Rawne cried, trying to staunch the blood gushing from his leg wound. Something catastrophic had just shaken the entire donjon. He could smell burning.

He heard Cirk yelp. She'd been hit. The shot-rate coming from the bastion troopers down the hall was increasing, and some were moving forward.

'Stay down!' he shouted again.

Rawne looked around. The partisan had vanished, and Feygor, last seen maimed and bleeding from at least three hits, had finally succeeded in dragging Larkin into the cover of an adjacent room. The only person in sight was Curth, crouched down in a doorway. She was still firing at the enemy, yelling out her rage. She had ditched her pistol and had grabbed hold of Feygor's fallen lasrifle.

'Ana!' Rawne yelled over the constant fusillade.

'What?'

'We have to get forward! We have to get forward now!'

'Why? What the feth for?'

Rawne staggered across the hall and fell down beside her. 'Cirk's pinned,' he said. 'We have to move forward and drive them back, or she's dead.'

'So fething what?' Curth snarled, firing again. 'She deserves to die. That bitch. She's a total bitch. You've seen the mark on her. She's Chaos filth!'

'I've seen it,' Rawne murmured. 'I see it everywhere.'

'What?'

He sat up and looked at her. She was still shooting.

'Ana. We can't leave her to die.'

'Why the feth not?' Curth asked.

'Because... because otherwise, the Archenemy has won.'

'What the feth are you on about, Rawne?'

Rawne coughed the smoke out of his gullet. 'She's helped us, Curth. Every step of the way, without question. She's got us through, risked her life. Feth it, we wouldn't have got in here without her. I don't like her either. I don't trust her. She's got the mark. But then again, I don't think I trust anyone any more.'

'I say we leave her!' Curth grunted and fired again.

'Ana,' Rawne whispered. 'The taint has got us. The poison of this fething world. You and me both. If we leave Cirk, we let it win.'

Curth stared at him. 'That's rubbish!' she said.

'No, it isn't. Whatever you or I think she is, she's got this far. This is our last chance, Ana. Our last chance!'

'Our last chance for what?'

'To prove we're still human. To prove we're loyal servants of the Emperor. Even now. Even though Gereon has done its worst.'

Curth lowered the rifle and gazed at him. Tears welled up in her eyes. 'You talk a lot of feth, you know that, major?'

'You know I'm right,' Rawne replied. 'I won't let this place beat me. How about you?'

'Do the right thing?' she asked sarcastically.

'Because the Emperor protects. And if he approves, he will protect us and let us know he is pleased with our service.'

'You make that shit up all by yourself?' she said.

'No. It was something Gaunt said.'

'All right,' said Curth. Rawne handed her his last fresh clip and she slammed it home.

'For the Emperor, then,' she said.

He shook his head. 'No, for Tanith, first and only.'

They got up, lasrifles blasting, and charged down the corridor side by side into the enemy fire.

THE TWO SONS of Sek had shoved Sturm into another apartment chamber. He was terribly agitated now, pacing up and down, the lexigrapher hobbling after him.

'Gaunt… no, that's not right. As I said, he can't be here. It makes no sense…'

Sturm paused. He glanced at Humiliti, who was still typing, and then walked through into the apartment's bedchamber, throwing the doors wide.

'I remember,' he said, sitting down on the bed. 'I remember now. Throne, I thought I'd remembered everything. Who I was, what I was. But there are deep, dark places in the mind that take a long time to resurface.'

Humiliti tapped and rattled his keys.

'I was a commander of men… did I say that before?'

The lexigrapher nodded.

'Men feared me. Respected me. But… oh, Emperor, I remember it now. Vervunhive. The bloody war. We were losing. The Zoican host was right at the gates.'

Sturm got to his feet and hunched down facing the lexigrapher. Humiliti looked up at him with bright eyes, his nimble fingers poised over the key-levers.

'I was afraid,' Sturm said. 'I was afraid for my life. I ran. I deserted my post. I would have left them all to die.'

Humiliti hesitated, wondering if he was supposed to record this.

'Take it down, you maggot!' Sturm cried, rising again. 'Take it all down! This is my confession! This is me! You and your foul masters wanted to know all about me! All my secrets! You wanted to pick my mind clean! Well, how about this one, eh? I thought I was a lord general. I thought I had power and strength. So did your masters. That's why they spent all this time and effort breaking me. And what do they get? What do they get, you little runt?'

Sturm turned and bowed his head. 'A coward. A man too afraid of death to do the right thing.'

Beyond the outer room of the apartment, shots rang out.

MKOLL AND CRIID pulled Varl and Brostin to their feet. Both men had blisters on their skin from the sucking fireball. Behind them, the entire staircase was ablaze. There were ominous rumbles as the structure of the bastion itself began to crumble.

'Nice one,' Criid grinned.

'Time to leave,' Mkoll said.

'WHERE'S THE WOUND?' Curth was yelling. 'Where are you hit?'

Cirk showed Curth her left forearm. A round had broken the bones and exploded the imago in its pus-filled blister.

'It's gone,' Cirk sighed.

'Come on,' Curth said urgently, helping her up. Rawne was behind her, raking las-fire into the doorway of the staircase, pushing the enemy back. Every muzzle flash seemed to form the stigma mark to him, but he didn't care any more.

'You came back for me,' Cirk whispered.

'Yeah, we did,' said Curth. 'How about that?'

THE TWO SONS of Sek turned and began to return fire, but Gaunt and Mkvenner had the drop on them. Gaunt stormed forward, a bolt pistol in either hand, firing at the frantic warriors. One toppled as his skull exploded. The other jerked back, a bolt round striking his right arm and disintegrating it. The soldier screamed and Mkvenner put a bullet through his open mouth.

Gaunt and Mkvenner prowled forward, their weapons smoking. The door that the Sons had been defending was wide open. Gaunt holstered his pistols, and drew his power sword. It throbbed as the blade ignited.

The chamber beyond was an anteroom, full of opulent furniture. An empty gilt frame hung on the wall, surrounding a blasphemous symbol. There was a doorway beyond, open. Gaunt could hear a voice talking.

He glanced at Mkvenner. Ven raised his autorifle. They crept forward.

And Desolane entered the room behind them.

TWENTY-NINE

THE LIFE-WARD pounced forward, its twin ketra blades scything at the two Guardsmen. Mkvenner reacted first, turning to block, his raised autorifle splintering apart beneath the life-ward's right-hand blade.

Gaunt turned too, bringing the power sword up. It met the left-hand ketra, and the blade glanced away.

He had never seen anything like this creature. A towering, slender, sexless body sheathed in a tight suit of blue-black metal-weave and draped with a gauzy black cloak that moved like smoke. The monster's long legs were jointed the wrong way below the knees and ended in cloven hooves. A smooth bronze helmet covered the thing's head, broken only by four holes: two for the eye-slits and two on the brow through which small white horns extended.

It moved like water, as if the rest of existence had been slowed down.

Gaunt blocked another stab, and another, then danced around to present again. The thing lunged forward, ripping Gaunt's coat with the tip of its left-hand blade, and then swung in a strike that left a long, lacerating stripe down Gaunt's torso.

Gasping in pain, weeping blood, Gaunt leapt back and swung the power sword of Heironymo Sondar around in a savage chop. The powered blade met Desolane's left-hand knife and shattered it.

Desolane lunged again, and stripped a deep gash through Gaunt's right arm with its remaining knife. The sheer impact threw Gaunt over onto the floor. His hands wet with blood, he scrambled for the sword. Desolane knocked it away with one cloven hoof, and then kicked Gaunt hard in the belly. Gaunt doubled up, choking and winded.

Desolane stabbed its remaining blade towards Gaunt's head.

Silenced pistol rounds, spitting like whispers, jerked the life-ward back-wards. Mkvenner rose, tossing aside the now-empty autopistol, and picked up the fallen power sword. It hummed and sang in his hands as he crossed and turned it.

Desolane went for him.

Mkvenner parried the first cut, swung wide, deflected the second and wheeled back to stop the third. Desolane snarled, swinging round to attack Mkvenner again. The life-ward scythed in low, and Mkvenner managed to turn the ketra blade away, but Desolane slammed its bodyweight into the Tanith scout, and sent him reeling back. Desolane checked and spun again, fending off the sword and splitting Mkvenner's cheek open from the lip to the jaw-line.

Mkvenner fell, blood pouring out of his face.

Desolane turned nimbly and stepped over to Gaunt, who was still trying to rise. The life-ward raised its ketra blade double-handed to deliver the killing stroke.

An iron quarrel hit Desolane in the ribs. As the life-ward staggered back, another went in through one of the eye slits in its bronze helmet.

Eszra ap Niht walked forward, reloading his reynbow. The partisan fired again, and planted an iron arrow in Desolane's chest. The life-ward stag-gered forward and smashed Eszrah across the room with one blow of its fist. The partisan lay where he fell, his segmented cloak in tatters. Desolane stumbled round, swaying. By now, the moth-toxin was flooding through its veins. It fell down hard on its face.

GAUNT GOT TO his feet, dripping blood. He limped through the doorway into the bedchamber, drawing a bolt pistol in each hand.

The hunched lexigrapher backed away.

Sturm sat on the end of the bed, staring at the floor.

'Commissar,' he said, without looking up.

'Lord general,' Gaunt replied.

'I'm glad it's you,' said Sturm. 'Somehow appropriate.'

'In the name of the God-Emperor–' Gaunt began.

'Please, no. Nothing so formal,' Sturm protested. 'I remember it all now, Gaunt. All of it. The fear. The… cowardice. It's not a pretty memory. Throne knows, it took long enough to come back.'

Gaunt raised one of his pistols. 'By the power of the Commissariat, I hereby declare–'

'Ibram? Ibram… please,' Sturm begged.

'Not this time, Sturm.'

'Please, in the name of the Throne! Give me a weapon!'

Gaunt stiffened, feeling the blood leaking out of him.

'I showed you that respect at Vervunhive. You turned it into an attack.'

'I know. I'm sorry. I beg you. Gaunt, you have two bolters, for Throne's sake.'

Swaying, Gaunt held out one of his bolt pistols and gave it butt-first to Sturm. He kept the other one raised to cover the traitor general.

'Final request granted. Or… another trick?' Gaunt asked.

Sturm shook his head.

'Final request accepted,' Sturm said. He put the barrel of the bolt pistol to his head and pulled the trigger.

Gaunt took a step forward, not yet believing it was over. Sturm lay at his feet, his skull exploded like a ripe melon.

Desolane burst into the bedchamber, swinging the ketra blade like a sickle. The life-ward howled when it saw the pheguth's corpse.

Gaunt flinched back.

A hotshot round disintegrated Desolane's midriff and threw the life-ward's corpse against the far wall.

Gaunt looked up. Feygor, his face streaming with blood, lowered Larkin's long-las.

Gaunt smiled at Feygor. 'You know,' he said. 'I knew there was a reason I brought you along.'

THIRTY

Behind them, against the early dawn, the bastion was burning. The fleeing Ghosts had regrouped in a dim valley below the fortress. Every single one of them was wounded. But every single one was also alive.

Curth was trying to dress Gaunt's wounds.

'See to the others, Ana. The more deserving,' he said.

'That would be you,' she replied.

Gaunt sent her away and limped down through the figures of the Ghosts sprawled amongst the rocks.

Larkin was moaning and seemed close to death. Feygor was now unconscious from blood loss.

Gaunt crouched down beside Beltayn.

'I'm so sorry, sir,' Beltayn said.

'For what?' asked Gaunt.

'My vox-caster, sir. I got it shot up. Now we can't call in the extraction.'

'Bel, we'll be fine. Nothing's awry.'

Gaunt rose, and walked on. Curth was excising the last shreds of the burst imago from Cirk's broken forearm. He watched for a moment as the steel pliers dragged black tendrils from the woman's flesh.

Under the skin. What matters is on the inside. In the heart. In the mind. The Saint used many instruments to guide those loyal to her, even some that appeared to bear the mark of Chaos.

Gaunt turned away. He wondered how he would tell them.

It had been the last thing Van Voytz had said to him before the mission. The one thing Gaunt had not shared with the chosen team.

'Ibram, please understand there's very little chance of getting you off Gereon again. You can transmit a call, of course, but the odds are you'll be left stranded. Getting you in will be hard enough. Getting a ship close enough to pull you back out...' Van Voytz had looked away.

'Are you saying, sir, that if we're still alive at the end of this suicidal mission, it's *still* a one-way mission?'

'Yes, Gaunt,' Van Voytz had said. 'Does that change your mind?'

'No, sir.'

Gaunt wandered down the slope to find Landerson.

'They fought and died with honour,' Gaunt said to him. 'The Gereon cells. They almost had the bastards on the ropes. The resistance did its very best.'

'Yes, sir, it did,' Landerson replied. 'But it wasn't enough, was it? And now they're all gone.'

Gaunt shrugged. 'Then we'll build the underground back up between us.'

'Between us?' Landerson asked.

Gaunt nodded. 'I think I'm going to be here for a while longer. What do you say?'

'That Gereon resists?'

'Gereon resists,' Gaunt replied. He looked up. From the back of his mind came a memory, strong and unbidden. Tanith pipes. Brin Milo, playing the tune he always played when the Tanith First retired from a battlefield. He tried to remember its name.

The mountain wind rose, cold and unforgiving. It blew the smoke from the fortress out across the heartland, another stain upon a wide, disfigured world.

HIS LAST COMMAND

FOR TANITH · FOR THE EMPEROR

for Matt Farrer

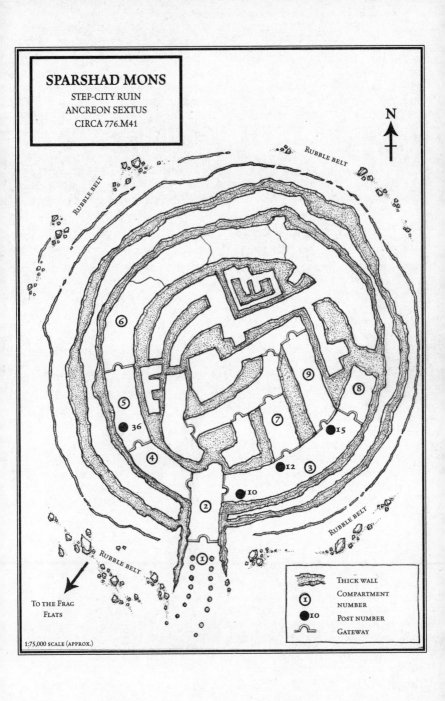

SPARSHAD MONS

STEP-CITY RUIN
ANCREON SEXTUS
CIRCA 776.M41

N

RUBBLE BELT

RUBBLE BELT

RUBBLE BELT

⑥

⑤
● 36

④

②

①

● 10

⑦

③
● 12

⑨

⑧

● 15

RUBBLE BELT

TO THE FRAG
FLATS

1:75,000 SCALE (APPROX.)

THICK WALL

① COMPARTMENT
NUMBER

● 10 POST NUMBER

GATEWAY

'By the middle of 776.M41, the twenty-first year of the Sabbat Worlds Crusade, Warmaster Macaroth's main battle-groups had penetrated extensively into the Carcaradon Cluster, and had become locked in full-scale war against the main dispositions of the Arch-enemy overlord, ('Archon'), Urlock Gaur.

However, to Macaroth's coreward flank, an equally savage war front was being prosecuted by the Warmaster's secondary battle-groups – the Fifth, Eighth and Ninth Crusade Armies – as they attempted to oust the forces of Magister Anakwanar Sek, one of Gaur's most ferocious warlord lieutenants, from the margins of the Khan Group.

The theatres of that campaign read as a roll call of Imperial heroism and endeavour: the glass beaches of Korazon, the black glaciers of Lysander, the high sierra forests of Khan Nobilis, the step-cities of Ancreon Sextus…'

– from *A History of the Later Imperial Crusades*

PROLOGUE

23.45 hrs, 185.776.M41
Imperial Internment Camp 917 'Xeno'
Southern Polar Plateau, Ancreon Sextus

'ARE YOU SURE about this, sir?' Ludd yelled above the storm as they crossed the yard, heads down into the knifing gale.

The wind was full of ice crystals that flashed like glass dust in the beams of the blockhouse stab-lights. Kanow had no intention of opening his mouth to reply.

They reached the iron porch of the assessment block, and pulled the cold metal hatches shut behind them. The wind-howl subsided slightly.

'I said–' Ludd began.

'I heard,' Kanow replied, brushing powder-ice off his leather coat. 'Sure about what?'

Junior Commissar Nahum Ludd shrugged. 'I was only wondering, sir, if we should wait.'

'For what?'

'Corroboration?'

Kanow snorted. 'This camp's at full capacity, Ludd. We must process, process, process.' With each repetition of the word, he slapped his hands together quickly. 'If I waste time checking each and every tall story these deserters and heretics spin, we'll be overrun. What's my motto, Ludd?'

'Fast appraisal, fast despatch, sir.'

'Fast appraisal, that's right. And in this case, are you in any doubt?'

The junior commissar hesitated.

'Well, I'm not,' Kanow said. 'Deserters and heretics. You can see that just by looking at them, and smell it just from the stink of their bodies. And that story? It doesn't deserve corroboration, Ludd. It's patently mendacious.'

'Yes, sir,' said Ludd.

'What are they?'

'Deserters and heretics, sir.'

'That's right. Did you actually think we should get this verified?'

Ludd looked at his feet. Pools of ice-melt were forming on the metal floor around his boots and coat-hem. 'There were certain aspects which I felt to be compelling and worth–'

'Shut up, Ludd,' Commissar Kanow said.

Kanow pushed through the inner hatch into the main hallway of the assessment block. Ludd followed. There was an animal warmth in the air, a cattle-bower stink. Laced with metal walkways and staircases, eight storeys of prison containment rose up on either side of the gloomy hall space, and from the shuttered rockcrete pens all around them, Ludd and Kanow could hear moans and murmurs issuing from thousands of incarcerated men. Dirty, degenerate wretches with ragged clothes peered out at them through the serried wire gates of the sorting cages on the ground floor.

'Please, sir! By the grace of the Throne, please!' one man called out, reaching a filthy hand out through the bars.

Kanow unholstered his bolt pistol and racked the slide. The wretch drew back immediately, and inmates in the nearby pens shrank away to the far walls with a muted wailing, like reprimanded dogs.

A nearby blast-hatch whined open and let in a fierce gust of icy air. The commissar and his junior both shielded their faces from the cold. Yelling and waving shock mauls, a gang of armoured troopers began herding in another batch of new arrivals from Outer Processing.

'Pen one seventeen!' a voice shouted, and a buzzer sounded as the electric cage door on one seventeen unlocked with a clack. The troopers drove the newcomers inside, enthusiastically beating the slowest or most reluctant amongst them.

Once the cage was locked again, the gang of troopers began to disperse to other duties.

'Trouble, commissar?' asked Troop Sergeant Maskar, noticing the drawn bolt pistol as he came over.

'Not yet, Maskar,' Kanow grunted. 'But I need you and an armed detail, if you've got a moment.'

'At your command, sir,' Maskar nodded, and turned. 'Squad six, with me!'

Maskar was a big man, shaven-headed and fleshy. Like all the Camp Xeno troopers, he wore leather-jacked steel armour that was articulated around his body and limbs in interlocking segments, so as to give the impression of well-developed but flayed musculature. He slid his shock maul into its belt loop and unlimbered his cut-down autorifle. The five troopers with him did the same.

Kanow ejected the magazine from his bolt pistol. The afternoon's round of executions had left it almost spent. He slammed home a fresh one.

'Pen three twenty-eight,' Kanow said, and the troopers fell into step behind him, arming their rifles.

'Summary kills, sir?' Maskar asked.

'I'll have the paperwork done by the morning, sergeant. The warrants too. But this can't wait. Follow my lead.'

'Sir, I–'

Kanow looked round at Ludd.

'What? What now?'

'Nothing, sir,' Ludd said.

The party clattered up two flights of metal stairs, their heavy tread shaking the steps, then turned right along the third deck gallery.

They reached the cage door of three twenty-eight. The chamber within looked empty.

'Pen three twenty-eight!' Maskar yelled, and the automated bolts shot open as the buzzer sounded.

Kanow entered. The third deck pens were larger holding tanks reserved for groups of up to thirty inmates. Several of the wall lights in three twenty-eight had apparently malfunctioned. Kanow could just make out some dark figures, a dozen or so, cowering in the shadows at the back of the pen.

'Were they armed?' asked Maskar.

'They were when they arrived,' Ludd replied. 'But they surrendered their weapons without protest.'

Kanow ignored his junior's pointed emphasis.

'Where is the leader here?' he called.

A figure walked towards him out of the shadows: tall, lean, feral. The man's clothes were a dirty patchwork of leather and canvas, stained almost black with dirt and dust. A vagabond. His angular face was masked behind a thick, grey beard of matted dreadlocks, but where it could be seen, it was lined with scars, and seemed to have a discoloured, grey cast, as if the dirt was ingrained. His hair was shaggy and long, and also matted grey. His eyes were piercing.

'Commissar,' he said, with a formal nod that was strangely at odds with his matted, shaggy appearance. His voice was dry, with a peculiar, alien inflection. 'I trust you have reviewed my statement and have made contact with–'

Kanow raised his pistol. 'You are a heretic and a deserter. You now face the justice of the Imperial Throne and–'

An immense and sudden force tore the pistol painfully out of Kanow's hand. Simultaneously, a knuckle-punch struck him in the throat and he fell back, gasping.

A vicing arm locked around his neck in a throttle-hold. Kanow felt himself being dragged back tightly against his assailant's body. Then he felt the cold muzzle of his own pistol brush gently against his temple.

'No one move,' said the man behind him, with that same, dry, curious inflection.

Maskar and all the other troopers were aiming their autorifles directly at Kanow and his captor. Ludd stood in the middle of them, bewildered.

'Put the gun down. Now,' Maskar snarled over his shouldered weapon.

'So you can shoot me?' replied the voice behind Kanow's head. 'I don't think so. But I'm a reasonable man. Look, sergeant. I had the stone drop on you just then, and yet no one's dead so far. Is that the act of a heretic or a deserter?'

'Drop the gun!'

'Put up your weapons, sergeant,' Ludd urged.

'That young man's got the right idea,' said the man with the gun to Kanow's skull.

'Not in a million years, you bastard,' Maskar replied.

'That's a shame,' the man choking Kanow said. Then, quietly, he added, 'Dercius.'

Figures moved out of the shadows. Either that, or shadows moved out and became figures, Ludd wasn't sure. All he knew was that in a heartbeat, Maskar and his men had been crippled and dropped by swift phantoms, their rifles ripped out of their hands.

Maskar and his men writhed on the deck, clutching bloody faces, snapped arms and broken noses. The shadows, now armed with the troopers' weapons, surrounded Ludd.

'What do you want?' Ludd asked quietly.

'Shut up, Ludd! Don't give them anything!' Kanow yelled. The choke-hold tightened.

'You were saying, Ludd?' said one of the shadows.

Ludd swallowed. 'What… what is it that you want?'

'What I asked for in the first place,' replied Ibram Gaunt, his arm locked around Commissar Kanow's neck. 'I want to talk to Lord General Barthol Van Voytz, and I want to do it *now*.'

ONE

HE HAD BEEN expecting to get a view of the infamous Sparshad Mons as they dropped into their shallow approach, but all he could see via his relay screen was a flat expanse of endless dust dunes baked bone-white in the merciless glare.

He fiddled with the screen's magnification, and zoomed in on the desert floor, glimpsing dark dots and tiny litters of black specks. The white flats were not so spotless as the distance had suggested. There were thousands of square kilometres of wreckage down below: the twisted shells of war machines, burned-out ruins, human bones, a dead city, the legacy of the previous year's fighting. The debris was covered with a coating of white dust, smoothing it into the flatness of the desert. Once, the entire zone had been the site of the mighty prefecture city of Sparshad Celsior. War had transmuted it into Frag Flats.

'Where's the Mons?' he asked.

'Directly ahead, sir,' the pilot's voice crackled over the intervox.

'I can't see… oh.' He still couldn't see the Mons, but he could now tell where it was. Where the flat, white land ended and the pitiless blue sky began, a vast bank of orange cloud covered the horizon, directly ahead. It looked like a natural weather pattern, or the haze of a gathering dust storm, rising like a cliff-face above the desert.

But it was smoke. A gigantic slab of smoke lifting from the battlefront and veiling the bulk of the Mons. He dialled up to maximum magnification and was able to detect tiny flashes in the base of the fume-bank, like sparks. Laser artillery, heavy ordnance, earthshakers, all assaulting the hidden edifice.

'Escort peeling off,' the vox reported.

He looked round, squinting out of the tiny window port, and caught a glint in the sunlight as the Lightning escort turned away, leaving the Commissariat Valkyrie alone for its final approach.

'Two minutes,' the pilot reported.

'Thank you,' he replied. He adjusted his viewer again, and lined up on the rapidly approaching HQ. It squatted like a reptile on the bleak, white landscape. Four Command Leviathans docked together in a cross, surrounded by the vast, regimented lines of ranked fighting vehicles, gun-platforms, extensive habi-tent camps, fuel and munition depots, and parked fliers. A vast assembly of Imperial Guard power, a mobile city: each Leviathan alone was an armoured crawler the size of a small town.

He switched off the viewer, and looked at his own face reflected in the blank plate. He put on his cap and adjusted the set of it, but despite the cap, and despite his splendid formal uniform, he still looked like a pale-faced youth. And a frightened one, too.

Junior Commissar Nahum Ludd sat back in his restraint web, closed his eyes, and tried to calm his nerves. He was the only occupant of the passenger section, and the vacant seating all around troubled him more than he cared to admit. The transport rocked slightly as it applied thrusters to decelerate hard. Ludd felt his stomach flop as they began to drop vertically.

'Thirty seconds to touchdown,' the pilot reported, his voice calm and expressionless.

Ludd swallowed. *My lord general*, he rehearsed for the umpteenth time, *I extend a cordial greeting from my commanding officer, Commissar Kanow, who apologises that he could not come here himself…*

THERE WAS A thump, a hard vibration, then all sense of motion fell away. The internal lighting flickered on, and the red runes on the bulkhead switched to green.

'Sparshad Zone HQ, sir,' the vox crackled.

'Thank you, pilot,' Ludd replied, unclasping his harness and rising to his feet. The cabin's air-scrubbers had switched to external circulation, and the slightly stale air blew fresher from the vents. Ludd walked over to the hatch, past the rows of empty seats. Since boarding at Camp Xeno, he'd not seen another human face. That fact continued to bother him.

There was a hand-written notice pasted to the inside of the hatch. It read 'GLARE-SHADES!'. Ludd smiled, took his glare-shades out of his coat pocket and put them on.

'Hatch, please.'

With a slight pop of decompression that hurt his ears, the hatch disengaged and began to slide away and out on its hydraulic arms.

Light flooded in, and heat too. Ludd gasped at the hard bite of the atmosphere outside. The light was as white and fierce as a laser. Without his glare-shades, he'd have been blinded.

Ludd looked out into the radiant world awaiting him. Then, with his data-case under his arm, he walked down the ramp.

The Valkyrie had set down on a landing pad on the hunched back of one of the vast Leviathans. Service crews in full sun-shrouds were hurrying forward into the shadow of the big transport to couple it up and attach fuelling lines. The landing pad was a flat disc of pale green metal, coated with a thin dusting of fine, wind-blown white sand, so that the crews' progress was recorded in smudged footprints and the smears left by trailing hoses.

Ludd wandered a few paces away from the Valkyrie. The dust-caked back of the Leviathan spread out around him in all directions, a grim vista of cooling vents, gun-turrets and sensor domes. Ludd had not been aboard a Leviathan before. It was immense. Turning, he could see the other three crawlers, docked with it, a vast cruciform of dirt-swathed steel.

There was a loud bang and a doppler scream of passing jet-wash as a pack of Imperial Interceptors streaked overhead. Ludd watched them as they turned north, jockeying into attack formation.

Ludd walked over to the guard-rail. On the Leviathan's back, he was as high up as if he'd been standing on the roof of a hive stack. It was a giddying drop to the desert below, but not so distant as it had been from the air. He could see the extent of the HQ encampment clearly now, the huge, marshalled assemblies of men and machines spread out around the Command crawlers. Brigades of fighting vehicles waited in the sunlight for deployment orders, tenders and armoury loaders moving amongst them. Vast forests of troop tents covered the desert like infestations of domed fungi, surrounding the large prefab modules of infirmaries, mess-halls and training barns. To the west, beyond the heavily defended mass of the supply dumps and the temporary hangars, lay a massive stretch of rolled-down hardstand matting lined with parked fighter-bombers and their smaller escorts. At the camp's northern perimeter, he could see a column of armour, kicking up dust as it moved out towards the front. Dozens of black vox-masts sprouted from the camp all around, like spears planted into the ground.

The heat was amazing. There was no shade. The sun was so hot it seemed to crackle and buzz in the sky. Ludd felt his exposed skin tingle. A tan, he thought. It would be good to go back to the camp with a tan, after all those months of polar night.

He looked north, at the towering smoke bank, at Sparshad Mons. Now he was outside, Ludd could distinctly smell the reek of fyceline bombardment. And the Mons was a good fifty, sixty kilometres away.

He could just make out the battery flashes, but he wanted a better look. He raised his hand to his glare-shades.

'I really wouldn't, if you're fond of your ability to see.'

Ludd turned. A man was approaching him across the landing pad. He was tall and straight-backed, and wore the dress uniform of an Imperial commissar.

Ludd made the sign of the aquila and saluted.

'Junior Commissar Nahum Ludd, Camp 917,' he said.

The man mirrored the sign and the salute, and then offered his hand. 'Commissar Hadrian Faragut. Welcome to Frag Flats, Ludd.'

Ludd shook the proffered hand.

Faragut had a commanding manner, but appeared only a few years older than Ludd. He evidently hadn't been a full commissar for long. What little Ludd could see of Faragut's face was lean, tanned and clean-shaven. But the black lenses of his glare-shades hid his eyes, and therefore his character and temperament. There was a slight crook to his lips, as if Faragut was amused by something.

'I'm the welcoming committee,' Faragut said. 'The commissar-general was going to greet you personally, but it was felt that might be too intimidating.'

'Indeed. I'm glad it's you.'

'First time at the Flats?'

Ludd nodded. 'First time on a Leviathan, too.'

'Throne, they have kept you locked away, haven't they? Xeno. That's a polar station, isn't it?'

'Yes. Deliberately removed from the war zones. It's pretty bleak.'

'Count yourself lucky. The zones are... demanding.' Faragut spoke with an increasing curve of smile, as if to suggest he had seen many things and, more importantly, done many things. Heroic, glorious things.

Ludd nodded. 'I often wish for something demanding,' he said.

'Careful what you wish for, Ludd,' Faragut replied, his smile disappearing. 'The Sextus Zones are hell. There's not a single man of my rank doesn't pray for a soft posting like yours.'

Ludd bridled slightly. Not only was Faragut teasing him for being out of the fight-zones, he was teasing him for landing an easy option. Camp Xeno wasn't easy. It was a bastard, bitter job. Thankless, punishing, relentless–

Ludd decided not to say anything.

'You were admiring the Big Smoke?' Faragut said.

'Excuse me?'

Faragut gestured towards the orange roil rising off the horizon.

'Oh, I just wanted to get a look at the Mons,' Ludd said.

'Not from here. The Big Smoke's been a permanent fixture since the assault began three months ago.'

'It's what... sixty kilometres away?'

Faragut chuckled. 'Try *two hundred* and sixty. Have you any idea how big the Mons is?'

'No,' Ludd replied.

'Shame you won't get to see it,' Faragut said, in a tone that suggested he enjoyed meaning the opposite. 'Sparshad Mons is so wonderfully impressive.'

They turned as they heard a clank and hiss behind them. A deck hatch had opened directly under the Valkyrie, and the entire cargo pod was lowering away on power hoists, disengaging from the transport and sliding down into the hull of the Leviathan.

'You're handling them like freight,' Ludd said, disapprovingly. 'It was bad enough they had to be transported that way. Won't you even let them disembark on foot?'

'That's not appropriate,' Faragut said. 'Not until we've had them checked out.'

'You do know who they are?' Ludd asked.

Faragut looked at him, his eyes unreadable behind his black glare-shades. 'I know who they want us to think they are, Ludd. That's not quite the same.'

'You've read my report, though?'

Faragut frowned. 'Yes, Ludd. And we've read your commanding officer's report too. Commissar Kanow, isn't it?'

'Yes.'

'So… you will allow us to be cautious, I hope? Kanow was quite specific. What was his last command to you?'

'To bring the prisoners to the person of the lord general,' Ludd said.

Faragut nodded, solemnly. 'Just so. Because we do want to handle this according to Commissariat rules.'

'Absolutely,' Ludd replied. He didn't like the way Faragut had emphasised the 'do' in his last sentence. The man was condescending, patronising. And Ludd didn't like the way Faragut was suggesting he was anything less than a true commissar because he didn't have a warzone posting.

Ludd decided he didn't actually like Faragut all that much.

All of which became academic when Faragut said, 'Well, let's not keep him waiting.'

'Who?'

'Why, the lord general, Ludd. Who else?'

Ludd's stomach turned to water at the idea he was keeping such a great man waiting even for a moment.

He followed Faragut to the deck-stairs, his pulse elevated.

TWO

12.02 hrs, 188.776.M41
Frag Flats HQ
Sparshad Combat Zone, Ancreon Sextus

'WAIT HERE,' FARAGUT instructed him, and Ludd did as he was told. They had descended together through the Leviathan's vast interior and, after almost fifteen minutes' brisk walk along armoured, air-cooled hallways and heavy, bulkheaded companionways, had come to a halt in a gallery that over-looked one of the main tactical command centres.

Ludd looked down through tinted and slightly inclined panels of glass into a massive, tiered chamber where scores of intelligence officers, Imperial tacticians and high-order servitors manned display consoles and logic engines. In the centre of the chamber, a strategium pit cast a large, pulsing hololithic display up into the air. A huddle of senior officers surrounded the pit display; evidently a briefing was just coming to an end. Ludd saw the uniforms of a dozen different divisions, including Navy Wing and Guard Armour. There was intense bustle down in the chamber, but the glass was soundproofed. Ludd could only imagine the constant racket of reports and data-chatter.

Faragut appeared in the room below, and dutifully approached a tall, striking man who wore the plain, dove-grey day-dress of a lord general. That would be Van Voytz, no doubt, Ludd thought. Lord General of the Fifth Crusade Army, commander in chief of this warzone operation, master of this theatre. Everyone in the strategium was deferring to him. Ludd had never anticipated having to meet with a man of such staggering seniority. It was one step away from meeting Warmaster Macaroth himself.

His mouth went dry and cottony. He tried to remember his rehearsed words.

Faragut spoke to the lord general, and got a brief nod and a pat on the arm for his trouble. *Oh, to enjoy such informality in those lofty circles,* Ludd thought. Van Voytz finished his conversation with two Navy squadron leaders, shared the knowing laughter of old comrades, then turned and followed Faragut from the chamber.

Half a minute later, Lord General Barthol Van Voytz was standing in front of Ludd on the gallery.

'Junior Commissar Nahum Ludd,' Faragut introduced. Ludd snapped to attention and made his salute.

The lord general was flanked by Faragut and a short, stern man wearing the black-and-red uniform of a senior Imperial tactician. Behind them waited an honour guard of six veteran soldiers in full ballistic plate.

'Van Voytz,' the lord general said, as if there were some doubt as to his identity. His voice was surprisingly soft and amiable, and there was the rumour of a smile on his lips. He stepped forward and offered Ludd his hand.

Surprised, Ludd hesitated, then shook it. 'Welcome, Ludd,' Van Voytz said. Then, still clasping Ludd's hand, he leaned closer and whispered in Ludd's ear.

'You're trembling, young man. Don't. I'm not a man to be afraid of. And besides, you don't want to show fear in front of that arse-kisser Faragut, or he'll never let you live it down.'

Ludd felt a little easier immediately. He nodded and smiled back. Van Voytz seemed to be in no hurry to let his hand go.

'As I understand it,' Van Voytz said aloud, 'I owe you a great deal, Ludd.'

'Sir?'

'I've read the reports, Ludd. Yours, and that of your commanding officer. Today, I will take great pleasure in welcoming back friends I had long since given up as dead. I cannot begin to imagine what they've been through, but it would have been a supremely tragic irony if they had been executed by mistake at Camp 917.'

'Yes, sir.'

'And I've you to thank for that.'

'I'm not sure about that, sir,' Ludd said.

'You listened. You listened when others did not. Kanow will hear from me about this. Later on, I'd like you to tell me all the details, the things you left unsaid in your report.'

'I wouldn't wish to betray Commissar Kanow's authority, sir,' Ludd said.

'That was an order, Junior Commissar Ludd.'

'Yes, sir.'

'Kanow clearly overstepped the mark. That much is evident even from your very diplomatic account. I won't have behaviour like that in my army, Ludd.'

'With respect, lord general,' said a voice from nearby, 'if Kanow needs to be reprimanded, that office will fall to me.'

A figure had joined them on the gallery deck, a woman of medium height and build who possessed quite the most austere face Ludd had ever seen. Her skin was white and drawn tight around her high cheekbones, her mouth a prim slit with a thin top lip. Her right eye was violet and keen, her left a compact augmetic embedded into a snowdrift smooth fold of scar-tissue that ran down across her brow onto her alabaster cheek. She wore the long black leather robes and cap of a commissar-general.

'Hello, Balshin,' Van Voytz sighed.

Ludd hadn't needed the name to know who this was: Viktoria Balshin, Lady Commissar-General of the Second Front theatre, one of the few women ever to ascend to such a rank in the Commissariat. She was a legend and, if the stories were true, a scourge to friend and foe alike. It was said that in order to thrive in such a male-dominated service, she had compensated for her gender by being the most ferociously hard-line political officer and disciplinarian imaginable. If Ludd had realised who Faragut meant when he'd referred to the 'commissar-general' he'd probably have just got straight back aboard the Valkyrie and fled.

'We will see for ourselves if Kanow overstepped the mark,' Balshin said. 'Personally, having reviewed the intelligence, I don't believe he did. You're fooling yourself, my lord general, if you believe that the individuals escorted here by this young man are... how did you put it? Your friends.'

'I know who they are, Balshin,' Van Voytz retorted, bristling slightly. 'I've known Ibram and his boys for years. I sent them off on this damn mission personally, and by the Throne, they have done me proud. I won't have them coming home to mistrust and accusation. They're heroes of the Imperium.'

Balshin smiled. 'Barthol, I don't refute any of what you say. Fine soldiers, yes. Brave souls who undertook a vital and thankless mission, yes. Heroes, why yes, that too. But precisely because of what they have endured, they may no longer be the soldiers you knew. I advise caution.'

'Noted,' Van Voytz said.

'And I advise you dispense with fond sentiment. You must think with your head, not your heart.'

'In that, Balshin, I'll follow your example,' Van Voytz said. 'How is your heart, these days? Still in a drawer somewhere, gathering dust?'

Balshin snorted.

'I'm not going to let you spoil this moment, Viktoria,' Van Voytz said. 'A great hour of victory has just been reported by the senior commanders. The fifth compartment of Sparshad Mons has just been breached, and we are advancing to the gates of the sixth.'

'Praise be the God-Emperor,' Balshin nodded. 'That is wonderful news.'

'Indeed,' Van Voytz said. 'And to top it off, a courageous friend of mine has just come back from the dead, when all hope was gone. So don't you go pissing on my parade, lady commissar-general.'

There was a frosty moment. Ludd dearly wished he was somewhere else. Then the Imperial tactician stepped forward and said, 'Senior staff in forty-five minutes, my lord.'

Van Voytz nodded. 'Indeed, Biota. Then let's get on with this. Ludd? Take me to greet your charges, please.'

* * *

THE FREIGHT SILO, deep in the bowels of the Command Leviathan, was unnaturally cold. Vapour from the landing jets was still swirling out of the overhead extractor vents. The cargo-pod from the Valkyrie sat quiet and still in its hoist supports.

'If you please, Ludd,' Van Voytz said.

Ludd hurried forward to the pod's hatch. Faragut went with him. The commissar eased his laspistol out of its holster.

'There's no need for that,' Ludd said.

'Do your job, Junior Ludd, and I'll do mine.' Like Ludd, Faragut had removed his glare-shades upon entering the command crawler, and now Ludd saw his eyes clearly for the first time. Cold, white-blue, uncompromising.

Ludd glanced nervously back at the lord general, Balshin, the Imperial tactician, and the veteran escort waiting on the deckway behind them. Van Voytz nodded, encouragingly. Ludd tapped the numeric code into the hatch lock.

Nothing happened.

He tapped it in again.

Still nothing.

'Do it right, for Throne's sake!' Faragut hissed. 'This is embarrassing!'

'I am doing it right!' Ludd whispered back. 'There's something wrong with the lock.'

He tapped a third time. The readout remained blank.

'Stand aside,' Faragut said. 'You must be making a mistake. What's the code?'

'Ten-four-oh-two-nine,' Ludd replied.

Faragut pounded the numerals in with the index finger of his left hand. Still nothing.

Faragut reached out and tugged at the heavy hatch. It swung open, free, unlocked.

'What the hell?'

The veteran guards immediately raised their weapons and prowled forward.

Pistol braced, Faragut peered into the open pod.

'Lights!' he commanded, and the bank of glow strips along the pod's ceiling flickered on, bathing the interior with a hard white glare.

The pod was empty.

'Oh, God-Emperor...' Ludd murmured.

'Sound general quarters!' Balshin yelled. 'Full security lock down, my authority! Now!'

The Leviathan's internal klaxons began to whoop.

THREE

12.29 hrs, 188.776.M41
Frag Flats HQ
Sparshad Combat Zone, Ancreon Sextus

'YOU CHECKED THE pod was sealed when you departed Camp Xeno?' Balshin demanded as she strode along.

'Yes, ma'am,' Ludd replied, struggling to keep up with her pace. 'The security detail locked the container, but I double-checked it before it was stowed on the transport.'

'And it was locked?' Balshin asked dubiously.

'It was, ma'am. On my life it was.'

'Bad choice of words,' Faragut muttered privately to Ludd. 'Your head's going to roll for this.'

They were rushing down one of the inner companionways behind Van Voytz and Balshin. As security squads swept the Leviathan deck by deck, Balshin's priority was to get the lord general safely sequestered in his private quarters.

'We didn't even have time to bio-scan them,' Ludd heard Balshin say over the noise of the blaring alarms. 'The intruders could be anyone, posing as the missing guard team to gain entry.'

Ludd was sweating. This was down to him, just as Faragut had taken pleasure in noting. Not only had Ludd been in charge of the transfer, he'd also been the one to advocate trusting the prisoners.

Had he just facilitated getting a team of Archenemy assassins into the lord general's central command post? *Everything will be all right,* he tried to assure himself. The Leviathan was swarming with armed, vigilant troopers. Everywhere he looked, he saw fireteams running point-and-cover searches down hallways and along through-deck walks, or conducting stop-and-search examinations of passing crew members. No intruder, no matter how determined, was going to get far under these conditions.

The hurrying party reached the heavy blast hatch of Van Voytz's quarters. 'Stay with his lordship,' Balshin told Faragut, and then marched away to take direct charge of the manhunt. Faragut followed Van Voytz and Tactician Biota in through the blast hatch.

'Come on,' he said, beckoning impatiently at Ludd. Ludd hurried after them. The guard escort took up station outside, and the heavy hatch sealed and locked. The air pressure changed immediately. Amber runes lit up to show that the lord general's chamber, a virtual bunker at the heart of the huge crawler, was locked down and running on its own independent systems.

They were in an ante-room, well-appointed with seating and a table for debriefing sessions. An inner hatch led into Van Voytz's office, and they followed the lord general in that direction. The office was functional and service-issue, but piled with books, pictures and trophies from Van Voytz's worthy career. There was a desk with a high-backed chair at the far end, a couple of couches, and a side door into the sleeping pod.

'Dammit,' Van Voytz muttered. 'Dammit all.' He glanced at Ludd. 'Locked, you said?'

'Yes, sir.'

Van Voytz shook his head. He seemed to bear no particular anger towards Ludd. It seemed more as if he were puzzled, disappointed.

Faragut was listening to the security channel traffic on his earpiece. 'Sweep has now reached deck six and seven. Internal scanners still show no sign of the intruders.'

Biota muted the alarm blaring in the office. The hazard light panels continued to flash. Van Voytz was pacing.

'Sir,' said Ludd, suddenly and very quietly.

'What?' Van Voytz replied, looking round at him.

'I think you should remain very still, sir,' Ludd said, his voice trembling.

Ibram Gaunt, bearded, thin and dishevelled, had slowly risen to his feet from behind the high-backed chair. He was holding a chrome and silver ceremonial laspistol. It was aimed at Faragut, the only one of them with a drawn weapon.

'Lose your sidearms,' Gaunt said. 'Onto that couch. Now.'

Ludd unholstered his laspistol and tossed it onto the couch. Biota took out his small service auto and threw it down too.

'I said lose them,' Gaunt told Faragut, his aim not wavering. Faragut's gun was pointed at Gaunt.

'Don't be a fool,' Gaunt said. 'Do you really want to start a firefight in the presence of the lord general?'

Faragut slowly lowered his weapon and slung it onto the couch cushions.

Van Voytz took a step towards Gaunt.

'Ibram.'

'My lord general. Not quite the reunion I was hoping for.' The more Gaunt spoke, the more they could all detect the odd, alien cadence in his accent.

Van Voytz stared at Gaunt, bewildered. 'Throne, man. What happened to you?'

'I followed your orders, sir. That's what happened to me.'

'And those orders included holding me hostage with my own sidearm?'

'It was all I could find.'

'Ibram, for the love of Terra, put the gun down.'

'Only when I'm assured of my safety, and the safety of my team.'

'How could you doubt that?' Van Voytz said. He sounded hurt.

'Being herded up for summary execution at that processing camp didn't help,' Gaunt replied. 'Neither did having my honour and loyalty ignored. That boy there was the only one who had any faith at all.' Gaunt indicated Ludd with a nod of his head. 'But I'm not sure I can even trust him now. We were put into a cargo pod, *locked* into a cargo pod, and brought here like animals.'

'There were security issues, colonel-commissar,' Biota said. 'You must understand. You were brought here for formal identification and debrief.'

'Like animals, Antonid,' Gaunt replied. 'By the time we were being unloaded, I didn't feel I could trust anything or anybody. I had to make provisions for the good of my troops.'

'How did you get out of the pod?' Ludd asked.

'Does it matter?'

'It's a fair question,' said Van Voytz.

'My men developed many skills on Gereon. Resistance tactics. I don't think there's a lock made that can beat either Feygor or Mkoll.'

'Where are your men?' Faragut demanded.

Gaunt seemed to smile, but the expression was obscured behind the caked, grey mass of his beard. His wary aim still favoured Faragut. 'Hidden. Where no security sweep will find them. Hiding's something else we've got very good at.'

'How can we resolve this, Ibram?' Van Voytz asked.

'Your word, sir. An assurance of safety for me and my team. I think you owe us that.'

Van Voytz nodded. 'My word. You have it, unconditionally.'

There was a long moment of stillness, then Gaunt lowered the weapon, flipped it over neatly in his hand, and held it out to the lord general, grip-first.

Van Voytz took the pistol and put it down on the desk. Faragut hurled himself forward to tackle Gaunt.

'No!' Van Voytz bellowed. Faragut stopped in his tracks.

'I gave this man my word!' Van Voytz roared at him.

Faragut stammered. 'Sir, I–'

Van Voytz slapped Faragut hard across the face and knocked him to his knees.

'I'm going to send a signal, Gaunt. All right?' Van Voytz said. Gaunt nodded. The lord general crossed to his intercom.

'This is Van Voytz on the command channel. Stand down general quarters and cancel the search.'

'Balshin here. Please clarify.'

'The situation is contained, commissar-general. Follow my orders.'

There was a pause. Then the vox crackled. 'My lord, are you under duress?'

'No, Balshin. I am not.'

'Please, sir. I need the clearance.'

'Clearance is "Andromache".'

'Understood. Thank you, sir.'

The hazard lights stopped flashing, and the distant howl of klaxons outside faded. Heavy bolts automatically retracted and the outer hatch of the general's quarters opened. The escort detail stationed outside hurried in. Gaunt stiffened.

'Shoulder arms!' Van Voytz ordered, and the men did so immediately. Van Voytz pointed at Gaunt.

'Now salute him, damn you!'

THEY FOLLOWED GAUNT down to the huge enginarium in the belly of the Leviathan. In every hallway they passed through, personnel turned to stare, some so bemused by what they saw, they quite forgot to salute the lord general. A tall, shaggy, filthy man in ragged, leather clothes, wrapped in the torn remnants of a camo-cloak, leading the supreme imperial commander, two commissars, an Imperial tactician and a vanguard of troopers.

The turbine hall of the enginarium was cavernous and gloomy, dominated by the vast whirring powerplants that drove the Leviathan's systems. The air smelled of promethium and lubricants. Van Voytz ordered the tech-adepts and engineers out of the chamber.

'Here?' he asked, raising his voice above the machine noise.

'The heat and machine activity mask bio-traces,' Gaunt said. 'The best interference you can get when it comes to beating internal sensors. We learned that taking out a jehgenesh at the Lectica hydroelectric dam.'

'I don't know what that means,' Van Voytz said. 'I trust you'll debrief fully.'

'Of course, sir,' Gaunt said, as if surprised there might be any doubt. He walked over to a wall-set vox, adjusted the dial to speaker, and said, 'silver.' His amplified voice echoed along the engineering bay.

The Ghosts came out of hiding. It was unnerving to have them appear, one by one, out of shadowed cavities that didn't seem deep enough to conceal a human being. The Tanith troopers didn't so much emerge as materialise.

All of them were as underfed, grubby and ragged as their commander. Their eyes were bright, wary, cautious. Their beards and long hair were caked into dreadlocks with what looked like grey mud.

'Holy Throne,' Van Voytz said. 'Major Rawne.'

'Sir,' Rawne replied, making an awkward salute as he came out into the light.

'And Sergeant Varl. Sergeant Mkoll.'

The two men also saluted as they came forward, Mkoll unwilling to look the lord general in the eye. The others approached. Van Voytz greeted each one as they appeared.

'Trooper Brostin. Sergeant Criid. Trooper Feygor. Vox-officer Beltayn. Scout-trooper Bonin. Marksman Larkin.'

Gaunt looked at Van Voytz, quietly impressed. 'You... you know their names, sir.'

'I sent you and these soldiers on a mission we both thought you'd never come back from, Ibram. What kind of lord general would I be if I couldn't be bothered to remember a handful of names?'

Van Voytz turned to face the group of tattered Ghosts. 'Welcome, all of you. Welcome home.'

Two more figures emerged from the shadows.

'And these I don't know,' Van Voytz said.

'Major Sabbatine Cirk,' Gaunt said. The tall, dark-haired woman stepped forward and bowed to the lord general.

'Cirk was a principal leader of the Gereon Resistance. She's come with us to supply High Command with full intelligence concerning the situation on Gereon.'

'Welcome, major,' Van Voytz said. 'The Emperor protects.'

'And Gereon resists,' Cirk replied sardonically.

The other figure was abnormally tall and slender: a disturbingly tribal, grey shape in a long, feathered cloak, who seemed more uneasy than any of them.

'Eszrah ap Niht,' Gaunt said. 'A warrior of the Untill Nihtganes, a Sleep-walker.'

'Welcome, sir,' Van Voytz said. The Sleepwalker made no movement or response. The skin of his thin, moustachioed face seemed to have been stained with grey clay, and oval patches of iridescent mosaics surrounded his deep-set, apprehensive eyes. Van Voytz glanced at Gaunt. 'And he's here because?'

'Because I own him and he refused to remain behind.'

Van Voytz raised his eyebrows. 'Two are missing. Scout-trooper Mkvenner and Medicae Curth.'

'Last I knew, both lived,' Gaunt said. 'But Mkvenner and Curth elected to stay behind on Gereon in support of the Resistance. Ana Curth's medical skills were proving invaluable, and Mkvenner... Well, let me say briefly that Ven and the Sleepwalker partisans have become the elite commandos of the Gereon Underground.'

'You'll make a full report?' Van Voytz said.

'Again, as I said, of course, sir.'

'Good.' Van Voytz stepped towards the Ghosts and shook each one by the hand, though he didn't even attempt to take the hand of the mysterious tribesman. 'I understand that your mission was accomplished... and more besides. The Emperor will never forget your efforts, and neither will I.' He glanced round. 'Balshin?'

Lady Commissar-General Balshin came out of a nearby access, flanked by armed Commissariat troopers. More troopers, rifles levelled, surged in through the enginarium hatchways on all sides and formed a ring around the battered Ghosts.

'No...' Ludd gasped. Faragut began to snigger, despite his bruised cheek.

'Take them into custody,' Balshin said.

Gaunt stared at Van Voytz in furious disbelief. 'You bastard. You gave me your word!'

'And it stands. And it will not be broken. I assure the safety of you and your team. But that is all. I attested to nothing more than that, Ibram. You threatened my life, the security of this HQ, and the very core of Imperial Command here on Ancreon Sextus. Take them to detention.'

The troopers closed in and began to manhandle the Ghosts away.

FOUR
09.01 hrs, 189.776.M41
Frag Flats HQ
Sparshad Combat Zone, Ancreon Sextus

LUDD WALKED INTO the small interview cell and heard the hatch lock up behind him. The cell was crude and stark: just scuffed bare metal and rivets, glow-globes recessed in cages, a small steel chair and table in front of the wire screen cage. Pict units mounted high in the corners of the cell recorded the scene from multiple angles. The air was stale and stuffy. On the far side of the wire screen stood another empty steel chair.

Ludd put the plastek sack he was holding down on the deck, took off his gloves, and laid them on the small table along with his data-case. Then he sat down, opened the case, and took out two paper dossiers and a data-slate.

A buzzer sounded and the door inside the cage opened. Ludd rose to his feet.

Gaunt entered, and the door closed automatically behind him. He glanced briefly at Ludd and then sat down on the empty chair.

'Commissar Gaunt,' Ludd said, and took his seat again so he was face to face with Gaunt through the wire screen.

'I'd like to begin by apologising,' Ludd said.

'For what?'

'You said yesterday, during the altercation in the lord general's quarters, that you didn't believe you could trust me any more. I want to assure you that you can. If I gave you any cause that provoked yesterday's incident, I apologise.'

Gaunt's hard gaze flickered up and down Ludd. 'You locked us up in a cargo pod,' he said.

'In order to placate Kanow, who would have had you shot. Besides, can we start to be realistic, sir? You have served the best part of your career as a commissar and a discipline officer. Given the circumstances, would you have handled it differently?'

Gaunt shrugged.

'Let me put it more plainly. You encounter a dozen armed renegades. No idents, no warrants. Their story is difficult to believe. They are… not attired to regulations. Indeed, they are shabby. Barbaric. At the very least they have suffered hardships. Perhaps they have gone native. It is also entirely possible that they are tainted and corrupt. And they demand a personal audience with the most senior ranking Imperial officer in the quadrant. Do you not agree that any Imperial commissar would be duty-bound to exercise the utmost caution in dealing with them?'

There was a long silence. Gaunt shrugged again, and stared at the floor behind Ludd as if bored.

Ludd was about to continue when Gaunt spoke. 'Let me put it plainly, then. You are a unit commander. Your team has been sent on a high priority mission behind enemy lines on the personal request of the lord general commander. The secrecy of the mission is paramount. Against the odds, after the best part of two years in the field, you get your team out again. Whole, alive, mission accomplished. But you are treated like pariahs, like soldiers of the enemy, mistrusted, abused, threatened with execution. Do you not agree that any Imperial officer would be duty-bound to do everything to safeguard his men under such circumstances?'

Ludd pursed his lips. 'Yes, sir,' he said. 'Within the letter of regulation law. Threatening the person of the lord general–'

Gaunt shook his head sadly. 'I didn't threaten him.'

'Please, sir–'

'I did not aim the weapon directly at him, nor make any personal threat against his life.'

'Semantics, sir. Regulation law–'

'I've fought wars in the name of the God-Emperor most of my adult life, Ludd. Sometimes regulation law gets bent or snapped in the name of victory and honour. I've never known the God-Emperor object to that. He protects those who rise above the petty inhibitions of life and code and combat to serve what is true and correct. I don't much care about myself, but my men, my team… they deserve better. They have given everything except their lives. I will not permit the blunt ignorance of the Commissariat to take those from them too. I am a true servant of the Throne, Ludd. I resent very much being treated as anything else.'

Ludd sighed. 'Candidly, sir?'

Gaunt nodded.

'You don't have to convince me. But therein lies your problem. I'm not the one you have to convince.'

Gaunt leaned back in his seat, stroked his long, dirty fingers down through his heavy, woaded beard and then folded his hands across his chest, almost forming the sign of the aquila. 'So what are you doing here, Ludd?' he asked.

Ludd opened one of the dossiers on the table in front of him, and weighed down the corner of the spread card cover with the data-slate. 'There is to be a tribunal,' he said. 'You, and each member of your team, will be examined by the Office of the Commissariat. Individually. It is being called a debrief, but there is a lot at stake.'

'For me?'

'For all of you. Lady Commissar-General Balshin suspects taint.'

'Does she?'

'Sir, it would be suspected of any individual or unit exposed for such a length of time on an enemy-occupied world. You know that. Chaos taint is a very real possibility. It may be in you and you don't even know it. It might also–'

'What?'

Ludd shook his head. 'Nothing.'

'Say what you were going to say.'

'I prefer not to, sir.'

Gaunt smiled. There was something predatory about the way the expression changed his face. Like a fox, Ludd thought.

'You'd prefer not to. Because you fear what you have to say might enrage me. Or at the very least piss me off.'

'That would be a fair assessment, yes, sir.'

Gaunt leaned forward. 'You know what a wirewolf is, son?'

'No, sir, I do not.'

'Lucky you. I've killed six of them personally. Say what you have to say. I'm big enough to take it.'

Ludd cleared his throat. 'All right. You might be tainted with the mark of Chaos and not even know it. Furthermore, a subconscious taint like that might also explain your paranoia and your volatile, desperate behaviour.'

'Like waving a gun in Van Voytz's face, you mean?'

'Yes, sir.'

Gaunt leaned forward a little further, and hooked his grubby fingers through the mesh of the wire screen. He glared at Ludd. His voice became a tiny, dry crackle. 'So you think my mind might have been poisoned by the enemy, corrupted without me even knowing about it, and that's why I'm a... what? A loose cannon?'

Ludd shrank back slightly. 'You asked me to be frank...'

'You fething little–!' Gaunt snarled, and threw himself at the wire screen, his teeth bared.

Ludd leapt up so fast his chair toppled over. Then he realised that Gaunt was sitting back, laughing.

'Ludd, you're too easy. Throne, your face just then. Want to go change your underwear?'

Ludd righted the fallen chair and sat back down. 'That sort of display isn't going to help,' he said.

'Can't take a joke?' Gaunt asked, still amused with himself. 'A little gallows humour?'

'No, sir,' said Ludd. Gaunt nodded and folded his arms, his amusement subsiding.

'And if I can't,' Ludd added, 'you can be sure as hell Lady Balshin won't. Pull a stunt like that during the tribunal and she'll have you ten-ninety-six in a flash.'

'I have no doubt. It was clear to me the woman had a little too much starch in her drawers.'

'Again–' Ludd began.

Gaunt waved a hand dismissively and looked away. 'Ludd, you're talking to me like you're coaching me. Are you coaching me?'

'I'm trying to prep you for the examination, sir. Understand, the examination will be both verbal and medical. You will have to submit to all manner of analysis scans and investigative procedures. All of you will. Balshin will be thorough. The merest hint, be it verbal or physiological, that any of you are unsound... she will declare Commissariat Edict ten-ninety-six on all of you.'

Gaunt looked at the deck.

'I take it you recall what that edict is?'

'Of course I do. Do you intend to prepare every one of my team for the hearings?'

'Provided I have the time, yes. I'd appreciate it if you passed the word along to your team members to cooperate with me.'

Gaunt looked up. 'I'll recommend it. It's up to them. Be advised, you'll have trouble with Cirk, Feygor, Mkoll and Eszrah especially. In fact, I'd like to be present when you handle Eszrah. He's... not Guard. He's not like anything you or this tribunal will have ever handled.'

Ludd made a note on the dossier with a steel stylus. 'So noted. I'll see what I can do.'

'So why do we get you as an advocate, Ludd?' Gaunt asked.

'You're permitted one under the rules of the tribunal, sir,' Ludd replied.

'And we don't get to pick?' Gaunt asked.

Ludd put his stylus down and looked squarely through the cage at Gaunt. 'No, sir. It's a voluntary thing. The tribunal appoints an advocate if no one volunteers, of course. No one did besides me.'

'Feth,' said Gaunt, with a sad shake of his head. 'How old are you, Ludd?'

'Twenty-three, sir.'

'So a twenty-three year-old junior is the only friend we've got?'

'I could stand aside, allow the tribunal to appoint. You'd probably get Faragut. I didn't think you'd want that, so I put my name forward.'

'Thank you,' said Ibram Gaunt.

Ludd turned a few pages in the open dossier and replaced the data-slate to weight them down. 'I need to clarify a few points, sir. So I'm up to speed for the hearing. I will be a greater asset if I'm not taken by surprise.'

'Go on.'

'This mission you refer to. You mentioned it back at Camp Xeno too. But without specifics. It was on Gereon, right?'

'That's right.'

'What were the parameters?'

'The parameters were encoded vermillion, Ludd. Between me and the lord general. I can't divulge them to you.'

'Then that makes it hard for me to–'

'Go to Van Voytz. If he gives you written clearance, I'll tell you. If he comes and gives me a direct order, I'll tell you. Otherwise, my lips are sealed… to you and the tribunal.'

'I'll do that,' said Ludd. He closed the dossiers and put them away. 'The hearings begin tomorrow at 16.00 hours. As mission commander, you'll be called first. Your testimony may take a day or two to hear. I'll be back at 18.00 hours, sooner if I can get the waiver from the lord general. We may be prepping into the night.'

'If that's what it takes.'

'One last thing,' Ludd said, picking up the plastek sack from the floor beside his chair and dropping it into the hopper basket built into the wire screen at knee height. 'I need you to shower and put on this change of clothes. Your team will have to do the same. I'll provide kit for them as necessary.'

Gaunt looked dubiously at the sack of clothes. 'What I'm wearing,' he said firmly, 'I've been wearing through it all. It's my uniform, though I don't suppose you'd recognise it any more. Patched, repaired, sewn back together, it's been on me from start to finish. It's like my skin, Ludd.'

'That's exactly the problem. You're filthy. Ragged. You smell. I can smell you from here, and I can tell you, the smell isn't pleasant. I'm not talking dirt, sir, I'm talking a sweet, sickly stench. Like corruption, like taint. And that grey hue to your skin.'

'That won't come off easily.'

'Try. Scrub. And shave, for Throne's sake. Don't give the commissar-general any reason to suspect you more than she does.'

Gaunt took the plastek sack out of the hopper.

'So I stink?'

'Like a bastard, sir. Like a daemon of the Archenemy.'

THE COMMISSARIAT GUARDS led Gaunt back along the cellblock of the Leviathan's detention deck. Grim bars of lumin strip made a ladder of light along the low ceiling. The air was damp and musty. Patches of green-white corrosion mottled the iron walls.

They were walking past a row of individual cages. Each one contained a Ghost. Young Dughan Beltayn was in the first cage, sitting close to the bars. He nodded to Gaunt, a little eager, a little hopeful, and Gaunt tried to put some reassurance into the half-smile he sent back to his adjutant as he passed. Next in line was Cirk. She simply followed Gaunt with her caustic gaze as he went by, then looked away as he tried to make eye contact.

Flame-trooper Aongus Brostin, thuggish and hairy, was in the next cage. He was standing at the back, leaning against the far wall, with his meaty, tattooed arms folded and his eyes closed. Dreaming of lho-sticks, no doubt. Then came Ceglan Varl, sitting on his cell's fold-down cot. The sergeant was stripped to the waist, displaying his dirty, lean torso and his battered augmetic shoulder. He flipped Gaunt a laconic salute.

'Just keep walking,' said one of the guards.

In the next cell sat Hlaine Larkin, huddled in a corner, looking more like a tanned leather bag of bones and nerves than ever. He watched Gaunt pass with a sniper's unblinking stare. Larkin's neighbour was Simen Urwin Macharius Bonin, Mach Bonin, the darkly-handsome and preternaturally fortunate scout-trooper. Bonin was standing at the cage front, leaning forward and clutching the bars with raised hands.

'Any luck?' he asked.

'Shut up,' one of the guards said.

'Screw you too,' Bonin called after them.

Gaunt passed the cell holding Tona Criid. She'd not cut her hair since the start of the mission, and it had grown out long and straight, returning to its original, brick-brown colour, stained with Untill grey. She'd taken to wearing it loose, swept down to veil the left side of her face. Gaunt knew why. As he passed her cage, she made the quick Tanith code-gesture that was Ghost shorthand for 'everything all right?'

Gaunt managed to reply with a quick nod before he was marched on out of sight.

Eszrah ap Niht, or Eszrah Night as they had all come to know the Untill partisan, stood in the next cell, silent and staring, his mosaic-edged eyes hidden behind the old, battered pair of sunshades Varl had given him so long ago.

'Histye seolfor, soule Eszrah,' Gaunt called out quickly in the Sleep-walker's ancient tongue

'Be quiet!' the guard behind him cried, and prodded Gaunt between the shoulder-blades with his maul.

Gaunt stopped in his tracks and looked round at the three armoured guards. 'Do that again,' he began, 'and you'll–'

'What?' taunted the guard, patting his maul into the palm of his glove.

Gaunt bit back, tried to counsel his temper, tried to remember what Ludd had told him.

He turned round and continued to walk. The next cage in the line held Scout-Sergeant Oan Mkoll. The grizzled, older man remained staring at the floor as Gaunt went by.

Murtan Feygor lay on the cot in the next cell. He sat up as Gaunt passed and called out 'We dead yet, Ghostmaker?' His voice had a rasping, monot-onous quality thanks to the augmetic larynx in his corded throat, the legacy of an old war wound.

One of the guards kicked the bars of Feygor's cage as they went by.

'Oh, you think so? You think so?' Feygor called after them. 'Come back here, you feth-wipe, come back here and I'll make your momma weep.' The threat was curiously dry and flat uttered in that monotone. It was almost comical.

Rawne was in the final cage they passed. He was sitting on the floor, near the front, his back against the left-hand cell partition. He didn't even bother to look up.

At the last cage on the block, the guards slid the barred gate open. Gaunt looked at them.

'Shower pen?' he asked.

'We'll be back in twenty minutes,' one of the guards replied. Gaunt nodded, and stepped into the empty cell. The guards slammed the cage shut with a reverberating clang of metal on metal, locked it, and walked away.

Gaunt dropped the plastek sack onto the cell floor, then walked across to the right hand partition and slithered down, his back to it, near the cage mouth.

'So what's the story, Bram?' Rawne asked quietly from the other side of the wall.

'We're in it up to our necks, Eli,' Gaunt replied. 'My bad call, I think. I pushed them way too far.'

There was a long pause.

'Don't beat yourself up,' Rawne said. 'We all knew why you called it like you did. They were treating us like shit. You couldn't take chances.'

'Maybe I should have. We're facing a tribunal. Balshin's in charge. Van Voytz may not be on side any more, after what I did.'

'Combat necessity, Bram,' Rawne replied, stoically. 'If we'd stayed in that fething pod…'

'We might be all right now. Or in a better situation. I should have trusted Ludd.'

'That feth?'

'We're all going to have to trust him now, Elim. That feth's our only friend. Pass the word along. We have to comply with his every instruction and recommendation, or we're blindfolded with our backs to a wall.'

'Why?'

Gaunt sighed. 'The accusation is Chaos taint.'

'Hard to prove.'

'Harder to disprove. Eli, as a commissar, I'd always err on the side of caution.'

'Shoot first, you mean?'

'Shoot first.'

'Feth.'

'Ludd's in our corner, and I may be able to swing Van Voytz round, if I can get any time with him. But make sure the Ghosts cooperate with Ludd. Whether you like him or not, he's the only decent card in our hand.'

'That an order?'

'More than any other I've ever given you.'

'Consider it done.'

Gaunt looked over at the sagging plastek sack nearby. 'Ludd wants us to shower and clean ourselves up. Get new fatigues on. Get fresh, shaved and scrubbed for the hearings.'

'I'm fine as I am.'

'Rawne, I'm not kidding. We stink of filth and corruption. We reek of what they think is taint. Everyone does this, or they'll answer to me.'

'Eszrah won't like it.'

'I know.'

'And Cirk...'

'I know. Leave her to me.'

'You gonna follow my advice?' Rawne asked.

Gaunt shook his head. Rawne's advice, repeated two dozen times through the last few days, had been to sell Cirk out, to give her to the Commissariat in exchange for the Ghosts' lives. He'd never liked her. And that was crazy, because in the last ten months she'd given Rawne so many reasons to do so. Sabbatine Cirk was a brave, driven officer. But there was just something about her that was inherently untrustworthy. On Gereon, she'd suffered under the Archenemy occupation too long. She'd learned that essential skill of the die-hard resistance fighter, that quality that was both a blessing and curse: no one, not a friend, not a family member, not even a life-partner, was beyond betrayal if it benefitted the cause. That made her as mercurial and unpredictable as a razor-snake.

Cirk had been Elim Rawne's lover for the past eight months. Rawne desired her, but he still didn't like her much, or trust her even slightly.

'So what happens now?' Rawne asked.

'They'll start with me. You'll be next, I'm guessing. Stick to the facts. And observe our clearance unless I tell you otherwise.'

'Got it. Feth, I can't believe I'm thinking this, but... we'd have been safer staying on Gereon.'

Gaunt grinned. 'Yes, maybe. But we had our chance and we took it. We had to get off-world with the news about Sturm. And about the Sons. Demands of duty, Eli.'

'And this is how they thank us,' Rawne said bitterly. Gaunt heard him slide closer to the edge of the wall. Rawne's dirty hand appeared through the bars.

'I never wanted to go to Gereon,' Gaunt heard him say. 'I thought it was madness, I thought it was suicide, and it so nearly was. But I did what you ordered and what the God-Emperor deserved. And by feth, I never expected it to turn out like this. We're loyal soldiers of the Imperium, Bram. After all we did, and all we sacrificed, where the hell did justice go?'

Gaunt reached his own hand out through the bars and clasped Rawne's.

'It's coming, Eli. On my life, it's coming.'

'I WANT THIS quashed,' Van Voytz said.

'After what they did?' Balshin replied.

Van Voytz waved his hands as if brushing crumbs away from his lap. 'We treated them badly. I owe them—'

'Nothing, sir. You owe them nothing if they are tainted. That's the bottom line. Whatever mission they accomplished, whatever great service they did for you and the Crusade, if they've come back tainted, it's the end. We can take no chances. We would be derelict in our duty to the Golden Throne if we did.'

'You're such a bitch, Balshin,' Van Voytz said.

'Thank you, Barthol. I try.'

Seated at the long debrief table in his chambers, Van Voytz looked sidelong at Biota. 'Are they tainted, Antonid?' he asked.

Biota keyed open a data-slate. 'Medical scans say no, though there is a significant degree of obscurity. For all their filth and organic corruption, they seemed to have survived exposure to what we might think of as actual taint–'

Balshin raised her hand. 'Point of order, lord general. Master Biota, with respect, is a member of the Departmento Tacticae Imperialis. Since when did he get to render psycho-biological evidence? It's not his field.'

Van Voytz got to his feet and went to the sideboard to pour himself an amasec. As an afterthought – and a silent gesture of solidarity – he filled a thimble glass with sacra instead.

'Antonid is my right hand man. He also knows Gaunt and the Ghosts of old. I've asked him to bring his close scrutiny and eye for detail to their case. Go on, Biota.'

Biota cleared his throat. 'I am not an advocate or a specialist martial lawyer, madam commissar-general, as you indicate. But my mind is trained to a superior level in the processing of evidence and intelligence. As far as I can determine from the medicae and psychologicae reports, Gaunt and his men are not tainted. They are genuinely damaged in many ways: they are tired, scared, traumatised, unappreciated. But there is no sign of actual taint. Medicae and toxicological scans agree. They are physically infested… lice, worms, bacteria… and they show perplexing registers of some kind of toxin or venom that they have built up a resistance to. They are scarred, they are battered, they are strung out, and they may never again be the fine warriors we once knew. But they are not tainted.'

Balshin nodded. 'I don't agree. At least, I'm not convinced. Lord general, you trusted your man Biota here to process the data on your behalf. I saw fit to call upon the services of another expert.'

'Did you?' Van Voytz asked.

Balshin turned and gestured to Faragut, who was waiting by the door.

Faragut opened the hatch and a short, thickset figure walked in. He was wearing a dark brown leather coat reinforced with patches of chainmail. His greying hair was receding, but a tight black goatee covered the chin of a face that was pugnacious, almost sunken in aspect. His eyes were entirely dark blue, without a hint of white.

'Lord General Van Voytz,' Balshin began, 'may I present–'

'Lornas Welt,' Van Voytz finished. 'Lornas and I know each other of old, Balshin. How fare you, master inquisitor?'

'Very well, my lord general,' Welt replied in soft, clipped tones.

Van Voytz turned to Biota. 'Inform Junior Ludd that the Inquisition is now involved.'

Biota got to his feet.

'I don't believe that's necessary, my lord,' Balshin said.

'I do, Viktoria,' Van Voytz snapped. 'You've just upped the ante. Ludd needs to know that. Throne, Gaunt needs to know that.'

'This is acceptable,' Welt said, politely.

Biota left the room. Welt took a seat at the table beside Balshin.

'I've reviewed the data,' the inquisitor said. 'It's a tough call. These people have served the Imperium creditably. They have given their all. However, for the safety of us all, I believe they should be put to death quickly and quietly.'

Van Voytz glared at the inquisitor. 'That is a brutal–'

'It is the price you pay, my lord. The price of the mission you had them undertake. They did what you ordered them to do, and for that, they should be celebrated. But there is no way they could have come out of that nightmare untouched. It would have been better for them if they had died on Gereon. You sent them to their deaths, after all. The only nagging problem is that they've come back and now you're faced with doing the dirty work Chaos failed to do for you. You must execute them.'

'If they survived the hell I sent them into,' Van Voytz said, 'then I'll give them a chance.'

Welt nodded. 'Hence the hearings. We will be compassionate.'

'I hope so,' said the lord general.

Faragut approached Balshin and handed her a slip of paper.

'My lord, I am called away briefly.'

Van Voytz nodded.

Following Faragut out of the hatchway, Balshin asked quietly. 'Is this true?'

'Yes, ma'am.'

THE CAGE-HATCH of the detention deck slid open and Balshin walked down the block, Faragut tailing her. The lady commissar-general stopped at one of the cages.

'You wanted to see me?' she asked.

Sabbatine Cirk got to her feet and walked to the cage-front. 'Yes. I want to cut a deal.'

FIVE

16.03 hrs, 190.776.M41
Frag Flats HQ
Sparshad Combat Zone, Ancreon Sextus

THE GUARDS STATIONED around the hearing chamber came to attention with a rattle of armour, and the eight senior Commissariat officers seated around the semicircular dais rose to their feet. Commissar-General Balshin swept in through the main hatch, her long gown billowing out behind her, accompanied by Faragut, Inquisitor Welt, and an Imperial Guard colonel in a dark blue dress uniform. The four of them marched to their seats at the centre of the curved dais.

'Be seated,' the colonel said. 'This hearing is called to order on the one hundred and ninetieth day of 776, by the grace of the God-Emperor. Let us commence without delay.'

The main hatch opened again, long enough to allow Ludd and Gaunt to enter, side by side. They strode smartly across to the small desk facing the half-circle of the dais, came to a halt beside it, and stood at attention.

'Junior Commissar Nahum Ludd, advocating for the defendant,' Ludd announced.

'So noted,' replied the colonel. 'Have a seat, junior commissar. The defendant will remain standing.'

Ludd glanced at Gaunt, who was ramrod stiff, staring down the tribunal, then sat down behind the small desk.

'The defendant will identify himself,' the colonel called.

'Ibram Gaunt, colonel-commissar, Tanith First, serial number–'

'Your name is sufficient, Gaunt,' the colonel cut in. 'At this stage, you have no recognised rank in the eyes of this tribunal. I am Colonel Gerrod Kaessen, and I will be presiding over the hearing today.'

'Was the lord general too ashamed to face me?' Gaunt asked.

Ludd jumped to his feet. 'The defendant withdraws that remark, sir.'

Kaessen raised an eyebrow. 'Do you, Gaunt?'

'If that's what my advocate advises, sir.'

'For your information, Gaunt,' Kaessen said, flipping through some papers in front of him, 'Lord General Van Voytz is unavoidably occupied at this hour, and has asked me to represent High Command interests in his stead. It would be unusual, don't you think, for the supreme commander of this theatre to be directly involved in a comparatively minor tribunal hearing?'

'It depends what you mean by "comparatively minor", sir,' Gaunt replied.

'Well, let's see,' the colonel shot back. 'Compared to… the ongoing prosecution of this war, for example?'

'The point is taken, sir,' Ludd replied.

'The point is also that Lord General Van Voytz is the sole reason I'm standing here today,' Gaunt said.

'How so?'

'Because he personally sent me on the Gereon mission, and only on his word have I not been executed for accomplishing said mission and returning alive.'

'Please!' Ludd hissed at Gaunt.

'I withdraw my last remark,' Gaunt said.

Colonel Kaessen pursed his lips. 'Gaunt, do you recognise the authority of this tribunal?'

'I think, colonel,' said Inquisitor Welt quietly, 'that is essentially what we're here to establish.' Several of the commissars around the dais chuckled. Balshin leant over to whisper to Faragut.

'Very well,' said Kaessen. 'The defendant may be seated. Junior Commissar Ludd, you may begin with your opening remarks.'

Gaunt crossed to the desk and sat down beside Ludd. Gaunt was dressed in high black boots, black breeches and a simple black vest, all unadorned by rank pins or insignia. The cut sleeves of the tight vest showed the lean, corded power of his arms and upper body, and also the dozens of old scars, large and small, that decorated his flesh. He'd showered three times since his first meeting with Ludd, but still the dark grey stain of the Nihtganes' camouflage paste lingered in his pale skin, like a faint, all-over bruise. He'd also shaved. The thick, stiff dreadlocks of his beard and long hair were gone, leaving a severe crewcut and a neatly trimmed goatee. The hair on his head and chin were a pale, dirty blond, like faded, slightly stale straw.

Ludd stood up with a dossier in his hand and cleared his throat. 'If it please the tribunal, I would like to begin by reading a transcript record of the colonel-commissar's career to date, making reference to the many meritorious–'

Faragut got up quickly. 'Objection, colonel. Copies of the transcript record have been circulated to all the members of the tribunal. We are all perfectly familiar with it. Reading it aloud will simply occupy valuable time.'

'Colonel,' said Ludd. 'The record attests to the past character of the defendant.'

'The defendant's past character is not in question,' Balshin put in.

'Duly noted,' said Kaessen. 'The objection is sustained. Move along, please, junior commissar.'

Ludd frowned and put the dossier back on the desk. He selected another. 'In that case, colonel, I should like to read the defendant's own, detailed statement regarding his mission to Gereon.'

Immediately, Faragut was on his feet once more. 'Again, colonel. Cause as before. We have all been copied with this statement, and we have all read it.'

'Duly noted,' Kaessen repeated.

'With respect, sir,' Ludd insisted, 'the matter of the Gereon mission under-pins the entire nature of the hearing today. It cannot be glossed over.'

'The statement runs to one hundred and forty-seven pages,' Faragut said. 'I must object to a simple recitation of–'

'Colonel?' Inquisitor Welt put in softly. 'I have read Gaunt's statement in full, as have, I'm sure, my worthy fellows. I've really no wish to hear such prepared material repeated out loud. However, I believe Junior Ludd's point to be well taken. Perhaps, as a compromise, and pursuant to the interests of fairness, the defendant might be permitted to make a brief summary of the salient facts in his own words?'

'That sounds fair and practical, inquisitor,' Kaessen replied. He looked at Balshin. 'Objections?'

'None, colonel.'

'Junior Ludd?'

Ludd bent and exchanged a few whispered comments with Gaunt before rising again to face the dais.

'The defendant is happy to comply with the inquisitor's suggestion.'

Ludd sat down. Gaunt rose to his feet and began to speak.

'In the latter part of 774, my unit arrived here on Ancreon Sextus as part of the Fifth Army's liberation contingent. We'd shipped in from Herodor after the scrap there. Shortly after our arrival, I was contacted by the office of the lord general, and summoned to meet with him. He told me he had a high-category mission that needed to be undertaken immediately. It was classified vermillion, and was on a volunteer-only basis. It involved the covert deployment of a specialist mission team onto the enemy-occupied world of Gereon. I agreed to lead the mission.'

'Just like that?' asked one of the ranking commissars.

'Naturally, I reviewed the requirements first,' Gaunt replied sardonically.

'Once you had, you accepted?'

Gaunt nodded. 'It was clear the matter was potentially vital to the con-tinued success of the Crusade on this front. Besides, I felt the lord general was asking a personal favour of me.'

'Why was that?' Faragut asked.

'The nature of the mission suited the skills of my regiment. The Tanith are experts at stealth infiltration.'

'Wasn't there another reason?' Faragut pressed.

Gaunt shrugged slightly. 'I believe it's possible the lord general had a decent regard for my abilities, and the abilities of my soldiers. I'd like to think he asked me because he trusted me.'

'You had worked directly with the lord general before, isn't that right?' Ludd put in.

'Yes,' said Gaunt. 'Most particularly on Phantine in 772, and a year later on Aexe Cardinal.'

'In both instances, you served him well?'

'As far as I know, he was satisfied.'

'It's fair to say then,' Ludd continued, 'that you had become one of the lord general's favoured commanders? He regarded you highly, and counted on your expertise during special circumstances?'

'I was honoured to enjoy the favour and friendship of Lord General Van Voytz,' Gaunt said.

Balshin rose. 'None of that is disputed. General Van Voytz has imparted to me on several occasions that he considers the defendant both a close comrade and a friend. However, I believe Commissar Faragut was pressing at something else.'

'Such as, my lady?' Kaessen asked.

Balshin looked down at Gaunt on the main floor below her. 'Perhaps the defendant might describe the specific parameters of his mission?'

'I was just getting to that,' Gaunt said, totally at ease. 'The mission was to infiltrate the occupied planet Gereon, broker contact with the local pro-Throne resistance, and then locate and eliminate with extreme prejudice an individual held in custody by the Archenemy forces.'

'And that individual was?' Balshin asked.

'The Imperial traitor General Noches Sturm.'

'Why was this important?' Balshin added.

'Sturm had been disgraced and was awaiting court martial when the Archenemy captured him. He had been carefully mindlocked, so that the information in his brain could be reopened during the trial. It was a distinct possibility that the enemy might penetrate that mindlock and recover all manner of sensitive information from Sturm. Fleet codes, ciphers, deployments, tactics. If he could be opened up, he would surely betray significant Crusade strengths to the Archenemy, resulting in catastrophe for our cause.'

'Indeed,' said Balshin. 'Tell the tribunal, if you would, why General Sturm was facing court martial?'

'For dereliction of duty during the siege of Vervunhive,' Gaunt said.

'Who found him so wanting at that time?'

Gaunt coughed slightly. 'I did, ma'am.'

'You were the one who placed Noches Sturm under arrest and saw that he was charged?'

'Yes.'

'You were a colonel and he was a militant general?'

'Yes. I found him wanting in my capacity as an Imperial commissar, and removed him from command.'

'I see,' said Balshin. 'And in your capacity as an Imperial commissar, were the charges against him valid?'

'Absolutely.'

'Let me get this straight,' Balshin smiled. 'In the middle of a quite notorious siege, in the extreme heat of combat, you removed General Sturm from command... in your capacity as a commissar?'

'Yes, as I just said.'

'Under such intense circumstances, Gaunt, did you not consider that summary execution was more appropriate? In your capacity as a commissar, I mean?'

'I did not.'

'But it was quite within your power. Instead, you stretched vital reserves of manpower to keep him a prisoner.'

'An objection to the commissar-general's tone and inference!' Ludd called out.

'Overruled,' said Kaessen.

'Gaunt?'

'It was also quite within my power to order his internment,' Gaunt said quietly. 'I do not shrink from execution where it is needed, but I felt that Sturm deserved to face full court martial because of his status and rank.'

'So he was alive because of your judgement?' Balshin said. 'Let me rephrase that... Noches Sturm was only alive *to be captured by the enemy* because you had let him live?'

'Yes.'

'The entire jeopardy he represented when he fell into enemy hands was *your* fault?'

'Another objection!' Ludd cried.

'I made no error,' Gaunt growled. 'Perhaps the fault lies with the office of the Commissariat for guarding him so unsuccessfully.'

'But isn't it true that you undertook the Gereon mission because you felt it a personal failing that he had got away?'

'Objection!'

'Isn't it true,' Balshin urged, 'that Van Voytz asked you to undertake the Gereon mission because he wanted to give you the opportunity to clean up your own mess?'

'Objection! Colonel, please!'

'My last remark is withdrawn,' Balshin said, and resumed her seat.

Ludd had been on his feet throughout the last exchange. 'Sir,' he said to Gaunt. 'Who won the battle at Vervunhive?'

'The forces of the God-Emperor,' Gaunt said.

'And who was in command of them?'

'I was.'

'If you would,' Ludd said, 'remind the tribunal of the official rating the Departmento Tacticae gave to the Gereon mission.'

'The status was *EZ*.'

'Which is?'

'I believe the definition is *"extremely hazardous/suicidal"*.'

'There were twelve mission specialists on the team including yourself,' Ludd said. 'How many did you lose?'

'None.'

'And was the mission successful?'

'Yes. We eliminated Noches Sturm at the Lectica Bastion. A confirmed kill.'

Ludd looked back at the tribunal panel. 'Perhaps the defendant might resume his account of the mission?'

'So requested,' Kaessen said, with a nod to Gaunt.

'My stalwart advocate has rather ruined the ending, colonel,' Gaunt smiled. Despite themselves, several of the senior commissars on the dais smiled. So did Welt.

'That wasn't the end of it, though, was it?' Faragut asked. 'Once Sturm was dead, I mean.'

'No, commissar,' Gaunt said softly. 'Before we set off, Lord General Van Voytz had made it plain to me that there was very little chance of extraction. It had been hard enough getting us in. Even if we survived, it was likely to be a one-way mission.'

'So you were stuck there?' Faragut pressed.

'Yes. Most of us were injured–'

'In what way?'

'The usual way. Enemy fire. Some of my team were severely hurt. We had also expended most of our munitions and supplies. We had little choice but to throw in our lot with the Gereon underground and serve the Imperial cause by adding our abilities to the resistance efforts. But we did this, I think, gladly. We had seen much of the privation levied on the planet. The Gereon underground was a proud, defiant, valiant force. We were honoured to help.'

'Isn't it true you did more than help?' Ludd asked.

Gaunt shrugged.

'This is not a moment for modesty, Gaunt,' Inquisitor Welt called out.

'Very well, sir. The Gereon underground – which, I might add, had sacrificed great portions of itself to help us achieve our mission – was principally an under-equipped force of local citizens, reinforced by the military skills of a few surviving PDF officers. My team and I were able to spread our knowledge and our combat abilities. We restructured the underground in the Lectica area, and also in neighbouring provinces. We trained them in stealth warfare. For that, I would especially commend my scouts Mkoll, Bonin and Mkvenner. Trooper Brostin supervised the steady manufacture of makeshift flamer weapons. Sergeants Criid and Varl, along with myself, taught them cadre and fireteam drills. Major Rawne and Trooper Feygor travelled the cells, instructing them on demolition and explosives know-how. Vox-officer Beltayn, my adjutant, pretty much rebuilt the underground's communication network. Trooper Larkin hand-trained a school of marksmen using captured las-locks, teaching them how to make the one, sure killshot you need with single-action weapons like that. Medicae Curth's training became utterly indispensable to the underground's needs. I would also, before this hearing, commend Gerome Landerson and Sabbatine Cirk, officers of the resistance, for their courage and determination at all times.'

'You paint a heroic picture,' Welt said.

'What about the partisans?' Ludd nudged.

'The Nihtganes, or Sleepwalkers, of the Untill region—' Gaunt began.

'The what?' asked Kaessen.

'The Untill, colonel,' Gaunt explained. 'The untillable or un-navigable regions of Gereon, deep marshes mostly. The Sleepwalkers are surviving communities of the original colonists. Infamously separatist, they had been the bane of Imperial authority for many years. But Chaos was a common foe. A tribe of Nihtganes assisted us in our initial actions on Gereon, and later, principally through the work of Scout Mkvenner, we were able to enlist them in the resistance as elite troops. Without the Sleepwalkers, we would have failed on Gereon, both in our attempt on Sturm, and in the guerilla war that followed.'

'I've seen your pet Nihtgane,' Faragut said. 'Eszrah, isn't it? Not the model Imperial citizen.'

'I would ask that you take that slur back, commissar,' Gaunt replied. 'Eszrah ap Niht is the most loyal soldier of the Throne I have ever met.'

'Why do you say that, Gaunt?' asked Kaessen.

'Because he is loyal to me, sir.'

'This period of operation with the Gereon resistance, it was hard, wasn't it?' Faragut asked.

'Yes,' said Gaunt.

'Demanding, I mean,' Faragut continued. 'From your appearance alone, on your return... you were undernourished.'

'Food was in short supply. For everyone.'

'And you were deprived of many things. Soap, for example.'

'I won't dignify that with a response.'

'Your clothing too, ragged...'

'As far as I'm aware, the nearest functioning Guard quartermaster was eight light years away.'

'Colonel,' Ludd said. 'Please, is the defendant under scrutiny here because of his dishevelled appearance? That length of time behind enemy lines, it's hardly surprising he was not parade muster.'

'A fair point,' Kaessen said. 'Where are you going, Commissar Faragut?'

'There's more to it, sir,' Faragut said. 'There is the question of taint. We all know that's the heart of the matter. Dirty, bearded, ragged... that's one thing. Gaunt and his team were living rough with the resistance. In many ways, the fact that they seem to... how shall I put it best? The fact that they seem to have *gone native* is understandable.'

'Under the circumstances,' said Gaunt, 'it was vital.'

'But there are other, more concerning matters. The grey staining to your skin and hair—'

'We all adopted the Nihtgane practice of using *wode*. That's their word for it. Essentially, it's a skin-dye paste ground from the wing-cases of the swamp moths. It's excellent for camouflage. Not only visually, but it masks scents too. We would treat our hair, clothes and skin with it. It has other prophylactic properties too.'

Gaunt noticed that Welt was making some hasty notes.

'But it's difficult to get out. Even by scrubbing with carbolic.' Gaunt paused and looked at Welt.

'Does it explain the elevated toxin levels found in your bloodstream and in the systems of your fellows?' the inquisitor asked.

'The moths are venomous, sir, yes,' Gaunt said. 'The paste allowed us to build up a tolerance to local poisons.'

'And anything else?' Welt asked.

Gaunt shrugged. 'The Nihtgane believed that a more concentrated form of the paste could actually fight off Chaos-related infections. I wouldn't know about that.'

'Did you see that done?'

Gaunt nodded. 'Yes, with Trooper Feygor. To startling effect.'

'But "you wouldn't know about that"?' Faragut asked.

'I'm no medicae,' Gaunt said. 'I know what I saw. I know what it was like. Maybe the paste helped Feygor, all of us perhaps. But it may also have been a placebo. I believe the best way to fight Chaos taint is to be sound and determined of mind.'

'Are you saying,' said Faragut, 'that you and your team came off Gereon untainted because you mentally refused to allow yourselves to become so?'

Gaunt looked at Ludd, who shrugged.

'Answer the question please,' Kaessen called.

'Yes,' Gaunt said. 'That's an oversimplification, but I think it's essentially correct. Though we suffered, and we were sorely tested, we rejected the corruption of the Ruinous Powers by force of will.'

Faragut glanced at Welt, who shook his head. Balshin rose instead. 'If you were sitting in judgement here, Gaunt,' she asked, 'would you believe a word of what you just stated to the hearing?'

'Knowing it to be the truth, lady commissar-general, I'd like to think I would.'

'And supposing you didn't?'

'I don't know. It's an aspirational idea. One based on the notion of the essential incorruptibility of true Imperial souls.'

'Indeed. And that is how you see yourself and your team?'

'Yes,' said Gaunt.

'It's interesting,' Welt said, rising as Balshin resumed her seat. 'As you say, Gaunt, an aspirational idea. But isn't it true that even the greatest and purest of men have, through the course of our history, been corrupted by the warp despite their soundness of heart?'

'History speaks of such things. But I think I'm right in saying that Urbilenk wrote that: "Chaos merely unfetters the dark quarters of the mind, unlocking that which was always there. True, pure minds have nothing that curse may use".'

'You quote him well.'

'One of my favourites, inquisitor. I would also cite Ravenor, who said in *The Spheres of Longing*: "Chaos claims the unwary or the incomplete. A true man may flinch away its embrace, if he is stalwart, and he girds his soul with the armour of contempt."'

'Fine words,' said Welt.

'I think so,' Gaunt replied.

'Even so, statistically–'

'My team and I were not tainted.'

'Because you and your team are somehow special? Exempt?'

'I believe the Ghosts of Tanith have been blessed by their interaction with the Saint,' Gaunt said.

'On Herodor, you mean?'

'Then, and before. I think perhaps… we're especially hard to taint.'

Welt smiled. 'You took inhibitors with you?'

'A fair supply. They ran out.'

'Before you left on the mission,' Welt said, consulting a data-slate, 'is it not true that you consulted Tactician Biota for information as to how long you might reasonably last on a Chaos-held world before taint became inevitable?'

'Yes, inquisitor.'

'And to answer that, Biota referred himself to the Ordo Malleus, correct?'

'I believe so.'

'And what was the answer?'

'About a month,' said Gaunt.

'About a month. And how long were you and your team on Gereon?'

'Sixteen months.'

'It's evident that your accent has changed, Gaunt. It has a timbre. A quality.'

'It's the same for all my team. Living amongst the Nihtgane inevitably caused some alterations.'

'Do you acknowledge that the change in your accent is disconcerting?'

Gaunt shrugged.

'Do you acknowledge that it makes you sound like the Archenemy?'

'No,' said Gaunt. 'Though we all speak Low Gothic, the accents of the Imperium are many and varied. Ever spoken to a Vitrian, inquisitor? '

'I have.'

'What about a Kolstec? A Cadian? A Hyrkan? Ever heard the burr of a Phantine voice? The wood talk of the Tanith in full, mellow flow?'

'Your point?'

'Accents prove nothing. Would you execute us for a twang in our voices?'

Welt put the data-slate down. 'Voi shet, ecchr setriketan.'

'Hyeth, voi magir, elketa anvie shokol,' Gaunt replied.

An ugly murmur ran around the room. Ludd stared at Gaunt with a queasy look on his face.

'You speak the language of the Ruinous Powers,' Welt said.

'One of them.'

'Fluently and naturally, it seems.'

'How long do you suppose the underground would have lasted if it didn't learn the language of the enemy, sir?' Gaunt asked. 'It was a vital tool of resistance.'

'Even so–' Balshin began.

Gaunt stared up at Inquisitor Welt. 'You speak it well,' he said. 'Why aren't you down here with me?'

Welt laughed heartily. 'Touché, Gaunt,' he said. He sat back down.

Immediately, Faragut stood again, opening his dossier. 'You were embedded with the resistance for a considerable time,' he said.

'As I said, we were resigned to our situation.'

'Why, then, did you leave?'

'Because we had the opportunity to do so.'

'For what purpose, if you were performing such a vital service leading the underground?'

'I felt it was necessary to get the intelligence concerning Sturm off-world as soon as the chance arose. I also wanted to communicate other information to High Command.'

'Such as?'

'Such as the fact that the foul Magister Sek was using Gereon as a proving ground for his own elite shock troops. They are modelled on the Blood Pact. If anything, they are more vicious.'

'You know this how?'

'From fighting them and killing them,' said Gaunt.

'You think they present a tangible threat to the crusade?'

'How tangible is the Blood Pact, Faragut? If the Sons of Sek, as they are known, are marshalled into a proper fighting force, we will be in a shit-storm of trouble.'

Faragut paused, lost for another question. From his seat, Kaessen said 'Tell us about your evacuation from Gereon, Gaunt.'

'Gladly, sir. We had been planet-side and dug in for about sixteen months,' Gaunt said. 'By then, the Archenemy hold on Gereon had fractured a little. Not much, but enough to allow independent and rogue traders access to remote portions of the planet, conducting black-market runs. Also, they extracted civilian refugees who could pay. Beltayn and Rawne had developed this connection, in order to supply the underground with munitions, but the trade grew, even though the occupying forces dealt harshly with any traders they captured. I've seen more than one far trader ignite in orbit. However, it became possible for people to leave Gereon, if they were prepared to take the risks.'

'And you chose to take that route?' Faragut asked.

'I felt I owed it to my mission team. As I said, I felt I needed to bring word of Sturm's death to High Command. Most particularly, I felt the Crusade forces needed to know about the Sons of Sek before it was too late.'

'So you left Gereon?'

'It was hazardous. We procured a rogue trader, who then let us down five nights running. On the sixth evening, we managed extraction, but it was compromised. Enemy warships pursued us to the limits of the system.'

'And then?'

'Then a month's transit to Beshun. The trader deposited us there, unwilling to risk the Imperial blockade at Khan Nobilis. We had no access to astropath communications, but I knew we needed to reach Ancreon Sextus.'

'Why?'

'We needed to reach Van Voytz. He was the only one who could vouch for us.'

'And what happened?'

'Liberty ships were coming in to Beshun, carrying refugees and survivors fleeing Urdesh and Frenghold. We got passage to Ancreon Sextus as part of a host of Guardsmen trying to rejoin the Crusade main force. On arrival, we were transported to the internment camp for processing. No one I spoke to would believe our story, or allow us contact with Van Voytz. We were told that the opportunity would arise at Camp Xeno, during processing.'

'Did that happen?' asked Ludd.

'It did not. But for the extremis actions of my team... and the interjection of my advocate here, we would have been executed without hesitation.'

'An objection!' Faragut cried.

'Withdrawn,' said Balshin.

An aide had entered the hearing room, climbed the dais and whispered into Inquisitor Welt's ear. Welt looked at Colonel Kaessen.

Kaessen nodded. 'That's enough for now. We'll resume at oh-eight hundred tomorrow. Hearing is in recess.'

SIX

THE FOLLOWING MORNING, Balshin and Welt were late. Kaessen himself arrived almost ten minutes after the appointed start time, and apologised to the waiting commissars. 'An unavoidable hold-up,' he said. 'We will begin shortly.'

Gaunt and Ludd had been sitting at the defendant's desk since just before eight. Ludd was sorting through various papers from his document case, and seemed ill at ease.

'Do you know what this delay is about?' Gaunt whispered to him.

'No,' said Ludd, a little too firmly. 'They choose not to tell me anything.'

Gaunt raised his eyebrows thoughtfully. He could tell Ludd was tense. For his own part, Ludd was trying to maintain a veneer of calm. He didn't want his own edginess to rile Gaunt into further outbursts. But the night had not passed well. Three times he'd been summoned to see Balshin, each time quizzed on various aspects of Gaunt's testimony. He'd spent half an hour alone reviewing the medical records. Something was going on, but the defence advocate was being kept out of the loop.

'When they put me back in the tank last night,' Gaunt said quietly, 'I saw that Cirk had been removed. She wasn't back this morning, either. Any idea what that means?'

Ludd shook his head. 'I'm sorry. I asked, and was told she'd been removed for questioning by Balshin.'

'Isn't that counter to the terms of the tribunal, Ludd? They said they'd be starting with me.'

'I know. It's frustrating.'

'This is increasingly feeling like a scam to me,' Gaunt said. 'Is there something you're not telling me, Ludd?'

'No,' Ludd replied. 'Except that there's something they're not telling either of us.'

Behind them, the heavy door of the hearing chamber drew open with a scrape of metal, and Commissar-General Balshin entered, escorted by Inquisitor Welt. Ludd and Gaunt rose to their feet, and the chamber guards came to formal attention.

'My apologies to the tribunal,' Balshin said as she stepped onto the dais. Then she turned aside and engaged Kaessen in a quiet, intense conversation. Welt took his seat. He was staring at Gaunt, and when Gaunt met his eyes, nodded briefly.

Balshin handed Kaessen a data-slate and then sat down. The colonel reviewed the slate's contents and remained standing to address the hearing.

'I'll keep this brief and simple,' he said. 'I'd like to bring to the tribunal's attention this edict.' Kaessen indicated the data-slate. 'It was issued by the Commissariat at oh-seven forty-five this morning, and personally ratified by Inquisitor Welt on behalf of the Holy Ordos. It states that all charges and suspicions against Gaunt and his mission team are to be dropped with immediate effect.'

There was a chatter from the commissars around the dais. Ludd looked at Gaunt.

'The defendants will be released shortly into the hands of the Munitorum for dispersal. The members of the tribunal are thanked for their time and attention.'

'Sir?' Ludd said. 'Are there terms to this edict?'

Kaessen nodded. 'Gaunt and his team must submit to a full round of psychometric tests and interviews to assess mental health and combat readiness, and they must all make themselves available for thorough debriefings with Military Intelligence. There will then be a probationary period at the discretion of the Commissariat. Other than that, no. Junior Ludd, perhaps you'd stay with Gaunt until he's been issued with appropriate credentials for this HQ.'

'Yes, sir.'

'By the grace of the God-Emperor, this hearing is closed.' Kaessen declared, and the commissars on the dais immediately rose and started talking in huddles as they left the chamber.

'I wanted to ask why the sudden change of heart,' Ludd confided to Gaunt, 'but I didn't want to tempt fate.'

'I know what you mean,' Gaunt replied. 'But I think I'll find out in due course.'

Colonel Kaessen approached. He saluted and held out his hand to Gaunt. 'A good result, if unexpected,' he said as Gaunt shook his hand. 'I'd not have been happy to be the man presiding over your demise, colonel-commissar.'

'Thank you, colonel. Any idea what happened to change events?'

Kaessen smiled. 'I think you have a good deal of influence, sir. Powerful allies.'

'I see,' Gaunt replied. He looked past the colonel, but Balshin and the inquisitor had already left the chamber.

'The lord general's waiting to see you,' Kaessen said.

LUDD LOCATED A watch officer, and had him issue a pass warrant for Gaunt. Gaunt fixed the small plastek badge to the front of his vest and then allowed Ludd to accompany him as far as the outer hatch of the lord general's quarters.

Ludd paused at the doorway, anticipating – or at least hoping – that Gaunt might offer him some acknowledgement, perhaps even thanks. Gaunt merely glanced at him, a brief, almost dismissive look, and then walked on through the hatch without a word, leaving Ludd alone in the hallway.

Ludd looked down at the deck, ran his tongue around the front of his upper teeth thoughtfully, and turned to leave.

'Junior commissar?'

Ludd looked round. It was Balshin.

She beckoned to him with a curt hook of her fingers.

'A word with you, please.'

VAN VOYTZ WAS at his desk in the inner office of his quarters, reviewing reports. As Gaunt entered, Van Voytz dismissed the group of aides and servitors and got to his feet as soon as they had left the room.

He walked around the desk until he was face to face with Gaunt.

'Shall we start again?' he said.

'I'd appreciate the chance, sir,' Gaunt replied.

'Any weapons you'd especially like to threaten me with?' Van Voytz asked.

'My lord, I never threatened you directly. I–'

Van Voytz held up his hand. 'Lighten up. I'm joking. It's over, Ibram. Done with.' The lord general gestured, and they sat down on the battered leather couches beside the desk.

'This is how it should have been,' Van Voytz mused. 'Mission over and done, you reporting back to me, a quiet moment to savour your success.'

'Events conspired against that,' said Gaunt.

'They did. Look, if I could have spared you any part of that tribunal, I would have done. I have authority, Ibram, extraordinary amounts of it, in some areas. But not in others. Discipline and security are not in my remit. You know how it works.'

'I remember how it used to work,' Gaunt said.

'Once you'd pulled that stunt in here, Ibram, it was out of my hands. I had no choice but to give you to Balshin. There would have been hell to pay, otherwise. I had to give you to Balshin, and while she was busy with you, find ways to get you cleared.'

'You did that?'

'I pulled some strings, called in a few favours. My last few favours, probably. Viktoria Balshin is possibly the most fanatical person I've ever met where it comes to issues of Imperial purity. She's devoted her career to the suppression of taint, and won't even let the slightest rumour of it pass her by. Admirable, of course, and understandable given the way things have gone this last year. But even she has a price. I had to give her something to make her drop the case.'

'What was that?' Gaunt asked, uncomfortable.

Van Voytz shrugged. 'It doesn't matter. You'll be better off not knowing. All you need to know is… I made her a proposition. I contacted the office of the Warmaster himself, and got his personal endorsement for my proposal. Inquisitor Welt also supported it, which helped a great deal. I think Welt likes you, Ibram. Admires you.'

Gaunt frowned. 'I don't know why, sir.'

'Neither do I,' replied Van Voytz. 'Who knows how the curious minds of Inquisitorial servants operate? He has his own agenda. Whatever, with the Inquisition and the Warmaster himself backing me, I had the sort of leverage that Balshin couldn't ignore.'

'Are you saying the Warmaster himself vouched for my case?' Gaunt asked.

'On my recommendation. You look surprised.'

'I didn't think he was even aware who I was,' Gaunt said.

'You've met him?'

'A handful of times, but I'm not senior staff, and I–'

'You'd be surprised what he remembers,' Van Voytz said. 'Macaroth might be a very different animal to old Slaydo, but he's still a Warmaster. He has the same skills, the same eye for detail, the same memory for those who serve the cause well, whoever they are. He remembers you all right, and he was fully appraised of the Gereon mission.'

'I see,' said Gaunt.

'About the Gereon mission,' Van Voytz said. 'With Macaroth's approval, I have requested citation for you and your team. A special honour or decoration may be approved eventually. Throne knows, you deserve it. But the matter's knotted up in larger, political issues, and these things take time anyway. In a few months, there might be an official recognition. I'm telling you this because for now, and perhaps for always, you'll receive only private thanks.'

'I didn't do it for the glory,' said Gaunt. 'The Emperor knows there was precious little in it anyway. I'd simply like to get back to active line duties as soon as possible.'

'That was my next question. It's in my power to retire you from the front for the duration. A little soft duty in the rear echelons might do you the power of good. But I expected that wouldn't appeal, knowing how you're made. As soon as you're cleared fit, I can get you into the field again, if that's what you want.'

'It is, sir,' Gaunt nodded.

'Well, then…' Van Voytz began. Gaunt could see that the lord general seemed unsettled. Van Voytz had changed too, from the man who had sent the Ghosts off on their mission. The change was perhaps not as dramatically obvious as the alterations hardship had wrought upon Gaunt and his men on Gereon. But it was there, nevertheless. Van Voytz was older, more haggard, more worn than Gaunt remembered him. He'd lost weight too, so his crisp day uniform hung limply from his frame. The stress of command seemed to have eroded his robust physique.

'Sir,' Gaunt said. 'May I ask what you meant when you said "the way things have gone this last year"?'

Van Voytz shrugged. 'Tough times, Ibram. The Second Front's facing especially bitter resistance from Sek's forces, right across the coreward Khans. Macaroth expects results, but they're just not coming fast enough. Here alone, we should have been done six months ago.'

'Particular problems?'

'Enemy fanaticism is especially high. Plus the special terrain here and on a couple of other key worlds. That's a killer. Here, it's the damn step-cities. Clearing them is a nightmare. There's also the issue of taint.'

'That again?'

'In the last twelve months, the Second Front has lost thirty-two per cent more to taint or suspected taint than during the previous phase. Whole units are deserting the field. Some are even changing sides.'

'Hence the commissar-general's particular obsession with that heresy?'

'Indeed. It's endemic. Oh, there are reasons, I'm sure. Men break easier when the going's hard, and it's certainly hard here. We're making nothing like the palpable inroads the Main Front's achieving in the Carcaradon System. It also doesn't help that the majority of troop units in the Second Front armies are fresh and inexperienced. Most of them are new-founded regiments sent to us from the rear to replace lost strengths. Macaroth took most of the veteran regiments with him for the main push. I'm left with boys, Ibram. Untried, innocent, naive. Their first experiences of real combat are against ferocious cult units lousy with corruption, heresy and the marks of the Ruinous Powers. Suicide is up, mental collapse, desertion…'

'Is the enemy using psykers to magnify the effect?'

'Jury's out on that one, Ibram. Possibly. All we know is, the corruption of the foe is sweeping through our ranks like a plague, right across the Second Front. Morale is at an all time low, and that can only lead one way.'

'The collapse of the Second Front.'

'Unless Second Front Command can turn the tide. Or unless the Warmaster decides we are not leading and inspiring the men in a manner appropriate to our authority, and replaces us.'

'Is that a real possibility?' Gaunt asked.

Van Voytz did not reply. Clearly it was. Clearly he was under immense pressure to dig his command out of a deep, dark hole.

'So, your field posting,' Van Voytz said, at length. 'It'll be good to have another experienced officer on the line.'

'I am anxious to return to the Tanith First,' Gaunt said. He'd deliberately not thought of that possibility for a long time. In the dark days on Gereon, it had been too much to hope for, too painful a hope to cling to. Gaunt allowed himself the pleasure of anticipation for the first time in months.

It was short lived.

'That... look, I'm sorry, Ibram. There's no easy way into this. That's not going to happen.'

'What? Why?'

'There are two reasons, really.' Van Voytz got to his feet and helped himself to a small amasec. He didn't offer one to Gaunt. 'The first is you. I've moved heaven and earth to get you reinstated, Ibram. Called in favours, like I said... and, like I said, I'm down to my last few. Particularly with Macaroth regarding my performance with mounting displeasure. I had to compromise. It was a condition demanded by Balshin and the senior Commissariat. You may return to the line in the capacity of commissar, with a purview to reinforce and support unit discipline. They don't want you given a command posting again.'

'I can't believe this,' Gaunt said.

'I don't like it. Not at all. But it's the hand we're dealt. You must come around to the idea that the future of your career lies with the Commissariat, not with command. A separation of powers. I'm sorry. New duties await you, new challenges. The Tanith First was your last command.'

'Can I file a protest?' Gaunt asked.

'To whom?' Van Voytz laughed, mirthlessly.

'Then... then what was the second reason, sir?'

Van Voytz cleared his throat. 'Simple enough, Ibram. You can't go back to commanding the Tanith First, because the Tanith First doesn't exist any more.'

SEVEN

06.19 hrs, 193.776.M41
Fifth Compartment
Sparshad Mons, Ancreon Sextus

ONCE THEY HAD made him, they named him Crookshank. Crookshank Thrice-wrought, in honour of his twisted form and the complexity of his making. It was a name he could recognise – sometimes – but could not say. In the barking cant of the wrought, he was known simply by the depth and timbre of a particular throat-roar.

The sun was rising, but no daylight had yet penetrated the vast black gulf of the fifth compartment. High overhead, the visible sky was blue-white, suffused with smoky light, and the rays of the sun were illuminating the faces of the towering stepped walls of the inner Mons to the east. Where the sunlight touched the stone, far away and high above, it glowed like amber.

The deep floor of the colossal fifth compartment was a blind, cold place, trapped in the shadow of the western wall. The pre-dawn temperature was minus three, and a chill mist shrouded the jumbles of wet, black stones and deep crater pools. It was quiet and still: just the occasional skitter of vermin in the rubble, or the distant grumbling roars of other wrought ones echoing down the compartment's long canyon.

Crookshank Thrice-wrought was hunting. The urge to do so was knotting his omnivorous stomach and needling at the tiny, primitive lump of his brain. Quietly, he clambered his great bulk along a ridge of broken ruby quartz. The only sounds he made were the slight clicks of his thick claws against the quartz, the low wheeze of his phlegmy lungs.

The end of the ridge overlooked a sunken watercourse. He could see it clearly, despite the blackness. His eyes resolved the details of the world as pink phantoms, and he could smell and taste the shapes of it too. He snorted twice, pulling rushes of cold air in through the blood-rich olfactory passageways of his long skull. He smelled the texture of stone, the feeble

319

flow of the shallow water in the sunken course, the damp lichen clinging to the underside of granite boulders.

There were two wrought ones behind him. He'd been well aware of them for the last fifteen minutes, but had made no show of acknowledging them. They were little, once-wrought, immature things, lacking the display decoration of a mature bull, their lank black hair plastered damply over their pink, sutured scalps. They were following him unbidden, hoping he'd lead them to a kill, hoping to share in his success. The once-wrought often did that. They tailed the elders to learn skills from them and benefit from their protection.

Crookshank ignored them. They were making too much noise. One was panting hard as the adrenaline rose, and it was causing his throat tubes to hoot involuntarily.

Crookshank moved forward. His massive hands and feet read every notch and crevice of the rock, but he felt no scratch or graze or pain, just as his body registered it was cold but knew no discomfort. He could smell something new now. He could smell meat.

There was a sudden bang. The thump of it echoed down through the darkness, and made distant voices hoot and bark. Five minutes run ahead of him, Crookshank saw flames. A fierce spot of fire, bright like a star in the darkness, painfully bright to his straining dark-sight.

His blood began to course. Engorged, the fighting spines of his hackles rose up. Crookshank did not choose this reaction. It was bonded into the flesh of him, wired into his bones. The killing instinct that motivated him to do the things for which he had been made. Already, his dark-sight had clouded from pink to red. He felt the flush on his skin, the wetness as his throat tubes distended and vibrated with the rapid gusts of his exhalations.

He stood upright, swung his huge arms back and then forward, and pulled that momentum into a great forward leap which carried him down into the watercourse. He landed in the mud, and began to hurtle along the littered shore on his feet and his knuckles, bounding like a giant simian.

His two followers came after him eagerly. Both leapt off the promontory and landed in the shallow water itself, splashing after him on all fours. One left the water and began to chase Crookshank down the muddy shore, but the other – which was now hooting loudly with every overexcited breath – continued to crash and spray through the shallows.

Crookshank slid to a halt and turned suddenly. The once-wrought on the bank quailed back in alarm, but the other one came on, whooping and splashing. Crookshank ploughed into the stream and swung for him. The blow connected with the once-wrought's head and neck, and lifted him clean out of the water. He landed on the far side of the watercourse, twitching and convulsing, black blood pumping from the lacerations Crookshank's claws had left in his throat. But the throat wound wasn't the killer. The convulsions were just nerve-spasms. The immense force of Crookshank's blow had crushed the once-wrought's skull.

Crookshank turned and resumed his charge. He saw only red now. Red, and the bright white star of the flames. He shredded his way through a stand of stiff black thorn-rushes, snapping their stems, came in over a low ridge, and saw the prey. Little meat figures, struggling around a burning metal box. One of them saw him coming and screamed. Darts of light flickered at him.

Crookshank unleashed the full fury of his roar through his throat tubes, shaking the world. As he pounced, throwing all eight hundred kilos of himself forward into the air, arms outstretched, his massive jaws opened on their hinges and the steel daggers of his teeth slid out and locked in place.

'CONTACT!' THE COMPANY vox-officer was yelling, but that much was obvious. A kilometre ahead, the pre-dawn dark in the compartment was lighting up with flashes and flame-light. They could hear the chatter of weapons, and another sound. A roaring sound.

Wilder ran across the ice-clagged track to where Major Baskevyl crouched beside the vox-officer.

'Report!'

'It's not entirely clear, sir,' Baskevyl replied, making dragon breath. He was pressing the vox-set phones to his left ear. 'Sounds like the Hauberkan push has found a mined zone. At least one vehicle crippled. Now they seem to be under attack.'

'Oh, for Throne's sake!' Wilder said. 'I thought the area had been swept?'

'Last night, before dark,' Baskevyl shrugged.

'What are the Hauberkan doing?'

'Their commander's just signalled a halt, citing danger of mines.'

Wilder cursed again. 'Patch me through,' he said to the vox-officer. The man nodded and handed Wilder the horn.

'This is Wilder, Eighty-First Bellad–' He paused, and corrected himself. 'Wilder, Eighty-First First. Request confirmation. Are you moving?'

'Uh, negative on that, Wilder.'

'In the Emperor's name, Gadovin, if you sit still, they'll find you and gut you. Tank or no tank.'

'The zone is mined. We are holding as of now.'

Wilder tossed the horn back to the vox-man. 'What the hell's wrong with these idiots?' he asked Baskevyl. 'Didn't they have this explained to them?'

'The Hauberkan just got here, sir. I don't think they yet appreciate the jeopardy.'

'Did they think we were explaining it because we like the sound of our own voices?' Wilder asked.

'I think that's exactly what it was, sir.'

'Here's what we're going to do,' Wilder said, adjusting the gain of his low-light goggles so he could study a plastek-sheathed chart. 'We're going to move forward in a broad line and come up in support of these morons.'

'The order was to hold these trackways for the second wave,' Baskevyl advised.

'A second wave is going to be as effective as quick piss through a furnace grate if the forward line remains stalled. We'll leave six companies here on the trackways. The rest go forward. Tell the commissars I'll need them with me when we reach the Hauberkan command section. Tell them to bring sharp, pointy sticks.'

'Yes, sir.'

'That's if the Hauberkan are still alive when we get there. Bask, if we advance in the current disposition, which company's going to make that contact point first?'

'Best guess, E Company.'

Wilder nodded. 'Let's get to it,' he said.

Baskevyl saluted and crunched down the frosty track, ordering the men of the Eighty-First First up out of their cover. In their black camo, the troops flooded like shadows down the trackway and up across the open ground to the left.

'Get those support weapons moving!' Wilder heard Baskevyl shouting. 'Slog it! Look alive now!'

Wilder watched the fast deploy for a moment, and was satisfied. Moving together, no shirking. Still, blessedly, no sign of an enthusiasm problem in this newly alloyed force. There hadn't been a single serious issue of morale since the mix. He wasn't sure if he should feel flattered or simply lucky.

He adjusted his micro-bead link. 'Wilder to E Company lead. Talk to me.'

'Receiving. Go ahead, sir.'

'Chances are your first troop are going to reach that contact, captain. I'm relying on you to deal with it.'

'Understood, colonel. No problem,' the voice of the young captain crackled back.

'Thank you, Meryn. See you on the far side.'

THE FIRST SPEARS of intrusive daylight were stabbing down over the high, black crest of the western wall. A sort of twilight gathered in the depths of the compartment.

This was a bad time of day. Too dark for eyes, too light for goggles. Meryn removed his goggles anyway. According to scout philosophy, the sooner you got your eyes adjusted, the better.

The forward elements of E Company were pushing ahead through stands of black rushes thriving on a strip of wetland between the line of a trackway and a low watercourse. They were following the crushed and trampled pathways left by the Hauberkan armour. Ahead, all sounds of fighting had ceased, but they could still see fire, lifting into the air beyond the sticky, black undergrowth. The sight of the flames seemed to emphasise how cold it was.

Dark shapes loomed up ahead. Three Hauberkan treads, parked and immobile. Meryn heard the voice of his adjutant Fargher rising angrily.

'What's the problem?' Meryn demanded as he came up.

Fargher gestured to the vehicle commander in the open hatch.

'He won't budge, captain,' he said.

'I've got orders,' the armour officer said.

'Feth your orders,' Meryn told him. 'Those are your boys in trouble up there.'

'I was told not to move,' the man protested.

'Feth you too, then,' Meryn spat. 'Fargher, take a note of this tread's stencil plate. Put it in the book.'

'Sir.'

'Let's close it up!' Meryn called, turning to the advancing troopers. 'Sergeant?'

Caffran jogged over to him. 'Sir?'

'Move your troop around to the right,' Meryn pointed. 'Come in along those rocks. I'll sweep in from the left, with Arlton's mob at the flank.'

Caffran nodded. It was still as strange to be taking orders from Meryn as it was to be wearing the silver badge with 81/1(r) on it. Times change, war didn't. Neither did men. Flyn Meryn was as fond of giving orders now as he had been as a lowly squad leader. In Caffran's opinion, Wilder hadn't made many mistakes during the mix, but Meryn's promotion was surely one.

They ranged forward, moving fast and low through the rushes. Caffran kept an eye on his troop. Five of them were Belladon, but they'd got the hang of the camo-capes pretty well. Besides, they had their own rep to uphold.

Crossing the rocks, they reached the contact.

A Hauberkan Chimera had churned out of the rushes onto a stretch of shingle and mud, and gone right over a mine. The blast had burst it wide open, scattering the mud with debris and fragments of armour. Fire was boiling fiercely from the machine's exposed guts. Two other Chimeras, moving in just behind, had evidently halted. Open hatches showed where the crews had exited in an effort to help the stricken tread.

Then something else had happened. The ground around the vehicles was littered with torn remains that steamed in the cold air. Caffran swallowed. They'd been hit hard, slaughtered. He knew what must have done this. The deep, terrifying roars of the spooks had echoed down the compartment valley all night.

Lasrifle raised, Caffran edged down onto the mud. Leyr and Wheln followed, then Raydee and Mkard. Caffran waved the others out into firing positions along the edge of the rocks, then gestured Neskon up. The flame-trooper slithered down the rocks to join them, gently pumping the stirrup of his burner. The little naked trigger light hissed blue in the gloom.

The state of the bodies was chilling. None of them was intact. Limbs had been stripped of flesh, torsos emptied. Bloody stumps of ribcage poked through torn, soaked cloth.

Leyr made a quick hand signal for stillness. Caffran moved up close to his scout until he could hear what Leyr had heard. A snuffling, a wet crackling. Until now it had been indistinguishable from the pop and crack of the burning Chimera.

Round there, Leyr indicated. They raised their weapons to their shoulders, and edged on. Deftly, silently, Wheln and Neskon followed them. Mkard, and the Belladon, Raydee, moved around to cover the other side of the burning wreck.

The once-wrought had not learned from the example set by the mature bull he had followed. Crookshank had attacked, slaughtered, fed quickly and savagely, and then vanished into the dark again. The once-wrought had killed nothing. He had whooped and roared plenty as he charged in, but Crookshank had already finished the work. Hungry, and twitching with the huge adrenaline rush, the once-wrought had lingered to feed on the parts of the kill Crookshank had spurned and left behind.

He was sucking on the marrow of a Hauberkan officer. Vaguely humanoid, with stunted legs and vast arms and shoulders, the once-wrought weighed around four hundred kilos. The raw, pink flesh of his broad chest was smeared with blood, and tatters of meat dangled from his huge, under-biting snout. Patches of long, black hair trailed from a flat, almost indented scalp that still showed the healing scars of surgery, and hung down across tiny, pig-eyes that glinted behind an implanted iron visor. He raised his massive head as he detected movement.

'Holy feth!' Caffran gasped. He and Leyr began firing immediately, full auto bursts of las from their mark III carbines. The stalker was already coming for them, powering forward on knuckles like tree-roots, jaws opening. It roared a wet, choking roar, gusting a mist of blood and saliva from its slack throat tubes.

Caffran and Leyr saw their shots cutting into the spook's hide, but it didn't even flinch. Blood streaked down it from the multiple puncture wounds.

They feel no pain, Caffran thought. *How do you stop a thing like–*

It was just three metres from them when Neskon caught it in a long, howling spear of flame. The beast fell back, thrashing at the living fire that engulfed it. Neskon kept the pressure on.

Wild, demented, the once-wrought turned and lurched away around the other side of the wreck. Raydee and Mkard met it head on.

Raydee almost managed to get out of the way. He went sprawling, and the once-wrought trampled him, crushing his left foot into the mud and snapping his ankle. The monster grabbed Mkard around the body with its gigantic left hand and slammed him back against the rear-end of the burning Chimera so hard it pulped the Tanith-born's torso.

The flames had died down. The once-wrought's hair was burned off, and his skin bubbled with fat blisters. He roared, his throat sacs vibrating.

A hot-shot round exploded his cranium. The shot had been aimed right down the once-wrought's yawning gullet. There was a stringy burst of gore that left nothing behind except the heavy lower jaw, and the nightmare pitched over dead.

'Move in! Move in and secure the area!' Caffran yelled.

Meryn's troop began to emerge from the rushes. In cover, Jessi Banda lowered her long-las and ejected the spent hot-shot pack.

'Nice shot,' Meryn said, and kissed her roughly on the mouth. Their faces were cold against each other.

'I aim to please,' she smiled.

Meryn grinned and hurried forward to join the others.

DAWN WAS COMING up fast. Light was creeping down the eastern wall of the compartment. The wind was picking up too.

Wilder felt the breeze against his face, like the cool decompression rush of a flooding airgate. No one in Guard Logistics or Intel had yet been able to explain why the winds picked up in daylight, though Wilder had sat through three or four lengthy briefings filled with talk about ambient cooling, rapid-rise solar heating, pressure change and inter-compartment windshear effects.

In the grey light, Wilder saw the stands of thorn-rush and lime swaying and hissing. The landscape ahead, split by outcrops of granite and a quartzy rock, looked like wet hair. Through it, the black figures of his men advanced in a wide fan.

Good spacing, good unit protocol, Wilder thought. Excellent noise discipline. Mongrel or not, he was growing proud of the Eighty-First First (recon), with its proud battle-song of–

Well, that was the sort of area where things weren't perfect. He doubted any of the influx would be happy learning the words to 'Belladon, Belladon, world of my fathers', and he couldn't blame them. Likewise, he was sure, the Tanith and Verghastites had songs of their own that would not easily swell the breast of a true-blood Bel-boy. Where it was relatively easy to combine regimental titles, things became clumsy when it came to songs and traditions. And warcry mottos. 'Fury of Belladon, for Tanith, for the Emperor, and, by the way, remember Vervunhive!' Full marks for effort, but still dead in a slit-trench before you'd said it all and actually started fighting.

Things would come, evolve, but it would take time, and it certainly wouldn't be forced. Braden Baskevyl, Wilder's number two and a keen promoter of esprit de corps, had spent most of the last evening in camp encouraging a little improvisation between the regimental musicians. Belladon fifes and Tanith pipes. It sounded like a disenchanted cat being elaborately stabbed in a sack.

Wilder smiled to himself, but it was not smiling weather.

'Coming up on the Hauberkan line,' Captain Callide reported over the vox. 'Got them in sight, fifty metres.'

'Pull in slow,' Wilder ordered on the wide channel. 'Make yourselves known. The tankers are going to be jumpy. Anyone touch off a black cross, I'll kick their arse. Even if they are dead.'

Black cross. The mark made in Munitorum ledgers to indicate a Guard-on-Guard firing accident.

Major Baskevyl hurried up out of the gloom. He'd pushed his low-light goggles up onto the brim of his helmet.

'How can you see?' Wilder asked.

'It's an accustomisation thing, sir,' Baskevyl said. 'The Tanith scouts reckon it's best to let your eyes adjust as soon as possible.'

Wilder frowned, then took of his own goggles, blinking hard. It had been his experience so far that the Tanith knew what they were talking about, especially the ghostly scouts.

'Got a signal from E Company,' Baskevyl said. 'Meryn's secured the contact. A spook had ambushed some treads that had been stopped by a stray mine.'

'They get the bastard thing?'

'Yes, sir.'

'Casualties?'

'No details yet.'

The officers turned as they heard a flutter of polite, whispered greetings from the men behind them. The commissars were approaching, and as they moved up the line, the troops were greeting them with formal respect.

'Over here,' Wilder called.

Commissar Genadey Novobazky had been with Wilder and the Belladon for five years. Grizzled and lithe, he was a stern man, a fair man, and one disapproving glance from his grim demeanour was usually all that was needed. When it wasn't, Novobazky really came into his own. He was the best talker Wilder had ever met, the best rabble-rouser, a real burning det-tape when it came to igniting battlefield spirit: funny, loquacious and inspirational. His predecessor, Causkon, had been a real sap, which hadn't mattered much as the Belladon had never needed much field discipline, but Wilder had counted himself lucky to have an asset like Novobazky assigned.

The other commissar, Viktor Hark, he'd inherited from the Tanith. Bulky, heavy-set and impassive, Hark seemed a decent sort, and his augmetic arm spoke of heroic effort on the field of war. Hark had proved good at sorting out matters of petty theft, uniform code violations and mess-hall spats, but he'd yet to reveal any true potency as a commissar. There were the odd hints that Hark had some subterranean strengths, but he seemed to Wilder to be curiously reserved and hesitant, as if used to a subtler style of command. A legacy of the Great Lost Commander, Wilder supposed. Big boots to fill, and Wilder's own boots were quite tight enough, thank you. He pitied the Tanith First for the body-blows it had taken on Herodor and afterwards, but sometimes he was secretly a little glad the other guy was dead. His job would have been so much harder if any hope had remained.

'I want to get the armour moving,' Wilder told them.

'And they're not moving why?' Novobazky asked.

'Mines,' said Baskevyl.

'Nerves,' Wilder corrected. 'They've had a little hiccup, and now they've frozen up.'

'We can impress them with orders,' Novobazky said. 'It was perfectly clear last night. Ridge eighteen is the objective, with an open, covered corridor for the second wave. We're a long way short of that, and Gadovin knows it.'

'He's saying the orders are void because the orders supposed the zone had been cleared of mines,' Baskevyl said.

'Mine. Singular,' Wilder said. 'Boo hoo, that's war. Gadovin is overreacting. And if he sits there much longer, he'll be inviting all sorts of hurt.'

'And you're not happy about that?' Novobazky asked.

'How do I sound?'

'Let's have a word with him then,' Hark said. Hark didn't say much, and when he did, it was low-key, but this was one of those hints that Wilder had learned to pick up on. A muted suggestion that Hark was quietly polishing something large and spiky.

Wilder nodded. 'This they then do,' he said. He turned to Baskevyl. 'Get F Company moving onto that rise around the right flank. And tell Varaine to pick up L's pace before we leave them behind.'

A vox-officer ran up. 'Colonel Wilder, sir. Signal from Frag HQ.'

Wilder took the message wafer and started to read it. Some business about a personnel transfer.

There was the sudden suck-hiss of an inbound ballistic object. A hot, hard fireball burst amongst the line of stationary tanks. Two, three more fell, then a sustained salvo, ground-bursts erupting furiously along the Hauberkan position, throwing soil up into the air. The wind blew the grit back across Wilder's advance.

'Shit!' Wilder cried. He started to run forward. 'Into it! Into it!'

As he ran up through his scrambling troops, Wilder shoved the wafer, half-read, into his coat pocket.

EIGHT

07.56 hrs, 193.776.M41
Fifth Compartment
Sparshad Mons, Ancreon Sextus

WILDER LED THE charge up the slope, through the rushes and the sickly limes, into the wind, into the concussion of the falling shells. He saw at least three Hauberkan vehicles on fire. The quivered air was full of blown soil, dust and fragments of rush-stem. None of the tanks had begun firing, but at least some were restarting their engines. Wilder heard starter-motors whining and coughing. They'd been sitting in the cold for forty, fifty minutes. Some of these old treads would need a lot of nursing and blessing to get going again.

The shells continued to drop – brief shrill whistles, followed by heavy, splattery detonations. Some of the Eighty-First First had reached the spaced formation of tanks and got in between them, firing down across the brow of the slope into mist and shell-vapour.

'Auspex!' Wilder yelled over his link, panting as he struggled through the wet undergrowth.

'No fix yet, working.'

'Faster!' Wilder barked.

He was coming up behind a Chimera that had its turbines running. It was snorting plumes of blue vapour out of its exhausts. An Exterminator, three vehicles to his left, took a direct hit, and went up in a prickling sheet of flame. The concussion jarred Wilder's innards against his ribs. He almost fell.

'Open fire!' he yelled up at the Chimera. 'Open fire, damn you!'

For a second, Wilder thought his shout had actually penetrated the machine's thick armour and made some sense. The Chimera revved its engines hard.

And started to reverse.

Wilder was so amazed, it nearly ran him down. He threw himself out of the way.

'Scatter! Scatter!' he yelled at the men nearby. Other Hauberkan tanks were starting to back violently down the shallow gradient. The men of the Eighty-First First, drawn up between and behind the fighting machines, struggled to avoid them, some falling, some crying out.

Wilder heard a high-pitched scream that could only mean one of his men had been caught under treads.

Colonel Lucien Wilder, Belladon born, proud and decorated commander of the Belladon Eighty-First since Balhaut, was known as a genial, humorous soldier: a soldier's soldier. He had an infectious wit that often earned the disapproval of his superiors, and a track record that had won him nothing but plaudits. Well-made, dark haired, clean-shaven, he had a wry, handsome face and a sort of permanent, knowing, lady-killer squint. When he raised his voice, it was so orders could be understood, or so that the troopers at the back of the mess-hall could hear the punchline.

And, occasionally, when fury drove him. Like now.

As the Chimera reversed past him, splashing him with cold mud and twigs of reed, he hammered against its sponsons and track guards with the butt of his autopistol and screamed 'Halt! Halt, you bastard! Halt!'

It did not.

Raging, Wilder grabbed a netting hawser and scaled the side of the moving vehicle. Up on top, rolling with the lurch of the Chimera, he kicked at the squat turret. A shell went off nearby and threw dirt and debris across him.

'Halt! Halt!' His voice had become a scream. He saw that the top-hatch cover was loose. Wilder yanked the hatch wide open, let it fall with a clang, and lunged inside. In the dim, instrument-lit interior, the pale face of the vehicle commander looked up at him in dismay, and reached for a sidearm.

'Bastard!' Wilder shouted and slapped the gun away. Then he grabbed the tanker by the hair and slammed his head repeatedly against the metal bars of the roll-cage. 'Bastard! Bastard! Tell your driver to halt now! Now!'

'Do it! Do it!' the commander yelled, wincing at the tearing grip on his scalp. The Chimera bounced to a stop.

'Vox-link!' Wilder demanded, and ripped the headset out of the man's hands. Then he smacked him in the mouth for good measure.

The headset was crazy with nonsense traffic, panic-calls, hysteria. The Hauberkan had broken completely.

'Gadovin! Gadovin! This is Wilder! Cease your retreat now! Now, Throne damn it! Gadovin!'

The squealing nonsense was all that answered.

'Gadovin, so help me, stop your line moving and throw down some fire or, by the Emperor, I will hunt you to the ends of everywhere and shoot you a new arsehole! Gadovin! Respond!'

Nothing. Wilder threw the headset back at the dazed commander. 'Use your pintle mounts,' Wilder told him. 'Fire into that mist bank. I have a gun and, so far, you look like the enemy to me.'

The tanker nodded furiously. He activated turret power, wound up the autoloader, and then the heavy linked bolters in the low-profile turret began to blaze away, gouting flame-flash from the muzzle baffles.

Wilder switched his commlink to the wide channel. 'Wilder to troop leaders. Be advised that the Hauberkan should now be regarded as without line of command. I am assuming control. Their orders are to hold and fire. Do whatever you can to impart that order. Any refusal must be considered a failure to follow officer directions.'

The shells were still raining down. More than a dozen armour units were ablaze, destroyed, and the undergrowth at the crest of the rise was burning too. From his raised vantage point, Wilder saw that half a dozen tanks had already retreated right back down the slope to the lower trackway. The noise of the barrage was deafening. Wilder wondered how much of his order had been heard.

Nearby, the six crew members of an Exterminator had abandoned their machine and were fleeing down the slope. Wilder was about to leap down after them when he saw Commissar Hark appear out of the smoke wash. Hark had drawn his sidearm, a plasma pistol.

'You men!' he yelled, the loudest thing Wilder had ever heard him utter. 'Get back to your stations!'

The tankers hesitated, then continued to run.

Hark turned away.

Wilder jumped down. 'What the hell was that?' he demanded.

Hark glanced at him. 'If they're scared enough to ignore me, my rank and my weapon, then they're too scared to be of any use. Why? Would you like me to have shot them?'

'Hell, yes!'

'What, to assuage your current anger?'

'You and I are going to have a conversation, Hark.'

Hark nodded. 'As you wish, colonel.'

'Now rally the men!'

Wilder ran down the left wing of the broken line. Some of the Eighty-First First were in place at the crest of the slope, sniping into the mist. He passed Novobazky, who had expertly grouped most of D Company's first troop into firing positions and was delivering a variation on one of his favourite themes, The Shores of Marik.

'On the Shores of Marik, my friends,' Novobazky declaimed, head-high as he walked the line, oblivious to the whizzing shells, 'the fathers of our fathers made a stand under the flag of Belladon. Shells fell like rain. Were they afraid? You bet they were! Were they trepidatious? Absolutely! Did they break and run? Yes! But only in their minds. They ran to friendly places and loved ones, where they could be safe... and then, by the providence of the God-Emperor, they saw what those friendly places and loved ones would become if they did not stand fast, and so stand fast they did! How do you feel?'

There was a throaty murmur.

'I said, how do you feel?'

Louder shouting.

'Belladon blood is like wine on the Emperor's lips! Belladon souls have a special place at his side! If we spill our blood here today, then this is the soil He has chosen to bless and anoint! Oh, lucky land! Rise up and load, my friends, rise up and load! If they're going to have our precious blood, then they'll find the cost is dearer than they can afford! Fury of Belladon! Fury! Fury!'

A piece of art that. Honed over the years. The skilful acknowledgement of fear, the patriotic strand, the unexpected sucker-punch of 'Did they break and run? Yes!'. A piece of art. The thundering cadence and gathering rhythm. Simple words that carried over the tumult. Too many commissars told men they were invulnerable when they patently weren't. Too many commissars harangued and scolded, stripping away pride and confidence.

Or turned their backs on fleeing cowards, Wilder thought.

'Commissar!' Wilder called.

'Colonel, sir,' Novobazky answered, hurrying over.

'Good work. We're in a patch of hell here.'

'I noticed.'

A shell struck twenty metres away and they both winced.

'I want you down the left flank. I need you to pull the sections down there in tight. If the enemy start a ground push, we'll be exposed at the base of the hill.'

Novobazky nodded. 'I'll get to it.'

'Fury of Belladon, Nadey.'

'Fury of Belladon, Lucien.'

Novobazky hurried off down the slope.

Wilder turned and took stock. He hoped to see Baskevyl or Callide, but neither Belladon was in view. Little was in view, in fact, apart from flames, roiling smoke-fog and scattering figures. Wilder comforted himself that at least a half-dozen Hauberkan machines were now firing, including an Exterminator, which shattered the thickened air with the hammer of its heavy autocannons. Wilder doubted any order had been given. He was fairly confident that once he'd got the Chimera firing, others had joined in because they supposed that was what was meant to be happening.

Whatever works, Wilder thought.

He came up on a troop section dug in around the cover provided by a shattered and smoking Chimera. They'd got their field support weapons set up: two thirty calibre cannons and a trio of light mortars.

None of them was firing.

It was G Company. Wilder read that from their shoulder flashes.

He ran across, ignoring the raining dirt and biting wind.

'Where's Daur?' he yelled.

Captain Ban Daur, tall, solemn and good-looking, clambered up from a slit trench to face him.

'Colonel?' he saluted, his head hunched down in that 'shrapnel's flying and I'd rather I wasn't so tall' attitude.

'Nice position, Tanith,' Wilder said.

'Thank you, sir. It's Verghastite, actually.'

Wilder smiled humourlessly. He should have known that. The influx from the First-and-Only had been allowed to retain their patriotic badges, which they wore next to the 81/1 (r) silver emblem of the mongrel unit, just as the Belladon retained their brass carnodon head. A skull and single dagger for the Tanith-born, an axe-rake motif of the Verghast miners. Ban Daur wore the latter.

'My apologies.'

'No need, sir.'

'Much as I'd love to spend the rest of the day in genteel conversation with you, Daur, might I ask, since we're being shelled, why the hell your troop isn't firing?'

'Because we're being shelled, sir,' Daur replied.

'Make this good.'

Daur turned and gestured out at the fog-bank lapping the far edge of the slope. 'We're being shelled, colonel. Whatever's lobbing these munitions is well beyond our small-arms or even light support range. Four or five times that, maybe more. If there are hot-body targets out there too, well, they're likely to be two or three times beyond our range too. Any closer, and they'd stand the risk of taking the back-creep of their own artillery. I've got a limited amount of ammo and mortar loads. I'd rather not waste any of that until I can be sure of a target.'

Wilder frowned, turned away, and then looked back at Daur. He was grinning. It was that grin that had made Daur like him on the first day of the mix.

'You're smart, Ban,' Wilder said. 'You after my job at all?'

'No, sir.'

'Sure?'

'I'll admit to nothing, sir.'

'That's fine. Good job here. I like sense. Sense is good. Hold this just as you are… but you'd better start wailing on them the moment they show.'

'It's my purpose in life, sir,' Daur said. 'Correction, it's G Company's purpose in life.'

There was an enthusiastic roar from the men.

'Keep doing what you're doing, then,' Wilder said, moving away. 'You need a piper or anything to get you going?'

'No, sir. Unless you can produce Brin Milo out of nowhere.'

'Who?'

'Never mind. We're fine.'

'Yes, I think you are, captain. Carry on, G Company.'

* * *

COMMISSAR NOVOBAZKY SCRAMBLED down the lank, wet grasses to the base of the slope at the left end of the Hauberkans' disastrous line. Fyceline smoke billowed down from the hammering shell-strikes, and the skyline looked as if it were on fire.

The Eighty-First First troops on the left flank had accumulated in the long ditch watercourse at the foot of the hill. They seemed unformed, un-unified, cowering in the lapping water.

'My friends!' Novobazky cried as he moved in amongst them. They looked at him. 'On the Shores of Marik, my friends,' he continued. The text had worked earlier, and it was fresh enough for another go-get. 'The fathers of our fathers made a stand under the flag of Belladon. Shells fell like rain. Were they afraid?'

'Who?' asked a man nearby.

'The sons of Belladon!' Novobazky smiled.

The man looked the commissar up and down. 'My name is Caober. I'm a scout, born and raised on Tanith. I honestly don't know what you're talking about, but I'm sure it matters somehow. Why don't you talk to the captain?'

A big man approached them, drawn by the voices. He studied the commissar for a moment. Novobazky shook his head at his own mistake. This was C Company.

'Commissar?'

'Major Kolea. Wasting my time with the whole Shores of Marik riff, right?'

Gol Kolea half-smiled. 'Not the best crowd to try that material on. Pretty much Ghosts here, through and through.'

'Can I retain any sense of cool at all?'

'I doubt it. You entered like a pantomime chorus. I'd love to hear the story, mind you. Where's Marik?'

'Damned if I know. I wasn't there.'

Gol Kolea chuckled. 'Gaunt never told stories, you know that?'

'I'm sure he did,' Novobazky said.

'Well, maybe. I don't remember any to tell. Derin? You recall any of Gaunt's stories?'

'Only the ones we lived through, major,' a trooper nearby called out. 'I've still got the scars from Hagia.'

'Yes, yes, all right,' Kolea said. He looked back at the commissar. 'You got a reason for being here, sir? Apart from pantomime, that is?'

Novobazky nodded. 'Instructions from the colonel. Get tight.'

'Any tighter and we'd be spitting pips.'

'Good. You don't seem tight.'

'We're tight. We're tight, aren't we?' Kolea called to the crouching figures along the watercourse.

'Tight as tight can be, Gol!' someone called back.

'That's good,' said Novobazky. 'Wilder's anticipating a ground push.'

'Nice to hear he's on the same page,' Kolea said. 'So are we. The moment the shells stop.'

'Well...' Novobazky began. He paused. An ominous, lingering silence, broken only by the crackle of flames and the cries of the wounded, had fallen across the slope. The shelling had stopped.

'I...' he continued, but Major Kolea waved him to silence.

'Saddle up,' Kolea hissed.

With a clatter of weapons and munitions belts, C Company rose and steadied.

The first las-shots began to pink out of the smoke. Small-arms fire pattered across the position. On the slopes, the dug in sections of the Eighty-First First began firing, supported by the heavy guns of the few Hauberkan machines that had not fled or died.

Enemy infantry was slogging up out of the mist, assaulting the slope. They emerged one by one, but soon became hundreds strong, thousands. They came yelling and baying, bayonets fixed.

'All right, C Company,' Kolea said. 'Like Gaunt himself would have wished, up and at them.'

The enemy troopers came forward out of the mist. Dawn light was now filtering down across the floor of the compartment, enough to glint off black and red armour, steel blades, and iron grotesques.

At brigade strength, the echelons of the Blood Pact assaulted the hill.

NINE

08.17 hrs, 193.776.M41
Frag Flats HQ
Sparshad Combat Zone, Ancreon Sextus

DRESSED IN A clean field uniform and a black leather jacket, a heavy kit-bag across one shoulder, Nahum Ludd stopped in front of the cabin door, paused for a moment, then knocked smartly.

He waited. Officers walked past along the quarters deck hallway. There was a faint smell of breakfast coming up from the mess-deck, mixed with the caustic odour of rat poison that always seemed to build up in the Leviathan's air systems over night.

Ludd was about to knock again when the door opened. He found himself staring up at Eszrah ap Niht. The sheer size of the partisan was intimidating enough, but now Ludd took a step back in surprise. Complying with orders, Eszrah had bathed and shaved. Or had *been* bathed and shaved. The tangled hair and the long, wode-matted moustache had gone, as had the iridescent mosaics around his eyes. His bald skull, regally and firmly domed at the back, his wide shoulders and his long neck gave him a noble aspect. His skin was entirely dark grey, as if that was its natural pigment, or as if the Nihtgane paste was simply too chronically ingrained to come off. The feathered cloak and tribal trappings had gone too. Eszrah was wearing laced boots, fatigue trousers and a woollen sweater, all Guard issue, all black. They served only to emphasise his height and slender build.

'I'm here to see the commissar,' Ludd said.

Eszrah's dark face was impassive. His grey, creaseless skin had a polished sheen to it, like gun-metal. His eyes were invisible behind an old, scuffed pair of sunshades.

'The commissar?' Ludd repeated, a little louder.

Eszrah stepped aside to let Ludd past, then closed the door behind him. Gaunt had been given high-status quarters in the officers' wing. The room Ludd stood in was part of a suite. Through an open door across the room, Ludd could hear a whipping sound, as if a flogging were underway.

Ludd put his kit bag down beside the door, and dropped his cap on top of it. The Nihtgane had returned to a chair in the corner of the room, and was busy cleaning some kind of ancient weapon that looked for all the stars like a crossbow. Around the room, equipment had been laid out, most of it still in the plastek wrap it had come bagged in, fresh from the quartermaster's stores. Ludd saw a fleece bedroll, a field-dressing pouch, a leather stormcoat, a ten-to-sixty field scope, and a brand new commissar's cap, the brim gleaming, still half-wrapped in cushion paper. On a side table, in an open steel carrier, a matched pair of chrome, short-pattern bolt pistols lay in moulded packing. Ten spare clips were fastened into the carrier's lid with elastic webbing.

On the main table lay a pile of data-slates and open dossiers. Walking past, Ludd noticed one slate was a set of current data codes and protocols. Another was loaded with the tactical charts of Sparshad Mons. With particular interest, Ludd noticed a brand new paper copy of the *Instrument of Order*, the Commissariat's 'rulebook'.

Ludd stepped through the doorway. The room beyond, larger, was the bedchamber, but the cot and all other furniture had been pushed back against the walls, and the twin-ply matting on the floor had been rolled up.

Gaunt was in the cleared centre of the room. He was wearing highly buffed black boots and a pair of dark grey jodhpurs with green piping down the legs. High-waisted, the jodhpurs were held up by a tight pair of black, service-issue braces. Apart from the straps of the braces, Gaunt was unclothed from the waist up. His lean, muscular body was flushed with perspiration. He held a beautiful, polished power sword in a two-handed grip, and was executing masterful turns, sweeps, blocks and reprises, circling and crossing, never putting a foot wrong, each motion exact and severe. As it moved, the blade made a hard, whistling sound like a whip.

Ludd watched for a moment. He had no wish to interrupt. Gaunt was evidently a brilliant swordsman who took practice very seriously. As he swung round, Ludd noticed with a slight intake of breath the huge and old pucker of scar-tissue across Gaunt's washboard stomach. It looked like he'd taken a hit from a chainsword or–

'Ludd.' Gaunt stopped mid-stroke and lowered the sword. 'Can I help you?'

'Good morning, commissar,' Ludd said. 'I came to tell you we've been routed. Transport will be made available at noon.'

'So soon?' Gaunt said. He picked up a hand towel and scrubbed it across his face and neck.

'They want you in the field as soon as possible.'

'I'm sure she does,' Gaunt said. 'Noon. All right. Do we have a deployment?'

Ludd reached into his jacket and handed Gaunt a message wafer. Gaunt took it, deactivated his sword and passed it to Ludd.

'Hold that, would you?'

Ludd took hold of the weapon. It was old, superb, deliciously heavy. The grip was worn from use, and the hilt patinaed with age, but the perfectly-balanced blade shone like a mirror. Switched off, it was still warm, and gave off a scent of heated oil and ozone.

Flopping the towel over his left shoulder, Gaunt tore open the wafer and read the tissue-thin form inside. 'Third Compartment Logistical Base. Uhm hum. Good as anywhere, I suppose. We're to report to the staff office of Marshal Sautoy. Know him?'

Ludd shook his head.

'I do,' Gaunt said, and left it at that. He balled up the wafer and dropped it into the little incineratum on his nightstand.

Gaunt turned back to Ludd and held out his hand for the sword. 'Like it?'

'It's a very fine weapon, sir,' Ludd replied, handing it over carefully.

'The ceremonial blade of Heironymo Sondar,' Gaunt said, flicking the blade back and forth one last time before returning it to its leather scabbard. 'A trophy, Ludd. It was awarded to me by the ruling families of Vervunhive as a mark of respect.' Gaunt looked at Ludd. 'It's just about the only thing I took to Gereon with me that came back intact. It's been in holding since I arrived here. They just sent it along to me. I'm glad to have it. I missed it.'

'I requested that all of the effects taken from you during processing at Camp Xeno be forwarded,' Ludd said.

'Processing,' Gaunt smiled. 'How nice you make it sound.'

Ludd blushed.

'Forget it, Ludd,' Gaunt said, pulling down the straps of his braces and towelling his armpits and shoulders. 'If we're going to work side by side, I can't have you going a shade of puce every time I make a dig about the circumstances of our meeting.'

Ludd nodded and tried to look happy. 'I want to say, sir... I want to say that I consider it a real honour to be assigned to you.'

Gaunt stared at Ludd as he finished rubbing down. 'I didn't request you, you know.'

'I know, sir.'

'You were appointed to me.' Gaunt tossed the towel away and reached for the clean vest and tunic shirt hung over a nearby chair back.

'You could have requested an alternative, sir,' Ludd said.

Gaunt pulled the vest over his head and tucked the hem into his jodhpurs. 'I suppose so. But after that bang-up job you did at the tribunal...'

Ludd sighed. 'Do I take it, sir, that I should expect this kind of ribbing to be an everyday aspect of serving as your second?'

'Yes, why not?' Gaunt said, buttoning his shirt. 'It'll keep you on your toes.'

Ludd nodded.

'I appreciate the sentiment, though,' Gaunt added, tucking the shirt in and pulling up his braces. 'The fact you think it's some kind of honour. I was under the impression it was more like a duty. Aren't you supposed to be my watcher?'

'Sir?'

'Come on, Ludd. I can deal with the idea you're watching my every move, reporting back, making sure I'm on the level. But I can't abide dissembling. You're Balshin's appointed spy. I know that. You know that. Let's be open about it, at least. I can't stand deceit, Ludd. Be a man and be frank about it, and I won't have to kill you.'

Ludd cleared his throat. 'Another example of your trademark humour, I take it?'

'Oh, let's hope so,' said Gaunt. He'd carefully pinned two small badges to the breast of his shirt, and now was searching for something on the dresser.

'Lost something, sir?' Ludd asked.

'More than you could possibly imagine, Ludd,' Gaunt replied. He squatted down, peering under the cabinet. 'Feth it, where the hell...'

Looking around, Ludd noticed something small and shiny down beside the night stand. He went over and picked it up. It was a regimental crest, a skull surrounded by a wreath, with a blade transfixing it top to bottom. There was a motto on it, but age had worn it indecipherable. The badge had rough edges, as if parts of it had been broken off.

'Is this what you're looking for, sir?' he asked.

'Yes,' said Gaunt. He took the badge and pinned it beside the other two on his shirt.

'May I ask...?' Ludd began.

Gaunt pointed to the emblems in turn. 'The pin of the Hyrkan 8th. The axe-rake of Vervunhive. The badge of the Tanith First-and-Only. All lost to me now, Ludd, but I'll not wade into war without them about my person.'

'Lucky charms?' Ludd said.

'I suppose. Ludd, have you ever lost anything that really mattered to you?'

Ludd shrugged. 'Not really, I... yes. Yes, sir. I lost my father at Balhaut.'

'Really? Was he a commissar?'

'Yes, sir. Serving with General Curell's staff at Balopolis. As far as I know, he was slain in a gas attack during the first few days of the battle.'

'What was his name?'

'The same as mine, sir. Nahum Ludd. Commissar Nahum Ludd. I'm Junior Commissar Ludd in so many ways.'

Gaunt nodded. 'I didn't know him. I was up at the Oligarchy during Balhaut. I know Balopolis was a bad show. The worst. I knew Curell, though. A little.'

'The Oligarchy,' Ludd said. 'That was the heart of it, wasn't it? You were with Slaydo?'

'Yes, I was.'

'Holy Throne. Is that where you–'

'What, Ludd?'

'The scar on your belly, sir...'

Gaunt shook his head. 'I won that a long time before Balhaut. In honour of my father. We have something in common then, I suppose. Following in our fathers' footsteps.'

'Yes, sir.'

'Careful where they lead, Ludd,' Gaunt said.

He walked back into the outer room where Eszrah was still cleaning his antique weapon. They exchanged a few words Ludd didn't understand. Gaunt pulled his fresh, new stormcoat out of its plastek wrap and put it on. It had been bundled up so long it still had fold creases in it as it hung from his shoulders. The room was filled with the pervasive smell of new leather.

Gaunt crossed to the main table and started to work through the dataslates and dossiers. He called up a plan of the third compartment and studied it for a while.

'The *Instrument of Order*?' Ludd asked, picking the book up.

Gaunt glanced over. 'I thought I should refresh myself. I'm a rogue, Ludd. I've been in the wilderness for a long time. I thought it was as well that I reminded myself of the actual rules.'

'And?'

'They're a nonsense. Starchy, high-minded, tediously prim. I find it hard to remember now how I ever managed to discharge my duties as a commissar without breaking down in tears of frustration.'

'You're a commissar again, now, sir,' Ludd said.

'Yes I am. And not that rare beast a colonel-commissar. I'll miss command, Ludd. Miss it dearly. Tell you what, you'd better slide that volume into your coat. I'll need you to remind me what the feth I'm supposed to be about.'

'Sir?'

Gaunt laughed and shook his head. 'A trooper is afraid for his life, as is quite natural in war. He breaks the line. What am I supposed to do?'

Ludd hesitated.

'Well, here's a clue, Junior Commissar Ludd. It's not speak to him, calm his fears, improve his morale and get him back in line. Oh no, sir. The correct answer, according to that vile text, is to execute him in front of his peers as an example.' Gaunt sighed. 'How did we ever build this Imperium? Death and fear. They're not building blocks.'

'This is another example of your off-beat humour, isn't it, sir?'

Gaunt looked at him. 'If it makes you sleep better at night, I'll say yes.'

Gaunt put down the data-slate. 'I want to see the Ghosts.'

'Sir?'

'The Ghosts. They're about to be reassigned too, right?'

'Yes sir. In a day or so.'

Gaunt nodded. 'They're going to be sent to join this new company?'

'The lord general thought that made the best sense, sir. Provided the company commander agreed.'

'I see. What's his name?'

Ludd thought for a moment. 'Colonel Lucien Wilder, sir.'

'Feth me,' Gaunt said. 'How truth seeps into dreams.'

'Sir?'

'Never mind, Ludd. I want to see the Ghosts. Before I go.'

'Is that wise, sir? Surely a clean break–'

'Too much history, Ludd. Too much blood under the bridge. I have to see them, one last time.'

'Barrack E Nine, sir. Awaiting dispersal.'

Gaunt walked to the door. 'Thanks. I'll be back before noon. Make yourself useful and pack up my kit for me.'

Ludd paused. 'Me?'

'I wasn't talking to Eszrah,' Gaunt said as he opened the cabin door. 'He has many fine qualities, but packing a Guard field kit as per regulations isn't one of them. I meant you, Ludd.'

'Yes, sir.'

'There's a place for Eszrah on the transport, right?'

'He's coming with us?'

'Of course.'

'Then I'll make sure of it, sir.'

GAUNT WALKED AWAY down the hallway, under the harsh bars of the lumin strips. He knew what was coming and he hated it. He'd never imagined, never at all, that he'd have to do what he was about to do…

Say goodbye.

He passed various fresh-faced young officers as he strode along. Most pretended not to look at him, but he could feel their eyes as he went by.

Scared. Wary. Unsettled.

Damn right. They should be scared.

Right then, Ibram Gaunt felt like the most dangerous fething bastard in the whole Imperium.

THE GHOSTS ROSE as he came in, but Gaunt waved them back down. They looked strange in their clean, black fatigues, like newly-founded draughtees. Only their faces betrayed their experience. All of them except Criid had shaved scalps. On various bare forearms, Gaunt noticed medicae skin-plasts, little adhesive patches that were releasing drugs into their systems to clean them of parasites and lice.

Gaunt sat down on one of the bunks, and they formed a casual huddle around him.

'I've been routed, and I'll be leaving this morning,' Gaunt began. 'So I probably won't see any of you again for a while.'

There was little comment. Rawne just nodded his head gently. Beltayn stared at the deck.

'Well, don't go all mushy on me,' Gaunt said. Varl and Brostin laughed. Bonin murmured something.

'Mach?' Gaunt said.

Bonin shrugged. 'Nothing. I just said… it's not how you expect.'

'What are you talking about?' asked Feygor.

'He's talking about the end,' Mkoll said, his voice low.

Bonin nodded. 'You never think about it,' he said.

'Except for the times you do,' Larkin whispered.

'Yes, except then,' Bonin agreed. 'And then all you can imagine is… oh, I don't know. A glorious last stand, maybe. Or a triumphal parade and a Guard pension. One or the other.'

'Dead or done,' Varl said, raising his eyebrows mockingly. 'Some choice.'

'Mach's right,' said Larkin. 'That is all you ever imagine. The two extremes. Not this.'

'Not this,' Bonin echoed.

'It all just seems so…' Beltayn began. 'So… mundane.'

'This is the real world, Bel,' Rawne said. 'The life of the Guard, hey ho. Forget the glory songs. Slog and disappointment, that's our lot.'

'Well,' said Gaunt. 'Now I've raised morale to a fever-pitch…'

More of them laughed, but it was generally hollow.

'You know where you're going?' Gaunt asked Rawne.

'We're waiting for despatch,' Rawne said, getting to his feet. He crossed over to his field pack and started rummaging inside it. 'But we know roughly. And we know what we are.'

He pulled a waxed paper pouch out of his kit and tossed it to Gaunt. It was heavy and it clinked. There was a Munitorum code-stamp on the wrapper. Gaunt shook the contents out into his palm. Shiny silver pin badges marked with the emblem 81/1(r).

'I don't know much about them,' Gaunt said, studying one of the pins. 'But the Munitorum will have tried to make sure that any mix of leftovers like this makes field sense. And Van Voytz gave the mix his personal approval.'

Someone snorted disparagingly.

'All right, I know he's not your favourite person. But I think he's still on our side, even now. I've been given to understand your new commander is a decent sort.' Gaunt looked over at Criid. 'His name's Wilder.'

Half-hidden behind her mane of hair, Tona Criid's eyes widened for a second.

'Yes, I wondered if you'd remember that, Tona.'

'What?' asked Varl.

'Nothing,' she said.

Gaunt slid the badges back into the pouch and handed it back to Rawne. He got up. 'I'm not going to make goodbyes, because that's a sure way to jinx us ever meeting again. And I'm not going to make any grand speech. This isn't the place, and it's not really in me anyway. And I don't want you thinking you've got to go out there and make me proud. You don't owe me anything. Not a thing. Do it for the Throne, and do it for yourselves.'

He walked to the barrack room door. He wasn't even going to look back, but at the threshold, something made him turn one last time. Silently, the Ghosts had risen to their feet. They hadn't formed a rank, or any kind of formal row, but they were all facing him, standing stiffly to attention.

Gaunt saluted them, and then walked away.

TEN

09.03 hrs, 193.776.M41
Fifth Compartment
Sparshad Mons, Ancreon Sextus

TWICE IN HALF an hour, they had pushed the enemy back from the top of the hill. Support weapons and well-disciplined rifle drill had done most of that work, but in places it had been brutal. Callide reported casualties from a face-to-face scrap where Blood Pact troops had come up along a blind defile and flanked his second section.

Wilder sensed they'd reached the tipping point in this particular scrap. Was the enemy going to break, or was it going to force a third attempt at the slopes?

It was hard to tell. Daylight had come, heavy and white, but the visibility was cut drastically by the waves of smoke running off the hill crest. Reports said his own line was still in position, but where the enemy stood was a matter of guesswork.

Wilder was finding it difficult to see anyway, because of the blood in his eyes. He'd been halfway along the escarpment when a nearby Hauberkan Chimera had taken a rocket. The vehicle had gone up like a demolition mine, and Wilder had been flung forward by the blast, gashing his forehead against the bole of a dead, splintered tree.

Now he had to keep blinking away the drops, dabbing his head. He could taste the salt in his mouth.

He reached the position commanded by one of the Tanith company officers, a Captain Domor, and his own Captain Kolosim. Throne, he had to stop thinking like that. They were *both* his own now.

'Are you all right, sir?' Domor asked as Wilder scrambled up. Domor was a solid, four-square man with a reliable air about him. His eyes had been repaired at some point in his career by heavy augmetic implants. The Tanith had a nickname for him, but Wilder couldn't remember it.

'I'm fine,' he replied. 'What have we got?'

'They've pulled back to the stream down there,' replied Kolosim, a burly redhead. 'Lot of cover sweeping that way. Lot of rocks. We've got a line of sight overlap with Sergeant Buckren's troop, but neither of us can determine what they're doing.'

'I've pushed two units down the flank,' Domor said. 'Raglon's and Theiss's. In case they suddenly stab that way, across the ditch.'

Far away to their left, the meaty chatter of an autocannon throbbed the air.

'Think they're coming back for another go, sir?' Kolosim asked.

'How stupid do they look, Ferdy?' Wilder grinned.

'Stupid enough we could be here all day,' replied Kolosim.

'What about those tankers, sir?' said Sergeant Bannard, Ferd Kolosim's adjutant. 'Coward-bastards!'

'We've all got our own words for the tank-boys, Bannard,' Wilder said, 'and I'll be having most of them with that leper-brain suck-pig Gadovin the moment I find him.' Wilder held up his hand suddenly. 'What was that?'

A low note, a machine noise, had just reached them.

'That's armour,' one of the Belladon troopers said with some confidence. Some of the men crawled forward to try and spot enemy vehicles in the smoke.

'It's behind us,' said Kolosim.

'No, that's just the echo roll. Backwash,' Bannard said.

Captain Domor had turned, and was gazing up into the smoke bank pluming off the hill behind them. 'Kolosim's right,' he said.

'What?' Wilder said.

'Oh feth!' Domor said suddenly, and grabbed the voice-horn from his vox-officer. 'Inbound, inbound, report your position!'

Static.

'Inbound, I say again! Report your position! If you are on approach, be advised we have troops in the grid!'

More static. A pause, then: 'Inbound at two minutes. We are hot for strike on grid target.'

To Wilder's eyes, the smoke was just smoke, but Domor's augmetics, enhanced beyond human vision, had picked up the heat trails chopping in at low level. He glanced at Wilder.

'Order retreat. Right now!' Wilder said. Domor started yelling into the vox. 'Up and back! Now!' Wilder yelled. 'Double time it! Get off this hill!'

Grabbing kit and weapons, the men started to scramble back down the slope, running between the burning shells of Hauberkan machines. All along the saddle of the hill, the troops of the Eighty-First First began a frantic pull-back towards the trackway.

About a minute later, with the men still running, the gunships slammed out of the smoke. The roar of their turbojets preceded them like the bow-wave of a ship. Twenty-five Vulture attack ships, boom-tailed, jut-jawed and painted in cream and tan dapple, burned in through the smoke-bank at tree-top altitude. Their vague shadows slid over Wilder's men in the hazed sunlight. He heard the *hiss-whoosh* as their underwing rocket pods began to fire. Spears of vapour shot out ahead of the thundering Vultures and the top of the hill disappeared in a necklace of fireballs that quivered the ground.

Wilder saw men on the slopes knocked down by the shockwave. 'They're coming in short!' he yelled at the nearest vox-man. 'Tell them they're coming in short!' The man started shouting into his link.

A second wave drummed over, rippling the hanging smoke with their powerful backwash. Another salvo of fragmentation rockets squealed out over the hill. Another riot of fire and hurled soil chewed up the landscape.

'I've got strike control,' the vox-officer reported. 'I think I've persuaded them to redirect beyond the hill.'

A third wave came in, or maybe it was the first on its reprise, Wilder couldn't tell. The third rocket strike went in behind the hill, detonating down the far slope. The thick black smoke from the first strike eddied in wild patterns as the Vultures travelled through it.

Wilder clapped the vox-man on the shoulder. 'Nice piece of fast-talk, my friend. What's your name?'

The man looked at him in surprise. 'Esteven, sir. It's Esteven.'

It was. Esteven, Belladon born and raised, vox-man in Baskevyl's troop. Wilder had become so overcautious about correctly identifying his new mix, he failed to recognise a man he'd known for years. Esteven's face was smeared with soot, but it was no excuse.

'Of course it is,' Wilder said. 'I was just testing,' he added, trying to joke it off. Esteven just laughed, and scooped up his vox-caster to head for the nearest ditch. It was indeed a laughing matter, but Wilder hadn't felt much like laughing all day.

'Hey, Esteven!' Wilder called. 'Did strike control explain the grid error to you?'

Esteven nodded. 'They said it wasn't an error. They were locked on the plot the Hauberkan had given them.'

THEY GOT THE signal to retire about half an hour later, and moved back down the trackway road to post 36, four kilometres back down the compartment. It was mid-morning by the time the Eighty-First First began to reassemble.

Post 36 was one of the field HQs set up at the friendly end of the fifth compartment. It lay close to the west wall and within sight of the gargantuan gateway leading back into the fourth compartment. The post covered about two square kilometres, most of which was taken up with supply dumps and field tents. Some of the post facilities, including the field hospital, had been set up in the crumbling house the Imperials had found as they pushed into the fifth. The house was a single storey stone structure, as old and ragged as the Mons walls themselves. Ruins like it could be found throughout the explored compartments of the step-city, some just wall-plans proud of the dirt, others still upright and flaking. No two were alike, and no purpose for them had yet been decided. There was some talk that they were the remains of primitive domiciles, that the compartments had once been filled with populated cities. Others said the houses were shanty relics built by local tribes who had come to scrape a living and dwell inside the walls long after the Mons itself had become a ruin. A third theory ran that the compartments had always been open areas of contained wilderness, constructed with some mystical purpose, and the houses were the temples and shrines left behind by the original builders of the Mons.

Wilder didn't much care. The place made a decent enough foothold camp from which the exploration and clearance of the compartment could be run.

Several regiments of infantry were gathered at post 36. On the high road up to the great gate, others could be seen moving in. An armour column. Supply vehicles. Valkyrie drop-ships were swinging down onto a wide table-rock of basalt, west of the post, dropping off wounded from the field. Some of those bodies on the stretchers were Wilder's men. Once they'd dropped, the Valkyries either lifted off and headed back out into the compartment for a second run, or flew on south, through the massive arch of the gate, heading to their landing fields at the fourth compartment forward posts.

Wilder walked off the roadway track and up the dusty slope into the post. Sunlight was burning off the grasses and the islands of scrub behind him, and the far wall of the compartment rose like a desert cliff. He looked up as a flight of cream and tan Vultures went over, heading home.

There was a bunch of armoured vehicles parked by the roadside, most of them black-drab numbers from a regiment Wilder didn't recognise. But amongst them were at least five Hauberkan treads, and other Hauberkan units were grumbling up the winding track out of the valley floor.

'Get the men rested and watered,' he told Baskevyl. 'Ration detail, and a weapons check by fourteen hundred. I want every one with a full load, no excuses.'

'Yes, sir.'

Wilder headed up the dirt causeway to the hospital.

MUNITORUM PIONEERS HAD roofed the house with precast armour-ply sheeting, and reinforced the walls with flakboard and sandbags. The north end contained the post command station in an area extended from the building with tent canopies. A pair of vox-masts had been set up nearby, trailing cables off to the bank of generators behind the building. The rest of the place was given over to the triage station and infirmary. There was a pervading smell of sawdust and new chip-panel that almost choked out the regular odours of a field hospital.

Neither the severely wounded nor the dead stayed there long. There was no facility for them. Regular transport runs ferried them away to main station compounds at Frag Flats and Tarenal, or to the gradually swelling cemetery out in the desert. Post 36's hospital was a processing point, superficial and efficient, treating minor wounds, illness, infection, and patching the less fortunate up for evac.

The *less fortunate*. Wilder thought about that. Were they? Were they really? He walked in under the low arch, stepping aside to let a procession of stretcher bearers inside. To the right lay a pair of rooms given over to triage, with an adjoining chamber fitted up as a field theatre. There were two more theatres in habi-tents outside on the causeway. To the left were three small wards where men with minor wounds could be given bedrest and treatment for a few days before returning to active duties, and the grossly injured could wait for transport.

The place was busy. It hadn't stopped being busy since the Guard had moved in and occupied the position five days earlier. Wilder saw a few of his men amongst the injured, most of them walking wounded with cuts and burns. He exchanged encouraging words with a few. So far there were about five more seriously hurt. Two were unconscious: one of them Sergeant Piven, who Wilder had always had a lot of time for. Piven looked like he'd been smacked in the face with a flat iron. The other, Trooper Boritz, had been shot eight or nine times. Lumps of his torso and legs were missing. Two corpsmen were busy intubating him.

Further down, Wilder found trooper Raydee on a cot. The Belladon was woozing in and out of consciousness, high on painkillers. His foot and ankle had been crushed by a stalker.

'Big bastard it was, sir,' Raydee said.

'You get it?' Wilder asked.

'Not me, no sir, but it was got.'

Wilder smiled. Raydee's injury would be a long time healing. He would soon be one of the *less fortunate*.

'Did Mkard make it, sir?' Raydee called out.

'Sorry?'

'Mkard, sir. He was with me when it happened. I hope he made it, sir,' Raydee said.

'I'll find out,' Wilder said. Raydee had expressed genuine concern, and for one of the influx. Mkard was a Tanith name. Maybe the alloy was strong already.

Nearby, Wilder spotted the elderly chief medicae who had joined with the Tanith. He was strapping up a Verghastite's arm-wound.

'Doctor?'

Dorden looked around. 'One moment, colonel,' he said, finishing up. Dorden seemed fragile and brittle to Wilder, too old for battlefield duty, but he had the seniority and the skill, and since the Belladon had lost most of its medicae staff, that counted for a lot.

'This way, colonel,' Dorden said. He led Wilder over to a vacant dressing table. 'Just tilt your head back, please.'

'What? Oh!' Wilder had almost forgotten his own injury. 'I'm not here for that, doctor. I just stopped in to get some idea of numbers. We had to pull out of the line in a hurry, and I've no idea what kind of hit we took.'

Dorden shrugged. 'I'm sorry, colonel, I can't answer that. They're still coming in, as you can see, and I've not been keeping a tally of badges. Just bodies to patch. The Kolstec 50th took a hammering early this morning up along the bluff. They've been airlifting them in for the past hour.'

'A bad hammering?'

'Is there a good kind? What about you?'

'Fairly intense. A mess, actually. I'll go talk to the men.'

'I'd prefer to treat that wound right now, actually,' Dorden said.

'Later. Get to someone who needs you more urgently.'

Dorden looked at him for a moment then turned away.

Wilder was about to cross over into the wards when he saw that the door at the back of the house was open. In the patch of sunlight outside, body bags lay on the dry earth. He went out, removing his cap despite the glare. Nearly forty bodies lay in neat lines, drill ground perfection. Orderlies were carrying more over from nearby trucks. Wilder walked down the line, looking at the tags tied off round the bag-seals. He found two Belladon, and a Tanith. *Mkard*.

An ancient, hunched man was slowly moving down the rows, reading from a hymnal and blessing each body in turn. Last rites, field style.

'Ayatani,' Wilder nodded.

Zweil peered at him. The old priest always struck Wilder as a little mad, but he was just another part of the influx.

'Colonel. Another day in the dust, unto which we will all return, most of us faster than we'd like, at this rate.'

Wilder wasn't quite sure what to say. The old man had a knack of blind-siding him.

'Some days, you know, I pray to the beloved beati for some skill that I can contribute. I don't fight, as you know, and I don't fix… not like Dorden. I often pray to her for the gracious ability to bring them back from the dead.'

'Who, father?'

Zweil gestured at the bodies on the ground. 'Them. Others. Anyone. But so far she's refused to grant me that knack. Can you do it, Wilder?'

'What?'

'Bring them back from the dead?'

'No, father.'

'It's funny, sometimes you look to me exactly like the sort of person who can bring them back from the dead.'

'Sorry, no. I'd like to think my area of skill lay in not getting them killed in the first place, and even that's not infallible.'

Zweil sniffed, and wiped his nose on his sleeve. 'None of us are perfect.' He stared up at Wilder, then, to Wilder's surprise, grabbed hold of Wilder's jaw with his less than clean fingers.

'You should get that looked at,' Zweil said, twisting Wilder's face around so he could scrutinise the head wound.

'Yes, I will. Thanks, father,' Wilder said, prying the priest's hand away. 'Dorden already offered to patch it, but I said it could wait.'

'Why?'

'Triage, father.'

'Exactly.'

'What?'

Zweil took a dried fig from his pocket and sucked it thoughtfully. 'Triage. Degrees of priority. Only a scrape, but you are the company commander. What if you leave it and it gets infected? That's the regiment, at this early, delicate stage, without a chief.'

'I suppose so, father.'

'So get it done. Priorities.'

'Yes, father.'

'Before the whole mob of them starts flailing around for the want of proper leadership with you in bed, feverish with blood poisoning–'

'Yes, father.'

'And gangrene of the eyebrows. And black pus oozing from–'

'Thank you, father. I'll go right away.'

'That's my other skill,' Zweil called out as Wilder turned away. 'I just remembered. It's to give sage advice and good counsel. I bless the beati for granting me that talent.'

'Yes, father.'

'Are you sure?' Zweil called out as Wilder reached the door into the house.

Wilder looked back. 'About what?'

Zweil was staring down at the bagged bodies on the dry earth. He was subdued again now. His sudden mood swings and skipping trains of thought had a bi-polar quality to them.

'You can't bring them back?'

'No, ayatani father, I can't.'

Zweil sighed. 'Carry on, then.'

'Lose the headset and the hat,' Dorden said, and Wilder obliged. 'Head back.'

Dorden washed the wound and pulled it shut with some plastek staples. 'I'd dress it, but it'd be better to get the air to it,' Dorden said. He handed Wilder a small tube of counterseptic gel. 'Put that on it every few hours, keep it clean, come back in a day or two.'

'Thanks,' Wilder said.

Baskevyl appeared in the triage bay doorway, and sighted Wilder. 'DeBray wants a field debrief, sir. I don't think he's too taken with the mess this morning.'

'He can join the queue behind me,' Wilder said. 'When does he want me?'

'At your convenience. I told him you were being patched.'

Wilder nodded. 'We got a tally yet?'

'Eight dead,' Baskevyl said. 'Thirty-eight wounded, twelve of those serious. That's so far.'

'Could have been a whole lot worse,' Wilder said. 'A whole hell of a lot worse. Pass on my compliments to Captain Domor, by the way. He's one of the reasons it wasn't.'

'Sir.'

'And we'll get the company leaders together and–' Wilder was tucking the counterseptic tube into his coat pocket, and his hand had just encountered the forgotten message wafer. He pulled it out and read it.

'Sir? Something the matter?' Baskevyl asked.

'What?'

'There's a look on your face like… like I don't know what.'

Wilder looked up at his first officer and was about to reply when Dorden interrupted. He was holding Wilder's micro-bead headset and cap.

'Your link's squawking,' he said.

Wilder pulled the headset in place, in time to hear a repeated call.

'Wilder receiving, go ahead.'

'This is Hark, colonel. Please come down to the dispersal area.'

HARK SALUTED AS Wilder and Baskevyl approached. The wide dirt-pan of the dispersal area was filling up with vehicles: treads returning from the front, and the inbound convoy from the gate. Hark was standing beside a trio of dirty Chimeras sporting Hauberkan livery.

'This way,' Hark said. A crowd of Hauberkan troopers had gathered around the rear of one of the AFVs. Wilder felt his fists tighten.

'Stand aside!' Hark snarled, and the tanker crews broke to let them through. Gadovin, the Hauberkans' commander, was cuffed by one wrist to a tie-bar on the Chimera's rear end. He was a sallow-faced man with thin, yellow hair. His tunic had half-moons of perspiration under the arms.

'Release me!' he snapped at Hark. 'This is ridiculous!'

'Ridiculous?' Wilder said.

Gadovin saw him for the first time and stiffened.

'You were supposed to advance, Gadovin,' Wilder said.

'The zone was mined.'

'Not so much you had to stop dead and cut engines. I warned you what would happen.'

'I listened to you!' Gadovin protested. 'When the assault came, I took immediate action–'

'You reversed.'

'To regain the trackway!'

'Through my men, who had moved in to support you. You nearly ran them down, and left them stranded, line broken. Then you called down an air-strike.'

'The situation was extremely dangerous! We might have been overrun. It was essential that–'

'It was dangerous all right. You'd seen to that. My men were still in the target grid, fighting your fight for you, when the Vultures came in. Didn't you think? Didn't you care?'

'I thought you'd pulled back too!'

'Why? Because you did? We're not all gutless worms, Gadovin.'

Gadovin didn't answer. He was staring over Wilder's shoulder. Marshal DeBray was approaching, led by Major Gerrogan, Gadovin's second in command.

The men drew back further, respectfully. DeBray entered the circle of tank troopers. A slightly-built man, with white hair and a permanently listless expression on his lined face, DeBray looked them up and down.

'Stand down, Colonel Wilder,' he said. 'This isn't your place to direct reprimand. Did you cuff this man, commissar?'

Hark nodded.

DeBray stared at Gadovin. 'I've been reading through the preliminaries, Gadovin. Not a pretty picture. In the first place, you should have pushed on. In the second, you should have held tight, like Wilder told you. Third, the air-strike was a fantastically bad call.'

'The situation was critical, sir,' Gadovin said. 'There were mines and–'

'Funny that, mines. It being a war. You're an arsehole, Gadovin. But you and your entire unit is new to this theatre and fresh-founded. You're off to a famously bad start, but I hope you can learn from this and get your bloody act together. Quickly. Be bold, be decisive, stick to the plan, and when an experienced officer like Wilder gives you advice, bloody follow it. Are we clear?'

'Sir.'

'Being cuffed up, humiliated and called an arsehole by me in front of your men is probably punishment enough. Uncuff him, please, commissar.'

Hark paused, then stepped forward and released Gadovin's restraint.

'Are you just going to let him–' Wilder began.

'Ub-bub-bup!' DeBray said, raising a hand. 'I appreciate your rancour, Wilder, but I did tell you this wasn't your place to direct reprimand.'

'Actually, marshal, it's not yours either,' said Hark bluntly. 'This man was found wanting in the service of the God-Emperor today. Sorely wanting.' He turned. A small autopistol had appeared in his hand. The single shot made everyone around start. Gadovin slammed back against the rear of the Chimera, a fern-leaf of blood from the back of his head decorating the plating. He fell on his face.

The Hauberkan men all around gazed in speechless horror. DeBray glared at Hark.

'Discipline and punishment are the provinces of the Commissariat,' Hark said clearly, so all could hear. 'We do not need to hear another word from you on the matter, marshal. The Hauberkan crews will learn from this demonstration that the Imperial Guard, Warmaster Macaroth, and Emperor himself will not tolerate incompetence or cowardice, especially from line officers. Major Gerrogan, I hope this is ample inspiration to you to be a much better regimental leader than your predecessor. Clean this up, and clean up your act.'

He holstered his pistol and walked away. DeBray sniffed, glanced humourlessly at Wilder, then stalked back to his command station. 'That report please, Wilder!' he called over his shoulder.

Wilder caught up with Hark half way to the Eighty-First First billet.

'What now?' Hark said.

'Nothing, I just…' Wilder shrugged. 'Men desert in the field, and you let them run, but you're quite happy to execute a ranking officer.'

'Yes. Let that be a lesson to you,' Hark said. He stopped walking and turned to face Wilder. 'I'm joking, of course. I'd like to think this might have illuminated you a little as to my approach. Men desert in the field. They're afraid. Why are they afraid? Because they're not being led soundly. Should they be executed, for a simple, human failing? No, I don't believe so. I think they should be given a solid leader so it doesn't happen again. An officer fails, then the whole structure falls down. Gadovin was why those men were running. Gadovin was the failure. So I reserved my censure for him.'

Wilder nodded.

'Are we good?' asked Hark.

'Yes.' Hark began walking again.

'Hark?'

'What, colonel?'

Wilder held out the message wafer. 'I received this earlier. I think maybe you should see it.'

Hark read the note. 'Is this confirmed, sir?'

'Yes.'

'Holy Throne. They're alive? After all we… Well, that's unexpected. Have you told anyone?'

'No. You're the first.'

Hark nodded. 'We'd better decide how to handle this. How do we tell the Ghosts that Gaunt's still alive?'

ELEVEN

12.32 hrs, 193.776.M41
Departing Frag Flats HQ
Sparshad Combat Zone, Ancreon Sextus

IN THE STARK NOON heat, the Valkyrie's turbojets whined up to power, shaking the airframe. The flight sergeant checked Ludd's harness with a tug, then Gaunt's, but drew back from doing the same with Eszrah's.

'He's fine,' Gaunt said.

The flight sergeant nodded, then signalled to the pilot. The roar of the engines suddenly intensified, as if they were going to burst, and then the assault carrier lifted off.

The flight sergeant had left the side doors of the cargo bay open, and he stood in the left hand doorway beside the swung-out heavy bolter mount, one hand raised to clutch a grip-bar. Past his silhouette and the shading arch of the port wing, Ludd could see the bright world flashing by. Low level at first, as they raced away from the Leviathans across the tent city and vehicle depots of Frag Flats, the jigging flags, the fence-post vox-masts, a blur of passing detail. Then they began to climb, bearing north. The view outside became the unbroken white expanse of the Flats themselves, a glaring vista of reflected light. The Valkyrie banked slightly in a wide, climbing turn, and through the mouth of the right-hand door, Ludd could see their tiny, hard shadow, a black dart, chasing them across the bright desert floor far below, flickering and jumping as it was distorted by dune-caps and ridges.

'Flight time's about fifteen minutes to the Mons,' the flight sergeant shouted.

Gaunt nodded and checked his wrist chronometer. Ludd noticed Gaunt was fiddling with the strap. The timepiece was Guard issue, chunky, well worn, but its bracelet strap had long since gone, replaced by a woven braid of what looked like leather and straw.

352

'We should have checked you out a fresh one from stores, sir,' Ludd yelled over the engine noise.

'It's fine,' Gaunt called back. 'It kept time on Gereon, it'll keep time here.'

Ludd glanced back at Eszrah. Arms folded, the Nihtgane looked like he was asleep. But with his old, battered sunshades on, it was impossible to tell. Ludd suddenly got a queasy feeling that Eszrah was actually staring right back at him. He looked away quickly.

Below, in the blinding white desert, he saw black dots, dark lines and twists of dust. Massed troop and vehicle columns moving up-country from Frag Flats to lend their muscle to the fight at the Mons. It was an immense undertaking. Ludd wondered quite what sort of obstacle could require such effort. Sparshad Mons was just one of eight step-cities on Ancreon Sextus currently under assault by Van Voytz's armies. Driven from the plains and the modern cities of Ancreon during the first phase of the liberation, the cult armies of the Ruinous Powers had taken refuge in the ancient monoliths, where they were now, reportedly, doing a very fine job of keeping the Imperium at bay.

There was a clack of vox, and the flight sergeant deftly slammed the side doors shut and locked the seals. The engine roar did not abate, but it changed tone and became deeper.

'Coming up on the smoke bank,' the flight sergeant explained. As if on cue, the small window ports in the cargo doors suddenly washed dark with ashen fumes, and the Valkyrie began to buck and tremble. They were flying through the vast smog field that veiled Sparshad Mons from view at Frag Flats.

The vibration eased, and after about three minutes, the flight sergeant reopened the side doors. Vapour still streamed off the sides of the carrier, but the air outside was clear again, and the sunlight dazzling.

The Valkyrie began to bank around again, and Ludd caught sight of new details on the ground below. Jumbles of rocks, slabs of tumbled stone, the occasional flash of sunlight on metal. Gaunt unstrapped, and got to his feet, moving to the door beside the flight sergeant. Ludd couldn't hear their conversation, but the crewman was pointing to various things out of the door.

Ludd snapped off his harness, and went to join them. It was harder to keep balance on the shaking, tilting metal deck than Gaunt had made it look. Ludd made sure he kept hold of the safety rail.

'Sparshad Mons,' Gaunt said to him, with a tip of his head.

From the open door, Ludd got his first sight of the Mons. He was expecting something big, but this dwarfed his expectations. The Mons was vast: wide, towering, cyclopean, not so much a man-made monument as a mountain peak cut into great angular steps from its broad skirts to its cropped summit. The stone it had been hewn from – not local to this desert region, but actually quarried in the lowland plains thousands of kilometres west, and conveyed here by means unknown – glowed pink and grey in the sunlight.

From the briefings, Ludd knew the Mons was a structure of concentric walls, ascending to the peak. The walls, hundreds of metres high and monumentally thick, enclosed the so-called compartments, significant tracts of wild country open to the sky. By some quirk of climate and topography, these compartments – some of them as much as twenty kilometres by ten – supported entire eco-systems of plant and wildlife, nurtured by untraceable underground water courses, defying the deserts outside. The encircling compartments were linked in chains, connected end to end by gigantic inner gateways, and the Imperial invaders had found, perplexingly, that the eco-system and terrain of one could differ wildly from that of its immediate neighbour.

The brief had also emphasised that there was no direct route into the heart of the Mons. A gateway compartment – dubbed, with the military's typical lack of imagination, the first compartment – allowed entry at the base level, and then connected to further compartments like a maze. Each area had been heavily defended, each compartment forming a walled-off 'lost world' that the Guard had to fight its way through to the next gate. So far, only seven of the compartments had been breached.

'What was it for?' Ludd shouted.

Gaunt shook his head, still staring out. 'No one knows. No one even knows if it was built by humans. But the multicursal plan suggests some ritual or symbolic purpose.'

'The *what*…?'

'Multicursal, Ludd. A pattern of alternate pathways, some leading nowhere, some to a dead centre.'

'Like a labyrinth, sir?'

'Actually, no. A labyrinth is unicursal. It has just one path, with no blind ends or alternates. A maze is multicursal. Designed as a puzzle, a riddle.'

'So the Archenemy is right inside the heart of that thing, and we have to find the correct way of getting to them? Since when was warfare so complex?' Ludd yelled.

'Since forever,' Gaunt called back.

'Why don't they just flatten the place from orbit and save all this bloodshed?'

'I was wondering that myself,' said Gaunt.

The Valkyrie dipped lower. The passage of time and the ministries of the desert had collapsed what had once been the outer rings of compartments around the base of the Mons. The white sand was densely littered with fallen stone blocks and the tatters of once-immense walls. Within these eroded ring patterns, Ludd could see the long emplacements of Imperial artillery, dug in and lobbing shells up at the higher steps of the inner Mons.

Lower still, they came in towards the bulwarks of the first compartment. The density of Imperial machines and manpower beneath them increased. There was other air traffic too now: carriers and gunships, passing them in formation.

The mouth of the first compartment was gone, its grand gate shattered into loose stones. Within its broken throat, lines of truncated columns, each ten metres in diameter, marched off into the scrubby wilderness of the compartment interior. Ludd saw field stations, seas of tents, marshaling yards of AFVs, the portable bridge units of the pioneer corps spanning streambeds and ravines. He saw tanks on the move, flashing in the light. The scene was starkly half-shadowed by the hard shade of the sunward wall.

They seemed to be flying straight towards the colossal end wall of the compartment, but Ludd realised that what he had taken to be part of the shadow was in fact a yawning gateway, black as pitch. It was a hundred metres high at least, almost as wide, coming to an arched top. As they closed in, Ludd found he could make out the worn marks of carvings and bas-reliefs around the giant gate, smoothed out by the ages and shrouded in massive drapes of dry creeper and lichen.

There was a sudden pressure hike and change of engine sound as they swept on into the gateway. They were plunged into cool darkness, a long cave of rock lit at lower levels by burner lamps and rows of stablights. The far end of the gateway shone ahead of them, an arch of sunlight in the dark.

With another suck of air, they were out into the second compartment. The immense floor space was a mat of brown undergrowth and islands of pink-ish scrub, interlaced with the white lines of roadways and the occasional stone jumble of an old ruin. There were areas where the undergrowth was black, where fires had scorched away great patches of the plant cover. Ludd saw the twisted hulks of war machines and other dead relics of the first fighting phase. To the north of them, far away down the compartment, an area was still on fire. Stray scuds and puffs of black smoke fluttered back past them on the slipstream.

They banked to starboard. About three kilometres along the right-hand wall of the compartment, another massive gateway loomed, its facade severely pock-marked and burned by shelling. Ludd glimpsed rocket batteries and artillery positions clustered around its mouth as they flew on through, into darkness, and out the other side.

'Third compartment,' the flight sergeant said.

This section of the Mons, as wide and vast as the previous two, ran north-east, and curved away to the left gently, following the orbit of the step-city. Below, the land was rough and irregular, with outcrops of jutting granite and wide pools or lakes that reflected the tiny image of their carrier back like mirrors. There were more trackways, more areas of damage and scorching. Ludd saw several large blast craters, hundreds of metres across, their shallow pits filled with dark water.

Gaunt nudged him and pointed ahead. On a large outcrop of lowland before them, an Imperial station of considerable size was spread out. Close-packed avenues of tents, net-covered depots, uplink masts, prefab structures, portable silos and hangar-barns, an extensive jumble of local ruins that had been converted for military use. Third Compartment Logistical base, also known as post 10. Even from the air, it was clear the station was heaving with activity.

In a stomach-rolling series of soft swells, the pilot dropped the carrier down, circling wide across the post before nosing in towards a wide patch of flat, baked earth to the south of the main complex where a giant eagle had been crudely stencilled in white paint on the ground. Two Vulture gunships and a Nymph-pattern recon flier were tied down at the edge of the field. A member of the ground crew ran out into the middle of the scuffed eagle, and cross-waved a pair of luminous paddles. The Valkyrie eased into its descent, jets wailing, and landed with a jolt. Immediately, the engine sound began to peter away.

Gaunt and Ludd jumped down into the sunlight and the dry, scented heat. Eszrah followed them, stepping out more cautiously, his head bowed low under the wing stanchions. The flight sergeant unloaded their kitbags and holdalls, and Gaunt tipped him a thank you nod. The sergeant nodded back with a quick salute, and then went to unstrap the freight of medical supplies and perishables that had ridden with them to the station.

Ludd went to gather up their bags, but Eszrah had already picked them up – all of them except Ludd's own kit bag.

'That too,' Gaunt said.

Effortlessly, the Nihtgane hefted Ludd's kit as well.

'Do you need a hand there?' Ludd asked him.

Eszrah made no reply. He just stood there, impassive, laden with bags.

'Maybe not then,' Ludd said. Gaunt was already walking away across the pad, and Ludd ran to catch up.

'I don't think he likes me, sir,' he said.

'Who?'

'Eszrah.'

'Oh. You're probably right. He doesn't take to people quickly. He probably thinks you're after his job.'

'His job, sir? What job?'

'Looking out for me. He takes it very seriously and he's very good at it.' Gaunt looked back at the Nihtgane following them. 'How many times, Eszrah? Preyathee, hwel many mattr yitt whereall?'

'Histye, sefen mattr, soule,' Eszrah replied, his voice thick and dense.

'Seven. Seven times he's saved my life,' Gaunt told Ludd.

They'd nearly reached the edge of the pad. Windspeed streamers and garish air-buoys fluttered on their wire-braced poles. An officer in a beige uniform was coming to meet them, escorted by two troopers. They stopped short and the officer, a captain, saluted Gaunt. He was a pale-skinned man with a narrow mouth and watery blue eyes.

'Commissar Gaunt? Captain Ironmeadow. Welcome to post 10. The marshal's waiting for you.'

'Thank you, captain. This is my junior, Ludd.'

'Sir,' Ironmeadow nodded. He paused and squinted at the Nihtgane. 'And that is?'

'Eszrah Night. He's with me, captain. Don't bother him and he won't kill you.'

'Well, that's excellent,' said Ironmeadow, trying not to show that he had no idea what had just been said to him. 'This way, commissar.'

They fell in step and headed up the flakboard walkway towards the main station post. It was a rambling local ruin, a house, as old as the ages, patched and shored up by the pioneer crews. Hydra batteries lurked in dug-out nests along the north side, their long barrelled autocannons slouched at the sky.

'What's your unit, captain?' Gaunt asked as they walked.

'Second Fortis Binars, sir,' Ironmeadow replied.

'Really? I'd heard Fortis had at last grown strong enough for a founding.'

'Three now, sir, actually. We're very happy to get into the fight. I have to say, I requested the honour of greeting you. Every man of the Binars knows the name Gaunt. From the liberation.'

'I was one of many, captain.'

'One of many without whom Fortis Binary forge world would still be under the yoke of the Archenemy.'

'It was a good while ago,' Gaunt said. 'I don't want you treating me like a hero.'

'No, sir.'

'Just with the abject fear and suspicion that is normally afforded an officer of the Commissariat.'

Ironmeadow blinked. He noticed Gaunt was almost smiling, so took that as permission to laugh at what he dearly hoped was a joke.

'Yes, sir.'

They entered the gloom of the house. The place, almost window-less, was lit by glow-globes and lumin strips. The hallway was piled with cargo and munitions cases, and the floor covered with metal grilles to overlay the extensive web of power and data cables. Ludd could hear the chatter of cogitators and the hum of equipment.

'This way, sir,' Ironmeadow said. 'The marshal's just down here.'

MARSHAL RASMUS SAUTOY rose from his chart table as they entered the station command room. Of medium build, he had a thick, grey goatee and soft eyes, and wore a row of citation ribbons across the left breast of his purple coat.

'Ibram Gaunt!' he declared, extending a hand as if welcoming an old friend.

'Marshal,' Gaunt returned, shaking the hand briefly. He had no particular wish to use first names. Sautoy clearly wanted to demonstrate there was some old history between them.

'Long time since Fortis,' Sautoy said.

'Long time indeed.'

'Quite a record you've notched up since then. Inspiring reading. Funny how fate brings us back together.'

'Fate is quite the comedian.'

Sautoy barked out a laugh. 'Have a seat, Ibram. Your junior too. Is this your man?'

'Eszrah, wait for me outside,' Gaunt said. Without even a nod, the Niht-gane stepped out.

'Can I offer you caffeine? Something stronger?'

'Just water, thank you,' Gaunt said. He could already feel the water debt from the heat of the trip in.

'Ironmeadow, some water, please.' The Binar captain scurried away.

'So, Ibram, welcome to this end of the war.' Sautoy resumed his seat, but turned the chair to face his guests. The command room was long and low-ceilinged. Away from the marshal's area, with its chart table, wall maps and stacks of document cases, the bulk of the room was filled with tactical cod-ifiers and cogitators, manned by Guard officers and advisors from the Tacticae Imperialis. There was a general background murmur.

'You've come to us in the capacity of a commissar, I understand,' Sautoy said. 'Throne knows, we need it. This theatre is plentifully supplied with men, Ibram, but for the most part they are new-mustered and green.'

'So I understand,' said Gaunt. 'What's the per capita ratio of Commissariat officers?'

'Roughly one in seven hundred,' Sautoy said. 'Woefully thin. It needs sorting out. Discipline, discipline. There's a lack of backbone and spirit. Desertion is high. Though it's fair to say this place would spook even experienced Guards-men.'

Ironmeadow returned with flasks of water and handed them to Gaunt and Ludd.

'Would you bring us up to speed on the situation in this compartment, sir?' Gaunt said.

Sautoy nodded, and cleared the surface of the large-scale chart on his table. 'Third compartment, so designated because it was the third section to be penetrated. Heavily defended in the early stages, though the enemy has dropped back. I've nine regiments here, infantry, plus armour support to the tune of three mechanised outfits. I've petitioned for more, but we'll have to wait and see. Main force concentration is here at post 10, here at post 12, and here, post 15. Now, the hot zones are as follows: we breached the gate in the north wall here four days ago so we're fighting up into the compart-ment designated "seven". Early days, very fierce. Then, about four kilometres further along the same wall, here, you see, is the gate to compartment nine. We're not through that yet. The country around the gate mouth is seriously defended and wooded. There's quite a tussle going on up there. In fact, I'm due to go up tomorrow to see first hand, if you'd like to join me?'

'I may well do that, marshal. I'd like to get orientated as quickly as possi-ble.' Gaunt pointed to the chart. 'There appears to be another gate here at the very north end of this compartment.'

'That's right. It leads through into compartment eight. Our scouts reached that early on. Eight's empty, a dead-end. The gate wasn't defended and the area's abandoned. We've found other dead-end spurs like it. We just crossed it off our list and concentrated on Seven and Nine.'

'What's the enemy disposition extant in Third, sir?'

Sautoy shrugged. 'Very little. Pockets of insurgents, the odd clash. Most have been wiped out or driven back. I'm not saying it's safe – patrols do run into firefights, but Third is pretty much ours. Oh, except for the stalkers.'

'Stalkers?' Gaunt asked.

'Nocturnal threat, Ibram,' Sautoy said. 'We can't work out if they are natural predators in this habitat, or something the Archenemy is able to unleash in the cover of darkness. They've been encountered in all the compartments, though more heavily the deeper in we reach. Bastard things. The boys have various names for them: stalkers, spooks, wights, ogres. Wretched, wretched creatures. The most puzzling thing is we've not been able to track them to their source. No lairs, no sign of where they go to ground during the day.'

Sautoy turned from the table and looked at Gaunt. 'So how do you intend to work things, Ibram?'

'I'll spend a few days getting the way of things, meeting with unit commanders and other commissars. Make my own deliberations, and then focus my efforts where they seem to be most useful.'

'And what do you need from me?'

'Accommodation here, just habi-tent space. Transport, and an authorised liaison, an officer, to start me off. Also, full clearance for the compartment, communication day codes, and an up-to-date disposition list.'

'No problem,' said Sautoy. 'I can give you the list right now.' He took a data-slate from the shelf over his desk and handed it to Gaunt. 'As you'll see, most of the units are as green as an ork. Fresh blood. Oh, Ironmeadow, don't look so worried. The Binars are new too, but they're proving themselves quite nicely, thank you very much.'

'Yes, marshal,' Ironmeadow nodded.

'Ironmeadow here can be your liaison, if you've no objections?'

'None,' said Gaunt.

'Well, I won't keep you from your work,' Sautoy said. He held out his hand again, and Gaunt shook it as briefly as he had the first time. 'My senior staff dines at twenty hundred local, if you'd like to join us. I'll make sure there's a seat if you make it.'

'Thank you, marshal.'

'By the way, Ibram?' Sautoy said. 'What happened to that unit of yours? You had command for a while, didn't you?'

'I lost them, sir,' said Gaunt.

BEHIND IRONMEADOW, WITH Eszrah in tow, Gaunt and Ludd headed to the logistics office at the far end of the house.

'Just wait here, sir,' Ironmeadow said. 'I'll get a billet assigned for you.' The captain disappeared into the office.

'You didn't drink all your water,' Gaunt said to Ludd.

'I wasn't that thirsty.'

'Drink it next time. All of it. Every chance you get. Water debt in this heat is going to be high, and I want you sharp, clear-headed and reliable.'

'Yes, commissar.'

They waited. 'You said you know the marshal, sir? He certainly acted like you were friends,' said Ludd.

'You'd be better off reading my body language than his. Yes, I know Sautoy. Back on Fortis Binary. I was serving under Dravere then. Odious bastard, cruel as a whip. Sautoy was a colonel back then, part of Dravere's oversized general staff. Toadies and runts, the lot of them. Sautoy was a desk-soldier, as I knew him, and I doubt he's matured. He's inherited his old commander's habit of wearing medals that mean little. And he's anxious to show himself well in with combat veterans like me. You heard how he kept using my first name, like we were pals? That was all for Ironmeadow's benefit. It'll get back to the rank and file.'

'You don't like him?'

'Sautoy's probably harmless enough, but that's just it. He's harmless. Toothless. He was so keen to impress on us how green the Guard strengths are here. Fresh-founded, draughtees, kids, most of them, getting their first taste of a real combat zone. What Sautoy neglected to mention was that the same can be said of the officer cadre, even the senior staff. Oh, there are exceptions... Van Voytz, naturally, and Humel and Kelso... but for the most part, Macaroth's taken the cream with him to the front line. This Second Front's being fought by children, commanded by inexperienced or unqualified commanders. No wonder the desertion and taint rate is so high.'

Ludd tried to look thoughtful, hoping that the conversation wouldn't come round to his own utter lack of combat experience.

'Damn,' said Gaunt suddenly. 'I completely forgot to ask Sautoy the key question.'

'Which one, sir?' asked Ludd.

'The one you asked.'

Ironmeadow returned. 'I've arranged a billet. It's alongside the Binar section. I'll show you to it.'

They stepped out into the bright sunlight. Ludd reached for his glare-shades.

'I wonder if you can answer a question for me, Ironmeadow?'

'I'll try, sir.'

'Why is the Guard prosecuting the step-cities this way? Why haven't they been neutralised from orbit?'

Ironmeadow frowned. 'I... I never thought to wonder, commissar,' he said. 'I'll find out.'

Ironmeadow led them a short way across the busy post into the neat files of the Fortis Binar billet area. In the row upon row of habi-tents, young troopers in beige fatigues relaxed and chatted, smoked, kicked balls around, or simply lay out of the sun in their cots, the sides of their habi-tents rolled up and secured. Many of the young men made to greet the captain, then backed off warily when they saw who was with him.

'Will this one do?' Ironmeadow asked, indicating an empty habi-tent near the end of one of the rows. It was a four-man model designed for officers.

'That'll be fine, captain,' Gaunt said, nodding Eszrah inside to deposit the kit. The habi-tent was close to the main through-camp truckway, and only five minutes' walk to the Command station.

'All right, captain,' Gaunt said to Ironmeadow. 'Give us an hour to settle in here. Go scare me up some transport. And get some water brought here.'

'Yes, sir,' Ironmeadow nodded, and went off.

Gaunt took off his coat and cap, and sat down on one of the small camp chairs inside the tent. He was flicking his way through the disposition list Sautoy had given him.

'Throne,' he said after a while. 'They weren't lying about the desertion rates. Nineteen troopers sequestered in the last week alone for suspected corruption and taint.' He looked at Ludd. 'Know how that feels. And look–'

Gaunt held the slate up so Ludd could see it. 'There's sickness too. Above the normal rate, I mean. There's an especially bad case at post 15. A serious attrition of manpower.'

He put the data-slate down. 'Let's go for a walk,' he said.

'Where to?'

'Just around,' Gaunt replied. He looked over at Eszrah. 'Restye herein, soule,' he said.

The Nihtgane lay back on one of the cots.

Outside, Gaunt turned to two Fortis Binar troopers playing cards under the awning of their own habi-tent.

'You men.'

They jumped up. 'Yes, sir!'

'No one goes to that tent or disturbs the man inside, got that? I'm counting on you both.'

'Yes, sir!'

THEY STROLLED THEIR way around the limits of post 10. It was a typical large-scale Guard encampment, the kind Gaunt had seen so many times before. The large prefab structures that housed field mess halls, the stores and work-shops, the canvas drum-tents of field stations, the ordered aisles of the billets, the rows of parked vehicles. Transports and light armour grumbled down the roadways, troopers hurried about their duties. On parade areas, companies were being drilled. Ludd saw a mob of newly-arrived infantry disgorging from a line of trucks while power lifters unloaded their equip-ment crates. There was a smell of cooking, and the chemical tang of well-maintained latrines. In front of one large tent assembly, a platoon of Guardsmen in full battle dress were kneeling to receive the benediction from a robed ecclesiarch.

'Hardly the horrors of war,' Ludd remarked.

'Those await up-country in the hot zones,' Gaunt said. 'And in here.' He tapped his own chest. 'The single most likely reason a man has to desert is fear of the unknown. In new recruits, that fear means everything. They've not seen combat, they've not seen injury or death. They've probably never left their home worlds before, and certainly not ever been this far away from their families and all things familiar. This post looks decent enough, but to most of them it's probably a lonely, alien place. And their dreams are full of the horrors to come. So they break and they run.'

'My heart bleeds,' Ludd muttered.

Gaunt smiled. 'For such a young man – and, forgive me for saying so, such an inexperienced person – you're quite a hard sort, Ludd. Are you past this, or were you always made of stern stuff?'

Ludd shrugged, delighted by the sort-of-compliment. 'I understand what you've said about these young men, sir, but I've never known those sentiments myself. I never had much attachment to any home. Since I was very young, I've wanted to do nothing except follow in my father's footsteps. And you seem to forget, I am a product of Commissariat training.'

'You know, somehow I do seem to forget that. Which scholam?'

'Thaker Vulgatus, like my father. You, sir?'

'Ignatius Cardinal, more years ago than I care to remember.'

They had paused on the edge of the vehicle pound, at the west end of the post site. Gaunt took off his cap, mopped his brow and gazed out at the granite outcrops and shimmering lakes of the third compartment.

'What a strange place to fight a war,' he said.

'We should be getting back,' Ludd noted, checking his time-piece. 'Ironmeadow will be checking back, and I doubt you'll want him left alone in Eszrah's hands.'

The thought made Gaunt chuckle. He checked his own chronometer, and then started reaching down the sleeve of his coat.

'Sir?'

'Wretched thing,' Gaunt grumbled, wrestling with his sleeve. He finally fished out his wrist chronometer. The primitive band had come loose and it had fallen back inside his cuff. He retied the instrument to his wrist.

'We should have–'

'Don't say it, Ludd.'

They started to retrace their steps to the Binar billets. Ludd suddenly realised he was walking alone. He looked round. Gaunt had moved into the shadow of a depot shed and was standing quite still, staring at something.

'What is it?' Ludd asked, joining him.

'Those men there,' Gaunt said. Across the truckway, which was busy with passing traffic, Ludd saw a hardstand where several cargo-8's were parked behind a Munitorum storage prefab. Seven troopers in khaki fatigues, the sleeves of their jackets rolled up, were loading ration boxes onto the back of one of the trucks.

'What about them?'

'They were doing that when we passed by ten minutes ago,' Gaunt said. 'How long does it take seven men to load a pile of boxes?'

Ludd shrugged. 'I don't see–'

'Then try, son. What exactly do you see? As a commissar, I mean?'

Ludd looked again, anxiously trying to identify whatever it was Gaunt's practiced eye had seen.

'Well, Ludd?'

'Seven men…'

'What company?'

'Ah, Kolstec Fortieth, Forty-First, maybe.'

'What are they doing?'

'Loading ration packs onto a transport.'

'Is that all you see?'

'They look... relaxed.'

'Yes. Nonchalant, almost. As if *trying* to look relaxed.'

'I don't think–'

'Where's the Munitorum senior, Ludd? In a depot, you can't move for a grader or a senior checking things off. And since when did combat troops load field supplies? That's servitor work.'

Ludd looked at Gaunt. 'With respect, sir, is that all? I mean, there could be hundreds of reasons to explain the circumstances.'

'And I know one of them. Stay here. Right here, Ludd. Come only if I call you.'

'Commissar...'

'That was an order, junior,' Gaunt snapped. He stepped into the road, paused to let an ammo carrier sweep past, then swung in behind it into the middle of the truckway, skirting round a dusty cargo-12 grinding the other way, and arrived on the hardstand before any of the men had seen him approach.

'Hot work, lads?' he said.

They stopped what they were doing and stared at him. All of them were wearing glare-shades, but Gaunt read their body language quickly enough.

'I said, hot work?'

'Yes, commissar,' said one of them, a thick-set man with the stripes of a gunnery sergeant. 'In this weather.'

'Tell me about it,' Gaunt said, removing his cap and making a show of wiping his brow. 'Does it need seven of you to shift these cartons?'

The sergeant tilted his head slightly, good-humoured. 'They're heavy, sir.'

'I'm sure they are.' Gaunt eyed two of the other men, who were still hefting a box between them. 'Please, lads, put that down. You're making me sweat.'

Uneasily, the men set the box down. The others stood around by the open tailgate of the cargo-8, watching.

'Oh, look, I'm making you jumpy,' Gaunt said apologetically. 'I know, I know, the uniform does that. Relax. I'm new at the post, just settling in. I came over because I recognised the uniform. Kolstec, right?'

'Yes, sir.'

'Which outfit?'

'Forty-First, True and Bold,' the sergeant said. Some of his men grunted.

'I served alongside the Hammers. At Balhaut. Great soldiers, the Kolstec Hammers. Big old boots for you young men to fill.'

'Yes, sir.'

'How are you finding it?' Gaunt asked. He started patting down the pockets of his storm coat. 'Damn it, where did I leave my smokes?'

The sergeant stepped forward and plucked a pack out of the rolled-up cuff of his fatigue jacket. Gaunt took a lho-stick and let the sergeant light it with his tin striker.

'Thanks,' Gaunt said, blowing out a mouthful of smoke. He took a step backwards, and his heel kicked the box the two men had set down. It slid back across the dry earth lightly. Gaunt back-kicked it again without looking. It slithered another good half-metre.

'Here's a tip,' he said. 'When you pretend to load heavy cartons, bend at the knees and make it look like it's an effort. Break a fething sweat. Just so you know, next time.'

He looked at the sergeant. 'Not that there's going to be any next time.'

The sergeant lunged at Gaunt. Gaunt slapped the approaching fist aside and stabbed the man in the cheek with the lit lho-stick. The sergeant staggered back with a yelp. The other men were moving. One swung at Gaunt, missing him entirely as the commissar ducked, and got a fist in the mouth. He stumbled back, spitting blood and fragments of tooth, and Gaunt spun round, his coat-tails flying out, to deliver a side-kick to the man's belly. Doubled up, the trooper slammed over onto the empty carton and crushed it flat.

Three more rushed in. One had a tyre iron in his hands.

On the far side of the truckway, Ludd started forward. 'Oh Throne!' he murmured. 'Oh Holy Throne!'

He ran out into the street, then jumped back, narrowly avoiding a personnel carrier that blared its horn at him. Ludd waited for it to pass, then ran out, dodging between transports and mechanised munitions carts. Halfway across, he was forced to stop dead to let a massive tread transporter grumble by the other way.

'Come on!' he yelled at the crawling load. 'Come on!'

His cap flying off, Gaunt ducked low and punched a trooper hard in the chest, grabbed him by the front of his tunic, and punched him again. As the man fell away, paralysed and winded, Gaunt swung round and kicked the legs out from under the next man running at him, then rose to tackle the trooper with the tyre iron. This man was big, big and young. For a second, he reminded Gaunt of Bragg, big, dumb and eternally innocent.

Gaunt crossed his arms to meet the youth's double-handed swing, and caught him in a tight, scissoring block. The trooper struggled back, trying to use the advantage of his size, but Gaunt had already kicked him in the kneecap and spilled him over. As the trooper slumped sideways, Gaunt wrenched him sharply around with his scissor grip, and the flailing blunt end of the tyre iron smacked into the face of the next attacker so hard his legs went up in front of him like he'd run into a tripwire.

'Come on!' Ludd yelped. The tread transporter was taking forever to move by.

A fist caught Gaunt's jaw, snapping his head hard round. Gaunt tasted blood on his tongue where he'd bitten his own lip. He feinted left, dummied the man, and then felled him squarely with a socking straight-armed jab that

Colm Corbec had once taught him. The old Pryze County Number One feth-your-face.

The Kolstec fell over, rolling up in a ball, wailing. Gaunt turned to the last one. The remaining trooper fell down onto his knees, shaking. 'Please, please, sir, please... they said it would work. They said we'd get out of here... please... I only wanted to...'

'What?' Gaunt snapped.

'My home, sir. I wanted to go home.'

Gaunt squatted in front of the blubbering boy and slapped his clumped hands away from his face. 'Look at me. Look at me! *This* is home now, trooper. This is the zone! It doesn't make friends and it doesn't like you, but by the Throne, it's where you are! The Emperor wants you, boy! Did no one ever tell you that? The Emperor wants you to make his glory for him! How can you ever do that if you run for home?'

'I'm scared, sir... they said it would be all right... they said...'

'You're scared? You're scared? What's your name?'

The boy looked up at him. His eyes were red and wet. He was no more than seventeen years old. Like Caffran, Gaunt thought. Like Milo, Meryn, Cader, on the Founding Fields at Tanith Magna.

'Teritch, sir. Trooper third-class Teritch.'

'Teritch, if you're scared, I'm terrified. The Archenemy is no playmate. You're going to see things, and be expected to do things your poor mother would have a fit at. But the Emperor expects and the Emperor protects, all of us, even you, Teritch. Even you. I promise you that.'

Teritch nodded.

'Get up,' Gaunt said, rising. The boy obeyed. 'I thought you were going to execute all of us,' he whispered.

'I should,' said Gaunt. 'I really should. But I think–'

'Lie still! Right where you are! No moving! Not a flinch!'

Gaunt looked round. Ludd was hurrying forward across the hardpan, head low, his laspistol aimed in a double-handed grip at the men sprawled and moaning on the ground.

'Not one move, you bastards!'

'Ludd?'

'Yes, sir!' Ludd replied, switching his aim from one supine form to the next, diligently.

'Put that weapon away, for feth's sake.'

Ludd straightened up and slowly returned his gun to its holster.

'Everything's under control,' Gaunt told him. 'Call up the post watch and get these men put into custody. I'll deal with them later.'

Ludd nodded. He gazed at Gaunt's handiwork. One boy, sobbing fretfully into his hands, and five able-bodied troopers rolling and groaning in the dust. Gaunt had taken on and felled seven men with–

One plus five equalled–

'Sir, where's the other one?'

Gaunt looked round at Ludd. 'What?'

'There were seven of them, sir.'

The gunnery sergeant was missing. Gaunt's crushed and bent lho-stick still sizzled on the ground.

'Ludd–'

The cargo-8's engine roared into life. It pulled out of the rank and started to turn wide across the hardstand towards the street exit.

'Hold these men here, Ludd!' Gaunt yelled, running after the transport. 'Wave your sidearm or something!'

Ludd drew his laspistol again. 'Everyone face down on the dust. You too, boy.'

Gaunt ran across the pan. The truck was kicking up dirt and exhaust plumes as it turned around the end of the next bank of parked transports, and headed towards the road.

Gaunt drew one of his brand new bolt pistols, shiny and clean, virgin and unfired, and ran out into the path of the cargo-8. He could see the gunnery sergeant at the wheel, driving madly.

Legs braced, Gaunt stood his ground and raised the bolt pistol.

'Pull up! Now!' he yelled.

The truck skidded to a halt ten metres short of him. The turbine engine continued to rev hard. Exhaust pumped from the stack like the angry breath of a dragon. Gaunt realised how small and flesh-made and vulnerable he was compared to eighteen tonnes of fat-wheeled transport.

'Engine off. Get out.'

The exhausts belched again, another rev.

'You haven't quite crossed the line yet, gunnery sergeant. But you will soon,' Gaunt yelled, squeezing back the hammers of his aimed weapon. 'Shut down, get out, and come quietly, and we'll deal with this like men. Keep going and I promise you, you'll be dead.'

The engines revved again. The cargo-8 jerked forward a pace or two.

Gaunt sniffed and lowered the bolt pistol to his side. 'Go on, then. You can run me down just like that. But then what? Where are you going to run to? There's nowhere to go except here, and here's where you stop.'

The engine revved one last time, then died with a mutter. Arms raised, the gunnery sergeant clambered down from the cab and lay on his face.

Gaunt walked over to him.

'Wise choice. What's your name?'

'Pekald.'

'We'll be chatting later, Sergeant Pekald.'

Horns were blaring now. Post security personnel were rushing in across the hardpan.

'My arrest,' Gaunt told one of the approaching troopers as he walked away from the spread-eagled Pekald. 'My name is Gaunt. Secure them all in the stockade pending my interview. And mine only. Understood?'

'Yes, sir!' said the trooper.

ESZRAH WAS WAITING for them as they came back to the habi-tent. The Nihtgane tilted his head questioningly

'Nothing for you to worry about,' Gaunt told him, and Eszrah stood aside. Inside the tent, Ironmeadow was waiting for them. He was sitting bolt upright in one of the camp chairs, taut and terrified.

'Hello, Ironmeadow,' Gaunt said as he came in and stripped off his cap and coat. 'Been waiting long?'

'Your man...' Ironmeadow murmured nervously. 'Your man there, Eszrah Night. He...'

'He what?' Gaunt picked up one of the water canteens and took a deep drink.

'He had this crossbow thing, and he waved it at me, and he made me sit down, and–'

'That's common pleasantry where Eszrah comes from, captain. I'm sure you weren't put out.'

'No, sir. Just a little frightened.'

'Frightened? Of Eszrah?' Gaunt said. 'Good. How's the transport coming?'

Ironmeadow cleared his throat. 'I've got a cargo-4 and a driver ready at your convenience, commissar.'

'That's fine work, captain, I appreciate your efforts.'

'I...' Ironmeadow coughed delicately. 'I understand there was an altercation–'

'It's done. Forget it, captain. Just another chore for the Commissariat.'

'I see. So everything's all right for today?'

'It is,' said Gaunt, sitting back on his cot. 'Get yourself off duty, Ironmeadow. We'll start again tomorrow. A tour of the stockade, I think.'

'Yes, sir. Well, goodnight.'

'Sleep tight,' said Ludd, removing his jacket and his webbing belt.

'Oh, commissar,' said Ironmeadow, swinging back in through the flaps of the habi-tent. 'I got an answer for that question you posed.'

Gaunt sat up. 'Indeed.'

Ironmeadow fished a data-slate out of his coat pocket and handed it to Gaunt. 'The tacticae prepped this for you. It's all there. We're not annihilating the step-cities from orbit because the Ecclesiarchy says there is a possibility they are sacred places.'

'They're what?' Ludd asked.

Ironmeadow shrugged. 'There's a lot of argument about what these structures mean and who built them. You'll see it all there in the text, sir. Some say they are relics of the Ruinous Powers, some say they are the vestiges of a prehuman culture. But there are signs, apparently, tell-tale clues that archaeologists have identified, that this Mons and the others like it are edifices raised in the name of the God-Emperor, circa M.30.'

'In which case...' Gaunt began.

'In which case they are preserved holy sites,' Ludd said.

'In which case they must be cleansed and not obliterated,' Ironmeadow finished. 'Does that answer your query, sir?'

TWELVE

11.23 hrs, 195.776.M41
Post 36, Fifth Compartment
Sparshad Mons, Ancreon Sextus

WILDER HAD BEEN at the observation point on the southern edge of the post for the best part of an hour. Officers from all the regiments housed at post 36 had gathered there, training the tripod-mounted scopes out across the grasslands and the broken, rocky terrain of the compartment. Five kilometres north, a battle was raging.

Just before dawn that day, scouts had reported a concentration of enemy war machines moving south. Best guess was that they'd used the cover of darkness to move forward through the gate from the sixth compartment. DeBray had sent out the newly-arrived 8th Rothberg Mechanised to meet them, with the Hauberkan squadrons, very much on probation, to establish a picket line at their heels. The engagement had begun rapidly, and escalated quickly, with the Rothbergers' Vanquishers assaulting the enemy treads across a series of water meadows east of the main trackway. The din of tank-fire had been rolling back ever since, and the wan daylight across the wide compartment had become tissue-soft with smoke. Numerous clots of solid, black vapour trickled up into the sky, marking the demise of armoured vehicles, friendly and hostile. The Rothberg commander had reported the fighting as 'intense, though the line is holding'. He had identified stalk-tanks, AT70 Reaver-pattern tanks, AT83 Brigands and at least two super-heavies. Many displayed the colours and emblems of the despised Blood Pact.

At the observation point, the infantry commanders waited nervously. If things went well, or if the enemy suddenly produced ground troops to support their push, units like the 81/1(r) and the Kolstec Fortieth would be rapidly moved forward to reinforce the armour. If things went badly, really badly, everything up to and including a withdrawal from post 36, and the other fifth compartment field HQs, was on the cards.

The one eventuality DeBray would not allow was withdrawal from the compartment itself. It had taken too much time and blood to force a way in through that ancient gate in the name of the Golden Throne.

Wilder was accompanied by Baskevyl and Kolea, respectively the senior Belladon and Tanith officers under his new command. Wilder liked Major Kolea immensely, and had admired his solidity and command-sense from the outset. He wondered if it was significant that the most senior ranking officer in the influx was not a Tanith at all, but a Verghastite. The Tanith, on whose bones the regiment had originally been composed, didn't seem to resent Kolea's position. Since the siege of Vervunhive that had brought the Tanith and Verghast together, the two breeds had bonded well. Wilder knew of other 'forced mixes' where the regiments had ended up at war with themselves, stricken with factions, feuds and in-fighting. Apart from a few rough edges and teething problems, the Tanith First – the so-called Gaunt's Ghosts – had meshed admirably, according to the records. Now the game of 'leftovers' was happening all over again, and so far it seemed to be going reasonably well.

That was until the news had arrived. After consulting Hark, Baskevyl, Kolea and a few others, Wilder had made the announcement to the Eighty-First First. It had been greeted with stunned silence. Wilder had looked out across the shocked faces of the Tanith and Verghastites, and sympathised completely. The news had done away with most of the key reasons for the mix.

As a consequence of the action on Herodor, and the classified Gereon mission, the Tanith First had found itself deprived of its key leaders. Colonel Corbec had died heroically on Herodor, and the beloved Verghastite Soric had been removed from active duty under difficult circumstances. Then the Gereon mission had apparently robbed the Ghosts of Gaunt, Major Rawne, and the scout commander Mkoll. Despite the valiant efforts of Gol Kolea and Viktor Hark, neither one of them Tanith founders, the Ghosts had been considered, by High Command, as woefully lacking in the charismatic and essential leadership that had made them strong in the first place. Gaunt, Corbec, Rawne, Mkoll: without those men, the Ghosts were a headless entity.

For its own part, the Belladon Eighty-First had also suffered. Founded two years before the start of the Sabbat Crusade, the regiment had once been eight thousand strong, and had enjoyed a series of notable victories during Operation Newfound and the push into the Cabal Salient. Then had come the hellstorm of Khan III, the war against Magister Shebol Red-Hand. As a victory, it would remain pre-eminent in the regimental honours of Belladon, but the cost had been great. Nearly three-quarters of the Eighty-First had been killed, almost a thousand of them in one stroke during the desperate stand-off at the Field of the Last Imagining. The Belladon Eighty-First had defeated the notorious 'Red Phalanx' elite there, destroyed the Rugose Altar, slain Pater Savant and Pater Pain, and put the Magister himself to flight, an act that led to Shebol's eventual destruction at the hands of the

Silver Guard at Partopol. But it had been a pricey trophy. Reduced to around two thousand men, the Belladon had been in danger of being redesignated as a 'support or auxiliary company'. However, their command structure was remarkably intact.

Thus, as Wilder understood it, the lord general himself had approved the mix. The two partial regiments – both light, both recon oriented – complemented one another. The Ghosts would swell the Belladon's depleted ranks, the Belladon officer corps – most especially Wilder himself – would provide the Ghosts with much needed command muscle. That was how the dry, distant decisions of staff office were made, that was how men were added to men to make the Munitorum ledgers add up.

That was how the Eighty-First Belladon and the Tanith First had become the Eighty-First First Recon, for better or for worse.

And now all of that was up in the air again. Gaunt was alive. The Ghosts had accepted the change, believing their singular leader dead. Now he wasn't any more. Whichever way you sliced it, Wilder thought, the Ghosts were going to resent the mix now. Resent the Belladon. Resent Wilder himself. It had all been for the best. Now there was another best that the Ghosts had never dared hoped for.

'You're over-thinking it,' Gol Kolea said.

'What?' Wilder looked around.

Kolea smiled. He was a big fellow, a slab of muscle and sinew, and his mouth seemed small and lost in the weight of his face. But the smile was bright and sharp.

'You're worrying, sir. I suggest you don't.'

Wilder shrugged gently. His body language was slow and amiable, one of the key things that had made him such a fine leader of men. 'I'm just worried about that, Gol,' he said, nodding his head at the distant thump of tank-war echoing up the compartment.

'No you're not,' said Kolea.

'No, he's not,' agreed Baskevyl, bending over to stare through a scope.

'What is this?' Wilder asked. 'You ganging up on me?'

'You're worried about the message, sir,' Kolea said. 'The one you read to us yesterday.'

'You're no fool, Gol Kolea,' Wilder said.

'Guess that's why I'm still alive,' Kolea replied.

'No, that would be luck,' Baskevyl commented, still staring through the scope.

'Actually, Bask's right,' Kolea said. 'Doesn't matter. I know you're sweating because Gaunt's turned up alive. You're worried about the effect that's going to have on the mix.'

'Wouldn't you be?' Wilder asked him.

'I would,' Baskevyl murmured.

'I'm not asking you, Bask. Wouldn't you be, Gol? I mean, in my place?'

'In your place? Sir, in your place, I'd have kept the name Tanith First and let the Belladon suck it up.'

'Of course you would.'

'That was a joke,' Kolea said.

'I know,' Wilder replied casually.

'I was just joking.'

'I know.'

Several officers from other outfits nearby were beginning to listen in. Kolea beckoned Wilder away to the back of the redoubt. Baskevyl joined them.

'Here's what I think,' Kolea said frankly. 'This mix made sense. It made absolute sense to you and it made absolute sense to us. Have you heard any complaints?'

Wilder shook his head.

'Feth no, you haven't. I'm not pretending it's been easy, but the Ghosts have gone along with everything. Losing their name, mixing in. They're experienced Guardsmen, they understand how it works. We all have to stay viable, combat-ready. In the Guard, you keep moving, or you die.'

'Or you go home,' Baskevyl said.

'Shut up,' Kolea and Wilder chorused.

Baskevyl shrugged. 'Just saying...'

'This mix made sense,' Kolea said. 'We got into it, we didn't complain. It's the way things work. And you know what made it easy? You. You, and the likes of Bask here.'

'Now you're just blowing smoke up my skirt, Kolea.'

Kolea smiled. 'Do I look like the sort of man who likes to make nice, Lucien?'

Wilder paused. Kolea didn't. Big as he was, he really, really didn't.

'No.'

'We were lost and we were hurting. You came along and we liked you. Liked Bask, liked Kolosim and Varaine. Liked Novobazky. Callide's an arse, but there's always one, right?'

'He's not wrong,' Baskevyl said, 'Callide is an utter arse. I'd shoot him myself if he wasn't my brother-in-law.'

Kolea looked mortified. 'Throne, I didn't know that. Sorry, sir.'

Baskevyl looked at Wilder and they both chuckled.

'I'm lying,' Baskevyl said.

'He's not your brother-in-law?' Kolea asked.

Baskevyl shook his head. 'He is an arse, though.'

Kolea ran his big hands across his shaved head. 'Throne, I had a point just then, and you with your jokes...'

'Sorry,' Baskevyl smiled.

'I think what I was going for,' Kolea rallied, 'was that the Ghosts have taken to you, *because* of you. This is starting to work.'

'But Gaunt–' Wilder said.

Kolea showed his palms in a 'forget it' gesture. 'When you told us the news, you know what I thought? I thought... well, I thought how happy I was. Ibram had made it. Come through. Done the gig. Like he swore to us he would. I was happy. I still am. The Ghosts are too. Ibram's a great man, sir, and the fact that he's done this and come back to tell the tale, well that's one more notch for us.'

'But he's alive,' Wilder said.

'Yes he is. But he's not a threat to you. You told us, the despatch was clear… Gaunt's been returned to Commissariat duties. Reassigned. He's not going to rock the boat.'

Wilder looked away. 'The very fact that he's alive is going to rock the boat,' he said. 'The Ghosts are going to want him back. Accept no substitutes.'

'I think they've moved on, sir,' Kolea said. 'And even if they do want him back, High Command has been emphatic. We can't have him back. End of story.'

Wilder nodded. 'I guess. What about the others? They're coming back. What about this Rawne guy? I hear he's a truck-load of trouble.'

'We'll make room,' Baskevyl said. 'I'd slide Meryn out to make a place for Rawne. What do you think, Gol?'

'Not Meryn,' Kolea replied. 'Meryn had become one of Rawne's inner circle and he won't like the idea of stepping out. I'd slide out Arcuda and give Rawne H Company. Better still, have a Belladon give up a company command. That'd send the right signals.'

Wilder thought about that and did some quick maths. 'If I did that, more of the companies would have Ghost leaders than Belladon.'

'Would that be so bad?' Kolea asked. 'I mean, as a gesture. A compromise?'

'It rankles,' Wilder said. 'I know my boys. Is this Rawne fellow that good?'

'He's a gakking son of a bitch,' Kolea said frankly, 'but Gaunt never did anything without Rawne in the front of it.'

Wilder looked at Baskevyl. 'What do you think? Kolosim? Or Raydrel?'

'Throne, neither!' Baskevyl said. 'Demote Ferdy Kolosim and he'll hunt you down like a dog. Raydrel's also an excellent officer. We're talking about pride, here.'

'I agree,' Kolea said. 'Not Kolosim or Raydrel. Look, if it helps, I'll step aside for Rawne.'

'No!' they both said.

Kolea grinned. 'I got a warm tingling feeling right then. So… Arcuda. He'll understand. Or maybe Obel. Or Domor, he's very loyal.'

Wilder sighed. 'This, gentlemen, is exactly what I was worried about. Not Gaunt himself. The others. Mkoll–'

'Oh, that's easy.' Kolea said. 'Form up a dedicated scout unit and give him power. You'll love what he does. He's like… I don't know. He's a wizard. Give him the Ghost scouts and the best of your recon men and he'll blow your shorts off.'

'My friend here meant that in a good way,' Baskevyl said.

'I know he did,' said Wilder. 'All right, all right… Rawne's still the problem. Leave that with me.'

The micro-bead link pipped. The three officers looked at each other.

'This is it,' Wilder said. 'Come with me, please, both of you.'

'You think I'd miss this?' Kolea said.

* * *

THE NORTH END of post 36 was strangely quiet. As the puff of dust on the highway track from the gateway slowly approached, the Ghosts got up from their sunbathing, their card games and their habi-tent cots and gathered around the roadway.

The trucks approached. Four cargo-10s carrying medical supplies and munitions, and a fifth one stripped out for troop transfer. Changing down into low gear, they grumbled up the escarpment into post 36, kicking walls of dust out behind them.

Wilder, Baskevyl and Kolea arrived a few moments before the trucks rolled to a halt. They joined Hark and Dorden, and stood waiting. Ayatani Zweil appeared, and scurried to join them, holding up the skirts of his robes.

'You lied to me, colonel,' the old priest said.

'What, father?'

'You swore blind to me the other day that you didn't have the power to bring people back from the dead. You were lying.'

Wilder chuckled and shook his head to himself.

The dust slowly billowed away and settled. Wilder looked around, felt the electric expectation in the air. He saw the Ghosts: Domor, Caffran, Obel, Leyr, Meryn, Dremmond, Lubba, Vadim, Rerval, Daur, Haller, DaFelbe, Chiria... all the rest.

Eyes wide. Waiting. *Waiting*.

The tailgate on the fifth truck slammed down. Dark figures jumped clear onto the track. There was a moment's pause, and then they began to stroll down into the post, in a loose formation, black-clad figures slowly looming out of the winnowing dust. Walking in step, slow and steady, weapons slung casually over their shoulders.

Rawne. Feygor. Varl. Beltayn. Mkoll. Criid. Brostin. Larkin. Bonin.

Their faces were set and hard. Their new uniforms, displaying the pins of the Eighty-First First, were bright and fresh. A slow smile dug its way across Lucien Wilder's face. He'd seen some bastards in his time, and many of the best were in the Belladon's ranks.

But he'd never seen such a casual display of utter cool. He liked these troopers already. Coming home when they were believed lost. Coming home, asking for trouble. The slow pace, the lazy stride. Throne damn it, they were heroes before they had even started.

Wilder heard a sound, a sound that started slowly then grew. Clapping. The Ghosts around the post were clapping and it became frenzied. Without really knowing why, the Belladon joined in, applauding the heroes home. Shouts, whoops, whistles, cheers.

Rawne and his mission team didn't react. They came striding in out of the dust towards Wilder, faces set hard and stern.

They came to a halt right in front of Wilder. The clapping rang on. The newcomers made no attempt at an ordered file, they just came to a stop in a ragged group. Then they came to attention in perfect unison.

'Major Elim Rawne, and squad, reporting for duty, sir,' Rawne said.

Wilder took a step forward and saluted. 'Colonel Lucien Wilder. Glad to meet you. Welcome to the fifth compartment.'

THIRTEEN

14.01 hrs, 196.776.M41
Post 12, Third Compartment
Sparshad Mons, Ancreon Sextus

THE CONTRAST BETWEEN posts 10 and 15 could not have been more striking.

They'd spent a couple of days in the relatively civilised and ordered environs of post 10, orientating themselves, but it had felt much longer to Ludd. Gaunt had insisted on conducting extensive interviews with company leaders, tacticae advisors, Munitorum seniors and Commissariat officers, and Ludd had become a little bored with either sitting in as a silent observer or waiting around. Ludd had been looking forward to beginning actual fieldwork as Gaunt's junior, but there seemed to be no particular direction to what they were doing. Gaunt moved with a purpose, but he didn't share it with Ludd. Ludd wasn't really sure what Gaunt was looking for, and when he pressed the commissar, Gaunt had a habit of replying in oblique riddles.

'We're looking, Nahum, for men carrying empty boxes and not bending their legs.'

Gaunt had also spent a long time in the stockade, talking with the prisoners. Ludd had expected some hard interrogations, but Gaunt had been very low-key and relaxed. He'd interviewed the Kolstec they'd rounded up on the first afternoon. Several of them had almost broken down as they confessed their fears to Gaunt.

'Just frightened boys,' Gaunt told Ludd. 'Totally without strong leadership, lost. They saw a chance to sneak out under cover of a faked freight run. It was all a little desperate and sad. I've arranged for them to receive eight days lock-up here, and then be transferred back to Frag Flats for basic support duties.'

'Shouldn't they just be... shot?' Ludd asked.

Gaunt pretended to search his coat pockets. 'I don't know. Should they? I can't find my *Instrument of Order*.'

'You know what I mean, sir.'

'If we start executing,' Gaunt said, 'Van Voytz will be fighting this war on his own. From what I've seen and what I've been told, the Imperial forces of the Second Front are plagued with fear and lack of resolve. Punishment has its place, Ludd, but what's needed here is a way to give the Guard some focus. Some resolve.'

'Because they've lost it?'

'Because they've never had it. These boys have no experience of war, nothing to insulate themselves with. Under other circumstances, the officer class and the commissars would whip some spirit into them and get them through the first weeks of doubt and fear until they found their feet. But the officers are no more experienced, and there aren't enough commissars. Summary execution is a commissar's most potent tool, Ludd. Used to effect in a situation involving a veteran unit, it reminds the men of their commitment. Used on units of fresh-faced boys, it destroys what little spirit they have. Worse, it confirms their fears.'

When, on the second morning after their arrival in the Mons, Gaunt announced it was time to visit post 15, Ludd had perked up. Fifteen was right inside the hot zone, close to the fight for the gate into the ninth compartment. They might even see some action.

As they drove down to post 15, Ludd realised the prospect of action was making him twitchy and nervous. Suddenly, he understood how the young Guardsmen had felt.

Ironmeadow had kept a transport and driver on standby for Gaunt's use, and came with them to act as liaison. The transport was a battered, open-top cargo-4 that had seen better days. Its engine made the most desperate clattering sound, as if there were stones in the manifold. The driver was a short, tanned Munitorum drone called Banx who had a slovenly attitude and bad hygiene.

'Only the best for us, eh?' Gaunt muttered to Ludd as they climbed aboard. Ironmeadow rode up front beside the driver, with Ludd and Gaunt in the rear seats. Eszrah, whom Gaunt insisted was to come along, sat sideways in the truck-back, leaning against the column of the roll-bars.

Post 15 lay some nine kilometres north-east of 10, in the sickly woodland around the mouth of the ninth compartment gateway. Ironmeadow insisted they could only make the journey in daylight, and had to get travel papers signed off by Marshal Sautoy.

The trip seemed to drag. The up-country trackway wound around the wide pools and lakes that characterised the third compartment, and passed through wide plains of ill-looking sedge and broken rock, and sudden gloomy forests of black larch, lime and coster.

There were signs of war everywhere: burned-out wrecks, cratered earth, and pieces of tarnished and forgotten kit beside the road. Three or four times, they had to pull over to allow a transit column to go by: big dark trucks and small freight tanks trundling south towards post 10. Once, about halfway to 15, the cargo-4 overheated, and they had to linger on the road-side while Banx nursed some life back into the tired engine. They had a good view of the towering compartment wall, and the massive gateway into the seventh compartment. Somewhere over there was post 12. Beyond the gate, an entirely new phase of warfare was going on.

Post 15 announced itself robustly before they even arrived. Above the grim, undernourished trees, they caught sight of thick smoke and fuel vapour, half-cloaking the massive cliff of the compartment wall and the contested gate. On the wind, Ludd heard the heavy report of energy artillery, and the dull thump of shell-launchers. His guts tightened. He realised he was afraid.

Then they noticed the smell. A rank, sick, organic odour that clung to the gloomy woodland like bad luck.

Banx slowed as perimeter guards appeared and demanded to see paper-work. The guards, hard-edged men with jumpy, nervous dispositions, became a little more obliging when they saw Gaunt.

'Go right on through, sir,' one said. 'We'll vox the post commander to let him know you're inbound.'

'Do me a favour, trooper,' Gaunt said, taking a couple of fresh cartons of lho-sticks out of his kit-bag and passing them to the men without any fuss. 'Let it be a surprise, all right?'

The men nodded. Banx drove on.

Post 10 had been a smart, regimented place, swept and formal, wound like a well-maintained watch. Fifteen was a hellhole. Sitting low in a spongy hollow under the gate, it was waterlogged and damp. The truckways were rutted mires, and the latrines had evidently become swamped. The place stank, and clouds of biting flies swirled in the wet air. They drove past rows of habi-tents that had become sodden with groundwater, huge scabs of mould and fungus caking the limp surfaces of the canvas. Dirty cooking smoke was thick in the air, and carried the gorge-raising hint of rancid meat and fat. All the men they passed were pale and hollow-eyed, tired and strung out. They stared at the passing transport with fretful, sullen expres-sions. Ludd began to feel still more anxious.

The north end of the post was a ring of artillery positions, actively ham-mering fire at the vast gate facade and washing fyceline fumes back over the post. The constant, earth-shaking thump of the guns was enough to put a man on edge. And it was like this every hour of every day.

Ludd jumped as a flight of Vultures went over them, turbojets screaming. The gunships banked wide and shot into the dark mouth of the gateway, disgorging their rockets in a blitz of sparks and smoke.

'Calm down,' Gaunt said.

'I'm calm,' Ludd said. 'Very, very calm.'

Gaunt had particular concerns at 15: the drastic desertion rates and the virulent sickness. The feel of the place reminded him unpleasantly of Gereon and the taint there. He felt his skin itch. It made him think for a moment of Cirk. He wondered what eventual fate had befallen her, and was surprised to realise he didn't care. He doubted he would ever see her again.

He spent a brief twenty minutes with the post commander, a harried colonel who was standing in for the marshal and had far too much on his mind. Ludd saw the medicae tents – five times the size of the infirmary complex at post 10; extra sections had been added on in the last few days to accommodate the Guardsmen stricken by illness. The chief medicae had wanted to ship the sick back to facilities away from the frontline, but the request had been denied for fear of spreading the infection to 'clean' posts.

'They say it's a Chaos taint,' Ironmeadow said to Ludd as they waited for Gaunt outside the command station. 'Something in the water, something in the air.' Ironmeadow had tied a neck scarf around his nose and mouth. Ludd thought the captain looked like a bandit.

He was not at all surprised that sickness had blighted the post. The conditions were dreadful: the damp, festering conditions alone could have incubated the infection, and Ludd was grimly sure that the leaking latrines had a lot to answer for.

Chaos taint? The answer didn't need to be anything like that fanciful. Even so, Ludd had the crawling sensation that infectious microbes were burrowing all over him. He wished he could stop jumping every time the massive cannons at the north end of the camp banged off.

Gaunt reappeared. 'What a hole,' he muttered. 'I'd run away from it myself.'

'I know what you mean,' Ludd said.

'I'll go and arrange some billets for us,' Ironmeadow said.

'Why?' asked Gaunt.

Ironmeadow shrugged. 'Well, sir. It's mid-afternoon already. if we leave in the next hour or so, fine. But if we leave it much later, we'll have to wait until tomorrow.'

'Because?'

'Marshal Sautoy's orders, sir. Under no circumstances are we to travel after dark.'

Gaunt glanced at Ludd. 'We won't be here long, Ironmeadow,' he said. 'Don't worry about it.'

'What do you know, sir?' Ludd asked.

'I have a hunch. I hope I'm badly wrong,' Gaunt replied.

Before he could explain in more detail, an especially violent explosion ripped into the air away at the gate mouth. The detonation shook the ground and threw curls of flame up at the sky.

'Holy Throne!' Ludd grunted. 'Shouldn't we be–'

'What, Ludd?'

'Running, sir?'

Gaunt shook his head. 'That was just a tank. A tank's munitions load cooking off.'

'How do you know?' Ludd asked.

'I've heard it before. Poor bastards. May the Emperor protect their souls. Right, let's head for the mess.'

Ludd stared quizzically at Gaunt. 'You want to eat?'

'No.'

'Sir, I've arranged for you to speak with the chief medicae.'

'That can wait, Ludd.' Gaunt had a data-slate in his hand. 'The post commander gave me this and I've made a quick scan. Hence my hunch. I want to check it out first. Ironmeadow?'

'Yes, commissar?'

'I want to apologise, captain.'

Ironmeadow looked baffled. 'What for, sir?'

'I think in the next half-hour I might wound your pride considerably.'

'I don't follow you, sir.'

'Doesn't matter. Just accept my apology now. Remember it was nothing personal.'

Ironmeadow looked at Ludd, who simply shrugged.

'This way, gentlemen,' Gaunt said, and headed towards the mess tent.

THE LONG ROW of open-sided mess-tents was busy with troopers chowing down, spooning stew out of dented tins. Smoke welled under the canvas awnings, and the smell of meat was ripe and heavy.

At the back of the main tent, a mix of Munitorum workers and Guard service workers ladled out the day's offerings onto the trays of waiting men, stirred the heavy vats sitting on the burners, mashed vegetables that were past their prime.

'Ludd?' Gaunt said. 'Go ask some questions. Engage the staff. Get some basic answers.'

'To what, sir?'

'To anything you can think of. Ironmeadow? Cap and coat, please.'

'What?'

Gaunt took off his commissar's cap and heavy leather stormcoat and swapped them for Ironmeadow's canvas jacket and bill-cap. 'You're pretending to be a commissar now. Say nothing, look aloof, and let Ludd do the talking.'

'Sir, this is highly irregular…'

'*I'm* highly irregular,' Gaunt replied, pulling on the bill-cap. 'And lose that damn bandana. You look like a bandit.'

Ironmeadow put on the coat and hat, and followed Ludd into the mess. They lost sight of Gaunt.

'Hello, there,' Ludd called across the vats of food.

'Meal for you, sir?' returned one of the line workers.

'No, thank you. I just wanted to ask a question or two. Actually, my senior here did, but he doesn't like to talk much.'

Ludd indicated Ironmeadow, who made an effort to appear remote and intimidating. Gaunt's coat was a little too large on him, and it made Ironmeadow look like he was a ghoul or vampire, lurking, about to strike.

'Doesn't he like the food?' asked the menial.

'Do you?' asked Ludd, having to raise his voice above the drone and clatter of the busy kitchen.

'Me? No, sir. I eat dry rations, me.'

'Who's staffing this canteen?'

The menial, a heavy, lumpy man in stained aprons and vest, thought about this. 'Munitorum, mostly. The charge cooks are from the local regiments. First Fortis Binars.'

Ludd looked at Ironmeadow, but the captain was so busy getting into character and frowning that he hadn't picked up on the mention of his kindred unit.

'Point me to one of them,' Ludd said.

The menial looked around. 'Hey, Korgy! Over here!' he yelled.

Another server approached. He was very solidly made, beetle-browed. He wiped his hands on his greasy apron and looked Ludd up and down. Ludd saw the Fortis pin dangling from the man's undershirt.

'Commissar? What can I help you to?'

'Just reviewing. You're Korgy? Something like that?'

The man nodded, wary and, to Ludd, far too defensive. 'Regiment Service officer, first class, Ludnik Korgyakin. Korgy for short. Is there a problem?'

'You run these kitchens?'

Korgy nodded. 'Me and Bolsamoy,' he said, indicating a tall, portly, bald-headed man hurrying past with a full kettle of stew.

'Any problems?' Ludd asked.

Korgy shrugged. 'Like what, sir?'

'I don't know. Camp's down with the fever, but you guys seem all right.'

'We eat well and we live clean, what can I tell you? The Commissariat's never been down here before, nosing. You got an issue?'

'No,' said Ludd.

'You got a warrant for this?' Korgy added.

'No,' said Ludd. 'I don't need one.'

'Well, you're backing up the queue,' Korgy said.

'Yes, we are rather backing up the queue,' Ironmeadow put in.

'Shut up and stay in character,' Ludd hissed.

'Only saying…' said Ironmeadow.

'He speaks,' noted Korgy.

'Ignore him. He's battle-damaged,' said Ludd. 'The queue can wait for a second. Why are you defensive, Service Officer Korgyakin?'

Korgy let his ladle flop loose against the side of his stew kettle. 'I have no idea. Maybe being quizzed by the Commissariat? That might do it.'

'It might,' said Ludd. 'You're real jumpy for a cook. Why is that?'

Korgy looked away at someone. A passing hint, a tip-off. Ludd saw it plainly. Korgy looked back. 'Look, do you want a meal or what? If you don't, move on. There are plenty of hungry guys behind you.'

Some instinct, some part of him that he had never known, brought Ludd up to reflex. Without thinking, he drew his laspistol and aimed it at Korgy.

'Back away and raise your hands!' he said.

'What are you doing?' Ironmeadow was bleating behind him. 'Put that away!'

Korgy took a step back, lifting his meaty hands away into the air and dropping his wipe-cloth. 'You shit-head,' he said.

'Ludd!' Ironmeadow yelled.

Ludd glanced sideways. The other head cook, Bolsamoy, had dropped his steaming kettle and pulled a heavy auto pistol, a Hostec 5.

Bolsamoy started to fire.

GAUNT SLIPPED BACK to the rear of the cook-tents, and waited until the foot traffic nearby had cleared. There was no door, so he pulled out his Tanith straight silver, and slit a line down the canvas back-vent.

Stepping through, he found himself in the meat chiller, a larder kept fresh by powerful freezer pods. Lank pieces of meat hung from hooks, or lay, turgid and slimy, in cooler-crates.

He took a step or two forward. Every ounce of him wanted his hunch to be wrong. He reached the back wall. Flakboards, tight-set, formed a heavy barrier around the rear of the mess area. He looked them over, and saw the scrape marks on the floor, the worn edges on one board that had been pulled out and replaced a number of times.

He pulled it open. It came away after a little effort. On the other side was a loading dock, and a prefab lean-to. It was quiet, a private little space in the heart of the busy camp. Gaunt caught the smell on the air.

'Oh, Throne, no…' he muttered.

He edged across the prefab hatch and opened it.

Cold vapour welled out through the door into the damp heat. Counterseptic stink. He took a glance, and all his fears were confirmed.

He almost threw up.

'You stupid bastards,' he said.

Behind him, in the mess tents, shots rang out, followed by screams and yelling.

Gaunt reached inside Ironmeadow's jacket and drew his twin bolt pistols. He started to run back towards the mess hall.

BOLSAMOY'S FIRST BURST had splintered the nearest tent support pole and killed a junior trooper who had been waiting in line, holding his mess tin. The boy simply tumbled down, his skull burst. Further shots wounded three more men in the canteen queue and caused everyone to flee in riotous panic.

Ironmeadow fell down and covered his head with his arms.

Ludd had thrown himself sideways, colliding with the canteen tables and spilling over several cauldrons.

Korgy was running, along with several other members of the cook-tent staff. Bolsamoy was firing into the tent, screaming.

Ludd rolled up, ducked under another flurry of rounds, and then trained his weapon.

'Commissariat! Drop it or drop!'

Bolsamoy fired again.

Ludd had a perfect angle. He prided himself on his marksman scores. He fired.

Bolsamoy staggered slightly. To Ludd, the world went into some kind of slow motion. The cook shuddered, so hard and so violently, Ludd was able to watch the fat of his belly and jowls quaking like jelly. A tiny black hole, venting smoke, appeared abruptly in Bolsamoy's right cheek. His face deformed around it. His right eye bugled and popped. His head hammered back like whiplash had cracked down his frame. Nerveless, his hand spasmed around the trigger of the auto, which tilted up as he went over backwards, punching holes in the canvas roof.

Ludd rolled up onto his knees, aiming his weapon. He heard a deep, throaty whine that went past his left ear and realised that someone had just shot at him and almost hit him in the face. Korgy was close to the tent flaps, amidst the frantic mass of fleeing service crew. He had a blunt 9 in his hand and was firing backwards on full auto.

For a split-second, Ludd believed he could see one of the bullets in the air, spinning towards him. He tried to turn. The round hit him in the head with a crack like thunder and he went down, slamming his right cheek against the leg of the service trolley beside him.

Ironmeadow was screaming like a girl. The troopers in the tent were fleeing en masse, yelling and shoving.

Gaunt appeared from somewhere out in the back, bursting through the tent flaps that screened the inner kitchens. He had a gleaming chrome bolt pistol in each hand.

Korgy saw him, and blasted away with his auto-blunt, backing away now, yelling out some obscene oath.

Gaunt skidded to a halt, raised his monstrous weapons and unloaded. There was a fury of muzzle flash and Korgy came apart, shredded in an astonishing shower of blood and meat.

'Halt where you stand!' Gaunt yelled 'No mercy! No choices! Run and I'll kill you all!'

The fleeing cooks and servers stalled in their flight and fell on their knees, their hands behind their heads.

One of them turned, reaching for a hide-away pistol.

'Idiot!' Gaunt snapped and shot the man through the back of the skull. He fell over on his folded knees, bent double.

'Ludd?' Gaunt called. 'Ludd?'

'I think he's dead, sir,' Ironmeadow called back.

HE WASN'T DEAD. The bullet had exploded his cap and put a crease of bruise along the top of his scalp.

'Are you all right?' Gaunt asked.

Ludd nodded. 'Did I… Did I just shoot a man?' he asked.

'Yes,' Gaunt nodded.

Ludd threw up.

'The station commander's in a rage,' Ironmeadow said. 'What the hell was this all about?'

'Remember my apology, Ironmeadow?' Gaunt said.

'Yes?' Gaunt led the captain into the back tent and beyond. He left Ironmeadow vomiting on the verge outside.

'I'm sorry the Binars brought this curse with them,' Gaunt said. 'Really, I am.'

'Shut up!' Ironmeadow growled between his retches. 'Shut the hell up!'

BANX, TRUE TO form, said nothing as they drove back towards post 10. The light was fading, but they still had time. Gaunt now rode up front beside the driver, Ludd and Ironmeadow sullen and sickly in the back seats. Eszrah, as always, was silent.

'I'm sorry,' Gaunt said over his shoulder.

'You were wrong,' Ironmeadow replied. 'The Fortis Binars never have–'

'I'm sorry, Ironmeadow, but they have. I was there. On Fortis Binary, food shortages got so serious that the Munitorum started to take corpses from the morgues and process the flesh for food. It was endemic in the hives at one point. A shameful secret your people put behind them.'

Ironmeadow threw up again, spattering yellow bile over the side of the cargo-4.

'I knew the smell as soon as I arrived. And once the base commander had shown me the spread on the data-slate, it was clear. The Fortis Binars are new blood, but their service staff isn't. The cooks and canteen workers are veterans from the old war on your homeworld, Ironmeadow. They know how to make a meal go round. More particularly, they can make a killing selling fresh food-stocks on the black market, filling in the shortfall with forbidden supplies.'

'You bastard!' Ironmeadow yelled.

'Sickness and plague, Ironmeadow, you do the maths. I'm sorry this tragic piece of Fortis Binary's history has followed you here.'

'Bastard!' Ironmeadow returned, and threw up in his mouth again. Ludd grabbed the captain as he leaned out to spit the sick away.

'All right, Ludd?' Gaunt asked.

'Peachy,' Ludd called back over the engine roar.

'You did fine, son. How's the head?'

'Sore.'

'You did all right.'

'Not good,' Banx said suddenly. The cargo-4's engine cackled and then died completely. They rolled to a halt in the shade of some black-trunked lime trees.

'Get it started,' Gaunt told the drone, climbing out of the transport. Banx hurried round to the front of the truck and lifted the hood.

'Dammit, we don't need this,' said Ironmeadow as he wandered up to Gaunt on the roadside. 'It'll be dark soon.'

'Just relax,' said Gaunt.

Ludd joined them. The sky above was still clear and pale, but the heavy shadow of the compartment wall was approaching fast as the sun sank.

'We'll be fine,' Gaunt said. He looked back at Banx.

A thready, fretful clatter was issuing from the cargo-4 as the drone tried to restart it. Five minutes passed. Ten. Thirty. The cargo-4 coughed and sputtered and refused to live. Banx cursed it colourfully.

The close woodland around them became heavy and mauve. The shadow was close now.

'Sir?' Ludd said, touching Gaunt on the sleeve to alert him.

Eszrah had suddenly got down from the transport, his reynbow in his hands. He was alert, listening, coiled. He took one look at Gaunt, then disappeared up into the undergrowth.

'Shit,' said Gaunt. 'Now we're in trouble.'

A deep roar cut the air, a predatory howl that echoed through the damp glades.

Twilight enclosed them. In the dark thickets nearby, something massive was moving closer.

FOURTEEN

18.47 hrs, 196.776.M41
Open Country, Third Compartment
Sparshad Mons, Ancreon Sextus

THE TEMPERATURE BEGAN to drop sharply as night set in. In the distance, the compartment began to echo with odd, inhuman calls, throaty and rough. Something closer by answered the calls with a whooping roar.

'Stalkers,' said Ironmeadow. 'Holy Throne, stalkers! They come out after dark and–'

Gaunt took him firmly by one shoulder. 'You've had a really bad day, captain. Keep your voice down and don't make it any worse. Get your weapon.'

Ironmeadow nodded, and went to the transport to fetch his lascarbine.

'You too, Ludd,' said Gaunt. 'Neither of you fire unless you hear me tell you to. Understood?'

'Yes, sir,' said Ludd, unholstering his pistol. 'Where… where did Eszrah go, sir?'

'Hunting, Ludd. My guess is before long we'll know who to feel sorry for: us, or whatever's lurking out there.' Gaunt went over to the truck, and took another look at Banx's efforts. The drone's hands were shaking so hard he could barely work.

'Calm down,' Gaunt told him. 'You've got four armed men covering you. We need to get this heap of junk rolling, so concentrate, work hard, and get it done.'

Banx nodded and wiped sweat off his brow with his cuff.

Something moved in the undergrowth beyond the track. Ludd turned smartly, aiming his weapon. Gaunt hurried to him. He had a bolt pistol drawn now.

'See anything?'

'Something's definitely circling us, sir.'

384

Somewhere a twig broke and leaves rustled. The distant calls echoed again. Like the forest wolves on Tanith, Gaunt thought, howling as they slowly circled in to pick off the stranded, the unlucky, the lost. He'd never heard them himself, of course, but Colm Corbec had liked to tell such tales by the campfire. 'I like the look on the lads' faces,' Colm had once said of those stories. 'I can see how the tales are reminding them of home.' *Scaring the crap out of them, more like*, Gaunt had reckoned.

He realised, suddenly, that he wasn't frightened. He was quite aware that they were in all kinds of danger, but fear refused to come. If anything, his pulse rate had dropped, and a terrible clarity had settled upon him. He tried to remember the last time he'd actually felt any fear, and realised he couldn't. Gereon had stolen that from him, and from all the members of the mission team. Terror had been such a permanent fixture, around them at every moment, that the fear response had simply burned out. So had everything else: desire, appetite, common feeling. All they had been left with was the simple, pure will to survive. Gereon had hardened them so drastically, Gaunt wondered if any of them would ever get back those basic human traits.

Another rustle in the dark foliage. Ironmeadow's carbine was jumping back and forth at every sound, or imagined sound at least. The cargo-4's engine rattled into life, revved, and then died again.

In the silence that followed, Gaunt heard an odd, rapid whispering. He traced it back to Ironmeadow. The Binar captain was muttering the *Litany of Faithful Providence* over and over to himself.

'I appreciate the sentiment,' Gaunt said, 'but under your breath, if you don't mind.'

There was a rather louder movement in the undergrowth. Boughs shook, shivering leaves. Pebbles skittered. All three men raised their weapons.

Something big suddenly moved in the treeline, crashing through bracken, splintering saplings. It sounded as if a Leman Russ were ploughing in from the outer woods. A dreadful, blubbering roar whooped out of the dark.

'Wait until you can see it!' Gaunt cried.

There was more thrashing, another roar, then a series of odd, muted barks. Something, possibly a tree, fell over with a crash in the outer darkness, and the thrashing stopped abruptly. Silence settled again.

'Oh my Emperor, there it is!' Ironmeadow shrieked.

'Idiot!' said Gaunt, and knocked the man's aim aside.

Eszrah Night emerged from the darkness and walked calmly towards them.

'Preyathee, soule?' Gaunt said.

Eszrah raised one hand to his mouth and made a plucking motion away from the lips with his long fingers. It was a Nihtgane gesture, the equivalent of a Guardsman running a finger across his throat. *The spirit of the foe has been plucked out.*

'It's dead,' Gaunt said.

'What?' said Ironmeadow.

'It's dead. Eszrah killed it.'

'Well, that's bloody wonderful!' Ironmeadow exclaimed. He was so relieved, he was almost in tears. 'Bloody wonderful! That's amazing! Well done, sir!' He held out his hand to the Nihtgane. Eszrah looked at it as if he was being offered a dead rat.

'Anyway, bloody good work!' Ironmeadow said, as Eszrah walked past him.

The cargo-4 made a nasty grinding sound, then roared into life. The engine sounded decidedly unhealthy, but it was running. As the engine turned, the headlamps came on, bathing Banx in bright yellow light. He slammed down the hood, and turned to them in the spotlights of the twin beams, arms spread, like a showman taking an encore.

'Slow but sure,' he called out to them, 'the Munitorum gets the job done. You can all thank me later!'

For Banx, later lasted about a second. A gigantic shadow rose up behind his lamp-lit form, leaned over into the glare, and bit his head off.

Arms still wide, what remained of the driver took two shuffling steps forward, shaking and jerking, and fell over onto the track. Violently pressurised jets of blood sprayed into the air from the ghastly wound, and now blood fell like rain.

Ironmeadow lost control of his bladder and dropped onto his knees.

'Holy Throne…' gasped Ludd.

The wrought one came forward into the light, hunched low, its throat tubes baggy and loose. Its huge arms, locked at the elbow, supported the titanic bulk of its head and upper body. Its flesh was florid and pink, and a mane of tangled brown hair draped forward over the segmented metal armour of its massive skull. Tiny, fierce eyes glowed in the deep recesses of the visor slits. They could smell it, smell the rancid sweat-stink of its mass, smell the sour blood and meat rotting in its vast maw.

The stalker's vast lower jaw thrust forward, underbiting the plated snout, and long steel teeth, as spatulate and sharp as chisels, rose up out of the gum slots and locked back into position.

'Hwerat? Hweran thys?' Eszrah murmured, evidently surprised. 'Ayet dartes yt took haff, withen venom soor, so down dyed yt!'

'Well, somehow,' said Gaunt, 'it got better.'

The creature gazed at them for a moment. Then its slack, heavy throat tubes began to swell and distend. It opened its mouth and let out a deafening, trumpeting roar, exhaling bad air and blood vapour in a mighty gust.

'Kill it. Right now,' Gaunt said. He had both of his bolt pistols out. They began to boom, lighting the gloom with vivid muzzle flashes. At his side, Ludd started firing too, his laspistol slamming off at maximum rate. Eszrah raised his reynbow and thumped another iron dart deep into the meat of the thing's shoulder.

The combined firepower would have felled most of mankind's known humanoid enemies. Even a dread Traitor Space Marine might have reeled from the force of two bolt pistols at such tight range. Certainly, the monster's flesh tore, burst, exploded. Grave wounds ripped across its upper torso and arms, and two deep dents appeared in its armoured snout.

But it didn't seem to care. It charged them.

'Move! Move!' Gaunt yelled.

Ludd threw himself to the left. Eszrah disappeared to the right. Gaunt went after Eszrah, and then remembered Ironmeadow.

The captain was still on his knees in the thing's path, weeping and helpless.

'Oh feth,' Gaunt snarled.

He turned back, skidded on the muddy track, almost fell, and then righted himself. Wrapping his arms around Ironmeadow, his pistols still in his fists, he yelled 'Move it! Now!'

Just about all of Captain Ironmeadow's higher functions had by then become devoted to emptying his body as quickly as possible. The frantic weeping was the most wholesome aspect of this evacuation. Gaunt felt the ground shake as the monster thundered in at them. He put all his strength into a desperate body throw.

Gaunt went over backwards, and Ironmeadow flew over him, landing on his back in the trackway mud. He slid on his shoulders for quite some distance and ended up beside the cargo-4. The massive beast thundered past, its quarry suddenly missing.

The wrought one turned heavily, grunting and snuffling. Its throat sacs puffed out and went limp, puffed out and went limp. Its vicious teeth retracted and then snapped back, bright and murderous.

It saw Gaunt, spread-eagled on his back.

Gaunt tried to rise. He saw the iron quarrels, eight of them, stuck in the beast's pink flesh. Eszrah hadn't lied. He'd put eight reynbow darts into the thing, loaded with Untill toxin, and still it was moving.

With another roar, the stalker came at Gaunt.

Gaunt had lost his grip on one of his bolt pistols, but, still on his back, he fired the other one at the hideous thing as it bore down.

Gaunt rolled hard, to his left. One of the stalker's huge paws, claws extruded, dug up a bucketful of mud as it struck at the place where Gaunt had been lying.

Gaunt leapt onto his feet. Just three rounds left in the clip. He put them all into the side of the beast's skull as he backed away.

Shaking its long, armoured head, the stalker turned to look at him with its glinting, piggy eyes.

Clip out. Another in his coat pocket. Two seconds to load, maybe? Three? Nothing like enough time for that.

Holy Throne, Gaunt thought. *I'm afraid. Great God-Emperor, I'm actually afraid!*

'Well done, you son of a bitch!' he cried into the monster's face.

It lunged forward at him, raising an arm so thick, so corded with reinforced muscle, Gaunt knew his bones would be pulped.

Before the blow could land, the stalker winced away, blinking. Las-rounds were striking it in the ribs. Heavy, hard, a sustained and serious assault.

'That's right, you bastard!' Ludd shouted. 'This way! This way!' He fired again.

With a raging, phlegmy rattle, the wrought one turned aside and went for the new target instead.

'Oh! Bugger...' Ludd said.

The empty bolt pistol flew up into the air, discarded. Gaunt ran forward, drawing the power sword of Heironymo Sondar. He lit it up and felt the crackle of ignition.

He sliced at the wrought one.

The amplified blade cut clean through the monster's body. If he'd hit the backbone, Gaunt was sure he'd have severed it and crippled or killed the beast. But he didn't quite manage that.

The wrought one let out a huge howl of pain that shook its flapping throat tubes. It turned back to find out what had hurt it so. A copious amount of black, stinking blood gushed out of the deep slice Gaunt's sword had put through its torso.

It swung at him. Gaunt guarded and sliced back, his blow deflecting off the monster's reaching claws. Several talons flew off into the air, sizzling from their cut ends.

The beast opened its mouth. The stink of it hit Gaunt like a body slam. It was going to lunge forward, a biting strike. Gaunt braced his blade in both hands. He was certain he could impale it, kill it, maybe. Of course, he would be dead in the same exchange, as the huge killing jaws snapped forward and closed.

There would be a symmetry to that, at least. To die, killing your killer. That might be enough. After all this time, all these battles, after the unremitting horrors of Gereon, it might be enough. Enough to die with. He almost welcomed it.

'Finally...' he sighed.

The wrought one fell on its face at his feet.

It gurgled once, then the breathing stopped. It was dead. Really dead, this time.

'Holy...' Gaunt said. He sank to his knees, leaning on his sword.

The potent toxins of Eszrah's bolts, quite enough to kill a regular human with the slightest scratch, had finally worked through the stalker's system.

'Sir? Are you all right? Sir?' Ludd called, coming closer.

'I'm fine. I'm alive,' Gaunt replied. He rose upright again. 'I'm alive. Still, I'm alive!' he shouted the words at the dark woods around them. Ludd took a step back. 'You hear me? I'm alive, you bastards! You can't kill me! You just can't kill me, can you?'

Gaunt held his arms up, holding the sword aloft, and slowly turned in a circle. 'I'm alive, even now! You bastards! What have you got left?'

He began to laugh, violently, full throatedly, his head back, almost manic.

Nahum Ludd had seen plenty during that day that had scared him, and the stalker had almost topped the list. But Gaunt's defiant laughter was the scariest thing of all.

ESZRAH NIGHT LOOMED out of the dark and placed a hand on Gaunt's shoulder.

'Restye, soule,' he whispered.

Gaunt nodded. 'It's all right, my friend. I'm all right. Ludd?'

'Yes, sir?'

'Good work there. I won't forget it. Get Ironmeadow cleaned up.'

'How exactly, sir?'

'Find a stream or a pool. Make him stand in it.'

'Yes, sir.'

Gaunt looked back at the partisan. 'Howe camyt be, soule? Sow suddan, sow vyle?'

Eszrah shrugged. 'Stynk offyt I hadd. Thissen steppe.'

The Nihtgane led Gaunt into the undergrowth. Away from the track, and the lights of the truck, huge slabs of granite loomed in the dark between the trees. They were slumped and fallen askew, like a monolith that had been sunk and toppled by the measures of eternity.

'Histye,' Eszrah said, touching parts of the stone and the foliage as he led the way. 'Herein, herein y twane. Thissen spoor, here alswer, yt maketh spoor, alswer, alswer over.'

He came to a stop before a massive slab of quartz, as big as a superheavy tank. The lump of rock reclined among the draping, sickly trees. Gaunt had to feel for its shape in the dark.

'And here's where the track stopped?' he asked.

'Namore stynk, namore spoor yt leaf. Comen fram Urth yt dyd.'

'Are you sure?' Gaunt asked, feeling the rock. Eszrah did not reply. Gaunt could feel the Nihtgane's reproach. Of course Eszrah was sure. He was partisan, a Nihtgane of the Untill. What he couldn't track was beyond the limit of measure.

Gaunt looked up at the night sky. In the cold, hard frieze of the air, stars twinkled beyond the trees. Somewhere out there, across the dim, distances of space, the proper face of this war was being fought, by experienced, determined men.

But it would be lost here. If he was right, and Gaunt was pretty sure he was, the Sabbat Worlds Crusade would be lost right here, in the step-cities of Ancreon Sextus. The Warmaster was going to get stabbed in the back.

He would get stabbed in the back and die.

And there was nothing Gaunt could do about it. After all, he was a loose cannon, a suspect officer, regarded as so dubious in his loyalties, he'd been issued with an observer to keep an eye on him. Regarded as so untrustworthy, he hadn't even been given back a command of men.

Just because they thought he was tainted. Well, it was that very poison essence in his blood that made him know this now. Know it for sure.

Somehow, despite all the odds against him, he had to find a way of getting the senior staff to take him seriously.

And there was one way he could think of...

'Let's get back to the transport,' Gaunt said to Eszrah. On the trackway below them, the cargo-4's engine was still running, and its lights were burning. The distant cries of hunting stalkers flooded the night.

'Ludd? Ironmeadow?' Gaunt yelled as he scrambled back down to the transport, Eszrah behind him. 'We're leaving. Now.'

FIFTEEN

RAWNE'S TEAM HAD been back amongst them for nearly two days, and Wilder was now convinced they should never have returned. It wasn't that he didn't know them – and by the Throne, he didn't – but he had been counting on the Tanith men to absorb them back into the company, to smooth over the transition, to welcome the squad's return. And that just wasn't happening.

There'd been an attempt at greeting on the first afternoon. Once they'd cheered and applauded their arrival, the Ghosts had mobbed forward around their long-lost comrades, shaking their hands, embracing them, asking the first of a thousand questions. Rawne's team had, for the most part, simply suffered this attention. They'd smiled back thinly, accepted the handshakes and embraces stiffly, quietly said hello to old faces.

Gol Kolea had marched straight up to his old friend Varl and squeezed the smaller man in a big hug. Varl had grinned an empty grin and patted Kolea on the back until he stopped.

'All that, and they still didn't get you?' Kolea said.

'So it seems,' said Varl. 'I suggested they tried harder, but their heart wasn't in it.'

'Holy Throne, it's good to see you,' Kolea admitted.

'Yeah,' Varl seemed to agree. He was simply looking around at the camp, anywhere but at Kolea's face.

'So… when do we hear all about it?' Kolea asked.

'Not much to tell,' Varl replied.

The Tanith scouts had surrounded Mkoll and Bonin. From what Wilder could overhear, those greetings were oddly muted too.

'What did you see, sir?'

'What happened?'

'Gaunt's alive, right?'

'What happened to Ven?'

'Good to see you all still breathing,' Mkoll had replied. This Mkoll, the famous Mkoll the scouts had boasted proudly about, didn't look like much to Wilder. Small, unprepossessing, tightly wound.

'But what did you see out there?' Leyr asked.

'Not much worth speaking of,' Bonin replied.

'Somebody give me a sit rep,' Mkoll had said, as if he'd just wandered in from a routine, half-hour sortie.

Trooper Caffran had pushed his way through the huddle towards Tona Criid, and stopped short in front of her. He started to move to embrace her, but there was something in her manner that seemed to persuade him not to.

'Tona,' he said.

'Caff.'

'I knew... I knew you'd make it back.'

'Glad someone did.' Then she'd moved on past him, heading towards the billets, leaving him alone, a puzzled expression on his face, the muscle in the corner of his jawline working tightly.

Only Brostin, Rawne's flame-trooper, had seemed in a remotely expansive mood. Greeted by company flame-troopers like Lubba, Dremmond, Neskon and Lyse, Brostin had accepted a lho-stick from a proffered pack.

'What was it like, Bros?' Dremmond asked.

'Well,' Brostin had replied, looking down at his smoke, 'there weren't enough of these for a start.'

A despondency had settled in. The returning 'heroes' appeared to want nothing more than to be left on their own. The day's celebratory mood ended up fizzling away as pathetically as a badly connected det-tape.

THE FOLLOWING MORNING, Wilder had called them all to a briefing at his field tent. He summoned other officers too, including Baskevyl, Kolosim, Meryn and Kolea. The down country squabble with the Blood Pact was still grumbling away inconclusively, the spat holding over from the previous day. Daylight in the compartment was a patchy grey that seemed as shiftless as the mood. According to the post advisors, DeBray was likely to order an infantry advance in the next thirty-six hours. This made sense to Wilder. The enemy armour wouldn't have been gripping on so tightly if they weren't trying to hold a door open for a ground troop push.

'Chances are we'll be moving into the compartment again tomorrow,' Wilder had said. 'Maybe even as soon as later today. Details to follow, but I'll be looking at a firm foot advance from the main companies, with scout units combing ahead. A secondary issue is getting you fixed into place neatly.' By 'you' he had meant Rawne's team. The major nodded.

'I've got various ideas about where to slot you,' Wilder said, 'but I think a little familiarisation is needed first. This is odd fighting country–'

'We're used to odd,' Rawne said.

Wilder paused. He wasn't accustomed to being interrupted, certainly not by a man he didn't know.

'Noted, Rawne. Thank you. I'm going to divide you up and post you with three forces. Sergeant Mkoll and Trooper Bonin, given your speciality, I want you moving in with the recon force, to get a good feel of the way we like to run scouting operations. Captain Kolosim is one of our recon leaders, so you'll be with him.'

Kolosim nodded a greeting to Mkoll and Bonin that was only just acknowledged.

'Varl, Criid, Brostin and Larkin. I'm sorry I don't yet know any of you better. I'm going to put you with C Company, that's Kolea's bunch, so you'll be in with the main infantry advance. Try and find your feet. I don't think you'll have much trouble doing that.'

'I'll keep them in line if they don't,' Kolea remarked, shooting for a good-natured quip. It fell flat.

'Major Rawne, I'd like to attach you to E Company, along with Feygor and Beltayn. E Company is Captain's Meryn's unit. If I can be frank for a moment, I know that might be a little strange, as Meryn was very much your junior when you left. Rub along, please. This is simply about acclimatisation. Meryn, you know Major Rawne is a seasoned and experienced officer. I think we all know we're lucky to have him back with us. I won't lie – there's every chance I'll be moving E Company to him before long. I know that'll feel like a demotion to you, but suck it up. If it happens, it'll be no reflection on you, Meryn. There will be other opportunities.'

'I understand perfectly, sir,' Meryn said. There was not even a hint that he was put out by the suggestion. He must have seen that coming, Wilder thought. Wilder saw how Kolea looked briefly unhappy that Wilder didn't seem to be following his recommendation about Meryn and Rawne.

'All right, that's it,' Wilder said, rising to his feet. 'Major Rawne, I'm sure you'll remind your team that this is all about getting to know your old comrades again, and getting to know your new ones as fast as possible.'

'Of course,' said Rawne.

'And may I take this opportunity to say that the Eighty-First First has nothing but admiration for what you've accomplished in the last eighteen months. We haven't been told everything, naturally. Parts of your mission details remain classified. But you don't have to prove anything to us... except that you can fit back into company level operations.'

NOW ANOTHER DAWN was on the way. Wilder woke and immediately felt uneasy again. It wasn't just the cold. The cool, aloof attitude of Rawne's team still bothered him deeply. There were only nine of them, but that was enough to unsettle the entire balance of the regiment. The Belladon didn't know what to make of these surly newcomers and their hard-as-nails reputation. For the Tanith and the Verghastites, it was just a huge disappointment. These people were heroes, back from the dead. They'd built them up so much in their minds, the reality was like a cold shower.

The Eighty-First First and the Kolstec Fortieth had mobilised in the pitch dark. The eerie hoots of stalkers echoed up from the blackness of the compartment. Baskevyl brought the signals up from the command station. A pre-dawn advance, just as Wilder had suspected, the Eighty-First First leading off the Kolstec into the eastern side of the compartment. By oh-nine hundred, DeBray wanted Wilder's regiment secure along Hill 56, preferably having made contact with the Rothberg armour.

Down on the trackway, and on the assembly areas, the companies were forming up: men, numb and cold from their billets, canteens full, adjusting webbing and the fit of battledress, checking weapons. The sky overhead was as clear as glass, and only the bright pattern of the stars showed where the black sky ended and the black shape of the high compartment walls began.

Twenty minutes to the go. Wilder buttoned up his fleece-lined coat, did a quick intercom test, and went to check a carbine out of the stores. He normally only carried the powerful laspistol strapped to his thigh, but today he had a feeling, and it wasn't pleasant.

On his way back out of the post, he saw Hark and Novobazky talking to Dorden.

'Morning,' he said, joining them.

'Just off to join the ranks, sir,' Novobazky said.

'Problem?' Wilder asked.

'We were just discussing Rawne and the others,' Hark said.

'Anything you'd like to share?'

Hark shrugged and looked at the old medicae. 'I can't imagine what they've been through,' Dorden said. 'I can't imagine, and therefore I have no real idea, because none of them are at all willing to talk about it. I checked each of them over yesterday, just the expected routine exam. I'd been so looking forward to seeing each one again, and they were like strangers. Not actually unfriendly, but… distant.'

Hark nodded. 'That'd be my reading too, sir.'

'Any conclusions?' Wilder asked.

Dorden frowned. 'They've been on their own for so long, it may take them a while to settle back into company. I mean, they're just not used to being around people they can trust. I think they've had to ditch a lot in order to survive as long as they have. In fact, that's all they have left. Survival. I don't know if they'll ever be the people we knew again.'

Wilder knew the old doctor was bitterly disappointed his beloved colleague, Curth, hadn't returned with the team. 'Are they fit?' Wilder asked.

'Physically, they're supremely fit. Even Larkin, who's the oldest one of them. And Larks is the one who gave me most pause, I suppose. He was never–'

'Go on,' said Wilder.

'Dorden is diplomatically trying to say that Larkin was a little poorly wired in the head department,' Hark said. 'He had personal issues, edgy and nervous. The only reason he made the cut for the Gereon mission was that there's no better marksman in the Tanith First.'

'Larks has got a hard edge to him now,' Dorden said. 'A lot of the old shakes and tics have gone. I'd have expected a horror show like Gereon to push him right over the edge. Maybe it did, and he got pushed so far, he came back the other way. Point is, if that's what it's done to the most psychologically weak member of the team…' his voice trailed off.

Wilder sighed. He checked his watch. 'All right, gentlemen, let's get this circus moving.'

THE SIGNAL TO advance came over their micro-bead links, quiet and simple. Standing with C Company, Larkin felt the pip in his ear and picked up his weapon. It was new, an Urdesh-pattern mark IV long-las, finished in satin black with dark plastek furniture. Quite a nice weapon, all things considered, but he was still getting to know it. He'd left his own weapon – the old nalwood-fitted long-las that had seen him through every firefight from Tanith to Herodor – back on Gereon. In fact, it was still hard for him not to think they'd left three friends behind on that arse-end world: Ven, Doc Curth and his sniper rifle. It had been a simple thing, in the end. About six months into the Gereon tour, he'd run out of hot-shot rounds, run out of even the means to manufacture or recook hot-shot rounds. Dead, mute, his old long-las had become about as useful as a club. He'd switched to a simple, solid-slug autorifle that Landerson had found for him, an old hunter's bolt-action.

As they moved forward down the trackway into the darkness, Larkin found himself walking beside a young Belladon soldier who was also carrying a long-las.

'Kaydey,' the youth said, offering his hand.

'Larkin.'

'Major Kolea's asked me to travel with you. Wants us up the front with the point men.'

'Lead on,' Larkin said. They double-timed for a couple of minutes, moving up the file of troopers.

'So, you take some shots on this Gereon place?'

'One or two.'

'What was it like?'

Larkin looked at the boy. 'Aim and squeeze, just like here.'

'No, I meant–' Kaydey began.

'I know what you meant.'

After that, Kaydey didn't say much.

KOLEA GOT HIS company moving north into the scrublands off the track. Dawn was still a while off, and most of them were using goggles, painting the world as a green image, as if they were underwater.

Kolea gave point to Derin and moved back, checking the company line, troop by troop. He saw Criid, and fell in step with her.

'You been avoiding me, Tona?' he asked.

'Yes, Gol. That's why I went to Gereon, to avoid you.'

'I don't suppose you got a chance to see the kids on your way in here?' he said.

Criid and her partner Caffran had rescued two young children from the Vervunhive warzone, and had been raising them as their own as part of the regimental baggage train of camp followers, support staff and non-combatants. It had turned out that the kids, in one of the more quirky examples of the God-Emperor's sense of humour, were Kolea's. The children he thought he'd lost back there. Kolea had let things be, left Criid and Caff in charge, not wishing to screw up the kids' minds any more than they already had been.

Since the regiment had arrived on Ancreon Sextus, the kids, Yoncy and Dalin, had been in the care of the regimental entourage back at Imperial Command.

'No,' said Criid.

'You going to?'

'Eighteen months since I've been gone, Gol. You seen them yet? You been to them and told them the truth that daddy's not actually dead?'

'No,' he said.

'You talk to Caff at least?'

'No,' Kolea said.

'Throne's sake, Kolea! He knows! I told him all about it. Feth it all, eighteen months and the two of you haven't even had a conversation? You're as bad as each other!'

'Tona–'

'Don't talk to me,' Criid said. 'Maybe later, but now you don't talk to me. We're in the fething field here, you dumb gak. Shut up and choose your moments better.'

She walked on. Some of the men nearby looked at Kolea. They hadn't caught much of the exchange, but they knew something spiky had just gone down.

'That's *major* dumb gak...' Kolea called after her.

E COMPANY, ALONG with Callide's H Company, were the last to move out from post 36. In the bitter darkness, lit by lumen paddles and lamp-packs, the Kolstec units that would follow them were already forming up and filling the assembly areas vacated by the Eighty-First First.

As he waited for the off, Feygor kept looking back at the Kolstec assembling on the hardpan thirty metres behind them. He tutted silently and shook his head. The Kolstec were making a fair bit of noise.

Rawne stood beside him, huddled deep in his new leather coat. He'd spent some time in the last few days working at the coat with oil and wool to soften it, but the new leather still creaked slightly as he moved.

'Murt?'

'Fething craphounds,' Feygor whispered. 'Zero noise discipline.'

Rawne nodded. He'd actually been fairly impressed with the manner in which the Eighty-First First had drawn together and moved out. Some noise, and some chat, but nothing too disgraceful. He had assumed the good practice of the Tanith had rubbed off on these Belladon people.

The Kolstec though, they just wouldn't shut up. He could hear whining and complaining and occasional bursts of laughter. And even though they clearly had low-light goggles as standard, they were flashing lamps and torch paddles like it was Glory of the Throne Day.

Rawne saw the Belladon commissar – what was his name again, Novobazky? – talking with Captain Callide and several junior officers Rawne couldn't name. He went over.

'Major Rawne? Good morning.'

'Commissar. I assume you'll be doing something about that?' He inclined his head towards the Kolstec forces.

'I'm sorry?'

'The noise and light. It's not acceptable.'

'They'll settle once we're underway.'

Rawne smiled. 'Will they? Oh, that's all right, then.'

'Besides, it's a matter for their own commissars to–'

Rawne stared into Novobazky's eyes. 'It will be our matter when those fething idiots bring down the hurt on our heads by yabbering at our heels. If you just assume something will get done, it never will. And somebody else's problem never stays somebody else's.'

'Are you telling me how to do my job, major?' Novobazky said.

'Yes, I fething well am. Someone has to.' He turned and walked away.

'Major! Get back here!'

'I don't think I will, fethwipe,' Rawne said, still walking.

'Major Rawne!'

Rawne ignored Novobazky and rejoined Feygor. 'We just got the signal to move,' Feygor said.

E Company began to stir. Ayatani Zweil was moving down the column, issuing a few last blessings to troopers. He reached Beltayn and smiled, about to speak the simple prayer of protection.

'Save it, father,' Beltayn said.

'Son, I'm only–'

'Just save it. I'm blessed or I'm cursed. Either way, a few words from you won't help.'

Zweil closed his mouth and watched the young trooper move away with the rest of the company. Dughan Beltayn had once been one of the most devout troopers in the regiment, always amongst the first to arrive for the daily service. But the look in his eyes just then...

Meryn was near the head of the formation, leading the men off into the darkness. For all he'd nodded along with Wilder's placement orders the previous day, he was twitchy and uncomfortable. He felt as if Rawne's eyes were boring into him wherever he went. Before Gereon, Meryn had styled himself on the Tanith's second officer, admired him, sided with him, and had benefited from being one of 'Rawne's men'. Now he was a captain and a company leader, and Rawne had come back from the dead, threatening to take that away. Meryn didn't blame Rawne; ironically, the situation made him focus ever more intently on the skills and philosophies Rawne had drummed into him: self-reliance, cunning, the desire to protect what was his with brutal and exclusive efficiency.

He'd make nice, he'd nod along with Wilder. But there was no fething way Flyn Meryn was going to let Rawne come in and steal this command from him.

Jessi Banda was up ahead of him, moving forward with the marksmen taking point. There was another little sticky point. It hadn't been common knowledge, but Rawne and the caustic, sharp-tongued sniper had been an item before the mission. Once Rawne had gone, Banda had chosen Meryn as a replacement partner. Meryn was no fool. He knew that Banda was an ambitious woman, who liked to keep the company of promising officers, or men on the rise. Like Rawne before him, Meryn was one of the sniper's trophies. He knew she didn't love him, and he didn't much care. They were good together, and had a hard-nosed, volatile relationship that seemed to cater for their basic needs.

The trouble was, Meryn had become terribly possessive. He didn't love Banda either, if he was honest, but he was intoxicated by her; intoxicated by her cruel wit, her laugh, her flirtatious manner, by the very heat and smell of her. She just had to look at another man – or another man look at her – and Meryn would brew up. Two days earlier, a Belladon sergeant called Berenbeck had wound up in the infirmary, badly beaten. Berenbeck was a loud-mouth, and it was presumed – even by Berenbeck himself – that he'd been jumped by Hauberkan tankers who had overhead him opining that a bullet had been too good for Gadovin. The truth was it had been Meryn, waiting for Berenbeck behind the latrine tents after dark with a sock full of stones. Meryn had heard the man telling his buddies how 'hot the Ghosty sniper girl' was.

Banda hadn't said anything about Rawne's return, nothing to get Meryn thinking, at any rate. But Meryn could barely fight down the furnace in the pit of his gut. His command and his girl. Fething Rawne wasn't going to take either one from him.

E Company, with H Company on their right flank, moved out across the scrublands, closing up on the Eighty-First First units already slogging up north through the compartment. Rawne thought they moved well. The Belladon were evidently a decent enough regiment. In all probability, the Ghosts were lucky to have been mixed with them. But Rawne felt empty and cold, and it wasn't just the biting chill of the pre-dawn air. There was nothing about this he engaged with any more, no point, no purpose, no sense of loyalty. The Tanith First was gone, even though so many familiar faces were around him. There was no longer any intensity, no passion. The world had become empty, its lustre gone, and Elim Rawne was simply going through the motions.

* * *

NORTH-EAST OF post 36, the landscape of the compartment was downland scrub for three kilometres, a stubbled expanse of tumbling rough ground speckled with stands of lime and thorn-bush. At its lowest point, the scrubland gave way to marshes and oxbows of brackish water, thickly clogged with black rushes and reeds. East of the depression, past a vestigial trackway overgrown with moss, the land rose again, becoming bare and flinty, the scrub broken by ridges of quartz and ouslite that looked like the gigantic exposed roots of the compartment's massive eastern wall.

Ridge 18, so marked on the charts, was a particularly high example, a hard-sided buckle of sharp rock that ran east-west for about half a kilometre, its upper surfaces thick with dogwood, bramble and flowering janiture. Kolosim's recon unit was about halfway up the southern side.

Four recon units had set out ahead of the main advance, one to the west, two across the central basin of the scrub, and the fourth, Kolosim's, around to the east. It had taken them about forty-five minutes to move down country from the post. Dawn was still not yet a glimmer above the western wall.

Ferdy Kolosim, red-headed and bluff, was Mkoll's equivalent amongst the Belladon. A recon specialist, he had risen to company command by dint of his experience and his leadership skills. He was well liked. Even the Tanith had warmed to him.

There were eight men in his unit. The Tanith Scouts Caober and Hwlan, the Belladon Recon Troopers Maggs, Darromay, Burnstine and Sergeant Buckren, and the newcomers Mkoll and Bonin. Already, Kolosim had made a mental note of the scary way the last two performed. He'd always believed the Belladon to be pretty good stealth artists, and it had been a wake-up call to witness the extraordinary abilities of the Ghosts when the regiments first amalgamated.

But Mkoll and Bonin were something else. Kolosim had to keep checking they were still there, and every time he did, neither Mkoll nor Bonin was where he'd last seen them.

It was to the Belladon's credit, as a recon division proud of its skills, that there had been no ill will when the Ghosts first came along. Rather than resenting the way the Ghosts showed them up, the Belladon had got busy learning all the woodcraft and battle-skills the Tanith could teach them. They'd got rid of the netting shrouds they'd been using since their founding, and adopted Ghost-style camo-cloaks. They'd stopped using their clumsy sword-form rifle bayonets for close work, and got hold of smaller, double-edged fighting knives. The knives were nothing like as handsome as the Ghosts' trademark straight silver, but they were far handier than the long bayonets. They'd even started dulling down their regiment pins and badges with boot black. Caober, pretty much the senior Ghost scout since Mkoll, Bonin and Mkvenner had gone, had taught Kolosim that himself. He'd pointed out the faintly ludicrous fact that the Belladon drabbed up buttons, blades, fasteners, bootlace eyelets, skin and uniform patches for stealth work, but still wore a shiny, scrupulously gleaming regimental badge on their tunics.

'It's a matter of pride,' Kolosim had said. 'Pride in our unit identity.'

'Pride's great,' Caober had replied. 'Great for a lot of things, except when it gets you seen and killed.'

Kolosim liked Caober's frank and fair attitude, and the two were forming a decent working relationship. He wasn't sure how things would sit now the famous Mkoll was back. Every tip and piece of advice Caober, or any of the other scouts, had ever imparted, came with a phrase like 'as Mkoll taught us' or 'like Mkoll always said'.

So far, Mkoll had said a dozen words to Kolosim, and six of those had been, 'You Kolosim? Right. Let's go.'

The unit reached the crown of Ridge 18 and slid through the bramble cover. From the top of the ridge, they got a decent view, via night-scopes, across the deep basin beyond, a steep-sided, scrub-choked vale that widened as it ran west. On the far side of the basin, parallel to them, ran Ridge 19, a lower and more jagged escarpment. At its western end rose Hill 55, and behind it, the broader, loaf-like bulk of Hill 56, where the Eighty-First First was meant to form up later in the day. Hill 56 was back-lit by a jumping, trembling light, brief flashes and bursts that lingered as after-images on their goggles. Even from half a dozen kilometres away, they could hear the crump and report of tankfire. The Rothberg armour had pushed the Archenemy back up the compartment, but the fight was still in them, even at this early hour.

Kolosim studied the area and made a few jotted notes with his wax pencil.

'At least they're where we thought they'd be,' he muttered. Buckren nodded. There had been a danger that the Rothberg would have been shoved backwards overnight, or worse, which would have made Hill 56 unviable as an infantry objective. One of the key objectives of the recon units was to make sure DeBray's orders still made sense. Thanks to the high ground and the efficiency of their advance, Kolosim's unit was the first to get a visual confirmation.

'Signal it in?' Buckren asked.

'Do that,' said Kolosim. Buckren crawled over to Darromay, who was carrying the vox-caster, and began to send in the details.

The other duty of the recon units was to assess the approaches. The tacticae advisors at the post reckoned there was a high probability that the Archenemy might use the distraction of a drawn-out armour fight to sneak infantry down the eastern side of the compartment.

Mkoll stared northwards. He studied the charts in detail, but there was nothing like seeing the land first hand. Feeling the lie of it. And there were so many lies here. For all it seemed like a natural landscape, the compartment was artificial. It was a giant box full of dirt and rock. He didn't trust any part of it. He turned his scope towards the far north end, and was just able to pick out the suggestion of the end wall, the great bastion enclosing the next massive gateway. That would be the real objective in the days to come: burning a path to that monumental gate and breaking through. What lay beyond that, none could say. Even orbital obs and spy-tracking had come up with nothing. The only thing anyone knew for certain was that the next compartment was another step towards the centre of this ancient puzzle, and that it was capable of launching forth armoured columns and companies of warriors to face them.

Hooting roars echoed up the ridge from the basin. Mkoll swung his scope to look down that way.

'You'll never spot 'em,' said Maggs.

Bonin looked across at him. 'The stalkers?'

'Yeah, you never see 'em. Not until it's too late.'

'That so?'

Maggs nodded, and patted the butt of his mark III. 'And one of these babies won't stop one, not even on full auto. Even if you do see it first. Which you won't. You never see 'em till they find you.'

'You maybe, not the chief,' Bonin replied.

Wes Maggs frowned. He was a short, well-built man with a broad, swimmer's back and heavy shoulders. His hair was cropped and brown, and he had a little vertical scar running down from the outside corner of his left eye. Maggs was one of Kolosim's best scouts, known amongst the Belladon as a likeable rogue and joker, who sometimes had too many words in his mouth for his own good. Bonin hadn't made up his mind about Maggs yet. Too much personality for his liking.

'I'd like to see your old man try taking a stalker...' Maggs began.

'Stick around,' said Bonin.

Kolosim was ignoring the quiet exchange. He was studying the ridgeways ahead of them.

'No way they'd bring a force this way on foot,' Buckren said.

'Too much like heavy going,' Burnstine agreed. 'The lateral ridges would slow them down. And if they got into trouble, they'd have no easy retreat.'

'The Blood Pact don't often think of things in terms of retreat,' Mkoll said.

'You think they'd come this way?' Maggs asked.

'I think it's possible. I think it should be checked,' Mkoll said.

'You're crazy–' Maggs remarked.

'Pin that lip,' Kolosim snapped. He rose to his feet and stood beside Mkoll. 'I was going to have us follow the line of this ridge west until we hit the open tableland, then hike up the escarpment to Hill 56. Something tells me that's not what you want to do.'

Mkoll shrugged slightly. 'Your unit. You call it.'

'We're meant to be getting to know one another, Mkoll. I'd like to hear what you have to say.'

'All right,' said Mkoll. 'The ridges break the terrain along this east wall. It wouldn't be the approach of choice. The enemy would be better off trying to cinch an infantry column around Hill 55, and come in on the trackway. But I think we should stop thinking about this like normal open country. We're boxed in by walls. We're enclosed. If I wanted to outflank us, I'd send in troops this way.'

'Over the ridges?'

'Over the ridges. They're steep, but we made the top of this one in, what? Under an hour from the post? It's well covered too. The densest undergrowth in the compartment. It would be hard going, but it would pay off. Besides, we don't know what's down there or behind the next ridge…' he gestured down into the basin. 'And we don't know how much better our enemy knows this place.'

'Meaning what?' asked Caober.

'Meaning tunnels. Meaning trenches. Meaning sally-ports we can't see. It's artificial.'

'There's been no sign of any tunnels or anything so far,' said Hwlan.

'Doesn't mean there aren't any there,' said Mkoll.

Kolosim pursed his lips. 'Let's take a look.'

'You're kidding me!' Maggs grunted.

'Darromay,' Kolosim said, ignoring Maggs. 'Signal post command we're moving onto Ridge 19. Maybe another hour. We'll vox them again when we're on site, and take it from there.'

'Yes, sir.'

Down in the dark, overgrown basin between Ridge 18 and Ridge 19, in a dank glade between lichen-heavy lime trees, Crookshank Thrice-wrought paused. Something was coming, something moving down the steepness to the south of him.

Other, lesser wrought ones, once-wrought or twice-wrought, were hunting in the damp groves nearby, but they all knew to give Thrice Crookshank a wide berth. The sun, and the time of going back, was a long way off.

Crookshank puffed breath through his floppy throat tubes and made a dull, idle rasp. He clambered forward, rolling his gait through all four, powerful limbs, head low.

He sniffed the air. He could smell it now for sure.

Something was coming, and it was called meat.

SIXTEEN

05.26 hrs, 197.776.M41
Fifth Compartment
Sparshad Mons, Ancreon Sextus

EVEN IN DAYLIGHT, the basin would have been dark. An off-set bowl between the two long ridges, it was choked with undergrowth that blocked out the sky. Back on Tanith, it was what the woodsmen would have called a combe.

The southern slope was steep, almost sheer in places. The ground was a mix of loose, flinty loam and exposed quartz. Thick gorse and bramble spilled down the slopes, hanging like frozen waterfalls. Resilient lime, and some form of tuberous, gnarled tree species, sprouted from the thicker deposits of soil, and provided handholds for the recon unit to brace against as they descended.

A musty smell of damp and mud and leaf decay welled up from the basin below. It was several degrees warmer out of the open.

The men moved with their weapons strapped over their right shoulders, right hands on the grips, left hands free to grip and grasp. Distant noises came up out of the darkness below. Scrabbling, snorting, the occasional half-heard grunt. Mkoll had no doubt there was at least one stalker loose down there.

Mach Bonin was listening carefully. The other members of the recon unit were making precious little noise, but it still sounded loud and clumsy compared to the total silence he and Mkoll were managing. It wasn't just the Belladon. Even Caober and Hwlan seemed to him to be heavy footed, and they were two of the Ghosts' best scouts. Had their technique really slackened off in Mkoll's absence?

No, he realised, watching them for a moment. They were as good as ever. The difference was with him. Heading to Gereon, Bonin hadn't thought he could get any sharper. The place had proved him wrong about that, like it had proved them wrong about so many things.

403

About halfway down the slope, Mkoll perched on a jutting crop of quartz and held up his hand for a silent halt. The others arrested their descents quickly, and waited, watching him.

Mkoll paused for a moment, listening, breathing in the air, working out what was there and what wasn't. No birds, no insects to speak of. Possibly burrowing worms and beetles, but nothing flying. Nothing chirruping and stirring. No small rodents, no lizards. Just the still, damp, stringy undergrowth.

He smelled wet stone, bark, musky leaves, humus. He smelled free flowing water, and he could hear that too: rills and rivulets gurgling down the slope below.

The noise of the stalker or stalkers had receded for a while, and the few louder sounds he heard were actually the echoing thumps from the distant tank battle beyond the hills, which were hard to screen out.

But he could smell blood. The rank sweat, body odour scent of blood, as from a poorly healing wound. The smell of rotting meat between the teeth that a carnivore carries with it.

He signalled them to move again. As they got up and carried on, Maggs shook his head, as if amused by Mkoll's painstaking manner.

Kolosim reached the bottom of the slope, where the depth of the basin began to round out, and was glad to have both hands back on his weapon. He began panning round, then jumped in surprise to find Mkoll right beside him.

'Shit!'

'Let's spread that way,' Mkoll whispered.

In a lateral line, they moved out across the basin floor, their boots sinking into the thick black mud, dense bramble and branches pushing in around them. Bonin could smell the blood scent too, and glanced at Mkoll.

The smell had changed a little, as far as Mkoll was concerned. It had become more like sweat, dirty human sweat.

Something moved up ahead. A tree shivered and there was a snort.

Weapons came up.

Mkoll took a step forward.

CROOKSHANK THRICE-WROUGHT salivated at the air's taste. He was close now, moving with astonishing grace and care for something so big and heavy, delicately parting gorse stems and saplings as he slid forward.

Nearby, off to his left, a lesser wrought one, a twice-wrought, was active, snuffling. Much longer, and the lesser thing would spoil it.

Crookshank opened his jaws and unslid his steel teeth. His dark-sight stained red. He could see the meat at last, twiggy shapes of pink heat in the red darkness.

His teeth locked into place.

RIFLE UP TO his cheek, Mkoll waved Maggs and Bonin to his left. Caober and Burnstine were just away on his right-hand side, and the others were coming in behind.

Maggs moved through the undergrowth as instructed, sliding his body this way and that, so it barely touched a twig. He'd had enough of the newcomers' showboating. They weren't the only ones who knew how things should be done.

Maggs came in under a twisted lime and looked back for Bonin. There was no sign of the man. Where the h–

A hand clamped over his mouth. Maggs stiffened in terror and then realised it was the Tanith.

Bonin took his hand away. Somehow, he'd come up around Maggs without Maggs noticing. How the hell did a man do that, unless he was a–

Ghost.

Maggs glared at Bonin. Bonin ignored the acid look, and pointed ahead. There was something there all right. Something stalking them as surely as they were stalking it.

Maggs swallowed. This was insane. The truth was, and Maggs wasn't about to admit this to Mr Know-it-all Bonin, he'd never actually seen a stalker. But he'd heard plenty of stories since the Eighty-First First had moved into the Mons. Horror stories of the bogeymen that stalked the compartments after dark. Bestial ogres that refused to drop, even when you were hosing them with full auto fire and saying please nicely. Everyone knew you didn't go looking for stalkers, even when you were part of a fire team. Kolosim should have turned back from the ridge, not come down here, not down here where–

Bonin was slowly lifting his weapon. From the dense, black undergrowth ahead, there came a wheezing snort. The crack of a root breaking under a great weight.

Maggs raised his rifle too. He toggled it to *full auto* anyway.

CROOKSHANK THRICE-WROUGHT tensed, muscles pulsing, his breathing short and sharp. He began to puff up his throat tubes. His fighting spines rose erect. Saliva oozed from the long, dagger-toothed line of his jaw.

WITH A LUNG-BURSTING howl, the wrought one tore out of the undergrowth and ploughed towards Maggs and Bonin. Maggs began firing at once, loosing a bright cone of energy flash as his weapon discharged at maximum sustain.

Twenty metres back, Mkoll started running forward, and the rest of the unit came after him. Mkoll couldn't see anything of the situation ahead, apart from the bright, flickering wash from the las-fire backlighting the undergrowth. He could hear the shooting, and the roaring.

Maggs kept firing as long as he dared. He had made a real mess of the stalker's armoured face and throat. His furious shots had chewed at it, ripped and stippled the flesh. But still it came on, bawling aloud, trailing flecks of blood and saliva into the air. *You never see 'em*, he heard himself saying, *not until it's too late*. It was too late now. The thing was a freaking *nightmare...*

Then Maggs realised something else. He was alone. Bonin had vanished. Somewhere between the thing bursting out at them and Maggs opening up, the Throne-damned runt-head spineless Ghost had just *disappeared*, without even firing a blessed shot. He'd run, and left Maggs to face the music.

'You lousy shithead bastard!' Maggs yelled, his voice all but drowned out by the whooping roar of the monster's throat tubes. He turned and ran. Maggs got about five metres, tripped on a root in his terror, and fell.

The wrought one came after him.

Maggs looked up, screamed, tried to untangle himself from the brambles. The thing was right on him, right on him, mouth agape, those teeth, those teeth, those f–

The wrought one abruptly flailed, and fell hard on its face, as if it had tripped too. It landed so suddenly that its lower jaw smashed into the loam and slammed its gaping mouth shut. It had come down less than a metre from Maggs's outstretched feet.

It wasn't even slightly dead. It thrashed and roared, reaching with its huge arms, its maw snapping and slicing the air. Maggs screamed again, and scrabbled backwards, out of reach. He fumbled for his lasrifle. Why had it fallen down? Why the hell had it fallen down?

And why in the name of the God-Emperor had its roaring, bellowing sound become so shrill and wretched?

Like it was… in pain.

The wrought one heaved itself forward again in a mighty surge, rising up on its massive arms, muscles bulging, veins prominent like cables. Curds of foam glistened around its drawn lips. It lunged at Maggs.

He found his weapon and fired into its gullet, glimpsing the scorched punctures his shots made in the ribbed, pink roof of its mouth. Then he rolled aside hard, lacerating his face and arms on spine-gorse and thorny bramble.

Bonin suddenly appeared in mid-air behind the wrought one, propelled by a leap that must have needed a run up. He was no longer holding his lasrifle. In one outflung hand, he clutched the Tanith trademark weapon, the straight silver fighting dagger. The blade of Bonin's dagger was black-wet with blood.

Bonin landed astride the wrought one's hunched back with a grunt of effort, and grabbed hold of the raised fighting spines for purchase with his free hand. Maggs realised that the stalker was half-prone on its belly, dragging its rear limbs.

The monster shook and bucked, trying to shake the man off its broad back. Bonin clung on, and thumped his dagger down into the base of the stalker's skull.

Thirty centimetres of straight Tanith silver punched into its brain case. Thick, dark blood squirted out, hitting Bonin like a pressure hose. He wrenched the knife out and stabbed again.

The wrought one quivered, spasmed, convulsed, and then fell over on its side with a jolt that seemed to rock the ground. Bonin was thrown off.

An almost silence fell. The only noise was the last, tremulous breathes rattling phegmatically in and out of the dead stalker's throat tubes, the gurgle of the blood weeping out around the hilt of the embedded knife.

'Holy Throne...' Maggs said.

'You all right, Maggs?' Bonin asked, getting to his feet and slicking the thing's blood off his face with the palm of his hand.

'Yeah, I'm dandy...' Maggs said.

'Bonin?' Mkoll said. He had suddenly appeared beside them, weapon raised. Kolosim and the others arrived a moment later.

'Golden Terra...' Kolosim murmured, gazing in astonishment at the stalker's huge corpse. 'I mean... Golden bloody Terra...'

'Was that you, Mach?' asked Hwlan.

'Oh, none other,' Caober chuckled. 'See the silver?'

'Yes. Good work, Bonin,' Mkoll said. He was still stiff, as if uneasy.

'Good work? Good work?' Maggs stormed. 'He left me to face it! He left me to deal!'

Bonin walked over to the stalker and plucked out his dagger. When he turned, Maggs was in his face. 'You ditched me, you bastard!'

'I killed it, didn't I?' Bonin asked.

'Yes, but–'

'Before it chomped on you.'

'Yes, you bastard, but–'

'You told me even full auto wouldn't stop a stalker,' Bonin said quietly. 'And so I took your word on that, Maggs. It's a hell of a beast, but it's still an animal. It has anatomy. Anatomy that obeys the simple laws of hunting.'

'What?'

'It has hamstrings. So I cut them. It fell down. It has a brain. That's where I stabbed it. See the skull there? The grafted armour plating at the front? That's why they can't be stopped, even by full auto. Whoever made them armoured their braincases at the front. You have to hit them from behind.'

Maggs stared at Bonin for a long moment.

'Wait a minute,' said Sergeant Buckren. 'Whoever *made* them...?'

Caober was about to speak when he saw that Mkoll had slowly raised his hand.

The Tanith chief scout pulled his weapon up to his chin and aimed back into the undergrowth behind them.

'Get ready,' he hissed. 'We're not out of this yet. Not at all.'

CROOKSHANK THRICE-WROUGHT was panting. The twice-wrought had rushed in early, and ruined his kill. It had almost spoiled the hunt with its inexperience and haste. Later, back under the Quiet Stones, once they had gone back in, Crookshank would have most definitely slain it for its insolence in depriving a thrice-wrought of its meat.

But such punishment was no longer necessary. The lesser thing was dead. The meat twigs had killed it.

Crookshank drew a breath. His throat sacs filled and swelled pink. The sun, and the time of going back, was close now, but he would still feed. The meat had no idea how close he was. They had no notion just how near his claws were to their–

No. One had. The smallest one. The one with no meat on his bones. That one had turned, and was looking directly at Crookshank Thrice-wrought.

Crookshank's blood-hunger was too enflamed by then for him to be troubled by such a curiosity. He extended his claws and pounced.

THE SECOND STALKER came out of the bramble screen like an avalanche. Lime stems cracked and splintered as its bulk pulverised them. It was massive, at least twice as large as the monster Bonin had brought down.

Kolosim, Hwlan, Buckren and Caober began to fire. Mkoll was already unloading at full rate. Bonin ran towards his fallen weapon. Maggs turned and gasped at the stupendous bulk of the new monster. Burnstine simply ran.

Darromay died.

The middle claw of Crookshank's splayed left paw cracked down into the top of Darromay's skull like an augur, right through the hardened steel helmet he was wearing. Then the weight of Crookshank continued to press down, crumpling Darromay into the ground, snapping him like a grass-stalk, breaking all his bones, and rupturing the splintered ends of them out through his deforming skin.

Darromay became a crushed, trampled mess in the loam, his burst blood steaming in the cool air. Crookshank hadn't even meant to kill him. Darromay had simply been underfoot.

The broken vox-set on Darromay's twisted back sparked and crackled.

Backing away, the unit fired together, hammering bright las-fire at the charging monster. Full auto from five Guard weapons wasn't even slowing it down. Maggs retrieved his gun and joined the fusillade. So did Bonin.

It wasn't anything like enough.

Oan Mkoll threw aside his spent weapon and drew his warblade.

'Let's go then, you ugly bastard,' he growled.

There was a sudden, piercing buzz that made all the Guardsmen wince and reach for their micro-beads.

Crookshank faltered, lifting his massive paws to the sides of his head.

He roared in frustration.

The call. The call to the quiet stones.

Mkoll yanked the micro-bead plug out of his ear. He could still hear the buzzing. It was in the air, all around them, so low and intense all the leaves were shivering. The rest of the recon unit were stumbling around, clawing at their intercoms to pull the plugs out.

Crookshank backed away a pace or two, fighting the command, twisting his massive head from side to side, and gouging at his ears. Shuddering with the queasy, infrasonic buzz, Mkoll took a step towards the monster.

It looked at him. Blinked. Grunted.

'Next time we meet, I'll kill you.' Mkoll said.

Crookshank Thrice-wrought roared, turned, and then vanished into the heavy sedge and bramble.

The buzzing stopped.

Slowly, the men of the recon unit straightened up.

'What the hell was that?' Caober asked.

'Some kind of call,' Kolosim said. 'Right, Mkoll? Some kind of call?'

Mkoll nodded. 'It reminded me of something,' Bonin said to him quietly.

'Yes, you too?' Mkoll asked, picking up his lasrifle and reloading it.

'It reminded me of the sound the glyfs made, back on Gereon.'

'That's what I thought,' Mkoll said. He turned back to the others.

'We have to find Burnstine,' Kolosim was saying.

'Burnstine? Burnstine?' Buckren began yelling.

'Shut up!' Mkoll spat. He looked at Bonin. 'Why would they call their monsters off, I wonder?'

Mkoll paused. He could smell it again. The smell of dry, soured blood that he had detected from higher up the slope. He had supposed the reek belonged to the stalkers, but now he knew different. The stalkers stank of sour-sweat, human meat.

This dry, blood smell was different.

Familiar.

'We need to move,' he said.

'What about Burnstine?' Kolosim asked. 'Dammit, Mkoll, what about Burnstine? And Darromay? We can't just leave the poor bastard's body there.'

'We can and we will. Forget him, captain, forget Burnstine. I'm not joking around here. I think the enemy's close. Very close. Just like we suspected.'

'What?'

'Let's go take a look, then get the word out if I'm right.'

'Without a vox?' Buckren said. The unit's caster had died with Darromay.

'We'll find a way,' Kolosim said. 'Do as Mkoll says.'

They clambered through the dense vegetation, heading north-east, cutting away fronds of strangling gorse that blocked them. Behind them, in the west, the first light of dawn was hazing in over the far wall, slowly turning the sky red.

'What's that?' Kolosim asked, coming to a halt, whispering.

'Machine noise,' Hwlan responded.

Clack-clack-clack the noise went, drifting through the vegetation. There were footsteps too. A lot of them, crunching and squishing on mud and grit. Kolosim waved the unit into cover. They dropped down, fast and obedient, skulking in behind tree boles and dense thorn, their weapons gripped ready.

Into view, into the realm of their lambent night vision, figures appeared, advancing through the tangled undergrowth of the basin, a column of men moving down from the northern ridge.

Men wearing dark grotesque masks. Men sporting the signs of the abominable and the forbidden.

Mkoll knew he had smelled that dry-blood aroma before. Too often before, in fact.

It was the stink of the Blood Pact.

From his vantage point, Mkoll estimated at least a hundred Blood Pact infantry, probably more. With them – *clack-clack-clack!* – came stalk-tanks, rattling along on their calliper legs, light and nimble enough to manage the steep terrain of the ridges.

Kolosim signalled the unit to stay low and silent. They didn't even dare dropping back.

Nice and quiet, let them go by, then slip away and–

'Captain? Captain? Respond, please…' Burnstine's anxious voice suddenly crackled over the intercom. Kolosim quickly muted his mic, but the damage was done.

One of the stalk-tanks shuddered to a halt, its body raised. The head turret tracked round until it was pointing towards the undergrowth where the scouts lay concealed. They could see the tank's operator, a surgically augmented human, prone in the fluid-filled blister cockpit under the tank's tail, making adjustments to his controls. The cannon mounts on the tank's head clattered as they autoloaded.

'Voi shet tahr grejj!' The command echoed out of the stalk-tank's external speakers. Immediately, two squads of Blood Pact troopers broke formation and began moving towards the scouts' hiding place, weapons ready. Almost at once, one of them spotted Buckren.

The warrior called out. As he raised his weapon to fire, a las-shot took him off his feet.

'Concealment's no longer an option,' said Mkoll, firing again and taking down two more troopers. 'Hit and run.' The rest of the recon unit joined in his gunfire.

In reply, the Blood Pact began shooting, blasting into the undergrowth with their rifles as las-bolts began to rip into their ranks.

And then the stalk-tank's cannons opened fire too.

SEVENTEEN

06.10 hrs, 197.776.M41
Fifth Compartment
Sparshad Mons, Ancreon Sextus

AT FIRST LIGHT, Wilder allowed himself a little, satisfied glow of content-
ment. The bulk of the Eighty-First First was still advancing across the
tableland scrub, but Hill 56 was less than a kilometre away, and Baskevyl's
company had already reached it. They were well ahead of schedule.

It was going to be a cold, grey start to the day. Mist still lingered in the
lowlands. Beyond the soft curve of Hill 56, the thumping drone of the tank
fight echoed like distant thunder. Occasional flashes lit the sky.

Wilder called up his vox-officer and got himself patched through to
Baskevyl. He walked along beside the vox-man, talking into the speaker
horn.

'Tell me what you've got, Bask.'

'...see some business...' Baskevyl's voice came back, chopped and sliced
by atmospherics. Sunrise did that sometimes, though this seemed worse
than usual.

'Say again, Bask. You're phasing on me.'

'I said I think we'll see some business this morning, sir. The Hill's secure.
I can see the Rothberg line, and I've had a brief connect to their commander. It's a hell of a tussle down there. The–'

'Repeat that last, over.'

'I said it's a hell of a tussle. The armour's holding, but from what I can see,
the enemy's throwing a lot this way. The Rothberg mob have brought the
Hauberkan in to support them now.'

'Are they behaving, over?'

A wash of static.

'Baskevyl? Baskevyl? Come back, B Company lead.'

'...me now? I repeat, are you hearing me now, Eighty leader?'

411

'Check on that, Bask. The air's bad today. I asked how the Hauberkan were doing.'

'According to the Rothberg commander, the Hauberkan have raised their game. I can see a line of their treads over to my north-west, guarding the trackway. Lot of smoke, lot of dense smoke. The trouble seems to be that the Rothberg have been at this for the best part of three days. The crews are dog-tired. A signal's gone to post command for more armour to relieve them. I understand some Sarpoy treads are due to join us around noon. That will be the critical time. The enemy may try to push for the advantage if they see the Rothbergers breaking off.'

'Understood,' Wilder replied. That would be when a picket line of well dug-in infantry would come into its own. Anticipating armour, both the Eighty-First First, and the Kolstec Fortieth behind them, had come loaded for a spot of tank-hunting. Every fireteam unit had been issued with at least one anti-tank launcher, devices which Wilder had learned the Tanith referred to as 'tread-fethers'. He consulted his chart again. They'd have to hold the hill and the adjacent trackways, and also the watercourse along the west side. Tread-fethers, crew-served weapons. They had about six hours to dig in effectively. That was doable.

'You still there, Eighty leader?'

'Reading you, Bask. I want you to start scoping the land there for good, defensible positions. I want a breaker line, you understand me? A breaker line to stop anything we don't like the look of.'

'Understood. I'm on it,' Baskevyl's voice crackled back. A 'breaker line' was Belladon shorthand for a defensive position constructed to maximise cross-fire support, so that every element was backed up by the enfilading cover-fire of its neighbour.

'Bask, any sign of foot advance?'

'Not at this time, sir, but like I said, dense smoke. Likelihood is they've got infantry massing in the wings to storm up once the tank fight's done.'

'You got the recon units there with you?'

'Two of them. Raydrel's unit's still over in the west, circling through the marshes. He checked in about ten minutes back and says there's zero chance of the enemy trying anything that way.'

'Like we supposed. What about Kolosim?'

'Negative on Ferdy, Eighty leader. Nothing from him since the routine check over an hour ago.'

'Understood. Get to work. I'll be with you in about twenty minutes. Eighty leader out.'

Wilder handed the speaker horn back to the vox-officer, who shrugged the harness of the heavy caster set on his back to make it sit more comfortably.

'Get Kolosim for me.'

'Yes, sir.'

Still walking, the vox-officer adjusted his earpiece and began to tune through the channels using the caster's secondary control panel, which was strapped around his left forearm. Wilder heard the man test-calling for Kolosim on the channels reserved for recon forces.

Wilder turned and looked east across the tableland towards the distant compartment wall. Beyond the dotted lines of his men trudging north, long-shadowed, through the broken scrub, the land fell away and became jagged and jutting along the steep rock ridges. The woodland was deep there, dark pockets still smoking with mist. Somewhere over in that direction, Ferdy Kolosim's recon unit was supposed to be cutting around west towards Hill 56.

Wilder tried to shake off the nagging feeling that had entered his head. It wasn't like Kolosim to miss a check, and he should have been on or near the hill by now.

'Nothing, sir,' the vox-officer reported. 'Zero return from the captain's designated channel.'

'Try the other bands. He may be having reception trouble.'

'I have, sir. Nothing. Post command says he voxed in just before five and reported his position as Ridge 18. He told them he was going to scout the next ridgeline before turning west.'

Wilder nodded. He scratched the corner of his cheekbone where two hours of wearing low light goggles had started to chafe.

'I want you to keep trying him, every five minutes.'

'Yes, sir.'

'Before that, get me the Kolstec commander. Then I'll want a general patch to our company leaders.'

'Yes, sir.'

The field commander of the Kolstec Fortieth was a man named Forwegg Fofobris. The Fortieth was a fine bunch of experienced heavy infantry, packing some serious crew-served support pieces, which would be useful come noon. However, Fofobris had come across as a bit of a blowhard to Wilder in the brief encounters they'd had. Baskevyl and Wilder had taken to referring to Fofobris as 'Foofoo Frigwig', which was a bad habit, because it was all to easy to slip and call a man by his nickname to his face. The pair of them had once developed the name 'Jonny Frigging Glareglasses' in reference to a archly posing Volpone officer they'd had to deal with on Khan III. When Wilder had called the man that by accident during a briefing, he'd been challenged to an honour duel.

He'd got out of it, thanks to Van Voytz. A formal apology and a case of amasec. Funny thing was, Baskevyl, who usually coined these derogatory terms, never slipped. It was always Wilder. Wilder wondered if Baskevyl had a nickname for him too.

Most probably.

Foofoo Frigwig came on the line. 'Wilder, is that you, sir?'

Wilder suddenly got a fit of the giggles. He remembered a moment in the post 36 billets, several nights earlier, when Gol Kolea and Ban Daur had introduced the Belladon officer cadre to the mysteries of home-brewed sacra. A Tanith tipple, evidently. One sip made you smile like a lovely bastard. It was during that little session that Baskevyl had come up with the name 'Foofoo Frigwig', adding that the 'foofirst class arsehole' was in command of the 'Kolstuck Foofortieth' fighting 'foofor the Golden fooFrigging Throne.'

Ah well, it had been foofrigging funny at the time, and such childish humour had a habit of sticking in places where it was no longer funny or appropriate. Unless you'd been there.

'Fofobris? This is Eighty leader.'

'What's the matter with this link, man? It sounds like you're giggling.'

Wilder covered the vox-horn and looked at the comms officer. 'Slap me real hard, Keshlan.'

'Sir?'

'Across the cheek. If you don't mind.'

'Sir… uh, what?'

Wilder shook his head. 'Never mind.' He looked out east towards the ridges and the thought of Kolosim straightened his face pretty quick.

'Sorry, Kolstec lead, the atmospherics here are bad. You're at our tail, I understand?'

'Affirmative, Eighty leader. Forty minutes from the hill at this time.'

Fooforty minutes. Really, still funny.

'The Rothberg are going to be pulling out around noon, Fofobris. By then, we're going to need to be providing serious ground cover. Are you good for that?'

'As soon as we're on site, Eighty leader.'

'That's good to hear, Kolstec lead. We're going to need tread-fethers and–'

'Say again?'

Throne, how easy to fall into slang. *I'm my own worst enemy*, Wilder thought. 'Anti-tank, Fofobris. A lot of it. Expect heavy shit. Patch to my number two, Baskevyl, on 751. He's scouting the terrain now. I want you placed as per his recommendations.'

'Not a problem. Understood, Eighty leader.'

Wilder handed back the horn to vox-officer Keshlan. 'Now the company leaders, please.'

Keshlan hooked him up, and Wilder briefed the officers of the Eighty-First First on the bare bones of the gig ahead.

All the while, he stared east.

Where are you, Ferdy, and what's the problem?

C COMPANY HAD reached the foot of Hill 56. 'Double time it, you slugs!' Kolea shouted. 'Up the slope now. You can rest when you're dead.'

The troopers began jogging up the scrubby incline.

Kolea turned, and saw Varl. Varl had stopped moving. He was standing on the slope, looking west, his hand to his left ear.

'Varl?'

It took a moment for Varl to look round. When he did, there was no hint of the man Gol Kolea had once known.

Varl adjusted his micro-bead plug. 'You hear that?'

'What?'

'It's clipping in and out. Through the static.'

Kolea shook his head. 'Atmospherics, Ceg. Just atmospherics. The weather's bad for that today. Solar radiation, or something.'

'No,' said Varl. 'It's the chief. He's in trouble.'

'Mkoll?'

Varl looked at him.

'You know, you're going to have to tell me some stories, sometime, Ceg,' Kolea began gently. 'I mean, you and me. We were friends once. And the Ceglan Varl I knew was the biggest blabbermouth storyteller I ever met. I'm beginning to think the Archenemy sent us back a copy that looks all right, but is actually–'

'That some kind of joke?' Varl growled. His eyes were suddenly hard.

'Gak, yes!' Kolea said, taking a step back, mortified. 'A joke, Varl. A fething joke. You remember them, right?'

Varl breathed deeply. A tiny smile crossed his face. 'Sorry, Gol. Sorry, man. It just seems like everyone I meet suspects me. Thinks I'm tainted, because I was there so long. I had the fething Inquisition on me, you know.'

'I know.'

'We all did. How fething right is that, after what we did? A tribunal? I served, for Throne's sake! I fething served!'

Kolea blanched. He held out his hand. 'Gak it, Ceg. What happened to you? What did they do to you on Gereon?'

Varl laughed. 'Nothing, Gol. *They* did nothing. I did it all to myself. Just to survive…'

Varl's voice trailed off. He looked at his old friend. 'Sometimes, you know…'

'What, Ceg?'

Varl shook his head. 'Nothing. It's just that sometimes I wish my old Ghost buddies had the first fething clue about what we had to deal with on Gereon.'

'So tell me. Then I will.'

Varl laughed again. It pained Kolea to see his old friend so conflicted. 'Tell you? There's nothing I can tell you. Gereon didn't make for anecdotes and war stories. Gereon was fething hell on a stick. Sometimes I want to scream. Sometimes I just want to cry my heart out.'

Kolea smiled. 'Either. Both. It'd just be between you and me.'

'You're a good man, Gol. How are the kids?'

'The what?'

'Tona told us all about it. You have to see your kids, Gol.'

Kolea turned away, bruised with anger. 'You better watch your lip, Varl.'

'All right. Whatever you say, poppa. Stings, does it? Close to home? I tell you what, Gol, Gereon's closer than that to me. To all of us that were lost. It fething hurts, it's so close.'

Varl looked east again. 'The chief. He's in trouble. I know it.'

* * *

CAPTAIN MERYN RAN back down the scrubline and summoned his troop leaders out of the advancing mass of E Company.

'Coming up on 56 now,' he told them as they huddled around him. 'Wilder wants us into a line, with close support to the front. Fargher, Kalen, Guheen, Harjeon, that means your teams. Into position, quick smart, and listen for Baskevyl's instructions.'

'Yes, sir,' they chorused.

Meryn paused and looked around. 'Where's Major Rawne?'

Guheen pointed back to a gaggle of figures down the slope.

'All right,' said Meryn, 'move it up. I'll be there in a minute or two.' He hurried back down the slope towards Rawne.

Rawne was standing with Feygor, Caffran and Beltayn. The vox-officer was fiddling with his set's dials.

'Is there a problem here?' Meryn demanded.

Rawne looked at Meryn as he approached them. 'I think so, captain.'

Throne, how Meryn hated the way Rawne said '*Captain*'.

'And it is?'

Beltayn looked up at Meryn, fiddling still with his caster dials. 'Something's awry.'

Meryn managed a smile. It had been a Throne-awful long time since he'd heard that refrain.

'Like what?' he asked.

'Mkoll's in trouble,' Feygor rasped, his voice issuing flat and bald out of his metal throat-box.

'How the feth can you know that?' Meryn asked. 'Come on, Tanith. We're meant to be setting in at the top of this fething hill and–'

'Mkoll's in trouble,' Rawne repeated. He stared at Meryn. 'Beltayn tells me so. How much more do you need?'

Meryn squared up to the major. 'I need to know,' he said, 'why you think that. I need to know the details. Don't push me around, sir, I still have command here.'

Rawne gestured towards Beltayn. 'I'm getting static shunts, pulse, three after one,' Beltayn said, adjusting his set.

'It's just the atmospherics,' Meryn said. 'Wilder just warned us about that. Solar radiation. It's just futzing the link.'

'No, sir,' Beltayn said. 'It's a signal.'

'Oh, come on now, please, we've–'

Meryn shut up quickly as Rawne grabbed him by the lapels. 'Listen to him, you little jumped-up fethwipe,' Rawne snarled. 'It's a signal we learned on Gereon.'

'What?'

'Pulse three after one. That was our signal for trouble. Back on Gereon, my young friend, we often didn't have full gain vox. We had to improvise. Pulsing static, shunting vox burps. Three after one was the signal for trouble.'

Meryn pulled himself away from Rawne. 'Is that true, Beltayn?' he asked.

'Yes, it's true,' the vox-officer replied.

'All right, all right,' Meryn said. 'Maybe I can spare a couple of troops to head east. Maybe.'

'Do it quick, or I'll tell Banda you let the chief hang out to dry,' Rawne said.

'You bastard.'

'Yeah, yeah, whatever.'

'It's coming again,' Beltayn called, working his set.

THREE PULSES, THEN ONE. It was hard to manage on the run. Mkoll had torn off his micro-bead and split the plastek casing open so that he could trigger the vox-send key manually. Finger and thumb.

Three, then one. Just the way they had done back on Gereon. Improvisation. It created a hell of a lot of interference, binding out the main vox-channels, but Mkoll knew it was worth it.

Three, then one.

The recon team scattered through the undergrowth of the basin. Buckren was already dead, and Hwlan had been hit so badly he was limping and falling behind.

Into the dense vegetation, the Blood Pact chasing them, weapons firing. Clinking and clanking, the stalk-tanks scurried in pursuit, their gun-mounts blasting into the thickets, spraying out leaves and charred bark.

Three, then one.

Three, then one.

'COLONEL WILDER?' VOX-OFFICER Keshlan said.

'Yes?'

'I'm getting reports, sir.'

'Of what?'

'I'm not sure, sir… Uh, it seems that C and E companies have turned east.'

'They've *what*?'

Keshlan shrugged. 'Like I said, I'm not sure, sir. They seem to have turned east, both of them.'

'They realise that they're supposed to be on that hill right now?' Wilder asked.

'Yes, sir. I've spoken to both Kolea and Meryn. They apologise. But they're heading east.'

Wilder held out his right hand and slapped the fingers against the palm repeatedly. 'Give me that vox-horn, mister. Give it to me right now.'

EIGHTEEN

06.59 hrs, 197.776.M41
Fifth Compartment
Sparshad Mons, Ancreon Sextus

THE RECON TEAM ran clear of the gloomy basin into the pale, misty daylight. The ground ahead was barren, a flinty slope of sedge and thin gorse. Blazing las-bolts followed them out of the thickets, whining in the cold air.

'Cover would be good,' Kolosim said, almost casually.

Mkoll pointed. Five hundred metres up the open slope, the land levelled slightly, and there were what appeared to be boulders or part of a wall.

'That'll do!' Kolosim agreed. They started running. Hwlan fell behind again, limping and stumbling. Mkoll tossed his rigged micro-bead to Bonin. 'Keep sending!' he ordered, and ran back to the wounded scout. Hwlan was a good deal taller and heavier than Mkoll, but the Tanith chief scout didn't hesitate. He stooped, grabbed Hwlan around one thigh with his left hand, and hoisted him up over his shoulders. Then he started running towards the promised cover.

'Ditch me...' Hwlan gasped.

'Shut up,' Mkoll grunted, taking quick, short steps, trying not to fall. Several powerful las-bolts hit the dirt nearby, coughing up powder ash and dust. A couple more hissed past.

Kolosim and Bonin had reached the litter of rocks. It proved to be the ruin of one of the Mons's curious house structures. This particular relic was beyond the hope of reconstruction: little more than a plan of the walls that had once stood there, sketched out in rubble amid the patchy grass. In places, enough of the walls remained for them to kneel behind. Kolosim and Bonin leapt the ragged stones and took position, firing back down the slope to cover the others. Maggs joined them, then Caober. Mkoll and his burden were still a little way back.

'Come on!' Kolosim yelled. 'Come on!'

The first of the pursuers had broken from the dense undergrowth behind them. At least a dozen Blood Pact troopers, their heavy kit and battle plating rattling as they ran up the slope, began firing their weapons from the hip.

'Pick 'em off!' Kolosim roared.

The four scouts in cover started blasting single shots. Las-bolts whickered up and down the slope, crosshatching the air. Caober hit one of the Blood Pact in the chest and walloped him heavily down on his back, then immediately hit a second of the enemy number in the head. The shot exploded the trooper's leering black iron mask and sent pieces of it spinning away as the man toppled onto his front. Kolosim got another, who fell down in a sitting position, clutching his throat, before he slumped over backwards. Maggs and Bonin managed to kill the same target.

'There's a waste,' said Maggs grimly, resighting and blasting again.

Bonin made no reply. He tapped another pulse on the micro-bead, then took up his weapon again and dropped two more of the enemy troopers.

Mkoll reached the ruin. Kolosim and Maggs threw down their rifles and grabbed him and Hwlan, hauling them in over the wall. Shots smacked into the stones.

Hwlan cried out in pain as he landed. He'd been shot in the right hip, and in the side of the torso just above it.

'I've got him!' Maggs yelled, his head low as he went to work. Kolosim and Mkoll joined Bonin and Caober at the wall, and started firing. A great deal more Blood Pact infantry had begun to spill out of the undergrowth behind the front runners. Three, four dozen, perhaps more. Some ran forward, others dropped to their knees, or onto their bellies, and started loosing aimed shots. Las-bolts filled the air like sleet.

Maggs yanked open one of his webbing pouches and pulled out his field kit, spilling paper-wrapped dressing wads onto the ground.

'Hold on, you hear me?' he murmured at Hwlan. Hwlan, on his back and going into hypovolaemic shock, nodded weakly, his face drawn and pale with pain.

Maggs ripped open the leg of Hwlan's fatigue trousers and loosened the scout's webbing belts. The wounds were messy. The flesh had burned and cauterised, the usual consequence of super-hot energy hits, but the concussive impact had ruptured the flesh and caused severe secondary bleeding. Hwlan's skin was sickly white and beginning to bruise. Maggs's hands became slick with blood.

'Hold on,' Maggs said again. 'Hwlan? Hwlan! Don't you grey out on me! Hwlan!'

'I'm here, I'm here!' Hwlan insisted, snapping back awake. 'Feth, Wes, it hurts.'

'No, really?' Maggs was washing the wounds with counterseptic gel. 'Come on, stay with me. Talk to me.'

'What about?'

'Tell me something. Anything. Tell me about your first time.'

'What, getting shot?'

'No, you dipstick. Your first time with a girl.' Maggs had packed adhesive dressing across both injuries, and was now using Hwlan's belt to tourniquet his leg around the groin.

'Hwlan?'

'What?'

'Your first girl.'

'Oh. Her name was Seba.'

'Sabre? Like a sword?'

'No. No. Seba. Feth, she was sweet. Oww!'

'Sorry. It's got to be tight.' Maggs wiped his hands on his jacket and pulled the cap off a single-use plastek syringe.

'Seba, eh? Was she any good?'

'I don't know. Yes. I was only sixteen. I didn't know what I was doing.'

Maggs stabbed the needle into the meat of Hwlan's thigh. 'Story of my life,' he said. 'Hwlan?'

'Uhn. Yeah.'

'The shot should take the edge off the pain, but you might get a little woozy. I've got another shot if you need it.' Each of them carried a field kit with two doses of painkiller, but the medicaes never advised using more than one at a time.

'I feel better already.'

'Good. I got to get to it now. You lie here and don't move.'

'Prop me up by the wall. I can fire my weapon.'

'Oh, be quiet. You a hero now, too? Shut up and lie there.'

Maggs crawled back to the wall. 'What did I miss?' he asked.

'Just another highlight of life in the poor fething Guard,' Caober said, snapping off shots.

Maggs looked down the slope at the distressingly large number of enemy troopers massing there. Between them, the scouts had killed more than twenty, littering the patchy soil with the jumbled bodies. But more than a hundred were now shooting their way up the slope towards the ruin. The density of las and hard rounds flying up at the scouts was frightening.

'How's Hwlan?' Mkoll asked, between shots.

'Stable,' Maggs replied. 'At this rate, he'll outlive us.'

An explosion just beyond the wall line tossed grit and soil into the air. The Blood Pact warriors were starting to hurl stick grenades, though they were falling short. Kolosim saw one Blood Pact trooper rise, arm back to throw, and put a las-round into his chest. The warrior fell, and a second later the four or five troopers around him were knocked flat by the blast of his grenade. Two more grenades dropped in front of the wall and flung dirt and flame up.

Bonin grunted as a las-round sawed across his right shoulder.

'Mach?' Caober called.

'I'm all right. Just scratched me,' Bonin replied, though in truth his shoulder throbbed like it had been struck by a red-hot sledgehammer.

Another shot, a hard slug, exploded part of the wall top and ricocheted off into Kolosim's face. He staggered backwards, blood pouring from his mouth. The deformed bullet had torn his upper lip and philtrum. Spitting out blood, he continued shooting.

'I don't like the sound of that,' Bonin said suddenly. Maggs cocked his head. 'No, me neither,' he agreed.

The first stalk-tank lumbered out of the undergrowth, trailing vines and brambles from its spidery legs. Behind it came a second one. The Blood Pact sent up a fierce cheer.

The sound of the cheer roused Hwlan from his stupor. 'Are we winning?' he asked.

Maggs and Caober laughed. Even Bonin cracked a grin.

'No,' said Mkoll sadly. 'I don't think we are, this time.'

Striding forward, the stalk-tanks began to fire.

'BASKEVYL!' WILDER SHOUTED into the vox. 'You've got command, you hear me?'

'Reading you, Eighty leader.'

'Form up the defence here and get this hill secure. Don't take any shit from anyone.'

'Understood. What's going on? Where are you?'

'No time to explain. Get on with it.'

Wilder tossed the speaker horn back to his vox-man. 'Follow me,' he ordered, and set off down the slope, heading east. 'And patch me to Meryn, Kolea or Rawne. Any of them. Immediately.'

'Yes, sir.'

The pair of them were running cross-country, against the tide of advancing men. 'Keep moving up the hill! Keep moving!' Wilder yelled at the troops as he pushed through. 'Novobazky!'

The commissar, marshalling squads near the foot of the hill, turned at the sound of his name.

'Yes, colonel.'

'Come with me.'

Novobazky hurried over and ran along with Wilder and Keshlan. 'What's going on?'

'In a nutshell, Rawne. We've got two companies breaking formation and heading east.'

'What? Why?'

'Like I said, I think this is Rawne's doing. Why the hell did he have to come back?'

'I wasn't going to mention it, sir, but he gave me some crap first thing this morning.'

'Then you've got my permission to shoot the bastard.'

The three of them were out in the empty scrub land now, pressing away from the Guardsmen deployed on the hillside. Wilder had to slow down to let the heavily-laden vox-man keep up.

'Major Rawne, sir,' Keshlan reported, panting. The three men stopped and Wilder took the horn.

'Rawne? This is Wilder. What the hell is going on?'

'We've got a situation, sir,' Rawne's voice came back. 'Contact from the missing recon unit. They've run into trouble.'

'What kind of trouble?'

'Can't say. The contact was non-verbal.'

'It was what?'

'Emergency pulse code, improvised. I know it's Mkoll. I know the code.'

'Rawne, I'm fit to choke you with your own genitals. What the hell happened to chain of command? Why in the name of the Golden Throne did you not run this by me?'

'No time, sir. This was priority.'

Wilder lowered the horn from his mouth for a second. 'That bastard's going to be the death of me,' he told Novobazky. 'I can just about imagine him pushing Meryn into this, but what the frig is up with Kolea? I thought that man was sound.'

'Old loyalties,' Novobazky said. 'This Mkoll, he's a pretty big deal to the Ghosts. Almost as big a deal as Gaunt, as I understand it.'

'And what am I? Dried rations? This is no way to run an army. I'll have them all up on charges. *You'll* have them all up on charges. Things are hard enough without these idiots...' He trailed off, shut his eyes, and cursed.

'Rawne?' he said, trying to inject a little calm and control into his voice as he raised the speaker horn again. 'Where are you?'

'Moving south-east of Hill 55, towards Ridge 19.'

'Find it,' Wilder told Novobazky, who pulled out his chart and began examining it.

'And where do you think the recon unit is?'

'Somewhere near the ridge. There's a lowland ahead. We can hear shooting. Heavy gunfire.'

'Rawne, I'm heading to join you. When you know anything for certain, tell me. And do not, repeat *do not* engage without my express permission. Wilder out.'

'Come on,' he said to Novobazky and the vox-officer. They had to run to keep pace with him.

RAWNE PASSED THE vox-horn back to Beltayn.

'What did he say?' Feygor asked.

'He's coming to join us,' Rawne said.

'What else did he say?' Meryn asked.

Rawne shrugged. 'I really don't remember. Atmospherics kept cutting him off.'

'You're lying,' Meryn said.

'Yes, but I outrank you, so live with it.'

They were moving as they talked. E Company was slogging double-time across the rough scrub. The body of C Company was about fifteen minutes behind them, to the north.

'Lot of shooting ahead,' Caffran called out. 'Down under the ridge, about half a kilometre. Serious exchanges.'

Rawne came to a halt. 'Give me a scope, someone.' One of the Belladon sergeants, Razele, handed Rawne a set of magnoculars. Rawne played them left and right.

'Feth,' he said. The swell of the land was obscuring much of the view, but Rawne could see a shroud of gun smoke leaking up into the sky, and serious back-flashes of las-fire. 'Caff wasn't kidding. Someone's started a little war down there in private.'

He handed the scope back. 'Line advance!' he shouted. 'Straight silver! Weapons live!'

There was an answering clatter as the company fixed their bayonets.

'I thought Wilder said we weren't to engage?' Meryn said.

'Meryn, if you know what he said, why the feth do you keep asking me?'

'Company ready, sir,' Feygor said.

'Let's get busy,' Rawne yelled. 'Company advance! For the Emperor and for Tanith!'

'What about Belladon?' Razele demanded.

'Screw Belladon,' Rawne told him. 'This is a family thing.'

THE DEVASTATING FIRE of the advancing stalk-tanks disintegrated another section of the ruined wall. Flame and stone debris showered into the sky. Crouching down, Mkoll, Kolosim and Bonin crawled back from what remained of the wall cover, still firing. Caober and Maggs dragged Hwlan between them.

A third stalk-tank had now emerged from the undergrowth. This one had an oversized head turret, like a deformity, and appeared to be armed with a plasma weapon or a multi-laser. With that in play, the game really would be done. Cheering and howling, the Blood Pact, now two hundred-strong, was on its feet, advancing at the pace of the rattling tanks. Two minutes, and they'd be at the wall.

'You're a piece of work,' Maggs said to Mkoll. 'I've known you about twenty-four hours and you get me into this shit.'

'Just think what I could do if I was really trying,' said Mkoll.

Another salvo hit the feeble barrier of stones, blowing a stretch of it onto them in a spray of stones and chipped fragments. Then the lead stalk-tank rose into view over the ruined wall, its gun-pod head lifted high on greasy hydraulics, smoke gusting from the exhaust vents of the heavy cannon.

There was a loud, sucking woosh of air and something screamed in low over the heads of the cowering scouts. It struck the stalk-tank squarely between the gimbal-joints of its front pair of legs and exploded. The entire forward section of the stalk-tank vaporised in a blinding orange blur. Concussive overpressure flattened the scouts into the soil.

Shrouded in smoke, coughing, they struggled back up.

'All right,' said Kolosim. 'Which of you jokers had a rocket launcher in his pocket all along?'

'Eighty-First First!' Maggs yelled out. 'Eighty-First First!' He was pointing back into the open country behind them.

'Holy feth,' said Caober.

The soldiers of E Company were yelling as they came charging in around either side of the house. The cry they made was incoherent, but the intent, the passion, unmistakable. Warriors of the Imperium, blood up, with the enemy in sight. The scouts saw the flash of fixed blades against the dark battledress of the running figures.

'Now that's a sight,' said Bonin.

THERE WOULD BE no time for finesse, Rawne realised. This was going to be a pitched battle in the antique sense of the word, infantry line against infantry line. There was no cover, no terrain for ranged fighting, and no room for flanking moves. Face to face, hand to hand, the way wars used to be fought.

E Company had the slope on their side. They poured over the rim of it, running towards the enemy, firing shots from weapons that they were brandishing like spears. The Blood Pact seemed to balk en masse, as if they could not quite understand what was happening. Those at the top of the slope froze in dismay, those further back hesitated because they couldn't see what was coming.

The lines struck with a visceral, crunching impact of bodies, helmets and battle-plating. The sounds of shooting, shouting and striking became frenetic.

Caffran and Guheen ran into the ruin with the scouts. Both were lugging launcher tubes. Dunik followed, carrying a drum of rockets.

'Welcome to my world,' Caober said to Guheen.

'That your handiwork?' Bonin asked Caffran, who was loading up another rocket.

Caffran glanced at the headless stalk-tank smouldering beyond the wall. 'Yes. Bit of a risk at the range I had, but I thought you'd appreciate the effort.'

Guheen had already shouldered his tread-fether and taken aim at the second tank. 'Ease!' he yelled. The men around him opened their mouths to help with the discomfort of the pressure punch. Guheen's tread-fether barked out a hot backwash of flame and spat a rocket into the shoulder of the second tank. It shook with the impact, badly damaged but still active.

'Load me!' Guheen shouted to Dunik.

Caffran was crouching by the wall with his own tube. 'Ease!' he warned, and fired. His streaking rocket hit the second tank and finished the work Guheen had begun. The main body section blew apart with huge force, probably helped by the detonation of the tank's own munitions, and dozens of the Blood Pact around it were roasted in the firewash.

'Aim for the third tank,' Mkoll told Caffran. The formidable plasma mount had opened up, slicing beam-energy mercilessly into the ranks of E Company. The air was suddenly ripe with the smell of cooked blood and bone.

Rockets squealed out from several points in the E Company spread. A Belladon trooper called Harwen scored the winning shot. The third tank went up, its oversized head spinning away, decapitated, still firing plasma beams wildly like a firecracker as it bounced amongst the Blood Pact lines.

Rawne and Feygor were right in the thick of it, lost in the punching, whirling, deafening violence of the fight. Rawne shot those he could shoot, and smashed his bayonet into those who were too close. The last proper action he'd seen had been back during the last days on Gereon, and he'd briefly forgotten the way killing had come to feel. This slaughter quickly reminded him.

Once, combat had been about pride and fury for Elim Rawne, the honest, hot-blooded endeavour of a fighting infantry man. Such a romantic notion, that seemed to him now. He recalled Gaunt and Colm Corbec debating the styles and types of combat, as if it came in different flavours or intensities, like love or sleep.

Today, his blood was cold, his pulse barely elevated. His blood was always cold. Gereon had done that to him. On Gereon, every single fight, from the full-blown open battles to the savage blade-brawls of infiltration missions, had been about survival, merciless survival, totally undressed of sentiment, honour or quarter. He'd learned to use everything, every opening, every advantage. He kicked, stabbed, crushed, stamped, bit and gouged; he ripped his straight silver into backs and sides and buttocks, he'd butchered men who had already fallen wounded, or who had turned to run.

Rawne had never been a particularly honourable man, but now his soul was cold and hollow, utterly devoid of honour or courage. Fighting had simply become a mechanical absolute; it no longer had degrees. Rawne either fought or did not fight, killed or did not kill. Combat's purpose had been reduced to a point where it was simply a way to ensure he was still alive when everything around him was dead. He had no use for caution, no use for fear.

Feygor, fighting at his commander's back, was much the same. Death was no longer something he feared. It was something he used, a gift he dished out to those that opposed him. Death was just a tool, an instrument. The only thing Murt Feygor was afraid of any more was being afraid.

Near to them, struggling in the melee, Meryn became aware of the sheer fury he was witnessing. It took his breath away to see the two men, so completely unchecked by fear. When Mkoll and Bonin broke through the scrum of bodies to lay in beside Rawne and his adjutant, Meryn faltered completely and backed away. He hated the Archenemy with a passion, but his own courage and intent seemed to leak away when he saw the Blood Pact broken apart by these daemons.

Daemons. *Daemons!* Not Ghosts at all. Not even human.

THE BLOOD PACT broke. Engulfed and overwhelmed, surprised by a foe it had not expected to meet, it scattered back towards the deep cover of the basin. E Company, enflamed by Rawne's brittle fury and example, gave chase.

Meryn limped back up towards the smoking stones of the house. He'd taken a gash in the knee somewhere along the line, he couldn't remember how. The ground was carpeted with bodies, the vast majority of them crimson-clad Blood Pact. Steam rose like mist. The air was clammy and smelled like a butcher's hall.

In the house ruin, and along the ridge beside it, E Company teams were setting up crew-served weapons. Leclan, the corpsman, was treating Hwlan. Maggs and Caober had vanished into the fight. Kolosim was sitting against a pile of stones, a dressing pressed to his torn mouth.

'What's the matter with you?'

Meryn glanced round. Banda had been using part of the stone wall as a sniper nest, but the enemy was out of range now.

'Nothing,' he said.

'Are you just going to let him do that?' she asked, stripping out her long-las to take a fresh barrel.

'Do what?'

'Just come in and take over. Last I heard, you were E Company's commander.'

Meryn sat down on part of a stalk-tank's buckled undercarriage. He tore off his helmet and threw it on the ground.

'It's Rawne,' he said.

'So what?' she asked.

'You think I could have done this?'

'You give the order, captain, E Company jumps,' Banda said.

He really wasn't enjoying her tone. 'Jessi,' he said, 'if it had been up to me, I wouldn't have even broken us east. Rawne recognised the signal, I didn't.'

'Wilder's going to be pissed.'

'I know.'

'You want Rawne to get E Company?' Banda asked.

'He'll be up on charges for this.'

'You think, Flyn?' she asked. 'You really think so?' Jessi Banda's face was unusually beautiful and expressive, but when she got angry, it became ugly and repellent to Meryn. 'Take a look, Flyn. Take a long look,' she said, gesturing down the body-littered slope towards the dark basin. E Company was near the line of undergrowth now, picking off the enemy troopers as they tried to escape.

'Rawne just picked up on a counter-offensive and squashed it flat. Wilder may have words with him, but that's a commendation in the eyes of high command. Maybe a pretty medal.'

'So what?'

'So you just stood there and let him do it,' she said, getting to her feet and slamming a fresh hot-shot pack home.

'Something's happening,' Kolosim said abruptly, rising to his feet.

'You're right. They're coming back,' Leclan agreed, getting up from beside Hwlan.

Meryn turned. Down the long slope, E Company was suddenly pulling back. Heavy fire was driving them into reverse out of the undergrowth. Plasma fire, lancing beams of blistering force.

Meryn realised he was smiling, despite the situation. Rawne had taken a big bite, and it had proved too big. The Blood Pact force Mkoll's scouts had alerted them too was a great deal bigger than they'd first imagined.

'Shit,' said Kolosim again, coming to stand beside Meryn. 'We thought it was a small strike brigade. They must have been pushing a whole frigging army along the east side.'

Meryn took a deep breath and reached for his dangling micro-bead. Now he could take charge and settle in a proper defence. Now he could make Rawne look like an impulsive idiot for–

'We heard there was a party. Are we too late?'

Meryn looked around. Gol Kolea calmly strolled up beside him. Behind him, C Company had fanned out in a wide line, covering the top of the slope. Support-weapon teams were assembling their pieces.

'Fix your silver,' Kolea called out, casually.

His words were answered by a clatter.

'Looking good, digger,' Banda called out to Kolea with a cheeky grin.

'I always look good, girl,' he called back. 'C Company! Get your act together. Let Rawne's people come back to us and then we'll get busy.'

Rawne's people. Meryn glared at Kolea.

'Come on, C Company!' Kolea was shouting. 'Let's get some torches up to the front.'

Brostin, Lyse, Mkella and a Belladon called Frontelle hurried forward out of the C Company line, their heavy flamer tanks clanking.

'I spy undergrowth,' Kolea said. 'It looks flammable to me. What do you say, Bros?'

Brostin smiled. The last stub of a lho-stick dangled from the corner of his mouth. He reeked of promethium, as if he'd been bathing in it.

'I say good morning flammable undergrowth, sir. Just say the word.'

'Heat 'em up,' Kolea said.

Brostin moved forward, trudging down the long slope. 'Line up on me, torches, wide spacing,' he called out. 'Fat-blue, wide-wash, keep it near the ground. And keep your pressure up.'

Lyse, Mkella and Frontelle came forward with him, adjusting their regulators. The stink of promethium jelly was now sharp and acute.

'Hey, Larks!' Brostin called out as he went forward. Larkin emerged from the C Company line, toting his long-las. The Belladon, Kaydey, came with him.

'Yeah?'

'Little airburst special?' Brostin said.

Larkin nodded. 'Whatever makes you happy.' He toggled off his long-las and shook out his shoulders, following the flame-troopers down the slope.

'What are we doing?' Kaydey asked him.

'I'm taking a shot,' Larkin said. 'You're watching and learning.'

'Hey, sniper,' Banda said as Larkin walked past her.

'Hey yourself, doll,' Larkin replied, smacking hands with her.

'Go do some hurt,' she called.

'I intend to,' Larkin replied, snuggling his long-las up into his shoulder as he walked forward, like a gamekeeper seating his shotgun.

E Company was coming back up the slope. It wasn't so much a retreat as a survival measure. Whatever was massing in the undergrowth behind them was angry and well-armed.

The C Company flamers, tooling down the slope in a wide spread formation, as if they were on a country walk, met the men of E coming back up. Rawne, spattered with blood, came up to Brostin.

'Good to see you,' he said.

'Trouble, major?' Brostin asked.

'The hostiles we just minced were only the forward section of something a lot bigger. They're right behind us and about to come calling.'

Brostin nodded. 'Fine. Mister Yellow is at home for visitors,' he replied. 'Got a smoke on you, boss?'

'Feygor?' Rawne called.

Feygor hurried over and pulled out a pack of lho-sticks. With the troops of E Company flooding past back towards the top of the slope, Feygor drew a stick out and posted it into Brostin's mouth.

Brostin lifted his flamer gun up and lit the stick off the blue pilot flame sizzling beside his weapon's regulator. Bubbles of promethium were dripping from his torch's hoses.

'Ah, yes,' Brostin said. 'That draws nice. A fine brand, Mister Feygor.'

'Only the best,' Feygor smiled.

Brostin exhaled. 'Flamers? Let's get this done.'

As the last tail-enders of E Company ran back past them, the flame-troopers plodded down the slope, spreading wider. The tanks on their backs were gurgling and sputtering, and their pilot flames hissing. Larkin, his gun half-raised, tailed them, Kaydey behind him.

Twenty metres from the edge of the undergrowth, Brostin brought his team to a halt. He took a flamboyant drag on his smoke and then flicked it away.

'Wait for a heartbeat,' he called out. 'Let's see their faces.'

Blood Pact troopers began to emerge from the edges of the undergrowth cover. They raised a cry, a howl. Weapons cracked and barked. Behind them, machine noise betrayed the approach of more stalk-tanks.

'All right,' said Brostin. 'That's enough faces. Cook 'em. Fat-blue, wide-wash, keep it near the ground. Let's do it.'

The four flame-troopers triggered their weapons and sent searing plumes of fire down the slope. Caught in the sudden inferno, the front line of the Blood Pact shrieked and staggered, enveloped. A moment later, the edges of the dried undergrowth caught too. A mess of flames boiled up the basin, storming and furious.

Brostin squeezed his flamer's paddle gently, nursing out gouts of liquid flame. 'Easy does it,' he urged.

The hem of the undergrowth was a blitz of fire now. Screams and shrieks rang out of the furnace. Several Blood Pact troopers emerged, stumbling, encased in fire.

'Now, that's real nice,' Brostin said.

Something big exploded in the undergrowth – a stalk-tank's munitions cooking off – and the fire spread.

Brostin shrugged off his flamer tanks and glanced at Larkin. 'Larks?' he said.

'I'm ready,' Larkin replied, raising his weapon. Brostin uncoupled his feeder tubes and dropped his gun.

'Wind it up,' Larkin said. He and Brostin had pulled the 'airburst special' more than once back on Gereon.

Brostin was a big, hulking man with a heavy upper body. He began to turn slowly, picking up speed as he rotated, like a hammer thrower. His flamer tanks were in his right hand, spinning out as a counter weight.

With a grunt of effort, he released them, and the heavy prom tanks flew up into the air over the basin undergrowth. Larkin tracked them, and, as they began to dip, he fired.

The hot-shot round smacked into the pressurised tanks and ignited them. A torrential rain of liquid fire fell across the basin and brought it up in searing flames.

'Holy crap,' Kaydey said.

Brostin turned away from the crackling heat of the firestorm in the basin. The screams and popping explosions drifted back with the smoke.

'Say hello to Mister Yellow,' he said.

A THICK BELT of black smoke was climbing into the sky when Wilder reached the scene of the battle. Keshlan sat down to catch his breath. Novobazky wandered in beside Wilder, gazing at the litter of the fight.

C and E Companies had taken up a heavy defensive position facing Ridge 19. A large portion of the lowland countryside was on fire.

'The God-Emperor protect us...' Wilder said, surveying the devastation. Kolea approached and threw a salute.

'I want full details, including casualties, later, Kolea. Right now, the short version.'

'Kolosim's recon party picked up hostiles in the woods thataway. E Company moved in and pretty much crushed them before we got here.'

'This would be the E Company that I ordered specifically not to engage without my permission?'

'I'm guessing yes, sir.'

'Go on, Kolea.'

'But the hostiles were just part of a much larger force.'

'How large?'

'Eight, nine hundred troops, maybe more, with stalk-tank support. The enemy was definitely out to mount a major offensive through the difficult terrain in the east compartment while our attention was on the tank fight.'

Wilder nodded. 'And you've held them?'

'Flamers did a lot of damage. Drove them back. We assume they're either in retreat, or they're waiting to come at us along the ridge there.'

Wilder looked around. 'Understand me, Kolea. You, Meryn, Rawne and I will be having a serious talk about this later. I know it's going to be hard for me to tear you off a strip when the results are this good, but believe me, this will be settled.'

'Yes, sir.'

'You stay in my command, you follow my orders, or I throw you to the commissars.'

'Yes, sir.'

Wilder walked over to Keshlan. 'Get me post command,' he said to the vox-man. 'We'd better tell DeBray that the enemy's just gone proactive on us.'

'Not just here, sir,' Keshlan said. 'From the reports coming in, the whole Mons has gone crazy.'

NINETEEN

THE SOUND OF gunship engines woke Gaunt from a curious dream. Dawn had come, grey and damp, and a cold wind flapped the seams of the habi-tent. Ludd was still sound asleep, but Eszrah was crouching in the flapway of the tent, looking out into the camp. There was a lot of activity out there. Trucks and transporters were revving, and men were shouting. Another squadron of Vulture gunships droned low overhead, snouts down, heading into the north-east and the bleak morning.

Gaunt stepped past Eszrah, who rose to follow him. Gaunt shook his head, and motioned that the Nihtgane should stay where he was.

He went outside into the billet area. Most of the habi-tents around had already been vacated. There really was a hell of a lot of activity going on. Gaunt pulled his shirt and vest off over his head and walked to the stand-pipe of the nearest service bowser. He cranked the pump handle, and sluiced out cold water to wash his armpits, his neck, and his face.

More attack ships went over, Valkyries this time. Gaunt stood upright and shook the water off his face like a dog as he watched the gunships slide past. Twenty of them, then another fan of at least thirty. Their combined engine noise was deafening.

Something about them, or about the cold, grey sky behind them, reminded Gaunt of his dream. He'd been in a room, a small, oblong room, with a door in each of the shorter walls. The room had been open to the sky, lacking a roof. Every time he'd looked up, he'd been able to see a vast stretch of wild heavens, deep and florid with banks of cloud that were ominously edged with a fiery russet.

In the dream, Gaunt had been aware of a deep compulsion to get out of the room. Some odd part of the dream's internal logic told him that if he

431

didn't leave the roofless room, he wouldn't be able to do any good. Any good at what, the dream wasn't particularly bothered to identify.

But every time he walked towards one of the doors, it was no longer there. The doors wouldn't stay put. He'd move towards a door, and suddenly it would be in another wall.

For a few weeks on Gereon, early on, he'd been plagued by a recurring dream where he'd been stuck in a stone chamber that had no doors or windows. It had bothered him deeply, scared him, back at a time when he still could be scared. The claustrophobia, the sense of imprisonment, had lingered on him each morning, long after he'd woken. Ana Curth had told him it was simply an anxiety dream, a nightmare about being trapped on Gereon. After a few weeks, it had passed.

This new dream didn't scare him, but it left him with an unsettled sensation that fed uncomfortably into his current troubles.

Gaunt was pulling his vest and shirt back on when Ludd appeared, bleary-eyed.

'What's going on, sir?' he asked.

'I don't know. Something big. I'll go and see Sautoy. I have to report to him, after all.'

They'd arrived back late the previous night after their bloody encounter on the road. Ironmeadow had wanted to file a full report at once, but Gaunt had told him to get some sleep. He'd assured the captain he'd make his damning report about post 15 in the morning.

'I'll come with you,' Ludd said.

'No. Stay here and get some caffeine brewed. We both need some. I'll be back soon.'

GAUNT PUT ON his coat and cap, and headed down the truckway to post command. There was activity all around. Young troopers, their faces pale and anxious, were boarding transporters or loading munitions onto cargoes and armoured cars. A line of Chimeras grumbled past. The sky was overcast and grim, and there was a real wind picking up. It was hard to tell, but Gaunt was sure he could hear heavy, booming blasts echoing from far away.

Post command was busy. The place was heaving with officers and tacticae advisors, message runners and technicians. Briefings were underway in some of the side chambers, and a constant flow of shouted updates rang from the bustling vox station.

Gaunt pushed inside. There was a smell of fear. Stale sweat, morning breath, the ugly odour of men who had been living in the field and now had been roused early, unwillingly, to face a cold, unfriendly day. Faces were pinched, troubled, unwelcoming. The younger men in particular looked like a slow horror was dawning on them.

Sautoy was in the station command room. He looked harried and bothered. The start of his day had evidently been so brusque that he hadn't even had time to pin his handsome collection of medals to his purple coat. Officers had gathered around his chart table, and Sautoy was throwing orders and directives left and right as he sorted through an increasing pile of status forms and message papers that the runners were bringing in from the vox-station.

'Gaunt!' he called as he saw the commissar in the doorway. No false bonhomie this morning. 'Come in. I just sent Ironmeadow to find you.'

'I must have crossed him on the way,' Gaunt said. 'It's busy out there.'

Gaunt stepped inside and took off his cap. Half a dozen of the junior officers around the marshal's chart table hurried out to get on with their orders. The others remained, bent over the table in a serious huddle, conferring and pointing out various details on the underlit map image.

'I wanted to file a report, sir,' Gaunt began. 'My visit to post 15 yesterday. Serious code violations led me to–'

Sautoy held up his hand. 'I know all about it, Gaunt. Ironmeadow came to see me last night.'

'I see.'

'He was shaken, Gaunt. Understandably. What you found there was vile.'

'Symptomatic of an underlying–'

'It's academic now, anyway, Gaunt.'

'Why, sir?'

'Because a total crap-storm broke about two hours ago, Gaunt. Post 15's gone. Twelve's maybe about to fall too. The Archenemy has decided, this morning, to mount a full scale counter-offensive.'

He led Gaunt over to the chart table. It took Gaunt very little time to make sense of the markers and deployments on display.

'Significant enemy forces struck through compartments seven and nine just before first light,' Sautoy said anyway. 'They stormed out of the ninth compartment and overran post 15. Our forces there abandoned the site rather hastily. They've also pushed us entirely out of the seventh compartment. We're currently throwing everything we've got into this compartment to try and establish some resistance in the lowland sector here, behind post 12. Trouble is, as it stands, post 12 is pretty much cut off and taking the brunt of both advances. We've had no contact with them for thirty-eight minutes.'

Sautoy beckoned Gaunt away from the junior officers and lowered his voice. 'We've not seen anything on this scale since we first chased the bastards into this step-city. It's barely credible that they've got such resources built up in here. Our boys are rattled. Seriously rattled, and on the back foot. There's a real danger we could get pushed right back out of the third compartment unless we rally soon.'

A vox-officer came in, saluted Sautoy and gave him a message wafer. Sautoy's face darkened as he read it. 'Throne above,' he whispered, and handed the slip to Gaunt. Post 36 in the fifth compartment was reporting a major enemy offensive too.

Gaunt sighed. He'd had a plan that morning. He'd intended, one way or another, to find a way of persuading Sautoy to allow him to transfer to fifth compartment operations. It was a long shot, and Sautoy was certainly no ally.

Gaunt had already debated with himself at least a dozen possible excuses or reasons for the transfer, none of them satisfactory. He'd even considered contacting Van Voytz and going over Sautoy's head. But now this had happened, and everything, as Sautoy had remarked, was academic. There was no point even asking.

Gaunt did, anyway.

'I'd like to request permission to transfer to the fifth compartment, sir,' he said.

Sautoy blinked. 'Out of the question, man. Why would you even ask that?'

Gaunt paused. In the light of the current situation, he quickly decided which of his excuses sounded the most plausible. 'My old outfit, the Tanith First, is up in the Fifth, sir. If this is as bad as it sounds, I'd like to be with them and try–'

Sautoy shook his head. 'Admirable, Gaunt. Very admirable. Loyal. I like that. It's why I've always liked you. But the answer's still no. I need you here, for Throne's sake. I need you right here, you and every experienced cadre officer I've got. I want you forward in the line as soon as possible. Intelligence says the greener regiments, especially those falling back from 15, are in total disarray. We have to rally these young men, and that'll take veterans like yourself.'

'I understand, sir.'

'Get into the field and start whipping those boys back into shape. Get them forming up a proper line of resistance. I'll be sending all the officers I can forward to help get the situation under control.'

'Will… you be joining us, sir?' Gaunt asked.

Sautoy stared at him. 'Damn you, Gaunt. Of course I will. Now get about it.'

Gaunt saluted. 'My apologies, marshal. I intended no slight.' He turned for the door, then looked back at Sautoy. 'Why today, sir?'

'What?'

'Why is this happening today, I wonder?'

'I have no idea, Gaunt!' Sautoy snapped.

'Then you might want to relay that question back to Frag Flats Command and get the tacticae advisors thinking about it. Historically, ritually, there may be a reason the Archenemy is stirring in such force this morning.'

GAUNT LEFT THE command room. Instead of heading outside, he pushed through the men hurrying to and fro along the internal corridor and entered the vox room. Twenty-five vox-officers worked at independent high-gain sets, all of them speaking at the same time as reports came in and went out.

Gaunt wandered to the nearest one. The operator, a small man with a pencil moustache, looked up and took off his heavy earphones.

'Commissar, can I help you?'

'I need you to patch me a link, operator,' Gaunt said.

'On what authority?' the officer asked.

'On the authority I'm wearing, soldier,' Gaunt said. The operator swallowed. 'Yes, sir. Sorry, sir.' Gaunt told him the comm-code he required. The operator tuned it in. He didn't look entirely comfortable.

'This is… non-standard, commissar,' he said as he adjusted the dials. 'It will have to be recorded in my day-book.'

'You do what you have to do,' Gaunt said. 'By all means note it was a direct order from the Commissariat.'

'I have contact, sir,' the operator reported. He indicated a spare set of headphones on the desk, and keyed the channel through as Gaunt put them on.

'Unit receiving,' said a voice on the line, cut by static. 'Identify sender, over.'

'This is One. That you, Beltayn, over?'

A pause. 'Yes. Yes, it is, sir. Didn't expect to hear your voice, over.'

'Sorry I don't have time to catch up, Bel,' Gaunt said. 'I need to talk to Rawne or Mkoll. That possible, over?'

'Stand by, over.' Gaunt waited, listening. Burbles and fluting wails of distortion echoed over the channel.

'This is Rawne. That you, Ibram, over?'

'Affirmative. What's the situation, over?'

'A fair mess, Bram. Hell in a handcart. Where are you, over?'

'Not as close as I'd like to be, Eli. Listen up. I've got very little time to explain this to you, but I need you and Mkoll working on something, over.'

'Copy that. We're a little busy right now, but go ahead, over.'

'All right. Listen to this, and tell me what you think…'

ONCE HE'D FINISHED the brief conversation, Gaunt handed the phones back to the vox-man, thanked him, and left the command post. The operator, a little bemused, wrote up the track in his day-book, and was about to resume his work when another voice said, 'May I see that, operator?'

The operator looked up and saw a second commissar standing by his caster set. What *was* this?

'Your day-book, please,' the second commissar said. The operator handed it to him. 'This was a confirmed patch?'

'Yes, sir.'

'Authority?'

'The commissar's own, sir. He said it was Commissariat business.'

'And this is authenticated? The code?'

'Yes, sir. A field vox-caster. Ident 11012K. That's with the Eighty-First First.'

'Patch me to Commissariat command, Frag Flats. Immediately, please. Use this code.' The commissar wrote a numeric serial down on the vox-man's message pad.

'Channel open,' the vox-officer announced a moment later.

The commissar picked up the speaker set. 'Command, this is Ludd. Put me through to Commissar-General Balshin.'

* * *

GAUNT RETURNED TO his billet.

'Where's Ludd?' he asked Eszrah. The Nihtgane shrugged.

'Get your stuff together,' Gaunt told him. 'We'll be leaving shortly.'

The wind was quite strong now. There seemed to be spots of rain in it. Gaunt touched his cheek where he'd felt the droplets land. Rain? The sky was a mass of crinkled grey cloud above the towering walls.

Ludd appeared, hurrying down the track between the habi-tents. Empty, they stood on either side of him like an honour guard, their door flaps rippling like cloaks in the rising air.

'Where did you go?' Gaunt asked him.

'I went looking for you, sir,' Ludd said.

'I told you to stay here, Ludd.'

'Yes, sir. I know. But Ironmeadow came by just after you'd left. He had transport placings for us. We're to move up because–'

'I know, Ludd. Where is he?'

'Waiting with our transportation, sir. So I came looking for you. I thought you'd want to know.'

Gaunt looked at him. Ludd seemed a little more tense than usual, but then this day was doing that to everyone. 'Where did you look, Ludd?'

'Oh, in the command station. Around there. One of the Binar officers said they'd seen you heading back this way.'

Gaunt held Ludd's gaze a little longer. 'All right, Ludd. Grab your things.'

They took only their weapons and basic field kit. Eszrah zipped the rest of their kit up in the habi-tent, and then hurried after Gaunt and Ludd.

The main assembly yards were packed with transports filing out along the east trackway. Most of the transports were carrying men dressed in the beige battledress of the Fortis Binars.

Ironmeadow waved them over to a pair of Salamander command vehicles, both of which had been newly painted in Binar livery.

'Sir!' Ironmeadow said, saluting and handing over a message wafer. 'The marshal asked me to find you and–'

'Old news, Ironmeadow, I've spoken with him.' Gaunt read the paper slip. It was a brief, curt order-tag requiring Gaunt to advance with the Second Binars into the hotzone, and 'accomplish the maintenance of decent battlefield morale and discipline.'

Gaunt handed the wafer to Ludd. 'Keep that for me, Ludd. If I get a chance later I may want to choke Sautoy with it.'

'You and your sense of humour, sir,' Ironmeadow laughed.

'Did you think I was joking, Ironmeadow?' Gaunt asked. Ironmeadow half-laughed again, then blinked. Gaunt could tell how desperately scared the young officer was. He remembered how little combat experience Ironmeadow had – how little anyone of his regiment had. Sautoy was sending novice, frightened boys up country to assist novice, frightened boys. On top of that, Ironmeadow was most likely still very rattled by the events of the previous day.

Just for a moment, Gaunt reminded himself who and what they all thought he was. 'Things will be fine, Ironmeadow,' he said. 'Our spirits may be tested today, but if we keep our faith in the Throne and remember our training, we will prevail.'

'Yes, sir,' Ironmeadow nodded.

'Make it known that I regard it as a privilege to be advancing alongside the men of the Second Fortis Binars.'

That actually got a flush of pride into Ironmeadow's face. 'Thank you, sir. I will.'

One of the open-topped Salamanders had been reserved for Gaunt, with a driver, gunner and vox-operator assigned. The other belonged to Major Jernon Whitesmith, Ironmeadow's direct superior. He was a slender, craggy man in his fifties, with receding hair, and the look of a veteran about him.

'PDF?' Gaunt asked him as he was introduced. Whitesmith smiled, as if impressed that Gaunt should notice. 'Yes, sir. It was my honour to serve in the liberation war.'

In founding their regiments to assist the Crusade, the people of Fortis Binary had selected some of their planetary defence force veterans to serve as line officers. That was something at least, Gaunt mused. It would be the experience and steadiness of the few older men like Whitesmith that would keep the rookie companies together.

There was no time for further conversation. Whitesmith climbed into his Salamander and set off down the truckway, the vehicle's heavy track sections clattering. Gaunt, Ludd and Eszrah followed Ironmeadow aboard the second machine, and rattled off after him, the light tanks skirting swiftly around the column of slow-moving troop trucks on the road. Heavier tanks and armour pieces formed the bulk of the column's front portion, including Trojan tractor units tugging heavy field artillery.

The inky grey storm clouds were firmly settled above the compartment, leaching most of the daylight away. Again, Gaunt felt the cold spits of rain in the air. It was so overcast that many vehicles had activated their head-lamps and running lights.

'Damned weather!' Ironmeadow said, raising his voice over the roar of the Salamander's engines. 'It's getting as black as night out here!'

He's right, Gaunt thought. As black as night. Then he wondered if anyone in high command or the senior staff had considered just how *literally* nocturnal the stalkers were.

LESS THAN AN hour later, powering north-east into the middle lowlands of the third compartment, they met hell coming the other way.

It was an astonishing sight. The scrubby, shelving landscape that Gaunt and Ludd had driven up through the previous day was masked with wind-driven smoke-banks, great tidal waves of choking black soot and ash that billowed off firestorms raging across the central compartment. From wall to wall, it seemed that the whole landscape was ablaze, except where it was broken by the lakes and deep ponds, stretches of water that now flashed back the reflected flame-light like mirrors. There were men and machines moving everywhere, not just on the trackways. Thousands of Guardsmen and a ramshackle multitude of vehicles were crawling back across country, chased by the firestorms.

As the Salamander slowed, Ludd got to his feet and stared out over the cabin top. He'd never seen anything like it.

The column was bunching up ahead. The relief forces from post 10 were coming up against the exodus from the north. There was panic and confusion. Over the Salamander's vox-caster, Gaunt could hear frantic chatter. Calls for help, calls for clarification, calls for orders. He knew the sound only too well. It was the sound of defeat. It was the terrible sound the Imperial Guard made when it fell apart.

'Post 12?' he asked the Salamander's vox operator. The man shook his head.

'Sir!' Ludd called out sharply. Gaunt joined him at the front of the Salamander's compartment and took up a scope. The ragged edge of the firestorms lay about three kilometres in front of them, and through it, the first enemy units had just emerged. Tanks, some churning fire, scrub and earth ahead of them with massive dozer blades; self-propelled guns, lurching out of the smoke; platoons of troops in rebreathers. Gaunt could see the flash of shells landing amongst the fleeing Imperial forces. He saw the bright surge-fires of the flamer weapons the Blood Pact was using to drive all before it. A quick estimate put the number of enemy vehicles at three hundred plus, and that was just what he could see. There was no telling the infantry strength.

'Throne, this is awful,' Ludd said.

'Nothing gets by you, eh, Nahum?' Gaunt replied. He jumped down from the Salamander and hurried on up the track on foot to the brow of the hill. There, Whitesmith stood in conference with some of his senior unit officers.

'Situation?' Gaunt asked.

'We've just had an unconfirmed report that Colonel Stonewright has been killed.' Stonewright was the Second Binar's commanding officer, who had led the support forces in an hour in front of them. Whitesmith's orders had been to move in to support him.

'That puts you in charge, Whitesmith,' Gaunt said. 'These men are waiting for your orders.'

Whitesmith straightened himself up, as if he'd only just realised that. 'Yes, commissar, of course.' He paused. 'I've called in for more air cover.'

'That's good. That's about the only advantage we have right now.'

Whitesmith gestured to his left. 'The bulk of our armour is down that way, though Throne knows it's hardly deployed properly. Beyond it, towards that lake, I think we've got auxiliary light armour, the Dev Hetra 301, but I've no idea what shape they're in.'

'Other side?' Gaunt asked, glancing south.

'The bulk of our infantry, and two columns of Sarpoy armour. See for yourself, though. It's a shambles.'

Whitesmith looked at Gaunt. 'I can't raise Marshal Sautoy. I can't even get a clean patch through to the Sarpoy or Dev Hetra commanders. And I'm afraid I can tell for a fact that my boys are close to breaking. They've had no experience of this. Line discipline has gone and–'

'Line discipline is my job, Major Whitesmith. Stop worrying whether the men will do as you tell them, and start worrying about what it is you're actually going to order them to do.'

Whitesmith shook his head. 'I believe I have two options on that score, sir. The first is to hand command to you.'

'Whitesmith, I'm a commissar, not a command officer. It's my place to advise, muster control and make sure orders are followed. It's not in my remit to decide strategy.'

Deep, rolling booms echoed in across the lowland floodplain. The enemy tanks were shelling with more fervour. 'With respect, Gaunt,' Whitesmith said soberly, 'you were a line officer and a commander for a long time. A successful, decorated commander. You've had a damn sight more experience of front-line engagement than me or any of my staff, and you've lived to carry that wisdom forward. For pity's sake, sir, I hardly think this is a moment to stick to some feeble rule of authority. Are you honestly going to stand by and watch while I struggle and lead these young men into a shambolic disaster?'

'No, major. In my capacity as an agent of the Imperial Commissariat, I am going to support you in the implementation of your command decisions. You were given your rank for a reason. You are an officer and a leader of men, and your training should tell you what to do under these circumstances.'

Whitesmith smiled sadly. 'Then there's the second option, commissar. My forces are in disarray. The enemy's right upon us. I must order an immediate retreat in order to salvage what lives and materiel I can.'

'What about a third option, major?' Gaunt said.

'Dammit, there is no–'

'There's always another option, Whitesmith!' Gaunt snapped. 'Think of one! You were kind enough to remember I was once a successful commander in war. Do you think for a moment those successes came easily? That I never had to wrack my brains and think beyond the obvious? Tell me, quickly, what would you do if this was more to your liking?'

'What?'

'Ignore the immediate problems. Imagine you've got the Jantine Patricians here under your command, or a phalanx of Cadian Kasrkin. Battle-hardened veterans, ready and eager for your orders. What would those orders be, Whitesmith?'

'I'd…' Whitesmith began. 'I'd order them to hold this ridge line, and the open fen down to the lake there. That would give us the best defensive file.'

'Good. Go on.'

'I'd spread the infantry out, right along the line, and swing two squadrons of armour up over the ridge onto the right flank. I'd deploy artillery in the low land behind us and start shelling the enemy before they got any closer. And I'd make damn sure the Dev Hetra and Sarpoy understood that I needed their firm support.'

Gaunt smiled and smacked the Binar on the shoulder. 'That sounds like a plan to me, sir.'

'But–'

'Call up your officers. Finesse that plan for five minutes, get it solid and workable, make sure everyone knows what they're supposed to be doing.'

'Where will you be?' Whitesmith asked.

'Holding up my side of the bargain,' Gaunt replied, 'by making sure your orders are followed when they come.'

Gaunt hurried back down the dirt track to Ludd and Ironmeadow. Eszrah lurked behind them, gazing dubiously at the creeping curtain of fire and smoke approaching like doomsday across the scrubby landscape.

'Ironmeadow,' Gaunt said. 'Your services as a liaison are no longer required.'

'Sir?'

'Look about you, man. Whitesmith needs every officer he can get. Go to him, listen to him, obey him. You've got rank there, Ironmeadow. Use it. Give an example to your men and they will follow you. Whitesmith's counting on you.'

'Yes, sir!' Ironmeadow said.

'I know you're young and this is new to you, Ironmeadow, but I have faith. You faced down a stalker last night and lived to tell the tale.'

'Only because you saved my bloody life, sir,' Ironmeadow groaned.

'It doesn't matter. You've looked death in the eyes, and survived. That's more than any of these young men can say. That makes you special, tempered, like any good officer or fine piece of steel. It almost makes you a veteran. Strength of character, Captain Ironmeadow.'

Ironmeadow smiled.

'Tell every Binar you meet that Ibram Gaunt is with them, and Ibram Gaunt expects to be honoured by the company he keeps. And Ironmeadow?'

'Yes, sir?'

'I expect to read your name in despatches tomorrow, you hear me?'

'Yes, sir!' Ironmeadow replied, and ran up the slope to where Whitesmith was convening his officers.

'Ludd?' Gaunt said, turning to his junior. 'I want you to go find every commissar on this hillside and get them assembled here in the next ten minutes.'

'Sir?'

'The Binars have at least three, Ludd. Find them for me.'

Ludd hesitated. The sound of shelling was rolling ever closer. There were dark strands of smoke in the wind.

'What are you waiting for?'

'Nothing, sir. I'm on it.' Ludd hurried away.

With Eszrah at his heels, tall and ominous, Gaunt crossed the trackway to the left and hurried down a slope of patchy grass onto a muddy strand beside a long pool. Almost a hundred Binar troopers were gathered there, gazing at the oncoming horror. Behind them, several Binar treads had come to a halt, bottled up.

'You men!' Gaunt yelled. Some of them turned and straightened up at the sight of an approaching commissar.

'What the hell are you doing?' Gaunt demanded, splashing closer. There were a few, miserable answering grunts. Gaunt leapt up onto a limestone boulder at the edge of the pool so that they could all see him.

'You see the emblem on my cap?' he cried out. 'Commissariat, that's right! You know what that means, don't you? It means bully! It means discipline master! It means the lash of the God-Emperor, driving you cowards to a miserable end! Let me show you something else...'

He drew a bolt pistol in one fist, his power sword in the other, and held them both up so that the crowd of men could see. 'Tools of my trade! They kill the enemy, they kill cowards! Either one, they're not fussy! Now listen to this...'

Gaunt dropped his voice, made it softer, but still injected the well-practiced projection qualities he had honed over the years, so that they could all still hear him. 'You want to run, don't you? You want to run right now. You want to get out of here. Get to safety. Throne, I know you all do.' He sheathed his sword and reholstered his gun. 'I could wave those about some more. I could tell you, and Throne knows I wouldn't be lying, that whatever it is coming this way in that wall of smoke is nothing compared to my wrath. I could tell you I'm the thing to be frightened of.'

He jumped down off the boulder and walked in amongst them. Some of the men backed away. 'If you want to run, men of Fortis Binary, then go ahead. Run. You might outrun the Archenemy, bearing down on us now. Feth, you might even outrun me. But you will never, ever outrun your conscience. Your world suffered under the yoke of the Ruinous Powers for a long time. You're only here today, as free men of the Imperium, because others did not run. Your fathers and uncles and brothers, and young men, just like you, Imperial Guardsmen from a hundred scattered worlds, who had the courage to stand and fight. For your world. For Fortis Binary. I know this because I was there. So, run, if you dare. If you can live with it. If you can face the dreams, and the pangs of conscience. If you can even bear to think of the fathers and uncles and brothers you lost.'

He paused. There was a strained silence, broken only by the booming sound of the shelling behind him.

'Alternatively, you can stay here, and follow Major Whitesmith's orders, and fight like men. You can stay, and honour the memory of your fathers, and your uncles and your brothers. You can stay and stand with me, for the Imperium, for the God-Emperor. And for Fortis Binary.'

Gaunt walked back to the boulder he had vacated and climbed back onto it. 'What do you say?' he asked.

The men cheered approval. It was hearty, and just what Gaunt had been looking for. He smiled and raised a fist. 'Squad leaders form up! Get this trackway cleared so the treads can roll through! Unit commanders! Where are you? Come on! Get yourselves up onto the trackway so Whitesmith can brief you! Support weapons, through to the front and get set up! Let's move!'

The men started moving. Gaunt jumped down. He turned to Eszrah. 'Come on,' he urged.

They splashed across the edges of the pool, onto the far slope and ran towards the next gaggle of Binars, milling purposelessly on the adjacent ridge top. The men there had seen the activity below, heard the sudden cheer, and stood bewildered.

'Histye, soule!' Eszrah called.

'What?' Gaunt looked back over his shoulder, still running.

'Preyathee, wherein wastye maden so?'

'Blood,' said Gaunt simply. 'My blood. My father.'

Eszrah nodded, and followed Gaunt up the slope. The Binars crowded there spread back from the commissar. Gaunt hurried to a parked Chimera and clambered up the access rungs onto its roof. He stood there for a moment, looking down at the huddled men. So young, all of them. So scared.

'Sons of Fortis Binary,' he began, 'I'll keep this simple. I'll tell you what I just told your comrades down in the vale…'

It was almost fifteen minutes before Gaunt and Eszrah returned to the trackway. The enemy line, indeed the firestorm itself, was much closer. The forward edge of the Binar formation was now less than a kilometre from the advance, and the rain of shells from the Blood Pact armour had begun to find range. Binar and Sarpoy tanks started to open up in reply. From behind the Binars' forward position, the artillery commenced barrage firing, lofting shells over into the Blood Pact lines.

Gaunt checked in with Whitesmith. The man was pale with tension, but also enervated. 'I've lined them all out,' he told Gaunt. 'And the armour's all but deployed. Some slackness from the infantry. Most of them are still scared. It's the ones in flight, you see.'

By then, the exodus of troops and machines fleeing before the invasion had begun to trickle through the reinforcement line. The sight of them, and the stories they were bringing with them, were steadily eroding resolve.

'Tell your officers to let them come through,' Gaunt said. 'Don't oppose them. They're running anyway, nothing's going to change that. Let them through and ignore them.'

'That an order, sir?' Whitesmith smiled.

'No,' Gaunt smiled back. 'Just an informed suggestion. It's going to get bad in the next half-hour or so, major. I won't lie. Keep the line, and trust your men. The Emperor protects.'

Whitesmith saluted Gaunt and ran back to his Salamander. Shells were now whistling down and impacting on the lower slope of the rise where the track fell away. Gaunt hurried back down the roadway to Ludd.

Ludd had assembled five commissars. An elderly senior attached to the Sarpoy called Blunshen, two of the primary Binar commissars – Fenwik and Saffonol – and two young juniors.

'Gentlemen,' Gaunt said as he came up to them.

'The state is parlous,' Blunshen said at once. 'With such woeful measure of resolve, and such feeble unit connection, we must supervise an immediate fall-back and–'

'Blunshen, is it?' Gaunt asked.

'Yes, commissar.'

'Chain of command places Major Whitesmith in charge of this action. I am Major Whitesmith's commissar, and so that gives me authority here. Do you agree?'

'I suppose so,' said the old commissar.

'Good. No more talk of retreat. From anyone, especially someone wearing that badge. Marshal Sautoy's last orders to me were to accomplish the maintenance of decent battlefield morale and discipline along this line. That's right, isn't it, Ludd?'

'To the letter, sir.'

'Good,' said Gaunt. 'There will be no falling back. Not on my watch. Whitesmith has devised a scheme of resistance. Are you all familiar with it?'

'I made sure the major's orders were circulated,' Ludd said.

'The Archenemy has us on the ropes here,' Gaunt said. 'They must not be allowed to prevail. If we break now – or fall back, Commissar Blunshen – then the third compartment will be forfeit. Do you know what that means?'

'A severe setback to our advance into the Mons structure–' Blunshen began.

'No, Blunshen, It means Lord General Van Voytz will be angry. I happen to know him, and I do not want to be on the receiving end of that anger. The seven of us will make the difference between success and failure today. The Guardsmen here are well-armed, well-trained, and capable. The only thing they lack is discipline. They're scared. It's up to us to enforce the control they need. It's up to us to make sure Whitesmith's entirely workable strategy pays off. The Guard needs inspiration and motivation, gentlemen. Few though we are, we have to accomplish that. Blunshen, I'd like you to return to your Sarpoy units and make sure they hold the right flank. A great deal depends on their crossfire and support. Explain to them if you have to, that the Fortis Binars in the middle width of the line will be slaughtered if they don't maintain fire-rate.'

Blunshen nodded. 'I'll see to it at once.'

Gaunt turned to the others. 'What's your name? Fenwik? And you? Saffonol? Good to meet you. Whitesmith has drawn his armour line out across this ridge, and laced the infantry in between it. We have to hold that echelon stable. Fenwik, go south. Maintain firing discipline there, keep the tanks shooting. Range is all we have. Saffonol, head forward, take charge of the units at the head of the rise. Do not, and I emphasise, do not, allow the troop units to charge and lose the advantage of gradient. Use your crew-served support weapons.'

Both men nodded.

'You juniors, step up. What are your names?'

'Kanfreid, sir.'

'Junior Loboskin.'

'Move to the rear, sirs. We won't survive this without the artillery support, and artillery units have a habit of getting edgy and pulling out because they're too far away from the visible line to understand what's happening. Assure them everything's fine. Dissuade them from leaving. How you do that I leave up to you. Just keep your cool, and keep the rate up. Even if we break, we'll need the field guns to cover us. They must keep firing. In the event of a rout, they can ditch their cannon and run at the last minute.'

'Yes, sir,' the young men echoed.

'Get on with it!' Gaunt cried with a clap of his hands. The commissars hurried away. Gaunt turned to Ludd.

'I'm intending to cover the northern flank of the Binars,' Gaunt said. 'I need you to press on further north and link up with the Dev Hetra units. I need you to keep them solid.'

Ludd paused. 'Sir,' he began.

'What is it, Ludd?'

'Sir… I'm not supposed to leave you. I mean, my orders are that I should stay with you at all times.'

Gaunt glared at him. 'Throne's sake, Ludd! Feth, I'd forgotten you didn't actually take orders from me.'

Ludd pulled back, stung. 'That's not fair, sir. Not at all.'

'Really? You're Balshin's spy. You never denied that. You're my… what is it? Minder? That was all fine when this was just a game, but it's not a game any more, Ludd. You see what's going on out there? You see what's coming?'

'Yes, sir. Yes, I do.'

'Then show some wit, Ludd,' Gaunt snarled. 'Us commissars have got to spread thin, to maximise our effect. Are you really telling me that Mamzel Balshin's orders are so intractable you're going to stick with me like a bad smell instead of getting the job done?'

'No, sir.'

'Louder so it means something, Ludd.'

'No, sir!'

'Find the Dev Hetra, Ludd. Get them into formation. This is war now, lad. Not politics. Not games.'

'Yes, sir.'

'Get on with you. You're an Imperial commissar, Ludd. Act like one. And if Balshin chews your ear, send her to me.'

'Yes, sir,' Ludd shouted, scrambling down the wet, grassy bank.

'Ludd?' Gaunt called after him.

'Sir?'

'Don't die, all right?'

'No, sir.'

IT WOULD TAKE a two kilometre dash, cross-country, to reach the Dev Hetra 301. Ludd ran as fast as he could, stumbling through the loose, plashy mires of the lowland belt. He crossed behind the drawn-up retinues of the Binar

infantry, behind the hasty dug-outs where they had secured their infantry
support weapons. He dodged through lines of battle tanks, squirming
through the mud to their deployment positions.

By some miracle, he realised, Gaunt and Whitesmith were bringing the
Binar line together. It was strong and it was firm. Men were singing battle-
songs that had last rung out over the field of war between the ruined
refineries of Fortis Binary. Behind the Guard front line, a kilometre south-
west, artillery positions were thumping shells into the air with maintained
vigour.

Shells sang back. The enemy was dreadfully close. That roiling belt of
smoke and flame. Huge explosions ripped into the Guard line, hurling bodies into the air, rupturing tanks. The Blood Pact was at the door and their
assault was slicing mercilessly into the ranged forces of the Emperor.

Ludd ran on, slipped, and righted himself. A shell dropped just behind
the next rise and lifted a huge column of water, fire and mud into the air.
Drenched by it, Ludd sprinted forward. There was a buzzing sound, which
got louder, and then much louder still. A wave of Vultures flocked overhead,
fifty or more machines, wrenching off rocket fire into the closing enemy
line. A long, snickering wildfire of overlapping explosions crackled along
the target spread. The Vultures peeled away. A second wave went in, another
fifty or so. Ludd could hear their rocket pods banging like snare drums, and
their autocannons grinding like whetstones. Less than half a kilometre away,
he saw Blood Pact AT70s disintegrate in twitchy puffs of smoke and fragmenting metal.

Las-fire from the advancing enemy infantry started to kiss into the Imperial lines.

Ludd reached the upland above the Dev Hetra position. Something hit
the ground behind him, and turned the whole world into fire.

GAUNT DREW HIS powersword and ignited it. In his right hand, he clutched one
of his paired bolt pistols. The sky was as black as a coal-star now, and thick
smoke billowed in from the ends of creation. All along the line beside him,
Fortis Binar officers blew whistles and demanded order. Gaunt could hear
mumbled prayers and frightened moans addressed to mothers and loved
ones. Shells wailed down. Gritty blasts tore the air and quaked the earth.

'Men of Fortis Binar, stand firm!' he yelled.

It was no use now. They couldn't really hear him.

The first of the Blood pact AT70's were in view. Gaunt could hear the distinctive whistle-whoop of their main weapons discharging. He saw figures
in crimson battledress massing forward alongside the tanks, running in
through the smoke towards the raised ground where the Imperials had chosen to meet them. He saw the black masks, grotesques, like faces frozen in
agony, the glint of bayonets.

'Rise and address!' he yelled. Whistles blew in answer. The young, virgin
troopers of the Second Fortis Binars stepped up to meet the onrushing tide
of the Blood Pact.

Gaunt leapt over the ledge of the hastily dug slit-trench and greeted the enemy head on. Binar troops either side of him buckled and died under sudden, hailing gunfire.

Gaunt's blade cleanly decapitated the first Blood Pact trooper to reach him. The second and third fell victim to his booming bolt pistol.

Mayhem descended. Bodies clashing in the smoke, blood flecking the air. Gaunt fired his bolt pistol at point-blank range, right into the chest of a charging Blood Pact soldier. He leapt over the fallen body and fired again, knocking another of the Archenemy host onto his back. Figures rushed in around him: the Binar boys, yelling, firing, stabbing with their bayonets.

'For the Throne!' Gaunt bellowed. Two rifle rounds punched through his coat. Gaunt twisted round and shot a Pact trooper to his left, hurling the man into the air in a tangle of limbs. The sloping ground was treacherous. He found himself sliding into a scrum of enemy troopers that was trying to scale the muddy bank. Gaunt stroked left and right with his power blade, sliced off a trooper's arm at the shoulder, took out the throat of another. A third fell over in the mire in his frantic effort to dodge the slashing blade.

A Blood Pact officer, barking orders and curses, ploughed up the low bank and assaulted Gaunt with a keening chainsword. Gaunt deflected the first stroke with his power blade, and then was driven backwards, knocking aside the demented, hacking cuts that swung at him.

'Bastard!' he yelled, throwing the force of his arm into a ripping cross-cut that caught the chainsword halfway down its length and buckled it. As the enemy officer attempted to defend with the broken weapon, Gaunt sliced back in a reprise, and the tip of his blade found the side of the warrior's face. The officer recoiled and fell, blood pouring from his head, his silver grotesque hanging off to one side.

Guardsmen in the charging line dropped and sprawled as las-shots streaked across the mud and hit them. Shells detonated with huge, sucking roars. Explosions plumed like geysers across the miasmal fen.

Gaunt strode on. He buried his blade into the helmet of a Blood Pact trooper, wrenched it free, and shot another, who was wading in with his bayonet. A hard round skimmed his right shoulder and knocked him down for a second.

Strong hands grabbed him. Gaunt looked up and found Eszrah Night dragging him back to his feet. The partisan had streaked his face with wode, a ritual symbol of his intention to make war.

'I told you to stay back!' Gaunt yelled over the din. Eszrah put a hand to his ear as if to sign he couldn't hear. The Nihtgane turned and aimed his reynbow. The electromag weapon spat out a quarrel that dropped a nearby enemy trooper. Eszrah reached into his satchel and loaded another barb, sliding it down the reynbow's tube. The partisan weapon fired the iron darts with such force that they would easily kill a man if they hit squarely, but the fact they were tipped with powerful Untill venom meant that even a scratch was lethal.

Eszrah fired again. What little sound the reynbow made was lost entirely in the roar of battle. Another Blood Pact trooper collapsed, an iron quarrel jutting from an eye slit.

Gaunt picked up his fallen sword and resumed his advance. Almost immediately, he lost contact with Eszrah as the smoke swirled in. There were stalk-tanks ahead, trotting through the filthy air, hosing laser fire from their gun-pods. Gaunt saw one of them blow out as a rocket struck it. The flash was so bright, it left an afterimage on his retina.

Another wave of vile figures emerged from the hellish smoke. Blood running from his shoulder wound, Gaunt urged the Binar infantrymen into them. Bodies slammed together along the course of the ditch, clubbing and stabbing.

Gaunt broke free, breathing hard. His clip out, he holstered the pistol and dragged out its twin. He looked around for the next enemy to kill. Nearby, three Vanquisher tanks lurched and splattered forward, their hulls bouncing. The support weapons on the tanks chattered, licking out brilliant tongues of ignited gas. Several dozen enemy troopers fell back before the approaching tanks.

Beams of light lanced through the smoke wall ahead of them. Gaunt saw one of the tanks simply disintegrate in front of him.

Churning out of the vapour, clearing a path for the Archenemy advance, the stumble-guns had arrived.

TWENTY

10.29 hrs, 197.776.M41
Third Compartment
Sparshad Mons, Ancreon Sextus

WHEN HE WAS a boy, Nahum Ludd had been particularly taken with the frescoes on the ceiling of the scholam chapel. He'd loved all pictures of war, and pored over old books and military texts, but the frescoes had been special. The domed ceiling had been a wide, cloudy blue, an imitation sky through which Imperial angels of war had flown on golden wings, swords aloft. With them, depicted in that quaint, slightly primitive style of old murals, there had been gunships and strike fighters, the hosts of the air, radiant and mighty.

He opened his eyes, and thought for a moment that he was still a boy, still in the old chapel. The roof above him, swollen with white cloud, full of gunships and angels.

His hearing returned like a hammer blow. Ludd sat up quickly. He'd been lying on his back in the muddy grass. A blast had knocked him down, he remembered that now. He was numb and cold, but there seemed to be no obvious signs of injury.

Ludd looked around. Overhead, Vulture gunships were making approach passes, chasing low and hunting for surface targets. To the east, the vast horror of the battle spread out against the encroaching black cloud. It was turmoil. Ludd took a moment to accept the scale of it, the blinding flash and blast of the shelling, the stink of mud and fyceline, the juddering buffet of overpressure.

Individual figures were almost too small for him to make out, but he saw dark, sparking lumps that were evidently tanks engaging as they thundered into the lowland belt. He saw the fiery breath of flamers, the strafing blizzards of autolaser fire in the sky, detonations of extraordinary violence. In the thick of the fighting, he could make out obscene banners and battle standards, waving aloft, mocking the sanctity of the Emperor and the purity of man. He saw rockets fly like sparks from a bonfire.

A bonfire. That's what it looked like: a gigantic, blazing bonfire, filling the entire compartment, crackling with sparks and embers, lashing with tongues of yellow flame, choking out the sky to the east with a mountainous block of charcoal smoke.

He realised that this was finally it. This was war. He'd yearned for it, trained for it, prepared for it, and worked hard to earn a place for himself in the ranks of the Imperium so he could pursue it. This, ridiculously, was what he had been searching for all his life. This madness, this chaos, this calamity.

It had no sense or shape, no structure or meaning. It was simply a maelstrom of hurt and damage, a sundering whirlpool laced with fire and blood and splintering metal. It was as if Ludd had been let in on some giant, private joke. Men trained for war, rehearsed, honed skills, solemnly studied military teachings, as if warfare was something that could be learned and controlled and conducted, like a formal banquet or a great country dance. But here was the raw truth of it. All theories of combat perished immediately in the furnace heat of real war.

How foolish lord generals seemed, plotting in their back rooms and command cells, dreaming up principles and schemes of battle. They might as well be trying to govern and contain a supernova.

Ludd had almost forgotten why he had been running north, or what it was Gaunt had demanded of him. Surely he could serve no purpose now? The frenzy of war was feeding itself, fire into fire. It just *was*, and no man could alter that.

Ludd wondered where Gaunt was. He tried his micro-bead, but there was nothing except sizzling distortion. Gaunt had to be somewhere down there, in the jaws of the beast.

And probably dead by now. Could anything human survive in that horror?

He wondered where to go, what to do. Binar tanks and infantry groups were advancing past him on the flanks of the ridge. He could see where the foremost sections were entering the battle, riding forward into the fierce gunfire. Shells were slamming into the fenland, and showering water up from the long, wide lakes.

On the far side of the ridge lay the Dev Hetra positions. Over two hundred units, most of them Hydra and multi-laser mobiles, along with some bulky Thunderer siege tanks and heavy Basilisk platforms. There was very little fire coming from them.

Ludd began to head down the slope towards the light support line. There was an abrupt bang overhead, as if the vault of heaven had finally split. Ludd looked up, and watched in helpless awe as a Vulture gunship fell out of the air, trailing ochre smoke. Sub-assemblies disintegrated off it as it dropped. It hit the fenland short of the main line and tumbled over and over, ripping apart, leaking fire.

Ludd turned and ran on into the Dev Hetra position. Motors were running, and gun-crews were stacking munitions and power-chargers. The Dev Hetra machines were of the finest quality, and polished like they'd just rolled out of the forge silos. The uniforms the men wore were almost regal in their decoration: dress white with gold braiding, with gleaming silver crest-helmets for the officers, and black fur shakoes for the rank and file. They looked like the ceremonial escort detail of a sector governor. Ludd had never seen such resplendent troops.

'Who's in charge here?' Ludd shouted. His voice was hoarse from the smoke. The men, magnificent in their regalia, looked at him archly, as if he was some filthy low-life blundering uninvited into their midst. 'I said who's in charge here, dammit?'

The men around still didn't answer. They continued to regard him with what appeared to be utter disdain. No, he thought, they're just dazed, frightened. That was it. Despite their finery, the soldiers here, all of them young, all of them no doubt first-timers and fresh recruits, were simply too shocked by the spectacle of the battle to form any coherent reply. Ludd knew how that felt. He swallowed hard, tried to clear his throat a little and put some authority into his words.

'Who's in charge?'

A sergeant came forward. He wore a blue sash and carried a silver power-sabre. He bowed curtly.

'Who may I say is asking?'

'Ludd. Commissar Ludd.'

'Do you not have a hat, sir?' the man enquired.

Ludd realised his cap had come off somewhere, probably when he'd been knocked down. He tried to stroke back his hair, and felt it was caked with mud. His coat was torn and smeared with drying dirt. He realised his first instinct had been correct. The haughty Dev Hetra had chosen to ignore him because of his dishevelled appearance.

'No, I don't have a hat! I've also not got much patience! Get me a ranking officer! Now, if you please!'

The sergeant bowed again, and led Ludd over to a gun platform where a very young officer, a captain, was working a vox-caster set. The sergeant had a few quiet words with the captain. The captain put down the vox-horn, and turned to face Ludd. His white uniform was frogged up the tunic front with gold braid, and his high peaked cap was a sumptuous affair of silverwork and yet more braiding. He wore a mantle of black fur around one shoulder, secured by a golden clasp.

'Are you really a commissar?' he asked. He was handsome, in a fey, high-born way, his slightly-slanted eyes disapproving.

'I fell down,' said Ludd.

The captain looked Ludd up and down. 'Did you? How unfortunate.'

'Who am I addressing?' Ludd asked.

'Captain Sire Balthus Vuyder Kronn.' The young man was very softly spoken, and his accent betrayed fine breeding. Ludd remembered his briefing. The Hetrahan came from a highly structured world ruled by an aristocratic elite. They appointed officers by merit of birth and breeding.

'Why aren't you engaged, Kronn?' Ludd asked.

'I would prefer it if you used my full nomenclature when addressing me,' the captain said, and began to turn away.

'I would prefer you answered my frigging question, Kronn,' Ludd said. 'Why isn't this unit engaged?'

Ludd might as well have slapped him by the look on Kronn's face. 'At this time,' Kronn said, 'it has been deemed inappropriate for us to engage.'

'Really? By whom?'

'My commander, Colonel Sire Sazman Vuyder Urfanus.'

'Well, I'd better have a word with him, then.'

'He has gone. He has already quit the field. I have been given charge of the withdrawal of the war machines.'

'He's gone? Your commanding officer has left you here?'

Kronn raised his eyebrows. 'Of course. There is some jeopardy here. Sire Vuyder Urfanus is a high-born man, first cousin to the Hzeppar of Korida himself. His security takes precedence.'

Ludd began to laugh. He couldn't help it. The sheer insanity of it all had got to him. Behind him, the amoral, elemental fury of war was loose, defying comprehension and logic. In front of him, stood men hidebound by tradition and breeding, who were packing away for the day like their garden party had been rained off.

'I do not like the way you laugh,' Kronn said. 'It is uncivil.'

'I don't much like anything about anything at the moment,' Ludd replied. 'Look, you were given orders.'

'The communication systems are inoperative,' Kronn said, gesturing to the vox.

'You were sent orders. By runner. Orders from the Fortis Binar commander.'

'The orders were garbled, and the runner refused to address Sire Vuyder Urfanus with a correct measure of formality. Sire Vuyder Urfanus will only respect orders given to him by the marshal.'

'Listen to me carefully, *captain sire*,' Ludd said. 'If he survives today, Sire Vuyder Urfanus will find himself in deep trouble with the Commissariat. This will be because he has disobeyed orders. Most likely, he will be shot without trial.'

Kronn began to speak, outrage in his face.

'Continue with your intent to retreat now, and you... and all your fellow officers... will suffer the same, ignoble fate. If that doesn't appeal, get your arses in gear, and start doing what you're supposed to be doing.'

'You are uncouth,' Kronn announced. He unbuttoned his leather glove and smacked Ludd round the face with it. Then he threw the glove on the grass.

'You have grossly offended my honour, the honour of my sire, and the honour of Hetrahan. I will be pleased to settle this matter in a bout of merit at your convenience.'

'Did you...' Ludd paused as he fought to get his head around it. 'Did you just challenge me to a duel?' he asked, rubbing his smarting face.

'Are you such a base thing you do not know common manners? Of course I did. By the Code Duello, we will–'

Ludd punched Kronn in the face and broke his nose. The young captain staggered back a few steps and fell down against the tracks of the weapon platform.

'Duel's over.' said Ludd. 'You did say it would be at my convenience. That was a good time for me. Now, get the hell on!'

Kronn looked up at Ludd. There were tears in his eyes, but that was probably just pain.

'Throne's sake!' Ludd cried. 'How far have you and your men come to be here, Kronn? How many frigging light years have you travelled? Your war machines are shiny and new, your uniforms pressed and clean. What are these, gold buttons? You come all this way, dress up in your finest, get to the front line... and then just decide to go home again without firing a shot?'

'It was deemed inappropriate–' Kronn gasped. He paused, and swallowed. Ludd realised the tears were real. For all his bluster, the captain was embarrassingly young, just a precocious child. Kronn looked up at Ludd, and his voice became thin and piteous. 'Look at it out there! Look at it! It's simply madness! Just blind madness! Tell me you do not think so!'

'No,' Ludd lied. He dragged Kronn to his feet, and jerked him round to face the calamitous battle. 'Break now, and you simply postpone your deaths. Break now, the line breaks, the line breaks, the city falls, the city falls...'

He looked at Kronn. '...the city falls, the world falls. Death and glory, Kronn. Or cut down running away. What does your breeding tell you a man should choose?'

Kronn wiped the blood from his face. His hand was shaking. 'I am afraid,' he said, simply.

'So am I,' said Ludd. 'And there'd be something wrong with us if we weren't. But it's worth remembering that the Imperium of Man, which has endured these thousands of years, was forged by men who were afraid, yet who faced down the daemons anyway.'

He let go of Kronn, bent down, and picked up the captain's fallen cap. It was heavy with gold thread and finely-worked bands of silver. He dusted it off and handed it to Kronn. 'Let's begin again, Captain Sire Vuyder Kronn.'

Kronn turned to the men who had gathered nearby. 'We will engage, Sergeant Janvier. Make ready.'

'Yes, captain sire!'

'Crews to your platforms! Load munitions! Connect power cells!'

Ludd followed Kronn back to his command vehicle, a gleaming super-Hydra with twin quad turrets. Standing before the machine, Kronn paused and looked back at Ludd. 'What do we do, commissar?'

'The line's left us behind a little. I suggest you move forward in formation about five hundred metres, maybe a touch more. We have to seal up this side of the line. More importantly, we have to start hitting the enemy sections.

You may not have a large complement of treads, sir, but your Hydras and multi-laser carriages pack a serious fire rate. We need to lay down a blanket of sustained firepower across that stretch there.' Ludd pointed. 'Carve into them, and maybe even split up their spearhead phalanx.'

Kronn nodded and clambered up onto the footplate. 'I would appreciate your advice as we progress,' Kronn said. 'As you so easily detected, this unit is new to war. We are... novices. We have never seen anything like this. We would benefit from your experience in these things.'

Ludd was startled for a second. 'My experience?'

'Whatever it is that allows you to remain so calm, so centred. Assist me, please, commissar. I'm sure you can sympathise with our situation. You must remember your own first taste of battle.'

Ludd climbed up onto the riding board. 'As a matter of fact, I do,' he said. 'You never forget your first time.'

STUMBLE-GUNS WERE virtually spherical frames of plated steel, three metres in diameter. The muzzles of plasma-beam cannons jutted out from their carcasses like the spines of a sea-urchin. They rolled and bounced across the field of war, heavy and relentless, propelled by some kind of inertial drive, spilling out random beams of destructive energy.

Gaunt had never seen one in the flesh, but he'd heard far too many reports of their devastating effect in other conflicts. They were like murderous playthings, gewgaws rolled out of the Archenemy's toy-box, blitzing out slaughter wherever they bounced.

Phalanxes of cult troopers followed the tumbling advance of the stumble-guns. The cultists were heavily armoured in black plate, and brandished flamers to scour the ground wracked by the ball-weapons. The cultists also carried heavy censers, bearing them along like litters. The censers were vomiting out the dark, black cloud that marked the Archenemy advance, sheeting up swirling cover that amplified the smoke of the firestorms.

'Hold fast! Form a line here!' Gaunt yelled

Some of the Binars obeyed. Others broke. The lead stumble-gun rolled in across a line position, massacring men with its lancing blasts, crushing others under its metal frame. Gaunt saw men die. Too many men.

The stumble-guns weren't solid. Well armoured and heavily plated, as well as being wrapped in rusty razor wire, they were still frameworks. Gaunt glimpsed the operators inside the balls, supported in stabilized, gyro-mounted cockpits that remained upright against the turn of the ball-cages around them.

They made a terrible sound as they advanced: a clanking, rattling noise overlaid by the screech and whine of the sputtering weapons.

Gaunt turned to shout another rallying cry, and a plasma beam destroyed the ground beneath him. He fell, squirming, into the mud, into a jagged furrow where the ground water steamed, super-heated.

Explosions burst overhead. Gaunt clambered up from the furrow, drenched in muck. He saw a stumble-gun buffet past, and ducked as more plasma beams speared his way. The Binar line had broken back. Men were running. Some caught fire and fell as the randomly lancing beams touched them. Others were cut in half, or decapitated, by direct hits. A direct plasma beam, especially the crude, stream-blasts of a stumble-gun, severed a human body quite thoroughly. A bright beam ripped along an entire platoon of fleeing men, and their torsos left their legs behind. Gaunt saw a Fortis colour sergeant trying to struggle out of a ditch. A beam touched him, bright as the sun, and the man fell in two directions, bisected vertically down the length of his spine.

Gaunt got up, and began to run back towards the broken Binar formation. Men were milling around him, running. A Binar Vanquisher stormed forward over the ditches, and hit one of the stumble-guns squarely with a shot from its turret weapon. The stumble-gun rocked back, over and over, like a kicked ball, and then began to rotate towards the tank again. It squealed and fired.

The tank's armour caved in like wet paper and it began to burn.

'Hold fast!' Gaunt yelled.

'They're killing us!' a man protested.

'So kill them back!' Gaunt shouted.

But how? The line had crumpled. All the precious gains they had made in the first few minutes of the battle were slipping away. How did you even begin to kill machines like that?

Gaunt found himself wishing he had Larkin with him. The grizzled marksman would have had the wit and ability to put a round in through the stumble-gun cages and kill the operators, at least.

But the Ghosts weren't with him any more, nor would they ever be again. He was surrounded by frightened youths, who were fleeing and soiling themselves in the face of death.

And he couldn't blame them.

'Someone give me a grenade!' he yelled.

The nearest stumble-gun suddenly stopped firing, and rolled to a halt. Gaunt ran towards it, expecting at every step to be incinerated. He approached the smoking ball. Even from a few metres away, through the frame and plating, he could see that the operator was dead, bent over in his cradle.

An iron dart transfixed the operator's throat.

'Eszrah! Eszrah!' Gaunt yelled.

The tall, slender figure of the Nihtgane appeared, bounding towards Gaunt across the mud. He reloaded his reynbow.

'Hwat seythee, soule?'

'You did that?'

Eszrah plucked his fingers from his mouth again. The Nihtgane's kiss of soul-taking.

'Do it again, if you please.'

He might not have Hlaine Larkin, but he had the hunter skills of an Untill's partisan.

Gaunt and Eszrah ran towards the next stumble-gun. It had rolled past them into the soft footing of the fen. Men were running before it. A few of the Binar troops had taken cover behind some scorched boulders.

'You! What's your name?' Gaunt yelled.

'Sergeant Tintile, sir. Georg Tintile.'

'Good to know you,' Gaunt said as he ran up to the man. 'My name is Gaunt.'

'We all know who you are, sir,' Tintile said.

'I'm flattered. Listen to me, sergeant. Our line's broken, but the day's not lost. I want you to send a runner to Whitesmith and tell him you're advancing.'

'Why, sir?'

'Because you are advancing. The stumble-guns are terror weapons. See for yourself, they've already burst through our ranks. The enemy believes that when that happens, we'll break like fools. Prove them wrong. Advance. Hit those bastards coming in.'

'But the stumble-guns, sir...' Tintile began.

'Leave them to me. Do this for me, please, Tintile. The Emperor protects.'

'Yes, sir.'

'Do you have grenades, Tintile?'

The sergeant handed his last two hand-bombs to Gaunt.

'Good luck, sir,' he said.

Tintile rallied his men and continued to advance. Piecemeal at first, then more urgently. The rattled and broken structure of the Binar line re-formed and pushed ahead again.

Gaunt and Eszrah approached the next stumble-gun. It had trampled into a break of larch and coster, and was slicing out plasma beams at the Binar armour as it revved its inertials to clatter free.

Eszrah killed its operator with his second shot. As the stumble-gun died and rolled back into the mud-wash, Gaunt ran up close and tossed one of Tintile's grenades into the cage.

The stumble-gun blew out with such force that Gaunt was thrown flat. Eszrah helped him up and away from the burning sphere.

'That's two,' Gaunt said, looking around for the other terror-weapons.

'Histye,' Eszrah said, and pointed.

Away to the north, a monumental rain of shells and las-fire had begun to sweep across the Archenemy advance. The phalanxes of cult warriors shrieked and fell as multi-laser fire, at a fabulous rate, rippled across them. Censer-bearers collapsed. A deluge of shots, like torrential flame, was engulfing the enemy's right flank.

The Dev Hetra had moved forward and, at last, brought their gun-platforms into the fight.

TWENTY-ONE

15.50 hrs, 198.776.M41
Fifth Compartment
Sparshad Mons, Ancreon Sextus

FOR A WHOLE day, they held them off.

About three hours after Rawne's unilateral repulse of the Blood Pact, the enemy struck again from the east, using the quartz bastion of Ridge 19 to shield its approach onto the compartment floor. By then, following consultation with DeBray, Wilder had brought the entire bulk of the Eighty-First First into position on the eastern flank in anticipation of just such an event, leaving the Kolstec Fortieth to assume responsibility for Hill 56.

At that point, the day seemed to turn spectacularly bad. Massed in much more considerable numbers than before, the Blood Pact poured out into the scrub, resolutely determined not to be denied a second time. The Eighty-First First became locked in place, rigidly defending a two-kilometre line of rough ground from hasty dug-outs, relying heavily on its crew-served weapons.

In apparent coordination with the Blood Pact's attempt at an eastern breakthrough, the Archenemy armour brigades beyond Hill 56 renewed their assault. All possibility of the fatigued Rothberg tankers withdrawing evaporated. With the Hauberkan reserves, they became tangled in an increasingly feral struggle, which was only relieved by the arrival of the promised Sarpoy armour, the force that had been supposed to replace them on the field. More Kolstec infantry was rapidly sent down from post 36 to reinforce both Hill 56 and Wilder's line, and strings of Valkyries began flying urgent munition runs back and forth across the southern compartment to keep both fighting zones supplied.

By nightfall, it became evident that the Archenemy was not going to back down from either fight.

Through the course of that long, wearisome day, Wilder had kept himself updated with news from the Mons as a whole. From the sound of things,

456

the third compartment was in an even worse state. Both Wilder and Fofobris had sent requests to high command, via DeBray, for reinforcement, but got little satisfaction. Significant reserves had been sent through to the third compartment, where the situation was described as 'grave'. After a while, even that choked off. Wilder listened to frantic and disheartening vox-traffic describing mayhem in the first and second compartments, where relief columns were becoming boxed in by personnel fleeing the third compartment fighting. There were also ominous reports that some of the relief forces themselves had broken back, too scared of what they had heard was happening ahead of them. Some of these units were actually reported to be 'in flight'. Others, more cautious perhaps, were declaring 'mechanical problems' and other set-backs that were preventing them from moving.

It was an ugly picture. The two key 'hot' compartments, three and five, were enduring massive offensives, and the rest of the Imperial strength was milling around in headless confusion, unable or unwilling to come to the aid of either.

It had been Wilder's professional experience that warfare ebbed and flowed. Quiet days, quiet months, could be suddenly disrupted by angry flares of enemy activity. He did not see anything especially sinister in the fact that the enemy had chosen that particular day to coordinate and unify its defence of Sparshad Mons. In many ways, he'd been waiting for it to happen.

But there was no denying how successful the Archenemy had been. No one knew for sure how centralised the enemy command was in the mysterious heart of the Mons, but by whatever means, it had orchestrated a shatteringly well-timed attack on all sides. And the systems and discipline of the vaunted Imperial Guard had seized up, paralysed, as a result.

In the fifth compartment, fighting continued after nightfall. As the temperature dropped, the ferocious tank battle behind Hill 56 raged on, lighting up the low horizon and painting the looming black walls of the compartment with a shadowplay of coloured flashes. At Wilder's line, the intensity dropped a little, but all through the night the support weapons of the Eighty-First First continued to hammer away at invasive attempts by Blood Pact strike teams to edge their way forward in the darkness. Just after midnight, one force almost broke through, but it was denied by Callide's Company after a brutal, forty-minute gun battle across the frosty scrub.

Other dangers lurked in the darkness. Stalkers appeared again, some inexplicably, haunting the darkness behind the Imperial front, as if they had somehow lurked hidden during daylight in dens or lairs in the southern part of the compartment. Two munitions convoys were attacked, and men lost, and Fofobris's Kolstec troops on the hill suffered a series of predatory raids from the rear.

The next day dawned, but the sun was only a little bruise of light against the black undercast. The unnaturally dark smoke rising off the third compartment war zone was blanketing the entirety of Sparshad Mons. The surreal twilight it created seemed like the product of some foul sorcery.

Along the Eighty-First First's position, things were quiet for the first few, chilly hours of the day. Vox distortion levels rose, and the inexplicable daylight winds groaned across the scrub and clumpy thorn-rush. Then the Blood Pact renewed its assault on the eastern flank.

This time they sent stumble-guns to shatter the infantry line that had repelled them time and again the previous day. Wilder had been forewarned about these things via the garbled reports flowing out of the third compartment. They were supposed to strike down everything before them like skittles, random and wild, and make a path for the ground forces.

There were three of them. They came down across the escarpment of Ridge 19, rattling like pebbles in a mess can. At a distance, they seemed so odd, so unthreatening, Wilder's troops just stared at them. Steel balls, trundling in across the damp, gritty soil. Then their spines started to glow and they began to flash out searing plasma beams in all directions, like jumping firecrackers.

The men and women of the Eighty-First First, veterans all, did not break in panic as the inexperienced Binars had done the day before in the third compartment. They held their line. That resolve cost them nearly thirty lives in the time it took to kill the stumble-guns.

The worst of the losses were amongst L Company, Varaine's troop. Oblivious to the stupendous rally of gunfire they sent at it, the stumble-gun rolled into them and crushed those that it did not dismember and char with its beams. Corporal Choires, one of Varaine's toughest, finally halted its progress. Luck, more than anything else, had left Choires unscathed as the ball-weapon rolled past, and he bowled a grenade in through its armoured structure, annihilating the operator. Choires did not live to celebrate. As it expired, one of the stumble-gun's final, spasmodic plas-beams vaporised his head.

Commissar Hark led an attack on the second weapon, determined to stop it before it reached the Eighty-First First's position. Despite the loss of four of the troopers bold enough to go with him into the reach of the lethal device, Hark blasted shot after shot into it with his plasma pistol, and managed to kill the operator. Directionless, the stumble-gun rocked to a halt, smoking.

Caffran, Guheen and the Belladon Gespelder, each of them armed with a tread fether and supported by anxious teams of loaders, used up fourteen rockets between them stopping the third. One of the last two rockets managed to penetrate the heavily armoured sphere deeply enough to touch off its plasma vats or cause some kind of critical weapon failure. The stumble-gun exploded like a miniature star. Guheen and Gespelder argued amiably over which of them should claim the kill.

The Eighty-First First line rippled with mingled cheers at the sight of the last stumble-gun's demise, but the relief was short-lived. With stalk-tanks and modified cannon platforms to the fore, the Blood Pact main assault came in.

Three hours of intense fighting followed. More than once, Wilder was afraid they would be overrun and slaughtered, but Hark and Novobazky, along with the company leaders, kept the position firm. Even Rawne, Wilder noted, with a mix of satisfaction and annoyance, led from the front, spurring the Guardsmen on.

Just before noon, a phalanx of Hauberkan treads, part of the reserve element from post 36, arrived in support. The formidable range and effect of their main weapons crippled the coherence of the Blood Pact front, and forced it into retreat.

Wilder was amazed. He'd never thought he'd be glad to see a Hauberkan tank.

AFTER THE BATTLE, an uneasy lull settled. Keeping a careful eye on the ridge, the Eighty-First First took advantage of the quiet spell to eat rations, service weapons, and even catch a few, quick minutes sleep. Though it was long past the middle of the afternoon, conditions had not improved. The day was still lightless and dismal, the air bitter cold, and the ground hard as lead. Wrapped in camo-cloaks and bedrolls, troopers huddled down beside boulders or nested in patches of stiff grass. Some just sat, looking out across the scrubland, where hundreds of corpses, and the wrecks of fighting machines, lay scattered all the way back to the jagged quartz of Ridge 19.

The Hauberkan treads had taken up position on the left flank of the Eighty-First First position, and Wilder went to liaise with the crews, leaving Baskevyl to supervise munition distribution from a pair of Valkyries that had just arrived from post 36.

'I think we should go now, while it's still quiet,' Mkoll said. 'If we leave it much later, it'll be dark.'

Rawne nodded. They'd found a place to talk away from the others, behind some broken lime trees about thirty metres away from the E Company slit trenches. Criid, Varl, Feygor and Larkin were with them.

'All right. Everyone gather what you need and meet up out beyond those rocks in fifteen minutes,' Rawne said. 'We–'

Varl suddenly made a brusque, throat-cutting gesture with his finger and Rawne shut up. Gol Kolea and Ban Daur were approaching.

'Everything all right?' Kolea asked.

'Fine,' said Rawne.

'Just taking a breather,' Varl said.

Kolea glanced at Daur. 'See? They're just taking a breather. I told you there was nothing dodgy going on.'

'You're right,' said Daur, leaning against the trunk of a lime and folding his arms.

'And you said they looked conspiratorial,' Kolea said to Daur.

'I did. I did say that.'

Kolea looked at Rawne. 'There's nothing conspiratorial going on here, is there?'

Rawne said nothing. Kolea looked at Mkoll instead. 'Is there, chief? Just a bunch of comrades, taking a breather, hanging out. I shouldn't read anything into the fact that all of you are lost souls who went to Gereon?'

Mkoll held Kolea's gaze without any sign of discomfort. 'There's nothing going on, Kolea,' he said.

Kolea pursed his lips and looked up at the sky for a moment, as if watching the black clouds chase. 'I got roasted a little bit,' he said at length. 'For siding with you yesterday, Rawne. Wilder was pretty gakking pissed off we pulled C and E out of the line without his say so, even though it turned out we had a good reason. I don't blame him, either. If I was Wilder, I'd be mad as hell. This is a good unit, and most of that is down to his hard work pulling it together.'

'Noted,' said Rawne. 'Why are you telling me this?'

'Because I'd hate to see that happen again,' Kolea replied. 'It's a great thing all of you made it back to us, but if you refuse to settle, it's going to cause problems. If you're chasing secret agendas, for instance. It'll be divisive. How will Wilder maintain authority if you constantly refuse to work with him? The Eighty-First First will suffer. And everything and everyone that used to be the Tanith First will suffer too.'

'I understand that,' Rawne said. 'But there are just some things…'

'Like what?' asked Daur.

Rawne inhaled deeply before replying. 'Some things that won't fit into your nice, ordered boxes. Gut instincts. Feelings. I don't dislike this man Wilder. And I honestly have no intent to damage this unit. But there are just some things.'

'Are they important?' Daur asked.

'Feth, I think they are,' Rawne replied.

'So bring Wilder in. Get him on your side, instead of sneaking about behind his back, pissing him off, and undermining his command.'

'Wilder won't–'

'How do you know what Wilder will or won't do, Elim?' Kolea asked. 'Have you asked him? Have you given him a chance? Ban's right, Wilder's a good man, and when us Ghosts thought you and Mkoll and Gaunt were all dead and gone, we counted ourselves lucky to get him as a commander. I say you go talk to him.'

Rawne looked at the others. None of them made any comment.

'Gereon really messed you lot up, didn't it?' Kolea said softly. 'I think you all got so self-reliant, you've forgotten how to trust anyone.'

'You don't know what it was like,' Feygor growled.

'No, I don't. You bastards still won't tell me. But I think I just hit a nerve, didn't I? You've forgotten how to trust.'

'We trust each other,' Rawne said. 'And we trust Gaunt.'

'Is this about Gaunt?' Daur asked.

'Perhaps,' Rawne said.

'So where do your loyalties lie?' Kolea demanded. 'To this regiment or to Gaunt? Because if the answer's Gaunt, this isn't ever going to work.'

'Do you remember his last command?' Criid asked. They all looked at her. The wind gusted and lifted her long hair away from her face, and they all saw the ugly scar across her left cheek, the blade wound she'd grown her hair to hide.

'His last command to the Tanith First,' she repeated. 'Before we left for Gereon, Gaunt told the Ghosts that if he didn't come back, they were to serve whoever came in his place as loyally as they had served him. We should tell Wilder, Rawne. As soldiers of the Imperium, we're obliged to, because that's what Gaunt ordered us to do.'

'GOOD NEWS,' BASKEVYL said to Wilder and Novobazky. 'We just got a signal from 36. We should expect some serious reinforcement by dawn tomorrow. Van Voytz has committed the entire Frag Flats reserve to the front line.'

'Everything?' Wilder said.

'The full works,' Baskevyl confirmed. 'I guess he's getting as tired of this place as we are.'

'Don't look now,' Novobazky said. Rawne, Mkoll and Kolea were walking across the scrub towards them.

'Great,' said Wilder. 'Don't go far, either of you. I've seen friendlier looking mutinies.'

He took a few steps forward, and Kolea and Mkoll fell back a little so that Rawne came up face to face with Wilder.

'Major?'

'Colonel. I think there's a good case to be made for us starting over.'

'Really?' Wilder raised his eyebrows.

'The situation is difficult, and the return to this regiment of the Gereon mission team, particularly myself and Sergeant Mkoll, must have unsettled loyalties.'

'You could say that.'

'My actions yesterday can't have helped much.'

That brought a smile to Wilder's face. 'All right, Rawne. And don't think I'm not appreciating you making this effort, but I get the feeling there's something more to it.'

'You'd be right. There's something that has to be done. I was just going to go ahead and do it, but Major Kolea took the trouble to remind me that I am an officer of the Imperial Guard and have a responsibility to clear things with my commander.'

'Bonus points for Major Kolea,' Wilder said. 'All right, shoot. What's this thing?'

'It'll be dark soon,' Rawne said. 'After last night's experience, we should form a secure rearward perimeter to prevent any stalker trouble.'

'Agreed. Absolutely. See, that wasn't too hard, was it Rawne?' Wilder said. He paused and saw the look on Kolea's face. 'There's more, isn't there?' Kolea nodded.

'Sir,' Rawne said. 'I'd like to take advantage of the current lull not only to set up a perimeter, but also to try tracking these stalkers.'

'Tracking them?'

'Mkoll's pretty sure he can do it.'

'Tracking them?' Wilder repeated.

'To find out where they're coming from,' Mkoll said.

'You mean dens or lairs or whatever?'

'Or whatever,' Mkoll agreed.

'Why?' Wilder asked.

'That's the part you're not going to like,' Kolea said.

'We've not had that already, then?' asked Wilder.

'I received a message from Gaunt,' Rawne said.

Wilder took a casual step backwards and looked sidelong at Novobazky and Baskevyl. 'You know that feeling?' he asked them. 'When you find out your girl's still writing letters to an ex-lover?'

Baskevyl sniggered.

Wilder looked back at Rawne. 'Rawne. Rawne, I couldn't feel much more undermined if you... if you got hold of a frigging land mine and... and put me under it.'

'That probably sounded better in your head, didn't it?' Rawne said.

'Yes,' said Wilder. 'Really, much, much better.'

'Listen to me, Wilder,' Rawne said. 'As everyone – including high command, the Commissariat, the Inquisition, and our old comrades in the Tanith First – has been quick to point out, the team that went to Gereon came back different. You don't spend that long on a Chaos-held world and not have it affect you. It changed the way we fight. It changed the way we live and think, the way we trust. All of those changes were alterations forced on us by the simple need to survive. Gereon left its mark on us.'

'Like a taint?' Novobazky asked. He was only half joking.

'Yes,' said Rawne. 'But not the kind you mean. Just to stay alive, we developed a... a hunch. An instinct. What would you call it, Mkoll?'

'A sensitivity,' Mkoll said.

'Yes, a sensitivity. A little inkling that rang alarm bells when things weren't right. When the ruinous powers were playing tricks or about to strike. I've got that inkling now. So's Gaunt. We've had it since we first set foot in this place.'

'And what does it mean?' Wilder asked.

'We don't think Sparshad Mons is what it seems to be. It's not just an old ruin with the Archenemy hiding inside it. Something else is going on. Think about the stalkers. Where in the name of feth do they keep coming from at night?'

'I don't know,' said Wilder.

'No one does. Gaunt suggested it was high time someone did. He contacted me because he thought it was a job ideally suited to the Tanith scouts, to Mkoll and Bonin especially. If they can't track these things to their source, no one can.'

'And what does he expect you'll find?' asked Baskevyl.

'Let's hope lairs and dens,' Mkoll said. 'Burrows, maybe. Natural hiding places that no one has yet detected.'

'But your inkling tells you...' Wilder began.

'That they're getting in a different way. That this place isn't what it seems.'

'If that's true,' said Novobazky, 'it could change everything.'

'All right, you've convinced me,' Wilder said. 'I'm not happy, but you've convinced me. Assemble a team, Rawne. Not just Gereon survivors, though. Include Novobazky and at least a couple of Belladon scouts.'

'Yes, sir.'

'And keep checking in with me.'

'Yes, sir.' Rawne saluted and walked away. Wilder turned to Baskevyl and Novobazky.

'That was right, wasn't it?' he asked.

Baskevyl nodded. 'If there's even a shred of truth,' Novobazky said, 'this is important.'

'And if there's not, at least it gets Rawne out of my face for a few hours.' Wilder grinned. 'Who knows, we might get lucky. Something might eat Rawne.'

THE HUNTING PARTY left the Eighty-First First position half an hour later, and headed south into the broad scrub of the compartment's centre. Rawne had brought Mkoll and Bonin, Varl, Criid and Beltayn, and left the choice of Belladons to Commissar Novobazky. Novobazky selected Ferdy Kolosim, Wes Maggs and two recon troopers Rawne hadn't met called Kortenhus and Villyard.

They moved south in a wide circle, through thickets of gorse and thornrush, and across fields of loose flint and ashy soil. Three times in the first hour, Mkoll announced he'd detected a trail, but each one was at least two or three days cold, in his opinion, and too vague to bother with.

'I don't see anything,' Maggs complained each time.

'Why am I not surprised?' muttered Bonin.

Mkoll led them on through a belt of dead trees: leafless, desiccated costers, bleached by the elements, clawing at the sky with gnarled branches. Massive boulders slumped between the trees every few dozen metres, mossy blocks of misshapen granite that looked as if they might have tumbled down from the compartment walls generations before. Mkoll and Bonin studied each one.

'What's the interest in the rocks?' Novobazky asked Rawne.

'Gaunt told me he'd tracked a stalker in the third compartment, and its trail seemed to go dead at the foot of a large rock.'

'He tracked one?' the commissar queried.

'Actually, the tracking was done by Eszrah Night, a Gereon partisan who kind of attached himself to Gaunt. Excellent tracker, mind you. Quite brilliant.'

'If this Night fellow is so good,' said Novobazky, 'why has Gaunt got us doing this?'

'Gaunt wants to support his theory with clean evidence,' Rawne said. 'If you were high command, Novobazky, who would you trust? The heathen claims of a primitive hunter, or the authenticated findings of an Imperial Guard recon expedition?'

'Point,' said Novobazky.

'Here's something!' Mkoll called.

They hurried over. Criid, Varl and the Belladons formed a perimeter.

'It's getting dark!' Varl called out, weapon raised.

'I know,' replied Rawne. Mkoll was crouching beside the foot of a large rock.

'Trail here,' Mkoll said. 'Pretty fresh too. It seems to go right in under this rock.'

'How can that be?' Kolosim asked.

Maggs bent down beside Mkoll. 'I see it this time. Throne, Mkoll, your eyes are good. No doubt about it, it runs right in under this rock.'

'Here's another!' Bonin called.

The main group moved across to where he was kneeling in an open patch of rush-grass. The troopers on watch moved with them, rifles steady.

'Really, getting dark now!' Varl called.

'I know,' said Rawne.

'Just saying,' said Varl.

'Fresh. Moving that way,' Bonin said, examining the trail. 'Maybe last night or this morning, early.'

Mkoll nodded. 'This way.'

'Hang on,' said Kolosim. His voice had an amusing lisp to it because of the swelling around his split lip. 'I thought Bonin said it was moving that way?'

'I did,' said Bonin.

'So… why are we going in the opposite direction?'

'Because we don't want to know where it went, Ferdy,' Maggs said. 'We want to know where it came from.'

'Say what you like about Maggs,' Bonin said to Mkoll, 'he's a quick learner.'

'He is,' Mkoll agreed. 'He really is.'

Criid suddenly held up her hand. The party froze. From not too far away, a whooping roar rang through the dead forest.

'Oh, tremendously not good at all,' said Varl.

'Full auto,' Rawne said. 'Safeties off.'

'Never mind that,' Novobazky said. He drew a pistol from under his coat. Heavy, matt-black and ugly, it was unmistakably a plasma weapon. 'Hark lent me this. Thought we could do with the extra oomph.'

'I've always loved Commissar Hark,' Varl said. Beltayn grinned.

Criid signed. *Something moving, thirty metres.*

Mkoll nodded, and signed the party to move on anyway. Criid and Varl brought up the rear, walking backwards, rifles aimed into the gathering dark.

The trail led into another clearing. At the centre lay yet another big rock, a three tonne ovoid, gleaming with a varnish of glossy green lichen.

'Stay back,' said Mkoll. The party halted at the edge of the clearing.

'What is it?' asked Novobazky.

'You feel that?' Mkoll asked.

Bonin and Beltayn nodded. 'I sure as feth do,' Rawne said. 'It's faint, but it's there. A tiny buzzing.'

'Like a glyf,' said Beltayn.

'Exactly,' said Rawne. 'Exactly like the sound a glyf makes.'

'What's a gliff?' asked Kortenhus.

'You don't want to know,' said Bonin.

'Damn, it's making my skin crawl,' said Rawne.

'It's making my tongue itch,' said Varl.

'I can't feel anything,' said Novobazky. 'Except… except a sense of unease. Is that just me?'

Rawne shook his head.

'Not the first time I've heard this on Ancreon Sextus,' Mkoll said. 'You heard it last time, Maggs. You too, Major Kolosim.'

'That buzzing?' Kolosim replied. 'That was deafening.'

'This is much more low level, but it's the same thing,' Bonin said.

'Oh shit,' said Villyard. 'Look!'

The Belladon scout was pointing towards the boulder in the clearing. Something *wrong* was happening to it. It was distorting: bending and twisting, as if they were seeing it through a ripple of heat haze. The buzzing increased in intensity until all of them could hear it.

There was a noise like cloth tearing, the sudden pop of a pressure change, like an airgate opening, and the lifeless trees around them shivered in an exhalation of cold wind.

The boulder was no longer there. Occupying its precise space and shape was a doorway. A gate. A simple, impossible hole in the fabric of the world.

The hole shimmered. Mist, frost white, slowly drifted out of its dark, yawning gulf. Reality had somehow folded up on itself to allow this hole to be.

'There's Gaunt's answer,' Bonin said.

'I don't understand what I'm seeing,' Novobazky murmured.

'What you're seeing is a very bad thing, commissar,' whispered Mkoll.

'Hate to correct you, chief,' Varl began.

The stalker, thrice-wrought, eight hundred kilos, emerged from the hole as if it was sliding out of the surface of a mirror. It prowled forward on its knuckles, shoulders hunched and rolling loose. It sniffed the air.

'Yeah,' said Varl. 'See, *now* it's a very bad thing.'

TWENTY-TWO

18.01 hrs, 198.776.M41
Fifth Compartment
Sparshad Mons, Ancreon Sextus

'Novobazky!' Rawne yelled

'What?' the commissar stammered.

'Novobazky! The weapon!'

Genadey Novobazky, quite unmanned by his first glimpse of a mature stalker, slowly remembered who and what and where he was, and started fumbling with the plasma pistol Hark had given him.

'Hit it!' Kolosim bellowed. The stalker was coming forward, increasing speed. Its throat sacs puffed out like bellows, and its vast jaws opened to allow the steel teeth to engage.

The hunting party opened fire. Ten lasrifles on full auto lit up the clearing with a blitz of laser fire.

Shrugging it off, the monster came on, turning its bounding progress into a pounce.

The Guardsmen scattered in desperation. Maggs managed to smash Novobazky over in a side-tackle that saved both of their lives. The stalker went over them, and caught Villyard in its mouth.

The Belladon screamed the most appalling scream any of them had ever heard as the stalker's massive bite sheared him apart. Varl turned and began firing at the huge brute. Varl was no fool. He knew full well he couldn't kill the creature with his mark III. He was trying to hit Villyard. He was trying to spare the poor bastard any more agony.

Busy with its kill, the stalker lashed out with its left paw and smacked Varl into the air. He hit a tree, snapped it, and tumbled onto the cold ground.

Maggs rolled off Novobazky. 'The plasma gun! The plasma gun!' he yelled.

'I can't work the safety!' the commissar babbled, fighting with Hark's favourite weapon. 'I can't get it to–'

Maggs snatched the pistol out of Novobazky's hands. He slid the toggle and aimed it at the stalker.

The huge beast turned, its muzzle slick with Villyard's blood. It hooted and roared, and began to charge the Belladon scout like a fighting bull.

'Eat this,' said Maggs, and fired. The searing beam from the pistol vaporised the stalker's enormous skull in an astonishing burst of blood and bone chips.

But the sheer momentum of the thrice-wrought's attack carried its mammoth, headless carcass on. It slammed into Maggs, and knocked him backwards through the air.

Limbs flailing, a look of despair on his face, Maggs fell backwards into the hole and vanished. The headless stalker collapsed onto the soil in front of the shimmering gate.

'Maggs!' Bonin shouted, and ran towards the hole. Mkoll was behind him.

'Feth!' Bonin said, coming to a halt in front of the hole. He reached out his hand and the light rippled like water around his finger tips. 'Maggs! Maggs!'

Bonin looked at Mkoll.

'Never leave a man behind,' Mkoll said, and leapt through the portal.

'Mkoll! No!' Bonin roared.

There was a shout from behind him. Criid had opened up. A second stalker, the one that had been trailing them, exploded out of the treeline and came lumbering across the clearing towards Bonin.

The Tanith scout dived away, coming up to spatter las-shots into the thing's flank as it turned. It wasn't as big or mature as the beast that had come out of the hole, but it was still big enough. Three hundred kilos plus, thick with muscle, its plated skull half a metre long, its teeth the size of fingers.

It made for Bonin, roaring. Rifle fire smacked into it from the left and forced it to turn away. Kolosim and Criid were coming forward, firing at it, trying to distract it from Bonin.

Their efforts worked. It went for them instead.

Dughan Beltayn landed on its back. He stabbed his straight silver down into the rear of the monster's skull. Black blood burst up across his hands and forearms. The stalker convulsed and bucked, throwing Beltayn off its back like an unbroken horse.

Hurt, panting, its throat sacs swelling in and out like a respirator pump, the stalker took a few, unsteady steps. Beltayn's dagger was still buried in the back of its head.

Rawne stepped towards it. There was something in his hand.

'Hello, you,' he said. The beast turned, blood dripping from its gigantic mouth. It gurgled and opened its jaws, slotting its teeth in and out of position as it tasted a new target to bite.

Rawne threw the tube-charge into its wide open smile.

The stalker's jaws closed. There was a brief rumble, and then it blew apart, showering the whole clearing with greasy blood and lumps of meat.

Rawne wiped the hot, rank gore off his face. 'All right, Mach?'

Bonin got to his feet and nodded.

'Criid? Kolosim? Bel?'

'I'm fine,' said Beltayn. He looked at Bonin. 'Back of the skull, that's what you told me. Back of the skull, you said.'

'You did fine,' Bonin replied. He wasn't really interested. He was gazing at the boulder.

The gate had closed. It was just a boulder again.

'MKOLL? COME BACK. Maggs? Respond.' Beltayn delicately adjusted the dials of his vox-caster. 'Mkoll. This is hunting party. Do you receive?'

'Maybe you broke the caster jumping on that thing's back?' Bonin suggested.

'Well, I wouldn't have done an idiot thing like that if you hadn't told me the back of the skull was the weak spot,' Beltayn snapped.

'It worked for me,' Bonin said.

'Children, hush,' said Rawne. 'Bel? Any joy yet?'

Beltayn shook his head. 'Something's awry. I'm not picking up Maggs or the chief, but they're close. I mean, I've got their signals. I'm picking up their micro-beads.'

'Why can't we talk to them?' Kolosim asked.

Beltayn shrugged. 'Micro-bead links have a range of about ten kilometres, tops, major. This baby–' he patted his vox-caster set, 'well, she's good for global work. The point is, look here.'

Beltayn indicated a particular gauge on the vox-set. 'That's the range finder. We call it the booster. See, see how it's hunting?'

'What does that mean?' Criid asked.

'It means… it means something's awry,' Beltayn replied. 'I've got signals from their micro-beads, which suggests they're somewhere within a ten-kilometre spread from here. But the set is hunting madly for a fix. Like they're also out of range.'

'Out of range?' said Rawne. 'Out of *global* range?'

Beltayn shook his head. 'I can't explain it. They're close by… but they're also not actually on…' his voice trailed away.

'Not actually on Ancreon Sextus any more?' Rawne finished.

'Um, yes, sir. I said it was awry.'

Rawne turned away. 'How's Varl?' he asked Kortenhus.

'Sore,' said the Belladon. 'He'll live.'

'All right, Novobazky?' Rawne said.

'I froze,' Novobazky said. 'I'm sorry. I've never seen anything like that before. I still can't–'

'No blame,' Rawne said. 'That was a shock to us all.'

'Sir!' Beltayn cried. 'I have something. Throne, it's coming through like it's on a delay. Why would it be on a delay?'

'Speaker!' Rawne demanded.

Beltayn threw a switch on the vox-caster. They all stood silently as the crackling, distorted voices breathed out of the vox-set.

'–shit hole now!'

Crackle. 'It's not good, is it?'

'Is this what you meant? The shit you could get me in if you really tried?'

'Shut up, Maggs.'

Indistinct garbage followed for a while.

'–the sky? What the hell's wrong with the sky?' That was Maggs. '–the frigging stars are wrong. They're just wrong. It's so frigging cold.'

'Shut up.'

'So cold. Look at the roof.'

Crackle.

'Why?'

'It's like a roof. I mean, a ceiling. Stones. Huge stones. What's holding it up?'

'Shut up.'

Crackle.

'Mkoll, Mkoll, we're picking you up,' Beltayn said. 'Respond!'

Crackle.

'–are we? I mean where the f–'

'–swear Maggs, if you don't shut u–'

Crackle.

'Beltayn? Beltayn? Is that you? This is Mkoll. I can read you, but you're not clear. Say again.'

Beltayn keyed the send button. 'Mkoll, this is Bel. We're reading you, over.'

Crackle.

'–can no longer hear you. If you can hear me, get Rawne to the set.'

'I'm here,' Rawne said.

'–getting nothing over the micro-beads. I hope you can hear me. Tell Rawne we're not on Ancreon Sextus any more. Tell Rawne–'

Crackle.

'–place is like a vast chapel. There's no supports for the roof. Stones hanging in the air. It makes me want to cry. It's all so impossible. Maggs has lost it. There are stalkers here. All around us. Hundreds of them, climbing the rocks towards us. I think they have our scent.'

Crackle. A long whine of distortion.

'–me the pistol! Give me the fething plasma pistol, Maggs! They're coming for us! Give me–'

Crackle. Distort. Whine.

'–come on! Move! Don't–'

'–this way! Keep–'

'–right behind us! Keep moving now for feth's sake or we–'

A hideous roar burst out of the vox-caster speakers. Then the channel went dead.

Flat noise droned out of it.

'Oh, Throne,' Criid said.

All of them winced as a bomb went off three hundred metres west. With Rawne in the lead, they started running towards the blast, weapons raised.

Varl, Bonin and Criid fanned out ahead, scouring the woodland, rifles at their shoulders.

'Clear!'

'Clear this way!'

'Over here!' Bonin cried out. The hunting party ran to him.

He was hunched over in another clearing, beside another huge stone. Mkoll and Maggs were sprawled at his feet, lifeless, caked in frost. The corpse of a stalker lay nearby, its skull destroyed by a tube-charge.

Rawne knelt down beside Mkoll and cradled his head.

'Chief?'

Mkoll's eyes opened, slowly blinking. 'Gaunt was right,' he gasped. 'Gaunt was right.'

TWENTY-THREE

01.05 hrs, 199.776.M41
Third Compartment
Sparshad Mons, Ancreon Sextus

GAUNT WOKE TO find Eszrah shaking him by the shoulder. For a moment, he thought he was still on Gereon, in the gloom of the Untill. But this was a different kind of darkness. He remembered where he really was.

He peered at his chronometer. Its glass had been shattered some time during the previous two days. It was still the dead of night. He'd been asleep in the back of the Salamander for less than three hours. He remembered climbing in to rest for a minute, and then nothing. Exhaustion had overwhelmed him.

'What is it?' he asked.

Eszrah pointed. A young Binar corporal was waiting beside the command tread. His uniform was torn and blotched with mud.

Gaunt slid down from the tread's bay. Every atom of him ached, and some pieces of him hurt a great deal more than that. He was slightly dizzy and disorientated.

'Yes?' he said.

The corporal saluted. 'Commissar Gaunt?'

'Yes.'

'A message for you, sir. It came through to my vox station. It says it's urgent.'

Gaunt nodded and rummaged for his cap. He followed the young soldier back down the rutted trackway.

A kilometre behind them, the battle still raged. It was just entering its third day. Somehow, they had endured thus far, somehow they had held that narrow, precious line and kept the enemy at bay. The previous afternoon, reinforcements had begun to arrive. By the evening, the Fortis Binars and their allied units had finally been able to retire from the front and rest.

471

Gaunt glanced back as he walked down the track. The blackness of the night had been thickened into an almost solid mass by the smoke, and this darkness was underlit by a throbbing orange glow from the vast firezones along the front line. The crackle and shriek of munitions continued to echo up from the fenland positions. Gunships swirled through the murk overhead.

All down the long trackway, men slept or rested in the jumbled troop trucks and fighting vehicles. Most of them were Binars, many of them were wounded. The worst of the injured had been evacuated out in slow-moving processions to post 10.

Gaunt and the corporal reached the vox station, set up in one of a cluster of habi-tents beside the trackway. Figures, mainly junior officers, milled about, dead on their feet from fatigue.

The corporal showed Gaunt over to one of the casters, where the operator made some deft connections, and handed a headset to Gaunt. He removed his cap and slid the set on.

'This is Gaunt.'

'Rawne. We've got what you need, over.'

'Confirm that, Rawne. You have proof, over?'

'Corroboration, Bram. It's solid, over.'

'Where are you, over?'

'Post 36, fifth compartment. That's 36 in the fifth, over.'

'Stay there. I'm coming to you. Gaunt out.'

Gaunt handed the set back and left the tent.

ESZRAH WAS WAITING for him outside. Despite the fact that he'd been in the thick of battle for as long as Gaunt, the Nihtgane seemed untroubled by any sign of fatigue.

'Come on,' Gaunt said to him, and began to walk south down the track, away from the boom of war.

'Restye!' Eszrah called out. Gaunt turned. The partisan was hanging back, glancing behind him up the track.

'What?' Gaunt asked.

'Ludd?' Eszrah said. The last time Gaunt had seen Ludd, the young man had been unconscious from exhaustion in the seat of a cargo-10 parked off the road.

Gaunt shook his head. 'Not this time. Come on.'

THEY FOLLOWED THE track for about a kilometre, stepping out of the road from time to time as heavy transports and armoured cars went by, moving up towards the line. The landscape on either side of them was clogged with troop trucks and munition freighters, along with tanks and Chimeras preparing to advance. A broad patch of bare earth was being used as a forward landing strip for gunships and Valkyries. Six of the machines were on the ground, surrounded by prep crews and fuel bowsers.

Gaunt led Eszrah past a team of bombardiers off-loading tank shells from the payload bay of one battered Valkyrie, and approached the next in line.

The pilot, who had been resting on the ground beside his machine, jumped up when he saw the commissar approaching.

'You fuelled and prepped?' Gaunt asked.

'Yes, sir, but–'

'But what?'

The pilot explained that his Valkyrie and the three next to it were on standby for Marshal Sautoy and his senior officers. Sautoy had finally graced the front line with his presence four hours before, to 'oversee the reinforcement phase'.

'The marshal, who's a personal friend of mine,' Gaunt said, 'will have to spare you. I need transit right now. Urgent Commissariat business.'

'It's… irregular, sir,' the pilot said.

'Look around, my friend,' said Gaunt. 'Everything's irregular right now. I can't exaggerate the importance of this. If I hang around and try to go through proper channels to get a bird assigned, I'll be here the rest of the night. If it helps, I'll sign off on a k46-B requisition slip to say that I've commandeered you. You can always show that to your flight controller.'

The pilot studied Gaunt for a moment. There was no doubting his rank, but the commissar was a mess. His clothes were ragged and filthy, and he had fresh scratches and contusions on his dirty face and an agony of fatigue in his pale eyes. He also appeared to have a shoulder wound. The pilot concluded this was probably not a man to cross.

'I'll clear off the fitters and get us up, sir,' the pilot said, buttoning up his flight suit. 'Destination?'

'Fifth compartment,' Gaunt told him. 'Post 36.'

FROM THE AIR, Sparshad Mons was a sprawling, monstrous shadow twitching with ten thousand spots of fire. They flew through reeking banks of smoke that blotted everything out, forcing the pilot to fly by instruments. In clearer patches, once they were over the second compartment, Gaunt could see the columns of troop and armour advance threading up into the stepcity: long, winding rivers of lamps and headlights flowing through the dark. Everything was coming. Van Voytz had committed everything he had.

Beyond, to the north, the towering heart of the Mons rose, full of secrets and malice. Implacable, immense, as solid as a mountain peak, it lowered above the outer compartments, half-visible in the night, as ugly as a death threat.

The Valkyrie flew on, down the long fourth compartment, where yet more mighty rivers of military traffic flowed onward. A significant portion of Van Voytz's commitment was heading for the bitter fifth compartment hot zone. Gaunt understood that the Imperial forces were at least making some headway in the fifth. Given the weight of the reinforcement coming through, he was hardly surprised.

They came in under the cyclopean arch and entered the fifth. Far ahead, down country, the baleful glow of a battle lit up the night, amber and red. Gaunt sighted the post, brightly-lit by radiant ground lights and stab-beams, over to the left of them. Another long column of armour and transportation was moving north below.

The Valkyrie circled in, and began its descent towards the wide table of basalt west of the post that served as a landing pad. They touched down with a gently controlled thud and the engines cycled down.

Gaunt slid open the side hatch and jumped out, Eszrah behind him.

'Do you want me to stay on site, sir?' the pilot called out.

Gaunt nodded. 'Yes, thank you. As long as you can.'

'Turn-around checks, please!' the pilot shouted to the approaching ground crew. 'Ten minutes!'

Gaunt and Eszrah hurried up the path towards the house that served as the focus of the post. The low, hillside area around it was encrusted with thousands of habi-tents, like barnacles on the skin of some sea-monster. There was a din of engines from the nearby trackway as the relief column rolled past, without beginning or end. The post itself was bustling with personnel.

'Who's the post commander?' Gaunt asked a passing Kolstec NCO.

'That would be Marshal DeBray, sir.'

'Where can I find him?'

'He's already gone forward to the front line, sir.'

'So who's in charge here?'

'Colonel Beider, sir. Sarpoy 88th.'

'And where would he be?'

The NCO shrugged. 'Maybe in the main dug-out? Or you could try–'

'Never mind,' said Gaunt. He walked past the NCO towards a figure he'd just spotted in the crowd. An old man, all on his own, watching, waiting.

Gaunt began to walk faster, pushing through the crowds. The old man turned, and saw him coming.

Gaunt took a few, last steps, and dropped to his knees in front of him.

'Ayatani father,' he whispered. Zweil bent down and laid his hands on Gaunt's shoulders, gently urging him back onto his feet. The priest gazed up into Gaunt's face. There were tears welling in Zweil's ancient eyes.

'I've seen plenty, life I've had,' Zweil said. 'But the sight of you here gives me the most joy.'

'It's good to see you too,' said Gaunt. He swallowed hard. 'I've been a long time without blessing, father, too long. My sins are heavy on me. Sometimes, I think they're too heavy now to be lifted away, even by the beati.'

'She's a strong lass,' Zweil said. 'I'm sure she'll be up to the job.'

Zweil continued to stare into Gaunt's face. 'By all that's holy, Ibram, you have been to hell, haven't you?'

'It wore a different name, but yes.'

'I like the beard, though,' said Zweil.

ZWEIL LED GAUNT up towards post command, his arm linked around Gaunt's for both comfort and support. Ayatani Zweil, permanently ancient, had become much more old and frail since the last time Gaunt had seen him.

'Rawne's here?'

'Yes, yes. You've lost weight too. Have you not been eating?'

'Father...'

'And you're hurt. These scratches on your face.'

'Yes, father. There was a battle.'

'And your shoulder. What's wrong with your shoulder?'

'A wound. A flesh wound.'

Zweil tutted. 'Flesh wound? Flesh wound? They're all flesh wounds! No one ever says "Ooh, look! I've just been shot in the bones, but it missed my flesh completely!" It's a load of old nonsense, is what it is. It's a phrase you heroic warrior types trot out so you can sound manly and stoic. "Bah, it's just a flesh wound! Only a flesh wound! I can carry on!" Nonsense!'

'Father–'

'I've heard men say that when a leg's come off!'

'Father Zweil...'

Zweil suddenly leaned close and whispered up into Gaunt's ear. 'I don't want to worry you, Ibram my dear boy, but there's a very large man following us. Very large. Great tall fellow. He looks pretty sinister to me, but I'm sure you're aware of him, ever-vigilant coiled spring that you are.'

Gaunt halted and turned.

'Eszrah? Come here.' The Nihtgane approached.

'Eszrah ap Niht, of the Gereon Untill. This is my old friend Father Zweil of the Imhava Ayatani.'

The towering partisan nodded slightly in Zweil's direction.

'Biddye hallow, elderen,' he said.

'What did he say?' Zweil asked, sidelong to Gaunt.

'He greeted you.'

'He's very tall. Alarmingly tall. I say, you're very tall, sir.'

'Hwat seythee?'

'I said, you're very tall. Tall!' Zweil gestured with his hand above his own head. 'Tall? You know? Not short?'

'Hwat, elderen?'

'Is he simple in the head, Ibram? He doesn't seem to understand.'

Eszrah looked questioningly at Gaunt, nodded towards Zweil and plucked his fingers away from his lips.

'No, that's all right,' Gaunt said. 'I've suffered him this long.'

'That was a rude gesture, wasn't it?' Zweil whispered to Gaunt. 'He just made a rude gesture towards me.'

'No, father. He was just concerned for my welfare.'

'Hnh! Tall is one thing, rude is quite another. Strange acquaintances you pick up in your travels, Gaunt.'

'I've often thought so,' Gaunt smiled. 'Now, where's Rawne?'

'In here, in here,' Zweil muttered, pushing open the doors into the wards of the infirmary. A smell of counter-septic and body waste suddenly filled the air. Medicae personnel were treating the latest batch of wounded shipped back from the fifth compartment front line.

'This way!' Zweil called breezily, apparently oblivious to the suffering around him. He strode on into the field theatre.

Gaunt followed him and came to a halt. The massive, badly damaged corpse of a semi-mature stalker lay on the theatre bed. A masked surgeon was in the middle of a rigorous autopsy.

The surgeon looked up at the interruption and slowly set down his bloodied instruments. He struggled for a moment to take off his gloves and mask, and then came quickly across the room to Gaunt and embraced him.

'Throne of Terra, Ibram!'

'Hello, Tolin.'

Dorden took a step back. 'Let me look at you,' he said. 'Feth, is it really you?'

'In the flesh.'

'That's why I brought him to you first, doctor,' Zweil said. 'So you could look at him. He has a flesh wound, he says. In the flesh, precisely, *in corpus mortalis*. He blusters he's fine, but you know these warrior types. Off comes a leg and they blither on regardless.'

'You're hurt?' Dorden said. 'Leg, is it?'

'Just ignore Zweil for a moment. I've scraped a shoulder. You can look at it later. Rawne's here, isn't he?'

Dorden nodded.

'Was this his idea?' Gaunt asked, gesturing to the autopsy.

'One of your lot suggested it, actually. A commissar, Novobazky. He's with Rawne. They dragged this carcass out of the scrubland with them.'

'Find anything?'

Dorden shrugged. 'Yes. Things I'd rather not have found. But I'm still collating data.'

'I need to see Rawne. Do you know where he is?'

THE HUNTING PARTY was waiting in one of the larger habi-tents outside the infirmary. Dorden led Gaunt across, with Zweil and Eszrah behind them. Gaunt went inside the tent, and embraced Criid, Varl and Beltayn. Bonin shook him firmly by the hand. The Ghosts greeted Eszrah warmly too, though the partisan made no response. Rawne waited, facing Gaunt.

'Bram.'

'Elim. Same old, same old. eh?'

'There's only war, sir.'

'Show me what you have.'

'Introductions, first,' Rawne said. 'This is Kolosim, Eighty-First First.'

'I've heard a lot about you, sir,' Kolosim said.

'And this is Commissar Novobazky.'

'Gaunt,' Novobazky nodded.

'Commissar,' Gaunt nodded back.

'Over there,' said Rawne, 'that's Recon Trooper Kortenhus. On the cots there, Recon Trooper Maggs and, well, Mkoll.'

'Poor devils,' said Zweil.

Mkoll and Maggs were supine on simple bed frames. Both of them were hooked up to intravenous drips and bio-feeds. Both looked unconscious, cold, pinched.

'What's wrong with them?' Gaunt asked.

'They went through,' Rawne said. 'They left this planet entirely for a few minutes. Dorden says they're hypothermic and run-down, but they'll live.'

'They left this planet entirely for a few minutes?' Gaunt repeated.

'The proof you were asking for,' Rawne said.

'Start at the top,' Gaunt said.

RAWNE RECOUNTED THE hunting mission for a few minutes. What detail he left out was readily reinforced by Varl, Novobazky and Beltayn.

'Bonin said the back of the skull was the weak point, so that's what I did,' Beltayn complained. 'He'd already killed a stalker that way.'

'You killed a stalker by stabbing it in the back of the head?' Gaunt asked Bonin.

'Yeah. Sure,' said the scout. 'They're not armoured in the back.'

'That's not the point I was trying to make, sir,' Beltayn continued. 'I tried it, on good faith, and–'

'Let's move along,' said Gaunt. 'Commissar Novobazky? Maybe you'd like to report?'

Novobazky nodded. 'I can only confirm what these people have told you, Gaunt. The stalkers clearly enter the compartments via portals. Warp gates. I don't know what you'd call them. They're like trap doors, letting the bastards out after dark, right in amongst us.'

'This is a character of the Mons, you think?'

Novobazky shrugged. 'The various standing stones in the inner terrain seem to be the focal points of the gates. Throne, I don't know. I'm no expert in these things. In my opinion, the Mons is wired to let them through. It's built into the architecture. Established warp gates, networked to I don't know where. This isn't a level playing field.'

'And the stalkers themselves?' Gaunt asked, looking at Dorden, who was standing in the doorway of the habi-tent.

'Tissue samples say they're ogryns,' Dorden said, 'with some human genetic material. The creations of some vicious eugenic program. Their brains are modified for absolute aggression. We're talking about human and ogryn specimens who have been stripped down, rebuilt and programmed just to kill.'

'You've proof?'

Dorden shook his head. 'I'm still collating. I don't have the right instrument back-up here to be conclusive. This is just a field hospital. Maybe if I had access to the body scanners and biopsy vaults at Frag Flats or Tarenal. Right now, it's just a hunch.'

'We do hunches,' Rawne said. 'Inklings too.'

Gaunt looked at Dorden. 'But from what you've seen, doctor, you'd say these were modified human or human-allied troops?'

Dorden nodded. 'The corpse I was autopsying, it had dog tags buried in the flesh of its throat. I mean overlapped by skin graft and regrowth. The tags identified a Trooper Ollos Ollogred, Fifth Storm Faction (Ogryn), 21st Hurgren Regiment. I checked it out. The 21st is currently in action on Morlond.'

'They're sending our own people back to fight us,' Novobazky said.

'It seems so,' Gaunt replied. 'And they're sending them back through punctures in the warp. Anyone here remember the *jehgenesh*?' he asked.

Rawne, Varl, Criid and Bonin nodded. Beltayn moaned at the memory.

'The what?' asked Novobazky, but Gaunt had already moved on. 'Mkoll and…what was his name? Maggs? They went through?' he asked.

'And came back alive,' Rawne replied.

'I want to talk to them,' Gaunt said.

DORDEN INJECTED SOMETHING powerful into Mkoll's drip, and nursed him back into consciousness.

'Five minutes,' he told Gaunt. 'That's all I'll allow.'

Gaunt nodded. He crouched down at Mkoll's bedside. 'Oan? Hey, Oan? It's Gaunt.'

'…never come back…'

'Mkoll?'

'Thought you'd never come back,' Mkoll slurred, opening his eyes.

'You're going to be fine, Oan. Dorden says so. I just want to talk to you.'

'So talk. I'm not going anywhere.'

'What did you see, Oan? What the feth did you see?'

Mkoll rolled over and stared at the roof of the habi-tent. 'Maggs went through, so I followed him. Never leave a man behind, that's what you always taught me.'

'I did. I did.'

'So I went after him. It was cold, that place. Really cold. I knew at once that I'd stepped off Ancreon Sextus completely. I was… somewhere…'

'Oan?'

'Sorry sorry, drifting off. I was somewhere else. The stars weren't right, that was the first thing I noticed. The constellations were entirely different. I navigate by the stars. I notice these things.'

'Go on, Oan.'

'It was cold. Did I mention that? I mean really cold. Rocks, slabs. Everywhere you looked. Maggs was shouting about the sky, and I noticed that too. I could see star patterns, but directly overhead, it was a roof. A ceiling. Massive blocks of stone hanging in the night sky. It made no sense. How could stones be just hanging there? And they were so quiet.'

'Quiet?' Gaunt asked.

'Really quiet,' Mkoll whispered. 'They should have been making a huge noise, a sky filled with stone slabs. But they were quiet.'

His voice faded away. Dorden reluctantly pushed another vial into the drip.

'No more,' he told Gaunt.

Gaunt nodded. 'Oan? Tell me about the place. Was it empty?'

'No! No, no, no. Hordes of stalkers, massing to attack. Inhuman things too. Machines. War machines. Blood Pact. We ran, and we tried to hide. The stalkers came after us. The wrought ones. I saw legions of the damned, assembled, en masse, waiting for the gates to open.'

'The gates?' Gaunt asked.

'You have to understand,' Mkoll murmured. 'There's nothing inside the Mons. It's empty. It's just a gateway. A massive gateway, sucking us in so it can open and destroy us. The gates in each compartment don't lead into the next compartment along. I saw them. Laid out in a row. They open into some-where else....'

'Mkoll?'

'That's enough!' snapped Dorden. 'He's passed out again.'

Eszrah suddenly unharnessed his reynbow and moved to the entrance.

'What is it?' Varl asked. He and Criid switched round, training their weapons on the mouth of the tent. Bright lights were flickering outside. Gaunt rose, hearing the whine of a gunship.

'Put your guns away,' he said. 'You too, Eszrah. I've been waiting for this.'

The tent flaps pulled aside and Commissariat troopers came in, firearms raised.

'Nobody move!' the squad leader said, playing his hellgun around the tent.

Nobody did, not even Rawne.

His pistol aimed squarely at Gaunt, Faragut entered the tent. Behind him came Commissar-General Balshin, Inquisitor Welt and Nahum Ludd.

'You will surrender yourselves to the authority of the Commissariat!' Faragut barked.

'End of the road, Gaunt,' Balshin smiled.

'I'm really very sorry, sir,' Ludd said.

TWENTY-FOUR

04.10 hrs, 199.776.M41
Post 36, Fifth Compartment
Sparshad Mons, Ancreon Sextus

'WE GAVE YOU a chance, Gaunt,' Balshin said smoothly. 'I was against it, but the lord general insisted. We gave you the chance to prove yourself. And as is usually the case when someone is given enough rope...'

'All the things you could be focusing your attention on, commissar-general,' Gaunt said, 'and you fixate on me. I really bother you, don't I?'

'My foremost task is the removal of the heresy of taint in the Imperial Guard, Gaunt,' she replied. 'It is endemic on this front of the Crusade. I have never seen its effects so pernicious, so deep-rooted. Of course I am bothered when a senior commissar, a man of influence and authority, walks free amongst us, riddled with the touch of ruin.'

Gaunt almost laughed out loud. 'Based on what?'

Balshin stared at him levelly, as if scolding a recalcitrant child. 'I was never satisfied with your testimony at the tribunal. It was hollow. To be exposed for such a length of time to an afflicted world? The notion you remained untainted is laughable. Since returning to duty, your behaviour has been wayward to say the least. You have meandered from duty, pursued your own private agendas. There have been unauthorised communiqués, conspiratorial exchanges conducted under the guise of official Commissariat business...'

Gaunt shook his head. 'Is that all you've got?'

She smiled blandly. 'Let's consider the fact that just a few hours ago you deserted your post, broke your orders, misappropriated an Imperial transport, moved from one location to another within a martial cordon without clearance or validation... and here I find you, plotting again, in a little huddle with some of the very people who stood accused of taint beside you.'

'I suggest you modify your language, madam general,' Novobazky said sharply. Ignoring the Commissariat troopers all around them, he took a step towards her.

'That's close enough!' Faragut warned.

'I take issue with your characterisation of us as tainted or heretics,' Novobazky said. 'There are matters here that–'

'Novobazky,' Balshin said. 'I always thought of you as a dependable man. Thank you for demonstrating how odiously and malignantly Gaunt's contamination can be spread.'

Novobazky's face hardened and his cheeks flushed with fury, but he kept his mouth shut. Gaunt looked directly at Inquisitor Welt, who had not spoken a word. 'Inquisitor? Do you go along with this? I took you to be far less blinkered than Balshin.'

'Say something to convince me,' said Welt.

Gaunt gestured around the theatre tent. 'I can tell you plenty. Everyone in this room can tell you plenty. There is taint here, inquisitor. It's the city itself. The place we're fighting for is sick.'

'That's ridiculous,' said Balshin. 'And borderline heresy. The step-cities of Ancreon Sextus are revered monuments that date back to–'

'Tell me about the stalkers,' Gaunt said.

'What?' Balshin snapped.

'The Ordo Xenos has established, through analysis of recovered specimens, that the so-called "stalkers" are augmetically enhanced humans and, more often ogryns,' said Welt. 'This information has been suppressed for reasons of morale. The unauthorised autopsy you have been conducting here, and all evidence bearing from it, will be sequestered by the Inquisition.'

'And tell me about the warp doors,' Gaunt said.

'What are you talking about?' Balshin asked.

'Tell me about the warp doors that riddle the compartments. Explain to me how the stalkers get in and out during the night.'

'I don't know what you mean. We have assumed burrows, perhaps...'

'There aren't any fething burrows,' Rawne said. 'My team and I witnessed a warp door in use last night, less than five kilometres from where we're standing. We saw a stalker come through. Those two men there passed through the gate themselves and re-emerged through a second one.' Rawne pointed at the unconscious forms of Maggs and Mkoll on the cots.

'They must be examined and interviewed,' said Welt.

'That will have to wait,' Dorden told him. 'They are in no condition.' Welt half-smiled at Dorden, as if amused at the medicae's defiance of an Inquisitorial order.

'The structure of the Mons is unsound, Balshin,' said Gaunt.

'The structure of the Mons has been extensively studied and surveyed,' Balshin exclaimed. 'It is under constant scrutiny from the Fleet and the Tacticae. Do you really expect me to believe that you and a few of your fellow deviants can come here and, in just a few days, uncover secrets that everyone else has missed? If there was a system of warp doors here as you claim, they would have been detected months ago.'

'They are pretty much invisible to standard sensory systems,' Gaunt replied, 'and to regular human senses too.'

'But not to you?' sneered Balshin.

'No, not to me,' Gaunt said. 'Nor to any of the Gereon mission team.'

'He's practically confessing to taint!' Faragut blurted.

'I'm repeating what I've told you all along,' Gaunt said. 'I'm admitting to a sensitivity, an awareness of the vibrations of Chaos. We could not have survived our time on Gereon without developing an affinity. The very instincts that kept us alive there are showing us the truth now.' He stated directly at Balshin. 'The fact that we have worked to expose this danger, the fact that we are telling it to your face... Does that alone not prove whose side we're fighting for?'

Balshin was about to answer back, but Welt raised a hand. 'Commissar-general, perhaps you and your team would be so good as to record full statements from the individuals here. Doctor? Please prepare those two men for transportation back to Frag Flats. Gaunt, walk with me.'

Gaunt glanced at Rawne, and then followed Welt out of the theatre tent. There was a moment's silence.

'That went well, I thought,' said Varl.

GAUNT AND THE inquisitor walked together through the habi-tent rows of the post, and came to a halt on a patch of higher ground, looking north. The air was still black, but the compartment was lit by the moving lights and the distant radiance of fire.

'Balshin is under pressure to produce results,' Welt said. 'The Crusade Second Front is truly ailing. If your claims are validated, it will make a big difference to the way the war goes here on Ancreon Sextus.'

'They'd better be validated soon,' said Gaunt. 'Mkoll said he witnessed vast hosts massing beyond the gate. Did no one ever stop and wonder how the enemy was able to keep producing so many troops and fighting vehicles from out of the heart of this Mons?'

Welt paused, as if wondering whether to let Gaunt in on classified information. 'It's not just here, Gaunt. The situation here at Sparshad Mons is being replicated, right now, at every other step-city on the planet.'

'A unified offensive? In cities thousands of kilometres from each other?'

Welt nodded.

'It's because the enemy isn't in the cities,' Gaunt said. 'The cities are just delivery systems to bring them through. The Blood Pact armies are not waiting for us in the next compartment or the one after that. They're simply coming out of the gates. Mkoll suggested that the main compartment gates are large scale versions of the doors the stalkers use.'

'So the enemy gets our attention, draws us into laying siege to these haunted rocks, gets us to commit all our forces deep inside the walls...' Welt let the words hang.

'And then fully opens the gateways.' said Gaunt. 'I sometimes think we're guilty of underestimating our old foe, inquisitor. The Ruinous Powers operate with levels of guile and sophistication that we scarcely credit. On Gereon, we witnessed them using *jehgenesh*. Gigantic warp creatures that were bred to consume a planet's natural resources, such as fresh water or mineral ore, and excrete them via the warp to supply planets light years away. They are not destroyers, they are users. If they work on that kind of scale, why should it surprise us if they deploy entire armies that way, in places like this, where the ancient mechanisms for such transmission still exist?'

'I subscribe to the theory that the Imperium's worst enemy,' said Welt, 'is its own ignorance.'

Welt looked at Gaunt, and studied him curiously for a moment. 'Inquisitor?'

'It's an unhappy position you're in, Gaunt. Despite all the great service you've done for the Imperium, you're regarded as a difficult, dangerous man now.'

'I don't know about difficult,' said Gaunt. 'Dangerous is right, though.'

'You're this close to summary execution,' Welt said baldly. 'And there's only one thing keeping you alive.'

'What's that?'

'Me,' Welt said. 'If you and your team could survive as long as you did on that hell-hole world without succumbing to taint, then for the sake of the Imperium and the protection of our species, I have to find out why.'

WELT RETURNED TO the theatre tent to assist with the interrogations. Two Commissariat troopers were detailed to Gaunt, and kept him secluded in one of the rooms in the post. He sat alone for a few minutes, and then fell into a deep sleep. Ludd woke him four hours later. Outside, a thin light was announcing the day.

'What's going on?' Gaunt asked.

'Commissar-General Balshin's finished here. Rawne's team has been debriefed. They're to return to their unit at the front. Maggs and Mkoll will be shipped back to Frag Flats.'

'How are they?'

'Still unconscious, but showing signs of recovery. I've been sent to collect you, sir. You're to come back with us.'

Gaunt got to his feet.

'Sir, I want to say… I'm sorry,' Ludd said.

'For what?'

'For reporting your actions. Balshin made it quite clear I was to report to her any… unorthodox behaviour on your part. It was my duty. But I didn't like doing it.'

'I was counting on you, Ludd,' Gaunt said.

'What, sir?'

'When I realised something was wrong here, I knew there was no point me trying to convince Balshin. She has no time for me. I needed her to believe I was up to something, that I had something to hide. That way she'd come looking and wouldn't be able to dismiss what I had to show her.'

'So… you expected me to–'

'I expected you to do your duty, Ludd. And luckily, you did.'

TWENTY-FIVE

14.10 hrs, 199.776.M41
Frag Flats HQ
Sparshad Combat Zone, Ancreon Sextus

HE'D BEEN WAITING for hours, almost but not quite a prisoner in a spartan chamber aboard one of the command Leviathans. He kept looking at his pathetic, broken chronometer, watching time creep on slowly.

The chamber doors folded inwards on electric motors. Commissar Faragut stood in the doorway. Faragut stared at Gaunt contemptuously.

'Did you draw the lucky straw, Faragut?' Gaunt asked. 'You must be very happy. Back of the head, please. I don't want your face to be the last thing I ever see.'

Faragut tensed, but didn't take the bait. 'The lord general is waiting for you,' he said.

VAN VOYTZ WAS in the Leviathan's main tactical command centre. Intense activity was taking place all around him. Hundreds of voices speaking all at once, hundreds of logic engines chattering and whirring. The hololithic displays above the main strategium pit were changing fast: coloured patterns and contours symbolising the effects of enormous coordination work.

Van Voytz saw Gaunt approaching.

'Ibram,' he said, and gestured around himself. 'All this, Ibram.'

'Sir?'

'That's all, Faragut,' Van Voytz said, and the commissar left them.

Van Voytz led Gaunt through to a quieter side vault where eight tacticians, including Antonid Biota, were softly discussing their art around an active display table.

'Can I have the room, gentlemen?' Van Voytz asked. 'You stay, Biota.' The other tacticians filed out.

'There's been some preliminary investigation, Gaunt,' Van Voytz said. 'Ordo Xenos, various astropaths. No solid proof can be found of any warp network within the Mons.'

'I see,' said Gaunt.

'But it's all rather hasty, preliminary, as I said. Time is not on our side.'

'No, sir.'

Van Voytz sighed. 'And that's when a lord general earns his pay. Proof or no proof, a decisive tactical decision has to be made, based on the best information. You should have heard the arguments amongst the senior staff this morning. I nearly shot a couple of them. Whatever else, there are two Guardsmen in the infirmary – one a "tainted" Ghost from your Gereon team, the other most definitely not – who are well enough to testify about what they saw last night. I spoke to them both myself…'

Van Voytz looked at Gaunt. 'I know when men lie, and these men are not lying. Their words chilled me. And when I read substantive evidence, written statements from men like Novobazky, I know I'd be a fool to dismiss what you've stumbled upon.'

The lord general glanced across at Biota.

'Thirty-eight minutes ago,' the tactician said, 'formal order was given for the immediate staged withdrawal of Imperial Guard forces from Sparshad Mons and all other step-cities on this planet. Orbital manoeuvres are now underway to deploy the Fleet in geo-synchronous positions for surface bombardment. It is estimated they will have firing solutions in eight hours.'

'I expect to give the order at around midnight tonight,' Van Voytz said.

'You're going to destroy the cities…' said Gaunt.

'I'm going to wipe them from the face of creation,' Van Voytz said. 'As I wanted to, incidentally, all along. Damn this siege work.'

'It is the prudent thing to do,' Biota said.

'A swift and total victory here could be just what the Second Front needs,' Van Voytz said. 'A robust statement of Imperial domination. An end to a long, slow, drawn-out wrestling match that has sapped and shredded morale.'

'In my opinion, sir,' said Gaunt, 'the problems the Guard has had here on Ancreon Sextus – the desertions, the sickness, the psychoses – much of that can be attributed to the taint in the cities. Exposure to these places has twisted men's minds and souls, even if they haven't been aware of it. The taint Balshin is so desperate to root out is real here, just very, very subversive. But on the Second Front in general, the problem is simply that Macaroth has given you a young, inexperienced army. They're scared, they're improperly supported, they're learning to make war as they go along. In the field here at Sparshad, it's been my honour to serve alongside young men who have never seen battle before. They have brave hearts, general, I can vouch for that. They simply lack the confidence to use that courage.'

'The Imperial Victory of Ancreon Sextus,' said Van Voytz, banging his fist on the edge of the display table. 'That'll put some fire into their bellies. They'll see that the Second Front is capable of accomplishing something.'

Gaunt looked at the display's schematic images of the outer compartments. 'You intend to order the start of bombardment around midnight, sir?' he asked.

'Thereabouts, as soon as it practicable.'

'It will be quite a logistical exercise getting such a huge commitment of troops and machines clear of the cities by then. Especially in situations where they are engaging the enemy.'

Van Voytz glanced uncomfortably at Biota. 'We will orchestrate as full a withdrawal as is feasible,' said the tactician. 'It is regrettable that there may be some losses.'

'Black cross losses, you mean?' said Gaunt.

'Yes.'

'So any Guard unit too slow getting clear of the cities by the deadline... or any that can't break free of enemy engagement...'

'Will be sacrificed,' said Biota calmly. 'Such losses are unfortunate, but, up to a certain proportion, considered acceptable when stacked against the over all strategic advantage.'

'What Antonid means,' grumbled Van Voytz, 'is that if we stick with the siege, we'll most likely lose a hell of lot more men than the ones who'll give their lives in a good cause tonight.'

'I understand what he means,' said Gaunt. 'The poor rearguard will suffer the worst.'

'Don't they always?'

Gaunt turned away from the display and faced Van Voytz. 'Sir, I request permission to return to the field. Discipline will be the deciding factor in how quickly and cleanly the withdrawal can be managed. There will be fear and panic, and also carelessness. You need every commissar you can find to supervise.'

'I expected you to say as much,' Van Voytz said. 'If you must, then–'

'I want to go to the fifth compartment, sir.'

Van Voytz let a slight smile turn his lips. 'Yes, I thought you might. That's where they are, isn't it?'

'Yes, sir.'

'Carry on, Commissar Gaunt.'

GAUNT REMOVED ESZRAH Night from the holding cell where the Commissariat had put him, and together they recovered their confiscated weapons and possessions from a duty officer.

The hull-top flight platforms were seething with activity in the glaring sunlight. Lifters, gunships and fliers were already relaying personnel back from the Mons. Servitors unloaded equipment, and fitter teams in sunshrouds worked on quick turn-arounds. Gaunt found a deck supervisor, who consulted his checklists and told Gaunt there'd be spaces on one of the Destrier-pattern heavy carriers in fifteen minutes.

Gaunt and Eszrah waited by the guard rail. Other passengers, mostly officers and medicae staff, gathered. From the high vantage, Gaunt could see the Frag

Flats camp below, spread out under the white sun, baking in the heat. After days in the Mons's drab, dank micro-climate, obscured by smoke, it felt like another world.

The camp was striking. Even the Frag Flats HQ was going to withdraw to a greater distance from the Mons before the midnight deadline. Gaunt watched the temporary city slowly deconstructing itself.

A pair of Valkyries lifted off the pad behind him, and he turned to watch them go. They arced away in the bright blue air towards the great, dark cloud on the horizon.

The deck supervisor called them, and they walked with the other waiting men towards one of the bulky Destriers. It was an ugly, obese flier, its hull flaking grey. The side hatch was open, and they clambered into the battered, bare metal hold and made themselves comfortable in the small, wall-mounted strap-downs.

Another of the Destriers lifted away in a huge din of thrust and flying grit. Their own transport's engines began to turn over.

'Two minutes!' the deck supervisor called.

A figure appeared in the sunlight outside, and climbed into the hold, a last-minute addition to the passengers. He walked across to Gaunt and Eszrah.

'Hello, Ludd,' Gaunt said.

'I heard you were… I mean, I thought I should…'

'Strap yourself in,' Gaunt said.

'This is going to be hard work, isn't it?' Ludd said. 'It's going to be tough getting the men out of there in time.'

'Especially if they're rearguard,' Gaunt said. 'First in, last out.'

Ludd looked over at Eszrah Night.

Slowly, carefully, as a matter of ritual, the partisan was smearing wode across his face, ready for war.

TWENTY-SIX

15.05 hrs, 199.776.M41
Fifth Compartment
Sparshad Mons, Ancreon Sextus

SOMEWHERE, SOME GOD or similar higher being, possibly one seated upon a Golden Throne, was having a good laugh at Lucien Wilder's expense. Ordinarily, Baskevyl believed, his friend and superior officer had a refined appreciation of good irony, but the special irony of this particular situation was simply making Wilder curse and swear.

They had come so very close.

Wilder darted across the dry gulch and ducked in behind the broken chunks of quartz where Baskevyl and a fireteam were in cover.

'Can you believe that arse?' Wilder spluttered.

'Which particular one now?' Baskevyl asked. 'Are we still on Van Voytz?'

'No!' Wilder growled. 'DeBray! Bloody shithead DeBray!'

'Because?'

'He's only ordered B and C munition trains to pull out! Both of them! That leaves us–'

Wilder broke off as a stream of tracer rounds ripped across their position. Some hit the tops of the quartz boulders, pummelling powdered rock into the stale air.

Wilder looked up and yelled 'Will somebody please kill that stubber for me?'

Two crew-served weapons nearby immediately kicked off, blasting away.

'DeBray's ordered B and C trains out of the zone already,' Wilder continued. 'Which leaves us with what's left of A. And according to the chief armourer with A, that's mostly tank shells and mines, anyway.'

'Not good news,' Baskevyl agreed.

'How does DeBray expect to maintain a successful breakaway?'

Three heavy detonations, in rapid succession, went off close by, and shook them violently. Dirt rained down.

'Dammit,' Wilder said, 'I need to be able to see better. Come with me.'

Wilder and Baskevyl left cover, heads down, and ran around the back of a low ridge where a good portion of Callide's company was dug in. They kept going into slopes of larch and coster on the north side of the ridge. There were Eighty-First First troopers down amongst the trees, N Company. Wilder could hear Captain Arcuda shouting orders.

Baskevyl and Wilder ducked down, and Wilder got out his scope. Stray shots were hitting the tops of the dead trees around them, clattering and rattling like scurrying woodland animals.

'Where's Kolea?' Wilder asked.

Baskevyl pointed. 'To the west there, in support of Obel's mob. Varaine's Company is trying to cover the open stretch there, but it keeps getting pounded by the gun platforms they've got over by the... over on the approach there.'

Wilder swung his scope round, and caught sight of the ugly, multi-barrelled cannon platforms thumping away in the middle-distance, wreathed in white smoke. He knew full well that Baskevyl had said 'on the approach' because he didn't want to use the phrase 'over by the gate'. Baskevyl didn't want to remind Wilder of the irony.

The gun platforms were indeed 'over by the gate'. Throne, they had come so very close.

The battle on and around Hill 56 and Ridge 19 had been curtailed in the small hours by the arrival of the promised reinforcements: huge levels of field reinforcement, with more on the way. DeBray himself had come forward with the advance. Word was that Van Voytz had finally committed the entire reserve into the Mons. Through the end of the night, and into the morning, the reinvigorated Imperial wave had surged forward, making large gains in the fifth compartment. In places, enemy resistance seemed to melt away completely. By midmorning, the towering gate into the sixth compartment had been clearly in view. By midday, the Imperial forces had arrived within a half kilometre of it.

DeBray had offered the Eighty-First First, along with the Kolstecs and the armour groups, the opportunity to stand relieved and retire. They had, after all, been holding the line since the start of the offensive. What remained of the Rothbergers left the field, exhausted and ground down. But for the rest of them, their blood was up. The arrival of the mass reinforcement had bolstered their spirits, and Wilder had certainly not been about to walk his men away from a fight and let somebody else get the glory of finishing it. Fofobris of the Kolstec had been of the same opinion, as had Major Garrogan of the Hauberkan armour. DeBray had graciously allowed them to continue, and together, the three units had made the best of the forward push. There had even developed a sense of friendly rivalry as to which of them would get the honour of taking the gate as a prize.

Then that special god had started laughing. The general order had been relayed forward. Van Voytz had commanded a complete and immediate staged retreat, to be accomplished no later than midnight. He had ordered the Imperial Guard to abandon Sparshad Mons. DeBray had immediately begun the systematic withdrawal of the fifth compartment strengths, starting with the backline reinforcement columns that hadn't even seen action yet.

Wilder wasn't entirely sure what was going through the lord general's mind. Very little, was his best guess. He simply was at a loss to fathom why, after all this time and effort and sacrifice, the Crusade was going to give up on Sparshad Mons.

On top of everything else, one did not simply fall back from a fighting line. A proper breakaway was called for. Certain units had to stay in position until the bitter end, covering the main retreat and holding back the enemy, or they would be inviting a massacre. Standard Guard tactics dictated that any such rearguard action should fall to the units in the most advanced position. For the Eighty-First First, the Kolstec and the Hauberkan, the glory of victory was no longer a prospect. What faced them now was a gruelling, backwards fight, as they covered the main retreat until such a time as they could themselves break off and run.

Simply run. The end of this ludicrous expedition would see them running for their lives. If he got out alive, Wilder swore he would find Van Voytz and–

'Stalk-tanks!' Baskevyl said. Five of them had just emerged from the gate itself, advancing down the rough incline in support of the Blood Pact units along the lower ridge. Fierce gunfire licked up and down the incline. Wilder heard rockets banging.

'Who's down in the rockline there?' he asked.

Baskevyl peered. 'E Company,' he said.

Meryn's lot, thought Wilder. 'I hope they have some live tread-fethers left, because those stalks are going to be on them in about ten minutes.'

More loose shots snickered through the dead trees. Pieces of dry branch fluttered down. Away to the east, AT70's were booming away as they tried to prise Garrogan's treads off a shelving escarpment.

'Colonel!' Wilder turned, and saw his vox-man, Keshlan, running towards him down the wooded slope.

Small-arms fire pattered through the trees, and Keshlan fell with a sharp cry.

'Dammit! Keshlan!' Wilder was up and running. More shots pinged down, shattering bark and twigs. Some bastard somewhere had a damn good angle.

'Cover fire!' Baskevyl yelled down to Arcuda, and N Company began to lay las across the enemy positions.

Wilder reached the vox-officer.

'I'm all right, sir,' Keshlan said. His face was white with shock.

'Where'd they get you?'

'Just caught my body armour, sir. Shoulder plate's pretty smacked up, but I'm all right.'

Wilder examined him. A hard round had torn clean through Keshlan's shoulder plating and broken the skin. A few centimetres to the right and Keshlan would have taken it in the throat.

'Teach you to go running about,' he said. 'They *are* armed, you know.'

'Yes, sir.'

'You needed me?'

Keshlan picked himself up. 'Yes, sir. Signal from the marshal, sir. The Hedrogan Light is just pulling out behind us now, and we are to expect the last of the Sarpoy to follow them in the next forty minutes.'

'There'll be no one left to talk to at this rate,' Wilder said. He could see the young man was frightened, and he wanted to keep him steady. But no, it wasn't fear. Something else.

'What is it, Keshlan?'

'Signal from I Company. Captain Raydrel was shot dead about fifteen minutes ago, and both his adjutant and Sergeant Favre were killed trying to rescue him.'

'Holy Throne…' Wilder breathed hard. Favre, and the adjutant, Vullery, were fine men and old comrades. Raydrel had been a friend, one of the best officers in Wilder's command. 'Who's… who's heading up I Company now?'

'Uh, Sergeant Haston, sir.'

'Patch me to him.'

Keshlan started setting his vox. Baskevyl scurried up.

'Raydrel's dead,' Wilder said simply.

Baskevyl looked away, then at the ground. 'We all will be at this rate,' he said. 'The hand Van Voytz has dealt us. Breakaway's going to be nigh on impossible. Throne, if I could plug that gate, just for an hour.'

'Right. Or magically transport us all to a safe world full of wine and flowers. I need practical bloody solutions right now, Bask, not–' Wilder paused. 'All right, that wasn't me talking just then. And it wasn't you listening.'

'Don't apologise, Luc. I know how you feel. I want to kill something just at the moment.'

'Well, as luck would have it,' Wilder grinned, 'we happen to be in the middle of a frigging battle. Take it out on the damn Blood Pact.'

'No response from Sergeant Haston, sir,' Keshlan reported.

Wilder looked at Baskevyl. 'Bask, head down to Meryn and make sure his company is ready for those stalks. If you see Hark anywhere, tell him I need him at I Company immediately. We have to get them rallied.'

'On it.'

'Try Hark on your micro-bead too,' Wilder called after him. As he moved off, Baskevyl pointed back up the slope. 'More bad news,' he joked.

Wilder looked round. A group of figures was approaching, heads down.

'It's Major Rawne,' said Keshlan.

'That's all I need,' sighed Wilder.

It was Rawne, all right. Novobazky, too, and Ferdy Kolosim, along with most of the infamous 'hunting party'. Wilder scrambled up the bank to meet them.

Throughout the previous night, Kolosim had kept Wilder appraised of the hunting party's movements, though it had all been rather vague and brief. The last Wilder had heard, Rawne's team had been heading for post 36 with 'urgent information'.

'What are you doing here?' Wilder asked.

'We were sent back up the line to rejoin you this morning,' Novobazky said. 'By the time we heard about the general order, we were as good as here, so we kept going.'

'You should have turned back,' Wilder said.

'I'd prefer to withdraw alongside my regiment,' Rawne said. Wilder studied Rawne's face, and realised the man was completely serious. He nodded.

'Are you going to tell me what happened?' he asked. 'I see Kortenhus, Criid, Varl, Beltayn and Bonin. Where are the others?'

'Abe Villyard didn't make it,' said Kolosim. 'Maggs and Mkoll were shipped out, injured.'

'What the hell did you get into?' Wilder asked.

'Gaunt was right,' said Rawne simply.

'He was right?' Wilder said. 'You mean this place isn't... isn't what it seems?'

'No, it's not,' said Ferdy Kolosim.

Wilder felt a sudden rush of understanding, so swooping and immense, it made him feel giddy. 'Is this why... Throne! Is this why Van Voytz has ordered a general withdrawal?' he asked.

'I honestly don't know,' said Rawne. 'We weren't told. We were questioned by the Commissariat, and then sent back to the line.'

'Gaunt,' said Wilder. 'Frigging Gaunt! Ever since he came back from the dead, he's made my life a crap storm of problems and disappointments!'

There was a smack, flesh on flesh. Wilder realised Rawne had swung a fist at him. The scout, Bonin, had stopped Rawne's blow, blocking it tightly in his own hand.

'Don't, Eli,' Bonin hissed, squeezing.

Rawne let his hand drop.

'Oh, please. Go ahead,' Wilder said. 'Give it your best shot. I know you've been itching to, from the moment we met.'

Rawne shook his head. 'That's not true, Wilder. I have great respect for you, believe it or not. But no one bad-mouths Bram Gaunt in my hearing.'

Wilder thought for a moment. Close by, a series of shells exploded in a rippling line, and the air shivered with overpressure. Renewed gunfire began to crackle below them.

'Enough of this,' Wilder said. 'If you're back, you're back. Start doing some good. Ferdy, take Kortenhus and get back to your company. We'll need the left flank trim and tight in the next two hours, so that the FooFoo Frigwig and his beloved Kolstec can fall back.'

'Sir!'

'Nadey? Head along to I Company and perform your miracles. We lost Raydrel.'

'No!'

'Just do what you can.'

Novobazky nodded and hurried away.

'The rest of you come with me. E Company's in a fix. That's *Meryn's* company, Major Rawne, just so you remember, all right?'

'I understand,' said Rawne.

They hurried down the slope into the rocks. Ahead, the stalk-tanks had begun to spatter las-fire into the Eighty-First First's position.

CAFFRAN RISKED A run between boulders that brought him up behind a particularly large lump of granite. Tank fire crackled past, and Caffran could smell burning stone. The clattering strides of advancing stalk-tanks echoed around the shallow incline.

Nearby, troopers were huddled low, clipping off shots at the enemy ground troops advancing behind the tanks. Caffran could see Larkin, Osket, Kalen and Mkillian close by, obscured by their camo-capes. Several Belladons too. He wished he could remember their names.

Tank fire sizzled in again in great, slamming blasts, and Caffran ducked. He glanced up again in time to see that three of the Belladons had been cut down. Their mutilated bodies lay smouldering on the burned soil. Now he *really* wished he could remember their names.

He took a look out. One of the tanks was very close, waddling along on its slender, insectoid legs, pistons hissing and wheezing. Caffran hefted up his rocket tube, checked the load, and armed the rocket by removing the priming pin. He muttered a little blessing as he did so. Just to make it fly right.

It was his last load. He looked back the way he had come and yelled, 'Guheen! Where the feth are you?' Guheen had his back. And the heavy canvas holder with the last three rockets in it.

'Little hairy!' Guheen shouted back, ducking as small-arms fire licked past.

'Move your Tanith arse!' Caffran shouted. The tank was firing again. It sounded like masses of shingle slithering across a wet beach. It reminded Caffran of the storm landing at Oskray Island. Feth, how many years ago was that now?

'Any time soon, Caff?' Kalen shouted. Caffran shouldered the launcher tube, snuggled it close, and placed his fingers around the trigger spoon.

He swung out of cover and raised the snout of the tube. The tank was right there. Right on them, gun-pods traversing as it hunted for live targets. He clenched his fingers and depressed the metal spoon. The tube jumped violently against his shoulder as the rocket left it. There was a sucking rush, a fart of flame.

The rocket rushed out, trailing white smoke across the air behind it, and smacked into the stalk-tank head on. The blast tore off the stalk's head and thorax, burst the operator's cocoon, and smashed the whole machine over onto its back. It lay there, burning, its long metal legs twitching at the sky.

A cheer went up. *Premature*, Caffran thought. There were still four more stalk-tanks plodding towards E Company's line, and plenty of Blood Pact with them.

He knew he needed a better angle on the next tank. He tensed, then ran out across the open stretch towards the rocks where Larkin was huddled. A squall of gunfire chased him. He threw himself flat and crawled in beside the sniper.

'Very dainty,' Larkin said.

'They were shooting at me.'

'I don't blame them. Look at the mess you made of their nice tank.' Larkin smacked in a fresh hot-shot clip and settled his long-las. 'Speaking of tanks,' he began.

They were getting close. Caffran didn't need the old marksman to tell him that. What he needed was a rocket load. His launcher was smoking and empty.

'Guheen! Any time soon!'

Guheen shouted back something incomprehensible. Lugging the rocket bag, he started to run, and made it to the boulder that had previously given Caffran shelter.

'You know,' Larkin began, conversationally, as if they weren't actually in the middle of a horrendous firefight. 'Those kids. Nice kids. Kolea really ought to wake up and do something. They deserve to know.'

Caffran blinked at him. 'Feth, does everybody know?'

Larkin shrugged. 'Tona told me. On Gereon, there wasn't any place for secrets.'

'Gereon, Gereon, Gereon... I'd give real money if you lot would shut up about that place. It was just a place. Just a fething place.'

'You weren't there,' said Larkin. 'You don't know.'

'I know I'm sick of hearing about it,' Caffran turned. 'Guheen! I need those rockets!'

'One moment you're alive, the next you're dead. In this game, I mean,' Larkin rambled on.

'Shut up, you old bastard!'

'And what are secrets worth then? Even secrets made with the best intentions. Your son and your daughter deserve to know about their other father, Caff. And Gol deserves to–'

'Shut up, Larkin! Shut the feth up! We're in trouble here!'

Heavy-duty las-fire screeched over their heads from the lead tank.

'Guheen! Load me!'

Guheen looked left and right, halted as shots whipped past, and then started his run to Caffran's side, the heavy rocket bag over his shoulder.

He got three metres, and a hard round from the Blood Pact infantry went into the side of his head. Everything inside his skull came out in a shower on the other side. Before he'd even started to fall, two more shots had ripped into him, screwing his flailing body around, forcing it to lose all structure and semblance of humanity.

He hit the dry ground and rolled, one hand clawing impulsively at the sky.

'Oh feth!' Caffran whispered. He started to move forward, but Larkin grabbed him and yanked him back. Gunfire raked the open space, jerking and twitching Guheen's pathetic corpse. The rocket sack was well out of reach.

The Blood Pact troopers were running in close. E Company met them with a flurry of las. Larkin dropped an officer with a perfect kill shot. But still the small-arms fire rattled in relentlessly.

'I can't load,' Caffran said. 'I can't stop those tanks.'

'That's not good,' Larkin agreed casually, thumping home another hot-shot.

'Larks!' Caffran said, keeping his head down. 'Aim for the operator. There, man! In the bubble! Kill him!'

Larkin cosied his new rifle up to his cheek, and drew aim on the nearest stalk-tank. Through his scope, he could see the mutated, augmented operator in his liquid cocoon under the arched, mantis tail.

'Larkin!'

'You don't rush these things,' Larkin said. He exhaled and pulled the trigger. The cocoon burst. The stalk-tank took another few, stuttering steps, and rocked to a halt, dead on its caliper feet.

The Blood Pact wave was almost on them. Caffran dropped his tube launcher and drew his laspistol. He started to fire at the enemy troopers running in. Nearby, Mkillian cried out as a las-round killed him and knocked him back off the rocks.

A torrent of las-fire cut a swathe across the advancing Archenemy. They buckled and fell.

'Get up! Up and into them!' someone shouted.

It was Tona Criid, running forward, her weapon on full auto. Beside her came Varl and Bonin. They seemed oblivious to the danger, just running into the zipping fire.

Varl reached the rockline beside Caffran, put one boot up on it to brace himself, and let rip from the hip.

'Having a little trouble?' he asked.

Criid ran forward, shot a Blood Pact trooper in the neck, and scooped up the fallen rocket bag from beside Guheen's body.

'Catch!' she cried, throwing it to Caffran.

'First-and-Only!' Varl shouted as he unloaded. 'First-and-fething-Only!'

Caffran grabbed the bag and began packing a rocket into his tube. 'Tona!' he yelled. 'We need to–'

'Shut up, I'm working here!' she shouted, ripping rounds through a trio of Blood Pact troops.

One moment you're alive, the next you're dead. And what are secrets worth then? Caffran briefly looked at Guheen's body. All the way from Tanith, then just gone. Just gone, like that.

He latched a fresh rocket into the launcher, primed it with a quick blessing, and raised the weapon onto his shoulder.

SEVENTY METRES BEHIND him, Wilder was confronting Baskevyl, Feygor and Meryn.

'This isn't the time,' he was saying.

'I think it is,' Baskevyl said. 'Luc, I came down here and I happened to repeat my flippant comment about how I wished I could plug that gate. And Feygor said we could.'

'It's possible,' Feygor said.

'This is crazy talk,' Wilder said.

'No, sir,' said Baskevyl. 'Hear the man out.'

'We could blow it,' Feygor said. 'If we got sufficient charge in there.'

'And how do you hope to–'

'Mark IX land mines,' Feygor smiled. 'There were plenty of them on the munition train last time I looked. Packed with compressive diotride D-6. Explosive putty, very nasty. Give me half an hour and a decent trigger mechanism, and I could rig up a device that would bring that whole fething gate down.'

'No,' said Wilder. 'This is not an option.'

'It really is,' said Rawne, from behind Wilder.

Wilder looked round. 'Your adjutant is a demolitions expert now, is he? You don't mess around with land mines, and you certainly don't mess around with D-6. If I had an authorised bombardier here, or a tech priest, maybe I'd–'

'Feygor knows this stuff. Always has. And since Gereon–'

Wilder groaned. 'Oh, Rawne! Don't *since Gereon* me. Not now.'

'I think I will. How do you suppose we conducted our sabotage operations there, Wilder? Did we give up the idea because we didn't have an authorised bombardier with us? Feygor knows this stuff.'

'I do. I can handle it,' Feygor said.

Wilder hesitated. Up ahead, rockets were slamming into the advancing stalk-tanks.

'So, Feygor builds us a device. Then what?'

'We get it into the gateway,' Meryn said. 'Sneak it in.'

'What else?' Wilder asked.

'Someone has to carry the device,' Feygor said. 'It'll be heavy. Really heavy. I'd need someone strong.'

There was a clatter of metal tanks hitting the ground. 'I'm up for that,' Brostin said, coming forward. He had let his flamer set slide off his broad shoulders.

'Bask?'

'I think this could work, Luc,' Baskevyl said.

'Get to it, Feygor,' Wilder said.

'I'll assemble a strike team to–' Rawne said.

Meryn cut Rawne off. 'I'll assemble a strike team to get the device in place. This is an E Company initiative. Last I heard, I was still in charge of that.'

Rawne nodded.

'Then it'll be me leading that team,' Meryn said.

'No question, captain,' Wilder replied. Meryn hurried away.

Wilder realised that Rawne was looking at him. 'What?'

'You have to understand about the gateways, Wilder. The enemy isn't coming through from the next compartment. It's simply coming out of the gate. It's warping out of that archway.'

Wilder shrugged. 'Whatever, Rawne. But if we plug that gate, the result's the same, right?'

Rawne nodded. 'I think so.'

As Meryn strode off, Banda caught his sleeve.

'What are you doing?' she asked.

'Getting it done, Jessi,' he said.

'I heard you overrule Rawne just then. Are you trying to prove something?' He looked at her. 'What if I am?'

'If you are, try not to make me miss you when you're gone,' Banda said.

HALF AN HOUR turned into an hour and a half. The enemy continued to emerge from the gate. Each time it did, sighing winds from another world gusted out across the compartment.

'Feygor?' Wilder called over the micro-beads.

'It's ready. A real job. Coming in now.'

'Bask!' Wilder yelled. 'Full spread across the gate mouth! Obel? Domor? Varaine? Company fire for support!'

Near the mid-point of the Eighty-First First line, Novobazky had managed to rally I Company. They had taken up position in and around a long island of thorny scrub, which gave them a good angle on the gate. 'Fire for support!' Novobazky shouted. He could see an alarming number of crimson figures in amongst the broken granite seventy metres ahead. Stray tracer shells sailed by, high overhead, like lost birds.

'Commissar!'

Novobazky turned to see Hark running up.

'We're going to need to rise and push,' Hark told him. 'Sitting here and firing isn't going to cut it. You can't see it from this angle, but there's a mass of hostiles around behind that outcrop. This company needs to come forward to that line and lay down a field of fire, or the bastards are going to cut right down our centreline.'

Novobazky nodded, and relayed instructions to the section leaders. Then he remembered the plasma pistol, and offered it to Hark.

'Yours.'

'Keep it,' said Hark.

'Thank you. It served us well,' Novobazky said.

'It's about to again,' Hark said sourly. 'I understand you met Gaunt.'

Novobazky nodded. 'Briefly. He seemed to me to be an admirable man.'

'I'm glad you think so,' Hark nodded. 'I always believed that was the case.'

The combined companies of the Eighty-First First were now hosing the gate mouth with fire.

'Company up to address!' Novobazky yelled. 'Advance and fire at will!'

MERYN'S STRIKE TEAM, twenty-strong, ran forward, cutting through the Blood Pact resistance on the east side of the gate. Meryn had chosen the east side because it was particularly cluttered with loose rock and fat slabs of stone that had fallen from the walls over the centuries. There was plenty of cover, and for the most part they would be shielded from the main Blood Pact retinues.

It was still murderous. Wildfire sizzled between the rocks, and every few metres, hostile troops would suddenly appear from behind boulders. In the first fifteen minutes, two of the Tanith fell, then three of the Belladon Meryn had selected from E Company.

'Come on! Come on!' Meryn yelled out. They had a brief window of opportunity, all the while the heavy fire from the Eighty-First First line was driving the Archenemy backwards towards the end wall of the compartment.

Meryn ran ahead, firing short bursts around the rocks. Behind him came Brostin, struggling under the weight of Feygor's jury-rigged device.

'Keep up!' Feygor shouted, lugging the detonator pack.

'Feth it, Murt, you try carrying this!' Brostin growled back.

Shells slammed in around them. The air stank of scorching las-fire.

Meryn reached the crest of rock in front of the gate. A las-round smacked into his head, and he fell.

Vision blurred and in pain, he reached up and found a wet gash across his scalp. *Almost* a kill shot.

'Advance!' he yelled.

The Archenemy had spread wide, out of the gate. Growling armour was now advancing towards Callide's position, and sweeping east towards the Hauberkan line. The gate itself was empty, vacant like the cavity of a skull.

Brostin staggered into the vast, black mouth of the gate.

'How deep?' he yelled back, his voice echoing.

'Into the throat of it!' Meryn shouted. Shots were winging up from the Blood Pact in the lower basin. They had suddenly realised that a recon force had sneaked around behind them. Cager fell, dead. Mkeln toppled over, his chest torn apart.

'Quickly now!' Meryn yelled. His head hurt.

A las-round hit Meryn in the arm, and exploded his bicep in a shower of bloody meat.

Feygor grabbed him and kept him upright. 'Run!' Feygor said.

'But–'

'Just fething run, Meryn!' Feygor screamed. 'Brostin's set the charge.'

Brostin came running back out of the gateway. Las-fire hit him. He fell, and then got up again, blood streaming from multiple wounds

'Set and down!' he shouted. Two more members of Meryn's strike team were hit and killed.

'Go! Go on!' Feygor yelled, setting down the makeshift detonator pack. Meryn began to sprint, las-rounds whistling after him.

'Open wide,' Feygor said, slamming down the plunger.

For a second, nothing seemed to happen. The force of the blast was so severe, its noise and violence were off the scale of human senses. There was a solid, heavy slam, like an immense weight had hit the earth, then a gigantic, volcanic shower of mud and rock and smoke sprayed out of the gate mouth.

Feygor began to laugh. He threw aside the detonator pack and rose to his feet.

A las-round smacked into his chest. He fell down onto his knees, gurgling and coughing blood.

'Murt! Murt!' Brostin cried out as he reached him.

Murt Feygor murmured something, and slumped onto the ground.

Brostin scooped his limp body up and began to run.

'SEE THAT?' BASKEVYL cried out. 'They did it!'

Wilder waited. He watched the huge, dense cone of smoke rise from the fire-ball engulfing the gate. He thought he might almost be ready to start smiling.

He felt the cool breeze of a pressure change sweep across him, as if a door had opened somewhere, letting in the cold. The smoke billowed and the flames seethed away as chilly air fanned through them. A line of crimson battle tanks, rusted and heavy, began to roll out of the sixth compartment gate, spilling the debris and dying flames in front of them.

They *hadn't* done it. Not even slightly.

TWENTY-SEVEN

18.11 hrs, 199.776.M41
Fifth Compartment
Sparshad Mons, Ancreon Sextus

THE TRAITOR HOSTS of the damned and the insane vomited out of the gate mouth in a swollen tide. It seemed to the men on the ground as if the warp itself had torn open and scattered its contents forth. The charging formations of war machines and troops, of mobile guns and fluttering banners, made everything that they had faced so far seem trivial and slight. The forces they had struggled and fought with over the last few days had been just an advance guard.

Night was falling, but the black filth coiling out of the sixth compartment gate around the arriving hostiles reached upwards and accelerated the descent of darkness. The arcane door had opened so wide this time, weather swept through with it from the climate systems of whatever fell world these creatures had embarked from. Not just cold winds, but fog and moisture. Lightning discharge crackled around the tops of the compartment walls, and covered the stone face of the Mons's towering heart like luminous ivy. Ice rain began to fall, hissing into the fires.

The Kolstec forces took immediate heavy losses and fell back in a desperate, scrabbling retreat. Then fire fell upon the Eighty-First First too. Callide and almost his entire company were cut down and destroyed. Hundreds of bodies in black battledress lay amongst the burning scrub.

Wilder drew the Eighty-First First back, through the rain, through the belts of scraggy woodland and outcropping granite. The temptation was to flee, but that would hasten yet greater disaster. The Archenemy had to be slowed. They had to be harried and delayed. The Kolstec, half-breaking to the west, seemed unable to accomplish this, but the remnants of the Hauberkan treads were still operating in support of the Eighty-First First.

The sound of gunfire was constant and deafening. Wilder caught up with Keshlan at a dry watercourse.

'Signal DeBray!' Wilder yelled above the noise. 'Tell him the retiring line has got to move faster! As fast as it can. Tell him they've got to get out of the compartment! Tell him all hell is coming after them!'

Half a kilometre back, in a stretch of burning woodland, Rawne, Kolea and Baskevyl had established decent bounding cover between the men they brought with them. Two sections would sustain fire while the third fell back. It worked against the foot troops and the ranks of grotesque mutants that poured into the treeline. But there were tanks coming, heavy Brigands by the sound of their engines, perhaps something even bigger, and the sections had no rockets left.

Rawne saw men move past him in the smoke, stragglers trying to rejoin the retreat. Many were badly hurt. He saw Meryn, covered in blood, helped along by two Belladon troopers.

He saw Brostin, trotting as fast as he could, a limp figure in his arms.

'Brostin!' Rawne ran to him. The flame-trooper was smeared in blood. He'd been hit himself several times. Feygor was just a loose bundle, blood soaking his tunic.

'Put him down,' Rawne said.

'I can carry him. I've got to get him to a medic. I've got to get him to Dorden. He'll patch him up.'

Rawne put his hand against Feygor's neck. It was impossible to tell if there was a pulse left, or any sign of respiration. Even if Feygor was still alive, he wouldn't be by the time Brostin had carried him back down the compartment.

'Put him down,' Rawne repeated.

'No!' Brostin was agitated by the idea. 'We didn't come all the way through fething Gereon to wind up dying in a place like this! I can carry him!' he moved on, blundering through the smoking trees. 'I can carry him!'

WILDER REACHED AN area of rising, open ground, and tried to take his bearings. To the east, at least four companies of the Eighty-First First, along with some Hauberkan armour, was cutting along the scrublands, moving steadily south. Directly behind him, Daur's company and parts of Obel's, along with an assortment of men from Kolosim and Varaine's commands, were caught in a brutal firefight with the leading edge of the Blood Pact units.

Wilder realised the western flank of the breakaway was yawning dangerously. If the enemy overlapped, they'd catch Daur, Obel and the others quickly and simply. What had happened to his formation?

He looked around again, calling A Company up around him into a firing line. His throat was sore from smoke. The rain was getting heavier, and the ground was turning to mire. To the south of him, the ground shelved away and rose into a significant hill. With a little surprise, Wilder realised it was Hill 56, the very site they'd been assigned to at the start of this punishing and pointless expedition. If he could retain cohesion long enough to get a force onto its back, he'd have a commanding field of fire right across the scrub. To the west of the hill, the main trackway ran wide. It was choked with a portion of the fleeing Kolstec units. He saw, to his dismay, that in the mayhem, both Domor's and Sabrese's companies had fallen back too far, right onto the track. That was where the gap had formed.

'Keshlan!' he yelled. 'Get me Sabrese, quickly! We've got to get him to move up a little.'

The vox-officer obeyed, but he looked dubious. The distance was significant. Persuading those men to turn back into the teeth of the enemy advance was going to be a tall order. Fierce shelling and heavy weapons fire was coming out of the ruined scrub to the left. Even the most loyal soldiers would falter from an effort like that.

A curious thing began to happen. Keshlan had yet to secure a clear channel, but Sabrese and Domor's men were beginning to move back anyway. They were advancing into the fight, covering the trackway. The gap was actually starting to close.

'Link up with those men!' Wilder shouted to A Company. 'Across the slope! Give them covering fire as they close up!'

Blood Pact and mutant troopers swarmed out of the scrub, but the supporting companies drove them back again with a blistering rate of shots. Wilder could hear shouts coming from Domor's men, and Sabrese's too. Battle cries. Passionate, almost eager.

He saw two figures amongst them. Two commissars, directing the steady flow of the regroup. One had a sword raised aloft.

'GHOSTS OF TANITH! Men of Belladon!' Gaunt shouted. 'Close the line! Deny the enemy!'

'First-and-Only!' the men were shouting.

'Domor! Get some men onto those rocks,' Gaunt yelled as he strode forward through the men. Eszrah came with him, reynbow raised. The men seemed as astonished at the sight of Gaunt as they were by the towering warrior at his heels.

'Yes, sir!' Domor barked. Despite the enclosing horror, there was a renewed vitality in the troops. 'Gaunt's with us!' Domor shouted. 'Gaunt's with us! Chiria, Nehn! Get men into those rocks! Raglon, section to the left, rapid fire!'

'We can do this,' Gaunt said to Domor. 'We can't win, but we can hold them back.'

'Yes, sir,' Domor said. He couldn't quite accept the sight of the man in front of him. Even with his augmetic eyes, Gaunt didn't seem real. 'Sir, are you a ghost?' he asked.

Gaunt smiled. 'Always have been.'

Ludd ran up. 'Sections are holding to the right, sir.'

'Go to them, Ludd. Keep them together and keep them strong.'

'How, commissar?'

'Improvise. Sing them a song, tell them you're my clone-son, whatever works.' Ludd nodded, and rushed away. Wounded stragglers from the rear of the breakaway stumbled past. The Tanith and Verghastite amongst them blinked when they saw Gaunt. Some stopped, and despite their injuries, came to him.

'Keep moving,' Gaunt called out. 'Get onto the track and get away from here. We'll drink to this day together, later on.'

Gaunt saw Brostin amongst them, Brostin and the sad bundle he carried. He went over to the bulky flame-trooper immediately. Brostin sank down to his knees, tired, hurt and barely able to go on. He clutched Feygor's limp body tightly in his hefty arms.

'Let him go,' Gaunt said. 'Let him lie on the ground.'

'Sir…'

Eszrah knelt down and examined Feygor. He looked at Gaunt and shook his head.

'He's gone, Brostin,' said Gaunt. 'I'm too late for him, but not the rest of you.'

Brostin gently laid Feygor's body on the wet grass. Rain streamed off his beard like tears.

'Get moving, Brostin. I'll catch you up.'

Gaunt straightened up and turned back to face the fight. Eszrah touched his arm lightly and pointed. An officer was approaching.

'Commissar Gaunt?'

'Colonel Wilder?'

They stood facing each other in the rain. Gaunt put his sword in his left hand and held out his right.

'My compliments, colonel. The lord general has ordered me back to the line to assist with the rearguard.'

Wilder shook his hand. 'We don't seem to need much help dying right now,' Wilder said.

'You've executed a fine breakaway action, Wilder,' Gaunt said. 'A great number of lives have been spared by–'

'It's not over,' Wilder said bluntly. 'You have no idea of the weight of hostiles at our heels.'

'Nevertheless, I believe we should still call the day done. Move the men onto the trackway and get them out to–'

'You're not listening!' Wilder snapped. 'There is a nightmare coming and we must check it for as long as we can. I intend to get a force up onto that hill, at least a company strong. From there, they should be able to hold the scrubland long enough to allow the rest to get away.'

Gaunt regarded the hill. 'It would be possible, I suppose…'

'Look, Gaunt. I know you just want to get your men out.'

'My men? They're not my men, Wilder. They're yours. The Eighty-First First. And a fine regiment too. Give me command of a company, and I'll hold that hill for you. I'll buy you enough time to get the rest of your men clear.'

Wilder smiled and shook his head. 'I'll not order a man to die while I run for home. Nor do I expect you to do a job I wouldn't do myself. My regiment, you said. My men. My job.'

'Wilder–'

'I believe I outrank you, commissar. You don't hold a command rank. I will hold the hill with A Company. My orders to you are to take field command of the remainder of the regiment, and conduct them to a place of safety while I cover your backs.'

'Throne's sake, Wilder, don't be so awkward! This isn't some contest to see which of us is the bigger man, this–'

'Actually, it almost is. This way, we both win and we both lose.'

'Colonel, I'm not–'

'Are you disobeying direct orders, Gaunt? I'd heard you'd come back from that place with an unruly streak to you. A touch of taint, they say. A lack of proper discipline. No place for that in the Imperial Guard. I've given you your orders. Are you going to follow them?'

Gaunt glared at Wilder. 'Yes, sir,' he said, and saluted.

'Excellent. Carry on.' Wilder saluted back and turned away.

'The Emperor protects,' Gaunt said.

Wilder snorted. 'Some of us he does.'

THE ANGLE OF fire from the top of Hill 56 was as good as Wilder had hoped. He formed A Company up, and began laying fusillades down across the scrub, where the enemy formations were now in sight, toiling forward through the scorched and smoking land.

'Keep the rate up, A Company!' Wilder yelled. There seemed to be a near impossible number of targets crossing the valley below, hordes of red and black figures, machines that rolled or walked. The woods beyond burned like a blast furnace and threw smoke up the towering compartment wall. Stalkers had appeared in great numbers too, no doubt from their mysterious doorways. Many were bounding ahead of the enemy troops like gigantic attack dogs, hooting and roaring. Some were gigantic things.

Down on the trackway to the west of A Company, the last of their comrades moved away, south, into the enclosing darkness.

Genadey Novobazky strode down the A Company line, his voice firm and defiant. 'On the Shores of Marik, my friends,' he declaimed, 'the fathers of our fathers made a stand under the flag of Belladon. Did they break and run? Yes! But only in their minds. They ran to friendly places and loved ones, where they could be safe… and then, by the providence of the God-Emperor, they saw what those friendly places and loved ones would become if they did not stand fast, and so stand fast they did! How do you feel?'

There was a triumphant bellow from the ranks.

'Belladon blood is like wine on the Emperor's lips!' Novobazky stormed. 'Belladon souls have a special place at his side! If we spill our blood here today, then this is the soil He has chosen to bless and anoint! Oh, lucky land!' He took out the plasma pistol, and carefully toggled off the safety. No mistakes this time. 'Stand firm and fire, my friends, stand firm and fire! If they're going to have our precious blood, then they'll find the cost is dearer than they can afford! Fury of Belladon! Fury! Fury!'

Wilder grinned as he heard the surge of Novobazky's speech. A piece of art that, he'd always thought. And never more so than now.

'Keshlan!' The vox-officer ran to him.

'Yes, colonel!'

'Wilder beckoned for the vox-horn. 'Speaker broadcast, please, Keshlan. All the volume you've got.'

'Yes, sir!'

THE FIRST OF the Archenemy warriors began to charge up the slopes of Hill 56, into the hail of gunfire. Hundreds fell, but there were thousands behind them to take their places. The Blood Pact horns bellowed into the night air. Blades flashed, banners swung. Feral mutants and wrought beasts led the attack.

Crookshank Thrice-wrought was at the very front of the storming line, shrugging off the flashes of light that stung at his hide. He came up the long slope, roaring through his throat sacs. He could see and smell the meat ahead of him. The rows of little meat figures who curiously refused to flee at the sight of him.

Bounding forward, the thrice-wrought opened his mouth and engaged his teeth.

WILDER THUMBED ON the vox-horn and raised it to his mouth. When he spoke, his voice boomed out from Keshlan's vox, distorted with volume.

'Stand firm, A Company! Fury of Belladon! Hold this line and deny them!'

His amplified voice echoed out across the bleak hillside, carrying his command away into the rain and the raging night.

His last command.

EPILOGUE

00.07 hrs, 200.776.M41
Ancreon Sextus

THE SUN CAME out, in the middle of the night, and the step-cities died. Even from a great distance, it was impossible for observers to look directly at the bombardment without filters or glare-shades. Devastating pillars of white light came down from the top of the sky and burned deep, black holes into the world.

It took the warships of the Imperial Navy five hours of sustained orbital bombardment to wipe the ancient and cursed stones of the monolithic cities from existence.

In the days that followed, all that remained at the sites where the step-cities had once stood were gaping wounds in the earth, some a kilometre deep. Within these slowly cooling cavities, jewelled beauty lurked. The fury of the weapons had transformed the rock and sand, fusing it into swathes of glass that glinted and swam with colour in the bright sun.

JUST AFTER MIDNIGHT, Gaunt was amongst the many hundreds of Imperial officers congregated on the hull-top landing pads of one of the command Leviathans to watch the distant doom of Sparshad Mons. Zweil stood by his side. He'd borrowed Eszrah's glare-shades, and winced and gasped at every flash of light.

'You did that, Ibram,' Van Voytz said, coming up to Gaunt and nodding in the direction of the fearsome lightshow. 'Hope you're proud of yourself.'

'Proud of something, sir.'

'I understand they're yours again?' Van Voytz said.

'It's a field command only,' said Gaunt. 'Just temporary.'

'We'll see,' said Van Voytz.

'He said he couldn't, but he could, you know,' Zweil said after Van Voytz had moved on.

'What?' Gaunt asked.

'He said he couldn't bring things back from the dead, but it turned out he could.'

'Who are we talking about, father?'

'Wilder,' Zweil said.

'Oh.'

'You and Rawne and the others all came back when we thought you dead. And now the unit has too.'

'I don't–'

'It's yours again. Wilder gave them back to you. Not his Ghosts. Yours again. Gaunt's Ghosts, back from the dead.'

'You know, you talk a lot of nonsense sometimes, father,' Gaunt said.

THE HATCH OF the holding cell opened and Inquisitor Welt entered the chamber. Commissar Faragut got up from the table to make room for the inquisitor.

Welt sat down beside the commissar-general. 'How are we doing?' he asked.

'I think we're getting somewhere,' Balshin said, looking across the table at the interview subject.

'Good, good,' said Welt. 'Shall we go back over the main areas, in case there's something we missed?'

'Fine with me,' said Balshin. Welt looked questioningly at the interview subject.

Sabbatine Cirk shrugged. 'Just tell me what you want to know.'

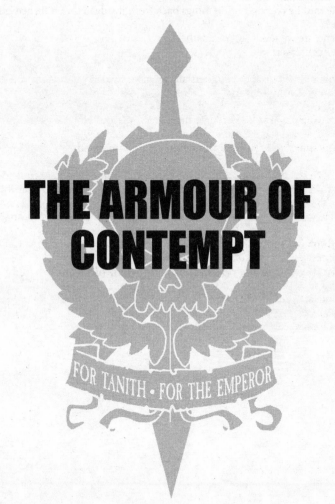

THE ARMOUR OF CONTEMPT

FOR TANITH · FOR THE EMPEROR

*For my friend Richard Collins
on the occasion of his fortieth birthday*

'Chaos claims the unwary or the incomplete.
A true man may flinch away its embrace,
if he is stalwart, and he girds his soul
with the armour of contempt.'

— Gideon Ravenor,
The Spheres of Longing

'T HE TWENTY-SECOND *year of the Sabbat Worlds Crusade saw a period of renewed fortune for Warmaster Macaroth's main battle groups. Flush from swift and decisive victories at Cabal Alpha, Gerlinde and Zadok, the Warmaster's forces made a vigorous advance into the disputed Carcaradon Cluster, and threw the principal hosts of the Archenemy overlord ('Archon'), Urlock Gaur, into hasty retreat. Macaroth's intention was to scatter and destroy the Archon's musters before they could form a cohesive line of resistance in the Erinyes Group.*

'*To Macaroth's coreward flank, and increasingly left behind, the Crusade's secondary battle-groups – the Fifth, Eighth and Ninth Crusade Armies – maintained their efforts to drive the forces of Magister Anakwanar Sek, Gaur's most capable lieutenant, from the margins of the Khan Group.*

'*Weakened by problems of morale and logistics, and the fact that the bulk of its manpower came from new and recently founded regiments (the majority of experienced and veteran Guard units had been routed to the main line), the second front had begun to stagnate by the start of 777.M41.*

'*To compound the problems, the armies of the second front often found themselves outclassed by the highly proficient ground forces fielded by Sek. It is likely many of the second front commanders would have incurred Macaroth's severe displeasure, had the Warmaster not been so singularly occupied with his own objectives. However, General Van Voytz of the Fifth made strenuous efforts to rally the second front, in particular by promoting a series of uncompromising actions to liberate certain worlds previously regarded as 'lost causes'.*

'*Van Voytz dubbed his strategy "Crush and Burn", and its purpose was to restore pride to the second front through the systematic purging of worlds that had, until then, seemed incontrovertibly the possessions of the Archenemy.*

'*"Crush and Burn" had the desired effect, though the vast expenditure of resources necessitated by the policy was later questioned by the Munitorum. Confidential position papers also reveal that, in one particular case, there was an altogether different motive behind these costly liberation efforts.'*

– from A History of the Later Imperial Crusades

WALKING GLORY ROAD

I

RIP WAS AN acronym, and it happened in the Basement. There were two hundred and forty-three scalps in the detail, the majority of them there for the 'P' part of the name. On the first day, Criid didn't know anybody, and stood alone, hands in pockets. That earned a few words of elucidation from the instructor, Driller Kexie.

'No bloody Guardsman, not even a wet-fart scalp like you, parks their hands in their pockets!' Kexie opined. Kexie was two-twenty tall, and looked as if he had been woven out of meat jerky. He spoke in a slow measure, as if he had all the time in the world to wither and abuse, and the words came out of his dry, lipless mouth like tracer-shot: hot, bright and burning. If he shouted at night, you'd see his words stitch up the dark like phosphor tears.

Driller Kexie had a stick. For reasons no one in the detail ever fathomed, he called it 'Saroo'. It was a thick spar of turned hardwood, forty centimetres long, and resembled both an officer's baton and the leg of a chair. Kexie liked to reinforce certain words and phrases with Saroo. At 'wet-fart scalp', Kexie stroked Saroo against Criid's left hand, which was still in its pocket. A flash flood of acute pain flared across the knuckles of Criid's fist. On 'like you', Saroo visited Criid's right hand. The words 'parks hands' brought Saroo right up between Criid's legs. Criid dropped onto the metal decking, sucking air.

'Upright, hands at your sides. No other posture is acceptable to the God-Emperor, to me, or to Saroo. Are we clear?'

'Yes, driller.'

'Ech,' Kexie said, tilting his head on one side. He had, they would discover, a habit of punctuating his speech with that particular sound. 'Ech,

515

call that a clean loader?' 'Ech, what a shit-soft attempt!' 'That the best you offer, ech?'

'Ech,' he said, 'I don't believe that Saroo can hear you, scalp?'

'Yes, driller!' Criid shouted. 'We are clear, driller!'

'Get up,' Kexie sniffed, and turned back to the others.

Some of the others were greatly amused. The first day was scarcely ten minutes old, and already one of their number was prone on the deck with pain-wet eyes.

They were an ugly lot, most of them the flotsam of various regiments. Criid had already put a name to three or four of the most prominent. A nickname, at least. There was Fourbox, who was a tall, heavy-set joker from the 33rd Kolstec. He was on RIP, he had proudly declared to them as they gathered, for being 'rubbish at everything'. Lovely was a female tanker from the Hauberkan. She was on her third repeat of RIP, though this was her first taste of Driller Kexie. 'I don't like orders,' she had replied when Fourbox asked her what her reason for being there was, and left it at that. Lovely had a real edge to her. Dark haired and tanned, she seemed as risky as an unsheathed knife in a kitbag.

Boulder, as was often the case with Guard nicknames, belonged to a youth who didn't deserve it. Boulder was small and scrawny, a stick-thin go-nowhere, another Kolstec like Fourbox. Criid supposed the sledgehammer irony of the Imperial Guard had stuck Boulder with his handle. Though he was small, and looked picked-on, it was hard to empathise with him. He had a shrill cackle, and used it to signal his delight at the pain of others. Boulder had been sent on RIP by his commanding officer 'for fixing a bay-onet to a rocket launcher, haw-haw-haw.'

In Criid's opinion, less than ten minutes old, Wash was the real poison in the detail. Wash reminded Criid of Major Rawne: tall, dark, handsome and venomous. He knew he looked good, even in the faded RIP issue fatigues, and he regarded all of them with a dismissive silence. When, as they first assembled, Fourbox had asked him 'what he was in for', Wash simply hooded his eyes and turned his back.

'Oooh, hard man, haw-haw-haw!' Boulder had sniggered, and Fourbox and some of the others had laughed along.

Wash had turned, extended the index finger of his left hand, and inserted it into Boulder's mouth, pushing the fingertip up over the front teeth until it wedged, painfully, in the roof of the gum, tenting the lip and philtrum against Boulder's nostrils. Boulder had snorted in distress but, like a fish on a hook, had been unable to pull free.

'I am not "hard man",' Wash had said. 'I am not your bloody friend. You want me, you ask for Wash. And you never, ever want me.'

With that, he let Boulder's lip go. Everyone was suitably respectful of Wash from that point.

'Tanith takes a dive!' Fourbox chortled when Driller Kexie put Criid on the deck. 'First and only, they say. First and only to get a smack!'

'Tanith's tearing up,' Boulder joined. 'Look, look! Like a little girl! Boo hoo! Haw-haw-haw!'

'Go home to mama, little Tanith!' Fourbox sang out.

'She'll wipe your eyes and make it all nice again,' Lovely sniggered. 'Mwah! Mwah!' she added, pantomiming kisses. 'All better now!'

'My mother...' Criid began, getting up. 'My mother would gut you fethers...'

'Oh, *I'm* so bloody scared!' announced Boulder. 'So scared, I wet myself haw-haw-haw!'

'I know your mama,' Fourbox called. 'She wriggled a bit, but she was all right. She still writes to me. "Oh, Boxy, when can we be together again? I long for your hot–"'

'Enough!' Driller Kexie tracered. 'Staple your lips, you wet-farts. Ech, I've seen some details in my time, but you take the brass arse. Muscle up, in a line! Come on, come on! Get up and get in it, Criid. Drill order. Is that a drill order, shit-wit? Get to it! Six lines, now! Come on!'

Kexie walked the lines, twirling Saroo in his calloused hands.

It was cold in the echoing vault of the Basement. Their breath made smoke in the air. Like all bilge spaces, the Basement was unheated and raw. Its walls were a ferruginous stain of rust and metallic gangrene, and the air smelled of the stale urine and solvents that had leaked down-hull.

'All right, ladies and ladies,' said Kexie. 'I'm assuming that's the best you can do. Frig, I've seen foundees dress a better rank. You are *shit*, you hear me? The lowest of the low. You are RIP, and making your life a misery is my purpose, given to me expressly by the God-Emperor of Mankind himself. Ech, I have to turn you into proper bloody Guardsmen. You come to me as wet-farts, and I send you back as real soldiers. Or... you die.'

He paused and ran his gaze along their silent rank.

'Anyone got anything funny to say about that? Come on, now. Speak openly.'

'Well, you can try,' Lovely suggested.

Saroo struck her in the throat, and then across the back of the head as she went down.

Lovely lay on the decking, choking. Criid moved to help her.

'No one bloody move. No one! Let her soak it up. Anyone else got a comment? No? *No?*'

Kexie stopped pacing and stood facing them. 'Welcome, you sons and daughters of bitches, to RIP detail. Let us be sure we understand what those letters stand for. "R" is... I'm waiting?'

'Retraining, driller,' they murmured.

Kexie smacked Saroo into his palm. 'I don't believe Saroo can hear you...'

'Retraining!' they yelled.

'And the "I" is for...?'

'Indoctrination, driller!'

'Getting there. Good. And the "P"? You all know what that means?'

'Punishment, driller!'

Kexie nodded. 'Good and good. Ech. So let me do a head count. I'm guessing most of you scalps are here for "P" purposes. Show of hands.'

Most of the detail, including Boulder, Wash and Lovely, raised their hands.

Kexie nodded again. 'And who's in for "R"?'

A handful, including Fourbox.

Kexie swung Saroo in his hands. 'Imagine my surprise if any of you are here for "I". Anyone?'

Eight hands rose. Criid was one of them.

'Shit,' said Kexie. '*Eight* of you? All right, you eight. Front and centre.'

Criid came forward alongside the other seven. They looked like boys, all of them, with that long-limbed, round-shouldered, malnourished air of puberty.

'Look and learn, you wet-farts,' Kexie told the rest of them. 'These eight are virgins. Cherry bloody scalps. Never seen a day of hot war. Never fired in anger. You'd bloody well better make sure none of them do better than you, or I will personally take a bolt pistol to the sides of your heads and grin when I twitch the trigger.'

Kexie regarded the eight 'I' candidates.

'Deck-thrusts, fifty reps,' he said. 'Now.'

AFTER AN HOUR of reps, the detail ran ropes for three hours or so, and then did circuits of the Basement with weight loads. By the time five hours were done, they were numb and mindless with fatigue.

'Switch, ropes!' Kexie yelled.

Fourbox, sweaty and flushed, could no longer haul himself up the knotted ropes to the Basement's roof.

'Anyone fails, the whole detail repeats!' Kexie informed them.

'Spit on your palms,' Criid whispered across to Fourbox. 'Spit on your palms and you get a better grip.'

Fourbox did so, and began to ascend.

'Who taught you that?' he grunted.

'My father,' said Criid, several metres higher and going strong.

'What's his name?'

'Which one?' asked Criid.

II

THE LIGHTS DOWN the roof of the Basement began to switch off, each bank dying with a loud *rr-chunk*. The members of the detail were scattered like battlefield dead on the practice mats, panting and moaning. Their sweat-soaked fatigues stuck to their bodies. They lay on their backs, holding their hands out like faith healers, away from any contact. Fat with friction blisters, their palms were too inflamed to bear touching anything.

'Right here, tomorrow, at oh six hundred,' Driller Kexie told them. 'Not a minute later, or Saroo will want to know why. Assemble and salute me.'

Drill Instructor Kexie stood, slapping Saroo against his right thigh, as the RIP detail slowly got to its feet and formed ranks.

'Six weeks,' Kexie said. 'Six weeks walking Glory Road to planet-fall. God-Emperor, I'll have turned some of you into fighting bloody Guardsman by then. Today was a disgrace. Tomorrow, you'll do better. Dismissed.'

Kexie wandered over to Criid as the detail broke up.

'Sorry about the hard whacks, Criid,' he whispered. 'I didn't realise you were here on indoctrination.'

Criid nodded. 'That's all right, driller. You weren't to know.'

'No, I wasn't. Shame. Now put the bloody mats away.'

The rush-woven practice mats were heavy, and twelve metres square. Hauling and rolling them into their lockers would have been a significant feat for anyone, let alone a person with brutally blistered hands.

'You're kidding?' said Criid.

'Are you refusing an order, scalp?' Kexie asked.

'No, but–'

Saroo paid Criid a rather more prolonged visit, smacking into places where the bruises wouldn't show.

After Kexie had gone, Criid lay on the deck for a long while, drenched in pain, and then got up and put the mats away. It took a long while. Fourbox, Lovely and half a dozen other members of the RIP detail were lingering by the hatch. They'd all seen what the driller had done. Finally they came over and helped Criid with the mats.

'I can do it,' Criid said.

'Driller really beat on you,' Fourbox said. 'You all right?' The mischief had been robbed from his face. He looked genuinely worried.

'Yes. Look, I can do this.'

'Be quicker if we help,' said one of the others, a thin boy called Zeedon.

'Kexie's a bastard,' Lovely said. 'Think I might stick him good.'

'Yeah, sure you will,' Fourbox said.

'I got a blade,' Lovely snapped. 'I'll stick the bastard, he comes near me with that rod again.'

'Don't,' said Criid.

'Why not?' Lovely asked. 'He's got it coming…'

'Don't be stupid. Attack an officer?' Criid said. 'You''ll be executed. Summary shots behind the ear.'

'Be worth it,' Lovely said, but she no longer sounded so sure.

'Driller's doing his job, don't you get that?' Criid said. 'This is the Imperial Guard. Drill discipline and hard knocks. That's what gets us to the grade and keeps us there. If you expect any different, Throne knows why you ever signed up.'

'You sound like a bloody commissar,' one of the others said.

Criid smiled. 'First compliment I've had today.'

'What's your name?' asked Fourbox.

'Criid.'

'What, like the holy Imperial creed?'

'No. Double "i" not double "e". It's a Verghast name.'

'I'm going to call you "Holy",' said Fourbox, alighting on a nickname in the time-honoured Guard way of zero consideration. 'Yeah, "Holy". Got a good ring to it.'

'Whatever you think best,' said Criid.

'Who's that?' asked Lovely suddenly, pointing. On the far side of the Basement deck, a figure was standing in the shadows of the main entry hatch. A woman, tall and slender, wearing dark combat gear and the pins of a sergeant.

'Feth,' muttered Criid.

'Who is that?' asked Lovely.

'Just my—' Criid began. 'My supervising officer, come to fetch me. Tomorrow, all right?'

'Same time, same pain, Holy!' Fourbox laughed out as Criid hurried away.

'Holy?' the woman asked as Criid joined her.

'I won a nickname.'

'Is that a bruise?' she asked, reaching out to touch Criid's face.

'Don't!' Criid hissed, slapping her hand away.

'Who did that to you?'

'I fell. During an exercise.'

'You're limping.'

'Leave it alone. What are you doing here?'

'I came to see how you'd got on. First day and everything.'

'Well, I wish you hadn't.' Criid pushed past her and limped on down the service way.

'Dalin!' she growled.

Nearly eighteen years old, tall and strong, Dalin Criid was afraid of nothing in the cosmos apart from the sound of her voice. He halted.

'Someone beat you?' she asked.

'The driller was making a point. That there are no favourites in RIP.'

'Bastard. I should kill him,' Tona Criid said. 'Want me to kill him?'

'No,' he replied, 'but if you come here to find me again, ma, I want you to be sure and kill me.'

III

FOOD CYCLE. THE swelter decks were heaving. Grease smoke and steam wallowed out of the mess wells, and rolled along the roof above the milling crowd. The grilles of the vent ducts were matted with ropes of solidified fat. There was a smell of boiled greens, mashed squash and pith oil. Hand bells were ringing. Various vendors called out their bills of fare to the passing tide.

For an issue scrip, a trooper could eat basic heated rations in the Munitorum halls, but the promise of something different drew hundreds of them to the swelter decks at the end of every day cycle. That, and the fact you could get drink here, and indulge other vices, if you knew who to ask.

The swelter decks existed because of the 'followers on the strength'. Every Guard regiment trailed after it an entourage of attendant personnel: wives, children, girlfriends, whores, faith healers, preachers, beggars, tinkers, hucksters, tooth-pullers, contrabandeers, scribes, loan-sharks and a whole panoply of shadowy souls who lived, like parasites, like fleas, on the coat-tails of the military. Hark had been told that some regiments doubled in size when you factored in the hangers-on.

The swelter decks were where they lived and ate, and dealt and traded. He'd once heard a junior commissar suggest the camp followers be purged from the fleet. 'It would reduce Munitorum costs by nearly fifty per cent,' the junior had announced brightly.

'Yes,' Hark had smiled, 'and the following day, every Guardsman in the quadrant would desert.'

As they wandered down through the press of the main gangway, Viktor Hark noted with some satisfaction that his companion showed no signs of voicing any similarly naive comments. Ludd's eyes were wide, for this was Junior Commissar Nahum Ludd's first experience of a carrier's fringe areas. But he was bright and sharp, and Hark could see why his superior had arranged Ludd's formal transfer to the re-formed First-and-Only.

They ducked under a gibbet rack of swinging, salted waterfowls, and then sidestepped to avoid the steam outflow from a rack of broiling vats. Eager voices were raised as dirty hands held out currency to be exchanged for fried meat on wooden sticks and parcels of spiced mince wrapped in cabbage leaves.

'Hungry?' Hark asked.

'I've eaten, sir,' replied Ludd, raising his voice over the din.

'Munitorum basics?' Hark wondered.

'I ate at the early shift. It comes out of our pay, after all.'

'What was it tonight?'

'Ah, some kind of pickled fish, and a starch pudding.'

'Nice?'

'The, ah, fish was piquant, you might say,' Ludd said.

A tender hurried by with a shoulder paddle laden with steaming pies. Ludd turned and watched them go past. Hark could almost see the young man salivate.

Viktor Hark was powerfully built with thick dark hair and a clean-shaven face. His head rose from his thick neck like the tip of a bullet. He had an easy, casual manner about him that Ludd found disquieting, particularly as Ludd knew Hark could be a savage and ruthless disciplinarian. At some point in his life – Ludd had never had the balls to ask about it – Hark had lost his left arm and had received an augmetic replacement.

Hark raised that augmetic now and clicked the fingers. The flick of the mechanical digits sounded like a boltgun being racked.

The tender stopped in his tracks.

'Sir?'

'Two of those,' Hark said, pointing a V-fork of his real fingers.

'Sweet or sour, sir?' the tender asked, sweeping his wooden paddle round to proffer his wares.

'What is it?'

'Spiced fowl, or sugar ploin, sir.'

'Ludd?'

'Ah, ploin, sir?'

'One of each, then,' Hark said, fetching coins from his coat pocket.

They took the hot pies. The tender gave them sheets of grease paper to fold them in.

They began to walk and eat. Ludd was evidently hungry. He was enjoying his pie so much his eyes were watering.

'Thank you, sir,' he said.

Brushing crumbs from his mouth, Hark made a dismissive gesture. 'What are we now, Ludd?' he asked.

Ludd had to hurriedly swallow a hot mouthful to answer. He winced. 'I... ah, I'm not sure I know what you mean, sir.'

'Well, Nahum, what were we before I bought the pies?'

'Ah... two commissars patrolling the rude quarters?'

'Swelter decks, Ludd. That's what the camp followers call them. I know "low quarters" is the official term, but for Throne's sake, it sounds like the start of a barrack room joke.'

'Yes, sir.'

'Eat up.' Hark took another bite of his pie. He had to chew and wait until his mouth was clear enough to continue. 'You're right, anyway. Two commissars, wandering the swelter decks. You're a ne'er-do-well trooper with something to hide. You see the likes of us, you know we're looking. But two commissars, eating pies... and, by the way, getting crumbs and juice down the front of his uniform...'

'Mhm! Sorry!'

'Now what does that say?'

'That we're here for food cycle? And therefore... not on any official duty?'

Hark bowed his head. 'Exactly. A trick of the trade, Nahum. If you can't hide, hide in plain sight.'

There was a sound of music, of reed pipes. Hark looked around with a start. A troupe of entertainers capered past, playing pipes and viols and hand drums. Five acrobats were turning handsprings in their wake along the main aisle. Jugglers ran like skirmishers around the fringes, snatching hats, fruit and other items like spoons and half-eaten skewers from unsuspecting passers-by, and were spinning them in the air once or twice before returning them to their laughing, baffled owners. A small child followed the troupe, her eyes huge in a face smeared lime green with camo-paint, collecting coins in a battered Guardsman's helmet that she held out, like a bucket, by the chinstrap.

Hark drew Ludd back to let them go by. Junior Ecclesiarchy adepts with ink-stained fingers were moving through the crowd, circulating Lectitio Divinitatus texts still damp from the block-presses. Beggars and invalids offered wares of candle stubs and balls of bootblack. At a nearby cook stand, two Guardsmen, one a Kolstec, the other a heavy-set Hauberkan, were arguing over who was next to be served. It looked like a brawl was about to start.

'Ignore it,' Hark said to Ludd. 'Break it up and we show our hand. We're here on other business.'

Ludd nodded, scoffing down the last of his pie. He wiped his mouth on his cuff.

The press around them was getting thicker. Ludd could smell liquor. A scrawny preacher, either half-mad or half-cut, had got up on a handmade pushcart pulpit, and was yelling to any who might care to listen about the 'jubilation of the dying soul'.

Hark wasn't listening. He could still hear the sound of the pipes, fading through the crowd as the troupe moved away. It reminded him of something, in the way that a dream forgotten from the night before sometimes catches up suddenly and becomes memory again. As with such dreams, Hark couldn't define or reconnect the memory. But there was a feeling buried there. Sadness. Regret.

'Sir?'

'What?'

'Sir?' Ludd asked.

Hark blinked. Foolish to be so distracted. That just wouldn't do. Glory Road was always a long walk, and a commissar had the best of his work there. 'Well,' he said, quietly and carefully, 'what did your source say again?'

'Pavver's Place,' Ludd replied. 'It's where Merrt's been seen most. My source says he's over three hundred in the hole.'

'You have to wonder why he keeps going back,' said Hark.

'You do have to wonder,' Ludd said. 'I think there may be more to it than the money.'

Hark nodded. He knew Rhen Merrt of old, one of the original Tanith foundees. War had been cruel to him, and dealt him a bad hand. Seemed like fortune was continuing the spell.

'Are we to execute him?' Ludd asked bluntly.

'What? No!' Hark said. 'Throne, no! You think I'm that hardline, Ludd?'

'I don't know you, sir,' said Ludd. 'I wanted to understand your thinking.'

Hark nodded. 'Sound, then. Decent question. No, I won't shoot him. Unless he gives me real cause. He's one of our own, Ludd, and we've come to save him before he tips over the brink. For the good of Trooper Merrt *and* the regiment. Morale and discipline dance a delicately balanced polka, Ludd. You know what a polka is?'

'Like a... leopard?'

'No. Is that Pavver's Place?'

'Yes, sir.'

'Good. Give me your cap and coat,' Hark said.

'My cap and coat?'

'Come along. Take this.' Hark held out a fold of dirty bills. 'Go and take a look.'

Ludd handed over his cap and coat. Without them, he looked like a junior trooper in his grubby fatigues. He took the fold, tucked it in his hip pocket, and headed towards Pavver's Place.

Pavver's Place liked to think of itself as some kind of 'establishment'. In truth, it wasn't. It lay a few steps down from the deck gangway, a dark, smoky gaming den fashioned into the stanchion holes between hull supports. Most of the roof was a tent made of stolen tarpaulin. There was a charge pending in that alone, Ludd thought.

Music was playing, loud 'pound' music issuing from battered vox-horns wired up in the tent roof. Several lightly clad girls sashayed through the crowd, hoisting trays of drinks, moving their skinny hips in time to the beat. There was no joy in their eyes, nor any bounce in their step. Pavver paid them to swing their bodies to the music as part of their jobs.

Ludd entered, crossed to the makeshift bar, and ordered an amasec.

The barkeep regarded his apparent youthfulness dubiously, until Ludd slapped a bill on the counter. His drink was served in a little, thick-milled, dirty glass.

Without looking around, Ludd had made out Trooper Merrt at a side table, amongst a card school. There was no mistaking him. A round to the mouth on Monthax years ago had blown his jaw out, and he now sported a crude augmetic implant. Merrt had once been a sniper, one of the Tanith's better marksmen, but the injury had put paid to that career speciality. Since the forests of Monthax, Merrt had tried six times to rejoin the sniper cadre. Every time he'd been unsuccessful.

He was scowling as the cards came down, though he always scowled with his face. Around the table with him were four other players: two Kolstec, a Binar and, Ludd noticed, a Belladon. Sipping his drink, Ludd fought to remember the Belladon's name. Maggs. That was it. Recon Trooper Maggs. Bonin spoke highly of him. What the feth was he doing here?

Merrt seemed distracted. The flop clearly hadn't gone his way, but he was raising anyway.

Ludd looked around the place. There, in the corner, was Pavver, with four of his strong-arms. 'Pander' Pavver, lean and nasty, with a thick, crusty fork of beard and a glassy eye. Ex-Guard. In 'the strength', ex-Guard were usually the worst kinds of predator. Pavver and his lackeys were watching Merrt, and talking low. Another loss to the house, another loss Merrt couldn't cover, and they'd skin him.

Ludd reached into his trouser pocket and felt the comfortable grip of his auto-snub. This was going to get ugly. Uglier than Rhen Merrt himself.

He wanted to be ready.

OUTSIDE, VIKTOR HARK thought about another pie. Ludd was taking his time. The heavy-set Hauberkan loomed into his field of vision.

'You Hark?' asked the trooper.

Hark narrowed his eyes. 'I think you'll find I'm referred to as *commissar*, trooper,' he said.

'Yeah, yeah. Commissar Hark, right?'

'What do you want?' Hark asked. 'I'm busy.'

'We've got a problem, Commissar Hark. I think you'll want to deal with it,' the trooper said, ushering Hark on.

Hark sighed and followed. He folded Ludd's coat and hat under his arm. 'What sort of problem?' he asked.

The Hauberkan trooper led Hark down some grille steps behind the mess wells. It was dark and steamy down there. Molten fat dribbled down the walls.

'I said what sort of problem?' Hark demanded.

There were suddenly five Hauberkan troopers around him. One held a knife.

'You're the bastard who executed Gadovin,' said one of them. 'You're gonna pay.'

'Oh, you stupid boys,' Hark said.

IT WAS ABOUT to go off. Finishing his drink, Ludd made a hasty exit onto the gangway. There was no sign of Hark.

'Sir?' he called out. Some of the passing crowd cast him curious looks.

Ludd turned and ran back down into Pavver's place. There was a small pocket of frantic activity that every one else, even the girls, was trying to ignore. Pavver's men were dragging Merrt out through the back door. Merrt had raised on a bet that even the house refused to cover. He was crying out, but his cries, strangulated through that awful augmetic jaw, seemed comical.

What was he saying? 'Sarat'? 'Sabbat'? *Something*.

Patrons in the vicinity were laughing at him. Just some poor old damaged fool, risking too much.

One of the serving girls, a pretty thing with short black hair, was urgently following Merrt out.

'What are you going to do?' she was yelling. 'What are you going to do?'

'Get away and serve!' spat one of the strong-arms, kicking out at her.

Merrt cried out again as he disappeared through the back doors.

Ludd pushed through the crowd. He saw the other men who had been players at Merrt's table. They were on their feet. Wes Maggs, the Belladon, looked like he was about to follow Merrt. When he saw Ludd, he halted, and sat back down sharply.

'Stay there!' Ludd yelled at him, and ran on towards the back doors.

They were still ajar when he reached them. He peered out. Beyond was an undercroft, a dank box of dead space that stank of piss and rotten vegetables. Against the far wall, the strong-arms were already busy beating Merrt to a pulp. Ludd took a deep breath and stepped out.

'That's enough!' he yelled.

The strong-arms stopped hitting Merrt. Glazed and semi-conscious, the Tanith trooper sagged and slid slowly down the wall. The four pieces of muscle turned to regard Ludd with narrow eyes.

'Who the hell are you supposed to be?' one of them asked.

Ludd knew they weren't about to wait for an answer.

* * *

IV

THE KNIFE CAME first, a glint of steel.

It was early. If the Hauberkans had been drinking at all, they hadn't been drinking much. They were still sharp, quick, confident. It was also likely they had been planning this ambush for a long while, and were therefore coiled tight like clip-springs.

The knife came first, and Hark simply caught its blade in his augmetic grip. He squeezed. It snapped with a sound like a dull bell.

'Well, that broke,' said Hark. He let go of Ludd's coat and hat, and punched the knife wielder in the face with his real hand. The man dropped hard. The impact was satisfyingly dense, even though it hurt his knuckles.

This again. This was old news. Since Ancreon Sextus, Hark had found himself in three brawls with Hauberkan troopers, all of whom hated him for his execution of their incompetent leader, Gadovin.

Well, tough feth to them.

The moment unspooled. They were on fight time now, that unreal measure of passing moments that seemed an eternity while it lasted but in reality was just a handful of seconds. Fight time. Instinct time. One of the others swung at him. Hark sidestepped the telegraphed blow, and thumped his augmetic fist into the man's chest, breaking ribs. The fool stumbled away, gasping, aspirating blood. The rest were on his back. Hark used his elbows. He heard a nose crack, and felt something soft give. He was released.

Hark rotated on the balls of his feet, the tails of his leather storm coat floating out. It was a surprisingly graceful move for someone so solid. He surveyed his work.

One Hauberkan was on his knees, his hands clamped to a ruptured nose from which blood was pouring. The other was on his back, curled up, hands clamped to his throat gasping. Hark tutted, then kicked the first one in the head and laid him out on his back. He looked at the second and decided he'd done enough there.

The fifth Hauberkan was off to his left. Hark had presumed the man would bottle and run, seeing as how all his cronies were down and broken. Mob mentality worked that way.

But it wasn't going to happen, Hark realised. Fight time was still unravelling the moment according to its own curious tempo. The fifth man was wearing a chain fist. It had undoubtedly cost him a great deal on the black trade. He'd bought it to do Hark, and he was going to use it. It started snarling as it swung towards Hark's face.

Hark deflected the strike with his augmetic hand. Drilled chips of steel and black plastek flew off his hand-plant as the buzzing weapon wrenched away.

A knife was one thing, but you didn't fool with a chain fist. It offered no latitude, no second chances. The moment the chain fist appeared, the situation stopped being aggravating and became serious. Fight time spun faster.

The man was saying something. Hark didn't let him start or finish. He kicked the man in the groin, punched him in the mouth, then gripped him around the throat and slammed him back against the filthy wall of the mess well. He kept the grip tight, reinforcing it with his knee and the rest of his body weight. His augmetic arm pinned the chain fist out, helpless.

'Drop it,' Hark instructed.

'Ghhk!' the man choked.

'Now would be good.'

'Gnhh!'

'Two or three more seconds will make the difference between penal service and summary execution. Write your own sentence.'

The man shook the chain fist off his hand. It dropped onto the ground, bounced twice, and lay there, twitching like an insect, eating into the deck.

'Penal service it is,' Hark said. He stepped back and let go. The man staggered forward, regaining his breath.

'One last point,' Hark added. He punched the man in the side of the head with his augmetic. The man tumbled the length of the wall and fell on his face. His skull was probably fractured. A mercy, Hark considered. Thirty years on a penal colony would probably pass a lot easier if you were simple from brain-damage.

Fight time ceased. Breathing hard suddenly, Hark took a step backwards and checked himself. No damage. No wounds. You could take a lot in the unreality of fight time and only learn about it afterwards. He'd been taught that on Herodor. When the loxatl had blown his arm off, he hadn't realised at first.

He looked around at the grunting, coughing bodies around him.

'You stupid bastards,' he said. He reached into his coat pocket and hooked out his vox.

'Hark to Commissariat control.'

'Reading you, commissar.'

'Verify my position via vox-link.'

'Verified, commissar. One eight one oh low quarters.'

'Thank you. Despatch a handling team to that location. Five, repeat five Hauberkan troopers for detention. Zero tolerance. I'll file charges later.'

'Handling team on its way, commissar. Do you require medicae attention?'

'Yes, for them.'

'Also despatched. Will you remain on station, sir?'

Above, at gangway level, the troupe was passing by again. Hark heard the pipes, and the tune got into his head for a second time. Like a dream when–

'Sir, will you remain on station?'

Hark shook himself. He saw the coat and cap lying on the ground.

'Feth... Ludd...'

'Sir?' the vox crackled.

'No, I won't. Deal with this.' He started to run, towards the stairs, up them two at a time. He came up onto the busy gangway, and knocked his way through the capering troupe. The piper stopped playing.

'Hey!' he complained.

'Not now,' Hark warned.

* * *

LUDD TOOK HIS auto-snub out of his pocket and aimed it at the strong-arms.

'That's close enough,' he said. He wondered what was wrong with them. He had a gun to them, and they weren't backing down.

The pound music behind him had got louder suddenly.

'We have a problem?' asked a silky voice.

His eye and aim still on the circle of strong-arms, Ludd glanced sideways and saw Pavver beside him. Pavver was calmly standing there, side on to Ludd, looking at the muscle.

'Yes, we have a problem,' Ludd said tightly.

Pavver nodded. 'You, I don't know,' he said, still not looking at Ludd. 'You, you're new to me.'

'Nahum Ludd, Commissariat,' Ludd said.

'Well, they all say that, don't they?' Pavver chuckled. The strong-arms nodded.

Ludd gently took a step or two backwards until he was covering Pavver and the thugs. Pavver turned slowly to face him.

'I am Junior Commissar Nahum Ludd,' Ludd stated.

'Junior commissar, is it?' Pavver nodded. 'That's nice. A nice touch of reality. A nice detail. More credible. *Junior* commissar. Here's a tip. Next time you play the part, get yourself a cap and a coat. Live the role.'

'I'm going to reach for my insignia now,' Ludd said, his left hand straying towards his breast pocket. 'No one do anything stupid.'

Pavver shrugged in a 'take your time' kind of way. 'Only one of us here doing that,' he said.

Ludd flashed his warrant card.

'All right then,' Pavver admitted. 'You're a commissar. I don't want any trouble. I run a decent establishment and–'

'Stop talking,' said Ludd. 'This place persists thanks to the tolerant attitude of this vessel and its Commissariat function. In fact, it's not an "establishment". It's a hole in the wall. It's a den. You so much as cough wrong and we ship you out. You have no rights, no influence, and feth all authority. So stop pretending like you run the finest saloon on Khan Nobilis.'

Pavver nodded. 'I understand my place, *Junior* Commissar Nahum Ludd. I am a little man, and I scrape by. Let us reach an understanding. What is the nature of your problem?'

'Your men were busy killing one of my troopers,' Ludd said.

'That ugly shit?' Pavver shrugged. 'You even care what happens to him? He broke house rules. He staked too high against the bank. My cash hurts me when someone plays rough with it. Yes, my boys were going to kill him. A lesson.'

'You admit it?'

'Where's the point in denying it?'

'You wouldn't get away with it,' Ludd said.

Pavver brought out a lho-stick and lit it. He exhaled smoke. 'You know the turbine halls, *Junior* Commissar Nahum Ludd?'

'By the reactor engines? Yes.'

'Furnace domes down there. Big and hot. Melt skin and bone in a second. We kill a trooper or two who insults my establishment, there's no trace. All gone in a puff of ash. No awkward questions. No come-back. Tidy. This I do to keep the peace.'

'You're admitting to murder?'

Pavver shrugged.

'Why would you do that? To me? I'm a juni– I'm a commissar! I've got you at gun-point. I–'

He hesitated. The strong-arms laughed. Pavver smiled.

'You've got *me*, haven't you?' Ludd asked.

Ludd felt the cold nudge of a pistol's muzzle at the nape of his neck. Pavver hadn't emerged from his den alone. Another of his boys stood behind Ludd, gun aimed at the back of his head.

'One body into the furnace domes? Two? Makes no odds to me. I'm a business man, *Junior* Commissar Nahum Ludd. I've got a hole in the wall to run.'

Pavver pinched the lho-stick between his lips and took out a roll of notes. 'If you'd like to walk away,' he said, edging the words out around his smoke. 'I can make it worth your while. How much does your blind eye cost?'

'If I took your bribe,' Ludd said, 'I could still report you.'

'Ah,' said Pavver, halting his shuffle of cash. 'You've seen the flaw in my argument. You know too much.'

Something odd happened. Time seemed to dilate. Ludd flinched, expecting to feel the hot round scorch through his brain case from behind, and his finger began to squeeze the trigger of his auto-snub. A gunshot rang out, and something hot and wet splashed across the back of Ludd's head and shoulders.

Pavver was yelling. The strong-arms were moving. Ludd fired, and dropped the first of them with a bullet to the chest.

'Balance of power restored,' said a voice. 'Get your hands on your heads, you feth-wipes.'

Viktor Hark stepped into Ludd's field of vision. He was aiming a large combat automatic at Pavver. The muzzle was breathing smoke.

'On your knees!' Hark growled. Pavver and his men obliged quickly. The man Ludd had shot lay on his face in a slick of blood.

'All right, Ludd?' Hark asked.

Ludd nodded. He looked behind him. A body lay on the ground, a pistol in its hand. The headshot had blown most of its cranium away. Ludd realised what was dripping down his back.

'Commissar Hark,' Hark announced, routinely. 'This is the end. Expect no mercy and resign yourselves to a life of misery.'

Pavver started to wail. Hark kicked him in the ribs.

Ludd stepped past the cowering men and reached Merrt. 'We need a medicae,' he said, after a quick inspection. 'Right now.'

Hark nodded and reached for his vox.

Pavver's Place closed forever about fifteen minutes later. It wasn't the first establishment on the swelter decks to come and go so fast, and it wouldn't be the last. As the Commissariat troops led Pavver and the strong-arms away in chains, the girls grabbed their things and fled.

'What about Merrt?' Ludd asked.

'What about you?' Hark answered. 'You sure you're all right?'

'It was weird for a moment,' Ludd confessed. 'Back there, I mean. Thank you, sir. I thought I was dead.'

'These things happen. Weird how?'

'Ah, well… everything seemed to speed up and slow down, all at once.'

Hark nodded. 'Fight time,' he said, as if that explained everything.

V

LARKIN LET THE view through the sniper scope drift and settle until the reticule was framing his target. The young man. A boy really. How old was he? Eighteen standard? The very thought made Larkin feel as old and leaden as a dying sun. He couldn't remember being eighteen himself. *Wouldn't*, actually. Trying to remember being an eighteen year old required him to recall a place and a time, and that place was Tanith, in the deep woods. Larkin didn't like to think about Tanith. After all these years, it was still too bleak and private a loss.

He remembered the boy, though. The kid must've been about ten when he'd come to them. That had been after Vervunhive, after that grinding war, when the First-and-Only's ranks had been swelled by the Verghastite intake. Just a refugee kid, with a baby sister, another two souls dragged along with the followers on the strength. A pair of orphans rescued and protected with maternal fury by a bleach-blonde hiver girl with too many piercings and too many tats.

The hiver girl's name had been Tona Criid. Now she was Sergeant Criid, the regiment's first female officer, a comrade and a friend, her military record outstanding, her worth proved ten times over. Larkin owed her his life, more than once, and had returned the favour, more than once. Seeing her that first time, on the embarkation fields outside Vervunhive, scrawny, dirty, full of rage and spite, dragging two filthy children into the landers with her, Larkin would never have imagined befriending her, or admiring her.

How times changed. He admired her now. For everything she'd done, and everything she was, and every charge she'd led against the Archenemy of Mankind. But most of all, he admired her for being a mother to two kids who weren't hers. For raising them in this squalid, itinerant life.

She'd done a good job. The boy was tall, strong, good looking. Like his father. He had a confidence to him, and smarts, and an easy way with others. And it wasn't just what he was. It was what he represented.

Larkin watched Dalin Criid approaching through his scope for a while longer, then lowered it and pretended to clean it. He had sat himself down outside the main hatch of the barrack hall, his back against the khaki metal of the wall. The excuse was that the uninterrupted length of the concourse outside gave him the chance to test and recalibrate his gunsight.

He took out a patch of vizzy cloth, and began polishing the lenses. His longlas, broken down, lay on the deck beside him in its bag.

People came and went down the echoing concourse. Dalin came up to him.

'Keeping your eye in, Larks?' he asked, coming to a halt over the cross-legged man.

'Never hurts,' Larkin replied.

Dalin nodded. He paused. He didn't expect much, but he thought there might be something. A comment about his first day, perhaps.

'You all right?' Larkin asked looking up.

'Yes. Yeah, I'm fine. You?'

'Golden as the Throne itself,' Larkin said, and returned his attention to his work.

'Well. Good. I'll see you, then,' Dalin said.

Larkin nodded. Dalin waited a second longer and then walked away through the hatch into the barrack hall.

Larkin touched his micro-bead link. 'He's coming,' he said.

'HE'S COMING,' SAID Varl. 'Are you coming?'

Gol Kolea sat on the edge of his cot, turning the pages of an instructional primer on spiritual faith.

'He won't want me there, getting in the way,' Kolea replied.

'Yes, he will,' said Varl, arms folded, leaning on the frame of the billet cage.

'Why?'

Varl shrugged. 'Dunno. Perhaps because you're his father? Stop pretending to read and get off your arse.'

Kolea scowled. 'How do you know I'm pretending to read?'

Arms still folded, Varl very slowly and very gently tilted his upper body over until his head was almost upside down. 'You're holding that book the wrong way up.'

Kolea blinked and stared at the primer in his hands. 'No, I'm not.'

Varl straightened up. 'Yeah, but you had to check. Stop prevaricating and get off your arse.'

Kolea tossed the book aside and got up. 'All right,' he said. 'But only because you used a word like "prevaricating" and now I'm scared to be alone with you.'

'HE'S COMING,' SAID Domor.

'Already?' Caffran replied.

'Larks just voxed.'

'Did you get it?' Caffran asked. He was busy folding the blanket back on the billet cage's cot.

Shoggy Domor's eyes would have twinkled in an avuncular manner if they hadn't been oversized augmetic implants. He reached into his musette bag and slid out the bottle of sacra. The bottle, a re-used water flask, had a handwritten label 'Try Again Finest'.

'The real stuff,' said Domor, tossing it to Caffran. Caffran caught the bottle and smiled at the label.

'Not fresh and burn-your-belly out of Costin's still,' Domor added. 'That's the real thing. Matured. Vintage. Laid down.'

'Laid down?'

'In Obel's foot locker, for "future pleasures", but it's the stuff.'

'It cost?'

Domor shook his head. 'When I told Obel what it was for, he just handed it over. "Wet the baby's head", he said.'

'He's not a baby.'

'He's not.'

'He's *not.*'

'I know he's not.'

'Just so we're clear. How do I look?'

Domor shrugged. 'Like a tight-arse feth? What did you do, starch your uniform?'

Caffran paused. 'Yes,' he confessed.

Domor sniggered. 'Then you have succeeded in looking like a tight-arse feth.'

'Thanks. Why are you my friend again?'

'Pure fething accident,' Domor smiled.

A head poked round the cage door. It was gnarled and ugly, like the protruding head of a startled tortoise.

'Hello, father,' said Domor.

'He's coming!' announced Zweil.

'We know, father. So are we,' Caffran replied.

'Big day,' Zweil added. He looked at Caffran and frowned. 'Tight-arse feth. Was that the look you were shooting for, son?'

'Be quiet,' said Caffran.

BARRACK HALL 22 was a vast enclosure given over to the billets of the Tanith First-and-Only. Across the concourse, the Kolstec 15th were housed in similar conditions. Something over four thousand troopers, packed away for the long voyage, for the long walk down Glory Road.

The billets themselves were metal-framed boxes five storeys deep. Each trooper had a cage-walled cell, like animals in a battery farm. Every cell had a cot and locker, and most troopers improved privacy with strategically arranged ground sheets and camo-cloaks.

It was sweaty-hot and noisy. A fug of smoke hung in the chamber roof from the lho-sticks and pipes. A chemical stench issued from the latrines at the southern end. The Tanith lay around, relaxing, leaning on staircases, playing cards and regicide, basking on folding chairs. In the open space beyond the billet cages, troopers were playing a loud game of kick-ball, stripped to their vests. Tanith, Verghastite, Belladon. Three races now bound together as one fighting unit.

Dalin walked in through the campsite. He felt a vague despondency. No one acknowledged him, not even the men who he regularly chatted to. A few 'hellos', a few nods. No one asked how his day had gone.

That was all right, though. He didn't want a fuss. He had been one of them for a long time, but not one of them. Now, finally, he was turning eighteen, and training for his tags. This had been his aspiration, his whole life. To be one of them, equal, an Imperial Guardsman.

Dalin sometimes wondered if he would have aspired to the Guard if his life had followed a different path. If war hadn't blown out the home-hive he grew up in. He probably would've become a seam miner, like his dad. His real dad. But war had embraced him, and warriors had carried him away, and their calling was all that appealed to him now. To be a Guard. To be a Ghost, more importantly. One of Gaunt's chosen.

To fight and, if necessary, die, in the name of the God-Emperor of Mankind.

He hurt. Damn Kexie and Saroo. He hurt, and all he wanted was to collapse on his cot and sleep the pain off.

He walked around the end of the fifth cage block and into the circulating space where troopers dozed and gamed. He heard a strange sound, staccato, like gun-fire.

It was applause.

To a man and a woman, the Ghosts had risen to their feet all around him, and were clapping wildly. He stopped and blinked.

'Dalin Criid! Dalin Criid! First day in "I", everyone! Dalin Criid!'

Dalin blinked again and looked around at the smiling faces surrounding him. They looked... proud. Connected to him, like they owned him, in the very best way.

Mach Bonin stood on an upper landing, leading the cheer. 'Dalin Criid! Show him we approve!' he was shouting.

'This...' Dalin grinned. 'This is...'

'The way Ghosts welcome one of their own,' said Domor, coming forward. 'Dalin, this is a rare moment, so you'll excuse us if we make the most of it.'

He shook Dalin's hand.

'Your dad's here,' he said, over the clapping.

Dalin looked around, and saw Caffran smiling at him.

'Oh, you mean Caff,' he said.

'All right, then?' Caffran asked, coming forward.

Dalin nodded. 'What did you do to your uniform?' he asked.

'Don't you start. Look, I did a thing. I hope you like it. I set you up with a billet cage, right upstairs, two down from mine. Guard issue, all proper.'

'I'm not Guard yet, Caff.'

'I know, but you will be.'

Dalin smiled and clamped his hands around Caffran's.

Dermon Caffran wasn't old enough to be Dalin's biological father, but, as Tona Criid's partner, he had raised the boy and his sister as his own, as far as Guard life allowed that to be possible. Then complications had set in.

'I got you this,' Caffran said, producing the sacra. 'To toast you.'

'Thanks.'

Dalin turned in a slow circle, acknowledging the applause. He saw all the faces: Obel, Ban Daur, Wheln, Rafflan, Brostin, Lyse, Caober, Nessa Bourah. Larkin was there. Larkin winked. The old dog.

Zweil came forward, holding a psalter and bless-bottle. 'Heavens, Dalin Criid. You're very tall suddenly,' he exclaimed. 'I thought I might bless you, but I fear I won't reach!'

Dalin grinned and bowed.

The crowd hushed as Zweil made the sign of the eagle on Dalin's fore-head. 'In the name of the God-Emperor who watches over us, and the Saint whose work we do, I vouchsafe your soul against the horrors of the dark,' Zweil announced. He sprinkled some holy water over Dalin's shoulders.

'The Emperor protects,' he finished. There was more applause.

Tona Criid had appeared at Caffran's side. 'Enjoy this,' she told Dalin. 'The Ghosts don't make a fuss much.'

'They didn't need to make a fuss at all, ma,' Dalin said. She smiled, and touched her fingertips to his cheek briefly. Truth of it was, when the Ghosts gathered like this, it was usually to say goodbye, not hello. To bid farewell to another friend or comrade lost in the grinder. This was an expression of welcome, a salute to the living. Criid's heart was heavier than her smile suggested. They were welcoming her son into the Imperial Guard, into a way of life that had only one conclusion. This, too, was as good as saying goodbye, and she knew it. From this moment on, sooner or later...

'There's someone here who wants to say a few special words,' Varl said, appearing from the crowd.

Varl beckoned. In the shadows behind the cage wall, Kolea stiffened and cleared his throat. Then he pulled back as a tall figure strode past him.

It was Gaunt.

VI

'I wouldn't miss this,' said Ibram Gaunt. Silence had fallen.

'How did you go?' Gaunt asked.

'Good, sir. Good,' Dalin replied. 'Just starting out.'

'You'll be a good trooper,' Gaunt said. 'Is that sacra, Caffran?'

Caffran froze, half-hiding the bottle. 'It might be, sir.'

Gaunt nodded. 'You know there's a charge related to illicit alcohol?'

'I'd heard something of that, sir,' Caffran admitted.

'We'd better drink it before someone sees then, hadn't we?' Gaunt said.

Caffran smiled. 'Yes, sir.'

'Get some glasses, Caff,' Gaunt said. 'By the way, what the feth is going on with your uniform? A starch accident?'

'That might explain it,' Caffran said.

Shot glasses were produced. The bottle emptied as it filled as many cups as it could.

Gaunt raised his. 'To Dalin. First and next.'

They slugged it down. Dalin felt his torso go warm.

'We're walking Glory Road,' Gaunt told him, handing his empty glass to Domor. 'You know where that leads?'

'Well, glory?' said Dalin.

Gaunt nodded. 'I have complete confidence you'll be a trooper by then, Dalin. I'll show you glory, and I'll be proud to have you stand at my side.'

Gaunt looked around. 'I know I'm not wanted here. But I needed to come. That's it done. Carry on.'

He walked away.

The troopers closed around Dalin, shaking his hand and scrubbing his hair.

'Come on!' Varl hissed.

'Not now,' replied Kolea. 'He's happy. I don't want to go walking in there…'

'Gol…'

Kolea turned and walked away.

'VERY CLEVER, SIR, if I might say so,' Beltayn said, following Gaunt through the billet.

'How's that, Bel?'

'Sharing the grog out like that.'

Gaunt nodded. 'Dalin will need a clear head in the morning. Anything awry?'

Beltayn smiled and shook his head. 'Nothing right now, sir.'

'Dismissed then, Bel. Thank you.'

Gaunt had reached the medical tents. Dorden, the regiment's venerable chief medicae, stood in the doorway of the main surgery.

'You don't look happy,' said Gaunt.

'Do we still not know where we're going?' Dorden asked. Gaunt shook his head.

'Then come and look at this.'

Dorden led him into a freight space that was piled high with wrapped boxes from the Munitorum.

'These just arrived,' he said. 'Standing order is to distribute them throughout the regiment, double dose.'

Gaunt picked up a packet and read the label. 'Anti-ague drench?'

Dorden nodded. 'Remind you of anything?'

'I'll assemble an informal,' he said.

VII

SERAPHINE. THE LETTERS were inscribed into the heavy ironwork of the vent duct, and again on the duct beside it, and again on the duct beside that. Eszrah ap Niht traced his fingers across the bas-relief letters. *Seraphine*. It was, he understood, the name of the great boat they flew in. It wore its name on metalwork all about the place, as if acknowledging that it was so vast, a person might forget where he was, and need reminding.

Eszrah had been on a great boat before, but not as great a boat as this. It was so mighty, it was a world within a world. Gaunt had told Eszrah that it was a 'mass conveyance', a carrier ship. Several dozen regiments were being carried in its belly, more people than he'd seen in his whole life before leaving the Untill.

There was no sense they were moving. No soaring sensation of flight. Just a dull vibration in the deck, a harmonic in the heavy iron of the ducts and walls and plating.

He touched the word again, following the letters left to right as Gaunt had taught him. His lips moved.

'S... sera... serap... hine...'

He heard a noise and stopped, withdrawing his hand sharply. He was struggling to master the out-tongue, but it was hard, and he didn't like people seeing how hard he found it.

He was Nihtgane, Sleepwalker, bow-hunter of the Untill. It did not do for people to see his weaknesses.

It was bad enough they had to see him without his wode.

Ludd was approaching down the companionway. Ludd was all right, because Gaunt trusted Ludd, and Ludd and Eszrah had bloodied together in the hollow city.

Nahum Ludd saw Eszrah Night waiting for him as he came up. Gaunt's private quarters lay at the end of Barrack Hall 22, accessible via the narrow companionway flanked by ductwork. Eszrah had taken to guarding this narrow approach, like a warrior-spirit guarding a secret ravine in some ancient myth. In the months since they'd met, Ludd had begun to relax around the towering Nihtgane partisan, although his initial impression that Eszrah was about to kill him in some particularly silent and effective manner was never far away. When he'd first met him, Eszrah had been a fearsome giant of dreadlocks and painted skin. Gaunt had tidied him up, disguising the savage a little. The wode had gone, as had the shaggy mane and beard, and the eye mosaics, but still Eszrah stood out. Unnaturally tall, rake thin, he wore black, Guard-issue fatigues, heavy laced boots and a camo-cloak. His skull was shaved, and had a regal sculpture to it. His skin was gun-metal grey. His eyes were hidden behind a battered old pair of sunshades Varl had once given him.

Everything about Eszrah ap Niht, in fact, was hidden. Hiding was what the Nihtgane did. They hid themselves and their thoughts, their emotions, their hopes and their fears. Ludd knew Eszrah, but he didn't *know* him at all. He doubted anyone did. Not even Gaunt.

'Histye, soule Eszrah,' Ludd said. With a little tuition from Gaunt, Ludd had been practising the Nihtgane's tongue, just a few phrases. It seemed to Ludd unfair that only Gaunt could converse with him.

Eszrah nodded, faintly amused. Ludd's accent was terrible. The vowels were all too short. Ludd had almost said *histyhi*, the word for swine mash, rather than *histye*, the greeting.

'Histye, soule Ludd,' Eszrah replied.

Ludd grinned. This was almost a proper conversation by Eszrah ap Niht's standards. The over-long vowels of Eszrah's accent amused Ludd, especially the way he made his name sound like 'Lewd'.

'We're gathering for an informal,' Ludd said. 'More people will be coming this way.'

And I'd rather you didn't kill them, was the unspoken end of that sentence. Eszrah considered himself to be Gaunt's property, and for this reason alone had followed the colonel-commissar all the way from the deep Untill of Gereon. As Ludd understood it, Eszrah didn't regard himself as a slave. Gaunt owned him as one might own a good sword or a balanced rifle. As part of this relationship, Eszrah protected Gaunt's person and his quarters with what Gaunt's adjutant Beltayn had described as 'maternal fury'. A few days earlier, a Belladon NCO had been hurrying down the companionway to bring an order slip to Gaunt, and Eszrah had pounced on him from the shadows, presuming him to be, perhaps, an assassin. It had taken quite a while before Eszrah could be convinced of the man's innocence enough to let go of his throat, and a good deal longer for the NCO's breathing to return to normal.

Eszrah nodded again. He understood. Ludd was warning him, decently, that others were coming, giving him time to melt away. He disliked company.

Voices could be heard at the mouth of the companionway. Ludd glanced round. 'That'll be the rest,' he began, 'so we–'

He turned back. Eszrah ap Niht had vanished, as surely as if he had never been there.

Ludd sighed, shook his head, and walked on.

THE OTHERS CAME. From the shadows of the ducting, the Sleepwalker watched them, his reynbow loaded and aimed. Major Rawne first, walking with Dorden, the old surgeon. Eszrah didn't know Dorden well, but he had warmed to him. The Nihtgane respected the seniors of their tribe, and Eszrah showed the same courtesy to the elders of the Ghost clan. Rawne was different. Of the out-worlders who had come to the Untill, Rawne was one of the most ferocious warriors, and for that alone, he had earned Eszrah's respect. Gaunt valued Rawne too, and that counted for a great deal.

But there was a quality to Rawne. A malice. Eszrah's people had a word – *srahke* – which they used for people like Rawne. Literally, it meant the keenness of a newly-whetted dagger's edge.

Next came Major Kolea and Major Baskevyl, and Beltayn, the adjutant. They were chatting convivially. Kolea, a Verghastite, was a big man, physically imposing, with an air of reliability and determination about him as heavy and hard as a block of ouslite. But his weight of personality was leavened with a good humour. Baskevyl was a Belladon, a well-made, compact man who, like Kolea, married a stern reliability with a refreshing brand of confidence. Beltayn, a Tanith man, was small and bright and so lightly built it seemed soldiering was entirely the wrong profession for him. But Eszrah had seen Beltayn fight, and seen him survive the Untill. Along with Gaunt and Ludd, Beltayn was one of the few Ghosts Eszrah considered to be friends. Though, in the Nihtgane tongue, the words for 'friend' simply meant 'someone I consider to be a trustworthy hunting partner'.

Belladon, Verghastite, Tanith… this was where things became complicated for Eszrah. Gaunt had explained it many times, but still it seemed peculiar. The fighting clan was the Tanith, the Tanith First-and-Only. At some point in their history, after, so Eszrah had been told, a mighty battle, the Tanith had agreed to accept men from another clan into their order. These were the Verghastites, and some of them were females. The two clans had bonded into one. This, in Eszrah's experience, never happened amongst the tribes of the Untill. Unless disease or famine had ravaged one tribe, and breeding partners were needed.

Then had come the matter of the hollow city. Eszrah had been there and seen it, following Gaunt to war. During Gaunt's expedition to Gereon, his fighting clan had been given to another leader, and had bonded to yet a third clan, who were called the Belladon. Following Gaunt's return, and the death in war of the other leader, all three clans had unified under Gaunt, taking the name Tanith First-and-Only.

This, as far as Gaunt and the others seemed to think, had been a good thing.

Eszrah wasn't sure. In the Untill, clans seldom combined successfully. For a start, there was the scent. No clan smelled alike. How could they bond when their bodies gave off such different scents? With his eyes closed, Eszrah could tell them apart quite easily. The resin sap of the Tanith, the mineral dust of the Verghastites, the hard steel of the Belladons. Eyes open, it was even more apparent. Tanith were lean and hard, pale skinned, dark haired. Verghastites were more solid, flat-faced and fairer. Belladons were between the two in their average build, darker-skinned, lighter in voice.

Eszrah didn't understand how such a compact of fighting clans could work. It wasn't even a fact that these could. At the hollow city, they had fought to victory together due to the extremities of circumstance. Genuine bonding had yet to be proven, and that test would happen wherever they were going, wherever the great boat was taking them.

To complicate matters further in Eszrah's mind, Gaunt wasn't Tanith, Verghastite or Belladon. He was other, with a scent of good, oiled hide. So too was Ludd (fire ash and flint), and Hark (bone dust and chemicals). And the old man Zweil too, though as Eszrah understood it, the clan kept Zweil around so they could be amused by a capering madman. Untill chieftains often allowed a simpleton to live for exactly the same purposes. The name for that was *jestyr* or *foole*.

Gaunt, Ludd, Hark. They were Tanith, but not Tanith. It was perplexing. A fighting clan, already intermingled in blood and scent, allowed itself to be led by men from other clan territories.

Eszrah decided he would never understand it, not even if he lived to be forty years old.

Kolea, Beltayn and Baskevyl had passed down the companionway into Gaunt's quarters. After a moment, Gaunt himself went by, alone, striding purposefully.

Eszrah lowered his reynbow. Then he raised it again, quickly, as a final figure passed by.

Mkoll. The master of scouts. The master of hunters. Tanith, so Tanith that his Tanith scent was stronger than any, though Eszrah doubted any could ever track the man's spoor.

Mkoll stopped suddenly, halfway down the companionway, turned and looked directly into the shadows at the place where Eszrah was concealed. He smiled.

'All right, Eszrah?' he asked.

Eszrah froze, then nodded.

'That's good,' Mkoll grinned. 'Carry on.' He walked away into the commander's quarters.

The Nihtgane had a word for people like Mkoll too. It was *sidthe*. It meant ghost.

THE ROOM WAS quite small, just a steel box, with a table in the centre of the floor. Beltayn had, over the days since they'd boarded the carrier, begged, borrowed or robbed a number of seats to furnish the place into some semblance of a briefing room. Pew benches with sagging upholstery, a few stools, a couple of high-backed chairs, both of which were so loose on their spells that they creaked and swayed.

'Hello to all,' Gaunt said, taking off his storm coat. 'Take a seat.'

The officers of the regiment had been standing out of courtesy. Now they took their places. Kolea and Rawne reclined on one pew, Dorden and Hark on another. Baskevyl scooted forward on one of the creaking high-backs, and Mkoll settled himself on its twin. Beltayn perched his backside on a stool. Ludd withdrew to a corner of the room and remained standing.

The room was dark, lit only by the outer light shafting through the door and high window slits. Gaunt nodded to Ludd, and the junior commissar activated the overhead lamps.

Holding his coat up by the collar loop, Gaunt brushed it down as he carried it over towards a row of wall hooks.

'Let's start with basics. Any reports?'

'The men are bedding down well, sir,' Kolea said. 'Good transit discipline.'

'Gol's right,' said Baskevyl. 'No nonsense. Smooth ride.' He leaned forward as he spoke, and his feeble chair let out a screech of wood.

'Eli?' Gaunt asked over his shoulder, hanging his coat up.

Elim Rawne was the regiment's second officer, the senior man in the Tanith-Verghastite-Belladon command pyramid formed by himself, Kolea and Baskevyl.

He stayed reclined, arms folded, and shrugged. 'I've no reason to refute those statements. The Tanith have always conducted themselves perfectly during carrier transits. In my experience, the Verghastites have too. I can't speak for the Belladon.'

That was pointed. Gaunt looked around sharply.

'Eli...'

Baskevyl snorted and sat back. Another terrible groan issued from his chair. He said, 'Major Rawne and I are reaching an understanding. He goads me and mine, sir, and I let his scorn drip off me like rain. Come the zone, the Belladon have agreed to allow Rawne to buff our medals.'

Gaunt sniggered. 'Providing he asks nicely?' he inquired.

'Naturally,' Baskevyl said. His chair complained again.

'I seem to remember,' Gaunt said, 'I asked you to work hard to welcome the Belladon into our company, Eli.'

'This is me working hard,' said Rawne. 'You should see me when I'm being a bastard.'

'We've all seen *that*,' scoffed Mkoll. When he moved in his seat, for some reason his chair, as ailing as Baskevyl's, made no sound at all.

'There is one thing, sir–' Ludd began.

'Not now,' Hark warned.

Ludd shut up and pursed his lips.

'I've time on my hands,' Gaunt said. 'Let's hear it.'

Ludd cleared his throat and took a step forward, producing a sheet of paper from his pocket. 'There was an incident earlier, sir. On the swelter decks... see, as it says?'

He handed the paper to Gaunt. Gaunt read it quickly.

'Merrt?'

'I dealt with it,' Hark said.

'You dealt with it?'

'Yes, Ibram. It's old news.'

Gaunt nodded. He handed the paper back to Ludd. 'That's a shame. A man like him. Get any reasons?'

Hark's eyes were more hooded than ever. 'He's a broken man. Has been since Monthax. Men like that run off the rails.'

'You've set him on charges?'

'Yes,' said Hark. 'Full stretch. All six weeks. I'm assuming this is still a six-week voyage?'

'As far as I know,' Gaunt said.

'Not wishing to gloat,' muttered Gol Kolea, 'but very much wishing to support Baskevyl... may I just say, ho ho, it's a Tanith that steps out of line?'

'You may,' said Gaunt.

Baskevyl grinned so broadly his chair creaked.

'Funny,' said Rawne. 'You Verghastites are as funny as the Belladon and they're, let me tell you, funny.'

Kolea looked sideways at the man on the pew beside him. 'You kill me, Eli. You and your sense of humour. You kill me.'

'Oh, for a dark night and the opportunity,' replied Rawne.

There was general laughter. Smiling, Gaunt reached into the pocket of his hanging storm coat and pulled out a box stamped with the seal of the Departmento Medicae.

He set it down in the centre of the table top so they could all see it.

'This is why I called an informal.'

Rawne, Hark and Kolea leaned forward to inspect the object. So did Baskevyl, with a protest from the spells of his chair. Mkoll nodded.

'Anti-ague?' he asked.

'Anti-ague,' Gaunt replied. 'Inhibitors. Full shots.'

'Double-dose standard,' Dorden said. 'That was my instruction. Double-dose courses for all personnel, starting now.'

'We get ague drench before every planet-drop,' Baskevyl said, looking round at Gaunt with another noise from his chair.

'We do,' Gaunt agreed.

'But not double-dose and not a course,' Dorden said.

'It's like before Gereon,' Mkoll said, leaning forward and picking up the box to examine it. His chair made not a single sound.

'Gereon?' asked Baskevyl. 'Is there a point?'

'Aside from the one on the top of your head?' Rawne asked.

'Yes, there's a point,' Gaunt said. 'When I led a mission team to Gereon, it was full insertion, enemy territory. They dosed us up real good, double shots. They knew we'd need to survive as long as possible on a world lousy with Chaos taint. Now, let's think, your standard infantryman gets a shot in the arm or buttock every few weeks during transit, and never asks why. I know better. I'm asking.'

'You think?' Kolea began.

'Always,' smiled Gaunt. 'I think this means we're being routed to a liberation effort. We're going to be deployed against a Chaos-held world. High Command still hasn't confirmed our destination, but I believe the brass expects us to go in against a hard target.'

'I thought combat policy was to ignore the worlds too tough to break?' Mkoll said.

'I think policy has changed,' said Gaunt. 'I think they want us to break the tough worlds we can't ignore.'

Mkoll sat back and let out a long, plaintive whistle. His chair let out no noise at all.

'What does that mean, practically?' Kolea asked.

'It means double-hard preparation,' Gaunt said. 'It means tight drop training, around the clock. It means, if we can, slipping the hint to other regiments, so they can begin the same.'

'I can do that,' said Hark. 'I know the commissars in the Kolstec and the Binars. We can spread the word.'

'Do you understand the meaning of the word "subtle", Viktor?' Gaunt asked.

'It's my middle name,' Hark smiled. 'Viktor bloody subtle Hark.'

'Bear it in mind,' Gaunt replied. 'I don't want to be accused of starting a scare. There's something else.'

He looked round at his adjutant. 'Bel? Course correction added in, how many hostile-held worlds are there approximately six standard weeks transit rimward of Ancreon Sextus?'

'Two, sir,' replied Beltayn.

'Their names?'

'Lodius, sir. And Gereon.'

Gaunt looked back at his senior staff. 'I fancy, gentlemen, we might be heading back to Gereon. For the liberation they never thought we'd bother to bring.'

'Gereon resists,' Rawne muttered.

'Let's hope so,' said Gaunt. 'Well, that's it. Carry on and be ready. Anything else?'

'I have a question,' Baskevyl said. 'When I move, my chair creaks, but when Mkoll does, there's no sound. What the frig is that about?'

'Scout training,' Mkoll chuckled, getting to his feet and patting Baskevyl on the arm.

The meeting broke up.

'I hear your son's started basic,' Dorden said to Kolea.

'What? Yes. Yes, he has.'

'That's good. He'll do well, I think.'

'I hope so.'

'A father and son in the ranks again,' Dorden mused. 'That's wonderful. Like a new start.'

'I'm not so much his father, doc,' Kolea said. 'His blood father, yes. But then there's Caff. Two fathers and one son, you might say.'

Dorden nodded.

'Dah!' said Kolea suddenly. 'Gak it, that was clumsy of me. I'm sorry, doc.'

'For what?' asked Dorden.

Once there had been a father and son in the Tanith ranks. Dorden, and his son Mikal. Mikal had been killed during the defence of Vervunhive.

'I didn't think...' Kolea began.

Dorden shook his head. 'My son died on Verghast. Coincidentally, that's where your son joined our ranks. Now he's training to be a Ghost. A son lost and a son gained. One father bereft, one... sorry, *two* fathers made proud. I think there's a certain completeness to that, don't you, Gol? A certain symmetry?'

'I hope so,' said Kolea.

'One thing,' Dorden added. 'Gol, in the Emperor's name, look after him.'

THE SENIORS HAD gone. Gaunt sat at the table in one of the terribly creaking chairs, reviewing order papers. Beltayn brought him a cup of caffeine.

'Anything else, sir?' Beltayn asked.

'No, that'll be all, Bel. Thanks.'

Beltayn left. Gaunt worked his way through the papers.

'Geryun?' asked a voice.

Gaunt looked up from his work. Eszrah stood in the doorway.

'Iss...' he said slowly, mangling his words. 'Iss ite true, soule?'

'That we're going to Gereon?' Gaunt replied. 'I'm not sure, Niht. But I think so. You were listening in? Of course you were.'

'Geryun, itte persist longe, foereffer,' Eszrah said.

'Yes,' said Gaunt. 'That's what I've always believed.'

VIII

ANOTHER DAY-CYCLE, another slog, another step along Glory Road, another RIP drill. Eight days since the start of RIP, and something different that morning.

'New body,' said driller Kexie. 'New body. And you are, apart from shit-on-my-toecap ugly?'

'Merrt.'

Kexie looked the newcomer up and down and began the long and ritualistic process of bagging him out in front of the detail. Nothing was taboo. Kexie spent a particularly long time likening Merrt's face to a number of things, a bilge hatch, a grox's rectum, and so on.

Dalin tried not to look or listen. He stared at a fixed point far away on the opposite wall of the Basement, and waited for reps to begin.

'Hey, Holy! One of yours, isn't he?' Fourbox whispered.

'What?'

'Tanith?'

'Yeah.'

'He's in for P?' Fourbox probed. 'What he do?'

'I dunno.'

'I mean, what he do to his face?'

'Got shot,' whispered Dalin. He didn't know much about Merrt's story. Merrt was a loner and didn't mix much. For as long as Dalin could remember, Merrt's face had looked like a bilge hatch.

'Someone yapping?' Kexie asked, turning from Merrt suddenly to regard the rest of the detail. 'Someone yapping there in the file?' He aimed Saroo at them and panned it along the line, as if the baton could sniff out malfeasance like a sentry dog.

'Some wet-fart scalp exercising his lip, ech?' Kexie wondered. Wise to the driller's tricks after eight days of RIP, no one made the mistake of saying 'No, driller'.

'Let's start it, then,' Kexie announced, stroking Saroo in a way that suggested the baton was disappointed not to have doled out clouts. 'Five laps, triple time! Move!'

THREE DAYS LATER, Kexie took the detail up to the range deck, a converted hold in midships. It was a serious space, and made the Basement seem like a foot locker. They trooped in over grille bridges as the previous mob drained out of the place via lower walkways: a river of shaved scalps and laughter down below. Range officers in flak coats and ear protectors issued them with rifles that had been marked with big, white serial codes.

Off to the left, a combat-certified unit was conducting clearance drills in an area of the range that had been faked up into streets and buildings by the use of cargo crates and conveyance pallets. The unit was maintaining its hard-edge frontline readiness, determined not to let the slow days of a long haul make them slack and dull. RIP could hear their back-and-forth shouts, the corner by corner call and return, the bursts of gunfire.

Kexie yelled this and that. RIP milled about, trying to look useful, checking over their weapons, while the range officers led them up to the shooting line in groups of forty. At the line, in a grubby dugout made of flakboard and tarps, they were each handed a live clip, and began rattling away at tarpaper targets at the far end of the sandbox.

The air became thick with heat exhaust and the cracking sounds of multiple discharge. It was a sound like kindling being split, like a hundred greenstick fractures all together, an uneven, brittle racket that rolled up and down the line of shooters.

A buzzer sounded. The shooters gave up their clips and stepped back to make way for the second batch.

So the rotations went for the whole shift.

Dalin took the gun he was issued with great reverence. He'd fired plenty before. You didn't grow up in the middle of the Ghosts and not know one end of a las from the other. But he wasn't in RIP for punishment or retraining, so he hadn't dropped back out of the ranks for this. He'd never formally been issued with a weapon.

It was a loaner for the afternoon, and Dalin was pretty glad of that. It was old, a scabby mark I with a chipped and flaking khaki paint job, a broken bayonet lug, and a folding skeleton stock that had belonged to another weapon in an earlier life. The range officers kept a cache of weapons like it for drill use: scrap weapons or battlefield flotsam that the Munitorum regarded as unfit for service issue.

He went up to the line when his turn came, and popped home the cell the instructor handed him. The las made a noise like a cane switch, and pulled badly to the left. He compensated. The nearest range officer was walking the row, shouting advice at them in turn, but Dalin blocked that out and heard a voice of his own. Caffran, teaching him to shoot, teaching him the basics of rifle drill and firing discipline in a campsite field on Aexe Cardinal, or out on the obsidae of Herodor, or amongst the nodding windflowers on Ancreon Sextus.

The buzzer rang. Dalin ejected the clip, handed it back to the officer, and withdrew to the assembly area. Behind him, a fresh round of gunfire caught up, like the *rat-a-tat-tat* of a company snare drum.

'Anyone,' Kexie was yelling, striding through the company, 'anyone who scores less than a thirty gets three days of punishment reps.'

There were some groans.

'Anyone got a comment? Ech, address it in writing to me, care of Saroo.'

Dalin went to one side. Now he had some time between shoots, he could take a rag to his weapon. The action was gummed up with dirt and old lube, and that made the trigger pull hard and snatchy. He worked to free it.

'What are you doing, Holy?' Boulder asked, regarding Dalin's industry with some amusement. Boulder and Lovely and a few of the others were using the lull between shoots to rest their arses on the ground and chat.

'Improving my score,' Dalin replied.

'When you get good, do me a favour,' said Lovely. 'Shoot Kexie in the brain.'

'Why wait?' Boulder asked. 'Why not do it now?'

'Because,' said Lovely, 'the driller's brain's so frigging small, you'd have to be a marksman shot to hit it.'

Dalin noticed that Merrt was in their batch. Merrt was the only other scalp apart from Dalin who was tending to his rifle. The older trooper was adjusting the fore- and back-sights, lifting the gun to his shoulder to check between each adjustment.

He spoke to no one, and no one spoke to him.

Dalin remembered, now he came to think of it, that Merrt had been a sniper once. A specialist. He should have no problems with this drill, Dalin thought.

AT THE END of the rotations, Kexie pulled them off the range and stood them in a transit hallway while he called out the score groupings from a data-slate that one of the range officers had handed him. Everyone tensed to hear their name alongside the magic thirty or higher. Thirty was combat standard, the acceptable average grade a man had to make if he wanted to be Guard, like the weight and height and vision requirements.

Either through lack of effort or incompetence, fifteen members of the RIP detail scored under the line, including Boulder. Even he couldn't raise a 'haw haw haw' to that.

Most of the rest got in a band between thirty and thirty-five, with the top five per cent of them hitting fifty and above. Merrt got forty-eight. When Kexie read this out, Merrt seemed to shudder, and he grated some caustic word under his breath.

Kexie peered at Merrt, eyes narrowed, wondering if there was a juicy infringement there to be pounced upon.

'You speak, scalp?'

'No, driller.'

Kexie regarded him for a moment longer, and then carried on with his list. He reached Dalin's name. Dalin had scored sixty-six, twelve points clear of the best of the rest. There were a few whoops and cat-calls when Kexie read the number out, but they quickly simmered down. Kexie went over to Dalin – using that easy, shoulders-back, hip-roll walk he had – and stared him in the face.

'No new body clocks a tally like that.'

Dalin didn't know what to say, so he said nothing and remained staring straight ahead.

'I said, this is a joke. You hear my voice, wet-fart? What'd you do? Bribe a range officer? Switch some numbers?'

'No, driller.'

'No?'

'No, driller.'

'Then how would you explain this, ech?'

Dalin wanted to say he'd fired a weapon before, that he had experience, but the same could be said for every 'R' and 'P' in the detail. He wanted to say he'd been well-taught, and his teachers were the best. He wanted to say that it was probably less to do with marksmanship skill and more to do with simple weapon discipline and method, and that most of them would be scoring in the fifties if they simply took the time to check, adjust and *listen to* their rifle.

But all he found himself saying was, 'Luck, driller?'

'No such thing as luck,' Kexie said. 'Allow me to prove that particular dictum.'

Kexie cracked Saroo across Dalin's knees, and then rammed the blunt end of the baton into the small of Dalin's back as he folded forward and crumpled. Teeth bared, Kexie whaled the stick down into the boy's ribs, glancing several loud, bony blows off Dalin's forearm as it came up defensively.

Kexie stepped back, planting his left toe-cap in Dalin's gut. Dalin, on his side on the deck, grunted and coiled up like a foetus.

'See?' Kexie crowed, loud and laughing. 'He got the top tally, but he don't look all that bloody lucky now, does he?'

No one responded.

'Does he?'

There was a muted answer. Annoyed, Kexie looked back at Dalin and laid in again.

'That ain't right.'

Kexie stopped and swung about. Merrt, hands at his sides, had stepped out of the pack to face the instructor.

'You what?'

'That… gn… gn… ain't right,' Merrt repeated, his clumsy jaw misfiring a couple of times over the words.

'What?' There was a high, almost querulous tone of disbelief in Kexie's voice. He craned his neck forward and cupped a hand around one ear. 'Bloody *what*?'

'You're too happy with that stick,' Merrt said plainly. 'You deal out the licks when someone needs punishment, that's how it goes, but he don't deserve it. What kind of fool punishes someone for gn… gn… getting it right?'

'The kind of fool that's in charge of your entire bloody life,' Kexie announced, and came forward at Merrt. Everyone else shrank back. They knew that mad-eyed look.

'Maybe, but I still say what's right,' Merrt said. He spread his hands wide, palms open, and tilted his chin back so he was looking at the ceiling. 'Come on, whack me. I spoke out of line, I gotta have something coming, but not him. He didn't do nothing.'

Kexie came up short, and lowered his baton slightly. No one had ever invited Saroo's attention before. That rather took the fun out of it.

Kexie allowed a grin to tear across his mouth like a slow knife-slit. This was going to be interesting.

IX

DURING TRANSIT, THE barrack deck chapels conducted their services at all the devotional hours, according to shipboard timekeeping. The principal act of worship was held immediately after the noon watch bell.

Aboard ship, the noon watch was the axle on which all timings turned. Standing orders were for all horologs and timepieces to be synched with the chime of the watch bell.

The 'bell service' lasted about forty minutes. It was the very least devotion a Guardsman was expected to make, duties permitting. The Ghosts used Drum Chapel, near the aft quarters, a medium-size hold space that had been converted and consecrated. The room was cold and spare, crudely dressed in wood and canvas. Worship was conducted by prefects and celebrants of the Ecclesiarchy using cheap, military issue incense that smelled stale and dusty. There was none of the pomp and regalia of a civilian ceremony, none of the opulence and heady perfume of a high-hive mass. Thin priests in threadbare robes exhorted the congregation to uphold the honour and tradition of the Guard, the glory of the Imperium and the spirit of Man.

Hark listened without hearing any of the content. From his place at the back, he was scanning the rows of kneeling figures, marking faces. No wonder turnout was so regularly poor. It was dreary. Hark's own past had been privileged, and he remembered occasions at temple in the cities where he'd grown up. Glory and splendour: ecclesiarchs in billowing silks carried to the podium on golden-legged walking platforms, the choirs singing hymns into the lofty rafters of the cathedrals, the light bursting radiant white through the colossal splinter windows behind the stalls.

He met up with Ludd outside as the congregation filed away. Ludd had the roll book.

'Many?' Hark asked.

'Mostly the same few,' Ludd replied. He showed Hark the book, turning pages and pointing to several names. 'Repeat absenters.'

Hark read and nodded. 'We'll root out the chief miscreants this afternoon, Ludd. Put a rocket up them.'

Hark looked around and scanned the thinning crowd. 'He wasn't here, was he?'

'No, sir.'

'Some example. Leans on us to boost attendance, and then doesn't bother himself. I didn't miss him, did I?'

Ludd shook his head. 'That's the third day in a row. If he... I mean, if he was anybody else, he'd have a red tick beside his name by now.'

'I should, I think, explain that to him,' Hark said. 'Carry on, Ludd.'

* * *

HARK WALKED THE rusting, water-stained half-kilometre of companionway back to the regimental office, a suite of chambers and cabins midship. Most of the staffers were Munitorum officials, or officers from the support battalions and company command. The Commissariat had a presence too. In some of the larger chambers, ranged at folding desks in the low light, commissars and line officers sat written exams on battlefield theory, tactics and discipline, or engaged in simulation tests around chart tables.

He saw faces he recognised around one of the stations. Ban Daur, Kolosim and Obel were working through a tactical problem with a trio of Kolstec officers. They all straightened as he approached. He glanced at the glowing hololithic projection that covered the console top between them.

'Line assault?' he asked.

'Principles and applications of bounding cover,' replied Daur.

'Intermediate level, lesson three,' added Kolosim snidely.

Hark chuckled and nodded. The simulation confronting them was complex and demanding. 'Time sensitive?'

'On a real-time clock,' replied Daur.

'Then I won't spoil your rate any longer. Have you seen the colonel?'

Daur checked his wrist-chron. 'Won't he be coming back from bell service?'

Hark shook his head.

'I saw him about an hour ago in 22,' said Obel. 'I don't know where he was going, but he had his sword with him.'

'Thank you,' said Hark. 'Good luck with that.'

HARK FOUND GAUNT ten minutes later in one of the individual practice rooms. Gaunt had signed the chamber out on the chalkboard outside, and added 'NOT TO BE DISTURBED'.

Hark went inside anyway. Just inside the door there were racks of training blunts and some target dummies. Past that, open and dormant, was a mobile practice cage shaped like a clamshell.

Gaunt was in the main part of the room, duelling with four training drones: multi-legged machines with lashing weapon limbs. They circled him, jabbing and striking. Gaunt was stripped to the waist, sweating hard, ducking and spinning, lashing out with his power sword. Every clean hit he made to the pressure-sensitive pads on the bellies and heads of the drones shut them down for ten seconds. After each count, they jerked back to life and resumed their attacks.

Four drones. Four at once. That seemed excessive to Hark. He'd always admired Gaunt's blade skill, and knew it took a lot of practice to keep such close-combat skills honed. But four...

He watched for a moment longer. He noticed a mark on Gaunt's back, low down, just left of the spine. A tattoo, or...?

Hark started in surprise. The mark was blood, blood streaming from a deep cut. He realised what he was seeing.

All the drones had untipped blades. Between them, the four machines were engaging Gaunt with sixteen double-edged, half-metre long blades.

'Feth!' Hark breathed. 'Shut down! Shut down!'

The rattling machines continued to mill and strike. All Hark had managed to do was distract Gaunt, who glanced around for a moment and was then forced into a frantic, defensive back-step to avoid a slicing blade-arm.

Hark rushed forward. 'Shut down!' he ordered. 'Vox-control: shut down! Cut! Power out!'

Sensing his movement, the nearest drone broke away from Gaunt and came for him, skittering its metal legs off the practice mat onto the hard metal deck. Its weapon arms rotated and scissored.

'Feth!' Hark said again, backing up quickly. 'What the feth is this? Shut down!'

Gaunt let out a curse. He exhaled as he ducked sharply and turned his body in a low spin under the lunging blades of one of the drones. Then he came up clear and parried the weapons of another aside with his sword. He kicked out savagely and sent the deflected drone stumbling backwards. The third was close on him. Gaunt turned and sliced under its guard, drawing the power sword clean across its torso and out through its head unit in a flurry of sparks. The edges of the sheared metal glowed brightly as the head section fell away.

Gaunt leapt past the dead machine.

The fourth drone was right in Hark's face. Hark drew a plasma pistol from under his coat and raised it to fire.

But Gaunt had reached the cut-off switch on the far wall of the chamber and punched it. The three remaining drones went slack as they made power-down whines.

Hark lowered his pistol, re-engaged the safety and put it away. He looked across the room at Gaunt. The colonel-commissar was breathing hard. He deactivated his power sword as he reached for a towel to mop his face and chest.

'Unsafe weapons and a cancelled voice override?' Hark asked.

'I believe in diligent practice.'

'A trainee must have a second and a medicae present if he intends to make the practice drones capable of actual injury. Standing order–'

'57783-3. I'm aware of the rule.'

'And the punishment?'

Gaunt glared at Hark.

'The voice safety is never to be shut off,' Hark said. 'You could have been killed.'

'That was the point.'

'How was this drill supposed to end, Ibram?'

'When I'd had enough, I'd break free and hit the wall switch. You pre-empted things, Viktor. What do you want?'

'I want you alive to lead the Ghosts when we reach the next zone,' Hark replied.

'I believe in diligent practice,' Gaunt repeated. 'I believe in pushing myself and testing myself.'

'So do I,' Hark said. 'I put time in on the range, run a few sparring sessions and exercise. What you're doing is tantamount to obsessive.'

Gaunt shrugged. He threw the damp towel aside and reached for his shirt. 'Then let's just hope you never have to fight me, Viktor,' he said with a wolfish grin. 'What do you really want?'

'You missed bell service.'

'Did I?'

'Yes. It's regrettable because we're trying to whip the malingerers back into attendance and, frankly, you're not setting an example.'

Gaunt pulled his wrist-chron out of his trouser pocket and looked at it. It was an old, battered thing, the strap long since replaced by a hand-woven bracelet.

'According to this, it's another seventeen minutes to noon watch bell.'

'Then that's slow,' said Hark. 'About sixty-five minutes slow.'

'It kept good enough time on Gereon.'

'It's not keeping good enough time now, Ibram. What? You're smiling.'

Gaunt was strapping the chron to his wrist. 'I've kept this set and wound since we embarked. Fifteen days' transit and I've not synched it to the noon bell.'

'So?'

'Diurnal settings, Viktor.'

Hark frowned. It was standard Guard practice, during long voyages, to adjust the length of shipboard day/night cycles to match those of the destination world, so that over a mid-to-long duration voyage, the troops would become accustomed to a different circadian rhythm. It helped with acclimatisation. The changes weren't made in one fell swoop. Time was shaved off or added incrementally over a period of days. Synching to the noon watch kept everyone in step.

'So you're running on Ancreon Sextus time?'

Gaunt nodded. 'And the ship's set to a daylight cycle that's about an hour shorter.' He walked over to where his coat was hanging from the rail of the practice cage and slid a data-slate out of the pocket. 'I consulted a compendium of sector ephemera to check,' he said as he switched the slate on and scrolled through the data, 'but I was pretty sure anyway. It was familiar.'

He showed Hark the screen. Tight-packed data showed tide charts and seasonal daybreak and sunset tables, grouped into geographic regions, for a number of worlds in the local group. One was highlighted.

'Gereon,' said Hark.

'Pretty much the confirmation we wanted,' Gaunt said, snapping the slate off and putting it away. 'That's why I shut off voice safety, Viktor. We're going back, and I wanted to remind myself what it was like.'

* * *

X

THE MEMBERS OF RIP who failed the range grade, and that included Dalin and Merrt, got circuit marches for the next three nights.

A circuit march involved full kit, weighted backpacks and a heavy spar of pig iron as a substitute for a rifle. It involved looping the ship, end to end and back, following outer hull-skin corridors, twenty times. Kexie, who had paced the route, assured RIP that this was the equivalent of fifty kilometres.

Kexie did not march the whole distance with them. He'd go with them a way, and then cross the ship laterally via transit halls while they were toiling round the prow, or slogging through the low ducts over the enginarium, and meet them coming back up the far side.

There was a temptation to shave corners off the route, a temptation that Boulder had all but planned, but Kexie had set up a dozen servitors as checkpoints. Miss any one of these way-markers, fail to let one register your tag as you went by, and you got to spend some quality time with Saroo before repeating the march.

Most of the route wound through scabby metal ducts and long, unpainted, unheated tunnels where few people had any business being. They jogged through the canyons behind the heavy hull skin plates, behind the riveted shield of the dust sheath. They ran through the clear spaces between oily field generators that stank of ozone, and splashed through rusting compartments waterlogged by condensation. They pounded across empty holds where greased chains swung from ceilings invisible in the shadows. They struggled through the stinking chambers of the husbandry and livestock section and the sweaty, marsh-gas fug of hydroponics.

They'd started out quite upbeat, intending to take the march in their stride and let Kexie suck on it. Boulder had even tried to get a round of call and chorus cadences going to keep the rhythm. Before they'd completed even one circuit, those good intentions had soured. Breathlessness, blistered feet, bruised elbows and knees from impacts with bulkhead obstructions, and, most of all, a sick realisation of exactly how far twenty circuits was, had strung them out into a long, toiling line, grinding its way, dead-eyed and hopeless, around the course.

Every time he appeared, grinning, at some point in the route, Kexie would wave them by, and tell each straggler in turn precisely how useless he was. He'd learned some new insults for the march, or else had been saving up some particular favourites for this special occasion.

Dalin didn't complain about his inclusion. He'd grown up understanding there was a basic strand of unfairness running through a soldier's life. Soldiering was about the whole, about the unit, and about the way that unit functioned in terms of discipline and coherence. Once an individual got used to the disappointment of being levelled out whether he was right or wrong, he began to function with the unit, and life got easier.

He also understood the importance of examples.

Kexie had not beaten Merrt after the range drill. Even his attack dog logic had recognised it was unproductive to beat a man who was asking to be beaten.

Such an act would also weaken him in the eyes of the detail. Kexie was determined to remain above these affairs, untouched and unscathed by the numbers his charges pulled. It was possible he thought of himself as inscrutable.

Kexie put Merrt on the march. Then he told the others that the ten circuit marches they owed for failing to score above thirty were now going to be twenty circuit marches, thanks to what he called Merrt's 'lip'.

On the third circuit, Dalin dropped into step with Merrt. It was the first time he'd ever spoken to him.

'I wanted to–' he began.

'Skip it,' Merrt replied, without looking round.

'Was it...' Dalin hesitated. 'Was it a Ghost thing?'

That made Merrt glance round, his sunken eyes bright and curious above the awful facial prosthetic. 'A gn... gn... Ghost thing?'

'Because I'm regiment, I mean.'

Merrt shook his head. 'The fether was just wrong. I'd have spoken up no matter who it was.'

'Oh.'

They ran on, through a loading hatch and out across the grille floor of a port stowage bay. The mesh rang with their footfalls.

'How did you end up on RIP?' Dalin asked.

'The traditional way.'

'Yeah, but how?'

Merrt pulled up to a stop and Dalin stopped with him. Bodies clattered past them, slogging onwards.

Merrt stared at Dalin for a moment, right in the face. 'Do I know you?' he asked.

'I–'

'Do you know me?'

'No, but–'

'Then I'll thank you to keep your fething personal questions to yourself. I'm gn... gn... not your friend.'

'Sorry,' said Dalin. He felt himself blushing, and that made it worse. Merrt turned away and started to pace up to a jog again.

Suddenly he stopped and looked back at Dalin. 'If you must know,' he said, 'I raised my head out of gn... gn... cover during a firefight on Monthax.'

'No, I meant–'

'I know what you meant. That's still the answer.' Merrt turned again and began to run.

After a moment, Dalin followed him.

XI

OUT ON THE clear deck beyond the billet cages, a crowd had gathered to watch a team of Ghosts kick a ball with some troopers from the Kolstec barrack hall. There was a lot of good-natured shouting and cursing.

Kolea watched the game from one of the upper landings, his arms leant on the railing. Varl was with him, smoking a hand-rolled lho-stick. Every now and then, they exchanged a few philosophical remarks about the relative skills on display, especially Brostin's reluctance to pass the ball to anyone useful.

'It's like he has a disability.'

'More than the ones we know about.'

'Right.'

Down in the crowd, some of the Belladon had begun to thump out a rat-a-tat-tat on some hand drums to urge the Ghosts on. It was a fast, pacy beat. It sounded like the urgent drum march of an execution detail.

'This place we're going to–' Kolea began.

'No one knows for sure where we're going,' Varl replied.

'Yeah, but if. What's it like?'

Varl had been one of Gaunt's original mission team to the occupied world of Gereon almost three years before. The fact that any of them had come back alive was a major miracle. A garrulous man ordinarily, Varl had seldom spoken of the matter.

'It's a bad place,' he told his friend. 'Bad as can be. And I can't imagine it's got any better since I was last there.'

Kolea nodded.

'I'll be glad to go back, though,' Varl admitted.

'Really? Why?'

'Ven and Doc Curth. We left them both there. Their choice. We all meant to go back for them if we could.'

'Do you think they'll still be alive?'

Varl shrugged. 'The Doc? I dunno. But Ven… you imagine anything in this cosmos having the stones to kill Ven?'

Kolea grinned and shook his head.

Varl pinched the ash off his lho-stick and slipped the extinguished remainder behind his ear. 'I gotta go do something about that game,' he said. 'Shoot Brostin, maybe.'

Kolea had been alone on the landing for a few minutes when Tona Criid came up beside him. He nodded to her, but said nothing for a while.

At last, he said, 'How's the lad doing?'

'He's doing well, 'specially given the mongrel squad he's in.'

'That's good.'

'He's fitter than I've seen him,' Criid added, 'though his feet are hurting him right now. Last few weeks, a lot of circuit marches.'

'Yeah?'

'Punishment.'

Kolea frowned. 'Punishment for what?'

'For being too good. For showing the driller up. He's being made an example of, and he's sucking it up.'

'Maybe this driller needs–' Kolea began.

She shook her head. 'No, no, Gol. It's fine. It's the way Dalin wants it. He knows how the Guard works, and he's toeing every line. The driller's on him because he's never had such a model recruit and he can't shake the feeling that it has to be a trick.'

Down below, there was a sudden whoop and the drums picked up their beat again.

'You could ask him how he's doing yourself,' she said.

'I don't want to get in the way.'

'You're his father.'

'I'm his surviving biological parent,' Kolea replied. 'He's got a father and a mother.'

'You're his father,' Criid repeated. 'There's nothing normal about the lives we lead, so I don't believe it matters how you, me and Caff fit together, so long as we do. Dalin wouldn't mind if you showed an interest.'

'Maybe.'

'I'd go as far as to say he'd like it if you showed an interest.'

Kolea pursed his lips and thought about that. He didn't look at her. His eyes remained fixed on the game below them.

'Do it before it's too late,' Criid suggested.

'Too late?'

'We're walking Glory Road,' she said. 'Sooner or later, we get to the end of that, and you know what's waiting there. Leave it till then, and it could be too late.'

XII

THEY WERE IN the Basement, cleaning kit. Each one of them had their stuff laid out on their ground sheet. Kexie would come by, occasionally kicking a meal-can or a cup the length of the chamber if it wasn't up to regs. Sometimes he'd pick up a tin, toss it lightly into the air as he straightened up, and use Saroo like a bat to swat it into the roof.

Dalin could see the distant figures of several comrades down the far end of the Basement, recovering their launched kit items.

Kexie came up to Dalin. As he arrived, Dalin stood at attention, the ground sheet at his feet.

Find a fault with that, he willed.

He heard Kexie grunt – the slight disappointment of finding nothing to pick on.

'Pack it up. Carry on,' Kexie hissed, moving to inspect the next candidate.

It was the end of the fifth week of RIP detail. At the close of the day's cycle, they would hand in the battered practice kit they'd been caring for over the last three weeks and get issued with service materials. The following day, they would get their weapons. Then, a last three days of tight drill and prep.

It had been getting tougher every step. Kexie had been supplemented by Commissariat officers to hone the mindset alongside the body drill. There was a feeling of order, of discipline. No one played up any more.

Just looking around, Dalin could see how most of the detail had changed. Intense exercise had worn them all lean and tight, even Fourbox. The patched hand-me-down fatigues they were wearing were loose. There wasn't a pick of fat on their frames. Their hands and feet were hard and calloused. Their scalp-cuts were just growing back in, hard-edged. Their minds were wound tight like wire. Off detail, they walked with a swagger and a presence.

In just under four days they would be cycled back into their home regiments to return to duty or, like Dalin, pass out of Basic Indoctrination and become a Guardsman.

Not everyone in RIP would make it. Statistically, Caff had told Dalin, a reasonable chunk of any RIP detail got folded in again for another shakedown. The rate was higher on the Second Front, where the abnormally high percentage of sub-standard troop quality was the Crusade's shame.

Some fethers just never made the grade. That was true of this bunch. There were slackers who couldn't meet the physical grades and idiots who couldn't perform, and there were individuals like Wash who *wouldn't* rather than *couldn't*. Wash had got fit enough, but his attitude still stank. Dalin was fairly confident that Wash was one of thirty or so of them who would fold back.

Sooner or later, the repeat malingerers just got kicked out of the service, which is what most of them wanted, or got executed by the Commissariat, which is what most of them didn't.

Dalin cinched his kitbag and carried it over to the group that had finished packing. Amongst them were Fourbox and Lovely, and Hamir, one of the detail's other 'I' candidates. He and Dalin had bonded particularly well.

Hamir was a tall, olive-skinned youth from Fortis Binary. He'd followed his father and uncles in the Binars off-world after their founding and, like Dalin, had lived amongst the followers on the strength until he was old enough to take the aquila. Hamir had intelligent eyes and a slightly learned manner about him, so Fourbox had dubbed him 'Scholam'.

'No Saroo for you, Holy?' Lovely asked.

'He knows when he's beaten,' Dalin replied, looking across the chamber at Kexie, who was clubbing a candidate's shoulder blades for the incorrect fastening of a bed roll.

'Nearly there,' Hamir said.

'What?' asked Dalin.

Hamir looked up at the lights. 'We're nearly there. Can't you feel it?'

'Where?'

'The end of training. The start of Guard life. Wherever this transport is going. Take your pick.'

'I'm going to miss this,' Fourbox muttered ruefully.

Dalin, Hamir and Lovely stared at him. He beamed. 'That was a joke,' he said.

As THE DETAIL assembled, the last stragglers running to their places pursued by Saroo, Dalin caught sight of Merrt. He hadn't spoken to him since the night on the circuit march weeks before. Not before or since. Merrt had kept himself to himself.

Dalin felt terrible pity for Merrt, which he was sure the older man wouldn't appreciate. The pity came from the fact that the bulk of the RIP were all youngsters. Merrt was an old man in their midst. It seemed cruel to see him forced to repeat the mindless drills of basic 'I', like an adult forced to play along in children's games. He was above it, beyond it. He'd seen real life and felt its lash. He didn't need a refresher course.

Dalin wasn't sure what it was that Merrt needed. Merrt simply got on with RIP duties and never uttered a word of complaint. He hadn't stood up to Kexie over anything again. In Fourbox's opinion, this was because 'with a mouth like that' Merrt hated to have to speak, but Dalin believed it was that Merrt didn't have to. After that day on the range, although he had beaten many of them since, Kexie had never pulled a stunt so vindictive and unfair.

'All right?' Dalin said, stepping up alongside Merrt.

Merrt looked around, then nodded.

'Can I ask you a question?' Dalin said.

Merrt shrugged.

'On the range–' Dalin began.

'We've spoken about that,' Merrt said quickly.

'No,' replied Dalin. 'No, not then. I mean since. On the range, you're regularly getting, what, sixty, sixty-two?'

'Yeah.'

'You never seem happy with that.'

'What are you rating, son?'

'Around seventy-one.'

'You gn… gn… gn… happy with that?'

'Feth, yes. Of course.'

Merrt sighed. 'Know what I used to get? On an average day, I mean?'

'No?'

'Ninety-seven,' Merrt said. 'Ninety-seven, without any trouble. It was just in me. Range best was ninety-nine on three occasions.'

A consistent, sustainable ninety-four got a man a marksman's lanyard. Dalin knew specialists the likes of Raess, Banda and Nessa Bourah, even Larks himself, were happy with a steady ninety-five.

'Now I'm scraping sixty-one. You think I'm gn… gn… gn… happy?'

XIII

TONA WOKE WITH such a shock that her hands clawed at the coop-wire of the cage-wall and made it shake and rattle. There were muffled complaints from nearby billets.

It was dark, and there was the heavy body smell of night cycle. Caff was asleep. She went out onto the cage landing. The barrack hall was dim, just deck lighting on, but the overheads were warming up. Day-cycle was close.

She looked at her hands. They were pale in the spare blue light. She couldn't see them shaking, but she knew they were.

SHE WALKED DOWN the companionway towards Gaunt's quarters and heard the sounds of a blade striking another blade. She drew her warknife and stepped forwards cautiously.

Eszrah appeared, magically, from the shadows, and shook his head. She put the knife away again.

At the end of the companionway, in a small open space of deck in front of the hatch into Gaunt's private accommodation, two men were duelling with swords, by lamplight.

Gaunt and Hark, both in breeches and shirts, were swinging sabres. The swordplay was intense, and from the sweat on them, they'd been at it for a while.

Leaning against some ducting, his arms folded, Rawne was watching them.

'What is this?' Criid asked.

Rawne glanced at her. 'Just sparring. They've been doing it just before the start of day-cycle for weeks now.'

'Why?'

Rawne shrugged. 'Practice. Hark said something about improving his blade skills.'

'Has he?'

'Well, if I wanted to take him, I'd choose a gun,' Rawne replied. Tona watched the combatants. Gaunt had always been skilled with a sword, and she reckoned these last few years she'd seen none finer. But Hark, who she'd always thought of as heavy and slow, was holding his own.

'Why are you here?' she asked Rawne.

'I was just watching. You never know. He might slip and kill him.'

'Which one are you talking about?' Tona asked.

Rawne grinned. 'I don't care.'

Gaunt and Hark broke off and saluted one another.

'We've got an audience,' Gaunt remarked. Hark nodded and took a swig of water from a flask on a nearby stand.

'Word is, orders are about to be sent down,' Rawne said. 'I just came to tell you that.'

Gaunt nodded. 'You need something, Criid?'

'A private matter,' she said.

'Give me a moment,' Gaunt said, sheathing his sword and fetching himself a drink.

'Rawne tells me you wanted to improve your blade skill,' Criid said to Hark.

'The colonel-commissar was recently good enough to remind me of the importance of diligent practice, sergeant,' Hark said. 'A little reminder against complacency. He's been good enough to offer some instruction.'

She nodded. Gaunt waved her over and she joined him, while Hark struck
up a conversation with Rawne.

'What is it, Tona?' Gaunt asked.

'I feel stupid saying this, but–'

'Just say it.'

'I dreamed you died.'

'I died?'

'Yes.'

'Are you sure it was me?'

She hesitated. 'I think so. It mattered that much.'

'And you told me this because of the dream on Gereon?'

'Yes, sir. I dreamed of Wilder there, and that was true. I wonder if it's
something about Gereon.'

'Thank you, Tona. I appreciate that this was an odd thing to confess. Tell
you what, though… Gereon didn't kill me the first time. I'm not going to
give it a second chance.'

She nodded, faked a smile and realised Gaunt was looking past her.
Beltayn had appeared.

'Bel?'

'Just issued, sir,' Beltayn said, saluting and handing a wafer envelope to
Gaunt. Gaunt tore it open and pulled out the tissue-thin paper inside.

'It's what we've been waiting for,' he said. 'We'll be translating in ten
hours, at which time the ship will be marshalling with others at a designated staging area. All units are to make themselves combat ready and
prepare for dispersal.'

'I'll get on it,' Rawne said.

'With you,' Hark said, following him out.

'Is that all?' asked Criid.

'What?'

'You hesitated when you were reading the orders, sir,' she said. 'Was there
something else?'

'Just a list of disposition details,' he said. 'Nothing to worry about.'

XIV

THE BRIDGE AND sub-bridge levels were about the only locations aboard the
vast spaceship where a man might be afforded a look outside. Most occupants spent the long passages stacked blind, deck after deck, inside the
armoured hull, like seeds in a case, but the bridge decks were furnished with
cabin ports and windows.

Since translation from warp-space, the ship had been on a steady deceler-
ation, and armoured shutters had been peeled back from those ports like
eyelids from waking eyes.

A strange, silvery light shone in from the void outside, a light quite at
odds with the hot glow of the instrumentation and decks lamps. As he
waited, his cap under his arm, Gaunt crossed to the nearest cabin port and
peered out.

He always misremembered the sheer blackness of space. He would think of it as a rich, solid, substantial black, and picture it in his mind's eye, and then when he saw it again, he was always surprised. It was a black like no other, admitting no form or variance, but of impossible depth. The light of stars and other objects, simply sat against it, hard and contained and tiny. Starlight itself ran off the background black like water down a wall.

There was a star nearby, a cone of silver smoke, bright as a flashlight, even through the metre-thick porthole, and Gaunt could feel the faint impulse through the deck as the ship turned in towards it. This was the staging area. They were moving in through a silent shoal-pattern of other ships, all of them sharply lit at their sunwards ends and silhouetted at the others, some of them breathing furnace glows from idling drive systems.

Many of the cathedral-like ships were massive, massive like the carrier on which he stood, some more massive still: manufactory vessels, Munitorum supply ships, bulk conveyances. Great and ancient cruisers and frigates lay off to sunward like fortified broadswords. In places, transport ships and tankers were lashed together in long drifts, like the seed-purses of sea creatures. Small craft – luggers, shuttles, cutters, lighters and tugs – flitted between and around the great warp-going vessels, sometimes bright specks in the sunlight, sometimes trace-glimmers of exhaust in the lee of some cyclopean hull shadow.

Gaunt began to count the ships and lost the tally at seventy-three. Sunflare and the hard lines of shadows made it hard to differentiate shapes. This was a fleet, however. A fleet massed for invasion on a vast scale.

Gaunt wondered which of the basking giants out there contained Van Voytz.

'Sir?'

Gaunt turned from the port and found a junior deck officer waiting for him. The officer, a subordinate of the ship's Master Companion of Vox, offered Gaunt a sheet of message foil and waited politely while he read it. Gaunt balled the foil up in his hand.

'Will there be a reply, sir?' asked the officer.

'No. Just re-send my original request.'

'With respect, sir, that has now been declined three times,' the officer ventured tentatively.

Gaunt was well aware of the two other scrunched up foils in his coat pocket. 'I know, but repeat it, please.'

The officer hesitated. 'The Master Companion has made it known that he will not have all signal bands tied up with traffic during the manoeuvring phase.'

'One more try, please.'

Gaunt waited twenty minutes for the man to come back. During that time, with a series of deep thumps and heavy vibrations, the carrier came to a standstill alongside another ship whose bulk all but occluded the window ports. The dull noise of machine drills and unspooling cables began to echo up from the lower levels, along with the occasional distant rasp of a hazard siren.

The junior officer reappeared, trotting up the wide iron screwstair from the vox hub. The gabbling of the deck crew running post-dock crosschecks filled the sub-bridge air. The officer presented a foil to Gaunt, but the commiserating look on the man's face told Gaunt what to expect.

'Very well,' Gaunt sighed, casting his eyes over the repeated form message: BY ORDER OF THE LORD GENERAL'S OFFICIUM, REQUEST DECLINED.

'Your name is Gaunt, sir?' the man asked.

'Yes. Why?'

'There was a separate message for your attention.' The officer consulted a data-slate. 'A party is en route to meet with you, and requests you wait for them at the aft 7 airgate.'

IT WAS THE first time he had seen Commissar-General Balshin since the Ancreon Sextus campaign. She stood on the extended ramp for a moment until she caught sight of him, and then strode swiftly in his direction. Two men in the dark uniform of the Commissariat flanked her.

The airgate was cold, and stank of fumes and interchange gases. Steam from the pneumatic clamps hung like fog, and billowed occasionally in the sharp gusts of directional vents.

Gaunt bowed his head and made the sign of the aquila across his breast. 'Lady commissar-general.'

'Gaunt,' she replied with a curt nod. Her face was hard and pale, like white marble, and no warmth whatsoever flickered around her thin mouth. Her violet right eye, beady and bright, was utterly unmatched by the augmetic embedded in her left socket.

'I had not expected my remonstrances to draw a personal visit by so august a person as you,' Gaunt said.

'Remonstrances?' she asked.

'Yes, concerning the activation of the reserves.'

Balshin frowned. 'I know nothing of such matters, Gaunt. That's not why I'm here.'

'Ah,' Gaunt murmured. He had suspected as much.

'I'm here to brief you, Gaunt, and supply you with your specific orders. The armada's objective–'

'–is Gereon.'

Balshin allowed herself a tiny, mocking smile. 'Of course. You will have worked that out.'

'Commissar-general, if I hadn't been certain before now, your arrival would have been all the confirmation I needed. You'll have a special objective for the Ghosts, no doubt?'

'Indeed.'

'Due to their skill specialisations, and to my prior knowledge of the target world?'

'Invaluable prior knowledge, Gaunt.'

'You flatter me.'

'Not my intention, sir,' she said. 'Gaunt, you are uniquely placed to perform a great service to the God-Emperor.'

'May He protect us all,' one of the commissars at her side muttered. Gaunt glanced at him and recognised the man as Balshin's efficient but unctuous lackey Faragut.

'May He protect us all indeed,' Gaunt echoed.

'There is a chance here,' Balshin said. 'A chance to make a quick breakthrough. I will not allow that opportunity to be missed. Months of planning, Gaunt. I think it's time you got up to speed.'

She looked around the air gate. 'Is there somewhere private we can discuss this?'

Gaunt nodded. 'If you'd care to follow me?'

Balshin turned and looked over her shoulder. 'This way!' she snarled back at the open side-hatch of the lander.

A figure emerged and came to join them through the thinning steam.

It was Sabbatine Cirk.

XV

In full battledress, the Ghosts came to order in company blocks. As he walked out to inspect them, setting his cap on his head brim-first, Gaunt could hear Rawne and Hark yelling commands to dress the outer ranks, but such instructions were purely cosmetic. There was a background whine of loading hoists, and muted fanfares and drum-play from the nearby Kolstec barrack hall.

Gaunt came to a halt at the head of the ranks, took a salute from Rawne, and turned on his heel to face the troops. He cleared his throat.

'We've walked the road,' he announced, 'now glory's just another step away.'

There was a robust murmur of approval. Some of the Ghosts beat their hands against the furniture of their rifles.

Gaunt raised his own hand for quiet. 'In two hours and fifty minutes, we will board drop-ships for descent. Descent will be five hours' duration. Planetfall will be into a hot zone. You are to expect serious opposition from the moment you disembark. Stay in your company groups after this to receive briefing specifics.'

He ran his gaze along the ranks. Stock still, not a man wavering.

'Target world is Gereon,' he called out. 'I told you I'd show you around one day. Dirtside objective is the market town of Cantible. I won't tell you what I expect of you, because you know what I expect of you.' He paused. 'Soldiers of the Imperium,' he cried, consciously altering a phrase that had once begun 'Men of Tanith...', 'do you want to live forever?'

There was a huge cheer. Gaunt nodded, and made the sign of the aquila. 'The Emperor protects!' he yelled. 'Dismissed!'

The ranks broke up into company groups for discrete briefings. Gaunt saw some of the section leaders – Obel, Domor, Meryn, Varaine, Daur and Kolosim – drawing their commands into huddles and opening map cases.

Dorden approached him, medical pack slung around his body.

'Doctor?'

'Would you talk to him, please?' Dorden asked, gesturing to Ayatani Zweil. The old priest, in his full regalia, was kneeling down to tie the laces of a pair of oversized – and evidently borrowed – Guard boots. A rood topped with an eagle lay on the deck to his right, a golden censer to his left, its swinging chain slack.

Gaunt nodded. 'Father–' he began.

'Stick it up your arse,' Zweil said.

'I beg your pardon?'

The laces lashed in place, Zweil rose to his feet, hauling his bony self up by the haft of the rood. He shook out the skirts of his blue robes to cover his gnarled knees and scrawny shanks.

'Your suggestion, Gaunt. Up your arse with it.'

'That's very ecumenical of you, father. Now what suggestion would that be?'

'The same one as Dorden made, of course. That I should bless the men and do my "holy, holy" schtick and then wave farewell to you all and stay here.'

'And you don't want to do that?'

Zweil pouted and tugged at his long, white beard. 'Don't want to, don't intend to. Dorden says I'm too old. Says I'm "medically" too old, as if that is a completely different kind of too old. I'm as fit as a Tembarong grox, I am! I'm as fit as a man half my age!'

'Even so,' Dorden put in, 'a man half your age would need to have his food mashed up for him.'

'Shut your fething trap, sawbones,' Zweil returned, and stamped his feet. 'I'm coming with you, that's the up and down of it, and the side to side. I'm coming with you to minister to the needs of the regiment.'

'Father–' Gaunt tried to interject.

'I've got boots, if that's what you're worried about,' Zweil said, raising his skirts to prove it.

'It wasn't,' said Gaunt.

'I'm coming with you,' Zweil hissed, seizing Gaunt's sleeve with his claw-like fingers. 'That place we're headed for, that poor place… it's been unholy for too long. Perhaps it's past redemption, but I have to try. I happen to think it needs a man of the cloth like me more than it needs a soldier like you, Ibram, but I accept there are gunfire issues to consider.'

Gaunt held his stare for a few seconds. Then he looked at Dorden. 'Ayatani Zweil will be accompanying us.'

Dorden shrugged and rolled his eyes skywards.

'Sir?'

Hark had joined them. Criid and Caffran were with him. Their eyes were hard, hurt. Gaunt breathed deeply. He had been dreading this moment.

'Can they have a word?' Hark asked.

'Of course. Carry on, doctor. You too, father.'

Gaunt led Criid and Caffran away to the edge of the assembly area.

'Is it true?' Criid asked.

'About the reserve activation, you mean?' Gaunt asked. 'Yes, I'm afraid it is true.'

'Is there anything we can do?' Caffran asked.

Gaunt shook his head. 'I've been trying to fix it myself, but I'm not getting any joy.'

'It's not right,' said Criid. Gaunt had never seen her quite so brittle.

'No, it's not, but reserve activation is standard military practice. It's one of the Warmaster's regular tactics when manpower is needed, and Throne knows it's needed here. Departmento Tacticae and the Commissariat both approve. I will keep trying, until the moment we make the drop. After that too, if necessary. But you've got to accept right now that the Guard is a huge and grinding mechanism, and it rolls blindly on over individual requests and objections. It loves expediency and mass effect and hates exceptions. What I'm saying is, we may not be able to affect this decision.'

'It's not right, Criid said again.

'He should have been a Ghost,' said Caffran.

'Yes,' said Gaunt. 'He should.'

XVI

HE FELT AS IF he had been hit somewhere between the head and gut with the flat edge of Saroo. He was numb, almost dazed. His eyes were hot. He looked around and saw the same hurt and surprise in the faces of others.

Strange. He had been so sure today was going to be the best day of his life: passing out of Basic Indoctrination, becoming a Guardsman, taking ownership of his rifle from the armourer. Getting his trooper pin, his aquila, his sew-on patches...

...becoming a Ghost.

The gun in his hands felt like a dead weight. No thrill of pride came from gripping it.

'What's going to become of us, Holy?' Fourbox asked.

Wash and some of the others were voicing their disbelief. Candidates like Dalin had at least expected, and wanted, to see active service after RIP. Wash and his kind had done all they could to dodge activation for another cycle. This was devastating news to them.

A sour-looking, middle-aged commissar named Sobile had come to share the news with them just before they'd been issued with their kit and weapons. He stood up before them under the Basement's lights, and took half an age to unfold the notice.

'Hereby order given this day of 777.M41 that to meet the imperative drive for able troops in the coming theatre, High Command has committed to the activation of all reserve units, including punishment details, whereby they are to retain formation, be given designation, and be fielded as battlefield regulars. No individual currently on reserve status, be it for reasons of punishment, retraining or indoctrination, is to return to, or join, any other tactical element. For the present purposes, this detail will be afforded the name Activated Tactical 137, that is AT 137. Section details will follow. May the God-Emperor protect you. That is all.'

'GOL?'

Gol Kolea didn't look up.

'Gol? Shift your arse, the buzzer's gone.' Varl came down the walkway between the empty billet cages. Down below, the assembled Ghosts were emptying out of the barrack hall like water draining from a tank.

'Gol? Hark'll have your knackers if you don't move,' Varl said. Both men were bulked up with full webbing and battlegear, packs on their backs, helmets slung from their belts. Both carried their rifles in their right hands.

'I'm coming,' Kolea said. 'I was going to give him this. I meant to give it to him before, but today seemed like the right day.'

He looked at Varl, and held out his left hand. A Tanith cap badge, deliberately dulled with soot, lay cupped in the palm.

'Come on,' Varl said.

Kolea nodded. He slipped the cap badge into his breast pocket.

'It's like Tona warned me,' he said. 'I left it too late.'

PLANETFALL

I

THEY DIDN'T WAIT for daybreak. They didn't wait for clement weather, or a favourable turn in the tides. They didn't wait because they were greater than the weather and more powerful than the tides. They were brighter than the daybreak.

Along the west coast, down the line of seaboard towns and cities that had been linked and fortified into one long snake of battlements called K'ethdrac, or K'ethdrac'att Shet Magir, the sky went white. It was off-white, a sour white, and the whiteness pressed down on the high roofs and machicolations. Hot, dry clouds rolled in off the sea, and pooled wire-rough fog in the lower parts of K'ethdrac, as if the ocean were evaporating.

There was no wind, and everything was hushed. Visible static charges gathered like ivy around the raised barrels of the weapon assemblies standing ready all along the seventy-kilometre long fortress.

A door opened out to the west, out over the ocean, and cool air rushed in. In seconds, it had grown into a gale, a blistering, eastward-rushing belt of wind that lashed across the ramparts of the city-fort, and blew soldiers off the battlements, bent the stands of coastal trees into trembling right-angles, and stacked the sea up, white-top wave upon white-top wave, before driving it at the rockcrete footings of K'ethdrac.

As the huge wind reared up over the coast, the earth below shook, as if a terrible iron weight had been dropped upon it, and there was a noise, the loudest noise any man has ever heard and it not kill him. It was the sound of the atmosphere caving in as billions of tonnes of metal fell into it like rocks into a pool.

Less than a minute later, the first strikes seared into K'ethdrac'att Shet Magir. They were not pretty things, not the lusty, romantic blooms of fire a

567

man might see delineated on a triumphal fresco; they produced no halo of purifying light, no magnificence to backlight a noble hero-saint of the Imperium.

The first strikes were like rods of molten glass, blue-hot, there and gone again in a nanosecond. The cloud cover they came through was left wounded and suppurating light. Where they touched, the ground vaporised into craters thirty metres wide. Bulwarks, armoured towers, thick barriers of metal and stone all vanished, and with them, the gun batteries and crews that had been stationed there. Nothing was left but fused glass, lignite ash and deep cups of rock so hot they glowed pink. Each strike was accompanied by a vicious atmospheric decompression that sucked in debris like a bomb-blast running backwards.

The strikes came from the batteries of giant warships hanging above the tropopause. Their ornate hulls glowed gold and bronze in the pearly light of the climbing sun, and their great crimson prows parted the wispy tulle of the high, cold clouds, so that they resembled fleets of sea galleys from the myths of legend. So thin and peaceful was that realm of high altitude, their massive weapons systems blinked out the rods of visible heat with barely an audible gasp.

Other vessels, bulk carriers, had emptied themselves into the sky, like swollen insectoid queens birthing millions of eggs. Their offspring fell in blizzards from the scorched and punctured clouds, and were picked up and carried by the hurricane winds slicing in from the sea. Countless assault ships spurted like shoals of dull fish. Clouds of drop-pods billowed like grain scattered from a sower's hand.

The defenders of K'ethdrac began to fire, although their efforts were merely feeble spits of light against the deluge. Then heavier emplacements woke up, and sprawling air-burst detonations went off above the coast. At last, substantial orange flames began to splash the sky, twisted into streamers by the monstrous gales. Bars of black smoke streaked the air like a thousand dirty finger marks.

To its occupants, K'ethdrac had always seemed horizontally inclined: the long parapets and curtain walls running for kilometres, bending and twisting around the curves of the coast, with the flatness of the tidal mud beyond, the hinterlands of marsh and breeze-fluttered grasses and the undulating plane of the grey sea. It was a place of wide angles and vistas, of breadth.

In five minutes, that inclination had changed. It became a vertical place, where that verticality was emphatically inscribed down the sky by the beams and stripes of glaring energy jabbing out of the clouds. The sky became tall and lofty, illuminated by inner fire. The fortified blocks of K'ethdrac were reduced to just a trimming of silhouette at the bottom of the world, as the towering sky lit up above it, like some vision of the ascent to heaven, or the soaring staircase that leads up to the foot of the Golden Throne.

Shafts of light, so pure and white they seemed to own the quality of holiness, shone down from an invisible godhead above the sky, and turned the clouds to polished gilt and the smoke to grey silk.

The blizzard of crenellated assault ships fell upon K'ethdrac's burning lines. They came in droning like plagues of crop-devouring insects, and struck like spread buckshot. Furious scribbles of light and pops of colour lit up the seventy kilometres of wall in an effort to repel them. Thousands of tracer patterns strung the air like necklaces. Sooty rockets whooped up in angry arcs, trailing hot dirt. Rotating cannons drummed and pumped like pistons and turned the sky into a leopard skin of black flak smoke.

In the steep fortress wall, gunports oozed with light like infected wounds as energy weapons recharged and then sprayed out their ribbons of light.

Drop-ships burned in mid-air. Some melted like falling snowflakes in sudden sunlight and some blew out in noisy, brittle flashes and pelted the battlements with metal hail. Some fell into the sea, trailing plaintive smoke, or buried themselves like tracer rounds in the towers and tuberous spires of K'ethdrac. One great tower, at the southern end of the city region, half collapsed after such a collision, and left just a part of itself standing above the billowing dust, a finger of stone with a broadening crest like the trochanters of a giant thigh bone rammed into the ground.

Some drop-ships made it to the ground intact.

II

DALIN CRIID SAW nothing of this.

He suffered the awful turbulence of descent, rattled like a bead in the bare-metal casket of the lander. He heard the shrill whine of the engines, like spirits screaming to be freed. He smelled and tasted the fear: acid sweat, rank breath, bile, shit.

Fear made some men weep like babies, and others as silent as marble. The company pardoner, a flat-faced, gone-to-seed fellow called Pinzer, was reciting the Sixtieth Prayer, the *I Beseech*. Many of the troopers were saying it along with him, some gabbling fast and loud, as if they were anxious that they wouldn't get to the end before they died, or before they forgot how it went. Others spoke it like they meant it, meant every word with every fibre of their wills; while others said it like a charm, a superstitious rhyme you recited to bring you luck. They spoke it carelessly, as if the words themselves were meaningless and the act of saying it was all that mattered.

Others just murmured the lines, probably not even knowing what they were saying, just fastening their scalded minds to something other than mad panic.

Criid saw a dead look in Fourbox's eyes, in Hamir's too. It was a sunken look, and it showed how totally hope had left them, and how deeply their personalities had withdrawn to hide in the very kernels of their heads. All around him, there were eyes that looked the same. Criid was sure his own eyes shared that dead look too.

The turbulence was unimaginably violent. There was simply no let-up in the shake and slam, the jump and rattle, and no relief from the howl of the engines. At particularly catastrophic lurches, some of the company would shriek, assuming the sudden death they had been anticipating.

The shrieks made Pinzer forget his words. He kept having to go back and pick up. He didn't seem scared – unlike the scalps of AT 137, he'd done this before. But Criid could tell it was an effort for the pardoner to keep expression from his face. This didn't come easy, no matter how many times you did it.

The shaking and lurching became so intense that Criid could no longer bear it. There was no escape, no exit from it, and he became so desperate that he thought he might rip open the deployment hatch and step out, and let the thundering windshear snatch him away.

A clear voice was speaking the Sixtieth Prayer. 'God-Emperor, in whose grace I persist and in whose light I flourish, I beseech thee to lend me the strength to endure this hour…'

He realised it was his own voice.

Sobile, the commissar, sat silently in his restraint harness, watching the rows of troopers from the end of the cabin. He looked like he was attending a particularly tedious dinner.

Beside the commissar, Kexie – Sergeant Kexie, as he was now – listened to his intercom and then reached up and yanked on the bell-cord vigorously. Kexie was in charge. Major Brundel, their newly appointed CO, was riding in another lander.

'Company, stand up!' Kexie bellowed over the row.

Zeedon, the trooper two seats down from Criid, bowed forward and spewed watery sick onto the steel floor between his boots.

'Ech, I said stand up, not throw up,' Kexie barked.

Criid released his restraint and took hold of his lasrifle.

Thirty seconds.

He saw Commissar Sobile take something out of his pack and lay it, ready, across his lap. It was something he'd never seen Gaunt carry, or even heard of him using.

It was a whip.

III

ZEEDON WAS THE first to die. The first Criid saw, anyway. Fourbox told him later that a Kolstec called Fibrodder had got scragged while they were still in the lander. A piece of white-hot debris, probably a piece off another drop vehicle, had punched through the hull wall two seconds before the hatch opened. Flat, sharp and rotating, the object struck Fibrodder in the back of the head with an effect similar to a circular saw, and opened his skull in a line level with the tops of his ears.

The screaming and retching of the blood-drenched troopers strapped in around Fibrodder's corpse was lost in the tortured hammer blow of landing. The landing was so brutal that Criid felt like his bones were shaking free of their tendons, his teeth flying loose from his gums. His jaw flapped and made him bite his tongue.

His mouth filled with blood, but the pain kept him sharp: the preposterous, tiny, impertinent pain, the indignation. *I've got enough to worry about and now I've bitten my fething tongue?*

Kexie and the other officers were blowing whistles. The air was hot, and it filled entirely with acrid yellow smoke as soon as the hatch opened. Noise blasted in from outside. It was gunfire, mostly; the unrestrained, unstinting chatter of an autocannon mowing at the sky.

Criid got out into cold air, felt grit beneath his boots, solid ground. The smoke was thick, and big, deep thumps of overpressure kept dulling his hearing. Head down, they were all running, weapons across their chests. There was a loud *pock-pock-pock* sound, and the patter of pebbles pinging off nearby metal plating. *Not pebbles, not pebbles…*

Criid didn't know if he was running the right way or not. He didn't know how they could tell which way to run. The smoke had swallowed both Kexie and the sound of his whistle. They were in some kind of rockcrete canyon. Slabby grey-green towers rose up on either side.

He looked back. The lander lay like the carcass of an animal kill. In its final few seconds of flight it had barged through a fortified wall and augured into the yard behind it. Criid didn't know if this could be reckoned a good landing or a bad one.

He realised there was an awful lot of things he didn't know. He was starting to form a list.

He spat out the blood he'd been holding in his mouth since he'd bitten his tongue. He heard Sobile's voice, barking about 'cover spread'.

He looked up.

Through a roof of moving smoke, he could see the sky. It was full of fire, choked with giant feathers of yellow and amber flame. For as far as he could see, the sky was blistering with explosions, big and small: airbursts, shells, tracers, rockets. It seemed random and bewildering.

There were black dots visible in the sky – other ships, other aircraft. Two more landers, flying in formation, suddenly swept low overhead, crossing the fortified wall, and disappeared around the far side of the towers. The downwash roar of their engines was painful. Far more painful was the bombardment that opened up from the top of the towers, and swept around chasing them.

Soot flakes ambled through the smoke. Criid took his eyes off the sky and tried to get some sense of the deployment. Given how many hours they had spent in the Basement learning the rudiments of unit cohesion, there was precious little sign of it now.

Commissar Sobile appeared from the smoke about a hundred metres away. He was pointing urgently with one hand and cracking his whip with the other. A gaggle of troopers rushed past him, preferring, it seemed, to Criid, to dive blindly into the drifting smoke than stay anywhere near his lash.

Criid started to follow them. They were heading towards the base of one of the towers. As he turned, the air shivered and another lander screamed in low overhead. He looked up involuntarily.

The lander was much lower than the previous two. Criid could see the detail of its underside and landing gear. Its tail section was on fire. He looked at it with a sick fascination, knowing exactly what was going to happen, while simultaneously knowing that there was nothing he could do to prevent it.

The lander rushed over him. It was thirty metres up, but it made him duck anyway. It hit the side of the nearest tower, the one he and the other troopers had been running towards.

It hit with annihilating force. One moment there was the moving bulk of the lander and the immobile face of the grey-green tower; then there was a huge and spreading fireball, a bulging fiery cloud that swallowed the lander as if it was drawing it into the tower's interior. Debris – huge pieces of stone, mortar and reinforcement girders – scattered outwards, trailing dribbles of smoke and fire.

The troopers who'd reached the base of the tower ahead of him turned and ran back. He saw the nearest of them clearly. It was Zeedon. There was still a speckle of puke on his chin. He was shouting *'Get back, get back!'*

Huge chunks of masonry and burning sections of the demolished lander – one of them, a whole engine pod, clearly still running – came down in a torrent. The avalanche caught the running troopers and enveloped them in a bow wave of dust.

Zeedon was ten metres from Criid and still running towards him when the stone block landed on him. It was a large block of ouslite, bigger than two men could have lifted between them. One face was still caked in grey-green plaster. Zeedon didn't fall beneath it or even fold up. It simply flattened him in the most total and abrupt way. He was there and then he was gone, and all that was left behind was a block of stone with a man's leg stuck out flat on one side, and another stuck out on the other. The force of violent compression had sent a powerful and curiously directional jet of blood out more than twenty metres. It left a dark red, glittering trail, like gemstones, on the dust for a moment. Then more dust filmed and tarnished the red beads, covering them over.

IV

BEYOND THE TOWERS, that particular sector of the fortress of K'ethdrac'att Shet Magir was a wilderness of fire and rubble. Kexie and Sobile gathered up the squads and managed to link up with some of the company from the second AT 137 lander, which had come down inside the perimeter wall. There was no sign of Major Brundel.

They were closer to some of the area's major gun emplacements, and subjected to the side-effects of their bombardment.

The emplacements, mainly anti-air and long range anti-orbit weapons, were firing at full rate. Their flashing concussions tore the sky overhead, and the ground shook continuously. It overcame the senses. It was too loud for the ears, too bright for the eyes and no voice could penetrate it. Criid tried to find cover. In the open, the bombardment was as crude a sensory experience as having a high power lamp pack pressed against each eye socket and then switched on and off rapidly. Even with his eyes closed, the flashes came through white and traced with capillary threads.

Criid half-jumped, half-fell into a rockcrete drainage trench, a culvert running along the edge of the yard. Rubble littered its dry bed. He passed the body of a Guard trooper, curled up in the culvert as if he was asleep, but not even the deepest sleep relaxed a body that much.

At the end of the culvert, he caught up with a squad led by Ganiel, a Hauberkan who Kexie had made corporal. Boulder was amongst the troopers. They crossed a smoke-washed concourse and came up towards what Criid was certain were the munitions silos for two of the thundering emplacements. Somewhere along the way, Kexie joined them. He took them as far as a low wall, and then got them down into cover.

Criid wasn't sure why at first. Then he saw puffs of stone dust lifting off the top of the wall, and realised that they were under ferocious small-arms fire, the noise of it lost in the bombardment. Lip, a Kolstec girl on RIP for arguing with a superior, was slow getting down. She walloped over onto the ground and lay there with her legs kicking furiously for a few seconds. Then her limbs went slack.

When the firing became sporadic, Kexie led them over the wall. He did this with a simple gesture and a certain look on his face. It seemed clear from both that ignoring him was a more dangerous proposition than breaking cover into a fire zone.

Criid started to run, leading Boulder, Ganiel and a Binar called Brickmaker. Criid felt the movement of air against his face as rounds tore past.

They reached the cover of an upturned slab of rockcrete that a rocket had scooped out of the yard, got down, and started firing. It felt satisfying, somehow, to be firing back at last. His first shots in anger, although he couldn't see where he was shooting.

Kexie got to the cover of a mangle of engine debris five metres away. Socket, Trask and Bugears slithered up behind him. Three others weren't so fortunate. Landslide was cut up messily by las-fire the moment he left cover. His broken body lay on the ground, the jacket on fire. Likely, a diligent little Binar who had been, with Criid and Hamir, one of the few 'I' candidates in RIP, had covered half the distance when he was hit in the knee and went sprawling. He rolled over, clutched his ruined knee, and was immediately shot in the same knee a second time. This shot had to pass through his clutching left hand to do so and blew off three fingers.

Likely screamed in pain. Bardene stopped and turned to help him, and was killed outright by a bolt round to the base of the spine that left him spread-eagled on his face. A second later, cannon fire put Likely out of his torment.

Criid reloaded. Stone dust and fycelene stung his eyes. A horn sounded, deep and long and loud, like a manufactory hooter.

'Ech, look at that,' Kexie bawled.

Criid turned to look. Behind them, the god-machines were moving in.

V

AGAINST A SKY ragged with fire, Titans were coming in off the shore to raze K'ethdrac'att Shet Magir. Criid had seen them before – in books and picts, and also for real at several victory parades. He'd once nursed an ambition to be a princeps when he grew up, until the honest aspiration to be a Guardsman took over.

At that second, he could no longer recall why he'd made that choice. If nothing else, being a princeps high up in an armoured thing like that would have been a lot safer.

Criid knew Titans were big; he was just utterly unprepared for the scale of their violence. It was the way they strode along, demolishing walls and roofs without effort, and the way their weapon limbs unleashed apocalyptic doom at targets great distances ahead.

There were two assaulting the fortress wall about a kilometre to Criid's left, but his attention was transfixed by the third one, the nearest, coming in through the walls behind him.

It was matt khaki, its flanks inscribed with big white numerals. Its movements were ponderous and arthritic, like a heavy old man shambling after his grandchildren. Its head and torso rocked backwards and forwards gently on its hips as it took each step. There was a sound of gears, of giant hydraulics, of creaking metal. The volcano cannon, its right arm, tracked slowly, fired out salvos of rapid, shrieking shots, and then tracked again and repeated. Criid saw tiny lights high up under the beetle brow, and felt as if he'd glimpsed the thing's soul, even though it was surely only the cockpit lights.

It was on his side, but it terrified him, and it terrified the men around him. It was a war machine, and this was its natural habitat. Criid felt he had no business being anywhere near it. For a start, how would it know that the screaming dots around its feet were loyal soldiers of the Imperium? How could it make that subtle differentiation when each blundering step it made brought curtain walls tumbling down in cascades of bricks or ripped through razorwire fences like they were long grass? Criid believed that if he was a princeps, commanding that power, he would trample over everything in his way and, afterwards, if he was told he'd crushed friends on his way to the foe, he'd say 'But we have a victory, that's what counts.' It was preposterous to think that a Titan should be bothered with the details of what lay under its feet. You unleashed it, and then you got out of its way.

The sergeant had clearly arrived at a similar opinion. At the top of his parade ground voice, he was yelling at the squads to move clear, to move right. Small-arms fire was still raining down on them like summer drizzle, but the Titan at their backs was approaching like a tidal wave. Another barrier wall came down around its shins, filling the air with the clopping sound of loose blocks tumbling together, filling their nostrils with the fresh, dry stink of masonry dust. The volcano cannon ululated again, shredding the air above them with fizzling javelins of light. Criid felt his skin prickle and the hairs on his arms lift as the close energy blasts altered the ionisation of the air.

He could smell ozone and oil, and hot metal. Steel plates shrieked, dry and unlubricated, as they took another shuddering step forward. A horn blared. The manufactory hooter noise was the thing's voice, its warning, not to the foe but to its own kind. *Out of my way, I'm walking here. Out of my way, or die.*

They started to run, to the right, as Kexie had instructed. The sergeant was running too. Again, Criid felt the stinging breeze of rounds cutting the air beside him. He saw las-bolts soar and flicker past. A flying pebble hit him in the leg. He saw a trooper running a few paces ahead twist and fall over. He got down in a shell hole.

The ground trembled with the tread of the Titan as it passed. Down in the shell hole, small rocks and sand trickled down with each quiver.

A body fell into the hole on top of him. It was Boulder. He kicked and struggled to get the right way up and dropped his rifle more than once.

'Holy?' he said, realising who he'd fallen in on. That made him laugh, although Criid couldn't hear it above the Titan's horn. *Haw-haw-haw*, went Boulder's mouth. He had a cut over one eye, and his left cheek was covered with soot. Criid signed to ask if he was all right, but Boulder didn't understand. Caff had taught Criid how to sign. It was a stealth thing, a Ghost thing.

The reminder made Criid wince. There was nothing heroic or exciting about the situation he found himself him, nothing even remotely sensible or purposeful. It was a mad, ragged scramble, full of fear and shocking glimpses of mutilation, and with no clear purpose. He had dreamed of a Guardsman's life, wanted a Guardsman's life, and if this was it, it was wretched and idiotic. He felt cheated, as if Caff and his ma and Varl and all the others had been lying to him all these years. No one would want this. No one would choose this.

Except, maybe, if he had been going through this as a Ghost, instead of as a member of the arse-wipe detail AT 137, maybe all those qualities would have been there… the excitement, the heroism, the purpose.

'What do we do?' Boulder was yelling, his manner part whining, part sarcastic. 'What do we do? Can we go home now, haw-haw-haw?'

Criid took a look up out of the hole. He looked for Kexie, or the commissar. He saw Ganiel in a ditch nearby with Fourbox, Socket and Brickmaker. He saw a body, out on the open rockcrete, half-turned on its back, leaking blood into the dust. Who was that? Did it matter?

Criid didn't know which way to go, or what to do if he got there. He could discern no value whatsoever in the Imperial Guard's investment in bringing him and his comrades to this place.

'You've been shot,' Boulder shouted.

Criid looked. The calf of his fatigue pants was holed and bloody. It hadn't been a pebble that had bounced off his leg. He'd been shot and hadn't realised it.

The Titan passed by fifty paces to their left. Its shadow, cast by the seething fireball of a burning fuel tank, had slid over them. The ground continued to tremble with each step, and the air was still rent with the horn, the shriek of metal plating and the squealing of the cannon.

Criid craned around to see it. It was tearing into the inner yards, passing the munition silos on its advance towards the main emplacements. It was trailing part of an electrified wire fence from one ankle, like a shackle, and the bouncing, jangling wires sparked and fizzled. Criid was suddenly struck by what the Titan really reminded him of. The bear.

Years ago, with the followers on the strength of another transport, there had been a dancing bear, a big black ursid from some backwater world that one of the regiments had kept as a mascot. It was shackled to a post by one of its rear feet, and the handler would stab it with a goad to make it rear up and dance to tunes played on a tin whistle. The bear could shuffle about well enough. It reared tall and huge, forearms bent at its sides, rocking from side to side in a manner that amusingly mimicked a man, but it was no biped. As soon as it was able, it would stop pretending to be human and drop back down onto all fours to become a big, simple beast again.

That's what the Titan reminded him of: a wild beast, a giant carnivore, taught to roar and shamble on two legs, plodding slowly, uncomfortably, yearning to drop back into its natural stance.

Boulder tugged at his sleeve.

'What?'

'See that?' Boulder pointed. Sobile had reappeared, leading twenty members of the company in across the smouldering rubble. There were more troops too. Several dozen figures in brown battledress were clambering into the compound through the gap that the Titan had made in the outer wall.

The dozens became hundreds, the hundreds thousands. Criid blinked. He saw regimental banners rise and bugles sound. Androman Regulars, he made out from the gilt thread of one banner, Sixth Regiment. Regular Imperial Guard at battalion strength, swarming in from shore landings. The tide of men flooded the concourse and advanced behind the Titan like the train of a cloak. Criid could see the white and yellow tinder strikes of their rifle fire as they aimed up into the blockhouses. Rockets whooped upwards on erratic arches of smoke.

'Get up,' Criid told Boulder. 'Get up. Let's go.'

VI

THEIR CONFIDENCE TEMPORARILY lifted by the company of so many others, AT 137 moved forwards. Commissar Sobile hardly had to use his whip. They surged out onto a vast yard or parade ground beneath the network of emplacements, following the plodding Titan.

The enemy guns were still pounding. All down the coast, for kilometres in either direction, the defences of K'ethdrac ripped into the morning sky, pummelling the air with concussion and echoes of concussion. A shroud of fycelene vapour clung like a sea fog.

The sky seemed, to Criid, to be the greatest casualty of all. It was swollen with smoke and the light from massive fires. Great black and orange mushrooms welled up into it. To the north, thick squadrons of attacking aircraft swirled around like flocks of birds gathering to migrate.

One of the more distant Titans, visible over the line of burning roofs, took a direct hit from a super-heavy emplacement. The centre of the torso and the head blew up in a vast fireball that rose, writhing and expanding, and finally separated into a crowning ring of flame that wobbled into the sky. Its structure shorn through, the torso plating failed and the heavy weapon limbs, the Titan's arms, fell away and tore the folding halves of the body with them. The rest of the machine remained standing: locked, frozen legs and a black iron pelvis gutted by fire.

A great moan of dismay rose from the foot troops at the sight. The Androman Regulars began to charge the emplacements, bugles and drums sounding.

Criid was caught in the surge for a moment and was carried along. Men in brown uniforms were all around him and he couldn't see another shape in the drab grey of his own unit.

'Keep going, boy!' one of the Androman troopers told him. He was a big fellow with sallow skin, as hirsute as the rest of his breed. He grinned at Criid. 'Come on! The Emperor protects!'

Criid wasn't so sure. He was pretty certain he ought to be linked to his own company. He searched for his comrades, but his foot caught on a slab of rubble and he fell.

The Guardsmen charged past him. Some were yelling battle cries. He tried to get up again, but was knocked over twice by barging men. Some cursed him.

Enemy fire began again. It fell like sleet on the Imperial force from gun nests and strongpoints up on the looming emplacements. The spirit that had driven the men forward en masse left them. The advancing flow recoiled.

Criid got up and started to run. A series of mortar shells planted themselves into the rockcrete not far from him and sprouted into cones of fire and grit. Two or three men were thrown bodily into the air and came down heavily like sacks full of rock. Others were cut down as they turned back, smacked into by whining cannon fire. Each shot wailed for a split second before it arrived and made the *thwuck* of impact that brought a man down in a mist of blood.

Criid saw the big Androman who had spoken to him. He was staggering about, sneezing, spitting and aspirating blood through a face that had lost its nose, top lip and upper teeth. The man flailed past him and Criid didn't see what happened to him after that.

Criid ran across the concourse. It was littered with bodies. The Androman Guardsmen were now flooding off to the left, shrinking back from the killing ground below the emplacements. The Titan strode on, oblivious to the tidal changes in the infantry around its feet, oblivious to the small-arms fire and mortars pinging off its hull.

Some parts of AT 137 had taken cover in a rockcrete gulley leading to a heavy loading door. The loading door, riveted metal, was shut and had resisted attempts to open it.

Sobile saw Criid approach along with other stragglers, and cracked his whip at them agitatedly.

'Watch the unit and stay together, you worthless morons! Stay together and stay focused! How can we achieve our objectives if we don't have unit cohesion?'

Criid wanted to answer back. He wanted to ask how they were supposed to achieve their objectives if they didn't know what their objectives were. He wanted to ask if Sobile had a fething clue what the objectives were himself. Criid had a long list of questions.

One of Sobile's petulant whip cracks caught him across the right shoulder and the corner of his jaw and he forgot about his questions and his lists. The corded leather sliced right through his jacket and drew blood along his collar bone. It felt like his jaw had been dislocated.

'Get up!' Sobile ordered, generally disinterested in Criid's plight. The pain was so sharp that Criid could barely move. His eyes filled with hot tears.

'Get up!' Sobile snarled and then turned to the others. 'I'll damn well skin the next moron who forgets to focus. Are we clear?' He coiled up his whip and glanced at Sergeant Kexie. Kexie was rubbing a scratch on his gnarled cheek. The troopers were all gathered in the shadow of the gulley, panting, trying to draw breath. Some were sobbing.

'Sergeant?' Sobile said.

'Break into squads, advance that way across the yard,' Kexie said, indicating with his lasrifle. 'Come at the nearest emplacement from the side, see if we can't storm it and shut it down.'

'Instructions are clear, 137,' Sobile thundered. 'Get into position!'

Artillery, a kilometre or so away, was suddenly thumping like the drums of a giant marching band. The skyline lit up with pulsing flashes. Beyond the gulley, the Androman troops were massing for another attempt to get across the parade ground.

Criid got up. Blood was leaking out of the split flesh at the corner of his jaw, and his shoulder throbbed. He could feel the tissue stiffening and swelling. The fingers of his right hand were numb. Getting into position was a joke. Of the two hundred and fifty individuals that made up AT 137, about forty were gathered in that dank gulley. Criid didn't know if that meant the rest of them were dead, or were simply somewhere else, equally bewildered. Another question for his list. This chunk of AT 137 seemed to qualify as the 'main section', because it happened to have both the commissar and the sergeant with it.

There were barely any surviving vestiges of predetermined fire teams or squads. People just joined up with people they knew into assault teams that had roughly the right number of bodies. Criid got in with Ganiel's mob, along with Bugears, Socket, Trask and Fourbox. He saw Boulder in another gaggle with Corporal Carvel. Boulder was looking confused and dazed. The cut over his eye had begun to bleed more freely.

'Where is your weapon? Where is your issued weapon, trooper?' Sobile shouted.

Boulder suddenly realised that the commissar was speaking to him. He looked around and blinked. His hands were empty, and they'd been empty for a long time, and he hadn't noticed. The last time Criid had seen Boulder's rifle, he'd been busy dropping it in the shell hole. It was probably still there.

'I think I dropped it,' Boulder began. He tried to curl his lips into a smile, but the full, trademark laugh wouldn't come.

No, no, no, Criid thought. Boulder had no idea what he was heading for. He wasn't thinking.

You didn't drop your rifle. You didn't lose your rifle. A Guardsman protected the rifle issued to him with his life, and vice versa. It was basic and fundamental.

'Gross infringement, article 155,' Sobile said and shot Boulder through the head. Boulder jerked as if he'd been told surprising news. It obviously wasn't funny news, because he didn't laugh. He pitched over, slack and heavy, and hit his sagging head against the gulley wall on his way down.

There was a moment when even the artillery seemed silent. It was the first ten-ninety Criid had ever witnessed. He felt sick. In a day filled with waste and hopelessness, this was the most obscene thing yet.

'Anyone else?' Sobile asked holstering his pistol.

Everyone looked away. They didn't want to catch Sobile's eyes, or look at Boulder.

'Ech, you soft-shit scalps!' Kexie snapped. 'You want to be proper bloody Guardsmen, you better show me and the Emperor what you've got. On the whistle...'

The sergeant's whistle blew. They broke from cover and ran, leaving Boulder alone in the shadows with steam gently rising from the wound that had killed him.

VII

CORPORAL GANIEL'S SQUAD reached the western corner of the large emplacement without incident. They were all out of breath from the dash across the open, and wired from the fear of making that dash. Behind them, smoke wreathed the scattered rubble. A noisy, widespread firefight was raging beyond a row of warehouses, spraying tracers and backflash into the lowering sky, and they could see Corporal Carvel's team spread out and running for the building's eastern end. Sporadic, almost tired cannon fire barked lazily from the roof high above, and kicked up dirt around them.

Up close, the building was dead and dark. It was built not from stone but from some synthetic or polymer, faced with pitched wooden boards. Criid could see sections of the chipped resin in places where gunfire had shredded off the wood. On close examination, it looked less like polymer and more like bone or fossilised tissue. There was a smell to it, up close. It was a warm, animal smell, slightly rancid, slightly spicy. It wasn't entirely unpleasant.

The sergeant came up behind them, with another of the squads.

'Move up!' he grunted.

'There's no door, sergeant,' said Ganiel.

A missile squealed overhead and caused a large explosion beyond the ruptured sea wall. Two fighters – Thunderbolts, Criid guessed – swept in past the emplacements at rooftop height and peeled out towards the northern districts of K'ethdrac'att Shet Magir. The cityscape was dense with thousands of columns of smoke like trees in a woodland.

Sobile moved up with another squad. He'd found the pardoner somewhere. The man, unfit and unhealthy, was wheezing as he muttered the words of grace and benediction to a wounded man.

Carvel's squad moved around the eastern end of the emplacement. They'd been gone about thirty seconds when there was a fizzling crump that tore the air like dry paper, and a flash lit up behind the corner where they'd vanished.

Kexie ordered Ganiel's team forward to investigate. They had no man-to-man vox. Either there hadn't been spare micro-bead kit available for issue at AT 137's sudden advancement to active status, or a rat-tail dreg outfit like AT 137 didn't deserve such costly luxuries. They had a unit vox-officer with a field set, a Kolstec called Moyer, but Criid hadn't seen him since boarding. He was probably dead along with Major Brundel.

Covering each other with jerky, nervous switches of their lasrifles, Ganiel, Criid and Trask reached the eastern corner. Bugears and Fourbox were close behind.

Around the corner, a wide service lane led up to loading shutters built into the back of the emplacements, access for the heavy carts of the ammunition trains coming up from the silos. The area had been hit comprehensively during the first phase strikes. The Navy bombardment had missed the blockhouse gun emplacements but had expertly flattened a row of empty bunkers behind them. The service lane was littered with debris and rubble from the bunkers. It was quiet back there, just some drifting smoke. The heavy weapons within the emplacement had been silent for some minutes.

'Where's Carvel?' Ganiel asked.

One patch of the rockcrete roadway was smoking with particular vigour. The smoke rose from a wide, tarry puddle of debris. It was organic debris. Criid smelled burned meat and took a step back.

'Carvel…' he gagged.

The remains of the five men lay in the dark, smoking scorch mark. They'd been incinerated, although some parts of them were still identifiable: skulls, ribcages, long bones, heat-twisted rifles. The bones were black-wet with sticky meat and cooked blood.

'Get back,' Ganiel said.

'Good idea,' Kexie muttered. He'd arrived behind them to take a look. 'Ech, get running.'

He said something about a tank that Criid didn't hear properly because of the sudden roar of a flamer behind them, and a gust of heat singed the back of his neck as he ran.

He never saw the tank, but he heard and smelt it – the deep, grinding rumble of its engines, the clatter of its treads, the stink of its oil. According to Kexie, it had been hull-down in the ruins of the bunkers, guarding the service lane with its hull-mounted flamer.

They ran from it. Disturbed, it roused from its lair and came after them.

'Back up. Back up. Find cover!' Kexie yelled as they rejoined the others. 'Bandit armour right behind us!'

Sobile started to run. They all started to run, to scatter, but Sobile ran in a way that suggested to Criid that he no longer cared about his duties and responsibilities, and certainly didn't care to risk his skin any longer trying to preserve either unit cohesion or the moronic lives of any of the rejects he'd been lumbered with.

Criid heard the flamer roar again as the tank cleared the emplacement. He looked for cover, any cover, spotted a shell hole in the rockcrete and threw himself into it.

He'd been there before. In the oily seepage at the bottom of the hole lay Boulder's rifle.

VIII

HE STAYED IN the hole for what seemed like a year or two. He wrapped his arms around his head, but they didn't block out the increasing volume of the clattering tracks and the throbbing motor. The gushing roar of the flamer sounded like an ogryn's wet snarl.

There were screams. There were a lot of screams. Some lasted longer than a scream should decently last.

He tried to block it all out. All he could see was the blood-red sky above, filmed with driving smoke, and the occasional afterglow of a big flash. He kept expecting it to be blocked out by the black, oiled belly of the tank as it rattled over the top of him.

Rolled up like an unborn child, Dalin Criid felt more mortal than he'd ever felt in his life. All the self-deceiving vitality of youth drained from him and left just a silt of pain behind. His needs reduced to an undignified, simple level, and became the sorts of things that grown men scorned as weaknesses in the mess hall or the bar room, and cried out for shame in extremis. In a hole in the ground, in the path of a tank, for instance.

In that moment, he knew with astonishing clarity that this happened, sooner or later, to every man or woman who became an Imperial Guardsman. It was the moment when a person faced up to the fact that everything he'd bragged about wanting – action, glory, battlescars and reputation – was, without exception, chimerical and of no value or reward, and everything he'd disparaged as weak and soft, and cowardly was all that genuinely mattered.

He wanted the noise to stop. He wanted to be elsewhere too, but the noise was the key thing. It was relentless and he needed it to stop. He wanted the pain in his face and shoulder to go away. He wanted to see his ma. He wanted to be eleven years old again, playing paper boats with his baby sister in the deck gutters of a troop ship.

In that hole in the ground, so like a grave, these things acquired a sudden and resonating value that went far beyond comfort or escape. There was something else he yearned for too, something he couldn't quite resolve. A face, maybe.

He understood that he was experiencing the soldier's universal epiphany, but he didn't know what would happen next. Was it fleeting? Was it a mood that came and went, or was his heart now hollowed out, his courage permanently compromised? Had his fighting mettle perished? Was he of no use as a soldier?

What actually happened next was a loud detonation, fierce and visceral, that sounded like two anvils colliding at supersonic velocities. The metallic impact physically hurt, jarring his bones and making his sinuses ache.

Then there was a second explosion, much richer and throatier with the sound of flames than the first.

Criid heard the sergeant's muffled voice, as if from a long way off. '137! 137, regroup! Regroup!' The whistle blew.

He raised himself up out of the shell hole and saw figures moving through a dense heat-haze. The haze was rippling off a vast bonfire twenty metres away, a huge stack of black material the size of a revel fire, swollen with leaping orange flames.

Criid got out of the hole. He looked at Boulder's rifle and wondered if he should take it with him. In the end, he decided to pop the power cell and take just that.

He walked through the washing heat towards his regrouping unit. There were bodies on the ground, charred and smouldering. One was the trooper Fourbox had given the name Socket. His whole form had been wizened and shrunk by extreme heat, but Criid could tell it was Socket because, mysteriously, Socket's face had remained untouched, like a mask tied to a pitch-black dummy.

Kexie was drawing the unit together. There was no sign of Sobile, which was the only decent thing that had happened since they'd arrived.

'What happened to the tank?' Criid asked Brickmaker.

The Binar nodded to the big bonfire.

'That's it?'

It was, apparently, it. No one could say exactly what had killed the tank, but the best guess was 'a stray shot from something big a long way off. According to the sergeant, 'This kind of shit happens on the battlefield sometimes.'

Commissar Sobile turned up alive a few minutes later, so that kind of shit happened on a battlefield too apparently. He got busy with his whip, and tore two troopers new exits for losing their helmets.

They moved north, up the line of the emplacements, towards an enormous firefight about a kilometre away. The Titan, now long gone, had flattened the emplacements on its way past. Most were burning and broken open to the sky. Some had burst, leaking dark, sticky fluid out in wide lakes around their foundations. It was as if the buildings were bleeding. Kexie warned them not to go near the stuff, but no one had the slightest inclination to anyway, and nobody wanted to take a look inside the ruins.

They reached a main thoroughfare that thrust east up through the gloomy city. A river of Imperial tanks and light armour was flowing inland, heading towards the gourd-shaped super-towers at K'ethdrac's heart. Vs of fighter aircraft skimmed up the line above the tanks. The city district on the far side of the thoroughfare, a region of dark towers and strange, crested structures the colour of tungsten, was being pummelled into extinction by pinpoint orbital fire. The ribbons of light, eye-wateringly bright, jabbed down through the stained cloud cover and, with chest-quaking concussion, reduced habitation blocks to swirling storms of ash.

Back the way they had come, more Titans stalked the burning skyline, visible from the waist up behind the roofscape as if they were wading a river. They were booming silhouettes against the amber twilight, their hands flickering luminously with laser discharge.

To Criid, it seemed like the entire city was on fire.

Another wave of drop-ships began pouring in overhead.

On the debris-strewn pavements, AT 137 encountered a fast-moving stream of Guardsmen, a Kolstec regiment, pushing inland behind the armour thrust. There were hundreds of Kolstec, all regular troops moving quickly and urgently, with drilled precision and fixed, unruffled faces. Kexie and Sobile spoke briefly to their white-haired commander, who indicated something on a hand chart.

'Listen up!' Sobile shouted as they returned. 'Listen to your sergeant. He speaks with the voice of the Emperor!'

Criid wasn't sure Driller Kexie did speak with the voice of the Emperor. From the look Kexie gave Sobile, Kexie wasn't sold on the idea either.

'Moving in support,' Kexie drawled, pitching his voice above the factory clatter of the tanks. 'The enemy is thick in this district, so we're going in with the Kolstecs to clear it. By squads, now. Watch closely for my signals, and watch the Kolstec officers too. I don't want no soft-shit fraghead mistakes from you morons.'

The sergeant had adopted Sobile's generic term for them which, while unflattering, was one step up from 'scalps', the lowest of the low, the newest of the new, heads fresh shaved by the Munitorum barber.

The sergeant did a time check, and they moved off. Criid was sure his chron was broken, because there was something wrong with the time check, but there was no pause to adjust it. Halfway down the next cross street, gunfire lit up from a towering grey building that was already extensively ablaze. Flames gushed from the upper storey window slits. Multiple cannon fire ripped across the street and mowed down the front ranks of the Kolstec advance. Everybody scrambled for cover. Fire was returned, but too many Kolstecs were caught out in the open, and were simply scythed down like corn.

Criid got into cover as the full force of the street fight got going. The Guard sections opened up with everything they had, and the hidden enemy seemed to increase its rate of fire to match. Criid took a shot or two, but was forced down by a series of close impacts that chopped deep grooves in the stone wall above him. He could feel the fear rising in him again, the trapped, pinned terror that had found him in the shell hole.

It was at that point it started to rain bodies.

It was so horrific, so unreal, he didn't believe it at first. The living bodies of men in full kit were dropping out of the sky and hitting the street or cracking off the faces of buildings. Each impact was shockingly solid: a writhing, living man struck flagstones and instantly became a splattered mass of gore wrapped in split cloth. There were screams, cut short.

Only when Criid understood what he was witnessing did he believe it. An incoming drop-ship had been hit by enemy fire and the side of its fuselage torn off. As it shrieked down on its swan dive, the troops inside were wrenched out by the slipstream and showered across the streets.

Criid saw the stricken drop-ship for a second before it hit a tower and vaporised. Some of the men falling from it seemed to be jumping.

The bodies rained down, striking like bundles of ripe fruit. Several Kolstecs on the ground were hit and killed by falling bodies. There was an abominable stink of raw meat and excrement. A fog of blood steamed off the street.

It made Criid gag.

He bent low and rubbed at his face, feeling the sharp pain of the whip-cut on his jaw. He began to murmur the *I Beseech* again and took a look at his chron. It wasn't wrong after all. The time check hadn't been wrong at all.

His mind refused to accommodate it, but he'd only been a Guardsman for an hour. It didn't fit. It seemed like days – vile, barbaric days – had passed, but just an hour before, he'd been clean and tidy, riding the platform hoist up through the two metre-thick carrier deck with the rest of AT 137, while the military bands played and the dropships lit their engines.

One hour. One hour of insanity and blood. One hour more savagely extreme than all the other hours of his life added together.

And he hadn't even seen the enemy yet.

ENEMY COUNTRY

I

EVEN AT A distance, they could hear the fetch-hounds baying in the pens inside the town. The dogs could smell them coming. They shivered the pale daylight with their yowling.

'Dogs,' remarked Ludd, crunching across the dry moorland grasses.

'Big dogs,' Varl corrected with an unhappy look. 'Fething big dogs.'

Ludd looked over at Gaunt. 'Have they got our scent, sir?'

'Oh, I'm sure they have,' Gaunt said, 'but it's more than that.' He nodded in the direction of the horizon. Far away, across the rolling moors, there was a tremble of light in the west, a fluttering wash of radiance brighter and whiter than the wan daylight and the overcast sky. It was as if a giant mirror was being waggled just behind the horizon to catch and dance the sun.

It was coming from the coast, four hundred kilometres away. It was coming from a place that Navy Intel had named K'ethdrac'att Shet Magir, one of the eighteen primary objectives earmarked on Gereon.

'That's one feth of a song and dance,' Varl murmured, looking at the light show.

Cantible was not one of the eighteen primary objectives. It wasn't even one of the six hundred and thirty secondary objectives, or one of the five thousand and seventeen second phase objectives. On High Command's complex logistical diagrams, it appeared amongst a list labelled *Tertiary/recon*. Light scout, reconnaissance and intruder regiments were being dropped forward of the main assaults to secure bridgeheads and clear lines of advancement. Cantible, the municipal and administrative hub for an agri-belt province called Lowensa, defended one of the main west-east running corridors between K'ethdrac and the Lectica heartlands.

But even that wasn't the main reason they had been sent there.

Gaunt took a look left and right. The entire strength of the Tanith First was advancing in a wide spread across the rolling grassland from their dropsite higher in the moors. Supporting light armour was chugging to meet them along a pasture route to the south.

There were woods ahead, then broad stretches of farmland, and then the town itself. Gaunt could see the chubby finger of the guildhall tower above the trees.

He'd always vowed to return. He'd always vowed to come back and deliver what the resistance and the people of Gereon had deserved from day one, from the very first Day of Pain. He had no idea what Day of Pain it was now, though he estimated somewhere in the low two thousands. Far too long. Far too late, perhaps.

Gaunt hadn't visited this part of the country on his previous stay, so he couldn't compare directly, but it seemed like everything had fallen into dismal ruin. Everything was spoiled somehow, stained, contaminated. The sky, the ground, the vegetation, the weather. The noxious imprint of the invaders permeated everything.

It was early spring in this part of Gereon, but the sky was hot and frowzy. The moorland grasses were yellow and parched. There was a dull, persistent crackle in the air as if the sun was sizzling. Radiation was spiking. vox-links were wandering and full of squeals and phantom voices.

The woods ahead looked like they consisted of eshel and talix, but they had grown wrong and sickly, sprouting deformed limbs out of true. Leaf cover looked autumnal, in its shades of red and yellow. The seasons of the world had been unravelled.

The farmland was also corrupted. Vile black crops, the product of intensive xenoculture, covered the far side of the valley. Gaunt could smell the maturing fruit. Other patches, overworked and rendered barren by chemicals, lay scorched and brown in the sun. Rusty pink crusts of nitrate scummed the edges of the blighted acreage. The fallow fields and dead land had a stink to them too.

'Untillable,' Cirk murmured as she gazed at the fields. Her heavy flak coat was pulled in around her. 'They bleed us dry and make it all Untill.'

Gaunt nodded, although he was still not comfortable having her around. He'd told Faragut to keep 'specialist' Cirk with the rear echelons, but both she and Faragut had wandered out to the front of the line the moment the drop-ships emptied.

'We'll have to burn it all,' Gaunt told Rawne.

'The farm land?'

'The crops. All of it.'

'Brostin will be pleased. Presumably you want this to happen once we've taken the town? The fields catching fire will be a bit of a giveaway that we're here.'

Gaunt gestured into the breeze, as if he could catch hold of the travelling sound. 'Listen to the dogs, Eli. They know we're here.'

* * *

II

So THIS, CAFFRAN thought, is the famous Gereon at last. The site of the one big Ghost operation most of the Ghosts hadn't taken part in. The ones who had gone, and come back alive, had spoken of it afterwards in secretive, reverential tones, as if it was a dark mystery they wished to forget.

It wasn't all that. Just another place that the Archenemy had fethed up. Of course, it must have been hard digging in here, hiding with the resistance on an occupied world for all that time. Caffran didn't doubt that. Maybe that was why Rawne, Varl and the rest spoke about it as if it was some exclusive trial or initiation that they had gone through and no one else had managed. The members of the Sturm mission still kept themselves a little aloof.

No, Caffran didn't doubt it had been a tough tour, but other things in the cosmos were tough too. Missing Tona for all that time, for example, and friends like Bonin, Varl and Larks. Thinking they were dead and never coming back. Thinking Gaunt was dead. Command had taken the Ghosts apart because of that, and only put them back together again when he returned like a...

'Ghost,' Caffran said aloud, softly. The woodland around him was quiet. Dry leaves rustled in a slight breeze and cold, watery sunlight filtered through the canopy. He held his lasrifle across his chest and stopped walking.

In the distance, he could hear and smell the burning fields. As the wind changed every few minutes, soot and ash blew back through the trees. It was pungent. Something bad was burning.

The advancing troops were almost silent. There was no way to guess the scale of the infantry force closing on Cantible.

This place had a lot to answer for. Things had not been the same since Gaunt and the others had come here the first time, and they hadn't been the same since they had come back. It wasn't just the forced influx of the Belladon leftovers. They were good men and the fit was fine, as good as the fit between the Tanith and the Verghastites had been after the hive war. In fact, Caffran missed Colonel Wilder, and regretted his loss on Ancreon Sextus.

The differences that really mattered weren't the big things. It was the small stuff. It was months spent getting over Gaunt's death only to find out that he was back. It was like reverse grief. Caffran almost resented it, and he wasn't the only one.

Tona and he hadn't been as close since Gereon. Things had got a little better of late, but it still wasn't the same. She was withdrawn from him, altered. He had wondered at first if it was some kind of Chaos taint, but it wasn't that. She had just changed. She'd seen stuff that he hadn't. He wasn't someone she could talk to any more, not about the things that mattered to her anyway.

Well, that would change, starting from right now. He was going to taste the infamous Gereon for himself. He was going to know it like she knew it, and that would help him lift its shadow off the two of them. They'd exorcise Gereon together, and get back to where they had been.

Caffran knew others had experienced the same thing. Varl and Kolea had been close for ever, and Varl was the biggest mouth in the company, but since Varl had come back, even Kolea hadn't managed to get him to open up about Gereon.

Ghosts moved up past him. Caffran realised he was slowing the line. He started forward through the dappled sunlight.

'All right there, trooper?' Hark asked, moving by.

'Yes, sir,' Caffran said, getting back in the game.

Hark looked at him with an almost sympathetic expression. 'I know what you're thinking about,' he said.

Caffran blinked. He did? About Tona and Gereon and resenting Gaunt and–

'He will be all right,' Hark nodded, and headed on.

Caffran cursed himself, guiltily and silently. Hark had been wrong, because Caffran, so lost in thought, had not had his mind in the right place at all. Not at *all*.

Dalin. *Feth*!

FIFTY METRES AWAY through the woodland, Eszrah ap Niht paused, slowly removed his sunshades and blinked at the light. He touched the fingers of his left hand against the bark of a tree.

Gaunt had told him this was Gereon, that they were going back to Gereon, but this wasn't Gereon. It was a dead place. He could smell the death-stink in it, as surely as a man could smell the death-stink from another man raddled with disease.

If this was Gereon...

Eszrah put his sunshades back on, and loaded his reynbow.

III

'RERVAL?' GAUNT ASKED quietly.

Kolea's adjutant listened to his vox-caster for a moment longer, then slipped the earphones down.

'Whipcord reports they'll be in position in another ten minutes, sir,' he said.

'And when they say position, we can confirm we're both talking about the same place?'

'I'm cross-checking their coordinates now,' Rerval said.

'All right then,' Gaunt nodded. 'Bel?'

Nearby, his vox-caster leaning against a gnarled tree bole, Gaunt's own adjutant Beltayn was delicately adjusting the set's dial. Retrofitted with a bulky additional power cell and an S-shaped low frequency transmitter, his vox was decidedly non-standard.

'Beltayn?'

Beltayn shook his head. 'Nothing, sir.'

'Still nothing?'

'I've tried Daystar and Mothlamp. Nothing.'

'Keep trying, please. Stay here and keep trying.'

Beltayn nodded.

Gaunt waved up Captain Meryn of E Company. 'He's your responsibility, Meryn,' Gaunt said. 'Stick a guard around him. Six men at all times.'

'Sir,' said Meryn.

Gaunt turned and walked a few paces to the edge of the clearing. Baskevyl handed him his scope.

'There could be all sorts of reasons why they're not transmitting,' Baskevyl said.

'I know,' Gaunt said, panning the scope round for a good view of the town.

'And not just bad ones,' Baskevyl went on. 'Power failure. Vox breakdown. Atmospherics...'

'I know. We'll pick them up soon enough. Are we set?'

Baskevyl nodded. 'I've had taps from Rawne, Kolea, Daur and Kolosim. Varaine, Kamori, Domor and Obel are on the facing slopes. Arcuda's mob's covering the ford.'

'Mkoll?'

'Since when was Mkoll not in position?'

'A good point.'

The sky south of them was a haze of smoke from the blazing fields. The town, a wide cluster of grey-green blocks and towers behind a wall at the hill crest, was quiet. The dogs had fallen silent.

Ludd and Hark came up through the woodland behind Gaunt and Baskevyl, and stood with them.

'Set?' Hark asked mildly.

'Whipcord's position confirmed,' Rerval called.

Gaunt pursed his lips. *Whipcord* was the operational call-sign for the Dev Hetra light armour supporting them.

'Tell them to load and stand by. They don't fire without a direct order from me.'

'Understood, sir.'

'Make sure they do.'

'Whipcord,' Hark mused. 'You know, Ludd, in some theatres, it is still common for commissars to carry lashes.'

'For purposes of encouragement, sir?' Ludd asked.

'Naturally. What other purpose would there be?'

Ludd shrugged. 'Spiritual mortification?' he suggested.

Hark sniffed. 'You've far too much time for thinking, Ludd.'

Gaunt looked at them both. 'If it's all right by you, can I commence the attack?'

'Of course. Sorry,' Hark said. 'I was just telling the boy. A commissar with a whip–'

'Had better not show up when I'm around,' Gaunt said. 'This isn't the Dark Ages.'

'Oh,' smiled Hark blithely, 'I rather think it is.'

Gaunt thumbed his micro-bead.

'Mkoll?

'At your service.'

'Go.'

'Gone.'

Gaunt turned and drew his power sword. Activating it was all the signal Baskevyl required. He pointed to Rerval, who immediately sent the code for advance.

Across the tangled field and brush in front of the woods, the first rows of Ghosts got up, weapons aimed, hunched low, and began to scurry towards the town.

IV

THE MOST GHOSTLY of the Ghosts melted through the sunlight towards the foot of the town wall. They made no sound, and their signing was so under-stated that even their hands were whispering.

Without haste or rush, Mkoll, master of scouts, stepped from one shadow to another, pouring himself out of one dark space and into the next. He had a good view of the wall. Guard post, two guards in sight. He raised his hand, twitched his fingers and spread the information.

Bonin moved forwards five metres to his left. Their skills were identical, but their methods of silence were totally different. It was an odd detail that only real recon experts would pick up, but each Tanith scout had his own 'flavour' of silent movement. Mkoll flowed like liquid, running through the levels of dark-ness. Bonin had a dry drift to him, like a shadow moving with the sun.

Caober, for his part, seemed always in the periphery of vision, always there until a second before you looked. Caober, who'd been a scout since the Found-ing, had held the regimental specialty together while Mkoll, Bonin and MkVenner had been away on the Gereon expedition. He'd done a good job, and brought on several newcomers. Mkoll owed him a good deal.

Jajjo was one of those newcomers, elevated to scout operations after Aexe Cardinal, the first Verghastite in the specialty. His hard-learned skills were more industrial and mechanical than those of the Tanith-born. He would never have their instinctive grace, but Jajjo was all concentration. It was as if he stayed silent and unseen by force of will.

What appeared to be market gardens or allotments covered the slopes outside the town wall. The patches had gown wild with weeds and grox-eye daisies. Vermin scurried under the dry nets of foliage. Jajjo ducked under a broken gate, and crossed between a row of wooden lean-tos and an over-grown cultivator. He was low, twenty metres down and right of Mkoll. He spotted, and marked, five more guards on the run of town wall above him. He signed it to Mkoll.

Right of Jajjo's position, there were patches of scrub and a bone-dry paddock littered with the mummified carcasses of livestock. Hwlan, who moved like smoke, took up a spot by the gate and held cover as Maggs and Leyr crossed up the paddock to a woody clump of wintergorse. Leyr was Tanith, and moved as secretly as slow thawing ice.

Wes Maggs was Belladon, one of the Eighty-First's primary recon special-ists. Immensely good at what he did, he'd had to learn the rules from scratch to keep up with the Tanith experts. He was still a little in awe of Mkoll, and that respect tended to blind him to his own abilities.

Maggs was short and broad-shouldered, and had a scar that dropped vertically from the corner of his left eye. Off duty, his mouth could give Varl's a decent race. He had his own style too. It was 'try damn hard not to get seen and killed'.

He came up into the gorse on his belly, rolled into a dry dirt cavity around the dead root, and peered out. *Clear*, he signed to Leyr, who relayed that down the line.

Maggs worked his shoulders round for a different look. The town wall was made of stone, dressed in some kind of planking, a grey-green material. There was a door ten metres away from him. Not the main gate or even a minor one, some sort of sluice or storm hatch. Maybe a waste outlet.

Too much to sign. He sent 'minor entry' and its position.

Mkoll nodded this.

Maggs made the dash as soon as the nod came back to him. A second out in the sunlight, and then down in the cool shadow at the foot of the wall, pressed in close to the cold, smelly boards. He edged along. The town was awfully quiet. The place had to be on alert because of what had hit from space that morning.

The hounds had whined, the fields had burned, but the place was quiet.

He arrived at the door. It was a wooden hatch, half-height for a man, badly built into the wall covering. It was bolted shut and the bolt secured with an ancient padlock, but the wood was damp and fibrous. Maggs began to work it with his warknife, levering the bolt away from the soft board.

Back from him, in the gorse, Leyr saw the guard coming. A single enemy trooper in dirty green combat armour strolled through the overgrown ditches around the wall, running a sight-check of culverts and drains.

Leyr tapped his earpiece and Maggs looked up and saw the guard approaching. Recommended practice at that moment would have been for Maggs to curl up and hide where he was and let Leyr nail the guard from behind.

Maggs had other ideas. He rapped the blade of his warknife against the rusty door bolt, clinking it like a little metalwork hammer.

What the feth, Maggs? Leyr blinked, toggling off to make the shot he was certain would be called for.

The guard heard the clinking, and headed right over to the source. As he came down the ditch to the door, Maggs just got to his feet to meet him in one smooth motion and buried the blade through his neck. Maggs caught him in an embrace and pulled his body back down into cover with him. A blink of an eye and they were both out of sight again.

Maggs forced back the bolt and gently flopped the door open. He kept having to prop the guard's limp body up out of the way now they were sharing the same ditch. He peered inside.

It was the soak away of a stream or sewer outflow built to run out under the wall and into the ditch. The door was simply a lid over a much smaller cavity, a sump under the wall base blocked, along its course, by three heavy wrought iron grates. Even without the bars, the soak away was far too small to allow a man to crawl through.

The ground, however, was parched and dry. The soak away had shrivelled and enlarged in the months without rain, and become a dusty, desiccated hole, pulling away from the underpinning of the stone wall like a diseased gum from a tooth. Maggs could easily reach in and wiggled the nearest iron grate free.

He signed to Leyr. *Tell Mkoll. We're in.*

V

TEN MORE MINUTES ticked by. At Baskevyl's instruction, the first wave of Ghosts advanced again, closer to the wall slope, keeping low and using the brittle, dead undergrowth for cover.

One of the wall guards finally noticed them, or at least noticed movement in the lower scarps and terraces below the wall. There was a shout, and then an ancient stubber began spitting slow, desultory shots down the slopes. The shells tore into the brambles and dried leaves, showering up papery fragments. The shots made high pitched buzzing hums as they flicked through the ground cover. In a moment, a second gun had opened up, then a third. Las-locks cracked from the wall platforms. Then the spring-coil *tunk! tunk!* of mortars started up, lobbing shells over from the yards behind the wall. The mortar bombs dropped short into the allotment patches and kicked up hot, gritty spumes of smoke and soil, each one with a rasping fiery heart, each one turning to thready smoke that wafted away down the hill.

The mortar rate increased.

'Permission to engage?' Baskevyl asked Gaunt.

'Granted,' Gaunt said.

The Ghosts fanning out on the slopes below the town began to fire. Las-shots rained off the wall tops. The range was bad, but the effort was more to suppress the enemy shooters. The light support teams, bedded in ahead of the woodline, opened up. Seena and Arilla, Surch and Loell, Belker and Finz, Melyr and Caill, gunners and feeders. Their large calibre cannons began their *tukka-tukka-tukka* rattling, like giant sewing machines. the heavy fire festooned the main gate with thousands of little curls of smoke.

'Start making it personal,' Gaunt voxed, moving forwards.

The regiment's marksmen had been waiting for that nod. All were bedded down and all had selected targets. Jessi Banda was watching the heads of the enemy sentries on the wall top through her sniper scope.

'Like tin cans on a stump,' she murmured as she lined one up.

The head popped in a puff of red. Banda blinked to make sure she'd seen it right.

Close by, Nessa Bourah looked up from her long las. 'Like tin cans on a stump,' she grinned, speaking the words with the slightly nasal flatness of the profoundly deaf.

The snipers set up a steady rate of fire, notching every figure fool enough to appear on the walls. Larkin's rate was the highest of all. Five kills in three minutes. He left one target draped forwards over the parapet.

Something considerable exploded behind the wall and the mortars shut up. The scouts were plying their trade inside.

BEHIND THE WALLS, the old market town was a sick, dishevelled place. Filth littered the streets, and the buildings were all in miserable repair, though many, like the town walls, had been refitted or converted using a patchwork of unpleasant materials that weren't immediately identifiable. There was a grey-green sheeting that was halfway between flakboard and tin, and odd, resin-like substances. Walls had been reinforced with struts and beams of iron that had begun to rust, and many roofs had fallen in. Civic statues had been smashed and, in places, stretches of wall were pock-marked from old gunfire. The occupiers had decorated the place with lurid scrawlings in their own, hideous script, sickening graffiti that unsettled the mind.

There was an odour in the air, cloying close and sickly, and human remains – most of it bone – scattered everywhere. It was as if, rather than taking the town over and occupying it, the Archenemy had nested in it.

Working in silently from the entry point Maggs had provided, the scouts set to work. Jajjo and Caober threaded the shadows in a series of side streets until they emerged at the edge of a wide cobbled yard under the walls, where eight mortars had been set up on flakboard pallets. Tall servants of Chaos were crewing the weapons. They were rancid creatures in grey scale armour, the high brass collars of mechanical speech boxes covering their mouths and noses. Most had implants sutured into their eye sockets. Some were using goads and lashes on a team of half-naked, emaciated human wretches – skin and bone and rags – forcing them to ferry shells from a supply stack to feed the weapons. The wretches were prisoners, captives, grotesquely malnourished and abused, the stigma rune branded on their faces.

Caober signed to Jajjo to draw attention with a little gunfire and get the slaves clear while he moved in with tube-charges to blow the weapons.

Jajjo nodded, and moved forward, skirting some iron scaffolding, into the open yard. Without any hesitation he opened fired, squirting bursts of las fire into the mortar crews. Two of the armoured creatures dropped. The others turned, scattering, reaching for las-locks. Jajjo fired some more and blew another off his feet. The slaves, halfway through their plod between ammo dump and weapons, stopped in their tracks and just stared at the Ghost.

'Come on! Come on!' Jajjo called, firing his lasrifle one-handed from the hip as he gestured wildly with his other hand. 'This way!'

None of them moved. They simply stared, dull-eyed, blank. Some still clutched mortar bombs in their arms like babies.

Caober readied his tube-charges and hurried around to the side. He was concerned that the human captives weren't moving. They were still well inside the blast radius that he was about to lay down.

'Come on!' Jajjo yelled again.

More blank looks.

Cursing, Jajjo moved towards them, firing between a pair of them at one of the crew who had got hold of a las-lock. Grey scales flew up from the being's broken armour as Jajjo's laser bolts sliced through him and knocked him onto his back.

'Come on. Move!'

Two more of the enemy crew had seized weapons and returned fire. One las-lock shot skimmed over Jajjo's head. The other, hasty, struck one of the motionless slaves in the back. The man, elderly it seemed, though the abuse he had suffered may have aged him mercilessly, toppled forwards dead. The mortar bomb he had been clutching rolled free and ran, clinking, across the cobbles.

The slaves remained stationary. They didn't run forwards to his aid, they didn't scatter for cover in fear. They turned their heads slowly and looked blankly at the body for a moment.

Jajjo ran right up amongst them, still snatching off shots at the enemy.

'Come on!' he shouted, pulling at reluctant arms and limp shoulders. 'Move, for gak's sake! Move yourselves!'

This close, he could smell them. The stench made him gag. The filth caking them was unbelievable. He could see the lice and the ticks. Their skin felt like cotton, thin and loose on frames where all body fat had gone.

'Move!'

Another las-lock blast blew out the skull of the woman he was pulling at. Her body had been masking his. As she fell, wordlessly, Jajjo brought his lasrifle up to his shoulder and furiously belted full auto across the mortar stand, raking all the enemy creatures he could see. Two fell back, spread-eagled. One spiralled sideways, knocking an entire mortar off its tripod with a dull clang.

Jajjo backed away, squeezing off more shots. There was no more time. No more time for compassion.

'Do it!' he yelled, desperately.

Caober plucked off the strip of det tape and bowled the bundle of charges over arm into the midst of the weapons. He and Jajjo dived for cover.

When they got up, in the billowing smoke, the mortars were trashed. The slaves were all on the ground, flattened by the blast.

'I w-' Jajjo began. Caober grabbed him and pulled him back. There was no point checking if any were alive. The effort would be as futile as trying to save them in the first place. They had to keep moving.

There was still work to be done.

MKOLL HEARD AND felt the blast that gagged the mortar fire. He was two streets from the yard, with Hwlan, heading for the gate. He'd expected to encounter more resistance inside the town. The place was half-empty. They saw a few of the enemy guardsmen, the scale-armoured spectres that Mkoll had learned to call excubitors on his last visit to the occupied world, and kept out of their way. The excubitors were hurrying towards the walls, summoned to face the external attack that had broken out five minutes earlier.

There were enemy troopers too, men dressed in polished green combat armour. They were double-timing in squads, under the command of excubitors or sirdar officers. Some rode on battered trucks or wheezing steam engines. Cantible was mobilising its defences, but where were the people? Most of the dwellings and commercial properties the scouts darted past were empty and abandoned.

It occurred to Mkoll that there were no people because, like any resource, they had been used up. He'd seen the process half-done before he left the first time. The occupation had progressively exploited and consumed Gereon's raw materials: manufacturing, minerals, crops, water, flesh. Vast swathes of the country had been turned over to xenoculture producing gene-altered or warp-tainted crops that depleted the land by strip-mining the soil of its nutrients. The crops fed the occupying forces, but were harvested in such gross abundance that they could be transported off-world to supply the ravenous armies of the Archon. For a few years, until the process killed its fertility, Gereon would be one of the Archenemy's breadbasket worlds in this region. Fuel and metal reserves went the same way. With his own amazed eyes, Mkoll had witnessed two jehgenesh, warp beasts deliberately unleashed into Gereon's water supply by the occupiers. These... *things* drank lakes, seas and reservoirs, and excreted the water via the warp to distant, arid worlds in the Archenemy's domain. He had helped to kill both of them.

Flesh was just another commodity. Those of Gereon's human population who had not become proselytes and converted to the new faith had been made slaves, robbed of all rights and dignities. More literally, others had been fed to the meat foundries, where the flesh of their bodies had been cut apart to supply the enemy with a source of spare parts and transplants. The dead, the useless and the unviable were fed into the ahenum furnaces which powered much of Gereon's abominable new industries and lit the sky red at dusk. Ultimately, the furnaces awaited everyone.

In the long months and days of pain since he had last been there, Mkoll realised, the human supply, like all finite resources, had begun to dwindle. Gereon was close to exhaustion. As Gaunt had feared, and privately confided to Mkoll, they were bringing liberation far too late.

Mkoll and Hwlan scurried through the dry, dead husks of homes and workplaces. Every room contained a warm, stale atmosphere and a yellowed cast of neglect. Everything had shrivelled and flaked. Window glass, where it still existed, was stained the colour of amasec. Dust mould and a virulent fungus, violet and blotchy, were endemic across walls and ceilings. Heaps of dead blowflies, like handfuls of coal dust, lined every windowsill.

They came up through a tomb-like building that must once have been a butcher's shop. In the workshop, the gouged wooden counters were stained dark brown, and traces of dried meat clung to the iron hooks that swayed slowly on their long black chains.

Hwlan reached the back door and checked outside.

Main gate, he signed, *sixty metres*.

Mkoll nodded. He pulled the canvas satchel he had been carrying off his shoulder and put it on one of the chopping blocks. One by one he took out the tube-charges, checked each one, and laid them out side by side. Twenty, and one, Rawne had put it, 'for luck'. Major Rawne, who knew about these things thanks to what he described as a 'misspent youth', had built the detonator himself. It had a simple switch, triggered by mercury in a gravity bottle, a glass phial the size of Mkoll's little finger. Dislodged by impact or a change in attitude, the mercury would flow down the phial and make the connection.

Mkoll bound the tubes into a bundle and taped the switch to them, twisting together the wires that ran from the switch to the tubes' detonation caps. Only a little slip of labelled parchment, wedged between the trigger phial and the feeder reservoir full of quicksilver, kept the weapon safe.

The shooting war outside had picked up pace. To Mkoll's experienced ear, they had about ten minutes left before the wild card of a stealth intrusion ceased to have any value. Ten minutes to achieve their goal and prove the tactical worth of the scouts.

'Vehicle,' he said.

Hwlan, down at the back door, looked at him in surprise. It was the first time either of them had spoken aloud in twenty-five minutes.

'We need a vehicle,' Mkoll expanded. He'd been expecting to commandeer a truck, a traction engine or something similar. Now they were there, inside, he saw how limited resources were.

Hwlan moved to the butcher's side door. There was a yard out the back, adjoining several sheds that he presumed had been used for smoking or salting meat. What appeared to be a handcart was visible in one of them.

'Let me check, chief,' he said, and went outside.

Mkoll waited. He heard marching footsteps on the road and ducked down behind the butcher's table. The shadow of a squad of excubitors travelled over the dirt-clouded windows.

The hand cart was useless. It was missing its back wheels. Hefting his lasrifle up under the crook of his right arm like a gamekeeper, Hwlan walked down the sheds and discovered that they backed onto the annexe of a neighbouring property. He crossed the narrow, shadowed yard and stood on tiptoe to look in through the window lights.

Hwlan sighed.

It was a nursery. The place had been ransacked some time before and left to rot in disarray, but he could see small wooden blocks, painted bright colours, scattered over the floor, the tattered remains of dolls, and some rather less identifiable piles of rubbish.

And, on its side, a baby carriage.

He tried the door. The lock had been kicked off a long time before. Inside, there was a terrible, musty smell of enclosed air, of dry rot, of decay. For the first time he realised, with a strange start, that there were no cobwebs at all. Arachnids, like rats and lice, had accompanied mankind out into the stars and had permeated all his living spaces. What had happened to all the spiders here? Was there something about Chaos that drove them out or – and Hwlan had always had a thing about spiders – was the absence of webs a sign that spiders enjoyed some sort of collusion with the Ruinous Powers? He wouldn't put that past them, filthy little wrigglers.

Contemplating the essential evil of all eight-legged things, Hwlan crossed the room to the overturned carriage. Effortlessly and skilfully, his feet avoided every loose object in his path. He stooped to move aside a pile of rags to get to the baby carriage.

The pile of rags was alive.

IN THE BUTCHER'S, Mkoll froze when he heard the shrill wail echo from the neighbouring building. With smooth, expert calmness, he picked up his satchel and the tied package of tube-charges, and slid them out of sight under the counter. Then he ducked down behind a large galvanised vat.

The back door opened. Two excubitors, alerted by the cry, stepped inside from the roadway and peered around. Down in cover, Mkoll could smell the sweet perfume of the oils and unguents they used to dress their flesh. It was a smell he hadn't known in a while, but he hadn't forgotten it. He closed his grip around his lasrifle.

'Eshet tyed g'har veth?' one of the excubitors said to the other. *What was that sound/noise in here/in this place?* The sounds crackled from the speaker boxes in their brass collars.

'Voi ydereta haspa cloi c'shull myok,' the other replied. *You go join the others/attend to duties while I look/check/search.*

Like Gaunt, and the rest of the Sturm mission team, Mkoll had learned the basic elements of the enemy language as a survival skill.

'Desyek? Seyn voi shet?' *Are you certain/sure/confident?*

'Syekde. Jj'jan fer gath tretek irigaa.' *Go/I'm sure. This is nothing, but I should check nevertheless.*

One of the excubitors turned and went. The other moved into the room, his las-lock aimed from his chest.

Mkoll stood up, leaving his lasrifle out of sight. The excubitor started, turning to aim at him.

'Eletreeta j'den kyh tarejaa fa!' Mkoll said. *Thank goodness you're here! Look here/look at this thing I have!*

'Jabash je kyh tarej?' said the excubitor, taking a step closer. *What thing must I look at/must I inspect for you?*

'Straight silver,' Mkoll said, and plunged his Tanith warknife into the excubitor's forehead. The excubitor dropped his las-lock and reached both hands up to his impaled skull. Mkoll hugged the excubitor down onto a chopping block table top, his left hand cupped behind the thing's scalp, pulling the head deeper onto the knife. Foul, septic blood poured out around the wound over Mkoll's knife hand. The excubitor spasmed and went limp.

Gently, Mkoll lowered the body to the floor rather than let it fall. He jerked the knife out.

The other excubitor reappeared in the doorway.

VI

THE EXCUBITOR FROZE. It saw the fresh blood spilt across the worktop, and the body of its comrade curled on the floor. It began to speak and, at the same time, began to lift its primed las-lock.

Mkoll flicked his wrist and threw the blood-wet dagger. It planted itself, blade-first, in the excubitor's left eye, so deep that the hilt bars were stopped by the rim of the socket. The excubitor swayed for a moment, its head rocked back by the impact. Then it fell on its face.

Mkoll started forwards, dragged the corpse fully indoors, and quietly closed the back door.

THE PILE OF rags was something vaguely human. An old man, an old woman, Hwlan wasn't sure. Something half dead and bone-thin. As he moved it, and it came to life and wailed, he struck out involuntarily, and knocked it aside. It fell, turned and ran away back into the house.

Hwlan followed it knowing, if nothing else, that he had to silence it, but it had vanished, and it wasn't making any more noise. He picked his way back through the shuttered, abandoned rooms to the nursery and the baby carriage.

He was just righting it and checking it over when Mkoll appeared behind him. The master scout's right sleeve was soaked with blood.

'What the feth are you playing at?' Mkoll whispered.

'Vehicle,' Hwlan replied.

HALF A TOWN away, Bonin and Maggs were heading deeper into Cantible, hugging the shadows and not staying anywhere for long. They both turned as they heard the rolling boom of Caober's tube-charges.

'Temple?' Maggs whispered, pointing.

Bonin shook his head. *Iconoclave,* he signed carefully.

'What's that then?' Maggs whispered with a smile.

Do you not know how to sign? Bonin signed angrily.

Yes, Maggs signed back, and to prove it elaborately signed, *You are a total feth-wit.*

Bonin tried not to smile. Maggs was all right, for a non-Tanith. Feth, he was all right for a non-Verghastite.

They ducked into cover as a troop of soldiers rushed past, followed by a long, gawky procession of excubitors, heading towards the gate.

The building Maggs had mistaken for the temple was a long, new structure raised of heavy dressed stone. An iconoclave was where the forces of the enemy pressed citizens into the wholesale destruction of any icon, statue or motif that honoured the Imperium. The town temple was two streets away, a grand but wrecked edifice.

They hurried to it. There was meant to be a sign here, a contact. Navy Intel had said there would be. Maggs and Bonin could find nothing except miserably defaced temple dressings and the sacrilegious handiwork of the enemy. The great mosaic of an aquila in the temple floor tiles had been damaged with hammers.

Maybe there's another temple, Maggs signed. Before Bonin could reply, a lasshot passed between them, narrowly missing both of them. Several more followed, but Maggs and Bonin were already rolling for cover.

Occupation troops in green armour were surging in through the main doors of the derelict temple, firing their weapons. Bonin wondered if this was just an unlucky mischance, or if the enemy had kept the temple under surveillance.

Laser bolts splintered into the old wooden seating and high-backed chairs. Maggs and Bonin, both on the cold floor, raised their rifles and began to fire back. Bonin's first burst dropped the leading trooper, and his second burst killed the two men behind him. The enemy was fanning out around the sides of the fane, taking cover behind pillars and the stone tombs of ancient grandees. Though temporarily protected by the fragile shield of the congregation seating, Maggs and Bonin would shortly find themselves outflanked on both sides. There was no cover for them to drop back to.

'Not good!' Maggs yelled.

'You can say that again,' Bonin replied. He fired another burst that caught an occupation trooper in the neck and the side of the head. The man's frame twisted around violently. A spigot of blood emptied out of his throat as he crashed over into a bench.

Maggs tried to move, but gunfire from the side of the fane chewed at the tiled floor and drove him back. Thick smoke from the weaponsfire began to clog the air and catch the bars of weak sunlight stabbing in from the clerestory windows.

Bonin fired selectively, but there were too many targets to hit, too many targets to drive back.

The situation had just become very lousy indeed.

A FULL-SCALE battle raged beyond the town walls and the main gatehouse. In answer to the Imperial onslaught, the forces occupying Cantible had filled the wall tops with troops and opened up with the heavy weapon nests built into the high towers and gatehouse. Though it had taken the Archenemy a while to properly rouse itself, as if from a cold-blooded torpor, the resistance was now considerable.

Inside the main gate, reinforcement squads of occupation troops clambered out of trucks and hurried up the gatehouse stairs to take position. More troops from the town's garrison were arriving in vehicles that came speeding down the hill from the town hall.

Thirty metres from the gate, Mkoll peered out from an alleyway and looked down the cobbled slope to the gatehouse. He waited while two decrepit army trucks went by, let go of the wooden handle and stepped back into cover beside Hwlan. There was a little scrap of parchment in his hand.

Occupation troops were scrambling down from revving trucks by the gates when the baby carriage appeared. It was rolling free, jiggling over the cobbles, picking up speed as it came down the long slope of the road. A couple of troopers looked at it in frank puzzlement, others called to friends and comrades. The baby carriage rolled right past a few mystified troopers, past a truck, heading for the gates themselves.

One officer, a sirdar, cried out, recognising the sinister subtext to the curious apparition that his men had missed. He shouted for someone to stop the carriage, to grab it, to prevent it from reaching or hitting the gates.

No one moved to obey. Puzzlement was slowing them. So the sirdar leapt from the flatbed of the truck where he was standing and lunged at the carriage as it rolled by.

He stopped it three metres from the gates. He stopped it with a violent jerk. The jerk snapped quicksilver along a glass phial.

There was a click.

VII

THE BLAST HURT, even from a distance. The tarnished moorland air outside the town seemed to snap, as if the day had fractured suddenly. All of the advancing Ghosts felt it deep in the warm cavities of their bodies and the tight knots of their joints.

The main gates of Cantible rose up off their giant iron hinges on a luminous cloud of fire, and spread like great wings as they disintegrated. Only small burning slivers were left to flutter back to the ground. The gate blockhouse vanished in a swift, roiling, rising mass of fire-threaded smoke, and collapsed, spilling outwards in a noisy torrent of loose stone and tiles.

As a downpour of ash, cinders and burning flecks rained across the hill slopes and approaches, a considerable cheer issued from the Imperial forces. The charge began at once.

Heads down, Ghosts began to flock up the main trackway to the burning ruin of the gate, heading in under the billowing swathe of black smoke that climbed above the town and made a broad stain across the pale sky.

They met no resistance at first. All the enemy personnel in the vicinity of the gate had perished in the blast, or had been injured so fearfully that they died in minutes. Others, especially wall defenders further down the curtain from the gate, were knocked down by the shockwave, or hit by debris, or simply stunned into temporary immobility by their sudden misfortune. The Ghosts poured in through the ragged breach unopposed.

Captain Ban Daur's G Company was the first inside, closely followed by Ferdy Kolosim's F Company. Daur's approach was methodical and efficient. He brooked no dallying in the initial advance, but urgently pushed his platoons into the main street network to secure strongpoints before the reeling enemy could recover. Ban Daur was a tall, clean-cut and youthful man of good breeding and polite manners. Meeting him, it was easy to forget he was a veteran of the Vervunhive War and had first-hand expertise in siege warfare and city fighting. Gaunt often thought Daur was the most underestimated of his unit commanders. Daur didn't trail a robust air of soldiering about him like Kolea, Obel or Varaine, nor did he have the air of a killer like Rawne or Mkoll. It was too easy to mistake him for an affable, well-mannered chap who could run a neat camp but who left war to the grown-ups.

G Company invaded Cantible with well-drilled grace. Daur's principal squad leaders – Mohr, Vivvo, Haller, Vadim, Mkeller and Venar – pushed their troops forwards in overlapping fan formations, securing street corners and likely buildings. Sporadic fighting broke out as the advancing Tanith met pockets of bewildered excubitors.

Within five minutes, Daur's beachhead had opened the way for Kolosim's company to push forwards, followed by Rawne's and Kolea's. The last two were the heavyweight, thoroughbred companies of this new model First, rivalled as warriors only by Mkoll's scout pack and the fighting companies of Obel and Domor. They began to claw into the town where Daur had stabbed.

In their cover position thirty metres from the gate, Mkoll and Hwlan slowly picked themselves up. The shockwave had smashed across the entire area and blown out every window and door. His ears ringing, Mkoll quietly cursed Rawne's 'one for luck'. The two scouts started to move in time to link up with Daur's advance.

'Nice work,' Daur commented as he met Mkoll.

'Let's make the most of it,' Mkoll replied.

Within ten minutes of the blast, the picture had changed a little. Waking up from the explosion that had slapped it into a daze, Cantible began to fight back. The unseen commander of its garrison realised little mattered except that the enemy was now inside the walls, and had directed all of his forces through the town streets to engage and repel. Squads of green-armoured troops appeared, along with armoured carrier vehicles and a few light tanks. The narrow streets of the lower town began to ring and shake with gunfire and cannon shot. Gaunt, entering the town himself for the first time, ordered up the armour support, and the first of the Dev Hetra units began to roll in across the smashed gateway and clatter up into the town.

THE BLAST TEMPORARILY saved Bonin's life, and Maggs's too. The enemy troops had been pouring into the temple, surging inside to overwhelm them. Maggs had taken two las-burns across the left arm, and Bonin had suffered a hit to the back that had burned a deep gash in his flesh but which had glanced off the surgical plate of his old spinal wound.

Both of them knew, without saying it, without conferring – and there was no opportunity to confer in that hell-fight – that they had two or three minutes left to live at the most optimistic guess.

Then Rawne's present went off across town. The ground shook and all the south facing windows of the temple blew inwards in a cascade of glass. Caught by the flying shards, several enemy troopers screamed and fell, lacerated and shredded.

Low, in cover in the heart of the place, Bonin and Maggs were the best protected. Seeing the momentary confusion, the fleeting advantage, both seized the initiative.

Maggs rolled to his feet and began a headlong dash towards the heavy wood and stone of the altarpiece at the back of the temple.

Bonin began to sprint towards the base of the nearest screw stair, a stone-cut arch on the far side of the congregation space that led to a narrow twist of steps to the temple gallery.

Collecting their wits and realising their quarry was in flight, the enemy troopers resumed shooting. Las-bolts and hard rounds chased Maggs across the floor of the temple, scratching tiles and chipping stones. He threw himself bodily forward into cover, but a shot struck him in the left heel and slammed him against the altarpiece rather than behind it. The heavy frame of inlaid wood and its ouslite base went over with him. He fell, dazed for a second, under the lancet windows of the nave. Three enemy troops rushed forward across the open heart of the temple, their boots scuffing over the desecrated mosaic of the aquila on the floor. They had, for a second, clean kill-shots on the fallen Maggs.

However Mach Bonin had reached the carved stone cover of the stairway. Turning, face set like an angel bringing solemn notice of death, he emptied half of his last power clip in a flurry of shots that blazed across the echoing chamber.

The shots struck – and chopped into – the three troopers like hacking axe blows. One of the enemy troopers was hit in the knee by a shot that severed his leg. Before his toppling body could fall, he had been sliced through the torso twice, and the shoulder, and the neck. The second pitched over as two shots entered his back above the waistline and incinerated his gut and lungs. He fell, foul steam exhaling from his screaming mouth. The third was hit in the ankle and calf of his left leg, the hip and the side of the head, and went over as if run into from the side by a truck.

The rest of the considerable enemy force turned their guns on Bonin, but immediately had to duck and find cover as Maggs rose behind the felled altarpiece and opened fire.

Briefly guarded by Maggs's frantic support, Bonin turned and ran up the narrow stairs onto the gallery. This balcony of stone ran around the upper level of the temple dome, supported by the ring of pillars. As he came up onto the gallery deck, Bonin could feel the heavy pulse of the gunfire below as the enemy turned its attention back to Maggs.

Bonin ran to the edge of the gallery and unloaded the last of his clip down at the gathering enemy. They scattered backwards through the smashed and overturned seating, leaving several dead, twisted and still, behind them.

Bonin ducked down and ejected his dead clip. There was abrupt slience in the fane as the enemy regrouped. Clattering footsteps and boots crunching over glass and wooden splinters replaced the whine of gunfire.

'Wes!' Bonin voxed from his vantage point. 'I'm out. Chuck me something.'

'Where the hell are you?' Maggs replied.

'Upstairs. Gallery, to your left.'

Down in cover, Maggs took out one of his last clips, weighed it up and hurled it towards the gallery. It struck the rim and fell back into the main space of the fane. Several enemy troopers fired at the movement.

'Feth! Do better!' Bonin snarled. He drew his laspistol. It wouldn't do the job his rifle could, but it might have to do.

Maggs had two clips left. During the ferocious firefight, he'd been more economical than the Tanith scout. He kept one for himself and put his back into launching the other up at the gallery. It flew in over the balcony's edge and disappeared.

Realising their original advantage had been lost, the occupation troopers attempted to rush the Imperials again. Some charged out across the fane floor towards Maggs's hiding place, firing wildly. Others headed towards the three sets of stairs up to the gallery.

With one clip left each, Bonin and Maggs met them. Bonin swung up over the balcony lip and decimated the figures charging Maggs's position. Simultaneously, Maggs lit up and fired at the hostiles heading for the stairwells. In ten seconds of sustained firing, they laid out thirty of the enemy.

Then they were out. They fell back into cover, and dropped their empty rifles in favour of pistols and straight silver. The fight had entered its final, most brutal stage.

During the melee, Bonin had seen something from the vantage of the gallery as he'd fired down. Something that was more important than his life.

He cued his micro-bead. The enemy was creeping forward, ready to smother the pair of them with their numbers. He had seconds left.

'Bonin to Gaunt. Bonin to Gaunt. Urgent. Respond. Respond.'

VIII

RECEPTION WAS POOR. Bonin thought he heard Gaunt's voice replying, but it was hard to tell in the midst of all that crackle. He started to send his message anyway.

The enemy troopers rushed the gallery. They came up one set of stairs to begin with. Later, Bonin could not explain how their first few shots missed him. He could only presume that the enemy's haste to storm the stair head caused their aim to be rushed. He felt the sucking heat of shots passing his face and began to squeeze off bolts in reply with his laspistol.

Cornered, his efforts were desperate and his aim was no better than that of the soldiers trying to kill him. He hit nothing living, but at least managed to wedge the enemy into the cover of the stair head, seriously restricting their field of fire. That was fine... until troops started to emerge from the other staircases.

There was a sudden and unexpected halt in the attack. Firing ceased. The only sounds were the throb of the street fight raging in the town outside, and the slithering bump of the troops inside the fane moving about. Bonin waited. He heard boots crunching on broken glass and boards creaking. His mind envisaged the enemy quietly manoeuvring into place to spring one final, sudden death trap.

Nothing happened.

'Wes?' Bonin voxed a whisper.

'I hear you.'

'Still alive down there?'

'Less alive than I was when we started,' Maggs replied, his breathing short and laboured over the link, 'but, yeah.'

'What's happening?'

'Dunno. I think... I think they just fell back. I think they broke off and made an exit from the building.'

'All of them?'

'I think so. I don't really want to stick my head up to find out.'

That was a sentiment Bonin could sympathise with. Slowly, very slowly, and very quietly, he crawled forwards under the sheltering lip of stonework until he had reached the edge of the gallery. With a muttered prayer to the God-Emperor for protection, Bonin slowly raised his head and peered down.

The temple, already in great disrepair when they first arrived, had been shot to pieces. The stone walls and pillars were chipped, flecked and scorched in a million places, and the wooden seating banks had been pulverised into lacy, punctured shells. The bodies of the occupation troopers they had killed in the frantic gun battle littered the floor, the tumbled-down seating, and the main aisle all the way back to the front doors. Discharge smoke hung like mist in the profaned air.

There was no sign of anything alive.

Bonin was about to call to Maggs when the handles of the temple doors rattled and the doors opened. Bonin dropped down again, pistol raised.

Dark figures with steadied rifles melted in through the doorway. Bonin knew that style at once.

'Straight silver!' he called out.

'Who's there? Mach?' a voice answered.

'Major?'

Flanked by half a dozen Ghosts, Rawne stepped out of the shadows and looked up at the gallery.

'I think we scared them off,' he remarked. 'You boys finished making a mess in here?'

Bonin stood up and holstered his pistol. 'See to Maggs. He's down behind the altar. I think he's hit.'

Rawne gestured two of his men forward.

'I was trying to reach the colonel,' Bonin said. 'I believe I've found what he was looking for.'

'What?' asked Rawne.

Bonin pointed. 'Sir, you're standing on it.'

THE BATTLE OF Cantible didn't so much end as tail off like an unfinished sentence. Three and a half hours after Gaunt had given the 'go' command to Mkoll, the fighting was done, and the principal locations within the hilltop town captured.

The enemy was dead or fleeing. Gaunt had heard such abandonments likened to the frantic exit of rats so often in his career it had become a stale cliché, but the sentiment had never seemed more appropriate. In headlong flight, the occupation troopers and some of the excubitors and higher dignitaries threw open the northern gates of the market town and ran off into the decaying countryside. Some literally ran: troopers discarding weapons and armour in an effort to make themselves more fleet. Their bobbing shapes slowly disappeared into the stands of sickly corn and overgrown fields. Some of the more senior enemy personnel attempted flight in vehicles, tracked machines and motor carriages laden with ransacked spoils and valuables.

Gaunt was not in the best of moods. He felt dispirited and dissatisfied. The last few years of his life had been inextricably linked to Gereon, and its redemption mattered to him a great deal. In the preceding weeks, and that very morning before and during the drop, he had been energised by a driving force of satisfaction: at last, at long last, he was going to contribute to the liberation of a world he cared about with particular intensity.

He hadn't even objected to the low priority site that High Command had selected for his regiment. However, the battle for Cantible – 'battle' was itself a laughable term – had been muzzy and half-hearted. The Ghosts had performed commendably, and particular appreciation was owed to the scouts, but it all seemed so oddly colourless. Liberating Cantible was like putting a sick animal out of its misery.

He walked up through the steep heart of the town. A swarthy belt of smoke was rising off the place and smearing along the white moorland sky. He had just ordered the most mobile Dev Hetra machines and two of his companies to pursue and finish the fleeing enemy stragglers beyond the town.

Gaunt tried to pinpoint the source of his unhappiness. The defence of the town had been second-rate, but no commander should regret an easy, low-cost win. His Guardsmen had done a perfect job. According to Rawne, who seldom exaggerated, Bonin and Maggs had been heroes for a brief, shiny moment, facing down superior numbers in the temple, in a stand-off that wouldn't have shamed any of the battles on the Tanith First's roll of honour.

But where were the people they had come to save? Where was the relief and the release? Where was the point of liberation if a place, emptied of its sordid, inhuman occupiers, was just empty?

Gaunt had heard great things in the early reports from the main theatres. Colossal war, and the endeavour of the Imperial Guard. Less than half a world away, real battles were being fought against real enemies. Real victories were being won.

Not here. There was only death in Cantible. Literal, messy death and a more general, lingering sense of demise. They had come to save a place that was too far gone to save. Gaunt hoped, prayed, that Cantible was not a representative microcosm of Gereon as a whole.

He walked in through idling Hydra carriages and gaggles of relaxing troops, accepting salutes and nodding greetings. There was relief amongst his own, relief of a task less than had been feared, and he had no right to extinguish that. He approached the town's temple, the site of Maggs and Bonin's admirable combat. Rawne was waiting for him.

'Find what we need?' he asked.

'Bonin says so,' said Rawne and looked into the shadows of the temple porch. Bonin, hunched over Maggs's prostrate body with a tending corpsman, saw the look and came over to join them.

'Maggs?' Gaunt asked.

'Shot to the ribs,' Bonin said. 'Nasty. He needs to be seen by Dorden.'

'Dorden's down in the lower town,' Gaunt replied. He looked over his shoulder and yelled, 'Ludd!'

The young commissar ran up obediently. 'Sir?'

'Can you escort Trooper Maggs down to the field hospital?' Gaunt asked.

Ludd nodded. He went over to Maggs and helped him get to his feet. They hobbled off together.

Gaunt looked back at Bonin. 'So?'

'In here, sir,' Bonin replied. He led Gaunt and Rawne into the devastated fane and they picked their way between the enemy dead until they were standing on the wide mosaic of the aquila.

'It's been desecrated,' Bonin said. 'Just beaten up and dirtied. It was only when I was up there that I saw it.' He pointed to the gallery.

'Saw what?' Gaunt asked.

'The aquila,' said Rawne.

Gaunt looked down at the mosaic. Evil, corrupt hands had gleefully defaced the Imperial bird, paying particular attention, and effort of pick-axe, to the twin heads. However, the left-hand head had been repaired. Long after the torrent of abuse, the left-hand head had been quite carefully repaired and re-cemented, sometimes using stray mosaic chips that hadn't been components of the original head.

'The head's been put back together,' Gaunt said.

Bonin nodded. 'It's a signal. It's pointing.'

'To what?'

'There's a section of fresh plasterwork on the wall over there,' Rawne said. 'You follow the way the beak's pointing, that's what you come to. We hacked it off.'

Gaunt walked across to the wall. The removed stretch of plaster lay in dusty pieces on the floor. On the exposed wall, they could see six digits, cut there with a tightly narrowed flamer.

'Six eight one nine seven three,' Gaunt read.

'It's got to be a frequency,' said Rawne.

'Have we tried it?'

'As soon as Beltayn gets here,' Rawne replied.

GAUNT WALKED BACK into the open while they waited for his adjutant to arrive. Cirk and Faragut were approaching, strolling up from the lower town like a couple on an afternoon constitutional.

Gaunt was surprised by how pleased he was to see her. For reasons he had never been able to explain, he could not contain Sabbatine Cirk in his mind. She was dangerous and she was untrustworthy, yet he had learned to trust her completely during his first venture on Gereon. She exuded considerable sexual appeal, and that appeal was contaminated by her aura of damage. No one embodied Gereon in his mind more than Cirk. She was a living victim, the planet personified, beautiful, appealing, but damaged and abused.

Most of the time, he tried not to think about her. Now, he had to and he allowed himself to. He found he felt great kinship with her. She, and she alone, understood the sense of disillusion he felt.

Cirk had done more than anyone to bring about the liberation of Gereon, more than even Gaunt knew. She had been on the brink of tears since the dropships had launched – first tears of anticipation, and then tears of dismay.

'Colonel-commissar,' she said smartly as she came up to him.

'Are you all right?'

She glanced at him, quizzically, taken aback by his unusual warmth.

'Yes, I'm fine. A little strung out. I hope you've some good news.'

'We may have a link to the resistance. We're about to try raising them.'

'That's good. You'll want me to talk?'

'We'll need your ciphers,' Gaunt said.

'I should be present,' Faragut said. They both looked at him as if he was an intruder.

'My brief was very specific,' Faragut said, smiling to diffuse the hostility.

'Of course,' said Gaunt, softening, knowing the man couldn't be blamed for his masters. 'Of course.'

'We're on the same side,' Faragut said sweetly. 'I mean, that's the point, isn't it?'

'AM I HURTING you?' Ludd asked. They took another shuffling step.

'No,' said Maggs.

'Are you sure?' Ludd cinched his arm up tighter under the scout's armpits. 'You can lean on me more heavily, if you like.'

'I'm fine,' Maggs grunted. They were about ten minutes away from the field hospital and progress was slow.

'Really,' said Ludd. 'I could–'

'With respect,' Maggs said, exhaling with pain, 'could you talk about something else, son? Walking's really hard, even with you propping me up. Can't you take my mind off it?'

'Oh, yes, yes,' Ludd reassured, thinking frantically. He ransacked his memory. He had no stories to tell about battles or girls, certainly not any that a heartbreaker and woundmaker like Wes Maggs would be impressed by. He'd once known a man who'd owned a cat, and the funny thing was... no, no that wouldn't do.

'Merrt,' he said.

'What?'

'Merrt. The Tanith with the fethed-up face. The ex-sniper who–'

'I know who you mean.'

'The day Hark and I busted him on the swelter decks. Dragged his backside out of trouble. You were there. I saw you in that dive.'

'I was there.'

'Coincidence?'

'No, Ludd.'

'Want to tell me about that?'

Maggs groaned. 'Sit. I need to sit,' he said, clutching his bandaged ribs. Ludd helped him over to the doorstep of a derelict hab. Maggs sat down.

'We should get to the field hospital,' Ludd said. He was edgy. He'd never done well at first aid drills and he was worried that Maggs might start toppling over with a swollen blue tongue. Or worse.

'Just give me a moment to catch my breath,' Maggs said, leaning back against the scorched doorpost. 'I'll be fine for another walk once I've caught my breath.'

Ludd nodded and waited. 'So, Merrt?' he asked.

Maggs was leaning back, fingering his blood-heavy bandages. 'Merrt. Right. We look after our own, you know.'

'What?'

'First-and-Only. It might surprise you to hear that, given that I'm Belladon and fresh into the mix, but it's true. When a bunch of soldiers come together and bond – I mean, really bond – they stick tight. The Tanith were lucky to find us Belladon, and we were lucky to find them. I'm not going mushy but shit, we make a good pack. You know what I mean?'

'I think so.'

Maggs nodded. 'Leftovers, dregs, remnants. Tanith, Verghast, Belladon. The bits they couldn't kill. Mix us together, we come from the same place and we stick like glue.'

'That's good to hear,' Ludd said.

Maggs leaned forwards and sighed. 'Merrt. We knew he was in trouble. Gambling. In well over his head. Varl noticed it first, and he got us together. Drew us in. Told us we needed to look out for Merrt. Well, we couldn't clear his debt. Even clubbing up, we didn't have anything like the cash. So – and this was Bask's idea – we drew lots to follow him and keep an eye on him. If he got into shit, one of us would be there to bail him out. We drew up a rota. That night on the swelter decks, it was my turn. I knew something dark was about to happen, and I was going to move when you showed up.'

'What would you have done?' Ludd asked.

'Something stupid, probably,' Maggs replied. 'Something that would have got me up on charges, even got me a ten-ninety, but I would have done it. It's that sticking together thing, you see? If we don't stick up for one another, if we don't stick our necks out for one another, what's the point? I mean... what's the fething point? Merrt's one of us, and us is all that counts.'

Ludd nodded.

'What's up?' Maggs asked. 'You look far away all of a sudden.'

'I was just thinking,' Ludd said. 'I was just thinking if I could bottle the regimental spirit you just expressed, I'd be the best commissar in the history of the Guard.'

Maggs grinned, and then his smile slowly faded. 'I hadn't thought of Merrt until just now. Shit. I wonder where he is. That poor ugly bastard.'

FACE-TO-FACE

I

EVERYWHERE, THE DEAD were smiling at him.

Firestorms had scorched through the district of streets and small squares, and left the crisped shells of habs behind. The sky was low and black, and lay like night. Heat radiated from the stones and the rubble, and there was a powerful chemical stink of the burned, the oxidised and the transmuted. Many fires were still burning.

Dalin Criid could feel the warmth of nearby flames against his face, and feel his own sweat trickle through the dirt of his face like tears. He didn't move. He just stood for a while in the jumping shadows of the ruined street, and stared into the flames.

Fire had reduced all of the corpses in the area to scrubby black things made of twigs. They were barely human, barely humanoid, just scorched stumps of driftwood. The only things the fire could not reduce were the eyes and the teeth. Indeed, it magnified both. All eyes became huge, staring sockets of darkness, at once mournful and hating. With the flesh burned away, all teeth became wide, white smiles, part amused, part clenched in pain. From the ground, from doorways, from windows, and from heaps of rubble spoil, they smiled and stared at him as he went past, sometimes several side by side, all smiling at the same joke.

There was something about their smiles. They were rueful, as if so taken aback by the suddenness and ferocity of their demise that there was nothing they could do except put a brave face on it and chuckle. *Look what happened to me in the end, eh? Oh well, what can you do...*

They were so denuded of anything except stares and grins that it was impossible to tell who the dead were. Local people, citizens of the coastal towns, engulfed by the fury of war, or Imperial Guardsmen who had got

613

there some time ahead of AT 137 and found death waiting with a tinder-box?

The other possibility was that these smiles of chagrin and welcome were the smiles of the enemy. Were these his enemy, these blistered black-tar mannequins with their gleaming teeth? If they were, they were the first he'd met.

'Holy.' A word, not even a question. He turned his head. Hamir came close, through the smoke, carrying his rifle across his stomach. Criid fell into step with him and they moved down the street, picking over the smoking rubble.

A quiet had fallen with the darkness. There was the immediate crackle of the flames, the scurry of falling masonry and the distant rumble and thump of something important happening somewhere else. Generally, though, there was a warm quiet, the sound of aftermath.

Criid knew it was no aftermath. He'd become reluctant to check his chron, because the maddeningly slow passage of time was sapping his will, but he knew they'd been down for about five hours. K'ethdrac was an immense target and it could not have fallen yet, even considering the fury of the assault. As with so many great cities and hives, the Imperial ground forces might be picking their way from street fight to street fight for weeks, for months.

For years. That wasn't unheard of. Criid wondered, if he lived that long, whether he would survive mentally. If his body avoided being shot or blown apart or cut into pieces, would his mind withstand a length of time like that here? He doubted it, if the passage of time continued to be so heavy and prolonged. He would end up mad, with a rueful smile on his face.

Hamir gestured ahead of them with a nod. A trio of troopers, Fourbox amongst them, was edging forwards behind a low remnant of wall. On either side, they could make out other members of the company advancing through the rubble and the lazy smoke. In the last, creeping hour, their numbers had grown. Crossing a road bridge into the deeper parts of the city, they had encountered about thirty-five members of the AT 137 drop under the command of Corporal Traben. They'd come off a dropship that had overshot and ended up in some kind of manufactory compound. Wash and Lovely were among the troops. Like Kexie's group, they'd seen nothing of Major Brundel.

A blurt of gunfire rang in from their right. Some of the troopers turned to peer into the smoke.

'Should I find Kexie?' Hamir asked Criid.

'Don't bother,' said another voice from just behind them.

It was Merrt. He'd been with Traben's party too.

'Shouldn't we…?' Criid began.

'In this?' Merrt asked. 'Surrounded by this? You report in every bit of gn… gn… gn… gunfire you hear, Kexie'll be chasing his tail the whole day checking it. Best to keep moving, keep your formation. If it turns out that gunfire needs to involve you, it will.'

It was almost reassuring just to ignore it, to just get on and get through without looking for trouble. There was enough to go around anyway. It did the element more harm jumping at every last thing than it did keeping firm with the deployment.

To prove the point, they went on for another twenty minutes, and the gunfire got personal.

II

THEY HAD ENTERED a part of the fortified city where the air was so black and the smoke so dense that it felt subterranean. Buildings on either hand – some ruined, some intact, and all empty – loomed like the smooth, grey walls of cyclopean caves. It was hot and dank, like the centre of the earth. Moisture dripped out of the noxious smoke. It was not rain or climate damp, but the condensing vapours of warfare: fuel oil, lubricants, accelerants and volatiles. It was sticky and brown like a lho-smoker's phlegm, and the air coughed it out like spittle.

To the west of their position, about five kilometres away, a firestorm blazed through eight or nine city blocks like a communal fire at the centre of the cave. It made the faint light russet and gold. When they stopped to wait and listen, the members of AT 137 resembled gilded statues on a victory arch.

To the south of them, at a similar distance, an emphatic battle was raging, either between armoured forces or duelling batteries of artillery. It was evidently a formidable clash and raised a huge, slightly muffled, noise. They could see nothing of it, however, not even the merest hint of a flash or shell burst.

They had been some time without taking fire, so when the first shots came upon them, they seemed mystifying and unfamiliar. The trooper known as Gyro suddenly fell and rolled violently backwards across the ground as if he had been unrolled briskly out of a carpet. The sergeant yelled everyone to cover, but as they scrambled, Splits, a Kolstec with an unpopular, nasal voice, was also hit.

Unlike Gyro, his wound wasn't fatal. He started to scream, tortured by the pain. His cries became strangulated and high-pitched. Criid had never heard such sounds come out of a person before.

Sergeant Kexie was pinned near the rear of the group, so Commissar Sobile ordered the first men forward. He fired his pistol into the dark and cracked his whip so they could hear it.

'Take out that shooter!' he yelled.

Everyone wondered who he was talking to.

Criid had found cover behind the thick exterior wall of a hab. Ganiel and Fourbox squashed in behind him.

'Can you see it?' Ganiel asked.

Criid couldn't see much of anything. It was all he could do to think of anything apart from the awful screams coming from Splits. Occasionally, a shot whined past the corner of the wall.

'I'll take a look,' Fourbox announced, and peeked around the corner. Almost immediately, he jerked back, banging his head against the bricks in his haste to withdraw.

'Fourbox?'

Fourbox was doing a little stamping dance, his hands to his head.

'Fourbox?'

'How bad is it?' Fourbox asked, turning his head so that they could see his right ear. A hard round had punched it clean off, nicking the rim of his helmet as it deflected. He had a scorch mark burn across the top of his cheek, and a bloody rosebud of tissue and cartliege where his ear had been. Blood streamed down his neck.

'How bad is it?' he asked again. He was in a little discomfort, but didn't seem genuinely distressed.

'Get a dressing on it,' Ganiel said. Fourbox sat down and fumbled with a belt-pack.

Splits was still screaming. Gunfire was coming from several places in the Imperial spread. It sounded like they had half a dozen shooters firing at them.

'Somebody move forwards!' Sobile yelled. 'In the name of the Golden Throne, advance and engage, or by Terra I will flog you all for cowardice!'

Criid started to run. He was running before he'd even realised he'd decided to. He vaguely heard Ganiel, left behind, cry out, 'Criid, no!'

He was out in the open. Several shots hit the ground near his feet like firecrackers, and a las-round shrieked over his head. He reached the far side of the street, rolled down behind a flight of stone steps, and started firing. Other figures followed him. He heard running footsteps, hard boots thumping over grit, the sound of voices cursing.

All the while, Splits was in the background, wailing like a child.

Las-fire was coming from directly above him. Looking up at the gloomy face of the building he was cowering against, he saw the sparks and fizzles of muzzle flash from an upper window.

Moving without thought or hesitation, he rose and ran up the steps into the building's entrance. It was hard to tell what the place had originally been. Wall tiles had been chipped away and littered the floor. Rot discoloured the ceilings of the unlit hallways. He moved from doorway to doorway, swinging his aim around, lugging the heavy barrel of the lasrifle from one imagined target to the next. He climbed a flight of creaking, decaying steps, his back sliding against the wall, and then turned a landing onto a second flight.

On the next landing, he finally met the enemy face-to-face.

III

HE HAD JUST come out of a room, as if breaking from some activity and casually heading off in search of a smoke or a latrine. Afterwards, Criid was able to remember in astounding detail the specifics of the man's clothing and equipment. He was wearing dark green combat armour of an exotic style not worn by any Guard unit Criid had ever seen. The armour was well-finished and well-made, and had once been polished to a good shine, but dust had caked its surfaces badly. It looked light and wearable. It had insignia marked in red and green on the breastplate, and some kind of ornate shoulder braid. The marks were vulgar and alien, and made no sense.

The man's webbing, his boots and most of all his lasrifle, were Imperial issue. His kit closely resembled the equipment Criid was carrying. Criid could even see the little yellow Munitorum stencil, half worn off, on the rifle butt that had denoted the theatre of issue. He had been told, time and again in briefings, and anecdotally by his extended family in the Ghosts, that the enemy frequently used the weapons, uniforms and vehicles they appropriated from the Imperial Guard.

Of course, sometimes they even used the men themselves, if the men could be turned.

They were face to face on that dingy stairhead for less than a second, although the frozen moment embedded itself in Criid's memory forever. Two things broke the hesitation. First, the man began to raise his rifle. Second, the man wasn't a man at all.

He wore no helmet or head covering, except for a padded canvas hood that tied beneath the chin, the sort worn by a tank driver under his wide-bowl helm. With the exception of the insignia, from the neck down, the man might be mistaken in every respect for an Imperial Guardsman. His face, however, was a rancid, distorted mass, so bloated that its original structure was gone. It was as if the hood had been tied in place simply to hold the face together. There was no nose, just a raw socket, and the eyes under the deformed brow were the staring, circular eyes of a large bird. The wet mouth hung open to reveal teeth like quills.

The horror of the face was the last thing about the figure that Criid noticed, as if he was blocking it out and absorbing all the non-disturbing details until he couldn't put it off any longer.

Criid exclaimed in disgust and shot the enemy soldier three times with his lasrifle. The shots lifted the creature off the floor and bounced it off the corridor wall.

Two more equally depraved creatures stormed out of the same room. One had a drooling snout, full of yellow peg teeth, that wouldn't close. The second, draped in a long Guardsman's greatcoat, looked perfectly human except that his left eye socket was shared by two eyes.

The snout had a laspistol and was firing it in a wild, panicky manner. Splinters blew out from the wall behind Criid and from the banister posts in front of him. Yelling, Criid ran up the last few stairs, squeezing the trigger of his lasrifle. The snout with the laspistol was hit so hard that it flew back through the doorway with a sharp jerk, as if someone had yanked it back inside. The other thing, which seemed to have no weapon, turned and ran down the landing, arms wide, greatcoat tails flapping, desperately yelling something in a language that made Criid's brain sizzle. Criid dropped to one knee, the rifle up to his cheek, and fired two aimed shots to bring the fleeing thing down. It fell flat on its face, halfway down the mouldering hall, with an impact that puffed dust up from between the floorboards.

Criid got up slowly. There was a lot of noise down below where others from AT 137 were following him into the building. Around him, on the second floor, sound seemed suspended. Dust, disturbed by the brief but frenzied exchange, wafted in the air. Criid took a few steps forwards gingerly, his heart punching at his ribs, his hands shaking. Everything seemed to be alive around him. Out of the corner of his eyes, shapes seemed to scurry and shuffle behind the grey wallpaper, or fidget and gnaw behind the skirting. Patches of mould and decay seemed to spread while his back was turned. There was a buzzing, like flies. A comb-on-teeth clicking of dusk bugs.

Another step, another. Was that all of them? Where had the thing in the greatcoat been running to? What had it been shouting? Was there anything else in the rooms at the far end of the hallway?

Criid tightened his grip on his rifle and took another few steps along the landing. He was a metre or two short of the place where the corpse in the greatcoat lay, just drawing level with the half open door that all three of the enemy had emerged from.

His attention was fixed on the end of the hallway. Where had the thing in the greatcoat, the thing with the nightmare eye, been running to? The hall ahead – bare dusty boards, stained walls, rot-infested ceiling – led to a foggy, soot-stained exterior window at the far end. Adjacent to that, two doors on opposite sides of the hall were both closed.

Something was in there. In one of the rooms. Criid knew it. His nerves sensed it more acutely with every step he took. Something. Left or right? Left or right? Another step, another. What was that? A movement? Did something just move in the shadows under the right-hand door? Was–

'Get down,' Caff said.

Criid obeyed without even thinking about it. He hit the boards prone as the right-hand door flew open and a squealing pig-thing came out.

It was huge, as tall as Criid, but four or five times the body-mass. It wore old, unlaced Guard boots and ragged battledress trousers belted under the girth of its distended belly. It was bare from the waist up, a sagging barrel of hairless pink flesh smeared with dirt and sweat. Its shoulders and arms were massive, massive like old Corbec's used to be. It was carrying a heavy autocannon, greasy and black, like a normal-sized man would carry a combat shotgun. Its head was tiny, a puckered, bald, pink ball with dot eyes and brown tusks. It made a shrill, bleating squeal as it opened fire.

Fed by a long, swinging belt of ammunition, the cannon thundered, its muzzle crackling with fierce flash jags. Each rapid sound was a blend of numbing boom and metallic ping. The hallway behind Criid tore apart under the onslaught.

From the floor, beneath this concussive rain, Criid fired back. He hit the huge, shuddering torso three times, and then his fourth made a definite kill-shot as it struck the thing's squealing face. The pig-thing toppled backwards, the cannon tilting with it, the last of its belt of shots firing blindly into the hall ceiling. The impacts ripped out the centre of the ceiling in a violent flurry of plaster, dust and splintered lathes.

Collapsing, the thing struck the hall-end window and shattered it, but did not fall all the way out. It crashed to the floor, its right arm hooked up on the broken glass of the window. The cannon barrel, sobbing smoke, hit the floorboards like a piece of lead piping. A long gurgling sigh issued from the dead bulk.

Criid slowly regained his feet, still aiming at the pig-thing. The air was dirty with cannon-smoke. Pieces of ceiling kept fluttering down like autumn leaves. He moved towards the pig-thing to make sure that it was dead.

Something slammed into him from behind and drove him against the far wall of the hallway. Criid struck his chin and his cheek against the wall as he fell, and pain flared, but he was more undone by confusion and shock. Something was screaming in his ear. Everything was blurred. Something was on top of him, pinning him to the floor.

He managed to half-roll over. Another enemy trooper, his howling face a diseased wreck, was astride him, raining fists down on him. This wretch must have sprung from a side room that Criid hadn't checked. Criid tried to block the repeated blows. He'd lost his grip on his rifle, and he couldn't raise his own arms to defend himself properly. The enemy was intent on beating him to a pulp.

A las-shot cracked out and the enemy trooper folded up with a judder. The body slumped sideways, and Criid was able to heave himself out from underneath. Three or four metres back down the hall in the direction of the stairs was Merrt. The Tanith lowered his lasrifle.

'All right?' he asked.

Criid's head was swimming. His face throbbed and he could taste blood and feel it running down his lips. He nodded to Merrt, and made an attempt to stand.

He was almost on his feet when there was a commotion. Yet another enemy trooper had rushed out of the side room to grapple with Merrt. They were struggling face-to-face, Merrt pressed against the hallway wall, his rifle pinned impotently between his chest and his aggressor's. With snapping needle fangs, the trooper was trying to get at Mertt's throat while its hands tried to wrestle Merrt's weapon off him.

Dizzy, Criid tried to move. He looked around for his own weapon, or something else that he could club Merrt's attacker off with.

At his feet was the sprawled figure of the enemy that had been beating him. Merrt's shot had punched clean through its torso, and it was leaking a wide puddle of stinking black blood across the dusty floor.

It wasn't dead.

Unable to stand, barely able to move, it was hacking out its last few breaths and, with trembling fingers, pulling the pin from a stick grenade.

* * *

IV

CRIID THREW HIMSELF at the dying soldier, clawing at its hands to win ownership of the grenade. Lying on its side, the enemy trooper cried out, and blood gushed from its mouth. It struggled with Criid for a moment more, and then suddenly expired.

It had pulled the pin out.

There was no way to put it back. Criid simply snatched the stick grenade out of the dead thing's hands and threw it through the open doorway opposite. There was some vague hope in his head that the wall of the room would take the brunt of the blast.

In the two or three seconds it had taken for Criid to wrestle the bomb away, Merrt had fought with the other soldier. Locked together, grappling face to face, they had struggled frantically until Merrt butted the enemy in the face with his augmetic jaw. The soldier reeled away, finally, by accident, tearing Merrt's rifle out of his hands, and staggered backwards through the doorway a fraction of a second after Criid had hurled the grenade in that direction.

The blast was dull and flat and rough, and filled the air with spinning tatters of debris and clouds of dust.

Coughing hard, Criid rose and looked around. Merrt's attacker was half-visible through the smoke gusting out of the room. He'd taken the force of the mangling blast. The room's door was stoved in. Merrt himself had been thrown back as far as the stairhead.

'Are you all right?' Criid called out, still coughing. Merrt nodded and began to pull himself up.

Voices were calling out from below. 'Clear?' a voice was calling. 'Clear?'

'Clear!' Merrt yelled back.

'Make way! Who's up there?' the voice asked. Merrt and Criid realised it was Sobile. Sobile was on the stairs. He was coming up. His boots were thumping on the steps.

Merrt had no rifle.

Criid looked at Merrt, and then put his foot on his own lasrifle, which was lying on the ground, and slid it as fiercely as he could across the landing to the Tanith.

Merrt grabbed it.

'Report? Who's taken this building?' Sobile demanded as he came up the final flight to join them with his pistol drawn. Criid looked from side to side and snatched up the nearest fallen lasrifle.

'Report!' said Sobile. He looked at Criid. 'You clear this?'

'Yes, commissar.'

'What's above?'

Criid shook his head. Sobile shouted to the gaggle of troopers coming after him to sweep the upper floors. He looked at Criid again. 'Don't just stand there!' he snapped.

* * *

THE UNIT WAS moving again in less than half an hour, back into the blackness of the night-afflicted city. A Krassian division was pushing in left of their position. Their gunfire and flamers lit them up like a river of lava in the darkness. Aircraft swooped in overhead to support them. Criid heard the distant voice of a Titan.

They appeared to be fast approaching some kind of inner city wall or second line of defences. Criid glimpsed huge bulwarks dotted with gunports, and flamer towers that periodically dressed the face of the cliff-like wall with curtains of sheet flame. High towers and hab blocks loomed massively behind the inner wall.

'Halt!' Kexie ordered, and made them crouch down along a bombsite street while the area ahead was scoped. From where they were crouched, Criid could see parts of the defence wall above the nearby ruins. The scene was lit up by intense firelight, the ruins in the way just fragile silhouettes.

They waited. Criid dabbed at his bruised face. His whole head, face and collar bones ached and throbbed from the frenzied beating he'd taken. His jaw, mouth and one eye were swollen, and his lips were split and sore. Blood from grazes and abrasions had dried on his skin. It felt as if he'd torn a muscle in his neck in his efforts to twist his face away from the fists.

He replayed the fight in his head several times. Each time he ran through it, he hoped that the faces of the enemy soldiers would diminish in their horror, fading through repetition and familiarity. They refused to. He'd met the enemy at last, and it had scarred his mind.

The squealing pig-thing with the heavy gun was worst of all. If he hadn't dropped to the ground when Caffran gave the warning, he–

Criid thought about that. Caffran wasn't with them. He was hundreds, maybe thousands of kilometres away. Yet it had been his voice, clear and distinct.

Hadn't it?

Perhaps it was the blessing of the God-Emperor that allowed Caffran to watch over Criid. Criid didn't object, but he wondered why Caffran? Why not his ma, or his real father?

'Rise up!' Sobile ordered, and the unit got up with a clatter of kit. 'Ready to advance!'

They began moving forwards again. The fight ahead sounded loud, like the loudest fight they'd been drawn into yet. Criid ran his tongue around his teeth. Several felt loose.

'Hey,' said Merrt, falling in step beside him. He held out his lasrifle.

'You gave me yours,' he said.

'Oh,' said Criid. They quickly exchanged weapons. Merrt looked his up and down.

'That *is* yours?' he asked Criid.

'Yeah. What's the matter?'

'Nothing.'

Kexie was shouting. The unit was starting to run forward, clearing the jagged ruins and coming out onto the approaches of the huge defensive bulwark.

It was immense, bigger than Criid had even imagined. The flame light was so bright, it was like a grounded sun. Furious blizzards of gunfire billowed in the air under the great wall. The streets and transit ways of the outer districts met the wall, both at ground level, and by way of giant road bridges that crossed the trench in front of the wall, and entered the wall through huge, defended gates. Hundreds of thousands of Imperial Guardsmen were sweeping forwards in fast flowing rivers of bodies along the roads and out across the bridges to assault the wall.

AT 137 went with them.

HUNTERS

I

'WHAT'S THIS ONE called?' Zweil asked.

'Syerte,' Eszrah replied. The old ayatani sniffed, nodded and wrote the word down on his flap of parchment.

'And this one? This one here?'

Eszrah cocked his head and stared. Then he frowned and shrugged.

'Is that a "no" or a "not sure"?' Zweil asked.

Eszrah shrugged again.

'Well, far be it for me to condemn an entire genus of plant to eternal damnation,' said Zweil, 'so I'll play safe for now and describe it under "others".'

Eszrah didn't seem particularly bothered either way. Zweil scratched down a brief description of the dull, unimpressive plant in question, and then moved further along the overgrown ditch.

Tona Criid jogged up the curve of the parched field to join them. Cantible, still exhaling smoke into the glassy sky, lurked on the neighbouring hill. There was a general bustle of activity coming from the town: a distant clatter of armour, the hum of Valkyrie engines, a very occasional gunshot.

Noa Vadim, the Ghost assigned to watch the ayatani out in the open, saluted as she approached. She looked down at the priest in the tangled field trench, the Nihtgane standing over him at the edge of the field, watching him diligently.

'What's he doing?' she asked.

'Don't ask,' replied Vadim. He yawned expansively.

'Tired?' she asked. He shrugged. 'You should have taken the rest while you could,' she said. Some of the regiment had been given a few hours' sleep overnight.

'I slept all right,' Vadim replied. 'Thought I wouldn't, bedding down in a place like that…' Vadim shot a sour look in the direction of Cantible. 'But, no. I slept all right. It was just the dreams.'

Criid nodded. 'The dreams'll get you here, every time. Keep saying your prayers. So… what is he doing?'

'I'm not entirely sure. When I asked, he said something about a "systematic benediction", and left it at that.'

'I've come to get Eszrah.'

Vadim shrugged again. 'You'll have to take it up with him,' he said.

Criid slid down the dusty bank into the weed-choked ditch. It was part of the old field system, an agricultural divider, but the neglect and abuse Gereon's most recent masters had imposed upon the land had allowed it to run wild, and then wither. She picked her way over to where the priest was bending.

'This one?' Zweil called.

'Syerte,' replied Eszrah from the bank.

'Ah, yes. That's come up before, hasn't it. And here, this one, this one down here, this ugly fellow?'

'Unkynde,' the nightwalker said.

'You sure now?' Zweil asked.

'Unkynde.'

'Unkynde… khhaous?'

Eszrah nodded. Zweil scratched down a few words on his long flap of parchment, and then stopped to pull up the offending plant vigorously and toss the scraps up onto the edge of the dead field. The recently pulled remains of other plants already littered the field rim.

'Father,' said Criid. 'Your errand here seems rather botanical.'

'This world's been a long time without the ministry of the Throne,' Zweil said. 'It needs a damn good blessing, every last soul and beetle and pebble and wildflower. The tall fellow is acquainting me with the local flora, so that I can be quite specific in my prayers.'

'You're cataloguing the flowers you have to bless?'

'Flowers, plants… we'll get to trees this afternoon, I hope.'

'This afternoon?'

Zweil looked at her. 'You think it might take longer?'

'I think it's possible you haven't undertaken a comprehensive bio-survey of a planet's indigenous plant life before,' she said.

He held up his flap of parchment. 'So, what you're saying is, I'll need a bigger piece of paper?'

'That is what I'm saying,' she replied.

He turned back to the weeds around his legs. 'You see, Tona, what I don't want to do is bless something unworthy of the Emperor's grace. I've only got a limited amount of spirituality inside me, you see, so I don't want to waste any. The Archenemy, damn his hide, the Archenemy brought plants with him, you see. Crops and spores and other alien things.'

'Yes, I know,' said Criid.

'They've infested the whole place. Parched the soil. Choked off the local crops. Filthy things. The tall fellow's helping me to identify those and root them out so I don't go blessing them by mistake.'

'Are you going to weed the entire planet?' she asked.

'Don't be stupid, woman, I'm not an idiot. It's just if I see them, they offend me and I pluck them out. The tall fellow, he calls them... what is it you call them?'

'Unkynde,' said Eszrah.

'Unkynde. That's it. Means sort of alien. Not of this place. Not from round here. An outsider. A–'

'I understand,' said Criid. 'Father, I came here because the colonel-commissar needs Eszrah for a while.'

'But I'm still working here.'

'I know, but it's important.'

'Well, I'm not going to get to trees this afternoon at all now, am I?'

'It's a shame, certainly,' she agreed. She looked up at the Nihtgane. 'Gaunt,' she said. Without a word or another sign of notice, Eszrah turned and headed down the field towards the town.

Zweil puffed out a tired, disappointed breath and sat down on the bank of the ditch. He pulled up his skirts and fiddled with his large army-issue boots.

'My boots are too big,' he said. Then he complained, 'What am I going to do until the tall fellow gets back?'

Criid hesitated. 'Father, there was something.'

Zweil looked her in the eye sharply. 'Dalin,' he said. 'I hadn't forgotten. You know, I mention his name at all the sacred hours.'

'I think it's me,' she said. 'I need more than this morning's regimental prayers.'

He took her by the hand and knelt her down amongst the weeds. 'Here?' she asked.

'As good a place as any,' he replied. 'He's somewhere on this dirt, and so this dirt connects us. Mr Vadim?' Zweil held up his bony hand and gestured to Vadim to fetch the stole and rood and antiphonal that he had left on the edge of the ditch to go rooting in the weeds.

'Now then,' Zweil said, turning the pages of the old book. 'The prayer of a mother, for her offspring, under the eyes of the God-Emperor...'

II

'Ears on,' Gaunt said as he strode into the middle of the group assembled in the town square. The senior officers came to attention.

'I'll make this brief, because we've all got work waiting,' Gaunt said. 'Item one, remind the men in your commands that daily shots are essential. Dorden tells me there were quite a few who forgot to report to him this morning for anti-ague. No excuses. Let's get into a habit. Item two, Cantible's going to be our operational base for the next few days at least. For our own security we need to move ahead with the search patterns. Street by street, hab by hab, thorough flush searches. I don't want to find enemy scum holed up amongst us, and I certainly don't want reprisal cells managing to stay hidden. Basements, cellars, attics. Got it?'

There was an affirmative chorus.

'Any sign of glyfs or wirewolves yet?' Gaunt asked.

'No, sir,' replied Mkoll.

'Well, that's a part I don't understand,' Gaunt said. 'Anyway, remain vigilant. Anything strange, anything, vox it in. Make sure your men understand. Those are things they simply will not be ready for, or be able to deal with. That's why we brought tanks.' He glanced politely at the Dev Hetra officer present, who made a respectful nod.

'Indigenous survivors?' Gaunt asked.

'We've found about two hundred and seventy humans who appear to have been enslaved townsfolk,' said Hark. 'All of them are seriously sick, malnourished, and implanted with a thing in their arms. What did you say that was called? Consented? Some refuse to talk, or are unable to talk. Those that can, affirm their allegiance to the Emperor and bless us for rescuing them.'

'Which could just be them saying what they think we want to hear,' said Faragut. 'We will, of course, have to keep them interned. Envoys of the Inquisition will be arriving in the next few days.'

Gaunt frowned. He didn't like it, but he understood that there was no other way.

'After examination by the Inquisition, and the appropriate medical treatments, they have every reason to expect to be freed,' Faragut said. 'They may be exactly what they seem to be. Slaves. There is, after all, a precedent,' he added pointedly, 'for Imperial subjects surviving on this world for some time without becoming tainted.'

'But we've only located two hundred odd?' asked Cirk.

'Two-seventy,' said Hark.

'Out of a population of what? Thirty thousand?'

'About that.'

'What in the name of the Throne happened to the rest of them?' Cirk asked.

'I doubt we will ever know,' replied Faragut. 'Or want to know.'

'Item three,' Gaunt said, before the meeting lost its way, 'we seem to have made initial contact, which was our primary objective, so I'll be leaving this site shortly to pursue that. Mkoll will lead my escort detail. Is that drawn up?'

'Ready to go, sir,' Mkoll said.

'Good. In my absence, Major Rawne has the baton. Any questions?'

THEY SET OUT on foot about an hour later, a section of thirty men along with Gaunt, Cirk, Faragut and Eszrah, and moved north. Their route followed a farm road up through the devastated agricultural zones of Lowensa Province in the direction of a smaller town called Vanvier.

The day was warm and still, the sun climbing slowly behind a blanket of hazy white. Deep, scraping, doom-laden sounds reached their ears as if from vast distances, suggesting they could hear echoes of the main conflicts across the continents, although Faragut dismissed this as wishful thinking and blamed a trick of the wind.

'There is no wind,' Larkin said to Brostin.

Another trick of the wind, perhaps, was the sizzling static crackles that blistered the air from time to time, and appeared to be associated with the glare of the sun.

The rolling landscape was shrivelled and dead. It had once been a lush arable region, similar to the part of the country around Ineuron Town where Cirk had grown up and where her family had owned agricultural land. Her own lands, already plundered and razed before she left them, probably resembled this now: a dust bowl, where only the roughest, coarsest grasses and vile, imported fungi still grew, where homesteads and lonely farms stood empty and dead, and the dry bones of livestock littered the cracked earth.

It was a distressing sight. Cirk said little as she walked along, but Gaunt could empathise with the grief she was hiding. It hadn't been that long since he'd lived on this world, and it had been suffering then. The land, the climate, the plant and animal life had all begun to suffer, as if diseased, and natural cycles had begun to fall apart. It was nothing compared to this. Gereon was no longer a place afflicted with the brutal early onset of a disease or an infection. This was the terminal phase of waste and corruption.

As they marched, Gaunt checked with Beltayn. The vox-officer, using the new codes that Bonin had found, had finally managed to raise Daystar early that morning. Daystar was code for one of the few underground contacts the Navy had managed to establish prior to the liberation. Gaunt's force had been meant to join up with them at the temple at Cantible. Plans had evidently changed.

'The resistance only survived by being as secretive as it could,' Cirk said. 'Unlocking it may be slow going. Even though we're not the enemy, getting them to let go of their secretive habits might be tough.'

'We'll manage. It's the task High Command has set for us, after all. It doesn't matter how much hot metal we throw at the main theatres, we can't properly take Gereon back until we open it up from the inside. For that to happen, the underground is vital.'

Cirk nodded, but it was a strange expression, as if she was trying to convince herself. Faragut, by her side, smiled. He looked as if he was about to say something.

'What is it?' Gaunt asked.

'Nothing, sir,' said Faragut.

Up ahead, Criid suddenly shouted, 'Down! Off the road!'

The section dropped off the roadway immediately and took cover in the low roadside ditch. The land around was rolling flat, and covered with a thick expanse of pinkish grass that grew to the height of cereal crops.

Gaunt crawled along to Criid and Mkoll.

'What did you see?'

'Something out there in the grass, about half a kilometre off. Something big, prowling low.'

'What sort of something?' Gaunt asked.

'A big animal. A predator. Just a shape, really, too low in the vegetation for me to make it out. It was like it was stalking us. As if we were a herd of game.'

Mkoll and the other scouts in the section crept out to sweep. When they came back reporting no traces, Gaunt moved the section on again.

'Must've been my imagination,' Criid said, not sounding as if she believed it. She was thinking of the hideous stalkers, the wrought ones of Ancreon Sextus, which had come and gone, thanks to the twisting influence of Chaos, in ways that a mortal man could not.

THEY CAME IN sight of their destination, a small farming hamlet called Cayfer. It was a ramshackle collection of stone buildings set on a low hill amid the pink, invader grasses, in an area studded with the dead remnants of talix and keltre trees. Several kilometres beyond the hamlet, a thicker belt of sickly woodland began.

There was no sign of life. The hamlet seemed dead, and turned over to the elements. Through his scope, Gaunt could see that stone walls were broken down, and habs and outhouses were missing their roofs. The bones of dead livestock spotted the stony ground amongst the rusting farm machinery. The ruin of an air-mill sat in the centre of the place, its still vanes like tattered wings. Air-mills were common in the agri-provinces. They'd seen several ruined mills during their march. Gaunt remembered a row of giant air-mills marking the border of Edrian Province, a place where Brostin had once performed a particularly spectacular stunt with a tanker load of promethium. That seemed like an awfully long time ago.

'Try the link,' he said to Beltayn.

Beltayn knelt down and set the dials of his non-standard vox-caster. 'Daystar, Daystar, this is Skyclad. Please respond.' He sent the message as a verbal signal and a simultaneous non-verbal code pulse, tapped out by hand on the transmitter's key bar.

Nothing came back.

'What the feth is wrong with them?' Gaunt muttered.

'They weren't exactly chatting this morning, sir,' Beltayn said. It was true. The sum total of the previous message, aside from the verification ciphers, had been 'Cayfer mill, by tonight.'

'They could be watching us,' Cirk said. 'Making sure we're who we say we are.'

'I'd know it,' said Mkoll.

'Or maybe you wouldn't,' Cirk told the scout.

'They could be lying low,' said Beltayn. 'I mean, if something had spooked them. Maybe they think something's awry and they don't want to come out until it's safe.'

Gaunt was panning his scope around, taking in the hamlet and the surrounding vista of the countryside. He stopped suddenly.

'What, sir?' Criid asked.

'I think Bel's right. I think something is awry.'

'How do you mean?'

'You know you thought you saw something stalking us?'

'Yeah?'

'I think I just saw it too.'

III

THE BUILDING HAD once been a college or a hospital, and it stood in the south-west corner of Cantible. Early patrols had reported it to be empty, but now Kolea had charge of the search pattern in that part of the streets and he wanted to make sure.

'Something that big's going to have a basement,' he told Varl. 'Storerooms, cellars, vaults. We'll check it room by room.'

The squads moved in.

The sky had turned a fulminous yellow hue. Despite their care, the Ghosts' footsteps clattered noisily through the wreck-strewn courts and cloisters of the old place.

'Sir?'

Kolea crossed a quadrangle to an open door where Domor and Chiria were standing.

'What have you got, Shoggy?'

'Just a hall,' Domor said. Kolea peered inside. It was indeed a large assembly hall or congregation room. The walls had been defaced, and the floor was covered with broken glass and shattered wooden stalls. At the far end, large, smeary lancet windows were backlit by daylight, and showed the fuzzy shapes of trees outside.

'Any hatches here? Doors?'

'No, sir,' Chiria told Kolea.

'All right, then,' Kolea said, stepping back out into the quad. 'Carry on.'

His link pipped. It was Meryn.

'Yes, captain?'

'The habs are clear to the end of the street, sir. We found some bodies in one. Old kills. Nothing else. Shall I move on into the next row?'

'No, stay put. We'll be there presently. I want to keep the sweeps overlapping.'

'Understood.'

Varl trudged towards him across the quad followed by half a dozen other Ghosts.

'What's that way?' Kolea asked.

'An undercroft,' said Varl. 'It's derelict. There's a few storerooms, but they've been trashed.'

'And what's behind that wall?' Kolea asked him. The far side of the quad was enclosed by a tall stone wall.

'The street,' said Varl.

Kolea nodded and then paused. 'No,' he said, 'it can't be.'

'I'm sure it is,' said Varl.

'Were there any trees in the street?' asked Kolea. 'Do you remember any trees?'

'No,' said Varl.

Kolea thumbed his micro-bead. 'Uh, Meryn? You still in the street?'

'Yes, sir. Covering from the north end.'

'You see any trees?'

'Say again?'

'Trees, Meryn? You see any trees?'

A pause. 'Negative on trees, major.'

'What's going on?' asked Varl. Kolea pointed at the end wall. 'It can't be the street behind that. The street runs further over to the left. If there was any doubt, that wall screens off whatever this hall backs onto. You can see trees through the hall windows.'

They walked over to the high wall. The stones were dirty and black, as if soot had been baked on and then varnished. Kolea felt his way along, followed by Varl and some of the other squad members.

'Door,' Kolea announced.

'Feth,' said Varl. 'Who missed that?'

'Doesn't matter,' Kolea replied. 'I don't think this place wants us to know its secrets.'

The door, narrow and wooden, was painted black and set flush into the stonework. Even close to, it was virtually invisible.

'Ready weapons,' Varl started to say to the others. 'We're going to hop through and–'

But Kolea had already opened the door.

'Feth!' Varl said, and followed him.

There was a yard beyond, a small, dark courtyard bordered on all sides by high, black walls except for where the hall adjoined.

The ground was covered with human bones. Thickly covered. The bones were loose and jumbled, stacked deep in places, piled against the walls. There was a smell of old rot, and mould growth caked the inner walls. It was like an ossuary, or a foul, anatomical rubbish tip.

'Gak,' Kolea sighed. 'I think we found out where all the people went.'

Beside him, Varl stared in bleak horror at the disarticulated relics of the dead, the staring sockets, the gaping mouths, the brown ribs. The other troopers, no strangers to death, were similarly transfixed.

'Trees,' Kolea mused suddenly, swallowing hard and trying to get his brain moving again. 'Why could I see trees?'

He looked up and saw the three, tall, slender gibbets in front of the hall windows. The wood that they were made from was dark, as if stained with blood. Skeletal metal mannequins hung from steel strings, silent and empty and stark.

Varl saw what Kolea was looking at. The shock lingering on his face melted into fear.

'Gol,' he whispered, backing away very slowly and trying to make the others come with him. 'Gol, for Throne's sake… those are wirewolves.'

IV

THEY ADVANCED UP through the tousled pink grasses and tumbled stones towards the boundaries of Cayfer. Mkoll lingered at the back, watching the grasslands for signs of the thing stalking them.

'It was low down in the grass,' Gaunt had said, 'gone before I could see it.'

'A beast?'

'A hunting beast,' Gaunt had nodded. He refused to speak the word *daemon*, but what else might be haunting the moorlands of a world embraced by the Ruinous Powers?

The slopes approaching the hamlet were melancholy. Pink grass and violet lichens clung to the low stone walls and withered gates, and the trees were dead and desiccated like the bones of giant hands. Within the sagging walls, amongst the collapsing farm machinery and scattered animal bones were tiny shreds of human evidence: a tin bucket full of wooden clothes pegs, bleached by the sunlight; a row of odd boots and shoes, the leather cracked and worn like old flesh, mysteriously lined up along the top of a stone wall; a broken trumpet, lying in the weeds; a rag doll with one button eye; mismatched pots and drinking cups and other receptacles, laid out in a curious pattern in the grass, each one half-full of stagnant rainwater; a chopping block for splitting firewood, and a pile of cut wood beside it, but no axe.

The sky had darkened, and a low wind had got up, brushing the grasslands like an invisible hand and making the dead trees creak. A door banged somewhere. Cloth strung to the air-mill's ragged vanes began to flap.

They were closing on the main hamlet now. Gaunt drew his bolt pistol and waved everyone down. The section, spread wide, got down in cover around walls and outbuildings.

'Bel?'

Beltayn tried the vox again. This time the answer to his send was squealing distortion.

'Atmospherics,' he said. Gaunt nodded. No surprise. It felt as if there were a storm coming. The colour of the sky said as much, and the change in the light. The rising wind was cold, as if it was air displaced from some polar latitude. The warm stillness that had surrounded them since the drop was blown away.

Gaunt was about to move forwards again when they all heard a long, purring growl. It came from a distance away, and travelled on the wind, which suggested it had been loud to begin with. Eszrah started and raised his reynbow.

Gaunt looked back at Mkoll. The scout pointed. The sound, as far as he was concerned, had come from the swaying grassland.

'Criid,' Gaunt said. 'Hold the position here. Larks, Mktass, Garond… with me and Mkoll.'

The designated troopers picked themselves up and scurried down the slope after Gaunt.

'It's moving like a felid,' Mkoll whispered as they got into cover with him. 'Belly down, ears flat.'

'It's got ears?' Larkin asked.

'I haven't even seen it,' Mkoll confessed, 'but I can feel it. I can feel it watching us and getting closer.'

Another purring growl came up on them in the wind. It was almost a coughing, hacking sound.

'And we can hear it,' Mkoll added.

'Keep that loaded,' Gaunt told Larkin, pointing to his longlas. 'If it's big and fast, we're going to need to be able to put it down hard.'

'If I can see it, I'll blow its fething head off,' Larkin assured them.

'Right,' said Gaunt. 'Garond and Mkoll, split left. Mktass with me to the right. Larks, you move forwards from here, and we'll see if we can't pincer it.'

'Were there big predators on Gereon?' Garond asked.

'No,' said Gaunt. 'In the Untill, maybe, but not out in a place like this. This is trouble. This is something the enemy brought. Let's go.'

The two prongs hurried off, heads and backs low, through the nodding grasses. As he ran, Gaunt thought he heard the growl again, but realised it was the rumble of thunder approaching. He waved Mktass low, and they crept forwards. Gaunt felt for the grip of his sheathed power sword. It would be cumbersome to draw, in cover, but the time might come. It had a taste for warp-beasts.

Seventy metres away across the shivering pink crop, Mkoll and Garond slithered on their bellies to the base of one of the dead trees.

'Smell that?' Garond whispered.

Mkoll nodded. 'Blood. Dried blood.'

'What the gak is this thing?' Garond hissed.

'It's dead, that's what it is,' Mkoll whispered back. 'I don't care how big and ugly you are, you don't ghost the Ghosts.'

Mkoll peered out. There was still nothing visible. The coughing growl came again, a little surging purr. Then it was gone.

'Where are you?' Mkoll murmured.

LARKIN EDGED FORWARDS, nursing the long-las. He'd got a tingle, the sniper's tingle that divined the location of a target when it still couldn't be eyeballed. Eighty, ninety strides ahead, in the downroll of the long grass, between the two forked trees. Larkin would have put money on it if Varl had been around. It was a gut thing, and Larkin had been a hunter for a long time. He snuggled his rifle up to his cheek.

'In that dip, between the trees,' he voxed quietly.

'Specify,' Gaunt replied.

'Make the two trees to your left. Tall skinny one with no branches, curved like a swan-neck? And the ragged one like a woman bending in a high wind and her skirts going up?'

'Got them.'

'Ground dips away there, pretty deep. Down there.'

'You certain?' Mkoll voxed in.

'My gut is.'

'Good enough for me,' Mkoll noted.

Larkin settled his aim. Through his scope, he tightened in on the nodding grasses. For the first time, he thought he could see a shape, a dark shape. He was lined up.

There was another growl, a sputter, a snorting sound, and the thing moved. It began to come up out of the grass, as if it was rising to pounce. Larkin saw its eyes, bright, yellow and glowing. His aim was set directly between them. Headshot. He took it.

The hot-shot round sizzled across the pink grass and struck between the beast's eyes. There was a scorching, metallic crack.

With a further hacking, coughing roar, as if goaded by pain, the beast rose up out of the dip in a sudden, violent surge. Now they could see it.

Now they could see what kind of beast it was.

'Oh feth,' said Mkoll.

V

'MOVE!' GAUNT BELLOWED. 'Stay low!'

They scattered. Roaring and snorting, the beast reared out of the dip, flattening the long grass in its path. Chugging geysers of black smoke streamed from its hindquarters straight up into the air as it exerted itself to move forwards. Its enormous engine revved. It was a machine, but it was a beast and a daemon too. It was an enemy tank.

The battered, wounded armour was crimson, the paint flaking off to bare grey metal in places. Twisted sheet plating and skeins of rusted barbed wire reinforced its skirts. Rivets covered it like barnacles. Strung trophies knocked and clattered against its flanks. On its turret side was a single painted mark, a runic symbol of cosmic malevolence. Yellow headlamp eyes glowed from the front of the hull.

The beast came up out of the dip with alarming speed, and set off across the flat ground with a steady clatter of tracks. It was heading directly for Larkin's position.

Gaunt was still moving. He looked back.

'Larkin?'

The autocannon hard point built into the left-hand side of the beast's forward hull began firing. Large calibre rounds wasped across the swishing grass. Clumps of earth sprayed up into the air. A small, dead tree splintered into dry kindling.

'Larkin!'

There was no sign of the master sniper.

The beast abruptly slewed around to its left, one set of tracks braking as the other raced on. Dirt and soil sprayed out behind it as it dug in. Bouncing, it rolled around in the direction of Gaunt and Mktass.

As if it had heard his voice.

The beast's main gun, lolling with its motion like a slack limb, was angled down steeply, slightly below the horizontal. The turret clamp squealed out above the brute thunder of the engine as the turret began to traverse.

Gaunt and Mktass were already down in the grass. Gaunt turned his head to the side and glimpsed Mktass a few metres away through the grass stalks, scurrying forwards on his hands and knees.

'Stay still–' he was about to say.

The beast spoke.

The sound of its main gun firing was painfully loud, like a sledgehammer striking an anvil. The range was so short that there was no space to hear the whistle of the shell. Twenty metres ahead of Gaunt, a large lump of moorland disintegrated in a cone of smoke and flame. The blast shook the ground.

The beast lurched to a halt, and another metal-on-metal squeal sounded as the turret traversed back in the other direction. It stopped.

Gaunt wrapped his arms over his head and clenched his teeth, waiting for the–

Again, the beast spoke. Another volcano of dirt and fire erupted out of the moorland.

Gaunt had heard tankfire hundreds of times before, both close to and from far away, and it wasn't just the proximity of the threat that made the beast's voice particularly monstrous.

It was the fact that it *was* a voice. It was the boom of a heavy gun, but in that boom, in that sledgehammer on anvil clash of main gun mechanism and shellfire, there was an organic note. A howl. A roar of lust and rage and glee. A rumble of hunger.

The engine revved again, and the beast swung about, track links rattling. It began to rock and bounce in the direction of Mkoll's position.

Its behaviour was extraordinary. Gaunt knew the use and value of armoured weapons, for power and strength, for psychological force. Tanks were a vital tool of warfare as unsubtle monsters that could roll in and deliver stupendous firepower.

This beast wasn't behaving like a tank. It wasn't just advancing inexorably towards them, firing its weapons. It was hunting them, and it had been hunting them since they'd first become aware of it earlier in the day. Since before that, most probably. They'd become convinced there was a big predatory animal shadowing them on the moors, and there had been. When the beast first emerged, it was all Gaunt could do to remember that it had been hull down in the dip and the long grasses, and not *belly* down.

Since when did tanks act like wolves or felids?

The beast trundled towards the area where Gaunt had last seen Mkoll. Its hard point spat out a few lazy shots, and then it lurched to a sudden halt. Braking hard, its hull rocked nose to tail on its suspension. The trophies decorating its flanks – mostly human skulls and Guard helmets strung on wire like beads – swung and clattered for a moment. The big turbine throbbed, idling. Little gusts of black smoke dribbled up out of the exhaust pipes.

What was it doing? What was it waiting for?

The turret began to traverse again, turning slowly to the beast's left. The metal turret collar made a laborious screech of unoiled joints, like a stone slab being dragged off a tomb. The turret stopped, facing the hill slope where the hamlet sat. There was an electric whine and the tank barrel elevated slowly until it was twenty-five degrees off the horizontal, aiming directly at Cayfer.

Not aiming. Gaunt raised his head out of the grass and risked a look. The beast sat thirty metres away, its heavy back end towards him. The main gun wasn't aiming at Cayfer, Gaunt thought. It was... sniffing, scenting the hamlet. Scenting the wind, like a cat.

Slowly, Gaunt drew his power sword. While it was occupied, maybe he could crawl towards its hindquarters and get in really close at its blind spot. Armour plating or no armour plating, the power blade of Heironymo Sondar could stab in through a vent grille or an exhaust slot and cripple the engine.

Providing someone was smiling down on him from a golden throne...

He edged forwards. He didn't activate the blade, for fear that the energised hum might give him away... for fear that the tank might hear it. The idea would be funny if it weren't so horribly real. To his right, he saw Mktass, still down in the grass, signalling frantically that Gaunt shouldn't try it. *Too much of a crazy risk,* said Mktass's gestures and wide, staring eyes. *You'll get yourself killed. You'll get us all killed.*

Gaunt kept going. He flexed his fingers around the grip of the power sword, down low beside his thigh. His nostrils were assaulted by the exhaust wash of the idling beast, the rank oil and soot, the smell of dried blood from the grisly battle trophies strung about it.

He was ten metres from the beast's rear when things changed. He saw a little flurry of sparks light up on the slope directly below the ruined hamlet, coming from behind one of the tumbled pasture walls. From a distance, it looked like tinderbox sparks. In a second, las-bolts sang overhead. Someone on the slope was firing a lasrifle at the beast on full auto.

The range was poor, and even point blank, a lasrifle couldn't penetrate tank armour. Gaunt knew what it was. It was somebody's attempt at distraction. It was somebody's attempt to draw the tank off them. Gaunt recognised this with a mixture of warmth and annoyance. Someone in the section was risking their life to distract the tank, and that was selfless. In the section, Trooper Gonry had been carrying a tread fether and, presumably, whoever was shooting was hoping to lure the beast into range for a rocket kill.

Gaunt was very close, however, and this was spoiling his chance.

He broke cover and began to run, igniting the power sword in the hope that he could get a crippling thrust into the beast-machine before it moved.

The engine blitzed into life, pumping out a torrent of black exhaust, and the beast spoke again.

It spoke three times. Sledgehammer-anvil-howl. In dismay, Gaunt saw the three shells land in the slopes below Cayfer, shredding a wall line into a rain of stones, demolishing a pair of dead trees, and blasting a raw scab of earth out of the grass.

The beast started to surge forwards, tracks chattering like fast percussion. Dirt and stones and tufts of grass like small scalps spattered up and out from its rear as it moved, and Gaunt had to shield his face. He couldn't reach it. It was pulling away.

'No!' he spat.

The beast heard him.

VI

THE BEAST SWUNG right around, chewing the ground as it dragged its dark tonnage about. Exhaust smoke farted upwards in a sudden blurt of effort as it turned. It turned to face Gaunt. Its staring headlamps pulsed with yellow light.

Gaunt was gone. There was no one behind it.

The beast revved its engine, sounding like an angry growl. The hard point clattered and let off a burst of shells that raked the grasses ahead, and caused a cloud of shredded plant fibre to waft into the wind.

The beast sped forwards, grinding back across the track of flattened stems that it had left in its wake.

Something had knocked Gaunt flat just as the beast began to turn. Where Mkoll had come from, Gaunt wasn't sure. *Stay flat*, Mkoll had signed.

They lay on their backs in the deep grass, hearing the snorting, growling frustration of the beast nearby. They heard it fire its hard point, and heard the close whip and slice of the shells. Then they heard it start forward, coming closer.

Gaunt twitched involuntarily, but Mkoll put a firm hand flat on his chest. *Stay flat. Don't move.*

The din of engine and treads got louder and closer. It was increasing speed.

Don't move.

The beast passed by less than three metres from Gaunt's left side. Its noise receded behind them. They waited for what seemed like an eternity for the noise to change, for the beast to make its next turn, but the noise simply faded away.

Mkoll and Gaunt lifted themselves slowly and took a look across the nodding grass.

There was no sign of the beast. No sound. No smoke.

They rose to their feet. Garond and Mktass appeared, from different points in the weed cover.

'Where the feth did it go?' Gaunt asked.

'That way,' Garond pointed. A trampled path of pink grass led away down the slope, following the base curve of the hill on which Cayfer stood. Already, the stiff pink grass stalks were beginning to spring back up.

Mkoll ran forwards a short way and leapt up into the lower branches of one of the dead trees. He pulled himself up to get a good view.

'It's gone,' Larkin said.

Mkoll looked down. Larkin was curled up against the bole of the tree, sheltering behind its withered trunk. The sniper pointed down the slope. 'Last I saw it, it was rolling down into cover again. Past that cairn of stones into the small valley.'

Mkoll leapt down out of the tree. 'I'll go after it. Track it,' he said.

'And do what when you find it?' Gaunt asked. 'No, we regroup. We know it's out here and we know how it moves. We'll keep watch, and when it shows itself again, we'll be ready.'

THEY WORKED THEIR way back up the hill to the fringes of Cayfer, past the three still-burning shell pits that the beast had scarred the slopes with. Criid appeared to meet them.

'That you shooting?' Gaunt asked.

She nodded.

'Brave. Maybe foolish, but thanks.'

'I wanted to pull it close so Gonry could slag it with the fether,' she said, pretending her actions had had nothing to do with pulling Gaunt's skin out of the fire.

'Decent idea.'

'Where did it go?' Criid asked, following him up the slope.

'It didn't,' said Gaunt. 'It's still out there. Post a watch. Feth, what's this?'

They had rejoined the main group, which had been sheltering in the dusty yard behind a row of outbuildings. Faragut was bolt upright against a pen wall, his pistol at his feet. Eszrah was patiently aiming his reynbow at him. The rest were grouped in, watching, many amused at the commissar's discomfort.

'There was an incident,' Criid said lightly.

Gaunt walk up to Eszrah and gave a nod. The Nihtgane raised his bow and stepped back. Gaunt looked at Faragut.

'What happened?' he asked.

'The bastard was going to shoot Criid,' Beltayn snapped.

'Yes, that's right,' Faragut snorted. 'Hear them tell it. That'll make for an accurate picture.'

'You tell me then,' said Gaunt. 'Did you threaten my sergeant with your weapon?'

'I drew my pistol for emphasis because she refused a direct order.'

'Your order?'

'A direct order. I told her I would be forced to shoot her if she persisted in insubordination, as per the *Instrument of Order*, paragraph–'

'Oh, please don't, Faragut,' Gaunt said. 'What was the order?'

'She intended to fire upon that tank. I told her not to. I ordered the section to hold fire and stay in cover.'

Gaunt nodded. 'I see. You had the tank rocket up here, and Criid wanted to bring the enemy in range, but you saw it differently?'

'I saw it realistically!' Faragut replied. 'The chances of us taking a tank were slim. Very slim. The chances of that tank destroying this team before it could achieve its mission objectives were greater, in my judgement. Contacting the resistance is vital. I could not permit anything to prejudice our chances.'

'Even if it meant leaving me and the others to die?' Gaunt asked.

'Even that. You know the stakes, Gaunt. You know what necessary sacrifice is.'

'You fired anyway?' Gaunt asked Criid.

'With you and Mkoll down there, I had section command at that point. The tank needed to die, in my judgement.'

'She fired. I went to reprove her,' Faragut said. 'I may have had my gun in my hand at that time. Then your partisan aimed his weapon in my face.'

'Eszrah's only got a few friends in the whole universe, Faragut,' Gaunt said. 'Aiming your gun at one of them is a bad idea. Let's get on. Pick up your damn gun.'

'Watchposts!' Mkoll called. 'I want a lookout spread along the rise in case that tread shows again!'

'Gonry, get the tube ready,' said Criid. 'Someone stand by to load him.'

Everyone was moving. Gaunt walked up through the farm buildings towards the air-mill. He realised that Cirk was walking with him.

'Gaunt?'

'Yes?'

'Faragut is–' she began.

'Faragut is what?' he asked.

'There is a broad agenda,' she said. Her voice trailed off.

He stopped walking and turned to look at her. 'I don't know quite what you're trying to tell me,' he said.

Cirk shook her head sadly. 'I don't know either. I haven't been told anything. You haven't been told. They don't have to tell us. We're just pawns.'

'Who are "they"?' Gaunt asked.

She shrugged. 'I don't know that either.'

Gaunt snorted. 'You're not doing much except sound terribly paranoid, Cirk.'

She smiled. She had hugged her arms around her thin body, as if she was cold. 'I know. Listen, have you ever wanted something so much you'd give everything to have it? Have you ever prayed for something that much?'

'I don't know.'

'You'd know if you had. You want something so much it hurts. You give everything, *everything*, away just to have it. Only… when you gave up everything, you gave it away too and so there's nothing.'

The wind caught her hair, and she screwed up her eyes while she brushed it aside and wiped her nose on her sleeve.

'Cirk? What can't you tell me?'

'It cost the resistance dear to get us off Gereon.'

'I remember.'

'A lot of time, a lot of materiel and a lot of lives, but it was worth it, because we swore that if we got away, if we got back to Imperial space, we'd return. We'd bring liberation back with us. That was the deal.'

'That's right. That's what we've done.'

'Just remember that's all I'm saying. Just remember that's how it's supposed to work.'

Gaunt frowned, and was framing another question when he heard Beltayn shouting. He looked round. His adjutant was standing at the top of the yard beside Criid and some other troopers. He was pointing, pointing up over the low, broken roofs of the hamlet, towards the air-mill.

In the rising wind, the vanes were beginning to turn.

VII

RAWNE STROLLED BACK across the quad to join Kolea and Varl. He looked back at the high wall, and the small black door that he'd just emerged from.

'I think they're dead,' he said. 'Just junk hanging there.'

'But–' Kolea began.

'Last time we were here,' Rawne said smoothly. 'Those things would go live at the slightest provocation.'

'I know. You briefed us,' Kolea replied.

'Well, they didn't wake up when we hit this place, and they haven't woken up yet. I don't know why they're dead, but that's what they are.'

Varl scratched his scalp behind his left ear. 'Yeah, but given they're not actually alive, there's a chance that's not a permanent state.'

'There's a chance,' Rawne agreed. 'For now, we cordon this whole area, put a round the clock watch on it, and level it with everything we have if something so much as twitches. There's been another signal from the Inquisition forces. They're on their way. They can deal with it when they get here.'

Rawne turned and looked up at the dark clouds chasing across the pearly sky. There was a wind in the air. Gaunt was overdue signalling, although the old blight of Gereon's atmospherics could explain that. 'For what it's worth,' Rawne said, 'I think they are dead. I think they're dead for the same reason that there are no glyfs around. Set up a cordon here and let's get on with the sweeps.'

Rawne left the quad to rejoin his party. Varl put Chiria's section in charge of watching the grim, walled secret.

Kolea had something on his mind. He stayed apart, sitting on a chunk of fallen masonry in the corner of the quad, musing and turning something over in his hand.

'Ready to move?' Varl asked once the place was secure.

'I suppose so.'

'What?'

'That was dumb,' said Kolea.

'What was?'

'What I just did. I just walked in there. We found the door and I just walked in there. You were getting a cover team ready, but I didn't wait. I just walked in.'

'No harm done,' said Varl.

Kolea looked up at him. 'No actual harm, but there could have been. It was real enough. The wirewolves were there. We've been briefed. We'd been told what to look for and how careful we had to be, and I just walked in. I might as well have been whistling.'

Varl grinned. 'And your point? 'Cause I know if I stand here long enough, you'll eventually make one.'

Kolea stood up and brushed off the dusty legs of his battledress pants. 'We take a lot of risks,' he said.

Varl pursed his lips as if stifling amusement. 'We're soldiers. We're the Emperor's Guardsmen, true and faithful. Risks are the job.'

'I know. I just don't think sometimes. I charge in. I take the plunge…'

'That's your style,' said Varl. 'You led from the front, which is why you're a major and I'm not. At the moment.'

'It's going to get me killed. That's what I'm saying. Nearly has more than once.'

'Life's going to get you killed,' said Varl. 'Come the feth on with you.'

They wandered back across the dusty quad to where Domor had the search team waiting in the street archway. A dry wind chased eddies of soot and sand around the quad flagstones.

They started to head down the street, past the derelict faces of burned-out habs and slopes of rubble dotted with nodding weeds. Meryn's section was ahead of them, leading the way into the tattered produce barns of the old town commercia.

'Know what I've been doing since we started on this?' Kolea asked Varl as they walked along in the breeze-stirred quiet.

'Getting on my wick?'

'I'm serious.'

'So am I.'

'Since we dropped, all I've thought about is the lad, how he is, if he's safe, how gakking unfair it is that he isn't with us. He must be scared, wherever the gak he is. The big zones must be bad.'

'That's natural enough.'

'I've never once wondered… is he alive still?'

'Well, you can't think that way.'

'I know.' They had reached the gates of the produce area. Kolea fanned the section out in support of Meryn's advancing Ghosts.

'It just occurred to me, there's something else I should think about.'

'What?' Varl asked.

'When we're all done with this place, maybe I'll see the lad again, and that will be fine, but what if I die? What if I do something dumb and just die? How will that be for him?'

Varl shrugged.

'I left it too late before this started. My fear was, I'd left it too late full stop. Because the lad might die, I'd never get the chance to put things right. Never occurred to me it might work the other way around.'

IT WAS ANYONE'S guess how long the excubitor had been holed up in the outhouses behind the silent, boarded habs. The area was a maze of small yards and narrow alleys, dotted with store huts and privies, and it stretched all the way down to a row of market gardens inside the town wall.

Osket, Wheln and Harjeon had just shifted left, and Kalen, Leclan and Raess to the right. Caffran moved his fingers and gestured Leyr and Neskon up behind him.

'We'll go through that way,' he said, pointing to a dingy alley.

Neskon shifted his flamer tanks higher onto his shoulder. 'This is a waste of time.'

'I'll tell you when it's a waste of time,' Caffran advised. 'Now stay sharp.'

The whole place was too enclosed and too dirty to be anything but oppressive. They jumped at shadows, or shrank back from tiny pieces of horror. Bones were common, and so were the daubings and scratchings of the enemy. Glass pots of blood had been left in various locations as offerings, and their contents were starting to putrefy and separate. Not for the first time, Caffran saw evidence of vermin eating vermin. That was a testament, if one was needed, of how low Gereon had slipped. It was so spent and exhausted that the only thing left for the rats to eat was other rats.

They'd gone about ten metres along the narrow alley when the sound of a las-lock boomed to their right and the shouting started. There were several bursts of las fire.

'Report!' Caffran yelled into the link.

'Man down!' Leclan crackled back. 'Hostile came out of hiding. He's coming your way!'

Leyr and Neskon immediately raised their weapons. Caffran ran forwards a little way and looked around. He could hear footsteps echoing in all directions, but the alley walls and the sides of the outbuildings were too steep to see over.

'Get me up!' he said to Leyr.

Leyr cupped his hands and boosted Caffran up a wall. He scrambled onto the roof of an outbuilding, ran along it and leapt onto an adjacent roof. He saw a figure darting along the crookback alleys to his left.

Caffran turned and shouted down to Neskon, 'Fire up the left-hand turn!'

Neskon hurried forwards, nursed his coughing flamer for a moment, and then sent a spear of fire down the left-hand path of the alley junction. The boiling flames filled five metres of alleyway for several seconds. There was a stifled cry. Driven back by the surging flames, the excubitor reappeared, running back the way he'd come.

Standing on the flat roof, legs braced firmly, Caffran fired from the chest. Two shots and the vile figure dropped.

'Hostile is down,' Caffran said. 'Pull this place apart and make sure he was alone.'

CAFFRAN SAT DOWN on a kerbstone and pulled off his left boot. The dust and grit got into everything. He ached. His limbs were sore. The sky over the town was turning to evening and looked like marble.

Nearby, the rest of his section was resting. Leclan was checking the dressing on the grazing wound Kalen had taken from the excubitor.

Caffran leaned back against a wall and closed his eyes. He scooped out the silver aquila he wore on a chain around his neck and said a silent prayer. Two prayers. One for each of them, wherever they were.

'Caff?'

He opened his eyes and looked up. It was Kolea.

'Major?' he said, rising.

'Bask said I'd find you here. Busy afternoon?'

'Yeah. The work of the Emperor never ends.'

'Praise be to that.'

'Can I help you?'

Kolea nodded. He fished something out of his pocket. It was a Tanith cap badge. 'I'll make this simple. I was going to give this to the lad when he finished RIP, and I never got the chance. My mistake. I'd like him to have it.'

Caffran nodded. 'That'd be good.'

Kolea held it out. 'Please, could you give it to him? When you see him?'

'You can do that,' Caffran said.

'I just got this feeling, Caff. Like I'm tempting fate by hoping on this. His fate and mine. All the while I'm hoping I can give him this, I'm daring fate to stop it happening. So here's an end to it. I don't have to think about it any more. If you don't mind?'

Caffran smiled and took the cap badge. 'I don't mind,' he said.

'Thanks.' Kolea managed a smile too. 'Thanks. That's a relief. Feels like it… improves our chances a bit.'

'MAJOR?'

At Baskevyl's call, Rawne left the map tent and hurried over to the entrenchment that the Ghosts had built across the ruins of Cantible's main gate.

'What it it?'

Baskevyl pointed. 'They're here,' he said.

Out across the moors, three black landers were speeding in towards the town, riding low, hugging the rolling terrain in formation.

As they came closer, Rawne could see the insignia on the hull of each one. The stylised 'I' of the Inquisition.

* * *

VIII

THE AIR-MILL smelled of old dust and starch. The slowly turning vanes made a low creaking that came and went with a dying fall. The shadow of the vanes passed over them at each sweep, like clouds across the sun.

Gaunt held off for a second. Mktass and Fiko appeared from around the side of the mill and Fiko nodded. Burone and Posetine held cover from across the dry yard in front of the mill.

Gaunt went inside. Mkoll followed, and then Derin and Nirriam. The floor was well-laid stone, but the structure was wood. The turning gears of the mill system made a painful, heavy rhythm through the floor above, like solid furniture being moved. Violet mould had infested the plasterwork and bleached some of the exposed beams. The place had been stripped, and nothing had been left except for some pieces of sacking and a litter of rope scraps. Mkoll crossed to the turning post of the mill.

'Deliberate,' he said. The mill's vanes weren't just rotating because the wind had picked up. Mkoll pointed to a heavy iron handle that had been thrown to release the bearings. Gaunt nodded, and walked slowly around, looking upwards. Through slots and grooves in the plank flooring, he glimpsed the cobwebbed upper spaces of the mill: shadows and shafts of thin sunlight.

'Check upstairs,' he told Mkoll and Nirriam. He turned to Derin. 'Bring Cirk in.'

'Sir,' said Derin, and ducked out.

'Nothing upstairs,' Mkoll voxed. 'Unless you're interested in seeing more dust.'

'Sweep the nearby buildings,' Gaunt voxed back. 'Whoever set this going can't be long gone. They may be watching us.'

'They're gone,' said Cirk, stepping in through the door. Faragut came in behind her.

'They're gone?' Gaunt asked.

'They wouldn't stay around to be followed or discovered. Far too cautious for that.'

'But this is a sign? A... signal?'

Cirk started looking around. What clues or evidence she was searching for was beyond Gaunt. She had far more experience than he did of the esoteric practices of the Gereon resistance.

'It's got to look accidental so the enemy won't notice it, but it will also be very precise. There–'

She pointed to a part of the floor where several handfuls of rope off-cuts lay in the dust.

'I don't see,' said Gaunt.

'Compare,' she said, raising her pointing finger and aiming it at a part of the mould-covered wall. Random marks had been scratched in the mould. Gaunt would never have noticed it, but now she showed him, he saw that the pattern of scratches matched exactly the pattern of the scattered rope strands.

'They repeat the pattern so we know it's not random,' she said. She crouched down beside the rope strands and began to examine them, turning her head to one side, and then the other. Mkoll and Nirriam returned from the floor above.

'It's a map,' she said at last.

'Of what?' Faragut asked.

'This area, I would imagine, but it's encrypted.'

'Encrypted?' laughed Faragut. 'It's just bits of string...'

'It's encrypted. We're not meant to use all of it. Some of the rope used has a blueish fleck in the weave. The rest has red. Please look around. Can you find more examples of either?'

'Here,' said Mkoll immediately. He indicated the heavy iron handle. There was a short tuft of rope tied around the metal spoke. It had a red fleck to it.

Cirk smiled. She reached down and quickly picked up all the blue-flecked strands and threw them to one side.

'There. The red is all that matters. There's our map.'

'I still don't see...' Faragut began. Gaunt shushed him and took out his pocket book. He quickly copied the lines and shapes down.

'The aspect will be accurate, won't it?' he asked Cirk as he drew.

'I would think so. This is aligned the way it is in the real world.'

Gaunt finished drawing and put his stylus away. He hurried up the creaking wooden steps onto the boarded first floor, and then up a quivering ladder into the second, a dusty loft in the narrower upper part of the structure. Ducking under part of the noisy, rotating vane assembly, he found another ladder and clambered up. Cirk, Mkoll and Faragut were following him.

The third storey was a very cramped space, and there was a real danger of being snagged by the turning wheels, and dragged into the crushing embrace of the mill's machinery. Gaunt poked around cautiously until he located some metal rungs bolted to the wall. The rungs led up to a small trapdoor in the roof.

He climbed out onto the roof. It was a precarious, small space, a rough platform of pitch-treated wood with no guard rail. The air-mill seemed very much taller outside than in. Gaunt had a good head for heights, but he steadied himself. The sloping sides of the mill dropped away, and below them, the roofs of the hamlet, the sides of the hill and the spread of the countryside beyond. He had a commanding view of the area, and that was deliberate. This vantage point was why the resistance had led him to the mill and left the map there.

Cirk and Mkoll clambered out beside him. Both showed no alarm at the height, and moved about casually. The wind was quite considerable now, and buffeted at all three of them. Every few seconds, another of the mill's vanes would swish past like a scything blade, which Gaunt found disconcerting. He took his hurried sketch out of his pocket and tried to align himself.

'About... so?' he asked, holding the map out and orienting his body. Mkoll nodded, and took out his scope. He began to play it over the distances.

The sky was blotchy and very threatening. The thunder that had been grumbling ever closer was now a regular rumble, and the clouds along the western skyline had an underbelly full of hazy, ugly light.

Cirk stood by Gaunt's shoulder, comparing the map lines with the landscape. 'That's the line of the hill, and that's the large escarpment,' she said, her pointing finger moving between map and distance. 'That's the stand of trees to the right, and that's got to be the line of the watercourse.'

Mkoll agreed. He didn't seem to need to look at Gaunt's sketch. The lines of the map were already imprinted on his mind. 'I think the intention is to get us to head north-east. About three kilometres takes us to the edge of that woodland. Whatever is marked by that cross would seem to be about another kilometre further on.'

'Would they expect us to make that by nightfall?' Gaunt asked.

Cirk shook her head. 'I doubt it. The original message told us to be here by tonight.'

'But this fits with our expectations,' Gaunt mused. Mkoll knelt down and slid his copy of the mission chart from his thigh pocket. He unfolded it enough to study the section covering their location. The Departmento Tacticae had produced their charts using orbital scans, supplemented by detailed governance surveys of Gereon held on file by the Administratum.

'Yeah, it does. Untill,' he said, looking up at Gaunt. 'Eszrah will be pleased.'

'I'm sure he will,' Gaunt replied. During his time on Gereon, and thanks to his efforts, the partisans of the Untill had linked with the struggling underground resistance, and the fathomless wastes of the Untill itself had been a vital hiding place. Even the Archenemy found it difficult to penetrate those untillable swamps and marshes. 'So we're really that close?' he asked Mkoll.

'Well, the main tracts of the Untill are two, three hundred kilometres further east, but the limits of it extend out this far. That woodland we can see is the borderland. A day's march beyond it, you get into Sleepwalker territory.'

Mkoll got up and put the chart away. 'What do you think? Stay here overnight, or move–'

He cut off. Gaunt had raised his hand for quiet, and Mkoll knew that sign. Gaunt was staring west, down across the hamlet of Cayfer, down the hillside, onto the rippling pink moorland.

'We're about to have a problem,' he said.

'What?' Cirk asked.

Down below, half a kilometre from the hamlet at the base of the hill, the beast was back.

* * *

IX

GAUNT WAS ABOUT to trigger his link when the vox-net came alive. Three of the troopers left on look out – Larkin, Brostin and Spakus – had spotted the tank and called it in.

'Hold your positions,' Gaunt sent back. 'Keep your eyes on it. Criid, get Gonry front and centre, and for feth's sake, keep him covered and safe.'

'Understood.'

Gaunt, Mkoll and Cirk scurried back down the ladders into the mill.

WITH GONRY RUNNING, head down, behind her, Criid crossed the inner yards of the hamlet and moved down through the derelict outbuildings. A sagging length of old wall fenced the sloping backfield from the rest of the hillside. Larkin was snuggled up there, long las resting on the lip of the wall. He was calmly watching the tank through his scope. Brostin was nearby, smoking a lho-stick as if he was waiting for his discharge papers. His flamer and its tanks lay on the grass next to him.

Brostin was a phlegmatic type. He knew when his area of expertise wasn't going to be called on. A flamer was no weapon to use against armour. Even the 'airburst special', a little party trick he and Larkin had improvised during their previous stay on Gereon, had no application here.

Criid dropped in beside Larkin. Gonry, a scrawny little Belladon, fell over beside her. 'Load that tube,' Criid told him. 'I'll stand by with the spares for cut and come again.' The satchel Gonry was carrying contained five rockets. That was their lot. He nodded to Criid and set to work setting the launcher and slipping the first rocket into place. Gonry was a sweet sort, and she knew he had a little bit of a crush on her. That helped. He did everything she told him as quickly as he could.

'Larks?'

'Just taking the evening air,' he replied.

'What?'

'Not me, lady. The tank,' Larkin snorted. He passed her the scope. 'Take a look.'

She swung up and panned the scope, being careful not to knock it against the wall top. This was Larkin's scope, after all. The master sniper had trusted her with a lend of his precious instrument.

She looked down the hill slope, past two runs of wall and several dead trees, skeletal-white in the changing light. The tank was down in the vale bottom, close to the place where it had played cat and mouse with Gaunt and the others earlier in the day. It was entirely visible to them, but it had decided to go hull-down in the grass, gun lowered, headlamps off. This attitude seemed insouciant to her. Something that big couldn't hide in open landscape, but it seemed to be pretending to do just that, as if all that really mattered was if the wind changed and its prey caught its scent and scattered.

She could hear its idling engine throbbing. No... panting.

'Two fifty metres,' she said, slipping back into cover and giving Larkin back his scope.

'Two sixty-two, with crosswind making the effective range three plus,' Larkin replied.

'Too far for a rocket either way,' Gonry said. 'I wouldn't waste anything over a hundred.'

He was right, but cautious. Criid bridled. 'Caff would smack it at three,' she said. She was boasting, but not much. Caffran was the best rocket lobber in the regiment.

'Caff's not here,' Gonry said. He said it with a smile that made Criid understand that he was happy about that fact.

'More's the fething pity,' she said, letting him know the score. She touched her link. 'Boss? We need to buy a little range to kill that gakker. Permission to sting it?'

'Refused,' Gaunt came back. 'Keep holding.'

'But sir–'

'Tona, that big thing on its topside is a high-calibre cannon. If it decides to start firing, it has the range and force to wipe us out. Don't go taunting it.'

'Understood.'

There was a repeated clicking sound. Larkin, Criid and Gonry looked around.

Brostin was playing with his igniter. 'Feth,' he said blithely, shaking it. 'Anyone got a light?'

GAUNT, CIRK AND MKOLL emerged from the mill.

'Shall I issue orders to retreat?' Faragut asked.

'Retreat?'

'We are overcome by armour,' Faragut said. 'We should withdraw and regroup. For the good of the mission.'

'Throne, you're scared,' Gaunt said, turning from his path to look at the young commissar. He stepped up until they were face to face.

'I'm not. How dare y–'

'Before with Criid, and now… it makes sense. Faragut, how much action have you actually seen?'

'I served on Ancreon Sextus and–'

'Yes, but how much?'

'Sir, I–'

'How much?' Gaunt snarled. 'Nothing? You haven't seen any real combat, have you? Not like this. Not in the thick of it?'

Faragut stared at Gaunt, so angry he was trembling slightly. 'How dare you question my courage, Gaunt.'

Gaunt took a step back. 'Holy Terra, I'm not. That's not what I'm doing. I'm questioning your humanity, Faragut. If this is new to you, tell me! I need to know. It's all right to be scared, but I need to know!'

Hadrian Faragut blinked. 'I… I've not yet… I mean…'

Gaunt took hold of Faragut's upper arm tightly and stared into his eyes. 'Faragut. Get down and get ready. Believe in yourself, and, for the sake of us all, believe in me. I'll keep you alive. Do you believe me?'

'Yes, sir.'

Gaunt slapped him on the upper arm and turned away, running. 'Larks?' he voxed. 'What's it doing?'

THE BEAST HAD been still for a good ten minutes. Dug down in the shuffling grass, it had grumbled its engines and kicked up the occasional spurt of noisy exhaust, as if clearing its throat.

Thunder stomped in the distance, and then a spear of lightning stabbed at a nearby hilltop for one brilliant second.

With an grinding whir, the main gun came up, and then the turret traversed, the raised gun chasing the source of the sudden sound. The turret almost turned back on itself before returning to face front.

The engine revved. Once, twice, three times.

'Feth on a stick,' Larkin whispered.

The yellow headlamps flicked on like eyes opening wide. The beast engaged drive and thundered forwards. It came out of its scrape like a hunting dog, and began to charge up the slope. Black smoke squirted out of its exhaust pipes as it made the surge.

'Here it comes,' Criid said to Gonry. 'You're about to get your range.'

The beast came up the hillside, driving a wake through the long, pink grass. It reached a wall, and the wall went over under its clattering treads.

'I would like to be somewhere else,' Brostin remarked, lighting another smoke.

'Relax,' Criid said. 'Gonry's got the bastard. Haven't you, Gon?'

Gonry hefted the tube up onto his shoulder and grinned at Criid.

The beast came on. The second stone wall collapsed beneath it, and a tree folded over as it was sideswiped by the machine's track guard.

'I think now might be a great time...' Larkin said.

'Almost,' said Gonry, aiming carefully. 'Ease!'

The enemy tank filled his sights. Gonry squeezed the trigger spoon.

Trailing a fat wake of white smoke, the rocket barked off from his launcher and missed the advancing tank entirely. It went off so wild, anyone would have thought Gonry was working for the enemy.

'What the feth was that?' Criid screamed.

'I'm sorry! I'm sorry!' Gonry exclaimed. 'I thought– I wanted– I–'

'Down!' Larkin snapped.

A banging, rattling noise cut the stormy air. The charging tank was firing its hard point cannon.

Gonry reached down for his satchel of rockets and his head vanished. Criid was facing him as it happened, and it seemed like one of Varl's conjuring tricks. A puff of red, and bang, no head. Gonry's headless body slowly fell away and hit the ground.

Something hard hit her in the mouth and also in the right cheek. Criid fell over. Larkin grabbed her and picked her up.

'Was I hit?' she slurred through split and bleeding lips.

'You're all right.' Larkin said. 'You'll live. Skull shrapnel.'

Pieces of Gonry's exploded skull had struck her. She shook her head, grateful that Larkin was holding her upright, and looked down at Gonry. A high-calibre shell had atomised his head and painted blood on everything in a five metre radius.

Dazed, unsteady, she bent down and dragged the tread fether off Gonry's corpse. The strap caught and Larkin had to help her.

'Load me,' she said.

'Tona–'

'Load me!'

Larkin ripped open the satchel and slammed a fresh rocket home in the back of the tube.

'Go!'

She swung it up onto her shoulder.

'Ease!' she yelled.

The beast was just ten metres away, thundering on. Caff had taught her all the tricks. Aim low, because the rocket will lift on its initial burst of propellant. Keep steady, because a tube doesn't aim like a rifle. Aim for seams, like the turret/body seam. Maximise that piercing shell head, and all the spalling you can get.

It was as if he was standing beside her, coaching her.

She fired.

The swishing rocket struck the top of the beast's turret, spun off and exploded in the air.

Criid suddenly forgave Gonry entirely. This wasn't half as easy as it seemed, or as Caffran made it look.

'Load me!'

'Feth, Tona!' Larkin replied. 'I want to be running. Bros has the right idea.'

Criid looked around. Brostin, tanks slung over his wide shoulders, was thumping up the hill into the hamlet.

'Just load me!' she said.

Larkin slotted another shell into the tube.

'Ease!'

Criid fired. A wide blossom of hot fire ripped across the beast's hull. It jerked to a halt. Flames rippled and flickered off its bodywork. A strange, mewling, sobbing sound came up from its engines. It began to roll backwards.

Then its main gun fired. The first shell it lobbed went right over Cayfer. The second hit the top of the mill and disintegrated it. The spinning vanes tore out of the structure and crashed down into the yard, turning and fragmenting as they rolled like a giant wheel into the outbuildings. The third round blew out the lower stages of the mill tower.

Wounded, hurt, the beast sat back and fired on the hamlet of Cayfer until it was reduced to smoking rubble.

X

IN THE DISTANCE behind them, in the failing daylight, the beast's gun was demolishing Cayfer. Gaunt's section scurried away through the grasslands towards the woods.

As they closed on their destination, they saw how scabby and thin the trees were. Poisons had stunted the wood. The Ghosts advanced, spread wide and moving slow, into a wasteland of parched, twisted trees and invader grass.

Behind them, a bright fire lit the encroaching night as the hamlet died.

The daylight was really fading when they reached the rendezvous point. They waited for an hour, and suddenly Mkoll rose, his gun aimed.

Two figures detached themselves from the enclosing darkness and came forward. They were thin, scrawny, dressed in rags, bearing las weapons strapped together with tape and cord.

'Gaunt,' Gaunt said. 'Daystar?'

The men stopped and stared at him. They lowered their rifles.

'My name is Dacre,' said one, extending his hand.

Gaunt took it. He could feel the bones. He could feel how thin it was.

'Gereon resists.'

'Just about,' said Dacre. 'Is this really it?'

'Yes,' said Gaunt.

Dacre nodded, and other figures emerged from the shadows. Some of them were Sleepwalkers.

Eszrah stepped forwards to greet them eagerly. They pulled back, reluctant.

'Unkynde,' announced one of them. Gaunt winced.

'Follow us,' Dacre said. 'There's something you have to see.'

In silence, the section followed Dacre for two hours through the dimming woodland. Behind them, thunder rumbled and the funeral pyre of Cayfer lit the sky.

They entered a dark tract of woodland. The trees there were especially bent and deformed. Dead leaves covered the dark ground.

'I was told you should see this,' Dacre said simply.

'Told by whom?' Gaunt asked.

Dacre didn't answer. He was pointing towards a cairn of rocks.

Gaunt stepped towards it. Mkoll was beside him.

The stones had been piled up in a makeshift manner, but the purpose was clear, even in the dying light. It was a tomb, a barrow for the fallen.

'Oh, great Throne above me,' Mkoll whispered.

He had seen the inscription. It was cut into a block in the middle of the heap.

'Feth,' Gaunt murmured as he read what Mkoll had seen.

The inscription was simple.

MkVenner.

GRINDER

I

'The thing is about nightmares,' Fourbox said, 'the thing is, is that they end. Sooner or later, eventually, they end. But this doesn't, you see? So I don't see how you can keep saying this is a nightmare, because it's nothing like a nightmare. When you wake up from a nightmare, the nightmare's over, and there's a whole rush of relief, but not here. There's no relief here. It's just non-stop.'

'Perhaps we haven't woken up yet,' said Lovely.

Fourbox seized on this. 'Now that's a good point!' he exclaimed. He was almost, as if this was possible, cheery. 'Maybe we haven't. Maybe the waking up is yet to happen.'

Dalin was pretty convinced he knew what was yet to happen. The river of meat was going to strike the wall of iron for the third time in ten hours. Something would give. If the last two occasions were anything to go by, it would be the meat.

'Perhaps we haven't…' Fourbox said, significantly. War changed men, so it was said. It had changed Fourbox into a philosopher, just not a terribly good one. Dalin wanted to tell him, frankly, what an idiot he was, but his voice was wedged up inside him like a jammed round, unable to clear.

The thing about nightmares, in Dalin's opinion, was neither the unpleasantness nor the relief of waking, though both were component parts. The thing about nightmares for him were the tiny, little bits of surreal or mundane nonsense that laced through them and rendered the horror all the more horrible. He'd once had a nightmare where he and his sister were being chased by a chair that was going to eat them. He'd been very young at the time, and very scared of the chair and its shuffling legs. But what had made the nightmare truly terrifying was that, all the way through, Aleksa, a

nice woman from the followers on the strength who looked after them
sometimes, kept appearing, smiling, and asking, 'Have you tied your
shoelaces?' She'd had a drowsy, fidgeting hen tucked under her right arm.

If his current situation could be properly called a nightmare, the elements
were certainly in place. They were assaulting the giant bulwark in the company
of hundreds of thousands of Guardsmen. They were moving forwards, under
a sky of flame, under increasing fire, in a flood of bodies, across the bridges and
up the trench approaches, towards the gates. They were running, without cover,
into death, with only the flimsy odds of their great numbers to protect them.

Fourbox, all the while, was having a conversation about whether or not
the circumstances were like a nightmare.

On the first two assaults at the mighty bulwark, AT 137 hadn't even come
close to the front of the charge. Carried along in the midst of the press, they
had surged towards the gateways and then been drawn back by the tidal
retreat. Many of the dead came back with them, held upright by the density
of bodies, and only falling, hundreds of metres from where they had died,
once the pressure eased and the spacing increased.

The great surge was building momentum to rush forwards for the third
time. They were beginning to press together. A tangle of shouts rose from
the moving troops and became one loud, commingled howl.

The whole scene was lit by flames. As they came out onto one of the great
bridges, Dalin saw the thousands of faces around him tinged with gold, and
down below them, another wide bridge crossing at a deeper level, streaming with golden faces. Other bridges stood to his left and right, heaving with
moving troops. Far beneath, in the approach trenches, thousands more. Aircraft and lancing rockets swept in over his head, jewelled with light.

The bulwark wall rose up hundreds of metres above them. Its flamer towers were the main source of the blazing orange light, but the wall was dotted
with gunloops and emplacements that were crackling with gunfire. It looked
as if the giant wall was ablaze in a million places, but it was the fire that the
wall was sending at them. Blue and white las-bolts showered like sparks.
Tracer fire wound and clung like climbing ivy. Shells airburst in flowers of
smoke that trailed fingers of burning debris beneath them like the strings of
jellyfish. The exhaust trails of rockets left arcs from ground to wall, or wall
to ground, each lingering trace describing some aspiration of ascent, like the
diagram of a proposed attack drawn in smoke. The great structure of the
wall itself glowed amber, and looked as if its heavy battlements and bas-
relief emblems had been plated in copper and bronze.

A nightmare was something you woke up from, but this was a horror he
was waking up to. Every minute since the drop-ship had launched had been
a minute too long, every horror a horror too much, every effort an effort too
far. This, this senseless mass effort to dash bodies against a solid wall, over
and over again, exceeded everything.

He heard Sobile shouting, 'Forwards!'

Sobile said it as if it were obvious, as if there was no choice. Logic
screamed that forwards was the last way they should be going.

* * *

II

SHOTS SEARED DOWN into their ranks almost vertically from high above. Teaser died. So did Bugears and Trask. Mumbles caught fire, became a screaming torch, and ignited the men around him in his thrashing despair. A Binar close beside Dalin had the top two-thirds of his head demolished, right down to the lower lip and jaw, and then stayed beside him, lolling back and forth, propped up by the crush around them. Ledderman died slowly, shot twice, unable to drop back. Boots, and then Frisky, both disappeared under foot. Corporal Traben was hit in the eye and died with smoke coming out of his half-open mouth.

The great gates were looming ahead, as heavy and immovable as a dwarf star. The front of the streaming charge was striking them, breaking around them like a wave against a quayside. Cascades of fire poured down from upper crenellations: wide, spattering torrents of burning promethium.

The Guardsmen were struggling uphill. They were stumbling and struggling up a ramp that was built out of corpses. Its steep slope, stacked against the gates by those that had come before and died already. It was so ridiculous, that Dalin wanted to scream and laugh. This was not the proud warfare his parents had raised him to admire and expect. This was nonsensical behaviour, quite without merit or point. Dalin felt a huge hatred for Sobile, in as much as Sobile embodied the insane Guard mindset that had brought them all to this astonishing futility. *Climb a mountain of bodies under heavy fire to a dead end.*

Why would we do that, sir?

Because the Emperor tells you to.

Dalin's foot slipped on a leg or an arm. He clawed at those jostling around him to stay upright, as they in turn clawed at him. Clothing tore. Bruises overlaid bruises which overlaid bruises. Elbows and gunstocks and knees and helmet rims knocked into him. There was a stink of fear-sweat, bile-breath, dirt and offal, and ordure.

Because the Emperor tells you to.

Dalin wondered, in a moment of sacrilegious epiphany, if he was the first Guardsman ever to wish the God-Emperor dead. It wasn't Sobile he felt hatred for, or the commanders, it was the lord above all others that they served. He wanted to kill the Emperor for this. He wanted to slay the God-Emperor for driving humanity out across this bloodstained galaxy.

It was a liberating thought. Pain and fear helped him to slough off a lifetime of loyalty and conditioning, and think the unthinkable. War had carried him past the end of all that was rational and showed him the empty imbecility of the stars.

Unless...

Dalin slipped, and rose again, and slipped once more.

Unless...

Unless he'd been made to think that way by this place. Perhaps it was no epiphany, but rather the malign touch of the Ruinous Powers. He had been steeped in Gereon's taint for some time. Perhaps he had been led astray.

The idea made him gag in self-doubt and revulsion. Out loud – though no one could hear him over the outrage of war – he begged and prayed to be forgiven. The pain and the anger of his ordeal had made him wish harm on the God-Emperor, nothing more! A moment's weakness, not a taint. Not a taint. Please, Golden Throne, not a taint!

He threw himself forwards, galvanised by some overriding impulse to purge himself and prove his loyalty.

'The Emperor protects! The Emperor protects!' Dalin yelled at the churning bodies packed in around him. The man beside him smiled, and seemed to agree, but the man beside him had no arms nor any back to his head.

Dalin turned, looking back across the faces, trying to see anyone from his unit. He glimpsed Fourbox, Ganiel, and Trenchfoot, although Trenchfoot was gone a second later in a flash of light. He saw Lovely and several others, further back, swept close to the side of the bridge.

'Come on! Forwards! Forwards!' he yelled.

A rocket or mortar bomb from the wall above hit the side of the bridge, shaking the entire structure. The limbs of some unfortunates caught directly in the blast flew through the air. A large section of the bridge's guard wall collapsed, taking part of the roadway with it. Dozens of Guardsmen fell into space, tumbling down amongst burning fragments of stone. Dalin saw some land on the bustling bridge below, or rebound brokenly off that bridge's rail and continue down into the abyss of the trench.

The pressure of bodies forced those on the outside off the side like a leak in a hose. Some tried to stop themselves falling by grabbing the troopers beside them. As the bridge crumbled further, groups of figures, clinging together, fell away, the first to fall dragging the last. Dalin saw Lovely. She was screaming, reaching out to grab someone or something as she was dragged backwards by the frantic hands of those behind her.

He lost sight of her in the smoke, and never saw her again.

The press of the charge wrenched him forwards again, close into the killing zone of the gates where the flamers swept and washed, and the las-bolts fell like torrential rain.

The world went white.

III

SOUND RETURNED FIRST. A voice was yelling above a background world of noise. Then light and colour came back to him too.

'Get up and get forwards! Get up and get forwards, dogs! You morons! Get up and fight on in the Emperor's name!'

Commissar Sobile was bellowing at the top of his lungs, his face flushed, his neck thick with veins, phlegm specking the corners of his mouth.

'Get up, you laggards! You wastrels! Fight on! Get up and repay the God-Emperor what you owe Him! Fight on!'

Dalin heard the lash crack. He got up, his head swimming, one of several men struggling to their feet from a smoking slope of dead and injured. He glanced around, unable to concentrate, unable to focus. What was different? What was–

They were inside the gate.

The immense bulk of the wall rose up over him, but the gates themselves had gone. What great force or accident had destroyed them, he had no idea. The impact had surely cast him down, and scattered his senses. The gates had fallen and, with them gone, the awful spoil heap of bodies that had built up against them had been released, and had gone tumbling and sliding forwards into the gatehouse like water from a broken dam, carrying the injured and unconscious alike with it. Dead men had borne him into the heart of K'ethdrac'att Shet Magir.

Storm parties of Guardsmen, most of them Krassian, were pouring in over the slumped heap of the dead. Dalin checked the load of his lasrifle and began to move ahead with them. Someone grabbed him by the arm.

'Fix your blade, scalp!' Kexie snarled at him, before releasing Dalin's arm and rushing on. 'Fix blades! Fix blades!'

Dalin drew his combat blade and attached it to the bayonet lug of his lasrifle. He ran forward with the rest. Visibility was hazy in the gatehouse, but greater radiance beckoned ahead of them.

They were running as they came out into the open. Some men were yelling unintelligible war cries. They burst from the smoky gloom onto a vast public square overlooked by threatening towers and skeletal steeples. The enemy awaited them in force.

Momentum carried him forwards, moving with the pack, but suddenly there were impacts all around: heavy, meaty thumps as men ran into obstacles. Bodies crashed into bodies as the charging Imperial line met with the surging rows of the enemy. Men tumbled and fell, slammed clean off their feet, crunched into the air by body-to-body blows. There were grunts and exhalations of effort, and grunts of pain. Shots fired, point blank, and, one by one, the men in the assaulting tide were halted by jarring collisions and crippling bodychecks. Shields and body-armour met. Bayonets jabbed and trench axes flashed. Dalin slammed into a figure in green, and punctured it with his bayonet, and the pressure of bodies behind him pushed him on. His bayonet tore free, and the enemy soldier disappeared underneath him. He was immediately into the next one.

More jarring impacts. Near to Dalin, a man was struck so hard that his helmet flew into the air. Sprays of arterial blood feathered across their faces. Dalin was shoved face to face with some feral thing with augmetics plugging its eyes and mouth. Yelling, he lunged with his blade, and fired for good measure. The thing fell backwards and then was knocked limply forwards into Dalin again by the swell of the mob. The Krassian beside him cried out as a bayonet slashed his arm guard. The man's own bayonet was lodged in the chest armour of the enemy soldier facing him, a diseased wretch in decaying black wargear. Dalin desperately hooked round with his own weapon, tearing out the enemy soldier's throat with the tip of his bayonet. The Krassian grinned at Dalin in gratitude. Ten seconds later, a bullet from somewhere had felled the Krassian with a solid *www-spakk!*

Dalin felt adrift in the stormy sea of bodies. Above their heads, out over the seething mass, banners and flags swayed and flourished. las-rounds zipped. Half a kilometre away, one of the other huge gateways on the bulwark trembled and blew out in a gargantuan sheet of flame. From the raging fire, through the breach, a Titan strode forwards, its armour scorched black by the fireball. A vast cheer went up from the men.

The tide moved forwards with renewed vigour. The resistance ahead gave way, and they advanced with greater speed, free to move apart and spread out, free to find breathing space. The flagstones underfoot were cracked by weight and impact, and stained brown with blood. Bodies lay everywhere, amongst a litter of debris and pieces of equipment.

Dalin ran. He found an enemy trooper in his path, a man with copper armour plates on his green cloth battledress. Dalin charged into him, and they grappled. Dalin swung the butt of his rifle up, brought the man to his knees, and delivered the death stroke with his bayonet.

Raising his weapon, he saw another man running at him with a sword. He fired two shots from the hip, and the man turned around as he fell, spun by torque. Small explosions blew stones and grit into the air nearby. He met another warrior face to face, and they locked bayonets. The enemy, a grotesque mutant beast with sunken features, screeched at him as it struggled. Dalin couldn't wrest his blade free. A passing bolter round blew out the warrior's midriff, and Dalin tore clear.

As far as he could see, the Guard was engaging hand-to-hand in furious skirmish fights right across the city square. The enemy warriors they were fighting were things he would spend the rest of his life trying to forget: bizarre things, some armoured and ugly and brutal, some strange and almost beautiful in their weird forms. Some seemed diseased, and so dependent upon their armour and augmetics that they were fused, flesh and metal, into one whole. Others were resplendent in bright wargear, flying banners from long spears on which the ignominy of Chaos was spelled out.

An entire catalogue of corruption, decay, mortification, mutation, mutilation and decoration was on display. The Archenemy faced mankind's assault armed with lasweapons, cleavers, autoguns, swords, talons and teeth. Dalin saw a man with a festoon of thin, barbed tentacles billowing from his open mouth. He saw a cyclops woman with a single jagged tooth curving down over her deformed lip. He saw bat-faced things, wailing and chirruping as they hacked with chain blades. He saw horned ogres, and men with the backwards legs of giant birds. He saw gleaming black flesh like sharkskin; bone fingernails worn on engraved metal hands; slitted eyes the colour of embers; grossly distended, encephalitic heads supported on sagging shoulders; cloaks of beaded, winking eyes; secondary faces blinking and mewling through gaps in garments and cloaks.

Shells landed with a woosh of fractured air and Dalin ducked instinctively. Heavy rounds fell across the square, hurling bodies off the ground in explosive swirls.

'Holy!'

Fourbox appeared. He had been drenched in blood and then dusted with fine stone powder.

'You're alive!' Fourbox cried, as if telling Dalin something he didn't know. 'We've got to move!' he cried, over the din. 'The armour's coming!'

The wide body of Guardsmen pouring into the square was parting and separating. Snorting plumes of smoke, Imperial tanks clattered forward from the sundered gates, firing their raised main weapons up into the towers and spires of the malevolent city. The first tanks were Leman Russes of the Rothberg division, puzzle-painted in beige and brown scales. Soot and dust jumped off their hulls every time they fired their main guns. Guardsmen ran along beside them, cheering and whooping at every tank round shot off.

The skirts of the city ahead were burning. Incendiary shells had created blistering firestorms that wrapped up the nearest towers and gutted their structures. The assaulting tanks moved out ahead of the expanding infantry line.

One tank rolled right past Fourbox and Dalin. They cheered as if it was a passing carnival float.

'Come on,' Dalin said, and they ran along behind it, joining others following the armour in. When its main gun fired, the sound was so loud and close that it made them all jump and then laugh. Dalin saw the mangled corpse of a commissar laying on the rubble. He wondered if it was Sobile. He hoped it was.

'Look!' he said to Fourbox. Nearby, the bodies of several Krassians lay around their fallen banner, a tattered aquila on a cross-spar square.

'Help me!' Dalin said, running towards it. Fourbox followed, along with two Krassian privates from the mob following the tank.

Together, they gathered the banner up and raised it. It took a moment to straighten the main flag and make it hang properly. Then they hustled it back to the file of men jogging after the tank. More cheers went up. The tank up ahead sounded its horn.

The smoke wafting in from the towers was getting thicker, draping across the square like a fog. Dalin suddenly spotted Merrt amongst the advancing lines.

'You made it!'

Merrt nodded and moved in to join them. His fight up from the gatehouse had been tough. The lasrifle he had ended up with, having swapped with Dalin, was poor: an unreliable old unit marked with a half-faded yellow Munitorum stencil on the butt. It had misfired twice, and each time that had almost got him killed. It was in poor condition, mechanically, and Merrt had a nasty feeling it was an old weapon recaptured from the enemy.

With Merrt were Amasec, Spader, Effort and Wash, four other members of AT 137. All of them were in a dirty, dishevelled state. Then Pinzer, the company pardoner, appeared. Dalin had assumed he'd been killed hours before. Pinzer held a laspistol in one hand and an open prayer book in the other, reading aloud as he walked along. The members of AT 137 cheered him as if he was a long lost relative. Pinzer looked up vaguely, but didn't seem to recognise them.

Wash spat on the ground and made the sign of the aquila. He'd seen something else. He nodded across the square.

Amid the advancing Guard ranks, Dalin could see gnarled dark figures coming forwards. Some were clad in stormcoats, and walked with the aid of long staffs. Others were bent, hunched forms in shackles who waddled along, linked to pairs of Commissariat guards by chain leads.

High Command had sent the sanctioned psykers forwards.

'Filthy bloody things,' Wash said, and spat again.

Dalin peered at the distant figures curiously. The daylight, admittedly sheened with smoke and dust, seemed especially murky around them, as if the air had been stained brown like the fingers of an old lho smoker. There was a slight flicker to the walking figures too, so they looked like an old pict recording, running slightly fast, with jerks and jumps on the file.

He felt his skin crawl, and imagined powerful, inhuman minds glaring at him, glaring at them all, and seeing inside them. He wondered how the psykers perceived the world. Were they looking into his mind? Where they seeing through his flesh to his weary bones? Did they even notice him?

Could they see into his head and read how scared he was of them?

He felt a touch, like light fingertips on his skin, and he jumped, and then reassured himself that it was his own imagination.

The sound of a fierce blow came out of the smoke ahead of them. The sound had been very loud, and expressed some considerable collision, like a wrecking ball striking a blast hatch. It was followed immediately by an impact that quaked the ground, and then by a long, drawn-out shrieking, scraping sound of metal on stone that grew louder.

A Leman Russ tank appeared out of the smoke. It was one of the Rothberg units, in beige and brown, part of the vanguard that had plunged ahead into the burning city.

It was half overturned, turret towards them and tracks away from them. The uppermost track section had been broken, and the loose tread segments trailed down like a lizard's loose scales. The hull armour on the raised flank was deeply dented, by some colossal force.

Sparks and scraping squeals came out from under it. On its side, the tank was sliding across the flagstones towards them.

IV

SEDATELY, ITS HULL still grinding on the ground, the tank slid past them and the Leman Russ they were following, and slowed to a halt. As it stopped, two heavy tread sections fell lumpenly onto the ground. There was almost a moment of silence.

'What in the name of hell could–' Fourbox started to say.

There was something in the smoke, something that had met the tank and struck it such a blow that it had knocked it over and sent it sliding across the square. The something was tall, the height of a two-storey hab, and it was barely moving. They could see it in the smoke, a grey shadow in the paler cloud. They saw it take a single, slow step. They heard a long, wet, rasping purr.

The advancing infantry lines had stopped. Banners flapping in the wind, they were staring at the bank of smoke and shadow inside it. The tanks had stopped too.

Another deep, wet purr came out of the smoke.

Along the line, officers and commissars were shouting orders and encouragement.

'Present your weapons! Firing ranks!'

'Hold order, hold order!'

An officer that Dalin didn't know ran past them down the line. 'Steady guns! Two files!'

'What is it?' Wash murmured. 'What is it?'

The shadow moved again. It began to have a form. Dalin almost swallowed his tongue in terror as he gazed up at the two giant horns that topped the wedge-shaped skull. A vast cloven hoof clopped the flagstones as it took a step. There was a stench of burned sugar and volcanic gas, thunderstorms and shit.

'Daemon...' said the pardoner, looking up. 'D-daemon...'

Several men fainted. The Guard line broke and fled like a stampede of timid veldt grazers. Voices suddenly rose in a hubbub as men turned and scrambled for their lives. Banners fell, forgotten. Commissars yelled and threatened, and were knocked down. Hatches clanged open and tank crews leapt out, abandoning their vehicles in an effort to flee with the rest.

The daemon came for them. Though he stared, and was one of the last to run, Dalin didn't really see it. He glimpsed the tusk-like horns, the massive, quasi-humanoid shape, the back-jointed legs, and a mouth full of ragged teeth inside a mouth full of ragged teeth inside a gaping, fang-fringed maw. He glimpsed the round, black, glossy eyes.

He wanted to see the daemon. He wanted to steel himself and witness his greatest fear made flesh, and bear the sight and be stronger for it, or die. But the daemon possessed a quality beyond all those enumerated in the Ecclesiarchy's texts and warning sermons.

It was fast.

Its speed was as unnatural as all of its other ghastly aspects. It was not fast like a man or animal might be fast. When it moved, reality folded around it and allowed it to pass from place to place in an eye-blink. There was a sound like screaming, gale-force winds. Dozens of fleeing Guardsmen were suddenly hurled upwards into the air, as if thrown aside by a violent wake. The crew had only just abandoned the tank in front of Dalin when it flipped up sharply into the sky like a toy, turned over, and came crashing down thirty metres away with an impact that jarred Dalin off his feet.

He struggled onto his hands and knees. Dismembered dead lay everywhere. Bodies, stripped and flayed in a second of fury, sprawled in lakes of blood. Dalin screamed in helpless rage and terror. Wash sat on the ground near to him, hands in his lap, weeping and sobbing. Fourbox was still standing behind them, staring at the place where the tank had been. Pinzer wandered past. Dalin looked up at the pardoner. The man was gazing at the crumbling Imperial lines around them, at the great, horned blur of smoke and stinking air that ripped through them, casting bodies into the sky.

Pinzer looked away. He turned his back on the slaughter and sat down on the ground beside Dalin. His prayer book fell from his hand and landed on the gritty flagstones.

'There's no ham here,' he said quickly, his voice thin and perplexed. 'None at all. I checked. Bad eggs. You ran too fast for me to count. Preposition.'

'What?' asked Dalin.

Pinzer put his pistol in his mouth and pulled the trigger. His body flopped back from the waist onto the ground.

'Get up!'

Dalin turned. 'Get up!' Merrt told him. He looked at Wash. 'Get him on his feet.'

'We're all dead!' Wash moaned through his sobs.

A flicker of light caught the corner of Dalin's vision. It made his teeth itch, and he felt a nasty liquid pulse in his gut. He thought he was going to lose control of his bowels. Fourbox felt it too, and Merrt. The sensation made Wash, hard man Wash, squeal like a girl.

'What was that?' Fourbox complained, apparently unaware or unwilling to acknowledge the full extent of what was happening.

'The psyks,' growled Merrt. 'They've engaged the gn... gn... that fething thing.'

They could all feel it, like someone was squeezing their internal organs. Wash dry-heaved. Tears streamed down all their cheeks, unbidden. Dalin felt the mother of all headaches gnawing at him, and tasted the iron tang of blood in his mouth. All the cuts and gashes he had taken since landing spontaneously reopened.

Filthy yellow light spread out across the vast, disputed city square. The haze was like a rainstorm vapour, and obscured the bulwark and the distant skyline. Forking traceries of energy lit up the frothing darkness like veins. Some of the larger flagstones under their feet spontaneously cracked, as if exposed to cosmically low temperatures.

Merrt put a hand to the side of his head. 'Let's move,' he said. 'Let's move before it kills us.'

V

FOR TWO HOURS, some form of combat rolled around the darkened square. A foul mist, busy with flies, breathed into the side streets, and screams echoed from the noisome dark. There were strange, inexplicable crashes and thumps.

The streets nearby were burning. Some Guardsmen from the advancing line had fled forward into the ruins, and this had probably saved them, from the daemon and the telepathic conflict at least.

Dalin, Merrt, Fourbox and Wash fled that way. Two Krassians, one called Firik, the other Bonbort, ran with them. Firik had lost his left hand. He either didn't know how he'd lost it, or was too traumatised to remember. Merrt bound up the stump, and Firik sat alone, making little gagging sobs of pain every now and then.

They had taken shelter in the bombed-out shell of a building. Nearby, one of the grotesque city towers, a monstrous thing of spiked architecture and insectile buttresses, burned, long into the night.

They sat in silence in the flickering shadows, flinching at every howl or crash. They were too tired and numb to speak. Fourbox took out a ration pack, but his fingers were too stiff and trembling to tear it open. Merrt seemed content to sit and check his weapon, examining it carefully as if trying to correct some fault with the foresight.

Dalin sat still for as long as he could, knowing he needed the rest, but there was a ticking impatience inside him. They weren't out of this, and every step seemed, triumphantly and incredibly, to be worse than the last. He got up and paced the ruin, peering out of the broken windows. The street to one side was full of dead enemy vehicles that looked as if they had been burned out in one flash firestorm while in procession. White ash covered their hulls like snow.

'Eat something.'

He glanced around and saw Merrt. He shook his head.

'You need food,' Merrt said. 'It's a miracle any of us are still functioning after the last few hours. Lack of food's the last thing you're noticing right now, but you're gn... gn... gonna know it when the crash comes. Eat something and you might stay useful for a little while longer.'

Dalin took a ration pack out and picked at it. Merrt helped Fourbox to tear open his pack, and then gave the others the same advice.

Sucking reconstituted broth through a straw, Merrt rejoined Dalin.

'Worst thing you've ever seen, right?'

Dalin wondered which particular aspect of the last day Merrt was referring to. He simply nodded.

'Actually, there was a chair once,' Dalin said.

'What?'

'I had a nightmare when I was a kid,' Dalin said. 'Me and my sister were being chased by a chair that was going to eat us. Aleksa from the strength was there, with a chicken under her arm, asking me if I'd tied my bootlaces.'

Merrt raised his eyebrows. 'Why'd you tell me that?'

Dalin shrugged. 'Because I honestly can't think of a single fething subject for sane conversation just at the moment.'

'That's the truth,' Merrt agreed, and turned to look out at the ash-covered street. 'Probably symbolic,' he said.

'What?'

'Your dream.'

'How so?'

Merrt glanced back at Dalin. 'A chair? That's gn... gn... got to be a symbol, right? Of the Imperium. The Throne. No matter how hard you try to prolong it, sooner or later the Imperium's going to eat you and your sister up, like it eats everyone up. The Imperium gn... gn... gets us all in the end. It consumes us all.'

Dalin frowned. 'If you say so. What about Aleksa and the hen?'

'That part's the Imperium too. Feeding you and clothing you and looking out for you for as long as it can.'

'Does everything in your scheme of interpretation represent the Imperium?' Dalin asked.

'Usually,' said Merrt. 'The Imperium or sex. It makes it easier.'

'You have no idea what you're talking about, have you?' Dalin smiled.

'Not a single fething notion.'

They both ducked back from the window as someone, just a dark ragged shadow, ran up the street and vanished into the ruins at the top of the road.

'You know,' said Dalin., 'I can't believe I've spent my entire life wishing to be here.'

Merrt snorted.

'So, you going to tell me?' Dalin asked, looking around.

'What?'

'We know how I wound up here. I was so gakking desperate to be a Ghost. What about you? Don't give me some shit answer this time.'

'Because I was stupid, and desperate,' Merrt said quietly, 'because I had it all and it was taken from me and I wanted it back. Oh, and there was a girl involved.'

He turned to face Dalin. 'Look at me,' he said. 'Take a good luck. I was a gn... gn... good looking bastard once. Maybe not a stud like some, but I did all right. Plus, I had that eye on me! Marksman's lanyard. That was something. Then I got the wound.'

He looked away. 'Took my face off. Took my voice. Took my skill away. I got a shake in the hand I can't steady, and I just can't settle to aim with this jaw. I ended up at the bottom of life.'

Dalin wasn't sure what to say.

'A drink helped. No girl'd go near me, though. I worked out that if I could maybe get my hands on some cash, I could fix things. Not completely, you know, but make them better. Gn... gn... get a better prosthetic than this furnace box. Maybe a graft. On the hive worlds, they say you can buy a whole new you, if you've got the cash.'

'They do say that,' Dalin agreed.

'But where was I going to get cash? Earn it? No, sir. Steal it? I'm no crook. Only way I could think was to win it. So I started to play the tables.'

'Yeah?'

Merrt made a sound that Dalin realised was a laugh. 'Turned out I had the same sort of luck there. I've played the tables for years, lost much more than I've won. Sooner or later, that swallows you up.'

'What happened?'

'I got in over my head. Got caught in a fight. The commissar saved my life–'

'Gaunt?'

'No, I mean Hark. He saved my life, the merit of which is debatable. But I got a charge. Gambling, affray, disreputable conduct. Six weeks RIP. That's how I got here.'

Dalin nodded.

'Didn't you see where you were going?' he asked after a while.

'You see where we're gn… gn… going now?' Merrt asked.

'No.'

'But you know how bad it's going to be, don't you?'

Dalin nodded.

'And you can't stop it. That's how it was for me. Oh, and there was a gn… gn… girl.'

'A girl?'

'She worked in the gambling parlour I used. A place on the swelter decks. Her name was Sarat. Prettiest thing. Since I took the wound, I've looked at girls, of course, but she was the only one ever looked back at me. This face didn't scare her. She'd talk to me, and see how I was doing. We weren't together, you understand. She was just… I don't know, maybe she was doing her job. Pavver paid them to act nice to the gn… gn… punters. She seemed genuine. Got so I'd go there as much to see her as play cards. I started thinking I could make that big killing, raise the cash to get my face fixed up, and she'd–'

He shrugged. 'That's where I thought I was going. Somewhere where I'd have the guts to ask her to be mine, and she wouldn't laugh at my face.'

VI

A FEW HOURS later, night ended and day crept out.

They'd lost all track of time. Since the psyk-flare on the city square, their chrons had been dead or spinning wildly. They couldn't tell if it was real dawn, or just a change in the wind, clearing the smoke-cover that had been making the world nocturnal.

Dalin had been hoping for light. Wishing for light. Light would make things better.

It didn't. It just made things different.

The night, real or artificial, had been hard to bear. After the noises in the dark, there had been laughter, high and manic, that had come and gone like the wind in the eaves, and echoed out of empty stairwells and broken plumbing. More than once, they heard shuffling in the street and found no one there. No one visible.

Bonbort, one of the Krassians, ran off in the night. No one saw him go. No one knew why he ran.

The light, when it came, was white and flat. It made the sky over the city appear to hang low, like the ceiling of a theatre not yet dressed with a scene. The light was as thick and lazy as it was colourless. There was a fogginess to the visibility at street level. White dust and ash lay everywhere and, once a breeze had picked up, the dust began to mist the air like smoke.

Dalin and Merrt went outside. The war was still raging, because they could hear its roar, blunt and muffled, from all directions. Fat pillars of black smoke rose into the sky over the rooftops from parts of the inner city still ablaze.

There was a smell in the air of spun sugar.

They ate a little more and drank the last of their water. Firik, the other Krassian, was running a fever from the infections that had set into his amputation. There was nothing they could do to help him.

When they heard whistles blowing in the nearby streets, they gathered Firik with them and moved out. Within a few minutes, they had found a column of Krassians moving up through the fire-blackened streets, collecting up the infantry remnants they encountered. The Krassians took Firik into their care. The officer could tell Dalin and the rest little of what was going on. They'd just been sent into the area to retake control.

The four of them trudged on through the ashy city. Sporadic gunfire coughed and chattered from nearby streets. They found a crashed Imperial Thunderbolt, its matted, crumbled fuselage embedded at the end of a long gouge in the ground. It had died with one wing raised to the sky, like a swimmer breaking the water with a stroking arm.

Then they found Hamir. They didn't know it was Hamir at first. They saw a lone figure in filthy battledress wandering along an empty street, looking up at the flakes of ash floating from the eaves like snowfall.

Wash raised his lasrifle at once, and so did Merrt, but Fourbox suddenly said, 'It's Scholam! Look, it's Scholam!'

Wash frowned. Dalin saw that Merrt was still ready to fire and knocked his gun muzzle aside. Merrt blinked and looked at him.

'What?'

'You nearly shot him!'

'I didn't. Gn. I…' Merrt looked down at the old rifle in his dirty hands, his brow furrowed.

Hamir heard them shout and stopped walking. He stared at them as they jogged to him. A dusting of white ash had settled on his shoulders and scalp like icing sugar.

'Hamir!' Dalin called as he came up to him.

Hamir smiled slightly, but acted dazed. He kept blinking as if he was having trouble focusing.

'Holy,' he said. 'Holy. There you are. Oh, that's good. Fourbox too.'

'How did you get here?' Merrt asked him.

Hamir sniffed and thought about it. He turned around, hesitated, and then turned back again. He put a grubby finger to his lips pensively.

'I don't– I don't remember. I don't remember which way–' Hamir glanced about again. 'The streets look the same. They all look the same.'

Dalin peered at Hamir. There was a crust of dried blood behind his right ear, below an ugly dent in the rim of his helmet. Hamir kept blinking. One of his pupils was a pinprick, the other dilated and black. Dalin wondered if he should take Hamir's helmet off. He decided he really didn't want to.

'Sobile sent me,' Hamir said suddenly.

'That bastard?' growled Wash.

'Sobile sent me,' Hamir repeated.

'Where is he?' asked Merrt.

'He'd gathered up some of the section. With the sergeant. He'd gathered up some of the section, what was left of the section, what he could find of the section–'

'Hamir? Where is he?' Dalin asked.

'Close by,' Hamir nodded. 'He told us to sweep the streets and see if we could find any other stragglers.'

'He sent you out?' Dalin asked.

'He sent me out to sweep the streets and–'

'He sent you out?' Dalin repeated. 'He didn't get you to a medicae or a corpsman?'

'We should try and find him,' Dalin said.

'Why?' Wash asked contemptuously.

'You got a better idea?' asked Merrt.

'Plenty,' Wash replied.

HOWEVER HE DIDN'T share any of them, and seemed content to fall into step as they started walking again. Dalin had hoped Hamir might be able to guide them, but it became clear he was following them.

Except, that was, for the many occasions when he stopped dead and looked up at the falling flakes of ash and soot as they descended silently.

'Hamir? Keep up.'

'Yed.'

'You all right?'

'Yed.'

He would start walking again obediently enough, but his words were becoming slurred, as if he had a blocked nose, or all his 'd's and 's's had become interposed. He remained standing in the middle of a street when a terrible, increasing rumble sent the rest of them scurrying for cover. The droning volume grew steadily, until they could feel the quiver of it.

'Scholam!' Fourbox hissed from cover. 'Scholam, get in here!'

There, in the middle of the road, Hamir stared up at the sky. He raised an arm and pointed.

Warplanes went over. They were the source of the deafening drone. Imperial warplanes, Marauder fighter-bombers. They were flying in mass formation at a height of about a thousand metres. Row upon row of their cruciform silhouettes passed overhead, chasing their shadows across the ash-whitened streets, darkening the sky like an immense travelling flock of slowly migrating wildfowl. The combined noise of their engines was so great, the men couldn't hear one another shout for the duration of the flypast.

It lasted ten minutes. Dalin couldn't even estimate the number of planes involved. The formation was heading north, coming in over the infamous bulwark and heading for the inner city, the central wards and high-hive of K'ethdrac'att Shet Magir. It was quite a spectacle, all in all, but during his brief yet intense career as a Guardsman, Dalin Criid had witnessed plenty more extraordinary sights.

They came out of cover while the warplanes were still roaring overhead and started walking again. Dalin took Hamir by the sleeve and led him along. Hamir was fascinated by the planes. He kept tripping because he was looking upwards instead of where he was going.

They started moving south, Merrt reasoning that direction was more likely to bring them into Imperial controlled zones, or at least some form of safety. Their boots sifted quietly through the deep, white dust.

They came along a particular street flanked on either side by blackened ruins. Half a dozen men appeared at the far end and turned their way.

'It's Sobile! It's Sobile and the others!' Hamir exclaimed, and started to run towards them, waving his hand and calling out.

It wasn't Sobile. The half-dozen men were big fellows, swathed in ochre clothing and black iron armour. They saw Hamir running towards them, calling cheerfully.

'Hamir! No, no! Hamir!' Dalin cried.

The enemy troopers opened fire.

VII

They fired quick bursts of las-fire. Hamir was still running towards them when they hit him. He crumbled and fell, face down, in the street, one waving arm still outstretched. His body looked especially forlorn, his blood splattered out across the white dust around him.

'Hamir!' Dalin cried. His voice was hoarse. He had unshipped his weapon. By his side, Merrt was taking aim.

The enemy was still firing. They began to advance too, apparently unfazed by the sight of four armed Guardsmen.

'Throne save us,' Fourbox yelped.

Each one of the enemy warriors was massive. Their upper bodies, shoulders and arms were thick with muscle, making them look slightly comical and top heavy. There was nothing comical about the speed or determination with which they were advancing. The bright yellow hue of their battledress contrasted, with an aposematic punch, against the gloss black of their body armour. Emblems of Ruin were welded to their chest plates, and long strings of beads and amulets rattled around them. Their heads were shaved and bare, and stained or dressed with a white pigment over which delicate black designs had been inscribed across the cranium and the brow. Their body armour rose up onto a broad neck guard which concealed their mouths behind a lip fashioned from black iron to resemble a cupping hand, as if they each had a hand placed over their mouths.

There had been enough briefings in the past year for even a no-gooder like Wash to know what they were. There was no doubt at all in Dalin's mind. These were Sons of Sek.

las-rounds zipped past the four Imperials. Dalin and Fourbox began to fire. Merrt cursed as his gun jammed again. 'Get to cover! Cover!' he boomed. Wash was already running.

The notorious Sons of Sek, the briefings said, were a fighting cadre raised by a local Archenemy warlord. They had started out as just a rumour, based on descriptions and warnings brought back from Gereon by Gaunt's team. Few Imperial forces had yet engaged them in the Sabbat Worlds, but they already possessed the same menacing reputation as the vicious Blood Pact.

Dalin wasn't sure if he'd managed to hit anything. He hadn't seen any of the hostiles go down, but the range had been good. He blamed himself. In his panic, he'd been snatching his shots. He, Merrt and Fourbox started to run, breaking off the dusty street through the ruins. las-shots struck the charred doorway and facade of the ruin behind them.

The interior was dark and jumbled with wreckage and charred objects. Everything was black with fire damage and there was no relief with which to judge distances. Merrt and Dalin both tripped and almost fell. They sprinted forwards, crunching over the debris. Wash was well ahead of them, a darting shadow between the heavy pillars.

The first of the Sons of Sek crashed into the building behind them, clawing in through window holes and sections of collapsed wall. They were moving fast too, clambering in and leaping down. Dalin could hear their guttural voices calling to one another. Renewed gunfire tore through the ruin, chasing their heels.

The three Imperial troops came out of the far side of the ruin onto another street where the remains of an iron portico stood. They'd lost sight of Wash. Two burned-out troop carriers sat on one side of the thoroughfare. A large part of the road was covered in rubble from a hab that had been flattened by a bunker-buster bomb. The running footsteps of the enemy came closer, through the ruin behind them. Several more shots whined past.

Lasrifle in hand, Dalin swung back to face the doorway they had emerged from.

'Go!' he said to Merrt and Fourbox. 'Go!'

GEREON RESISTS

I

THE STORM BLEW up into the night, and they struggled through it into the deep, dead woods.

The storm cured the sky a kind of dark, reptilian green, almost the colour of the world when seen through night scopes. The wind, which had turned the vanes of the mill at Cayfer, grew stronger, and lashed the stands of tall, mummified trees. The brittle branches swished and rattled like bone beads in a shaker. Dry leaf litter and dust swirled up from the soil.

The lightning chased them. White and thready, it sizzled in the sky, leaving brief, fragile traces like the filaments of light bulbs. There was no real thunder, just a pressure of air and a crackling, fizzling hiss of radiation.

Gaunt's section trudged along, wrapped in their camo-cloaks, following the resistance fighters into the strobing dark. It was hard going, but Dacre showed no inclination to stop and ride the storm out. Besides, any camp would have been swept away by the gale. They struggled on through blizzards of fossil leaves strewn by the wind.

The storm loaded their weapons and metal kit with static charge. Men jumped and baulked as guns tingled in their hands. Brostin spread a huge grin as he watched a crackling blue thread of electricity wander around the sooty muzzle of his flamer. He turned the torch in his hands slowly, watching the charge dance and jump, as if he was allowing a large insect to crawl around his weapon.

'Move up!' Criid scolded him.

Lambent curds of bright corposant lit distant trees, fuming and glowing, and making closer trees into skeletal silhouettes. The lightning also struck into the woods around them, and split ancient tree trunks like a forester's axe. Dry boles caught alight, husk branches burned. Sparks billowed up and were carried by the knifing wind.

At the tomb, two hours before, Dacre had refused to be drawn.

'Mkvenner? This is Mkvenner?' Gaunt had demanded. Dacre had shrugged.

'How did he die?' Mkoll had asked.

'I don't know. I didn't know him. He fought with the local cell and the Lectica cell. They thought highly of him. They said whoever came would want to see this, so I did as I was instructed and brought you here.'

'Who told you to?' Gaunt had asked Dacre.

'I'm not going to tell you that,' Dacre had replied. 'I don't even know who you are.'

'I'm Gaunt!'

'So you said. I don't know that.'

THEY'D BEEN TREKKING for three hours when the rains came. There was no warning, just a sudden assault of fast, fat raindrops. Within seconds, they were drenched. Within minutes, the deluge had killed off the dust and the skittering leaves. The thirsty earth became a quagmire. The white, dead trunks of the murdered woodland washed black.

The rain provoked the first emotional reaction they'd seen from Dacre and his men. The resistance fighters gazed up into the pelt, or took off their hats to bask in the streaming water.

'First rain this area's seen in two years,' Dacre said, brushing the running droplets off his face with a calloused hand.

Gaunt nodded. He knew it was the invasion that had triggered the storm. You didn't dump such a catastrophic amount of mass and energy into an atmosphere without the weather patterns flying apart. He remembered Balhaut, Fortis Binary and, most recently, Ancreon Sextus. It wasn't just the heat exchange of weapons use, it was ship drives in low orbit, gravity generators, overpressure and atmospheric insertions. This rainstorm in Lowensa Province was due, in part, to the null fields of capital ships squeezing the air over the ocean at Gereon's tropics, to the global warming of orbital barrage, to the rapid air displacement of a hundred thousand drop-ships.

They squelched onwards, water pouring off their weatherproofs and capes. Dacre led them down the line of a valley, and then took them across a stream swollen by the sudden rain. They moved upland after that, to a crest, and then sharply down, into a wet hinterland of dead and partially fallen trees. The rain showed no sign of letting up. Cascades of flash-flood water boiled down the slopes around them.

They arrived at a platform made of dressed stone. It extended out into the bend of a suddenly fast-flowing river. There was no explanation for the platform except that it might have once been the foundation of a building no longer in existence.

Dacre bade them all sit down.

'What now?' Gaunt asked.

'We wait,' said Dacre.

Gaunt moved through the settling figures of his section and found Beltayn.

'Can you raise Cantible?' he asked.

Beltayn shook his head.

'Keep trying. Try and get a signal to Rawne that we're all right.'

'I will, sir.'

Gaunt sat down and drew his cloak around his throat against the fierce rain. It was cold and clammy.

He looked out across the platform, and the surging, dark river, at the trees. Rain seasons usually brought life back to woodland and forest, but here it was too late. This forest had perished and dried, and the rain was simply washing the corpse.

II

TIME BEGAN TO lose its meaning. Every wrist chron in the section started to misbehave during the night, all except, as Gaunt believed, his own: the battered, junk timepiece he'd brought through Gereon once already. It continued to tick steadily when everyone else's was stopping, or spinning their hands like the vanes of an air-mill in a gale.

The storm subsided in the slow hours before dawn. For a long time, in the enclosing dark, the only sounds were the gurgle of the swollen river and the *plick-plack* of water dripping from the dead trees. The sky became pale before sunrise, and the light turned grey and turgid. When true daylight came, it suddenly became darker. The sky was a lowering roof of gunmetal clouds, knotted like brain tissue.

A hand touched Gaunt's arm and he started, realising he had fallen asleep. He'd been dreaming. He'd been in a house at the lonely edge of some world. Tanith pipes had been playing. Tona Criid had come up to him from some dim hallway and punched his chest. Her face had been stained with tears. 'You're dead! You're dead! You're dead!' she wailed, beating at him. He'd tried to embrace her and calm her, but she'd pulled away.

There had been a repetitive clicking. Gaunt had looked around and seen Viktor Hark sitting by a window, racking the slide of a bolt pistol.

'Look, I'm sorry,' Hark had said, rising to his feet. 'I really am, but you're dead and I can't let this go on. You're killing my men with your ghosts.' Hark had raised the bolt pistol towards Gaunt's face and–

The hand touched his arm. He woke with a snap.

It was Eszrah.

The Nihtgane was standing over him, his reynbow tucked under his arm. Gaunt noticed immediately that the weapon was loaded.

'Hwat seyathee?' he whispered.

'Gonn thesshaff,' Eszrah whispered.

Gaunt looked around and rose to his feet from his cross-legged stance. He reached for his weapon. Dacre and the resistance fighters had vanished. The

Ghosts of his section sat hunched and slumbering on the platform around them.

'Feth!' Gaunt hissed.

'Seyathee feth?' Eszrah whispered back, sweeping the woods on the far side of the river with his reynbow.

'Yes I fething well do seyathee feth!' Gaunt spat. 'Oan?'

'Already awake,' Mkoll replied, materialising suddenly at Gaunt's elbow. 'Dacre's gone.'

'No, really?'

Mkoll gazed at Gaunt steadily to diffuse the colonel-commissar's anger and sarcasm.

'I was awake,' he said, 'although they didn't realise it. They were talking. I listened. They were worried about us. They don't trust us, and the storm overnight spooked them.'

'Why?'

'Oh, come on. You remember what it was like here. We mistrusted everything. They haven't seen rain in two years, so that freaked them out. The whole idea of liberation–'

'What about it?'

'Well, I don't think they believe in it. It's what they've been praying for. Now it's here…'

'Now it's here what?'

'It's too good to be true.' Mkoll looked up at Gaunt. 'That's what they were saying. Anyway, they left, about an hour ago.'

'Why didn't you wake me?'

'Because we've been under observation ever since.'

'We have?'

Mkoll nodded. 'Besides, you could use the sleep.'

'Who's watching us?' Gaunt asked.

'Dunno,' said Mkoll, 'but they're out there.' He nodded in the direction of the trees on the far bank of the swirling, peaty river. 'They're safe enough.'

'How can you tell?'

Mkoll shrugged. 'We're not dead yet.'

'Get everybody up,' Gaunt said.

Mkoll and Eszrah roused the section. They woke and stood up, groaning and bemused. Larkin roused so suddenly, his long-las fell on the ground with a clatter that echoed through the dripping glade.

'Sorry, sir,' he said. 'Bad dream.'

Gaunt smiled. He knew about such things. His own recent dream still hadn't left his memory. He was especially locked on the image of Tona Criid, thumping at him. She'd had a dream too, he remembered, on the transport just before they'd come in. She'd dreamed that he had died. Gaunt believed in the power of dreams. They'd spoken the truth to him more than once. He'd fobbed Tona off, but now it troubled him. On Gereon, last time out, she'd dreamed so accurately of Lucien Wilder, Throne bless his memory. She'd dreamed of Lucien Wilder long before she'd known any man of that name actually existed.

'What was your dream, Larks?' Gaunt asked.

'Cuu,' Larkin said. They both laughed, for although Cuu was a true nightmare, he was a nightmare long gone.

'Sir,' Mkoll whispered, touching Gaunt's arm.

Gaunt turned to look.

A skinny figure had emerged from the treeline on the far bank of the river, stumping forwards through the silt and mire. He was tall and scruffy, rake thin from malnourishment.

Gaunt knew him at once.

Gaunt hurried to the end of the platform and leapt down into the gurgling river with a splash. He waded across to the far side and came up the muddy shore to greet the man standing there.

'Gereon resists,' he said.

The skeletal man nodded. 'So it does, Ibram. Shit, it's good to see you.'

They embraced. Although drawn and haggard, there was no mistaking the man.

His name was Gerome Landerson.

III

'You CAME BACK,' said Landerson.

'I swore I would.'

'And you brought…' Landerson didn't finish the sentence. He made a nod with his head. He didn't mean the combat section on the platform behind Gaunt. He meant the invasion forces rolling into Gereon half the world away.

'I swore that too. As well as I could.'

Landerson smiled. His skin was like old leather, and a poor diet had lost him several teeth. 'When I first met you, Ibram, you broke my heart. I thought I was going to meet salvation itself, and you told me you had just come to silence some rogue high brass.'

'I remember.'

'But you *were* salvation. Eventually. You've got them on the back foot.'

'It's only been a couple of days.'

'We have lines of information,' Landerson said. 'Two, maybe three main strongholds have fallen. The south is yours. Unholy fights are going on at Brovisia, Phatima, Zarcus, K'ethdrac, a dozen other zones. We know the Plenipotentiary fled the planet two hours before the first drop, presumably forewarned by pre-translation patterning. And the power's gone.'

'What?'

'In all the outlying regions. No wolves, no glyfs, no sorcelment barriers. It's like they've sucked every shred of power they have back into the main fights.'

Gaunt nodded. 'It's a start. But this isn't settled by a long way. Even given the military strength Crusade Command has unloaded on Gereon, we could be weeks, months from liberation. Maybe even longer. We don't know what the enemy has up its sleeve.'

'I understand.'

'I need you to know that. Even if the end is coming, there may be a lot more days of pain to come.'

'I understand, Ibram.'

'That's why we needed to broker proper contact with the resistance as quickly as possible, to speed the process.'

Landerson spread his hands. 'Well, here we are. I guess we should group up and start sharing data.'

'That'd be good.'

'Look,' Landerson said, 'I want you to know… I stand here in simple gratitude. What you've done for me. What you've done for my world. I–'

Gaunt held up a hand. 'Don't, Landerson. I know what you want to say, and I don't deserve it. I fought for Gereon while I was here, and I fought for it when I got back. I don't know what it was I said that made High Command decide to resource this liberation and commit to it. Maybe it had nothing to do with me at all. Maybe they just decided it was time.'

'I don't–'

'Whatever the reason, I'm glad it's happening and I believe it's a crime that it has taken so long to begin this effort. If anybody should be thanked for ensuring Gereon's survival, it's men like you.'

GAUNT'S SECTION CROSSED the river, and Landerson brought his own team of cell fighters out of the trees to meet them. They were all in as poor a state as Landerson himself. Gaunt actually knew three of the men from his time with the resistance, but he had difficulty recognising them.

Landerson and his men greeted Cirk, and Larkin, Brostin, Beltayn, Criid and Mkoll, who had all been members of that original mission team. Landerson had been resistance even back then, and had guided them loyally through the entire hunt for Sturm. Effectively stranded on Gereon after the mission's completion, Gaunt and his team had put all their efforts into building the resistance to wage an underground war against the forces of the Occupation. Together, they had taken risks and faced horrors that were difficult to frame into words. Gaunt was a career soldier, and had served on some of the bloodiest battlefields of the Crusade. In terms of personal danger, privation and extremity, none of them compared to his time in the resistance war for Gereon.

But they had made their mark. Under the leadership of Landerson and the Ghosts, the resistance had become a strong, supple thing that defied the occupying forces. They had built a pact with the partisans of the Untill, Eszrah's people, and learned to use both the Nihtganes' stealth talents and their impenetrable territories. Mkoll, Bonin and Mkvenner had schooled them in covert actions. Varl, Rawne and Criid had taught the resistance fighters, many of them civilians, how to live and operate as soldiers. Beltayn had engineered their communication network. Feygor had taught them the tricks of explosives, Brostin had taught them how to use fire, and Larkin had taught them how to shoot. Gaunt had instructed them in fluid principles of leadership. They had personally destroyed eighteen garrisons, seven power stations, thirty-six communication hubs, seven airfields and a large number of daemonic machineries, including several of the abominable jehgenesh. And the Plenipotentiary that Landerson had reported fleeing Gereon just prior to the invasion was not the same being who had held that office when Gaunt's mission team had first arrived. Assassination was not beyond them.

As they travelled together into the deep woodlands, under the grey sky, the Ghosts and the resistance fighters said little to one another. Both, for different reasons, were used to being silent.

Landerson walked with Gaunt.

'I'm sorry about all the precautions,' he said.

'You don't have to be sorry. I understand.'

'We have to be wary, even now. These last few months, the Archenemy's become more skilful at infiltration. Face changers. Mind swaps. Remote psychic control. We've had losses. Just last week they cremated an entire cell in Edrian, deep in the Untill. Eighty dead, most of them Nihtgane families.'

Gaunt shook his head.

'It happens that way,' said Landerson. 'But you remember Carook?'

'Carook the Butcher?'

'The very same.'

'Feth, the time we spent trying to sanction him. The ambush outside Phatima. The bombs in his palace.'

Landerson nodded. 'We got him. Last month. Finally. We got word he was going to observe worship at the ahenum in Fruslind, but an insider source, a palace servant, leaked he was going to stop en route and oversee some Son training at the Peshpal Garrison. Diggerson took a four-man team in three days before. Hid themselves behind the rostrum, and laid low for sixty hours. When Carook sat down to observe the display, they sprung him.'

'Clean kill?' Gaunt asked.

'We were low on firearms anyway, but Peshpal was warded, so nothing metal could be slipped in. Diggerson and his men tunnelled under the wire, naked. They were armed with slivers of glass. I don't believe it was a clean kill, Ibram. But it was a definite kill.'

'And a long time coming. I'd like to shake Diggerson by the hand.'

'So would I. None of them came back. Carook's life-ward slaughtered them.'

Gaunt didn't reply. Such was the desperate nature of resistance war. Missions, especially those aimed to assassinate high-ranking monsters, were regularly suicide.

'Diggerson was a good man,' Landerson said. 'He would have liked today. Anyway, I'm sorry we strung you along.'

'I understand.'

'We were observing you.'

'I know. Since Cayfer.'

'Since before that, my friend. The coded exchanges with Navy Intelligence seemed solid enough, but we had to be certain. The code said it was you that was coming, to establish contact, but it would say that, wouldn't it?'

'So you sent Dacre?'

'I sent Dacre, so I could look at you, and make sure you were on the level, and make sure you weren't being followed. You'll forgive me for being over careful.'

'Rawne will be sad to hear Diggerson's dead,' Gaunt said. 'They worked well together.'

'Rawne's here, is he?'

'Back at Cantible.'

Landerson nodded, as if this small fact made his world a better place. He asked after the others, Bonin and Varl and Feygor.

'Murt Feygor's the only one who hasn't come back with me. We lost him, on Ancreon Sextus.'

'I'm sorry to hear that,' said Landerson. 'He was a good man.'

'You know,' said Gaunt, 'he really wasn't. He and Rawne were black-hearted devils when I first met them. Gereon changed them both. I still take a pause to think that Rawne's a friend of mine now. My best friend, to be honest. Time was, we'd have happily killed one another. I still hate him and he still hates me, but the necessity of Gereon bound us tight. Feygor too. Not a model soldier, but after Gereon, I'd have sold my soul for him and vice versa. He died well, Landerson. He died in combat, at the front. He died like Diggerson did, selfless, heroic.'

'Murt Feygor?' Landerson laughed.

'I will count him amongst the heroes I've known,' said Gaunt. 'Thank the God-Emperor, I now don't have fingers enough. Now, you tell me about Ven.'

'Ven?'

'You had Dacre show me his tomb.'

Landerson nodded. They were slipping their way down a deep slope, surrounded by tall, dark trees and thickets of lichen brush. Gaunt didn't have to be told that they were entering the edges of the Untill.

'Ven was a giant,' Landerson said, reaching out to steady Gaunt as they slithered down the rain-mushed earth. 'I mean, peerless. We owe him as much as we owe the Nihtgane. Shit, it always seemed like he was a Nihtgane. I've never known a man move so quiet and kill so hard. Before you'd even left us, he was making a reputation for himself, you remember. The Archenemy wanted him. After you went, he came into his own. He wasn't shy. He knew that word-of-mouth was as important a weapon as blowing shit up. He started to–'

'To what?'

'Take credit. Spread the myth. Scare the enemy. He was supernatural, unkillable. A ghost in the woods. An avenging phantom. He became a figurehead for the resistance. Just like you told him to.'

'I did,' said Gaunt, remembering his final conversation with Mkvenner.

'Ven did you proud, Ibram. He did what you told him to do. He became a legend. Everything the resistance did was attributed to Ven. Sabotage, assassinations, bombings. He became their bogeyman. When they got him, it was our blackest day.'

'How did they get him?'

Landerson shook his head. 'It was one of those things. He was operating out of the deep Untill with a hand-picked team of Nihtgane. They called themselves the Nalsheen. That mean anything to you?'

Gaunt nodded.

'They'd done three raids in three days. A Sons garrison, a vox-hub, and a provincial governor. I was in contact, via the network. I sent to Ven he'd done too much and that he should burrow down for a week or two. He responded he would, said he was taking the Nalsheen west into the coastal Untill. I can only presume they were intercepted. A few days later, I got word that the Nalsheen had been slaughtered in an ambush by enemy killteams.'

'Confirmed?'

'Yes, confirmed. So we built the cairn.'

'You recovered his body?'

'No. We just built the cairn. That was the point. After Ven's death, we kept attributing kills to him, as if he couldn't die. That's why we built the tomb up in enemy territory, so they'd know about it. The man they'd finally killed was still hurting them. It was propaganda. They became more afraid of Ven dead than they had been when he was alive.'

'He would have appreciated that,' Gaunt said. 'The irony. The economy. The–'

He stopped short. They were advancing through a glade where the trees had been stripped of their branches and rendered into stakes. The rotting heads of Nihtgane sat transfixed on the tops of the spikes.

'What the feth is this?' Gaunt asked.

'This is the edge of the real Untill,' Landerson replied. 'This is the boundary the enemy makes. A warning… to us, to stay in, and to them, to stay out.'

Solemnly, respectfully, Gaunt walked past the first stake. 'You never thought to take them down?' he asked.

'Why? They'd only want to put up more.'

There was a sudden commotion in the file behind them. Ghosts and partisans alike raised their weapons. A figure appeared, stumbling through the ruined woodland.

It was Dacre. At some point since they'd last seen him, he'd lost his right arm. He was clutching the shattered splinters of the limb's bone and meat to his chest, his jacket soaked in blood.

'Feth!' Gaunt exclaimed.

'They were followed!' Dacre gasped, falling to his knees in front of Landerson. 'They were bloody well followed!'

Landerson looked sharply at Gaunt.

'We were clean when we came in,' Gaunt said firmly. 'By the God-Emperor, man, you watched us.'

'Dacre?'

'They brought something with them,' Dacre moaned. 'I swear to you. Despite all our efforts, they were followed. Nine of my men are dead. And I–'

He stared down at his shredded arm and fainted.

'Pick him up!' Landerson yelled.

From a distance away, through the trees, there came a snort of exhaust.

Gaunt knew what that meant.

The beast still had their scent.

IV

'CROPPER!' LANDERSON CALLED out to one of his men. 'Take the party forwards to Mothlamp. We're doubling back–'

'No,' said Gaunt firmly.

'I'm not arguing about this,' said Landerson.

'Good,' said Gaunt, 'neither am I. Take the main party on, and link Cirk and Mr Faragut with your people. Beltayn has unit command. I'll take the rest and double back.'

'But–'

'This is my problem. We led it in here.'

'Ibram, let the Nihtgane–'

'You got a rocket tube, Landerson? The partisans still packing kit like that?'

'No.'

'Then do as I tell you. The mission is more important than any of us. We'll deal with this and then swing back around. Post a watch to look for us and pick us up.'

Landerson looked at Gaunt for a moment, then saluted quickly.

Gaunt looked around. 'Short straws… Criid, Larkin, Mkoll, Posetine, Derin. Let's go!'

The selected Ghosts followed Gaunt back up the trackway. The soil was sticky and black from the overnight rain, and the grey sky above the perished trees was threatening a further downpour. By the time they had passed the grotesque markers of the staked skulls, the rest of the party had vanished behind them.

Except for Eszrah.

'Go with the others,' Gaunt told him.

Eszrah shook his head. Gaunt wanted to argue. Having a fluent native speaker with the contact party would be useful. But when Eszrah became so tight-lipped he didn't even use his own language, there was no point debating with him. Gaunt knew he'd been dismayed at his sour treatment by the other Nihtgane, though such behaviour was hardly unexpected. Eszrah had been cut free of his roots, and had gone to places further away than any Nihtgane had ever gone. It wasn't a matter of cruelty or prejudice, he was genuinely 'unkynde' to them now. But it left him stranded and disenfranchised, adrift between worlds. The only place left for him was the place his chieftain father had given him: standing at Gaunt's side.

They spread out, off the trail they had followed into the Untill, hoping to lure the beast around in a wide loop. There had been no further sign of it since Dacre's appearance. They travelled silently, following the lines of ridges and the cover of stands of trees. It began to rain again, a fine, heavy torrent that twinkled in the sidelong light. Pungent odours of mud, mould, and woodrot were reawakened by the sudden rain. The air scent was cold and clear, and organic.

At last they heard sounds. From far away, the splash and spatter of movement in wet mud, the grumble of an engine revving to cope with mire. In the enclosed box made by the rain, the sound suddenly travelled much further than before.

Gaunt ranged them out in a wide line. Criid carried the tube. Gaunt signalled Mkoll and Larkin forwards to sweep and locate.

They had crossed about three kilometres of woodland since separating from Landerson's party. The area they now slipped through was dense, dead forest that had been punctured in several places by artillery fire. They passed the charred wreck of a troop truck in one clearing. It had been there a long time, possibly since the original invasion. Further on lay the rusted shell of a light armoured car. Fallen tree trunks were rotting back into the mulch around the wrecks. Pieces of kit – buckles and buttons and the occasional gorget or helmet – showed up in the mud, all that remained of the bodies that had fallen in that place years before.

There was a signal tap on the micro-bead, and everybody got down. Gaunt waited a moment in a stillness where there was only the chirring of the drizzle. He heard a grumble up ahead, a wet purr. He smelled a hint of oil, a whiff of exhaust.

Larkin reappeared and ran back to Gaunt, head low, long las like a spear at his side. He dropped into cover beside the colonel-commissar.

'Other side of that mound,' he whispered. 'We caught sight of it, just for a moment. Fething thing is stalking us again.'

'Which way?'

Larkin pointed.

'Spot for Tona, Larks,' Gaunt said and signalled through the rain to Criid. Criid and Larkin immediately got up and took off, weaving in and out of the dead trees as they made their way up the slope, past the rusty chassis of another troop truck.

Criid ducked down behind some fallen logs just over the top of the slope. The rain was getting heavier. She could see down through a depression, thickly wooded, and into a clearing beyond. Larkin came up level with her, and she nodded. They took off again, heading down the slope and into the trees, slowing and crouching as they came through the black husks of ground vegetation.

Criid knelt down. Past the rot-black trunks of trees ahead, she saw into the clearing. The beast was partly masked by the woods behind it, a black shape against black shapes. She could just make it out through the rain, hull down, side on, as if it was waiting.

She glanced at Larkin. He had his scope raised, but the rain kept spattering the lens. He rubbed at it with a vizzy cloth and looked again. The view was poor, even with his optics. It was just a dark shape, but he could get a decent range for her. He had no wish to get any closer for a clearer look.

Thirty-two metres, he signed to Criid. She nodded, carefully loading one of the last two rockets into the tube.

The target wasn't moving. Through the streaming veil of rain, she lined up on its shadow through the cross hairs of the tube's aiming reticule.

Braced, she squeezed the trigger spoon. On a noisy streamer of smoke, the rocket arced across the clearing. It struck the tank in the side armour, detonated, and penetrated, flooding the interior of the hull with superhot gas.

Direct hit. Killing hit.

Even so, it was the worst mistake of her career.

V

CRIID AND LARKIN rose up out of cover, staring at the burning wreck.

'Good kill,' he murmured.

'Made a strange sound,' she said, taking a step forwards.

'What?'

'It made a strange sound, when it hit.' She was walking towards her kill across the clearing. The sound of the impact had been dull and hollow, like a gong, like a hammer on scrap metal. Rain streamed off her as she closed on the blazing machine. She could hear the rainfall hissing and spitting off flames and hot metal. Steam and white smoke pumped out across the black mud of the clearing.

The tank was dead. The tank had been dead for years.

In the poor light, she had killed a rusted ruin.

'Of feth–' she began. She turned, and started to run. She saw Larkin's face, wide eyed, mystified, wondering why she was breaking towards him so suddenly.

'Go! Larks, go!' she yelled.

The beast came through the trees to her left. The sudden howl of its raging engine shattered the rain-drenched quiet. Its treads were kicking up divots of mud and wet soil. The forward mantle of its hull shattered through the boles of the dead wood in its path. Entire trees folded and collapsed, ripping down through the relic canopy of the extinct forest. One crashed down across the beast itself, and fractured as it rolled off the moving armour. Another toppled away and fell into the burning wreck, where the lacy branches began to smoulder.

The beast left stumps, fallen timber and wood-debris in its wake. It hit some standing trunks so hard they disintegrated into flurries of rotten wood fibres. Bouncing, it thundered after the fleeing Criid. Larkin was finally running, plunging through the wet undergrowth and rot.

'Move! Move!' he voxed, his voice high with panic and jarred by the violence of his motion. 'It's on us!'

Plumes of angry smoke snorted out of the beast's rear end as it clattered after Criid. It seemed intent on running her down, on crushing her into the forest floor. At some point since they had last seen it, it had lost one of its front lamps. Only one baleful yellow light shone from its hull. The other had been smashed and mangled, most likely by the rocket that Criid had smacked into it at Cayfer.

It moved like a half-blind thing. Did it know Criid was the one that had hurt it the night before? Was that why it was hunting her so intently?

She snapped right suddenly, turning faster than it could, leaping and sprinting into another break of trees.

Larkin was running parallel with her about fifty metres off. He could see the beast through the trees, and he could see her running, dodging between the decomposing trunks. Over the link, he heard the urgent voices of Gaunt and the rest of the squad, demanding information as they closed in.

'It's ignoring me!' he yelled. 'It just wants Criid!'

'Have we got a tank shell left?' Gaunt demanded, his voice close to incoherence over the micro-bead.

'One,' Larkin answered. 'But Criid's got it. She's got the tube too.'

Larkin slithered to a halt and looked down the slope. He could barely see Criid. She was bounding through the dense wood, moving away from him. The beast had come to a halt. She was putting some decent distance between herself and it.

The tank gun boomed. Larkin fell to the ground even though he knew the shell wasn't coming his way. The beast had fired its turret weapon at zero elevation. The tank round sliced through the woodland like a giant bullet, leaving a trail of atomised branches and pulverised boles behind it. It went off against a heavy, ancient tree five metres to the left of Criid. The blast smashed her off her feet. She went rolling over and over in the black mire.

'Tona!' Larkin yelled. 'Keep running!'

He saw her get up, and head off to the left. She seemed all right. She was running as fast as ever.

The beast fired again. Larkin glimpsed the hissing, fibre-spraying track of the shell as it passed through the trees. There was a big blast of impact, big enough to tear down several small trees nearby. When the flash died and the smoke began to melt away, Tona Criid was gone.

'Oh no,' murmured Larkin. 'Oh no no no.' He took a step forwards and began to slither back down the slope towards the beast. He was filled with an urge to do something, to obtain revenge, yet had no idea what that might be. He raised his long las, aiming it at the tank as he skidded down the muddy bank.

With a surge of engine revolutions and an acrid belch of smoke, the beast began to roll again, and turned to meet him.

VI

Larkin saw the single yellow lamp swing round to regard him. He stumbled backwards, lowering his weapon for a moment. The beast came for him, spraying black mud out on either side as it hammered across the clearing. Larkin raised his long las again and fired directly at it. The shot blew out the remaining lamp.

The beast shuddered to a halt, slewing around slightly. A high, strangled note rose from the thrashing engine, which sounded to Larkin like a gurgle of pain and rage. Had he blinded it, or was that just his imagination?

The beast lurched forwards once more, swinging the front of its hull from left to right. Its main gun came up above horizontal and the turret traversed back and forth. Larkin started to run.

The hard point cannon began to fire. Heavy gauge shots chopped the air behind the Tanith sniper. Dead vegetation was chewed up and disintegrated like mist. Larkin heard the shells smack into the mud behind him. He'd chosen to run back up the slope, and that was foolish.

Eszrah appeared from behind a tree trunk and dragged Larkin to the ground. Down low, they bellied through the leaf mould and dead branches. Eszrah put a finger to his lips so Larkin would be in no doubt. The beast came up the slope behind them, felling more decomposing timber. They crawled quickly between the trees, heading for the top of the rise.

They reached the ridge top about ten seconds in front of the lurching, squirming beast. With line of sight cover provided by the terrain, they both leapt up and started to run down the far bank towards the rusting troop truck.

They both felt the wet ground quiver beneath them as the beast reared up over the rise at their heels. It came at speed, angry, hungry. As soon as its huge bulk had flopped over the crest, its treads dug in and it slalomed down the muddy slope after them. Larkin and Eszrah had just passed the rotting truck when the beast fired its main gun at them.

Liquid mud fountained into the air in a gout like a hot spring. Larkin felt himself lifted into the air by the shockwave. He landed hard, with dazing force, and in the blurry moments that followed, registered a terrible pain in his left leg.

He tried to snap awake. He felt the rain hitting his face and the ooze squelching beneath him. The snorting of the approaching beast was in his ears.

'Eszrah?' he called out, hoarse and choked by fumes. The blast had thrown Eszrah four or five metres away into the treeline. Larkin could see the sleepwalker, sprawled unconscious in the dead bracken. Larkin tried to get up and run to him. He wanted to drag Eszrah into better cover.

He couldn't. Pain flared through his left foot and leg. Larkin struggled round to identify the source of the pain.

The blast that had knocked him flat and cast Ezsrah across the glade had thrown the shell of the rusting truck too. The scabby metal bulk had rolled over and pinned Larkin's left foot beneath it.

He tried to pull free, but the weight of the wreck was far to great. All he got for his efforts was a sear of agony from his damaged foot. He began to scrabble feverishly.

The beast was thundering down on him, in a direct line that would bring the truck wreck, and Larkin himself, under its crushing tracks.

* * *

MKOLL COULD HEAR the beast's growling engine through the rain from the far side of the slope. He and Derin had cut around to the east as soon as Larkin's urgent call had reached them. Mkoll knew they had nothing to kill a tank with, unless the last rocket Criid had been carrying had survived.

'Look around!' he cried to Derin as they struggled through the brittle undergrowth. One of the tank rounds had punched clean through the dead trees, leaving kindling and rotting fibre strewn in a path. Mkoll located the half-cup of a shell hole bored into the black soil. He saw part of a Tanith issue sleeve hanging from a branch. A boot.

'Feth!' he cursed to himself. The tank had hit her so squarely, she–

'Chief!' Derin called.

Mkoll ran across to him. Derin was dragging back some of the black, tangled ground cover. He'd found Criid.

She was alive. Her battledress was torn, and burned in places, and she had suffered several deep gashes from zipping wood splinters. The force of the blast that had thrown her and left her unconscious in the undergrowth had torn one of her boots off and buckled her lasrifle.

Mkoll checked her throat for a pulse. 'Dress her wounds,' he told Derin. 'Stay with her and get her ready to move as soon as she comes round.'

'What are you doing?' Derin asked.

Mkoll was rummaging through the undergrowth for the fallen rocket tube and the remaining shell. He found the shell quickly, half-spilled from its torn satchel. Then he found the rocket tube. It was twisted and useless.

From up the ridge, the boom of a tank gun rolled.

LARKIN CRIED OUT as he dragged at his leg again. The pain from the crushed foot was immense, but it was eclipsed by his desperate desire to get clear. There weren't many ways Larkin fancied dying, but crushed under the treads of a predatory battle tank wasn't one of them.

His pinned foot wouldn't budge. He yowled again.

Running full tilt, Gaunt and Posetine slammed against the wreck beside him and immediately put their shoulders into moving it. The beast was almost on them, the roar of its engine quivering the air.

Gaunt grunted in effort. The truck wreck weighed several tonnes. They weren't even going to rock it far enough to yank Larkin free.

The old sniper was frantic. 'Don't let it crush me!' he stammered. 'Don't let it! Please, sir! Finish me quick! Finish me quick, I'm begging you! For the time we've served together, I'm begging you for this!'

Posetine's mud-spattered face was pale with fear. He glanced at the oncoming beast. 'Sir!'

'Please! Please!' Larkin was wailing.

'Oh feth,' Gaunt snarled. He wrenched out his power sword, activated it, and slashed down in a single stroke.

Larkin screamed. Gaunt and Posetine grabbed him under the armpits and hurled themselves towards the trees, dragging him between them. Not even a full second later, the beast went through, flattening the truck wreck like wet flakboard.

Gaunt and Posetine fell over into the wet undergrowth. Larkin had passed out. Gaunt scrambled around, his power sword still ignited. He stripped the remains of the boot and sock off Larkin's truncated leg and quickly pressed the flat of the blade against the stump to cauterise it. Larkin woke with a cry and then passed out again.

'Oh shit,' said Posetine.

The beast had overshot them, but now it was coming about, ripping through the weeds and stringy brambles.

'Carry him!' Gaunt said. Posetine nodded and hoisted Larkin up in a shoulder lift. 'Go that way! Into the trees!' Gaunt ordered. Posetine started to run, hauling Larkin's loose body into the darkness of the deep wood.

Gaunt ran to where Eszrah lay. The Nihtgane woke as Gaunt dragged him up.

'Come on!' Gaunt hissed. They struggled a few metres, and dropped into cover behind a pair of fungus-caked trees.

The beast had turned. It stood its ground, its engine throbbing. With an electric whine, the main gun rose slightly, and then the turret traversed slowly to the left with a dry squeal. It stopped, and traversed slowly back to the right. Rainwater streamed back down the raised gun.

Curled in cover, Eszrah looked around for his reynbow, but he'd lost hold of it when the blast overtook him. It was lying in the mud in the middle of the rain-dimpled clearing. Not far away from it, beside the flattened truck chassis, was Larkin's long-las, bent almost in half by the weight of grinding tracks.

Neither weapon would have done them any good anyway. The only chance they had lay with the power sword. Gaunt realised he had to kill the beast's engine the way he had tried to do on the moor land outside Cayfer.

Gaunt signed for Eszrah to stay put, and then began to crawl along the tree line. He was partly obscured by the truck wreck. The beast continued to sit where it was, rumbling and panting.

Gaunt had got about five metres. It was going to be a long, arduous crawl to get himself behind the thing. His left boot caught against something, a stone or a piece of bark, and made a slight sound.

The beast's turret tracked in his direction instantly and fired.

Gaunt dropped flat. He felt the air-burn and the shock of the round as it went over his position, heard it zip and punch and slice through the canopy. The round struck the exposed root-ball of a tree further up the slope and exploded. Debris pattered down in the fine rain.

The beast's gun tracked to and fro, edgy, wary. Its engine flared with revs and it jumped forwards a metre or two before it slammed to a halt again, rocking on its springs. The hissing rain steamed off its engine cover. Grey smoke lifted from the muzzle brake. It started forwards again violently, slewing slightly to its left, and then stopped once more, engine chuntering.

A small noise sounded off to its right, and the beast swung around, turret tracking, both sets of tracks driving in opposite directions to turn it around on its own body-length. The main gun swung slowly to cover the area of trees where the offending noise had come from.

Gaunt peered out. Eszrah was where Gaunt had left him, well hidden. He'd scooped some iron quarrels from his pouch, and was hurling them one by one into the trees behind the beast. It had already half-turned to face the sound. He was trying to make it turn right around.

Eszrah threw another dart. It thunked off a tree stump. With a snort of exhaust, the beast lurched around further, and swung its weapon. It fired. Water droplets jumped off its armour as the gun thumped. A large fireball burst through the trees on the far side of the clearing. Gaunt was already moving. He knew he wouldn't be able to reach the rear of the tank in one go, but he was sure he could get as far as the truck wreck, which now lay behind the beast.

He flopped into cover as the echo of the gun's blast rippled away. Eszrah threw another quarrel, but this time the beast did not respond to the lure. Slowly, it began to track its turret around to the left, gun raised, as if it was cocking its ear to listen to something behind it. Gaunt couldn't help anthropomorphising the machine's behaviour. It had behaved like a wild animal from the very start of their conflict. Blinded, it was hunting by sound, and by smell.

It had his scent. He was close to it, and it had his scent, or else it could hear him breathing, or simply feel his presence. Eszrah tried another dart, but it wasn't interested at all. Gaunt wondered if he had the time to break and run, or if it was simply toying with him, waiting for him to make a move.

He decided to try it. He tightened his grip on the power sword.

The beast's engine roared and it lurched backwards at speed to crush the truck wreck a second time.

VII

Gaunt threw himself headlong to the side as the beast ploughed into his cover. Already mangled, the wrecked truck twisted and sheared under the tank's weight, the metal screeching and pinging as it deformed. Gaunt rolled, praying that he would have time to manoeuvre back behind the enemy vehicle before it swung at him again.

It was already moving. Slipping in the ooze, Gaunt tried to get a footing and dash in close beside it. He reignited his power sword and plunged forwards. The tank bellowed and wheeled around on him. He had to dive and roll again to avoid its swinging track guard.

There was a clang. Gaunt looked up. Mkoll was perched on top of the tank, right on top of the turret. Gaunt didn't know if the scout had dropped out of a tree or had run up the beast's back while it had been busy with him. Mkoll clung on tight, his left hand clamped to a hand rail. The last tank rocket was in his right hand. He tapped the side of the rocket two or three times against the top hatch cover, as if he was knocking on a door.

The beast halted sharply, rocking on its springs once more. Mkoll fought to cling on and rapped again. The turret traversed one way then the other, with increasing vigour, like a man trying to turn his head to see something pinned to his back. The main gun came up. The muzzle of the hard point weapon jerked around blindly like a mole clawing up from the ground.

Mkoll rapped with the shell again. The beast's top hatches were armoured and locked. There was no way in, but there was no way it could get him off its back without one of the crew coming outside. He rapped again, deliberately goading it.

Gaunt got up, circling, waiting for a chance to lunge closer. The beast lurched forwards, stopped sharply, and then did it again, braking so hard the second time, it almost threw Mkoll forwards and off the hull.

He held on.

The tank abruptly powered backwards, spraying up mud, throwing Mkoll's footing the other way. He kept his grip and knocked again.

As if demented, the beast braked, and then threw itself forwards, picking up speed. Gaunt ran out of its path. The sudden acceleration threw Mkoll onto his chest, but he looped his elbow around the hand rail.

He clung on as the tank left the clearing and tore into the woods, demolishing a path as it went. Twigs and boughs raked and clawed at Mkoll as he was carried along. It was trying to scrape him off its topside.

Gaunt and Eszrah ran after it, following the trail of splintered stumps and exploded logs into the dead forest. Black leaf matter and wood fibres swirled down in the rain around them.

Deep in the tract of dark trees, the beast slewed to the left and scraped its starboard side against the mass of a big, old tree, like a hound scraping its flank against a post. The tree, soft and corrupted, folded over and crashed down onto the tank. Mkoll saw it coming down at him, and let go of the hand rail. He rolled sideways off the turret and landed on the top of the engine compartment as the dead tree broke like brittle honeycomb across the tank's topside.

The beast took off again, dropping nose-first into a hollow that bounced the rear end up and bucked Mkoll into the air. He grabbed the edge of an armour plate as he landed, and barely avoided a tumble off the side.

The enemy tank was nose in, gouging up the far side of the hollow in a spattering sheet of mud. It lurched to the left to find a better path, and churned through the undergrowth ahead of it, taking down another lifeless tree. Mkoll clambered back up onto the rocking turret top, and rapped the side of the missile against the hatch.

The beast thumped to a violent halt, unable to shake off its tormentor. Gaunt came sprinting out of the trees behind it, Eszrah close at his heels. Gaunt didn't break stride, but simply leapt up onto the tail plates of the big machine, clambered from there onto the engine compartment, and ran on up the engine cover to the turret.

Without hesitation, Gaunt sliced the power sword around and cut through the armoured lock and hinges of the top hatch. Sparks, a billow of steam, and a stench of burning metal accompanied the blow. Beside him, Mkoll kicked the severed hatch away with the heel of his right foot, jerked the detonation tape out of the rocket, and lobbed it in through the open hatchway.

Neither of them ever saw what was inside the beast. They got a quick impression of a lurid, infernal gloom, and a smell like an abattoir.

They leapt off the beast into the air, side by side, arms outstretched as the fireball gutted the tank and rushed up out of the hatch to chase them.

VIII

THEY TREKKED BACK into the Untill to the north-east, past the defining, warding line of partisan skulls on stakes. Criid had recovered well enough to limp, but she was battered and dazed. Posetine and Derin supported Larkin, who faded in and out of shock and consciousness.

'I'm sorry,' Gaunt told him. 'It was the only way.'

Larkin muttered something, but he was too woozy on the field kit shots Posetine had stuck him with to be coherent.

The rain cleared, and then came back with driving force. The sky darkened like wet cloth. Behind them, a ragged trickle of black smoke marked the beast's grave in the deep forest.

About two hours after the brawl with the tank had ended, they were met by partisan scouts in a glade at the edges of the marsh. Nightfall was beginning to add to the storm's darkness.

Silently, the Nihtgane led them on, into the swamp groves, along tracks and trails between the root masses and the filthy water, into a darkness that was darkness no matter the time of day or the weather.

In there, in the true Untill, Gaunt at last saw some remnant of Gereon as he had known it. The Untill, that most inhospitable and treacherous part of the world was now the only part that showed any sign of life. There were insects, small animals, some fish and lizards. The trees, and matting frond plants and climbers, were alive. The moths fluttered. It did not look so green and fecund as he remembered it – it was greyer and paler, and life was less abundant – but the Ruinous Powers had not encroached enough to kill it yet.

They trudged on into the green darkness, clouds of moths trailing them like confetti at some great triumph. Birds called in the canopy, and amphibians croaked and splashed in the marsh ways.

Mkoll paused at one spot, listening.

'What?' Gaunt asked him.

Mkoll was staring into the twilight distance of the Untill glades beyond them. 'I could have sworn,' he began. 'Something familiar, like…' he shook his head. 'No, there's nothing there.'

SOME TIME LATER, they arrived at the partisan encampment that Landerson had chosen for the operation. It was a large place, partly a Nihtgane village, partly a prefab camp, populated by underground soldiers and partisans alike. All told, some sixty people lived in the huts and habitents raised in clusters around a small island in the middle of the swamp, its limits extended by platforms and walkways. The division between Nihtgane and Gereonite, already eroding in Gaunt's time on the planet, had vanished. This was simply the resistance.

Landerson had brought the rest of Gaunt's section to the camp. Faragut, it seemed, had already begun discussions about shared tactical data. Cirk was present, helping to smooth the conversation between the commissar and the wary underground.

Landerson greeted Gaunt's party.

'We'd almost given up on you,' Landerson said.

'I thought you'd have learned not to by now,' Gaunt replied. He helped Criid onto the camp platform, and then made way for the two men carrying Larkin.

'It wasn't easy,' Gaunt said. 'It would be good to get a medic for Larkin. Do you have a medic?'

'Of course they have a medic,' said a voice from further up the platform. Ana Curth pushed her way down to reach Larkin.

'Ana?' Gaunt blinked.

'What did this?' Curth asked, examining Larkin. She was dressed in rags and scraps like all of Landerson's people, and was so thin that he barely recognised her.

'My power sword,' Gaunt said, staring at her.

'What?'

'His leg was pinned.'

Curth glanced at him. Whatever else had changed in her, changed or faded or perished, the fierce look in the eyes had not.

'Throne, Ana–' he began, taking a step forwards.

'Talk to me later,' she snapped. 'I've got to patch him up. Criid too, by the look of it. Talk to me later when I've finished.'

She gestured, and Posetine and Derin hoisted Larkin up and carried him after her into the camp.

'Ana Curth...' Gaunt murmured. 'I always hoped she'd make it and always feared she wouldn't.'

'She was always tough,' said Mkoll. 'A Ghost after all.'

And looking more like a Ghost now than ever, Gaunt thought. He followed Landerson into the camp.

'This Faragut's keen,' Landerson remarked.

'Cut him some slack,' Gaunt said. 'He doesn't know any better. Where's Beltayn?'

Landerson glanced around. 'I told him you had caught up. I don't know where he's got to.'

'Over in the hut there, sir,' said Garond.

Gaunt hastened over to the dwelling that Garond had indicated. It was a makeshift comms room and repair shop for weapons. By the light of a small prom lamp, Gaunt saw cannibalised rifles and two or three battered vox-sets.

Beltayn had his own, customised vox-caster up on a bench and was studying it.

'Bel?'

'Sorry, sir. I was about to come and meet you when I noticed something.'

'Something?' Gaunt asked, joining him.

'Yes, sir. Something's awry. I've been trying to raise Cantible or Command on the vox, but the conditions are as bad as ever. My guess is it's because of the storms kicked off by the invasion.'

He was fiddling with the back plate of his vox unit, using a dirty screwdriver to prise off the cover of the enhanced aerial.

'What are you doing, Bel?' Gaunt asked, peering closer.

'Well, last time I tried the set, I noticed there was a slight power drain, as if I'd left the channel booster on, which I hadn't.'

'So?'

'So there's a little power light here, at the base, that wasn't on before. There's some kind of system hidden in my caster that I didn't know about, and it's been switched on for about the last hour or so.'

'Wait a minute,' said Gaunt. 'Are you talking about sabotage?'

'I don't think so,' Beltayn replied. 'I hope not,' he added with a grin, 'or poking around with this screwdriver is going to be a bad idea.'

The backplate came away, and Beltayn pulled out some acoustic padding. They both stared into the small cavity. The device was about the size of a tube-charge, with activation lights glowing around its top end.

'Throne!' Gaunt spat. He wrenched the device out of Beltayn's caster and carried it outside.

'What is this?' he yelled. Underground fighters and members of the section alike looked around at the raised voice.

'What the hell is this?' he yelled again.

'Gaunt?' Landerson said, coming over.

'What's the matter with you?' asked Faragut as he strode in across the boards.

'This is what's the matter with me,' Gaunt said, holding the device out.

'That's a locator,' said Mkoll. 'That's a damn locator. High power, pulse-beam beacon. Feth, it's on. How long has it been on?'

'Since I switched it on,' Faragut said.

'What the feth have you done?' Gaunt snarled at the younger commissar.

There was a sudden, glittering blue light around them, and it expanded to fill the entire glade. Many of the underground, especially the Nihtgane, cried out in alarm. Long shadows fell across the camp and the waters of the swamp, cast by the sudden radiance.

The flare of the mass teleport beam died away. Gaunt stared at the squads of armed personnel ringing the camp. They wore black and gold armour, and the symbol of the Inquisition.

'My job,' Faragut replied.

RIP

I

ABOUT HALF AN hour after Caff spoke to him the second time, the Imperium loosed another deluge of wrath on Gereon.

It happened a long way away from Dalin, but he saw the flashes. Long-distance blinks of white light lit the sky, and he felt the hot wind pick up and brush his face a few moments later. A forest grew along the eastern horizon, a glade of giant, dark trees composed of smoke.

They had tall trunks and crowning caps of black vapour. They were evidently huge, because they were hundreds of kilometres away, and they stayed there for hours, unsmudged by the wind. Two other giant mushroom clouds elevated themselves in the far north-west.

Lost in the heart of K'ethdrac, he stumbled through the ash-white streets alone. The city skyline was smouldering, and to the south-east of him, several huge spires were burning up, consumed by extraordinarily ferocious fires that seemed to blaze with unnatural power. The silent, sentinel mushroom clouds formed a backdrop to these intense combustions.

Near at hand, the city was dry and still and empty, so caked in ash it looked like a town after a snowstorm. The bones of buildings rose above him like old, dry coral.

Dalin had killed the Sons of Sek. This thought alone contented him. He had killed three of them, single-handed. He had no idea what had happened to the rest of them.

He'd shot down the first two as they emerged from the building. They had been running, not expecting their quarry to turn and fight. He'd put three shots into each one, spilling them flat on the ground. The vaunted soldiers, the dreaded Sons, brought down so easily! Dalin felt elated. He felt as if he had passed some advanced test. Not only had he tasted battle and killed the enemy, he had killed the *best* of the enemy.

That was when Caff had spoken to him again. '*Watch yourself,*' was all he had said. Immediately, Dalin got a picture in his head of the other Sons of Sek inside the ruin. He saw them hearing the shots outside, and coming to a halt. He imagined how they would sneak out of the building, now that they had been forewarned, and get the drop on him.

He stepped back into the cover of the old iron portico, and got down, panning his weapon around. Little zephyrs of ash were dancing through the rubble, conjured by the ragged wind. Shredded plasterwork flapped in the breeze. Dalin remembered his breathing and his visual checking.

Sly and well-trained, the third of the Sons of Sek emerged from a window-hole twenty metres along the face of the building from the doorway, and slipped down into the shadows and the rubble. Dalin watched him for a minute or two, admiring the man's noise discipline and use of cover. The Son was moving around to flank any shooter covering the doorway.

Dalin watched and waited. He waited until the Son of Sek had drawn in close and entered a very reliable range band. Then he shot him through the forehead.

The enemy warrior grunted and fell face down onto the rubble. Dalin waited a while longer, but nothing else stirred.

He withdrew. He moved silently for a while, but after the flashes of light announced the crop of mushroom clouds in the sky, he relaxed. There was no sign of anybody around. He'd given Merrt, Fourbox and Wash enough time to get clear of pursuit. They were long gone. He called out a few times, shouting their names across the rubble and demolished lots.

His voice echoed, but the echoes were the only answers he got.

II

HE WONDERED WHY it was Caff's voice he had heard.

Obviously, it wasn't really Caff's voice. Dalin understood that well enough, and though he was as superstitious as the next Guardsman, he didn't believe in phantom voices or clairaudience. It was all in his own mind, and he was content with that fact. He'd been through a sensory onslaught in the past days, and he was exhausted, and stretched to the edges of his nerves. His combat instincts were pulled as taut as they could go. In the thick of the moment, his own mind had sent him subconscious warnings, and he had heard them as if they'd been spoken by Caff.

It was no big deal – men went an awful lot madder than that on the battlefield – and it was no mystery.

What vaguely puzzled Dalin wasn't that he heard a voice, but that it happened to be Caffran's.

He sat down to rest for a while, and thought about it a little longer. The light over the city had gone an odd, glazed colour, and the wind was chasing clouds across the sky, so that a rapidly moving pattern of shade and light dappled the landscape.

Why had his imagination chosen Caffran's voice? Why not his ma's, or his real father's? Technically, they were both more important to him. Dalin wished he had some water to drink. His throat was dry and he had a headache. He tried sucking on a small piece of one of his last ration bricks, but it didn't help.

He decided that his relationship with Caff was a particular thing. He had a bond with Tona of course, as close a bond as a real mother and son, as close as the harsh life of the Guard permitted. He and his sibling had come into her care on Verghast years before. Chance had thrown them together. He'd always assumed she'd never had much choice in the matter. They were small children, Yoncy a babe in arms, in the middle of a hive war, and she'd taken care of them. Without her, or someone like her, they would have died.

She hadn't been that old, probably not much older than he was now. She'd simply coped.

Sitting there, in the ruins, under the racing sky, he realised, properly for the first time in his life, how selfless her decision had been. Fate had given them into her care, and she hadn't hesitated. She hadn't hesitated in the rubble of Vervunhive, and she hadn't hesitated since. Perhaps it hadn't been fate. Throne, he saw that now. Perhaps it had been the strange ministry of the God-Emperor. Watching the chasing clouds, he felt a strong, unbidden sensation of the divine, stronger than he'd ever known it in temple worship, or daily blessing, or even during one of old Zweil's sermons. For a few minutes in that desolate place, he had an oddly intense feeling that the God-Emperor was watching over him.

He wondered if Tona had ever resented the responsibility she'd been landed with at Vervunhive. Certainly, she'd become a proxy parent for him and his sister, because there was no other option. Necessity had manufactured their relationship. She'd looked after them as fiercely as a she-wolf protecting her young.

His father, his real father, was different. Gol Kolea had believed his children dead for a long time until chance had revealed the strange twist of fortune that had kept them close to him. Kolea had never tried to remake his relationship with Dalin or Yoncy. Tona had explained on several occasions that Kolea had decided it best, for the children's' sake, not to upset their lives any further by stepping back into them. Dalin had little patience for this excuse. It felt like Kolea was washing his hands of them. He didn't understand it, and he'd never approached Kolea directly about it, because it made him angry. It wasn't as if you could have too many parents, especially in an odd social structure like the regiment. Plenty of Ghosts had been surrogate fathers and uncles and mothers and aunts over the years – Varl, Domor, Larkin, Aleksa, Bonin, Curth. His real blood father taking a role wouldn't have fethed up anything worse than it was already fethed up.

But Caff… Caff had chosen, where Tona had been offered no choice, and Kolea had backed off. Caffran had chosen to be a father figure to Dalin. Caffran could have stepped back at any time, the way Kolea had stepped back, and, unlike Kolea, no one would have thought badly of him for it. For the last eight years or so, Caffran had raised him. Caffran had been there.

This was why it was Caff's voice he had heard, he decided. He had been the one who had chosen, without duress, to care.

Caffran said, 'Don't be a fool, Dal. It's not a big deal. I wanted to be with Tona. It's not a thing. In the Guard, you just get on and you do it. You play it as it lays, that's what Varl says, am I right? If we don't look out for one another, what's the point?'

'Who's "we"?' Dalin asked.

'People,' said Caffran. His uniform was tightly pressed and funny looking, like he'd had an accident with the starch. He looked awkward, as if he was gussied up for dress review. He sat down beside Dalin in the dust and leant back against the wall.

'Clouds are fast,' he said.

'Really running by,' Dalin agreed. 'See how they paint the city. Like sunlight on running water.'

Caffran nodded.

'I'm thirsty,' Dalin said.

Caffran reached down and unhooked his water bottle. He passed it to Dalin.

The bottle felt light. Dalin unstoppered it. Something tugged at his right foot.

'Stop that,' Dalin said.

'What?' Caffran asked.

'Stop it with my foot.'

Caffran didn't answer. The water bottle was empty.

III

THE WATER BOTTLE was empty. It was his own water bottle. He let go of it and it fell off his chest.

The light had gone. The sky was petrochemical black. Cloaked by it, the half-seen sun glowed like a dirty lamp. His lips were dry and cracked, and his throat was like dry vizzy cloth.

He wondered how long he had been dead, and then realised he had only been asleep. He'd known little sleep since the drop, little of quality anyway. Just stopping for a moment, resting, it had stormed him and conquered him, like a drop-ship invasion. He'd been unable to resist.

He wiped his parched mouth, but the back of his hand was as rough as sandpaper from the ash. His lips bled. He sucked at the hot moisture. He looked around in the darkness for Caffran, but there was no Caffran, and there never had been any Caffran. Fatigue hallucinations had segued into dreams.

He was alone. Even the presence of the God-Emperor had withdrawn. Something tugged at his right foot.

That was no hallucination.

The dogs were big things. Scrawny dark shapes in the enveloping night, they closed their jaws around his right boot and worried. They were vermin dogs, scavengers loose in the ruins.

'Get off. Get away,' he said.

They looked at him reproachfully and whined.

'Get away!' he snapped, reaching for his rifle.

'Looking for this?' a third dog asked. It was sitting close by him, his rifle clamped under its paws.

'Give me my gun,' he said.

The dogs laughed. They rolled him over and started to search his pockets.

HE FELT HANDS on him. He was face down in the ash dust.

'Nothing. Just some food,' a voice said.

'His flask's empty,' someone replied.

Dalin groaned and rolled over.

'Shit! He's alive!'

Dalin opened his eyes. Three dirt-caked Krassians bent over him. They'd been stripping his body. Night had fallen when he hadn't been paying attention. The black sky was rimmed with orange fires around the horizon.

'What are you doing?' Dalin mumbled, but the words came out as another groan.

'He's bloody alive!' one of the Krassians said, and pushed Dalin back down.

'Croak him then, for Throne's sake,' said another.

Dalin saw the first Krassian reach for a long sword bayonet and draw it.

'Imperial Guard!' Dalin cried in alarm.

'Yeah, yeah,' said the Krassian. 'Welcome to the bloody war.'

The sword bayonet stabbed down at him, and Dalin rolled. The blade almost missed him. He felt the slick, hot pain of it as it sliced through the meat of his left hip.

'Bastard!' he cried.

'Hold the little shit!' exclaimed the Krassian with the knife.

Dalin kicked the man's legs out from under him, and the Krassian fell with a curse. Dalin's right boot, half undone, flew off with the effort. The other two Krassians pounced on him.

'What are you doing? What are you doing to me?' Dalin wailed. They struck at him. He felt their knuckles batter at his ribcage. He rolled the way Caff had taught him when they practised hand-to-hand on the billet decks. He broke free from one, and planted his fist in the other man's face. The Krassian lurched backwards, blood and mucus spraying from his crunched nose. He set up a loud cursing.

Dalin sprang up. The Krassian with the sword bayonet came at him. Dalin dipped to one side, caught the man's wrist, and broke it. Taking hold of the long blade, he slid it across the man's throat in a single, unsentimental sweep. Arterial blood squirted out and covered one of the others in such quantities that the man began yowling and spitting in disgust.

Dalin dropped the twitching corpse and slammed the sword bayonet down between the shoulders of the gasping spitter. Impaled, the man fell on his face.

'You little bastard,' sputtered the one with the broken nose. He was standing again, and aiming his lasrifle at Dalin with shaking hands.

A las-round hit him square in the back with such force that it cannoned his body into Dalin. Their heads struck hard with a crack, and they both went down.

Dazed, unable to move, Dalin watched as a fireteam of Sons of Sek approached out of the gloom to inspect the bodies.

The ochre clad figures moved slowly, stopping to check and examine each corpse in turn.

One of them got hold of Dalin's shoulder and rolled him. Dalin could smell the mysterious perfumes and oils that the Son had anointed his body with.

'A'vas shet voi shenj,' the Son said.

IV

'Please, get up.'

Dalin played dead.

'Get up, Holy. Get up, get up, get up…'

It was Fourbox.

Dalin opened his eyes.

It was still dark, and the only illumination came from the burning towers in the distance.

'There you go! Come on, Holy!'

'Fourbox?'

'We were looking for you.'

'Fourbox?'

'Yes, wake up.'

Dalin sat upright. There was a stinging pain in his left hip, and he felt a damp warmth around the side of his fatigue breeches and the side of his body.

'He all right?' Merrt asked from nearby.

'He's fine. Aren't you, Holy?' Fourbox said.

'But the Sons of Sek…'

'No Sons of Sek around here,' said Fourbox. He helped Dalin up. Dalin felt more bruises and pains that seemed fresh.

'But…?' he said.

'We gn… gn… gn… got to move,' said Merrt.

'Where's my boot?' Dalin asked. He looked down. His right boot was missing.

'Here,' said Merrt, tossing it to him.

Dalin sat back down, wincing from the pain in his left hip, and started to lace his boot on.

'Hurry it up,' said Merrt.

Dalin stopped lacing. He slowly looked around and saw the three dead Krassians crumpled in the white dust around him.

'What the feth is–?' he began, pointing.

'Deserters. They were trying to loot your body,' said Merrt. 'You'd stiffed two of them by the time we arrived.'

'What… what time is it?'

Fourbox waggled his chron. 'Who knows?'

'He's blowing for us,' Wash said, looming into vision. Dalin could hear whistles in the distance.

'Who is?' he asked.

'Sobile,' said Merrt. 'We found Sobile. Now get your boot on.'

SOBILE WAS WAITING with AT 137 in a neighbouring street. There were about ten men left, all told, all of them wounded or scraped in some minor way. They looked like beggars, like lepers in some underhive commercia. Kexie, more stringy and raw than ever, was blowing his confounded whistle.

Sobile stood on his own away from the huddle of exhausted men. His clothes were dirty, and there were tear stains on his soot-caked face where the dust had made his eyes run. He looked like the tragic clown prince in the Imperial mystery plays. His face was utterly without expression. He slouched. He seemed bored, or dismissively weary. Most of the men had lash marks on their scalps or shoulders. The cord of Sobile's whip was caked in blood.

Sobile stared at Dalin as he rejoined the section with Merrt, Wash and Fourbox. There was not a hint of recognition. There wasn't even a spark to show that Sobile was pleased to see that another of his charges had survived.

'Get in line, you moron,' he said. It was as if Dalin had only been out of the commissar's sight for a few minutes. The whole world had ended around them, but Sobile was acting like they were on routine manoeuvres. He was acting like there were more important things on his mind.

He glared at Dalin, but Dalin made no effort to hurry. Sobile let the cord of the whip flop free into the dust on the ground, its length played out to crack. Dalin held Sobile's gaze as he got in line. He stared back, defiantly. He knew that if Sobile used his whip on him now, he would shoot Sobile. He was sure of this fact, and quite reconciled to it.

Sobile rewound his whip and looked away. Perhaps he had seen the look in Dalin's eyes. Perhaps it was a particular look that he always watched for. *When a trooper glares back so hard you know he will shoot you if you strike him, then the trooper is ready and needs no further beating.* Maybe that rule was somewhere in the odious fething book the Commissariat worked from. Watch for the look of a beaten dog, then refrain from punishment.

'Check your loads,' Kexie said, walking down the line. 'Anyone choking?'

One of the men raised a hand.

'Share him some clips, you others. Anyone thirsty?'

Dalin raised his hand.

'Share him a bottle.'

Brickmaker passed Dalin a half-empty canteen.

'Ech, fit and square,' sad Kexie. He turned to look at Sobile. 'Fit and square, commissar. Awaiting yours.'

Screwing the cap back on Brickmaker's canteen, Dalin braced himself for Sobile's next utterance. It was as wholly inevitable as it was insane.

'Forwards,' the commissar said.

UNKYNDE

I

'START YOUR EXPLANATION NOW,' Gaunt growled. He had shouldered his way past several Inquisition troopers to reach Faragut. The troopers, visored and quiet, were rounding everybody up, partisans and Ghosts alike.

'Nobody do anything provocative until I've got to the heart of this,' Gaunt had told Mkoll.

'Once you have, it'll be too late,' Mkoll replied. They had looked at one another, and both had known Mkoll's words to be an untruth. Despite the reputation of the Inquisition's soldiery, the Gereon partisans were never to be underestimated, even when disarmed and 'restrained'.

'Faragut!'

Faragut was talking to a couple of the senior Inquisition officers. Cirk was nearby. She was looking washed out and not a little taken aback. The sight of armoured Imperial troopers herding members of the resistance was a hard thing for someone like her to see.

She caught Gaunt's eye and shook her head.

'Faragut!'

Faragut turned. 'I'm too busy to deal with you now,' he said. Gaunt grabbed him by the lapels.

'No, you're not.'

'Get off me!' Faragut snorted. Inquisition troopers nearby had stepped back and were suddenly aiming their guns at Gaunt.

'Get off me, now!' said Faragut. Gaunt slowly released Faragut's jacket. 'It's all right,' Faragut said to the guards. 'Lower your weapons.'

'What the hell is this?' Gaunt asked, his voice a whisper.

'This is the business of the Inquisition,' replied Faragut, who clearly seemed to be enjoying the situation. He reached into his jacket pocket and pulled out an identity module. When he activated it, it displayed the rosette of the Inquisition. 'I have been seconded to ordo operation with the permission of Commissar-General Balshin.'

'Of course you have,' said Gaunt. 'That bitch tricked me. I'm a fool. I should have known she had a deeper agenda.'

Faragut clicked off his module and put it away. 'Gaunt, you are a regimental officer. In almost every respect, you're disposable. There's no reason at all that you should have been kept in the loop on this. You didn't need to know, and you're not important enough to have an opinion.'

'My men were ordered to stage at Cantible, and then exploit our prior knowledge of the Untill and the resistance to establish a line of contact with the Gereon underground,' Gaunt said, 'so as to develop cooperation, and hasten the liberation effort. You've used us.'

'You're a soldier,' Faragut said, with a light, mocking laugh. 'What the hell did you expect, except that you were going to be used? You're such an idiot, Gaunt. You're far too liberal and highly principled for the Imperial Guard.'

Gaunt pulled back a little. 'I'll take that as a compliment. Now explain this. I will not stand by and watch these men and women manhandled like prisoners of war.'

'No, you'll not stand by. You'll stand down. Your job is done. Contact with the resistance is established. We'll take it from here. In fact, as soon as I've got clearance, you and your Ghosts can ship out back to Cantible.'

'No,' said Gaunt. 'You'll have to do better than that. I'm not going anywhere all the while it looks like I've sold these people out.'

Faragut smiled and leaned in close to Gaunt's face. 'You know, I used to quite admire you. High minded, strong, always with the right, brave turn of phrase ready to dish out for the benefit of the common dog-soldiers. But now I see it for what it is. It's just hot air, isn't it? What in the name of the Throne can you do about this? Have a tantrum?'

'He might kill you,' said a voice from behind them.

Gaunt and Faragut both looked around. Inquisitor Lornas Welt walked up the camp decking to join them.

'I thought you commissars were trained to read body language, Faragut?' Welt said. 'To know when to goad a man and when to refrain? Isn't that in your *Instrument of Order*?'

'Yes, lord,' said Faragut.

'I don't think you're reading Gaunt very well, Faragut. I think you were about twenty seconds away from a field execution. Wasn't he, Gaunt?'

'More like sixty. But, yes.'

'Hello, Gaunt,' said Welt. He smiled. 'Let's have a conversation.'

II

'LET'S BE CLEAR about this,' said Welt. 'Let's be clear so there is no misunderstanding. The Inquisition can be very heavy handed. The Inquisition *will* be very heavy handed. Here, in the next few weeks, the agents of the ordos will not be gentle. Which is unfortunate, because these brave people deserve better. However, don't expect me to apologise, and don't expect me to order restraint. What we are engaged in here is vital work. It's potentially the most important thing I've undertaken in my career.'

Gaunt blinked. 'What?' he replied.

'I'm not joking, Gaunt,' Welt said.

They had withdrawn to one of the upper habitat platforms, suspended in the tree canopy over the green waters. Down below, Welt's soldiers were securing the camp and watching over the bewildered partisans. Troopers with flamers were moving out into the swamp to fell trees and clear the canopy wide enough to form a landing zone.

'Why do you think the Crusade moved on Gereon, Gaunt?' Welt asked.

'Because the Second Front needed to start winning back territory to bolster its legitimacy. Because we could not suffer to have the Archenemy bedded in amongst us. Because individuals like Cirk and me have been petitioning for a liberation effort since we returned.'

'All valid reasons,' said Welt. He was a short, broad man with receding grey hair and a black goatee beard on his boxer's jaw. The pupils of his eyes were so large, the blue of the iris filled his lids to the edges, showing no white. He wore a brown leather storm coat, and the rosette of his office was strung across his breast on a pectoral. Like all the inquisitors Ibram Gaunt had ever known, Welt was frustratingly ambiguous. Commanding, authoritative, appealing in his great intelligence and polymath learning, yet treacherous and untrustworthy in that nothing was too precious to be sacrificed if it served his ends. Lilith had been like that. So had Heldane.

'But?' asked Gaunt, weighting the word.

'There is one other, better reason. The most compelling reason of all.'

'Which is?'

'You, Gaunt. You are the reason. The fact that you came back.'

Gaunt shook his head in disbelief and turned away. He walked to the edge of the platform and leant on the rope rail, staring down. The first time he'd ever been up on a camp platform like this, he'd been fighting for his life against the monster Uexkull. This conversation seemed somehow far darker and more dangerous.

'You still obsess with this?' Gaunt asked. 'I thought we'd laid it to rest. The tribunal–'

'Was just a formality.' Welt walked over to join him. He had a habit of looking people in the eye and not wavering. 'You and your mission team came here, to an enemy occupied world, and were here for sixteen times the recommended length of exposure. You were changed, of course. Such an ordeal would change anyone. But you were not tainted. You came away uncorrupted. This is a remarkable thing, Ibram. A remarkable thing.'

'So you have told me, inquisitor. I supposed I might have been dissected by now.'

Welt smiled. 'This isn't the Dark Ages,' he said.

'Oh,' said Gaunt, 'I rather think it is.'

'Your own theory was that you had survived corruption because you had been blessed by the beati herself,' said Welt. 'As theories go, it's reasonable. And not without precedent, historically. But there are other ways of looking at it. Ways that my colleagues and savants believe may repay examination.'

'You mean that this place is the reason?' asked Gaunt. 'That this place has some property that counters the touch of Chaos?'

The inquisitor nodded. 'Gereon... and, most specifically, the famously impenetrable Untill. You've spoken to me of this, and I've read your reports carefully. Cirk has also divulged a great deal. In the case of every single one of you, and especially in the case of Trooper Feygor, organic extracts derived from the Untill's singular, toxic biology appeared to combat the effects of taint.'

'Feygor died on Ancreon Sextus,' said Gaunt.

'I know. And his body was not recovered. If anyone should have been dissected, it was him. Alas, we never got the chance.'

'Are you saying the Imperial Guard and allied Crusade forces... millions of men and vast quantities of material... have been committed to the invasion of Gereon... because Murt Feygor died in battle?'

'That's an over-simplification.'

Gaunt laughed. 'Murt would have loved that. Say what you like about him, he appreciated good irony even if he couldn't voice it.'

He looked back at Welt. 'So you haven't come back for Gereon? You've done all this on the long shot that the Untill might be hiding something?'

'If the Untill has what we're after, it will change the course of history. It will change the destiny of the Imperium and mankind. It will liberate us from our greatest enemy.'

'A cure for Chaos?'

'Too trite. But yes. I suppose that's how it will be seen.'

'There's no such thing here,' said Gaunt. 'I could have saved you a great deal of effort. It's not here. It never has been. The Nihtgane may know of some extracts with strong medicinal properties, but not the miracle you're looking for. Mkvenner, one of my original team, had a notion. He reckoned Chaos didn't destroy us. It didn't taint and infect like a disease. It didn't work like that at all, which is why there could be no cure.'

'He believed in force of will, I presume,' said Welt.

'Precisely. Chaos isn't evil. It simply unlocks and lets out our propensities for evil and desecration. That is why it is so pernicious. It brings out our flaws. Force of will, determination, loyalty... these are the qualities that combat Chaos taint. If a man can remain true to the Throne, Chaos can't touch him. A hatred and rejection of Chaos becomes a weapon against it.'

'The armour of contempt,' said Welt. 'I am familiar with Inquisitor Ravenor's writings. The idea was not original to him.'

He stepped back from the rope rail. 'You may be right. It is an enobling notion. We might save mankind by strength of character, rather than by an extracted tincture of moth venom. History will like the former better.'

He looked back at Gaunt. 'But you'll forgive me for testing the moth venom.'

* * *

III

'It was a cellar,' Caffran told Rawne. 'Under the habs over that way. Street eighteen, I think.'

Leclan nodded as he took a swig from his canteen. 'Street eighteen.'

'I went in first, Leclan behind me,' Caffran continued. 'Black as pitch. I could smell something.'

'I said there was something,' Leclan put in.

'He said there was. I could smell it. I was pretty sure we'd run another excubitor to ground. I was all for lobbing a tube-charge in and sorting the bodies after.'

'You said that. You did,' Leclan agreed.

'But, you know, orders,' Caffran said. He scratched his chin and squinted up at the sun.

'Go on,' said Rawne.

'I almost shot him,' said Caffran. 'I had a lamp on, sweeping, and I saw movement. I just reacted. I almost put a las bolt through his head.'

'But you didn't,' said Rawne.

'I almost did. His face. He was so fething scared.' Caffran nodded across the ruined street to a nearby aid station. Under the close scrutiny of Inquisition troopers, Dorden and his corpsmen were treating the latest batch of emaciated civilians that the sweeps had flushed out of Cantible's hidden corners. The head count, according to Hark's tally, was now five hundred and fifty-eight survivors, all of them in a terrible condition. Dorden was treating a child, a boy of about ten standard, whose shrunken frame looked more like that of a five year old. The child was dazed, bewildered, in shock. That much was obvious, even from across the street.

'I don't know how long he'd been down there,' said Caffran. 'But he was too scared to come out.'

'This is happening a lot,' said Baskevyl. 'The survivors have been living in terror for too long. Most of them have been reduced to the level of animals. We're just men with guns, Rawne. They're too messed up to realise we've come to save them.'

'We have to finish the sweeps. We have to clear the entire town,' said Rawne.

'I know,' said Baskevyl.

'There's no other way.'

'I know,' Baskevyl nodded. 'But nobody wants to be the first to shoot one of these poor wretches by mistake.'

'Those fellows aren't helping much,' said Zweil. They all looked around. The old ayatani had squatted down nearby, resting his feet. He indicated the agents of the Inquisition nearby. 'We promise them they're safe, and we bring them out of hiding, and then those fellows take over.'

Some of the Inquisition soldiers were leading a troop of liberated souls away down the street towards the pens that had been erected in the town's main square. Under the direction of Interrogator Sydona, the agent in charge of the Inquisitorial forces that had arrived the day before, Cantible was being turned into a processing camp for the dispossessed. Sydona had made it clear to Rawne that the Ghosts were expected to act as security for the camp, and several sections had been seconded to help raise the wooden palisade fences of the pens. Sydona had also made it clear that Cantible would be expecting a further influx of survivors from the outlying districts over the coming weeks.

Rawne didn't like it much, and he knew none of the Ghosts did either. They were picking their way through the most miserable waste of a town, seeing small horrors everywhere they looked. The few people they found were dragged off for interrogation and internment. Rawne understood it had to be this way. No one who had lived on Gereon through the Occupation could be trusted. They had to be processed, and examined for taint or corruption. Many were likely to be executed. Quite properly, the Inquisition would take no chances whatsoever with taint. But it made the Ghosts feel as if they were staffing a concentration camp for Imperial citizens. It made Rawne wonder why they'd ever bothered with a liberation effort if this was all they could offer the people of Gereon.

'I'll speak to Sydona,' Rawne said. 'But I think this is how it's going to be. This is Imperial policy, and even if we did suddenly find ourselves in a topsy turvy world where the Inquisition listened to the opinion of the Imperial Guard, I'm not sure they're not right anyway. The Archenemy has held this place for too long. What was it Gaunt said? There's nothing left to save.'

'I don't think that attitude does much for morale,' said Baskevyl.

'Feth take morale,' snapped Rawne. 'I'd give most of all I have to help Gereon. This last year or so, I've dreamed of coming back and bringing the relief they begged us for. Now, I wish we'd never come.'

'Because they're not flocking out of their houses and cheering us, and crowning us with victory garlands for liberating them?' Zweil asked.

Rawne's face darkened. 'Because this is no more than a death bed vigil.' He strode away to find the interrogator. A couple of minutes later, the noise of a small explosion – a grenade or a tube-charge – rolled in from a neighbouring street, and Baskevyl set off to investigate.

Caffran remained where he was, staring across the street at the boy he'd almost shot.

'He's about the age Dalin was,' Caffran said.

'What?' asked Zweil.

'That boy. He's about the age Dalin was when Tona found him and Yoncy in the ruins of the hive. And I found all three of them a few days later. They were feral. Scared. Hiding. Just like him. I could have shot them by mistake. Like I nearly shot him.'

Zweil had been fiddling with his ill-fitting boots. He stood up, leaning on Leclan for support. 'Are you due off on another sweep?' he asked.

'Streets twenty-six and twenty-seven,' said Leclan. 'Another ten minutes, once the section has rested.'

'I'm coming with you,' Zweil said.

'I don't think so,' said Caffran.

'Well, I am. If you're just men with guns to them, maybe having a priest with you will help. I'd like to believe I can help diffuse their fears. Maybe coax them out of hiding a little less traumatically.'

'Father, there are still things hiding in this place,' said Leclan.

'So?'

'So you'll be in the line of fire,' said Caffran.

'And about time too,' Zweil replied. 'Do you know how old I am, Dermon Caffran?'

'No, father.'

'Neither do I. But it's high time I did something more useful than catalogue plants.'

Caffran and Leclan exchanged wide-eyed glances.

'This is why I came along,' Zweil said. 'To do real good. It's been a long time since I did any real good.'

'Whatever you like, father,' said Caffran. 'In truth, I could use the help. But if you get yourself killed, don't be blaming me.'

'I wouldn't dream of it,' Zweil grinned. 'If I'm killed, I'll just take the matter up with a higher authority.'

'JUST DO YOUR job, major,' said Interrogator Sydona. He was a tall, slender man in red and black garments, robed like royalty. He had a thin face and a thinner mouth.

'I assumed you'd say that,' Rawne replied, 'but for the sake of my own conscience, I had to ask.'

Sydona shrugged. 'I commiserate, major. Sometimes our holy duty is painful and ugly. But it must be done. Those we find who are still true, bless their courageous souls, will thank us one day.'

'I'm sure,' said Rawne, not sure at all.

'If I might say so,' said Sydona, signing a data-slate one of his aides held out for him, 'I find your concerns quaint. In a good way. I have had many dealings with the Imperial Guard. I have, most usually, found the soldiers of the Guard to be base and soulless. Your attitude does you credit.'

'I've kept good company over the years,' said Rawne.

'You mean Gaunt? I'm looking forward to meeting him. I've heard so much about him from my inquisitor. A rare creature, as I understand it. Honourable and highly principled. A total misfit, of course. They say when Warmaster Macaroth dines with his senior staff, he always asks to hear the latest stories of Gaunt and his ways. They amuse him so very much. Gaunt is a throwback to another era.'

'Which era would that be, sir?' Rawne asked.

Sydona laughed out loud. 'I have no idea. A better one, perhaps. One that progress has left behind. He is atavistic. Noble, yes, but atavistic. We may enjoy the luxury of admiring him, but his breed is dying out. There's no place for sentiment in the Imperium. No place for his kind of nobility either. If you're career minded, major, you might consider a transfer to a

unit with a more rational commander. Gaunt's wearisome honour will get
you killed.'

'I am an Imperial Guardsman, sir,' Rawne said. 'War will get me killed.
That is a matter of fact.'

'But Gaunt will get you killed worthlessly, over some idiotic point of
morality.'

'I spent a long time wanting to kill him myself,' said Rawne. 'Dying along
with him over some idiotic point of morality sounds like a death I would
be happy to choose.'

He turned to go, then paused. 'You speak of my commander as if you
expect to hear from him,' he said.

'Contact has been made with his section,' Sydona said, matter-of-factly.

'I wasn't informed. I've been trying to reach him for hours.'

'The weather has impaired vox-traffic,' replied the interrogator. 'But I have
it as a fact that my inquisitor has made contact with him in the Untill.'

'Who is your inquisitor?' Rawne asked.

'My lord Welt,' said Sydona.

'Ah,' said Rawne, nodding. 'Him.'

IV

STREET TWENTY-SIX was a commercial thoroughfare that began at the north
end of Cantible's main market square and ran west around the lower edge
of the town's central hill. The roadway was cobbled, though many of the
cobblestones had been displaced. A main sewer had been ruptured by a
tank shell, and the gutters had become stinking channels of waste.

The habs on either side were washed out and grey. Flamer teams had been
along already, burning off the worst of the heathen scrawl that the enemy
had written on the walls. Most of the windows had been broken or blown
out years before. Several buildings had been flattened by shelling from the
Dev Hetra armour in the last two days. On the street corner, a pyre had been
made of the bodies of the enemy recovered from that stretch of street. It
burned lazily, as if the immolation was some kind of cruel torture, or as if
the intention had been to slow burn charcoal from the corpses. Caffran's
section pulled their capes up around their noses as they went by.

They passed Domor and his squad, heading in to one of the habs, and
wished them luck. Then, a few buildings down, they encountered Kolea and
Varl with a ten-man unit.

Kolea nodded to Caffran.

'We're going to take the buildings at the end of the road,' Caffran told
him.

'Watch how you go,' Varl advised. 'We've smoked three excubitors out of
the basements along here already this morning.'

'One was wired. Packet bombs,' said Kolea, lightly.

'What did you do?' asked Caffran.

'Shot him before he could detonate. Why, what would you have done?'
Caffran smiled.

'What's the priest for?' asked Varl.

'Decoration,' replied Zweil.

'This is no place for a–' Kolea began.

'I've read him the rules,' Caffran interrupted.

'All right then,' said Kolea. 'Good luck.'

'The Emperor protects,' said Zweil.

Caffran moved his section on. He had eight men, plus the priest. Osket, Wheln, Harjeon, Leyr, Neskon, Raess, Leclan and Vadim. They spread out through the weed-engulfed rubble. Caffran kept having to stop to help the aged priest. He already regretted allowing the old man to come along.

They entered the portico of an abandoned hab. Someone had been using it as a latrine. The doors were broken, and all the tiles on the atrium floor had been prised up as if they were something someone wanted to collect. The word *PLEASE* had been written on one wall in whitewash. For some reason, Caffran found that especially chilling.

'Let me go first,' Zweil suggested.

Leclan and Leyr glanced at Caffran. Caffran paused and then nodded. Zweil limped along ahead of them, down the hallway. The building had skylights, but the shutters were broken and swinging limply in the wind, making the light in the hallway come and go, as if clouds were racing by overhead. Patches of grey and white light shifted uneasily around one another across the scabby walls and the ruined floor. Halfway down the hallway, they found a human collar bone lying on its own,

'Don't touch it!' hissed Caffran, seeing Zweil about to stoop.

'Poor soul,' whispered Zweil, recoiling.

'Poor soul my fething foot,' muttered Leyr.

Something banged somewhere far off in the empty hab. A loose door on its hinges, tugged by the wind, Caffran guessed. It banged again, and they jumped a second time.

'Hello?' Zweil called.

'Don't fething speak!' Wheln exploded. 'They'll know we're coming!'

'I want them to know we're coming,' said Zweil, tapping his nose. 'Trust me.' There was virtually nothing about the ragged old priest that seemed remotely trustworthy.

'Please be careful, father,' Caffran whispered, fiddling with his rifle. The word *PLEASE* on the wall behind him echoed uncomfortably in his mind.

Osket and Neskon pushed open some doors and found hab apartments in terrible states of ruin. The stink was appalling. There was debris on the floors that might have once been body parts. The skeleton of a large grox had been patiently and carefully reassembled in one hab room, the bones threaded onto wire.

'Why?' asked Leclan.

'If I knew why,' Caffran replied, 'I'd be insane.'

'Hello!' Zweil shouted. 'I am an ayatani of the Holy Creed. I've come here to help you. Show yourselves. Everything will be all right.'

'As if,' murmured Neskon.

Raess suddenly raised his long las and aimed it, sweeping.

'What?' Caffran barked.

'Saw something. Down the end.' Raess kept his aim steady. 'Something moved.'

They moved on slowly.

'I am an ayatani of the Holy Creed–' Zweil began to repeat.

Something moved. Caffran saw it this time. Something skittered through the shadows twenty metres ahead.

'Feth!' Raess exclaimed.

'Did you see that?' asked Caffran quickly. 'What do you th–'

Distantly, they all heard the *crack-crack-crack* of a lasrifle firing. They all tensed.

'What–' Zweil started.

'Shhhh!' Caffran hissed.

The link pipped. They could all hear a voice in their ear-pieces.

'–love of the Throne, feth… he just came at me… for the goodly love of the Throne–'

The channel went dead.

'That was Varl,' said Vadim. 'Shit, that was Varl.'

'Section eight, this is section five,' Caffran sent. 'Signal back. Kolea? Varl?'

There was a long pause.

Caffran waited and then began again. 'Section eight, this is–'

'Caff, it's Kolea,' the link suddenly crackled. 'The priest with you still?'

'Yes.'

'Feth's sake, Caff. Bring him here, would you?'

V

CAFFRAN'S SECTION LEFT the hab and hurried back to the block that Kolea's squad had been sweeping. Zweil, old and infirm, moved so slowly that Neskon finally stopped in frustration and, with Leclan, made a chair of their arms to carry him.

Kolea and several of his men were waiting in the atrium of the hab block.

'Down here,' Kolea said bluntly.

The rest of his section was thirty metres down inside the desolate shell, grouped around something on the floor. Varl was nearby, standing alone, clearly very angry or upset.

'He just came out of nowhere,' Varl growled. 'Out of the shadows. Feth. Feth! The stupid bastard!'

Caffran pushed his way through the huddle of Kolea's men. A man lay on the tiles, bleeding out from a ghastly las wound through the gut. He'd once been a fine figure of a man, an agricultural worker or a smith, some trade that had put bulk into his shoulders. He was dressed in rags, and weighed no more than half his proper bodyweight.

He was still alive.

'Black cross,' said Kolea simply. 'Varl got caught out. It's a bad thing.'

'The stupid fether came out of nowhere!' Varl yelled behind them.

'It's okay,' Kolea told him. 'It's not your fault.'

'Except I shot him!'

'It's not your fault, Ceg,' Kolea murmured. 'It's just a bad thing.'

Leclan had dropped to his knees beside the man, binding the bloody wounds, entry and exit. He worked fast, with a corpsman's practiced skill, struggling to stop the man's life from leaking away. He threw aside three or four field dressing packs as they became saturated with blood. The sodden bundles of lint packing splatted into the pond of blood on the floor and pattered drops up the wall.

His hands red and wet, Leclan looked up at Caffran and shook his head.

'Father?' Caffran called.

Zweil stepped forwards and touched Leclan on the shoulder, signalling him to step out. He knelt in the blood pooling around the civilian that Varl had accidentally killed, and cradled the man's head.

'I am an ayatani of the Holy Creed,' he said softly. 'Be calm now, my friend, for the God-Emperor of Mankind is rushing here to present you with the gift of peace you crave. Is there anything you wish to confess at this hour?'

The man made a gurgling noise. Blood bubbled around his drawn lips.

'I hear and understand those sins as you have confessed them to me,' Zweil said, 'and I absolve you of them, as I absolve you of all other sins you cannot enumerate. It is in my power to do this thing, for I am an ayatani of the Holy Creed. The winds have blown your sins away, and the beati has blessed you and, though there is pain, it will end, as all pain ends, and you will ascend without the pain of the mortal world to the place the God-Emperor of Mankind has set aside for you at the train of the Golden Throne of Terra. These last rites I give you freely and in good faith. Be at peace, Imperial soul, and may–'

Zweil stopped. Very slowly, he let the man's head rest back onto the tiled floor.

'He's gone,' he said.

VI

WELT'S FORCES CLEARED the partisan camp. Drawn by signal buoys, drop-ships landed in the clearing that the soldiers of the Inquisition had made in the canopy. More troops dismounted: troops, and interrogators, and sundry other agents of the Holy Inquisition.

Perched in the branches of a tree across from the camp, Mkoll watched. The order and authority of the Imperium was being restored. He understood that the process of that restoration would be fraught and uncomfortable, but this was a curious triumph. It felt as if some honourable compact had been betrayed. He could hear Landerson shouting, protesting.

He looked away.

A white moth fluttered around him, and came to rest on the back of his right hand. It stayed there for a moment, lifting and closing its furry wings.

'Gereon resists,' he whispered.

It flew away at the touch of his breath.

Mkoll waited a few minutes more, putting off returning to the camp. His senses were sharp. The sharpest. Only Bonin and Caober came close to his degree of skill in stealthing. Only one man had ever bettered it.

And that man was dead.

Mkoll looked around. Something had stirred, some slight sound, off to his right. He made no sound himself, but turned slowly in the crook of the branch.

The undergrowth of the Untill behind him was immobile and secret. The only movement was the flutter of the moths. He caught a scent, a very faint trace. He knew it, nevertheless.

'You're there, aren't you?' he called.

There was no reply.

'I don't expect you to answer. But you're there. You're out there, aren't you?'

There was still no answer. The scent had gone. Perhaps he had imagined it.

Mkoll dropped out of the tree and waded back towards the camp.

'CIRK?' GAUNT SAID.

'Ibram.'

He sat down beside her on the edge of the platform stage. Cirk had picked the most faraway part of the camp to sit, all alone in the edges of the swamp dark.

'Are you all right?' he asked.

She nodded. He could see that she had been weeping.

'You're not all right,' he said.

'I never meant this to happen.'

'This?'

'All of this. I cut a deal with Balshin and Welt.'

'When?'

Cirk shrugged. 'When we got back. On Ancreon Sextus, after the tribunal. I did it for your sake.'

'Oh, don't give me that.'

Cirk stared at him. 'You bastard. I did. I really did. You and the others had done so much for us and you were facing execution. I stepped up, and sold what little I had.'

'What exactly did you sell, Cirk?'

'The myth of our survival,' she replied with a sad smile. 'I told them that they had to liberate Gereon, because they'd find a way to proof themselves against Chaos. They found the idea deeply attractive. The mystery of how you came out of Gereon without taint infuriated them. And now, here we all are.'

'Here we all are,' Gaunt nodded. 'This isn't the way you thought it would go, though, is it?'

'Throne, not at all.'

She drew her feet up onto the edge of the platform stage and hugged her knees. 'Gereon's going to keep suffering. We suffered under the Archenemy, and now we'll suffer under the Imperium, as they take the planet apart looking for something that isn't there.'

'I take it you don't believe?'

Cirk began to laugh so hard that Gaunt almost had to steady her to prevent her from falling off the platform's edge.

'Sorry, sorry...' she sighed at length. 'I believe all right. I mean, we came through unscathed. But I think it's in here–'

She tapped her temple with a finger.

'It's in here. It's not something you can analyse and manufacture and stick in a pot. The very idea is so funny. But Welt and Balshin just seized on it. Those bastards. Such simple minds.'

She stared at her boots. 'It's such a bloody mess, isn't it, Ibram?'

'It's not exactly as I imagined it. I thought I'd be proud. I'm not proud of this. High Command didn't initiate this operation for the benefit of the people of Gereon. They're only bothering with Gereon because they think there's something valuable here.'

'I wanted them to rescue my world so much, I'd have told them anything. I never thought what the consequences might be.'

'Me neither,' Gaunt admitted. 'Be careful what you wish for... that's the lesson, isn't it?'

Cirk nodded.

'It's ironic, don't you think?' she asked, 'to want to save your world so much you end up killing it?'

BROSTIN TOOK OUT a crumpled pack of lho-sticks and wedged one in Larkin's mouth. He took one himself. He lit them both off his flamer.

Larkin sat back in the small cot. He was the only patient in the camp's small, makeshift infirmary.

'It's not so bad,' Brostin said. 'You could have been dead. The colonel did you a favour.'

'Cut my fething foot off.'

'Well, there is that.'

Curth appeared through a tent drape. She was carrying something bundled in rags.

'That's bad for your health,' she said, taking the lho-stick out of Larkin's mouth and clamping it between her own lips.

'Throne, it's been a long time,' she sighed, exhaling.

'I thought you said it's bad for your health?' said Larkin.

'It is.'

'So are power swords, I've discovered,' Larkin scowled.

'Not as bad for you as being killed by a tank, so shut up,' said Brostin.

'I've got something,' said Curth, putting the bundle down on the cot.

'What?' Larkin asked.

'Good medicine. It'll make you feel better.' Inside the rags, broken down into its component parts, was Larkin's old long-las, the nalwood-stocked rifle that Larkin had brought all the way from Tanith and had finally abandoned on Gereon for lack of ammo.

'Holy fething Throne…' Larkin whispered. 'You kept it.'

'I knew you'd need a reason to come back,' said Curth. She watched as Larkin began to fit the weapon back together.

'Get me some gun oil, Bros,' he said. Brostin nodded and got up. He passed Gaunt on his way out of the infirmary.

'Ana?'

She turned away from Larkin, who was lost in the act of rebuilding his precious gun, and walked with Gaunt into a small side room.

'How is he?'

'I think I've taken his mind off the injury.'

'That's good. I wish there had been some other way.'

She started cleaning some medical instruments.

'Ana,' he began, 'if I'd known the Inquisition–'

'Were you about to apologise?' she asked, glancing at him. 'There's no need. I've been expecting this.'

'You have?'

'Living and working with the resistance, you do tend to dream about the day of liberation. A reassuring fantasy. I happened to imagine what the reality would be like. Gereon will never be the same. It will continue to suffer. That's the way of things. The Imperium is a blunt instrument, Ibram, and Chaos is too dangerous a quality to take chances with.'

'The Inquisition believes there is a… a secret here in the Untill. That's why they moved in with such speed.'

'What secret would that be?' she asked.

'When I and the others got out, no one could understand why we hadn't been tainted. They think there's something here that protects against taint.'

'Something in the Untill?' she asked. 'Is that what this is all about? They'd have left us to rot, except there's something in it for them?'

'I'm afraid I think that's exactly what's happened. I think they're going to spend years, decades maybe, picking over Gereon, taking it apart, trying to find this secret thing.'

'I could save them some time,' Curth said, 'if they spoke to me. I'm a trained medicae, and I've been working here under these conditions for a long time. Various toxic compounds derived from natural sources here in the swamp habitat have remarkable properties that could benefit the Imperium. Anti-coagulants, counterseptics, and several extracts that have particular efficacy in dealing with agues and xenos-derived infections. But that's it. There's no secret here. No miracle protection against taint. You resist the touch of Chaos by resisting it. You resisted. I resisted. And Gereon resists.'

She stopped her cleaning work and faced Gaunt. She was so thin and so ill he found her painful to behold.

'You did a noble thing, Ana,' he said, 'staying here to help these people. I'm not leaving you behind again.'

'Good,' she said. 'I think I'm done. I think I'm worn out. I've prayed you would come back, Ibram. I know you promised, but there were no guarantees. It's just something that kept me going. But I've entertained no romantic follies of a happy ending. Just an ending, that's all I want now. An end to this. This place has nearly killed me.'

She sighed. 'Is Dorden with you? Is he still alive? I'd like to see him. It would be good to see him.'

'He's at Cantible.'

She nodded. 'Turns out, I have a limit,' she said. 'I've devoted my life to helping people, as a medicae. I left Vervunhive to serve the Guard, and left the Guard to serve the people here. They say that good works and selfless effort are their own reward. But this has been horror, without relief. It has taken me beyond a limit for selflessness I didn't know I had. I am not rewarded by what I have done. I do not feel a better servant of the God-Emperor for it. I hate this, Ibram.'

'It's over,' he said.

VII

BELTAYN REPORTED THAT the transports he'd signalled were inbound. A flight of Valkyries would be on station within a few minutes. Gaunt nodded, and went over to Criid and Mkoll.

'Is the section ready?'

'We're ready to go,' said Criid, her face bandaged. 'I'll be glad to leave.'

'Make sure Curth gets on board,' Gaunt said to Mkoll. He walked through the waiting Ghosts, speaking briefly to some, and reached Eszrah.

'Are you coming with us?' he asked.

The Nihtgane nodded. 'I am unkynde,' he said after a moment, struggling slightly to form his Low Gothic words, 'and this world is ending.'

'Geryun, itte persist longe, foereffer,' said Gaunt.

Eszrah shook his head, and walked away down the platform walkway, heading out of the camp.

'Ten minutes!' Gaunt called after him. 'If you are coming with us, you've got ten minutes!'

Eszrah looked back and nodded. Then he carried on his way, along the path into the swamp woods.

'WITH YOUR PERMISSION,' said Gaunt, 'I'm moving my force out and returning to Cantible.'

Welt was in one of the large habitents that the Inquisition had erected, reading through data-slates. Envoys, analysts and Inquisition troopers came and went. The place was well lit, and insect repellent devices hummed and crackled around the roof posts.

'The Emperor protect you,' the inquisitor replied. 'Thank you for your contribution.'

Gaunt shrugged.

'I believe the work here will take some time,' Welt said, still distracted by the documents. 'A grand undertaking, but a worthy one. Early results seem to confirm what we suspected.'

'Which is?'

'The resistance fighters, especially the Sleepwalkers, are the key. Their knowledge of the Untill's biology is a vital tool. That's why we needed you to make contact with them, of course. I'm sorry you felt used, Gaunt, but we needed to bring them out, and that meant utilising someone they would trust. I can't imagine how long it would have taken to locate them in this wilderness otherwise.'

'For the record,' Gaunt said, 'you're wasting your time.'

'I know your feelings, Gaunt,' Welt replied. 'If there's even a chance, a hint of a chance, I must pursue it. It would be a crime against the Throne if I didn't. Can't you see that?'

'I suppose so.'

'The liberation of Gereon was always going to be painful, Gaunt. A place that has suffered like this doesn't just pick itself up, dust itself down and get back on with it. It will take years. Centuries, perhaps. Gereon may never be what it was. But you must look at the positives. At least there has been a liberation. High Command regarded Gereon as an entirely lost cause until we presented good reasons for coming here. And if I find what I am looking for, the future of mankind will be more secure. Don't bother yourself with the whys and wherefores, colonel-commissar. You got the liberation you wanted.'

'I'm not sure what I wanted anymore.'

Welt sniffed. 'Carry on, then.'

Gaunt made the sign of the aquila, and left the habitent.

AWAY FROM THE illuminated camp, and the light falling through the canopy space cleared by the Inquisition, the Untill was dark and green and quiet. Amphibians called and plopped in the algae-surfaced water. Moths billowed in the mist-threaded air. Insects crawled on the dark root balls and gnarled branches.

Eszrah carefully collected bark samples into one of his old gourd pots. His jars of wode, moth venom and other tinctures were now almost full again. This, he knew, was his last chance ever to replenish them. What he collected now would have to last a lifetime.

He heard a splash, and looked around. Sabbatine Cirk was walking towards him, shin deep in the green water. He stood up and watched her coming closer.

She came to a halt facing him, and looked up at his face, his eyes screened by Varl's old sunshades. Eszrah had trouble reading people's expressions, but it seemed to him that she wanted to say something and apparently couldn't. After a moment, she reached out her hand, slipped it into his leather satchel, and drew out a single reynbow quarrel. It was a short iron dart, the point caked in venom paste.

She looked back up at Eszrah's face, and half smiled. Then she turned and walked away into the swamp.

Eszrah watched her until she was out of sight. He heard the sound of jets from the landing clearing, and knew he was running out of time. He crouched down to collect the last few things he wanted: a particular herb, a particular snail, a beetle with a red diamond on its wing cases.

He was busy sealing the last gourd flask when he realised he was being watched. There had been no sound, but he felt eyes upon him. He looked up.

The man was standing amongst the trees facing Eszrah, so still and green and quiet that he seemed to be a tree himself, or a hanging bough. He was very tall, and slender, and clad in the wode of a Nihtgane, but he was no Nihtgane that Eszrah knew. He held a fighting staff in one hand, and the filthy remains of a camo-cape were wrapped around his shoulders.

He was staring straight at Eszrah.

'Histye, soule,' Eszrah said, rising.

The man calmly raised one hand and put a finger to his lips. Eszrah nodded. The man was looking past Eszrah now, looking in the direction of the camp. Eszrah turned his head to see what the man was looking at in particular.

When he turned back, the man had vanished, as if he had never been there.

In the pale light of the clearing, the Ghosts splashed out to board the waiting Valkyries. The noise of the fliers' engines was shrill, and shook the glade. The water shivered. Brostin and Derin helped Larkin cross to the vehicles. Gaunt saw Criid escorting Curth. Inquisition officers with light batons were marshalling the Valkyries, and directing them to their take-off point. Lamp beacons had been bolted to the trunks of trees around the clearing.

Gaunt had wanted to speak to Landerson before he left, but the entire partisan contingent had been interned prior to interview. The Inquisition was keeping them in a series of huts, under guard, and Gaunt didn't want to jeopardise walking out with Curth by making a fuss.

'Eszrah?' he yelled over the jet noise. Mkoll shook his head.

'I told him we were going,' Gaunt shouted.

'There!' Mkoll yelled back. Eszrah had materialised in the trees, and was jogging to join them.

'Come on!' Gaunt called. 'We nearly had to extract without you!'

The three of them hurried to the nearest Valkyrie, where the Ghosts already on board reached down to pull them up through the hatch.

'What were you doing out there?' Mkoll yelled to Eszrah.

Eszrah calmly raised one hand and put a finger to his lips.

She heard the rising echo of the jet engines as the Valkyries climbed out of the landing clearing. The din faded, and the quiet of the Untill reestablished itself.

The camp was a smudge of light in the distance, like a swamp light flickering beyond the trees. Where she was, it was so black the trees were like anthracite and the air like oil. Tiny white moths fluttered in the air like blossom. There had been white blossom like that in her family orchards once, all those years ago.

Sabbatine Cirk took out the reynbow quarrel. She held it in her hand for a while, and then pressed the venomed tip against the palm of her left hand until the skin broke.

With no splash, no murmur, and hardly any ripple at all, she slid down beneath the glossy surface of the lightless water.

VIII

SQUALLY RAIN WAS beating down on Cantible when they arrived. The sky billowed with fat grey rainclouds, and seemed soiled and dirty. There was a smell of thunder in the wet air.

The Valkyries came in over the town and dropped into a paddock west of the walls. The downpour made the battered buildings of the town seem more drab and lifeless than before. The paddock, and the neighbouring fields were soaking into an unhealthy mire.

Gaunt jumped out of the flier onto a field covered in puddles that were splashed and rippled by the rain. From the air, he'd seen the changes that had occurred in Cantible since he'd left. Repaired defences, the extensive facilities of the camp, the habitents and vehicles of the Inquisition. As the other Ghosts dismounted, he hurried with Mkoll to the edge of the paddock where Rawne, Baskevyl and Daur were waiting.

'Welcome back,' said Rawne.

'Anything to report?'

'Business as usual, sir,' said Baskevyl.

'Not our show any more, anyway,' said Rawne. 'The Inquisition's in charge.'

'Speak of the devil,' said Daur quietly.

Interrogator Sydona was approaching, flanked by his aides.

'This one's in charge?' asked Gaunt.

'His name's Sydona,' said Rawne.

'Does he always look so pissed off?' Gaunt asked.

'Now you come to mention it, no,' Rawne admitted.

Sydona came to a halt in front of Gaunt. Both men made the sign of the aquila.

'Gaunt?'

'Colonel-Commissar Gaunt, yes.'

'I am Interrogator Sydona. You have come directly from the Untill site?'

'You know I have.'

Sydona paused. 'There have been urgent vox transmissions from the Untill site while you were in the air. My inquisitor, the Lord Welt, demands to know if you or any of your detail know anything about the events that have just taken place.'

'What events?' Gaunt asked.

Sydona looked a little awkward. 'As I understand it,' he said, 'at some time in the last hour, all the partisans detained at the Untill site for interview have gone.'

'Gone?'

'Yes. They have all disappeared. Despite the fact that the area where they were being kept was secure and under guard. Can you shed any light on this?'

Gaunt looked at Mkoll, who frowned and shook his head.

'I don't believe I can,' said Gaunt. He started to walk away with his officers, but hesitated and looked back at the interrogator. 'Tell your Lord Welt, I'm not finding them for him this time.'

IX

THE NEXT HAB in the line was just like all the others. Halfway down street twenty-seven, it was a four storey residential made of rockcrete and grey stone. The driving rain made the flaking rockcrete look like putty. A litter of broken furniture and discarded household possessions lay on the rubble in front of the property. Inside, the rain had brought out a dank smell.

The stairways and halls ran the depth of the building. Rain ran in through the skylights high in the roof space, and pattered down into pools along the tiled hall. Caffran watched the drips falling like tracer rounds, bright and silver in the gloom.

'Hello?' Zweil called out.

They were getting tired and cold. 'Lamp packs,' Caffran instructed. 'You three sweep that way. You three, up there. Stay in contact.'

The section divided up. Harjeon, Wheln and Osket moved up the stairs. Neskon, Raess and Leyr went off to the right. Caffran continued on down the hallway with Leclan, Vadim and the old priest.

'Hello? Hello? I am an ayatani of the Holy Creed. I've come here to help you. Show yourselves. Everything will be all right.'

The rain dripped down around them out of the invisible roof. Their moving lamp beams wobbled and danced across the floor and the stained walls. In the corner of one room, they found a nest of old blankets and torn clothes that looked as if someone had been sleeping in it. In the next room, a dead man sat in a chair at a table, the corpse untouched for months, mummified.

They moved on.

'You feel that?' Vadim asked.

'What?'

'Really feels like we're being watched.'

'Go slow,' said Caffran. Leclan crossed the hall to another doorway and his lamp flickered round to illuminate more debris and filth.

'Careful,' Vadim hissed.

Zweil shuffled forwards and cleared his throat. 'Hello? Hello? Is there anyone there? I am an ayatani of the Holy Creed and I've come to help you.'

They waited. Caffran held up a hand for quiet. They all heard the tiny scurry from beyond the doorway.

Caffran slipped through the door into the chamber beyond. The floor was covered with broken glass and torn paper scraps. The remains of a bed or couch rotted under a broken window. There was a door on the far side of the room, half closed.

Vadim swept in behind Caffran, panning his weapon.

'You smell that?' he whispered.

Caffran nodded. There was a slight scent of burning.

He moved across the room, and found something near the collapsed remains of the bed by the window. It was a small fire, made of twigs, still warm although the flames had been put out. A shrivelled Imperial Guard ration pack, stolen from somewhere, lay amongst the heaped twigs. Someone had been trying to warm up a meal.

Caffran was about to call Vadim over when something he had taken to be a heap of litter beside the bed moved and fled towards the other door. Caffran cried out, and tried to follow it with his lamp beam. Vadim raised his weapon.

'Don't shoot!' Caffran called out.

Leclan and Zweil had entered the room. With Caffran leading, they moved towards the second door. It led into a storeroom, a small chamber of rockcrete with shelves along one wall and an old cold store pantry beside them. There were no other doors, and the window lights were just slits high up near the ceiling. There was a powerful reek of human waste. Caffran saw there was nothing on any of the shelves, except a collection of buttons and bottle caps, laid out in rows in deliberate order of increasing size.

There was no sign of anybody. Caffran moved his lamp beam around. Leclan came in beside him.

'Pantry?' he whispered.

Caffran nodded. The pantry door was pulled to, but it was large, a walk-in larder where meat could be hung. They began to approach it.

'Feth!' Caffran exclaimed suddenly. Something moved under the lowest shelf. He swung around and aimed his rifle and his torch beam down at the floor.

The child was very small, twisted with starvation and disease. He was dressed in rags and his skin was brown with dirt. His eyes seemed fantastically big and wild, and he shielded them, whining, when the lamp found him.

'Feth! It's just a child!' Caffran said, bending down to get closer.

'Father!' Leclan called. Zweil and Vadim followed them into the storeroom. The child tried to climb deeper and deeper into the shadows under the shelving, making animal mews of fear.

'It's all right, it's all right,' Caffran called, reaching out his hand.

'Everything will be fine,' Zweil said. 'You come out of there, my young friend, and we'll look after you. Hello? Are you hungry? Do you want some food?'

Zweil glanced at the others. 'Anyone got a ration pack? Dried biscuit rations? A sugar stick?'

'I have,' said Leclan. He leant his lasrifle against his leg as he opened his breast pocket and fished around.

The pantry door opened.

The excubitor who had been hiding inside had a las-lock. When it went off, the noise in the confined space was huge. Zweil screamed in surprise and shock. The las-round hit Leclan, and took off the side of his head. He rotated slightly as he fell, and broke some of the shelves under him.

Caffran opened fire and cut the excubitor down with a flurry of close range shots. The impact threw the servant of the Anarch backwards into the pantry.

After the brief, furious gunfire, the silence was shocking.

Vadim went to the pantry, checked it was empty, and put an extra shot into the excubitor's head to be sure.

'Oh, feth… feth, feth, feth…' said Caffran. He crouched over Leclan's body.

'Is he–?' Zweil asked over his shoulder.

'Vadim! Get the others! Go and get the others!' Caffran yelled.

Vadim nodded and ran out of the room. A moment later they could hear him shouting.

'It's no good,' Caffran said. He sat back from Leclan. 'He didn't stand a chance.'

Caffran rose to his feet and looked at Zweil.

'What a mess.'

Zweil didn't answer him.

'Father?'

Zweil nodded, indicating something over Caffran's shoulder. Caffran turned.

The child, a boy of about nine or ten, had come out from under the shelves. Although it was much too big for him, he had picked up Leclan's lasrifle and was pointing it at Caffran and the priest.

'Get back, father,' Caffran breathed. He looked at the child and smiled encouragingly. 'Come on, little man, give me that.'

The boy fired three shots, the weight and discharge staggering him. Then he threw the weapon aside and ran.

'Caffran? Caffran!' Zweil yelled. He bent down and cradled the Ghost in his arms. There was blood everywhere, pumping from a huge, messy wound in Caffran's chest. 'Medicae!' Zweil shouted. 'Medicae!'

Caffran gasped.

'Hold on, you hear me,' Zweil demanded, trying to support Caffran and staunch the bleeding at the same time. 'You hold on. Help's coming.'

Caffran's eyelids fluttered. He looked up at Zweil for a moment. He tried to speak, but he couldn't. His left hand clawed at the vest pocket of his battledress tunic, trying to unbutton it.

'Medicae! Medicae!' Zweil yelled over his shoulder. 'Someone!'

He looked back at Caffran. He swallowed hard as he saw the distant look in Caffran's eyes, the receding light. As a priest in war, he had seen it before, too many times. Caffran's bloody left hand still fumbled with the pocket fastening. Zweil reached over and undid the pocket for him, and took out what was inside. It was a Tanith cap badge. Caffran's mouth tried to form words.

'I am an ayatani of the Holy Creed,' Zweil said softly. 'Be calm now, my friend, for the God-Emperor of Mankind is rushing here to present you with the gift of peace you crave. Is there anything you wish to confess at this hour?'

Caffran didn't respond. Zweil continued to hold him up, his hands and arms wet with Caffran's blood.

'I hear and understand those sins as you have confessed them to me,' Zweil said, his voice hoarse, 'and I absolve you of them, as I absolve you of all other sins you cannot enumerate. It is in my power to do this thing, for I am an ayatani of the Holy Creed. The winds have blown your sins away, and the beati has blessed you and, though there is pain, it will end, as all pain ends, and you will ascend without the pain of the mortal world to the place the God-Emperor of Mankind has set aside for you at the train of the Golden Throne of Terra. These last rites I give you freely and in good faith…'

PROPER BLOODY
GUARDSMEN

I

TWENTY DAYS EXACTLY after the initial wave of assaults had hit Gereon, the first retirement orders were sent through. Front-line units who had been on the ground since day one were drawn back, or switched out for fresh brigades from the carrier fleet. A quarter of a million new Guardsmen were dropped into the field. The exhausted soldiers they were relieving filtered slowly back along lines of transport to base camps, and then back to the fleet.

AT 137 was retired just before noon on the twentieth day, and moved back along the line with a Krassian division. The Krassians had taken especially heavy losses during the citadel war that had raged in the heart of K'ethdrac'att Shet Magir between days six and fourteen of the liberation.

In a single afternoon, AT 137 walked back the fourteen kilometres they had covered in the previous twenty days, through the gutted city, under a sky full of smoke, passing the newcomers marching in.

Brigade bands were playing, and colours were being carried high. The new arrivals they passed looked clean and healthy. They cheered and applauded the retiring troopers when they saw them. The retiring troopers tried to muster the effort to return the salutes.

Dalin wondered if the new blood knew what they were walking into. He wondered if he ought to stop and talk to them about the things he'd seen and the things he knew. There was a hell of fight left to be fought.

He decided to keep walking, because he believed Sobile might shoot him if he started telling people about the shit ahead. Bad for morale. Besides, no one had ever bothered to warn him.

They reached a dispersal point on the coast, and waited three more, leaden days in the Munitorum camp for extraction. Conditions were hot and dusty, but there was fresh food and clean water at least. Munitorum staffers processed each man in turn, and filled out forms and audits. Each man got a paper tag with his destination and redeployment details written on it riveted to his collar.

Dalin slept for a while in the grubby shared tents pitched along the shore behind the sea wall, lying in a bed roll that had been used by fifty men before him. It was hard to sleep, because he was wound up so tight, and though he tried, his mind and body would not unclench. He wondered if the tension would ever ease. It didn't feel like it would. He felt he would be two heartbeats from ducking and firing for the rest of his life. The instinct had been ground into him. Every sound from outside the tent made him reach for his weapon.

When he did sleep, it was a troubled slumber. Dreams plagued him, though on waking, he couldn't remember the details. The wounded were being processed through the area and, at night, he could hear their moans and screams coming from the hospital stations.

On the third day, they were directed to a row of drop-ships waiting on the hillside above the shore.

THE DROP-SHIP took them up out over the bay. Through the heavy armoured ports, Dalin saw the sea far below, like a sheet of chipped plate glass. He saw the city behind them, receding. The enemy city. The corpse of a city. Then it was gone in the haze, and it seemed as if Gereon had been entirely reduced to a realm of dust and smoke where nothing solid remained.

He fell asleep in his restraint seat, his head knocking and rolling limply against the backrest as the ship jolted. This time he didn't dream. This time his mind slid off the edge of some precipice and dropped into nothingness.

THEY RODE THE hydraulic platforms up through the decks of the carrier from the drop hangar. Most of them sat on the metal decking, their kit and weapons clutched to their chests, cold weather ponchos draped around their shoulders. The climate on the carrier was a good eight degrees colder than the surface, and the air had a metallic, chemical flavour.

Sobile stood on his own at the edge of the rising platform, hands clasped behind his back, watching the thick cross-sections of deck slide past. Downdraft air gusted down the riser shaft. There was a lot of noise from the repair decks: voices, machine tools, metal on metal. Dalin saw a row of fifty Leman Russ battle tanks drawn up ready for transportation. Twenty-three days earlier, he would have been thrilled by such a sight. He tried to remember what his twenty-three day younger self had been like, but all he could imagine was another young corpse face down in the white dust of K'ethdrac.

On the fifth deck level, they climbed down into the dispersal area. Munitorum officials mobbed around, sorting men and checking them off. The chamber was milling with personnel and ringing with chatter. Steam billowed up from under-deck vents.

'What does this mean?' Dalin asked, holding out the tag pinned to his collar. 'What does this mean?' The Munitorum staffers passing by ignored him.

'Company, form up!' Kexie yelled. 'Quick time, now!'

All that remained of AT 137 gathered in a row in the middle of the deck. It wasn't an impressive sight. Every one of them was dirtier than Dalin thought it was possible to be. They stank. Their kit was shredded.

'Stand to, stand to, ech,' Kexie said, walking the pitifully short line. He looked no better than they did.

Sobile had been talking to some Munitorum officials. He wandered over to face them.

He held up a data-slate and read from it.

'Attention. Hereby order given this day of 777.M41 that reserve activation has now been suspended. This detail, afforded the name Activated Tactical 137, that is AT 137, now stands deactivated, and the individuals here should report to their original regiments or divisions. So, you're free to return to your units. All obligation to RIP details is done with.'

Sobile lowered the data-slate and regarded them with a blank, humourless look. 'I can't see the good of that. You all started out morons and you're morons still. The likes of you give the proud tradition of the Imperial Guard a bad smell. I have never gone to war with such inadequate soldiers. In my opinion, you should be on RIP for the rest of your bloody lives. You're shit. I'm glad to wash my hands of you.'

He looked at Kexie. 'That's all. Sergeant, carry on.'

'Salute!' Kexie thundered.

They saluted. Sobile looked at them for a moment longer, and then turned and walked away.

They lowered their hands.

Kexie stood in front of them for a moment, chewing the inside of his cheek. His hands clenched and unclenched, as if imagining Saroo. Saroo was in a locker somewhere, waiting for him, waiting to greet the next RIP detail.

He looked at them, his eyes moving from one man to the next. Dalin hadn't realised that Kexie was quite so old. Perhaps it was the dirt caking his lined face.

With a final, diffident sigh, he saluted them.

The salute was straight backed and firm. They all returned it instinctively. Dalin felt something hot on his face, and realised that tears were rolling down his cheeks.

'Ech,' said Kexie, with a half smile. 'Proper bloody Guardsmen.'

He dropped the salute and walked away.

LEFT ALONE, THE row of them slowly disintegrated. Some of them sat down on the deck. Others wandered away. Fourbox was one of the ones who sat down. He dropped his kit and weapon beside him, and bowed his head, drawing his hands up over his scalp. Dalin saw that his hair was growing back in. The hard edges of his scalp cut were gone.

'Screw all this,' Wash said. Brickmaker sniggered. 'Screw all this and all of you,' Wash continued. 'I'll see you in the Basement.' He picked up his kit and walked off.

Dalin picked up his rifle and rested it across his left shoulder. He scooped up his filthy kit bag in his right hand.

'See you, Fourbox,' he said.

Fourbox looked up at him. 'Yeah, I'll see you.'

He called out as Dalin turned. 'Holy?'

'Yes?'

'We did it,' Fourbox said.

'Did what?'

'Whatever that was. We did it. We lived.'

'You say that,' Dalin replied, 'like it's a good thing.'

Dalin crossed the deck, looking for an exit. He'd gone quite a way before something occurred to him and he turned back. By then, Fourbox had disappeared.

'What are you looking for?'

Dalin looked around. Merrt was there, watching him.

'I was looking for Fourbox,' Dalin said.

'Why?'

'Because I suddenly realised I have no idea what his real name is.'

Merrt shook his head, amused.

'You know what?' Dalin said to him. 'All of this, all of this, and I don't think any of us have learned a single fething thing.'

'You have,' said Merrt. 'You just don't know it yet. Come on.'

'Where to?'

'We're supposed to report to our units,' said Merrt. 'I think you should follow me.'

'Why?'

'Where else are you gn… gn… gn… gonna go?'

Dalin walked alongside the Tanith soldier across the bustling deck.

'Hey,' said Merrt, pointing. 'Isn't that–?'

Through the press of bodies ahead of them, Dalin could see a figure waiting. A woman, tall and slender, wearing dark combat gear and the pins of a sergeant.

'Yeah,' said Dalin.

'Count yourself lucky,' said Merrt. 'My mother never waited on any dispersal deck to meet me.'

Dalin nodded, but he didn't feel especially lucky. As he walked towards Tona Criid, she spotted him and moved forwards to meet him. He saw the look in his ma's eyes, and felt even less lucky than before.

'Ma?' he whispered. His throat was dry and he dearly wished his canteen wasn't empty.

She had something in her hand.

It was a Tanith cap badge.

ONLY IN DEATH

FOR TANITH · FOR THE EMPEROR

For Steve Bissett (Master of the Blood Pact)

Only in death does duty end.
– old Imperial proverb

'I N 778.M41, THE *twenty-third year of the Sabbat Worlds Crusade,*
Warmaster Macaroth's main battle groups advanced swiftly and
thoroughly into the frontiers of the Carcaradon Cluster, driving the
hosts of the Archenemy overlord ('Archon') Urlock Gaur, before them.
Archon Gaur's forces seemed to fracture under the successive Imperial
assaults, though it now seems likely they were in fact withdrawing to estab-
lish a defensive cordon in the Erinyes Group.

'*To coreward, the Crusade's secondary battle-groups – the Fifth, Eighth*
and Ninth Armies – continued to combat the legions of Magister Anakwa-
nar Sek, Gaur's most capable lieutenant. The Second Front's avowed intent
was to hound Sek's rabble from the fringes of the Khan Group, and oust
them from the many fortress worlds of the Cabal System.

'*During this murderous phase of the Crusade, an especially bloody ban-*
ishment campaign took place on the ruinous fortress world of Jago…'

– from *A History of the Later Imperial Crusades*

Day two (out of Elikon M.P.). Sunrise at four, but dust-out til later. Progress fair (23 km). Am concerned about water rations, have mentioned matter to G. and R. Dust a factor. R. repeated his 'no spit' order, ~~weles~~ frankly unworkable in my opinion. G. assures objective has its own well/water supply. We'll see.

K. has once again ~~ras~~ raised questions re: dust jamming weapons. Inspect ordered for noon halt. To follow up. Good evidence for casing all weapons during march, though R. reluctant. Casing would slow unit response in event of ambush scenario.

~~Dreams getting worse, more troubl~~

Rumour persists. Have failed to winkle out origin. Suddenly everyone's a superstitious fething idiot. Bad form. Intend to get on top of it once we're installed at objective.

Don't like this place at all. Doing best to maintain morale. Dust and rumours not helping.

Sunset seven plus twenty-one. Light winds. Saw stars for first time. They looked a long ~~aw~~ way away.

- Field journal, V.H. fifth month, 778.

ONE

The House at the End of the World

I

DURING THE SIX-DAY trudge up-country, some bright spark (and no one ever found out who) started a gossipy piece of rumour that swept through the regiment like a dose of belly-flu. The rumour ran that a bunch of Guardsmen, maybe a pioneer unit or a scout reconnaissance, had come across a ravine up in the hills full of skulls with all the tops sawn off.

The Ghosts, both old and new, were tough fethers who had seen far, far worse than a few bleached bones in their days, but there was something about the rumour, that damned gossipy piece of rumour, that stuck like a splinter under the skin, and dug until it nagged.

Like all rumours, the art was in the detail. The skulls, so it went, were human, and they were old, really old. They weren't some relic of the present war, not even an atrocity perpetrated by the Archenemy who had, until the previous spring, been the undisputed master of Jago. Old, old, old and dusty; fossil-old, tomb-old; weathered and worn and yellow, evidence of some godless crime enacted in those wild, lonely hills in ages past. It smacked of ritual, of trophy taking, of predation. The meaning was long lost, erased by time and weather and the debrading dust, so that no clear detail could be discerned anymore, and all the awful possibilities imaginable came bubbling up in the minds of the marching troops.

More than anything else, the rumour seemed to cement the dim view every last one of them had formed about the place. Jago was a bad rock, and these lonely hills were the baddest, bleakest stretch of that bad rock.

Gaunt was having none of it. When the gossip reached him, he tried to have it stamped out, quick and neat, like a bug under a boot-heel. He told Hark and Ludd to 'have issue' with anyone caught using the words 'cursed' or 'haunted'. He told them that he wanted it made known that there would

743

be punishment duties available to any trooper found spreading the rumour.

Hark and Ludd did as they were told, and the gossip died back to a mumble, but it refused to go away.

'The men are spooked,' said Viktor Hark.

II

IT DIDN'T HELP that Jago was such a Throne-forsaken arse-cleft.

The northern mountains, an eight thousand kilometre-long range of buck and broken teeth, were possessed of three prevailing characteristics: wind, dust and craggy altitude. Those ingredients worked in concert to produce an environment that every single one of the Ghosts would have gladly said goodbye to at short notice, without regret.

The wind was cold and saw-edged, and banged around the tight valleys and deep ravines like a ricocheting las-round. It rubbed exposed flesh red-raw, and made knuckles as numb as ice. It tugged at capes, and whipped off hats without invitation. It slung itself about, and gnawed and bit and, all the while, sang like a siren; like a fething siren. It had had eons to practise its music, and it sang for the Ghosts of Tanith more keenly than any pipe or marching flute. It found crevices, split rocks, clefts, fissures and chasms, and wailed through them. It played the lonely hills like a templum organ, exploiting every last acoustic possibility of the mountainous terrain.

Then there was the dust. The dust got into everything, not least the singing wind. It sifted into collars and ears and cuffs; it invaded puttees and gloves; it clogged noses until they were thick with grey tar. It found its way into kit-bags, into weapons, into ration packs, into underwear even, where it chafed like scrubbing powder. Trekking up the narrow passes, the Ghosts spat lumpy grey phlegm, rinsing their mouths from their water bottles. Rifles fatigued and ailed, polished steel scoured matt, and mechanisms jammed, until Gaunt ordered weapons to be carried cased in weather-proofs. 'Up ahead' became an opaque mist, 'behind' a trail of boot prints that was erased in seconds. 'Above' was a vague suggestion of jagged cliffs. All around them washed the haunting song of the grit-laden wind.

Quickly, they all became very grateful indeed for the brass-framed goggles they'd been issued with by the Munitorum aides at Elikon Muster Point.

Dry skulls in a dusty valley, with all the tops sawn off.

'This is going to be trouble,' said Elim Rawne.

'Trouble's what we do,' said Ibram Gaunt.

III

PART OF THE trouble was that the war was taking place elsewhere. It might as well have been taking place in another century. At night, during the intervals when the wind died back and the dust clouds dropped away, they could hear the sky-punch of the artillery and the armour divisions south of Elikon. Sometimes they saw the flashes, like lightning on a different planet, pulsing like a watchtower beacon, far away. Once in a while, dropships droned overhead – Valkyries and heavy Destriers – zoning in towards the active killing grounds. The dropships courteously waggled their wings at the thread of troopers winding along the valley floors.

Jago was a fortress world, one of the infamous fortress worlds built along the trailwards salient of the Cabal System. Nahum Ludd hadn't known quite what to expect, so his imagination had run fast and loose with the words 'fortress' and 'world'. He had conceived of a planet built like a castle, all gun-slits and machicolations; a planet with bastion towers and square corners; an improbable, impregnable thing. The truth was rather different. Jago had been fortified long before the reach of mankind's memory. Its rocky, howling, fuming crust had been mined out and laced with thousands of kilometres of casemates, bunkers and structural emplacements. Ludd wondered what manner of long-forgotten war had engulfed the place so thoroughly that such formidable earthworks had been necessary. Who had the defenders been? Who had they been fighting? How could anyone tell where one fortress line ended and the next began? Elikon had been a bewildering matrix of sub-crust forts, a labyrinth of tunnels and hard points, a maze of armoured tunnels and cloche turrets, sprouting from the landscape like mushrooms.

'So, who fought here? Originally, I mean?' Ludd asked. 'Why was all this stuff built?'

'Does it matter?' replied Viktor Hark.

'Ask the skulls with all the tops sawn off,' mumbled Hlaine Larkin, limping up the gully behind them.

IV

THEY MARCHED FOR six days, following the rough country up into the waistline of the mountains. The dust billowed around them. General Van Voytz had been quite specific in his instructions. At Elikon, his gold braid fingered by the hillside wind, he'd climbed up onto the broad back of a scabby Chimera to address them all, like a serious but well-meaning friend. He'd been forced to raise his voice above the trundle of a passing convoy: heavy armour, troop transports, vox-trailers, and the guarded cage-trucks of battlefield psykers, all rolling out towards the front.

'The Archenemy may attempt to side-swipe us here,' Van Voytz had said, his voice planed smooth by the gritty breeze. 'I'm asking the Ghosts to watch our eastern flank.'

Asking. Gaunt had smiled at that: a dry smile, for no other kind was possible on Jago. His old friend and sometime mentor Barthol Van Voytz was an expert at making the average fighting soldier feel as if any given commission was either his own idea, or a favour for the boss. *Asking*. Show some spine, Barthol. What you're doing is called *ordering*.

'There is an end-of-line stronghold called Hinzerhaus at the far east reach of the fortress wall,' Van Voytz continued. 'It's up in the Banzie Altids, a spur of the main mountain range, eight days from here.'

More like six, the way my Ghosts march, thought Gaunt.

'Hinzerhaus is your objective. Find it,' said Van Voytz. 'Find it, secure it, hold it, and deny any attempt by the enemy to cross the line at that place. The Emperor is counting on you.'

They had all made the sign of the aquila. They had all thought *the fething Emperor doesn't even know my name.*

'Do we like this job?' asked Braden Baskevyl. 'Show of hands?'

'Does it matter?' replied Gol Kolea, as the regiment struck camp.

'You boys hear that thing about the skulls, then? The sawn-off skulls?' asked Ceglan Varl, as he wandered by.

V

SO THEY HAD trekked out into the back end of nowhere, into the most forgotten parts of the bad rock called Jago, into the Banzie Altids. The ravines grew deeper, the cliffs grew steeper, and the dusty wind sang for them at the top of its dry lungs.

'This is going to be trouble,' said Elim Rawne, spitting out a wad of thick grey phlegm.

'Oh, rot! You always say that, young man,' said Zweil, the old chaplain, plodding along beside him.

VI

DUST HUNG, LIKE a gauze veil, along the body of the deep valley. The wind had dropped for a moment, and ceased its singing, an eerie hiatus. Gaunt held up his hand. The fingers of his glove were white with dust.

'It's taking too fething long,' said Tona Criid.

'Give them a minute,' whispered Gaunt.

Ghosts materialised, ghostly figures, tracking back to them out of the veil of dust: Mkoll, Bonin, Hwlan. The regiment's best.

'Well?' asked Gaunt.

'Oh, it's up there all right,' said Mkoll, spitting to clear his mouth. His brass-framed goggles were covered in a residue of fine powder, and he wiped them with his fingers.

'We saw it,' said Bonin.

'And what does it look like?' asked Gaunt.

'Like the last house before the end of the fething world,' said Mkoll.

VII

THEY GOT UP and moved on; two and a half thousand troopers in a long, straggly file. The wind found its energy again, and restarted its song.

Thus it was the Tanith First-and-Only came to Hinzerhaus, the house at the end of the world.

'This is going to be trouble,' said Elim Rawne as they plodded up towards the main gate in the stinging haze.

'Any chance,' wondered Hlaine Larkin, 'any chance at all you could stop saying that?'

The wind shrieked around them. It sounded like the scream skulls would make if their tops had all been sawn off.

Day six (out of Elikon M.P.). Sunrise at four plus ten, considerable dust-out, increasing at eight (or thereabouts). Progress good (18km). Objective achieved at noon minus twenty. Can't get a good look at the place, due to dust storms. Advance moving up to secure as I write. Troop in holding pattern. G. has ordered cases off, to some general ~~complaint~~ complaint from the r & f.

I have dreamed again, this last night, of ~~voices noises someone who won't~~

I wonder if I should speak to Doc D. about my dreams. Would he understand? Maybe A.C.? She might be more receptive. It troubles me to reflect that, since Gereon, I have a difficulty knowing what to say to A.C. She has changed so. No surprise, I suppose. I am given to wonder where the Ana I knew went to.

It's hard to know what to do for the best. They're only dreams, after all. I'll wager if I could look into the dreams these Ghosts endure, night after night, I'd see a lot worse. I've walked the camp after nightfall. I've seen them twitch and fidget in their bedrolls, trapped in their own nightmares. ~~Still though I~~

Signals from the front. Scouts are returning.
Will record more later.

- Field journal, V.H. fifth month, 778.

TWO

Enter Here

I

THE GATEHOUSE HAS *been empty for nine hundred years. It is made of stone, close-dressed stone: floor, walls and roof alike. It is big. It has an echo that has not been tested in a while.*

The lights are still on. Glow-orb fitments sag from ancient piping, dull and white like a reptile's lidded eyes. The light issuing from them throbs, harsh then soft, harsh then soft, in tune with some slow, respiratory rhythm. The pulse of Hinzer-haus.

There is a rug on the floor. Its edges are curled up like the dry wings of a dead moth. There is a picture on the wall, beside the inner hatch. It has an ornate gilt frame. The canvas within is dirt-black. What is it a picture of? Is that a face, a hand?

Outside, through the thick bastion walls, the wind sings its siren melody.

Scraping, now. Shuffling. Voices. Scratching. Old, unoiled bolts protesting as they are wrenched back.

The outer hatch slides–

II

–OPEN.

The thick metal door swung open about half a metre and then stopped. No amount of shoving could persuade it to open any wider. Its hinges were choked with dust and grit.

Mkoll slithered inside, through the narrow entry. The wind came indoors with him, its song diminished, its dust inhaled by the gatehouse. Fine powder hung in the stilled air for a moment, as if surprised, before settling.

The rug fidgeted, tugged by the draught.

Mkoll looked around, sliding his lamp beam about him gently.

'Well? Anything? Have you been killed at all?' called Maggs, hidden behind the hatch.

Mkoll didn't dignify the question with a reply. He pushed ahead, crouching low, weapon braced, his lamp-pack chasing out all the corners and the shadows.

The shadows moved as his lamp turned. They dribbled and fell away, they altered and bent. The air was smoke-dry, not a hint of moisture in it. A pulse began to beat in Mkoll's temple.

'Chief? Is it clear?' the vox crackled. Bonin, this time, poised outside with Maggs.

'Wait...' whispered Mkoll, the pulse in his temple still going tap, tap, tap. He could feel his own nerves drawing tight. Why? Why the feth was he feeling so edgy? Nothing got to him, usually. Why did he have real misgivings about this place? Why had he suddenly got the strongest impression that–

this is going to be trouble

–he was being watched?

To his left, an alcove. A shadow. Nothing. To his right, a doorway. Another shadow. Wait, not a shadow, *a fething*–

No. Scratch that. Nothing. Just his imagination, reading shapes and forms in the gloom that weren't actually there.

'Feth,' Mkoll breathed, amazed at his own foolishness.

'Say again?' crackled the link.

'Nothing,' replied Mkoll into his micro-bead.

In that doorway, he could have sworn... *he could have sworn...* someone had been standing there. *Right there.* But there was no one. Just a trick of the shadows. Just his racing imagination.

This wasn't like him. Jumping at shadows? *Calm down. Calm all the way down. You've done this a thousand times.*

'Clear,' he voxed.

Maggs squeezed his way in around the hatch behind Mkoll and began to shine his muzzle-fixed lamp around. Mkoll secretly liked Wes Maggs: he liked the Belladon's spark and his wit, and admired his skill. Mkoll put up with a lot of mouth from Maggs, because of what he got back in soldiering.

But Maggs's famous mouth was unusually silent suddenly. Maggs was spooked, Mkoll could feel that. That compounded Mkoll's own edginess, because he knew Maggs wasn't like that either, ordinarily.

It took a lot to spook Wes Maggs. Six days marching through the shrieking dust, plus the–

Dry skulls in a dusty valley.

–rumour would have helped. This chamber, this dry gatehouse, did all the rest.

'Who–' Maggs began. 'Who puts a rug in a gatehouse?'

Mkoll shook his head.

'And a picture?' Maggs added, creeping over to the frame on the wall. The cone of his lamp beam bobbed and swung. Then he snapped around suddenly, his weapon up hard against his collarbone, aimed.

'Point that thing somewhere else,' suggested Bonin as he wriggled in through the hatch behind them. 'What are you, twelve? Simple?'

'Sorry,' said Maggs, dipping his gun.

'You knew I was behind you.'

'Sorry.'

'You knew I was coming in after you.'

'Sorry, all right?'

'Shut up, both of you,' said Mkoll. *This isn't like us. We're all over the place, scrappy and wound too tight. We're Ghost scouts, for feth's sake. We're the best there is.*

Bonin glanced around, and allowed his lamp beam to trickle over the walls and ceiling. 'This is charming,' he murmured.

He looked over at Mkoll. 'Shall I get the rest of the advance in?'

Mkoll shook his head. 'No.'

'Uh, why not?'

'I have a… never mind. Let's just poke about for a bit.'

Bonin nodded. 'You all right, chief?'

'Of course.'

'Look at this picture,' called Maggs. He had gone right up to the wall where the old frame was hanging, and reached out with his left hand to touch its surface. His glove was caked with dust as white as ash.

'What's it supposed to be a picture of?' Maggs asked. 'A woman, no… a man… no, a woman… a portrait…'

'Just leave it alone, Maggs,' Mkoll said.

'I'm only asking,' said Maggs, as he began to rub at the surface of the canvas with his gloved hand. The canvas shuddered in the frame. 'That's a woman, right? Am I right? A woman in a black dress?'

Mkoll and Bonin weren't looking. They were staring up at the sagging light fitments, the softly glowing, lidded reptile-eyes strung along the parched walls.

'There's still power here,' said Bonin, uneasily.

Mkoll nodded.

'How is that possible? After all this time?'

Mkoll shrugged. 'I think they're chemical lights. Chemical fed on a slow burn, not an actual generator or power cell. Anyway, they're almost dead.'

Bonin breathed out. 'Is it just me, or do they keep getting brighter, now and then?'

Mkoll shrugged again. 'Just you,' he lied.

'Hey, it *is* a woman,' announced Maggs behind them. 'It's some old dam in a black lace dress.' He'd rubbed a patch of filth off the painting with his glove. Mkoll and Bonin trudged over to his side. The pale, expressionless face of a woman gazed back at them from the blackened canvas.

'Fantastic,' said Mkoll. 'Can we get on now?'

'Oh!' exclaimed Maggs. He was rubbing at the portrait again, and the ancient canvas of the painting had suddenly perished beneath his persistent fingertips. It disintegrated like powder, and left a hole where the woman's gazing face had been. Through it, Maggs could see the stone wall the painting was hanging on.

'Happy now?' asked Mkoll, turning away.

Maggs pulled up his weapon abruptly, and aimed it at the painting.

'What the feth are you doing?' asked Bonin.

Maggs took a step backwards, and lowered his rifle. He shook his head, dismayed. 'Nothing,' he said, 'nothing, sorry. Being silly.'

'Start moving with a purpose, Maggs,' Mkoll instructed.

Maggs nodded. 'Of course. Absolutely, chief.'

For a moment, for a fleeting moment, the disintegrating portrait had appeared to bleed. Dark, clotted fluid had oozed out of the collapsed hole like black blood from a meat-wound. But it had just been trickling dust, and Maggs's imagination. He felt stupid.

Not blood. Not blood at all. Just dust. Dust and shadows and–

dry skulls in a dusty valley, with all the tops sawn off

–his own stupid imagination.

Mkoll and Bonin had crossed to the inner hatch. They began to haul on the elaborate brass levers.

'Let's get this open,' Mkoll grunted.

'Uh huh. Let's,' said Wes Maggs, as he hurried to join them.

III

'THEY'RE TAKING TOO long,' said Tona Criid. The thin song of the dust was all around them, and visibility was down to less than four metres. The forward companies had drawn up half a kilometre from Hinzerhaus, waiting for the scout advance to report back. Half a kilometre, but none of them could actually see the house.

'Just wait,' said Gaunt.

'Should I send up a support detail, just in case?' asked Gol Kolea. Like all of them, he wore his camo-cloak pulled up to protect his mouth and nose.

'Wait,' Gaunt repeated. He touched his ear-piece, took it out and checked it, and then glanced at his vox-officer.

'Anything, or am I dead?' he asked.

'You're showing live, sir,' Beltayn replied, adjusting the brass dials of his heavy vox-caster. 'Still nothing from advance.'

Gaunt frowned. 'Give them a vox-check, please.'

'Yes, sir,' said Beltayn. Pulling the phones around his ears, he unhooked the brass mic and held it close to his mouth, shielding it from the swirling grit with his cupped left hand. 'Ghost-ghost One, Ghost-ghost One, this is Nalwood, this is Nalwood. Ghost-ghost One, vox-check, please, come back.'

Beltayn looked up at Gaunt. 'Just static.'

'Keep trying, Bel,' said Gaunt.

'Ghost-ghost One, Ghost-ghost One, this is Nalwood, this is Nalwood...'

Gaunt looked over at Kolea. 'Gol, assemble a back-up anyway. Get them ready, but keep them in formation until I give the word.'

'Yes, sir.'

'Mkoll knows what he's about. This is just a vox glitch, nothing more.'

Kolea nodded, and shouldered his way back into the driving wind that was coming up the ravine. They could hear him shouting orders, and hear the clatter of men moving into position.

'This is going to be trouble,' Major Rawne growled.

'Eli, give it a rest,' said Gaunt.

Rawne shrugged a what-the-hell, but obliged.

Gaunt waited. It was slow, like waiting for his own inevitable death. He paced, head down, looking at the way his boots scooped out depressions in the dust, marvelling as they in-filled again instantly. The singing wind curated Jago. It had no desire to let anything change.

'There are certain–'

Gaunt turned around. Ludd had begun to speak and then, for some reason, had thought better of it.

'What were you going to say, Nahum?' Gaunt asked.

Ludd coughed, his voice muffled behind his cloak hem. 'Nothing, sir. Nothing.'

Gaunt smiled. 'Oh, I want to know, now. There are certain – *what?*'

Ludd looked sideways at the bulky figure of Viktor Hark beside him. Hark nodded. 'Just spit it out, Ludd,' Hark said.

Ludd swallowed hard. It wasn't just the dust in his throat. 'A-at times of stress, sir, I was going to remark, there are certain methods that may be employed to dampen a nervous disposition.'

'You think I am exhibiting signs of a nervous disposition then, Ludd?' Gaunt asked.

'Actually, sir, that was why I stopped talking. I realised, rather abruptly, that I had no business suggesting such a thing, openly.'

'Oh feth me backwards, Ludd,' Hark muttered.

'Well,' said Gaunt, 'in terms of morale and respect, you were probably correct to edit yourself. It doesn't look good when a junior ranker suggests to his senior officer that he might like to calm down.'

'Exactly my point,' said Ludd. 'I just arrived at it too late.'

'Let's hear the methods anyway,' said Gaunt, clearly in a playful mood. 'It might do some of us some good. Isn't that right, Eli?'

Nearby, Rawne inclined his head towards Gaunt, slowly. His eyes, behind his brass goggles, were hooded in the most sarcastic way.

'Y-you really want me to–?' Ludd stammered.

'Oh, Throne,' Hark breathed to no one in particular.

'I really do, Nahum. I think you should tell us all about these methods.' Gaunt looked around at the rest of them. 'Who knows? They might prove useful.'

'Could I not, you know, just shoot myself now?' Ludd asked.

'Surviving embarrassment is character-building, Nahum,' Gaunt said. 'Get on with it. Start by telling us where these methods originated.'

Ludd looked at the ground. He mumbled something.

'Louder, please.'

'My mother taught them to me.'

Tona Criid started to cackle. Varl, Beltayn and even Rawne, despite himself, began to laugh too, but it was Tona's brittle cackle that really cut the air. It made Hark wince. He knew that sound: the false laughter of bitten-down pain.

Gaunt raised his hand to quiet the chorus. 'No, really,' he said. 'Let Nahum continue. Nahum?'

'I'd rather not, if you don't mind, sir. I spoke out of turn.'

'Consider it an order.'

'Ah. All right. Yes sir. Well, there was this counting game she used to play to keep worry in check. You count one-two-three and so on, and take a deep breath between each beat.'

'In this dust?' snorted Criid. She pulled the ridge of her cape down, hawked, and spat out a gob of grey phlegm.

Ludd looked at Gaunt and lifted his shoulders. 'She used to say the words "Throne of Terra" between each count. One, Throne of Terra… two, Throne of Terra… three–'

'Can I ask you a question, Nahum?' Gaunt said.

'Of course, sir.'

'Was your mother an especially worried woman?'

Ludd shrugged. Gritty particles flecked off his leather coat. 'I suppose. She was always nervous, as I remember. Her nerves troubled her. She was frail. Actually, I don't know. I was eight the last time I saw her. I was being shipped out to the scholam. I believe she's dead now.'

Criid stopped chuckling abruptly.

'I was also young when I lost my mother,' said Gaunt. He may have been lying, but no one was in a position to refute him. 'Nahum, do I look to you like an especially worried woman?'

'Of course not, sir.'

'Of course not. But I am an especially worried commander. Do you mind at all if I use your mother's counting game?'

'No, I don't, sir.'

Gaunt turned and started back along the pass towards the invisible house.

'One, Throne of Terra… Two, Throne of Terra…' he began. At the tenth *Throne of Terra*, he turned and counted his way back to them.

The wind dropped, to a light breath. The dust sank. The sun came out.

Eszrah ap Niht, who had been silent all the while, placed his lean hand on Gaunt's arm, and nodded up the pass.

'Histye, soule.'

Ibram Gaunt turned.

They saw the house for the first time.

Elikon M.P., Elikon M.P., this is Nalwood, this is Nalwood. Objective achieved. Securing site as of sunset. No hostile contact to report at this time.

Nalwood out. (transmission ends)

- Transcript of vox message, fifth month, 778.

THREE

Ghosts in the House

I

IN THE TEN minutes of dust-less, song-less silence that followed, the Ghosts were afforded their first proper look at the place that would later ring with the sounds of their deaths.

Hinzerhaus.

There wasn't much to see: a fortified gatehouse, built into the foundations of the soaring cliffs and, above that, several tiers of armoured casemates and blockhouses extruding from the chin of the rock-face like theatre balconies. High up, along the cliff crest, there were signs of tiled roofs; of long, linked halls and blocky towers. To either side of the house proper, the ridge line was punctuated by cloche towers and budding fortifications, like warts and blisters erupting from wizened skin.

A fortress-house. A house-fortress. A bastion tunnelled and drilled out of the impassive mountain rock.

'Feth,' said Dalin Criid.

'Quiet in the line there!' his company officer called out.

Dalin bit his lip. Every man around him was thinking the same simple thought, but Dalin was the youngest and newest Ghost, and he was still mastering the stoicism and the field drill. For a flushed moment, he felt like a complete fool.

The worst of it was, he knew they were all looking at him. Dalin had acquired a special place in the regiment, one that he was not entirely comfortable with. Touchstone, lucky charm, new blood. He was the boy who'd made good, the first son of the Ghosts.

And bad rock Jago was his first combat posting as part of the Tanith First-and-Only, which made this more like a rite of passage, an initiation. Dalin Criid had a big legacy to uphold.

Two big legacies, in fact: the regiment's and his father's.

The vox-link clicked as signals came back from the command group. Senior officers were jogging back down the ravine, relaying the orders verbally to the waiting companies.

Dalin was part of E Company, which made him one of Captain Meryn's mob. Flyn Meryn was a handsome, hard-edged man, one of the youngest captains in the regiment, Tanith-born. Word was, Meryn was a Rawne in waiting, and styled himself on the number two officer's vicious manner. Time, Dalin had been reliably informed, had mellowed Rawne's notoriously sharp edges a little… well, if not mellowed then weathered. All the while, Meryn had been getting sharper, as if he was gunning for the top bastard prize. Dalin would have rather been assigned to any other company than Meryn's, even Rawne's, but there was a matter of duty involved. E Company had a vacancy and, in the opinion of everyone except Dalin Criid himself, only Dalin could fill it.

Meryn came back down the line.

'Advancing by companies!' he shouted, echoing the sing-song of the order as it had come to him. 'E Company, rise and address!'

The company rose, in a line. Behind them, G and L companies got up off their backsides and shook the dust out of their camo-cloaks as their officers called them forwards.

'Company uncase!' Meryn ordered.

Dalin stripped the field casing off his lasrifle. He'd done it a thousand times, drill after drill, and he was no slower than the men either side of him. The case, wound up like a stocking, slipped away in his webbing.

There was noise all around him: officers shouting instructions, and the chinking rattle of troopers rising to advance. Two and a half thousand Imperial Guardsmen made a considerable row just walking.

'Keep it low!' Meryn yelled.

More noise rolled back down the ravine. The command section, supported by A, B and D companies, was already beginning its advance up the gorge towards the gatehouse.

'Stand ready to move, company!' Meryn shouted.

'Are we expecting that much trouble?' Cullwoe whispered. He was next in line, on Dalin's right.

Dalin looked in the direction Cullwoe was nodding. The heavy and support weapon crews of the regiment had begun to set up along the sides of the ravine, covering the gatehouse. Locking brackets clinked and breeches clattered as team-served weapons were bedded and assembled in smart order.

'I guess so,' Dalin replied.

'I'm still hearing yap,' Meryn bellowed, moving back down the line. He approached.

'Was that you, Criid?'

Dalin saw no point in lying. 'Yes, sir. Sorry, sir.'

Meryn glared at him for a moment and then–

oh please, no, don't

–nodded. Dalin hated that. He hated the fact that Meryn cut him slack because of who and what he was.

'Just keep it low, Dalin, all right?' Meryn said, in a painfully avuncular tone.

'Yes, sir.'

Bastard, bastard, bastard, treat me like the rest, treat me like the others, not like some... not like I'm Caffran's fething ghost...

'That's got to be a royal pain in the butt, mister,' whispered Cullwoe side-long. 'Him doing that, I mean.'

Dalin grinned. It was a standing gag between the two of them. Khet Cullwoe was his buddy. They'd bonded early on, from the moment Dalin got himself plonked into E. Cullwoe was a Belladon, a bony, freckled, red-headed kid only four years older than Dalin. He had a grin you couldn't help but laugh with. Cullwoe was Dalin's sanity. Khet Cullwoe was the only one who seemed to get it, to get the very shitty place Dalin found himself in. 'Royal pain', in all its infinite variation, was their private, standing joke. The key was to make sure your sentence included the words 'royal', 'pain' and 'mister'.

On Dalin's left hand in the line was Neskon, the flame-trooper. He'd heard enough of the Cullwoe/Dalin interplay over the last few weeks to find it amusing. Neskon stank of prom-juice, the smell seeping out of his rind like rank, chemical sweat.

'Ready, boy?' he asked.

Dalin nodded.

The grizzled flame-trooper, his face and neck prematurely aged by the professional heat he deployed, let his tanks gurgle up and then flicked the burner. It coughed, and took with a belch of ignition.

'Happy sounds,' Neskon muttered, adjusting the fuel feed. 'You stand by me, boy. I'll see you right.'

Dalin nodded again. He felt strangely safe and looked after: a young buddy on one side, a friendly fire-ogre on the other, both of them looking out for him, because of who he was: Caffran's son. Criid and Caffran's son, brought up out of the fires of Vervunhive to be a Ghost in his adoptive father's place.

Neskon's flamer burped fuel and stammered. The flame-trooper adjusted it expertly, and brought the burn cone back to a liquid dribble.

'E Company! Make ready to advance!'

Dalin tensed, waiting for the order, the order he felt he had been waiting for all his life.

'Straight silver!' Meryn shouted.

Do it, now. Left hand down to the webbing, slide it out, spin it around, fix it to the rifle lug, *snap-snap!* Ten centimetres of fighting knife, locked in place. The trademark weapon of the Tanith Ghosts.

Dalin Criid felt a boiling surge of pride. His rifle was in his hands. He was a Ghost, and he had just fixed silver, straight silver, in anger for the very first time.

'Advance!' Meryn yelled.

'Come on then if you're coming,' said Neskon.

II

STRAIGHT SILVER DIDN'T apply to everyone. Marksmen weren't expected to fix. As the order ran down the company lines, Hlaine Larkin didn't move. His precious long-las, miraculously recovered from the swamps of Gereon, was already up to his chin and trained.

Larkin was old. With the exception of Zweil and Dorden, he was probably the oldest man in the regiment, and the best shot. Glory fething *be*, was he the best shot.

Larkin was skinny and lean, his face leathery like a tanned hide. He had been through every single battle the Ghosts had fought, and he had outlived many very good friends.

Larkin waited, sniffing the air. His head was clear for once, which made a change. He was a slave to migraines. He shifted uneasily. He still wasn't used to the foot. He'd opted for a prosthetic rather than an augmetic, but it had left him with a limp. A wooden foot brace – nalwood, thank you – Throne knew how the chief had pulled strings to make *that* happen. Larkin believed Gaunt felt guilty about the foot. It had been the right thing to do, of course, Larkin knew that, but he couldn't blame the chief for feeling guilty.

He *had* taken Larkin's foot off with his sword, after all.

Five seventy metres, panning, lock off. Larkin slowly travelled his scope. He ignored the foreground fuzz of advancing bodies, and played his sharp focus across the relief of the fortress walls and window slits instead. He was hunting for movement, hunting for danger with a well-practiced eye, hunting for the trouble Major Rawne had been so fething sure was waiting for them up there.

Larkin's breathing was very slow. Kill-shot at four thousand metres. He'd managed that once or twice. It was as if he had a special, holy angel watching over him, guiding his aim. A special angel. He'd seen her once.

Once was enough.

Larkin always believed he hadn't seen anything true until he'd seen it through his scope. As the Ghosts advanced, he watched to see what was real as much as he watched as a covering marksman.

There they went... Daur, Kolea, Kamori, driving their troops into the gate. Larkin swung his scope. There was Caober. There was Brostin and Varl. There was old father Zweil, up on a rock, using it like a pulpit to bless the advancing Guardsmen as they trudged past.

Larkin smiled. Zweil was a piece of work. Oldest man he'd ever known, and still full of it.

There was Wheln, and Melwid, there was Veddekin, Derin, Harjeon and Burone. There was Tona Criid and Nahum Ludd. There was Lubba, and Dremmond, Posetine and Nessa. There was Bragg and Noa Vadim and Bool. There was Vivvo and Lyse and sexy Jessi Banda. There was–

Wait. Pull up! Go back!

Feth, feth, feth, no–

In the midst of it all, all those moving figures... *Bragg*?

No, just a trick of the eye. A lie of the scope. A blip of the mind. Not Bragg. Some other fether. Not Bragg at all.

Come on, how stupid was *that*?

Larkin adjusted his sweep, his scope clicking.

III

COMMISSAR VIKTOR HARK heaved his not inconsiderable bulk through the wedged hatch and entered the old gatehouse. Men were gathering inside, waiting, looking around, chattering quietly. Captain Daur stood by the inner hatch, despatching men from the waiting mass a few at a time into the main house.

'Quiet!' Hark said. The chatter slid away like a sheathed blade.

'Next fire-team!' Daur called out, consulting a packet of papers he'd been carrying in his musette bag.

Five Ghosts moved forward from the gathered group, C Company men led by Derin.

'Up, forty metres, take the turn to your left. Reinforce the teams in the gallery and push forward.' Daur gestured up through the inner hatch as he gave out the instructions.

'Got it,' said Derin.

'Vox anything,' said Daur.

Derin nodded. He said 'Yes, sir,' but the look on his face was all about being indoors out of the dusty wind.

'Vox anything, Derin,' said Hark, coming up behind them. 'This is not a safe place until the chief tells us it is.'

Derin and his men suddenly had their game faces on.

'Absolutely, commissar, sir.'

'You so much as hear a mouse fart, you sing it in, Derin,' said Hark. 'Watch your backs and read the signs and don't tell me anything's clear unless you can personally guarantee it on your baby sister's unblemished honour.'

There were times when Derin would have felt bold enough to remind the commissar that any baby sister he might ever have had was long dead in the ashes of Tanith. This was not one of those times.

'Got it, commissar.'

'Off you go.'

Derin's team took off through the inner hatch. Hark could hear their footsteps thudding off the stone floor.

'Next fire-team!' Daur called. More men separated from the main body and moved forward.

'How accurate's the map, d'you suppose?' Hark asked Daur.

Ban Daur wrinkled his nose and looked down at the packet of papers he was holding. Several senior officers, Hark included, had been issued with copies of the objective layouts at Elikon Muster Point.

'Well, they're old and they look like they were done from memory,' said Daur dubiously. 'Or by someone guessing. So…'

Hark nodded. 'My thoughts exactly. We're going to be running into surprises in this place.' He took off his cap and removed his brass goggles. His eyes were sore.

'You all right, commissar?' Daur asked.

'Huh?'

'You look tired, if I may say.'

'I haven't been sleeping well. Get the next team moving. We're backing up.'

Ever more troops were coming in through the outer hatch, and assembling in the gatehouse space. Hark watched and waited as Daur brought up, instructed, and sent on three more teams into the house proper. While he waited, Hark pulled out his own packet of papers, and found the central floor plan. Ban Daur's description of the cartography had been kind.

'I'm keen to locate this place's water supply,' he told Daur.

'The well?'

'Yeah.'

'Bottom of the central level, I think. Supposed to be. I sent Varl's team in to section it.'

Hark nodded. 'I'll go find them. If anyone comes looking for me, that's where I've gone.'

'Yes, commissar.' Daur glanced at the big man. 'Do you want an escort, sir?'

'Do I look like I need an escort, captain?' Hark asked.

'You haven't looked like you needed an escort since the day I met you, sir,' said Daur.

'Good answer, captain. I'll see you later.'

Hark stepped through the inner hatch.

IV

A BROAD HALLWAY led back from the gatehouse's inner hatch into the heart of the house. It had an octagonal shape in cross-section, and the floor was paved. The walls and ceiling were panelled with a dark, glossy material which Hark imagined was either a weathered alloy or some time-discoloured, lacquered hardwood. A sheeny dark brown, at any rate, like polished tortoiseshell or tobacco spit. There was the faintest suggestion of etchings or engravings on the shoulder-level sections of the walls, but nothing that eye or touch could read.

Hark walked up the hallway. Every twenty or so metres, a short flight of stone steps raised the entire tunnel a metre or so, so it was impossible to see clearly the entire length of the passage.

For the first time in weeks, Hark felt genuinely alone. For the first time in *years*, perhaps. There was no sound except for his own footsteps and breathing, and the tiny crackle of his leather coat as he moved. There was no sound of movement or voices, and he was so deep in the rock, the song of the wind outside was gone.

The lights were strange: dull white chemical glow-orbs strung from fat, withered piping that looked like diseased arteries. The light came and went in slow pulse, brighter then softer. Unnerving. The satin-brown walls seemed to soak the light up too, so that the hallway was filled with a warm, white gloom, fuzzy and softly dense, like starlight on a summer's evening.

Hark stopped and watched the slow throb of the lights for a moment. It reminded him of something else. It reminded him of the bone-deep, heavy throb of pain, which was something he'd learned all about during the battle for Herodor five years earlier. Five years. Had it really been that long?

Hark realised he was sweating. Some other memory, unbidden, had just rekindled itself, and not for the first time. It wasn't the memory of the extreme pain he'd suffered at Herodor, nor was it the nagging phantom ache of the arm he had lost there. Yet it was both of those things, too. It was linked to them, sparked off by them. It was like a dream, forgotten on waking, that flashed back later, uninvited and formless. A sense of sadness, of regret and lingering pain. Oh yes, that too.

V

HARK SWALLOWED. HE dearly wished he could pin the sensation down, identify it, perceive it clearly for once. It had been coming to him repeatedly for months, perhaps years, more and more frequently. In his dreams mostly, waking him with a start and a sense of bafflement. Sometimes, it came when he was awake, an itch he couldn't scratch, a taste in the mouth, a taste in the mind. Dorden, the old medicae, had advised Hark that serious physical trauma of the type Hark had suffered often left an indelible residue on the victim. He hadn't just been talking about phantom limb syndrome. He had meant a mental scar, the burned pathway of synapses flared and fused by the moment of agony.

'Some patients report a metallic taste, Viktor,' Dorden had said.

'You've been to the mess hall, then?'

Dorden had smiled. 'A metallic taste. Sometimes a smell, a memory of a smell, from childhood perhaps. Soap. Your mother's preferred fragrance.'

'My mother was an all-comers wrestling champion in the PDF,' Hark had replied. 'She didn't go in for perfume much.'

'You're joking,' Dorden had said.

'Yes.'

'Joke all you like, if that's how you wish to cope. Everyone develops their own strategies, Viktor. You asked me for help.'

'I asked you for your medical opinion, doctor,' Hark had said. Then he had paused. 'Sorry. Sorry, doctor. You were saying?'

'Is it a taste? A smell? A memory?'

'It's… it's a dream, doctor. Just the faded echo of a dream that I cannot actually remember. It's just out of reach. Always just beyond my ability to recall it.'

'Do you dream it? Is it an actual dream, or just the sensation of a dream recalled?'

Hark had paused before replying. 'I dream quite a lot these days, doctor. My sleep is bothered and disturbed, but I cannot say what by.'

'It may pass in time,' Dorden had assured him.

It hadn't. Hark knew it wasn't going to. Sometimes he woke up biting his lip so as not to scream aloud. Sometimes, when he was wide awake, the feeling came to him: an amorphous, incomprehensible wash of softness, like smoke, like soft-filled pillows pressing in against him. But there was always something with a hard edge hidden inside the softness, pushing at him from behind the pillows.

The lights pulsed slowly, as if the house was breathing the slow breath of a sleeper. Exactly like that, *precisely* like that. What was it? What in Throne's name was–

VI

'HARK?'

Hark snapped around, his good hand on the grip of his holstered plasma pistol.

A fire-team led by Ferdy Kolosim had come up behind him. The men hung back as the Belladon officer came forward, his brow furrowed. Hairline sweat had made tracks down through the dust caked to Kolosim's forehead.

'What are you doing, standing there?' Kolosim asked.

'Just, erm, just getting my bearings, Ferdy,' Hark replied. He took out his floor plans and shook them out.

'You sure?' Kolosim was a good man, a worthy addition to the ranks of the First-and-Only.

'Oh yes,' said Hark, forcing a smile onto his lips. 'This place... quite a place.'

'Good to be out of that bloody wind, though, right?'

'I think that's just it, Ferdy,' Hark replied. 'It's suddenly so quiet, I quite lost myself.'

'I know what you mean,' said Kolosim, lowering his rifle and looking up at the tunnel roof. 'This place feels–'

'Don't say it,' Hark advised with a grin.

'I won't. I know what Gaunt ordered. But it does, doesn't it?'

Hark nodded. 'A little bit, yes. You carry on.'

'Sure?'

'Carry on, boys.'

The fire-team moved past him and rattled away up the hall. Hark looked down at his left hand. The skin of his wrist, under the heavy black glove, itched like a bastard. He wanted to tug the glove off and scratch. Except, as he knew very well, there was no skin under that glove, just augmetic bones and sinews, just wires and plasteks and solenoids.

Hark turned, trying to ignore it, and walked on.

VII

THE LONG HALLWAY led up into the base chamber of the house. Side galleries had opened to left and right as he walked the length of the hallway; long, drafty tunnels leading out into the base-level casemates and fortifications. The wind blew down them, thready and weak, forced in through distant apertures and slits. He could smell dust.

Hark reached a wide flight of steps. The hallway broadened out into a vestibule. The floor was no longer paved; it was tiled in the same sheened brown substance that clad the walls. It clacked under his boots, soft and gleaming, like polished leather. The steps went up under a huge wooden arch riddled with worm holes. The arch had been ornately carved, like the screen of a templum. Interlocking figures twisted into scrolling patterns, all sanded down by time until they had been rendered meaningless.

The base chamber was a circular stone vault fifty metres wide and four floors deep. A vast wooden screw-stair ran up from its centre into the upper levels of the house. At the ground floor level, and at each landing turn, hallways let out into the side sections of the house. Sentries had been placed on all the landings. The lights in the base chamber were hung from ceiling pipes, slack and heavy like eyeballs strung from optic nerves. They pulsed too: slowly, oh so slowly.

The wind was in the base chamber, gusting around from the doorways standing open on each level. It gave the air a dry, powdery smell.

'Where's that coming from?' Hark asked.

'There's a... gn... gn... shutter open somewhere, sir,' the trooper guarding the bottom of the staircase replied. Hark knew the voice and the messed-up face.

'A shutter, Trooper Merrt?'

Merrt nodded. He was cautious of the commissar. Hark had slammed Merrt down to RIP duties en route from Ancreon Sextus, though Merrt didn't hold it against him. Merrt knew he'd deserved it. As a result, Merrt had seen the Gereon liberation offensive from the sharpest end.

Rhen Merrt had once been a marksman, second only to Mad Larkin in skill. A headshot on Monthax, years before, had ended that speciality. Merrt was now the proud owner of an ugly augmetic jaw that made him look like a gruesome collision between a servitor and a human skull. The damage had ruined his aim, and he'd suffered for it. He was back at the bottom of the heap, his speciality a distant regret.

'A gn... gn... shutter, yes, sir,' Merrt said. He had trouble articulating his clumsy artificial jaw most of the time. His speech was slow and mannered.

Hark nodded. 'Well, we'll have to see to that. If any part of this fortress is open enough to let the wind blow through, Throne only knows what else it might let in.'

Merrt nodded. A couple more fire-teams clattered into the base chamber and headed off up the staircase.

'By the way, it's good to see you back, Merrt,' Hark said quietly.

'Sir?'

'This is where you belong. In the First. Try not to feth it up for yourself again.'

'I'm a gn... gn... changed man, commissar.'

'Glad to hear it. I'm heading for the well.'

'Back hatch, sir,' Merrt replied, jerking a thumb over his shoulder.

Hark walked around behind the massive staircase. There was a hole on the floor there, a brass hatch that had been levered open. Hark stood at the lip and peered down.

Darkness.

Packs of Guard equipment had been dumped on the deck beside the hatch. Hark went over and helped himself to a lamp-pack. He switched it on. The beam was hot and yellow, in strong contrast to the milky radiance of the house lights.

He went back to the hatch and played the light down. There was the rickety iron staircase. Hark lowered himself gently onto it.

VIII

'IF YOU FLICK 'em, they get brighter,' Trooper Twenzet remarked, flicking one of the wall-hung lights.

'Don't do that,' said Varl.

'Why not?'

'Because... I'll shoot you,' said Varl.

'Fair enough,' replied Twenzet.

The chamber was clammy and cold. It was the lowest part of the house, deep under the crust, or so the plans said. Varl had very little faith in the plans.

He was leading a fire-team of six men from B Company, Rawne's own boys: Brostin, Laydly, Twenzet (he of the lamp flicking), Gonlevy, LaHurf and Cant. Orders, straight from Gaunt in person, had been to find and secure the objective's water supply.

Ceglan Varl was old-school Tanith, one of the first of the few. He was popular, because he was a joker and a trickster, and unpopular, funnily enough, for precisely the same reasons. Varl was lean and taut, like a pulled rope. The men with him were mostly Belladon newcomers, except Brostin, the flame-trooper, who was old-school Tanith too, very old-school.

Brostin and Varl had done Gereon together, the first time round. They'd known tough, and had spat right back in its eye.

The orders had come with plans, flimsy things on see-through paper, which had led them down to what Brostin had delighted in describing as the 'butt-hole end' of the house.

Deep down, rock-cut, clammy-deep. Dew perspired off the rough, lime-washed walls. A shaky iron staircase had led them down into this pit.

They moved around, swinging their lamp-packs back and forth like swords of light in the gloom. The house lamps down in the well room were very feeble.

The chamber was roughly oval, and cut out of the deep rock. The floor was boarded with thick, varnished planks. A big cast iron tub with a brass lid stood in the centre of the chamber. A complex system of chains ran from the lid mechanism up to pulleys and gears in the roof space.

'So that's the well,' said Varl, aiming his lamp at it.

'Well, well, well,' said Twenzet.

'I do the jokes,' snapped Varl.

'Yeah, why is that?' asked Laydly.

'Because… I'll shoot you,' said Varl.

'Once again, fair enough,' replied Twenzet.

'Get it open,' Varl ordered.

Gonlevy and Cant began to wind on the levers on top of the lid.

'It won't budge, sarge,' said Cant.

'Why not?'

Cant paused. He knew full well what was coming.

'I… don't seem to be able to move the levers, sarge.'

'Because?' Varl asked.

Cant mumbled something.

'We can't hear you,' said Varl.

'Because I can't, sarge,' Cant said.

'Oh, you can't can you, Cant?' Varl said. All of them broke up in fits of laughter, again.

'Yeah, yeah,' said Cant, who'd long ago lost sight of the funny side of the joke. 'Just bloody help us with–'

'Tweenzy's right,' said Brostin, from across the dank chamber.

'Please don't call me that,' said Twenzet. 'I did ask you.'

'Tweenzy's on the money, Varl,' Brostin insisted.

Varl switched his beam over to pick out Brostin. Brostin was hunched down, flicking one of the wall lights with a sturdy index finger.

'They do get brighter when you flick 'em,' Brostin smiled.

'Stop it!' Varl snarled. 'All of you! We're meant to be–'

'Vaguely capable?'

They all froze. Commissar Hark clumped down the staircase into the chamber.

'Sir,' said Varl.

'This the well, Varl?'

'It is, sir.'

'Got it open? Secure?'

'Not yet, sir, sorry.'

'Open it up.'

'I was just saying how the levers were stiff, commissar,' Cant began. 'We can't–'

Viktor Hark put out his left hand. His augmetic fingers closed like a vice around the winding handle.

'Can't Cant, or won't?' Hark snorted.

'Oh, not you too,' moaned Cant.

Hark's arm turned. With a creaking, shrieking complaint, the gears turned and the lid began to open. Chains clattered in the darkness above them. A foul, dry stench oozed out of the well-head.

'Was that you, Brostin?' Varl asked.

'Not this time,' Brostin groaned, fingers pinching his nose shut.

Varl, Hark and Brostin went to the side of the well and looked down. Varl shone his lamp. The beam picked up moss and treacly black lichen. The drain-stench was unbearable.

Brostin took out a spare seal ring, a small knurled brass object, and tossed it down the well.

'One, Throne of Terra… Two, Throne of Terra… Three, Throne of Terra…' Hark began.

He got to sixteen, Throne of Terra. There was no plunk, no splash, just a dry, jingling series of impacts as the ring skittered away.

Hark looked at Varl. 'You see, this,' he said, 'this is what I was afraid of.'

Day seven (out of Elikon M.P.). Sunrise at four plus nineteen, wind storm all night. Got last of regiment in just before midnight local. No sleep. Squads working to secure objective. Place is a maze. Bears ~~litt~~ little or no resemblance to schematics. Keep finding new chambers, new halls. K. found whole new wing running east that wasn't on any version of charts.

Objective feels curiously dead and alive, both at the same time. Dry, empty, but power still on, and some signs of habitation. Major problem - no water supply despite promise. Well dry. Trying to contact Elikon for assist. G. annoyed. Local water supply essential if we are to stay on station here. Rumour of secondary well, which can't be found. Not only do our schematics not agree with ~~actal~~ actual layout of place, have discovered our charts don't even agree with each other. Will send official rebuke to office of tactics for this error.

I cannot shake the feeling that there's a ~~dream trying to wanting to something in my head that~~

Medics report high incidence of eye infection amongst troops, due to dust.

- Field journal, V.H. fifth month, 778.

FOUR

Written in Dust

I

THERE WERE STRANGE echoes in Hinzerhaus, echoes that took a while to get used to. Alone in one chamber, a man might hear the footsteps of a comrade two floors up and a hundred metres distant. Sound carried.

If the wind ever gets in here, Baskevyl thought, what a song it will sing.

He was moving down through the house in search of the power room. At every turn or junction, he consulted a scrap of paper. Mkoll had written out directions to the power room for him. The charts couldn't be trusted. Daur and Rawne had gone nose to nose the night before over the location of a room marked as the 'lesser hall'. It had nearly got ugly – Baskevyl was sure Daur had been on the verge of throwing a punch – until Gaunt pointed out that, for one thing, Daur's chart and Rawne's chart were appreciably different and, for another, they were having their argument *in* the lesser hall.

Looking back on it, Baskevyl reflected that perhaps the gravest cause for concern during the argument had been Daur's behaviour. Ban Daur, clean-cut and Throne-fearing, was a model officer, the last person you'd ever expect to see swinging for a senior man.

It's because we're spooked, every man jack. Some admit it, some don't, but we're all spooked by this bad rock and this labyrinth house. There's something in the air here, some–

dry skulls in a dusty valley

–thing palpable, an oozing tension.

Whatever it was, it wasn't in the water because there wasn't any. The well was dead. They were living off their own bottles, on quarter rations. Ludd had been detailed to mark all water bottles with a piece of chalk, and write up any man drinking too much. As a result, everybody *loved* Nahum Ludd.

Baskevyl's mouth tasted as dry as a storm coat's pocket lining, and his tongue felt like a scrap of webbing. He'd snatched two hours' sleep since they'd entered the house, and all one hundred and twenty minutes of it had been a dream about a fountain, gushing pure, bright liquid.

Baskevyl checked his crumpled paper. It told him to follow the next staircase down, and he obeyed. The walls were panelled in a dark, glossy material that had been overlaid in turn by a light coating of pale dust. The white wall lights pulsed slowly.

He heard footsteps approaching, and paused to see who was coming down the stairs behind him. No one appeared. It was just another echo, relayed through the warren of halls. During his ten-minute walk from the main staircase, he'd heard all manner of things: footsteps, voices, the bump and rattle of crates being stowed. Once, he'd heard a snatch of distinct conversation, three men complaining about the water rationing. The voices had come and gone, as if the men had been walking right past him.

When he arrived at the next landing, he found two troopers standing watch, Tokar and Garond from J Company. They both visibly jumped when he walked into view, then saluted with nervous laughs.

'On edge?' he asked.

'We thought you were another echo,' said Garond.

'We keep hearing noises, then there's no one there,' said Tokar. 'Feth, you gave us a scare.'

'My apologies,' said Baskevyl. 'The power room?'

'Down there, sir,' Garond said, indicating the narrow staircase behind him.

Baskevyl nodded. 'Anything to report? Apart from noises?'

Tokar and Garond shook their heads. Baskevyl nodded again, and took a quick look around the landing space. 'What about that?' he asked.

'What, sir?' asked Tokar.

Baskevyl pointed at the wall opposite. 'That.'

'I don't see anything,' Tokar began.

'In the dust,' Baskevyl insisted.

The troopers squinted.

'Oh!' said Garond suddenly. 'It's been drawn there! Gak, I didn't see that. Did you see that, Tokar?'

'First time I've noticed it.'

'Did either of you draw it?' asked Baskevyl.

'No,' they both answered together.

He could see they hadn't. It had been drawn in the dust on the satin-brown wall panel, but so long ago the lines themselves had been covered in dust. It was just a ghost image, a human face, neither specifically male nor female, open-mouthed. There were no eyes. It had been drawn in the dust with slow, lazy finger strokes. Somehow, Baskevyl felt certain they had been slow and lazy.

'What the gak is it?' Garond asked.

Baskevyl stared at the face. It was unsettling. 'I don't know.'

'Why,' Tokar began, 'why didn't we notice it before? We've been standing here two hours.'

'I don't know,' Baskevyl repeated. He took a deep breath. 'Wash it off.'

'With what, sir?' asked Garond.

'Spit?' Tokar suggested.

'Wipe it off, then. Use your capes.'

The troopers moved forward to oblige, scooping up handfuls of their camo-capes.

Baskevyl noticed how they hesitated. Neither one wanted to be the first to touch it.

II

'Not in here, please,' said Dorden as he entered the high-ceilinged room.

Gaunt paused in the act of emptying an appreciable quantity of dust out of his boot onto the floor.

'Why not? Is there a medical reason?'

'If this is going to be the field station, then I have to keep it swept of dust,' Dorden tutted, putting down an armful of medical cartons.

'The field station?' Gaunt asked.

'Yes,' said Dorden.

When Gaunt didn't reply, Dorden looked at him. He saw Gaunt's sarcastically arched eyebrows. He saw the old stuffed leather chair Gaunt was sitting in, the ancient desk behind him, the stacks of kit bags and munition boxes.

'Not the field station, then?' he asked.

'My office, I think you'll find.'

'Ah.'

'The field station is three chambers along, on the right.'

Dorden shook his head. 'These fething maps. Are they of use to any man?'

Gaunt shook his head. 'Not any I've met.' With some satisfaction, he poured the dust out of his boot. It drizzled out in a long, smoking shower.

Dorden looked around. The room was dark and tall, fast in the heart of the house. Dirty outlines on the sheened brown walls showed where paintings had once hung. It had been impressive once, a fine stateroom. Now it seemed like a cave, lit by the dim glow of the lamps.

With a slight start, Dorden realised they weren't alone. There was a third person in the room. Eszrah ap Niht was sitting in one corner, patiently reading an old book by the light of the wall lamp he had huddled up to. His fingertip was moving under the text, sticking at difficult words.

The Nihtgane had developed quite a thirst for knowledge and Gaunt had taught him his letters well. However, no one had yet convinced Eszrah that wearing sunshades indoors wasn't a good idea.

'What are you reading there, Eszrah?' Dorden called out. The old doctor still hadn't quite got the trick of pronouncing Eszrah's name.

Eszrah looked up from his book. 'Yt is ancallyd *The Mirror of Smoke*,' he replied.

'Ah,' said Dorden. He glanced at Gaunt, who was busy evacuating grit from his other boot. 'One of your favourites.'

Gaunt nodded. 'Yes, it is.'

'What's that phrase, that famous phrase? "By dying, we finish our service to the Emperor?" Or something?'

'I think you mean "Only in death, does duty end",' said Gaunt. The colonel-commissar was staring down at his bootless feet. His filthy toes poked out of the holes in his socks. He wiggled them.

'That's it,' said Dorden.

'Not original to the author, of course,' said Gaunt, preoccupied with his own feet. 'An old proverb.'

Dorden nodded. 'And rather disheartening.'

Gaunt looked up at him. 'Disheartening? Don't you intend to die in the service of the God-Emperor? Is there something you'd like to tell your commissar, Tolin?'

Dorden chuckled. 'Do you know how old I am, Ibram?'

Gaunt shrugged.

'Well,' said Dorden, 'let's just say if I'd chosen to muster out at Guard retirement age, as per the edicts, I'd have been a man of leisure for thirteen years now.'

'Feth? Really?'

Tolin Dorden smiled. 'Age-muster is, of course, voluntary. Besides, where would I go?'

Gaunt didn't answer.

'You know how I see myself ending my days?' asked Dorden. 'As a local doctor. A local doctor, serving some backwater community on a colony world. That'd be all right with me. The day comes I get too old, too slow to keep up with the pace of the Tanith First, that's where I want to end up. Leave me somewhere, would you? Somewhere I can treat sprains and flu and ague, and the odd broken bone or colicky newborn. Somewhere quiet. Will you do that for me, when the day comes?'

'You'll be with us forever,' retorted Gaunt.

'That's what I'm afraid of.'

Gaunt stared at him. 'Afraid?'

Dorden sighed. 'How much longer, Ibram? How many more years, how many more battles? We all die sometime. I saw my world die, and now I go from war to war, seeing out the last of my people, one by one. I don't want to be the last man of Tanith, Ibram, scrubbing blood off the surgery table as they wheel out the second to last man of Tanith in a body bag.'

'It wouldn't go like that–' Gaunt began.

'No, it wouldn't,' Dorden agreed. 'One day, I'll just get too old and doddery and you'll have to remove me from service.'

'Hardly. Look at Zweil.'

Dorden grinned. 'If that old fool makes a mistake, people don't die.'

Gaunt got to his feet. 'I'll find you that colony world, time comes,' he said. 'That's a promise. Maybe it'll even be the world the Tanith get to settle. Our reward for service.'

'Ibram, do you honestly believe that's ever going to happen?'

Gaunt was silent for a long time. 'No,' he said finally.

Warmaster Slaydo had promised Gaunt the settlement rights of the first world he won, as a reward after Balhaut. Gaunt had always intended to share that reward with the homeless Tanith. 'Somehow, I doubt Macaroth will honour a rash promise his predecessor made,' Gaunt said quietly.

'If he does intend to,' said Dorden, 'then just make sure we don't win here. The Tanith would lynch you if you won them this bad rock.'

Dorden looked up at the vacant places on the walls.

'I wonder what hung here,' he said.

'Do you?' Gaunt replied. 'All I seem to wonder is... who took them down?'

'What about you?' Dorden asked.

'Me? What about me?'

'How do you see your service ending?'

Gaunt sighed and sat down again. 'Tolin, we both know how my service is going to end, sooner or later.'

He gazed down at his socks. 'Do you have a needle and thread I could borrow? Of course you do.'

'You can darn, can you?' asked Dorden with a slight smile.

'I can learn to darn. This is unseemly for a man of my rank.'

'Don't you have spare socks?'

'These are my spare socks.'

'Dickerson.'

'What?'

'Dickerson, tall Belladon in Arcuda's mob. I hear he darns socks for a few coins. He's good. Used to be a seamster before the Guard. He'll probably do yours for free.'

'Thanks for the tip.'

Eszrah suddenly rose, his reynbow up and aimed. Gaunt and Dorden looked around.

Rawne entered.

'It's just Rawne,' Gaunt told Eszrah. The partisan didn't lower his bow.

'What's up?' Gaunt asked Rawne.

'Criid reckons she's found something,' Rawne said.

III

THE WARM STINK of energy greeted Baskevyl as he entered the power room.

The chamber was long and rectangular, with sloping ceilings. It was dominated by the bulk of the power hub, an iron kettle the size of a drop-pod. Power feeds ran off the kettle up into a broad roof socket, and grilled slits in the kettle's sides throbbed with a slow glow that matched the gentle rhythm of the house lighting. Baskevyl could feel the pulsing warmth. It made no sound. Whatever generative reaction was going on inside, it was a curiously silent one.

The fire-team assigned to guard the power room had been playing cards in a huddle at the foot of the entry steps. They stood when he came up, but he waved them back to their game with a smile.

'How are things here?' he asked Captain Domor.

Shoggy Domor was in charge of the fire-team detail. He walked over to the kettle with Baskevyl as the troopers resumed their quiet game. His bulbous augmetic eyes whirred quietly as they sharpened focus on the major.

'I can't really say, sir.'

'Meaning?'

'I don't know what this is. It's just running. It's been running for a long, long time, and it continues to run. I have no idea what the operating process is.'

'No idea?' Baskevyl frowned. If anyone in the Ghosts knew engineering systems, it was Shoggy.

'I think it's chemical, but I'm not sure.' Domor nodded at the pulsing, glowing kettle in front of them. 'I doubt the chief would thank me if I tried opening it up to find out.'

'There's no feed? No fuel supply?' Baskevyl asked.

'None, sir.'

'We need a tech out here, a tech-adept,' Baskevyl muttered to himself. He pressed his hands against the fat belly of the kettle, then took them away. The iron had throbbed under his touch, as if it was alive.

He looked around at Domor. 'Look, just keep watch on it, as per orders. We may not know how it works, but at least it does, and it's giving us lights. I'll get a detail down here to relieve you in... shall we say three hours?'

Domor nodded. 'What about the, er, noises, sir?'

'You too, eh?' asked Baskevyl. 'I think this place has some weird acoustic qualities. Sound carries. Just try not to let it spook you.'

Domor seemed less than convinced.

'What?' Baskevyl asked.

Domor tilted his head to indicate they should take a walk. Casually, they skirted around the throbbing kettle together and put its bulk between them and the huddle of troopers by the steps. Domor dropped his voice so his boys wouldn't hear.

'Footsteps and voices, right?' he asked softly.

'I've heard both. Like I said, I think sound ca–'

'What about the other noise?' asked Domor.

'What other noise?'

Domor shrugged. 'It comes and goes. A sort of grinding, scraping sound.'

'I haven't heard anything like that,' said Baskevyl.

'Come with me,' said Domor quietly. He stepped aside and called out to his troop. 'Chiria? You're in charge. I'm going to show Major B. the workshops.'

'Right you are, Shoggy,' she called back.

There was a door in the rear wall of the power room. Domor drew back the rusted bolts. He led Baskevyl into a series of four, small stone rooms that had once been workshops. The air within was much colder than it had been in the main hub room. It was chilly and stale, like an old pantry. Old wooden benches lined the walls, their surfaces worn. Wall racks had once held tools, but the tools had long gone. The sooty outlines of saws, pliers and wrenches hung under the old pegs.

Baskevyl peered along the row of workshop rooms. They were linked by stone arches. Domor pulled the door shut behind them.

'Listen,' he said.

'I don't hear anything,' replied Baskevyl.

'*Listen,*' Domor insisted.

IV

GAUNT FOLLOWED RAWNE up a long, rickety wooden staircase into the very summit of the house. They came up into a room shaped like a belfry: a circular, domed chamber into which the wind shrilled through partially open metal shutters. The wind whined like–

dry skulls in a dusty valley

–a scolded dog.

'Can't we close them?' Gaunt asked, raising his voice above the sound.

'No,' Criid called back. 'The mechanisms are jammed.'

Gaunt looked around. The base of the roof dome had eight large shutters around its circumference, all of them operated by brass winders. Years of dust had choked the gears. The shutters were frozen in various positions, like the half-closed eyelids of dying men. Eddies and scoots of dust billowed in around the sills and covered the floor like powdered snow.

'What is this?' Gaunt called.

'Criid called it a windcote,' Rawne cried back. 'Look.'

The centre of the chamber was dominated by a huge perch: a rusted metal tree of fat iron rods where things had once roosted. There was bird lime on the floor, and the remains of food baskets.

'I think they kept birds here, sir,' Criid called out, holding her cloak hem up over her mouth and nose. 'Messenger birds. You know, for flying messages.'

'I grasp the concept,' said Gaunt. He looked at the size of the shutters, imagining them wound back and fully open. 'Big birds,' he muttered.

He went over to the nearest shutter and bent down, trying to peer out of the wedged open slit. Windborne dust gusted into his face.

Coughing, he pulled back. 'This'd make a great lookout, if it wasn't for that fething wind.'

Rawne nodded. He'd thought the same thing.

'That wasn't what I wanted you to see,' Criid called out to them.

'Then what?'

She pointed upwards. Something was hanging from the uppermost branch of the roosting perch.

'That,' shouted Criid.

It was a black iron face mask, swinging gently by its head straps in the swirling wind. The mask had a hooked nose and a snarling expression.

It was a Blood Pact grotesk.

Gaunt said something.

'What?' Rawne asked, against the scream of the wind.

'I said there's that trouble you were on about,' said Gaunt.

V

BASKEVYL TURNED IN a small slow circle, gazing up at the ceiling of the workshop.

'You heard that, right?' Domor whispered.

Baskevyl nodded. His mouth was dry, and it wasn't entirely due to the short-rationed water. He'd heard the noise quite clearly, a grinding scrape, just like Shoggy Domor had described. It had sounded like… well Baskevyl wasn't sure he could honestly say *what* it had sounded like, but the moment he'd heard it, an image had filled his mind, an image he hadn't really wanted. It was the image of something vast and clammy, snake-like, all damp bone and glistening tissue, like a gigantic spinal chord, scraping and slithering along some deep, rough, rock-cut tunnel far below them, like a daemon-worm in the earth.

Lucien Wilder, in days long gone, had always said Baskevyl had been born with an imagination he'd have been better off without.

'What does it sound like to you?' asked Domor quietly.

Baskevyl didn't reply. Urgently, he tried to banish the image from his head. He walked under the stone arch into the next workshop, then into the next, until he was standing in the end chamber. The walls were panelled, like everywhere else, in that satin brown material.

The noise came again. Gnarled vertebrae sleeved in wet, grey sinew, dragged across ragged stone. It slipped along rapidly, fluidly, like a desert snake. Baskevyl could hear loose pebbles and grit skittering out in its wake.

There was cold sweat on his back. The noise died away.

'Well?' Domor asked.

'Vermin?' asked Baskevyl. Domor stared at him. His augmetic eyes whirred and clicked, as if widening in scorn.

'Vermin?' he replied. 'Have you seen any vermin?'

Baskevyl shook his head.

'The place is dry and dead,' said Domor. 'There's no vermin here, no insects, no scraps of food. If there were ever any vermin here, Major B, they've long since given up on the place.'

He was right. Baskevyl felt stupid for even suggesting it. There was no point trying to fob off smart men like Shoggy Domor with patent lies.

He heard the noise again, briefly, a wriggling scratch that faded away almost instantaneously. Baskevyl stepped towards the wall, and reached out. The satin brown panelling felt warm and organic to his touch. He tapped at it, at first hearing the dead reply of the stone wall behind it.

Then, as he moved his hand along, he got a hollow noise.

He glanced back at Domor, who was watching him.

'There's nothing behind this panel,' he said.

'What?'

'There's nothing behind this panel. Listen.'

He tapped again. A hollow dullness. 'Get your team in here,' Baskevyl began. The noise came back again. Baskevyl stiffened. Throne, but he could not help visualising the awful, clammy spine-thing, snaking through the dark.

'Shoggy, would y–' he started to say.

He heard another sound suddenly: a brief, leaden *pop*, like someone cracking a knuckle. How odd. Baskevyl looked up and down, studying the sheened brown patina of the wall panel.

There was a hole in the wall at chest height just to his right, a small hole, half a centimetre in diameter, that had certainly not been there before. The edges of the hole were smouldering slightly.

'Shoggy?' he said, and then registered a sudden, sharp sensation of pain. He glanced down at his right arm. A flesh wound was scorched right across the outside of his upper arm. It had burned through his jacket and shirt, and into the skin beneath, leaving a gouge of cooked, black blood.

'Oh shit!' he announced, stepping backwards. 'Shoggy! I think I've just been shot.'

He turned around, slightly head-sick with shock. The las-round had come clean through the wall, sliced across the side of his right arm, and…

Domor was leaning back against the workbench behind them in a slightly awkward pose. He was staring at Baskevyl with his big, artificial eyes, which whirred and turned, unable to focus. He was trying to say something, but all he was managing to do was aspirate blood.

There was a black, bloody puncture in the middle of his chest.

'Oh, Throne. Shoggy?' Baskevyl cried, and stumbled towards him.

Domor, lolling sideways, finally managed to find a word and speak it. The word was, 'down.' It came out of his lips in a ghastly mist of blood.

Baskevyl grabbed Domor and dragged him over onto the workshop floor.

A second later, more holes began to appear in the satin brown panel: two, three, a dozen, twenty, forty.

On the other side of the wall panel, someone had just opened up with a las-weapon on full auto.

Elikon M.P., Elikon M.P., this is Nalwood, this is Nalwood.
Hostile contact! Repeat hostile contact at this time!

Nalwood out. (transmission ends)

- Transcript of vox message, fifth month, 778.

FIVE

Vermin

I

It suddenly got very noisy indeed in the tiny end workshop. Bright daggers of las-fire punched through the wall panel, zipped across the shop and hammered into the opposite wall, blowing apart the empty racks and obliterating forever the smudged outlines of hanging tools.

Baskevyl tried to drag Domor in under the heavy workbench. He fumbled for his laspistol. His arm hurt like fire. Domor had gone limp, dead limp.

'Shoggy!' Baskevyl yelled.

More shots tore through the wall, shredding holes through the rims of previous holes, filling the close air with the stink of las-fire and singed fibres. Baskevyl started shooting back, one-handed, his other arm pulling at Domor's dead-weight. He wondered if he should risk reaching for Domor's lasrifle, which was lying nearby on the floor. Bad idea, he decided. He fired again, making his own holes in the wall.

'Contact! Contact! Hostiles!' he yelled into his micro-bead. The interlink went crazy, voices gabbling and yelling over one another.

The outer door to the workshops burst open and Domor's fire-team scrambled in, led by the redoubtable Corporal Chiria. The old battle scars across her face had long ago put paid to any looks she'd ever been proud of, but now she looked especially unlovely. Surprise and alarm, in equal amounts, had twisted her damaged features into a pink grimace.

'What the feth–?' she began.

'Help me!' Baskevyl yelled at her. He was intending for her to come and help him drag Domor out of the way.

Chiria had other ideas. She swung her lasrifle up to her shoulder and hosed the punctured wall, pricking the gloom with barbs of full-auto light.

781

'Get Shoggy up. Drag him back!' she yelled as she lit off. Domor was dead, she knew that much. One glimpse had been all she'd needed to know. A round to the body, heart shot.

Those bastards would pay.

Ezlan was beside her, Nehn and Brennan too. Their four lasrifles blasted furiously into the splintered panelling. They made a dull, echoing crack, like a length of cane being smacked repeatedly against a stone floor.

'Hold it, hold it! Hold fire!' Chiria yelled.

The Ghosts around her stopped shooting.

'What?' Nehn asked.

'Wait...' said Chiria.

Nothing, no return of fire, just a gusty moan of wind weeping through the hundreds of holes in the smoking, shot-up wall panel.

'Help me with him,' Baskevyl said, trying to get up and pull Domor clear. Nehn and Chiria hurried over. Ezlan and Brennan kept their weapons aimed at the perforated wall.

Baskevyl's hands were slick with Domor's blood. He'd been trying to compress the wound.

'Guard this,' he told Chiria. 'Anything stirs, you nail it. I'll carry Shoggy–'

'*You* guard this,' said Chiria, bluntly. 'I'll carry Shoggy. Nehn, get his feet.'

She handed her lasrifle to Baskevyl. He didn't argue. Sometimes, Major Baskevyl was wise enough to recognise, when it came to loyalty and bonding, orders sat better if they ran against the chain of command. It was right Chiria should carry Shoggy Domor.

Moving fast, Chiria and Nehn carted Domor's limp body out of the workshop. Baskevyl adjusted Chiria's weapon, and checked the clip. The air was full of dust, scorched and burned dust. The wall was a cratered mess of holes, like the backboard at the end of a practice range.

Baskevyl looked at Ezlan and Brennan.

'Either of you got a grenade? A tube-charge, maybe?'

'Why?' asked Ezlan nervously.

'Just asking,' said Baskevyl.

II

'HERE. OVER HERE. Set him down!' cried Ana Curth.

She'd been drawn out of the field station by sounds of commotion in time to see Chiria and Nehn struggle into the base chamber with what appeared to be the corpse of Shoggy Domor. Chiria and Nehn laid Domor down on the decking by the stairs, as instructed. Curth knelt over him.

'What happened?' she demanded as she stripped Domor's shirt and tunic off with scissors from her field satchel.

'Hostile contact,' replied Chiria, leaning on the banister and panting hard. She'd carried her captain's body a considerable way at speed. She could barely talk.

'Make sense please,' Curth snapped. 'From the top, corporal.'

'They were in the walls,' Chiria replied, gasping, her voice hoarse. 'In the walls like vermin.' She looked at Curth: 'He's dead, isn't he?'

Curth was too busy to answer. In the absence of a bone saw, she'd reached up and helped herself to Nehn's warknife. Nehn hadn't had time to object. He winced at the sight of Curth carving into Domor with his blade. Curth's hands were slippery with blood. There was an ugly crack as she sectioned the sternum. 'Chayker! Lesp! Where are you?' she shouted. 'We're going to have to get him into the field station right now!'

Chayker and Lesp, the orderlies, ran into the base chamber, lugging a stretcher and a surgical kit. Dorden materialised behind them, puzzled and half asleep.

'What's going on?' Dorden asked, groggily. He woke up very quickly. 'Sacred feth, is that Shoggy?'

'Upper torso puncture,' replied Curth as she worked frantically, tossing aside Nehn's warknife and trying to insert rib-spreaders from the kit Lesp had passed to her. 'Swabs! Forget moving him. I need swabs. Lots more of them!' she called out.

Dorden elbowed his way in beside Curth and sank to his knees.

'Oh, that's a mess…'

'You can clamp that shut with your fingers or you can get the feth out of my way!' Curth barked at him as she hastily prepped the tissue weaver from the kit.

Dorden snapped on a glove, reached in and clamped. 'There's a secondary hole in the aorta,' he began, peering down.

'Thank you for stating the obvious,' Curth replied, ripping the backing-pack off a field swab. 'These aren't going to be enough!' She looked up. 'I said I need more! More! Counterseptic too!'

Lesp took off towards the field station.

'Losing rhythm,' Dorden muttered.

'I've nearly got it!' spat Curth, trying to aim the tissue weaver.

'Auto patch it there. There, woman!' Dorden barked.

'Move your fingers, then!' Curth leaned into the bloody cavity with the buzzing surgical tool.

Calmly holding Domor's barely beating heart together as Curth heat-bonded its punctures shut, Dorden looked up at Chiria.

'How did this happen?'

'We got some hostile contact,' Chiria said.

'Where?' asked a dry voice from behind them.

Chiria looked around. Larkin limped into the base chamber towards them, accompanied by Raess, Nessa Bourah and Jessi Banda. All four of them had their long-las sniper weapons hefted over their shoulders. The marksmen had been touring the house, sniffing for decent vantage points or, better still, targets.

'Under the power room,' Chiria said.

Larkin took his long-las off his shoulder and armed it. He glanced at his fellow marksmen. 'Let's go shoot something, shall we?'

His fellow marksmen nodded.

Larkin glanced over at Curth. For a fleeting moment, she looked up from her bloody work and noticed his stare. Hlaine Larkin had believed that his precious sniper rifle had been lost forever during the grim trials of the Gereon mission. But the previous year, he'd been part of the extraction team that had finally rescued Curth from the Gereon Untill. To his amazement and delight, he had discovered that she had been keeping his beloved long-las safe for him all the while, in the hope of his eventual return.

Larkin gave her a brief nod that said he was about to make her thoughtful custody of the antique piece worthwhile.

Footsteps clattered down the staircase from above. Gaunt, followed by Rawne, Criid and a bunch of Criid's P Company, hurtled down into the base chamber, taking the steps two at a time.

'Report!' Gaunt commanded.

Dorden nodded down at the sprawled body of Shoggy Domor. 'We've been hit,' he said.

Gaunt stared at Domor's spread-eagled form. He could actually see the man's heart, beating like a red leather pump as Dorden and Curth worked on him.

'Will he live?' he asked.

'You better fething believe it,' replied Curth. 'Suture gun. Now, Chayker!'

Gaunt took a deep breath. 'Someone tell me exactly what's happened.'

'Hostile contact in the workshops under the power room, sir,' Chiria said, stepping forwards. 'Major Baskevyl is on site.'

'Show us! Go!' ordered Gaunt. Rawne, Criid, and Criid's men were already moving.

Gaunt hesitated and looked back at Curth. She'd never really regained the body mass she'd lost during her stay on Gereon. She was stick-thin frail, and her cheek bones stood out.

'Are you all right?' Gaunt asked.

'I'm not the one who was shot,' she told him, acidly, too busy to look up.

Gaunt paused, nodded, and then turned to run after Rawne and Criid.

III

CHIRIA LED THE way. Her hands were stained with her company officer's blood.

'The power room,' she repeated. 'Come on!'

'Wait! Wait!' Larkin shouted.

They all came to a halt, silent, listening.

'What?' asked Gaunt.

'Larks?' Rawne pressed.

Larkin shook his head, holding up a finger for silence.

Then they heard it: the distant crack-ping of las-fire.

'That's not the power room,' said Larkin. 'That's coming from somewhere above us.'

* * *

IV

THE LONG, DRAUGHTY hallway had seemed empty.

It ran as far as the eye could see: a broad, brown-panelled passageway, its roof interrupted by the domes of fortification cloches spaced at regular intervals.

The E Company fire-team was high up in the house, right under the spine of the mountain ridge, where the wind wheezed along cold, dormant hallways. Each cloche turret they came to was a dome of dead iron. The intricate manual winders on the walls were seized with grit and age. No amount of effort could induce them to turn and open the shutters overhead.

The fire-team had paused under each cloche dome in turn, gazing up at the jammed shutters, playing their lamps around, exchanging dead-end suggestions.

Meryn had inspected every set of winders they came to carefully. 'They have to open,' he announced at length. 'These winders are designed to open the shutters, so shooters can get up on the fething fire-step and aim out.' He leant on a brass handle that stolidly refused to budge. 'Feth it! Why won't they turn?'

'Because they're jammed,' said Fargher, Meryn's adjutant. It wasn't the brightest observation Fargher had ever made, but it matched his average. It would be the last idle suggestion he'd ever offer.

'Thank you, Mister Brains,' Meryn replied. 'I can see that. Why the feth would anyone build a fort this way, in this dust?'

He glanced back at the team. One of his troopers had muttered something.

'What was that? Was that a comment from you, Trooper Cullwoe?'

'No, sir,' said Dalin, 'it was me. I said maybe this place was built before there was any dust to worry about.'

'That's just daft talk!' sniffed Fargher.

'No, the boy could be right,' said Meryn, gazing wistfully up at the calcified shutter-gears of the cloche above them. 'Who in their right mind would construct a fortress with screw-open shutters in a fething dust bowl?'

'We could grease the gears,' suggested Neskon. 'I got prom-jelly. That's nice and greasy.'

Meryn thought about that.

'Maybe–' he began to say.

And just like that, like a conjuror's trick, the hallway ahead of them wasn't empty anymore.

Dalin blinked. Time seemed to slow, a phenomenon he'd once heard Commissar Hark call 'fight time'. The cold air was suddenly lousy with streaming shots: las-rounds and hard slugs, whizzing around them like a firework display. Swaythe grunted and spilled sideways as he took a round in the arm. Fargher let out a slight, sad sigh as he slammed over onto his back. As the adjutant landed, his limbs juddering, Dalin could see that Fargher's skull case had been forced out through the back of his shaved scalp in thick, white splinters. There was a black scorch mark on the ghastly, slack flesh of Fargher's forehead where the demolishing shot had entered.

Dalin started firing back several seconds before Meryn gave the order. Cullwoe joined in. Meryn's own las was up and blasting. The other six men in the team began to rake too, all save Neskon, who was frantically prepping his flamer.

There was no cover, no cover at all. Shots crisped past them on either side. Cardy smashed over onto his back with a dry cough as a las-round exploded his neck. Seerk squealed as he was hit twice in the stomach. He fell down on his hands and knees, and his shrill noises ceased abruptly as another round blew the top of his head in.

'Holy fething shit!' Meryn was roaring. 'Kill them! Kill them! Pour it on!'

They couldn't even see what they were supposed to be killing. Ahead of them, it was just dark and empty, ominously dark and empty, apart from the glittering gunfire spitting their way.

Dalin Criid crouched down and did as he had been instructed by Driller Kexie in RIP. He chased his aim towards the source of the shots, the muzzle flashes, and squeezed off round after round. Wall panels blew out either side of him. Venklin slowly backed into a wall and slid down it, blood and smoke leaking out of his surprised mouth.

'Stand back! Flames, flames!' Neskon shouted out, pushing forwards, his flamer finally prepped and raised.

'Duck and shield!' Meryn ordered. 'Flamer up!'

They dropped their weapons and put their faces in their hands. Neskon's torch sputtered for a second before it spoke, before it howled.

Brute fire surged out down the hallway in a fierce, licking cone. Dalin was sure he heard screams.

When the fire died back, dripping and sizzling off the scorched wall panels, there was silence.

'Feth…' said Meryn. He looked around. Cardy was dead, so were his adjutant, Fargher, Venklin and Seerk. Swaythe was hurt bad.

'Contact, contact, contact!' Meryn began to stammer frantically into his link. 'Hostile, hostile, hallway… where the feth are we? Fargher?'

'He's a little bit dead, sir,' Cullwoe said.

Dalin bent down and pulled the bundled schematics out of Fargher's pocket. The adjutant's dismantled head lolled unpleasantly as Dalin dragged the papers free.

'Dalin? Come on!' Meryn urged.

Dalin turned the papers over, searching for some kind of sense. 'Hallway… upper west sixteen, sir.'

'Upper west sixteen? You sure?'

'Yes, sir.'

'Hostile contact, hallway upper west sixteen,' Meryn told his micro-bead. 'Requesting immediate support!'

Meryn looked at the remains of his fire-team. 'Support's coming,' he said.

'What do we do now, sir?' asked Cullwoe, his hands shaking as he reloaded.

Meryn hesitated. His team strength had been pretty much slashed in half in less than fifty seconds. He was blinking fast, and showing a little too much white around his pupils.

Before he could think of something to say, they heard footsteps approaching from behind them and snapped around, weapons braced. The echo of half a dozen sets of boots rang towards them, running fast. They waited. No one came into view.

The footsteps seemed to go right past them and fade.

'What the feth?' Neskon muttered.

'Below us,' whispered Dalin. 'It must have been below us, on a lower level.'

Meryn nodded. 'Yeah, yeah. Below us. That's what it was.'

Neskon held up a grimy paw. 'Listen.'

More footsteps, further away, came and went.

'That was right above us that time,' said Cullwoe.

'Yeah, except there *isn't* anything above us,' Dalin replied quietly.

'Meryn?' a voice said. They all jumped in their skins like idiots. Captain Obel was standing right behind them, at the head of a support fire-team whose approaching footsteps hadn't echoed or carried at all. Obel and his seven troopers had just marched up behind them without any of Meryn's men noticing.

'Where the feth did you come from?' Meryn snapped.

Obel glanced over his shoulder uncertainly, as if suspecting a trick question. The open hallway behind them was long, and visibly empty.

'We came in support,' he said.

Obel glanced at the chewed up walls and the bodies of the fallen Ghosts with unsentimental efficiency. 'You decide to start the war without us, Meryn?' he asked. 'What the hell happened?'

Meryn jerked his head in the direction of the hallway ahead. '*They* happened,' he remarked acidly.

'Let's take a look,' Obel decided. Obel made swift, deft gestures of instruction with his free hand. *Advance, wary.* He left one of his men to look after Swaythe and dress his wound. The rest of them moved forwards, with Meryn and Obel at the front.

The hallway was as empty as it had been before. A sliver of wind sang in through some half-closed shutter. It moaned softly. Dust kicked and eddied along the bare floor. They could see a tidemark of burn residue on the walls and roof where Neskon's flamer had left its lasting impression.

'They fired on you?' Obel asked.

'Feth, yes,' Meryn answered.

'And you fired back, right?' asked Obel, keeping his voice low.

'Of course we did!' Meryn replied.

'Then where are the bodies?' asked Obel.

Day eight. Sunrise at four plus thirty-two, first light shows white out. Hit hard in two locations last night. Four men dead, two wounded, one critical.

Enemy unseen during both attacks.
They ~~or ein~~ are in here with us.

Regiment on full alert condition. Defensive sectioning of Objective has begun. G. has ordered some spurs and outer tunnel/hallways closed off and barricades erected. Deep sense of unease. Like waiting for a storm to break.

G. has sent signal to Elikon requesting water supplies and reinforcement.

Have bided time touring main positions to ~~kep~~ keep morale up. Uphill battle. We may see desertions before long.

Since when did Ghosts get haunted?

- Field journal, V.H. fifth month, 778.

SIX

Shooting at Shadows

I

GAUNT TOOK THE message wafer Beltayn handed to him, read it quickly, and gave it back. He continued on his way across the base chamber to the corridor spur that led to the lesser hall.

The base chamber was bustling. Ludd, Daur and Kolosim were coordinating fresh troop deployments to the outer hallway wings. Men were trailing up out of the empty side chambers that had been designated as billets. They were dead-eyed from too little sleep and too little water. Gaunt nodded to a few as he went by. Many were lugging wooden boards and wall panels liberated from unused rooms to help bulk up barricades in the outer wings. Other details were trudging in from the gatehouse, hefting musette bags and sacking they had shovelled full of dust as makeshift sandbags. The bagging details were dusted white from head to foot, and the stack of sandbags they were building on the lower deck area resembled the loading bay of a flour mill.

The senior officers were waiting for him in the lesser hall. It was a dark, hollow room, the sagging ceiling panels supported by six large, timber posts. Something had once been bolted to the floor in the centre of the room, but there was no longer any way of telling what it might have been.

Rawne had carried in a table the night before, so they'd have somewhere to hold briefings, but the table had already gone, requisitioned for a barricade somewhere. The officers stood around in an awkward huddle. Gaunt noted them: Rawne, Hark, Kolea, Mkoll, Baskevyl, Kamori and Theiss. All the other officers had duties that demanded they be elsewhere. This would have to do. Gaunt trusted the attending group to feed the business of the meeting back to the other officers of the regiment.

'Signal from Elikon,' Gaunt began without preamble. 'We're promised a water drop in the next twenty hours. We'll get specifics nearer the time.'

'What about additional strengths?' asked Theiss.

Gaunt sniffed. 'Nothing confirmed. The signal was terse. I think things may have got hotter up the line. Beltayn's hearing a lot of combat traffic, some serious armour duels in the main zone. Elikon requires us to make a full threat assessment before they consider releasing any reinforcements our way.'

'That could take days,' said Rawne, 'weeks, even. Don't they understand we can't even see what we're fighting?'

'I've got a direct vox-to-vox with Van Voytz scheduled for this afternoon,' Gaunt replied. 'I will attempt to explain the situation to him at that time.'

'I'll talk to him, if you like,' Rawne murmured.

Several of the officers laughed quietly.

'I want to make things better,' said Gaunt, 'not worse. How's Domor?'

'Stable,' Baskevyl replied.

'And Swaythe?'

'Broken limb, some tissue damage, but he's all right.'

'How's your arm?'

Baskevyl's arm had been patched, but he'd refused a sling. 'It's nothing.'

'So, any sign of the force strength that surprised Meryn's team?' Gaunt asked.

'Not a trace,' replied Kolea. 'Meryn's lads must have hit something, the response they put up, but there's no sign, not even blood stains where bodies were dragged out. I took a team right along upper sixteen personally. If it wasn't for the fact they got cut to ribbons, I'd have said they were shooting at shadows.'

'Where does upper west sixteen end?' Gaunt asked.

'It just ends in a box casemate,' said Kolea, 'about half a kilometre further on from the attack site.'

'Any access on that stretch?' asked Kamori.

'Two ladder wells and a staircase down to lower sixteen, and a ramp down to lower fourteen,' Kolea replied. 'But both spurs had men stationed on them when Meryn's team was hit. Any hostiles fleeing in either direction would have been picked up.'

'They're moving in the walls, then,' said Baskevyl with solemn certainty. 'False panels, tunnels.'

'Not any we can find,' said Mkoll. 'And we've looked. That was the first notion that occurred to me after your scrape in the power room, Bask. But my scouts simply can't find any false panels or sally ports anywhere in Hinzerhaus.'

'You'd better look again,' Gaunt told him.

There was a pause. It seemed unthinkable for Gaunt to question his chief scout's work. Mkoll, however, nodded. If there weren't any secret access points, the only alternative was something Gaunt had ordered them not to speak about.

'What about the power room?' Gaunt asked.

'Criid's ready for you to take a look,' Hark said.

II

P COMPANY HAD spent several hours barricading the workshop end of the power room. They'd stacked up double lines of sandbags and planking, one to cover the door into the workshops, the other to protect the power hub kettle. Two support weapons, crew-served .30s on blunt iron tripods, watched the doorway.

The Ghosts on duty saluted as Gaunt, Mkoll, Kolea and Baskevyl entered the power room.

'Criid?' Gaunt asked.

One of the men pointed towards the workshop door. 'In there, sir.'

Baskevyl led the way with a sense of trepidation. He didn't trust the walls any more, none of them. He kept waiting to hear the scratching, slithering sound again. The little run of workshops was cold, a draught running through them. Another manned barricade had been set up in the third shop along, facing the arch into the fourth and final chamber. Criid and some of her men were waiting for them there.

Baskevyl stiffened. For a second, all he could see was the blizzard of shots popping through the wall panel at him and Domor. Then the other image came again, the ghastly, glistening snake of the daemon-worm, sliding across dry rocks in the dark.

'You all right?' Kolea asked.

'Yeah,' said Baskevyl.

The shot-up wall panels had been crowbarred away, exposing a black socket in the rock wall behind. The hole was about the size of a door hatch, and cold air gusted out of it. Sandbags had been piled up to half block it. The hole didn't seem to have been dug or cut. It appeared to be a naturally eroded void in the mountain rock.

'You just tapped along and found it?' asked Mkoll.

Baskevyl nodded. 'It was hollow. It rang hollow.'

Mkoll glanced at Gaunt. 'We haven't got a hollow response off any other wall panel in the place,' he said. 'Everywhere else is just solid. Believe me, I've tried.'

'Has anyone been in there?' Gaunt asked Criid.

Hwlan, the lead scout in Criid's company, nodded. 'Me and Febreen, sir. Not far in, just a little way.'

'And?'

'Very rough passage, sir, quite low, running west.'

'No other routes? Divergences?'

'None we could see, but we didn't think it smart to go too far just yet.' Hwlan paused. 'Strong breeze coming through there,' he added. 'I think it may go out to the surface.'

Mkoll unshouldered his rifle. 'Let's find out,' he said.

* * *

III

GOL KOLEA FOLLOWED Mkoll into the hole. Gaunt slithered in after them.

'Sir–' Criid began.

'I'm just taking a look,' Gaunt told her.

Baskevyl hesitated. He had absolutely no wish to climb into the dark cavity. He'd heard what was down there, the grunting, scratching thing in the dark. He wavered.

'Bask?' Gaunt called.

'Sir?'

'Stay here and stay sharp,' Gaunt said as he vanished from view. Baskevyl let out a long sigh of relief. He'd never refused an order in his career, but if Gaunt had ordered him to follow, Baskevyl wasn't sure exactly what he would have done.

As Hwlan had described, the tunnel was low and rough. It seemed unnaturally dark. Gaunt bent low, his boots scrabbling for purchase on a dry, loose floor. His fingertips made dust and pebbles patter down out of the tunnel walls as they groped for support. A cold stream of air touched his face, gusting up from the depths before them.

Mkoll and Kolea switched on their lamp-packs. Two ribbons of yellow light picked up the swimming dust in the air ahead of Gaunt.

'Drops away here,' Mkoll hissed back. 'Watch your step.' Gaunt heard flurries of scattering pebbles as Mkoll and Kolea tackled the slope.

It was indeed steep. Gaunt almost lost his footing as he gingerly followed them down. At the foot of the slope, Kolea turned and shone his lamp back for Gaunt's benefit.

'All right, sir?'

'Fine.'

Kolea paused, and then played his lamp beam up along the slope, tracing the walls.

'What is it?' Gaunt asked.

'This has been mined out,' Kolea said.

'Mined out? You mean *dug?*'

'Yes,' said Kolea. He reached out and touched part of the crumbling, granular wall. 'Those are pick marks.'

'And you'd know,' said Gaunt.

Kolea nodded. 'I would. Look here.'

Near the base of the wall, his light picked out something metal, then another identical object further up. They were iron pins with loop heads. They ran at intervals right back up the slope.

'They set them in as they went,' said Kolea. 'No doubt ran a cord or rope through the loops to help them scale the slope more easily.'

They turned and carried on after Mkoll. The tunnel levelled out a little and ran for another ten metres or so. It remained low, so they had to stoop all the way.

'Watch yourself here,' Mkoll announced as they caught up with him. Part of the tunnel floor and wall had caved in, revealing a deep, impenetrable cleft. A man would have to crawl head first to get into it.

'That's deep,' said Kolea. 'I can smell it. A natural fissure that fell in while this was being dug.'

They stepped carefully around the cleft.

'That suggests this rock isn't especially stable,' said Mkoll.

'It absolutely isn't,' Kolea replied. 'If this was a new working, I'd order the crews out of it until it had been properly propped and braced.'

Somewhere, something rattled. Something scratched and shirred in the darkness.

'What was that?' asked Gaunt.

IV

BASKEVYL HAD BEEN listening at the hole. He pulled back sharply.

'What's the matter?' Criid asked him.

'Nothing,' Baskevyl told her. He was lying.

He'd just heard it again.

V

HARK HAD TAKEN a walk to inspect the gatehouse. As he moved down the long hallway from the base chamber, he passed men toiling in the opposite direction moving sacks filled with dust. He exchanged a few encouraging words with them. Most were from Arcuda's company, which had been detailed to dig and fill the sacks. They were powdered white from their labour outside in the wind.

The floor of the gatehouse, and the gatehouse end of the hallway, was tracked with white footsteps and dusty drag marks. Hark could hear the wind shrilling outside the open hatch.

Arcuda's men had dug out the hatch so it would open more fully, but that had simply allowed dust to billow in more thoroughly. A curtain of camo-capes had been pegged up around the mouth of the hatch to act as a dust screen.

'Your idea?' Hark asked Maggs, who was in charge of gate security.

'It was either that or get buried in the stuff,' Maggs said. The curtain parted as several Ghosts elbowed their way in, sacks on their shoulders. Arcuda was with them.

'I don't know how much longer we can be expected to keep this up,' Arcuda said. 'Without water…'

'I know,' said Hark. He thought around for something supportive to add.

'Feth!' said Maggs suddenly. Hark and Arcuda looked around. The scout had taken off towards the curtained hatchway with his weapon raised.

'Maggs?' Hark called. 'What is it?'

The Belladon didn't answer. He pulled back the undulating curtain and disappeared outside. Hark and Arcuda glanced at one another and followed him.

Outside was a hellish white-out of dust. They fumbled to get their goggles on. The gritty wind sizzled around them and, though it was luminously bright, actual visibility was down to a dozen metres. Hark could make out the shapes of the men toiling to fill sacks in the area in front of the gate-house. If it hadn't been for the fact there was an urgent need for sand bags, it would have been an insane activity, the whim of a sadistic commander setting some soul-destroying punishment task.

'Holy Terra,' mumbled Hark, raising a hand to stave off the gale. Maggs had gone forward, out into the open, his lasrifle up. He was hunting for something.

'Maggs? Maggs?'

Maggs dropped to his knees, inspecting the ground, as if he might determine tracks or spores.

'Maggs? What the feth are you doing?' Hark yelled as they reached him.

'I saw something,' Maggs called back. He was still looking around.

'You saw what?' Arcuda asked, raising his voice over the howling wind.

Maggs replied something that sounded like *she came this way*.

'She?' Hark yelled.

Maggs rose and cupped his hand around his mouth so they could hear him. 'Someone I didn't recognise,' he bellowed. 'They came this way from the gatehouse.'

Hark shook his head. He hadn't seen anybody. Why was he so sure Maggs had said *she*?

'Maggs?'

Wes Maggs didn't reply. He felt excessively stupid, and embarrassed that Arcuda and the commissar had witnessed his apparently irrational behaviour.

He could hardly tell them the truth. He knew they wouldn't believe him.

But it wasn't the first time he'd seen the silent figure in black, and he had the ugliest feeling he'd be seeing her again before long.

VI

Eszrah ap Niht walked into the lesser hall, scanned around once with his reynbow tucked at his shoulder, and walked out again.

Nahum Ludd was huddled up in a corner of the hall, checking duty rotas off his data-slate in an effort to forget how thirsty he was.

'Eszrah?' he called. Ludd got up and hurried to the chamber door in time to see Eszrah striding away down an east-running passageway.

'Eszrah? Wait!'

Ayatani Zweil came out of Gaunt's room and almost collided with Ludd. 'What's wrong with Eszrah, father?' Ludd asked.

'That's what I want to know, young man,' Zweil replied. 'We were happy as you like, reading. I was teaching him the pluperfect. Then up he jumps, snatches his uncouth bow from the table, and runs out.'

'Stay here, father,' Ludd said, and made off after the partisan.

'I'm not going to just stand here–' Zweil began.

'Then keep up!' Ludd called back over his shoulder.

Zweil sighed and came to a halt. 'Ah, see? You've got me there too.'

'Find someone and tell them what's going on!'

'Like who?'

'Someone useful!' Ludd shouted.

Eszrah had a good lead on the cadet, and was moving with the typical speed and stealth of a Nihtgane. Ludd realised it was no good shouting at him. Running, he managed to gain ground, mainly because Eszrah stopped to inspect a side chamber. Varl appeared out of it a moment after Eszrah had gone past.

'What's up with Ez?' Varl asked as Ludd ran up. 'He came in, aimed his bow at us, bold as brass, and then left again.' Varl's company was billeted in the side room. Several of the men were getting up off their bedrolls, bemused.

'He's seen something,' said Ludd. 'Or heard something. I don't know.' Varl grabbed his weapon and gave chase with Ludd. He called out for a fire-team to follow on the double. Ludd heard the clatter of boots coming after them.

They reached a junction. The main spur ran east, and a side hallway forked to the south. A stairwell climbed into the upper galleries.

Varl and Ludd came to a halt. 'Where did he go?' Ludd asked.

Varl shook his head. The fire-team – Twenzet, Kabry, Cant, Cordrun and Lukos – came running up the hallway behind them. Varl clicked his micro-bead. 'Listen up, sentries on the upper east galleries and east main. Anybody got anything? Anybody got sight of the Sleepwalker?'

There was a crackle of negative responses.

'Maybe he just had a funny turn,' suggested Twenzet.

'No,' replied Varl firmly.

'Why not?'

'Because… I'll shoot you,' said Varl.

'Oh sacred feth!' Lukos suddenly exclaimed.

Eszrah had silently reappeared out of the south-east spur without warning. He regarded them for a moment from behind his sunshades, his reynbow against his chest.

'Eszrah?' Ludd asked.

Without replying, the Nihtgane turned and started up the stairs towards the upper galleries.

'Follow him!' Varl ordered.

They ran up four flights in the weird, white gloom. The partisan left the stairs at the top, and turned east along upper east twelve, one of the highest fortified spurs on that side of the house. The spur was punctuated at regular points by casemate blockhouses and the roof domes of armoured cloches. They could feel a breeze from somewhere.

In a thunder of boots, a second fire-team joined them from the west. Six men, led by Rawne.

'Old man Zweil said Eszrah was acting up,' Rawne said bluntly.

Ludd nodded. 'He's gone this way.'

The Sleepwalker was almost out of sight. The two fire-teams started to move, jogging down the hallway. Rawne got on his link and ordered other teams to move up from the galleries below and cut off the spur ahead at the next staircase junctions.

'Where's he gone?' Varl asked. 'I can't see him anymore.' They slowed to a walk.

'He can't have got past us,' said Ludd. 'Or them.'

He pointed. Thirty metres away, a group of figures was moving towards them, evidently another fire-team, coming up and west from one of the other stairlinks.

'Then where the feth is he?' Varl asked.

'Forget the fething Nihtgane,' Rawne growled. 'Those aren't ours.'

VII

THE DARKNESS MELTED. Rough light seeped into the gloom. Gaunt could smell raw, cold air, and feel the airborne particulates pin-pricking off his face.

The tunnel grew wider as it bottomed out. There was a jagged, vertical scar of white in the blackness ahead.

'Leads right out into the open,' said Mkoll.

They scrambled up towards the jagged opening, negotiating a slope of tumbled boulders and dry, flaking earth. The wind made a low, eerie sigh as it blew into the cavity.

Mkoll reached the lip of the cave mouth, and leaned back to help Kolea and Gaunt up. They were in daylight now. A narrow shelf had choked with drifting dust in the entrance, and sprays of grit were winnowing in around the edges and chinks of the rock.

They clambered out into the open. It took them a moment to adjust their goggles and look around. They had emerged through the steep cliff wall on the far side of the crag that contained Hinzerhaus. The ground dropped away below them into a wide ravine, jumbled with boulders and scree. Beyond that, through the dust haze, they could see a broader plain of rough ground.

Gaunt turned and looked up, appreciating the northern face of the fortress rock. The cliff ran east and west, as indomitable as a city's curtain wall. He could just make out cloche towers and casemates on the cliff tops a hundred metres above. The scale was vast, far grander and more overpowering than it had been on the southern side when they'd approached the main gatehouse. The great rock ridge of the Banzie Altids dropped away like a gigantic step into the hostile flatlands behind. Flatlands – badlands, more like, badlands on a bad rock. Gaunt felt small, diminished. The three of them were just tiny specks at the foot of the soaring, dusty buttress.

Gaunt heard a dog barking in the wind, somewhere far away. He was about to remark on it when he realised it couldn't be a dog, and wasn't a dog.

It was the whining bark of a heavy support weapon.

Shots pummelled against the cliff face above them, making the brittle sound of a rock drill.

'Get down!' Mkoll yelled, but Gaunt didn't need to be told.

Elikon M.P., Elikon M.P., this is Nalwood, this is Nalwood. Requesting immediate assistance. Multi-point attack, unknown strength. This objective cannot be considered secure. Repeat, requesting immediate support at this time.

Nalwood out. (transmission ends)

- Transcript of vox message, fifth month, 778.

SEVEN

The First Assault

I

THE VOLLEYS OF shots striking the cliff face behind them were heavy and sustained. The scabby stone surface became riddled with black dents that vanished as fast as they appeared as the swirling dust retouched them. Gaunt, Mkoll and Kolea were pressed down behind a pile of loose rocks and scree. Occasionally, the enemy's aim dropped lower, and explosive impacts rattled along the top of the pile, blowing stones into fragments.

'Well, we're pinned,' groaned Kolea.

Mkoll scurried forwards on his hands and knees, searching for a way to move clear.

'No good,' he reported.

Gaunt had drawn his bolt pistol. He reached up over his head and fired off a couple of blind shots.

The enemy fire stopped. Gaunt looked at Kolea. Kolea shrugged. A second later, they both winced as the enemy fire resumed, more urgently.

'Great,' muttered Gaunt. 'Made them angry.' He clicked his micro-bead. 'Baskevyl? We've got hot contact. Support, if you please!'

II

BASKEVYL GLANCED AT Criid. She was staring at him.

'Read you, sir. Where are you?' Baskevyl said into his bead.

'The tunnel runs all the way to the outside,' his link hissed in his ear. 'We got caught in the open. We need cover fire from the cave mouth if we're going to get back in.'

'Understood.'

'Come carefully,' Gaunt's voice warned.

'Understood.'

Criid was still staring at Baskevyl. 'Well,' she asked, 'what are you waiting for?'

What am I waiting for, Baskevyl asked himself? What am I waiting for? Any possible excuse not to have to crawl into that bloody hole, that's what.

Criid shook her head in bafflement and headed for the hole herself, cinching her lasrifle tight around her body. 'You six, with me!' she ordered.

'Hold on, hold on!' Baskevyl called out. He drew his pistol and pushed his way to the front of the assembling team. 'Follow me,' he said.

He paused for a moment, one hand clutching the ragged edge of the hole. Darkness yawned in front of him.

He took a deep, steadying breath. 'Come on,' he said, and swung down into the blackness.

III

RAWNE WAS RIGHT.

Thirty metres away down the gloomy hall, the figures advancing towards them came to a halt. They were just shadows, half a dozen silhouettes, almost insubstantial. But they weren't Ghosts. Ludd felt that in his gut as a certainty. They absolutely weren't another fire-team responding to Rawne's order.

Rawne and Varl opened up without hesitation. Their las-rounds cracked away down the hallway. The Ghosts on either side of them began firing too. The fusillade was deafening and made Ludd's vision flash and blink. He pulled himself in against a wall and fumbled with his holster, trying to get his sidearm out. He couldn't really see the figures any more. It was as if they had gone, dissipated like smoke.

They hadn't.

Answering fire ripped towards the Ghosts. Somebody cried out as he was hit. Hard rounds and las-bolts dug into the ceiling and walls, some of them ricocheted off wildly, pinging almost comically around the tight box of the hallway like angry insects trying to escape. A wall light burst in a shower of white sparks.

'Hostile contact!' Rawne yelled. 'Hostile contact upper east twelve!'

IV

OUTSIDE THE GATE, in the gruelling wind, Hark turned his head sharply.

'Say again! Say again!' he yelled. The signal in his ear was little more than whooping static noise.

'Contact in the house!' Arcuda shouted, and set off in the direction of the gate hatch.

Hark turned back towards the work crews. 'Stop work! Stop work! Back into the gatehouse!'

The men could barely hear him over the wind. Some looked up, puzzled, sacks and entrenching tools lowered.

Hark waved his arms as he ran towards them. 'Come on! Stop what you're doing and get back!'

Some of them began to move, understanding his meaning at last. They grabbed tools and bundles of sacking, and started to hurry in the direction of the gatehouse.

One of them fell over.

'Get up! Come on, get up!' Hark yelled as he reached the man. Five metres away, Wes Maggs started firing.

'Maggs? What the feth are you–'

Hark looked down at the fallen man and understood what Maggs had already realised.

The fallen man was caked white with dust, but the wind hadn't yet obscured the wet, red mess in the small of his back.

'Contact!' Hark yelled. 'Contact, main gate!'

V

BASKEVYL COULD HEAR the scratching in the dark. He could hear the slither of knotted skin and twisted bone, scraping on the rocks.

'Can't you go any faster?' Criid complained from behind him.

No, he *couldn't*. It was all Baskevyl could do to stop himself turning around and knocking them out of his way in a frantic effort to return to the workshops.

He told himself it was his imagination. He told himself it was the wind, or the oddly echoed noise of the gunfire outside, or the scrape of his boots curiously magnified by the claustrophobic little tunnel he was squeezing his way down.

But if it was boots, or wind, or gunfire, why could he hear snuffling? Why could he hear a slick, mucus noise of wet tissue on dry rock? Why – in the Emperor's name – could he hear breathing?

'You keep slowing down. For feth's sake!' Criid exclaimed.

'All right, all right!' Baskevyl replied. He pushed his way forwards with renewed speed.

He was going to meet the daemon-worm, sooner or later, he reasoned. It was going to find him eventually, and when it did, well, that would be that.

He might as well get it over with.

VI

HARK PULLED OUT his plasma weapon as he ran up to Maggs.

'Where?'

'All around us!' Maggs replied. 'I can't get gun sound or muzzle flash in this wind… I can't see anything. But they're there, all right!'

'Drop back. Now!' Hark ordered. 'We're too exposed!'

They started to run. Odd, truncated sounds buzzed past them: stray, passing shots they could hear for only a split-second. Hark glimpsed the bright barb of a las-bolt as it exploded the dusty ground ahead of them.

Most of the bagging crews had reached the safety of the gatehouse and bundled inside, but enemy fire had picked off two more on the way. Arcuda and Bonin were standing outside the curtain, firing off into the wind. Maggs and Hark dropped in beside them. The arch of the hatch offered them a little better cover at least.

'You see anything?' Hark demanded.

'Not a damned thing,' replied Bonin with a shake of his head. 'I think it's snipers, up in the rocks.'

'On the basis of what?' asked Hark.

'The way our guys fell down,' Bonin replied simply. 'The way they jerked and dropped... they were hit from high angles.'

'I've voxed for marksman support,' said Arcuda. 'Larkin's coming.'

'He won't be able to see anything either!' complained Maggs.

'Sometimes he doesn't have to,' replied Hark.

'Are all our boys inside?' Bonin asked.

'Yes,' replied Arcuda.

'Then who the feth is that?' asked Bonin.

Fifty metres beyond the gate, the figures of men were shambling and lurching out of the gritty storm towards them, moving as fast as they could across the thick, loose dunes of dust. Dozens of figures, charging, yelling. Hark heard the raw war cries of feral voices, and the harsh blare of battle horns.

'We're about to have a busy day,' he said.

VII

THE FIREFIGHT IN upper east twelve was a mad, brief affair. Afterwards, Ludd wondered why everyone wasn't just killed in a second. Shots spanged and spattered in all directions, a lethal combination of directed fire and hopeless deflections. Smoke swirled around with nowhere to go. Muzzle flash made the light and shadow flicker and dart. There was nothing except a battering concussion, the kind of noise you'd hear if you stuck your head in a marching drum while someone played a rapid, endless roll. Rawne was shouting orders, as if a situation like that could be tempered or controlled by orders.

'Cease! Cease fire!' Varl cried.

They stopped shooting. The Ghosts were all crowded in against the hallway walls, or lay flat on the floor where they had been firing prone. Bars of smoke rolled lazily through the quietened air.

'Either we killed them...' Varl whispered.

'Or they've fled,' Rawne finished. He voxed to the other teams on upper east twelve, warning them to guard against hostiles moving east.

Three teams acknowledged in quick succession.

'Straight silver,' Rawne ordered. They fixed their blades to the lugs under their hot barrels. Two of Rawne's fire-team were dead, and one of Varl's – Twenzet – was wounded. 'Help him,' Rawne told Ludd.

Twenzet had been hit in the ribs, a grazing but bloody wound. He grinned sheepishly as Ludd helped support him, but his brave grin was punctuated by sharp flinches of pain.

At a wave of Rawne's hand, the team advanced.

'Looky, look, look,' whispered Varl.

Now there were bodies. In contrast with Meryn's similarly tight and brutal encounter the night before, the enemy dead had not vanished this time. Four corpses sprawled, twisted and limp, on the hallway deck twenty-five metres away. Each one wore filthy, mismatched Guard fatigues and webbing. Each face was hidden behind a leering black metal mask.

Blood Pact.

'Four of them,' muttered Cant. 'I counted more than that.'

'Me too,' said Varl.

Rawne clicked his micro-bead and repeated his warning to the other teams further along the spur. He listened to their responses, and then glanced at Varl.

'Next team east of us is Caober's, at the top of the next stairhead. There're no exits or ladder wells between him and us, so we've got the rest of them boxed.'

Varl had been listening to his own vox-link. 'Major, there's… I'm hearing there's an attack underway at the main gatehouse. Full-on assault.'

Rawne made an ugly face, his lips curled. 'Feth! Well, somebody else is going to have to be enough of a big boy to handle that. We're committed here.'

Varl nodded. 'Close file,' he told the men. 'Slow advance.'

Rawne snap-voxed Caober's group to warn them they were coming.

'Nice and slow,' Varl repeated, his voice a whisper. 'When we find 'em, it's going to get all sudden and messy.'

'Trail us,' Rawne told Ludd.

Ludd tried to shift his grip on Twenzet so he could support him more comfortably.

'Take my las,' Twenzet whispered to him.

'No, I–'

'Take my las. I can't shoot it one-handed, and your pop gun isn't going to be worth shit when this happens. You heard Varl. We've got them cornered and it's going to be a riot.'

Reluctantly, Ludd put his sidearm away and hung Twenzet's rifle over his left shoulder.

'Blood,' reported Cant.

Spatters on the floor. A trail, winding away from them.

'Got to be close now,' whispered Varl. 'Why can't we see them?'

Rawne touched his micro-bead. 'Caober? Anything?'

'Negative, sir.'

Varl held up a hand. They halted.

'Forty metres,' Varl hissed, head down. 'I see movement.' He brought his rifle up to his cheek and took aim. 'Fire on three.'

The Ghosts raised their weapons and aimed.

'Three, two–'

'Wait!' said Rawne.

'What's the matter?' Varl whispered.

Rawne called out, 'Caober?'

There was movement far ahead. 'Major?' a voice floated back.

'Throne, we nearly opened up on Caober's mob!' said Kabry.

'Then where the feth did they go?' asked Rawne. 'I mean, where the feth did they fething well go?'

VIII

BASKEVYL FELT A breeze on his skin and heard a rattle of gunfire from close by. It almost, but not quite, obscured the scraping slither of the thing waiting for him in the dark.

'Get ready,' he heard Criid instruct the men behind them.

Baskevyl swallowed hard. His lamp-pack was shaking in his hand. He drew his laspistol. Treading carefully over the rough black earth of the tunnel floor, a treacherous surface almost invisible in the dark, he edged on. The tunnel dropped a little more, and then widened out.

And he could see it at last.

His breath sucked in with a little gasp. It was right in front of him, rearing up in the gloom: a giant, twisted column of white bone and gristle, uncoiling from a writhing mound on the floor. Its knotted body segments – scabby, glistening flesh the colour of pale fat – dragged against the dry black rocks as it uncoiled, smearing with dust and mould. It let out a dry, bony rattle, like a bead in a husk. He felt its worm-breath strike his face, an exhalation of cold, ammoniac vapour.

'Major?' Criid called, pushing at him.

Why couldn't she see it? Why wasn't she shooting at it? Was it just a daemon spectre meant only for him?

'Major Baskevyl!' Criid shouted.

And, just like that, there was no daemon-worm: no daemon-worm, no rearing column of ghastly, white flesh like a gigantic, animated spinal cord.

There was simply an opening to the outside world, a jagged, vertical slit of white daylight against the black cave shadow.

'The mind,' Baskevyl whispered. 'It plays such tricks.'

'What?' Criid asked.

He didn't answer. He ran towards the slit of daylight. 'Move up close, two at a time,' he called out. 'Make ready to provide suppressing fire. Follow me.'

Baskevyl ducked down in the cave entrance and peered out. The bright air outside was a dancing haze of white dust, but he could see down across the rock spoil and boulders below the cave.

'One, this is Three. Come back,' he said into his bead.

'Three, One. Good to hear from you. Position?'

'Cave mouth, so above you, I'm guessing.'

'Three, we're under you and to your left.'

'There,' said Criid, crawling in beside Baskevyl and pointing down.

Gaunt, Kolea and Mkoll were pinned behind a pile of stones about twenty metres below and to the left of the cave fissure. Streaks of fire – tracer and las – spat horizontally out of the rocky plain beyond them and struck against the cliff wall with a sound like slapped flesh.

Baskevyl looked around. Two large boulders provided immediate cover in front of the cave. Tactically, he knew he had to get as many guns out and firing as he could. The cave mouth was only really wide enough for two shooters, side by side. He wanted all eight of them, if it was humanly possible.

'Go right of the big rock,' he told Criid. 'Take Kazel and Vivvo with you. Don't fire until you hear me tell you.'

Criid nodded, and bellied her long, lean body away from him; very much like a serpent, he thought, and quickly shook the idea away. Vivvo and Kazel followed her. Baskevyl signed Starck and Orrin to take the gap between the two rocks. He glanced to Pabst and Mkteal, and beckoned them to follow him.

Baskevyl crawled up on the left side of the left-hand rock. He took a look from this improved vantage. Now he could see what they were dealing with. Belches of muzzle flash from a heavy gun, something on a tripod he presumed, winked a hundred metres beyond the chief's position. Snap shots from shooters scattered in the surface rocks added their support.

'Heavy stub, one hundred left and out,' he voxed quietly.

'I see it,' replied Criid. 'There was another one, fifty right of it. It's stopped firing now. Changing boxes or barrels, is my guess.'

'Fifteen… no sixteen… other guns,' reported Vivvo.

'Eighteen,' came Mkoll's voice over the link. 'I've been listening. Two sources to my right stopped blasting about five minutes ago. Watch for them, they're probably trying to flank us.'

'That's your task for the day, Criid,' Baskevyl voxed. 'We'll hit the firing cannon. Starck, Orrin? Just make sure everybody else ducks, please.'

'Got it,' came the vox-clipped answer.

'First and only,' said Baskevyl.

They all started firing. Baskevyl, Pabst and Mkteal trained their shots directly on the source of the heavy fire, peppering the rocks around the origin point of the chunky muzzle flash. Starck and Orrin raked punishing rapid fire across the whole area. Baskevyl saw a figure rise, twist and fall. One kill, at least, probably Orrin's to claim. Criid, Vivvo and Kazel began taking speculative, selective shots down at the right-hand portion of the scree slope, trying to flush something out.

After about a minute of sustained shots from Baskevyl's group, the heavy gun stopped firing. The sporadic shots from the rock waste around it were now coming up at the two big rocks where the newcomers were sheltering.

'Hello,' said Pabst, and squeezed off a double-snap of las. 'Well, he's dead, then,' he remarked. A few moments later, Orrin made another kill.

Then fresh gunfire began to zip in from the right. Criid hunched down, hunting the flash source. Two flanking shooters, down in the bed of the ravine. She grinned to herself. Mkoll had been right, as usual. She snuggled in her aim and waited. One muzzle flash, a burp of burning gas. That determined location and range. A second, to confirm. A slug round whined past her ear. A third.

'Bang,' she said, and unloaded a stream of six tightly grouped las-shots that blew the shooter out of cover and left him sprawled across the rock litter.

Immediately, she rolled, to prevent the shooter's partner replicating the same trick on her. Two las-bolts clipped off the side of the boulder where she had just been crouching.

'Be advised,' she voxed. 'They're good.'

'Maybe, but they're one fewer now,' Starck voxed back, flush from a kill of his own.

'Don't get over confident,' Gaunt cut in over the link.

'Oh, as if,' Criid retorted, hunting for the give-away flashes of the other flanker.

The second heavy gun started up again abruptly, mowing fire up at the boulder shielding Baskevyl, Pabst and Mkteal, forcing them to duck. Coughing bursts of dust and rock chips stitched up across the boulder and then continued to smack a line up the face of the cliff above the cave mouth as its aim was frantically over-adjusted. The bulk of the enemy fire was now targeting the cave mouth area.

'Shall we?' Kolea asked Gaunt, hearing the distinct change in the whine of gunfire.

'Of course.'

They scrambled up the pile of stones, bellied down, and began firing, bolt pistol and lasrifle side by side. Gaunt saw dark shapes moving amongst the rocks, and checked his aim. He fired again, and saw a red and black figure smash backwards against the face of a boulder and slump.

'Uh, when did you last see Mkoll?' Kolea asked suddenly.

Gaunt smiled and fired again.

IX

OUT OF THE dust, like howling beasts, the Blood Pact assaulted the main gatehouse of Hinzerhaus.

'We're going to need support here,' Hark voxed. 'As much as you can spare.' His plasma gun beamed out from the doorway, incinerating the torsos and heads of three oncoming assault troops in quick succession. Their ruined bodies dropped like bundles of sticks into the dust. Beside Hark, Maggs, Arcuda and Bonin were sowing out las-fire in tight, chattering bursts.

'I knew this was going to be a bad rock,' Arcuda complained.

'Love the Guard and it'll love you back,' chastised Bonin.

Maggs was oddly silent, as if uncharacteristically cowed by the extremity of the situation.

'Support! Support to the main entrance for the love of the Throne!' Arcuda yelled impatiently into his mic.

The Blood Pact came in like a tide along a shore. As they loomed out of the dust storm's soft white blanket, they seemed shockingly black and ragged, as if they had been cut out of some dark, dirty matter utterly inimical to Jago, where everything was stained white by the eternal dust.

They were screaming, shrieking and bellowing through the slit mouths of their awful iron masks. Torn strands of fabric, leather and chainmail trailed out behind their stumbling forms. Several of them bore vile standards: obscene, graven totems or painted banners mounted on long poles, adorned with long black flagtails that fluttered back in the wind. Others blasted raucous notes on huge brass trumpets that curled around their bodies. Some brandished pikes, or halberds, or trench axes; others lugged heavy flamers with long, stave lances. The majority fired rifles as they came on.

'You know,' muttered Hark, quite matter of factly, 'we could learn a lot from these heathens.'

'In terms of what?' Arcuda snapped, pumping out shots.

'Oh, in terms of, you know, *terror*.'

'I've learned more than I need already,' said Bonin, crimping off a double-snap that felled a charging standard bearer.

Wes Maggs said nothing. He aimed and fired, aimed and fired, with mechanical efficiency. He was watching for her in the enemy ranks, quite certain she would be there, that old dam in the black lace dress. He knew her, oh he knew her all right. He knew her business, the oldest business of all. She'd be coming, of that he had no doubt. She'd been lurking about in this rat-hole place – he'd glimpsed her coming and going ever since they'd arrived, out of the corner of his eye. She wouldn't miss a chance like this. She'd come, and then they'd all be–

dry skulls, with all the tops sawn off

–reduced to dust, like all the other poor bastards who had tried and failed to stay alive on bad rock Jago over the centuries.

Unless Maggs saw her first. Unless he saw her coming, and had enough time and courage to punch a las-round into her appalling meat-wound face.

By his side, Hark fired again and vaporised the legs of a trumpet blower. The man fell, tumbling, his horn still barking out discordant squirts of noise like the cry of an animal in pain.

The curtain behind them raked back so hard it was dragged off its pegs. Ghosts rushed out.

'At last. Make a line!' Arcuda ordered. 'Spread out!'

Guardsmen, their rifles coming up to firing positions as they moved, fanned out to meet the oncoming tide.

'Make room,' Seena yelled as she and Arilla carried their .30 out through the hatch. Maggs began to help them bed it down and fix its tripod into the dust. 'We can do it,' Arilla told him sharply, fixing the first ammo box expertly against the receiver.

'All right then,' Maggs replied, turning to fire again. 'Just make sure you shoot her if you see her.'

'Who?' asked Arilla, snapping the receiver cover shut.

Maggs didn't reply. He had returned to his position and was busy firing again, and there was too much noise for idle chatter.

The wave of attackers was close now, just ten metres. Hark knew that, despite the number the Ghosts had already picked off, they were about to reach *the Crunch*.

Arcuda knew it too. 'Straight silver!' he ordered.

The .30 opened up. It made a clinking whirr, like a monstrous sewing machine. Its clattering hail cut a swathe through the front rank of the charging enemy. As Arilla fed it, Seena expertly washed the heavy cannon from side to side. It mowed the Blood Pact down. It ripped them apart, mangled limb from mangled limb.

Hark sighed. Fight time. They were on fight time, at last. He'd been expecting it. He'd been waiting for it to begin. Everything in the world seemed to slow down. Las-rounds trembled like leaves of fire, suspended in the air. Blood Pact warriors, struck by Seena's fire, fell backwards ever so slowly, arms flung wide, fingers clawing at the air as if trying to hold onto it. Blood bloomed like flowers opening lazily in the sun. A grotesk, torn from a face, flipped over and over in the air like a ponderously turning asteroid. Even the swirling dust seemed to slow down and stagnate.

Hark braced himself. He felt curiously content as if, despite the situation, the galaxy was at last behaving the way it was supposed to behave.

At the edges of the line, beyond the .30's cone of fire, the rushing tide of Blood Pact finally met the Ghost file head on.

This was *the Crunch*. This was the point at which an assaulting enemy could no longer be fended off by fire alone. This was the point of impact, of body on body, and mass on mass.

The wave struck the Ghost line. There was a palpable, shivering clash. Straight silver met chainmail, and trench axes and spears met moulded body plating. Blades struck and dug and stabbed. Bodies were impaled, hacked down or thrown back by the impact of momentous collisions. Not every falling body was a Blood Pact warrior.

Bonin found himself in the thick of it. He speared a Blood Pact soldier on the end of his silver, and then was forced to kick the next one to death because his blade was wedged in the spinal column of the first. Twisting it free at last, he swung it hard, and slashed through a windpipe. Hot blood squirted into his face. He turned again and narrowly avoided a lunging spear. Ducking, he rolled and destroyed knees and shin bones with a burst of fire.

Hark melted a grotesk – and the skull behind it – with a single shot from his potent energy weapon. The tip of a lance plunged through his left arm, but he felt no pain, and flexed his augmetic arm sharply, breaking the spear haft. He turned and finished the business by killing the owner of the broken spear with another single burst of streamed plasma.

For a moment, in the middle of it all, he suddenly thought he could make out a distant melody, like a pipe playing. Some brazen enemy battle pipe, he decided, breaking a man's neck with a chop of his left hand.

But it wasn't. It was an old tune, a fragile thing, an Imperial hymn. No, no, a *Tanith* song…

What the f–

There was no time to ponder it. A gust of heated, tortured air swept into his face, and the two Ghosts beside him went up in fireballs, shrieking as they perished. Hark fell over, flames leaping up the tails and back of his storm coat.

'Flamer! Flamer!' someone yelled.

Hark rolled frantically in the dust, trying to extinguish himself. Somebody landed on top of him, beating out the fire.

It was Arcuda.

'Get up, commissar! They've got range with their burners!'

Arcuda heaved Hark to his feet. The commissar was dazed. Fight time had suddenly taken on a strange, unwelcome flavour. He felt dislocated, unready. His back throbbed. He was hurt. He realised he was going into shock.

Hlaine Larkin limped out through the torn curtain of the gate hatch and took a moment to observe the sheer mayhem before him. Then he knelt down and swung his long-las up to his chin, where it belonged. Through his scope, he surveyed the close-quarter fighting in front of him.

'Flamers!' someone was yelling.

Yes, there was one, squirting fire into the Ghost ranks with his long burner lance. Larkin took aim. The long-las bumped against his shoulder.

'One,' muttered Larkin.

He changed clips, one hot shot for another, and panned until he saw another long, burning stave.

He aimed. Headshot. Bump. 'Two.'

He reloaded, panned, spotted on a third flamer.

'Tank shot,' he breathed. Bump.

Twenty metres away, a warrior's backpack tank punctured and exploded, showering the Blood Pact around him with ignited promethium. Blood Pact soldiers fell, writhing and shrieking, wrapped in cocoons of fire.

'Three.'

Larkin reloaded, panned, and aimed. 'Trumpet,' he decided, and fired.

A horn blower convulsed as the top of his head blew off. He fell. His trumpet made a strange, half-blown noise.

Nothing like as satisfying as hitting a flamer, Larkin decided, and went back to that sport.

Reload, aim, fire. *Five.*

Reload, aim, fire. *Six.*

'Keep 'em coming, Larks,' a voice said beside him.

Larkin looked over at the speaker. Try Again Bragg smiled reassuringly at his old friend. 'Go on, keep it up,' Bragg said. 'Reload, aim, fire. You know the drill.'

Larkin felt his guts knot up tight with fear. He forced himself to look away from the kind, smiling face and into his scope.

'Not now,' he breathed. '*Please*, not now.'

X

'No one came this way?' asked Rawne.

'No one, sir,' replied Caober.

'I don't understand it,' said Rawne.

A thin, sharp wind blew along upper east twelve. The wall lights faded softly and then came back.

'Walk it back,' Rawne told Caober. 'Walk it back to the next set of stairs. We'll go back the way we came. Feth, they have to be somewhere.'

'What about–' Caober began.

'What about what?'

'The main gate's being attacked. From what I hear on the link, it's pretty intense.'

Rawne stared at Caober. 'Scout, if there's any chance, just so much as the slightest chance, that the Blood Pact is magically inside this place with us, defending the main gate becomes a rather secondary objective, doesn't it?'

Caober nodded. 'Put like that, Major Rawne.'

'Let's get on with it,' said Rawne.

With Varl at his side and the rest of the fire-team following, Rawne retraced his steps along the draughty hallway. Ludd brought up the rear, supporting Twenzet. Behind them, Caober's fire-team turned the other way.

They'd been walking for a couple of minutes when Varl groaned.

'What?' asked Rawne.

'Where are they?' asked Varl.

'Where are who?'

Varl gestured at the floor. 'The four dead bastards we left here,' he said.

Rawne stared at the empty deck. There was no doubting their position, but there was no sign at all of the enemy corpses they had left in their wake.

'This is beginning to feth me off,' Rawne said.

At the back of the group, Twenzet nudged Ludd.

'What's that smell?' he asked.

'Smell?' replied Ludd, finding it an increasing effort to keep the wounded trooper upright. Ludd wasn't even sure if Twenzet should be upright.

'Smells like… blood. You smell it too?' Twenzet asked.

Ludd hesitated. He didn't like to point out that Twenzet was the most likely source of the odour.

'I–' he began.

The Blood Pact warrior made a snuffling noise as he came out of the shadows towards them. His trench axe ploughed down at Ludd, but Ludd fell, letting go of Twenzet, and the jagged blade missed his ear by a very short distance.

Ludd scrabbled frantically to protect himself, and grabbed at Twenzet's lasrifle, strung awkwardly over his shoulder. He brought it up to defend himself.

The Blood Pact warrior, leaping forward, impaled himself through the neck on the upraised straight silver. His trench axe made a loud *thunk* as it dropped onto the decking. He gurgled and collapsed on his side. The weight of his body snatched the lasrifle out of Ludd's hands.

Twenzet, sprawled where Ludd had dropped him, was moaning in pain. Ludd crawled across to him, looking around, bewildered as to why no one had come to aid them.

He realised that everyone else was too busy with their own problems.

Eight Blood Pact warriors had ambushed the fire-team, pouncing out of the shadows with axes and cudgels. Everything had turned into a frenzy of movement that seemed, at the same time, oddly tranquil.

What was it Commissar Hark had called it? Ludd thought as he reached Twenzet's side. *Yeah, fight time.*

Rawne gasped in surprise as the first grotesk came out of the darkness at him. Snap instinct alone allowed him to greet it with his rifle, and the fixed blade was swallowed up by the grimacing mouth of the iron mask. Rawne kept pushing until the back of the hostile's head smacked against the hallway wall.

Varl, reacting as fast as ever, ducked under a swinging spike-mace, and fired two shots, point-blank, into its owner's belly. The hostile dropped, hard.

Varl started to yell, 'They're on us! They're on us!' He turned, but far too slowly to block the hanger slashing down at the back of his neck.

There was a sound. A *phutt!*

The warrior with the hanger suddenly staggered backwards, an iron dart embedded in his left eye slit. He half-turned and then collapsed like a felled tree.

The sound repeated. *Phutt! Phutt! Phutt!*

The Blood Pact ambusher intent on Kabry suddenly doubled up, a thick dart in his belly. Cant flinched, unable to react in time, then saw the cudgel aimed at his face drop away as the Blood Pact warrior hefting it took a dart through the neck. Cordrun felt a trench axe bite into the body armour encasing his back, and then, abruptly, felt it snatch free again as its Blood Pact owner was hurled over by a dart that transfixed the middle of his grotesk's forehead.

Rawne and Varl quickly killed the two remaining hostiles with brutal bursts of fire that left their targets splattered against the hallway wall.

'What the holy gak was that?' Varl gasped.

Eszrah ap Niht dropped lightly down in the middle of them, out of nowhere. He was holding his reynbow.

'Where the feth did you come from?' Rawne demanded.

Eszrah pointed up at the cloche dome above them, as if that explained everything.

'Ygane ther, soule,' he said.

XI

MKOLL CROUCHED DOWN behind the two Blood Pact warriors manning the heavy cannon. One was diligently feeding belts of ammunition while the other aimed and fired the antique weapon. Mkoll observed them for a while, admiring their technique and discipline, kneeling down close behind them like a third member of the gun crew.

Then he killed them and the gun fell silent.

The Master of Scouts waited for a moment, huddled down in the position amongst the rock spoil. The sound of guttural voices reached him. A Blood Pact warrior, his filthy uniform stinking of fresh sweat and the stale blood of old rituals, scrambled in along a gully on his hands and knees, arriving to investigate why the cannon had stopped shooting. Mkoll killed him. He killed the second man who came to look for the first. Then he carefully removed a tube-charge from his musette bag, plucked out the det-tape, and tossed it over in the direction of the other cannon, which had begun to chatter again.

The shock of the blast drifted back to him, along with handfuls of loose pebbles that rained down out of the air.

There was a silence that lasted for about a minute, except for wind wafting dust around the place.

Mkoll clicked his micro-bead. 'I think we're all done here,' he said.

GAUNT AND KOLEA scrambled up the slope towards the cave mouth, where Baskevyl, Criid and the fire-team were waiting for them by the pair of rocks.

'Thanks for that,' said Gaunt.

Baskevyl nodded back. 'Sorry to be the bearer of bad news, but there's a hell of a fuss at the main gate,' he said.

'Fuss?' asked Kolea.

'I'm just getting it now. A frontal attack.'

Both Kolea and Gaunt checked their earpieces and listened.

'Feth,' muttered Gaunt after a moment. 'So they're able to come at us from both sides of the objective? What kind of rat-trap has Van Voytz sent us into?'

'The worst kind,' suggested Criid.

'Is there any other?' asked Mkoll, trudging up the slope to join them.

'Good work,' Gaunt told him.

'It was nothing, sir,' Mkoll replied. He was lying. It was everything. From the moment he'd led the way into the gatehouse two days before, Mkoll had been on edge. A daemon had been stalking him, a daemon made of fear and uncertainty, two qualities generally alien to Mkoll's state of mind. He'd begun to feel himself incapable. He'd actually begun to distrust his own skills. It had been good to get out there and test himself.

'Let's get inside,' said Gaunt.

'And set charges in this cave to block it?' Kolea asked.

'Oh, absolutely,' Gaunt replied.

XII

IN THE END, there seemed to be no clarity or determination, no win or lose. The howling tide of the Blood Pact broke and retreated back into the dust clouds that had unleashed it.

And that was that.

Hark panted hard, his plasma pistol slack in his right hand. He was exhausted. Fight time was re-spooling back into real time, and that was always tough, especially as, on this occasion, real time brought the pain of his burns back with it.

The dunes outside the gatehouse were littered with bodies. At a rough estimate, five-sixths of them were enemy corpses. Hark looked around, recognising a few old comrades amongst the dead. He wasn't quite sure which was worse – seeing the corpse of a man you knew by name, or seeing a corpse so atrociously damaged you couldn't identify it.

There were both kinds at the gate of Hinzerhaus. Forty Ghosts dead, at least. It had been a hell of a fight for a skirmish, and Viktor Hark knew, in his heart of hearts, that a skirmish was all that it had been: an opening skirmish, a melee, a prelude.

Hinzerhaus would be the death of them all. Holding onto this place, they'd all end up as–

dry skulls in a dusty valley, with all the tops sawn off

–defunct names checked off in the Imperial annals. He shivered.

'Viktor?'

He glanced around. Curth was beside him. The medics were arriving to handle the wounded. Lesp and Chayker hurried past with a man on a stretcher.

'Viktor, you're hurt. Burned,' Curth said.

He nodded. 'Just a second. Arcuda?'

Arcuda looked up from the Ghost he was field dressing. 'What, sir?'

'Was somebody playing the pipes?'

'What?'

'Was somebody playing the pipes, Arcuda, during the attack. Tanith pipes?'

'During the attack?'

'Yes.'

'I don't believe so, sir.'

Hark turned back to Curth. 'I may be going mad,' he told her. 'Can you treat that?'

'Let me dress your wounds first,' she said, and led him back towards the hatch.

As he walked back across the blood-mottled dust, Curth's thin hand pulling at his thick paw, Viktor Hark began to shake. The wind picked up, and drove the dust at them.

'It's all right,' Curth said. 'It's going to be all right.'

Hark saw Larkin, huddled down beside the hatch, his long-las hugged against his chest, his eyes wide behind his goggles. Hark saw Wes Maggs, standing ready, twitchy, gun in hand, as if watching for something.

'No, Ana,' Hark said. 'No, it really isn't.'

Are we the last ones left alive? Are we? Someone, anyone, please? Are we? Is there anybody out there? Are we the last ones left alive?

(transmission ends)

- Transcript of vox message, fifth month, 778.

EIGHT

Bad Air

I

THE VOICE COMES *out of nowhere. It betrays no origin or source. It is only a whisper, a dry hiss that seems as old as the house itself. It sounds as if it has been mute for a long time, and is only just now remembering how to speak.*

Where is it coming from? Is it in the building's stonework? Is it imprinted in the very fabric of the house? Has contact disturbed it, woken it up, caused it to play back like an old recording? Or is it leaking into the vox from somewhere else? The past? The present? The future? Whose future?

It is a static murmur, a lisping echo at the back end of the frequency. It fades, and comes back, and fades again, incoherently. It fades and comes back in time with the harsh then soft throb of the house lighting. It pulses in tune with some slow, respiratory rhythm, the pulse of Hinzerhaus.

Are those words, or just sounds? If they are words, what are they saying? Who are they speaking to? Is the voice telling lies or some awful, vital truth?

The frequency tunes out, skipping from channel to channel in groans of noise and snatches of message. A hand reaches to the dial and turns it–

II

–OFF

Beltayn lowered his headset and sat back from his vox-caster. He swallowed.

'What the feth?' he whispered. He leaned forwards again, and switched his set back on. He pushed one cup of the headset against his right ear and listened as he twiddled.

'Hello? Who is that? Who's using this channel?'

Nothing. Just base-line static and wild noise.

'Something awry?' Gaunt asked, tapping Beltayn on the shoulder.

815

Beltayn jumped out of his skin.

'Sorry,' said Gaunt, genuinely surprised by his adjutant's reaction. 'Calm down, Bel. What's got you so spooked?'

Beltayn breathed out. 'Sir, it's all right. Nothing. Just a… glitch.'

'What sort of glitch?'

Baltayn shrugged. 'Nothing, really, sir. Just bad air. I'm getting ghosting on the Elikon freak.'

'What sort of ghosting?' Gaunt pressed.

'A voice, sir. It comes and goes. It's pleading… asking for help.'

'Where is it?'

'No site or status code. I think it's a vox echo.'

'A vox echo?'

'That happens, from time to time, sir. An old signal, bouncing back off something.'

Gaunt paused. 'Old or not, what does it say?'

Beltayn heaved a sigh. 'It keeps saying "Are we the last ones left alive?" Variations on that particular theme. It keeps repeating.'

'It's not Elikon?'

'No, sir. I'm getting Elikon signals layered over it. It's background. I had to tune the vox right back to sandpaper wavelengths to hear it properly.'

Gaunt frowned. 'Well, keep doing that and let me know what you find. Right now, I need my scheduled link to Van Voytz.'

'I'll get it, sir. Take it in your office.'

Gaunt wandered away across the base chamber as Beltayn began to adjust the knobs and dials of his caster.

The mood in the place was grim. It had been a bad day, and Gaunt cursed himself for missing the worst of it. Forty men dead at the gate, according to Arcuda's report, and twelve hurt, including Hark. The regiment was on alert condition red.

Varl was waiting for him at the door of his room. The sergeant saluted Gaunt as he approached.

'Major Rawne's compliments, sir,' Varl said. 'He requests your urgent attention in upper east twelve directly.'

'Tell him I'll be there in thirty minutes, Varl,' Gaunt said. 'I've only just got back in. I've got this mess to deal with, and a vox-to-vox with the general.'

Varl nodded. 'I'll tell him, sir. It's important, though. He wanted me to make sure you knew that.'

'Consider me aware,' said Gaunt. 'Upper east twelve? You had a scrap up there, didn't you?'

'Saw off an infiltration attempt,' said Varl. 'We think we know how they're getting in.'

'Really?' Gaunt hesitated. 'Look, I've got to make this call. I'll be with you as fast as I can.'

Varl saluted again and hurried away.

Gaunt walked into his office. There was no sign of Eszrah. The place was cold and empty. The lights faded softly and swam back up again. Gaunt wished with every fibre of his being they'd stop doing that.

He sat down at his desk. He could hear a man wailing in pain down the hall, one of the wounded in the field station.

Gaunt saw the red light winking on the vox-set on his desk. He got up, walked back to the office door and closed it, shutting out the sound of the screams. Then he walked back to his desk, sat down, and put the headset on. He pressed the connection key.

'Sir, I have the general for you,' Beltayn said, a fuzzy distortion in his ear.

'Thank you. Switch him through,' Gaunt said into the chrome mic, holding it close to his mouth.

'Hello, Elikon, hello, Elikon? Yes sir, this is Gaunt. Yes, I can hear you quite clearly...'

III

'WILL HE BE all right?' Ludd asked.

Dorden looked up at the junior commissar and smiled reassuringly. The smile fanned patterns of age lines out around the old doctor's eyes. 'Of course,' said Dorden.

Trooper Twenzet lay on the cot between them, stripped to the waist, his ribs dressed and wrapped. Dorden had given Twenzet some kind of shot, and the trooper was woozy and smiling.

'Thanks, friend,' he said to Ludd.

'It's all right.'

'Thanks for looking after me, though. Thanks. You're all right, you are.'

'Couple of days' bed rest, and Mr Twenzet will be right as rain,' Dorden told Ludd. 'In the meantime, I will keep him pharmaceutically happy and pain free.'

'This stuff's great,' said Twenzet. 'I feel wonderful. You should try it, friend.'

'It's not recreational, Twenzet,' said Dorden. 'Let's hope Mr Ludd doesn't find himself in a position where he needs to try it.'

'Course not, course not,' Twenzet nodded. 'Anyway, thanks. Thanks, friend. You're all right.'

'I've left your weapon in the store,' Ludd told the Belladon. 'You can reclaim it when you're signed off fit again.'

'No, no, you keep it,' Twenzet insisted. 'Please, friend, you keep it. You might need some stopping power to see you through this.'

Ludd smiled, believing a smile would do the trick.

'I shouldn't call you friend, though, should I?' Twenzet rambled on, suddenly troubled. 'Sorry, sorry, I didn't mean no disrespect. You being Commissariat and all that. This stuff the Doc's given me is making me all groggy and smiley. I should show you proper respect. Throne, I hope you're not going to put me on a charge for being over familiar.'

'Twenzet,' Ludd said, 'get some rest. I'll check back on you later, how's that?'

'That'd be nice, friend. I mean, sir. I mean–'

'Nahum. My name's Nahum.'

'Is it? Is it? Well, I'm Zak. Like a las-round, me old dad used to say. Zak. Like a las-round.'

'I heard the men in your squad call you Tweenzy,' said Ludd.

Twenzet frowned. 'Zak,' he said. 'I bloody hate it when they call me Tweenzy.'

'Zak it is, then. Get better. I'll come back and see you.'

Ludd moved away from Twenzet's cot. The field station was busy. Over a dozen men lay on the makeshift cots, all of them, except Zak Twenzet, casualties of the battle at the gatehouse. Dorden had moved away to help treat a man who was screaming and thrashing in pain. The man had lost a leg. The stump was jerking around as if trying to plant a foot that was no longer there.

Ludd looked away.

He saw Hark.

The bulky commissar was prone on his face on a cot in the far corner of the chamber. He had been stripped to his underwear, and Ana Curth was applying wet dressings to burns on his back and legs. His flesh was unnaturally pale. Ludd crossed to his bedside.

'Don't stand in my light,' Curth told him. Ludd stepped aside.

Hark seemed semi-conscious. Out of his clothes, his augmetic was plainly visible. Ludd recoiled slightly from the sight of it, the bulky black and steel armature of the limb that had been plugged into Hark's shoulder stump. Exposed servos whined and purred as the artificial hand clenched and unclenched. Ludd had always wanted to know how Hark had lost his arm. He had never had the guts to ask.

'How is he?' he asked quietly.

'How does he look?' Curth replied, busy.

'Not great,' said Ludd. 'I was asking for a specific medical diagnosis.'

Curth looked up at him. Her eyes were hard. 'He was caught by a flamer. Thirty per cent burns on the back and legs. He's in a great deal of pain. I'm hoping we can preserve the flesh without the need of a full graft.'

'Because?'

'Because I can't do a graft here, with these facilities. If it turns out Viktor requires a graft, we'll have to ship him out to Elikon, or he'll die. How's that for a diagnosis?'

'Fine,' Ludd replied. 'Might I point out your bedside manner leaves a lot to be desired, doctor?'

'Meh,' said Curth, going back to her dressings.

'One thing,' Hark groaned. '"He" can hear what you're saying.'

'Sir?'

Hark waved Ludd close. 'Ludd?'

'Yes, sir?'

Hark slapped Ludd's face.

'First of all, the doctor's doing the best she can, so don't harass her.'

'Understood, sir,' Ludd answered, rubbing his cheek.

'Ludd?'

Ludd leaned close again. Hark slapped his face a second time.

'Don't make friends with the troops, for feth's sake. Don't bond with the likes of Twenzet. He's rank and file, and you're Commissariat. You don't mix. Don't make him your new best friend. You have to preserve the separation of authority.'

'Yes, sir. I didn't mean to. I mean, I was only–'

Hark slapped his face again.

'I heard you. First name terms. He's a dog-soldier, and you're the moral backbone of the outfit. He's not your friend. None of them are your friends. They're soldiers and you're their commissar. They have to respect you totally.'

'I... understand, sir.'

'I don't,' said Curth, peeling the backing off another dressing strip. 'Why can't the boy make friends? Friendship, comradeship, that's a bond amongst your lot, isn't it?'

'My lot?' Hark chuckled. 'You've been around the Guard for so long, Ana, and you still don't get it.'

'Enlighten me,' she replied, tersely.

'Nahum is a commissar. He needs to command complete and utter authority. He needs to be a figure of fear and power to the troop ranks. He cannot afford the luxury of friendships or favouritism.'

'Actually, sir,' Ludd said, 'I'm just a junior commissar, so– ow!'

Hark had slapped him again.

'Ludd,' said Hark, 'do I look like I'm going anywhere fast? Curth is plastering my arse with bandages, and the chances are I'm going to die.'

'Just wait a minute!' Curth protested.

'Shut up, Ana. I'm out of action, Nahum. The regiment is without a functioning political officer. This is your moment in the sun, lad. Field promotion, effective immediate. You're the Ghosts' commissar now, Ludd. You keep them in line. I can't do it from a sickbed.'

'Oh,' said Ludd.

'I'm counting on you. Don't feth it up.'

'I won't, sir.'

'You'd better not.'

Curth ripped off her blood-stained gloves and discarded them into a pan for Lesp to collect. 'I'm done,' she announced. 'I'll be back in four hours to change the dressings.' She looked back at Ludd. 'Congratulations on your promotion, commissar. I hope you can handle the responsibility.'

She unceremoniously stuck a painkiller bulb into Hark's left buttock. 'There, that'll help you sleep.'

'Ouch,' said Hark.

'You'll take good care of him, won't you?' Ludd asked Curth as she walked away. Curth looked back at Ludd with a narrowed expression that said *are you suggesting I don't take good care of all my charges?*

'Oh. Of course you will,' Ludd said.

'Ludd?'

'Sir?'

'Do it right, will you?'

'I'll do it the best I can, sir,' Ludd said.

Hark was slipping away into the same happy void Twenzet had entered. 'Ludd?' he slurred.

'Sir?'

'Pipes.'

'What, sir?'

'Pipes. Tanith pipes. Listen for them.'

'The Tanith have no pipers, sir, not any more.'

'Listen for the pipes, Ludd…. listen… the pipes, that's the sign, the sign…'

'Sir?'

Hark had passed out. Ludd got up and walked out of the field station.

Behind him, the man without a leg was still screaming.

IV

'I BEG YOUR pardon?' said Dalin.

'I said, I need an adjutant, someone capable, now Fargher's dead,' Meryn said. 'I need a sharp man at my right hand. You read those charts in upper west sixteen yesterday, worked out where we were.'

'Sir, I–'

'Are you turning me down, Dalin?'

'No, sir.'

'It'd mean a bump in your wages, trooper.'

'Captain, that's not why I'm hesitating. I'm the most junior and inexperienced member of your company. I'm a scalp compared to the rest. Why not Neskon or Harjeon? Or Wheln?'

'Neskon's flame-troop. They're all out, bug-eyed crazy men, you know that. Harjeon, him I don't trust. Vervunhive civ. Too much of a starch arse. Wheln is old-school, but… feth, too much stiff nalwood in him. He's not adjutant material, never will be, despite his veteran status. You, you know the ropes. You're smart. I'm asking you, Dalin.'

Dalin shrugged. *And my father was Caffran and my mother is Criid and making me adjutant wins you points in the regiment, right?*

'This certainly isn't about who your father was,' said Meryn. 'I mean, get that idea out of your mind right now. I don't care who your fething dad was, or who your fething mum happens to be. I want you because you're the best choice.'

'I just hope this decision won't come around and bite you on the backside,' Dalin said.

Meryn grinned. 'Then make sure it doesn't, adjutant,' he said.

V

'THIS OBJECTIVE–' GAUNT repeated.

'Ibram, bear me out,' the vox said back to him. 'All I'm asking you to do is watch the eastern flank.'

'Barthol, please understand me. This is a doomed enterprise. The Blood Pact has already scaled the fortress wall. We just took a hit on our main gate. Our main southern gate.'

There was a pause. 'Please confirm your last remark.'

'I said we have just been attacked on the southern side of the objective. The enemy is surrounding us. We're holding an objective that is already compromised.'

The link was silent for another long moment. There was just the wheeze of dead air.

'Are you still there?' Gaunt asked. 'Elikon, are you still there?'

'Sorry, Ibram, I was consulting the tactical officers. Look, it's not going well, this banishment campaign. The bastards are holding their line with depressing success. We're pushing hard from here, but the front is broadening and they don't seem ready to break.'

'That's bad news, sir,' Gaunt said into the mic, 'but that's not the problem I'm left looking at here. The intelligence you based our orders on must have been inaccurate or out of date. The eastern line is already porous. The Blood Pact had penetrated the mountains long before we secured the objective. I don't believe the enemy is here in any great strength yet, but it won't be long. A week or two, they'll sweep west and hit you from the side, and this fortress will not be the instrument you were hoping would stop them.'

'I understand your predicament, Ibram. To be frank with you, I feared as much.'

Gaunt didn't reply. *You as good as knew you were sending us to our deaths, Barthol. Didn't you, you bastard? The intelligence wasn't inaccurate or out of date. You knew.*

'Ibram? Are we still linked? Confirm?'

'I'm still here, sir. What are your orders? Do we have your permission to withdraw at this time?'

'Uh, negative on that, Ibram. I simply can't conscience leaving the eastern flank open.'

'We're just one, small regiment, Barthol–'

'Agreed. I'll get you some support.'

'Please elaborate.'

'I can't. This link may not be safe and we've said too much already. Stand by as you are. Consider your mission profile as changed. Explore all possibilities offered by Hinzerhaus and its surrounding geography to harass and delay the enemy.'

'You want us to… keep them busy?'

'As best you can. I'm asking this as a personal favour, Ibram. Keep them busy. Delay them.'

'And you can't tell me any more?'

'Not on this link.'

'Understood. But I need stuff if we're going to survive.'

'Define stuff?'

'Water. And support, as I said. Heavy support.'

'I've organised a water drop for you tonight or tomorrow. Further information will be conveyed at that time.'

'All right. My men will be grateful for water, at least.'

'I have to go, Ibram. The Emperor protect you. Keep the bastards busy.'

'If it's the last thing I do,' said Gaunt.

But the link was already dead.

VI

UPPER EAST TWELVE was cold and breezy, and stank of expended las-fire and an underlying, organic odour that Gaunt had been around long enough to recognise as burnt blood.

As he strode along the hallway, under the cloche domes of the useless defences lining the roof space, Gaunt saw the blast marks and wall scars of the recent fire fight. Ludd and Baskevyl walked with him. Their clattering footsteps echoed back dully in the flat-roofed stretches of hallway, and rolled over them with a sharper sound as they passed under each cloche.

'Officer approaching!' Baskevyl called out.

Up ahead, a waiting fire-team turned to greet them: Rawne, with Varl, Mkoll and a dozen Guardsmen.

'Barthol send us his warmest regards, then?' Rawne asked.

'I'll fill you in later,' replied Gaunt. 'What did you want to show me?'

'We've identified how the enemy is slipping in and out up here,' said Mkoll.

'Wall panels, right?' asked Baskevyl. 'I knew it. I knew it was wall panels.'

'It's not wall panels,' said Rawne.

'Tap at the walls, if you like,' Mkoll offered. It was the closest thing to sarcasm anyone had ever heard from him. Not like Mkoll, thought Gaunt. Not like him at all. If Oan Mkoll's bent out of shape, we'd better put our gun barrels in our mouths now and say goodbye.

'Not the walls, then?' asked Gaunt. 'So?'

Mkoll turned his eyes upwards at the cloche above them. The wind outside blew skims of dust in around the slits of the almost, but not quite, closed fighting hatches.

'It's so horribly obvious, it's not funny,' said the chief of scouts quietly.

'Except, you have to laugh, don't you?' said Varl. No one seemed likely to. 'Or not,' Varl added glumly.

'I was told the shutters didn't work,' said Gaunt. 'I read Meryn's report. The winding gear is seized with dust.'

'The winding gear *is* seized with dust,' said Mkoll. 'That's not the same thing. I'll show you. Rawne, give me a boost.'

'Of course,' said Rawne, not moving. 'Varl?'

Varl sighed, slung his rifle over his shoulder, and bent down with his hands locked in a stirrup.

Mkoll placed a foot in Varl's hands and hoisted himself up into the dome of the cloche. He reached above his head and pushed his hands against the nearest shutter cover. It swung outwards without protest. Mkoll took a grip, and lifted himself up and out through the shutter. The shutter swung back shut.

'Holy Throne,' murmured Gaunt. 'It's that fething simple?'

Rawne nodded.

'The gears are jammed, see?' said Varl, pointing at one of the winding mechanisms on the collar ring of the cloche. 'But they've been disengaged from the shutters. The shutters themselves swing free.'

'All of them?' asked Baskevyl.

'No,' replied Varl. 'Nothing like, and not on every cloche, but a good few, right down this hallway. And the other fortified hallways too, probably.'

'We have squads checking,' said Rawne.

'They've systematically been in here and disengaged gears to provide themselves with entry and exit points?' Gaunt asked, wide-eyed at the notion.

'They must have been in here for weeks, months maybe,' said Varl. 'Tinkering with the winding gears, poking about.'

'Am I the only one worried about what else they might have "poked about" at?' Baskevyl asked.

'You're not,' said Gaunt. He shook his head. 'This place is like a sieve. A sieve would be easier to defend. Throne of Earth, and I thought this was a bad job already. How the feth does Barthol Van fething Voytz expect us to–'

'Expect us to what?' Rawne asked.

'Never mind. How did you find this?'

'As a consequence of our recent action against the Blood Pact up here,' said Rawne.

'Oh, tell the man the truth!' Varl snorted. Rawne glared at Varl. 'Eszrah Night found it,' Varl told Gaunt.

'Eszrah?'

'Yeah,' said Rawne. 'He got the spooks in his undershorts and came up here. We followed him.'

'I followed him,' said Ludd, quietly. No one paid much attention.

'I think Ez heard something,' said Varl. 'You know, that sleepwalker fifth sense.'

'Fifth, Varl? How many senses do you have?' asked Gaunt.

'Ah, I mean sixth, don't I?'

'I fething well hope so,' said Rawne.

'Anyway, we got jumped,' Varl went on. 'Blood Pact all over us like a camo net. Then Ez just drops in out of nowhere like… well, like a Nihtgane, really. Reynbowed their arses to the wall, he did.'

'He'd gone out through a shutter?' Gaunt asked.

'He'd figured it,' said Rawne, grudgingly. 'He came back in the way they did. Ambushed their ambush.'

Gaunt smiled. Beside him Ludd stepped forwards, gazing up at the dome. 'So that's it?' he asked. 'I was still trying to work out where Eszrah had come from.'

He looked at Gaunt. 'If they've been in here, the Blood Pact, I mean,' he began, 'if they've been in here all this time, why didn't they take the place?'

'What?' asked Rawne, scornfully.

'Why didn't they take the place?' Ludd asked, turning to stare at the major. 'They had all the time in the world. Why didn't they secure it and occupy it? We could have marched up that valley three days ago and found Hinzerhaus fully defended against us.'

'I don't know.'

'Ludd's got a point,' said Gaunt.

'Maybe they wanted to play games with us?' Varl suggested.

'Maybe there's something in here they don't like,' said Baskevyl. 'Maybe there's something in here they're scared of.'

'That's just crap,' said Rawne. Baskevyl shrugged.

'If there's something in here the Blood Pact is scared of,' said Varl, 'we're totally fethed.'

Gaunt looked up at the dome. 'I want to see. I want to see where Mkoll went.'

'I don't think–' Ludd began.

'That was an order, not an idle reflection.'

Rawne clicked his micro-bead. 'Mkoll? The boss wants to take a look for himself.'

'I expected he might,' the vox crackled back. 'All right. We're clear out here. Goggles, no hats.'

Gaunt took off his cap and handed it to Ludd. He put on the brass-framed goggles Baskevyl handed to him.

'Rawne? Give me a boost,' he said.

'Of course,' said Rawne. 'Varl?'

Varl sighed, slung his rifle over his shoulder again, and bent down with his hands held ready.

'Major Rawne,' said Gaunt. 'Give me a boost.'

Varl straightened up, disguising a grin. With malice in his eyes, Rawne bent over and linked his hands.

'Thank you, Eli,' said Gaunt, and hoisted himself up.

VII

THE SHUTTER FLAPPED shut and Gaunt was gone. Standing below the dome, looking up at it, they waited.

'So, I understand you're acting commissar, what with Hark hurt and everything,' Baskevyl said conversationally to Ludd.

'Uh, yes, that's right, Major Baskevyl.'

There was a long silence.

'That can't be easy,' said Baskevyl.

'No, sir,' replied Ludd.

The wind blew.

'So, er, you men had better start behaving yourselves,' Ludd added.

Varl started to twitch, as if afflicted with a tickling cough or an itch. It took about ten seconds for the twitch to turn into a full blown snigger.

'Sorry,' Varl said. 'Sorry! I just–'

The snigger turned into laughter. The Guardsmen behind Varl started to laugh too.

'Would you like me to shoot them,' Rawne inquired of Ludd sweetly, 'for discipline's sake?'

'That won't be necessary,' Ludd said, and turned away.

VIII

IF THERE WAS a forever on bad rock Jago, you could see it from there.

Gaunt got to his feet. The wind, as if anticipating his entrance, had dropped to a whisper. The dust had died. In the west, down along the spiny backbone of the Banzie Altids, a goblin moon was rising. The sky was a dirty yellow, the colour of wet peat. Clouds gathered in the north, low and banked like meringue. Down below the vast cliff of the mountain range, blankets of white fog covered the landscape.

It was cold. Gaunt moved and his feet skittered away loose rocks that tumbled off down the sheer wall into the blanket of dust far below.

'Watch your step,' said Mkoll, appearing beside Gaunt and placing a steadying hand on his arm. 'You want to see this, you do so on my terms.'

'Understood.'

On previous excursions out through the shutters, Mkoll had pegged a network of cables around the cloche. He clipped a safety line to Gaunt's belt. Mkoll was supported on one of his own.

'It's a long drop,' he said.

'It is, it really is.'

They stood for a moment and looked out over the canyon behind the mountain ridge into the dust-swathed badlands.

'You sort of have to admire their balls,' Mkoll said.

'Yes,' said Gaunt.

'We found evidence of some climbing tackle, some pinned-up stuff, but they've been pretty much coming up here and getting in by fingertips and effort alone.'

'Right.'

'That's got to be some ugly upper body strength.'

'Definitely.'

The drop was huge and the rock wall sheer. Gaunt looked down. The distance was immense and dizzying. Just a few hours before, he had been at the bottom end of this aspect, pinned down with Mkoll and Kolea. He remembered looking up. If he'd been trying to take Hinzerhaus from the north, the last thing he'd have suggested to his men was scaling the cliffs. He wouldn't have expected them to even think of it, let alone try it. The tenacity of the Blood Pact was an object lesson. They had no fear, or limitation on their endurance.

So how are we supposed to stop them? Or even delay them?

He looked to his right. The top of the sharp ridge curled around, slightly north and then in a slant to the south-west. Its length was dimpled with cloche turrets and casemates, iron domes and boxes that dotted away for at least two kilometres. On the outside, the cloche turrets, like the one he was secured against, were worn matt and rough by the scouring action of the wind and grit.

Gaunt looked to his left. There, the ridge rose up to a peak. Cloche turrets and casemates dotted up the rise of the peak and down the other side. At the apex he saw the windcote from the outside, a brass cupola, the summit of Hinzerhaus. The windcote supported a broken finial of metal. A proud flag or standard had once flown there, Gaunt thought.

'You don't like this place, do you?' Gaunt asked Mkoll.

Mkoll sighed. 'Not at all. I honestly can't think of another site I'd care to defend less. There's something about it.'

'And that something's getting to you?'

'You noticed? Yeah, this damn place makes me edgy, I don't know why. Never known a place get under my skin like this. I didn't think I was the sort of bloke to get the spooks. Now I've got 'em, it's making me doubt myself.'

'I know.'

Mkoll looked at Gaunt. 'I feel sloppy and off form. I keep second guessing myself, and jumping at shadows. I hate that. I can't trust myself. This place is making a fool out of me. And fools die faster than others.'

Gaunt nodded. 'If it helps, it's not just you. Everyone feels it. Well, except Rawne maybe, as he feels nothing.'

Mkoll smiled.

'There's something about Hinzerhaus,' Gaunt went on, 'and it's playing on our nerves. We just have to learn to ignore it. It's just an old fortress at the arse-end of nowhere.'

'Perhaps,' said Mkoll. 'I just wish I could shake the feeling that none of us is going to be getting out of here alive.'

'Would it trouble you to know that I have the same feeling, Oan?'

'It would, sir, so you'd better not tell me.'

IX

THEY HEARD A cry, like the cry of a bird, and Gaunt thought for a moment that the denizens of the windcote might have returned.

But it was a human voice, hollowed out by the wind. Three figures appeared beside a cloche a hundred metres west of them.

Gaunt squinted. 'Ours?'

'Yeah,' said Mkoll. 'I've had men searching the outside of the ridgeline, cutting free any traces of Blood Pact rope work.'

They detached their safety lines and edged along the natural rampart of the rock towards the others. Gaunt felt relief every time they reached another cloche or gunbox, where he could hold on and steady himself for a moment. The alarming drop into distant clouds reminded him of Phantine and the view down into the Scald. Despite the chill, he was beginning to sweat. He had no wish to be where he was, especially untethered, if the wind rose again.

A long five minutes of concentrated effort brought them over to the others. The scouts Caober and Jajjo nodded greetings as Mkoll and Gaunt joined them. Eszrah ap Niht waited silently behind them.

'Found much?' Gaunt asked.

Jajjo pointed to the west. 'A whole network of rope ladders and tether lines, about half a kilometre that way. Bonin and Hwlan have gone to cut them free.'

'Question remains, what do we do with the fortifications?' asked Caober. 'I mean, they're weak links unless we crew them.'

'We could try blocking them off,' suggested Jajjo.

'We crew them,' said Gaunt. 'If this place is a fortress, let's occupy it as such. Let's man these defences. If the enemy comes creeping back up here, he'll be in for a surprise.'

Gaunt looked at Eszrah. The partisan, wearing the sunshades Varl had given him long before, was staring up at the malevolent yellow moon.

'That was good work,' Gaunt said.

'Soule?'

'Good work, learning about the shutters. And I think Rawne's fire-team owes you a debt too.'

Eszrah shrugged his shoulders slightly.

'There was something else, sir,' said Caober. He led them around the grit-burnished rim of the cloche to the southern side of the mountain rampart. They were overlooking what Gaunt thought of as the front of Hinzerhaus. There was the narrow pass that led to the gatehouse, though the gatehouse was hard to make out at that distance. Immediately below them, the main sections of Hinzerhaus grew out of the sloping mountain face: sections of old tiled roof, the tops of casemates built into the cliffs, and small towers.

'There, sir,' said Caober, pointing. Gaunt could see something a long way down the slope, in the lower area of the house's southern aspect. It looked like a large, square roof surrounded by other, red-tiled roofs on two sides, and mountain rock on the other two.

'You see?' asked Caober.

Gaunt took out his scope and trained it for a better look. It wasn't a square roof at all. It was a paved courtyard, open to the sky.

Gaunt lowered his scope. 'Has anyone reported finding a courtyard so far?'

'No,' replied Mkoll.

'So there's a courtyard slap bang in the middle of the lower southern levels, and we didn't know about it?' Gaunt paused. 'That means there are still parts of this damned place we haven't even found yet.'

Day nine. Sunrise at four plus forty-one, white-out conditions. It has been explained to me that I am expected to maintain this field journal while H. is incapacitated.

Day's activities two-fold. Teams are continuing to secure the objective, which includes taking up defensive positions in the upper fortifications + those casemates covering the main approach/gatehouse. Other duty sections resuming search of objective to find 'hidden' areas, including some sort of courtyard space.

My own concern is my singular lack of authority. I cannot blame the men for it. I have followed on H's coat-tails so far, and exercised his authority. Until now the men only had to tolerate or ignore me. I frankly do not know what to do. I wish to discharge my duties as political officer, especially at this trying time, but I cannot force the men to respect me. Have considered consulting G.

Water drop now overdue.

— Field journal, N.L. for V.H. fifth month, 778.

NINE

034TH

I

THE WIND SKIRLED around the gunslits of overlook six. Larkin had propped the main shutter open with a block of wood. Goggles on, his mouth and nose wrapped up behind the folds of his camo-cape, he trained his scope out into the dust storm.

'See anything?' asked Banda snidely. She'd given up watching, and had retired to the back of the casemate to brush the dust out of her scope. Her long-las leaned against the stone wall behind her. It was cold in the bunker, especially with the shutter lifted, and dust blew in, filling the air with a faint powder. Banda shivered. She took a swig of sacra from her flask. A lot of Ghosts had begun filling their empty water bottles with liquor from contraband supplies. Something to drink was better than nothing, now the water had all but gone.

'Want some?' she asked Larkin, holding the flask out. Larkin shook his head. 'That stuff'll just make you more thirsty,' he said from behind his dust-caked muffle. 'Rot your brain if you dehydrate and keep supping it.'

'Yeah, well,' said Banda with a shrug, and took another sip.

'Plus, you won't be able to shoot worth a damn.'

'Gonna write me up, Mister Master Sniper? Huh? Gonna put me on report?'

Larkin didn't answer. He didn't especially care if Jessi Banda went crazy drinking still juice. He certainly didn't want the bother of writing her up. What good would that do?

Overlook six was one of the main casemate towers above the gatehouse on the southern slope of Hinzerhaus. When the dust dropped back, it afforded an excellent, marksman-friendly line down the throat of the pass. When the dust rose, it afforded feth all.

829

Kolea came in through the hatch. Banda hurriedly tucked her flask away.

'Larks?'

'Hello, Gol.'

'Anything?'

Larkin shrugged. 'I think I saw some dust just now.'

Kolea managed a smile. Like most of them, his lips were cracked and dry, and dust infections were reddening his eyes. There wasn't enough fluid in the place to mix up counterseptic eye wash.

'Beltayn just got a squirt on the vox. We think it may be this mythical water drop, but he can't fix the signal.'

'I can't help you,' said Larkin. 'Sorry.'

Kolea nodded and turned to go. 'Make sure you don't work too hard there, Banda,' he remarked as he passed her. As soon as he was out of sight, Banda extravagantly gave him *the root*, a hand gesture popular amongst disenchanted Verghastites who found words failing them.

'Hey,' said Larkin suddenly. He set his scope up at the shutter again, focusing it. 'Hey, Gol! Gol!'

Kolea ran back in. Banda had risen to her feet. 'What is it?' Kolea asked.

'Wind just dropped,' said Larkin. 'We've got a calm. Air's clearing fast. Thought I saw... wait...'

His scope whirred.

'Yeah,' Larkin said with relish. 'Two contacts, airborne, about eight kilometres out, inbound from the south-west.'

II

'THIS IS NALWOOD, this is Nalwood. Say again, over.'

Beltayn listened hard to the crackle and hum of his vox-set. Gaunt, Daur, Criid and Kolosim stood behind him, waiting. Sections of troopers, forty in all, armed and ready to move, were congregating below them in the bottom level of the base chamber.

'Nalwood, this is Nalwood. Please re-transmit,' Beltayn said. The set snuffled like a snoring baby in a pram.

Kolea came clattering down the main staircase and ran across to Gaunt. 'We've got visual contact. Lifters heading this way.'

Gaunt nodded. 'Bel, can you–'

Not looking up, Beltayn raised his hand sharply for quiet.

A voice crackled out of the caster's main speaker grille. 'Nalwood, Nalwood, this is transport K862 inbound to your location. Estimate four minutes away. Water drop as requested, over.'

There was a raucous cheer from the Ghosts assembled on the staging below. Gaunt and his officers exchanged smiles.

Beltayn adjusted his caster. 'K862, K862, this is Nalwood, this is Nalwood. Good to hear you, over.'

'Hello, Nalwood. Need you to define LZ. Please advise. Pop smoke or display mag beacon, over.'

Beltayn glanced up at Gaunt. 'What do I tell him?'

'I've got smoke and a mag beacon ready,' said Ban Daur. 'What's it doing out there?'

'The wind's dead. We've got a clear window,' said Kolea. 'Let's not muck about. We'll bring them in outside the main gate and team the supplies inside, double time.'

Gaunt nodded. 'Go,' he said.

Kolea, Criid, Daur and Kolosim ran to join the sections waiting below at once, calling orders. The men began to file out towards the gatehouse.

'K862, K862, be advised we are popping smoke as requested,' Beltayn told the mic. 'Watch for it at the head of the pass. LZ is flat area in front of main gatehouse, repeat flat area in front of main gatehouse, over.'

'Thank you, Nalwood. Inbound, over.'

Gaunt clicked his micro-bead. 'All sections, this is One. Drop coming in, main gate. Full alert, full cover. This is going to get noticed. Any sign of trouble, you have permission to loose off.'

A FIRE-TEAM LED by Corporal Chiria was opening the outer hatch as Daur and the others arrived. 'Sections one and two, you're on portables,' Daur called out. 'Three and four, spread and cover as per brief.'

Daur stepped through the hatch and began to run out into the open. The sunlight was pale and bright, and only the faintest breeze stirred the surface dust. His heels puffed up plumes of the stuff as he ran.

He felt horribly exposed. Pieces of Blood Pact armour and weaponry still littered the dust from the day before, although the enemy had recovered their dead under cover of night. He was running right out into the open. The beige cliffs and outcrops of the pass loomed around him. In his imagination, they were full of enemy skirmishers, drawing aim. Daur was uneasily convinced his imagination wasn't wrong.

He couldn't see the transport, but he could hear the pulsing whine of lifter jets echoing around the tops of the cliffs.

Fifty metres from the gate, he dropped to his knees and swung the satchel off his shoulder. He pulled out the metal tube of the mag beacon, twisted the nurled grip and set it going. It began to emit a little, repeating chirrup, and a small light on its facing began to wink. Daur dug it into the dust, upright. Then he removed the smoke flares from the satchel, and pulled their det-tapes one by one, tossing the smoking canisters onto the ground in a crude circle. The smoke billowed up in bright green clouds and trailed off away from the gate.

'Ban, they're coming,' Criid voxed. Daur turned and jogged back towards the gate. The jet noise grew louder.

Two aircraft suddenly came into view, rushing in over the cliff top. Their hard shadows shot across the white basin outside the gate. They banked east around Hinzerhaus, disappearing from view for a second, and then swung around again in tight formation, dropping speed and altitude.

The larger aircraft was a big Destrier, a bulk lifter, painted drab cream and marked with a flank stencil that read 'K862'. It was making the most noise, its big engines howling as the pilot eased it down in a ponderous curve.

The other aircraft was a Valkyrie assault carrier, a hook-nosed machine one-third the size of the heavy lifter. The Valk was painted khaki with a cream belly. Its tail boom was striped with red chevrons and the stencil 'CADOGUS 52'.

'Get up and get ready to move!' Daur shouted through the hatch at the waiting men. The downwash from the fliers was creating a Munitorum dust storm in front of the gate area, and the green smoke was being forced upwards into the air in a strangely geometric spiral.

The Valkyrie stood on a hover at about thirty metres, and let the Destrier go in first. The big machine descended gently and crunched down in a fury of dust-kick, its cargo jaws immediately unfolding with a shrill buzz of hydraulics.

'Go! Go!' shouted Daur.

The sections led by Daur and Kolea ran out from the gatehouse towards the big lifter, heads down. They carried their lasrifles strapped across their backs. The other two sections, under Criid and Kolosim, simultaneously fanned out around the edge of the landing site, weapons in hand, watching the rocks for movement or attack.

Daur was first to reach the lifter. The idling engine was raising a tumult of dust, and the air stank of hot metal and exhaust. Three Munitorum officers stood on the payload area, manhandling the first of several laden pallets out through the cargo jaws.

Daur waved at them. 'How many?' he yelled.

'A dozen like this,' one of the handlers shouted back. The pallets were thick, flak board bases with rows of hefty fluid drums tight-packed and lashed onto them, twenty drums on each pallet.

'You got no cargo gear?' the handler yelled.

Daur shook his head. 'Gonna have to move them by hand!' he shouted back. Daur took out his warknife and sawed through the packing twine lashing the first pallet's cargo together. As his men came up, they each grabbed as many of the heavy, sloshing drums as they could manage, and headed back towards the gate. Most could carry two, one in each hand. A few of the biggest men, like Brostin, could just about lift three. It was a struggle. Everyone knew speed was of the essence.

'Let's go! Second load!' Daur yelled. He and Kolea tossed the empty first pallet clear as the handler crew slid the next one out through the jaws.

Too slow, too slow, Daur thought. The first troopers carrying drums had only just reached the gatehouse. The sheer weight of the drums, combined with the soft dust underfoot, made the process of unloading truly punishing.

Men came rushing back from the gate, empty handed, to take up the next load. They were already out of breath and flexing strained and tired arms.

'Come on!' Kolea shouted, taking the drums Daur passed to him and handing them out to each man in turn.

With the Destrier down, the Valkyrie came in to land to its left. It landed with a squeal of jets, inside Criid's perimeter.

'Derin! Watch those rocks!' Criid yelled, and jogged over into the dust-wrap surrounding the Valkyrie. A crewman had slid the heavy side door of the passenger compartment open and two men had jumped out into the dust under the hooked wing. They came forwards, bent down in the wash, hands shielding their eyes. One was dressed in khaki, the other in black. The man in black was carrying a heavy bag.

'This way!' Criid shouted, gesturing.

They hurried towards her. As they approached, Criid raised her arms and flashed a signal to the Valkyrie pilot. She saw him in his cockpit, his brightly painted helmet tipping her a nod.

The Valkyrie took off again, thrusters wailing as if in pain. It rose sharply, climbed hard, and began to turn at about three hundred metres, nose down.

Criid saluted the men as they came up to her. The one in khaki was short, slim and fair. For one awful moment Criid thought it was Caffran, back from the dead.

'Major Berenson, Cadogus Fifty-Second,' he yelled above the noise. 'This is my tactical advisor. I present my compliments to your commander, and request audience.'

'Criid, First-and-Only,' she replied, shaking his hand. 'Follow me, sir. We're a little exposed out here.'

She turned and ran towards the gate. The two men ran after her.

III

THEY WERE ONTO the third pallet. The Munitorum boys were shoving it out through the cargo jaws. Daur glanced at his chron. Four minutes. Too slow, still too slow. The men running back to collect the next load of drums were already panting and exhausted.

Kolea cut the twine with his knife, and started to pass out the drums as they slid loose, heavy and stubborn.

'Let's go, let's go, let's go!' he urged above the noise of the Destrier's engines.

Daur turned. 'What was that?' he asked.

'What?' Kolea shouted back, still handing the drums off to the relay of men.

'I heard a noise!' Daur yelled. It had been a dull thwack of a noise, a dense impact.

'Feth,' Daur murmured. 'We've got a leak here!'

Water, bright and clear, was squirting out of one of the drums on the third pallet, spattering copiously into the dust like a fountain jet.

'We've got a damn leak!' he yelled again, reaching the drum and trying to stopper it with his fingers.

There was another thwack. A metre to Daur's right, another drum began to hose water out of its side. Out of a *puncture* in its side.

Daur looked around at Kolea. 'We're–' Daur started to shout.

A las-round ricocheted off the cargo-jaw assembly. Two more spanked into the side of the Destrier. One of the Munitorum officers rocked on his feet as a red mist puffed out behind his back. He fell hard, crashing off the pallet and into the dust. A Ghost, a drum in each hand, turned and fell sideways, the side of his head shot off.

'Contact!' Kolea bawled. 'Contact! Contact!'

IV

RHEN MERRT TURNED. Something was up. He was part of Criid's section fanned out around the perimeter. The bulk lifter behind him was making one hell of a noise.

'What was that?' he yelled at Luhan.

'What?' Luhan shouted back.

'Kolea gn... gn... gn... yelled something!'

'I dunno,' yelled Luhan.

Merrt saw sparks in the rocks ahead of him. He knew what that was. They were taking fire from the crags of the pass. They couldn't hear the crack of discharge because of the lifter's engine noise.

'Contact!' Merrt yelled. He raised his rifle and blasted at the rock slope. Nothing happened. His lasrifle had jammed.

Shots whipped in across them. The enemy wasn't aiming at Merrt and his section. They were targeting the heavy lifter. Merrt saw las and tracer rounds sizzling through the air above him. He struggled to clear his weapon.

Merrt's lasrifle was a particularly battered and unreliable piece. He'd picked it up during the savage street fighting on Gereon after he'd lost his own. It was well-worn, and had a faded yellow Munitorum stencil on the butt. It was ex-Guard issue, but Merrt had a sneaky suspicion the weapon had been used by the enemy for a while.

A captured, recaptured piece, and not in particularly good order. He despised it. Merrt sometimes fancied that the time it had spent, literally, in enemy hands had left a curse on it. It was four kilos of bad luck swinging on a strap. He knew he should have exchanged it for a new issue at the Munitorum supply. He should have told the clerks the weapon's history and had them destroy it. But he hadn't, and he wouldn't have been able to say exactly why he hadn't if asked directly. Deep down, there was an unformed thought that he and the gun somehow deserved each other, an unlucky rifle for a fething unlucky man.

He worked to unjam it. It seemed to cooperate. Merrt trained it and fired. There was a jolt. The lasrifle emptied its entire load in one disastrous cough of energy. The blast threw Merrt down on his back. The blistering ball of discharge hit rocks twenty metres away and exploded like a tube-charge, throwing a drizzle of earth, dust and grit into the air.

Merrt rolled over, and looked around, dazed. He saw a Ghost go down, one of the men in the relay team running between the gate and the lifter. Full, heavy drums of water landed hard and askew in the dust either side of the body. Another member of the team fell as he was winged, got up, and fell again as a second shot burst through one of the drums he was carrying and into his hip.

Merrt got up and grabbed his las. He ejected the clip and forced home a new one.

'Work!' he snarled 'Gn... gn... gn... *work!*'

V

ENEMY FIRE WAS zipping and pinging in around them. The cargo jaws had been badly dented and the third pallet of water, half unloaded, was spraying out its contents through dozens of shot holes.

'We can't stay here!' one of the two remaining Munitorum officers yelled at Daur.

'You have to! We need this water!'

The officer shook his head. 'Sorry! The pilot says he's pulling out! Get back!'

'No!' Daur shouted, losing his footing. The Munitorum officers shoved the third pallet clear of the cargo-jaws and ducked back inside the lifter. The jaws whined shut and the Destrier lifted off in a storm of dust, shots thumping against its hull.

'No! Come back, you bastards!' Daur howled.

'Ban! Forget it!' Kolea told him, grabbing his arm and pulling him to his feet. 'We're dead out here! Get back to the gate!'

Daur ran, Kolea at his heels. The relay teams and the covering sections were scurrying back towards the gate, chased by shot. Above them, the southern casemates and gunboxes of Hinzerhaus had opened up. Heavy fire raked down from the open shutters and ploughed across the jumbled rocks of the escarpment.

Daur blundered up to the gate hatch. 'How much did we get?' he gasped. 'How much?'

'Two and a half pallets,' Kolosim replied.

'Out of a dozen?' Daur snapped. 'Feth's sake, that's not enough! We left half a fething pallet out there in the dust!'

'That's where it'll have to stay, Ban,' Kolea said quietly. 'We've got no choice. Get inside. We need to shut the hatch.'

VI

'K862, K862, WE need that load, over,' Beltayn said into the vox.

'I appreciate that, Nalwood, but the LZ is not secure. Am circling.'

Beltayn looked at Gaunt. Gaunt held out his hand and Beltayn put the vox-mic into it.

'Destrier K862, this is Colonel-Commissar Gaunt, commanding this position, over.'

'I hear you, sir, over.'

'We're out of water and we need what you're carrying, over.'

'No doubt in my mind that you do, sir, but that landing site was compromised. Heavy fire. It cost me one crew member. Another thirty seconds on station, and I'd have taken a round through my engine core. I couldn't stay there, over.'

'We need that water, K862, over.'

'Suggest we try an alternative drop point, sir, over.'

Gaunt glanced at Beltayn.

'Out the back, sir? Through the tunnel from the power plant workshops?'

'We sealed it last night,' Gaunt told his adjutant. He spoke into the mic. 'Stand by, K862.'

'Circling, Nalwood. Be advised fuel load will allow me to remain here for another six minutes only. Then we're out, over.'

'What about that courtyard?' Beltayn asked.

Gaunt raised the mic. 'K862, K862, suggest you try a courtyard in the lower southern face. You can see it better than we can from up there, over.'

'Turning in, Nalwood. The dust just blew up again.'

'K862?'

'Hold on, Nalwood, it's blowing up hard suddenly. All right, we see it. Coming around, over.'

'Thank you, K862, over.'

They waited. A wind rose and gusted through the base chamber.

'Nalwood, we have your courtyard in sight. Too small for a landing, over'

'K862, can you drop, over?' Gaunt asked.

'Not ideal, but we'll try, Nalwood. Stand by, over.'

Gaunt looked at Beltayn. They both waited in silence. It was taking forever. 'One, Throne of Terra... Two, Throne of Terra...' Gaunt began to whisper.

The vox coughed. 'Nalwood, Nalwood, this is K862, this is K862. We have dropped cargo at this time. View from here is that some of it may have burst. Did the best we could, over.'

'Thank you, K862. Go home, over.'

'Understood, sir. Hope it works out for you. K862 out.'

Gaunt handed the vox-mic back to Beltayn. 'So... all we have to do now is find that blasted courtyard,' he said.

VII

'I'M A LITTLE busy right now,' said Beltayn. 'What was it you wanted?'

Beltayn had been on his way out of the base chamber to work on charts in Gaunt's office when Dalin had stopped him. Dalin waved his hand. 'Nothing, adj. Just wanted to pick your brains.'

'Because?'

'Captain Meryn has appointed me as his adjutant and I'm not sure what I'm supposed to do, exactly. I thought I could ask you for advice.'

Beltayn shook his head. 'Meryn made you his adjutant? You poor bastard. What happened to Fargher?'

'He died,' said Dalin.

'Oh, yeah. Right. I heard that.' Beltayn looked Dalin up and down, thoughtfully. 'Can I ask you something, Dalin?'

'Of course.'

'Do you think Meryn asked you to do this because of who you are?'

'Are you kidding? I think it's safe to assume that was uppermost in his mind.'

Beltayn grinned. 'You don't care?'

'It irks me. It bothers me that no one can talk to me without the thought of who I am in their heads. On the other hand, I'll die of fatigue if I keep fighting it, so I'll live with it.'

'All right, then,' said Beltayn. 'So, apart from that, why do you think Meryn asked you to be his adj?'

'Because he knows I'm smart. Because he knows I can make him look good. Because I can read a map a feth of a lot better than he can,' Dalin replied.

'Read a map, eh?' Beltayn thought about that. 'You're good with charts?' he asked. 'Follow me.'

VIII

MERRT SLUMPED DOWN amongst the other members of his section. All four sections had been ordered back from the gatehouse into the base chamber. The sections that had been running the relay flopped down in exhausted heaps. Some had to move aside as the wounded were carried through by stretcher parties. From the upper levels of the fortress house, they could hear the crack and thump of continuing gunfire from the casemates.

Merrt sat and stared furiously at his rifle. The wretched bastard thing had jammed twice during the firefight. It *was* cursed, and it was jinxing him. He desperately wanted to get rid of it, but he knew he couldn't. He still had a lot to prove to the senior ranks, to men like Hark. Merrt was on unofficial probation, and he was determined not to screw things up. He'd promised Hark as much. If the likes of Hark, or Gaunt, or Rawne discovered he was carrying a weapon tainted by the Archenemy's touch, if he admitted it, and they found out he'd known about the rifle's dubious lineage all along, that would be it. He'd be lucky if he made a penal regiment.

And Rhen Merrt was not a lucky man.

He didn't know what to do. He was afraid of the gun, and was convinced it was enjoying his fear. *Don't be stupid, it's just a gun.*

He rubbed at the half-faded yellow Munitorum stencil on the butt. He hadn't really paid the stencil much attention before. It was just a Munitorum serial code, half worn out.

Except it wasn't. It said 'DEATH'.

Merrt blinked. He felt a cold anxiety fill his dry throat like a rod of ice. 'DEATH'. It actually said 'DEATH'. It–

No, it *was* just a Munitorum code. 034TH. Half flaked away, the numerals appeared to read 'DEATH'.

Merrt closed his eyes and rested his head back against the cold wall. *You stupid idiot. 'DEATH'. You idiot, scaring yourself. You've got to shake this off. You've got to forget this nonsense about the gun being cursed. It's just a gun. It's just a piece of junk.* Merrt heard voices and looked up.

'Good work, boys,' Captain Daur was telling them, walking down the line of them. 'Good work. That was tight, but you did well. I've just been told the rest of the water drop has been delivered. Drinks on me.'

Merrt ignored the insufferably good-looking Daur and placed his untrust-worthy rifle on the floor beside him. He looked down at it warily, sidelong, as if it was a poisonous snake.

We'll see, 034TH, we'll see. I'm going to beat your jinx and break your will. I'm going to master you and prove myself. Or you're going to be the death of me.

IX

'SIR, THIS IS Major Berenson,' said Criid, 'and this is Tactical Officer Karples.'

'Welcome to the fun,' Gaunt said. He shook hands with Berenson and took a quick salute from the aide. 'Let's talk in my office. Thank you, Criid, that will be all.'

Criid nodded and watched the three men walk out of the base chamber into one of the connecting hallways. Nearby, she saw Kolea staring at them too.

'Uncanny, isn't it?' she asked.

'Sorry, Tona, what is?'

'That Berenson. Dead spit for Caff, don't you think?'

Kolea raised his eyebrows. 'Gak, that's what it is! I couldn't put my finger on why he spooked me so much.'

'Dead spit. Could be a brother.'

Kolea looked at her. 'You all right?'

'I'm always all right,' she replied. 'So where's this water, then?'

'We're working on it,' Kolea said.

'I WASN'T EXPECTING a personnel transfer,' Gaunt said as he led Berenson and the tactical aide into his office. In one corner of the room, Beltayn was work-ing on a pile of maps spread out on a small table. Dalin, Rerval, Fapes and Bonin were huddled in with him.

'Do you need the room, sir?' Bonin asked.

'Please,' said Gaunt.

The group gathered up their charts, locators and wax pencils and left the office. Dalin cast an oddly lingering look at Berenson as he went out.

Gaunt led Berenson and the tactical officer over to his desk and offered them seats. Berenson and the tactical sat down on two mismatched wooden chairs. Gaunt perched on the edge of his desk.

'We can probably offer you some caffeine in a while, once we've found something to brew it with.'

'That's fine, sir,' said Berenson. He took off his cap and brushed the dust off the crown. Gaunt suddenly understood Dalin's lingering fascination. The man bore a startling similarity to Caffran.

'As I said, I wasn't expecting a personnel transfer.'

'Last minute thing,' Berenson explained. His voice bore the traces of a clipped accent. 'Elikon command was concerned about appraising you over the vox.'

'We've had penetration of code,' the tactical aide said bluntly.

'It was agreed I should follow the supply drop in and bring you up to speed in person,' Berenson continued.

'I appreciate that. We feel rather cut off out here.'

'I can see why,' said Berenson with a half-smile. He looked around. 'This is a curious hole, this Hinzerhaus. I must say, it has the most peculiar atmosphere. Not entirely pleasant. Sort of... menacing.'

'Its a bad place on a bad rock,' said Gaunt. 'I presume you were briefed by Van Voytz.'

Berenson nodded. 'He's fully aware of the plight he's placed you in, sir. Fully aware. He sends his regrets. In fact, he was most particular about that. The tactical summaries left something to be desired.'

'The enemy dispositions are hard to read,' the tactical officer put in, uncomfortably. 'We are revising.'

'Karples thinks we're getting at his department for doing a bad job,' Berenson smiled. 'I keep telling him it really wasn't Tactical's fault. The enemy surprised us all. They were disguising massive troop deployments along the Kehulg Basin.'

'Show me,' said Gaunt.

Karples got up and produced a hololithic projector from his bag. He set it on the desk and aimed the caster lens at the back wall of the office. The device hummed, and projected a hazy three-dimensional graphic into the air. Karples walked into it and began to point towards certain features.

'The main elements of our opposition were identified by early orbit sweeps and sat-scatter as accumulated here in the Jaagen Lowlands, and here in the lower provinces. Elikon was chosen as the optimum beach head for landing and dispersal. Fierce fighting at armour brigade level has been taking place here, and along here, and into the Lowlands. There was some concern that enemy elements might swing east and attempt a penetration through the Banzie Altids, which is why the Lord General deployed you to this site.'

Gaunt nodded. 'But that's not how it's playing out, is it? We've seen that much for ourselves.'

Karples looked back at Gaunt, his pinched, rodent face layered in streamers and patches of coloured light from the display.

'No, it's not, colonel-commissar. Undetected by the sat-scatter drones, the enemy had massed considerable forces here, here and here before we made planetfall, the Kehulg Basin in particular. These forces have swept around out of cover and achieved a pincer around the Elikon front.'

'That's seriously bad news, sir,' Berenson put in. 'The fighting along that stretch of the line is wicked. Be thankful you're out here.'

'I'm not that thankful,' said Gaunt. 'The enemy's here too.'

Karples nodded. 'Far more advanced than we first suspected. We now believe they have been planning this for months. Successive, surprise strikes along our eastern flank were the actual basis of their strategy. Hinzerhaus is the furthest projection of their swing attack, but crucial. They are not attempting to counter-strike here, sir. This is the path of their main offensive.'

'Imagine how pleased that makes me feel,' Gaunt said, sitting down in his chair.

'Clearly, we've disposed and positioned ourselves badly,' Berenson said. 'I'm here to tell you this isn't going to be your problem for much longer.'

'Really?'

Berenson smiled. So like Caff, Gaunt thought. 'The Cadogus Fifty-Second has deployed in total strength configuration. Twenty thousand men, plus armour and artillery, along with battlefield psykers. As luck would have it, we were delayed in transit, otherwise we'd have been placed along the Jaagen zone. Thank the Throne we weren't. It gives our side tactical flexibility. My regiment is operational and moving rapidly into the field east of Elikon, with the intention of meeting the enemy offensive head on. Show him, Karples.'

'Here, also here, here and here,' the tactical aide said, pointing at the 3-D light.

'The main business is likely to be at Banzie Pass,' said Berenson, 'but we can't ignore Hinzerhaus and its environs. Five companies of mechanised infantry will be arriving in the next three days. Full support. We'll take over from you then. We'll greet them and hit them hard. All your... Ghosts, I believe they're called... all your Ghosts have to do is hold this position until then and keep the enemy contained and occupied.'

Gaunt nodded.

'And I'm here to help you with that,' said Berenson brightly.

'I hope you can shoot, then,' said Gaunt.

Day ten. Sunrise at four plus fifty-three, white out conditions, or so I'm told by A.C. Bored out of my skull here in the field station. ~~WE~~ Wish I could move. Back hurts.

Face down on a gurney. This is how I will see out the rest of my career. L. comes in to visit me, once in a while. I can tell he's not happy. I imagine the men are being less than cooperative. Poor bastard.

There was a water drop yesterday, but it seems no one can now locate the damn water. I am so parched, it's killing me. My throat hurts worse than my back, and A.C. tells me I do not want to see my back.

Bad night. I ~~had the dream suffered the voices in my head the pipes~~ slept badly, and woke up a lot. Kept ~~hearing the pipes playing in my head~~ waking, troubled. There's something going on. G. came to see me, but he wasn't saying much.

Shoggy Domor died during the night. Twice. D. brought him back both times with cardiac paddles. I am scared for Shoggy. He needs proper care in a Guard hospital. Out here, in this cellar, he doesn't stand a chance.

Have begun to hate Hinzerhaus. Am increasingly convinced it is trying to kill us all.

- Field journal, V.H. fifth month, 778.

TEN

Five Thirty-Seven

I

IT WAS EARLY, very early. The house was cold and the lights seemed especially dim. Outside, the wind murmured.

The old dam in the black lace dress, she of the maggoty, meat-wound face, was walking about again. Maggs could hear her footsteps, and feel the chill of her.

Throne, how she wanted them dead, all of them. That was her business. When he closed his eyes, he could see her face, a face that wasn't a face any more.

Maggs had been sent to sit the small hours watch in a gunbox on upper west fifteen. At first, the six-man team had taken turns watching the shutters while the others rested, but there was nothing to see outside except dust, so they'd given up on that. They'd closed the shutters and rigged tripwires so they'd know if anyone was trying to prise them open from the outside.

Footsteps rolled along the quiet hallway behind them. Slow, shuffling steps. Maggs looked up, raising his gun.

'What's the matter?' Gansky asked him.

'Nothing,' said Maggs. He couldn't hear the footsteps any more. He got up and checked the tripwires.

'What time is it?' he asked.

'Five twenty-two,' said Lizarre, checking his chron sleepily.

Maggs walked down the hallway and looked around. Nothing, not a sign of anyone.

That was all right, though. He really, really didn't want to come face to face with her.

* * *

Dan Abnett

II

BASKEVYL WOKE AND rolled over with a groan. The floor beneath his bedroll was hard and unforgiving.

He remembered where he was.

Baskevyl sat up. He knew something had woken him: a noise. He wasn't sure if the noise had been in his dream or real.

He got up and left the billet chamber. A few Ghosts grumbled in their sleep as he picked his way out. There were sixty other men in the chamber, and he knew they needed all the rest they could get.

Out in the hall, he leaned against a brown satin wall and took out his water bottle. The water that had been taken in through the gate during the previous day's abortive drop had been carefully rationed out. It had tasted wonderful, but there was very little left in his bottle now. Another ration was going to be issued at breakfast. Estimates varied, but the reckoning was that, at strict ration levels, the water they had would last four days. No one had managed to find the bulk of the drop, or the elusive courtyard where it lay. Gaunt had already sent a request for supplementary supply drops to Elikon, a message that had not been answered.

The glow of the wall lights slowly faded. They seemed to take a long time to come back. Baskevyl watched them with fascination. The fade and return got slower at night, as if the house was breathing more slowly because it was asleep.

Something wasn't asleep. He heard a noise and knew it was the same noise that had woken him. He listened and heard, very far away, a scraping sound: a soft, wet, slithering sound coming from the depths of the earth.

It was still down there, the daemon-worm. It was still down there, and it was snuffling around, trying to get his scent.

III

'ARE WE–' THE link began to ask, and then the words were lost in a squall of loud vox-noise.

Beltayn adjusted his dials, the phones clamped to his sweaty head. 'Say again, source?'

Static. A drifting buzz.

Beltayn tried again, patiently. 'Elikon, Elikon, this is Nalwood, this is Nalwood. Requesting response to earlier transmission regarding future water drops, over?'

More static. When the dust blew up at night, it chopped the legs out of the vox-link.

Beltayn sat back and took off his headphones. It was five twenty-three. He'd promised Gaunt he'd rise early and check the vox.

The grand base chamber was empty and quiet around him. He could just hear the footsteps of a sentry moving about on one of the landings above. Soft, shuffling footsteps. The poor bastard is tired, Beltayn thought. We're all tired.

He kept looking at his water bottle. Half of his last night's precious ration was still in it. He was pacing himself.

'Adj?'

Beltayn looked around and saw Dalin wandering in, yawning. Dalin was holding a bundle of charts in his hands.

'What are you doing up?'

'Couldn't sleep,' said Dalin, sitting down beside Beltayn. 'Been thinking about the maps all night.'

'Oh, don't,' said Beltayn. The frustration of the previous night's efforts had almost driven Beltayn to snapping point. With Dalin, Bonin and a few of the other most accomplished adjutants and pathfinders, he'd gathered up all the maps of Hinzerhaus issued to the regiment and gone over them line by line, looking for the fabled courtyard. That's what they had begun calling it. The *fabled courtyard*. The true nonsense of the maps had quickly become apparent. None of them matched. Some looked like plans of entirely different fortress complexes. Beltayn wondered what the feth Tactical had thought they were playing at. How could they issue a dozen different schematics of the same objective? Hadn't they noticed?

Beltayn's team had worked on it for hours, sometimes walking the halls only to end up wandering aimlessly around in futile circles. Mkoll had joined them, trying to employ that ineffable Tanith woodcraft to the task. They knew where the *fabled courtyard* should be. They knew where it *had* to be, given the sight of it the scouts had got from the ridge two days before. But they just couldn't find the *fabled* fething *courtyard*, or any sign of a hall or spur that might lead to it.

Sleep had caved them in at last and they'd given up. 'The water's not going anywhere,' Mkoll had said, stoically. 'Let's get some rest.'

Beltayn had been particularly disarmed by Mkoll's manner. He had realised the chief scout simply hated being useless, and since when had Mkoll not been able to find anything? It was as if the house was deliberately hiding the courtyard from them.

That, of course, was utter nonsense, because to believe that, you'd have to believe the house was somehow... *alive*.

Dalin spread some of the maps out on the deck beside Beltayn's vox-caster. 'I had an idea,' he said. 'What if they're *all* right?'

'What? You need some sleep, lad.'

'No, no, listen. What if they're all correct? I mean, what if they all have some *parts* correct, as much as they all show stuff that's wrong too. We should look at the bits that agree, and that agree with the actual layout of this place.'

'We tried that,' said Beltayn, 'Remember?' He wasn't in the mood for this. The boy was trying hard to impress, and Beltayn had to give him credit for that, at least, but Dalin was wasting his time.

'Hear me out,' Dalin insisted. 'This was keeping me awake. No matter how wildly different the charts are, they have certain features in common. Gaunt's map shows the base chamber and the halls along here, so does Rawne's. Hark's has got them too, but not the lower hall or these galleries here. Kolea's got galleries all over the place that aren't marked on any other charts. All of them show the well, and six of them show the power room, although–'

'You have been busy.'

'Thanks. Daur's shows the power room on the wrong level, but that is the only chart that shows an area that could be the courtyard.'

'The fabled courtyard. Dalin, we worked out that Daur's chart was the craziest of the lot last night. Apart from a couple of details, it might as well have been made up. It might as well be a different fething site altogether.'

'Yeah, I know, but what if they're *all* correct?'

Beltayn sighed. 'You keep saying that. What do you mean?'

'How old is this place?'

'I don't know.'

'But old, right? Really old?'

'Yeah,' Beltayn conceded.

'It's probably been changed and altered and rebuilt a lot. Just suppose that all of these charts were correct and accurate… when they were drawn.'

'I thi– *What*?'

Dalin grinned. 'Maybe each chart accurately reflects the layout of this place at the time it was made. Maybe *this* one–' Dalin picked a map at random. 'Maybe this one is two hundred years old, and this one five hundred. Who knows? Anyway, none of them show how things are *now*, just how things looked when the particular map was made.'

Beltayn hesitated. 'That's actually not the maddest thing I've ever heard,' he began.

'Yeah, Dalin's got a point there,' said Mkoll.

Both Beltayn and Dalin started. They hadn't heard him approach.

'Feth, you scared me!' exclaimed Beltayn.

Mkoll nodded. 'Good. I haven't completely lost it then.' He sat down with them. His face was drawn and pale, as if sleep had been eluding him for months. He reached out and took some of the charts from Dalin.

'So you're suggesting these were made at different times, in different periods? A gallery on this chart, let's say, may have been built after this other chart here was made?'

Dalin nodded. 'That's what I was thinking. Bits get built, or demolished and closed off. Rooms get added or changed. Plus, of course, there may be genuine mistakes. These are hand-drawn.'

'That's good thinking,' said Mkoll.

'The boy's sharp,' said Beltayn.

'Takes after his dad,' said Mkoll.

'It still doesn't explain why we were issued with them,' said Dalin.

Beltayn shrugged. 'An archiving error? Tactical requested maps of Hinzerhaus for our use and someone pressed the wrong key code, so we got the history of the place in chart form, rather than a dozen copies of the most recent version.'

Mkoll nodded. 'Makes sense – actual, practical, non-spooky sense. Feth alive, I'm glad *something* about this tomb is starting to make some sense.'

'Don't say tomb,' said Beltayn.

'Sorry.'

'So... can we use this?' Dalin asked. 'I mean, can we make practical use of this?'

'Yeah,' said Mkoll. 'Dalin, go wake up Bonin and get him to assemble a scout detail.'

Dalin paused. 'Wake Bonin?'

'That's right.'

Dalin swallowed. The idea of trying to rouse a Tanith scout from slumber seemed vaguely suicidal.

'All right, I'll do it,' said Mkoll. He got up. 'Meet me on west four in five. Bring the charts.'

He left the base chamber. Beltayn looked at Dalin. 'You did good, Dalin. Mkoll's impressed.'

'He is? He didn't really show it.'

'Are you kidding? That was as close as the chief gets to whooping and thumping you on the back. Mark my words, you've made a good impression.'

Dalin grinned.

Beltayn got to his feet. 'Well, come on, then. Grab those maps.'

Dalin began to gather up the unfolded sheets of paper. Beltayn turned to check his caster. He saw that one of the needles on an input gauge was jumping. He scooped up his headset, tuning.

'What is it?' Dalin asked.

'Got something at last. A signal,' said Beltayn, tweaking a dial. He listened.

'Are we the last ones left alive?' the vox whispered into his ear.

Beltayn froze.

'Who are you, sender? Who are you?'

'Are we? Are we the last ones left alive?'

'Respond! Please, respond!'

The voice faded. Beltayn took off his headset.

'Did you get something?' Dalin asked.

'No,' said Beltayn. 'Nothing important.'

IV

034TH LOOKED HIM in the face, in the *ugly* face. Merrt got up, gripping his lasrifle.

It was early, five twenty-five. The house was as quiet as a graveyard, but there was something in the air. Merrt had a gut feeling, a vague glimmer of the old combat smarts he'd once been so proud of. Just the taste of that lost instinct made his heart sing.

He'd been awake for hours, staring at the 034TH stencil in the half-light of the billet chamber.

He walked out into the hall and waited. A figure loomed out of the shadows to his left, moving with a soft, almost silent shuffle.

It was the Nihtgane. He approached, his reynbow ready in his hands. Eszrah regarded Merrt through his sunshades.

'You too, eh?' asked Merrt.

Eszrah nodded.

'Gn... gn... gn... let's go,' Merrt whispered. Eszrah nodded again, but Merrt had actually been speaking to his gun.

V

BRAGG HAD SAT with him for an hour or two through the middle part of the night, just like he'd always done when the pair of them had pulled night watch.

Bragg hadn't said anything, and Larkin hadn't spoken to him. Larkin hadn't even looked at him. Larkin had just sat there in overlook six, watching the shutters as the wind outside tugged them, aware of the presence behind him. His back had gone cold with sweat. He'd been able to hear Banda snoring from the back of the room, as well as his own amplified pulse, along with a third sound of breathing, slow and calm, comfortable.

Bragg. Definitely, unmistakably Bragg. Larkin had recognised the smell of him, the sacra in his sweat, the particular musk of his body odour. It had been such a long time since he'd seen his dear friend, part of him wanted to turn and greet him, to embrace him and ask him where he'd been.

But Larkin knew where Bragg had been, and he didn't dare turn around for fear of what he might see. Bragg had been dead since the Phantine operation, killed by a rat-bastard monster that Larkin had finally plugged with his long-las on Herodor. Bragg simply couldn't be there behind him in the overlook. He *shouldn't* be. It was against all the laws of reason, but Larkin could smell him and hear his breathing anyway.

Larkin had missed his old friend over the years more than he could say. The idea of meeting him again was wonderful.

But not like this. Not like this, please Throne, no.

Not like this.

Just before five, Larkin had heard Bragg get to his feet with a grunt and walk out. Larkin had waited a while, then slowly turned. There was Banda, asleep in the corner. No one else.

Larkin got up and eased his leg stump. He'd been sitting far too long, pinned by fear.

He saw the bottle. It was sitting on the gritty floor of the casemate a few metres behind him. He limped over and picked it up, uncorking it.

Sacra. Sweet and wonderful, the very best. No fether in the regiment had cooked sacra this fine in years. Larkin knew what it was: a gift.

'Thanks,' he said, and took a little sip.

Glory but it was good.

Banda woke up and looked at him. 'What's going on?' she mumbled.

'This yours?' Larkin asked, showing her the bottle.

'No.'

'Didn't think so. Go back to sleep.'

She did so. She was strung out and hungover. She began to snore again. Larkin took one last little sip, then re-corked the bottle and put it into his musette bag. He sat down again.

He checked his chron. Five twenty-six.

Someone leaned into the casemate behind him and called out, 'Get ready, then!'

Larkin looked around. There was nobody there, but he had known the voice.

Clammy fear blew up and down his spine. In his whole life, he'd only known one person who'd been that cheery and wide awake at five twenty-six in the morning; only one person who'd been up to do the rounds, prep the picket and check on sentries; only one person who had owned that voice.

That person's name had been Colm Corbec.

VI

'WHAT'S THE TIME?' Hark asked.

'It's... it's five minutes since you last asked me,' Ludd replied. 'It's five twenty-seven.'

'Oh,' said Hark. The field station was quiet around them. The other casualties were asleep naturally, or were mercifully drugged up against pain. From where he was sitting at Hark's bedside, Ludd could see one of the orderlies, Lesp, asleep in a chair. Ludd knew the medicae personnel had been up most of the night.

'Look, this is too early,' said Ludd. 'You should be sleeping. I can come back at a better hour.'

'No, no, sit down,' Hark replied. 'I only asked because the time passes so slowly in here. It moves like a glacier. I'm glad of the company. I don't seem to sleep much.'

'All right then.'

Hark lay face down on his bed, a thin sheet rudimentarily propped up over his back and legs to provide some warmth. Ludd could see the dark shape of soiled dressings through the sheet, and smell the odours of burncream and charred flesh.

'Finish your report, Ludd.'

'There's not much left. No one needs writing up, general discipline is good, despite the situation.'

'Are they giving you a hard time?'

'What? No, sir.'

'Is that because you're not putting yourself in a position where they can give you a hard time?'

Ludd didn't answer immediately.

'You can't be meek, Ludd. You've got to get up in their faces and keep them tight.'

'That's... that's my intention, commissar.'

'They'll walk all over you if you don't,' said Hark. 'I mean it. They'll walk all over you. You have to show them who's in charge.'

Ludd nodded.

'What?'

'Nothing, sir.'

'Oh, give me something to think about, for feth's sake!' Hark exploded. 'Give me a problem I can solve while I'm like this!'

Curth stepped into the field station and looked disapprovingly at Ludd. Ludd raised a hand to her and smiled. She frowned and left again.

'You'll disturb the others,' Ludd whispered.

'Then talk to me.'

Ludd sighed. 'You said I had to show them who's in charge. Well, Gaunt's in charge... Rawne... Kolea... not me. '

'The officers will support their commissar,' Hark said.

'The officers think I'm just a kid. They laugh at me.'

'Who laughs?'

Ludd shrugged.

'Rawne?'

'Yes, and he's malicious. The others, even Gaunt, I don't think they mean to be disrespectful, they just can't help it. I have no authority.'

Hark shifted on his cot, wincing. 'That's just weak talk, junior commissar. Give me some paper and a pen.'

'Sir?'

'Give me some paper and a pen, and something to lean on.'

Ludd handed the items to Hark. He gave him the field journal to lean on. Hark lay on his belly, writing furiously on the slip of paper and grunting with the effort. Ludd could see raw burns on Hark's exposed, organic arm.

'What are you writing, sir? May I ask?'

'Shut up.'

Hark finished, folded the paper up and handed it back to Ludd with the pen.

'Next time you feel unable to exert your authority, give that to Gaunt.'

'May I read it?'

'No. Just give it to him.'

Ludd put the pen and the folded paper away in his coat pocket.

'Have this too,' Hark said, tossing the field journal aside.

'Ah, I wanted to ask you about that, sir,' Ludd said.

'About what?'

'The field journal, sir. I've been trying to keep it up to date, as instructed.'

'And?'

Ludd swallowed. 'I read back, naturally, to acquaint myself with your method and style of content. I noticed... how can I put this?'

'Soon?' Hark suggested.

'I noticed some scratchings out. Some changes, where you had written and then changed your wording.'

'It's a journal, Ludd,' said Hark, 'that's how it works. The final draft report will be clean.'

'But I couldn't help reading... some of the things you had excised. The words were legible. About your dreams, sir.'

'They were private remarks that I deleted because they had no place in the record.'

'Still, they concern me. Your comments about the dreams, and your disquiet. You said you couldn't sleep and–'

'That's enough, Ludd. Forget what you read. It isn't your concern.'

Ludd got to his feet, saluted, put his cap on, and turned to go.

Then he sat down again. 'Actually, you know what? I'm going to take your advice. Yes, it *is* my concern. It's my concern as the acting senior political officer that you are troubled by your dreams so much you can find no release. For the good of the regiment, I require you to explain yourself.'

There was a long silence.

'Finished?' Hark asked.

'Yes.'

'Go away.'

'No, I don't believe I will.' Ludd leaned closer, his voice a hard whisper. 'What's going on, Hark? What's been troubling you, from before we even got here?'

'You have no right to ask–'

'I have authority, Hark, over you. You gave it to me, remember? Now start talking!'

Hark began to chuckle. 'That's good. That's actually quite good, Nahum. I'm impressed. That's how you stand up to Rawne and the others.'

'Thank you. I'm still waiting.'

Hark went quiet.

'Do I have to write you up?' Ludd asked.

Hark turned his head and looked sidelong at Ludd. His dark eyes were darker still from lack of sleep and something else.

'I haven't slept well in years, Nahum. On and off, five years, at least. Dreams come to me and ruin my sleep.'

'Nightmares?'

'No, nothing so grandiose or obvious. Just a bad feeling. The pattern has varied. There have been periods without it – wonderful, clear patches, months on end. But it's been back again of late, these last few months, and it's grown worse since we put into Jago, worse still since we got here, to this damn place.'

'Go on. Can you remember anything about the dreams?'

'No,' said Hark, closing his eyes. 'It's like... when you remember a dream, hours after you've woken up?'

'I know that feeling.'

Hark nodded. 'Like that. A sudden memory of sadness and pain.'

'Have you told anyone?'

'I've talked to Dorden. He thinks it's a trauma effect from when I lost my arm.'

'How did that happen?'

Hark opened his eyes and stared at Ludd again. There was a brooding misery in his pupils. 'The battle of Herodor, fighting alongside the Saint. We were jumped by loxatl mercenaries. They blew it off.'

'Oh.'

'You never asked me before, Nahum.'

'I never liked to, sir.'

Hark shifted on his belly, looking away. 'Well, anyway, it's not that. It's not the arm. I wish it was. It's something else. Sometimes, more frequently in these last few weeks, it's come when I'm awake too. Out of nowhere, while I'm awake. That's when I hear–'

'Tanith pipes?' Ludd asked.

'You're sharp, Ludd. Did I tell you that?'

'When you were drowsy from the drugs, sir.'

'Tanith pipes,' Hark sighed. 'I hear them, and when I hear them, I know that killing is about to start.'

There was a long silence. One of the casualties across the station aisle woke up and started to moan.

'What's the time, Ludd?' Hark asked.

'Five thirty-one,' said Ludd.

'Go do your rounds.'

Ludd got up.

'Before you go,' Hark said. 'Give me back that piece of paper.'

Ludd took the slip out of his pocket, unfolded it, and read it.

It read, in scratchy handwriting, 'To Colonel-Commissar Gaunt. If Nahum Ludd gives you this note, it indicates he is hopelessly unable to execute his duties as your regimental commissar. Please shoot the sorry fether through the head and throw his miserable carcass out for the carrion birds. Yours, V.H.'

'That's funny,' said Ludd.

'I meant it,' Hark replied.

'That's why it's funny.'

'Give it to me.'

'Oh no,' said Ludd. 'I don't want you passing it to anyone else. I think I'll keep it. And maybe, just maybe, I won't write you up for it.'

Ludd could tell Hark was laughing, even though his head was turned away.

'I'm going to give you an order,' Ludd said, bending down over Hark.

'Oh, really?'

'Yes. By my authority as regimental commissar, I order you to stay here. Think you can do that?'

Hark told Ludd exactly where his order might be inserted.

Ludd smiled. 'Good. I think we both know where we stand,' he said, and left the chamber.

* * *

VII

THE TRIPWIRE PULLED tight for a moment, then slackened. It pulled tight again.

Wes Maggs rolled over to find a more comfortable part of the wall he was sleeping against.

VIII

MKOLL RAISED HIS lamp and shone it ahead of them. The wall lights in that stretch of the house seemed to have died completely.

'Well?' he asked.

Dalin and Beltayn rifled through the charts they were carrying by the light of the lamp-pack Dalin held in his hand.

'Hold on,' Beltayn said. 'Something's awry.'

'Again?' asked Bonin, stifling a yawn. 'You woke me up for this?'

'Just wait,' Mkoll told him.

The five-man scout detail, led by Hwlan, reappeared from the hallway ahead.

'There's nothing there, chief,' Hwlan said, wearily.

'But the chart–' Beltayn began.

'Maybe it's hidden, a hidden door,' said Dalin. 'We could try tapping on the walls.'

'Oh, not you too,' said Mkoll. 'You're as bad as fething Baskevyl.'

'Wait, wait, wait!' Beltayn said. 'This is east eight central, right?'

'East nine central,' said Bonin.

'No, east eight,' Hwlan objected.

'Shut up, shut up!' Beltayn cut in. 'Look here, match these two up.' He held out two of the charts for their inspection. 'There should be a junction right here, to the south.'

'There's nothing!' Mkoll growled.

Dalin flinched. He hated the idea of getting the chief of scouts riled, and this had all been his idea.

'Nothing!' Mkoll barked again, slamming his fist against a satin brown panel. 'See?'

'Er, chief?' said Bonin.

Mkoll turned slowly and rapped his knuckles against the satin brown wall panel again.

It gave off a hollow sound.

'Oh, Holy Throne,' Mkoll said, swallowing hard. 'I don't believe it.'

'Pry bars!' Bonin called out. 'Pry bars, right now!'

IX

FIVE THIRTY-THREE. Larkin went to the shutters of overlook six and raised one of them. Outside, the wind had dropped to a vague murmur. The dust was gone. He played his scope around. He could see right down the approach pass clearly, the crags backlit by a cold, rising sun. Everything was hard shadow and as still as ice.

Down there, something–

No, just the remains of the water drop, left in the open from the day before. And some bodies, the frozen corpses of friends and comrades.

Larkin limped back to the doorway of the gunbox and looked out, left and right. An empty hall, the lights coming and going softly. No Bragg. No Colm Corbec. No ghosts at all.

He picked up his long-las, clacked his scope into place on its foresight lock, and kicked Banda.

She stirred.

'Get up,' he said.

'Gak off.'

'Get the feth up. It's coming. I can feel it.'

'Uh-huh, feel this.'

Larkin pulled out his water bottle, sloshing around the last of his ration from the previous night. He tossed it to her. 'Drink that, for feth's sake. You need to hydrate. I need you sharp.'

She drained the bottle and got up. Larkin was already at the shutter.

Banda slid her long-las up next to his and unpopped her scope's cover.

'What did you see?' she asked, huskily.

'Nothing yet. Just keep watching.'

X

WEST THREE CENTRAL, just off the base chamber, was quiet. Merrt crept his way along the hallway to the junction, 034TH in his hands.

It twitched suddenly.

Merrt snapped around sharply and aimed his weapon from the shoulder.

'Gah!' cried Ludd, appearing around the corner and coming to a sudden, startled halt. 'What the bloody hell are you playing at?'

Merrt's bulky, augmetic jaw made a guttural sound as he quickly swung his rifle away.

'Gn... gn... gn... sorry, sir.'

Ludd took a step backwards, blinking. 'I asked you a question, trooper. What the feth did you think you were doing?'

'I gn... gn... gn... heard something.'

'Yes, me,' snapped Ludd, tapping his own chest with an index finger. 'Trooper, who gave you permission to stalk the halls with a lasrifle... an armed lasrifle, I notice... at fething daybreak?'

'I heard something,' Merrt repeated.

'You'll have to do better than that,' Ludd exclaimed. 'You could have shot me.'

Merrt knew he could have. Or, at least, 034TH could have. 'I was concerned there was some gn... gn... gn... activity. I was investigating.'

'And you didn't think of voxing it in straight away?'

Merrt stood up straight and lowered his weapon to his side. It twitched again. 'No. That was remiss of me, I realise.'

'Trooper Merrt, right?' asked Ludd. He knew full well who Merrt was. Ugliest bastard in the regiment with that jaw. During transit to the Gereon liberation, Ludd had worked alongside Commissar Hark to get Merrt out of gambling troubles on the troop ship's swelter decks. As a result, Merrt had ended up on RIP duties.

Ludd had always felt sorry for Merrt, sorry for his injury, sorry for his bad luck, sorry for the RIP detail and the inflexible ordinances of the Commissariat that had demanded that punishment.

Ludd didn't feel particularly sorry now.

'I could discipline you for this, Merrt,' Ludd said, summoning up some force of anger into his voice. 'I could. Right now, summary discipline.'

Merrt stared at him. 'Yeah, right.'

'I'm acting commissar, Merrt! You will address me correctly and with respect!'

'Oh, shut up, you're just a gn… gn… gn… boy.'

Ludd felt a singular rage. He'd left Hark's side full of buoyant confidence. Merrt had picked the wrong moment to disrespect him. If Ludd had thought about it, he would have recognised the irony of Merrt's unerring bad luck. But Ludd wasn't thinking. He was fired up. He pulled out his pistol. 'Get up against the wall, trooper!'

Merrt didn't move.

Ludd aimed his pistol. What was it Hark had said? Be firm? Exert and emphasise his authority? *You've got to get up in their faces and keep them tight.* As a commissar he had every right to shoot this man where he stood. The list of charges was more than enough: Lack of respect for a senior officer. Failure to obey a direct order. Demeaning a senior officer. Endangering a senior officer with an armed weapon. Carrying an unsafe weapon in post without permission. Failure to signal a suspected alert… more than enough. But–

'You're not gn… gn… gn… gonna shoot me, boy.'

That last 'boy' did it. Ludd snapped. 'By the authority of the Holy Throne, I–' Ludd began.

Eszrah swooped out of the shadows behind Ludd and pinned him against the wall. Ludd squirmed, but Eszrah somehow managed to pluck the pistol from his hand.

'Ow! Ow!' Ludd cried.

'Be thee quiet, soule,' Eszrah said. 'Lysten…'

XI

BASKEVYL TURNED AND walked back down the hallway. The scuffing, scraping sound was growing louder. It was coming, burrowing up under him.

The worm in the dark that–

Shut up! Baskevyl willed. He drew his laspistol anyway.

XII

'Now CAN YOU see them?' Larkin said, squinting into his scope.

'Oh yeah,' Banda replied.

'Poacher one, poacher one,' Larkin said into his micro-bead. 'Poacher one to all watches. Contact main gate. Time is five thirty-seven. Move your arses.'

He glanced at Banda.

'Shall we? On three?'

XIII

THE TRIPWIRE PULLED tight, and the cloche shutter slowly lifted open, prised up from the outside. A face peered in at them. For a moment, it looked like the meat-wound face of the old dam in the black lace dress.

But it wasn't. It was the cruel, glaring iron grotesk of a Blood Pact warrior. Wes Maggs shot it anyway. The face exploded.

XIV

MKOLL STEPPED OVER the shredded strips of satin-brown panelling and peered into the hole.

'I smell air,' he said.

'So? Let's go,' said Beltayn.

'He gives the orders around here, Bel,' Bonin told the adjutant.

'It's open air,' remarked Mkoll. 'Dust.' He looked at Dalin. 'I think you might have found it, lad.'

Dalin smiled.

His elation was short-lived. Mkoll brought his lasrifle up to his chest suddenly and looked at the roof.

'That was las-fire,' he said.

'Oh, yeah, without a doubt,' Bonin said.

'Move!' yelled Mkoll.

XV

'HERE THEY COME,' Larkin murmured, settling himself in for his first shot.

'Oh Throne, there are so gakking many of them!' Banda gasped.

'Just take them down one at a time,' said Larkin, and fired.

Day ten, continued,
I heard the pipes again. It's five thirty-six. I think
we are about to be ~~Hacked~~ attacked.

Please, Throne, make me wrong.

- Field journal, V.H. fifth month, 778.

ELEVEN

The Second Assault

I

IN THE COLD, early light, the Blood Pact hit the House at the End of the World on two fronts. A force of over three thousand men came pouring out of the crags on either side of the approach pass and charged en masse towards the gatehouse and the southern elevation. Simultaneously, an assault force numbering at least four hundred attacked the cloches and casemates of the summit galleries from the north side, having scaled the steep cliffs behind Hinzerhaus.

Waking rapidly from a light sleep, Gaunt pulled on his storm coat and assessed the situation as rapidly as Kolea's adjutant, Rerval, could feed it to him.

'C company forward to the gate,' Gaunt ordered. 'H and J to the upper west line. Any spare support weapons to the southern casemates.'

Rerval relayed the orders quickly into his vox-caster. Streams of running Guardsmen thundered through the base chamber, heading for both upper and lower levels. The house was waking up with a jolt. There was a lot of shouting.

From outside and above, there was a lot of shooting too.

'Conditions?' Gaunt asked.

'Clear, sir. Dust dropped away just a few moments before the attack began,' replied Rerval.

'Why the hell did they wait for a clear patch?' Gaunt asked out loud. 'The dust is their main advantage. They could have moved up under cover and jumped us.'

'I believe that may have been their intention, colonel-commissar,' Karples said, arriving in the base station with Berenson.

'Explain?'

'The principal attack on the gate was probably scheduled to commence only when the assault elements scaling the northern cliffs had signalled they were in position and ready,' said the tactical aide in an off-hand tone. 'Scaling the cliffs may have taken longer than predicted because your scouts cut away their lines and ladders. By the time the assault elements had achieved position, the sun was up and the dust had died. They evidently decided to press on anyway.'

'Let's hope that compromise costs them,' Berenson grinned. He was clutching a brand new, short-pattern lascarbine with a bullpup grip. 'Where do you want me?'

'Where I can see you,' Gaunt replied distractedly. 'Kolea?'

'Moving!' Kolea yelled back from the floor of the base chamber.

'Rawne?'

'Units heading to station!' Rawne replied with a shout from the main staircase.

'You've got the front door, Eli!' Gaunt cried. 'I'll take the attic!'

'Live forever!' Rawne called back as he vanished up the stairs with his men.

Rerval was packing up his caster to follow Kolea.

'Where's Beltayn?' Gaunt asked him.

'I don't know, sir. His caster's here, though, where he set it up.'

'I need a vox with me,' Gaunt said, exasperatedly.

'I can manage that,' said Karples.

'Good. Grab that caster and move with me. Criid!'

'Sir!'

'Scramble your company and follow me up top!'

II

DEEP IN THE heart of the house, Mkoll stopped running and turned.

'Go back,' he said.

'Gaunt needs me,' Beltayn objected.

'I'll square it with Gaunt,' Mkoll said. 'No matter what's going down, we need to secure that water. Take Dalin and go find that fething courtyard while we take care of business. Bonin, go with them. Hwlan, Coir, you too.'

Beltayn and Dalin turned with the three scouts and headed back the way they had come.

'Let's move with a purpose!' Mkoll told the remainder of the team.

They reached a stairwell and ascended two levels. On the second landing, the roar and chatter of gunfire from above them became alarmingly loud.

'Upper west,' Mkoll said. 'Attic levels.'

They ran on, taking the stairs two at a time. When they reached the landing that linked with the spur of west three central, they met L Company moving upstairs. They stood aside to let the troop body move up.

Mkoll saw Ludd, Merrt and the Nihtgane tagging along behind the unit.

'Commissar!' he called.

Ludd ran over, dodging in and out of the hurrying stream of troopers.

'Sir?'

'I'm going aloft,' Mkoll said. 'Beltayn may have found the water drop we've been searching for. Might I suggest you back him up and make certain?'

'Of course,' said Ludd. He was secretly pleased that the chief of scouts was addressing him with proper respect. There was no question in Mkoll's manner that Ludd was anything but the regiment's commissar. 'Where is it?'

'Mklane!' Mkoll called to one of his scouts.

'Chief!'

'Show the commissar the way.'

'Yes, sir.'

'We need that water,' Mkoll said quietly to Ludd. 'Men can't fight dry.'

'I understand,' said Ludd.

'Excellent news, sir.'

Ludd smiled and hurried after Mklane.

Mkoll nodded to Eszrah as the Nihtgane whispered past him. 'Look after Ludd,' Mkoll hissed.

'As a certayn thing, soule,' Eszrah breathed back with a look of mutual understanding.

Mkoll turned and gestured to his remaining scouts to follow the deploying company up the house.

'Where should I gn... gn... gn... go, sir?' a voice asked.

Mkoll looked over his shoulder. He saw Merrt.

Mkoll shrugged. In his experience, there wasn't much the poor bastard was good for, these days. 'Stick with the commissar. He could probably use some muscle shifting water drums.'

'Yes, sir,' Merrt replied.

Merrt turned. Mkoll and the scouts had already disappeared up the staircase, and the last of L Company was following them.

He was alone. The sound of distant gunfire echoed down the empty hallway. Merrt raised his rifle and headed down the stairs the way Ludd had gone.

III

THE SOUTHERN CASEMATES and towers of Hinzerhaus were lit up wildly with discharge flashes. Torrents of concentrated shots streamed down from the firing slits in the cliff face fortifications and hammered into the oncoming infantry ranks.

The Ghosts exacted their price for the surprise assault. In the first four minutes of action, the marksmen, gunners and support teams positioned inside the defence buttresses mowed down the charge. Hundreds of Arch-enemy troopers fell. Crew-served weapons, pumping and chattering out of casemate slots, cut down entire platoons. Bodies toppled and sprawled onto the pure white dust. Launchers spat squealing rockets down into the wave assault, and those rockets tossed burning figures into the air every time they struck. The hot shots of the expert snipers zipped into the charging host and took out warriors one at a time, blowing the running figures apart.

For about ten minutes, the fortress of Hinzerhaus performed its role admirably. Secure inside its ancient casemates, the Ghost defenders made a killing ground outside the front door, and slaughtered each wave that came rushing in.

'I'm out!' Banda cried, dropping back from the firing slit. 'Ammo!'

'Use mine,' Larkin spat, dropping down too. His long-las had just refused to fire. Time to change barrels.

Banda grabbed four of Larkin's clips and slammed the first one home. She resumed her fire position and banged it off.

'Shit!' she said.

'Miss?' Larkin asked, rummaging in his field bag for a fresh barrel section. 'Focus, you silly bitch. And learn... don't drink on watch.'

'Shut the gak up!' Banda replied, clacking in another hot shot load. She fired again. 'Oh shit! Shit! Shit! Shit!'

'You're wasting ammo,' Larkin snarled as he slid a fresh barrel into position. He wound it tight. 'Don't be so useless, or I'll strip you of that lanyard.'

'Gak you, Larks,' she returned, reaching for another clip. 'I can do this.'

'So show me,' Larkin replied. He checked his weapon. Ready to go. 'Ammo here!' he yelled, over his shoulder. 'Barrels too! Move it!'

He loaded from one of the handful of specialist clips remaining, and swung up to the gunslot. He took aim and dropped his breathing rate.

The long-las bumped at his shoulder. A howling standard bearer, far below, jerked backwards and fell spread-eagled on the dust.

'That shut him up.'

'Bang!' Banda announced beside him. She slid her weapon back in through the slot and beamed at Larkin. 'See? See that? Clean kill.'

They both reloaded.

Trooper Ventnor, who was acting as ammunition runner on level six, burst into the overlook through the hatchway behind them. He was panting, out of breath. He dumped a heavy musette bag on the floor. 'Clips!' he announced.

'And barrels?' Larkin asked, taking aim and not looking around.

'No,' replied Ventnor.

'I need barrels! Move!' Larkin ordered. *Bump.* Another fine headshot.

'Keep your fake foot on,' Ventnor spat, exasperated, and disappeared.

'Bang!' said Banda with a great deal of satisfaction. 'See that? See him go over?'

'Yeah,' Larkin replied, slotting in his next clip and chasing for targets through his scope. 'Good.'

'Gak. My barrel's carked,' Banda announced, dropping back from the slot.

'Two more in the bag there. Get one,' Larkin replied. *Bump.* Over went a Blood Pact officer, sword raised, mid-yell. No amount of labour would ever piece that iron mask back together.

Banda knelt down and struggled to unwind her burned-out barrel.

'Hurry up,' Larkin called out, taking another shot. Too low. he'd misjudged. A Blood Pact warrior lost a pelvis instead of a skull. Still...

'Gak!'

'What?'

'It's jammed in! It won't pull out!'

Larkin turned from the slot to help Banda. Her exchangeable long-las barrel was truly spent, and the carbon scoring had fused it into the body of her weapon. They fought with it until it came free.

Banda screwed a new barrel home.

'Ammo and barrels!' Larkin yelled out. 'Ventnor? We're down to our last one!'

Banda and Larkin chocked clips in simultaneously, and went back to the slot. *Hunting, hunting…*

'Bang!' Banda rejoiced.

Bump went Larkin's long-las.

The runner burst into the gunbox behind them again. 'Barrels!' he yelled.

'At last,' Larkin said.

'Get down,' the runner added.

Larkin turned. 'What?' he began. His voice drained away.

Colm Corbec grinned at him. 'Get down, Larks. Get the lovely lass down too, all right?'

'Oh feth,' Larkin groaned. He threw himself at Banda and smashed her away from the slot in a clumsy body tackle.

'Hey! Ow!' Banda complained as she landed.

A second later, the top of the casemate, right above the gunslot, took the full force of the first artillery shell.

IV

AT THE SUMMIT of the fortress, along the cloche and casemate domes of the ridge line, the fight was a much closer affair.

The Blood Pact raiders had tried at first to enter the shutters quietly, the way they had done many times in the previous days. They found the cloches manned, armed and ready. The waiting Guardsmen did not hesitate. As shutters flew open, small-arms fire blazed out, cutting down the nearest raiders at point-blank range. With nowhere to run to, and just a sheer drop at their backs, the enemy tried to rush the domes and overcome them with weight of numbers.

Inside each strong point, the noise and smoke was hellish. The Ghosts had hastily constructed stages and firesteps during the night, most often out of flak board laid across sand bags, so that they could present at the shutters at head height. Unit officers had little visibility, and were forced to rely on voxed commentaries from the men firing frantically through the wedged-open shutters. The officers attempted to create zones of fire between adjacent cloches and casemates to deny the assault, but most of the strong points, especially those on the upper west levels, were quickly choked with mobs of Blood Pact warriors and mounds of corpses.

Where the ridge defences were stepped, with three banks of cloches overlooking the cliff drop in some places, the men posted in the higher levels attempted to range their fire down onto the raiders attacking the lower positions. There was, however, little opportunity for proper, directed fire. The summit fight was frenzied: a frantic whirl of desperate shooting and hasty reloading.

About seven minutes into the brutal confrontation, the enemy achieved penetration. A Blood Pact warrior, already wounded, leapt from behind the piled dead outside a cloche on upper west sixteen and managed to launch himself onto the dome. Rolling forwards on his blood-soaked belly, he lobbed a bundle of stick grenades in under the flap of the nearest shutter.

The blast killed all eight Ghosts manning the dome. Before the thick, sweet fyceline smoke had even begun to clear, Archenemy raiders were pouring in through the blackened shutter slots and spreading out along the interior hallway. In the confusion, they took out the Guards manning the next cloche along, cutting them down off their makeshift firestep from behind. A second entry point was created as a result.

Two minutes later, a lucky grenade deflected in through a shutter on upper west fourteen and blew the defenders off their platform. Once again, the enemy came scrambling inside, slaughtering the Ghosts maimed and dazed by the explosion. Fierce fighting, some of it bloody hand-to-hand business, was now boiling along two separate spurs of the summit galleries.

By the time Gaunt reached the upper levels of the house, the Blood Pact had sunk its teeth in and was biting down hard. Gaunt moved down upper west sixteen with Criid's company, bolstering each cloche he came to with sections of Criid's force. He had to shout to be understood. The rain of shots pummelling the lid of each dome sounded like hail striking sheet tin. A backwash of discharge smoke had built up like smog in the ancient hallways. Every few seconds there was the dry, gritty *crump* of a grenade detonation, and hot air billowed down the confined spaces, driven by overpressure. The voices of men, shouting in dismay, or confusion, or pain, were as loud as the gunfire.

'Did you hear that?' Berenson yelled.

Gaunt glanced at him, scowling at the notion there was anything except total noise around them.

Berenson's face was wide eyed. 'Listen!' he shouted.

Gaunt heard them. Distant sounds, contrapuntal to the incessant din of war nearby: *whistle-krump, whistle-krump,* the unmistakable signature of shelling, coming from the southern face of the house.

Instantly, the vox-link was alive with shouts and reports.

'Rawne?' Gaunt called urgently into his micro-bead. 'Rawne! Two, Two, this is One, this is One.'

'–barrage coming in!' Rawne came back, his signal crumpled by distortion. 'Artillery ranging us from the pass. Repeat, artillery re–'

'Two? Two? Say again!'

'–in hard. Really hard! Feth, we–'

The link went dead, flat dead, no signal at all. Gaunt heard more shells striking the other side of the fortress. This time, he felt the floor shake slightly.

'Dear Throne,' said Karples. 'This is madness—'

He began to add something else, but Gaunt could no longer hear him because Criid, Berenson and some of the other troopers alongside had started firing. Screaming out their uncouth warcries, warriors of the Blood Pact were rushing towards them along the smoke-filled hall.

Gaunt drew his sword, the sword of Heironymo Sondar. It had been gifted to him after his successful defence of another bloody siege: the hive clash at Vervunhive.

'Men of Tanith!' he bellowed.

There was no time to say anything else. With trench axe, billhook, bayonet and pistol, the enemy was upon them.

V

DALIN COULD SMELL fresh air. He could also hear the wail and blast of artillery shells a lot more clearly than Gaunt could.

'They're giving us all kinds of feth,' he said.

'Sounds like it,' replied Beltayn. 'Keep moving.'

Dalin glanced at Bonin, Coir and Hwlan. The three scouts Mkoll had sent back with them were exchanging uneasy looks. Dalin knew they were dearly wishing they were somewhere else, somewhere they could be useful. They were three of the regiment's finest, and they were missing a full-on battle in order to run what was, essentially, a supply mission.

'Why don't you go?' Dalin suggested.

'What?' Bonin asked.

'Beltayn and me, we can find the water drop. Why don't you get going?'

'Mkoll gave us an order,' said Coir.

'But—'

'Mkoll gave us an order,' said Bonin. 'That's the start and the finish of it.'

They had passed through the hole where the wall panels had been pried away earlier, and had entered a corridor that had not seen life in a very long time. It was dry, and the polished floor was covered in a thick layer of undisturbed dust. There was something odd about the wall lights in this section. They were of the same style and arrangement as the wall lights in other parts of the house, strung along the wall panels almost organically on their heavy trunking, but these lights shone with an unremitting amber glow, not fading and returning. They burned like old lamps reaching the clamped-end of their wicks.

'Guess how much I don't like this?' Beltayn murmured.

'Guess how much I don't care?' Bonin replied.

They walked forward slowly, leaving five sets of footprints in the dust behind them. The air stirred like a cold breath. From somewhere ahead of them, they heard the rich, reverberative blasts of falling shells. The sound was not in any way baffled or dampened by intervening walls or doors.

'This match anything on the charts?' Hwlan asked.

Dalin studied the collection of maps he was carrying. 'It's hard to say…' he began.

Hwlan glared at him.

'I'm sorry,' Dalin said.

'Sorry's not good enough,' said Hwlan.

The hallway ahead bent to the left and widened slightly. They went down a short flight of steps. The walls were clad with the same satin brown panels that lined all of the house's walls, but there were more engravings and markings along the shoulder-height strips.

Beltayn ran the beam of his light along them. None of the decorations made any sense.

'I wish I knew what those meant,' he said.

'I wish you knew what those meant too,' said Bonin.

'Doors,' Hwlan said.

Up ahead, at the very limit of their lamp beams' reach, there were two doors, one on either side of the hall.

'Let's look,' said Bonin, his voice down to a whisper.

They approached the door on the left. It was solid and wooden. Bonin went first, his lasrifle cradled in a one-handed grip as he reached for the door's brass handle. Coir moved to his right, his own weapon up and aimed. Hwlan stayed behind Bonin, a grenade ready in his hand.

Bonin threw open the door and rolled inside, coming up onto his knees in a firing crouch. Coir swept in behind him, aiming up. Hwlan had their backs.

'Feth!' Bonin muttered, rising to his feet and lowering his aim. 'Look at this! Bel?'

Beltayn and Dalin scurried in past the scouts.

'Oh my word,' Beltayn gasped.

The chamber was long and high, and slanted slightly to the south halfway along its length. It was lit by the steady amber glow of the wall lights. From floor to roof, the room was lined with shelves, shelves laden with dusty books, manuscripts and matching volumes. Reading tables ran down the middle of the chamber.

'It's… it's a library,' Beltayn said.

They entered, looking around, playing their lamps up into the corner shadows of the roof, where the amber light did not reach. Slow dust billowed and twinkled in the beams of the lamps.

Thousands of books, slates and curling scrolls were stuffed onto the slumping shelves.

'So, not a courtyard then?' asked Bonin.

'No, but quite a discovery,' Beltayn said, peering at the spines of the books on the nearest shelf. 'We have to–'

'We have to find the water,' said Bonin.

'Now wait,' Beltayn said. 'This is–'

'We have to find the water, adj,' Bonin told him. 'Books are books are books. They'll still be here when we're done fighting.'

Beltayn scowled at Dalin. 'Check down there,' Bonin instructed, and Coir and Hwlan went down the room on either side of the reading tables, searching for doors.

'Dead end,' Hwlan called back.

'No other way out,' Coir agreed.

'All right then, the other door,' Bonin ordered, and Coir and Hwlan headed back to the exit.

'We really should check these books,' Dalin began.

'Why?'

'We might learn something about this place,' Dalin said.

Bonin smiled at Dalin. It wasn't a very friendly smile. 'We've learned all we have to. This fething place is a death trap, and we're all going to die here unless we secure some basics like water and a decent perimeter defence. Let's learn about the history of this place later, Trooper Criid, when we're not getting our arses shot off.'

'But–'

'Oh, don't "but" me again, or I'll smack you.'

Dalin shut up quickly.

'The lad's right,' said Beltayn.

'Same thing applies to you, adj,' Bonin told him. 'Hwlan?'

'Ready, Mach.'

Hwlan and Coir had taken up positions either side of the door across the hall.

'Take it,' said Bonin, with a nod.

Hwlan burst through the second door, Coir behind him.

'Feth me! It's an armoury, Mach.'

'A what?'

'An armoury. Come and see.'

Bonin crossed the hallway with Dalin and Beltayn in tow, and entered the second room behind Coir and Hwlan.

Lit by the same amber glow, the long gun room was high-ceilinged and lined with racks. Rows of ancient guns, most of them huge, the size of .50s, waited upright in the wooden racks for long-dead warriors who would never return to use them. The middle space of the room was taken up with armoured bunkers.

Hwlan took one of the old weapons down, grunting with the weight of it. 'What the feth is this?' he asked.

'Las?' Bonin asked.

'Yeah. I think so,' Hwlan replied, opening the action of the gun he was holding. 'Single shot charge, old style, like a las-lock. Feth, this thing is heavy.'

'Wall guns,' said Coir.

'What?' Bonin asked.

'Wall guns,' Coir repeated, taking one down from the racks for himself. Dec Coir was well known in the regiment for his knowledge of antique firearms. He carried a single shot las-lock pistol as a back-up piece.

'Hmm. Big and clumsy. Definitely wall guns,' he said, examining the weapon. 'Rampart guns is another name for them. Big, heavy, long range bastards used for battlement defence.'

'That makes sense,' said Dalin. 'I mean, given the nature of this place.'

Coir nodded. 'The casemates were built for firing these bastards. They were built with an army *armed* with these in mind. I mean, that's what this place was constructed for.'

'To defend against what?' Bonin asked.

'I can't begin to imagine,' said Coir. He was studying the hefty weapon in his hands, intrigued. 'Throne, these would have kicked. And killed. Slow rate of fire, mind you, but the sheer kill power...'

'Ammo?' asked Bonin.

Hwlan had prised open one of the bunkers. It was full of pebbles, brown satin pebbles the size of a human eyeball. 'Is this the ammo?' he asked.

'Yeah, it is,' said Coir, gazing into the open bunker almost sadly, 'but it looks dead, inert. Too long in the box, I guess.'

Dalin took one of the pebbles out. It was heavy. As he held it, it began to glow faintly.

'Feth!' he exclaimed.

'The warmth of your hand is heating up the volatile core,' Coir said. 'Put it down, please, Trooper Criid.'

Dalin put the pebble back down in the bunker, and the light in the pebble died away immediately.

'This still isn't the water,' Bonin said.

'Yeah, but–' Coir began.

'Yeah, but nothing,' said Bonin. 'Put that down. Let's get on.'

Reluctantly, Coir put the rampart gun back into the rack. Hwlan did the same.

Bonin sniffed. 'Let's move towards fresh air,' he suggested.

VI

FURIOUS BLOOD PACT artillery slapped Hinzerhaus hard in the face. Orange flashes of fire, hot and rasping, lit up the southern cliffs as shells struck and burst. Parts of the casing rock blew away like matrix and exposed the hard corner angles of previously buried casemates. Two gunboxes suffered direct hits, and their fortified rockcrete frames cracked wide open. The fury of the barrage forced many of the Ghost defenders back from their firing slits into cover.

Suddenly, only a trickle of defensive fire was falling on the enemy's infantry charge in front of the main gate. The enemy took full advantage.

The first Blood Pact wave finally reached the gatehouse. A second wave rushed in behind them and began to clamber up the lower fortifications of the house's south face. A third wave came up, several dozen of them dragging a huge iron battering ram in across the white dust. They set it against the main hatch, teamed and lashed to forty men, and began to swing it.

The impacts sounded like the chime of a doom bell. Inside the gatehouse, and the long entrance hallway running back to the base chamber, sections of Ghosts waited, crouching against the walls, guns ready, wincing at the sound of every strike. Kolea, Baskevyl and the other company officers tried to keep their men in line.

'Hold steady,' Kolea yelled above the deep, booming clangs. 'Hold steady. They're not going to get past us.'

'The hatch will hold, won't it?' Derin asked.

'Of course it gakking will,' replied Kolea.

Clang! Clang! Clang!

Kolea looked at Baskevyl. 'Get the flamers up,' he said. Baskevyl nodded and turned to see to it.

They could all feel the concussive power of the shells striking the house above them. Dust and grit trickled down from the ceiling with each muffled blast. Some of the men moaned in alarm when excessive spoil poured down. Roof panels split or came away at their corners, as if the cliff above them was about to collapse.

'Keep it together!' Kolea yelled.

The shelling stopped.

The men packed in the tunnel exchanged wide-eyed looks. There was no sound except the trickle of dirt pattering from the roof and the *Clang! Clang! Clang!* of the ram driving against the outer hatch.

'Rawne?' Kolea said into his micro-bead. 'Rawne? Watch out up there. Rawne?'

VII

MAJOR RAWNE COULDN'T hear him. One of the first shells to strike the south face had thrown him off his feet and trashed his micro-bead.

'Give me a link! I need a link right now!' he had yelled to no one in particular as soon as he was back on his feet, and had spent the next few minutes running blindly from casemate to casemate. The air was thick with smoke, and shells were hitting every few seconds. Rawne blundered into panicking Guardsmen in the choked dark, and tried to get them contained. He stumbled through one doorway and saw a gunbox blown open to the sky, forming a broken, blackened cave littered with chunks of human body. Another shell struck nearby, and Rawne reeled back, sprayed with grit.

'Get on your feet!' he yelled. 'Get back to the slits!'

'They're shelling us, sir!' a trooper protested.

'I am fething well aware of that, you idiot! Get back to your position!'

He clambered into another overlook gunbox. The roofline above the gunslot was sagging loosely, internal steel reinforcement exposed through the broken rockcrete. Trapped smoke swirled around the tight confines of the wounded casemate.

'Larks?'

'I'm all right!' Larkin called back. He was dragging Banda's limp body back across the floor of the gunbox.

'Feth! Is she–?' Rawne began.

'Stunned. Just stunned. She'll be all right.'

'Are you all right?' Rawne asked, catching Larkin's arm and helping him move Banda. Blood was streaming from a wound across Larkin's scalp.

'Yes, I'm all right.' Larkin looked at Rawne. 'We're going to die, aren't we?' he said. 'We can't fight this.'

They ducked down as another shell whined in and exploded, perilously close.

'Forget the fething shells,' Rawne said. 'It's the foot troops we need to worry about.'

'Oh, right,' said Larkin, almost laughing.

Rawne ran towards the damaged gunslot and peered out.

'You think I'm kidding?' he asked.

The shelling stopped suddenly. Larkin joined Rawne at the slot and peered out.

'Oh, feth,' he said.

VIII

THE ENEMY WAS coming up the south face of Hinzerhaus, swarming like ants. The distant artillery had been suspended so that it wouldn't vaporise its own assault troops.

The Blood Pact raiders were equipped with spiked, folding ladders, like coils of barbed wire that they shook out before them as they came. The thin anchor-teeth of the ladders bit into the stern, rock face of the house and held firm. As soon as each ladder was secure, crimson-clad raiders came grunting up them towards the lower casemates and gunslits. The ladders squealed and jangled as they dug into the stone beneath the weight of the men mounting them.

Blood Pact warriors clambered up to the first few gunboxes and stormed them. Their buck-tooth axes and sabre-knives made short work of the few, dazed Ghosts they found inside. Gore dripping from their weapons, the raiders began to press in through the lower casemate halls.

Initially deafened and baffled by the shelling, the Ghosts rapidly woke up to the intrusion. Fire fights lit up along the lower halls as outraged Ghosts responded to the masked killers surging into their midst. Daur's company found itself in the thick of the brutal close action, killing raiders as they loomed out of the smoke and attempting to drive them back out through the casemate slits.

'Contact and intrusion!' Daur yelled into his micro-bead. 'Contact and intrusion, level four!'

He pushed his way along the support tunnel, coughing, smelling blood and las-smoke. He was half blind. His eyes were wretched with tears from the fyceline stink. 'Come on, you men!' he bellowed at the figures around him.

They weren't all Ghosts. A scowling grotesk came at him out of the haze and an axe swung towards his throat.

IX

RAWNE PEERED DOWN out of the gunslit. Through the grey pall of smoke, he could see the red-clad figures clattering up the spiked ladders towards him.

He reached out and attempted to push one of the ladders away. It was too deeply dug in, held in place on its spikes by the bodies struggling up it. Las-shots whined past him, fired vertically.

'Larks!' he yelled.

Larkin appeared beside him, throwing the top half of his body out through the damaged gun slot. Larkin aimed his long-las down and fired. The shot punched through the chest of the Blood Pact warrior climbing towards him, and the corpse fell back, knocking the two Archenemy troops below it off the ladder as it dropped. Larkin reloaded and fired again, hanging right out of the slit. He'd aimed his second hot shot at the spiked ladder, and had blown through several rungs and one side of the ladder frame. The remaining upright broke under tension with a loud *ping*, and a large stretch of the ladder tore free. Eight raiders tumbled away into the smoke below.

Larkin had over-extended himself. Arms thrashing, he began to slide. 'Grab me! Grab me for feth's sake!' he cried.

'I've got you,' said Banda, wrapping her arms around his legs and pulling him back through the slot.

'There're more!' Larkin cried.

'I know,' replied Rawne, moving to the slot's lip with a tube charge in his hand. He leaned out and pulled the det-tape.

'Thanks for coming!' he called, and dropped back into cover as the tube charge fell away.

It bounced off the helmet of the Blood Pact warrior uppermost on the second scaling ladder and went off as it spun over his shoulder. The searing blast killed three of the ascending raiders outright, and sheered through the ladder, so that it broke and fell away like an untied rope, casting a dozen more raiders down to their deaths on the rocks below.

Rawne looked at Larkin. 'Is your link working?'

'I think so.'

'Send for me. Authority Two/Rawne. Kill the ladders. Priority.'

Larkin keyed his micro-bead. 'Listen up, you lot...' he began.

X

UPPER WEST SIXTEEN. The name would, in time, be added to the roll call of the Tanith First's most hard-fought and savage actions, and take its place alongside the likes of Veyveyr Gate, Ouranberg or the Fifth Compartment as a name to be remembered and honoured by those who came later.

Gaunt was right in the thick of it. Tunnel warfare was the worst discipline a soldier could know. It was claustrophobic, insane, uncompromising. The confines of the location drove foe into foe, whether they wanted to engage or not. Reaction times dropped to the merest fraction of a second. Everything depended on instinct and reflex, and if either of those things failed a man, he died. It was that simple. There was no margin for error, no space to correct or try again. More than once, Gaunt glimpsed a Ghost miss his first shot or first blow at an enemy foot soldier and die before he could manage a second.

There were no second chances.

Fighting in a box added its own hazards. Not only was there fire, there was deflected fire. Ricochets danced their lethal dance in and out, often caused by the nerve spasm release of a dying man, firing as he fell. Obeying their own occult dynamics, shots also hugged the walls or slid around corners, in apparent defiance of the laws of ballistics.

Gaunt's bolt pistol had serious stopping power and he used it to full effect. Those raiders who came at him were hurled backwards by his bolt rounds, knocking down the raiders at their heels like bowling pins. Where the flow of the fight descended to its most barbaric, the level of straight silver and trench axe, his power sword sliced through arms, blades, helmets and grotesks.

His Ghosts had one advantage. The enemy had effectively penetrated at two points in the summit galleries, which meant they were boxed in with Ghosts on either side of them. As best he could, given the frenetic circumstances, Gaunt pulled his defenders tight, trying to pin and crush the insurgencies. It was a task beyond the limits of his micro-bead, but Karples relayed his commands via Beltayn's powerful caster.

Not that there was much time or opportunity for orders. Gaunt remembered that Hark had once observed a phenomenon he had called fight time. That state ruled now. Gaunt fired, moved forwards, hacked with his blade, and allowed others to come forwards with him and blast at the enemy surge as he reloaded.

Fight time was relentless, breathless, barely any time to think or move, but also slow, like a pict-feed set on frame capture. It was almost hypnotic. Gaunt saw las-rounds glide by him like paper aircraft. He saw arterial spray hanging in the air in undulating droplets. There was no sound any more except the beating of his own heart. He felt a las-round crease his left arm. He watched a bolt-round he had fired centuries before meet a grotesk between the eyes and fold it up like a closing book, pulped flesh and pulverised bone expanding out around it like the petals of a ghastly pink flower. He witnessed a las-round, fired straight up by a man falling on his back, glance off the roof and then walk away down the hallway, deflecting ceiling to floor, ceiling to floor, like a bouncing cursor on a cogitator screen, until it finally buried itself in the neck of a raider.

Crimson beasts, stinking of blood, ran at him, ponderously slow, it seemed, wet tongues poking out of their leering metal lips, blades flashing in the furnace gloom. He cut a head in half with his sword, and shot another raider in the chest.

Then he realised, quite calmly, that this was how he was going to die.

XI

TONA CRIID HAD lost sight of her commander. The fight had become such a storm of confusion she barely had any idea which way she was pointing.

'Gaunt? Where's Gaunt?' she yelled.

The trooper beside her smiled at her and didn't reply.

'Where's Gaunt?'

Still smiling, the trooper slumped against her, his body falling open where it had been split by a fighting axe. She stumbled backwards, spitting rounds from her lasrifle into two raiders who had come out of nowhere. They jerked back, arms flailing, and dropped. Ghosts moved past her. She looked down at the dead Guardsman and wished she could remember his name.

'Forwards! Forwards!' she yelled at the men shoving up around her, and then tagged her micro-bead. 'This is Criid! Where the feth is the commander? We have to protect the commander!'

It was useless. There was no way of imposing order on this madness. The two Ghosts ahead of her crumpled and fell on their faces, killed so fast they hadn't even been able to scream or utter a word. All Criid could see was the grotesk coming for her, sabre-knife raised.

She brought her rifle up and impaled the raider on her straight silver. The raider took a flapping, quivering moment to die, dragging her gun down under his weight. Criid put her left foot against him to try and pluck the blade free.

Something struck her on the side of the head.

It struck her so hard, she slammed sideways into the hallway wall, and bounced off the blood-speckled brown satin panelling.

Her vision went. She tasted iron, heard wild, dulled sounds, knew she was on the floor but–

'Get up!'

'What?' she murmured.

'Get up, girl! Get up! They're all over us!'

'What?' Tona still couldn't see. She knew she ought to be moving, but she'd forgotten how her legs worked.

'Oh, come on!' the voice yelled. 'Is that how a Vervunhive gang-girl fights? Get up!'

Her vision returned. The side of her head felt sticky. She heard the chatter of a lasrifle on auto.

Caffran was standing over her, guarding her, spraying las from the hip into the enemy.

He picked off the last two with perfect aim and bent over her.

'Tona? My love?'

'Caff–'

'Gonna be all right, girl. You took a knock there.'

'Caff?'

She looked up into his eyes. They were as kind as she remembered, as kind as they had been when she had first seen them all those years ago on Verghast.

'You died,' she said, simply.

'How's Dalin?' he asked. 'I've missed him. How's Yoncy?'

'You *died*,' she insisted.

'Sergeant? Sergeant Criid?'

'Caff?'

Berenson was bending over her. 'Are you all right? Can you hear me?'

'Major?'

'I said you've taken a knock. You're dazed. Fall back.'

'I saw Caff,' she said.

'Who's Caff?' he asked. 'Look, fall back. Get yourself to the field station. Criid? Criid?' Berenson looked around. 'Trooper! Someone! Help me here!'

XII

'DOWN HERE!' DALIN yelled. He ran down the short flight of steps towards the glow of morning light. Firm hands grabbed him from behind.

'Don't just rush out there, you little fool!' Bonin hissed in his ear.

'Sorry,' Dalin replied.

'Weapons?' Bonin asked.

'Check,' said Hwlan.

'Check,' said Coir.

'Uh, check,' added Dalin. The three scouts ignored him.

'Let's go, gentlemen,' Bonin invited.

Dalin glanced at Beltayn. 'Follow them,' Beltayn advised.

From the old, worn steps, they advanced out under a carved wooden archway into the open air. The courtyard was paved with grey stones, and surrounded on two sides by wings of the house. The face of the cliff formed the yard's other two sides. The archway they had emerged from was built into a cliff face.

The tinny whine and flat crack of fighting echoed through the open air. Despite that, it was almost tranquil in the courtyard.

'Feth me backwards,' Bonin smiled. 'See that?'

They had all seen it. Nine pallet loads of water drums sat in the middle of the yard. They hadn't arrived cleanly; there was evidence on part of the tiled roof opposite that suggested the heavy cargo load had bounced at least once on its way down. Some drums in the lower part of the cargo had burst on impact, and the courtyard floor was soaked with their run out.

'It's mostly intact,' Beltayn cried.

'Glory fething be,' said Bonin. He ran to the side of the heap, pulled a drum free and unscrewed the cap.

'Drinks on me,' he grinned.

They all came forward. 'Canteen cups, one at a time, come on,' Bonin said.

They each produced their tin cups in turn and Bonin filled them all, careful not to spill a drop from the heavy drum.

The water was the most delicious thing Dalin had ever tasted. He drained his cup too fast.

'No more,' Bonin told him. 'We've been on short rations so long, I let you guzzle and you'll be shitting yourself silly come evening.'

'Besides which,' said Hwlan, 'this has to be shared out.'

'Of course it does,' Beltayn smiled, treasuring his cupful.

'Good job, you two,' Bonin said to Beltayn and Dalin. Then he fell over.

He fell on his face and landed hard across the heap of water drums. He lay still.

'Bonin?' Dalin asked, baffled.

The second shot blew the canteen cup out of Dalin's hand. The third punctured a drum beside Hwlan.

'Contact!' Coir yelled out, raising his weapon. His lasrifle was almost to his shoulder when he abruptly jerked backwards and fell.

Dalin looked up, fumbling for his rifle.

Blood Pact raiders were scurrying over the red-tiled roofs towards the courtyard. Some of them were standing up to shoot. Las-rounds whistled in at them. Dalin heard the dull *thukk* as more drums punctured.

'Oh no you don't,' he growled, and returned fire.

Day ten, continued,
All hell is breaking loose without me. Casualties are flooding in. Someone just told me we were under attack from both sides of the objective.

I can't stand the helplessness. Tried to get up just now, but A.C. ordered me back into my bed. In truth, I don't think I would've got very far. Pain more than I can manage.

I believe A.C. may have stuck me with something to keep me quiet. Feeling quite

- Field journal, V.H. fifth month, 778.

TWELVE

The Last Bloody Minutes

I

THE RAM BEAT against the outer hatch, heavy and relentless. Through the gatehouse and along the entrance tunnel, the assembled Ghosts waited. There was no chatter, no whispering. The men sat in cold silence, every one of them flinching slightly at each beat that rang against the hatch. The house lights faded and came back, faded and came back.

Baskevyl realised they were doing so in time to the beat of the ram. Though the shelling had ceased, dust and grit continued to dribble down from the roof in places. The little falls made scratching, scuttling sounds, sounds that were unpleasantly familiar to Baskevyl. A little voice in his skull told him it wasn't a ram beating at the gate. It was the worm, flexing and striking with its massive, armoured head, trying to dig its way in.

Kolea had brought the flamers to the front. The gatehouse reeked of stirred promethium. The small blue ignitor flames burning at the snout of each weapon made a serpentine hissing. Baskevyl could see the tension in the flame-troopers, the slight twitch and shiver in their limbs.

The ram struck again.

'The frame's buckling!' someone cried from the front of the gatehouse.

'Hold the line!' Kolea called. 'Keep your formation and stand ready!'

'It's definitely buckling!'

Baskevyl looked at Kolea. 'Don't let them past you,' he said quietly.

'I won't if you won't,' Kolea replied.

II

DAUR'S GUN WAS dry. He'd drained the entire cell with one long pull on the trigger. There was no one left alive in the support tunnel except him. The bodies of raiders lay all around him, including the bastard that had nearly taken Daur's head off. He'd just experienced the most intense fifteen seconds of his life.

He shook himself out of his daze, ejected the clip and slammed in a fresh one. Gunfire rattled and cracked around adjacent halls and chambers. He moved forwards.

The tunnel joined a main hallway. That too was littered with bodies and fogged with smoke. The ugly, jumbled corpses were Ghosts and Blood Pact, side by side in death. *Only in death,* Daur thought.

He snapped around as figures appeared. He saw Meryn moving up the hall with men of his own company and some from Daur's.

'Daur!'

'What's the situation?'

'I was about to ask you that,' Meryn snapped. He was filthy and there were beads of blood across his cheek. 'Where have you been?'

'Busy,' Daur replied.

'They're coming up the fething walls,' Meryn said. 'Rawne wants every man available to the gunboxes to keep them off. We've just cleared lower eight and nine.'

'All right. You keep moving that way. I'll take anyone from G Company with me and head back to east seven.'

Meryn nodded. 'See you in the happy place, Daur.'

Daur took his men back down the tunnel. They heard a flurry of rapid fire behind them. Meryn's group had met something coming the other way.

Haller looked at Daur. They'd known each other for a lifetime, since their days in the ranks of the Vervun Primary. Daur understood what the look meant.

'We keep moving,' he told Haller. 'They have to handle it.'

They emerged onto lower seven, a stretch of hall that connected a row of overlook casemates. Sounds of shooting rang out of each casemate hatchway. Peering into the first, Daur saw Ghosts at the slot, firing down at sharp angles.

'Spread out,' he told his men. 'Go where you're needed. Keep them out.'

III

'Can I just say how much I'm not enjoying this?' Larkin remarked.

'No,' said Rawne.

Along with Banda, they'd been holding the overlook for a full ten minutes since the ladders first came up. It was nasty work. They had to lean right out of the gunslit to fire at the raiders below or knock ladders off with charges. Leaning out made a person vulnerable. Snap shots kept screeching up past them from the base of the cliff. Larkin had been creased twice, and Rawne had taken a deflection in the front of his chest armour that had split the plate in half.

In the last few minutes they had been joined by two of Rawne's men and a Belladon from Sloman's company. That allowed them to rotate at the slot and reload, and still keep the pressure on.

'I think they're losing momentum,' Rawne said.

'You think?' replied Larkin.

'A storm assault needs momentum, otherwise it just fizzles out. If they'd had us in the first few minutes, they'd be in control now, but they didn't.'

'They look like they're still trying to me,' Banda put in, pausing to reload. 'We need more ammo. The bag's almost empty.'

Larkin limped towards the door of the casemate. He'd called twice in the last ten minutes for a runner, but there had been no sign of Ventnor, or anyone else. All the other overlooks and boxes on their level were packed with Ghosts free firing from the slits, and the ammo drain was considerable.

'Ventnor?' he yelled. 'Ammo here! Runner!'

He waited for a moment, and then Ventnor came into sight, lugging a heavy canvas sack.

'What do you need?'

'Standards and specials, and a few barrels.'

'No barrels,' Ventnor replied, pulling a few clips of standard from his sack. 'I sent Vadim down to the stockpile ten minutes ago for barrels, but he hasn't come back. There's a lot of fighting in the lower levels. The bastards got inside.'

Larkin nodded. 'I trust we booted them back out again?'

'It's a work in progress,' Ventnor replied.

'What about up top?'

Ventnor shrugged. 'I haven't heard anything, except that it's hell on legs. Someone said–'

'Someone said what?'

'Nothing, Larks.'

'Someone said what?'

Ventnor sighed. 'I dunno. Someone said Gaunt was down.'

'Is that a joke?'

'No. There was a major frenzy in upper west sixteen, that's what I heard. Gaunt was in the meat of it, as usual. And, well, he didn't walk away.'

'Where did you hear this?'

'Ammo runner I know on eight heard it from a bloke who'd heard it from this other bloke who'd been on stretcher duty coming down from the summit. One of the wounded had told this bloke and–'

Larkin held up his hand. 'That kind of story, eh? Don't spread it, Ventnor. It's wrong and it's bad for the men. Now get on. I hear other boxes calling for you.'

Ventnor nodded.

'No barrels?' Larkin added as Ventnor moved off.

'Sorry.'

'Then you'd better find me something to shoot with!' Larkin yelled after him.

Clutching the ammo packs in his arms, he turned to re-enter the overlook.

'He *is* dead,' said a voice. Larkin froze. He knew the voice, and it made him gulp in fear. He forgot how to breathe. He shut his eyes. 'Gaunt, he is dead,' the voice went on, low and soft. 'We know, because we are the ones who've been sent to get him. Sure as sure.'

Larkin opened his eyes. There was nobody there. Shaking, he backed into the overlook.

IV

DORDEN TOOK A second to breathe deeply. The field station was in a state of pandemonium. The rate of casualties coming in through triage was way beyond their capacity to cope. It broke his heart to see these broken men, the last of his kind, carried in alongside the comrades they had made in the years after Tanith.

Foskin's last estimate was two hundred and seventy-two injured, of which thirty-eight were critical. The number was rising with every passing minute. Men were going to die because Dorden couldn't help them fast enough. They'd already had to open up a second chamber to accommodate the waiting wounded, and a third to house the dead.

I am too old to witness this, Dorden thought, so old, this is too painful to bear. I should have died years ago, with Mikal, with my dear son. That would have ended this pain before it overcame me.

A stretcher arrived in front of him, and Dorden shoved his anguish aside. 'Where do you want her, doc?' asked one of the bearers, panting and sweating with effort.

Dorden looked down. Tona Criid lay on the stretcher, unconscious, the side of her head matted with blood.

'Oh Throne,' Dorden said. 'Here, over here!'

The bearers slid Criid onto a bunk and hurried away with their stretcher rolled up. Going back for more, Dorden thought.

He checked the side of Criid's limp head carefully. It wasn't as bad as it had first appeared, thank the fates. She'd be all right, provided the wound was cleaned and properly tended.

'Tolin! I need you here!' Curth yelled frantically from the other side of the station. A man was screaming a deep, dire pain-scream.

'A moment!'

'Now, Dorden!'

'Can I help?' asked a voice beside him.

Dorden glanced around. Zweil stood there. Like the medicaes, the old ayatani priest had been brought to the station for the usual duties. He had a flask of blessed water in his thin hands and a look of grief burdening his eyes.

'There are men who need your rites, Zweil,' Dorden said.

'The dead will stay dead until I get to them. The living need more urgent help. Is there anything I can do?'

Dorden nodded. 'Take this and this. Bathe her wound and clean away all the blood and dirt. Do it gently, and use that stuff sparingly. We're low on fluids.'

'Tell me about it. I'm quite parched.'

Dorden hurried away. Zweil knelt down and began to clean Criid's head wound.

She stirred.

'You're all right, Tona. You're all right now,' Zweil crooned.

'He's dead,' she murmured.

'Who is?'

'He's dead.'

'Who's dead?'

'Gaunt,' she breathed.

'What did she say?' called the trooper in the next cot along. 'What did she say, father?'

'She's delirious, Twenzet, calm yourself.'

'She just told you Gaunt was dead, didn't she?' Twenzet cried.

The noise in the station dropped away. Heads turned in their direction. Muttering began.

'Get on with it!' Zweil growled. 'She's delirious.'

Activity resumed, but there was an undercurrent that hadn't been there before.

'How delirious is delirious?' Hark asked.

Zweil looked up. Hark stood behind him, wrapped in a sheet. He was not entirely steady.

'I'm not a doctor,' Zweil replied. 'Should you be up?'

'You're not a doctor,' Hark said.

'She said Gaunt was dead,' Twenzet said.

'You can shut up,' Hark told him.

Zweil rose to his feet stiffly and looked up into Hark's eyes. 'She's delirious,' he said quietly, 'but if she's also right, well, Viktor, we knew this day would come. We will manage. We will cope. We thought Ibram was dead on Gereon for a year or more, but he came back. He's hard to kill.'

'But not immortal.'

Zweil nodded. 'Then you'd better start preparing what you'll say to the men.'

Hark was breathing hard. 'I wouldn't know where to begin. You're right. We thought he was dead on Gereon, and the regiment grieved and moved on. It won't be that easy a second time. Not if there's–'

'If there's what?'

'A body.'

'Ah,' said Zweil.

'Missing presumed dead on Gereon was one thing. There was always hope, and that hope was fulfilled. But here…'

Zweil looked at him. 'It will break us, won't it?'

'It will break us,' said Hark, 'and we will die.'

V

MAGGS COULD SEE her, moving amongst the Blood Pact raiders at the far end of the hall, her long black skirts swishing through the smoke. The old dam with the meat-wound face had come to them. She had come to claim some-one. Maggs prayed it wasn't him.

The fire fight along the cloche tunnel was frenetic and fast. Maggs was low on ammo and had been forced to switch from his favoured setting of full auto to conserve. He hugged himself against the bottom of a short flight of steps and rattled away at Blood Pact storm troops, ten metres distant, obscured by drifting smoke. He aced one, that was certain, maybe a second.

His skin crawled. He'd lost sight of the old dam in the black lace dress, but he could still hear her footsteps above the gunfire, and feel the chill of her breath.

Leyr dropped in beside him and started to fire.

'How many?' Leyr asked.

'I counted eight, but you can bet your arse there're more,' Maggs replied.

'Did you hear?'

'Hear what?'

'Ten minutes ago on upper west sixteen. Gaunt.'

'What about him?'

'They got him, Wes.'

'Shit, are you sure?'

'It's what I hear,' Leyr said. 'It was murder up there, and he was right in it.'

'Who saw it?'

Leyr shrugged.

'It's wrong,' said Maggs. 'They're wrong.'

They began firing again.

They got him. Leyr's words circled Maggs's head. *No*, they *hadn't. She had. That was why she was here. She only came when a truly great man was destined to fall.*

The old dam with the meat-wound face had made her kill and they would all suffer as a result.

VI

DALIN THREW HIMSELF into cover behind the heaped pallets of the water drop. He hated to do it, because it would only draw fire onto the drums, but there was nowhere else to go in the courtyard. He fired back at the crimson raiders scurrying along the rooftop. He kept missing. He was being too hasty with his aim.

Coir was dead, dead on his back on the courtyard stones with a black pool of blood surrounding his head like a halo. Bonin was dead too.

Hwlan and Beltayn had dragged themselves behind the water canisters with Dalin and were hammering off return fire.

The worst part of it all, it seemed to Dalin, was the spatter of water leaking out of the punctured drums.

Hwlan rose a little, took a decent line, and smacked two of the raiders off the roof with squeeze-bursts. Another turned, exposed, and Dalin caught him with a group of three shots.

There was a loud bang. Dalin looked around, wondering where the noise had come from. He saw that a smoking hole had appeared in the tiled roof beside the south-east corner of the courtyard buildings. Blood Pact warriors were dropping into it.

They'd blown the roof with grenades to gain entry. They were inside the buildings.

'Watch it!' Dalin yelled. 'They're in! They're going to be coming from the yard doorways now!'

'I see it!' Hwlan called back.

Five Blood Pact raiders emerged from the yard's corner doorway, firing and running out into the open. Their shots forced Dalin, Beltayn and Hwlan to duck. Rounds smacked soundly into the drums of the precious water cargo. Water spurted.

Gunfire ripped into the raiders from the side, dropping three of them. Ludd, Eszrah and Scout Trooper Mklane appeared at the rear archway, blasting away. One of Eszrah's reynbow bolts took a raider right off his feet. Hwlan, Beltayn and Dalin immediately resumed their shooting from behind the water cargo.

A vicious gun battle kicked off between the two groups of Ghosts and the Blood Pact on the roof and inside the corner buildings. Las-shots criss-crossed and deflected off walls.

'Can we rush them?' Ludd asked Mklane in the shadow of the archway.

'Rush them? And you've been insane since when?'

'That water is vital!' Ludd protested. He paused. 'Where's Eszrah?' he exclaimed.

The Nihtgane had run out into the open. Ignoring the fire coming his way, he dashed to a wall and scaled it, hand over hand, his fingers and toes gripping the edges of the stones. He hauled himself up onto the roof and began to run along it straight towards the enemy.

They fired at him, bemused by his efforts and his native appearance.

Still running sure-footedly across the tiles, Eszrah swung his reynbow up and shot it. A raider went down, and slid clumsily off the roof. Eszrah reloaded, still running, and shot again. Another raider doubled up and fell backwards. Eszrah had shot two more of them dead before he reached the hole in the roof.

'He's making us look useless!' Hwlan roared, and got up, blazing away at the enemy. Dalin joined in, and together they shot another three Blood Pact raiders off the roof line. By then, Eszrah had dropped down into the hole.

'Come on!' Hwlan cried.

They left cover and ran towards the far corner of the yard. Ludd and Mklane quit the archway and came with them. In the corner doorway, they met two Blood Pact, but Mklane and Hwlan dealt with them quickly.

'Stay back!' Hwlan spat, looking at Dalin, Ludd and Beltayn. 'Guard the water!'

'But–'

'Guard the water!'

'May I remind you–' Ludd growled.

'No, you may not!' Mklane replied.

Ludd's head sank. 'Just go, then,' he said, bitterly.

Hwlan and Mklane pushed on. Dalin, Ludd and Beltayn returned to the water dump.

Bonin suddenly got to his feet.

'What did I miss?' he asked.

They stared at him.

'What?' he asked, reaching round to touch the back of his neck. His fingertips came away bloody.

'Oh. I got shot, didn't I?' he asked, and sat down again hard. Dalin ran to him and pulled out a pack of field dressings.

'That's nasty. Why aren't you dead?'

'I dunno, boy. Lucky?' Bonin suggested and passed out.

Dalin tried to make him comfortable.

'What about Coir?' he called out. Ludd was bending over the other scout. He shook his head. 'He's gone. Poor bastard.'

'Something's awry,' announced Beltayn behind them.

'What did you say, adj?' Ludd asked, searching Coir's pockets for his tags.

'Move!' Beltayn was yelling. 'Get into cover!' Dalin and Ludd turned, struggling to rise.

Four Blood Pact warriors were charging out across the courtyard towards them, roaring death cries in their ghastly alien tongue. They were big brutes, their shabby clothes stained with blood, their masks curved in cruel grins. They were already firing.

Ludd felt the super heated shock of a bolt hiss past his cheek. He was fumbling with his weapon. Beltayn, defiantly standing his ground, was shooting his autopistol at the oncoming raiders, apparently oblivious to the squall of las-rounds that miraculously streaked past on either side of him. Dalin saw the adjutant kill one of the raiders, and knew with sad certainty that it was the last thing Beltayn would ever do.

Dalin tried to squeeze off a burst, but was lurched violently sideways as a las-bolt splintered off his chest plating. The shocking impact knocked him off his feet and punched the air out of his lungs. He was on his back, looking back up at the colourless sky. Las-rounds whipped past above him. Rolling, gasping, he heard the brittle crack of sustained las-fire, accompanied by a bark of pain. That was Beltayn gone, surely Ludd too. Dalin tried to get up, gulping air into his winded body, braced for the kill shots he knew were about to find him.

He rose in time to see one of the raiders flopping over on his back, a hole through his chest. A second was already down, drumming his heels spastically against the flagstones as the life left him.

The remaining raider turned in time to meet a streaking las-round face on. His head blew apart in a cloud of blood and metal, and his body dropped.

'Any more for any gn… gn… gn… more?' Merrt inquired, walking out of the archway with O34TH in his hands.

Ludd nodded at him. 'Never thought I'd be pleased to see you, trooper,' he said, wide-eyed and pale with shock.

'No one ever is, sir,' Merrt replied, 'in my gn...gn... gn... experience.'

'You old bastard,' Beltayn chuckled, slowly lowering his pistol and blinking in stunned disbelief as he realised that not a single part of him had been shot off.

'Good timing, Merrt,' said Dalin with a broad grin of relief.

Merrt nodded back and patted the stock of his weapon. 'That's more like it,' he whispered.

VII

THEY WERE ALL dead. Every single Blood Pact trooper that Hwlan and Mklane found was stone dead, with a crude iron quarrel transfixing him. As the two scouts advanced through that unexplored part of the old house, they counted thirteen kills.

'Got to hand it to the Nihtgane,' Hwlan said.

'You fething have,' Mklane agreed.

A shadow twitched in front of them. Hwlan and Mklane brought their weapons up.

It was Eszrah.

'Peace, soules,' he said. 'Yts dunne.'

VIII

THE RAM STRUCK the outer hatch with a hammer to anvil shock.

Then silence fell.

The Ghosts waiting in the gatehouse entry shifted nervously.

'Stay ready, stay ready,' Kolea whispered to them.

He waited. All noise had dropped away, even the distant rattle of gunfire. The anxious breathing of the assembled men became the dominant sound, like the soft rustle of sliding material, like a lace dress brushing against the floor.

Nothing happened. Gol Kolea waited a moment longer until nothing had definitely happened again.

He glanced at Baskevyl and raised his eyebrows.

Baskevyl clicked his bead. 'This is Gate. Can I get anyone on overlook, anyone?'

'This is Daur, overlook nine, copy.'

'We're blind here, Ban. What can you see?'

There was a pause.

'Not much, Gate. Dust is suddenly coming up extra hard. But they're falling back en masse. Repeat, the enemy has been driven off.'

'Understood, good news. Thank you.'

Baskevyl looked back at Kolea.

'I think we got off lightly,' he said.

Day ten, continued,

I barely care to maintain this journal any more, but I know I am bound to. I don't know what to write.

I don't know what I'm going to say. Z. was perfectly correct. I have to say something. I have to say the right thing.

~~I can't believe~~ I find I have some difficulty fully appreciating this circumstance. I should be coping better. I have been well trained, and ~~prt~~ part of that training was to prepare for this. I suppose it may be the pain I'm experiencing, but it's weakness to blame my body for something my mind can't do.

I simply don't know what I'm going to say. I don't know if there's ~~anything~~ anything I can say to make this any better.

I need to be sure. I need to see a body, I suppose.

— Field journal, V.H. fifth month, 778.

THIRTEEN

Dead and Dying

I

'THIS AREA'S NOT secure!' Varaine called out. All around, men were coughing in the accumulated smoke, or moaning and weeping where they lay.

'Look at my face,' Dorden told Varaine as he walked past.

'Doctor!'

'You heard him, Varaine,' Rawne growled, following Dorden down the ruined upper hallway.

Night, the night of the tenth day, was closing in, and the dust was up outside. The wind swirled around the cloche domes and squealed in through the slits of hastily closed shutters.

With the shutters on the summit levels closed, they were locked in with the after-stink of battle. A trapped stench built up quickly in the armoured hallways, a smell composed of blood, smoke, fyceline haze, piss and burned meat. Rawne wrinkled his nose and wrapped his cloak up tight. Dorden, without breaking stride, popped a surgical mask over his nose and mouth.

The medicae was walking quickly, amazingly quickly for a man so old.

'You don't have to do this,' said Rawne.

'I fancy I do. I'm senior medicae regimentum.'

'Then slow down,' said Rawne.

'I don't think I will,' Dorden replied.

'Slow down for me, then,' complained Zweil, lagging behind them.

Dorden paused and allowed the old priest to catch up. The old man took the older man's arm.

'He'll laugh when he sees our faces,' Zweil said.

'Of course he will,' Dorden replied, his unsmiling mouth hidden by his mask.

* * *

II

THE SUMMIT LEVELS of the fortress had been devastated. Ignoring the mounting storm outside, men from five of the Ghost companies were attempting to clear and secure the levels. The raiders had been driven out after the most brutal of efforts, but pockets remained. Distant, sporadic gunfire echoed sharply down the hallways.

The satin brown panels on the walls were gouged and scored. Some had been blown away, revealing bare rock. Half the lights had been shot out. Bodies littered the ground, piled high in places. Corpsmen were recovering the friendly dead and the few remaining injured. Armed Ghosts with lamp-packs moved through the devastation, killing anything that moved and wasn't one of their own with quick, sure shots from their laspistols. Smoke wove shapes in the lamp beams. Condensation, stained pink, dripped off the steaming ceiling plates. Blood coagulated in pools at the foot of steps, or dried black as it dribbled slowly down the wall panels.

'How many, do you think?' Zweil asked.

Rawne shrugged. 'If we've lost four hundred, we should count ourselves lucky.'

'We're going to lose half that without water and better medical supplies,' Dorden said, still walking. 'The wounded are going to die quickly. Add that to your tally.'

'It's not a tally I started, Dorden,' Rawne replied.

Dorden didn't reply. He kept walking.

III

MAGGS HEARD SLOW, shuffling steps approaching along the hallway. His eyes were sore with the smoke. His heart ached.

Come on, then, if you're coming.

'Put that away, Maggs,' said Rawne.

'Sorry, sir. Can't be too careful. We think we've driven them all out, but there may be some survivors.'

'Understood. This is upper west sixteen?'

'Sir, yes sir. It's… it's a mess.'

'We'll see for ourselves, lad,' Dorden told Maggs, patting him on the arm as he pushed on.

IV

FAMOUS BATTLES DID not leave dignified remains. That had always been Tolin Dorden's experience. Battle, under any circumstance, was a savage, thrashing mechanism that ripped bodies asunder indiscriminately and left an unholy mess for men like him to clear up.

The sort of battles that might win a place in the records – famous battles – well, they were the worst. Dorden had found, to his distress, that any combat that was destined to be remembered and celebrated left in its immediate wake the most atrocious debris of all.

The rumours had already begun to spread: upper west sixteen, a place of heroes, toughest fight there ever was, locked in the tunnels, man to man, blade to blade. Dorden knew there would be more stories later on, and maybe decorations to cement their authenticity. Upper west sixteen had been a finest hour for the Ghosts, a make or break that would be honoured for as long as the regiment existed.

There was nothing heroic about the scene that greeted him.

The stretch of hallway was a charnel house. It looked as if a mad vivisectionist had gone to work and then burned all of his findings. The air was filled with steam and smoke. The smoke issued from the burning corpses and the steam from the wet. The floor was coated several centimetres deep with blood and mushed tissue.

Dorden took the lamp-pack from Rawne. Zweil moaned and covered his nose with a handkerchief. The lamp beam moved. There was not a single intact body. Bodies lay burned to a crisp, grinning out of blackened, heat-stiffened faces. Bodies lay burst like meat sacks, trailing loops of pungent yellow intestine across the soaked floor. Parts of bodies littered the floor space: a hand, a chopped off foot in a boot, a chunk of flesh, the side of a face, half a grotesk.

'Feth take you and your war,' Dorden whispered.

'It's not my war,' Rawne began.

'I wasn't talking to you.'

There had been flamers, at the end. Parts of the hallway were burned back down to the rock, and blood had cooked to sticky treacle in places. The soles of their boots adhered unpleasantly as they advanced.

Ghosts were picking through the dead, searching with lamp-packs and – once in a while – firing rounds. Dorden was fairly sure it wasn't just the Blood Pact they were finishing cleanly.

Mercy is mercy, he told himself.

'Can you help me?' asked a voice. It was Major Berenson. He had been shot through the right shoulder and his arm was hanging limply.

Dorden moved towards him. 'Let me see–'

'Not me, medicae. *Him.*'

Berenson nodded down at the man slumped beside him on a pile of corpses. The man had lost both legs to a chainsword or the like. The exploded remains of a vox-caster set was still attached to his back.

Dorden bent down. 'Kit!' he yelled. 'Tourniquets! Don't waste your time, medicae,' whispered Karples, blood leaking out of his mouth. 'I know I'm done.'

'I'll be the judge of that,' Dorden replied, reaching out for the medical pack Rawne handed to him.

'I am not a stupid man,' Karples gasped. 'I know I can't be saved. Is there an officer here? A Tanith officer?'

Rawne knelt down and bent in close. 'I'm Tanith.'

'He deserves a medal.'

'Who?'

'Your– *guh*! Your colonel-commissar,' Karples gurgled. 'He led the way, all the way. I have never seen so much–'

'So much what?'

Karples opened his mouth. Blood rolled out of it like lava from a volcano.

'Karples!' Berenson cried out.

'Shame,' sputtered Karples. 'Shame to give a medal posthumously.'

'What are you saying?' Rawne exclaimed.

Karples didn't answer. He was dead.

V

MAGGS LED THEM on by the light of the lamp-pack fixed under his rifle muzzle. They wandered past Ghosts despairing and weeping as they searched for evidence of the living.

A figure moved in the dark under a cloche dome ahead of them. Maggs started, raising his weapon. He saw a meat-wound face and a black lace dress.

He was about to fire when Zweil rammed his rifle aside.

'You idiot!' Zweil yelled. 'That's Varl!'

VI

'IT WAS SOMETHING,' Varl said. He was so completely covered in blood, it looked as if he had been deliberately painted. The whites of his eyes seemed very white against the red, the pupils very black. He was shaking. Dorden helped him to sit down.

'Where are you hit?' Dorden asked.

'I don't think I am,' Varl said. His voice was oddly quiet. He looked up at Rawne.

'It was going to happen one day, wasn't it?' he asked.

Rawne made no reply.

'What happened?' Zweil asked. 'Son?'

Varl shrugged. 'I can't really tell it as a story. It was all so mad, everything happening at once. I know he was hit. He was beside me and he was hit. I heard him cry out. He told me to keep going. Next thing... next thing I know, he's gone down. I tried to protect him, but I got pushed back down the hall by the bodies shoving forwards.'

Varl wiped his mouth. 'When we regained ground, he wasn't there any more. It was all a bit confused, but then I saw him. I saw him. The enemy had him. Six of them were just carrying his body away. I suppose they recognised his rank pins and decided to take a trophy. That's what I thought at the time.'

He shook his head sadly. 'I wasn't having that. I fething well wasn't having that. I went at them, me and a couple of the lads. We really got into it. It was just a blur for a bit. Then I saw him again. They were lifting him out through one of the shutters.'

Varl stopped talking.

'Finish the story,' said Rawne in a voice that seemed as old and tired as the house around them.

'I followed them,' Varl said bitterly. 'I fought my way in and followed them out of the shutter onto the peak top. The dust was up. I could barely see at first. There was fighting still going on in and out of the cloches. They were lugging him over onto their climbing ropes to carry him down the cliff. That was when I saw why. He was alive. He was still alive. He saw me. I tried to get to him, but there were too many of them. They were dragging him down, they had a rope on him. I think he knew what was going on. I think he knew what kind of fate awaited him if they took him away.'

Varl looked up at the men listening to him. 'He shouted to me. I don't know what he said. He still had his sword. Somehow he still had it. He killed one of them with it, but they were all over him. So he... he took his sword and cut the ropes.'

No one spoke.

'That was it,' said Varl. 'The whole lot of them just went. He took them all with him. They just went back over the edge and that was it.'

'Are you sure?' Rawne asked. 'Are you sure it was him?'

Varl lifted something up. They'd all assumed it was his lasrifle he'd been carrying, but it wasn't. It was the power sword of Hieronymo Sondar.

'This was left on the ledge, right on the edge of the cliff,' Varl said. Tears were running down his face, making tracks of white skin in the plastering blood. 'Gaunt's dead.'

Elikon M.P., Elikon M.P., this is Nalwood, this is
Nalwood. Reporting loss in action of commanding officer.
Repeat, commanding officer regimental has perished.
Objective remains secure at this time.

Nalwood out. (transmission ends)

- Transcript of vox message, fifth month, 778.

FOURTEEN

Death Songs

I

It took another four hours to make Hinzerhaus secure. A scattered handful of the Blood Pact, unable to retreat with their main forces, laid low in sub-chambers and the dark ends of lonely galleries, and dished out hell to any search teams that discovered them. None died without a bloody scrap. Those were the cruellest Ghost fatalities, Rawne thought. The battle was done and still his men were dying.

His men. The thought made him light-headed. After all this time, they were his men now.

II

As the night drew out, Jago's furious wind screamed around the house, unleashing the worst dust storm the bad rock had yet inflicted on them. Dust invaded through the many broken and damaged shutters, despite efforts to seal them. The wind moaned along the hallways and galleries, clearing out the smoke, making men shiver. It sounded like grief, like the moaning despair of a widow or an orphan.

Somewhere in the noise, late in the night, Tanith pipes began to play. Hark heard them calling, plaintive and clear. His bed had been shifted to a side chamber when the field station had become full. Pain had overcome him, he'd stood for too long. The flesh of his back throbbed.

When he heard the pipes, he tried to rise. A hand touched his shoulder gently and a voice urged him to lay still.

'I can hear the music,' he said.

'It's Caober,' said Ana Curth.

'Caober doesn't play,' Hark said. 'No one in the Tanith plays the pipes any more.'

'Caober had an old set,' she said, 'and he's playing them now.'

Hark listened again. He realised it wasn't the same music that had been haunting him. It wasn't very good. There were bum notes and poor shifts of key. It was the work of someone who hadn't played the pipes in a long time.

He was playing the old tune, the old Tanith marching song, but he was playing it so slowly, it was a dirge, a lament.

'They all know,' Hark said.

'Everyone knows,' said Curth.

III

RAWNE WALKED INTO the room that had been Gaunt's office. Charts lay on the desk, and Gaunt's pack was leaning against the wall. A few personal items lay around: a data-slate, a button-brush, a tin of metal polish, a tin mug. A bedroll was laid out neatly on the small cot. Under the cot, by one of the legs, lay a pair of socks in desperate need of darning.

Rawne put the power sword down on the desk. Then he sat down heavily. He picked up the tin mug and set it on the desk in front of him. He took out his water bottle, unscrewed the cap, and half-filled the cup with water.

They had water now, a tiny little success almost lost in the day's bad business. Ludd and Beltayn had been so proud of their achievement. Rawne had taken no pleasure in wiping the smiles off their faces and the triumph out of their hearts.

Gangs of Ghosts had spent three hours lugging the water drums into the house from the courtyard. A great deal had been lost, but there was enough for full rations, enough for washing wounds and cleaning bodies, enough to make up eyewash to treat the sore and dust-blind.

Rawne took a sip. The water tasted of disinfectant, of Munitorum drums, of nothing at all.

There was a knock at the door.

'Come.'

Baskevyl looked in. 'Company reports are coming through, sir,' he said. 'Casualty lists and defence reports.'

'Field them for me, please,' said Rawne. 'Gather them all in and then report to me.'

Baskevyl nodded. He hadn't said a thing about Gaunt all night, nor commented on Rawne's elevation to command. Under other circumstances, Baskevyl might have had every right to be considered. But Rawne knew that Baskevyl understood that it had to be him. It had to be Tanith.

'Berenson would like a moment,' Baskevyl said.

'Ask him to wait, please.'

'Sir.' Baskevyl closed the door behind him.

Rawne took another sip of water. He was numb, and painfully aware that he had no idea what he was supposed to do now. It was hard to think.

'Thanks a lot,' he said to the power sword on the desk, speaking to it as if it was Gaunt. 'Thanks so very much for leaving me to deal with this shit.'

Rawne had no expectations of a happy ending anymore. Another assault like the one they had just been through would probably finish them. Gaunt had informed Rawne of Van Voytz's instructions. *Keep them busy*. That amounted to *stay there and die*.

There was another knock.

'Go away!' Rawne yelled.

Hlaine Larkin limped into the chamber and closed the door behind him.

'Are you deaf?' Rawne growled.

Larkin shook his head. 'Just disobedient,' he replied. He came over to the desk and sat down facing Rawne. His prosthetic was clearly rubbing sore, because he winced with every step and sighed as he sat.

'Finish your water,' he said.

Rawne hesitated, and then swallowed the last of the water in the cup.

'Is there a point to you being here?' Rawne asked.

'A point? No. An angel responsible? I'd have to think so. You and me, Eli. There aren't many of us left now. Fewer with each passing day. Do you remember the Founding Fields, outside Tanith Magna?'

'Yes.'

'Seems so long ago,' Larkin said, pulling a tin cup out of his pocket.

'It was a long time ago, you fething idiot.'

Larkin chuckled. 'That row of tents. There was me and Bragg, and you, Feygor, Corbec. All set for a life in the Guard, we were. Young, stupid and full of piss and vinegar. Ready to set the galaxy burning.'

Rawne smiled slightly.

'Ready to set the galaxy burning and follow some off-world fether called Gaunt into the war. Now look at us. Bragg's gone, long gone, Feygor, dear old Colm, who always seemed like he'd live forever. Feth it, I'm not even here as completely as I'd have liked.'

Rawne's smile broadened.

'Just that little row of tents,' Larkin went on, pulling something else out of his jacket pocket, 'and we're all that's left of it. Does that make us lucky, or the unluckiest ones of all?'

'My money's on the latter,' said Rawne.

Larkin nodded and unstoppered the old bottle he'd produced. He poured a measure into each of the two tin cups.

'What's that?' Rawne asked.

'The really good stuff,' Larkin replied.

Rawne picked up his cup and sniffed it dubiously. 'That's sacra,' he said.

'That's not just sacra,' Larkin replied. 'Taste it.'

Rawne took a sip. A haunted smile transfixed his face. 'You old bastard,' he said. 'You kept a bottle of Bragg's recipe all this time.'

'No,' said Larkin, 'but if I told you where it really came from, you wouldn't believe me.' He took a sip. 'This is special stuff, for special occasions.'

'Who are we drinking to?' Rawne asked, getting to his feet with his cup in his hand.

Larkin got up to face him. A traditional Tanith toast took three parts.

'Old Ghosts,' said Larkin.

They clinked the cups together and drank.

'Staying alive,' said Rawne, and they clinked again. The stuff went down so smoothly, like velvet and liquid ice.

Larkin and Rawne looked at one another.

'Ibram Gaunt,' they both said at the same time.

'May the Emperor protect his mortal soul,' Larkin added.

They clinked again and emptied their cups.

IV

RAWNE WAS ASLEEP on the cot that had been Gaunt's. He didn't stir as Eszrah slipped into the room. The Nihtgane walked over to the desk and sat down. He stared at the power sword lying across the desk top.

It was the dead time before dawn. The wind was swirling around the fortress. Nahum Ludd had carefully explained to Eszrah what had happened, using those pieces of the partisan's ancient language that he'd studiously endeavoured to learn. Ludd's eyes had been red and tearful.

Eszrah had simply nodded and made no reaction. He had walked away softly and left Ludd to his misery.

Sleepwalkers showed no emotion. It was part of their way. There was no weeping, no grief, no mourning for a Gereon Nihtgane. Such behaviour was a waste of time.

Eszrah ap Niht understood he had failed. He had failed his father's last command to him. The man his father had given him to was dead because Eszrah had not discharged his duty to protect him.

That made Eszrah a dead man too, a shamed outcast, dishonoured. Eszrah wasn't sure why any of the Ghosts were still speaking to him, or acknowledging his presence. Surely they realised his state of disgrace and recognised that the only thing awaiting Eszrah was the *deada waeg*, the road of corpses. His life had no purpose any more, except that he should atone for the wrong he had allowed to happen.

Eszrah ran his fingers along the blade of the power sword. He knew what to do: recover the body for burial and avenge the death ten-fold.

He took off the sunshades that Varl had given him so many months before and laid them on the desk. He would need to see now, see like a hunting cat in the dark. He took up his reynbow and, as an afterthought, picked up the power sword too. Eszrah was no swordsman, but the nature and true ownership of the weapon was important to the ritual. It had to be the dead man's weapon.

Rawne snorted in his sleep and rolled over. He looked up, blinking.

He was alone in the room.

V

'I'M ASKING YOU just one thing,' said Dalin in a low whisper. 'Don't die too. Please, don't die too.'

He sat at Tona Criid's bedside, his head pressed against hers. She did not move.

'Come back to me. Caff's not going to, I know that, but you can. You gakking well can.'

Tona lay as she was, her mouth slack.

Noises disturbed the field station. The medics were still at work, treating the last and the least damaged of the casualties. Corpsmen hurried in and out with bundles of supplies, fresh dressings and bowls of water.

'It'll be all right, Dalin,' a man said. 'She'll be all right.'

Dalin looked up and saw Major Kolea standing beside him.

'Sir,' Dalin said, and began to rise.

'As you were, boy,' said Kolea.

Dalin knew the major had been close with his mother and Caff. There was something about Major Kolea that was at once reassuring and also alarming. Kolea treated Dalin oddly, not like Meryn and the other arseholes, overly respectful of Caffran's memory. Kolea was different. He reminded Dalin of someone he'd once known, long ago, an uncle or a family friend perhaps, back on Verghast before the war.

'Did my mother know you, sir?' he asked.

'What?'

'My birth mother, not Tona, back at Vervunhive, where I was born. You're Verghastite. Did you know my family?'

Kolea shrugged. 'Yes.'

'Really?'

'I knew them very well.'

'Why haven't you spoken to me about them before, sir? My memory of that time is only patchy, but if you knew them–'

'It's a long time ago, Dalin,' said Kolea, his voice thick. 'Tona's been your mother for as long as it counts.'

'I know that,' said Dalin, 'but... what were they like, my mother and father? You knew them. What were they like?'

Kolea turned away. He halted. 'They loved you,' he said. 'You and Yoncy both, very much. And they'd be proud to know a woman like Tona took you in and made you safe.'

'They died in the war, didn't they? My parents. They died in the Vervunhive war?' Dalin asked.

'They died in the war,' said Kolea.

VI

THE ELEVENTH DAWN came, without betraying any visible sign. The dust storm outside was so fierce that it blotted out the daylight and made the night linger. The whirring, almost buzzing moan of high wind and blowing dust droned along the hallways and corridors.

'Well, at least they won't be coming at us in this,' remarked Berenson, accepting a cup of caffeine from Baskevyl.

'Because?' Baskevyl asked.

Berenson shrugged, forgetting for a moment he had one arm in a sling, and winced. 'Zero visibility? They'd be mad to.'

'Have you fought the Blood Pact before, major?' Baskevyl asked, sipping from his own cup as he reviewed some transcripts his adjutant had delivered to him.

'Yesterday was my first time,' Berenson admitted.

'And did you see anything yesterday that remotely indicated they were sane?' Baskevyl asked.

Berenson was silent.

'They could come at any time, storm or no storm, dust or no dust,' Baskevyl said. 'They won't let anything stop them, unlike our own forces.'

'What's that supposed to mean?' Berenson asked.

'It means your reinforcements are supposed to be here in the next two days,' Rawne said as he joined them in the base chamber. 'This storm is bound to slow them down.'

Berenson frowned. His expression was alarmingly like the one Caffran used to display when his honour was insulted.

'Oh, relax,' said Rawne, pouring himself some caffeine. 'That wasn't a slur on your regiment's reputation or efficiency. This dust-out is going to slow any mechanised advance down to a crawl. No Guard commander's going to push on blind. They'd have to be mad.'

'I refer you to my previous remark,' Baskevyl said to Berenson.

Kolea, Mkoll, Daur, Theiss and Kolosim arrived in the base chamber, closely followed by Sloman, Kamori and Meryn. Rawne waited a few minutes more until all the company officers had congregated around him.

'Let's start,' he said. 'Munition status?'

'Not fantastic, sir,' said Arcuda. 'We're down to about forty-eight per cent of our supply. We're all right for the time being in terms of standard cells, and we can cook some up if necessary. But we expended solid ammo, charges and tube rockets like you wouldn't believe yesterday.'

'Running badly low on barrels for the long guns too,' Larkin put in.

'Order a supply drop,' Rawne told Beltayn, who was taking notes. 'Be very specific about what we need.'

'No supply drop's going to find us in this,' said Kamori darkly.

'And if it does…' Kolea began.

'If it does, *what*?' Rawne asked.

Kolea made a face. 'Dropping water into that courtyard was one thing. Dropping munitions? Charges and volatiles? That could turn out to be one feth of a big, bad idea.'

'So's sitting here without any support weapons or heavy firepower,' said Rawne, 'and that's where we'll be if we take another hit like yesterday's. Rifles and blades are not going to be sufficient disincentive against another storm assault.'

'Maybe we can find an alternate LZ?' Daur suggested. 'Providing the storm abates, of course.'

'Start working on alternative plans for safe receipt of a munitions drop,' said Rawne. 'Beltayn, request the drop anyway.'

'Yes, sir.'

'How's our link, by the way?'

Beltayn shook his head. 'We can't raise Elikon or… or anyone else at this time, sir, atmospherics are too harsh. I'll keep trying.'

'Do that,' said Rawne, 'and keep trying to link Major Berenson's mechanised, will you? An ETA would be appreciated.'

'Sir.'

Rawne took another swig of caffeine, savouring the novelty of something warm to drink. He cleared his throat. 'Secure and hold is the order of the day. Vigilance is páramount. You all know your places and your areas. I want every rat-run, shutter and basement in this fething edifice locked up tight. Any contact, any attempt to penetrate, must be denied with our trademark lack of tolerance. Another full assault would be bad enough, but I've a hunch they may try stealth again.'

The officers nodded.

'Tell the men, make it clear to them,' Rawne said. 'I know the mood is grim, but we have to be twice as hard now. I don't want excuses. Make sure the men appreciate that any slip up today means that Gaunt will have died for nothing.'

There was a nasty pause. Varl sucked his breath in through his teeth in disapproval.

'You think that was callous?' Rawne asked. 'Then none of you know me very well. I'm not playing around because *they're* not playing around. And before you ask, that's the way he would have wanted it.'

Mkoll nodded. 'I don't doubt that for a moment,' he said.

'Good,' said Rawne. 'Who's securing the new area?'

'Two company's under me,' said Baskevyl.

'I want it clean and locked up in three hours,' said Rawne.

'Unless, of course, we find more new areas beyond the new area,' Baskevyl replied.

'Granted. Take Beltayn with you. A full report on that library and armoury, please.'

Baskevyl nodded.

'Then let's get to it,' said Rawne. The officers hesitated for a moment. Rawne stared at them and then sighed.

'Oh, and the Emperor protects and you're all going to live forever and all that…' he said with a wave of his hand. 'I don't do rousing or uplifting. Just get on with it.'

The men turned to go.

'One last thing, before I forget,' Rawne added, pulling them back in. 'Someone took Gaunt's sword from my office last night. Souvenir hunter, I'm guessing, or some sentimental idiot. I want it back. No excuses. And there will be severe discipline for whoever took it.'

'I'll handle that, major,' said Hark. At some point during the briefing, he had joined the back of the group. He was fully dressed, with his storm coat on, resting his bulk on a crutch made out of a stretcher pole. He looked pale and sick.

'Should you be up?' Rawne asked.

'No,' said Hark, 'but I am. This situation isn't going to wait for me to heal. Curth stuck me with enough painkiller to make you all seem like a lovely, smiley bunch of people. That'll wear off, I'm sure. Don't expect any rousing speeches from me, either, but Major Rawne is quite correct. We have to get this right today, and the next day, and the next, without feeling sorry for ourselves. Gaunt would hate it if we went to pieces now. Everything he spent his life working to achieve would be wasted.'

'Everyone got that?' Rawne asked. 'Good. Carry on.'

Day eleven. Sunrise at five plus two, dust out conditions, total, storm maintaining from last night. Worst storm yet.

I have to admire R. He has already met the task head on, handing out heavy work and duty loads to distract the men and officers both from the mortal blow we have suffered. He's right. This is the only way to continue. The ~~offcers~~ officers cannot afford to be squeamish or weak. There is no time for grief or despair. If we are lucky - very lucky - we may get a chance to mourn later.

The fact that we have water now is a boon. The munition/communication/reinforcement prospects are not so glorious. Given the present situation, I believe we may withstand one further attack.

~~I continue to hear odd noises and sounds in~~ I believe the drugs A.C. has given me to allow me to operate without pain may be having some side effects of a hallucinatory nature. I will ignore all such distractions.

I expect the enemy to assault again before the day is out, whether the storm blows out or not.

- Field journal, V.H. fifth month, 7/8.

FIFTEEN

After the Storm, the Storm

I

BESIEGED BY THE storm, the house covered its eyes and mouth, and waited. Concussive waves of brown grit and loose white dust-vapour broke against the ramparts and sand-blasted the metal casemates. Shutters flapped and rattled, and some had to be tied down from within. From the vantage of the main gatehouse, the wind made a deep, raw voiced howl as it thundered up the approach pass.

In the base chambers, the vox-caster sets whined and yelped like injured animals as they hunted for a signal.

II

MERYN WAS CALLING to them. Dalin and Cullwoe finished checking the chamber with their lamp-packs and returned to the hallway.

'Anything?' Meryn asked.

'Empty, sir.'

'Move along. Keep it fast.'

'Yes, sir,' said Dalin. He led Cullwoe on towards the next doorway. Meryn stepped back to check the progress of the rest of his company, which had broken down into pairs to explore and secure the newly discovered sections of the house beyond the inner courtyard. He called out some instructions.

'Captain?' Baskevyl appeared behind him.

'Sir.'

'Find anything?'

Meryn shook his head. 'We've identified about eight or nine rooms so far, mostly leading off this hallway. There are more over that way, according to Sloman's men. We're mapping as we go.'

'Empty?'

901

'Everything's empty,' Meryn nodded. 'Not even any furniture.'

This area may have been abandoned, I suppose,' said Baskevyl. 'I mean, Mkoll had to go through a wall panel to find it.'

Meryn glanced at him. 'Or hidden,' he said, 'deliberately hidden. There's that library place, and the weapons store. Why board that off?'

'I wish I had an answer for you, Meryn,' Baskevyl said. 'Any sense of this area's limits yet?'

'No, sir. Different in here, though, isn't it?' Meryn said.

'Different how?'

Meryn gestured towards the nearest wall light.

'The lighting glows amber, not white. It's lower intensity, but it doesn't come and go. It's as if it's on a different power feed from the rest of the place.'

'Or shut back to some emergency, energy conserving level,' said Baskevyl.

'Right.'

Baskevyl wrapped his camo-cloak around his shoulders. 'I'm going back to the library. Keep going here, and report to me with anything you find.'

'Don't get blown away,' said Meryn as he turned to go.

Baskevyl snorted as he moved off in the opposite direction. To get back to the library and armoury and, from there to the rest of the house, a man had to cross the inner courtyard. In the storm, that was not any kind of fun. Baskevyl pulled down his goggles, and edged out into the fury of the gale. The dust ripped into him with minute claws and pinpricks. He had to hold on to the courtyard wall and feel his way.

The wind made an odd, whooping, scraping sound as it formed a vortex in the courtyard. It sounded like–

No, it doesn't, he told himself.

He glanced up. Most of the dust storms they had endured since their arrival on Jago had been white-outs: blinding hazes of ash-white dust back-lit by the sun's glow.

This was different, and had been different since springing up the night before. It was an abrasive darkness, the dust brown-black and noxious, and there was no light behind it, no promise of sun. High above, the sky seemed a tar-brown emptiness, banded and mottled with radiating bars of darkness. Though it was lightless, sparks of luminescence seemed to dart through it. Lightning, Baskevyl presumed, electrical discharge. The wind was making so much noise, he couldn't tell if he could hear thunder or not.

Just let it not be artillery, he thought.

He made it to the far side of the courtyard and blundered in between the two Ghosts posted there.

'Stay sharp,' he told them, and began to walk up the steps in the direction of the library and armoury, pulling off his goggles and shaking the dust out of his cape.

* * *

III

WHEN BASKEVYL WALKED into the gun room, Larkin and Maggs were busy examining some of the big antique weapons by the soft amber light.

'If only we had ammo,' Larkin was saying.

'We do,' said Bonin, leaning back against a rack on the far wall, his arms folded. He nodded at the armoured bunkers running down the middle space of the room.

'If only we had *useable* ammo,' Larkin corrected.

'Oh, there is that,' agreed Bonin. The back and left side of his neck were thickly dressed. The pain of his recent injury didn't appear to bother him.

Baskevyl knelt down and lifted the lid off one of the bunkers. He looked at the heap of brown satin pebbles inside.

'Do you think they charged them?' he wondered. 'Do you think they're rechargeable?'

'Coir reckoned they'd been in the coffers too long, Throne rest him,' Bonin replied. 'I reckon we could kill ourselves pretty quickly fething about with old, exotic ammunition.'

'Still,' said Larkin, picking up a brown pebble and holding it in his hand until it began to glow.

'Larks...' Bonin warned, pushing away from the wall and standing upright.

Baskevyl held up a hand. Larkin opened the heavy, mechanical lock of the rampart gun he was holding, dropped the glowing pebble into it, and snapped the action shut. He aimed the massive piece at the blank, end wall of the armoury, flexing his palm around the over-sized grip.

'This is not a good idea,' said Bonin.

'Coming to this bad rock wasn't a good idea in the first place,' Larkin replied. He adjusted his hold, judging how to balance the considerable weight of the wall-gun.

He pulled the trigger.

There was a perfunctory *fttppp!* and a disappointing fizzle of light around the gun's fat muzzle. Larkin clacked open the action and looked down at the dead, brown pebble inside.

'Well, it was worth a try,' Larkin said, lowering the hefty firearm. 'You'd need a slot too, to fire this beastie properly. A slot and a monopod stand.'

'Like this?' Maggs asked. The shelving under the main gunracks was full of slender brass tubes. He pulled one free. It telescoped out neatly to form a shoulder-high pole with a forked rest at the top.

'Exactly like that,' said Larkin.

'We've got everything,' said Maggs.

'Except ammunition, in which case we've got nothing,' said Bonin.

'Are you always such a glass-half-empty bloke, Mach?' Baskevyl asked.

'Actually, I'm a glass-half-broken-and-rammed-in-someone-else's-face bloke,' said Bonin.

'Good to know,' said Baskevyl. 'Keep looking around and see what you can find.'

'Hey,' said Maggs. He'd tugged at the brass gun rest again, and an additional fifty centimetres had telescoped out. 'Why would you want it this tall?' he asked.

'For aiming upwards?' Baskevyl suggested with a shrug as he left the chamber. 'Carry on.'

IV

BASKEVYL CROSSED THE corridor to the library chamber where Beltayn, Fapes and two other adjutants were at work.

Beltayn looked up from the pile of books he was studying on the reading tables. Baskevyl didn't like the look on Beltayn's face.

'We're checking book to book, but it's either an old or non-human script, or it's code.'

'Everything?'

Beltayn patted the stack of books on the desk in front of him and then rolled his eyes meaningfully at the thousands of volumes and scrolls on the shelves around them.

Baskevyl nodded. 'All right. That was a stupid question. You've only just started.'

'By all means, help,' said the adjutant.

Baskevyl stood for a moment, listening to the slurring, scratch of the wind outside, a sound that seemed somehow to be coming from below him. Anything to take his mind off that.

He walked the length of one of the walls, running a fingertip along the lip of the elbow-high shelf. A fine billow of dust rippled out in a drowsy wake behind his moving finger. The books were a jumbled assortment, the spines frayed, worn and old. In some cases, it was clear from a collapsed knot of papers wedged between volumes that whole bindings had disintegrated. A few of the volumes bore embossed titles on their spines, but Baskevyl couldn't read any of them. Others seemed to be adorned with emblems or decorative motifs. He looked around at random for a book to start with.

'Is everything all right, sir?' Fapes asked him.

'Yes. Why?'

'Nothing, sir. You just made a sound like you were surprised at something.'

'Just clearing my throat, Fapes. This dust.'

Screw the dust, dust had nothing to do it. Nothing to do with the mumble of shock he'd been unable to stifle. Baskevyl swallowed and looked back at the shelf. It wasn't just the emblem his eyes had alighted on, it was also the fact that he'd been picking at random – *at random!* – and it had been right there waiting for him.

He stared at the spine of the book. It was bound in what looked like black leather, sheened and smooth, like–

Stop it.

Too late to stop it. Too late to stop his mind racing. The emblem, embossed in silver on the spine, glared at him. A snake, a serpent, a worm, its long, segmented body curled around in a circle, so that its jaws clenched its tail-tip to form a hoop.

He swallowed again, and reached out to take down the book. Deep in the recesses of his mind, he heard the scratching grow louder: the grunting, sloughing, scraping beneath his feet, beneath the floor, beneath the mountain itself, increasing as the daemon-worm writhed in pleasure and anticipation.

Baskevyl's hand wavered a few centimetres from the spine of the book.

Take it. Take it. Take it down. Look at it.

His fingers touched the black snakeskin binding just above the silver motif.

'Major?'

Baskevyl snatched his fingers away. 'Beltayn? What did you want?'

Beltayn had a large, leather bound folio open on the reading desk.

'You might want to see this, sir,' Beltayn said, leafing through the pages.

Glad of any excuse to leave the snakeskin book where it was, Baskevyl moved around the desk behind Beltayn.

The folio Beltayn had found was big and loose-leaf, containing fragile pages almost half a metre square. Some were blocks of annotated text: copy-black blocks of script in an arcane tongue, decorated with faded penmanship that was even less intelligible.

The rest were illustrated plates. They were finely done, but the colours that had been used to hand tint them were just ghosts of their former strengths.

The plates were diagrams of fortress walls, bastions, emplacements, outworks for debauchment, casemate lines, trench systems, cloche groupings.

'Feth,' said Baskevyl. 'Is this... here?'

Beltayn nodded. 'I think it might be. Actually, I think this might be a record of Jago. That... that looks like Elikon, doesn't it?'

'Yes it does.'

'And that... that's way too big to be here. That's... well, it looks like a hundred kilometres long at least.'

'At least.' Baskevyl breathed deeply. 'Records of the fortress world, old records. I wonder how accurate they are?'

'Better than ours, I'll bet,' said Fapes, peering in over their shoulders.

'Throne bless you, Bel,' said Baskevyl, slapping Beltayn on the shoulder. 'You may have just found something truly important to the war. How many more volumes are there like this?'

'Er... four, six, eight...' Fapes said as he began to count. 'Twenty-three on this stack. There may be others.'

'Shit,' said Baskevyl.

'You're not wrong there,' said Beltayn. 'Look.'

He'd turned over another plate. This one wasn't a diagram, it was a picture, an illustration. It was a cut-away view, done in an antique style, of armoured men defending a casemate during action. Starry missiles, like ancient depictions of comets, arced down at them. Some lay dead, side on, at the foot of the page, their scale and attitudes disagreeing with the perspective of the picture. The men at the casemate were quite clearly armed with wall guns identical to the weapons stored not twenty metres away from where they stood.

'Fighting men,' said Baskevyl, 'at a gun slit.'

Beltayn turned another plate over and revealed another, similar image, a third. Then a fourth, which showed the warriors winding the shutters open for firing. The intricate shutter mechanisms were clearly shown.

'Are they?' Beltayn asked.

'Are they what?'

'*Are* they men?' Beltayn asked. 'Look closely.'

Baskevyl peered down. Beltayn was right. The warriors in the pictures were humanoid, but they were encased in intricate armour from head to foot. Their faces were covered with complex visors.

'They might not be men at all,' said Beltayn. 'Look how big they are in comparison to the casemate slots.'

'You can't say that. There's no perspective, no scale,' Baskevyl said.

'Then look how big they are compared to the guns,' said Fapes.

In the illustrations, the warriors at the casemate slots were holding the rampart weapons as if they were lasrifles. Some of them were shown using gun rests, but even so...

Baskevyl remembered Maggs slotting out that last fifty centimetres of telescoping brass pole.

'Oh holy Throne,' he murmured.

'What's the matter, major?' asked Fapes. 'You seem awfully jumpy today.'

Baskevyl touched his micro-bead. 'Sir, this is Baskevyl.'

'Go,' replied Rawne's voice.

'Can you get yourself down to that library we found? There's something I'd like to show you.'

'Ten minutes, Baskevyl. Can it wait that long?'

'It's waited I don't know how many centuries so far. I'm sure another ten minutes won't make any difference.'

V

HUNDREDS OF FOOTSTEPS echoed around the house. The watch shift was changing.

The wailing storm outside had outlasted the night and the first watch of the day. Mkoll strode down a corridor spur off the base chamber to check on the scout rotations. He passed the door to Gaunt's chamber. It was ajar.

Not Gaunt's, he told himself, not any more. Rawne's.

He stopped walking, and stepped back a pace or three until he could look in through the open door.

Oan Mkoll was a hard man, a man not given to displays of emotion. He would never have admitted to anyone how lost he felt without Gaunt. They were all feeling it, he knew that. Every last one of them was feeling the loss, and there was no point amplifying that misery. He certainly didn't want anybody commiserating with him.

But the centre of his universe had gone, just like that, even though he had always known it probably would one day. He'd give his life to the service of the Tanith First and, more importantly, to Ibram Gaunt. Mkoll knew war as more than a passing acquaintance. Given his particular role, Mkoll had always assumed he'd die long before Gaunt. Now that Gaunt had beaten him to the happy place, nothing seemed to matter any more.

He hated himself for feeling this way. He resented Gaunt for his passing. It wasn't right. All the while Gaunt had been alive, there'd been some purpose to living, some point to the endless catalogue of war zones and battles, some hope, some... *destination*.

Mkoll pushed the door open and walked into the room. He breathed in. He could smell Gaunt, the ghost of him. He could smell Gaunt's cologne, the starch of his uniform, his lingering body odour.

Rawne's belongings were strewn untidily around the room. Mkoll walked over to the desk. Rawne's announcement that morning that Gaunt's sword had been purloined had filled Mkoll with the deepest fury.

What a bastard, dishonourable thing to do. Steal a dead man's sword? That was low.

Mkoll stared down at the desk top. A few personal items lay on it: a dataslate, a button-brush, a tin of metal polish, a tin mug.

From the moment Mkoll had entered the gatehouse of Hinzerhaus, he hadn't been himself. He'd been jumpy, tense and terrified that he was off his game. He'd told Gaunt as much, that evening out on the crag top. Gaunt had tried to buck him up, but Mkoll had continued to feel it: the sloppiness, the doubt.

I can't trust myself. This place is making a fool out of me. And fools die faster than others.

That's what he'd said.

Mkoll was painfully sure that Gaunt would still be alive if Mkoll had been on form. Mkoll would have been up in upper west sixteen, leading the way, making sure Gaunt didn't *have* to lead the way.

I should have been there. I should have known where the real danger was. I should have been there and I should have saved Ibram, even if that meant I took a kill shot myself.

Mkoll sighed. *I failed you. I'm so sorry.*

He looked down at the desk again. Feth take Hark and his due process. *I'll find the bastard who lifted Gaunt's sword and I'll–*

Mkoll saw the sunshades. He picked them up and turned them over in his hands. They were cheap things, machine stamped out of some plastek mill on Urdesh or Rydol. He remembered Varl posing with them for a laugh on Herodor.

What he most clearly remembered was the fact that the sunshades had never once left the Nihtgane's face from the moment Varl had given them to Eszrah on Gereon.

'Oh, you stupid feth,' Mkoll murmured to himself. 'What have you gone and done?'

* * *

VI

RAWNE ENTERED THE library.

'This had better be worth my time,' he said.

'Oh, it is,' Baskevyl replied. 'Look at this.'

'Look at what?' Hark asked, limping in behind Rawne.

'I–' Baskevyl began. He paused, and looked at Hark. 'Commissar? What's the matter?'

Hark had frowned suddenly, as if hearing something. When he spoke, his words came out in a short bark.

'Brace yourselves!'

They felt the shudder of the first shells falling on the house. One salvo, another. Some burst nearby, causing the floor to vibrate and dust to spill down from the ceiling.

'The storm is still blowing!' Beltayn complained. 'How can they range us?'

'They had us yesterday. That range still applies,' Rawne shouted back. 'Even firing blind!'

'But–' Beltayn began.

The next salvo felt as if it struck the bulk of the house directly overhead. Chunks of plasterwork and sections of brown satin panels spilled down out of the roof space. The lights flickered.

Rawne's eyes narrowed. *How do we fight an enemy we can't see and we can't reach? How do we fight an enemy that can pick us apart one piece at a time?*

VII

THE SHELLING CONTINUED for ten more minutes and then eased off. In another ten, it began again, like a summer rainstorm that comes and goes with the chasing clouds.

The house jarred in its rocky bedding. Several overlook casemates took square hits and were demolished, but there were few casualties as the Ghosts had withdrawn into the fortified heart of the house. The shell impacts sounded through the wailing drone of the wind, shrill and raucous, like the bleats of livestock going to slaughter.

Zweil had been conducting a service in the base chamber when the first shells started to land. As the men around him looked up in consternation, he hushed them down and carried on with his reading as if nothing was happening.

Nearby, on a lower landing of the same chamber, Rerval, Rafflan and other vox-officers had continued to apply themselves to their caster-sets, their constant, murmuring voices becoming a liturgical chorus to Zweil's confident voice.

Daur was in command of the watch on the main gatehouse. He knew that what they were hearing – and feeling – was harassing fire at best, a constant plugging away to weaken their resolve. No one, not even the Chaotic enemy, used artillery during a full-scale typhoon with any expectation of accurate, productive results. It was a wonder anything was hitting the house at all.

But even the whine of shells passing overhead, or the sound of a barrage landing within earshot, was enough to unsettle dug-in troops. It made them feel helpless and even more vulnerable than usual. It whittled away their hope and eroded their confidence.

Daur walked down through the huddles of muttering, wary men in the gatehouse and stood in front of the main hatch. His fingers traced the slight crease in the seam where the ram had done its work the day before. It wouldn't take much more to break the seal.

He placed the palm of his hand flat against the metal of the hatch and felt a slight, continuous vibration beneath his touch. Was that the pressure of the storm driving against the other side?

The shelling persisted for another half an hour and then died away again. There was no respite from the storm. High in the house, along those ill-fated uppermost halls and galleries, the fiercely moving air and dust outside made sounds against the metal domes of the cloches like claws on glass. Hastily tied or wired-down shutters juddered in their sockets. Sentry fire-teams waited in uneasy groups, listening, talking softly, playing at cards or dice, or gnawing on dried rations.

Mkoll toured the upper galleries, checking on the sentry teams. The men were glad to see him. Mkoll was a reassuring figure. As the shelling came and went, he told them not to worry, and to keep a close watch on the shutters and the trip-wires.

More than once, as if in passing, he casually asked, 'Do you happen to have seen the Nihtgane today?'

VIII

'You KNOW WHAT this is?'

'A royal pain, mister?' answered Cullwoe.

'Feth, yeah,' Dalin smiled, though his smile was not confident. Exploring and securing the new-found sections of the house was taking longer than projected: empty rooms opened unexpectedly into other empty rooms, and then into more besides, just when they were expecting to find a dead end or an external wall. The crump and rattle of falling shells simply added to the nervous tension.

Lamp-packs, fixed on the lugs under the barrels of their weapons, hunted through the amber gloom. The come and go of the soft white lights in the rest of the house, a detail that had been disturbing to begin with, seemed infinitely preferable to the low, steady orange burn of the wall lights in the new section.

Their micro-beads clicked.

'Confirm click,' said Dalin into his mic. Atmospheric distortion had been causing false signals on the intervox all day.

'Confirm,' said Wheln. 'Can you get down here?'

They followed his signal along a boxy corridor that joined a larger hall-way at right angles.

'Down here!' Wheln called, seeing their lights.

The robust, older Tanith was waiting for them at the southern end of the hallway. His search partner, Melwid, was with him.

'What have you found?' Dalin asked.

'Take a look, adjutant,' Wheln said. It was so odd. Wheln, like many others, seemed to have no hesitation whatsoever in accepting Dalin's new role, despite the age gap.

The hallway opened out into a wide flight of steps, eight deep, that descended onto the brown satin floor of a large, oblong chamber. There were no other doors or spur-exits. It was a dead end. Amber wall lights glowed along the side walls, but the wall facing the steps was just a panelled blank.

'End of the line,' said Cullwoe.

'Maybe. Look at that,' Wheln replied. He raised his hand and pointed out the carved wooden archway over the steps. It had been eaten away in prehistory by worms, and the carved figure work was impossible to read.

'So what?' asked Cullwoe. 'Are we making a note of interesting architectural features now?'

Melwid shook his head. Wheln ignored Cullwoe and looked straight at Dalin. 'Seen anything like it?' he asked.

Dalin nodded. 'Twice,' he replied. 'There's one at the end of the hallway between the main gate and the base chamber.'

'And another on the way into this part of the house, just as you're coming into the courtyard,' Wheln agreed.

Cullwoe shrugged. 'So?'

'Shush for a minute, Khet,' Dalin said.

'But–'

'Don't you get it?' Dalin asked. 'The other two arches like this mark entrances.'

Dalin crossed to the far wall of the dead end chamber, and ran his hand across the brown satin panelling. Then he struck his knuckles against it. The sound was dull.

'No echo,' said Melwid.

'Even so,' said Dalin, and clicked his micro-bead. 'Captain Meryn? Criid here, sir...'

IX

No sentries had been posted in the windcote. The belfry had been deemed, by everyone including Mkoll, too inaccessible for a scale assault. The shutters had been wired down and secured. It was an empty, gloomy roost where the wind got in through slits and crevices.

Eszrah ap Niht sat on the deck with his back to the metal tree and carefully applied *wode* to his face. When he had finished smearing the grey paste on, expertly banding it across his skin without the need of a mirror, he took another little gourd flask out of his tunic pocket and unscrewed the cap. One by one, he took up the iron darts laid out on the floor beside him, and dipped their tips into the flask, charging them with the lethal moth venom of the Untill. Then he wrapped the poisoned darts back up in their quiver, put the flask away and sat for a while in silence. Four items lay on the decking in front of him: a spool of rope, a bag of climbing hooks and pins, his reynbow and Gaunt's sword.

The moan of the wind outside was easing slightly, as if the gigantic storm was finally running out of power. Eszrah ignored the sporadic rumble of shell fire that echoed up from the southern face of the house behind him.

He rose to his feet in one smooth, unsupported uncrossing of his legs. He strapped the sword to his back and tied the reynbow over it, cross-wise, to balance the weight. The bag went over his body so it hung down on his left hip. He put his right arm through the spool of rope.

The loose dust in the windcote air slowly began to settle. After several minutes, the faintest hint of pale daylight began to show around the lips of the brass hatches.

Eszrah walked over to a north-facing hatch, undid the wiring and opened it. He looked out into a cold twilight, a violet sky, smeared by cloud, hanging above a thick yellow blanket of slowly calming dust cover that obscured the mountainside below him and stretched out over the immensity of the badlands to the north.

The storm had ended. Daylight was fighting to take its place.

Eszrah slid out through the shutter without hesitation and let it flap shut behind him.

X

'STORM'S DROPPED,' DAUR was informed.

'Gate here,' he said, activating his intervox. 'Overlook? Anything?'

High in the house above, the spotters and lookouts were returning to their posts, and opening the shutters they had sealed against the storm to look out into the bruised half-light across a landscape that had not yet properly recovered its form.

'Nothing, gate. Will keep you advised.'

Daur took a swig of water.

'I don't like this,' he heard one of the troopers nearby murmur.

I know what I don't like, Daur thought. *I don't like the fact that the moment the storm died back, so did the shelling.*

In the base chamber, Rerval adjusted another dial and said, for the umpteenth time, 'Elikon M.P., Elikon M.P., this is Nalwood, this is Nalwood, do you receive, over?'

'Nalwood, this is Elikon, this is Elikon,' the vox-caster replied.

Rerval clapped his hands together. 'Someone tell Rawne!' he shouted. 'We've got a link!'

XI

SPLINTERING AND CRACKING, the old brown panelling came away. Wheln and Dalin levered at it with the pry-bars Meryn had brought. The void behind the satin brown panels was packed with dust and grit, and everyone was coughing and pulling their capes up over their mouths.

'It's just bare rock,' Meryn spat, 'just bare rock. It was worth checking, Dalin, but–'

Wheln reached into the space behind the partially demolished panelling. He pulled out a large chunk of dirty stone. 'It's not bare rock,' he said. 'It's loose rock. It's spoil packed in.'

'Clear it,' Meryn ordered.

They didn't have to clear much to see what was behind it. There was a metal hatch behind the wall, caked in crusts of earth-mould and dust, a hatch virtually identical in size and design to the one in the main gatehouse.

'A second gate,' said Dalin.

'Yes, but sealed up,' Meryn said.

'On *this* side, captain,' Dalin said.

'We didn't know this place had more than one gate,' Meryn said. 'Why would the enemy know any different?'

'Because they seem to know a lot more about this place than we do,' said Dalin.

'The boy's right,' said Rawne appearing in the hallway behind them. 'So we have to be sure. Captain, get three squads assembled in here, three squads with at least one flamer.'

'Sir.'

'On the double, Meryn. I want this hatch open.'

They all looked at Rawne.

'Anybody else know a way to find out what's behind it?' Rawne asked.

XII

HARK LET OUT a low whistle as he slowly turned the loose leaves of the folio over one by one.

'Important, right?' Baskevyl asked.

Hark nodded.

'Rawne didn't seem that impressed,' Baskevyl added.

'He's got more immediate problems,' Hark said. The images he was looking at were so astonishing, he'd almost forgotten about the throb of pain in his back.

He looked up at Baskevyl and Berenson. 'These need to be taken to Elikon M.P. as soon as possible.'

'Yes, commissar,' Berenson replied. 'I think it's vital.'

'Taken?' Baskevyl said.

'There's no other way of communicating them,' said Hark. 'We can't upload them.'

'No way of converting them at all?' Berenson asked.

'We may have a few pict-readers, but it would take weeks to scan all of the volumes. The quality would be poor.' Hark sighed. 'And our up-link isn't secure enough to transmit it, certainly not in this quantity. No, gentlemen, this is going to have to get to Elikon the old-fashioned way.'

'Rawne won't like it,' said Baskevyl.

'Major Rawne's going to have to lump it, then,' said Hark.

XIII

MKOLL CREPT UP the wooden stairs into the windcote. His keen senses were not mistaken. The Nihtgane was up there, or he'd been up there.

The dome space was empty. Mkoll looked around. There wasn't much to see. One of the brass shutters rattled in its frame as the breezes knocked at it.

He saw a faint grey smudge on the floor. He bent down, touched it, and sniffed his fingertip.

Wode, the smell of the deepest Untill.

He rose to his feet and went over to the rattling shutter. It had been unwired.

He stood for a long time, deep in thought.

XIV

'STAND BY, GATE,' the vox-link said in Daur's ear.

'Come on,' Daur fretted.

'There's still a lot of dust, gate,' the overlook observer said. 'Terrain is still obscured.'

'But you thought you saw something?'

'Can't confirm. Stand by.'

Daur breathed out. He was about to speak again when the hatch behind him shook. A deep, reverberative clang rang around the gatehouse.

'Never mind, overlook,' Daur said grimly. 'Rise and address!' he yelled to the men.

The ram resumed its steady beat against the other side of the hatch.

Elikon M.P., Elikon M.P., this is Nalwood, this is Nalwood. Request urgent munition resupply. Request urgent vox-to-vox link with field commander at earliest practical opportunity. Please advise soonest.

Nalwood out. (transmission ends)

- Transcript of vox message, fifth month, 778.

SIXTEEN

The Third Assault

I

'CLEAR IT THERE! There!' Rawne called out. 'No, those rocks. They're jamming the hinge!'

Melwid scrambled into the gap and dug the rocks out of the way with both hands, strewing them back into the chamber behind him like a burrowing animal.

'Good!' Rawne yelled. 'Pull it now!'

The dry metal hinges of the hatch groaned in protest at being forced to move after such a long time. A shaft of grey daylight speared in around the edge, and white dust blew in with it.

'Squads ready!' Rawne ordered.

'Ready to address!' Meryn relayed.

The hatch opened to a gap of about half a metre and the cold outside light leaked more comprehensively into the chamber.

'Enough!' Rawne called. He held up his hand for quiet.

No one moved. No one spoke. The only sounds were the trickle of disturbed dirt, the soft hum of the wind outside and the hiss of Neskon's waiting flamer.

Using gestures, Rawne pulled Wheln, Melwid and Dalin back from the hatch, leaving Cullwoe and Harjeon behind the bulk of the door, ready to heft it shut again at a moment's notice.

Nothing came from outside, no sound of movement, no shots.

Rawne looked over at Bonin with a nod.

Bonin moved forwards, followed by his fellow scouts Livara and Jajjo. They reached the gap. Bonin took a quick look around it using one of the little, makeshift stick mirrors that Mkvenner had developed.

He signalled *clear*. Jajjo slipped past him, then Livara. Bonin followed them.

Rawne was the fourth man at the hatch. He was about to follow the scouts out when Meryn put a hand on his arm.

'Sir, I don't think–' Meryn whispered.

'Not now, Meryn.'

'We can't afford to lose two commanding officers in as many days.'

Rawne met Meryn's eyes for a moment, then he slid through the gap anyway.

Outside was a bleak place. The air smoked with lightly blown dust and the sky far above was stained the colour of an old bruise. The hatchway opened into a gulley, a high-sided ravine with slopes made of loose scree and tumbled boulders that centuries of gales had brought down the mountainside.

Rawne picked his way down towards the bottom of the gulley. He could see the three scouts moving ahead of him, low and careful. He turned slowly. He could see the craggy shelves of the house and the cliff face rising behind him, above the hatchway. The hatch itself was half-buried in scree. Before the hatch had opened, there would have been no obvious clue that there was a gate there at all.

The gulley was quite broad at the mouth, and it evidently lay adjacent to and separate from the main pass leading to the gatehouse: a side entrance, a secondary port. The enemy clearly didn't know about it, or they'd have used it during the last assault instead of climbing up and coming in over the roofs.

Rawne's bead clicked.

He moved down the gulley towards the mouth, where the scouts were waiting. He had almost reached them when the intervox in his ear shouted, 'Contact! Main gate!'

Rawne didn't reply. He started to run, and joined the scouts. They'd bellied down amongst the jumbled stones at the end of the gulley, looking right.

Rawne got down with them. Bonin handed him a scope and pointed.

As Rawne had surmised, the gulley opened out into the eastern side of the dust bowl in front of the main gate. The approach pass, grim and high-sided, lay to their left. The gatehouse was about five hundred metres west of them.

It was under attack.

Despite the sobbing moan of the wind and the curious acoustics of the pass, Rawne had been able to hear the noise of the attack from the moment he cleared the end of the gulley, the steady, gong-like beat of a ram against metal, intoning like a bell, the snarl and shout of men, the batter of drums.

More than a hundred Blood Pact warriors had gathered around the main gate, chanting and shouting as the ram-team heaved and swung their heavy device. Banners flapped in the mountain air.

Additional packs of enemy warriors were trudging in across the dust bowl to join the mass. Rawne could see the spiked ladders they were carrying, or dragging, across the dust. They were preparing for another scale assault.

Rawne opened his intervox. 'This is Rawne. Any contact from the top galleries? Anything from the north?'

'Negative, sir. It's quiet up there.'

'Keep watch. Full alert. They may come at any time. Be advised, the enemy is about to mount a scale assault of the south face. All defences are ordered to open fire only when they have clear targets on the wall. No wasting ammo.'

'Yes, sir.'

'I mean it.'

'Sir.'

Rawne paused. 'This is Rawne again. Who's commanding the gate?'

'Captain Daur, sir.'

'Get him some support, another company at least. I think he's about to need it.'

Rawne glanced at the three scouts.

'We could move in around them,' Bonin said.

'Go on.'

Bonin gestured back down the gulley at the new gate. 'Bring a company or two out this way, we could be into them from the right flank before they know it, and do a lot of hurt.'

Rawne nodded.

'Well?' asked Bonin.

Rawne took a deep breath. The idea was deliciously tempting. He could imagine how much damage a surprise counter-strike might do.

'No,' he said.

'No, sir?'

'No, Bonin. We hit them like that, they'll know we've found another way out. They'll come back this way and find the other gate.'

'But–'

'That second gate is our little secret. It's an advantage we didn't know we had, but we're only going to get one use out of it, so we've got to make it count. We have to use it at the right moment, for the best effect.'

'Isn't this the right moment, begging your pardon?' asked Jajjo.

'Feth, I wish it was,' said Rawne. 'I'd like to get my silver wet today. But I think we need to save it. Tactically, it could be much more important later.'

The three scouts nodded, but they didn't seem convinced.

'It's how Gaunt would have played it,' Rawne said.

'Really?' asked Bonin sceptically. 'How can you be so sure?'

'Because if he was here, he'd be telling us to wait, and I'd be the one telling him he was a fething idiot.'

There was a sudden burst of noise from the main gate. The first ladders had hooked up the walls, and the Blood Pact storming up them had been met with gunfire from the casemates and the overlooks above. Las-bolts spat down from the gunslots like bright rain, and many red-clad figures jerked and tumbled back down the lower cliffs, rolling and bouncing limply. Explosions began to bloom like desert flowers, brief gouts of fire that left fox-tails of black smoke trailing off into the sky when they had gone. Two spiked ladders, laden with enemy troopers, tore free and went slithering and cascading down the steep revetment of the lower house. Rawne could hear screams and yelling, voices raised in both pain and war cry. The firing grew more intense. Rockets banged off from the ground outside the gate and curled in to strike the upper casemates. Blood Pact crews with mortars and bomb-launchers had set up outside the gatehouse, and began to crank their machines to lob explosives up the walls. Fire and shrapnel skittered back down the cliff.

'Let's go back and secure the new gate,' said Rawne. 'We'll keep it open and under watch so we can see what's out here, and close it if we need to.'

'I'll stay put,' said Bonin. 'We could use a spotter. First sign of trouble, I can double time back to the gate and get it shut.'

'Just stay out of sight,' Rawne told him.

He headed back up the gulley with Livara and Jajjo. Behind him, he could distinctly hear the *Clang! Clang! Clang!* of the iron ram striking the main hatch.

II

'WHERE DO YOU suppose you're going?' Hark asked.

He was limping down the hallway towards the main gate on his crutch, moving through the tail end of Daur's men. They were agitated, and some had risen to their feet instead of crouching by the walls as instructed.

'Get back down and get ready!' Hark ordered, thumping past. The repetitive slam of the ram up ahead was dismal and chilling, and he could appreciate why the men were close to snapping. Hark understood their fear, but lack of formation discipline simply couldn't be permitted. He drew his pistol.

'Get ready! Ready now! Glory of Tanith! Spirit of Verghast! Fury of Belladon! They're going to come at us and we're going to give them death! What will we give them?'

'Death!' the chorus came back.

'That's more like it!'

Some of the men cheered. Others shook themselves and tightened their grips on their weapons. Hark realised he was wishing, hoping, *begging* for the main gate *to just get on with it and cave in*. The waiting was the worst part. Give the Ghosts a fight and none of them would have time to think about running.

Brutal fighting was already underway. From above, through the thick rock of the roof, they heard the muffled noises of frantic las-fire and explosions reaching them from the scale assault. The floor shook occasionally, and dislodged dust seeped fitfully from the cracked ceiling.

Hark came up the tunnel to the gatehouse. The men were lined up against the wall. He saw Ban Daur, standing ready at the tunnel mouth. Daur had four flamers drawn up ready at his back, but there were over a dozen troopers positioned down in front of him around the tunnel steps and the inner hatch. Daur had cleared all his men out of the gatehouse chamber.

'Captain?' Hark said.

'Commissar.'

'Why the feth have you pulled out of the gatehouse, Daur?' Hark whispered in his ear. 'Why aren't your flamers front and centre?'

'Who's commanding this position, commissar?' Daur asked.

'Well, you, of course.'

'Thank you. I know what I'm about. The men know what's expected. Support me. Don't question me.'

Hark had never seen Daur so firm, so bloody determined.

'Absolutely,' Hark said, with a courteous nod.

The outer hatch was badly deformed. With each successive blow of the ram outside, it buckled even further, tearing away from its frame. They could hear, quite clearly, the shouts and bellows of the enemy right outside, clamouring to get in.

Clang! The hatch bent. *Clang!* The lip of it twisted inwards. *Clang!* A hinge began to shear. *Clang!* The middle of the hatch distended like a fat man's belly.

'We hold the outer hatch, we kill a few of them,' Daur whispered to Hark. 'I want to kill a lot of them. The gate chamber is our killing ground. It bottles them up and leaves them ready for slaughter.'

Hark nodded. He understood.

'You may tell the company to fix, commissar,' said Daur.

'G Company!' Hark yelled, turning to aim his voice back down the tunnel. 'Straight silver!'

A clatter of locking blades answered him.

'Fixed and ready!' Haller called back.

'Fixed and ready, captain,' Hark said.

'Any moment now!' Daur shouted. 'Remember who you are! And remember Ibram Gaunt!'

The company, to a man, roared its approval. The sound drowned out the beat of the ram.

The sound drowned out the metal screech of the hatch finally sundering.

Screaming like feral shades loosed from the depths of the warp, the Blood Pact stormed the gatehouse. The hatch had only partially fallen in, and they came pouring in, over and around its bulk, streaming, as it seemed to Hark, like rats, like a swarm of rodent vermin spewing out of a duct across the belly hold of a mass conveyance, flowing like a tide over any and all obstructions. Grim figures in red, their filthy uniforms adorned with strings of finger bones and human teeth, came scrambling through the opening, howling out of the mouth slits of their black iron masks, their eyes bright with bestial lust. Some fired weapons, others brandished trench axes and mauls. The reek and noise of them was appalling.

The first of their wild shots hit the floor, the roof, and the frame of the inner hatchway. A Ghost in the front rank went over.

'Fire!' Daur yelled.

The dozen or so Ghosts crouching around the inner hatchway opened fire, cutting into the front of the swarming tide as it surged towards them.

Enemy warriors buckled and fell, or stumbled, wounded, and were promptly smashed down by the brute men rushing in behind them. There was a sudden stink of blood and crisped flesh. The Ghosts kept firing. Daur was firing too. Hark raised his pistol and lanced energy beams into the oncoming mass, incinerating some, violently dismembering others. In seconds, the leading ranks of the storm force were dead, just corpses carried forward by the press behind.

The tide faltered slightly. The Blood Pact warriors began struggling to clamber over bodies to reach their foe. Some tripped and fell. Las-fire knocked others off their feet. The close confines of the gate chamber degenerated a bewildering blur of bodies and yelling, motion and shots, almost incomprehensible in its violent confusion.

In the first ten seconds after the fall of the hatch, the Blood Pact lost forty warriors in the gate chamber, for the cost of only two Ghosts. Daur's killing ground had been expertly achieved.

But Ban Daur's ambitions were greater. As the gate chamber filled to capacity with storming enemy troops, with more shoving in behind, and the front of their assault almost at the inner hatch, Daur turned.

'Switch! Now!' he yelled above the din.

The Ghosts at the hatch who had been holding the enemy at bay with rifle fire suddenly rose and fell back, firing as they went. Daur pulled Hark to one side.

The flame-troopers stepped up, line abreast, and took their places, facing the charge.

'Flames, flames!' Brostin yelled.

He triggered his burner. At his side, Lubba, Dremmond and Lyse did the same. The result was devastating. The heat wash shock-sucked back down the tunnel and made Daur, Hark and the Ghosts around them gasp and shield their faces. The four flamers stood side by side in the inner hatch and streamed liquid fire into the entry chamber of the gatehouse.

There was nowhere to run or hide. There was nowhere to escape from the conflagration. The seething inferno ripped back across the chamber all the way to the broken hatch, and then blasted outside into the open, into the iron-masked faces of enemy warriors packed tight and clawing to get in.

Inside the furnace of the gate chamber, the monstrous destruction was stoked by grenades and ammo packs touching off and exploding. Stumbling, burning figures, ablaze from head to foot, blew apart as grenades in their packs and musette bags caught and detonated.

The fire made a whining, keening sound as it swirled around the chamber, spinning up to scorch the roof. It was licking, leaping and surging as if it was alive. It was almost too bright to look at, and the writhing black shapes inside it almost too terrible to bear. The scream of the fire reminded Hark of the shriek of the wind that punished Jago, day and night, eternal, primordial and hungry.

The burns across his back ached in blistering sympathy. It felt good to pay back that pain with flames.

* * *

III

THE GHOST MANNING the slot to Kolea's left suddenly took three rapid steps backwards, swayed, and collapsed flat on his back.

'Medic!' Kolea yelled, continuing to fire down out of the slot at the enemy figures on the walls below him. His overlook wasn't the only one where someone was shouting for a doctor. Kolea had started the fight with five men in the box, and now only Derin and Obel's adjutant, Dafelbe, remained upright.

'Medic!' Kolea yelled again. 'Medic here!' He aimed out, saw a scrambling figure ascending through the smoke below, and squeezed off two shots. The enemy warrior crumbled and half fell, his arm snagging on the side of the storm ladder he'd been scaling. Hooked, the warrior struggled. Before Kolea could shoot again, the warrior's own comrades had heaved him off the ladder out of their way. He fell into the smoke. Derin put a round right through the face of the first man up behind him.

'Need ammo,' Derin growled.

'I know,' said Kolea.

'Soon,' Derin added.

A whooping rocket hit the top lip of their slot and showered them with grit as it exploded.

'Too close,' coughed Dafelbe.

Kolea looked out again, shots whining up past him. He saw the Blood Pact on the nearest ladder passing up another coiled length of scaling rungs, man to man, making ready to cast it up the next stretch of wall. Kolea fired at them.

The warrior at the top of the ladder, anxious to protect the ladder-bearers below him, unpinned a stick grenade and swung back to pitch it up at the slot.

'I don't think so,' said Kolea, taking a pot shot.

The warrior toppled back off the ladder, and his grenade dropped in amongst the men immediately beneath him. The blast took the ladder away from the rock face in a thud of smoke and sparks.

Kolea had no time to feel satisfied. Heavy fire began to chop in from the right. The raiders had succeeded in getting another scaling ladder right up under the overlook next to them. The Blood Pact warriors at the top of it were fighting hand-to hand with the men in the slot, hacking to gain entry. Those lower down on the swaying ladder section were shooting sideways at Kolea's position.

'Feth it!' Kolea said, trying to return fire. The angle was poor.

'Derin! Do what you can!' Kolea cried, backing away from the window.

'Where are you going?'

'Just do it!'

Kolea ran out of the overlook, along the connecting hallway and into the adjacent casemate box.

The gunslot there was full of hacking, flailing limbs and snarling grotesks. Pabst, Vadim and Zayber were fighting to keep them out, but Pabst was wounded in the arm and Vadim could barely see for the blood streaming down his face.

'Shoot them!' Kolea cried, coming in behind them.

'No ammo!' Vadim screamed. A trench axe crunched into Zayber's neck and he staggered backwards, spewing blood.

Kolea snapped his carbine to full auto. 'Ghosts drop!' he yelled. Vadim lurched aside, pulling Pabst with him.

Kolea raked the gunslot with rapid las, blowing chunks and lumps out of the rockcrete sills. The enemy warriors choking the slot screamed and jerked as rounds ripped into them. Some fell out and disappeared instantly, others yowled and held on, clawing at the edges of the firing position, weighed down by the dead and wounded.

'Run! Get some ammo!' Kolea shouted at Pabst. He kept firing, blowing off fingers and hands, dislodging grips. A Blood Pact warrior tried to lunge bodily in through the slit, and Kolea blew him open across the shoulder, dropping his corpse onto the firestep inside the slot.

Kolea ran to the step and pulled two stick bombs out of the corpse's webbing panniers. He yanked the pins out and posted them out over the slit edge. There was a meaty double *thud*.

Pabst came running back in with a bag of clips. He was closely followed by Merrt, Vivvo and Tokar.

'What are you?' Kolea asked them.

'Gn…gn… gn… reinforcements,' said Merrt.

'Rawne sent a company down from topside to back you up,' said Vivvo.

'Get to the slot. Good to see you,' Kolea nodded. He went back into the corridor, moving through the fresh troops joining the overlook deck.

'Spread out! Fill the gaps!' he heard Corporal Chiria yelling down the smoke-washed run.

He went back to his original position, and found that Derin and Dafelbe had been joined by two Ghosts. One was Kaydey, a Belladon marksman firing a long-las. The other was Tona Criid.

The side of her head was bandaged. With grim concentration, she was firing snapshots from the corner of the slot.

'Welcome back to the Emperor's war, sergeant,' Kolea said to her as he resumed his place.

'I can't tell you how glad I am to be here,' she replied sardonically.

Kolea risked a look out as the others rattled away on either side of him. No fresh ladders had been attached, and the enemy forces were milling around at the foot of the casemate buttress in a disorganised rabble, swathed in smoke, contenting themselves with firing up at the boxes. A vast plume of dirty black smoke was fuming out of the gatehouse far below.

'I think Daur's done a day's work,' Dafelbe muttered.

'Looks that way,' Kolea agreed.

'Either that, or the fething fortress is alight,' Derin added, never one to trust a bright side.

'They're falling back!' Criid called out.

It was hard to see clearly through the thick, accumulating smoke seething up the southern face of the house, but the enemy did appear to be in retreat. Gunfire and rockets continued to come up at the gunboxes, though the rate grew thinner. Kolea could see groups of distant figures fleeing back across the dust bowl into the throat of the pass.

The last few shots were exchanged.

'This is Kolea,' Kolea said into his micro-bead. 'Report – did we hold the gate?'

Traffic snatched to and fro in brief clips.

'Say again?' Kolea said.

'Overlook, this is Daur. We have held the gate.'

Kolea looked at Derin and they both allowed weary grins to cross their dirty, unshaved faces.

'Sir!' Dafelbe called out.

Kolea turned.

Dafelbe was bending over Tona Criid. She had sagged down quietly in the corner where she had been standing. Kolea hurried over.

'Was she hit?' he asked.

'I don't think so,' Dafelbe replied. 'I think she just passed out.'

Tona stirred. 'I'm all right.' she mumbled.

'On your feet too soon,' Kolea said. 'Let's get you up.'

She didn't answer. She had blacked out again.

Day twelve. Sunrise at five plus eleven, clear. No contact overnight, no sign of enemy at daylight.

We weathered the third assault yesterday with precious few casualties considering. I am certain that if they had hit us on two fronts, as per the previous ~~assualt~~ *assault, we would not have survived.*

As it is, I intend to recommend B.D. for decoration for his sterling command in defence of the main gate (see accompanying citation).

Ammo very low. R. trying to arrange supply drop. He has a plan that he is not sharing with anyone at this stage. I have impressed upon him the vital nature of the documents discovered in the so-called library. We must preserve and secure them, or transport them clear, before this fortress finally succumbs.

One minor but troubling footnote. Master of Scouts Mkoll seems to have disappeared. I am trying to account for his whereabouts.

- Field journal, V.H. fifth month, 778.

SEVENTEEN

The Ghosts

I

THE GHOSTS CLOSED in. *They have been there all the time, luminal things chained to the ancient place, just out of sight. Now they step closer, silent as whispers, elusive as voice fragments on a skipping vox-channel, soft as the brush of black lace against stone. They draw near.*

They are not invited. They are sent. They smell the mind-heat of the lost souls in the house at the end of the world and swoop down, like winged things returning to the windcote. They are the dust on the satin brown walls, the glow and fade of the lights, the scratch and rattle of something buried under the earth. They have the voices of friends. They are the voices of the dead. They are the darkest corner of the night, the coldest atoms of the cosmos, the moan of the wind. They are music, half-heard. They are dry skulls in a dusty valley.

The ghosts close in. Only in death may they move so freely. Only in the presence and the hour of death may they come so close.

They feel it. The end is coming: the end of Hinzerhaus and all those within its walls.

They gather in the empty halls and cold galleries. Slowly, slowly, they reach–

II

–OUT.

The light died. Rawne cursed, and flicked at the lamp-pack on his desk. He was sure the cell had been a fresh one, but it was dead.

'Rerval!'

His adjutant appeared at the door. 'Sir?'

'Get me a fething lamp-pack, would you?'

'Yes, sir.'

Rawne sat back. He was tired. He'd been studying some of the old books brought up from the library. Trying to work by the come and go radiance of the wall lights gave him a headache, so he'd trained a lamp-pack on the pages.

The books didn't interest Rawne much. He'd never had much time for history. History was dead, and Rawne was much more interested in being alive. However, the likes of Hark and Baskevyl believed the books to be important, so he'd made the effort.

It had also given him some occupation. The day had passed slowly, perhaps the slowest so far. Expecting attack at any moment, they'd all stayed on knife-edge nerves. That wore a body out. As Hark had said so often, waiting was the real killer.

The books, with their crumbling, loose leaf pages, had been diverting enough. Most of the plates made no sense, and Rawne had no way of knowing how accurate any of the charts were.

But he could see enough to know that Hark was right. The books had to be shown to someone who could assess their real worth. If there was any chance – *any chance* – that they were what they seemed to be, then they could be the difference between triumph and defeat.

A chill passed through the room, a draught from somewhere. Someone had come in, pushing the door open quietly.

'Have you got that fething lamp?' Rawne asked, looking up.

'One last fight,' said Colm Corbec, smiling sadly down at him.

Rawne got up so fast his chair fell over backwards with a bang.

He blinked fast. There was no one there. Rawne turned around sharply, shaking, then around again. The room was empty.

'Feth!' he hissed. 'What the *feth*...'

'Did you knock your chair over, sir?' asked Rerval mildly, walking into the room with a fresh lamp-pack in his hand.

Rawne strode right past him to the door, and glared up and down the hallway outside.

'Sir?'

'Was that someone's idea of a joke?' Rawne snarled.

'Was what, sir?' Reval asked, confused.

'That! The... the...' Rawne stopped talking. None of the men could have pulled that stunt. Only his mind could have played a trick like that. He was tired. That was it, just fatigue.

'Are you all right, sir?' asked Rerval.

Rawne walked back to the desk and righted his chair. 'Yes. Yes... just a little jumpy.'

Rerval held the lamp-pack out to Rawne. Rawne took it.

'Thanks.'

Rerval nodded. 'Beltayn says your link should be set up in the next half an hour.'

'Just give me a nod when it's ready. I'll take it here.'

'Yes, sir.'

Rerval walked out of the room and closed the door behind him. Rawne sat down and turned his attention back to the folio, clicking the lamp-pack on.

As he turned the pages, he kept one eye on the door.

III

THAT NIGHT, ALTHOUGH the weather had not turned, the house felt especially airless after dark. The air was dry and still, and the shadows seemed to be layered, as if they had piled up on top of one another like sheets of fine black lace.

Hark hobbled along a lower hallway, leaning heavily on his stick. His back hurt. He knew he'd been pushing himself too hard, and the pain was beginning to erode the sense of well being that Curth's drugs had briefly provided. His burns were not healing. They were still wet and raw, and moving made them worse.

He reached a short flight of steps and lowered himself carefully down onto them. Just sit for a minute, he thought, just a minute or two.

His skin was pale and clammy and sweat streaked his forehead. He breathed heavily. He heard the footsteps of an approaching patrol. Hark had no wish for any of the men to see him so ill-taken.

He drew his sidearm. The cell of his plasma pistol had been running low, so he'd taken a back-up from his holdall – a handsome, almost delicate bolt pistol of brushed steel with a saw-grip handle and engraved slide plates. He made a show of unloading and reloading it.

When the patrol came past, they nodded to him and he nodded back. Just Commissar Hark, taking five to prep his weapon.

He waited until they had gone. It seemed to take a long time, because apparently phantom footsteps rolled up and down the brown satin floor for several minutes after the men had disappeared.

'Is there anyone there?' Hark called out.

The footsteps stopped.

Hark shook his head. Since they'd taken up occupation of Hinzerhaus, he'd heard so many reports of ownerless footsteps.

'Throne take this place,' he muttered.

He put the pistol away, noticing how his real hand was shaking, not from fear. It was the pain doing that, the pain slowly gnawing away at his strength.

He got up and climbed the stairs like an old man. The scout billet was a little way along the next gallery.

Livara was standing by the doorway when Hark approached. He nodded to the commissar. Hark went inside. Most of the scouts present – Hwlan, Leyr, Caober and Mklane – were resting. Preed was playing a solo card game on an upturned box.

Bonin was sitting in the corner, cleaning dust out of his lasrifle with a vizzy-cloth. He saw Hark, put his weapon and cleaning kit down, and got up.

The skin of Bonin's face was raw, like sunburn. They'd had a scout out on watch at the end of the gulley since the discovery of the new gate, and Bonin had personally taken three of the shifts. The dust had scoured him relentlessly.

'You wanted to see me?' Hark asked as Bonin came over. Bonin nodded. 'On what matter?'

Bonin jerked his head and they went out into the corridor, away from the others. They walked along until they were out of earshot.

'Are you a man of honour?' Bonin asked. 'I've always assumed you were.'

'I'd like to think so,' said Hark.

'I need to report something. I need to report it to you as a man of honour, not as a commissar.'

'The two things are not separate,' said Hark.

Bonin sniffed. 'Do you understand what I'm saying? What I'm going to tell you, I won't have you jumping on it like a commissar.'

'I'll have to make that judgement,' Hark replied.

Bonin thought for a moment. Then he said, 'I hear you've been looking for Mkoll.'

'You hear correctly.'

As if it gave him great discomfort, Bonin reached his right hand into his grubby jacket and pulled out a crumpled piece of paper. He unfolded it and stared at it for a moment.

'I found this tucked into my bedroll this evening. Dunno how long it's been there. A day, maybe two.'

He handed the slip to Hark.

It was handwritten, a brief note. It said:

> *Mach–*
>
> *There is something that must be done, a matter of honour for the regiment. It is the sword, I mean. It must be got back.*
>
> *I have gone to get it. I know I have no orders to do so, but I have a moral duty. In conscience, I could not disappear without any word. I ask you to tell them where I've gone and what I plan to do. I hope they will understand the purpose of my actions.*
>
> *The Emperor protect you.*
>
> *Your friend,*
>
> *Oan.*

Hark read it twice. 'How long have you really had this, Bonin?' he asked.

Bonin didn't answer.

'Do you know where he's gone?'

'It says there.'

'I mean how and which direction?'

Bonin shrugged. 'There was rope gear and pegs missing from the store. North, I'd guess.'

'Why north, do you think?' asked Hark.

Again, Bonin didn't answer.

'He's gone after the sword,' said Hark, 'and the sword didn't leave by itself.'

'It doesn't say who took it,' said Bonin.

'It doesn't,' Hark agreed, 'but Mkoll's not the only one missing.'

Bonin looked sharply at the commissar. There was a long silence.

'What will you do?' Bonin asked.

Hark folded the paper up and put it in his coat pocket. 'I'll have to decide. This is troubling. By his own admission, Mkoll has abandoned his post and his duty. He's left the regiment's side without orders or permission. That's called desertion.'

'Feth you!' Bonin growled. 'I asked you if you were a man of honour! I didn't have to tell you this!'

'Oh, you really did.'

Bonin stared at Hark. 'Not his duty.'

'What?'

'You said he'd abandoned his duty. He hasn't.'

Hark sighed. 'I know full well that there was no one more loyal to Gaunt than Mkoll, but we can't afford to be sentimental. Gaunt's dead, his sword's gone, and we really, really needed Mkoll here, not away on some idealistic quest.'

Bonin shook his head sadly. 'You don't know the old man like I do. Since we arrived here, he's been off his game. Told me that himself. Hated the fact that he felt sloppy and ineffective. When... when Gaunt died, he took it personally. A personal failure. He doesn't believe he's any use to us here, not any more. A liability, more like. This is his way of making amends.'

'I will consider this carefully and decide what action needs to be taken,' said Hark. 'Without wishing to sound pessimistic, it may be rather academic. If Mkoll's gone north, alone, we'll probably never see him again. If that's the case, I won't tarnish his memory by going public with this. But I have to tell Rawne. I imagine he'll want you to take command of the scouts. He'll probably send for you before the night's out.'

'Yes, sir.'

Hark looked up at something.

'What?' asked Bonin.

'I thought I heard...' Hark began. 'No, my mistake.' He looked back at Bonin. 'As you were,' he said, and limped away.

IV

A CHOKE-HOLD was the last thing he expected.

Weary of the stifling air in the shuttered overlook, Larkin left Banda on watch and stepped out into the connecting hallway. It was no better out there. The air was cold, but still, unmoving, even though the wind crooned outside. Shadows clung to the walls, and the baleful white lights glowed and faded in a slow rhythm.

Larkin paced up and down, rubbing his hands. He took a sip of water from his flask, and was about to put it away again when an arm locked around his throat.

'You're dead, Tanith,' said a voice in his ear.

Larkin struggled but the grip did not slacken. He tried to speak. *Who…?*

'You know who I am, Tanith,' the voice whispered. 'Sure as sure.' Something cold and sharp pressed against Larkin's throat.

'We got Gaunt, so we did. Now I get to settle things with you.'

Larkin snarled and rammed backwards against the hallway wall, crushing the figure on his back against the brown satin panels.

Larkin landed on the ground.

'What the gak are you doing, Tanith?' Banda demanded, appearing at the door of the overlook. Larkin looked around. He was alone. On the floor beside him, his unstoppered water flask slowly glugged out its contents.

'Musta slipped,' he said.

Sure as sure.

Banda shook her head and went back to her post. Larkin struggled back up onto his feet.

A strong hand helped him up.

'I can't watch you all the time,' said Bragg.

Larkin turned. Bragg was just there, large as life. There was a great sadness in his genial eyes. He reached over and brushed dust off Larkin's shoulders and sleeves with his huge, gentle hands.

'I can't watch you all the time,' he repeated. 'You have to be careful, you know? Be careful, Larks, or the fether will get you.'

'Bragg,' Larkin whispered. He stretched out his hand, but there was nothing to touch. Bragg had gone, like a bubble bursting, like dust settling to nothing as a bad rock storm blew out.

Larkin bent over, his fists against his forehead.

'No, no, no, NO!'

He couldn't feel the headache or the nausea yet, but he knew they were coming.

It was the only explanation, the only explanation Larkin could tolerate, anyway.

V

'Do I HAVE to stay here?' Criid asked, toying with the bandage on the side of her head.

'You asked that the other day,' replied Dorden, unwrapping the blood pressure strap from her bared arm, 'and look what happened when I let you walk around.'

Criid shrugged and sat back on her cot. The field station was quiet. Far too many Ghosts lay silent and broken in the bunks on either side of her.

'What aren't you telling me?' she asked.

'It's concussion,' said Dorden.

'And?'

'Just concussion. But it's bad, and if you move around, you're going to feel ill and pass out. So you stay there, please, until I say otherwise.'

'Really? That's all?'

Dorden sat down on the edge of her bed. 'I won't lie to you, Tona. If we were in a proper medicae facility, with decent equipment, I'd run a deep scan to assess for oedema, meningial bleeds and pieces of skull pushing into your brain, just to be safe. But we're not, so I can't. And I am confident in my diagnosis: concussion. You still have pain?'

'It comes and goes.'

'Now?'

She nodded.

'I'll get you something,' he said.

Dorden walked down the length of the field station and crossed the hall into the side room where they had secured the drugs and dressing packs. It was gloomy, and poorly lit. He took out the lamp-pack he'd taken to carrying on his belt and clicked it on. It came on, then faded, as if the battery was drained. He clicked it on and off.

'Lesp!' he called.

He started to rummage in one of the dispensary cartons, looking for high dose tranq/anti-inflammatories.

He could hear something dripping.

'Lesp! Get in here! Bring a light!'

The orderly appeared in the doorway with a shining lamp.

'Doctor?'

'Get some light on me, I can't see a thing.'

Lesp shone his lamp down obediently.

'What's that sound?' he asked after a moment. He turned the beam away. 'Feth's sake, Lesp! I can't see!'

'Doctor?' Lesp murmured. 'Look.'

Dorden looked up. Lesp's lamp beam was illuminating the back wall of the little room. The wall was streaming with blood. It glistened black in the hard light.

'What in the name of–' Dorden stammered. 'Who did this? What fething idiot thought it would be funny to waste precious blood supplies?'

'It's coming out of the wall,' said Lesp.

'That's ridiculous! It's–'

Dorden stared. The blood was quite clearly oozing out between the brown satin panels.

'Get me a pry-bar,' said Dorden.

'What?'

'A pry-bar! A pry-bar!'

'What's going on in here?' Zweil snorted, entering the room behind him. 'You're waking the patients. Is that good medical practice? I don't believe so–'

'Get out, Zweil!'

'I will not!'

'Father, get out of this room now!'

'What are you staring at?' Zweil asked, pushing past them.

'The blood!' Lesp blurted. 'The blood on the wall!'

'What blood?' the old ayatani asked, touching the wall. 'It's just dust.'

Dorden snatched the lamp from Lesp's quivering hand and stepped closer. He could see it clearly. It wasn't blood running down the wall, it was dust, fine trickles of dust seeping out around the panels.

'Throne take me for an old fool,' Dorden muttered. He looked around at Lesp and punched him on the arm. 'And you for a young one.'

'It looked like blood,' said Lesp, ruefully.

It really had.

'Get me a ten mil dose of axotynide and shut up,' Dorden replied.

He walked back into the field station, aware that his pulse was still racing. Criid's cot was empty.

'Where is she?' he asked, looking around. 'She was just here. Where is she?'

In a nearby cot, Twenzet shrugged. 'She just got up and went out. I told her not to. She said–'

'What did she say, trooper?'

'I dunno,' Twenzet replied.

'What did she say?' Dorden snarled.

Twenzet's eyes widened. 'I… I think she said something like "He's calling me". I thought she meant her boy.'

Dorden didn't believe that for a moment. He hurried back into the hallway. 'Tona!' he shouted. 'Tona!'

VI

LUDD STARTED TO hurry the moment he heard the angry voices up ahead. Then there was a rattling crack of gunfire and he broke into a run.

He burst into the billet hall, into the middle of a riot. On all sides, troopers were shouting, backing away, waving their hands. Wes Maggs stood with his lasrifle in his hands in the centre of the room. He was shaking, his eyes wide, his teeth clenched. Scorched holes in the wall panels ahead of him showed where his shots had gone in.

'Give me the gun, Wes,' Varl was saying calmly, moving round to face Maggs, his hands extended.

'She was right there! Right there! You all saw her, didn't you?'

'Give me the fething weapon, Wes!' Varl ordered.

'She was right there!' Maggs yelled. 'Right in fething front of me! I must have hit her!'

'That's enough,' said Ludd. No one paid him the slightest attention.

'I said, that's enough!' Ludd bellowed.

'Give me the gun!' Varl repeated, facing Maggs down.

'Stand back, sergeant,' said Ludd, trying to interpose himself between them.

'Get out of the way,' Varl warned him.

'That's not how this is going to work,' Ludd replied.

'She was right there!' Maggs insisted, his voice strangled with tension.

Varl lunged at Maggs.

'No!' Ludd cried.

Varl got his hands around Maggs's weapon and they grappled. Varl's augmetic strength forced the barrel up. A flurry of rounds fired off into the ceiling.

Nahum Ludd was neither especially large nor especially strong, but the Commissariat had trained him well in methods of self-defence and disarmament. Training took over.

He leapt forward, scoop-kicking Varl's legs out from under him. Simultaneously, he took hold of Maggs's weapon in his left hand, and chopped Maggs in the throat with the side of his right. Varl crashed down on his back to Ludd's left, and Maggs went over, gasping, to his right. Ludd was left standing between them, Maggs's lasrifle in his hand. He swung it around deftly and aimed it at Maggs.

'Stay the feth down!' he instructed.

'I didn't do any–'

'Stay down! Varl, don't even think of continuing this.'

'Hey,' said Varl, getting up, his hands raised. 'I was just trying to help.' He looked at Ludd, impressed. 'That was pretty fancy stuff, Ludd.'

'Commissar Ludd.'

Varl nodded, grinning. 'Fancy fething stuff, eh?' He looked around.

The Ghosts around them began to cheer and clap.

'Thanks, but shut up,' said Ludd. 'Melyr. Garond. Remove Trooper Maggs's other weapons and get him on his feet.'

'She was right there!' Maggs protested as the two Ghosts scooped him up and took his warknife and pistol away. 'I was just trying to protect us all!'

'From what?' Ludd asked.

'The old dam! The old dam!' Maggs cried bitterly.

An armed fire-team slammed into the billet hall behind them, led by Kolea. They had their weapons trained.

'Shots reported,' Kolea growled looking at Ludd and the others down the foresight of his carbine. 'Do we have contact?'

'False alarm, major,' Ludd said. 'Just a little domestic incident.'

Kolea lowered his gun and clicked his micro-bead. 'Kolea to all stations. Stand down, stand down. False contact.'

He looked back at Ludd. 'What happened?'

'Nothing I couldn't handle,' said Ludd. 'Can we find somewhere we can make Maggs secure for the time being?'

Kolea frowned. 'Lock him up, you mean?'

Ludd nodded.

'Is he on charges?'

'I think it's safe to say yes,' said Ludd.

Kolea whistled.

'I was only trying to protect us all,' said Maggs, quieter and calmer now. 'You've seen her, haven't you, Gol?'

'What's he talking about?' Kolea asked.

'Who the feth knows?' Varl replied.

* * *

VII

HE HADN'T BEEN able to sleep, the air was so still. As he lay in his bedroll, it felt like he was being smothered. He got up and walked around, with no particular destination in mind.

That was a lie.

No particular destination at all.

The scratching under the floor knew he was lying.

Baskevyl wandered idly down through the lower levels of the house, nodding to sentry groups and watch positions as he went, stopping to share a few words.

All the while, he could hear the slithering underground, the mottled, slick, spinal cord thing moving through the rock beneath him, following him, following him.

No, not following, leading.

Baskevyl walked on, down a loop of stairs, passing lights that glowed and faded, glowed and faded, in time with the hideous scratching noise *down there*.

He reached the entry hole in the wall that led into the new section. The wall panels that had been pulled down had disappeared for firewood. Three troopers guarded the doorway: Karsk, Gunsfeld and Merrt.

'Quiet night, sir?' Gunsfeld asked.

'So, so.'

'We heard there was a thing just now, in one of the billet halls,' said Karsk.

'Nothing to worry about.'

'We thought it might have been another raid starting.'

'It wasn't,' said Baskevyl. 'You can relax. Not too much, mind. All right if I go through?'

Gunsfeld ushered him in. 'Help yourself, sir.'

Baskevyl smiled a thank you, and stepped through the hole into the amber glow of the new section. He'd gone a little way when he heard a voice call to him from behind. Trooper Merrt had followed him down the tunnel.

'What's up, Merrt?'

'I just gn... gn... gn... wanted to ask you something, sir,' Merrt said. He looked awkward and embarrassed.

'All right.'

Merrt held out his weapon. 'What does that say to you, sir?'

Baskevyl peered at the gun. 'It says... I think... er, "034TH".'

Merrt nodded. 'Right. Gn... gn... gn... thanks, sir.'

'Was that it?'

'Yes, sir.'

'Carry on, then.'

Merrt waited until Baskevyl was out of sight, then he looked at his rifle again. 034TH. That's what Gunsfeld had said too, when Merrt had asked him. Gunsfeld had looked as perplexed by the question as Baskevyl was.

The problem was, they were wrong. Merrt could understand that, because he'd been seeing 034TH too, for a long time.

But the more he'd studied the serial mark, the more he'd become convinced he'd been right all along.

It said DEATH. It absolutely, definitely said DEATH.

IT SLITHERED BENEATH him, so close to the surface, some of the brown satin floor panels seemed to lift slightly and drop back into place as it passed. He could hear it scratching and grinding, wet meat and bone on rock.

'All right,' he whispered. 'I'm doing it.'

The scratching fell silent.

Baskevyl entered the library. He walked along the stacks until he was facing the book. It was bound in black leather, sheened and smooth, with an emblem embossed in silver on the spine – a worm with its long, segmented body curled around in a circle, so that its jaws clenched its tail-tip to form a hoop.

He reached out to touch it. His fingers wavered.

He took the book off the shelf.

VIII

'WHAT DO YOU mean, you don't know where she is?' Dalin asked.

'She's just gone for a walk,' said Curth. 'We're looking for her.'

Dalin looked around at Cullwoe.

'She'll be all right,' Cullwoe said. 'She's tough.'

Dalin turned and walked back to where Meryn stood at the door of the billet.

'Permission to help search for Sergeant Criid, sir,' he said.

'Two fire-teams, out here with me,' Meryn called over his shoulder. 'Quick as you can.'

He turned back to face Dalin. 'We'll help you look, adjutant,' he said.

IX

'SO, IT'S TRUE then, Vawne?' Van Voytz's voice crackled over the poor link.

'That's Rawne, sir. Yes, it's true.'

Static hissed and buzzed. 'I'm losing you, general,' Rawne said, pulling the mic closer.

'I said that's a damn shame, Rawne. He was a good man, one of the best. I've known Ibram for years. Fine, fine officer. I'll miss him. How are you coping?'

'The circumstances here are not good. We need assistance urgently. Munitions mainly, but reinforcement would be very welcome.'

'It's coming, Rawne,' the voice on the link said. 'Hold tight. I'll try to arrange a munitions drop for you.'

'Sir, I've sent you particulars. Munition requirements, plus a plan for the drop.'

Static shrieked and moaned for a moment. '–in front of me.'

'Say again, Elikon?'

'I said, I've got your request right in front of me, Rawne. Looks do-able. You're sure about this drop site?'

'Confirmed, sir.'

'And you want an extraction too?'

'Yes, sir. If you read my communiqué, you'll see why.'

Rawne waited. The vox gurgled and fizzled like a dud grenade. The signal strength indicators kept dropping back to nothing.

'Did you hear me, Nalwood? Nalwood?'

'Here, sir.'

'I said I'll review this and try to set something up. I won't leave Gaunt's boys hanging out to dry. Expect contact from me around dawn.'

'Thank you, sir.'

'Ech'kkah.'

Rawne paused. 'Elikon, Elikon say again? Elikon, Elikon, this is Nalwood, this is Nalwood.'

The vox grunted and flared, letting out a sharp rising whine that made Rawne yank off his headset with a wince. The signal continued to flood out of the speakers.

'–ech'rakah koh'thet magir shett gohrr! Gohrr! GOOOOHHRRR! ECH'KHETT FF'TEH GOOOOHRRR ANARCH!'

The link went dead, cold and dead as hard rock.

'Beltayn!' Rawne yelled, leaping to his feet. 'What the feth was that?'

Fifty metres away in the base chamber, Beltayn urgently nursed his vox-caster, one headset cup pressed to his ear.

'Channel interference, sir!' he shouted back. 'I'm trying to recover the Elikon signal now!'

Rerval bent over Beltayn. 'Try 3:33 gain–'

'Thank you, I *am*.'

'That sounded like–'

'I know what it fething sounded like, Rerval!' Beltayn snapped.

Rerval went pale. 'Do you think… if we can hear them… can they hear us?'

Beltayn wasn't listening. He wound a dial over and threw two toggle switches. 'Think I've got it… I think I've got it back. Clean signal. Setting for balance.'

Beltayn sat back from the caster suddenly. 'Feth,' he said.

'Bel?' Rerval asked.

Beltayn handed him the headset. Rerval pressed it to his ear.

He heard the voice, distant but quite distinct. It said, 'Are we the last ones left alive? Are we? Someone, anyone, please? Are we? Is there anybody out there? Are we the last ones left alive?'

Rerval began to shake. 'Bel,' he said. 'That's *your* voice.'

'I know,' said Beltayn.

X

It seemed a long way back to the base chamber. Hark wanted to lie down. More than that, he wanted painkillers. More than that, he wanted sleep.

He was limping along a corridor in the middle range of the house on the southern side. Individual inset box gunslits formed a row of windows looking out down the pass. He sat down on the firestep under one of them, careful not to lean back. Shifting around he managed to peer out into the darkness. It was well past midnight, local. The night was virtually calm and very clear. He could see the black walls of the pass against the maroon sky, and the small, fierce moon hanging above them. The moonlight lit up the lower slopes of the house and made the dust bowl beyond the gate glow like a snowfield. He watched the wind chase zephyrs of dust across the shining dunes.

He heard footsteps approaching.

He took out his pistol, pretending to load it again.

Someone walked past him, stirring the air. He looked up, but there was nobody around. Hark tensed. The air had suddenly gone very cold. The pain in his back flared and he realised he was quite incapable of standing up. He distinctly heard the sound of Tanith pipes. Fear prickled across him.

Tona Criid appeared, padding along in bare feet. She looked like she was sleepwalking.

'Tona?'

She turned her head slightly, but didn't seem to recognise him.

'Tona, can you help me?'

She kept walking, her feet making small, slapping noises on the brown satin flooring.

'Sergeant Criid, please,' he groaned. 'I can't stand, and there's something badly wrong here, something terrible.'

She stopped in her tracks and looked back at Hark.

'He's here,' she said. 'He's here.'

'Who is?'

'Caff,' she said. 'Look.'

She gestured ahead of her. Down the corridor, in the dark, a light had appeared. It was tiny at first, but then it grew brighter until it had become a twisting, jumping, flickering snake of intense, baleful luminosity. It danced and crackled. Hark felt the hairs on his neck rise and smelled ozone. He knew it for what it was: corposant, freak electrical discharge.

'Tona, get back,' he said, trying to get up, but his legs were too weak. 'Tona Criid, get back, now!'

'Look,' she said, smiling.

The light wasn't a light anymore. It was a figure, a human figure, radiating light from inside its form. Tona began to cry. Tears raced down her thin cheeks.

'Caff,' she sobbed.

'That's not Caffran!' Hark cried. He tried to rack the slide of his bolt pistol. It jammed. He fought at it, grinding it back and forth.

'Tona!'

The figure turned to face them slowly. It was tall. Its clothing was torn and ripped, and soaked with blood. It was quite dead, Hark saw that instantly. Gore caked its face and matted its short, blond hair.

It was Ibram Gaunt.

Criid uttered a cry of pain and disbelief. She lurched forwards and beat at Gaunt's chest with her fists.

'You're dead! You're dead!' she wailed, thumping at him. 'Where's Caff? You're dead! You're fething dead!'

The bloody figure reached out its arms to embrace her. She pulled back, terrified.

Hark finally cleared his gun. He found his feet at last and rose, taking a step forward.

'He's dead!' Criid screamed.

'I know,' Hark said. He grabbed her by the arm and pushed her back behind him. She did not resist. He faced the figure and raised his pistol.

'I don't know what you are,' he said. 'I know what you'd like us to think you are. Leave us alone.'

The figure opened its mouth, as if to reply, but the mouth did not stop opening. The jaws extended wider and wider in a hellish, silent scream, and noxious light shone out of the throat. The skin, the bloody lips, pulled back away from the widening maw, revealing teeth, revealing skull. Flesh and meat scurried backwards like acid-eaten fabric, stripping the face, the scalp, the throat down to muscle and sinew, then down to bare bone. Clothing rotted in a split second, decomposing back to dust, stripping the skeleton until it stood before them, gaunt and stark.

Its mouth was still wide open in that silent, endless scream. Its arms were still extended, the last gobbets of liquid flesh and tufts of rag dripping off them.

Then, and only then, it screamed aloud. The sound stripped out their minds and shivered their organs. It was a sound neither of them would ever forget.

Hark dropped his pistol and pulled Criid into his arms to protect her with the bulk of his body.

The screaming skeleton exploded.

They felt the shockwave rock them. They smelled dust and fried bone and, worst of all, Gaunt's cologne. Every wall lamp in the hall blew out and the light died.

Hark released Criid. They blinked in the darkness. They heard footsteps running up through the house to find them.

'What the feth was that?' Hark gasped.

Outside, the heavens lit up. Huge booming sounds echoed down the pass, the sound of a martial god's boundless wrath. Hark staggered to the nearest window slit and looked out. Bombardment fire had lit up the sky behind the pass, making it a jagged silhouette, flash after flash.

'What the feth was *that*?' Criid asked him.

'I don't know,' Hark replied quietly, watching the giant flares of light eat up the dark. 'But I think this is the end for us.'

Day thirteen. Four sixteen, before sunrise. Conditions good.

What am I saying? Conditions good? I mean the wind is down and it's clear. Nothing else is good.

Madness descended last night. Things happened that can't be accounted for. Men saw things, felt things, heard things. I saw things. I will not record them here, because I do not ~~know how~~ have any way to explain them.

I had a feeling about this place from the very start, a feeling that the rational part of my mind put aside. I can't ignore it any more. This place, this damn house, is evil. There is a presence here that is growing in strength. I believe it poses as great a threat to us as the enemy itself.

When we came here, when the rumours first started, G. had us ban words like 'cursed' and 'haunted'. I do not think such words can be ignored any more. We are in trouble, more trouble than we ever imagined.

The war reached us a few hours ago, in the middle of the night, at the height of the madness. Some kind of huge artillery battle is taking place beyond the pass, lighting up the sky.

This may mean the promised reinforcements are moving up to relieve us. Or it may mean we are about to be annihilated in the middle of a full scale offensive.

— Field journal, V.H. fifth month, 778.

EIGHTEEN

The Last Chance

I

'THAT'S YOU THEN, is it?' Rawne asked, watching the light shock quake and shimmer the distant morning sky beyond the pass.

'Yes,' said Berenson. 'It's been confirmed, though details are scant. Vox-links are poor. But, yes. As of midnight local, last night, the advancing strengths of the Cadogus Fifty-Second engaged the enemy main force. At Banzie Pass, actually, just as predicted.'

'Throne bless the Tacticae,' said Kolea.

The three of them stood outside a cloche on the ridge line of the house, looking south through scopes. The day was bright and startlingly clear. The cloche domes studding the ridge on either side of them glowed gold like templum cupolas. The sky was selpic blue. Far away, beyond the crags and the western arm of the Altids, that blue buckled and quivered like silk in the wind. They could hear the *thoom thoom thoom* of heavy guns. It would have sounded like an approaching thunderstorm, except that the booming was too regular.

'Implications for us?' Rawne asked, lowering his scope.

'The prospect of relief at last,' said Berenson. 'If the Cadogus main force has reached Banzie Pass, then the reinforcement companies must be close at hand.'

'Right on time,' muttered Rawne. 'Three days, you said.'

'I did,' Berenson nodded.

'It's not going to be that easy,' said Kolea. 'They won't let us go that easily.'

'Why not?' asked Berenson.

'Because we've hurt them,' said Kolea. 'We've kept them out for days. They want this place, so they can secure the pass here. But that part is secondary. They'll want to make us pay.'

'You can read their minds, major?' Berenson sneered.

'I've fought them before,' said Kolea.

'Are we in a position to fight them now?' Berenson asked.

'No,' Rawne replied, 'but in a few hours, we might be. I've secured a munitions resupply. We can re-arm and hold on a little longer. As long as we have to.'

'When's the drop?' asked Kolea.

'Waiting for an ETA,' said Rawne. 'By noon, I hope.'

'Let's hope we're all still here come noon,' said Kolea.

Rawne looked around at him. 'What's that supposed to mean, Kolea?'

'You were here last night, weren't you?' Kolea replied. 'You saw the things that were happening. They're getting worse, these–'

'Are we ever going to use the word?' asked Rawne. 'Hauntings?'

'All right, hauntings,' said Kolea. 'They've been happening since the day we got here, but they're getting worse. And just because the sun's come up, it doesn't mean we're safe.'

II

ZWEIL PUT DOWN his psalter, licked his thumb and forefinger, and snuffed out the votive candle.

'You want me to do what?' he asked.

Hark sat facing him in the small room that Zweil had taken as his sanctuary.

'You heard me, father.'

'An exorcism? I'm an ayatani priest, not a wizard, you idiot.'

Hark breathed deeply. 'All right, setting to one side the fact you just called me an idiot – you really shouldn't do that, father, on account of the fact that I have a gun – I know what I'm asking is extreme. But you've seen what's going on.'

Zweil nodded. His gnarled, liver-spotted hands reached up and removed the ceremonial stole from around his neck, folded it and put it away in his satchel. 'I've seen,' he said. 'I've seen what I always see. Men in a dire circumstance. Men afraid. Men dying. Men *afraid* of dying. Tension, stress, battle fatigue...'

'It's more than that.'

'Piffle. This place is ghastly, the fighting's been miserable and we've lost a great deal. Worst of it is, everyone feels like we're penned in. Trapped, like we're in a cage. Like this house is our cage.'

'Father...'

Zweil glanced at Hark. 'There are no malign spirits here, Viktor. Just frightened soldiers in extremity. The human mind does all the rest. Last night, Dorden – a man as sound and sober as Dorden, Viktor – thought he saw blood running down a wall. It wasn't blood. It was dust.'

Hark drew his hand across his mouth and then, hesitantly, told the old priest what he and Criid had witnessed the previous night.

Zweil was silent for a long time after Hark had finished.

'Well, was that my imagination, father?' Hark asked.

'There will be some rational explanation,' Zweil replied.

Hark shook his head and rose to his feet. To do so, he had to lean heavily on his crutch. 'Let's say you're right, father, and it's all in our heads. Surely a blessing of prohibition from you would help psychologically if nothing else?'

'I don't do parlour tricks,' said Zweil. 'I won't have the Imperial creed diminished by empty theatrics.'

Hark turned and limped towards the chamber door. 'Your scepticism disappoints me, father ayatani. It's especially disappointing to hear it coming from a man who saw the Saint with his own eyes, and believed.'

'That was different,' said Zweil.

'Only because you wanted to believe then,' said Hark. 'You really don't want to believe in this, do you?'

III

BASKEVYL'S HANDS HAD been shaking as he'd opened the book for the first time. Now, as he closed it again, he felt like a fething idiot. His service pistol, which he had drawn and laid on the table beside the book just before opening it, only emphasised that idiocy. What exactly had he been expecting? That something was going to leap out of the pages at him? Had he actually been thinking he might have to shoot the book?

Idiot, idiot, idiot...

The book was nothing, an alien thing, as incomprehensible as some of the other texts Beltayn had pulled off the shelves to examine, a disappointment.

There had been pages of tightly packed text, which he couldn't read, and illustrated plates that seemed to be a mix of obscure diagrams, primitive zodiacs and charts. As he leafed through the pages, Baskevyl had turned the book the other way up several times, uncertain which end was the front and which the back. Neither way seemed convincing.

Baskevyl had borrowed Rawne's office for an hour while the commander walked his dawn tour of the house. Outside the door, the place was waking up. Men trudged past. Baskevyl heard glum, early morning voices, the voices of those who had woken up after far too little sleep mixing with the voices of those who had seen the small hours in, red-eyed, on watch. He smelled meal-cans warming on the cooking grate in the base chamber and caffeine steaming in metal jugs.

He got up and stretched. Maybe some food...

There was a knock at the door and Fapes came in. Hurriedly, foolishly, Baskevyl covered the book and the pistol with his jacket.

'Thought you might like a cup, sir,' said the adjutant, holding out a tin mug of caffeine.

'I'll have to report you to the Black Ships, Fapes,' Baskevyl smiled.

'Sir?'

'You're a mind-reader.'

Fapes grinned and brought the mug over to the desk.

'Last night, eh, sir?' he said. 'What was all that?'

'The barrage, you mean?'

Fapes shrugged. 'That, yeah. But the rest of the stuff. I heard Wes Maggs went nuts and there are all sorts of stories doing the rounds.'

'Stories?'

'Rumours, I suppose, sir.'

'You know the regiment's stance on rumours, Fapes.'

Fapes nodded.

Baskevyl picked up the mug and sipped. 'Still,' he said, 'between you and me?'

Fapes smiled again. 'They've been saying this place is, you know–'

'Haunted, Fapes?'

'I wouldn't like to comment, sir, but they've been saying it since we got here. Last night, feth, footsteps, lights, whispers. Bool swears he saw an old lady without a face.'

'A what?'

'Up in west six, sir. He told me himself. An old biddy in a long, black dress.'

'With no face?'

'Exactly.'

Baskevyl took another sip. 'How long has Bool been in charge of the regiment's sacra supply, Fapes?'

Fapes snorted, but Baskevyl could tell he was unsettled. The light-hearted approach, the easy manner, it was all Fapes's way of handling the matter. He was looking for reassurance.

Baskevyl was horribly afraid he wasn't in a position to offer any.

'Do you think,' Fapes began, 'do you think there really are ghosts here, sir?'

'Apart from us? Of course not, Fapes.'

Fapes nodded. 'If there are, sir, if there are… could they kill us?'

Baskevyl blinked. He wanted to blurt out *there's something under the rock here, right under us, that would kill us all in a second*.

Instead, he managed a simple 'No.'

'That's what Ludd said, sir. He said it was our imaginations getting to us.' Fapes didn't look particularly convinced.

'Ludd's right, Fapes,' said Baskevyl. 'One thing, though…'

'Sir?'

'It's *Commissar* Ludd.'

'Yes, sir. Of course, sir.'

There was a slightly awkward pause.

'Major Rawne has called a command briefing in half an hour,' Fapes said.

'In here?'

'Yes, sir.'

'I'd better clear my things. Go and get a pot of this stuff and some more cups. The officers will appreciate it.'

Fapes nodded and left the room. Sipping his caffeine, Baskevyl scooped up his jacket with his free hand. The sleeve caught on the book's cover and knocked it open.

Baskevyl put his cup down and pulled on his jacket. A draught slowly licked the open pages over like dry leaves. Baskevyl picked up his pistol and buckled it back into its holster.

He stopped and reached towards the book quickly. What was that he had just seen? He flipped back through the pages, reversing the draught's work. *Where was it? Surely he hadn't imagined it...*

He found the illustration. Baskevyl flattened the page with his hand and stared at it.

It was a drawing of a worm. A line drawing of a worm that, like the silver emblem embossed on the book's spine, had seized its own tail in its jaws to form a hoop with its lean, limbless body. The worm circle was surrounded by concentric rings of a certain design, and lines came in from various sides to intersect with the outer circles.

What the feth is this?

Baskevyl turned the page and saw another illustration. It seemed to show some kind of pin or bolt in cross-section, though it could easily have been a heraldic device. Further diagrammatic drawings showed other rings and systems of lines drawn in a rectilinear web and annotated.

He turned another page. Here was a diagram showing what appeared to be the hooded eye of a reptile.

But it wasn't. Baskevyl took a deep breath.

He knew exactly what it was a picture of.

IV

HALF AN HOUR later, with the ominous boom of the distant bombardment still echoing in the background, Rawne walked into the room. Hark, Ludd, and all the company officers who had survived well enough to stand were waiting for him.

'Commanding officer!' Ludd barked.

Everyone saluted without hesitation. Everyone shared the grim presentiment that this might be the last time the officers of the Tanith First gathered for such a meeting.

Rawne took the salute with a nod. Berenson was with him, and Rawne had also called in the senior adjutants.

'The sounds you've been hearing since midnight last night,' he began, 'are the sounds of the Cadogus Fifty-Second giving hell to the Archenemy in Banzie Pass.'

There was a general chorus of satisfaction.

'All that remains for us to do now is hold on,' Rawne said. 'Hold on and hold this fething place until they get to us.'

'How long will that be, sir?' asked Kamori.

Rawne glanced at Berenson.

'As soon as they can,' said Berenson. Several officers groaned.

'How many times have we been told that over the years?' asked Obel.

'Too many,' said Rawne. 'And it's always true.' He looked around at them all. 'We keep our heads and do what we do best, and we'll get out of this hole yet. That's my promise to you, and you know I don't make many promises.'

'Doesn't keeping that promise rather depend on the Blood Pact playing along?' asked Kamori, winning a few dark chuckles.

'No,' said Rawne. 'Maintain discipline and vigilance. Get ready to fight if you have to, and if you have to, fight like bastards. The Blood Pact can go feth itself.'

Larkin raised a hand.

'Is this a question about munitions, Larks?' Rawne asked.

'Yup,' Larkin nodded, lowering his hand.

'Then I've got good news. Beltayn?'

The senior adjutant stepped forwards. 'We received the confirmation signal from Elikon M.P. twenty minutes ago. Munition supply drop will be made in exactly two hours.'

Beltayn's announcement provoked a lot of chatter and noise.

'Quiet down,' said Rawne.

'How's that going to work, sir?' asked Daur. 'We land anything in the gate area, the enemy is going to be all over us in minutes. You know what happened with the water drop. I wouldn't want to be lugging munitions in under fire.'

'We're not going to be using the gate area, Daur,' said Rawne. He looked over at Bonin. The new chief of scouts frowned slightly, and then slowly nodded as he understood.

'This is that "right moment" you were talking about, isn't it?' Bonin asked.

'It is,' said Rawne. 'The transports have been instructed to set down in the gulley in front of the second gate. As far as we can tell, the enemy doesn't know about it, and the gulley gives us decent cover. The transport can land, and we can unload it in through the second gate before the enemy realises what's going on.'

Bonin nodded. 'That's good,' he said.

'It'll still be tight,' said Kolosim.

'Of course,' Rawne replied, 'but it's the best option and we'll make it work. I want volunteers. Two companies, one to unload, one to cover them and defend the gulley.'

Almost every hand was raised.

Rawne looked around. 'Thank you. Captain Meryn, your boys get defence. Captain Varaine, L Company will be unloading. Everyone else, full strength at every rampart, overlook and casemate, north and south. Kolosim, Obel? The main gate's yours this time. Talk to Daur, he knows how to hold a fething gate. Kolea, you get command of the south face. Baskevyl, upper galleries and north. Daur, Sloman, Chiria, I want your companies mobile and fluid, ready to move at short notice to any part of the house that needs support.'

The three of them nodded. Chiria, now holding the brevet rank of captain, had taken acting command of K Company in Domor's absence. She was taking her duties very seriously. She was determined not to let her beloved captain down.

'One last thing,' said Rawne. He looked over at Hark. 'The stuff we found in the library.'

'The stuff Beltayn found,' Hark corrected, shifting uncomfortably on his crutch.

'Indeed. Credit to him. Everyone needs to understand this. Getting that stuff out and clear is as important as getting the munition supplies in. The drop will be two transports, not one. The first bird will be empty, ready to extract a team carrying as many of those fething books as they can. In and out, fast scoop. Then the munitions lifter will come in and we'll get busy. The gulley's only big enough to take one transport at a time.'

'That's gonna spoil the element of surprise,' said Bonin.

'Yeah, a little, but we work with it. The books are too important,' said Rawne. 'I know this because Hark and Bask told me so.'

'Who gets to take the ride out?' asked Meryn.

'I've already chosen a team,' said Rawne, 'and I'm not going to brook any arguments on it. Hark.'

Hark frowned. 'I want to stay, major.'

'No arguments, I said. I need someone with clout to get those books to the attention of the proper people. Besides, and I hate to draw attention to this, Hark , you're hurting. Dorden says you need urgent graft work. Get the books to Elikon, and they can give you the treatment you need.'

'That's an order, then?' asked Hark morosely.

'Firm as any I've ever given,' said Rawne.

Hark shook his head sadly. 'I won't pretend I like it.'

'Major Berenson's going to ride with you. I need him to link up with command and fill them in. Criid, you're going too.'

Tona Criid glared at him. 'No way am I–'

'Did I imagine it, or did I say the "no arguments" bit out loud?' Rawne asked. 'Dorden advises me you need proper treatment too so, like Hark, you're going to be a courier.'

'There are dozens of Ghosts in the field station who need emergency evacuation to proper medicae facilities,' said Criid bluntly. 'I won't be chosen over them.'

'Oh, Throne,' said Rawne. 'I fething hate being surrounded by so many bloody heroes. You're going, Criid. The poor bastards in the field station will get evacuated soon enough.'

'Who else?' asked Hark.

'Twenzet, Klydo and Swaythe. I'm not being sentimental about this. They're all walking wounded, but they're able-bodied enough to carry stuff. I'd rather send men with light wounds than draw troopers from the active line.'

Hark nodded. 'Makes sense. All right.'

'Get ready. Beltayn, help Commissar Hark pack the books into kit bags. And do one last sweep of the book room to make sure we haven't missed anything vital.'

'Yes, sir,' Beltayn nodded.

'Ludd?' Rawne said.

'Yes, sir?'

'Once Hark's gone, you'll be more than acting commissar. You'll be commissar, plain and simple. You up to that?'

Ludd nodded.

Rawne turned to the others. 'Ludd's going to have an uphill battle. Help him. Reinforce his instruction and his authority. You see any trooper, any trooper, mock or piss-take or ignore him, come down on him like an Earthshaker shell, or I'll come down like an Earthshaker shell on you. Are we perfectly clear?'

'Yes,' the officers said.

Rawne smiled and half-frowned. 'I believe I'm in command. I'm in command, aren't I, Bel?'

'Last time I checked, sir,' said Beltayn.

'So?' asked Rawne, and let it hang.

'Yes, commander,' the officers said.

'Better,' said Rawne. 'Now get your arses moving and let's show the fething bastard enemy how to prosecute a war.'

V

THE OFFICERS FILED out, heading off to assemble their companies. Rawne pulled Ludd to one side.

'Yes, sir?'

'Get Maggs out of lock up. We're going to need every man we can get. Tell him he was an idiot, and tell him if he acts up again, I'll hunt him down and gut him like a larisel.'

'Yes, sir.'

'Something else, Ludd?'

Nahum Ludd shrugged. 'What's a larisel, sir?'

'Does it matter, Ludd? I think the simile speaks for itself.'

'Yes, sir. Thanks for–'

Rawne had turned away. 'Thanks for what, Ludd?'

'For speaking up for me, sir.'

'Just do your fething job and don't shame me, Ludd. Then I won't have to gut you like a larisel either.'

Rawne walked off down the busy hallway. He entered the base chamber. It was thronging with troops moving off to their positions. The last of the ammo was being doled out. 'That's it,' Rawne heard Ventnor shout. 'What you've got is all there is! Only things I have left are prayers and goodwill!'

Berenson stood on the main level. He held his left hand out to Rawne, his right still in its sling. Rawne took it.

'I may not get the chance later,' said Berenson. 'Good luck. Not that you'll need it.'

'Oh, we're going to need all the luck we can get,' said Rawne.

VI

BASKEVYL WALKED INTO the field station. He looked around, and then crossed to the bed where Shoggy Domor lay. Domor was a pale shell of his old self, thin and drawn by the pain of his wound and the traumatic surgery he had endured. The white skin of his chin and cheeks was prickled with black stubble. He looked asleep. No, he looked dead, dead and gone.

Baskevyl hesitated.

'You need something, major?' Curth asked as she hurried by.

'No, thanks. Just looking in,' Baskevyl replied.

When she'd gone, Baskevyl stayed a moment longer, staring down at Domor.

He turned away.

'Major?' a small, dry voice said.

Baskevyl looked back. Domor's eyes were open, half open, at least.

'Hey, Shoggy, I didn't mean to wake you.'

'I thought it was you.' Domor's voice was very thin and quiet, and his respiration made an awful, hissing sound, like a snake.

Baskevyl pulled up a rickety wooden chair and sat down beside the bed.

'How are things going?' Domor asked, his breath hissing in and out like old, dry, punctured bellows scratching and pumping. *Hiss-rasp. Hiss-rasp.*

'We're all right. Still here.'

'They won't tell me anything. They keep telling me not to worry.' *Hiss-rasp. Hiss-rasp.*

'Well, they're right about that. We'll be out of here soon. Trust me.'

'Is that what Gaunt reckons?' Domor whispered. *Hiss-rasp. Hiss-rasp.*

Baskevyl bit his lip. 'Yeah,' he nodded. 'That's what the commander reckons.'

Domor closed his eyes for a moment and smiled. *Hiss-rasp. Hiss-rasp.*

'Shoggy?'

Domor opened his eyes.

'Yes, major?' *Hiss-rasp. Hiss-rasp.*

'You feel up to looking at something for me?'

Domor made a slight, flinching movement that might have been a shrug. 'Like what?'

Baskevyl pulled the black-bound book out of his jacket and opened it. He thumbed through he pages to the ones he'd marked.

'What's that?' Domor asked. *Hiss-rasp. Hiss-rasp.*

'You're the closest thing we have to an engineer, Shoggy, right?'

'I suppose.'

'Then tell me, please,' said Baskevyl, holding the book open so Domor could see. 'What do you make of this?'

* * *

VII

THE MICRO-BEAD CLICKED.

'Airborne inbound. Two minutes,' Beltayn's voice said over the link.

In the doorway of the second gate, Varaine glanced at Meryn.

'Time to go,' he said.

Meryn nodded. He looked back in through the open hatch. 'E Company, get set!' he called. Behind him, Dalin relayed the order down the line.

Meryn looked down the gulley. The day was still clear and open, the sky blue and bright. Down at the end of the gulley, Meryn could see Preed and Caober, the scouts on watch.

'This is Meryn,' he said. 'Are we good?'

'Anytime you like,' Caober voxed back.

'E Company, go!' Meryn called. The Ghosts under his command began to flow out of the hatch and move down the gulley, jogging to their designated places. They huddled in along the west side of the ditch, some of them scrambling up the scree bank to take up firing positions, belly down.

Meryn shook Varaine's hand and hurried to join them.

'E Company is set,' Varaine voxed. He turned and looked back in through the hatch opening. 'L Company, stand ready. Commissar?'

Hark moved forwards and stepped out into the daylight. He was limping on his crutch, a heavy kit bag slung over his shoulder. Criid followed him, then Berenson, Twenzet, Klydo and Swathe, all bearing heavy kit bags of their own. There was no dust, but everyone was wearing brass goggles.

Hark looked at Varaine.

'Any time now, commissar,' Varaine said.

'See you at Elikon, captain,' Hark replied, with a thin smile.

'Yes, sir.'

Vox-click. 'Here she comes,' Caober called.

They heard the throaty howl of engines a second later. A lone Valkyrie shot into view over the cliffs of the pass, skimming low. Hark could see that its side doors were already slung open. It made no turn or preliminary pass around the site the way the water drop transports had done five days before. It had locked coordinates and it wasn't messing around. Hark could almost taste the pilot's desire not to stay on station any longer than necessary.

Halfway down the gulley bottom, a magnetic beacon was set up and began sending out its signal.

The Valkyrie droned in and began to bank around in a hover.

The cliffs facing the house across the dust bowl lit up. Most of it was small-arms fire, but there were rockets too. A storm of gunfire began to spit into the sky.

'They've seen it,' said Variane.

'Of course they have,' Hark replied.

The Valkyrie dropped lower, turbines squalling. Even at a distance, they could all hear the loose shots spanking and twanging off its hull and booms.

'Feth!' said Varaine.

Hark opened his link. 'Rawne, perhaps–'

'Already there,' Rawne replied. The Ghosts in the southern casemates and overlooks of the house opened fire, blasting out heavy cover in the direction of the cliffs. Hark heard hot shots and .50's rattling away.

So much ammo getting wasted.

The enemy shooting reduced slightly as the suppressing fire from the gun-boxes forced them to take cover. The house continued to unload on the cliffs.

The Valkyrie corrected, nose down and circled in, its downwash lifting tor-rents of dust from the gulley area. Its jets began to scream as it came to a dead stop hover and its landing claws slid out. Wailing like the Jago wind, it came down and settled in the gulley. Varaine winced. The Valkyrie's stubby wingtips seemed about to brush the scree slopes on either side. The gulley had looked big until someone parked a Valkyrie in it.

'Go, go, go!' Varaine yelled.

Hark, Criid and the others set off towards the waiting Valkyrie, lugging the kit bags. The cargo officer, his head dwarfed by the helmet/goggles/headphones combo he was wearing, pulled the team in through the side hatch, one by one, taking the heavy bags from them.

'Hark's in,' Varaine voxed.

'Good. They're coming,' Meryn voxed back.

Despite the fusillades raining down from the casemates, squadrons of Blood Pact troops were streaming out of the cliffs across the dust bowl, heading for the gate and the more distant gulley.

'Feth!' Meryn voxed. 'There are thousands of them!'

'Hold your fire until it counts,' Varaine voxed back, signalling his own company to get ready.

'I know what to do.' Meryn's vox-reply was petulant.

The cargo officer waved to Varaine. Varaine waved back. Ducking inside, the cargo officer made a hasty, urgent signal to the pilot.

The Valkyrie, with a bellow of underthrust, hopped up out of the gulley, kicking back a deluge of jet wash and dust. It cleared the gulley line and began to turn. Enemy fire pinged and clicked off its fuselage.

It rose higher, banking hard to make its exit turn around the steep battle-ments of Hinzerhaus.

Down in the dust bowl, a host of enemy warriors was rushing forwards, like insects spilling from a nest, most of them charging for the gulley. Fire from the house was dropping dozens of them, but still they came.

'Locks off,' Meryn voxed. 'Here we fething well go.'

Varaine looked up. A new, heavier note was vibrating the air. The Destrier appeared, slightly off target, rushing down the throat of the pass with its burners blazing.

'K862, K862, inbound,' they heard the pilot vox.

'Hello, K862. Good to see you again,' Beltayn called over the link.

'Wish I could say the same,' replied the pilot of the heavy transport, his voice clipped by the transmission chop.

The Valkyrie was climbing and turning out, haloes of white fire surrounding its jet vents as it hunted for lift and speed. Below it, the Destrier galloped in, slower, louder and more ponderous. The mass of Blood Pact warriors crossing the open field was firing up at it wildly. The big lifter took several solid hits and thousands of light clips.

It lowered itself, correcting its flight path, its engine roar growing louder the slower and lower it got. It looked huge. Its shadow covered the entire gulley floor.

'Feth, that's never going to fit!' Varaine gasped. He knew he had to trust that it would. He looked back in through the hatch. 'Come on, you cheerful bastards!' he bellowed over the jet noise. 'Get ready to move in and unload this bloody thing!' The men began to file out, heads down in the punishing downwash.

'Down in five,' the pilot voxed. 'Stand by. Three, two, one—'

A surface-to-air rocket struck it in the belly and blew the Destrier's ribcage open in a searing ball of white flame.

'Oh, shit!' Varaine yelled. 'Back! Back! Get back inside!'

His men started to turn. They started to run. Varaine was running.

The Destrier quivered and bucked, flames and smoke streaming back out of its belly. It began to turn, trying to rise, to abort. Its engines flared deafeningly. Then it fell.

It fell with a sickening doomsday crunch. It hit the western side of the gulley in a vast spray of scree, crushing and killing over a dozen of Meryn's men. Still moving, sliding and slewing, it made a long, tortured metallic shriek as it tore out its underside along the rocks and dipped into the gulley.

'Oh shit. We're dead,' Varaine heard the pilot whisper on the link.

No power in the galaxy could have arrested the Destrier's death slide. One straining engine blew out, vomiting smoke and sparks into the air. It came on like a steamroller, like a battering ram, crushing and destroying everything in its path in a lethal blizzard of flying rock and splintering metal, eighty tonnes of steel moving at nearly forty kilometres a second. Scree winnowed out behind it in a gigantic, dirty, clattering wake, tonnes of loose stones torn up and flung out in a fan.

'Get inside! Get inside!' Varaine yelled to his men.

He turned.

The ploughing bulk of the Destrier crushed him to pulp. A second later, the huge, burning mass rammed headlong into the second gate. Metal tore. Fuel lines broke. Stanchions snapped. The nose of the bulk lifter crumpled, and mashed the cockpit section to oblivion.

The transport gave one last shudder and finally stopped moving.

Then the munition payload it was carrying detonated.

VIII

RAWNE TOOK A step back from the casemate slot as if he'd been slapped. He lowered his scope from his wide eyes. He didn't need a scope to see the immense mushroom cloud of fire rushing up out of the gulley. They'd all felt the thump. It had shaken the stone walls and lintels of the house.

'Oh Holy Throne,' he whispered.

The enemy host down below let out a huge, exultant roar. It began to rain. The raindrops were stones and micro-debris streaming down out of the dry sky.

By Rawne's side, Kolea shook his head in disbelief.

'We were so close,' he said.

'Feth!' Rawne roared, and threw his scope against the casemate wall in rage. 'Feth! Feth! Feth!'

He looked at Kolea, his eyes wild and bright.

'It can't end like this,' Kolea told him.

'It won't,' Rawne growled. 'It fething well won't. I won't allow it!'

Kolea paused, hesitating. 'We could–' he began.

'We fight on with what we have,' Rawne said, cutting Kolea off. 'We fight on with what we have left, and then we keep fighting with fists and blades. We kill every fething one of them we can, and we hold this damn place until we're all dead!'

Kolea nodded. 'That's basically what I was going to say,' he replied.

'Spread the word, Gol,' said Rawne, snatching up his lasrifle. 'Spread the fething word. Make sure everyone understands. No quarter, no retreat, no surrender.' *One last fight*. That's what Corbec had told him. *One last fight*.

Kolea nodded again.

'And get Daur's company down to whatever's left of the second gate,' Rawne added. 'If that's been blown wide, the bastards will be inside before we know it.'

Kolea turned to go. Around them, the house was chattering with defensive gunfire and the sounds of squads running to their positions. Men were shouting. Some were moaning in loud dismay, having just seen their last chance go up in a ball of fire.

'What about–' Kolea said.

'What about what?' Rawne asked.

'The men left outside? Meryn's company?'

Rawne looked away. 'The Emperor protects,' he said.

IX

FOR ONE, DISTURBING moment, he couldn't remember his own name. His lungs were full of smoke and his mouth was full of dust. He woke up with a violent lurch, and coughed out blood and dusty grey phlegm.

Sounds rushed in at him as the ringing in his ears faded.

From nearby came the noise of crackling flames and the cries of wounded men. From further off came a swelling roar of animal howling.

Dalin got up. The north end of the gulley had become a crater, littered with burning shreds of debris and machine parts. There was no longer any sign of the gate. The destruction of the Destrier had blown a giant scar into the ground, and scorched the exposed rock pitch-black. Thick smoke plumed off the heart of the conflagration and made a kilometre-high column in the sky. Dalin coughed, his throat tightening at the stench of fyceline fumes and burnt propellants.

The transport's death slide had scored a deep furrow across and down the gulley. Sheared off hunks of fuselage and hull casing dotted the gouge, along with mangled bodies.

The transport had killed dozens of Meryn's company on its way in. Dozens more had been killed or crippled by the blast. Those Ghosts that, like Dalin, had been fortunate enough to survive were getting to their feet, stumbling around dazed, calling out, or trying to dress the wounds of the many casualties.

Fortunate. That didn't really seem to be the right word. Dalin picked up his rifle and struggled up to the top of the scree slope. He could see the enemy force through the smoke. Despite the heavy fire striking down at it from the house emplacements, the Blood Pact warhost was still rushing the gulley. They had faltered slightly at the blast, but now they gathered again, surging forwards, screaming.

'Get up! Get up!' Dalin yelled at the bewildered troops around him. 'Get up and get into position! They're on us! They're fething on us!'

A few men stumbled forwards and dropped on their bellies on the ridge top, aiming their weapons.

'Come on! Move it!' Dalin yelled. 'Form a line! Form a fething line!'

The first rounds sang over their heads from the charging mass. The remnants of E Company began to pick off shots in reply.

'Like you mean it!' Dalin bellowed. 'You men! Get up here! Find a place! Move your arses!'

'You heard him!' shouted Caober, running back down the gulley from the southern end. He was shoving men up the slope, kicking some from behind. 'Get in a line or die! Shift it!'

He caught Dalin's eye. They stared at one another for a second. There was no time – no point – in exchanging tactical suggestions. They both knew there was only one thing to do.

'Onto the ridge!' Caober yelled at the befuddled men scrambling to obey him. 'Onto the ridge! Fire at will!'

Dalin checked a couple of bodies for signs of life. He managed to rouse Luhan, who had been knocked out by a grazing head wound.

'Get on the ridge,' Dalin urged him. 'Don't ask questions. Just shoot.'

Dalin saw Meryn, lying face down near the bottom of the gulley where the blast had thrown him. He leapt down and shook Meryn roughly.

'Get up! Get up!'

Meryn stirred and looked blankly up at Dalin.

'Get up, sir! They're right on us!'

Meryn blinked. 'Ow,' he said.

Dalin saw his injury. Half a metre of thin metal tube, a piece of one of the Destrier's bristling UHF antennae, had impaled Meryn through the meat of his left thigh.

'Oh, feth,' Meryn whispered, looking down and seeing the wound.

'I'll find a corpsman,' Dalin started to say.

'Forget it. Just get me up. Just get me up there.'

Dalin hoisted Meryn to his feet. Meryn swore in pain. Dalin dragged him up the slope, sliding and slithering on the loose scree.

They reached the ridge line. Heavy fire stung in from the approaching enemy, slicing over their heads or scattering stones at the ridge crest.

'You woke me up for this?' Meryn groaned.

They both started to fire. Along the ridge, E Company blazed away with what was left of their ammunition.

The enemy was a rolling wall of dust with rushing red figures inside it. Banners and standards bobbed like jetsam carried along by a breaker. Weapons flashed and cracked. The Blood Pact was howling a victory chant as it closed on the side of the gulley, even though masked warriors bucked and twisted as E Company's shots found them. They fell and were trampled, their bodies left behind in the swirling dust.

'Full auto,' said Meryn.

'Full auto!' Dalin yelled out to the company.

'Straight silver,' said Meryn.

'Straight silver!' Dalin shouted at the top of his voice.

Meryn took aim. 'Time to die like men,' he said.

X

'DID YOU SEE that?' Hark shouted over the wail of the Valkyrie engines. 'Did you see that?'

'Stay in your seat, sir!' the cargo officer shouted back.

Hark was fumbling with his restraints. The lifter was banking hard in its climb, juddering violently, its turbines screaming. Wind rushed in through the open slide-hatches. The ground far below was brilliant white with glare. Twenzet and the other troopers, strapped in, were glancing around in alarm.

'That flash!' cried Hark. 'That was an explosion! That was the fething transport!'

'Get back into your seat!' the cargo officer bawled.

'Hark! Stop it!' Criid shouted. Occupying the seat next to Hark, she fought to keep his hands off the harness release. 'Stop it, for feth's sake!'

'Sit down, Hark!' Berenson shouted from his seat.

'That was the bloody transport!' Hark roared back. 'They got it! The bastards got the bloody lander!'

Criid grabbed Hark's chin with her hand and slammed his head back against the seat rest. 'Sit down! There's nothing you can do!'

The cargo officer undid his own harness and got up. Gripping an overhead rail, he glanced forwards. They could all hear the pilot's rapid chatter. The Valkyrie slowly turned until it came level, still bucking and shaking in the rough air.

An alarm sounded and a red light on the ceiling began to flash.

'What's that?' asked Swaythe.

'What the feth is that?' Twenzet demanded.

The cargo officer looked around. Criid saw fear in the eyes behind the large tinted visor.

'We–' he began.

There was a loud, stunning *thump*. The Valk lurched and dropped sharply. Part of the cargo section flooring blew in, and sparks ripped up in a flurry. The alarm note changed to a much more urgent shrill.

'Hold on!' the cargo officer cried.

A second explosion shook the airframe, a vicious *bang* that blinded them for a second. Hot metal shards whizzed around the compartment. One streaking nugget punched clean through the cargo officer's chest.

He let go of the handrail and fell out of the side hatch, his limp body instantly snatched away by the savage slipstream.

Smoke filled the compartment and rushed out through the hatches. Someone was screaming. The alarm shrieked.

The Valkyrie began to vibrate. The engines started to emit a terrible, labouring noise. Its nose tipped down and it fell into a steep dive, a dive that it would never pull out of.

Mach–
There is something that must be done, a matter of honour for the regiment. It is the sword, I mean. It must be got back.

I have gone to get it. I know I have no orders to do so, but I have a moral duty. In conscience, I could not disappear without any word. I ask you to tell them where I've gone and what I plan to do. I hope they will understand the purpose of my actions. The Emperor protect you.
Your friend,

Oan.

– Personal correspondence, Tanith 1st, fifth month, 778.

NINETEEN

The Daeda Waeg

I

NORTH OF THE Banzie Altids, and the curtain of rock encasing Hinzerhaus, the badlands stretched out for a million square kilometres. The badlands were a trackless waste, a mosaic of inhospitable terrains: zones of dust, plains of wind-blown scree and boulder rubble, dry salt licks, and gleaming basins of air-polished calcites that shone bone-white in the sun. In open areas, the dust had collected in great seas of rippled grey dunes, punctuated every few hundred kilometres by jagged crags that sprouted from the desert floor, forming lonely outcrops and mesas surrounded by islands of jumbled stones.

It was a place to be lost in. Despite the passage of the sun, and the lay of the land, there seemed to be no reliable directions. It was a landscape of dry hell, scoured by the constant, angry wind and bleached by the hard light.

Mkoll woke. Two days out in the wastes had taught him that the middle part of the day was no time to move about in the badlands, so he had chosen that period to rest, curling up in the lea of an outcrop boulder. Early morning, late afternoon and night were the best times for travel.

Something had woken him. Gun ready, he swept the rocks, fearing he had been discovered by a passing patrol or scout party. There was no one around in the crag, no sign of activity. The dunes beyond the outcrop were empty.

He looked south.

Despite the dust haze, Mkoll could see the saw-edged ramparts of the Banzie Altids a dozen kilometres behind him. A pall of dark smoke was rising from the mountains, the blaze plume of some catastrophic explosion.

Mkoll turned away. He took a sip of water, ate half a ration bar, and tried not to think about what might have produced the smoke.

He had learned to stay focused. The decisions he had made, the course he had taken, they were hard things to reconcile. Mkoll was a man of infinite and honest loyalty. He knew that the moment he started thinking about the comrades he had left behind would be the moment he turned and started the long trek back to rejoin them. So he shut such thoughts out.

That wasn't difficult to do. Out in the wastes, every scrap of a man's concentration went on survival. You had to pick every footstep carefully to avoid sand falls and dust-choked holes. In places, the surface regolith was so fine and powdery, it could swallow you whole in seconds. You had to read the loose rocks in the scree fields so as not to twist or snap an ankle. You had to watch the wind, and learn its clues so you could get into cover before it rose and carried you away like a dead leaf, or shredded the flesh off your bones with a dust storm. You had to pace your water consumption and avoid excess exposure to the hard sun. Every waking moment was filled up with deliberate, calculated activity.

There were live hazards too. The Blood Pact was out in the wastes in force. Mkoll lay low when motorised patrols throbbed by in the distance. Twice, he'd hidden on top of a mesa and watched as a unit of troops and armour trundled by. The Blood Pact was moving south in considerable numbers. It wouldn't be long before Hinzerhaus faced an assault on its northern ramparts again.

Mkoll checked his kit, cased his lasrifle and prepared to move off. He would have liked to stay put for another hour or two, but there was a faint smudge along the eastern horizon, a blur that rippled like heat haze. That was another dust storm, rising out of the deep heart of the badlands. Mkoll figured he had about ninety minutes before it hit, and ninety minutes would see him reach another lonely mesa just in sight to the north-west.

He started out, picking his way through the loose white boulders at the foot of the crag. His boots lifted powder as he left the rock line and began to walk out across the dust flats. A light wind was blowing, and little eddies of dust danced and scurried over the undulating dunes.

He glanced behind him and saw that the footsteps he had left were already filling in and vanishing.

That reminded him, uncomfortably, that there was something else he was trying not to think about.

II

HE HAD MISCALCULATED. He was only a few minutes out, but that was enough to doom him.

The dust storm, a dark band of racing cloud, began to overtake him while he was still a good half a kilometre from the mesa. The first few gusts tugged at him and made him stagger. The wind force was huge. He began to run, but the wind blew him over several times and rolled him across the dunes. As the storm bit down, he tried to crawl on his hands and knees.

The wind tore at his clothes. The dust particles stung his exposed skin and abraded it until it started to bleed. The light died as the roiling dust mass, two kilometres high, blotted out the sun.

There was no way he was going to reach the mesa. He couldn't even see the mesa any more. He could barely breathe, there was so much dust in his mouth and nostrils. It blocked his ears until there was nothing audible except a dull, moaning sound.

Mkoll clawed his way over onto the leeward side of a large dune and began to dig with his hands, scooping out a hollow he could pull himself into and curl up. He used his own bodyweight to pin his camo cape into the depression, then dragged the loose, flapping side around to cocoon him. That shut out the dust and made a little, airless tent like a womb, where all he could hear was the howl of the gale and the frantic gasping of his own breath.

Trapped there, blind and half buried, he began to think about the things he had banished from his mind before. There was one thing he could not leave alone.

Oan Mkoll, master of scouts, was the best tracker in the regiment. His skills with spore and trace were company legend. No one could follow a path or a trail better than Mkoll, and no one had a keener natural sense of direction. His gifts in these areas, most of them self-taught techniques, seemed almost supernatural to many of his comrades.

Mkoll had no idea how he was tracking the Nihtgane. He knew he was, and he had the keenest sense he was closing on him, but he had no idea how.

This terrified him.

Jago was a tracker's nightmare. The combination of dust and wind erased all traces of a man's passing. It allowed for no footprints, no worn trail, and there was no undergrowth to read for marks. Scent was sometimes a useful tool, but on Jago the wind stole that away too.

Mkoll wasn't sure what exactly it was that he was following. He just knew, somehow, knew as sure as he knew night from day, that he was going the right way.

It was as if there was a road, a clearly defined route set out for him to follow.

It was as if someone or something was leading him.

In the two days since he'd set out, he had not questioned it for a moment, because he hadn't wanted to think about it. He had climbed down the northern face of the fortress cliff and set off into the wastes without a moment's consideration as to where Eszrah might have gone.

Caught in the lea of the dune, with the dust beginning to bury him, he had no choice but to dwell on it.

The thought that something unseen might be guiding him frightened Mkoll more than the prospect of a suffocating death.

III

THE STORM DIED after an hour, clearing as rapidly as it had come down. The light returned as the dust settled and the grey film drained out of the air. In its wake, the storm left a landscape of resculpted, remoulded dunes and an aching, barren silence.

A hole appeared in the slope of one dune, soft dust sucking down into a cavity, like sand in an hour glass. The hole broadened.

A hand reached out into the dry air.

Mkoll rose up out of his shallow grave, the dust streaming off him and fuming away into the breeze like smoke. He shook the clogging particles out of his sleeves and fatigues, and flapped out his cape. It took a few minutes to clean his brass goggles and wash out his mouth and nose. His throat was dry. His sinuses felt impacted. His vision was blurred, as if his corneas had been abraded.

He sat down and emptied his boots. The mesa he had been heading for, a crooked, flat-topped rock surrounded by an island of boulders, seemed ridiculously close. Mkoll re-laced his boots and was grateful he had chosen to carry his rifle cased. He looked south once more. The pall of smoke, smaller now, was still clearly visible.

He heard a *pop*.

He looked around sharply and heard two more. *Pop pop*, just small sounds, carried by the breeze. He got up and began to head towards the mesa.

More popping sounds reached him. They were coming from the other side of the outcrop. He slowed down and began to uncase his rifle. He sniffed the air. *Motor oil, warm metal, unwashed bodies.*

Mkoll stuffed the rifle case into his pack and ran into the boulder scree, head down. He moved from rock to rock, staying low, listening and sniffing.

Pop. Pop pop. Pop. Pop pop pop.

Gunshots, hollowed out by the wind. He checked his rifle cell and flicked off the safety.

It took five careful minutes to circle the mesa to the northern side. The sun was no longer overhead and he had shadows to play with, hard shadows cast by the boulders and the crag.

He ducked down at the first sight of movement, his back to a large rock. He pulled out his stick mirror and angled it for a look, taking care that it didn't catch the sun.

In it, he glimpsed a Blood Pact warrior clambering through the rocks, rifle in hand. The brute was panting, and sweating so profusely that his stained jacket had dark half-moons under the arms. Mkoll could smell him, he was so close. He could smell the rancid sweat and the stale blood-filth the warrior had coloured his jacket with.

How many of them were there? He kept watching.

The warrior stopped, and called out something. An answering cry came back. The warrior raised his rifle and squeezed two shots off at the overhanging crag.

Mkoll drew his warknife.

The Blood Pact warrior got up on a large boulder and looked around. Four of his comrades were toiling up the scree slope in a wide line below him. Behind them, out on the dunes, a rusty half-track sat with its engine running. A patrol, on a routine sweep.

'Voi shett! K'heg ar rath gfo!' the warrior on the rock shouted. Three more warriors jumped down from the half-track, one of them an officer with a gilded grotesk.

'Borr ko'dah, voi!' the officer yelled, waving his pistol. The trio entered the rock line and followed the other troopers up into the slopes under the crag. One trooper remained behind aboard the half-track with the driver, manning a pintle-mounted cannon.

The warrior nearby jumped down off the rock and looked around for an easy path up through the scree. A hand circled his throat from behind and a blade slid up under his shoulder blade into his heart. He died without a sound.

Mkoll lowered the body silently. He wiped the blade on the warrior's coat and helped himself to the cell clips in his webbing. He could hear the officer shouting down below.

Mkoll darted between the rocks, head low. He heard the crunch of boots nearby and froze. Another warrior clambered past, just a few metres away, calling out.

Mkoll crept forwards and finished the warrior as quickly and clinically as before.

A lasrifle started firing and Mkoll dropped, fearing he had been spotted. But the shots were zipping up at the crag, stitching puffs of dust across the bare rock.

There was a squall of pain and the firing ceased abruptly. Mkoll peered out and tried to see what was going on. The squad of Blood Pact warriors, urged on by their officer, was scrambling up through the rocks more urgently, and all of them had started firing up at the crag.

Mkoll put his knife away. There was no more time for subtlety.

He rested his rifle across a sloping rock and took aim. A Blood Pact trooper came into view, bounding from boulder to boulder. He rose up to fire his weapon and Mkoll took him out with a single shot. The trooper dropped back off the boulder.

Confusion seized the enemy squad. They'd all heard the shot and seen their comrade fall. They started shouting at one another and firing randomly. Mkoll rotated away from his firing position, scampered down a gap between two large stone blocks, and aimed again. He got a decent line on one of the remaining enemy troopers, but the man dropped out of sight as Mkoll fired and the shot went wide. Las-fire suddenly scuffed and pinged across Mkoll's cover. He was pinned. They had an angle on him from two sides.

He slid down into the shadows and began to crawl. Shots slammed and *thukked* off the rocks above him. A deflected las-bolt whined past his face. Mkoll switched on his intervox and began to wind the tuning control. It took him about thirty seconds to find the channel the Blood Pact was using.

The officer's hoarse barks filled his ears. He translated slowly. His fluency in the Archenemy tongue had diminished somewhat since the long stay on Gereon. Something about '...more than one fugitive. Find them both or I'll...'

Some visceral threat followed that Mkoll was happy not to translate, as it involved trench axes and fingers.

'Voi shett d'kha jehlna, dooktath!' Mkoll voxed, and stood up. The officer and the three other troopers were all looking the other way. No surprise, considering someone had just told them 'Look and take heed, there's one of them behind you, you ignorant rectums!', although rather more colloquially.

Mkoll shot the officer in the back of the head, retrained his aim, and killed one of the troopers too, before the officer had even hit the ground. The other two wheeled around and opened fire. One dropped, mysteriously, of his own accord, as if he had slipped over. Mkoll flattened the last one with a spray of shots.

The pintle-mounted cannon started to blast fire out across the rocks. The half-track's engine was revving furiously, and black exhaust coughed out of the tail pipes, as if the driver was in a sudden hurry to leave.

Mkoll took aim. The range wasn't good, but he was no slouch. He squeezed the trigger and held it down, pumping half a dozen shots at the half-track. The first few kissed the bodywork and bent the small shield plate fixed to a bracket around the cannon housing. The fifth or sixth bolt hit the gunner in the head and smacked him back out of the vehicle. The half-track jolted and started to move, its track sections squirming up clouds of dust as it turned. Mkoll stood up and raked the driver's door and windshield with shots. The vehicle lurched, slewed on, and lurched again before coming to a halt. Its engine over-revved wildly as if a deadweight was pressing on the throttle. Then it stalled and the engine died away with an unhealthy clatter.

Silence. Mkoll picked his way through the rocks, checking the bodies of the dead and stealing their ammunition. He found one he hadn't killed, though the manner of the warrior's death was quite evident.

Mkoll stopped moving. Slowly, he raised his hands. He knew instinctively that someone was aiming a weapon at his back.

'Eszrah?' he whispered.

'Hwat seyathee, sidthe?' asked the voice behind him.

IV

MKOLL TURNED SLOWLY. Eszrah ap Niht stood behind him, his reynbow aimed.

The Nihtgane was the colour of Jago. His clothing and the wode on his face had absorbed the pale grey of the bad rock somehow. Eszrah had employed some camouflage technique that Mkoll would have paid real money to learn.

'It's me,' Mkoll said. 'Histye.'

Esrah nodded. 'Histye, sidthe,' he acknowledged. His aim did not stir.

'You've always call me that,' Mkoll said. 'I don't understand your language the way Ven did. What does it mean?'

'Ghost,' Eszrah replied.

Mkoll smiled. 'You don't have to point that at me, soule,' he said.

'Cumenthee taek Eszrah backwey,' Eszrah replied, maintaining his aim.

'No,' said Mkoll.

'Cumenthee sidthe, cumenthee taek Eszrah bye Rawne his wyrd.'

'For Rawne? You think he ordered me to come and get you?' Mkoll shook his head. 'No, soule, no, no. That's not why I'm here.'

'No?' Eszrah echoed. 'Seyathee no?'

'I've come for the sword,' Mkoll said, gently pointing to the weapon lashed to the partisan's back. 'It wasn't yours to take, my friend. It belongs to the regiment.'

Eszrah slowly lowered the reynbow. 'Eszrah's ytis.'

'No, it isn't.'

'Eszrah's ytis,' the Nihtgane insisted. 'Soule Gaunt, daeda he. So walken thys daeda waeg Y go, bludtoll to maken.'

'Blood toll? Do you mean vengeance?'

Eszrah shrugged. 'Not ken Y wyrd, soule.'

'Revenge? Retribution? Payback? You're going to take lives for Gaunt's life?'

'Lyfes for Gaunt his lyfen, bludtoll so,' Eszrah nodded.

There was a long silence, broken only by the mournful song of the desert wind. Mkoll felt sudden, immeasurable sorrow: for the partisan, for Gaunt, for himself. This was how it was all going to end, and a poor, messy end it was. Loyalty and devotion, duty and love, all stretched out of shape and malformed until they were unrecognisable and tarnished.

'You think you failed him, don't you?' Mkoll asked quietly.

'Seyathee true, sidthe soule.'

Mkoll nodded. 'I know. That's how I feel too. I should have been there. I should have been there and…'

His voice trailed off.

'Feth!' he said. 'Throne, how he'd have laughed at us!'

Eszrah frowned. 'Gaunt laffen he?'

'Yes, at us! Two idiots in the middle of nowhere, both of us thinking we're doing the right thing! He doesn't care! Not now! He's dead, and we've made fools of ourselves!'

Eszrah was still frowning. 'The daeda waeg yt is the last waeg.'

'The what? What is the daeda waeg?'

Eszrah thought for a moment, struggling to find the words.

'Corpse. Road,' he said.

'And where does that lead?' Mkoll asked.

Eszrah gestured out towards the dune sea beyond them.

'Out there?' Mkoll asked, looking around. 'Forever?'

The partisan shook his head. 'Closen bye, sidthe soule. Bloodtoll wayten.'

Mkoll looked at Eszrah. 'Will you let me take the sword? Will you let me take Gaunt's sword back to the house?'

The Nihtgane shook his head. 'Yt must…' he began, wrestling with his words again, '…yt must be his sword. His weapon. For the bludtoll.'

Mkoll sighed. He had no wish to fight Eszrah ap Niht. He wasn't entirely sure he would win.

'All right. Then will you let me walk the daeda waeg with you? Will you let me help you make the blood toll?'

Eszrah nodded.

'Good, then.'

Side by side, they clambered down through the rocks onto the desert floor.

'How many of them do we have to kill?' Mkoll asked. 'To make the blood toll, I mean?'

Eszrah grinned. 'All of them, soule,' he said.

Day thirteen cont.

Under attack from two sides. Munition carrier lost, and our hopes with it. Heavy casualties at second gate. Basic estimates put the enemy numbers ten to one in their favour.

Ammunition virtually exhausted. Even R. acknowledges this is the endgame. I had always imagined a last stand to be a heroic thing, but this is just brutal, senseless. I suppose heroism and glory are things perceived later by those who did not have to endure the circumstances. We are going to die in the next few hours, one by one, in the most violent manner. They will not show us — nor do we expect — any mercy. Once they get in—

I am wasting time with such self-serving remarks. I may not get the chance to record this later, so let me commit this to the record now. It has been my honour to ~~serve the~~ serve the Tanith First-and-Only. Every man and woman has my respect, Tanith, Verghastite, Belladon. I hope this record survives us. I want the masters of this crusade to know how dearly the Tanith cost the Archenemy, when the time came. They are the best and the most devoted soldiers I have ever seen. I stand beside them with pride.

I pray my master, Viktor Hark, has made it clear of the house with the material from the library. It has been reported to me that several men saw a Valkyrie taken out by a surface to air rocket over the Banzie Pass earlier. If that is true, then our deaths here will ultimately mean nothing.

— Field journal, N.L. for V.H. fifth month, 778.

TWENTY

The Lost

I

As THE THIRTEENTH day began to end, they went into the fire with no hope or expectation of seeing another sunrise.

The sky had gone dark with smoke. Even in the depths of the house, there was no escape from the constant thunder of weapons and the howl of voices.

The Archenemy had descended upon Hinzerhaus in a force over ten thousand strong. In a drab, red mass like an old blood stain, they spread down out of the cliffs and the pass and filled the dust bowl, pressing in at the main gate and southern fortifications. They brought hundreds of light field guns and auto-mortars with them, and bombarded the fracturing rockcrete bulwarks with shells and rocket-propelled munitions. A large assault force, spearheaded by warriors carrying long, stave-flamers, drove in against the main gate. Spiked ladders and extending climbing poles clattered up against the lower earthworks, and raiders began to scale the walls. Some of the raiders, equipped with a spiked mace in each hand and toe-hooks on their boots, came up the walls without the need for ladders, hacking and gouging their own foot– and hand-holds like human spiders. The drums and horns in the host made a din that echoed down the pass.

There was no shortage of targets for the Ghosts. Firing from the casemates, overlooks and gunboxes, the Tanith First made hundreds of kills, but the Blood Pact was not going to be deterred. Oath-sworn warriors of Archon Gaur, the elite storm troops of the Great Adversary, they were too far gone with bloodlust to care about individual lives. They had been goaded and roused to berserker pitch by their sirdar commanders, until they had achieved a feverish state of zealous devotion and feral glee. Gol Kolea had been quite right – the Blood Pact intended to make the Imperial forces pay

969

for their defiance. Some of the raiders had cast off their helmets and grotesk masks to reveal the ritual scars cut into their faces and scalps. They wanted the marks of their dedication to the Archon to be plainly visible to their victims.

'That's right, you mad fether,' murmured Larkin, 'take your shiny hat off. That'll make my job easier.'

Either side of him in the overlook, Banda and Nessa matched his rate of fire. Banda had already been forced to switch to a standard pattern las. There were no fresh barrels for the long-form variants left. Their ammo bag was alarmingly empty too. Out in the hallway behind the gunboxes, Ventnor and the other ammo runners had set up braziers to cook some life back into spent cells. It was risky work, and they could never hope to juice enough back into operation in time.

Kolea had placed the bulk of his flamers in the lowest level of embrasures, so that their weapons, short-range at best, could roast the scaling parties off the walls. In one gunbox, where the air was eye-stingingly acrid with promethium fumes, Brostin speared squealing gouts of flame down out of the slot while Lyse coupled a fresh tank to her set.

Brostin ducked back inside as las-bolts chipped off the lip of the gunslot.

'They seem awfully eager to say hello to Mister Yellow,' he said.

Lyse answered his grin with a thin smile.

'What's the matter?' Brostin asked.

'That was the last tank,' she replied.

FOUR FLOORS ABOVE, Kolea rushed along a busy, smoke-swamped communication hallway, coordinating the repulse. A mortar shell had just penetrated one of the casemates on seven, slaughtering the five Ghosts inside. Another gunbox had been blown out by grenade work, though thankfully without fatalities. Its defenders were now firing from the cover of the ruptured rockcrete socket.

The volume of fire striking against the outer walls sounded like a rotary saw eating through lumber. Corpsmen hurried by, carrying the wounded. Kolea saw Ludd.

'Is the gate holding?' he asked.

'I don't know,' Ludd replied numbly. Kolea saw the dazed look in Ludd's eyes. Everyone around him was beginning to look that way. It was the seeping shock of the noise trauma, the inexorable destruction of nerves and focus wrought by the constant aural assault.

'Get with it,' Kolea hissed to Ludd. 'You're no use to the men unless you're sharp.'

Ludd blinked. 'Yes, yes of course.'

'You know how you feel?' Kolea asked. 'Every last one of the Ghosts feels like that. You need to help them forget it, ignore it, shut it out, or this fiasco is going to end a lot sooner than it has to.'

Ludd summoned some reserve of willpower. He hadn't realised how far he'd flagged.

'I'm sorry, major,' he said.

'Don't apologise,' Kolea replied. 'Didn't Hark teach you anything? Commissars never apologise. That's why we hate them so much.'

Ludd laughed. It was the last laughter Kolea would hear that day.

Part of Chiria's company surged down the hallway, sent to reinforce the gunboxes. Ludd moved away smartly to oversee and direct their deployment.

The intervox suddenly clicked. 'Contact! Contact! Upper galleries!'

So they're coming in from the north side too, Kolea thought. *Fething fantastic.*

II

'PICK YOUR TARGETS!' Varl shouted, firing from one of the cloche slots. 'Conserve your fething ammunition or we might as well hold the shutters open and invite them in!'

The first Blood Pact grotesks had appeared over the cliff lip about two minutes earlier. Now all the cloches and casemates along upper east sixteen, east fifteen and west sixteen were busy firing on the raiders swarming up over the edge of the precipice.

'Seems a shame,' remarked Maggs, snapping off a shot that knocked a Blood Pact warrior twenty metres away back off the drop. 'Poor bastards have climbed such a long way.'

'My heart bleeds,' replied Varl.

He jumped down off the fire step and yelled down the hallway. 'Stay sharp! Don't give them a chance to establish a foothold!'

Kamori appeared, running down the hallway at the head of twenty men. 'Varl! Where's Baskevyl?'

Varl shrugged. 'I ain't seen him, sir.'

'But he's got command of this level!' Kamori exclaimed.

'Maybe he got a better offer,' Varl suggested. Kamori was not well known for his humour. Varl turned away quickly. 'Cant! Go and find Major Baskevyl!'

'Where will he be?' Cant asked, jumping down from the step.

'If I knew that, he wouldn't need finding, would he?' Varl replied. Cant hurried away down the hall. 'And don't come back if you're still an idiot!' Varl called after him.

'How's it looking?' Kamori asked him.

'Sunny, some cloud,' Varl said.

Kamori's eyes narrowed.

Varl sighed. 'Oh, come on, Vigo. If you can't make light in the face of certain death, what can you do?' he asked.

'Punch you in the face,' Kamori proposed, and pushed past Varl to the firestep. He got up and looked out. Maggs and the other men in the cloche were firing sporadically, but the hits ringing off the cloche dome were growing more persistent.

'They're on the cliffs right below us,' said Maggs. 'You can bet they've come in force. They're pushing over the top a few at a time, but all they need is one lucky break.'

'Or one lousy mistake,' Kamori replied. He jumped off the step and clicked his micro-bead. 'Commander? Kamori, topside. It's holding here, but it's going to get hotter.'

'What's Baskevyl's estimation?' Rawne came back.

'We can't actually locate him at the moment, sir.'

'Say again, Kamori. For a moment there, you sounded like a fething halfwit.'

'I said we can't locate Major Baskevyl at this time, sir,' Kamori stated flatly, grimacing at Varl.

'Not what I want to hear, Kamori,' Rawne replied. 'Take charge up there and keep me advised.'

'Looks like you get to do the shouting, then,' Varl said to Kamori. Kamori nodded. He turned to the men he'd brought with him. 'Fill some gaps! Come on, shift! Sonorote, get each of the cloches on this level and the one below to sound off with a situation report. Make it fast, man.'

Cant reappeared, looking glum.

'I can't find Major Baskevyl, sir,' he said.

'Oh, you can't, can you, Cant?' asked Varl.

'Go feth yourself, Varl!' Cant snapped.

'Shut up, both of you!' Kamori growled. 'Get to a hole and start shooting out of it!'

A gritty blast blew down the hallway as Blood Pact grenades found an open slot on a nearby cloche.

'Move!' Kamori yelled. 'Hold the line and deny them!'

III

'LUDD! LUDD!' RAWNE yelled, striding through the smoke of lower east six.

'Yes, commander!'

'Major Baskevyl has deserted his post.'

'Sir?'

'You heard me, Ludd!' Rawne snapped.

'Sir, I'm sure there must be some explanation. Major Baskevyl is–'

'Does this look like a game to you any more, Ludd?' Rawne yelled. 'I don't want to hear you make excuses! I just want you to nod! Can you do that?'

Ludd nodded.

'Good. Major Baskevyl has deserted his post. Deal with it.'

Ludd nodded.

IV

BASKEVYL PAUSED AT the top of a stairway to let a fire-team race past him, double-time, heading towards the upper level. As he stepped to one side, he set down the heavy kit bag he was carrying.

He was about to make his way down when another squad hurried up the staircase towards him.

'I need one of your men,' Baskevyl told Posetine, the squad leader.

'We're all directed upstairs, sir,' Posetine said apologetically. 'Commander's orders.'

'Well, I understand that, but here's one of mine. I need the help of one of your men.'

Posetine looked awkward, but he guessed he would be in trouble if he tried to argue with the senior Belladon officer. He looked back at his men reluctantly.

'Merrt, step out and go with Major Baskevyl.'

Merrt glowered and stood to one side. He knew Posetine had picked him because he was no bloody good.

'Thank you, Posetine,' Baskevyl said. He hefted up his kit bag and ran down the stairs past the troops. 'With me, Merrt.'

'Major!' Posetine called out after them. 'Major, do you know they're trying to reach you on the link? They've been calling for a few minutes now.'

'I know!' Baskevyl yelled back. He'd taken his micro-bead off and stuffed it into a pocket precisely so he couldn't hear the intervox. 'Carry on, Posetine!'

'But–' Posetine began. Baskevyl had vanished.

'Shift it,' Posetine told his squad and they began to move again. Posetine adjusted his own micro-bead. 'Squad eight six moving up to west five. If you're looking for Major Baskevyl, we just saw him heading down into the basement levels.'

'WHAT ARE WE gn... gn... gn... doing?' Merrt asked, jogging to keep up with Baskevyl.

'I'll explain when we get there.'

'What's that book?'

'Just follow me, Merrt.'

Merrt hesitated. 'This leads down to the gn... gn... gn... power room,' he said dubiously.

'Come on man!'

No one had been left to guard the power room. The chamber was as Baskevyl remembered it. He could smell energy, and feel the slow pulse of the glowing iron power hub. Baskevyl put his kit bag down, took a few steps forwards and touched the warm metal.

'Major?'

'Wait,' Baskevyl said, holding a hand up. He pulled the black-bound book out from under his arm, set it on the floor and knelt down over it, turning the pages.

He looked up abruptly. The scratching sound was quite loud. It was coming from just below them and through the walls around them.

'Merrt?' Baskevyl whispered. 'Do you hear that?'

'Yeah,' Merrt replied. 'Do you see that?' He pointed.

Baskevyl saw the faces that had been drawn in the dust on the walls, eyeless faces with open mouths. He knew they hadn't been there when he and Merrt had entered the room.

'This place is cursed,' he said.

'I know it,' Merrt replied.

'There's something here. It's been here forever. It's trapped us here.'

'It wants us dead,' said Merrt.

Baskevyl shook his head. 'I think it wants us to stay. I think it wants company.'

'Forever?' Merrt asked.

'Yeah.'

'Then isn't that the gn... gn... gn... same thing?'

V

SHE WAS STANDING on the cliff edge, right out in the open, staring in at the cloche hatches. The desert wind was tugging at her black lace skirts.

Maggs shot at the next few Blood Pact warriors attempting to rush the dome.

'Why don't you take them instead?' he yelled out of the shutter at the old dam.

'Who the feth are you yelling at, Maggs?' Varl shouted from the neighbouring slot.

'Her,' Maggs replied.

'Oh, don't start with the–' Varl started to say. He shut up. 'Feth me, Wes.'

'You can see her?'

'Shit, yes.'

'Then it must be time. Throne, this must be it.' Maggs leaned forwards and yelled out of the shutter at the dark figure waiting silently at the edge of the cliff. 'Is that it, you old witch? Is it time now? Is this the end of it all? Is it?'

Very slowly, the awful meat-wound face nodded.

VI

WHEN NESSA TOOK a hit to the shoulder, Banda dragged her out into the hall to find a corpsman and left Larkin alone in the gunbox. His long-las had finally given up and he was using a standard pattern rifle. Looking out of the slot, it was distressing to see how far up the outer walls and bulwarks the Blood Pact had managed to climb. They were attacking the lower casemates. Larkin heard grenades and the bitter zing of nail bombs. The enemy would be inside in minutes, if they weren't already.

He peppered those in range with shots. 'Fire support here!' he called out. 'I need shooters at this slot!'

'You're on your own, Tanith,' said the voice.

Larkin turned around. He knew what he would see.

Lijah Cuu stood in the doorway of the gunbox facing him. His thin, scar-split face was drawn in a leer. His uniform was filthy and marked with rot and smears of soil.

Cuu had his warblade in his hand.

'All alone, sure as sure.'

Larkin shivered. Sheet ice was creeping across the inside walls of the over-look, creaking like flexing glass. Larkin could smell rich putrefaction and decay.

'I've killed you once, you son of a bitch,' Larkin whispered. 'I can do it all over again.'

'It doesn't work like that, Tanith,' said Cuu. 'Not this time around.'

'I'll tell you how it fething works,' Larkin replied. 'You're just a phantom from my crazy old brain. You're not real, so get the feth away from me! I'm busy!'

He turned his back on Cuu and began to fire out of the slot.

Slowly, steadily, the footsteps came up behind him.

VII

ZWEIL HOBBLED INTO the field chamber. He had been drawn from his prayers by curious sounds, sounds that were more than the usual moans and cries of anguish.

In disarray, the chamber had come to an odd halt. The wounded men, in their cots, were staring out in bewilderment. Corpsmen and stretcher bearers, bringing in the latest casualties from the repulse, had also stopped in their tracks, open-mouthed. Some were making the sign of the aquila. Others had dropped to their knees.

Zweil felt his guts turn to ice.

The dead had come back to them. The lost were all around them, thin grey shapes, shadows made of dust, transparent spectral figures cut from twilight. They lingered by bedsides, or hovered in the central aisle of the chamber, like silent mourners gathering for a funeral.

Some men were speaking to them out loud, crying out in fear or wonder, greeting old friends and fallen comrades, weeping at the sight of long lost loved ones. To them, the vague figures were wives and sweethearts, parents and children, brothers and sister, warriors of Tanith, Verghast and Belladon who had fallen on the long march to this dismal last battle.

Zweil saw men close their eyes or cover their faces with their arms, saw others open their arms wide for embraces that would never come. Some of the wounded men were trying to get out of their beds to reach the shades standing over them.

'No,' Zweil whispered. 'No, no, no…'

Dorden was beside him, his eyes streaming with tears. He gripped Zweil's arm tightly. 'My son,' he gasped. 'Mikal, my son.' Dorden pointed. Zweil saw nothing except a shadow that should not have been.

Zweil stepped forwards, pulling free of the old medicae's grasp. He raised his rod and held up the heavy silver eagle he wore on a chain around his reedy neck.

'I abjure thee,' he began. 'I command thee, be gone hence and be at peace–'

Voices rose in protest all around him, calling him a fool, a meddler, begging him to stop.

'I abjure thee now, by the light that is the Golden Throne of Terra,' Zweil cried.

'It's my son!' Dorden yelled.

'No, it isn't,' said Zweil firmly. Hark had been right, feth him, and Zweil had been a fool not to pay heed. Hinzerhaus was a place of damned souls, where the dead gathered to drag the living down into the lightless places.

'I command thee, daemons, be gone from here!'

Dorden clawed at Zweil, and the old priest pushed him away. Someone was screaming.

The shadows were thickening, becoming darker.

Blood, not dust at all, was streaming down the chamber walls.

VIII

THEY HAD HELD on to the gulley ridge for fifteen minutes, a period that had felt like centuries. Only eighteen members of E Company remained, and most of them were wounded. Unable to maintain a viable line, the survivors had drawn back into the throat of the gulley, until they were in amongst the wreckage of the crashed transport.

Dalin was down to his last clip. He fired his rifle with one hand, holding Meryn upright with his other arm. Meryn was almost comatose from blood loss.

He dragged the captain across the scree, shots lacing the air around him. The Blood Pact was streaming in over the top of the ridge, crashing down across the bank of loose stones, sliding and running. The warriors were uttering loud war cries and brandishing pikes and axes.

Cullwoe closed in beside Dalin, snapping off rounds from the hip. He nailed two of the charging warriors and sent them sliding down the loose stone slope on their faces.

'You know what this is, right?' Cullwoe cried.

Dalin didn't have time to reply. The bolt from a las-lock exploded Khet Cullwoe's midriff. He collapsed in a spatter of his own blood, ribs poking from his smouldering abdomen.

'I know what this is,' snarled Neskon. 'It's a fething bastard way to die!' His flamer roared and enveloped six enemy troopers in a sheet of white-hot combustion. They ignited, thrashed, and fell. One wandered a long way on fire before falling to the ground.

'Come on, boy!' Neskon shouted, ripping off another cone of fire. His flamer was beginning to splutter, its tanks all but done.

Dalin emptied the last of his clip and threw his rifle aside. Steadying Meryn, he bent down and took Cullwoe's rifle, and the last fresh clip Cullwoe had tucked into his belt loop.

'Come the feth on!' Neskon yelled. His flamer dried. He pumped it and worked the feed, but it was dead.

'Help me with the captain!' Dalin cried.

Neskon turned, pulling off his tanks and dropping them with a clatter. A las-round hit him in the hip.

'Fething hell!' he barked. Neskon did not fall down. He drew his service pistol and showed himself to be a damn good shot with a regular firearm. No one ever expected subtlety from a flame-trooper. Neskon banged off two rounds and blew a warrior with a pike over onto his back.

Neskon grabbed hold of Meryn and slung the man over his shoulder.

'Back to the gate!' he said, his voice hoarse with pain.

'There is no gate, Nesk!'

'Oh, we can pretend,' Neskon advised him. Together, they backed away through the burning wreckage of the Destrier, firing at the oncoming line of raiders.

'You can do this,' Caffran said.

Dalin glanced around. His father smiled and nodded to him. Then he was gone, and Caober, Preed and Wheln were beside him, adding their firepower to the hopeless retreat.

'First-and-Only!' Wheln yelled.

All four of them sang out a response, blasting their last shots into the faces of the enemy. In all the noise and fury, it sounded to Dalin as if the entire regiment was with them, shouting the war cry at the top of their lungs.

'Come on! Make for the hatch! The hatch!'

Dalin glanced over his shoulder. He saw Ban Daur and an awful lot of Ghosts behind him.

'Sacred feth!' he whispered in disbelief.

'Come on!' Daur yelled to them. 'Have I got to come and get you?'

The Blood Pact surged down the gulley. G Company came pouring out of the second gate and waited there to greet them, weapons raised.

IX

TRYING TO IGNORE the sheet ice slowly caking the power room walls, the scratching from under the floor and the fizzle of corposant scudding over the ceiling, Baskevyl tried to lift the lid off the power hub.

'There's a gn… gn… gn…' Merrt said.

'A what? A bloody what? Spit it out, man!'

'A latch! There!'

'Yes, all right. I've got it. Now lift.'

The lid came up, It was heavy, and they struggled with it as they lifted it clear. Hot, fetid air, as musty as–

dry skulls in a dusty valley

–the most barren, sun-baked desert, wafted out of the kettle.

'Now what?' Merrt asked.

Baskevyl looked into the hub.

It was a deep, hemispheric cavity. The bowl of it was covered in a rind of dust that looked like limescale or some mineral deposit manufactured alchemically deep under the earth.

The worm was inside the kettle.

It was a circular band of machinery, about two metres in diameter, segmented like a snake's scaled body, and it sat inside the waist of the cavity. It was rotating very slowly, pausing and juddering hesitantly, emitting a soft glow. Each pause and judder corresponded to a dip in the brightness of the wall lights.

Baskevyl stared at it. Where the segmented hoop was joined, there was a metal clasp that looked for all the world like a snake biting the tip of its own tail. It matched exactly the embossed emblem on the spine of the book.

Baskevyl reached into the kettle and felt the slowly moving hoop brush his fingertips.

'It's dry,' he said.

'This entire fething bad rock is gn… gn… gn… dry,' Merrt retorted.

'No, the kettle's dry. It's run dry, after centuries, used up its… I don't know… fuel. Its working on the very last of its reserves.'

'How do you know all this?' Merrt asked.

'I don't,' said Baskevyl, 'but Domor, he can read schematics. Apparently, this is essentially a basic cold fusion plant.'

'What's that?' Merrt asked.

'Fethed if I know.' Baskevyl walked over to his kit bag. 'Help me with this,' he said.

'With what?'

Baskevyl started to pull canteen bottles from the bag. Merrt approached.

'What's in the bottles?' he asked.

'Water,' said Baskevyl.

They heard a sound behind them and turned.

Ludd came down the steps into the power room, aiming his pistol at Baskevyl.

'Major Baskevyl,' he began, 'you are found derelict of your post, and have acted contrary to the express orders of the commander…'

Elikon M.P., Elikon M.P., this is Nalwood, this is Nalwood.
Please respond. Please respond. We are under sustained and
massive attack. Cannot hold out much longer. Casualties high.
No ammunition remaining. Please, Elikon, can you hear us?

Nalwood out. (transmission ends)

- Transcript of vox message, fifth month, 778.

TWENTY-ONE

The Worm Turns

I

It was a camp, all right. In the dwindling daylight, with the mauve cast of evening covering the sky and lengthening the shadows, they watched the flickering fires from the cover of a salt-lick three quarters of a kilometre away.

'I see tents, prefabs,' said Mkoll, slowly scanning with his scope, 'about fifteen vehicles. There must be, I dunno, a hundred or more of the bastards in there.'

'Y haf an score bow shottes,' Eszrah replied.

'So do the maths.'

'Then thissen sword Y haf, afftyr bow shottes dun.'

Mkoll shook his head and laughed. 'You think we can take them? I admire your confidence, Eszrah.'

'Hwat seyathee, sidthe soule?'

Mkoll went back to his scope. 'Wait now,' he muttered, panning it around. 'That's a vox-mast they've got set up there. High gain amp. You don't need a UHF vox-caster unless you're giving orders out, long range. This has got to be a command station. Someone pretty important, maybe a sirdar commander. An etogaur, even.'

'Hwat seyathee?'

Mkoll looked at Eszrah. 'You want your payback, don't you?'

Eszrah nodded. 'Paye bak,' he smiled.

'And I just want to do something useful before I die.' Mkoll pulled off his musette bag and sorted through the contents: two clips, four tube charges, one small-pattern cell spare for his pistol, a spool of det-tape, a grenade. He placed the items one by one into his webbing and pouches for easy access.

Eszrah watched him closely, intrigued.

Mkoll scooped up a handful of dust from the rim of the lick and wiped it across his cheeks and forehead. Eszrah laughed, and took out a gourd flask.

'You can do better?' Mkoll asked.

Carefully, ritually, the Nihtgane smeared grey paste across Mkoll's thin, dirty face. Then he nodded.

'Are we done?'

Eszrah pointed to Mkoll's warknife and held out his hand. Mkoll gave him the knife. Eszrah wiped concentrated moth venom along the edges of the thirty-centimetre silver blade.

'Dun,' he said, handing it back to Mkoll.

'Let's do it, then,' Mkoll said. He held out his hand. Eszrah looked at the proffered hand and then clasped it, bemused.

'It's been good knowing you, Eszrah ap Niht,' Mkoll said.

'Seyathee true, soule.'

They got up, heads down and hunched, and tracked off across the dust towards the distant fires.

II

THE VALKYRIE WAS burning. It was just a shell, a cage of black metal wrapped in a turmoil of fire.

Hark got to his feet. He assumed he had been thrown clear at the point of impact. If so, the dust, the benighted dust of bad rock Jago, had saved him. He could remember plunging down, and then tumbling over in the thick, soft cushion of the regolith.

He was not quite intact, though. His back throbbed mercilessly, and he could feel blood weeping down his legs. His head was gashed. Something, Hark had no idea what, had severed his augmetic arm at the elbow, leaving a sparking stump of wires that dribbled lubricant instead of blood.

He limped towards the wreck. Several of the kit bags had fallen clear. Two had split open, and ancient pages were fluttering away in the wind. He knelt down and tried to gather them together.

'Need a hand?'

Hark looked up. Twenzet, his face covered in blood, stood behind him. When Twenzet saw the snapped stump of Hark's mechanical arm, he baulked.

'I honestly didn't mean anything by that, sir,' he said.

'I never thought you did, trooper,' Hark said. 'Help me.'

Twenzet dropped to his knees and started to gather the loose pages in, stuffing them back into the kit bags.

'Thrown clear?' Hark asked him.

Twenzet shrugged. 'I woke up over there, if that's what you mean,' he said. He looked at Hark. 'Where are we?'

'Couldn't say.'

'Are the others dead?'

Hark sat back on his heels and looked at the blazing wreck. Heat-stiffened, black silhouettes sat in their restraints in the heart of the fire. Hark looked away.

'Yes,' he said.

'Not all of them,' said Tona Criid, limping up behind them. She was clutching a lasrifle across her belly with her left hand. Her right arm hung limp and mangled. Most of her right hand was missing. Blood dripped out onto the dust.

'We came in hard,' she said.

'I remember that much,' said Hark.

'I threw you clear,' she told Twenzet. 'I tried to get back for Swaythe and Klydo, but–'

Her voice faltered. She sank down onto her knees.

Hark got up. They were in a broad valley, a pass surrounded by soaring walls of rock. Night was falling, giving everything a violet cast.

'Listen,' Twenzet said.

Hark heard nothing at first, then made out a sound like the hum of a voxcaster on standby. The hum became the grumble of faraway thunder, and then the thunder became the rumble of turbine power plants. Lights were approaching down the gut of the pass. Heavy, full beam lamps, shone in the dusk.

'Pick up the bags,' he said.

'Sir?' Twenzet asked.

'Pick up the bags and move,' Hark growled.

Twenzet hauled the bags onto his back. Hark helped Criid to her feet. They skirted the burning wreck of the flier, and headed up the shallow incline of boulders and drifted dust.

'Where are we going?' Twenzet asked, panting from the effort of carrying the heavy bags.

'Away from the wreck,' Hark replied.

The noise behind them grew louder. They could hear the clanking rattle of track sections.

'Up here,' Hark told them. They'd gone a decent way from the crash site. At his urgings, they clambered up onto a shelving outcrop of rock and got down.

Down below, two Leman Russ battle tanks rolled into view, lamps blazing. Dust wafted from their churning treads. Behind them, a Hydra flak tank, its quartet of long autocannons raised to the sky, clattered to a halt. Figures moved in the dust, infantrymen escorting the armour on foot.

'Fifty-two,' Twenzet said. 'Look, on the hull! Fifty-two. It's a Cadogus unit. Bless the Throne!' He started to get up. Hark pulled him down flat.

'Look again,' Hark whispered.

The hull plating on the two large tanks was gouged and scorched in places. Neither vehicle seemed to be in the best repair. They appeared to have kit bags or sacking strapped to their prows.

Twenzet peered more closely.

The objects weren't kit bags. They were the brutalised corpses of men in khaki battledress, strung across the front fenders of the tanks with barbed wire, like trophies. The bodies lolled and jerked as the tanks ground to a standstill.

The infantry moved on, past the waiting tanks, towards the burning shell of the Valkyrie. The twilight made their long coats and fatigue jackets look mauve.

Twenzet saw the iron masks covering their faces.

III

G COMPANY HELD its ground for ten minutes until the Blood Pact advancing down the gulley realised the futility of charge tactics. They began to pull back and take up static firing positions, intending to clear Daur's men out of the way with prolonged and concentrated shooting. They left dozens of their kind dead in the bottom of the gulley, or littering the slopes.

As soon as the pressure of the assault waves broke, Daur ordered his company to pull back under bounding fire towards the gate.

The gate hatch had not survived the demise of the Destrier, and the opening had been buried by rock debris. Daur's men had cleared the way to get out, and now Daur intended to bury it again.

'There's no door to shut in their faces,' he said to Caober as they clambered in through the ruined doorway, 'and we don't have the ammo to hold them off.' Vivvo, Haller and Vadim were busy setting tube-charges in the portico of the gatehouse.

Corpsmen had already carried Meryn away, and Neskon had wandered off somewhere. Dalin felt lost and aimless. He kept looking around for Cullwoe, forgetting he wouldn't be there any more. Dalin was exhausted. His hands were shaking and he was having to fight the urge to fold up and collapse in a corner somewhere.

The last of G Company came in through the gate. Heavy fire chased them. The Blood Pact outside were closing in, and they'd had time to bring up support weapons. Machine cannons pummelled the doorway with explosive shells, raising a fog of pulverised stone. The enemy was tearing through ammo box after ammo box. They were evidently not short of supplies.

'Set!' Vivvo called out.

'Clear the chamber!' Daur ordered. 'Fall back through, three rooms back at least! That's the way! Come on!'

The tail-enders, who had been maintaining a steady suppression fire from the doorway to keep the enemy back, picked themselves up and ran for the inner rooms.

Daur stayed until they were all moving and accounted for. 'Right the way back!' he yelled, repeatedly sweeping with his arm.

Daur touched his micro-bead. 'Commander, sealing the second gate at this time,' he reported.

'Understood,' Rawne voxed back.

Daur got into cover and nodded to Vivvo, who was clutching the trigger box.

Gunfire squirted in through the doorway, heavy and sustained. A moment later, the first Blood Pact warriors clambered in, scanning the empty chamber with guns ready.

The world blew out from under them in a flash of supernova light, and the mountain fell on their heads.

IV

'PUT THAT AWAY,' Baskevyl said softly.

'Up against the wall. Lose the firearm,' Ludd said. 'You too, Merrt.' His aim did not waver.

'I admire your dedication, Ludd,' Baskevyl said, steadfastly not moving, 'and I know you have a duty to perform and a lot to prove, but this isn't the time.'

'That's enough!' said Ludd. 'You left your post, Baskevyl. You ignored a direct order! In the middle of this shit-storm!'

'Listen to me,' Baskevyl said firmly, 'we're going to lose. We're going to die here unless something fething miraculous happens.'

'And that's why you came down here? To find yourself a miracle?'

'Maybe,' said Baskevyl. 'Perhaps not a miracle, but a long shot, at least. A chance.'

'Gn... gn... gn... listen to him!' Merrt growled.

'That's enough from you,' said Ludd.

'Look at the book, Ludd. Look at that book there,' Baskevyl pointed. 'I found it in the library. I showed it to Domor and he agreed with me. It's a set of schematics. It's the operation instructions for the house's power hub.'

Ludd glanced at the book open on the floor. 'It's gibberish,' he said.

'The text is. But the drawings are what matter. Look... let me show you.'

Ludd hesitated, and then gestured with his pistol. 'You've got one minute.'

Baskevyl bent down and picked up the book. He held it out to show Ludd. 'Look, here. That's the hub. See? It's quite clearly this hub. Here, that's a diagram of the locking mechanism holding the lid down.'

He flipped a page over. 'This is a plan of the light trunking systems. That's a wall light, see? It's unmistakable.'

'What were you... going to do?' Ludd asked.

'Restart it,' said Baskevyl, 'if I could. It's running on the very last dregs of its reserve. I think most of the systems have long since died, or failed. The lighting ring is running on low-level emergency power.'

'But how were you going to restart it?' asked Ludd.

'It's a cold fusion plant. It's pretty much dry. I was going to empty those canteens into it, give it something to start its reaction off.'

Ludd stared at him. He edged to the side of the open kettle and looked in at the labouring rotation of the hoop.

He holstered his pistol.

'Do it,' he said. 'You're not off the hook, Baskevyl, but you're right. This is worth a try.'

Baskevyl and Merrt hurried to the kit bag and gathered up armfuls of canteens. Ludd watched for a moment and then helped them. Baskevyl emptied the first canteen into the dry cup of the open hub and tossed the flask away. Merrt passed him another, the top already unstoppered.

The kettle took an astonishing quantity without seeming to fill. Eight canteens, and there was just a shallow puddle in the bottom of the basin.

'Keep going,' said Baskevyl.

Baskevyl had brought thirty canteens altogether. There was probably some charge pending for misuse of so much of the precious water ration. He emptied the last one into the kettle. The basin was barely a quarter full.

'Better than nothing,' Baskevyl said.

'Yeah, and nothing is what's happening,' said Merrt.

Baskevyl peered in again. The hoop actually seemed to be slowing down. 'Show me the book again,' he said.

Ludd passed the black-bound book over.

'All right,' said Baskevyl, studying the pages. 'Domor said we could expect this. Its probably been set, or has set itself, to conservation running. There's a…' he paused, turning the book on its side to follow the diagram. 'Yeah, there.'

Baskevyl reached into the hub again and adjusted the nurled calibrations on the head of the snake.

The hoop stopped spinning all together.

'No,' Baskevyl breathed. 'No, no, come on…'

They stared at it.

The hoop quivered slightly. Mechanisms deep inside the kettle base and its adjoining apparatus whirred and clicked. They made grinding, scratching noises that Baskevyl knew only too well.

The hoop started to turn again. It turned in the opposite direction to before. Its rotations were steady this time, and it gathered speed until it was spinning like a gaming wheel. The water in the bottom of the basin began to froth and gurgle. Then the water turned milky white and started to shine.

'Throne alive,' murmured Ludd.

'The lid,' said Baskevyl. 'Help me get the lid back on.'

The three of them manhandled the lid back into place and latched it shut. The kettle was humming quite loudly, and bright white light shone out of the grilled slits in its sides.

'What now?' asked Ludd.

'Well, here's the piece of this plan that's really an act of faith on my part. Follow me.'

He paused. 'Is that all right, commissar? Will you indulge me one last time? Or do you just want to shoot me now?'

V

THEY RAN UP the stairs from the power room and followed the inner hallways in the direction of the newly opened house sections. Outside and above them, the bedlam of the savage battle was quite distinct. Baskevyl faltered for a moment, looking up.

'Feth, you're right, Ludd. Listen to that. I should never have left my post in this. I was so… obsessed. I–'

Ludd held up his hand. 'Look,' he said. 'Look at that!'

The slow, mesmeric pulse and fade of the wall lights had stopped. All down the hallway, as far as they could see, the wall-strung lights were growing steadily brighter, replacing the satin brown gloom with a cool, bright radiance.

Merrt started to make a strange noise. Ludd and Baskevyl realised he was laughing.

Baskevyl broke into a run and they chased after him.

As they entered the new section of the house, they met Daur's company pulling back through. Daur had set five squads to watch the vulnerable courtyard, and was despatching the rest up to the main southern overlooks.

Daur's face was drawn and haggard. 'They're in,' he told Baskevyl. 'I just heard it on the vox. They're in at the main gate, and in some of the lower levels. It's hand-to hand now. Rawne says all munitions are pretty much spent.'

Baskevyl nodded. He pulled his micro-bead out of his pocket and plugged it back in. 'Did Rawne say anything else?'

'He told us to draw silver and become ghosts, ghosts in the house. Keep in the shadows and kill as many of the bastards as we could.'

'What shadows, captain?' Ludd asked.

Daur was so weary, so deadened by fatigue and the prospect of the final, bloody grind, he hadn't noticed the lights. The previously amber glimmer of the lighting in the new section had been replaced by a firm, bright white.

'What,' Daur began, 'what's going on?'

Baskevyl pushed past him and entered the armoury.

He opened the lid of one of the bunkers that ran down the middle of the chamber. The pebbles inside were all shining brightly, like tiny stars.

He clicked his micro-bead. 'This is Baskevyl,' he said. 'Daur, get the men in here.'

VI

Larkin's gun dry clicked. The cell was dead. He tossed the useless weapon aside and got up from the gunslot, drawing his blade. There were scaling ladders barely ten metres below the overlook that he could do nothing about, aside from spit at them.

The sound of the battle had changed. Larkin realised that there was virtually no gunfire coming from the casemates. It was all coming *at* them.

He turned around. There was no Cuu. The presence had remained behind Larkin for some minutes while he meted out the last of his shots, unwilling or unable to strike as it had threatened.

There was no Cuu, but Larkin could still feel him, the wretched essence of him, hanging around him like a mist.

'You don't frighten me any more,' he said out loud. 'You hear me? I'm not scared of you. You're just a ghost. Sure as fething sure. You want to kill me, you get in line, because there's a whole bunch of bastards at the gates after my blood.'

There was no answer. It seemed to Larkin that it was much brighter suddenly.

He limped towards the door. 'Stay out of my way, Cuu,' he growled at the empty air. 'I've got to go away and die with the real Ghosts now.'

VII

THE BLOOD PACT warriors were milling around the burning Valkyrie. Some of them were beginning to spread out, searching the immediate area. An officer got up from the turret of one of the captured tanks and shouted some orders.

'Stay down,' Hark whispered to the others. They were flat on their faces on the rock. Hark slowly reached for his bolt pistol.

A whisker of lightning laced the purple sky above the pass. Slow thunder rolled, like mountains grating together. Down below, the enemy soldiers were suddenly agitated. They shouted to one another.

The air temperature had dropped by several degrees.

Twenzet whimpered. 'W-what is that?' he whispered.

Hark didn't answer. He could feel it too, a creeping dread, unfathomable and unnameable, that made his flesh crawl and his ravaged back bleed.

Something terrible, some unutterable horror, was approaching.

Help me

TWENTY-TWO

Only in Death

I

THE VOX-MAST, poking up into the enormous night sky, was emitting a string of clicks and beeps into the darkness, like some fidgeting nocturnal insect. The dust-proof tents, pitched in a wide ring, were internally lit by oil lamps and small, portable lights, so they glowed golden like paper lanterns. Braziers had been lit on the outer rim of the camp and brass storm cressets hung from poles. Figures moved about in the fire-lit spaces of the inner encampment. Voices came out of the night, along with the smell of cooking.

Two perimeter sentries, their patrol circuits crossing, paused to exchange a few words, then carried on along their routes, moving away from one another.

One paused and looked around. There was no sign of his comrade. The grey desert flat stretched away, empty, into the night.

He began to retrace his path, about to call out, and that became the final action of his life: a foot raised to take a step, his mouth open to call a name.

Mkoll lowered the body into the dust and wiped his knife. He nodded once, though his fellow infiltrator was invisible to him.

Low to the ground, Mkoll scurried forwards, dropping onto his belly for the last stretch where the lamp light extended.

Veiled by the dust-shroud of a tent, Mkoll rose, and stepped carefully over the guy wires. He waited as two thuggish men with scarred faces passed by. They were talking casually. One had a long-necked bottle.

When they'd gone, he slipped between two more of the tents and entered a darker area where the vehicles were parked. Half-tracks and cargo-8 transports made angular blue shadows against the sky. Mkoll dropped down, slid under the first vehicle, and went to work. Feeling, blind, he found the fuel

991

line and cut a slit in it with his warknife. In under three minutes, two other vehicles had been bled in the same way, their fuel loads slowly, quietly pattering away onto the dust beneath them.

Mkoll prised the fuel cap off one of the crippled trucks and packed the pipe with strips of material sliced off the hem of his camo-cloak. Then he poked a strip of det-tape into the wadding with his finger.

He wondered how far Eszrah had got.

Mkoll fixed his warknife to the lug of his rifle and tore the ignition patch off the det-tape.

II

A CLAMMY SENSATION of evil engulfed them. The night air seemed to bristle with it, like a static charge. Twenzet started to moan, but Criid clamped his mouth shut with her good hand. She looked at Hark. His eyes were wide. A pulse was pounding in his temple.

Below them, the commotion amongst the Blood Pact warriors had died away. They were standing stock still, gazing into the distance with their rifles in their hands. They could feel it too. There was no sound except the idling murmur of the tank engines and the dying crackle of flames as the Valkyrie burned out.

The night wind stirred. The ground, the air, reality itself, seemed to tremble for a second.

They heard howling. It was a pitiful, yowling noise, like an animal in pain, and it appeared to come from all around them. The Blood Pact warriors started, turning, hunting for the source.

They began shouting again as they realised the howling was coming from one of their own. The stricken warrior tore off his helmet and his grotesk. He was shaking, as if experiencing the initial spasms of a seizure. Two of his comrades moved to help him.

He killed them.

His autorifle made a hard, cracking sound in the night air. He kept firing, cutting down two more men who were backing away, waving their arms in protest. Stray shots pinged off the sponson armour of the nearest tank. The tank commander, yelling in rage, stood up in his turret hatch and shot the howling maniac with his pistol. The man flopped over, arched his back, and died.

The officer continued shouting as he climbed down from his machine. Warriors who had ducked for cover when the shooting started slowly began to rise to their feet. The officer strode over to the lunatic's corpse, fiercely rebuking each cowering soldier as he went by. He stood over the body and put four more rounds into it.

A blinding fork of electrical discharge leapt out of the corpse and struck the officer's pistol with a shower of sparks. The officer was hurled backwards through the air by the massive shock. He hit the track guards of his tank with such force, his back snapped. The electrical discharge, blue-white like ice and as bright as a las-bolt, lit up the tank's hull in a crackling, sizzling display of raw voltage. Then it leapt again, striking the nearest warrior in the face.

The warrior bucked and twitched as the power overloaded his central nervous system. The energy let him go and, before his limp body had time to topple over, the forking blue charge had jumped to another victim, then another, then another. Each one died, his last seconds spent as a spastic, dancing puppet.

The commander of the second tank emerged from his hatch and started yelling at the rest of the foot troops to fall back. In the general panic, no one noticed the four, long barrels of the flak tank's cannon array slowly lowering to the horizontal plane.

The flak tank opened fire with a deafening, prolonged blurt of noise. Its quad autocannons were built for anti-aircraft operations, and delivered streams of explosive shells at an extremely high rate of fire. All four guns unloaded into the rear of the nearest tank from a range of about ten metres.

Despite its heavy plating and monumental chassis strength, the larger tank shredded. Its hull ripped like wet paper, and a billion slivers of torn metal flew out in a lethal blizzard. Less than a second after the tank began to disintegrate, auguring flak shells found its magazine.

The sun came out, and everything died.

THE OVERPRESSURE OF the gigantic blast knocked Hark and Twenzet off the top of the rock. Criid managed to hold on. An expanding fireball raced out and scorched the air above her, and dust slammed out in a shockwave wall. Small pieces of debris and rock rained down out of the night sky.

Criid got up. The area below was a litter of fire. All three armoured fighting machines had been obliterated.

'Hark?' she yelled. 'Hark?'

He was below her in the shadow of the rock. Twenzet was sprawled beside him. Hark clambered to his feet.

'Are you all right?' he shouted up.

'I can see lights!' she yelled back, pointing to the south. 'I can see lights coming this way!'

Hark got up onto a boulder and stared. Vehicles were approaching fast, their lights bobbing as they rode over the dunes and scree on their tracks.

'Throne help us,' Hark murmured, and wondered if his micro-bead still worked.

III

RAWNE COULD HEAR the squealing rasp of flamers echoing down the tunnel from the main gate. Ghosts, many of them wounded, were pouring back out of the tunnel into the base chamber all around him.

'Obel!'

Obel limped up the steps to the first landing where Rawne stood. 'Main gate's done for. It was all well and good while we had ammo left, but...' he shrugged and looked at Rawne. 'They're leading in with flamers, sir. We had no choice but to pull back.'

Rawne nodded. He had one clip left for his pistol. He was already holding his warknife.

'Anyone with ammo left, send them back to defend the field station for as long as possible. There are men there we can't move. Everyone else digs in. Tell them to spread out and go deep into the place. Find a corner, a nook, a hiding place, and stay there until something comes their way that they can kill.'

Obel saluted and turned to spread the instructions to his men.

'Beltayn!' Rawne roared. Below him, the vox-officers were packing up the last of the casters. 'Get them all clear, now!' Rawne yelled.

'Yes, sir!'

'Kolea?'

'Rawne?' Kolea replied over the link. His signal was patchy, and washed out by lots of background noise.

'How does it stand?'

'Lost east four, five and seven. It's hand to hand in the tunnels and getting worse. They're pouring in. Any word from topside?'

'Negative,' said Rawne. The signals from Kamori and the other officers running the cliff repulse had gone ominously quiet about six minutes earlier.

Rawne looked up at the deep stone vault of the base chamber, the vast wooden staircase rising like a mature nalwood in its centre, its landings extending into the adjacent hallways on each level like branches. Ghosts were running in all directions, fleeing into the house, carrying packs of supplies, caster-sets and wounded comrades. They were heading for bolt holes, for sub cellars and attics, for corridors and stairwells where they could make their final stands, alone or in small groups, stabbing their straight silvers in defiance at death as it overran the house at the end of the world. Whatever corner of Hinzerhaus they went to, Rawne hoped they would find endings to their lives that were as quick as they were brave. One thing was certain: none of them would find a way out.

There was no more time for reflection. The vocal roar of the enemy outside threatened to tear down the house all on its own.

Flames scoured into the base chamber from the tunnel. On the lower steps, Mkfeyd, Mosark and Vril were caught and engulfed. Their thrashing forms crashed backwards down the stairs. Flames caught at the wooden staircase and scorched the stained brown floor panels. An abandoned vox-caster caught light and blew up.

'Move!' Rawne yelled. 'Move!'

Another belch of flame came rushing into the base chamber. Then the first of the Blood Pact flame-troopers appeared, sooty devils in heavy smocks wielding long firelances. Storm troops followed them, cracking shots up into the landings. Wooden steps splintered. Railings exploded like matchwood. Struck by las-fire, a Ghost plunged from an upper landing.

Rawne turned and fired his pistol at the invading figures. The last remaining troopers around him, Beltayn included, opened fire with their handguns as they retreated up the staircase. Rawne's first shots clipped a flame-trooper, and he went over, his lance thrashing out of control like a fire-drake, scorching several warriors and forcing them back.

Blood Pact gunfire filled the air with ribbons and darts of light. Tokar, standing right beside Rawne, fell backwards, the top of his skull blown off. Folore collapsed on the first landing, almost cut in two by autofire. Pabst was hit so hard he smashed backwards through the landing rail and dropped out of sight.

'Get back! Back!' Rawne shouted. He scrambled back up the staircase towards the second landing, pushing men ahead of him. 'Out of the chamber! Out of the chamber!'

Creach fell on his hands and knees, blood gushing from his mouth. Beltayn tried to pick him up and carry him on. A hail of shots cut them both down.

'Bastards!' Rawne bawled, and fired down into the advancing raiders. He reached Beltayn and Creach. The latter was dead. Beltayn had been hit in the side and thigh, and his uniform was soaked with blood. He blinked up at Rawne, his face peppered with blood spots.

'Something's awry,' he said.

'You've been shot you silly bastard,' Rawne told him. He started to hoist Beltayn up.

'Major!' Rattundo yelled from a few steps higher. The Belladon was firing down over Rawne's head.

Rawne swung round, Beltayn over his shoulder, and saw the Blood Pact storm troops thundering up the flight behind him. He shot the first one in the belly, and the second one in the hand and the forehead. The third fired his carbine from the hip. A round creased Rawne's cheek with stunning force. Behind him, Rattundo took the full force of the burst and fell against the stair rail.

Rawne fired again, but his pistol was finally dead. With a bellow of fury, he hurled it at the storm-trooper and bounced the heavy sidearm off the man's face with enough force to knock him over.

Hands grabbed at Rawne and Beltayn from behind. Rerval, Nehn and Garond dragged them back up the staircase to the third landing. Bonin and Leyr, both of them firing a laspistol in each hand, hammered shots down the steps to cover them.

They made it into a side hallway and began to head in the direction of the field station. Nehn and Rerval took Beltayn from Rawne and carried him between them. The rattle of gunfire rolled after them, interspersed with the *crump* of grenades and the *rasp* of flamers. The air filled with the stench of burning.

They're going to burn the place down around us, Rawne thought, burn us like rats. And all that'll be left of us will be dry skulls in a dusty valley.

'Keep going,' Corbec said.

Rawne stopped and turned.

'Come the feth on, major!' Bonin yelled. 'What are you waiting for?'

Rawne stared into Corbec's twinkling eyes.

'You're just a ghost,' he said.

'No such thing as just a Ghost,' Corbec replied.

Then Corbec wasn't there. Las-bolts whipped along the hallway past Rawne. He started to run after the others. Blood Pact storm-troopers thundered down the hallway behind him, yelling and firing.

Rawne saw Daur, Haller and Caober ahead of him. They were facing him, blocking the hallway.

'Back!' Rawne yelled as he closed on them. 'Get back!'

'Get down,' Daur replied.

IV

THE PARKED VEHICLES at the edge of the encampment went up in a satisfyingly dramatic *whoosh* of flame. In the seconds that followed, the site went into a frenzy. Enemy troopers and support crews ran in all directions, shouting and assembling extinguisher gear. The glare from the blazing vehicles lit the whole camp and threw long, leaping shadows. A fourth vehicle caught fire as flames raced along the fuel-soaked dust.

In all the commotion, few of the rushing enemy personnel noticed that some of them were falling down. Iron darts shot silently from the shadows. A trooper fell on his face. A mechanic with a hose tumbled onto his side. A junior officer flopped back into the side-screen of a tent.

Eszrah kept moving. Weaving from point of cover to point of cover, he fired his quarrels one at a time and made every one count. Where possible, he reclaimed his darts, wrenching them out of dead flesh, and slotted them back into his reynbow's barrel. He ran past a large tent, pausing briefly to fire two bolts through the backlit canvas. The silhouetted men inside convulsed and went sprawling.

Eszrah kicked over braziers as he went, rolling the sparking, sputtering cans onto ground sheets and into the hems of tents where the spilled coals ignited the canvas. A warrior with a trench axe came barrelling out of one tent, and took a wild swing at the Nihtgane. Eszrah thumped a quarrel into his sternum at point-blank range.

Eszrah ran on. Behind him, another large blast split the night.

Mkoll was employing the first of his tube charges. He took out a storage tent with it and then ran on in the direction of the vox-mast. Every time an enemy figure appeared in his path, he fired snapshots from the hip, knocking them down. A few rounds of fire came his way as the enemy began to gather their wits.

Mkoll ducked behind a row of tents. At each one, he slit the back sheet open with his bayonet and shot at anyone inside. Halfway through this surgical, methodical exercise, Blood Pact troopers appeared at the end of the tent row and opened fire on him.

Las-rounds zipped past him. Mkoll leapt into a tent through the slit he had just ripped. Inside, an officer with a gruesome mass of scar-tissue for a face was reaching for his bolt pistol. Mkoll broke his head with the butt of his rifle and kept running. More las-rounds scorched indiscriminately through the flapping canvas wall behind him.

He came out through the front of the tent. A hard round hit him in the left shoulder and knocked him over. Mkoll rolled and raked off a quick burst of fire on auto that did for the pair of enemy troopers rushing at him.

He got up again. Several tents were alight. Random shouting and blurts of gunfire echoed around the camp. He heard pursuers crashing in through the tent behind him, and tossed his grenade in through the flaps. There was a flash and the sides of the tent bulged and tore. Smoke gusted out through the rips.

He had three tube-charges left. *Enough for the vox-mast*, he thought.

The encampment's main shelters, a pair of large prefabs, lay close to the mast, which was mounted on a lashed-down field carriage platform. Mkoll reasoned that while he was still alive, he could silence both the mast and the bastard issuing orders through it.

He ran towards the prefabs. As he ran, he realised, without a shred of doubt, that something was still urging him forwards. Something was telling him the prefabs were more important than anything else.

Eszrah was out of bolts. His last shot had slain a large mechanic who had tried to attack him with a sledgehammer. Eszrah dropped the reynbow and drew Gaunt's sword. It felt clumsy and unfamiliar. Swords had never been part of his arsenal. Still running, he lit the blade and felt it throb with power. An enemy trooper emerged from behind a burning tent, and Eszrah cut him down without breaking stride. The blade went clean through the man's torso. Two more troopers appeared, and one saw the partisan in time to squeeze off a shot with his rifle. The round ripped through Eszrah's left side just above the waist. Before either of them could take another shot, he was into them, swinging the bright blade. The first slice cut a rifle in half and the second decapitated its owner. Eszrah shoulder barged the other man onto the ground and ran him through. As a swordsman, he made up in efficiency what he lacked in finesse.

Shots ripped past him. The air was full of streaming smoke. Eszrah slashed open the side of a tent, ran through it, and cut his way out of the far wall. The fully armed warrior standing on the other side turned in surprise and Eszrah chopped the blade down through the crown of his helmet. The blade slid out easily. The warrior, split in two to the breastbone, folded up in a heap. One more for the bludtoll.

Eszrah saw a large, prefab structure ahead of him. The wound in his side was bleeding profusely. He didn't slow down. Slowing down just gave the enemy a better target.

He stormed into the prefab.

It was a long hut, a command space, filled with stowage chests, collapsible furniture and chart tables. Brass lamps hung from the support poles. A junior Blood Pact officer just inside the entrance turned in surprise to block the intruder, pulling his pistol out of its holster. Eszrah delivered a scything blow with both hands that sent the officer crashing backwards over a campaign chest. A second junior officer, yelling out in dismay, came at Eszrah with a punch-grip dagger and effectively ran onto Eszrah's turning blade.

The encampment commander held the noble rank of damogaur. He had absolute control over eight sirdar brigades, and answered only to the etogaur of his consanguinity, and the Gaur who ruled above them all.

He was a being of massive stature. Men only advanced through the ranks of the Pact if they were capable of fighting off any rivals. He rose from his seat at the far end of the hut and faced Eszrah. His crimson battledress was reinforced with steel plates and adorned with gold frogging and hundreds of pillaged and defaced Imperial medals. His face was hidden behind a smiling grotesk of polished silver.

The damogaur reached for the nearest weapon. It was a huge, two-handed chainsword, a type popularly known in the Guard as an 'eviscerator'.

Activating his weapon, the damogaur thundered down the hut, bellowing the challenge cry of his consanguinity.

Eszrah held his ground and brought the power sword up defensively.

In seconds, the partisan realised that while a good sword cuts well, a man with no proper schooling in bladecraft could never hope to best a formally trained swordsman.

Eszrah ap Niht had reached the end of the daeda waeg.

V

THE LEAD VEHICLES of the Cadogus Fifty-Second mechanised squadron rocked to a halt, their engines running. Dust spumed around, glowing like smoke in the headlamps. An officer jumped down from the tail-board of a Salamander command vehicle and ran forward.

'Commissar Hark?'

'Yes,' Hark called back, limping into the glare of the headlights, shielding his eyes. He could see that the lead vehicles were just the tip of a significant armoured column.

'Colonel Bacler, third mech, Cadogus Fifty-Second. I didn't think we'd find you alive.'

'You were looking for me?' Hark asked.

'We were advised your bird had come down in this vicinity, sir. Elikon Command diverted us this way in the hope of finding survivors.'

'I've got injured with me,' said Hark.

'Medics to the front!' Bacler yelled into his voice mic.

'It wasn't survivors Elikon hoped you'd find, colonel,' said Hark. 'We're carrying critical documents in paper form.'

'I understand, commissar,' said Bacler. 'Did any of it survive the crash?'

Teams of corpsmen were running forwards to help Criid and Twenzet. 'Those kit bags with my people,' said Hark. 'We managed to get that much out of the wreck.'

'My orders are to get it back to Elikon as fast as possible.'

'Carry on,' Hark told him. Bacler ordered some troopers to gather up the kit bags.

'What's the state of things, colonel?' Hark asked.

Bacler shrugged. 'In the balance. The Cadogus has slammed up the Altid passes and blocked the enemy in three zones. It's tooth and nail in all of them. There's a hell of a tank fight going on about six kilometres north of us. That's where we were heading when the call to divert came in. This whole valley is crawling with rogue enemy units that have slipped past the main line. As you discovered.'

'What's your strength?' Hark asked.

'Forty main, twenty-five light, plus a thousand troops in carriers and sanctioned support. It was the sanctioned support that saved you, you realise?'

'Yes,' said Hark. 'I understood that's what it was.'

'I'll split the group up and send most of it on down the valley to the sharp end,' Bacler went on. 'A fast, light section under my personal command will carry you and your documents back to Elikon.'

'Thank you,' said Hark. 'What about Hinzerhaus?'

'I'm sorry, sir, I don't know anything about that. I believe there was a relief section on its way there as of this morning, but I can't confirm.'

Hark was silent for a while. He felt light-headed and unworthy. The chances were suddenly good he would get out of the zone alive. That didn't feel right, not when the Ghosts… wouldn't.

'Are you all right, commissar?' Bacler asked, frowning at him.

'Yes. I just remembered. It is with regret I have to inform you that your Major Berenson was killed in the line of duty.'

'Yes, that was a bloody shame,' Bacler replied.

Hark nodded towards the blackened shell of the Valkyrie on the slope behind them. 'I wanted to pull him clear, but it was too late,' he said. Bacler looked at him oddly.

'Did I say something wrong, colonel?' Hark asked.

'Major Berenson was lost when his Valkyrie was brought down en route to Hinzerhaus five days ago,' said Bacler.

VI

DAUR, HALLER AND Caober raised the weighty, antique weapons they were holding and aimed them. Rawne threw himself flat against the hallway wall. The three men fired.

The wall guns made noises like the amplified shrieks of eagles. Each one spat a fat, continuous beam of white searing light. At the far end of the hallway, the beams struck the Blood Pact troopers charging them.

The enemy figures weren't simply hit, they were destroyed. Bodies vaporised in clouds of atomised tissue. The streaming beams blew clean through the front rank, explosively dismembering them, and atomised the row behind.

The three men stopped firing and the beams vanished. 'Reload!' Daur yelled. They opened the heavy locks of the old weapons, ejecting the spent, black pebbles inside, and dropped in glowing white lumps they'd taken from their pockets. The locks snapped shut. Rawne had scrambled in behind the three men.

'What the feth?' he stammered.

Stunned for a moment by the fury of the first strike against them, the Blood Pact were pressing their assault again, blasting wildly as they poured into the hallway.

'Fire!' Daur ordered.

The wall guns shrieked again. Bright beams flashed the length of the hall and bodies disintegrated in puffs of wet matter. The hallway air misted with blood particles.

Rawne leaned back against the brown satin wall, breathing hard. Behind the firing line, he saw dozens of other Ghosts from G Company moving forwards with wall guns in their hands. Other troopers, in paired teams, had fashioned slings out of their camo-capes and were lugging four or five wall guns at a time into the nearest stairwell like stretcher bearers. Guardsmen with water cans and cooking pots followed them. The pots were full of shining white pebbles.

'How did you get them to work?' Rawne asked.

Daur stepped out of the line and gestured for the nearest trooper to take his place. Merrt hurried forwards. 034TH hung on its sling over his shoulder. He took his place next to Caober and raised the massive wall gun in his hands.

Merrt squeezed the trigger and felt the heavy, pleasing kick of the old weapon for the first time.

'Baskevyl did it,' Daur said, ducking in beside Rawne. He held his wall gun upright, its stock resting on the floor. 'He powered the system up.'

'Holy Throne,' Rawne murmured.

'I'm trying to get them distributed through the house. Ammo too. Baskevyl's leading Sloman's company topside to get them armed. Chiria's trying to cut through the house on level eight to relieve the southern face. It's not over yet. This is probably just a stay of execution rather than a reprieve, but we can make it count. We can give those bastards one feth of a show before we're done.'

'Ban,' said Rawne.

'Yes, sir?'

'I want one of those things.'

'I thought you might,' said Daur.

THE RAMPART LINE of cloche domes and casemates along the top of the house was on fire. Several domes had been blown entirely open, and flames and sparks guttered up into the cold night sky. H and B Companies had held the enemy back for as long as possible, but once the Blood Pact had penetrated the first of the domes, things deteriorated rapidly. The raiders had no short-age of grenades. They'd even lugged flamers up the sheer north cliff face. They showed no signs of fatigue after their arduous climb. Varl suspected they were too high on bloodlust and glanded stimms.

Vigo Kamori was killed by a nail bomb in upper west sixteen about five minutes before the last of the rifle cells packed up. He died not far from where Gaunt had fallen. To Varl, it seemed like a curse repeating itself. He had witnessed both deaths. He tried to raise Rawne on his bead, but the intervox had been dead for some time.

Kamori had not flinched in his duty. He had commanded the action from the front throughout, even when it descended into bestial melees in the burning hallways. Varl, forced to rely on his service pistol, found the men looking to him for leadership.

'Kamori's dead! Kamori's dead!' Cant screamed. 'What do we do?'

'Well, stop yelling in my ear would be a start,' Varl growled, cracking off a round to stop a charging storm-trooper with an axe.

'Maybe we can hold them in the next gallery,' Maggs suggested.

'Yeah, good,' said Varl. 'Close up!' he yelled. 'Close up and fall back! Nice and steady! Do you hear me?'

Firing their pistols or clutching dead rifles with fixed blades, the men around him shouted back in affirmation.

'Just keep firing,' Varl called. 'Pick your targets and keep firing. You can do that, can't you, Cant?'

Cant looked at him. 'You fething watch me,' he replied.

'That's what I like to hear,' Varl grinned.

'You heard the sergeant!' Maggs yelled. 'If she wants us, she can bloody wait for us!'

She wanted them. Shots were punching into them. On either side of Varl and Maggs, men were falling and dying. Sonorote took a round in the mouth that blew out the back of his head. Fenix lost an arm and an ear to a raking line of tracer shots, and bled out before anyone could get to him. Ezlan was thrown backwards by an impact to the belly. When Gunsfeld reached his side to help him, he found that Ezlan had a live rocket grenade sticking out of his stomach wall. Ezlan was wailing in pain.

'It's a dud! Ezlan, it's a dud,' Gunsfeld yelled at him. 'It misfired!'

'Get it out! Get it out!' Ezlan screamed. Gunsfeld took hold of the pro-jectile and tugged.

It wasn't a dud. The blast killed Ezlan, Gunsfeld and Destra outright and blinded Dickerson, the famous seamster and darner of socks.

Varl's pistol dry clicked. He searched in his pockets, certain that he must have one last cell left. He always kept one around for what he called 'emer-gency work', which translated as a headshot for himself if the situation ever got too bad.

Like now, he thought.

His pockets were conspicuously empty. In the turmoil, he'd torn through every cell on his person. He reached into his hip pouch and yanked out the old autopistol he carried as a last ditch. He racked the slide. Nine rounds and one in the pipe.

'Come on, back! Back!' Varl shouted. He fired the pistol. The bullet deflected off the grotesk of an advancing storm-trooper.

'You useless fething object!' Varl shouted at his weapon.

Cant cannoned into Varl and pushed him against the hallway wall. 'What are you doing?' Varl began to exclaim.

There was a shriek like an eagle's call. A bright, colimnated beam of energy burned down the hallway past him and reduced two Blood Pact raiders to clouds of swirling organic debris. Several more beams followed it, bursting enemy soldiers like ripe ploins stuffed with det-tape.

The last thing Varl had expected to see was reinforcements. Baskevyl stormed past him, hefting a huge long-gun. Other men followed, similarly armed. One of them was Dalin Criid, a look of grim determination on his young face. They paused and sent more beams down the tunnel.

'Varl?'

Ludd appeared, leading a second block of men all armed with the antique weapons. Ludd was carrying his pistol.

'Commissar.'

'Pull your men back as best you can to the stairwell on fourteen. Preed's waiting there with weapons to hand out.'

'I like the sound of that,' said Varl.

Ludd turned and raised his voice. 'Men of Tanith!' he yelled. 'Do you want to live forever?'

VII

ESZRAH STAGGERED BACKWARDS. He was gashed on the right arm, the left thigh and the left shoulder. So much blood soaked his grey clothing, he might easily have been mistaken for a member of the Blood Pact cadre. He tried to swing the sword.

The damogaur clipped its threat away with his whirring chainsword and rammed the blade into the side of Eszrah's head. The Nihtgane crashed over, breaking a chart table.

The damogaur took a step forwards, holding the chainsword's elongated grip with both hands. He chuckled, a deep, throaty sound. He was playing with Eszrah. He had knocked him down with the flat of his blade. Eszrah clawed for the handle of the sword, but the damogaur put his foot down on Eszrah's forearm. Bones creaked. Eszrah gasped in pain. The damogaur, tiring of his sport, raised the eviscerator for the kill stroke. The teeth of the blade whirred.

A tiny silver point, no bigger than a fingernail, emerged from the damogaur's Adam's apple. A single drop of blood glittered on it. The damogaur pitched forwards, revealing Mkoll, teeth clenched, both fists clamped around the grip of the warknife he had rammed into the back of the damogaur's neck.

'Hwat seyathee, soule?' Mkoll asked.

Eszrah managed a feeble, pain-drawn grin. 'Y seyathee sacred feth,' he whispered.

Mkoll yanked his silver out of the corpse. 'I've set charges to the mast,' he told Eszrah as he helped him up. 'We've got four minutes.'

Eszrah nodded and picked up the sword.

'We can still get out of here,' Mkoll said. 'Get out of here and head out into the desert while this place burns and they all run around looking for their arses with both hands.'

Eszrah shook his head. He raised the sword and pointed towards the back of the prefab, where a canvas flap led through into the adjoining shelter.

Mkoll knew what he meant. He was feeling the same thing, the same urge.

They moved down the prefab. Mkoll had unslung his rifle and held it ready to fire.

Near the doorway, a man was cowering in the shadows. He was a plump, wretched thing with scars on his bloated face. He wore a stinking leather apron smeared with blood both old and fresh. His hands were cased in rough leather gauntlets. He looked like a worker from a meat processing plant; the denizen of some infernal abattoir.

As they approached, he whimpered and held out a dirty spiked goad to threaten them.

Mkoll shot him in the head.

They moved past his twitching corpse, pulled back the canvas drop sheet and smelled blood.

VIII

THE ROCKING SALAMANDER sped back down the length of the Cadogus column, kicking dust. Hark sat in a pull down seat in the cab, lost in thought. Criid and Twenzet followed in a second Salamander. Bacler, riding in the cab beside Hark, had told them they would pick up their escort at the rear of the column. Bacler was busy on the cab vox-set, issuing instructions to the officers who would be taking charge of the mechanised squadron when he left it.

In the distance, the night sky was underlit by the pummelling flashes of an artillery duel ten kilometres north. Tanks and armoured vehicles flashed past as they rode down the centre of the advancing lines of Bacler's battalion.

Hark was oblivious to the passing vehicles and lines of men. Pain and fatigue had all but conquered him. He swayed in his seat, burned out and lost, lost, like the Tanith First. His broken machine arm ached, and he found the pain faintly ridiculous.

Deep inside his head, the pipes started to play. They were Tanith pipes and they played as only Brin Milo could play them. They played the way they had often played in his haunted dreams those past few years.

He stood up, steadying himself.

'Commissar?' Bacler asked.

'Something's going to happen,' Hark said.

'What?'

'Tell the driver to stop,' Hark said. 'Something's going to happen. Whenever the pipes play, it's a sign.'

'Commissar, you're tired. You've been through a lot–'

'Stop the vehicle! I can hear the pipes playing.'

Bacler smiled awkwardly. 'There are no pipes, sir. I hear nothing.'

Hark looked at him. 'You're not supposed to, colonel. I think they've always been meant for me. Will you please tell the driver to stop?'

'Cut the engines,' Bacler called into the driver's compartment. The commissar was clearly deranged, but that was hardly surprising. There was no harm humouring him for a minute or two.

The Salamander came to a halt, rocking on its tracks. Criid's ride came to a halt behind it, engine revving. 'Everything all right, sir?' the officer aboard the second Salamander voxed crisply.

'Stand by, Leyden,' said Bacler into his mic.

Hark dismounted, jumping down into the dust. He took a few paces forward. The melody hung in the air, or in his head, he couldn't decide which. He felt a sudden, terrible feeling of sadness and regret. It was like a dream breaking, a buried dream he could finally remember.

He looked back at the other Salamander. Criid and Twenzet had dismounted and were staring at him.

'Hark?' Criid called out.

'Just… just a minute, Tona,' he called back. He started forwards, walking down the line of the column ahead, past rows of tanks with idling engines and Cadogus troopers sitting at ease on the tops of transports. They watched him walk by, amused by the sight of the ragged, one-armed commissar with the hopeless look on his face.

Hark.

Hark walked on, gathering speed, past the tank and transport elements into the next section of the waiting column. He walked between two rows of Trojan tractors towing canisters of fuel on low-loader trailers. Their engines throbbed, but did not drown out the thin, floating melody.

Hark.

The Trojan drivers, sitting up in the top hatches, watched him stride past through the dust. Several more Trojan tractors stood in a line behind the fuel carriers. The machines were painted black and towed a far more volatile cargo in their trailers. A cluster of men in caps and black leather coats stepped out in front of Hark. They were commissars wearing Special Attachment emblems on their collars and epaulettes.

'Let me pass,' said Hark.

They hesitated, and then stood aside.

Help me.

Heavy cages with thick, iron bars sat on the trailers towed by the ominous black tractors. Dark, spavined shapes lurked behind the bars, chained hand and foot, lashed to bare metal frames in the centre of each cage. Some of the cages were studded with spikes and barbs that pointed inwards. Despite the stink of exhaust wafting from the tractors, Hark could smell the pain. Blood, sweat, faeces, gangrene and the wretched tang of static filled the night air.

The pipes grew louder.

Each cage was attended by dark, silent figures: Special Attachment commissars, servitors, armed guards in black uniforms with curiously full helmets, their visors down, and men and women in dark robes armed with handling poles and electric prods. Pale, grim faces and closed visors followed him as he toiled along the line.

Help me, Hark.

Hark came to a halt. He realised there were tears running down his face. The sadness that had eaten away at him for years had finally broken out, cracking the frozen surface of his emotional reserve. He looked up at the cage in front of him. The inward turned spikes were matted with dried blood.

A hunchbacked man in black leather came and stood in front of Hark. 'You cannot approach the cage,' he hissed through rotten teeth.

'Go feth yourself,' said Hark.

A woman stepped forwards beside the hunchback. She was old and stiff, her thin face disfigured with a large red birthmark. She wore a long, austere dress of black lace that rustled in the desert wind.

'Custodian Culcus is quite correct,' she said. 'You may not approach the cage or the specimen. These are the rules of the Sanctioned Division. It is for your own safety, sir. Psykers, even sanctioned ones, are dangerous animals.'

'Get out of my way,' said Hark.

'Let him pass.'

Hark looked around. Bacler had followed him up the line of vehicles with Criid limping at his side. Criid had tears in her eyes. She can probably hear the frail, plaintive music too, Hark thought.

'Let him pass,' Bacler repeated.

The old dam in the black lace dress nodded and backed away, pulling the hunchback aside.

Hark clambered up onto the greasy bed of the trailer. He knelt down in front of the cage, his hands clutching the filthy bars.

'I'm sorry,' he whispered.

The thing inside the cage stirred. It was just a sack of meat, rotting and sagging. Heavy shackles pinned its wasted limbs to the cage frame. Hark could see that it had undergone extensive surgery. Sutured scars criss-crossed its dirty scalp and augmetic devices had been implanted in its neck, chest and throat. Its ears had been clipped off with shears and its eyes had been sewn shut. It slumped naked in a pool of its own waste. Open, weeping sores covered the flesh of its torso.

It's all right.

'No,' said Hark. 'It isn't.'

This is my life now.

'This is no life,' said Hark.

The thing in the cage stirred. The chains holding its cadaverous limbs rattled.

I felt you here.

'I know. I understand that now.'

I felt you close. All of you. My friends. My old friends. I tried to reach you.

'I'm afraid you hurt us. We didn't understand.'

I'm sorry, Hark. I just wanted to help you. Help you to survive.

'I know.'

I just wanted you to hear me.

'I heard you. We all heard you, in our dreams, in the things that haunted us.' Hark wiped his nose on his cuff.

I just wanted you to hear me. I just wanted to help you. You were so far away, in such danger, but I could feel you. I tried to reach you–

'You reached us,' Hark said.

The thing inside the cage shuddered. It gurgled. Slime dripped from the slit that had once been its mouth. It was laughing.

It's not a precise art, this thing I do. Not cut and dried, neat and tidy, like smeltery work or soldiering. I miss both of my old professions. What I do is not precise, Hark. You were so far away, I could only reach you through your memories.

'You reached us,' Hark repeated.

Thunder rolled. Frost had formed on the bars of the cage.

'That's enough now!' the old dam in the black lace dress called. Bacler put a hand on her shoulder and whispered to her. She fell silent.

My handlers are unhappy. They think I might act up now you're here. They think your presence might provoke me. They think I might kill you.

'I know you're not going to do that,' said Hark. 'Although if you did, I wouldn't blame you.'

I only wanted to help you.

'I know.'

I only wanted you to help me. Help me. Please, Hark, help me. I can't stand this any more.

The thing inside the cage rattled its chains again. Icicles had formed along the roof bars.

'I'll help you,' Hark whispered, pushing his face against the bars.

You have to make it look right, Hark. Commissar-style, you know? Otherwise they'll charge you for all sorts of crimes. They'll hang you out to dry.

'I know what to do. Trust me. And forgive me.'

There's nothing to forgive. Just help me.

Hark rose to his feet. He drew his engraved bolt pistol and racked the slide.

'By the grace of the Emperor!' he declared, loud enough for the handlers down below to hear him, 'You're dead and I can't let this go on. You're killing my men with your ghosts.'

He let the slide snap back and aimed the weapon between the bars of the cage.

'He can't do that!' the old dam cried.

'Yes, he fething well can,' snarled Criid behind her.

'Is there anything else you want to say to me?' Hark whispered, his hand trembling.

Only the same thing I've been trying to tell you all these last few days.

'What's that?'

He's alive. He's in terrible pain, but he's alive.

Hark paused.

'Be at peace,' he said.

The wretched thing that had once been called Agun Soric looked up at him with sewn-up eyes through the bars of the cage.

Hark fired.

HE JUMPED DOWN off the trailer. The sound of the pipes had faded, forever. Hark felt sick.

'What did you do?' the old dam screamed at him.

Hark shoved her aside.

'I gave him what he needed,' Hark said.

'You killed him!' the hunchback stammered, outraged.

'Only in death does duty end,' Hark replied, 'and he had done his duty a thousand times over.'

He walked away from the trailer, the bolt pistol hanging in his grip. Behind him, Bacler and Criid were arguing with the handlers.

Hark's foot disturbed something lying in the dust. He bent down.

It was a brass message shell.

Hark picked it up and unscrewed it.

There was nothing inside.

IX

MKOLL AND THE partisan entered the second prefab. The sour, metallic smell of blood hung in the air. A dozen prisoners were strung up on crude wooden frames along the tent space. It was obvious they had been subjected to intense interrogation under torture.

The scene was appalling, even to a hardened veteran like Mkoll. He stopped in his tracks, breathing hard. The limp, naked bodies suspended on the frames were slick with blood and covered with black, clotted wounds. The torture had been vindictive, cruel and utterly typical of Blood Pact methods. Some of the prisoners had suffered amputations or organ removal. Others had been nailed to the frames by their soft tissue. The hideous tools of the torturers' trade, goads and nails and skewers, lay in blood-stained trays on stands around the room. Branding irons stood in fuming braziers.

Mkoll went down the line of prisoners, quickly and mercifully putting each one out of his or her misery. The deep urge he had felt to come there and enter the place had vanished as suddenly and mysteriously as it had come. He just wanted to get out and make a run for it. But he wasn't going to leave before he'd spared these miserable beings further agonies.

It was simple to do. Just pressing the edge of his venom-smeared blade against an open wound let toxins into the blood stream. A swift, numbing death resulted, without the need for shots or further wounding.

He touched his blade against an open wound in the belly of a heavy-set man who had been partly skinned. The man opened his eyes briefly. He smiled at Mkoll as he died. Mkoll felt as if he was an ayatani priest, delivering a last comforting touch and a blessing.

He moved to the next dangling body and reached out with his ministering blade.

Eszrah caught his hand and pulled it back.

'What?' Mkoll asked.

'Not him,' Eszrah said.

Mkoll looked up at the hanging body. The man had been whipped and flayed several times. His skin was hanging off in places. His face, hanging low, was drenched in blood. The cords holding him spread-eagled to the frame were biting into his wrists and ankles.

'I need to help him,' Mkoll said. 'I need to end his pain.'

Eszrah shook his head. Mkoll looked at the ruined man again. He saw the old, deep scars across his belly, the mark of a chainsword wound suffered many years before.

'Oh feth,' he murmured.

They cut him down quickly, cradling his limp body. His eyes opened. He looked at them, blood trickling out of his mouth. Mkoll realised that he had been blinded.

'Are we the last ones left alive?' he asked, turning his head towards the sound of them. 'Are we? Someone, anyone, please? Are we? Is there anybody out there? Are we the last ones left alive?'

Nalwood, Nalwood, this is Elikon M.P., this is Elikon M.P.
Please respond. Please respond. Can you hear, Nalwood?
What is your status? Please respond.

Elikon out. (transmission ends)

- Transcript of vox message, fifth month, 778.

TWENTY-THREE

The End of the World at the House

I

LATE ON THE fourteenth day, the mechanised unit Berenson, or some warp-whisper they had known as Berenson, had promised finally fought its way up the pass to Hinzerhaus. Twenty items of armour, with troop support in the van, and air cover from a string of Vulture gunships, blasted into the rear of the Blood Pact host besieging the house and scattered it in a battle that lasted fifty-eight minutes. The last twenty minutes were little more than a massacre. The Blood Pact fled into the cracks in the mountains, leaving over four thousand dead on the dust bowl and the lower escarpments of the house.

Hinzerhaus itself was a dismaying ruin. Clotted smoke drifted up into the desert sky from a hundred separate fires. Overlooks and gunboxes had been blown out and destroyed. Several sections of the southern face had collapsed, exposing the rockcrete bunkers buried in the rock to the sky. The walls were pockmarked and chipped with hundreds of thousands of gunshots. The main gatehouse had been totally demolished. The topside ramparts along the cliff lay in ruins, each and every cloche dome ruptured and burst. Fire spewed steadily and out of control from slots of the lower casemates. The cliff walls were cratered and dimpled with the scorched impacts of heavy shelling.

Major Kallard, commanding the relief force, clambered down from his vehicle in front of the gates and gazed at the ruin. The Vultures shrieked overhead, making another pass before peeling off to hunt for fleeing enemy units in the upper gorges of the range.

'Holy Throne,' muttered Kallard, surveying the burning structure. He looked around at his adjutant, a boy-faced man named Seevan.

'Anything?' he asked.

Seevan tried his caster again and looked up at Kallard with a shake of his head.

'Nothing. Link's dead.'

Kallard spat a curse. He waved the first detachment of his infantry forward into the place, pretty certain he knew what they would find.

'Look, sir!' one of the point men yelled.

Kallard turned and looked.

Figures were emerging from the demolished ruin of the gatehouse. Their dark uniforms were in tatters and their faces were plastered in dirt. They carried strange-looking, heavy rifles, which some had hefted up on their shoulders like yokes. They walked out across the dust towards Kallard.

He watched them approach, straightening his cap. There was something about them that demanded respect.

They came to a halt before him.

'I didn't think there'd be anyone left alive,' Kallard spluttered.

'It comes as something of a surprise to me too,' replied the gaunt, dark-haired man in front of him.

'Major Kallard, Cadogus Fifty-Second Mechanised,' Kallard said, making the sign of the aquila. The bad rock wind moaned.

'Major Rawne, commander, First-and-Only,' the man replied, throwing a half-hearted salute. 'These are my men... Kolea, Larkin, Daur, Commissar Ludd, Baskevyl, Bonin.'

The men behind him nodded in turn, and showed no sign of lowering the hefty antique weapons they carried.

'How... how did you manage to hold out for so long?' Kallard asked.

Rawne shrugged. 'We just decided we wouldn't die,' he replied.

Kallard gathered his wits. 'What are your losses, sir?'

'Forty-seven per cent dead. Eighteen per cent wounded,' Rawne said. 'I have two medicaes in there fighting to cope with the casualties.'

'Medics forwards and in!' Kallard yelled, waving his hand. Corpsmen and surgeons from the column hurried past him into the house.

'Might I ask, sir, what are those weapons?' Kallard asked.

Rawne took the wall gun off his shoulder and held it out for Kallard's inspection. 'They're what kept us alive. I have a feeling the Ordo Xenos will want to look at them.'

'I think they might,' said Kallard. He crunched around on the dust and gestured. 'I have transports waiting to ferry you out,' he said. 'Will you follow me?'

Rawne looked around at Kolea and Daur. 'Lead the way. Get moving. I'm not leaving until the last man is clear.'

Behind Rawne, a chunk of the southern cliff collapsed with a crunch and a gust of powder.

'Go.'

Rawne turned and walked back towards the house. Ludd followed him.

'You can leave now, Ludd,' Rawne said.

'I'll leave when my duty's done, sir,' Ludd replied. 'Let's get the men out.'

* * *

II

THEY FILED OUT along the burned out corridor that joined the base chamber to the gatehouse. Man after man, carrying their wounded with them. Curth and Dorden escorted the procession, tending to the most severely injured.

In the base chamber, Zweil cast a final blessing to the walls, and turned to hobble out of the place.

Merrt was one of the last troopers to leave. He left 034TH leaning against a wall in the base chamber.

'Don't you want that?' Dalin asked.

'It doesn't belong to me,' Merrt replied.

III

'MAJOR! MAJOR RAWNE!' Kallard yelled, running up the pass towards the line of Chimeras.

Rawne turned.

'I'm sorry, major, I quite forgot. There was a signal for you, from Van Votyz at Elikon.'

Kallard handed the slip of paper to Rawne.

Rawne read it. He turned to look at the Ghosts mounting the transports along the pass.

'Gaunt's alive!' Rawne yelled to them. 'He's fething well alive!'

One by one, they began to shout.

EPILOGUE
Elikon

I

SEVERAL SETS OF boots came marching down the stone hallway. Sentries presented arms as the figures marched by.

The boots crunched to a halt outside a ward room. The medicae on duty saluted and opened the door.

'Is that you, Barthol?' the man on the bed asked, turning his head from one side to the other. His eyes were bandaged.

'How did you know, Ibram?' General Barthol Van Voytz asked, sitting down beside the bed.

'I could smell acceptable losses.'

'Uhm,' Van Voytz replied. He looked over his shoulder at Biota and the escort guards. 'Out,' he said.

They made themselves scarce. The door closed behind them.

'I'm glad you're alive, Ibram,' Van Voytz said.

'As I understand it, that's thanks to Mkoll and Eszrah and a five-hour desert drive in a captured enemy half-track.'

'You surround yourself with good people, good things happen,' the general said.

Gaunt sat back. It was going to take many months of skin grafts to repair his body.

'I have always surrounded myself with good people, Barthol. Why do think I've lived this long?'

Van Voytz chuckled.

'You sent me to the end of the world, Barthol. You sent me to a death trap,' Gaunt said. 'Me and all my men. Barely half of them came out alive.'

'I'm sorry, Ibram,' Van Voytz said. 'Listen, we've spared no expense. Your new eyes will be the best aug–'

'My Ghosts, Barthol. My Ghosts, and you saw fit to let half of them die.'

'It wasn't like that, Ibram. It was vital to hold the enemy back for as long as possible. A delay was ess–'

'Here's what I want you to do, Barthol. Never ask that of me and my men again.'

II

FARAWAY, THE HOUSE *at the end of the world expires. The worm ceases its subterranean scratching. The old dam stops walking fretfully along the empty halls, biding her time and waiting, her black lace dress brushing the satin brown floors.*

A standard-pattern infantry rifle, serial 034TH, standing in the corner of a smoke-blackened room, begins to rust.

HINZERHAUS FALLS SILENT. *The wall lights flare and then dim away to nothing. In death, the house sleeps, waiting for the next soldiers to arrive out of the wind and dust, and the next battle to begin, one day, in ages to come.*

Day eighteen.

Sunrise at ~~something~~ dawn. No dust.

According to sources at the Tacticae, the documents retrieved from the library archive have proven remarkably helpful to the Jago campaign. I am told the war to reconquer Jago might be shortened by two or three years.

I am tired of this bad rock. It has cost us too much. My arm hurts. My mouth is constantly dry. ~~I miss the music in~~

When I told Rawne that Gaunt was alive, he looked as if he was going to cry. Just the dust, I suspect. The dust got into everything on Jago.

— Field journal, V.H. fifth month, 778.

ABOUT THE AUTHOR

Dan Abnett is a novelist and award-winning comic book writer. He has written twenty-five novels for the Black Library, including the acclaimed Gaunt's Ghosts series and the Eisenhorn and Ravenor trilogies, and, with Mike Lee, the Darkblade cycle. His Black Library novel *Horus Rising* and his Torchwood novel *Border Princes* (for the BBC) were both bestsellers. He lives and works in Maidstone, Kent.

Dan's website can be found at *www.danabnett.com*

WARHAMMER
40,000

DAN ABNETT

Contains the novels
*First and Only, Ghostmaker,
Necropolis* and the short
story *In Remembrance*

'He makes war so real that you want to duck!' – Sci Fi.com

THE FOUNDING

A GAUNT'S GHOSTS OMNIBUS

ISBN 978-1-84416-369-4

WARHAMMER 40,000

DAN ABNETT

Contains the novels
Honour Guard, The Guns of Tanith, Straight Silver and *Sabbat Martyr*

'So believable you can almost feel the gut-wrenching G forces.' – SciFi.com

THE SAINT

A GAUNT'S GHOSTS OMNIBUS

ISBN 978-1-84416-479-0

WARHAMMER 40,000

DAN ABNETT

BLOOD PACT

A GAUNT'S GHOSTS NOVEL

UK ISBN 978-1-84416-825-5 US ISBN 978-1-84416-824-8

WARHAMMER
40,000

EMPEROR'S MERCY

"Crunchy, vivid and memorable...
next time I need a galaxy burned,
I'm sending for Mr Zou."
DAN ABNETT

HENRY ZOU

UK ISBN 978-1-84416-734-0 US ISBN 978-1-84416-735-7

WARHAMMER
40,000

A BASTION WARS NOVEL

FLESH AND IRON

HENRY ZOU

UK ISBN 978-1-84416-814-9 US ISBN 978-1-84416-815-6